7⁵⁰

THE MODERN LIBRARY
of the World's Best Books

FAMOUS
SCIENCE-FICTION
STORIES

Adventures
in Time and Space

FAMOUS SCIENCE-FICTION STORIES

Adventures in Time and Space

EDITED BY RAYMOND J. HEALY
AND J. FRANCIS MCCOMAS

THE MODERN LIBRARY · NEW YORK

THE MODERN LIBRARY

IS PUBLISHED BY

RANDOM HOUSE, INC.

BENNETT CERF · DONALD S. KLOPFER

Manufactured in the United States of America by H. Wolff

ACKNOWLEDGMENTS

For permission to reprint copyrighted material the following acknowledgments are gratefully made to:

Street & Smith, Inc., publishers of Astounding Stories, and to the Editors of that magazine for the following stories: "Requiem" by Robert A. Heinlein, "Forgetfulness" by Don A. Stuart, "Nerves" by Lester Del Rey, "The Proud Robot" by Lewis Padgett, "Black Destroyer" by A. E. Van Vogt, "Symbiotica" by Eric Frank Russell, "Heavy Planet" by Lee Gregor, "Time Locker" by Lewis Padgett, "The Link" by Cleve Cartmill, "Mechanical Mice" by Maurice A. Hugi, "V-2: Rocket Cargo Ship" by Willy Ley, "Adam and No Eve" by Alfred Bester, "Nightfall" by Isaac Asimov, "As Never Was" by P. Schuyler Miller, "Q. U. R." by Anthony Boucher, "Who Goes There?" by Don A. Stuart, "The Roads Must Roll" by Robert A. Heinlein, "Asylum" by A. E. Van Vogt, "Quietus" by Ross Rocklynne, "The Twonky" by Lewis Padgett, "Time-Travel Happens!" by A. M. Phillips, "The Blue Giraffe" by L. Sprague de Camp, "Flight into Darkness" by Webb Marlowe, "The Weapons Shop" by A. E. Van Vogt, "Farewell to the Master" by Harry Bates, "Correspondence Course" by Raymond F. Jones, "By His Boot Straps" by Anson MacDonald, copyright, Street & Smith Publications, Inc., 1937, 1938, 1939, 1940, 1941, 1942, 1943, 1945.

P. Schuyler Miller, author, for "The Sands of Time," from Astounding Stories, copyright, Street & Smith Publications, Inc., 1937.

Raymond Z. Gallun, author, and his agent, Julius Schwartz, for "Seeds of the Dusk," from Astounding Stories, copyright, Street & Smith Publications, Inc., 1938.

Harry Bates, author, for "A Matter of Size," from Astounding Stories, copyright, Street & Smith Publications, Inc., 1934.

Robert Moore Williams, author, for "Robot's Return" from Astounding Stories, copyright, Street & Smith Publications, Inc., 1938.

R. DeWitt Miller, author, for "Within the Pyramid" from *Astounding Stories*, copyright, Street & Smith Publications, Inc., 1937.

Henry Hasse, author, for "He Who Shrank" from *Amazing Stories*, copyright, Teck Publications, Inc., 1936.

Fredric Brown, author, and his agent, Harry Altshuler, for "The Star Mouse," from *Planet Stories*, copyright, Love Romances Publishing Co., Inc., 1942.

S. Fowler Wright for "Brain." Hitherto not published in the United States.

FOR ANNETTE AND MIDGE

CONTENTS

INTRODUCTION

A WORD ABOUT the creation of this book. It was conceived in 1944, underwent a gestation period of some fourteen months, and was born in the spring of 1946, half a year after the Atomic Age dawned over Hiroshima.

Critics have called this the "definitive" anthology of science fiction stories. We agree—not because that appraisal flatters us, but because it is an accurate judgment of the stature of the magazine editor who first published most of the stories in this collection.

That man was John W. Campbell, Jr. And perhaps no one man ever had a greater influence over a literary form, for Campbell single-handedly revolutionized the writing of and—possibly more important —the *thinking* in modern science fiction.

He created what all of us—readers, writers and editors—refer to as the Golden Age of twentieth-century imaginative literature. You are about to read the golden bests of that golden time.

Prior to Campbell's advent as editor of *Astounding Stories* in 1937, modern science fiction had badly deteriorated from the standards set by its great founders, Wells and Verne. While some editors strove for genuinely interesting scientific speculation, they allowed such challenging postulations to be presented in a framework of atrocious prose. Generally, however, magazines nominally presenting science fiction offered science that was claptrap and fiction that was graceless and dull.

Campbell changed all that. Previous to his appointment as editor of *Astounding*, he had, under the pseudonym of Don A. Stuart, broken contemporary barriers with stories that were first-rate fiction by any criteria. (You will find two of the best by "Stuart" in this anthology.) He applied his own writing formula to his editorial task, personally developed writers who could work within that formula and even improve on it . . . and the result was a thing of joy forever!

Like so many revolutionary ideas, Campbell's literary doctrine was quite simple. Science fiction, he argued, should be just that: a story wherein equal stress is placed on each of the two definitive words. In other words, if you were writing for Campbell, you couldn't get away with *anything*. Your science had to be a logical extrapolation of known fact; it had to be presented within a framework of literate, entertaining fiction. As far as "Campbell's law" is concerned, a clumsy sentence or weak characterization is just as taboo as confusing a planet with a star. (And you'd be surprised how many would-be writers still do that latter with appalling regularity.)

Again speaking generally, during the pre-Campbell era the emphasis was on the science and the devil take the fiction. Today, as will be noted later, we are—self-consciously perhaps—preoccupied with our prose and too neglectful of the imaginative potential in our science.

As a corollary to his main idea, Campbell demanded detail. If, for example, you were writing about a civilization of the far future on a Venus-type planet, he demanded an infinite variety of detail on such everyday minutiae of life as clothes, weather, eating habits, food, speech, housing, sports, money, politics and the like. That called for strenuous exercise of the imagination. It demanded intense concentration, for God help you if you slackened your grip just a trifle and allowed the slightest inconsistency to creep into your narrative. But this rigid obedience to Campbell's discipline produced some of the finest speculative writing ever published.

Perhaps the most radical of all his ideas was Campbell's belief that humor had a place, a big place, in science fiction. (See the zany romps of Lewis Padgett herein.)

Another of Campbell's mighty virtues was his liberality. A writer could speculate in any field and the editor egged him on, as long as the scribe's conjectures were plausible and ably presented. Robert A. Heinlein, possibly the greatest of the giants of those days, plotted a future history of the earth, from the twentieth to the twenty-seventh century. Within this framework, Heinlein wrote two novels, six novelettes and four short stories, on such varied subjects as selective breeding for human longevity, housing and religious fascism.

To digress a moment: Heinlein's "future history" wasn't enough to keep him busy. (Writers were prolific in those days!) He concocted a number of ideas that had nothing to do with his "history" and executed these under the pseudonym of Anson MacDonald. (You might compare the offerings of the "two" we have given you.)

Returning to Campbell's liberality: A. E. Van Vogt wrote novels on non-Aristotelian logic; Anthony Boucher, mystery novelist coaxed into science fiction by Campbell, brought an entirely new approach to robotics. Writing in 1942, Lester Del Rey described a blowup in an atomic power plant which, besides being a fine story, is regarded by today's experts as uncanny—and very disturbing prophecy.

It is almost impossible to describe to a later generation the eagerness with which we of that era grabbed each new issue of *Astounding* as it appeared on the newsstands or in our mailboxes. Each number guaranteed a feast of wonder. We gobbled up Heinlein's visions of the future, savored Bester's sadly lovely pictures of man's proneness to fatal error, choked with laughter over Padgett's caustic ribbing of all we held dear, then, the banquet over but still not sated, complained because the last course was finished so soon.

This happy time lasted from 1939 through 1945. Those dates are approximate, for no two devotees will agree as to precisely when it began and when it ended.

Now, by "ending" we emphatically do not mean that John Campbell suddenly lost his genius and that *Astounding*'s high quality disappeared over night. Campbell is still first editor in the field but now he has competition . . . created by himself. Many of the writers he discovered and molded have proved the quality of his teaching by their success in other, more lucrative fields of writing. Since *Astounding* has competition, generated by Campbell's protégés, it no longer can exercise first claim on the works of the titans it spawned, or, for that matter, on the efforts of the lusty youngsters that came after them. And John Campbell would be the first to affirm that this is a healthy situation.

The moving of many of the Campbell-created writers into other fields and the sudden spawning of *Astounding*'s rivals were almost simultaneous developments, and the tracing of their genesis is a confusing process, but we'll do our best to clarify.

Remember that the explosion of the atom bomb suddenly sparked the interest of the general reader in the, to him, hitherto mysterious world of science fiction. Publishers, movie makers and radio producers (there was no television then, remember?) seized upon this new-born interest and tried to make the most of it. (And in the beginning, too many made the worst of it!) There was an insatiable demand for writers and editors who knew something about this weird genre and, with a few exceptions, these could be found only within the ranks of the Campbell trainees.

In this pattern, consider the case of Heinlein. As a result of the popular demand for science fiction, the *Saturday Evening Post* bought several of his stories (well worth the *Post*'s high pay!) that could previously have found a home only in *Astounding*. Then he concocted Tom Corbett, the space cadet, sold the rights to that youth for a tidy sum and royalties, and finally wound up in Hollywood, helping produce his *Destination Moon*, one of the best science fiction films yet produced.

Heinlein wisely refused to stay in Hollywood, but moved to Colorado Springs, where he settled down to writing science fiction—all juveniles (a post atom bomb publishing development and a most lucrative one!), which are yet without a peer and just as enjoyable to adults as to their teen-age audience. Happily, he has been producing "adult" science fiction also within the past few years.

Cinematic rendering of science fiction, although a bonanza for long-neglected authors, was usually anything but that for the audience. While Harry Bates' *Farewell to the Master* was well done as *The Day the Earth Stood Still*, Campbell-Stuart's superb *Who Goes There?* was ignominiously butchered as THE THING! from another world. (We render it exactly.) After the brilliant *Destination Moon*, Hollywood quickly recovered itself and reverted to the old girl-meets-monster-and/or-mad-scientist formula and let it go at that.

While all this was happening, bear in mind that other Campbell stars seemingly had reached a peak in their development where it was urgent that they branch out, try the exercise of their craft in other types of fiction. Cleve Cartmill wrote a series of first-rate "slicks" for *Collier's*. Lewis Padgett and Fredric Brown tried the mystery field. Both have been highly successful, each having reached that financial heaven of the mystery writer—the paperbacks—with pleasing consistency. Anthony Boucher got tangled up in radio as a writer for the Sherlock Holmes and other radio shows and it was several years before he could work himself free.

Publishing of science fiction books followed a violently uneven course for some years after The Bomb, but, as of this writing, seems to have at last settled down to a comparatively small but high-quality annual production. Such Campbell alumni as Alfred Bester and Isaac Asimov regularly produce novels, in both hardcover and paperback, that, in leaner days, could have found a market only in *Astounding*. Certain "freshmen" are giving the old grads tough competition, but more about them later.

Publishing of science fiction books had one unhappy effect. So many of his novels and short stories were printed, reprinted and re-reprinted that A.E. Van Vogt has had, in recent years, no (financial, at least) incentive to go through the labor pains of original creation. And who can blame him?

But it was in the field of magazine publishing that Campbell created the destruction of his own (so richly deserved) "monopoly." By 1949, a massive group of readers, appetites whetted by *Astounding* primarily, a few good movies and books, an occasional decent radio or TV show, were clamoring for more and more fiction with a scientific twist. In that year Anthony Boucher, done with radio, and J. Francis McComas founded *The Magazine of Fantasy & Science Fiction*, a journal whose editorial policies were based firmly on the Campbell doctrine. After them, H. L. Gold, another Campbell pupil, established *Galaxy Science Fiction*. These, with *Astounding*, were once called the "aristocrats" of the field by *Life* magazine.

After *F&SF* and *Galaxy* came a spate of magazines; some dedicated to Campbell's precepts, some not; some died after an issue or two, some still publish regularly. They all had one thing in common— they were a *market* for the writer.

Moreover, tastes and policies of editors vary, no matter how much they have in common. And this is a healthy and stimulating thing for writers.

As editor of the one science fiction magazine, Campbell produced the Golden Age of science fiction. At the same time, he could have only so much time and space for the development of new writers. The birth of other magazines, edited by pupils of the master, more than tripled that time and space.

Many of these younger writers are worthy to stand beside the heroes of the Golden Age. After you have read this book, go to your bookstore or newsstand and read the work of Chad Oliver, Arthur C. Clarke, James Blish, Cyril Kornbluth, Robert Sheckley, Richard Mathesen, or Zenna Henderson . . . to name just a few.

They may be producing their own Golden Age right here and now. Are they? *Fiction*-wise . . . mmmn, could be. *Science*-wise, we have our reservations. If contemporary writing of science fiction is flawed—and mind you, we won't take our oath it is—we believe the flaw lies in the occasional limitations of the thinking of today's writers. Generally, they write first-class fiction. Stylistically, they're better artists than some of the people we've included in this volume. Yet even the best of them is not on a par with Heinlein, say, in the breadth and depth of their speculations about man and his universe.

It may be that his heirs—both writers and editors, and especially the latter—don't have Campbell's penetrating insight into the enormous imaginative potential of present-day scientific fact.

Whatever . . . here is the best of that best of all possible times

in science fiction and, if this is your first exposure to it—my! how we
envy you!

Editors of anthologies have many persons to thank for comfort
and counsel. With the unqualified consent of our Samaritans, we
forego naming them in this edition and instead, thank those writers
of the Golden Age of modern science fiction and, above all, we thank
John W. Campbell, Jr., who made them, and this book, possible.

Los Angeles and Orinda, California
April, 1957

FAMOUS
SCIENCE-FICTION
STORIES

Adventures
in Time and Space

REQUIEM

by

ROBERT A. HEINLEIN

One wonders how Columbus might have felt if circumstances had left him standing on the dock, watching his tiny fleet sail westward without him. Robert Heinlein has envisioned the man who made space travel possible forced by ill-health to stand earthbound and watch the first rocket ship, his ship, soar out through space to the moon. The story of the frustrated pioneer is a rare combination of realistic detail and poignant charm.

*

ON A HIGH HILL in Samoa there is a grave. Inscribed on the marker are these words:

> "Under the wide and starry sky
> Dig my grave and let me lie.
> Glad did I live and gladly die
> And I lay me down with a will!
>
> "This be the verse you grave for me:
> Here he lies where he longed to be,
> Home is the sailor, home from the sea,
> And the hunter home from the hill."

These lines appear another place—scrawled on a shipping tag torn from a compressed-air container, and pinned to the ground with a knife.

It was not much of a fair, as fairs go. The trotting races didn't promise much excitement, even though several entries claimed the blood of the immortal Dan Patch. The tents and concession booths barely covered the circus grounds, and the pitchmen seemed discouraged.

D. D. Harriman's chauffeur could not see any reason for stopping. They were due in Kansas City for a directors' meeting; that is to say, Harriman was. The chauffeur had private reasons for promptness, reasons involving darktown society on Eighteenth Street. But the boss not only stopped; he hung around. He didn't seem much interested in the racetrack or sideshows, though.

Bunting and a canvas arch made the entrance to a large inclosure beyond the racetrack. Red and gold letters announced:

This way to the
MOON ROCKET! ! ! !
See it in actual flight!
Public Demonstration Flights
TWICE DAILY
This is the ACTUAL TYPE used by the
First Men to Reach the *MOON! !*
YOU can ride in it! !—$25

A boy, nine or ten years old, hung around the entrance and stared at the posters.

"Want to see the ship, son?"

The kid's eyes shone. "Gee, mister, I sure would."

"So would I. Come on."

Harriman paid out fifty cents for two pink tickets which entitled him and the boy to enter the inclosure and examine the rocketship. The kid ran on ahead with the single-minded preoccupation of boyhood. Harriman looked over the stubby curved lines of the ovoid body. He noted with a professional eye that she was a single-jet type with fractional controls around her midriff. He squinted through his glasses at the name painted in gold on the carnival red of the body, *Carefree.* He paid another quarter to enter the control cabin.

When his eyes had adjusted to the gloom caused by the strong ray filters of the ports, he let them rest lovingly on the keys of the console and the semi-circle of dials above. Each beloved gadget was in its proper place. He knew them—graven in his heart.

While he mused over the instrument board, with the warm liquid of content soaking through his body, the pilot entered and touched his arm.

"Sorry, sir. We've got to cast loose for the flight."

"Eh?" Harriman started, then looked at the speaker. Handsome devil, with a good skull and strong shoulders—reckless eyes and a self-indulgent mouth, but a firm chin. "Oh, excuse me, captain."

"Quite all right."

"Oh, I say, captain . . . er . . . uh—"

"McIntyre."

"Captain McIntyre, could you take a passenger this trip?" The old man leaned eagerly toward him.

"Why, yes, if you wish. Come along with me." He ushered Harriman into a shed marked "Office" which stood near the gate. "Passenger for a check-over, doc."

Harriman permitted the medico to run a stethoscope over his thin chest and to strap a rubber bandage around his arm. Presently the doctor unstrapped it, glanced at McIntyre, and shook his head.

"No go, doc?"

"That's right, captain."

Harriman looked from face to face, his disappointment plain to see. "You won't take me?"

The doctor shrugged his shoulders. "I couldn't even guarantee that you would live through the take-off. You see, sir," he continued, not unkindly, "it's not only that your heart condition makes heavy acceleration dangerous, but at your age bones are brittle, highly calcified, and easily broken in the shock of take-off. Rocketry is a young man's game."

McIntyre added: "Sorry, sir. I'd like to, but the Bates County Fair Association pays the doctor here to see to it that I don't take up anyone who might be hurt by the acceleration."

The old man's shoulders drooped miserably. "I rather expected it."

"Sorry, sir." McIntyre turned to go, but Harriman followed him out.

"Excuse me, captain—"

"Yes?"

"Could you and your . . . uh . . . engineer have dinner with me after your flight?"

The pilot looked at him quizzically. "I don't see why not. Thanks."

"Captain McIntyre, it is difficult for me to see why anyone would quit the Earth-Moon run," said Harriman a few hours later. Fried chicken and hot biscuits in a private dining room of the best hotel the little town of Butler afforded, three-star Hennessey and Corona

Coronas had produced a friendly atmosphere in which three men could talk freely.

"Well, I didn't like it."

"Aw, don't give him that, Mac—you know damn well it was Rule G that got you." McIntyre's mechanic poured himself another brandy as he spoke.

McIntyre looked sullen. "Well, what if I did take a couple o' drinks? Anyhow, I could have squared that—it was the damn persnickety regulations that got me fed up. Who are you to talk? Smuggler!"

"Sure, I smuggled! Who wouldn't—with all those beautiful rocks just aching to be taken back to Earth? I had a diamond once as big as— But if I hadn't been caught I'd be in Luna City tonight. And so would you, you drunken blaster—with the boys buying us drinks and the girls smiling and making suggestions—" He put his face down and began to weep quietly.

McIntyre shook him. "He's drunk."

"Never mind." Harriman interposed a hand. "Tell me, are you really satisfied not to be on the run any more?"

McIntyre chewed his lip. "No—he's right, of course. This barnstorming isn't what it's all cracked up to be. We've been hopping junk at every pumpkin doin's up and down the Mississippi Valley—sleeping in tourist camps, and eating at greaseburners. Half the time the sheriff has an attachment on the ship, the other half the Society for the Prevention of Something or Other gets an injunction to keep us on the ground. It's no sort of a life for a rocket man."

"Would it help any for you to get to the Moon?"

"Well—yes. I couldn't get back on the Earth-Moon run, but if I was in Luna City, I could get a job hopping ore for the company—they're always short of rocket pilots for that, and they wouldn't mind my record. If I kept my nose clean, they might even put me back on the run, in time."

Harriman fiddled with a spoon, then looked up. "Would you young gentlemen be open to a business proposition?"

"Perhaps. What is it?"

"You own the Carefree?"

"Yeah. That is, Charlie and I do—barring a couple of liens against her. What about it?"

"I want to charter her—for you and Charlie to take me to the Moon!"

Charlie sat up with a jerk. "D'joo hear what he said, Mac? He wants us to fly that old heap to the Moon!"

McIntyre shook his head. "Can't do it, Mr. Harriman. The old boat's worn out. We don't even use standard juice in her—just gasoline and liquid air. Charlie spends all of his time tinkering with her at that. She's going to blow up some day."

"Say, Mr. Harriman," put in Charlie, "what's the matter with getting an excursion permit and going in a company ship?"

"No, son," the old man replied, "I can't do that. You know the conditions under which Congress granted the company a monopoly on lunar exploitation—no one to enter space who was not physically qualified to stand up under it. Company to take full responsibility for the safety and health of all citizens beyond the stratosphere. The official reason for granting the franchise was to stop the enormous loss of life that occurred during the first few years of rocket travel."

"And you can't pass the physical exam?"

Harriman shook his head.

"Well, what the hell—if you can afford to hire us, why don't you just bribe yourself a brace of company docs? It's been done before."

Harriman smiled ruefully. "I know it has, Charlie, but it won't work for me. You see, I'm a little too prominent. My full name is Delos D. Harriman."

"What? You are old D. D.? But, hell's bells, you own a big slice of the company yourself; you ought to be able to do anything you like, rules or no rules."

"That is not an unusual opinion, son, but it is incorrect. Rich men aren't more free than other men; they are less free—a good deal less free. I tried to do what you suggest, but the other directors would not permit me. They are afraid of losing their franchise. It costs them a good deal in—uh—political contact expenses to retain it, as it is."

"Well, I'll be a— Can you tie that, Mac? A guy with lots of dough, and he can't spend it the way he wants to."

McIntyre did not answer, but waited for Harriman to continue.

"Captain McIntyre, if you had a ship, would you take me?"

McIntyre rubbed his chin. "It's against the law."

"I'd make it worth your while."

"Sure, he would, Mr. Harriman. Of course you would, Mac. Luna City! Oh, baby!"

"Why do you want to go to the Moon so badly, Mr. Harriman?"

"Captain, it's the one thing I've really wanted to do all my life—

ever since I was a boy. I don't know whether I can explain it to you or not. You young fellows have grown up to rocket travel the way I grew up to aviation. I'm a great deal older than you are; maybe fifty years older. When I was a kid practically nobody believed that men would ever reach the Moon. You've seen rockets all your lives, and the first to reach the Moon got there before you were old enough to vote. When I was a boy they laughed at the idea.

"But I believed—I believed. I read Verne and Wells and Smith, and I believed that we could do it—that we *would* do it. I set my heart on being one of the men to walk the surface of the Moon, to see her other side, and to look back on the face of the Earth, hanging in the sky.

"I used to go without my lunches to pay my dues in the American Rocket Society, because I wanted to believe that I was helping to bring the day nearer when we would reach the Moon. I was already an old man when that day arrived. I've lived longer than I should, but I would not let myself die—I will not!—until I have set foot on the Moon."

McIntyre stood up and put out his hand. "You find a ship, Mr. Harriman. I'll drive 'er."

"Atta boy, Mac! I told you he would, Mr. Harriman."

Harriman mused and dozed during the hour's run to the north into Kansas City, dozed in the light, troubled sleep of old age. Incidents out of a long life ran through his mind in vagrant dreams. There was that time—oh, yes, 1910—a little boy on a warm spring night. "What's that, daddy?"

"That's Halley's comet, sonny."

"Where did it come from?"

"I don't know, son. From way out in the sky somewhere."

"It's beyooootiful, daddy. I want to touch it."

"'Fraid not, son."

"Delos, do you mean to stand there and tell me you put the money we had saved for the house into that crazy rocket company?"

"Now, Charlotte, please! It's not crazy; it's a sound business investment. Some day soon rockets will fill the sky. Ships and trains will be obsolete. Look what happened to the men that had the foresight to invest in Henry Ford."

"We've been all over this before."

"Charlotte, the day will come when men will rise up off the Earth and visit the Moon, even the planets. This is the beginning."

"Must you shout?"

"I'm sorry, but you—"

"I feel a headache coming on. Please try to be a little quiet when you come to bed."

He hadn't gone to bed. He had sat out on the veranda all night long, watching the full Moon move across the sky. There would be the devil to pay in the morning, the devil and a thin-lipped silence. But he'd stick by his guns. He'd given in on most things, but not on this. The night was his. Tonight he'd be alone with his old friend. He searched her face. Where was Mare Crisium? Funny, he couldn't make it out. He used to be able to see it plainly when he was a boy. Probably needed new glasses—this constant office work wasn't good for his eyes.

But he didn't need to see; he knew where they all were: Crisium, Mare Fecunditatis, Mare Tranquillitatis—that one had a satisfying roll!—the Appenines, the Carpathians, old Tycho with its mysterious rays.

Two hundred and forty thousand miles—ten times around the Earth. Surely men could bridge a little gap like that. Why, he could almost reach out and touch it, nodding there behind the elm trees.

Not that he could help to do it. He hadn't the education.

"Son, I want to have a little serious talk with you."

"Yes, mother."

"I know you had hoped to go to college next year"—Hoped! He had lived for it. The University of Chicago to study under Moulton, then on to the Yerkes Observatory to work under the eye of Dr. Frost himself—"and I had hoped so, too. But with your father gone, and the girls growing up, it's harder to make ends meet. You've been a good boy, and worked hard to help out. I know you'll understand."

"Yes, mother."

"Extra! Extra! Stratosphere Rocket Reaches Paris. Read aaaaalllllll about 't." The thin little man in the bifocals snatched at the paper and hurried back to the office.

"Look at this, A. J."

"Huh? Hm-m-m, interesting, but what of it?"

"Can't you see? The next stage is to the Moon!"

"God, but you're a sucker, Delos. The trouble with you is, you read too many of those trashy magazines. Now, I caught my boy reading one of 'em just last week and dressed him down proper. Your folks should have done you the same favor."

Harriman squared his narrow, middle-aged shoulders. "They will so reach the Moon!"

His partner laughed. "Have it your own way. If baby wants the Moon, papa will bring it home for him. But you stick to your discounts and commissions; that's where the money is."

The big car droned down the Paseo, and turned off on Armour Boulevard. Old Harriman stirred uneasily in his sleep and muttered to himself.

"But, Mr. Harriman—" The young man with the notebook was plainly perturbed. The old man grunted.

"You heard me. Sell 'em. I want every share I own realized in cash as rapidly as possible; Spaceways, Spaceways Provisioning Co., Artemis Mines, Luna City Recreations, the whole lot of them."

"It will depress the market. You won't realize the full value of your holdings."

"Don't you think I know that? I can afford it."

"What about the shares you had earmarked for Tycho Observatory and for the Harriman Scholarships?"

"Oh, yes. Don't sell those. Set up a trust. Should have done it long ago. Tell Mr. Kamens to draw up the papers. He knows what I want."

The interoffice 'visor flashed into life. "The gentlemen are here, Mr. Harriman."

"Send 'em in. That's all, Ashley. Get busy." Ashley went out as McIntyre and Charlie entered. Harriman got up and trotted forward to greet them.

"Come in, boys, come in. I'm so glad to see you. Sit down. Sit down. Have a cigar."

"Mighty pleased to see you, Mr. Harriman," acknowledged Charlie. "In fact, you might say we need to see you."

"Some trouble, gentlemen?" Harriman glanced from face to face. McIntyre answered him.

"You still mean that about a job for us, Mr. Harriman?"

"Mean it? Certainly, I do. You're not backing out on me?"

"Not at all. We need that job now. You see, the *Carefree* is lying in the middle of the Osage River, with her jet split clear back to the injector."

"Dear me! You weren't hurt?"

"No, aside from sprains and bruises. We jumped."

Charlie chortled. "I caught a catfish with my bare teeth."

In short order they got down to business. "You two will have to buy a ship for me. I can't do it openly; my colleagues would figure out what I mean to do and stop me. I'll supply you with all the cash you need. You go out and locate some sort of a ship that can be refitted for the trip. Work up some good story about how you are buying it for some playboy as a stratosphere yacht, or that you plan to try to establish an Arctic-Antarctic tourist route. Anything as long as no one suspects that she is being outfitted for space flight.

"Then, after the department of transport licenses her for strato flight, you move to a piece of desert out West—I'll find a likely parcel of land and buy it—and then I'll join you. Then we'll install the extra fuel tanks, change the injectors and timers and so forth, to fit her for the hop. How about it?"

McIntyre looked dubious. "It'll take a lot of doing. Charlie, do you think you can accomplish that change-over without a dockyard and shops?"

"Me? Sure, I can—with your thick-fingered help. Just give me the tools and materials I want, and don't hurry me too much. Of course, it won't be fancy—"

"Nobody wants it to be fancy. I just want a ship that won't blow when I start slapping the keys."

"It won't blow, Mac."

"That's what you thought about the *Carefree*."

"That ain't fair, Mac. I ask you, Mr. Harriman—that heap was junk, and we knew it. This'll be different. We're going to spend some dough and do it right. Ain't we, Mr. Harriman?"

Harriman patted him on the shoulder. "Certainly we are, Charlie. You can have all the money you want. That's the least of our worries. Now, do the salaries and bonuses I mentioned suit you? I don't want you to be short."

"—as you know, my clients are his nearest relatives and have his interests at heart. We contend that Mr. Harriman's conduct for the past several weeks, as shown by the evidence here adduced, gives clear indication that a mind once brilliant in the world of finance has become senile. It is, therefore, with the deepest regret that we pray this honorable court, if it pleases, to declare Mr. Harriman incompetent and to assign a conservator to protect his financial interests and those of his future heirs and assigns." The attorney sat down, pleased with himself.

Mr. Kamens took the floor. "May it please the court—if my esteemed friend is quite through—I suggest that in his last few words my opponent gave away his entire thesis. 'The financial interests of future heirs and assigns.' It is evident that the petitioners believe that my client should conduct his affairs in such a fashion as to insure that his nieces and nephews, and their issue, will be supported in unearned luxury for the rest of their lives. My client's wife has passed on; he has no children. It is admitted that he has provided generously for his sisters and their children in times past, and that he has established annuities for such near kin as are without means of support.

"But now, like vultures—worse than vultures, for they are not content to let him die in peace—they would prevent my client from enjoying his wealth in whatever manner best suits him for the few remaining years of his life. It is true that he has sold his holdings; is it strange that an elderly man should wish to retire? It is true that he suffered some paper losses in liquidation. 'The value of a thing is what that thing will bring.' He was retiring and demanded cash. Is there anything strange about that?

"It is admitted that he refused to discuss his actions with his so-loving kinfolk. What law, or principle, requires a man to consult with his nephews on anything?

"Therefore, we pray that this court will confirm my client in his right to do what he likes with his own, deny this petition, and send these meddlers about their business."

The judge took off his spectacles and polished them thoughtfully.

"Mr. Kamens, this court has as high a regard for individual liberty as you have, and you may rest assured that any action taken will be solely in the interests of your client. Nevertheless, men do grow old, men do become senile, and in such cases must be protected.

"I shall take this matter under advisement until tomorrow. Court is adjourned."

From the Kansas City *Star*:

ECCENTRIC MILLIONAIRE DISAPPEARS

—failed to appear for the adjourned hearing. The bailiffs returned from a search of places usually frequented by Harriman with the report that he had not been seen since the previous day. A bench warrant under contempt proceedings has been issued and—

A desert sunset is a better stimulant for the appetite than a hot dance orchestra. Charlie testified to this by polishing off the last of the ham gravy with a piece of bread. Harriman handed each of the younger men cigars and took one himself.

"My doctor claims that these weeds are bad for my heart condition," Harriman remarked as he lighted his, "but I've felt so much better since I joined you boys here on the ranch that I am inclined to doubt him." He exhaled a cloud of blue-gray smoke and resumed. "I don't think a man's health depends so much on what he does as on whether he wants to do it. I'm doing what I want to do."

"That's all a man can ask of life," agreed McIntyre.

"How does the work look now, boys?"

"My end's in pretty good shape," Charlie answered. "We finished the second pressure tests on the new tanks and the fuel lines today. The ground tests are all done, except the calibration runs. Those won't take long—just the four hours to make the runs if I don't run into some bugs. How about you, Mac?"

McIntyre ticked them off on his fingers. "Food supplies and water on board. Three vacuum suits, a spare, and service kits. Medical supplies. The buggy already had all the standard equipment for strato flight. The late lunar ephemerides haven't arrived as yet."

"When do you expect them?"

"Any time—they should be here now. Not that it matters. This guff about how hard it is to navigate from here to the Moon is hokum to impress the public. After all, you can see your destination—it's not like ocean navigation. Gimme a sextant and a good stadimeter and I'll set you down any place on the Moon you like—without opening an almanac or a star table—just from a general knowledge of the relative speeds involved."

"Never mind the personal build-up, Columbus," Charlie told him. "We'll admit you can hit the floor with your hat. The general idea is, you're ready to go now. Is that right?"

"That's it."

"That being the case, I could run those tests tonight. I'm getting jumpy—things have been going too smoothly. If you'll give me a hand, we ought to be in bed by midnight."

"O. K. When I finish this cigar."

They smoked in silence for a while, each thinking about the coming trip and what it meant to him. Old Harriman tried to repress the excitement that possessed him at the prospect of immediate realization of his lifelong dream.

"Mr. Harriman—"

"Eh? What is it, Charlie?"

"How does a guy go about getting rich, like you did?"

"Getting rich? I can't say; I never tried to get rich. I never wanted to be rich, or well known, or anything like that."

"Huh?"

"No, I just wanted to live a long time and see it all happen. I wasn't unusual; there were lots of boys like me—radio hams, they were, and telescope builders, and airplane amateurs. We had science clubs, and basement laboratories, and science-fiction leagues—the kind of boys that thought there was more romance in one issue of the *Electrical Experimenter* than in all the books Dumas ever wrote. We didn't want to be one of Horatio Alger's get-rich heroes, either; we wanted to build spaceships. Well, some of us did."

"Gosh, Pop, you make it sound exciting."

"It was exciting, Charlie. This has been a wonderful, romantic century, for all of its bad points. And it's grown more wonderful and more exciting every year. No, I didn't want to be rich; I just wanted to live long enough to see men rise up to the stars, and, if God was good to me, to go as far as the Moon myself." He carefully deposited an inch of white ash in a saucer. "It has been a good life. I haven't any complaints."

McIntyre pushed back his chair. "Come on, Charlie, if you're ready."

"O. K."

They all got up. Harriman started to speak, then grabbed at his chest, his face a dead gray-white.

"Catch him, Mac!"

"Where's his medicine?"

"In his vest pocket."

They eased him over to a couch, broke a small glass capsule in a handkerchief, and held it under his nose. The volatile released by the capsule seemed to bring a little color into his face. They did what little they could for him, then waited for him to regain consciousness.

Charlie broke the uneasy silence. "Mac, we ain't going through with this."

"Why not?"

"It's murder. He'll never stand up under the initial acceleration."

"Maybe not, but it's what he wants to do. You heard him."

"But we oughtn't to let him."

"Why not? It's neither your business nor the business of this damn paternalistic government to tell a man not to risk his life doing what he really wants to do."

"All the same, I don't feel right about it. He's such a swell old duck."

"Then what d'yuh want to do with him—send him back to Kansas City so those old harpies can shut him up in a laughing academy till he dies of a broken heart?"

"N-no-o-o—not that."

"Get out there, and make your set-up for those test runs. I'll be along."

A wide-tired desert runabout rolled into the ranch-yard gate the next morning and stopped in front of the house. A heavy-set man with a firm, but kindly, face climbed out and spoke to McIntyre, who approached to meet him.

"You James McIntyre?"

"What about it?"

"I'm the deputy Federal marshal hereabouts. I got a warrant for your arrest."

"What's the charge?"

"Conspiracy to violate the Space Precautionary Act."

Charlie joined the pair. "What's up, Mac?"

The deputy answered. "You'd be Charles Cummings, I guess. Warrant here for you. Got one for a man named Harriman, too, and a court order to put seals on your spaceship."

"We've no spaceship."

"What d'yuh keep in that big shed?"

"Strato yacht."

"So? Well, I'll put seals on her until a spaceship comes along. Where's Harriman?"

"Right in there." Charlie obliged by pointing, ignoring McIntyre's scowl.

The deputy turned his head. Charlie couldn't have missed the button by a fraction of an inch, for the deputy collapsed quietly to the ground. Charlie stood over him, rubbing his knuckles and mourning.

"That's the finger I broke playing shortstop. I'm always hurting that finger."

"Get Pop into the cabin," Mac cut him short, "and strap him into his hammock."

"Aye, aye, skipper."

They taxied on the auxiliary motor out of the hangar, turned, and started out across the desert plain to find elbow room for the take-off. McIntyre saw the deputy from his starboard conning port. He was staring disconsolately after them.

McIntyre fastened his safety belt, settled his corset, and spoke into the engine-room speaking tube. "All set, Charlie?"

"All set, skipper. But you can't raise ship yet, Mac. *She ain't named!*"

"No time for your superstitions!"

Harriman's thin voice reached them. "Call her the *Lunatic*. It's the only appropriate name!"

McIntyre settled his head into the pads, punched two keys, then three more in rapid succession, and the *Lunatic* raised ground.

"How are you, Pop?"

Charlie searched the old man's face anxiously. Harriman licked his lips and managed to speak. "Doing fine, son. Couldn't be better."

"The acceleration won't be so bad from here on. I'll unstrap you so you can wiggle around a little. But I think you'd better stay in the hammock." He tugged at buckles. Harriman partially repressed a groan.

"What is it, Pop?"

"Nothing. Nothing at all. Just go easy on that side."

Charlie ran his fingers over the old man's side with the sure, delicate touch of a mechanic. "You ain't foolin' me none, Pop. But there isn't much I can do until we ground."

"Charlie—"

"Yes, Pop?"

"Can't I move to a port? I want to watch the Earth."

"Ain't nothin to see yet; the blast hides it. As soon as we build up enough speed to coast up to the change-over point, I'll move you. Tell you what; I'll give you a sleepy pill, and then wake you when we cut the jets."

"No!"

"Huh?"

"I'll stay awake."

"Just as you say, Pop."

Charlie fought his way up to the nose of the ship, and braced himself on the gimbals of the pilot's chair. McIntyre questioned him with his eyes.

"Yeah, he's alive all right," Charlie told him, "but he's in bad shape."

"How bad?"

"Couple of cracked ribs, anyhow. I don't know what else. I don't know whether he'll last out the trip, Mac. His heart was pounding something awful."

"He'll last, Charlie. He's tough."

"Tough? He's delicate as a canary."

"I don't mean that. He's tough way down inside—where it counts."

"Just the same, you'd better set her down awful easy if you want to ground with a full complement aboard."

"I will. I'll make one full swing around the Moon and ease her in on an involute approach curve. We've got enough fuel, I think."

When they commenced to coast in a free orbit, Charlie unslung the hammock and moved Harriman, hammock and all, to a side port. McIntyre turned the ship about a transverse axis so that the tail pointed toward the Sun, then gave a short blast on two tangential jets opposed in couple to cause the ship to spin slowly about her longitudinal axis, and thereby create a slight artificial gravity. The initial weightlessness when coasting commenced had knotted the old man with the characteristic nausea of free flight, and the pilot wished to save his passenger as much discomfort as possible.

But Harriman was not concerned with the condition of his stomach. There it was, all as he had imagined it so many times. The Moon swung majestically past the viewport, twice as wide as he had ever seen it before, all of her familiar features cameo-clear. She gave way to the Earth as the ship continued its slow swing, the Earth itself, as he had envisioned her, appearing like a noble moon, eight times as wide as the Moon appears to the Earthbound, and more luscious, more sensuously beautiful than the silver Moon could be. It was sunset near the Atlantic seaboard—the line of shadow ran down Hudson Bay, slashed through the eastern coast line of North America, touched Cuba, and obscured the eastern bulge of South America. He savored the mellow blue of the Pacific Ocean, felt the texture of the soft green and brown of the continents, admired the blue-white cold of the polar caps. Canada and the great Northwest were obscured by cloud, a vast low-pressure area that spread across the continent. It shone with an even more satisfactory dazzling white than the polar caps.

As the ship swung slowly around, Earth would pass from view, and the stars would march across the port—the same stars he had always known, but steady, brighter, and unwinking against a screen of perfect, live black. Then the Moon would swim into view again to claim his thoughts.

He was serenely happy in a fashion not given to most men, even in a long lifetime. He felt as if he were every man who had ever lived, and looked up at the stars, and longed.

At least once he must have fallen into deep sleep, or possibly delirium, for he came to with a start, thinking that his wife, Charlotte, was calling to him. "Delos!" the voice had said. "Delos! Come in from there! You'll catch your death of cold in that night air."

Poor Charlotte! She had been a good wife to him, a good wife. He was quite sure that her only regret in dying had been her fear that he would not take proper care of himself. It had not been her fault that she had not shared his dream and his need.

Charlie rigged the hammock in such a fashion that Harriman could watch from the starboard port when they swung around the far face of the Moon. He picked out the landmarks made familiar to him by a thousand photographs with nostalgic pleasure, as if he were returning to his own country. McIntyre brought her slowly down as they came back around to the Earthward face, and prepared to land in Mare Imbrium between Aristillus and Archimedes, about ten miles from Luna City.

It was not a bad landing, all things considered. He had to land without coaching from the ground, and he had no second pilot to punch the stadimeter for him. In his anxiety to make it gentle he missed his destination by some thirty miles, but he did his cold-sober best. At that, it was rather bumpy.

As they scooted along to a stop, throwing up powdery pumice on each side, Charlie came up to the control station.

"How's our passenger?" Mac demanded.

"I'll see, but I wouldn't make any bets. That landing stunk, Mac."

"Damn it, I did my best."

"I know you did, skipper. Forget it."

But the passenger was alive and conscious, though bleeding from the nose, and with a pink foam on his lips. He was feebly trying to get himself out of his cocoon. They helped him, working together.

"Where are the vacuum suits?" was his first remark.

"Steady, Mr. Harriman. You can't go out there yet. We've got to give you some first aid."

"Get me that suit! First aid can wait."

Silently they did as he ordered. His left leg was practically useless, and they had to help him through the lock, one on each side. But with his inconsiderable mass having a lunar weight of only twenty pounds, he was no burden. They found a place some fifty yards from the ship where they could prop him up and let him look, a chunk of scoria supporting nis head.

McIntyre put his helmet against the old man's and spoke. "We'll leave you here to enjoy the view while we get ready for the trek into town. It's a forty-miler, pretty near, and we'll have to break out spare air bottles and rations and stuff. We'll be back soon."

Harriman nodded without answering, and squeezed their gauntlets with a grip that was surprisingly strong.

He sat very quiet, rubbing his hands against the soil of the Moon and sensing the curiously light pressure of his body against the ground. At long last there was peace in his heart. His hurts had ceased to pain him. He was where he had longed to be—he had followed his need. Overhead hung the Earth in third quarter, a green-blue giant moon. The Sun's upper limb crowned the crags of Archimedes to his left. And underneath—the Moon; the soil of the Moon itself. He was on the Moon!

He lay back still while a bath of content flowed over him like a tide at flood, and soaked into his very marrow.

His attention strayed momentarily, and he thought once again that his name was called. Silly, he thought; I'm getting old—my mind wanders.

Back in the cabin Charlie and Mac were rigging shoulder yokes on a stretcher. "There. That will do," Mac commented. "We'd better stir Pop out; we ought to be going."

"I'll get him," Charlie replied. "I'll just pick him up and carry him. He don't weigh nothing."

Charlie was gone longer than McIntyre had expected him to be. He returned alone. Mac waited for him to close the lock and swing back his helmet. "Trouble?"

"Never mind the stretcher, skipper. We won't be needin' it. Yeah, I mean it," he continued. "I did what was necessary."

McIntyre bent down without a word and commenced to strap on the wide skis necessary to negotiate the powdery ash. Charlie followed his example. Then they swung spare air bottles over their shoulders and passed out through the lock.

They didn't bother to close the outer door of the lock behind them.

Charlie looked toward the relaxed figure propped up on the bed of Lunar pumice, face fixed toward the Earth. "Well," he grunted, "he hit the Moon—"

FORGETFULNESS

by

DON A. STUART

Mr. Stuart's picture of the ultimate destiny of man is very nearly a mystical vision of human perfection. He writes of that dim, distant day when man shall not only have mastered his science, but himself. And the result is not teeming cities whose buildings tower to the sky. No. Cities need power and engines and tools. And man is tired of all these. In fact, he has forgotten most of them. But not all, as those well-meaning visitors from outer space discovered when they attempted to change the proper course of history.

*

RON THULE, the astronomer, stood in the lock gate and looked down across the sweep of gently rolling land. Slowly, he breathed in the strange, tangy odors of this planet. There was something of a vast triumph in his eyes, and something of sorrow. They had been here now scarcely five hours, and the sun was still low in the east, rising slowly. Out beyond, above the western horizon, a pale ghost of the strange twin world of this planet, less than a third of a million miles distant, seemed a faint, luminous cloud in the deep, serene blue of the sky.

It was triumph, for six long years of travel, at a speed close to that of light, lay behind them; three and a half light years distant was Pareeth, and the crowding people who had built and launched the mighty two-thousand-five-hundred foot, interstellar cruiser that had brought this little band of one hundred. Launched in hope and striving, seeking a new sun with new planets, new worlds to colonize. More than that, even, for this new-found planet was a stepping-stone to other infinities beyond. Ten years of unbroken travel was the maximum any ship they could build would endure. They had found a planet, in fact, nine planets. Now, the range they might explore for new worlds was extended by four light years.

And there was sorrow there, too, for there was a race here now. Ron Thule turned his eyes toward the little clustering village nestled in the swale of the hills, a village of simple, rounded domes of some opalescent, glassy material. A score of them straggled irregularly among the mighty, deep-green trees that shaded them from the morning sun, twenty-foot domes of pearl and rose and blue. The deep green of the trees and the soft green of the mosslike grass that covered all the low, rounded hills gave it a certain beauty; the sparkling colors of the little gardens about the domes added color and further beauty. It was a lovely spot, a spot where space-wearied, interstellar wanderers might rest in delight. A village, indeed, where anyone might rest in ease and enjoyment, after long, long labors.

Such it was. There was a race on this planet the men of Pareeth had found after six long years of space, six years of purring, humming atomic engines and echoing gray steel fabric that carried and protected them. Harsh utility of giant girders and rubbery flooring, the snoring drone of forty quadrillion horse power of atomic engines. It was replaced now by the soft coolness of the grassy land; the curving steel of the girders gave way to the brown of arching trees; the stern ceiling of steel plates gave way to the vast, blue arch of a planet's atmosphere. Sounds died away in infinitudes where there was no steel to echo them back; the unending drone of the mighty engines had become breezes stirring, rustling leaves—an invitation to rest.

The race that lived here had long since found it such, it seemed. Ron Thule looked across the little village of domes to the largest of them, perhaps thirty feet across. Commander Shor Nun was there with his archeologist and anthropologist—and a half score men of this planet. Rhth, they called it.

The conference was breaking up now. Shor Nun appeared, tall and powerful, his muscular figure in trim Interstellar Expedition uniform of utilitarian, silvery gray. Behind him came the other two in uniform —young, powerful men of Pareeth, selected for this expedition because of physical and mental perfection, as was every man of them.

Then came Seun, the man of Rhth. He was taller, slimmer, an almost willowy figure. His lean body was clothed in an elastic, close-fitting suit of golden stuff, while over his shoulders a glowing, magnificently shimmering cape of rich blue was thrown. Five more of these men came out, each in a golden suit, but the draped capes glowed in deep reds, and rich greens, blues and violets. They walked leisurely beside the men of Pareeth. An unconscious force made those trimly uniformed men walk in step between the great, arching trees.

They came near, and Shor Nun called out, "Is the expedition ready?"

From the forward lock, Toth Mour replied, "Aye, commander. Twenty-two men. What do these people say?"

Shor Nun shook his head slightly. "That we may look as we wish. The city is deserted. I cannot understand them. What arrangements have you made?"

"The men you mentioned are coming. Each head of department, save Ron Thule. There will be no work for the astronomer."

"I will come, Shor Nun," called out the astronomer, softly. "I can sketch; I would be interested."

"Well enough, as you like. Toth Mour, call the men into formation; we will start at once. The day varies in length, but is some thirteen hours long at this season, I am told."

Ron Thule leaped down to the soft turf and walked over toward the group. Seun looked at him slowly and smiled. The man of Rhth looked taller from this distance, nearly six and a third feet in height. His face was tanned to a golden color that came near to matching the gold of his clothing. His eyes were blue and very deep. They seemed uncertain—a little puzzled, curious about these men, curious about the vast, gray bulk that had settled like a grim shadow over the low hill. Half a mile in length, four hundred feet in diameter, it loomed nearly as large as the age-old, eroded hills it had berthed on. He ran a slim-fingered hand through the glinting golden hair that curled in unruly locks above a broad, smooth brow.

"There is something for an astronomer in all this world, I think." He smiled at Ron Thule. "Are not climate and soils and atmospheres the province of astronomy, too?"

"The chemists know it better," Ron Thule replied, and wondered slightly at his replying. He knew that the man of Rhth had not spoken, simply that the thought had come to be in his mind. "Each will have his special work, save for me. I will look at the city. They will look at the buildings and girders and the carvings or mechanisms, as is their choice. I will look at the city."

Uneasily, he moved away from the group, started alone across the field. Uneasiness settled on him when he was near this Seun, this descendant of a race that had been great ten millions of years before his own first sprang from the swamps. Cheated heir to a glory five million years lost.

The low, green roll of the hill fell behind him as he climbed the grassy flank. Very slowly before his eyes, the city lifted into view. Where the swelling curve of the hill faded softly into the infinite blue of the sky, first one little point, then a score, then hundreds appeared, as he walked up the crest—the city.

Then he stood on the crest. The city towered before him—five miles away across the gently rolling green swale. Titan city of a Titan race! The towers glowed with a sun-fired opalescence in the golden light of the sun. How long, great gods of this strange world, how long had they stood thus? Three thousand feet they rose from the level of age-sifted soil at their bases, three thousand feet of mighty mass, stupendous buildings of the giants long dead.

The strange little man from a strange little world circling a dim, forgotten star looked up at them, and they did not know, or care. He walked toward them, watched them climb into the blue of the sky. He crossed the broad green of the land, and they grew in their uncaring majesty.

Sheer, colossal mass, immeasurable weights and loading they were —and they seemed to float there on the grace of a line and a curve, half in the deep blue of the sky, half touching the warm, bright green of the land. They floated still on the strength of a dream dreamed by a man dead these millions of years. A brain had dreamed in terms of lines and curves and sweeping planes, and the brain had built in terms of opal crystal and vast masses. The mortal mind was buried under unknown ages, but an immortal idea had swept life into the dead masses it molded—they lived and floated still on the memory of a mighty glory. The glory of the race—

The race that lived in twenty-foot, rounded domes.

The astronomer turned. Hidden now by the rise of the verdant land was one of the villages that race built today. Low, rounded things, built, perhaps, of this same, strange, gleaming crystal, a secret half remembered from a day that must have been—

The city flamed before him. Across ten—or was it twenty—thousand millenniums, the thought of the builders reached to this man of another race. A builder who thought and dreamed of a mighty future, marching on, on forever in the aisles of time. He must have looked from some high, wind-swept balcony of the city to a star-sprinkled sky—and seen the argosies of space: mighty treasure ships that swept back to this remembered home, coming in from the legion worlds of space, from far stars and unknown, clustered suns; Titan ships, burdened with strange cargoes of unguessed things.

And the city peopled itself before him; the skies stirred in a moment's flash. It was the day of Rhth's glory then! Mile-long ships hovered in the blue, settling, slow, slow, home from worlds they'd circled. Familiar sights, familiar sounds, greeting their men again. Flashing darts of silver that twisted through mazes of the upper air, the soft, vast music of the mighty city. The builder lived, and looked out across his dream——

But, perhaps, from his height in the looming towers he could see across the swelling ground to the low, rounded domes of his people, his far descendants seeking the friendly shelter of the shading trees—

Ron Thule stood among the buildings of the city. He trod a pavement of soft, green moss, and looked behind to the swell of the land. The wind had laid this pavement. The moving air was the only force that maintained the city's walks. A thousand thousand years it has swept its gatherings across the plain, and deposited them as an offering at the base of these calm towers. The land had built up slowly, age on age, till it was five hundred feet higher than the land the builder had seen.

But his dream was too well built for time to melt away. Slowly time was burying it, even as, long since, time had buried him. The towers took no notice. They dreamed up to the blue of the skies and waited. They were patient; they had waited now a million, or was it ten million years? Some day, some year, the builders must return, dropping in their remembered argosies from the far, dim reaches of space, as they had once these ages gone. The towers waited; they were faithful to their trust. They had their memories, memories of a mighty age, when giants walked and worlds beyond the stars paid tribute to the city. Their builders would come again. Till then—naught bothered them in their silence.

But where the soft rains of a hundred thousand generations had drained from them, their infinite endurance softened to its gentle touch. Etched channels and rounded gutters, the mighty carvings dimming, rounding, their powerful features betrayed the slow effects. Perhaps—it had been so long—so long—even the city was forgetting what once it was. They had waited, these towers, for. . . .

And the builders walked in the shade of the trees, and built rounded domes. And a new race of builders was come, a race the city did not notice in its age-long quiet. Ron Thule looked up to them and wondered if it were to be that his people should carry on the dream begun so long ago.

Softened by the silence, voices from the expedition reached him. "—diamond won't scratch it, Shor Nun—more elastic than beryl steel. Tough——" That was Dee Lun, the metallurgist. He would learn that secret somehow. They would all learn. And Shor Nun, commander, executive, atomic engineer, would learn the secrets that their power plants must hold. The dream—the city's life—would go on!

Ron Thule wandered on. No duty his, today, no responsibility to study carefully the form and turn of sweeping line, the hidden art that floated ten millions of tons of mass on the grace of a line. That for the archeologist and the engineer. Nor his to study the cunning form of brace and girder, the making of the pearly walls. That for metallurgist and chemist.

Seun was beside him, looking slowly about the great avenues that swept away into slim canyons in the distance.

"Your people visited ours, once," said Ron Thule softly. "There are legends, the golden gods that came to Pareeth, bringing gifts of fire and the bow and the hammer. The myths have endured through two millions of our years—four and a half millions of yours. With fire and bow and hammer my people climbed to civilization. With atomic power they blasted themselves back to the swamps. Four times they climbed, discovered the secret of the atom, and blasted themselves back to the swamps. Yet all the changes could not efface the thankfulness to the golden gods, who came when Pareeth was young."

Seun nodded slowly. His unspoken thoughts formed clear and sharp in the astronomer's mind. "Yes, I know. The city builders, it was. Once, your sun and ours circled in a system as a double star. A wandering star crashed through that system, breaking it, and in the breaking making planets. Your sun circled away, the new-formed planets cooling; our sun remained, these worlds cooling till the day life appeared. We are twin races, born of the same stellar birth. The city builders found that, and sought your worlds. They were a hundred thousand light years distant, in that time, across all the width

of the galaxy, as the two suns circled in separate orbits about the
mass of the galaxy.

"The city builders went to see your race but once; they had
meant to return, but before the return was made they had interfered in the history of another race, helping them. For their reward
the city builders were attacked by their own weapons, by their own
pupils. Never again have we disturbed another race."

"Across the galaxy, though. The Great Year—how could they—
so many stars——"

"The problem of multiple bodies? The city builders solved it;
they traced the orbits of all the suns of all space; they knew then
what sun must once have circled with ours. The mathematics of
it—I have forgotten—I cannot develop it. I am afraid I cannot answer
your thoughts. My people have forgotten so many things the city
builders knew.

"But your people seek entrance to the buildings. I know the city,
all its ways and entrances. The drifting soil has covered every doorway, save those that once were used for the great airships. They are
still unblocked. I know of one at this level, I think. Perhaps——"

II

Ron Thule walked slowly back toward the group. Seun was speaking with Shor Nun, and now they angled off across the city. Their
voices hushed; their footfalls were lost in the silence that brooded
forever over the towers. Down timeless avenues they marched, a
tiny band in the valley of the Titans. The towers marched on and
on, on either side, up over low hills, beyond the horizon. Then,
before them, in the side of one of the milky walls a great opening
showed. Some five feet above the level of the drifted soil, it led
into the vast, black maw of the building. The little party grouped at
the base, then, laboriously, one of the engineers boosted and climbed
his way to the threshold and dropped a rope to a companion.

Seun stood a bit apart, till Shor Nun lifted himself up to the
higher level and stood on the milky floor. Then the man of Rhth
seemed to glow slightly; a golden haze surrounded him and he
floated effortlessly up from the ground and into the doorway.

The engineers, Shor Nun, all stood frozen, watching him. Seun
stopped, turned, half smiling. "How? It is the *lathan*, the suit I
wear."

"It defies gravity?" asked Shor Nun, his dark eyes narrowing in keenest interest.

"Defies gravity? No, it does not defy, for gravity is a natural law. The city builders knew that. They made these suits shortly before they left the city. The *lathan* simply bends gravity to will. The mechanism is in the filaments of the back, servant to a wish. Its operation—I know only vague principles. I--I have forgotten so much. I will try to explain——"

Ron Thule felt the thoughts parading through his mind: Nodes and vibrations, atoms and less than atoms, a strange, invisible fabric of woven strains that were not there. His mind rebelled. Vague, inchoate stirrings of ideas that had no clarity; the thoughts were formless and indistinct, uncertain of themselves. They broke off.

"We have forgotten so much of the things the city builders knew, their arts and techniques," Seun explained. "They built things and labored that things might surround and protect them, as they thought. They labored generations that this city might be. They strove and thought and worked, and built fleets that sailed beyond the farthest star the clearest night reveals. They brought here their gains, their hard-won treasures—that they might build and make to protect these things.

"They were impermanent things, at best. How little is left of their five-million-year striving! We have no things today, nor any protecting of things. And we have forgotten the arts they developed to protect and understand these things. And with them, I am sorry, I have forgotten the thoughts that make the *lathan* understandable."

Shor Nun nodded slowly, turned to his party. Ron Thule looked back from this slight elevation, down the long avenue. And his eyes wandered aside to this descendant of the mighty dreamers, who dreamed no more.

"Seek passages to lower levels," said Shor Nun's voice. "Their records, their main interest must have centered near the ancient ground level. The engineers—we will seek the lowest, subsurface levels, where the powers and the forces of the city must have been generated. Come."

The opalescent light that filtered through the walls of the building faded to a rose dusk as they burrowed deeper into the vast pile. Corridors branched and turned; rooms and offices dust-littered and barren opened from them. Down the great two-hundred-foot corridor by which they had entered, ships had once floated, and at the heart of the building was a cavernous place where these ships had once rested—and rested still! Great, dim shapes, half seen in the misted light that filtered through wall on translucent wall.

The room blazed suddenly with the white light of half a dozen atomic torches, and the opalescent walls of the room reflected the flare across the flat, dusty sweep of the great floor. Twoscore smooth shapes of flowing lines clustered on the floor, a forgotten company of travelers that had stopped here once, when the city roared in triumphant life. A powdery, gray dust covered their crystal hulls.

Slowly, Shor Nun walked toward the nearest of them, a slim, thirty-foot-long private ship, waiting through eternity for a forgotten hand. The open lock at the side lighted suddenly at the touch of his foot, and soft lights appeared throughout the ship. Somewhere a soft, low humming began, and faded into silence in a moment. "Drus Nol —come with me. Seun, do you know the mechanism of these ships?"

The man of Rhth hesitated, then shook his head slowly. "I cannot explain it." He sighed. "They will not function now; they drew their power from the central plant of the city, and that has ceased operation. The last of the city builders shut it down as they left."

The men of Pareeth entered the ship hesitantly, and even while they walked toward the central control cabin at the nose, the white lighting dimmed through yellow, and faded out. Only their own torches remained. The stored power that had lain hidden in some cells aboard this craft was gone in a last, fitful glow. Somewhere soft, muffled thuds of relays acted, switching vainly to seek charged, emergency cells. The lights flared and died, flared and vanished. The questing relays relaxed with a tired click.

Dust-shrouded mechanism, etched in the light of flaring torches, greeted their eyes, hunched bulks, and gleaming tubes of glassy stuff that, by its sparkling, fiery life must be other than any glass they knew, more nearly kin to the brilliant refraction of the diamond.

"The power plant," said Shor Nun softly, "I think we had best look at that first. These are probably decayed; there might still be some stored power in the central plant they could pick up and give us a fatal shock. The insulation here——"

But the city builders had built well. There was no sign of frayed and age-rotted insulation. Only slight gray dust lay in torn blankets, tender fabric their movements had disturbed.

Seun walked slowly toward the far end of the room, rounding the silent, lightless bulks of the ancient ships. The dust of forgotten ages stirred softly in his wake, settled behind him. The men of Pareeth gathered in his steps, followed him toward the far wall.

A doorway opened there, and they entered a small room. The archeologist's breath whistled; the four walls were decorated with friezes of the history of the race that had built, conquered and sailed a universe—and lived in domes under sheltering trees.

Seun saw his interest, touched a panel at his side. Soundlessly, a door slid from the wall, clicked softly, and completed the frieze on that wall. The archeologist was sketching swiftly, speaking to the chemist and the photographer as he worked. The torches flared higher for a moment, and the men moved about in the twenty-foot room, making way for the remembering eye of the little camera.

As Seun touched another stud, the door slid back into the wall. The room of the ships was gone. Hastily, the men of Pareeth turned to Seun.

"Will that elevator work safely to raise us again? You said the power was cut off——"

"There is stored power. Nearly all had leaked away, but it was designed to be sufficient to run all this city and all its ships, wherever they might be, for seven days. There is power enough. And there are foot passages if you fear the power will not be sufficient. This is the lowest level; this is the level of the machines, the heart of the city —nearly one thousand feet below the level at which we entered."

"Are the machines, the power plant, in this building?"

"There is only one building, here beneath the ground. It is the city, but it has many heads. The power plant is off here, I think. It has been a long time since I came this way. I was young then, and the city builders fascinated me. Their story is interesting and——"

"Interesting——" The thought seemed to echo in Ron Thule's mind. The story of the conquest of a universe, the story of achievement such as his race dreamed of now. They had dreamed—and done. And that, to their descendants, that was—interesting. Interesting to this dark, strange labyrinth of branching corridors, and strange, hooded bulks. Production machinery, he knew, somehow, production machinery that forgotten workmen had hooded as they stepped away temporarily—for a year or two, perhaps till the waning population should increase again and make new demands on it. Then great storerooms, bundled things that might be needed, spare parts, and stored records and deeds. Libraries of dull metal under gray dust. The unneeded efforts of a thousand generations, rotting in this quiet dark that he, Ron Thule, and his companions had disturbed with the moment's rush of atomic flame.

Then the tortuous corridor branched, joined others, became suddenly a great avenue descending into the power room, the heart of the city and all that it had meant. They waited still, the mighty engines the last of the builders had shut down as he left, waited to start again the work they had dropped for the moment, taking a well-earned rest. But they must have grown tired in that rest, that waiting for the resurgence of their masters. They glowed dimly under the thin blankets of grayed dust, reflecting the clear brilliance of the prying light.

Shor Nun halted at the gate, his engineer beside him. Slowly, Seun of Rhth paced into the great chamber. "By the golden gods of Pareeth, Drus Nol, do you see that insulation—those buss-bars!"

"Five million volts, if it's no better than we build," the engineer said, "and I suppose they must be busses, though, by the stars of space, they look like columns! They're twenty-five feet through. But, man, man, the generator—for it must be a generator—it's no longer than the busses it energizes."

"When the generator operated," Seun's thoughts came, "the field it created ran through the bars, so that they, too, became nearly perfect conductors. The generator supplied the city, and its ships, wherever in all space they might be." And the further thought came into their minds, "It was the finest thing the city builders had."

Shor Nun stepped over the threshold. His eyes followed the immense busses, across in a great loop to a dimly sparkling switch panel, then across, and down to a thing in the center of the hall, a thing——

Shor Nun cried out, laughed and sobbed all at one moment. His hands clawed at his eyes; he fell to his knees, groaning. "Don't look—by the gods, don't look——" he gasped.

Drus Nol leaped forward, bent at his side. Shor Nun's feet moved in slow arcs through the dust of the floor, and his hands covered his face.

Seun of Rhth stepped over to him with a strange deliberation that yet was speed. "Shor Nun," came his thought, and the man of Pareeth straightened under it, "stand up."

Slowly, like an automatum, the commander of the expedition rose, twitching, his hands falling to his sides. His eyes were blank, white things in their sockets, and horrible to look at.

"Shor Nun, look at me, turn your eyes on me," said Seun. He stood half a head taller than the man of Pareeth, very slim and straight, and his eyes seemed to glow in the light that surrounded him.

As though pulled by a greater force, Shor Nun's eyes turned slowly, and first their brown edges, then the pupils showed again. The frozen madness in his face relaxed; he slumped softly into a more natural position—and Seun looked away.

Unsteadily, Shor Nun sat down on a great angling beam. "Don't look for the end of those busses, Drus Nol—it is not good. They knew all the universe, and the ends of it, long before they built this city. The things these men have forgotten embrace all the knowledge our race has, and a thousand thousand times more, and yet they have the ancient characteristics that made certain things possible to the city builders. I do not know what that thing may be, but my eyes had to follow it, and it went into another dimension. Seun, what is that thing?"

"The generator supplied the power for the city, and for the ships of the city, wherever they might be in space. In all the universe they could draw on the power of that generator, through that sorgan unit. That was the master unit; from it flowed the power of the generator, instantaneously, to any ship in all space, so long as its corresponding unit was tuned. It created a field rotating"—and the minds of his hearers refused the term—"which involves, as well, time.

"In the first revolution it made, the first day it was built, it circled to the ultimate end of time and the universe, and back to the day it was built. And in all that sweep, every sorgan unit tuned to it must follow. The power that drove it died when the city was deserted, but it is still making the first revolution, which it made and completed in the first hundredth of a second it existed.

"Because it circled to the end of time, it passed this moment in its swing, and every other moment that ever is to be. Were you to wipe it out with your mightiest atomic blast, it would not be disturbed, for it is in the next instant, as it was when it was built. And so it is at the end of time, unchanged. Nothing in space or time can alter that, for it has already been at the end of time. That is why it rotates still, and will rotate when this world dissolves, and the stars die out and scatter as dust in space. Only when the ultimate equality is established, when no more change is, or can be will it be at rest—for then other things will be equal to it, all space equated to it, because space, too, will be unchanged through time.

"Since, in its first swing, it turned to that time, and back to the day it was built, it radiated its power to the end of space and back. Anywhere, it might be drawn on, and was drawn on by the ships that sailed to other stars."

Ron Thule glanced very quickly toward and away from the sorgan unit. It rotated motionlessly, twinkling and winking in swift immobility. It was some ten feet in diameter, a round spheroid of rigidly fixed coils that slipped away and away in flashing speed. His eyes twisted and his thoughts seemed to freeze as he looked at it. Then he seemed to see beyond and through it, as though it were an infinite window, to ten thousand other immobile, swiftly spinning coils revolving in perfect harmony, and beyond them to strange stars and worlds beyond the suns—a thousand cities such as this on a thousand planets: the empire of the city builders!

And the dream faded—faded as that dream in stone and crystal and metal, everlasting reality, had faded in the softness of human tissue.

III

The ship hung motionless over the towers for a long moment. Sunlight, reddened as the stars sank behind the far hills, flushed their opalescent beauty with a soft tint, softened even the harsh, utilitarian gray of the great, inter-stellar cruiser above them into an idle, rosy dream. A dream, perhaps, such as the towers had dreamed ten thousand times ten thousand times these long aeons they had waited?

Ron Thule looked down at them, and a feeling of satisfaction and fulfillment came to him. Pareeth would send her children. A colony here, on this ancient world, would bring a new, stronger blood to wash up in a great tide, to carry the ideals this race had forgotten to new heights, new achievements. Over the low hills, visible from this elevation, lay the simple, rounded domes of the people of Rhth—Seun and his little clan of half a hundred—the dwindling representatives of a once-great race.

It would mean death to these people—these last descendants. A new world, busy with a great work of reconquering this system, then all space! They would have no time to protect and care for these forgetful ones; these people of Rhth inevitably would dwindle swiftly in a strange, busy world. They who had forgotten progress five millions of years before; they who had been untrue to the dream of the city builders.

It was for Pareeth, and the sons of Pareeth to carry on the abandoned path again——

CONCLUSION OF THE REPORT
TO THE COMMITTEE OF
PAREETH
SUBMITTED BY SHOR NUN,
COMMANDER OF THE FIRST
INTERSTELLAR EXPEDITION

—thus it seemed wise to me that we leave at the end of a single
week, despite the objections of those members of the expedition
personnel who had had no opportunity to see this world. It was better
not to disturb the decadent inhabitants of Rhth in any further degree,
and better that we return to Pareeth with these reports as soon as
might be, since building operations would soon commence on the
twelve new ships.

I suggest that these new ships be built of the new material *rhthite*,
superior to our best previous materials. As has been shown by the incredible endurance of the buildings of the city, this material is exceedingly stable, and we have found it may be synthesized from the
cheapest materials, saving many millions in the construction work to
be undertaken.

It has been suggested by a certain member of the expedition,
notable Thon Raul, the anthropologist, that we may underestimate
the degree of civilization actually retained by the people of Rhth,
specifically that it is possible that a type of civilization exists so radically divergent from our own, that it is to us unrecognizable as civilization. His suggestion of a purely mental civilization of a high order
seems untenable in the face of the fact that Seun, a man well respected by his fellows, was unable to project his thoughts clearly at
any time, nor was there any evidence that any large proportion of his
thoughts were to himself of a high order of clarity. His answers
were typified by "I have forgotten the development——" or "It is
difficult for me to explain——" or "The exact mechanism is not
understood by all of us—a few historians——"

It is, of course, impossible to disprove the assertion that such a
civilization is possible, but there arises in my mind the question of
advantage gained, it being a maxim of any evolutionary or advancing

process that the change so made is, in some manner, beneficial to the modified organism of society. Evidently, on the statements made by Seun of Rhth, they have forgotten the knowledge once held by the mighty race that built the cities, and have receded to a state of repose without labor or progress of any kind.

Thon Raul has mentioned the effect produced on me by close observation of the *sorgan* mechanism, and further stated that Seun was able to watch this same mechanism without trouble, and able to benefit me after my unfortunate experience. I would point out that mental potentialities decline extremely slowly; it is possible that the present decadent people have the mental potentialities, still inherent in them, that permitted the immense civilization of the city builders.

It lies there, dormant. They are lost for lack of the driving will that makes it effective. The *Pareeth*, the greatest ship our race has ever built, is powered, fueled, potentially mighty now—and inert for lack of a man's driving will, since no one is at her helm.

So it is with them. Still, the mental capacity of the race overshadows us. But the divine fire of ambition has died. They rely wholly on materials and tools given them by a long-dead people, using even these in an automatic and uncomprehending way, as they do their curious flying suits.

Finally, it is our conclusion that the twelve ships under consideration should be completed with all possible speed, and the program as at present outlined carried out in full; i.e. seven thousand, six hundred and thirty-eight men and women between the ages of eighteen and twenty-eight will be selected on a basis of health, previous family history, personal character and ability as determined by psychological tests. These will be transported, together with a basic list of necessities, to the new planet, leaving in the early months of the coming year.

Six years will be required for this trip. At the end of the first year on the new planet, when some degree of organization has been attained, one ship, refueled, will return to Pareeth. At the end of the second year two ships will return from Rhth with all data accumulated in that period. Thereafter, two will sail each year.

On Pareeth, new ships will be manufactured at whatever rate seems practicable, that more colonists may be sent as swiftly as they desire. It is suggested, however, that, in view of the immense scientific advancements already seen in the cities of Rhth, no new ships be made until a ship returns with the reports of the first year's studies, in order that any resultant scientific advances may be incorporated.

The present crew of the *Pareeth* have proven themselves in every way competent, courageous and coöperative. As trained and experienced interstellar operators, it is further suggested that the one hundred men be divided among the thirteen ships to sail, the *Pareeth* retaining at least fifty of her present crew and acting as guide to the remainder of the fleet. Ron Thule, it is specifically requested, shall be astronomical commander of the fleet aboard the flagship. His astronomical work in positioning and calculating the new system has been of the highest order, and his presence is vitally needed.

Signed by me, SHOR NUN, this
thirty-second day after landing.

UNANIMOUS REPORT OF THE COMMITTEE OF PAREETH ON THE FIRST EXPEDITION TO THE PLANET RHTH

The Committee of Pareeth, after due consideration of the reports of Folder R127-s6-I1, entitled "Interstellar Exploration Reports, Expedition I" do send to commander of said expedition, Shor Nun, greetings.

The committee finds the reports highly satisfying, both in view of the successful nature of the expedition, and in that they represent an almost unanimous opinion.

In consequence, it is ordered that the ships designated by the department of engineering plan as numbers 18834-18846 be constructed with such expedition as is possible.

It is ordered that the seven thousand six hundred and thirty-eight young people be chosen in the manner prescribed in the attached docket of details.

It is ordered that in the event of the successful termination of the new colonizing expedition, such arrangements shall be made that the present decadent inhabitants of the planet Rhth shall be allowed free and plentiful land; that they shall be in no way molested or attacked. It is the policy of this committee of Pareeth that this race shall be wards of the newly founded Rhth State, to be protected and in all ways aided in their life.

We feel, further, a deep obligation to this race in that the archeological and anthropological reports clearly indicate that it was the race known to them as the city builders who first brought fire, the bow and the hammer to our race in mythological times. Once their race gave ours a foothold on the climb to civilization. It is our firm policy that these last decadent members of that great race shall be given all protection, assistance and encouragement possible to tread again the climbing path.

It is ordered that the first colony city on Rhth shall be established at the spot represented on the accompanying maps as N'yor, as called in the language of the Rhth people, near the point of landing of the first expedition. The near-by settlement of the Rhth people is not to be molested in any way, unless military action is forced upon the colonists.

It is ordered that if this condition shall arise, if the Rhth people object to the proposed settlement at the spot designated as N'yor, arbitration be attempted. Should this measure prove unsuccessful, military penalties shall be exacted, but only to the extent found necessary for effective action. The colonists shall aid in the moving of the settlement of the Rhth people, if the Rhth people do not desire to be near the city of the colonists.

In any case, it is ordered that the colonists shall, in every way within their aid, advance and inspire the remaining people of Rhth.

It is further ordered that Shor Nun, commander, shall be plenipotentiary representative of the committee of Pareeth, with all powers of a discretionary nature, his command to be military and of unquestioned authority until such time as the colony shall have been established for a period of two years. There shall then have been established a representative government of such nature and powers as the colonists themselves find suitable.

It is then suggested that this government, the State of Rhth, shall exchange such representatives with the committee of Pareeth as are suitable in the dealings of two sovereign powers.

Until the establishment of the State of Rhth, it is further ordered that ——

IV

The grassland rolled away very softly among the brown boles of scattered trees. It seemed unchanged. The city seemed unchanged, floating as it had a thousand thousand years halfway between the blue of the sky and the green of the planet. Only it was not alone in its opalescent beauty now; twelve great ships floated serene, motionless, above its towers, matching them in glowing color. And on the low roll of the hill, a thirteenth ship, gray and grim and scarred with eighteen years of nearly continuous space travel, rested. The locks moved; men stepped forth into the light of the low, afternoon sun.

To their right, the mighty monument of the city builders; to their left, the low, rounded domes of the great race's descendants. Ron Thule stepped down from the lock to join the eight department commanders who stood looking across toward the village among the trees.

Shor Nun turned slowly to the men with him, shook his head, smiling. "I did not think to ask. I have no idea what their life span may be. Perhaps the man we knew as Seun has died. When I first landed here, I was a young man. I am middle-aged now. That time may mean old age and extinction to these people."

"There is one man coming toward us now, Shor Nun," said Ron Thule softly. "He is floating on his—what was that name?—it is a long time since I heard it."

The man came nearer leisurely; time seemed to mean little to these people. The soft, blue glow of his suit grew, and he moved a bit more rapidly, as though conscious of their importance. "I—I think that is Seun," said the archeologist. "I have seen those pictures so many times——"

Seun stood before them again, smiling the slow, easy smile they had known twelve years before. Still he stood slim and straight, his face lined only with the easy gravings of humor and kindliness. He was as unchanged as the grassland, as the eternal city. The glow faded as he settled before them, noiselessly. "You have come back to Rhth, Shor Nun?"

"Yes, Seun. We promised you that when we left. And with some of our people as well. We hope to establish a colony here, near the ancient city; hope some day to learn again the secrets of the city builders, to roam space as they once did. Perhaps we will be able to occupy some of the long-deserted buildings of the city and bring life to it again."

"A permanent colony?" asked Seun thoughtfully.

"Yes, Seun."

"There are many other cities here, on this planet, nearly as large, equipped with all the things that made this city. To my race the quiet of the unstirred air is very dear; could you not as easily establish your colony in Shao—or Loun—any of the other places?"

Shor Nun shook his head slowly. "I am sorry, Seun. We had hoped to live near you, that we might both discover again those forgotten secrets. We must stay here, for this was the last city your people deserted; here in it are all the things they ever built, the last achievements of the city builders. We will aid you in moving your colony if you wish, to some other meadowland near the sea. All the world is the same to your people; only this city was built in this way; it was the last to be deserted."

Seun exhaled softly, looked at the ten men of Pareeth. His mind seemed groping, feeling for something. His deep blue eyes misted in thought, then cleared slowly as Ron Thule watched. Slowly, they moved from man to man of the group, pausing a moment at the anthropologist, catching Shor Nun's gaze for an instant, centering slowly on Ron Thule.

Ron Thule looked into the deep eyes for a moment, for a long eternity—deep, clear eyes, like mountain lakes. Subtly, the Rhthman's face seemed to change as he watched the eyes. The languor there changed, became a sense of timelessness, of limitlessness. The pleasant, carefree air became, somehow—different. It was the same, but as the astronomer looked into those eyes, a new interpretation came to him. A sudden, vast fear welled up in him, so that his heart contracted, and a sudden tremor came to his hands. "You have forgotten——" he mumbled unsteadily. "Yes—but you——"

Seun smiled, the firm mouth relaxing in approval. "Yes, Ron Thule. That is enough. I sought your mind. Someone must understand. Remember that only twice in the history of our race have we attempted to alter the course of another's history, for by that you will understand what I must do."

Seun's eyes turned away. Shor Nun was looking at him, and Ron Thule realized, without quite understanding his knowledge, that no time had elapsed for these others. Now he stood motionless, paralyzed with a new understanding.

"We must stay here," Seun's mind voice spoke softly. "I, too, had hoped we might live on this world together, but we are too different. We are too far apart to be so near."

"You do not wish to move?" asked Shor Nun sorrowfully.

Seun looked up. The twelve great interstellar cruisers hovered closer now, forming, almost, a roof over this conference ground. "That would be for the council to say, I know. But I think they would agree with me, Shor Nun."

Vague pictures and ideas moved through their minds, thoughts emanating from Seun's mind. Slowly, his eyes dropped from the twelve opalescent cruisers to the outstretched palm of his hand. His eyes grew bright, and the lines of his face deepened in concentration. The air seemed to stir and move; a tenseness of inaction came over the ten men of Pareeth and they moved restlessly.

Quite abruptly, a dazzling light appeared over Seun's hand, sparkling, myriad colors—and died with a tiny, crystalline clatter. Something lay in his upturned palm: a round, small thing of aquamarine crystal, shot through with veins and arteries of softly pulsing, silver light. It moved and altered as they watched, fading in color, changing the form and outline of light.

Again the tinkling, crystalline clatter came, and some rearrangement had taken place. There lay in his hand a tiny globe of ultimate night, an essence of darkness that no light could illumine, cased in a crystal surface. Stars shone in it, from the heart, from the borders, stars that moved and turned in majestic splendor in infinite smallness. Then faded.

Seun raised his eyes. The darkness faded from the crystal in his hand, and pulsing, little veins of light appeared in it. He raised it in his fingers, and nine of Pareeth's men fell back. Ron Thule looked on with frozen, wooden face.

A wave of blue haze washed out, caught and lifted the men and carried them effortlessly, intangibly back to the lock, through the lock. From the quiet of the grassland they were suddenly in the steel of the ship that clanged and howled with alarms. Great engines bellowed suddenly to life.

Ron Thule stood at the great, clear port light of the lock. Outside, Seun, in his softly glowing suit, floated a few feet from the ground. Abruptly, the great atomic engines of the Pareeth shrilled a chorus of ravening hate, and from the three great projectors the annihilating beams tore out, shrieking destruction through the air—and vanished. Seun stood at the junction of death, and his crystal glowed softly. Twelve floating ships screamed to the tortured shriek of overloaded atomics, and the planet below cursed back with quarter-mile-long tongues of lightning.

Somewhere, everywhere, the universe thrummed to a vast, crystalline note, and hummed softly. In that instant, the green meadowland of Rhth vanished; the eternal city dissolved into blackness. Only blackness, starless, lightless, shone outside the lock port light. The soft, clear note of the crystal hummed and beat and surged. The atomic engine's cry died full-throated. An utter, paralyzed quiet descended

on the ship, so that the cry of a child somewhere echoed and reverberated noisily down the steel corridors.

The crystal in Seun's hand beat and hummed its note. The blackness beyond the port became gray. One by one, six opalescent ships
shifted into view in the blackness beyond, moving with a slow deliberation, as though forced by some infinite power into a certain,
predetermined configuration. Like atoms in a crystal lattice they
shifted, seemed to click into place and hold steady—neatly, geometrically arranged.

Then noise came back to the ship, sounds that crept in, afraid of
themselves, grew courageous and clamored; pounding feet of men,
and women's screams.

"We're out of space," gasped Shor Nun. "That crystal—that thing
in his hand——"

"In a space of our own," said Ron Thule. "Wait till the note of the
crystal dies down. It is weakening, weakening slowly, to us, but it will
be gone, and then——"

Shor Nun turned to him, his dark eyes shadowed, his face pale, and
drawn. "What do you know—how——"

Ron Thule stood silent. He did not know. Somewhere, a crystal
echoed for a moment in rearrangement and tinkling sound; the universe echoed to it softly, as the last, faint tone died away.

"Shor Nun—Shor Nun——" a slow, wailing cry was building up
in the ship. Scampering feet on metal floors became a march.

Shor Nun sobbed once. "That crystal—they had not lost the
weapons of the city builders. Space of our own? No—it is like the
sorgan: It rotates us to the end of time! This is the space we knew
—when all time has died, and the stars are gone and the worlds are
dust. This is the end of the nothingness. The city builders destroyed
their enemies thus—by dumping them at the end of time and space.
I know. They must have. And Seun had the ancient weapon. When
the humming note of the crystal dies—the lingering force of translation——

"Then we shall die, too. Die in the death of death. Oh, gods—
Sulon—Sulon, my dear—our son——" Shor Nun, commander,
seemed to slump from his frozen rigidity. He turned abruptly away
from the port light toward the inner lock door. It opened before him
suddenly, and a technician stumbled down, white-faced and trembling.

"Commander—Shor Nun—the engines are stopped. The atoms

will not explode; no power can be generated. The power cells are supplying emergency power, but the full strength of the drive does not move nor shake the ship! What—what is this?"

Shor Nun stood silent. The ship thrummed and beat with the softening, dying note of the universe-distant crystal that held all the beginnings and the endings of time and space in a man's hand. The note was fading; very soft and sweet, it was. Through the ship the hysterical cry of voices had changed; it was softening with the thrum, softening, listening to the dying thread of infinitely sweet sound.

Shor Nun shrugged his shoulders, turned away. "It does not matter. The force is fading. Across ten million years the city buildings have reached to protect their descendants."

The note was very low—very faint; a quivering hush bound the ship. Beyond the port light, the six sister ships began to move again, very stealthily away, retreating toward the positions they had held when this force first seized them. Then——

Shor Nun's choked cry was drowned in the cries of the others in the lock. Blinding white light stabbed through the port like a solid, incandescent bar. Their eyes were hot and burning.

Ron Thule, his astronomer's eyes accustomed to rapid, extreme changes of light, recovered first. His word was indistinct, a cross between a sob and a chuckle.

Shor Nun stood beside him, winking tortured eyes. The ship was waking, howling into a mad, frightened life; the children screamed in sympathetic comprehension of their elders' terror.

White, blazing sunlight on green grass and brown dirt. The weathered gray of concrete, and the angular harshness of great building cradles. A sky line of white-tipped, blue mountains, broken by nearer, less-majestic structures of steel and stone and glass, glinting in the rays of a strong, warm sun with a commonness, a familiarity that hurt. A vast nostalgia welled up in them at the sight——

And died before another wave of terror. "Darun Tara," said Shor Nun. "Darun Tara, on Pareeth. I am mad—this is mad. A crazy vision in a crazy instant as the translating force collapses. Darun Tara as it was when we left it six long years ago. Changed—that half-finished shed is still only three quarters finished. I can see Thio Roul, the portmaster there, coming toward us. I am mad. I am five light years away——"

"It is Darun Tara, Shor Nun," Ron Thule whispered. "And the city builders could never have done this. I understand now. I——"

He stopped. The whole great ship vibrated suddenly to thwang like the plucked bass string of a Titan's harp. Creaks and squeals, and little grunting readjustments, the fabric of the cruiser protested.

"My telescope——" cried Ron Thule. He was running toward the inner lock door, into the dark mouth of the corridor.

Again the ship thrummed to a vibrant stroke. The creaking of the girders and strakes protested bitterly; stressed rivets grunted angrily.

Men pounded on the lock door from without. Thio Raul, Ton Gareth, Hol Brawn—familiar faces staring anxiously in. Shor Nun moved dully toward the gate controls——

V

Shor Nun knocked gently at the closed metal door of the ship's observatory. Ron Thule's voice answered, muffled, vague, from beyond.

The commander opened the door; his breath sucked in sibilantly. "Space!" he gasped.

"Come and see, come and see," the astronomer called softly.

Shor Nun instinctively felt his way forward on tiptoe. The great observatory room was space; it was utter blackness, and the corridor lights were swallowed in it the instant the man crossed the threshold. Blackness, starred by tiny, brilliant points, scattered very sparsely, in every direction.

"Seun took the telescope, but he left me this, instead. I understand now; he said that only twice had they attempted to alter a race's history.

"This is space, and *that* is Troth, our own star. Watch——"

The star expanded; the whole of this imageless space exploded outward and vanished through the unseen walls of the observatory. Troth floated alone, centered in the invisible room. Seven tiny dots of light hung near it, glowing in its reflected light.

"And that is our system. Now this is the star of Rhth——"

Space contracted, shifted and exploded, leaving one shining, yellowish star, attended by five brightly visible worlds.

"The other planets are too small or too dimly illumined to see. When I came there was a new system displayed. This one."

Another planetary system appeared.

"That is the system of Prothor."

"Prothor!" Shor Nun stared. "Five and a half light years away—and planets?"

"Planets. Uninhabited, for I can bring each planet as near as I will. But, Shor Nun"—sorrow crept into the astronomer's voice—"though I can see every detail of each planet of that system, though I can see each outline of the planets of Rhth's system—only those three stars can I see, close by."

"No other planetary systems!"

"No other planetary system that Seun will reveal to us. I understand. One we won on the right of our own minds, our own knowledge; we reached his worlds. We had won a secret from nature by our own powers; it was part of the history of our race. They do not want to molest, or in any way influence the history of a race—so they permitted us to return, if only we did not disturb them. They could not refuse us that, a breach in their feelings of justice.

"But they felt it needful to dispossess us, Shor Nun, and this Seun did. But had he done no more, our history was altered, changed vitally. So—this he gave us; he has shown us another, equally near planetary system that we may use. We have not lost vitally. That is his justice."

"His justice. Yes, I came to you, Ron Thule, because you seemed to know somewhat of the things that happened." Shor Nun's voice was low in the dark of the observatory. He looked at the floating planets of Prothor. "What is—Seun? How has this happened? Do you know? You know that we were greeted by our friends—and they turned away from us.

"Six years have passed for us. They wanted to know what misfortune made us return at the end—of a single year. One year has passed here on Pareeth. My son was born, there in space, and he has passed his fourth birthday. My daughter is two. Yet these things have not happened, for we were gone a single year. Seun has done it, but it cannot be; Seun, the decadent son of the city builders; Seun, who has forgotten the secrets of the ships that sailed beyond the stars and the building of the Titan Towers, opalescent in the sun; Seun, whose people live in a tiny village sheltered from the rains and the sun by a few green trees.

"What are these people of Rhth?"

Ron Thule's voice was a whisper from the darkness. "I come from a far world, by what strange freak we will not say. I am a savage, a rising race that has not learned the secret of fire, nor bow, nor hammer. Tell me, Shor Nun, what is the nature of the two dry sticks I must rub, that fire may be born? Must they be hard, tough oak, or should one be a soft, resinous bit of pine? Tell me how I may make fire."

"Why—with matches or a heat ra—— No, Ron Thule. Vague thoughts, meaningless ideas and unclear. I—I have forgotten the ten thousand generations of development. I cannot retreat to a level you, savage of an untrained world, would understand. I—I have forgotten."

"Then tell me, how I must hold the flint, and where must I press with a bit of deer horn that the chips shall fly small and even, so that the knife will be sharp and kill my prey for me? And how shall I rub and wash and treat the wood of the bow, or the skin of the slain animal that I may have a coat that will not be stiff, but soft and pliable?"

"Those, too, I have forgotten. Those are unnecessary things. I cannot help you, savage. I would greet you, and show you the relics of our deserted past in museums. I might conduct you through ancient caves, where mighty rock walls defended my ancestors against the wild things they could not control.

"Yes, Ron Thule. I have forgotten the development."

"Once"—Ron Thule's voice was tense—"the city builder made atomic generators to release the energy bound in that violent twist of space called an atom. He made the sorgan to distribute its power to his clumsy shells of metal and crystal—the caves that protected him from the wild things of space.

"Seun has forgotten the atom; he thinks in terms of space. The powers of space are at his direct command. He created the crystal that brought us here from the energy of space, because it made easy a task his mind alone could have done. It was no more needful than is an adding machine. His people have no ships; they are anywhere in space they will without such things. Seun is not a decadent son of the city builders. His people never forgot the dream that built the city. But it was a dream of childhood, and his people were children then. Like a child with his broomstick horse, the mind alone was not enough for thought; the city builders, just as ourselves, needed something of a solid metal and crystal, to make their dreams tangible."

"My son was born in space, and is four. Yet we were gone a single year from Pareeth. Shor Nun sighed.

"Our fleet took six years to cross the gulf of five light years. In thirty seconds, infinitely faster than light, Seun returned us, that there might be the minimum change in our racial history. Time is a function of the velocity of light, and five light years of distance is precisely equal to five years of time multiplied by the square root of minus one. When we traversed five light years of space in no appreciable time, we dropped back, also, through five years of time.

"You and I have spent eighteen years of effort in this exploration, Shor Nun—eighteen years of our manhood. By this hurling us back Seun has forever denied us the planets we earned by those long years of effort. But now he does not deny us wholly.

"They gave us this, and by it another sun, with other planets. This Seun gave not to me, as an astronomer; it is his gift to the race. Now it is beyond us ever to make another. And this which projects this space around us will cease to be, I think, on the day we land on those other planets of that other sun, where Seun will be to watch us—as he may be here now, to see that we understand his meanings.

"I know only this—that sun I can see, and the planets circling it. The sun of Rhth I can see, and those planets, and our own. But—though these others came so near at the impulse of my thoughts, no other sun in all space can I see so near.

"That, I think, is the wish of Seun and his race."

The astronomer stiffened suddenly.

Shor Nun stood straight and tense.

"Yes," whispered Seun, very softly, in their minds.

Ron Thule sighed.

NERVES

by

LESTER DEL REY

Nerves was written early in 1942, when atomic power was discussed publicly only in the science-fiction magazines. It presupposes a world where atomic power is an accepted fact, where atomic-power plants are as commonplace as automobile factories. Writing in a curiously prophetic vein, Mr. Del Rey has furnished some very plausible—albeit fictional—answers to the questions in everyone's mind. What is an atomic-power plant like? How does it operate? What would happen if things got out of control?

*

THE GRAVELED WALKS between the sprawling, utilitarian structures of the National Atomic Products Co., Inc., were crowded with the usual five o'clock mass of young huskies just off work or going on the extra shift, and the company cafeteria was jammed to capacity and overflowing. But they made good-natured way for Doc Ferrel as he came out, not bothering to stop their horseplay as they would have done with any of the other half hundred officials of the company. He'd been just Doc to them too long for any need of formality.

He nodded back at them easily, pushed through, and went down the walk toward the Infirmary Building, taking his own time; when a man has turned fifty, with gray hairs and enlarged waistline to show for it, he begins to realize that comfort and relaxation are worth cultivating. Besides, Doc could see no good reason for filling his stomach with food and then rushing around in a flurry that gave him no chance to digest it. He let himself in the side entrance, palming his cigar out of long habit, and passed through the surgery to the door marked:

PRIVATE
ROGER T. FERREL
PHYSICIAN IN CHARGE

As always, the little room was heavy with the odor of stale smoke and littered with scraps of this and that. His assistant was already there, rummaging busily through the desk with the brass nerve that was typical of him; Ferrel had no objections to it, though, since Blake's rock-steady hands and unruffled brain were always dependable in a pinch of any sort.

Blake looked up and grinned confidently. "Hi, Doc. Where the deuce do you keep your cigarettes, anyway? Never mind, got 'em. . . . Ah, that's better! Good thing there's one room in this darned building where the 'No Smoking' signs don't count. You and the wife coming out this evening?"

"Not a chance, Blake." Ferrel struck the cigar back in his mouth and settled down into the old leather chair, shaking his head. "Palmer phoned down half an hour ago to ask me if I'd stick through the graveyard shift. Seems the plant's got a rush order for some particular batch of dust that takes about twelve hours to cook, so they'll be running No. 3 and 4 till midnight or later."

"Hm-m-m. So you're hooked again. I don't see why any of us has to stick here—nothing serious ever pops up now. Look what I had today; three cases of athlete's foot—better send a memo down to the showers for extra disinfection—a guy with dandruff, four running noses, and the office boy with a sliver in his thumb! They bring everything to us except their babies—and they'd have them here if they could—but nothing that couldn't wait a week or a month. Anne's been counting on you and the missus, Doc; she'll be disappointed if you aren't there to celebrate her sticking ten years with me. Why don't you let the kid stick it out alone tonight?"

"I wish I could, but this happens to be my job. As a matter of fact, though, Jenkins worked up an acute case of duty and decided to stay on with me tonight." Ferrel twitched his lips in a stiff smile, remembering back to the time when his waistline had been smaller than his chest and he'd gone through the same feeling that destiny had singled him out to save the world. "The kid had his first real case today, and he's all puffed up. Handled it all by himself, so he's now Dr. Jenkins, if you please."

Blake had his own memories. "Yeah? Wonder when he'll realize that everything he did by himself came from your hints? What was it, anyway?"

"Same old story—simple radiation burns. No matter how much we tell the men when they first come in, most of them can't see why they should wear three ninety-five percent efficient shields when the main converter shield cuts off all but one-tenth percent of the radiation. Somehow, this fellow managed to leave off his two inner shields and pick up a year's burn in six hours. Now he's probably back on No. 1, still running through the hundred liturgies I gave him to say and hoping we won't get him sacked."

No. 1 was the first converter around which National Atomic had built its present monopoly in artificial radioactives, back in the days when shields were still inefficient to one part in a thousand and the materials handled were milder than the modern ones. They still used it for the gentler reactions, prices of converters being what they were; anyhow, if reasonable precautions were taken, there was no serious danger.

"A tenth percent will kill; five percent thereof is one two-hundredth; five percent of that is one four-thousandth; and five percent again leaves one eighty-thousandth, safe for all but fools." Blake sing-songed the liturgy solemnly, then chuckled. "You're getting old, Doc; you used to give them a thousand times. Well, if you get the chance, you and Mrs. Ferrel drop out and say hello, even if it's after midnight. Anne's gonna be disappointed, but she ought to know how it goes. So long."

" 'Night." Ferrel watched him leave, still smiling faintly. Some day his own son would be out of medical school, and Blake would make a good man for him to start under and begin the same old grind upward. First, like young Jenkins, he'd be filled with his mission to humanity, tense and uncertain, but somehow things would roll along through Blake's stage and up, probably to Doc's own level, where the same old problems were solved in the same old way, and life settled down into a comfortable, mellow dullness.

There were worse lives, certainly, even though it wasn't like the mass of murders, kidnapings and applied miracles played up in the current movie series about Dr. Hoozis. Come to think of it, Hoozis was supposed to be working in an atomic products plant right now— but one where chrome-plated converters covered with pretty neon tubes were mysteriously blowing up every second day, and men were brought in with blue flames all over them to be cured instantly in time to utter the magic words so the hero could dash in and put out the atomic flame barehanded. Ferrel grunted and reached back for his old copy of the "Decameron."

Then he heard Jenkins out in the surgery, puttering around with quick, nervous little sounds. Never do to let the boy find him loafing back here, when the possible fate of the world so obviously hung on his alertness. Young doctors had to be disillusioned slowly, or they became bitter and their work suffered. Yet, in spite of his amusement at Jenkins' nervousness, he couldn't help envying the thin-faced young man's erect shoulders and flat stomach. Years crept by, it seemed.

Jenkins straightened out a wrinkle in his white jacket fussily and looked up. "I've been getting the surgery ready for instant use, Dr. Ferrel. Do you think it's safe to keep only Miss Dodd and one male attendant here—shouldn't we have more than the bare legally sanctioned staff?"

"Dodd's a one-man staff," Ferrel assured him. "Expecting accidents tonight?"

"No, sir, not exactly. But do you know what they're running off?"

"No." Ferrel hadn't asked Palmer; he'd learned long before that he couldn't keep up with the atomic engineering developments, and had stopped trying. "Some new type of atomic tank fuel for the army to use in its war games?"

"Worse than that, sir. They're making their first commercial run of Natomic I-713 in both No. 3 and 4 converters at once."

"So? Seems to me I did hear something about that. Had to do with killing off boll weevils, didn't it?" Ferrel was vaguely familiar with the process of sowing radioactive dust in a circle outside the weevil area, to isolate the pest, then gradually moving inward from the border. Used with proper precautions, it had slowly killed off the weevil and driven it back into half the territory once occupied.

Jenkins managed to look disappointed, surprised and slightly superior without a visible change of expression. "There was an article on it in the Natomic Weekly Ray of last issue, Dr. Ferrel. You probably know that the trouble with Natomic I-344, which they've been using, was its half life of over four months; that made the land sowed useless for planting the next year, so they had to move very slowly. I-713 has a half life of less than a week and reaches safe limits in about two months, so they'll be able to isolate whole strips of hundreds of miles during the winter and still have the land usable by spring. Field tests have been highly successful, and we've just gotten a huge order from two States that want immediate delivery."

"After their legislatures waited six months debating whether to use it or not," Ferrel hazarded out of long experience. "Hm-m-m, sounds good if they can sow enough earthworms after them to keep the ground in good condition. But what's the worry?"

Jenkins shook his head indignantly. "I'm not worried. I simply think we should take every possible precaution and be ready for any accident; after all, they're working on something new, and a half life of a week is rather strong, don't you think? Besides, I looked over some of the reaction charts in the article, and— What was that?"

From somewhere to the left of the Infirmary, a muffled growl was being accompanied by ground tremors; then it gave place to a steady hissing, barely audible through the insulated walls of the building. Ferrel listened a moment and shrugged. "Nothing to worry about, Jenkins; you'll hear it a dozen times a year. Ever since the Great War when he tried to commit hara-kiri over the treachery of his people, Hokusai's been bugs about getting an atomic explosive bomb which will let us wipe out the rest of the world. Some day you'll probably see the little guy brought in here minus his head, but so far he hasn't found anything with short enough a half life that can be controlled until needed. What about the reaction charts on I-713?"

"Nothing definite, I suppose." Jenkins turned reluctantly away from the sound, still frowning. "I know it worked in small lots, but there's something about one of the intermediate steps I distrust, sir. I thought I recognized . . . I tried to ask one of the engineers about it. He practically told me to shut up until I'd studied atomic engineering myself."

Seeing the boy's face whiten over tensed jaw muscles, Ferrel held back his smile and nodded slowly. Something funny there; of course, Jenkins' pride had been wounded, but hardly that much. Some day, he'd have to find out what was behind it; little things like that could ruin a man's steadiness with the instruments, if he kept it to himself. Meantime, the subject was best dropped.

The telephone girl's heavily syllabized voice cut into his thoughts from the annunciator. "Dr. Ferrel. Dr. Ferrel wanted on the telephone. Dr. Ferrel, please!"

Jenkins' face blanched still further, and his eyes darted to his superior sharply. Doc grunted casually. "Probably Palmer's bored and wants to tell me all about his grandson again. He thinks that child's an all-time genius because it says two words at eighteen months."

But inside the office, he stopped to wipe his hands free of perspiration before answering; there was something contagious about Jenkins' suppressed fears. And Palmer's face on the little television screen didn't help any, though the director was wearing his usual set smile. Ferrel knew it wasn't about the baby this time, and he was right.

"'Lo, Ferrel." Palmer's heartily confident voice was quite normal, but the use of the last name was a clear sign of some trouble. "There's been a little accident in the plant, they tell me. They're bringing a few men over to the Infirmary for treatment—probably not right away, though. Has Blake gone yet?"

"He's been gone fifteen minutes or more. Think it's serious enough to call him back, or are Jenkins and myself enough?"

"Jenkins? Oh, the new doctor." Palmer hesitated, and his arms showed quite clearly the doodling operations of his hands, out of sight of the vision cell. "No, of course, no need to call Blake back, I suppose—not yet, anyhow. Just worry anyone who saw him coming in. Probably nothing serious."

"What is it—radiation burns, or straight accident?"

"Oh—radiation mostly—maybe accident, too. Someone got a little careless—you know how it is. Nothing to worry about, though. You've been through it before when they opened a port too soon."

Doc knew enough about that—if that's what it was. "Sure, we can handle that, Palmer. But I thought No. 1 was closing down at five thirty tonight. Anyhow, how come they haven't installed the safety ports on it? You told me they had, six months ago."

"I didn't say it was No. 1, or that it was a manual port. You know, new equipment for new products." Palmer looked up at someone else, and his upper arms made a slight movement before he looked down at the vision cell again. "I can't go into it now, Dr. Ferrel; accident's throwing us off schedule, you see—details piling up on me. We can talk it over later, and you probably have to make arrangements now. Call me if you want anything."

The screen darkened and the phone clicked off abruptly, just as a muffled word started. The voice hadn't been Palmer's. Ferrel pulled his stomach in, wiped the sweat off his hands again, and went out into the surgery with careful casualness. Damn Palmer, why couldn't the fool give enough information to make decent preparations possible? He was sure 3 and 4 alone were operating, and they were supposed to be foolproof. Just what had happened?

Jenkins jerked up from a bench as he came out, face muscles tense and eyes filled with a nameless fear. Where he had been sitting, a copy of the *Weekly Ray* was lying open at a chart of symbols which meant nothing to Ferrel, except for the penciled line under one of the reactions. The boy picked it up and stuck it back on a table.

"Routine accident," Ferrel reported as naturally as he could, cursing himself for having to force his voice. Thank the Lord, the boy's hands hadn't trembled visibly when he was moving the paper; he'd still be useful if surgery were necessary. Palmer had said nothing of that, of course—he'd said nothing about entirely too much. "They're bringing a few men over for radiation burns, according to Palmer. Everything ready?"

Jenkins nodded tightly. "Quite ready, sir, as much as we can be for —routine accidents at 3 and 4! . . . Isotope R. . . . Sorry, Dr. Ferrel, I didn't mean that. Should we call in Dr. Blake and the other nurses and attendants?"

"Eh? Oh, probably we can't reach Blake, and Palmer doesn't think we need him. You might have Nurse Dodd locate Meyers—the others are out on dates by now if I know them, and the two nurses should be enough, with Jones; they're better than a flock of the others, anyway." Isotope R? Ferrel remembered the name, but nothing else. Something an engineer had said once—but he couldn't recall in what connection—or had Hokusai mentioned it? He watched Jenkins leave and turned back on an impulse to his office where he could phone in reasonable privacy.

"Get me Matsuura Hokusai." He stood drumming on the table impatiently until the screen finally lighted and the little Japanese looked out of it. "Hoke, do you know what they were turning out over at 3 and 4?"

The scientist nodded slowly, his wrinkled face as expressionless as his unaccented English. "Yess, they are make I-713 for the weevil. Why you assk?"

"Nothing; just curious. I heard rumors about an Isotope R and wondered if there was any connection. Seems they had a little accident over there, and I want to be ready for whatever comes of it."

For a fraction of a second, the heavy lids on Hokusai's eyes seemed to lift, but his voice remained neutral, only slightly faster. "No connection, Dr. Ferrel, they are not make Issotope R, very much assure you. Besst you forget Issotope R. Very ssorry. Dr. Ferrel, I musst now ssee accident. Thank you for call. Good-by." The screen was blank again, along with Ferrel's mind.

Jenkins was standing in the door, but had either heard nothing or seemed not to know about it. "Nurse Meyers is coming back," he said. "Shall I get ready for curare injections?"

"Uh—might be a good idea." Ferrel had no intention of being surprised again, no matter what the implication of the words. Curare, one of the greatest poisons, known to South American primitives for centuries and only recently synthesized by modern chemistry, was the final resort for use in cases of radiation injury that was utterly beyond control. While the Infirmary stocked it for such emergencies, in the long years of Doc's practice it had been used only twice; neither experience had been pleasant. Jenkins was either thoroughly frightened or overly zealous—unless he knew something he had no business knowing.

"Seems to take them long enough to get the men here—can't be too serious, Jenkins, or they'd move faster."

"Maybe." Jenkins went on with his preparations, dissolving dried plasma in distilled, de-aerated water, without looking up. "There's the litter siren now. You'd better get washed up while I take care of the patients."

Doc listened to the sound that came in as a faint drone from outside, and grinned slightly. "Must be Beel driving; he's the only man fool enough to run the siren when the runways are empty. Anyhow, if you'll listen, it's the out trip he's making. Be at least five minutes before he gets back." But he turned into the washroom, kicked on the hot water and began scrubbing vigorously with the strong soap.

Damn Jenkins! Here he was preparing for surgery before he had any reason to suspect the need, and the boy was running things to suit himself, pretty much, as if armed with superior knowledge. Well, maybe he was. Either that, or he was simply half crazy with old wives' fears of anything relating to atomic reactions, and that didn't seem to fit the case. He rinsed off as Jenkins came in, kicked on the hot-air blast, and let his arms dry, then bumped against a rod that brought out rubber gloves on little holders. "Jenkins, what's all this Isotope R business, anyway? I've heard about it somewhere—probably from Hokusai. But I can't remember anything definite."

"Naturally—there isn't anything definite. That's the trouble." The young doctor tackled the area under his fingernails before looking up; then he saw Ferrel was slipping into his surgeon's whites that had come out on a hanger, and waited until the other was finished. "R's one of the big maybe problems of atomics. Purely theoretical, and none's been made yet—it's either impossible or can't be done in small control batches, safe for testing. That's the trouble, as I said;

nobody knows anything about it, except that—if it can exist—it'll break down in a fairly short time into Mahler's Isotope. You've heard of that?"

Doc had—twice. The first had been when Mahler and half his laboratory had disappeared with accompanying noise; he'd been making a comparatively small amount of the new product designed to act as a starter for other reactions. Later, Maicewicz had tackled it on a smaller scale, and that time only two rooms and three men had gone up in dust particles. Five or six years later, atomic theory had been extended to the point where any student could find why the apparently safe product decided to become pure helium and energy in approximately one-billionth of a second.

"How long a time?"

"Half a dozen theories, and no real idea." They'd come out of the washrooms, finished except for their masks. Jenkins ran his elbow into a switch that turned on the ultraviolets that were supposed to sterilize the entire surgery, then looked around questioningly. "What about the supersonics?"

Ferrel kicked them on, shuddering as the bone-shaking harmonic hum indicated their activity. He couldn't complain about the equipment, at least. Ever since the last accident, when the State Congress developed ideas, there'd been enough gadgets lying around to stock up several small hospitals. The supersonics were intended to penetrate through all solids in the room, sterilizing where the UV light couldn't reach. A whistling note in the harmonics reminded him of something that had been tickling around in the back of his mind for minutes.

"There was no emergency whistle, Jenkins. Hardly seems to me they'd neglect that if it were so important."

Jenkins grunted skeptically and eloquently. "I read in the papers a few days ago where Congress was thinking of moving all atomic plants—meaning National, of course—out into the Mojave Desert. Palmer wouldn't like that. . . . There's the siren again."

Jones, the male attendant, had heard it, and was already running out the fresh stretcher for the litter into the back receiving room. Half a minute later, Beel came trundling in the detachable part of the litter. "Two," he announced. "More coming up as soon as they can get to 'em, Doc."

There was blood spilled over the canvas, and a closer inspection indicated its source in a severed jugular vein, now held in place with a small safety pin that had fastened the two sides of the cut with a series of little pricks around which the blood had clotted enough to stop further loss.

Doc kicked off the supersonics with relief and indicated the man's throat. "Why wasn't I called out instead of having him brought here?"

"Hell, Doc, Palmer said bring 'em in and I brought 'em— I dunno. Guess some guy pinned up this fellow so they figured he could wait. Anything wrong?"

Ferrel grimaced. "With a split jugular, nothing that stops the bleeding's wrong, orthodox or not. How many more, and what's wrong out there?"

"Lord knows, Doc. I only drive 'em, I don't ask questions. So long!" He pushed the new stretcher up on the carriage, went wheeling it out to the small two-wheeled tractor that completed the litter. Ferrel dropped his curiosity back to its proper place and turned to the jugular case, while Dodd adjusted her mask. Jones had their clothes off, swabbed them down hastily, and wheeled them out on operating tables into the center of the surgery.

"Plasma!" A quick examination had shown Doc nothing else wrong with the jugular case, and he made the injection quickly. Apparently the man was only unconscious from shock induced by loss of blood, and the breathing and heart action resumed a more normal course as the liquid filled out the depleted blood vessels. He treated the wound with a sulphonamide derivative in routine procedure, cleaned and sterilized the edges gently, applied clamps carefully, removed the pin, and began stitching with the complicated little motor needle—one of the few gadgets for which he had any real appreciation. A few more drops of blood had spilled, but not seriously, and the wound was now permanently sealed. "Save the pin, Dodd. Goes in the collection. That's all for this. How's the other, Jenkins?"

Jenkins pointed to the back of the man's neck, indicating a tiny bluish object sticking out. "Fragment of steel, clear into the medulla oblongata. No blood loss, but he's been dead since it touched him. Want me to remove it?"

"No need—mortician can do it if they want. . . . If these are a sample, I'd guess it as a plain industrial accident, instead of anything connected with radiation."

"You'll get that, too, Doc." It was the jugular case, apparently conscious and normal except for pallor. "We weren't in the converter house. Hey, I'm all right! . . . I'll be—"

Ferrel smiled at the surprise on the fellow's face. "Thought you were dead, eh? Sure, you're all right, if you'll take it easy. A torn

jugular either kills you or else it's nothing to worry about. Just pipe
down and let the nurse put you to sleep, and you'll never know you
got it."

"Lord! Stuff came flying out of the air-intake like bullets out of a
machine gun. Just a scratch, I thought; then Jake was bawling like a
baby and yelling for a pin. Blood all over the place—then here I am,
good as new."

"Uh-huh." Dodd was already wheeling him off to a ward room, her
grim face wrinkled into a half-quizzical expression over the mask.
"Doctor said to pipe down, didn't he? Well!"

As soon as Dodd vanished, Jenkins sat down, running his hand over
his cap; there were little beads of sweat showing where the goggles
and mask didn't entirely cover his face. " 'Stuff came flying out of the
air-intake like bullets out of a machine gun,' " he repeated softly. "Dr.
Ferrel, these two cases were outside the converter—just by-product
accidents. Inside—"

"Yeah." Ferrel was picturing things himself, and it wasn't pleasant.
Outside, matter tossed through the air ducts; inside— He left it hanging, as Jenkins had. "I'm going to call Blake. We'll probably need
him."

II

"Give me Dr. Blake's residence—Maple 2337," Ferrel said quickly
into the phone. The operator looked blank for a second, starting and
then checking a purely automatic gesture toward the plugs. "Maple
2337, I said."

"I'm sorry, Dr. Ferrel, I can't give you an outside line. All trunk
lines are out of order." There was a constant buzz from the board,
but nothing showed in the panel to indicate whether from white
inside lights or the red trunk indicators.

"But—this is an emergency, operator. I've got to get in touch with
Dr. Blake!"

"Sorry, Dr. Ferrel. All trunk lines are out of order." She started to
reach for the plug, but Ferrel stopped her.

"Give me Palmer, then—and no nonsense! If his line's busy, cut
me in, and I'll take the responsibility."

"Very good." She snapped at her switches. "I'm sorry. emergency
call from Dr. Ferrel. Hold the line and I'll reconnect you." Then
Palmer's face was on the panel, and this time the man was making
no attempt to conceal his expression of worry.

"What is it, Ferrel?"

"I want Blake here—I'm going to need him. The operator says—"

"Yeah." Palmer nodded tightly, cutting in. "I've been trying to get him myself, but his house doesn't answer. Any idea of where to reach him?"

"You might try the Bluebird or any of the other night clubs around there." Damn, why did this have to be Blake's celebration night? No telling where he could be found by this time.

Palmer was speaking again. "I've already had all the night clubs and restaurants called, and he doesn't answer. We're paging the movie houses and theaters now—just a second. . . . Nope, he isn't there, Ferrel. Last reports, no response."

"How about sending out a general call over the radio?"

"I'd . . . I'd like to, Ferrel, but it can't be done." The manager had hesitated for a fraction of a second, but his reply was positive. "Oh, by the way, we'll notify your wife you won't be home. Operator! You there? Good, reconnect the Governor!"

There was no sense in arguing into a blank screen, Doc realized. If Palmer wouldn't put through a radio call, he wouldn't, though it had been done once before. "All trunk lines are out of order. . . . We'll notify your wife. . . . Reconnect the Governor!" They weren't even being careful to cover up. He must have repeated the words aloud as he backed out of the office, still staring at the screen, for Jenkins' face twitched into a maladjusted grin.

"So we're cut off. I knew it already; Meyers just got in with more details." He nodded toward the nurse, just coming out of the dressing room and trying to smooth out her uniform. Her almost pretty face was more confused than worried.

"I was just leaving the plant, Dr. Ferrel, when my name came up on the outside speaker, but I had trouble getting here. We're locked in! I saw them at the gate—guards with sticks. They were turning back everyone that tried to leave, and wouldn't tell why, even. Just general orders that no one was to leave until Mr. Palmer gave his permission. And they weren't going to let me back in at first. Do you suppose . . . do you know what it's all about? I heard little things that didn't mean anything, really, but—"

"I know just about as much as you do, Meyers, though Palmer said something about carelessness with one of the ports on No. 3 or 4," Ferrel answered her. "Probably just precautionary measures. Anyway, I wouldn't worry about it yet."

"Yes, Dr. Ferrel." She nodded and turned back to the front office,

but there was no assurance in her look. Doc realized that neither
Jenkins nor himself were pictures of confidence at the moment.

"Jenkins," he said, when she was gone, "if you know anything I
don't, for the love of Mike, out with it! I've never seen anything
like this around here."

Jenkins shook himself, and for the first time since he'd been there,
used Ferrel's nickname. "Doc, I don't—that's why i'm in a blue
funk. I know just enough to be less sure than you can be, and I'm
scared as hell!"

"Let's see your hands." The subject was almost a monomania with
Ferrel, and he knew it, but he also knew it wasn't unjustified. Jenkins'
hands came out promptly, and there was no tremble to them. The
boy threw up his arm so the sleeve slid beyond the elbow, and
Ferrel nodded; there was no sweat trickling down from the arm-
pits to reveal a worse case of nerves than showed on the surface.
"Good enough, son; I don't care how scared you are—I'm getting
that way myself—but with Blake out of the picture, and the other
nurses and attendants sure to be out of reach, I'll need everything
you've got."

"Doc?"

"Well?"

"If you'll take my word for it, I can get another nurse here—
and a good one, too. They don't come any better, or any steadier,
and she's not working now. I didn't expect her—well, anyhow, she'd
skin me if I didn't call when we need one. Want her?"

"No trunk lines for outside calls," Doc reminded him. It was the
first time he'd seen any real enthusiasm on the boy's face, and however good or bad the nurse was, she'd obviously be of value in bucking
up Jenkins' spirits. "Go to it, though; right now we can probably use
any nurse. Sweetheart?"

"Wife." Jenkins went toward the dressing room. "And I don't
need the phone; we used to carry ultra-short-wave personal radios to
keep in touch, and I've still got mine here. And if you're worried about her qualifications, she handed instruments to Bayard at
Mayo's for five years—that's how I managed to get through medical
school!"

The siren was approaching again when Jenkins came back, the little
tense lines about his lips still there, but his whole bearing somehow
steadier. He nodded. "I called Palmer, too, and he O.K.'d her coming
inside on the phone without wondering how I'd contacted her. The

switchboard girl has standing orders to route all calls from us through before anything else, it seems."

Doc nodded, his ear cocked toward the drone of the siren that drew up and finally ended on a sour wheeze. There was a feeling of relief from tension about him as he saw Jones appear and go toward the rear entrance; work, even under the pressure of an emergency, was always easier than sitting around waiting for it. He saw two stretchers come in, both bearing double loads, and noted that Beel was babbling at the attendant, the driver's usually phlegmatic manner completely gone.

"I'm quitting; I'm through tomorrow! No more watching 'em drag out stiffs for me—not that way. Dunno why I gotta go back, anyhow; it won't do 'em any good to get in further, even if they can. From now on, I'm driving a truck, so help me I am!"

Ferrel let him rave on, only vaguely aware that the man was close to hysteria. He had no time to give to Beel now as he saw the raw red flesh through the visor of one of the armor suits. "Cut off what clothes you can, Jones," he directed. "At least get the shield suits off them. Tannic acid ready, nurse?"

"Ready." Meyers answered together with Jenkins, who was busily helping Jones strip off the heavily armored suits and helmets.

Ferrel kicked on the supersonics again, letting them sterilize the metal suits—there was going to be no chance to be finicky about asepsis; the supersonics and ultra-violet tubes were supposed to take care of that, and they'd have to do it, to a large extent, little as he liked it. Jenkins finished his part, dived back for fresh gloves, with a mere cursory dipping of his hands into antiseptic and rinse. Dodd followed him, while Jones wheeled three of the cases into the middle of the surgery, ready for work; the other had died on the way in.

It was going to be messy work, obviously. Where metal from the suits had touched, or come near touching, the flesh was burned— crisped, rather. And that was merely a minor part of it, as was the more than ample evidence of major radiation burns, which had probably not stopped at the surface, but penetrated through the flesh and bones into the vital interior organs. Much worse, the writhing and spasmodic muscular contractions indicated radioactive matter that had been forced into the flesh and was acting directly on the nerves controlling the motor impulses. Jenkins looked hastily at the twisting body of his case, and his face blanched to a yellowish white; it was the first real example of the full possibilities of an atomic accident he'd seen.

"Curare," he said finally, the word forced out, but level. Meyers
handed him the hypodermic and he inserted it, his hand still steady
—more than normally steady, in fact, with that absolute lack of movement that can come to a living organism only under the stress of
emergency. Ferrel dropped his eyes back to his own case, both relieved and worried.

From the spread of the muscular convulsions, there could be only
one explanation—somehow, radioactives had not only worked their
way through the air grills, but had been forced through the almost
air-tight joints and sputtered directly into the flesh of the men.
Now they were sending out radiations into every nerve, throwing
aside the normal orders from the brain and spinal column, setting
up anarchic orders of their own that left the muscles to writhe and
jerk, one against the other, without order or reason, or any of the
normal restraints the body places upon itself. The closest parallel
was that of a man undergoing metrozol shock for schizophrenia, or a
severe case of strychnine poisoning. He injected curare carefully,
metering out the dosage according to the best estimate he could make,
but Jenkins had been acting under a pressure that finished the second
injection as Doc looked up from his first. Still, in spite of the rapid
spread of the drug, some of the twitching went on.

"Curare," Jenkins repeated, and Doc tensed mentally; he'd still
been debating whether to risk the extra dosage. But he made no
counter-order, feeling slightly relieved this time at having the matter
taken out of his hands; Jenkins went back to work, pushing up the
injections to the absolute limit of safety, and slightly beyond. One of
the cases had started a weird minor moan that hacked on and off
as his lungs and vocal cords went in and out of synchronization,
but it quieted under the drug, and in a matter of minutes the three
lay still, breathing with the shallow flaccidity common to curare
treatment. They were still moving slightly, but where before they
were perfectly capable of breaking their own bones in uncontrolled
efforts, now there was only motion similar to a man with a chill.

"God bless the man who synthesized curare," Jenkins muttered as
he began cleaning away damaged flesh, Meyers assisting.

Doc could repeat that; with the older, natural product, true
standardization and exact dosage had been next to impossible. Too
much, and its action on the body was fatal; the patient died from "exhaustion" of his chest muscles in a matter of minutes. Too little
was practically useless. Now that the danger of self-injury and fatal

exhaustion from wild exertion was over, he could attend to such relatively unimportant things as the agony still going on—curare had no particular effect on the sensory nerves. He injected neo-heroin and began cleaning the burned areas and treating them with the standard tannic-acid routine, first with a sulphonamide to eliminate possible infection, glancing up occasionally at Jenkins.

He had no need to worry, though; the boy's nerves were frozen into an unnatural calm that still pressed through with a speed Ferrel made no attempt to equal, knowing his work would suffer for it. At a gesture, Dodd handed him the little radiation detector, and he began hunting over the skin, inch by inch, for the almost microscopic bits of matter; there was no hope of finding all now, but the worst deposits could be found and removed; later, with more time, a final probing could be made.

"Jenkins," he asked, "how about I-713's chemical action? Is it basically poisonous to the system?"

"No. Perfecty safe except for radiation. Eight in the outer electron ring, chemically inert."

That, at least, was a relief. Radiations were bad enough in and of themselves, but when coupled with metallic poisoning, like the old radium or mercury poisoning, it was even worse. The small colloidially fine particles of I-713 in the flesh would set up their own danger signal, and could be scraped away in the worst cases; otherwise, they'd probably have to stay until the isotope exhausted itself. Mercifully, its half life was short, which would decrease the long hospitalization and suffering of the men.

Jenkins joined Ferrel on the last patient, replacing Dodd at handing instruments. Doc would have preferred the nurse, who was used to his little signals, but he said nothing, and was surprised to note the efficiency of the boy's co-operation. "How about the breakdown products?" he asked.

"I-713? Harmless enough, mostly, and what isn't harmless isn't concentrated enough to worry about. That is, if it's still I-713. Otherwise—"

Otherwise, Doc finished mentally, the boy meant there'd be no danger from poisoning, at least. Isotope R, with an uncertain degeneration period, turned into Mahler's Isotope, with a complete breakdown in a billionth of a second. He had a fleeting vision of men, filled with a fine dispersion of that, suddenly erupting over their body with a violence that could never be described; Jenkins must have been thinking the same thing. For a few seconds, they stood there, looking at each other silently, but neither chose to speak of it. Ferrel reached for the probe, Jenkins shrugged, and they went on with their work and their thoughts.

It was a picture impossible to imagine, which they might or might not see; if such an atomic blow-up occurred, what would happen to the laboratory was problematical. No one knew the exact amount Maicewicz had worked on, except that it was the smallest amount he could make, so there could be no good estimate of the damage. The bodies on the operating tables, the little scraps of removed flesh containing the minute globules of radioactive, even the instruments that had come in contact with them, were bombs waiting to explode. Ferrel's own fingers took on some of the steadiness that was frozen in Jenkins as he went about his work, forcing his mind onto the difficult labor at hand.

It might have been minutes or hours later when the last dressing was in place and the three broken bones of the worst case were set. Meyers and Dodd, along with Jones, were taking care of the men, putting them into the little wards, and the two physicians were alone, carefully avoiding each other's eyes, waiting without knowing exactly what they expected.

Outside, a droning chug came to their ears, and the thump of something heavy moving over the runways. By common impulse they slipped to the side door and looked out, to see the rear end of one of the electric tanks moving away from them. Night had fallen some time before, but the gleaming lights from the big towers around the fence made the plant stand out in glaring detail. Except for the tank moving away, though, other buildings cut off their view.

Then, from the direction of the main gate, a shrill whistle cut the air, and there was a sound of men's voices, though the words were indistinguishable. Sharp, crisp syllables followed, and Jenkins nodded slowly to himself. "Ten'll get you a hundred," he began, "that— Uh, no use betting. It is."

Around the corner a squad of men in State militia uniform marched briskly, bayoneted rifles on their arms. With efficient precision, they spread out under a sergeant's direction, each taking a post before the door of one of the buildings, one approaching the place where Ferrel and Jenkins stood.

"So that's what Palmer was talking to the Governor about," Ferrel muttered. "No use asking them questions, I suppose; they know less than we do. Come on inside where we can sit down and rest. Wonder what good the militia can do here—unless Palmer's afraid someone inside's going to crack and cause trouble."

Jenkins followed him back to the office and accepted a cigarette automatically as he flopped back into a chair. Doc was discovering just how good it felt to give his muscles and nerves a chance to relax, and realizing that they must have been far longer in the surugery than he had thought. "Care for a drink?"

"Uh—is it safe, Doc? We're apt to be back in there any minute."

Ferrel pulled a grin onto his face and nodded. "It won't hurt you —we're just enough on edge and tired for it to be burned up inside for fuel instead of reaching our nerves. Here." It was a generous slug of rye he poured for each, enough to send an almost immediate warmth through them, and to relax their overtensed nerves. "Wonder why Beel hasn't been back long ago?"

"That tank we saw probably explains it; it got too tough for the men to work in just their suits, and they've had to start excavating through the converters with the tanks. Electric, wasn't it, battery powered? . . . So there's enough radiation loose out there to interfere with atomic-powered machines, then. That means whatever they're doing is tough and slow work. Anyhow, it's more important that they damp the action than get the men out, if they only realize it— Sue!"

Ferrel looked up quickly to see the girl standing there, already dressed for surgery, and he was not too old for a little glow of appreciation to creep over him. No wonder Jenkins' face lighted up. She was small, but her figure was shaped like that of a taller girl, not in the cute or pert lines usually associated with shorter women, and the serious competence of her expression hid none of the loveliness of her face. Obviously she was several years older than Jenkins, but as he stood up to greet her, her face softened and seemed somehow youthful beside the boy's as she looked up.

"You're Dr. Ferrel?" she asked, turning to the older man. "I was a little late—there was some trouble at first about letting me in—so I went directly to prepare before bothering you. And just so you won't be afraid to use me, my credentials are all here."

She put the little bundle on the table. and Ferrel ran through them briefly; it was better than he'd expected. Technically she wasn't a nurse at all, but a doctor of medicine, a so-called nursing doctor; there'd been the need for assistants midway between doctor and nurse for years, having the general training and abilities of both, but only in the last decade had the actual course been created, and the graduates were still limited to a few. He nodded and handed them back.

"We can use you, Dr.—"

"Brown—professional name, Dr. Ferrel. And I'm used to being called just Nurse Brown."

Jenkins cut in on the formalities. "Sue, is there any news outside about what's going on here?"

"Rumors, but they're wild, and I didn't have a chance to hear many. All I know is that they're talking about evacuating the city and everything within fifty miles of here, but it isn't official. And some people were saying the Governor was sending in troops to declare martial law over the whole section, but I didn't see any except here."

Jenkins took her off, then, to show her the Infirmary and introduce her to Jones and the two other nurses, leaving Ferrel to wait for the sound of the siren again, and to try putting two and two together to get sixteen. He attempted to make sense out of the article in the *Weekly Ray*, but gave it up finally; atomic theory had advanced too far since the sketchy studies he'd made, and the symbols were largely without meaning to him. He'd have to rely on Jenkins, it seemed. In the meantime, what was holding up the litter? He should have heard the warning siren long before.

It wasn't the litter that came in next, though, but a group of five men, two carrying a third, and a fourth supporting the fifth. Jenkins took the carried man over, Brown helping him; it was similar to the former cases, but without the actual burns from contact with hot metal. Ferrel turned to the men.

"Where's Beel and the litter?" He was inspecting the supported man's leg as he asked, and began work on it without moving the fellow to a table. Apparently a lump of radioactive matter the size of a small pea had been driven half an inch into the flesh below the thigh, and the broken bone was the result of the violent contractions of the man's own muscles under the stimulus of the radiation. It wasn't pretty. Now, however, the strength of the action had apparently burned out the nerves around, so the leg was comparatively limp and without feeling; the man lay watching, relaxed on the bench in a half-comatose condition, his eyes popping out and his lips twisted into a sick grimace, but he did not flinch as the wound was scraped out. Ferrel was working around a small leaden shield, his arms covered with heavily leaded gloves, and he dropped the scraps of flesh and isotope into a box of the same metal.

"Beel—he's out of this world, Doc," one of the others answered when he could tear his eyes off the probing. "He got himself blotto, somehow, and wrecked the litter before he got back. Couldn't take it, watching us grapple 'em out—and we hadda go in after 'em without a drop of hootch!"

Ferrel glanced at him quickly, noticing Jenkins' head jerk around as he did so. "You were getting them out? You mean you didn't come from in there?"

"Heck, no, Doc. Do we look that bad? Them two got it when the stuff decided to spit on 'em clean through their armor. Me, I got me some nice burns, but I ain't complaining—I got a look at a couple of stiffs, so I'm kicking about nothing!"

Ferrel hadn't noticed the three who had traveled under their own power, but he looked now, carefully. They were burned, and badly, by radiations, but the burns were still new enough not to give them too much trouble, and probably what they'd just been through had temporarily deadened their awareness of pain, just as a soldier on the battlefield may be wounded and not realize it until the action stops. Anyway, atomjacks were not noted for sissiness.

"There's almost a quart in the office there on the table," he told them. "One good drink apiece—no more. Then go up front and I'll send Nurse Brown in to fix up your burns as well as can be for now." Brown could apply the unguents developed to heal radiation burns as well as he could, and some division of work that would relieve Jenkins and himself seemed necessary. "Any chance of finding any more living men in the converter housings?"

"Maybe. Somebody said the thing let out a groan half a minute before it popped, so most of 'em had a chance to duck into the two safety chambers. Figure on going back there and pushing tanks ourselves unless you say no; about half an hour's work left before we can crack the chambers, I guess, then we'll know."

"Good. And there's no sense in sending in every man with a burn, or we'll be flooded here; they can wait, and it looks as if we'll have plenty of serious stuff to care for. Dr. Brown, I guess you're elected to go out with the men—have one of them drive the spare litter Jones will show you. Salve down all the burn cases, put the worst ones off duty, and just send in the ones with the jerks. You'll find my emergency kit in the office, there. Someone has to be out there to give first aid and sort them out—we haven't room for the whole plant in here."

"Right, Dr. Ferrel." She let Meyers replace her in assisting Jenkins, and was gone briefly to come out with his bag. "Come on, you men. I'll hop the litter and dress down your burns on the way. You're appointed driver, mister. Somebody should have reported that Beel person before, so the litter would be out there now."

The spokesman for the others upended the glass he'd filled, swallowed, gulped, and grinned down at her. "O. K., doctor, only out there you ain't got time to think—you gotta do. Thanks for the shot, Doc, and I'll tell Hoke you're appointing her out there."

They filed out behind Brown as Jones went out to get the second litter, and Doc went ahead with the quick-setting plastic cast for the broken leg. Too bad there weren't more of those nursing doctors; he'd have to see Palmer about it after this was over—if Palmer and he were still around. Wonder how the men in the safety chambers, about which he'd completely forgotten, would make out? There were two in each converter housing, designed as an escape for the men in case of accident, and supposed to be proof against almost anything. If the men had reached them, maybe they were all right; he wouldn't have taken a bet on it, though. With a slight shrug, he finished his work and went over to help Jenkins.

The boy nodded down at the body on the table, already showing extensive scraping and probing. "Quite a bit of spitting clean through the armor," he commented. "These words were just a little too graphic for me. I-713 couldn't do that."

"Hm-m-m." Doc was in no mood to quibble on the subject. He caught himself looking at the little box in which the stuff was put after they worked what they could out of the flesh, and jerked his eyes away quickly. Whenever the lid was being dropped, a glow could be seen inside. Jenkins always managed to keep his eyes on something else.

They were almost finished when the switchboard girl announced a call, and they waited to make the few last touches before answering, then filed into the office together. Brown's face was on the screen, smudged and with a spot of rouge standing out on each cheek. Another smudge appeared as she brushed the auburn hair out of her eyes with the back of her wrist.

"They've cracked the converter safety chambers, Dr. Ferrel. The north one held up perfectly, except for the heat and a little burn, but something happened in the other; oxygen valve stuck, and all are unconscious, but alive. Magma must have sprayed through the door, because sixteen or seventeen have the jerks, and about a dozen are dead. Some others need more care than I can give—I'm having Hokusai delegate men to carry those the stretchers won't hold, and they're all piling up on you in a bunch right now!"

Ferrel grunted and nodded. "Could have been worse, I guess. Don't kill yourself out there, Brown."

"Same to you." She blew Jenkins a kiss and snapped off, just as the whine of the litter siren reached their ears.

In the surgery again, they could see a truck showing behind it, and men lifting out bodies in apparently endless succession.

"Get their armor off, somehow, Jones—grab anyone else to help you that you can. Curare, Dodd, and keep handing it to me. We'll worry about everything else after Jenkins and I quiet them." This was obviously going to be a mass-production sort of business, not for efficiency, but through sheer necessity. And again, Jenkins with his queer taut steadiness was doing two for one that Doc could do, his face pale and his eyes almost glazed, but his hands moving endlessly and nervelessly on with his work.

Sometime during the night Jenkins looked up at Meyers, and motioned her back. "Go get some sleep, nurse; Miss Dodd can take care of both Dr. Ferrel and myself when we work close together. Your nerves are shot, and you need the rest. Dodd, you can call her back in two hours and rest yourself."

"What about you, doctor?"

"Me—" He grinned out of the corner of his mouth, crookedly. "I've got an imagination that won't sleep, and I'm needed here." The sentence ended on a rising inflection that was false to Ferrel's ear, and the older doctor looked at the boy thoughtfully.

Jenkins caught his look. "It's O. K., Doc; I'll let you know when I'm going to crack. It was O. K. to send Meyers back, wasn't it?"

"You were closer to her than I was, so you should know better than I." Technically, the nurses were all directly under his control, but they'd dropped such technicalities long before. Ferrel rubbed the small of his back briefly, then picked up his scalpel again.

A faint gray light was showing in the east, and the wards had overflowed into the waiting room when the last case from the chambers was finished as best he could be. During the night, the converter had continued to spit occasionally, even through the tank armor twice, but now there was a temporary lull in the arrival of

workers for treatment. Doc sent Jones after breakfast from the cafe
teria, then headed into the office where Jenkins was already slumped
down in the old leather chair.

The boy was exhausted almost to the limit from the combined
strain of the work and his own suppressed jitters, but he looked up
in mild surprise as he felt the prick of the needle. Ferrel finished it,
and used it on himself before explaining. "Morphine, of course.
What else can we do? Just enough to keep us going, but without
it we'll both be useless out there in a few more hours. Anyhow, there
isn't as much reason not to use it as there was when I was younger,
before the counter-agent was discovered to kill most of its habit-
forming tendency. Even five years ago, before they had that, there
were times when morphine was useful, Lord knows, though anyone
who used it except as a last resort deserved all the hell he got. A
real substitute for sleep would be better, though; wish they'd finish
up the work they're doing on that fatigue eliminator at Harvard.
Here, eat that!"

Jenkins grimaced at the breakfast Jones laid out in front of him,
but he knew as well as Doc that the food was necessary, and he
pulled the plate back to him. "What I'd give an eye tooth for, Doc,
wouldn't be a substitute—just half an hour of good old-fashioned
sleep. Only, damn it, if I knew I had time, I couldn't do it—not
with R out there bubbling away."

The telephone annunciator clipped in before Doc could answer.
"Telephone for Dr. Ferrel; emergency! Dr. Brown calling Dr. Ferrel!"

"Ferrel answering!" The phone girl's face popped off the screen,
and a tired-faced Sue Brown looked out at them. "What is it?"

"It's that little Japanese fellow—Hokusai—who's been running
things out here, Dr. Ferrel. I'm bringing him in with an acute case
of appendicitis. Prepare surgery!"

Jenkins gagged over the coffee he was trying to swallow, and
his choking voice was halfway between disgust and hysterical laughter.
"Appendicitis, Doc! My God, what comes next?"

III

It might have been worse. Brown had coupled in the little freezing
unit on the litter and lowered the temperature around the abdomen,
both preparing Hokusai for surgery and slowing down the progress of
the infection so that the appendix was still unbroken when he was

wheeled into the surgery. His seamed Oriental face had a grayish cast under the olive, but he managed a faint grin.

"Verry ssorry, Dr. Ferrel, to bother you. Verry ssorry. No ether, pleasse!"

Ferrel grunted. "No need of it, Hoke; we'll use hypothermy, since it's already begun. Over here, Jones. . . . And you might as well go back and sit down, Jenkins."

Brown was washing, and popped out again, ready to assist with the operation. "He had to be tied down, practically, Dr. Ferrel. Insisted that he only needed a little mineral oil and some peppermint for his stomach-ache! Why are intelligent people always the most stupid?"

It was a mystery to Ferrel, too, but seemingly the case. He tested the temperature quickly while the surgery hypothermy equipment began functioning, found it low enough, and began. Hoke flinched with his eyes as the scalpel touched him, then opened them in mild surprise at feeling no appreciable pain. The complete absence of nerve response with its accompanying freedom from post-operative shock was one of the great advantages of low-temperature work in surgery. Ferrel laid back the flesh, severed the appendix quickly, and removed it through the tiny incision. Then, with one of the numerous attachments, he made use of the ingenious mechanical stitcher and stepped back.

"All finished, Hoke, and you're lucky you didn't rupture—peritonitis isn't funny, even though we can cut down on it with the sulphonamides. The ward's full, so's the waiting room, so you'll have to stay on the table for a few hours until we can find a place for you; no pretty nurse, either—until the two other girls get here some time this morning. I dunno what we'll do about the patients."

"But, Dr. Ferrel, I am hear that now ssurgery—I sshould be up, already. There iss work I am do."

"You've been hearing that appendectomy patients aren't confined now, eh? Well, that's partly true. Johns Hopkins began it quite awhile ago. But for the next hour, while the temperature comes back to normal, you stay put. After that, if you want to move around a little, you can; but no going out to the converter. A little exercise probably helps more than it harms, but any strain wouldn't be good."

"But, the danger—"

"Be hanged, Hoke. You couldn't help now, long enough to do any good. Until the stuff in those stitches dissolves away completely in the body fluids, you're to take it easy—and that's two weeks, about."

The little man gave in, reluctantly. "Then I think I ssleep now. But besst you sshould call Mr. Palmer at once, pleasse! He musst know I am not there!"

Palmer took the news the hard way, with an unfair but natural tendency to blame Hokusai and Ferrel. "Damn it, Doc, I was hoping he'd get things straightened out somehow—I practically promised the Governor that Hoke could take care of it; he's got one of the best brains in the business. Now this! Well, no help, I guess. He certainly can't do it unless he's in condition to get right into things. Maybe Jorgenson, though, knows enough about it to handle it from a wheel chair, or something. How's he coming along—in shape to be taken out where he can give directions to the foremen?"

"Wait a minute." Ferrel stopped him as quickly as he could. "Jorgenson isn't here. We've got thirty-one men lying around, and he isn't one of them; and if he'd been one of the seventeen dead, you'd know it. I didn't know Jorgenson was working, even."

"He had to be—it was his process! Look, Ferrel, I was distinctly told that he was taken to you—foreman dumped him on the litter himself and reported at once! Better check up, and quick—with Hoke only half able, I've got to have Jorgenson!"

"He isn't here—I know Jorgenson. The foreman must have mistaken the big fellow from the south safety for him, but that man had black hair inside his helmet. What about the three hundred-odd that were only unconscious, or the fifteen-sixteen hundred men outside the converter when it happened?"

Palmer wiggled his jaw muscles tensely. "Jorgenson would have reported or been reported fifty times. Every man out there wants him around to boss things. He's gotta be in your ward."

"He isn't, I tell you! And how about moving some of the fellows here into the city hospitals?"

"Tried—hospitals must have been tipped off somehow about the radioactives in the flesh, and they refuse to let a man from here be brought in." Palmer was talking with only the surface of his mind, his cheek muscles bobbing as if he were chewing his thoughts and finding them tough. "Jorgenson—Hoke—and Kellar's been dead for years. Not another man in the whole country that understands this field enough to make a decent guess, even; I get lost on Page 6 myself. Ferrel, could a man in a Tomlin five-shield armor suit make the safety in twenty seconds, do you think, from—say beside the converter?"

Ferrel considered it rapidly. A Tomlin weighed about four hundred pounds, and Jorgenson was an ox of a man, but only human. "Under the stress of an emergency, it's impossible to guess what a man can do,

Palmer, but I don't see how he could work his way half that distance."

"Hm-m-m, I figured. Could he live, then, supposing he wasn't squashed? Those suits carry their own air for twenty-four hours, you know, to avoid any air cracks, pumping the carbon-dioxide back under pressure and condensing the moisture out—no openings of any kind. They've got the best insulation of all kinds we know, too."

"One chance in a billion, I'd guess; but again, it's darned hard to put any exact limit on what can be done—miracles keep happening, every day. Going to try it?"

"What else can I do? There's no alternative. I'll meet you outside No. 4 just as soon as you can make it, and bring everything you need to start working at once. Seconds may count!" Palmer's face slid sideways and up as he was reaching for the button, and Ferrel wasted no time in imitating the motion.

By all logic, there wasn't a chance, even in a Tomlin. But, until they knew, the effort would have to be made; chances couldn't be taken when a complicated process had gone out of control, with now almost certainty that Isotope R was the result—Palmer was concealing nothing, even though he had stated nothing specifically. And obviously, if Hoke couldn't handle it, none of the men at other branches of National Atomic or at the smaller partially independent plants could make even a half-hearted stab at the job.

It all rested on Jorgenson, then. And Jorgenson must be somewhere under that semimolten hell that could drive through the tank armor and send men back into the Infirmary with bones broken from their own muscular anarchy!

Ferrel's face must have shown his thoughts, judging by Jenkins' startled expression. "Jorgenson's still in there somewhere," he said quickly.

"Jorgenson! But he's the man who— Good Lord!"

"Exactly. You'll stay here and take care of the jerk cases that may come in. Brown, I'll want you out there again. Bring everything portable we have, in case we can't move him in fast enough; get one of the trucks and fit it out; and be out with it about twice as fast as you can! I'm grabbing the litter now." He accepted the emergency kit Brown thrust into his hands, dumped a caffeine tablet into his mouth without bothering to wash it down, then was out toward the litter. "No. 4, and hurry!"

Palmer was just jumping off a scooter as they cut around No. 3 and in front of the rough fence of rope strung out quite a distance beyond 4. He glanced at Doc, nodded, and dived in through the men grouped around, yelling orders to right and left as he went, and was back at Ferrel's side by the time the litter had stopped.

"O. K., Ferrel, go over there and get into armor as quickly as possible! We're going in there with the tanks, whether we can or not, and be damned to the quenching for the moment. Briggs, get those things out of there, clean out a roadway as best you can, throw in the big crane again, and we'll need all the men in armor we can get—give them steel rods and get them to probing in there for anything solid and big or small enough to be a man—five minutes at a stretch; they should be able to stand that. I'll be back pronto!"

Doc noted the confused mixture of tanks and machines of all descriptions clustered around the walls—or what was left of them—of the converter housing, and saw them yanking out everything along one side, leaving an opening where the main housing gate had stood, now ripped out to expose a crane boom rooting out the worst obstructions. Obviously they'd been busy at some kind of attempt at quenching the action, but his knowledge of atomics was too little even to guess at what it was. The equipment set up was being pushed aside by tanks without dismantling, and men were running up into the roped-in section, some already armored, others dragging on part of their armor as they went. With the help of one of the atomjacks, he climbed into a suit himself, wondering what he could do in such a casing if anything needed doing.

Palmer had a suit on before him, though, and was waiting beside one of the tanks, squat and heavily armored, its front equipped with both a shovel and a grapple swinging from movable beams. "In here, Doc." Ferrel followed him into the housing of the machine and Palmer grabbed the controls as he pulled on a short-wave headset and began shouting orders through it toward the other tanks that were moving in on their heavy treads. The dull drone of the motor picked up, and the tank began lumbering forward under the manager's direction.

"Haven't run one of these since that show-off at a picnic seven years ago," he complained, as he kicked at the controls and straightened out a developing list to left. "Though I used to be pretty handy when I was plain engineer. Damned static around here almost chokes off the radio, but I guess enough gets through. By the best guess I can make, Jorgenson should have been near the main control panel when it started, and have headed for the south chamber. Half the distance, you figure?"

"Possibly, probably slightly less."

"Yeah! And then the stuff may have tossed him around. But we'll have to try to get there." He barked into the radio again. "Briggs, get those men in suits as close as you can and have them fish with their rods about thirty feet to the left of the pillar that's still up—can they get closer?"

The answer was blurred and pieces missing, but the general idea went across. Palmer frowned. "O. K., if they can't make it, they can't; draw them back out of the reach of the stuff and hold them ready to go in. . . . No, call for volunteers! I'm offering a thousand dollars a minute to every man that gets a stick in there, double to his family if the stuff gets him, and ten times that—fifty thousand—if he locates Jorgenson! . . . Look out, you blamed fool!" The last was to one of the men who'd started forward, toward the place, jumping from one piece of broken building to grab at a pillar and swing off in his suit toward something that looked like a standing position; it toppled, but he managed a leap that carried him to another lump, steadied himself, and began probing through the mess. "Oof! You with the crane— stick it in where you can grab any of the men that pass out, if it'll reach—good! Doc, I know as well as you that the men have no business in there, even five minutes; but I'll send in a hundred more if it'll find Jorgenson!"

Doc said nothing—he knew there'd probably be a hundred or more fools willing to try, and he knew the need of them. The tanks couldn't work their way close enough for any careful investigation of the mixed mass of radioactives, machinery, building debris, and destruction, aside from which they were much too slow in such delicate probing; only men equipped with the long steel poles could do that. As he watched, some of the activity of the magma suddenly caused an eruption, and one of the men tossed up his pole and doubled back into a half circle before falling. The crane operator shoved the big boom over and made a grab, missed, brought it down again, and came out with the heaving body held by one arm, to run it back along its track and twist it outward beyond Doc's vision.

Even through the tank and the suit, heat was pouring in, and there was a faint itching in those parts where the armor was thinnest that indicated the start of a burn—though not as yet dangerous. He had no desire to think what was happening to the men who were trying to worm into the heart of it in nothing but armor; nor did he care to watch what was happening to them. Palmer was trying to inch the machine ahead, but the stuff underneath made any progress difficult. Twice something spat against the tank, but did not penetrate.

"Five minutes are up," he told Palmer. "They'd all better go directly to Dr. Brown, who should be out with the truck now for immediate treatment."

Palmer nodded and relayed the instructions. "Pick up all you can with the crane and carry them back! Send in a new bunch, Briggs, and credit them with their bonus in advance. Damn it, Doc, this can go on all day; it'll take an hour to pry around through this mess right here, and then he's probably somewhere else. The stuff seems to be getting worse in this neighborhood, too, from what accounts I've had before. Wonder if that steel plate could be pushed down?"

He threw in the clutch engaging the motor to the treads and managed to twist through toward it. There was a slight slipping of the lugs, then the tractors caught, and the nose of the tank thrust forward; almost without effort, the fragment of housing toppled from its leaning position and slid forward. The tank growled, fumbled, and slowly climbed up onto it and ran forward another twenty feet to its end; the support settled slowly, but something underneath checked it, and they were still again. Palmer worked the grapple forward, nosing a big piece of masonry out of the way, and two men reached out with the ends of their poles to begin probing, futilely. Another change of men came out, then another.

Briggs' voice crackled erratically through the speaker again. "Palmer, I got a fool here who wants to go out on the end of your beam, if you can swing around so the crane can lift him out to it."

"Start him coming!" Again he began jerking the levers, and the tank bucked and heaved, backed and turned, ran forward, and repeated it all, while the plate that was holding them flopped up and down on its precarious balance.

Doc held his breath and began praying to himself; his admiration for the men who'd go out in that stuff was increasing by leaps and bounds, along with his respect for Palmer's ability.

The crane boom bobbed toward them, and the scoop came running out, but wouldn't quite reach; their own tank was relatively light and mobile compared to the bigger machine, but Palmer already had that pushed out to the limit, and hanging over the edge of the plate. It still lacked three feet of reaching.

"Damn!" Palmer slapped open the door of the tank, jumped forward on the tread, and looked down briefly before coming back inside. "No chance to get closer! Wheeoo! Those men earn their money."

But the crane operator had his own tricks, and was bobbing the boom of his machine up and down slowly with a motion that set the scoop swinging like a huge pendulum, bringing it gradually closer to the grapple beam. The man had an arm out, and finally caught the beam, swinging out instantly from the scoop that drew backward behind him. He hung suspended for a second, pitching his body around to a better position, then somehow wiggled up onto the end and braced himself with his legs. Doc let his breath out and Palmer inched the tank around to a forward position again. Now the pole of the atomjack could cover the wide territory before them, and he began using it rapidly.

"Win or lose, that man gets a triple bonus," Palmer muttered. "Uh!"

The pole had located something, and was feeling around to deter-mine size; the man glanced at them and pointed frantically. Doc jumped forward to the windows as Palmer ran down the grapple and began pushing it down into the semi-molten stuff under the pole; there was resistance there, but finally the prong of the grapple broke under and struck on something that refused to come up. The man-ager's hands moved the controls gently, making it tug from side to side; reluctantly, it gave and moved forward toward them, coming upward until they could make out the general shape. It was definitely no Tomlin suit!

"Lead hopper box! Damn— Wait, Jorgenson wasn't anybody's fool; when he saw he couldn't make the safety, he might . . . maybe —" Palmer slapped the grapple down again, against the closed lid of the chest, but the hook was too large. Then the man clinging there caught the idea and slid down to the hopper chest, his armored hands grabbing at the lid. He managed to lift a corner of it until the grapple could catch and lift it the rest of the way, and his hands started down to jerk upward again.

The manager watched his motions, then flipped the box over with the grapple, and pulled it closer to the tank body; magma was running out, but there was a gleam of something else inside.

"Start praying, Doc!" Palmer worked it to the side of the tank and was out through the door again, letting the merciless heat and radia-tion stream in.

But Ferrel wasn't bothering with that now; he followed, reaching down into the chest to help the other two lift out the body of a huge man in a five-shield Tomlin! Somehow, they wangled the six-hundred-odd pounds out and up on the treads, then into the housing, barely big enough for all of them. The atomjack pulled himself inside, shut the door, and flopped forward on his face, out cold.

"Never mind him—check Jorgenson!" Palmer's voice was heavy with the reaction from the hunt, but he turned the tank and sent it outward at top speed, regardless of risk. Contrarily, it bucked through the mass more readily than it had crawled in through the cleared section.

Ferrel unscrewed the front plate of the armor on Jorgenson as rapidly as he could, though he knew already that the man was still miraculously alive—corpses don't jerk with force enough to move a four-hundred-pound suit appreciably. A side glance, as they drew beyond the wreck of the converter housing, showed the men already beginning to set up equipment to quell the atomic reaction again, but the armor front plate came loose at last, and he dropped his eyes back without noticing details, to cut out a section of clothing and make the needed injections; curare first, then neo-heroin, and curare again, though he did not dare inject the quantity that seemed necessary. There was nothing more he could do until they could get the man out of his armor. He turned to the atomjack, who was already sitting up, propped against the driving seat's back.

"'Snothing much, Doc," the fellow managed. "No jerks, just burn and that damned heat! Jorgenson?"

"Alive at least," Palmer answered, with some relief. The tank stopped, and Ferrel could see Brown running forward from beside a truck. "Get that suit off you, get yourself treated for the burn, then go up to the office where the check will be ready for you!"

"Fifty-thousand check?" The doubt in the voice registered over the weakness.

"Fifty thousand plus triple your minute time, and cheap; maybe we'll toss in a medal or a bottle of Scotch, too. Here, you fellows give a hand."

Ferrel had the suit ripped off with Brown's assistance, and paused only long enough for one grateful breath of clean, cool air before leading the way toward the truck. As he neared it, Jenkins popped out, directing a group of men to move two loaded stretchers onto the litter, and nodding jerkily at Ferrel. "With the truck all equipped, we decided to move out here and take care of the damage as it came up— Sue and I rushed them through enough to do until we can find more time, so we could give full attention to Jorgenson. He's still living!"

"By a miracle. Stay out here, Brown, until you've finished with the men from inside, then we'll try to find some rest for you."

The three huskies carrying Jorgenson placed the body on the table set up, and began ripping off the bulky armor as the truck got under way. Fresh gloves came out of a small sterilizer, and the two doctors fell to work at once, treating the badly burned flesh and trying to locate and remove the worst of the radioactive matter

"No use." Doc stepped back and shook his head. "It's all over him, probably clear into his bones in places. We'd have to put him through a filter to get it all out!"

Palmer was looking down at the raw mass of flesh, with all the layman's sickness at such a sight. "Can you fix him up, Ferrel?"

"We can try, that's all. Only explanation I can give for his being alive at all is that the hopper box must have been pretty well above the stuff until a short time ago—very short—and this stuff didn't work in until it sank. He's practically dehydrated now, apparently, but he couldn't have perspired enough to keep from dying of heat if he'd been under all that for even an hour—insulation or no insulation." There was admiration in Doc's eyes as he looked down at the immense figure of the man. "And he's tough; if he weren't, he'd have killed himself by exhaustion, even confined inside that suit and box, after the jerks set in. He's close to having done so, anyway. Until we can find some way of getting that stuff out of him, we don't dare risk getting rid of the curare's effect—that's a time-consuming job, in itself. Better give him another water and sugar intravenous, Jenkins. Then, if we do fix him up, Palmer, I'd say it's a fifty-fifty chance whether or not all this hasn't driven him stark crazy."

The truck had stopped, and the men lifted the stretcher off and carried it inside as Jenkins finished the injection. He went ahead of them, but Doc stopped outside to take Palmer's cigarette for a long drag, and let them go ahead.

"Cheerful!" The manager lighted another from the butt, his shoulders sagging. "I've been trying to think of one man who might possibly be of some help to us, Doc, and there isn't such a person —anywhere. I'm sure now, after being in there, that Hoke couldn't do it. Kellar, if he were still alive, could probably pull the answer out of a hat after three looks—he had an instinct and genius for it; the best man the business ever had, even if his tricks did threaten to steal our work out from under us and give him the lead. But— well, now there's Jorgenson—either he gets in shape, or else!"

Jenkins' frantic yell reached them suddenly. "Doc! Jorgenson's dead! He's stopped breathing entirely!"

Doc jerked forward into a full run, a white-faced Palmer at his heels.

IV

Dodd was working artificial respiration and Jenkins had the oxygen mask in his hands, adjusting it over Jorgenson's face, before Ferrel reached the table. He made a grab for the pulse that had been fluttering weakly enough before, felt it flicker feebly once, pause for about three times normal period, lift feebly again, and then stop completely. "Adrenalin!"

"Already shot it into his heart, Doc! Cardiacine, too!" The boy's voice was bordering on hysteria, but Palmer was obviously closer to it than Jenkins.

"Doc, you gotta—"

"Get the hell out of here!" Ferrel's hands suddenly nad a life of their own as he grabbed frantically for instruments, ripped bandages off the man's chest, and began working against time, when time had all the advantages. It wasn't surgery—hardly good butchery; the bones that he cut through so ruthlessly with savage strokes of an instrument could never heal smoothly after being so mangled. But he couldn't worry about minor details now.

He tossed back the flap of flesh and ribs that he'd hacked out. "Stop the bleeding, Jenkins!" Then his hands plunged into the chest cavity, somehow finding room around Dodd's and Jenkins', and were suddenly incredibly gentle as they located the heart itself and began working on it, the skilled, exact massage of a man who knew every function of the vital organ. Pressure here, there, relax, pressure again; take it easy, don't rush things! It would do no good to try to set it going as feverishly as his emotions demanded. Pure oxygen was feeding into the lungs, and the heart could safely do less work. Hold it steady, one beat a second, sixty a minute.

It had been perhaps half a minute from the time the heart stopped before his massage was circulating blood again; too little time to worry about damage to the brain, the first part to be permanently affected by stoppage of the circulation. Now, if the heart could start again by itself within any reasonable time, death would be cheated again. How long? He had no idea. They'd taught him ten minutes when he was studying medicine, then there'd been a case of twenty minutes once, and while he was interning it had been pushed up to a record of slightly over an hour, which still stood; but that was an exceptional case. Jorgenson, praise be, was a normally healthy and vigorous specimen, and his system had been in first-class condition, but with the torture of those long hours, the radioactive, narcotic and curare all fighting against him, still one more miracle was needed to keep his life going.

Press, massage, relax, don't hurry it too much. There! For a second, his fingers felt a faint flutter, then again; but it stopped. Still, as long as the organ could show such signs, there was hope, unless his fingers grew too tired and he muffed the job before the moment when the heart could be safely trusted by itself.

"Jenkins!"

"Yes, sir!"

"Ever do any heart massage?"

"Practiced it in school, sir, on a model, but never actually. Oh, a dog in dissection class, for five minutes. I . . . I don't think you'd better trust me, Doc."

"I may have to. If you did it on a dog for five minutes, you can do it on a man, probably. You know what hangs on it—you saw the converter and know what's going on."

Jenkins nodded, the tense nod he'd used earlier. "I know—that's why you can't trust me. I told you I'd let you know when I was going to crack—well, it's damned near here!"

Could a man tell his weakness, if he were about finished? Doc didn't know; he suspected that the boy's own awareness of his nerves would speed up such a break, if anything, but Jenkins was a queer case, having taut nerves sticking out all over him, yet a steadiness under fire that few older men could have equaled. If he had to use him, he would; there was no other answer.

Doc's fingers were already feeling stiff—not yet tired, but showing signs of becoming so. Another few minutes, and he'd have to stop. There was the flutter again, one—two—three! Then it stopped. There had to be some other solution to this; it was impossible to keep it up for the length of time probably needed, even if he and Jenkins spelled each other. Only Michel at Mayo's could—Mayo's! If they could get it here in time, that wrinkle he'd seen demonstrated at their last medical convention was the answer.

"Jenkins, call Mayo's—you'll have to get Palmer's O. K., I guess—ask for Kubelik, and bring the extension where I can talk to him!"

He could hear Jenkins' voice, level enough at first, then with a depth of feeling he'd have thought impossible in the boy. Dodd looked at him quickly and managed a grim smile, even as she continued with the respiration; nothing could make her blush, though it should have done so.

The boy jumped back. "No soap, Doc! Palmer can't be located—and that post-mortem misconception at the board won't listen."

Doc studied his hands in silence, wondering, then gave it up; there'd be no hope of his lasting while he sent out the boy. "O. K., Jenkins, you'll have to take over here, then. Steady does it, come on in slowly, get your fingers over mine. Now, catch the motion? Easy, don't rush things. You'll hold out—you'll have to! You've done better than I had any right to ask for so far, and you don't need to distrust yourself. There, got it?"

"Got it, Doc. I'll try, but for Pete's sake, whatever you're planning, get back here quick! I'm not lying about cracking! You'd better let Meyers replace Dodd and have Sue called back in here; she's the best nerve tonic I know."

"Call her in then, Dodd." Doc picked up a hypodermic syringe, filled it quickly with water to which a drop of another liquid added a brownish-yellow color, and forced his tired old legs into a reasonably rapid trot out of the side door and toward Communications. Maybe the switchboard operator was stubborn, but there were ways of handling people.

He hadn't counted on the guard outside the Communications Building, though. "Halt!"

"Life or death; I'm a physician."

"Not in here—I got orders." The bayonet's menace apparently wasn't enough; the rifle went up to the man's shoulder, and his chin jutted out with the stubbornness of petty authority and reliance on orders. "Nobody sick here. There's plenty of phones elsewhere. You get back—and fast!"

Doc started forward and there was a faint click from the rifle as the safety went off; the darned fool meant what he said. Shrugging, Ferrel stepped back—and brought the hypodermic needle up inconspicuously in line with the guard's face. "Ever see one of these things squirt curare? It can reach before your bullet hits!"

"Curare?" The guard's eyes flicked to the needle, and doubt came into them. The man frowned. "That's the stuff that kills people on arrows, ain't it?"

"It is—cobra venom, you know. One drop on the outside of your skin and you're dead in ten seconds." Both statements were out-and-out lies, but Doc was counting on the superstitious ignorance of the average man in connection with poisons. "This little needle can spray you with it very nicely, and it may be a fast death, but not a pleasant one. Want to put down the rifle?"

A regular might have shot; but the militiaman was taking no chances. He lowered the rifle gingerly, his eyes on the needle, then kicked the weapon aside at Doc's motion. Ferrel approached, holding the needle out, and the man shrank backward and away, letting him pick up the rifle as he went past to avoid being shot in the back. Lost time! But he knew his way around this little building, at least, and went straight toward the girl at the board.

"Get up!" His voice came from behind her shoulder and she turned to see the rifle in one of his hands, the needle in the other, almost touching her throat. "This is loaded with curare, deadly poison, and too much hangs on getting a call through to bother with physician's oaths right now, young lady. Up! No plugs! That's right; now get over there, out of the cell—there, on your face, cross your hands behind your back, and grab your ankles—right! Now if you move, you won't move long!"

Those gangster pictures he'd seen were handy, at that. She was thoroughly frightened and docile. But, perhaps, not so much so she might not have bungled his call deliberately. He had to do that himself. Darn it, the red lights were trunk lines, but which plug—try the inside one, it looked more logical; he'd seen it done, but couldn't remember. Now, you flip back one of these switches—uh-uh, the other way. The tone came in assuring him he had it right, and he dialed operator rapidly, his eyes flickering toward the girl lying on the floor, his thoughts on Jenkins and the wasted time running on.

"Operator, this is an emergency. I'm Walnut, 7654; I want to put in a long-distance call to Dr. Kubelik, Mayo's Hospital, Rochester, Minnesota. If Kubelik isn't there, I'll take anyone else who answers from his department. Speed is urgent."

"Very good, sir." Long-distance operators, mercifully, were usually efficient. There was the repeated signals and clicks of relays as she put it through, the answer from the hospital board, more wasted time, and then a face appeared on the screen; but not that of Kubelik. It was a much younger man.

Ferrel wasted no time in introduction. "I've got an emergency case here where all Hades depends on saving a man, and it can't be done without that machine of Dr. Kubelik's; he knows me, if he's there

.—I'm Ferrel, met him at the convention, got him to show me how the thing worked."

"Kubelik hasn't come in yet, Dr. Ferrel; I'm his assistant. But, if you mean the heart and lung exciter, it's already boxed and supposed to leave for Harvard this morning. They've got a rush case out there, and may need it—"

"Not as much as I do."

"I'll have to call— Wait a minute, Dr. Ferrel, seems I remember your name now. Aren't you the chap with National Atomic?"

Doc nodded. "The same. Now, about that machine, if you'll stop the formalities—"

The face on the screen nodded, instant determination showing, with an underlying expression of something else. "We'll ship it down to you instantly, Ferrel. Got a field for a plane?"

"Not within three miles, but I'll have a truck sent out for it. How long?"

"Take too long by truck if you need it down there, Ferrel; I'll arrange to transship in air from our special speedster to a helicopter, have it delivered wherever you want. About—um, loading plane, flying a couple hundred miles, transshipping—about half an hour's the best we can do."

"Make it the square of land south of the Infirmary, which is crossed visibly from the air. Thanks!"

"Wait, Dr. Ferrel!" The younger man checked Doc's cut-off. "Can you use it when you get it? It's tricky work."

"Kubelik gave quite a demonstration and I'm used to tricky work. I'll chance it—have to. Too long to rouse Kubelik himself, isn't it?"

"Probably. O. K., I've got the telescript reply from the shipping office, it's starting for the plane. I wish you luck!"

Ferrel nodded his thanks, wondering. Service like that was welcome, but it wasn't the most comforting thing, mentally, to know that the mere mention of National Atomic would cause such an about-face. Rumors, it seemed, were spreading, and in a hurry, in spite of Palmer's best attempts. Good Lord, what was going on here? He'd been too busy for any serious worrying or to realize, but—well, it had gotten him the exciter, and for that he should be thankful.

The guard was starting uncertainly off for reinforcements when Doc came out, and he realized that the seemingly endless call must have been over in short order. He tossed the rifle well out of the man's reach and headed back toward the Infirmary at a run, wondering how Jenkins had made out—it had to be all right!

Jenkins wasn't standing over the body of Jorgenson; Brown was there instead, her eyes moist and her face pinched in and white around the nostrils that stood out at full width. She looked up, shook her head at him as he started forward, and went on working at Jorgenson's heart.

"Jenkins cracked?"

"Nonsense! This is woman's work, Dr. Ferrel, and I took over for him, that's all. You men try to use brute force all your life and then wonder why a woman can do twice as much delicate work where strong muscles are a nuisance. I chased him out and took over, that's all." But there was a catch in her voice as she said it, and Meyers was looking down entirely too intently at the work of artificial respiration.

"Hi, Doc!" It was Blake's voice that broke in. "Get away from there; when this Dr. Brown needs help, I'll be right in there. I've been sleeping like a darned fool all night, from four this morning on. Didn't hear the phone, or something, didn't know what was going on until I got to the gate out there. You go rest."

Ferrel grunted in relief; Blake might have been dead drunk when he finally reached home, which would explain his not hearing the phone, but his animal virility had soaked it out with no visible sign. The only change was the absence of the usual cocky grin on his face as he moved over beside Brown to test Jorgenson. "Thank the Lord you're here, Blake. How's Jorgenson doing?"

Brown's voice answered in a monotone, words coming in time to the motions of her fingers. "His heart shows signs of coming around once in a while, but it doesn't last. He isn't getting worse from what I can tell, though."

"Good. If we can keep him going half an hour more, we can turn all this over to a machine. Where's Jenkins?"

"A machine? Oh, the Kubelik exciter, of course. He was working on it when I was there. We'll keep Jorgenson alive until then, anyway, Dr. Ferrel."

"Where's Jenkins?" he repeated sharply, when she stopped with no intention of answering the former question.

Blake pointed toward Ferrel's office, the door of which was now closed. "In there. But lay off him, Doc. I saw the whole thing, and he feels like the deuce about it. He's a good kid, but only a kid, and this kind of hell could get any of us."

"I know all that." Doc headed toward the office, as much for a smoke as anything else. The sight of Blake's rested face was somehow an island of reassurance in this sea of fatigue and nerves. "Don't worry,

Brown, I'm not planning on lacing him down, so you needn't defend your man so carefully. It was my fault for not listening to him."

Brown's eyes were pathetically grateful in the brief flash she threw him, and he felt like a heel for the gruffness that had been his first reaction toward Jenkins' absence. If this kept on much longer, though, they'd all be in worse shape than the boy, whose back was toward him as he opened the door. The still, huddled shape did not raise its head from its arms as Ferrel put his hand onto one shoulder, and the voice was muffled and distant.

"I cracked, Doc—high, wide and handsome, all over the place. I couldn't take it! Standing there, Jorgenson maybe dying because I couldn't control myself right, the whole plant blowing up, all my fault. I kept telling myself I was O. K., I'd go on, then I cracked. Screamed like a baby! Dr. Jenkins—nerve specialist!"

"Yeah. . . . Here, are you going to drink this, or do I have to hold your blasted nose and pour it down your throat?" It was crude psychology, but it worked, and Doc handed over the drink, waited for the other to down it, and passed a cigarette across before sinking into his own chair. "You warned me, Jenkins, and I risked it on my own responsibility, so nobody's kicking. But I'd like to ask a couple of questions."

"Go ahead—what's the difference?" Jenkins had recovered a little, obviously, from the note of defiance that managed to creep into his voice.

"Did you know Brown could handle that kind of work? And did you pull your hands out before she could get hers in to replace them?"

"She told me she could. I didn't know before. I dunno about the other; I think . . . yeah, Doc, she had her hands over mine. But—"

Ferrel nodded, satisfied with his own guess. "I thought so. You didn't crack, as you put it, until your mind knew it was safe to do so —and then you simply passed the work on. By that definition, I'm cracking, too. I'm sitting in here, smoking, talking to you, when out there a man needs attention. The fact that he's getting it from two others, one practically fresh, the other at least a lot better off than we are, doesn't have a thing to do with it, does it?"

"But it wasn't that way, Doc. I'm not asking for grandstand stuff from anybody."

"Nobody's giving it to you, son. All right, you screamed—why not? It didn't hurt anything. I growled at Brown when I came in for the same reason—exhausted, overstrained nerves. If I went out there and had to take over from them, I'd probably scream myself, or start biting my tongue—nerves have to have an outlet; physically, it does them no good, but there's a psychological need for it." The boy wasn't convinced, and Doc sat back in the chair, staring at him thoughtfully. "Ever wonder why I'm here?"

"No, sir."

"Well, you might. Twenty-seven years ago, when I was about your age, there wasn't a surgeon in this country—or the world, for that matter—who had the reputation I had; any kind of surgery, brain, what have you. They're still using some of my techniques . . . uh-hum, thought you'd remember when the association of names hit you. I had a different wife then, Jenkins, and there was a baby coming. Brain tumor—I had to do it, no one else could. I did it, somehow, but I went out of that operating room in a haze, and it was three days later when they'd tell me she'd died; not my fault—I know that now—but I couldn't realize it then.

"So, I tried setting up as a general practitioner. No more surgery for me! And because I was a fair diagnostician, which most surgeons aren't, I made a living, at least. Then, when this company was set up, I appled for the job, and got it; I still had a reputation of sorts. It was a new field, something requiring study and research, and damned near every ability of most specialists plus a general practitioner's, so it kept me busy enough to get over my phobia of surgery. Compared to me, you don't know what nerves or cracking means. That little scream was a minor incident."

Jenkins made no comment, but lighted the cigarette he'd been holding. Ferrel relaxed farther into the chair, knowing that he'd be called if there was any need for his work, and glad to get his mind at least partially off Jorgenson. "It's hard to find a man for this work, Jenkins. It takes too much ability at too many fields, even though it pays well enough. We went through plenty of applicants before we decided on you, and I'm not regretting our choice. As a matter of fact, you're better equipped for the job than Blake was—your record looked as if you'd deliberately tried for this kind of work."

"I did."

"Hm-m-m." That was the one answer Doc had least expected; so far as he knew, no one deliberately tried for a job at Atomics—they usually wound up trying for it after comparing their receipts for a year or so with the salary paid by National. "Then you knew what was needed and picked it up in toto. Mind if I ask why?"

Jenkins shrugged. "Why not? Turnabout's fair play. It's kind of complicated, but the gist of it doesn't take much telling. Dad had an atomic plant of his own—and a darned good one, too, Doc, even if it wasn't as big as National. I was working in it when I was fifteen, and I went through two years of university work in atomics with the best intentions of carrying on the business. Sue—well, she was the neighbor girl I followed around, and we had money at the time; that wasn't why she married me, though. I never did figure that out— she'd had a hard enough life, but she was already holding down a job at Mayo's, and I was just a raw kid. Anyway—

"The day we came home from our honeymoon, dad got a big contract on a new process we'd worked out. It took some swinging, but he got the equipment and started it. . . . My guess is that one of the controls broke through faulty construction; the process was right! We'd been over it too often not to know what it would do. But, when the estate was cleared up, I had to give up the idea of a degree in atomics, and Sue was back working at the hospital. Atomic courses cost real money. Then one of Sue's medical acquaintances fixed it for me to get a scholarship in medicine that almost took care of it, so I chose the next best thing to what I wanted."

"National and one of the biggest competitors—if you can call it that—are permitted to give degrees in atomics," Doc reminded the boy. The field was still too new to be a standing university course, and there were no better teachers in the business than such men as Palmer, Hokusai and Jorgenson. "They pay a salary while you're learning, too."

"Hm-m-m. Takes ten years that way, and the salary's just enough for a single man. No, I'd married Sue with the intention she wouldn't have to work again; well, she did until I finished internship, but I knew if I got the job here I could support her. As an atomjack, working up to an engineer, the prospects weren't so good. We're saving a little money now, and some day maybe I'll get a crack at it yet. . . . Doc, what's this all about? You babying me out of my fit?"

Ferrel grinned at the boy. "Nothing else, son, though I was curious. And it worked. Feel all right now, don't you?"

"Mostly, except for what's going on out there—I got too much of a look at it from the truck. Oh, I could use some sleep, I guess, but I'm O. K. again."

"Good." Doc had profited almost as much as Jenkins from the rambling off-trail talk, and had managed more rest from it than from nursing his own thoughts. "Suppose we go out and see how they're making out with Jorgenson? Um, what happened to Hoke. come to think of it?"

"Hoke? Oh, he's in my office now, figuring out things with a pencil and paper since we wouldn't let him go back out there. I was wondering—"

"Atomics? . . . Then suppose you go in and talk to him; he's a good guy, and he won't give you the brush-off. Nobody else around here apparently suspected this Isotope R business, and you might offer a fresh lead for him. With Blake and the nurses here and the men out of the mess except for the tanks, there's not much you can do to help on my end."

Ferrel felt better at peace with the world than he had since the call from Palmer as he watched Jenkins head off across the surgery toward his office; and the glance that Brown threw, first toward the boy, then back at Doc, didn't make him feel worse. That girl could say more with her eyes than most women could with their mouths! He went over toward the operating table where Blake was now working the heart message with one of the fresh nurses attending to respiration and casting longing glances toward the mechanical lung apparatus; it couldn't be used in this case, since Jorgenson's chest had to be free for heart attention.

Blake looked up, his expression worried. "This isn't so good, Doc. He's been sinking in the last few minutes. I was just going to call you. I—"

The last words were drowned out by the bull-throated drone that came dropping down from above them, a sound peculiarly characteristic of the heavy Sikorsky freighters with their modified blades to gain lift. Ferrel nodded at Brown's questioning glance, but he didn't choose to shout as his hands went over those of Blake and took over the delicate work of simulating the natural heart action. As Blake withdrew, the sound stopped, and Doc motioned him out with his head.

"You'd better go to them and oversee bringing in the apparatus—and grab up any of the men you see to act as porters—or send Jones for them. The machine is an experimental model, and pretty cumbersome; must weigh seven-eight hundred pounds."

"I'll get them myself—Jones is sleeping."

There was no flutter to Jorgenson's heart under Doc's deft manipulations, though he was exerting every bit of skill he possessed. "How long since there was a sign?"

"About four minutes, now. Doc, is there still a chance?"

"Hard to say. Get the machine, though, and we'll hope."

But still the heart refused to respond, though the pressure and

manipulation kept the blood circulating and would at least prevent any
starving or asphyxiation of the body cells. Carefully, delicately, he
brought his mind into his fingers, trying to woo a faint quiver. Perhaps he did, once, but he couldn't be sure. It all depended on how
quickly they could get the machine working now, and how long a
man could live by manipulation alone. That point was still unsettled.

But there was no question about the fact that the spark of life
burned faintly and steadily lower in Jorgenson, while outside the
man-made hell went on ticking off the minutes that separated it from
becoming Mahler's Isotope. Normally, Doc was an agnostic, but now,
unconsciously, his mind slipped back into the simple faith of his childhood, and he heard Brown echoing the prayer that was on his lips.
The second hand of the watch before him swung around and around
and around again before he heard the sound of men's feet at the back
entrance, and still there was no definite quiver from the heart under
his fingers. How much time did he have left, if any, for the difficult
and unfamiliar operation required?

His side glance showed the seemingly innumerable filaments of
platinum that had to be connected into the nerves governing Jorgenson's heart and lungs, all carefully coded, yet almost terrifying in their
complexity. If he made a mistake anywhere, it was at least certain
there would be no time for a second trial; if his fingers shook or his
tired eyes clouded at the wrong instant, there would be no help from
Jorgenson. Jorgenson would be dead!

V

"Take over massage, Brown," he ordered. "And keep it up no matter
what happens. Good. Dodd, assist me, and hang onto my signals. If
it works, we can all rest afterward."

Ferrel wondered grimly with that part of his mind that was off by
itself whether he could justify his boast to Jenkins of having been the
world's greatest surgeon; it had been true once, he knew with no need
for false modesty, but that was long ago, and this was at best a devilish job. He'd hung on with a surge of the old fascination as Kubelik
had performed it on a dog at the convention, and his memory for such
details was still good, as were his hands. But something else goes into
the making of a great surgeon, and he wondered if that were still with
him.

Then, as his fingers made the microscopic little motions needed
and Dodd became another pair of hands, he ceased wondering. What-

ever it was, he could feel it surging through him, and there was a pure joy to it somewhere, over and above the urgency of the work. This was probably the last time he'd ever feel it, and if the operation succeeded, probably it was a thing he could put with the few mental treasures that were still left from his former success. The man on the table ceased to be Jorgenson, the excessively gadgety Infirmary became again the main operating theater of that same Mayo's which had produced Brown and this strange new machine, and his fingers were again those of the Great Ferrel, the miracle boy from Mayo's, who could do the impossible twice before breakfast without turning a hair.

Some of his feeling was devoted to the machine itself. Massive, ugly, with parts sticking out in haphazard order, it was more like something from an inquisition chamber than a scientist's achievement, but it worked—he'd seen it functioning. In that ugly mass of assorted pieces, little currents were generated and modulated to feed out to the heart and lungs and replace the orders given by a brain that no longer worked or could not get through, to co-ordinate breathing and beating according to the need. It was a product of the combined genius of surgery and electronics, but wonderful as the exciter was, it was distinctly secondary to the technique Kubelik had evolved for selecting and connecting only those nerves and nerve bundles necessary, and bringing the almost impossible into the limits of surgical possibility.

Brown interrupted, and that interruption in the midst of such an operation indicated clearly the strain she was under. "The heart fluttered a little then, Dr. Ferrel."

Ferrel nodded, untroubled by the interruption. Talk, which bothered most surgeons, was habitual in his own little staff, and he always managed to have one part of his mind reserved for that while the rest went on without noticing. "Good. That gives us at least double the leeway I expected."

His hands went on, first with the heart which was the more pressing danger. Would the machine work, he wondered, in this case? Curare and radio-actives, fighting each other, were an odd combination. Yet, the machine controlled the nerves close to the vital organ, pounding its message through into the muscles, where the curare had a complicated action that paralyzed the whole nerve, establishing a long block to the control impulses from the brain. Could the nerve impulses from the machine be forced through the short paralyzed passages? Probably —the strength of its signals was controllable. The only proof was in trying.

Brown drew back her hands and stared down uncomprehendingly. "It's beating, Dr. Ferrel! By itself . . . it's beating!"

He nodded again, though the mask concealed his smile. His technique was still not faulty, and he had performed the operation correctly after seeing it once on a dog! He was still the Great Ferrel! Then, the ego in him fell back to normal, though the lift remained, and his exultation centered around the more important problem of Jorgenson's living. And, later, when the lungs began moving of themselves as the nurse stopped working them, he had been expecting it. The detail work remaining was soon over, and he stepped back, dropping the mask from his face and pulling off his gloves.

"Congratulations, Dr. Ferrel!" The voice was guttural, strange. "A truly great operation—truly great. I almost stopped you, but now I am glad I did not; it was a pleasure to observe you, sir." Ferrel looked up in amazement at the bearded smiling face of Kubelik, and he found no words as he accepted the other's hand. But Kubelik apparently expected none.

"I, Kubelik, came, you see; I could not trust another with the machine, and fortunately I made the plane. Then you seemed so sure, so confident—so when you did not notice me, I remained in the background, cursing myself. Now, I shall return, since you have no need of me—the wiser for having watched you. . . . No, not a word; not a word from you, sir. Don't destroy your miracle with words. The 'copter waits me, I go; but my admiration for you remains forever!"

Ferrel still stood looking down at his hand as the roar of the 'copter cut in, then at the breathing body with the artery on the neck now pulsing regularly. That was all that was needed; he had been admired by Kubelik, the man who thought all other surgeons were fools and nincompoops. For a second or so longer he treasured it, then shrugged it off.

"Now," he said to the others, as the troubles of the plant fell back on his shoulders, "all we have to do is hope that Jorgenson's brain wasn't injured by the session out there, or by this continued artificially maintained life, and try to get him in condition so he can talk before it's too late. God grant us time! Blake, you know the detail work as well as I do, and we can't both work on it. You and the fresh nurses take over, doing the bare minimum needed for the patients scattered around the wards and waiting room. Any new ones?"

"None for some time; I think they've reached a stage where that's over with," Brown answered.

"I hope so. Then go round up Jenkins and lie down somewhere.

That goes for you and Meyers, too, Dodd. Blake, give us three hours if you can, and get us up. There won't be any new developments before then, and we'll save time in the long run by resting. Jorgenson's to get first attention!"

The old leather chair made a fair sort of bed, and Ferrel was too exhausted physically and mentally to be choosy—too exhausted to benefit as much as he should from sleep of three hours' duration, for that matter, though it was almost imperative he try. Idly, he wondered what Palmer would think of all his safeguards had he known that Kubelik had come into the place so easily and out again. Not that it mattered; it was doubtful whether anyone else would want to come near, let alone inside the plant.

In that, apparently, he was wrong. It was considerably less than the three hours when he was awakened to hear the bull-roar of a helicopter outside. But sleep clouded his mind too much for curiosity and he started to drop back into his slumber. Then another sound cut in, jerking him out of his drowsiness. It was the sharp sputter of a machine gun from the direction of the gate, a pause and another burst; an eddy of sleep-memory indicated that it had begun before the helicopter's arrival, so it could not be that they were gunning. More trouble, and while it was none of his business, he could not go back to sleep. He got up and went out into the surgery, just as a gnomish little man hopped out from the rear entrance.

The fellow scooted toward Ferrel after one birdlike glance at Blake, his words spilling out with a jerky self-importance that should have been funny, but missed it by a small margin; under the surface, sincerity still managed to show. "Dr. Ferrel? Uh Dr. Kubelik—Mayo's, you know—he reported you were short-handed; stacking patients in the other rooms. We volunteered for duty—me, four other doctors, nine nurses. Probably should have checked with you, but couldn't get a phone through. Took the liberty of coming through directly, fast as we could push our 'copters."

Ferrel glanced through the back, and saw that there were three of the machines, instead of the one he'd thought, with men and equipment piling out of them. Mentally he kicked himself for not asking help when he'd put through the call; but he'd been used to working with his own little staff for so long that the ready response of his profession to emergencies had been almost forgotten. "You know you're taking chances coming here, naturally? Then, in that case, I'm grateful to you and Kubelik. We've got about forty patients here, all of

whom should have considerable attention, though I frankly doubt
whether there's room for you to work."

The man hitched his thumb backward jerkily. "Don't worry about
that. Kubelik goes the limit when he arranges things. Everything we
need with us, practically all the hospital's atomic equipment; though
maybe you'll have to piece us out there. Even a field hospital tent,
portable wards for every patient you have. Want relief in here or
would you rather have us simply move out the patients to the tent,
leave this end to you? Oh, Kubelik sent his regards. Amazing of him!"

Kubelik, it seemed, had a tangible idea of regards, however dramati-
cally he was inclined to express them; with him directing the volunteer
force, the wonder was that the whole staff and equipment hadn't been
moved down. "Better leave this end," Ferrel decided. "Those in the
wards will probably be better off in your tent as well as the men now
in the waiting room; we're equipped beautifully for all emergency
work, but not used to keeping the patients here any length of time,
so our accommodations that way are rough. Dr. Blake will show you
around and help you get organized in the routine we use here. He'll
get help for you in erecting the tent, too. By the way, did you hear
the commotion by the entrance as you were landing?"

"We did, indeed. We saw it, too—bunch of men in some kind of
uniform shooting a machine gun; hitting the ground, though. Bunch
of other people running back away from it, shaking their fists, looked
like. We were expecting a dose of the same, maybe; didn't notice us,
though."

Blake snorted in half amusement. "You probably would have gotten
it if our manager hadn't forgotten to give orders covering the air approach; they must figure that's an official route. I saw a bunch from
the city arguing about their relatives in here when I came in this morning, so it must have been that." He motioned the little doctor after
him, then turned his neck back to address Brown. "Show him the
results while I'm gone, honey."

Ferrel forgot his new recruits and swung back to the girl. "Bad?"

She made no comment, but picked up a lead shield and placed it
over Jorgenson's chest so that it cut off all radiation from the lower
part of his body, then placed the radiation indicator close to the
man's throat. Doc looked once; no more was needed. It was obvious
that Blake had already done his best to remove the radioactive from
all parts of the body needed for speech, in the hope that they might
strap down the others and block them off with local anæsthetics; then
the curare could have been counteracted long enough for such in-

formation as was needed. Equally obviously, he'd failed. There was
no sense in going through the job of neutralizing the drug's block
only to have him under the control of the radioactive still present.
The stuff was too finely dispersed for surgical removal. Now what? He
had no answer.

Jenkins' lean-sinewed hand took the indicator from him for inspection. The boy was already frowning as Doc looked up in faint
surprise, and his face made no change. He nodded slowly. "Yeah. I
figured as much. That was a beautiful piece of work you did, too. Too
bad. I was watching from the door and you almost convinced me he'd
be all right, the way you handled it. But— So we have to make out
without him; and Hoke and Palmer haven't even cooked up a lead
that's worth a good test. Want to come into my office, Doc? There's
nothing we can do here."

Ferrel followed Jenkins into the little office off the now emptied
waiting room; the men from the hospital had worked rapidly, it
seemed. "So you haven't been sleeping, I take it? Where's Hokusai
now?"

"Out there with Palmer; he promised to behave, if that'll comfort
you. . . . Nice guy, Hoke; I'd forgotten what it felt like to talk to an
atomic engineer without being laughed at. Palmer, too. I wish—"
There was a brief lightening to the boy's face and the first glow of
normal human pride Doc had seen in him. Then he shrugged, and
it vanished back into his taut cheeks and reddened eyes. "We cooked
up the wildest kind of a scheme, but it isn't so hot."

Hoke's voice came out of the doorway, as the little man came in
and sat down carefully in one of the three chairs. "No, not sso hot!
It iss fail, already. Jorgensson?"

"Out, no hope there! What happened?"

Hoke spread his arms, his eyes almost closing. "Nothing. We knew
it could never work, not sso? Misster Palmer, he iss come ssoon here,
then we make planss again. I am think now, besst we sshould move
from here. Palmer, I—mosstly we are theoreticianss; and, excusse, you
alsso, doctor. Jorgensson wass the production man. No Jorgensson,
no—ah—ssoap!"

Mentally, Ferrel agreed about the moving—and soon! But he could
see Palmer's point of view; to give up the fight was against the grain,
somehow. And besides, once the blow-up happened, with the resultant
damage to an unknown area, the pressure groups in Congress would
be in, shouting for the final abolition of all atomic work; now they

were reasonably quiet, only waiting an opportunity—or, more probably, at the moment were already seizing on the rumors spreading to
turn this into their coup. If, by some streak of luck, Palmer could
save the plant with no greater loss of life and property than already
existed, their words would soon be forgotten, and the benefits from
the products of National would again outweigh all risks.

"Just what will happen if it all goes off?" he asked.

Jenkins shrugged, biting at his inner lip as he went over a sheaf of
papers on the desk, covered with the scrawling symbols of atomics.
"Anybody's guess. Suppose three tons of the army's new explosives
were to explode in a billionth—or at least, a millionth—of a second?
Normally, you know, compared to atomics, that stuff burns like any
fire, slowly and quietly, giving its gases plenty of time to get out of the
way in an orderly fashion. Figure it one way, with this all going off
together, and the stuff could drill a hole that'd split open the whole
continent from Hudson Bay to the Gulf of Mexico, and leave a lovely
sea where the Middle West is now. Figure it another, and it might
only kill off everything within fifty miles of here. Somewhere in between is the chance we count on. This isn't U-235, you know."

Doc winced. He'd been picturing the plant going up in the air
violently, with maybe a few buildings somewhere near it, but nothing
like this. It had been purely a local affair to him, but this didn't sound
like one. No wonder Jenkins was in that state of suppressed jitters;
it wasn't too much imagination, but too much cold, hard knowledge
that was worrying him. Ferrel looked at their faces as they bent over
the symbols once more, tracing out point by point their calculations
in the hope of finding one overlooked loophole, then decided to leave
them alone.

The whole problem was hopeless without Jorgenson, it seemed,
and Jorgenson was his responsibility; if the plant went, it was squarely
on the senior physician's shoulders. But there was no apparent solution. If it would help, he could cut it down to a direct path from brain
to speaking organs, strap down the body and block off all nerves
below the neck, using an artificial larynx instead of the normal breathing through vocal cords. But the indicator showed the futility of it; the
orders could never get through from the brain with the amount of
radioactive still present throwing them off track—even granting that
the brain itself was not affected, which was doubtful.

Fortunately for Jorgenson, the stuff was all finely dispersed around
the head, with no concentration at any one place that was unquestionably destructive to his mind; but the good fortune was also the trouble,

since it could not be removed by any means known to medical practice. Even so simple a thing as letting the man read the questions and spell out the answers by winking an eyelid as they pointed to the alphabet was hopeless.

Nerves! Jorgenson had his blocked out, but Ferrel wondered if the rest of them weren't in as bad a state. Probably, somewhere well within their grasp, there was a solution that was being held back because the nerves of everyone in the plant were blocked by fear and pressure that defeated its own purpose. Jenkins, Palmer, Hokusai—under purely theoretical conditions, any one of them might spot the answer to the problem, but sheer necessity of finding it could be the thing that hid it. The same might be true with the problem of Jorgenson's treatment. Yet, though he tried to relax and let his mind stray idly around the loose ends and seemingly disconnected knowledge he had, it returned incessantly to the necessity of doing something, and doing it now!

Ferrel heard weary footsteps behind him and turned to see Palmer coming from the front entrance. The man had no business walking into the surgery, but such minor rules had gone by the board hours before.

"Jorgenson?" Palmer's conversation began with the same old question in the usual tone, and he read the answer from Doc's face with a look that indicated it was no news. "Hoke and that Jenkins kid still in there?"

Doc nodded, and plodded behind him toward Jenkins' office; he was useless to them, but there was still the idea that in filling his mind with other things, some little factor he had overlooked might have a chance to come forth. Also, curiosity still worked on him, demanding to know what was happening. He flopped into the third chair, and Palmer squatted down on the edge of the table.

"Know a good spiritualist, Jenkins?" the manager asked. "Because if you do, I'm about ready to try calling back Kellar's ghost. The Steinmetz of atomics—so he had to die before this Isotope R came up, and leave us without even a good guess at how long we've got to crack the problem. Hey, what's the matter?"

Jenkins' face had tensed and his body straightened back tensely in the chair, but he shook his head, the corner of his mouth twitching wryly. "Nothing. Nerves, I guess. Hoke and I dug out some things that give an indication on how long this runs, though. We still don't know exactly, but from observations out there and the general theory before, it looks like something between six and thirty hours left; probably ten's closer to being correct!"

"Can't be much longer. It's driving the men back right now! Even the tanks can't get in where they can do the most good, and we're using the shielding around No. 3 as a headquarters for the men; in another half hour, maybe they won't be able to stay that near the thing. Radiation indicators won't register any more, and it's spitting all over the place, almost constantly. Heat's terrific; it's gone up to around three hundred centigrade and sticks right there now, but that's enough to warm up 3, even."

Doc looked up. "No. 3?"

"Yeah. Nothing happened to that batch—it ran through and came out I-713 right on schedule, hours ago." Palmer reached for a cigarette, realized he had one in his mouth, and slammed the package back on the table. "Significant data, Doc; if we get out of this, we'll figure out just what caused the change in No. 4—if we get out! Any chance of making those variable factors work, Hoke?"

Hoke shook his head, and again Jenkins answered from the notes. "Not a chance; sure, theoretically, at least, R should have a period varying between twelve and sixty hours before turning into Mahler's Isotope, depending on what chains of reactions or subchains it goes through; they all look equally good, and probably are all going on in there now, depending on what's around to soak up neutrons or let them roam, the concentration and amount of R together, and even high or low temperatures that change their activity somewhat. It's one of the variables, no question about that."

"The sspitting iss prove that," Hoke supplemented.

"Sure. But there's too much of it together, and we can't break it down fine enough to reach any safety point where it won't toss energy around like rain. The minute one particle manages to make itself into Mahler's, it'll crash through with energy enough to blast the next over the hump and into the same thing instantly, and that passes it on to the next, at about light speed! If we could get it juggled around so some would go off first, other atoms a little later, and so on, fine— only we can't do it unless we can be sure of isolating every blob bigger than a tenth of a gram from every other one! And if we start breaking it down into reasonably small pieces, we're likely to have one decide on the short transformation subchain and go off at any time; pure chance gave us a concentration to begin with that eliminated the shorter chains, but we can't break it down into small lots and those into smaller lots, and so on. Too much risk!"

Ferrel had known vaguely that there were such things as variables, but the theory behind them was too new and too complex for him; he'd learned what little he knew when the simpler radioactives proceeded normally from radium to lead, as an example, with a definite, fixed half life, instead of the super-heavy atoms they now used that could jump through several different paths, yet end up the same. It was over his head, and he started to get up and go back to Jorgenson.

Palmer's words stopped him. "I knew it, of course, but I hoped maybe I was wrong. Then—we evacuate! No use fooling ourselves any longer. I'll call the Governor and try to get him to clear the country around; Hoke, you can tell the men to get the hell out of here! All we ever had was the counteracting isotope to hope on, and no chance of getting enough of that. There was no sense in making I-231 in thousand-pound batches before. Well—"

He reached for the phone, but Ferrel cut in. "What about the men in the wards? They're loaded with the stuff, most of them with more than a gram apiece dispersed through them. They're in the same class with the converter, maybe, but we can't just pull out and leave them!"

Silence hit them, to be broken by Jenkins' hushed whisper. "My God! What damned fools we are. I-231 under discussion for hours, and I never thought of it. Now you two throw the connection in my face, and I still almost miss it!"

"I-231? But there iss not enough. Maybe twenty-five pound, maybe less. Three and a half days to make more. The little we have would be no good, Dr. Jenkinss. We forget that already." Hoke struck a match to a piece of paper, shook one drop of ink onto it, and watched it continue burning for a second before putting it out. "Sso. A drop of water for sstop a foresst fire. No."

"Wrong, Hoke. A drop to short a switch that'll turn on the real stream—maybe. Look, Doc, I-231's an isotope that reacts atomically with R—we've checked on that already. It simply gets together with the stuff and the two break down into non-radioactive elements and a little heat, like a lot of other such atomic reactions; but it isn't the violent kind. They simply swap parts in a friendly way and open up to simpler atoms that are stable. We have a few pounds on hand, can't make enough in time to help with No. 4, but we do have enough to treat every man in the wards, *including Jorgenson!*"

"How much heat?" Doc snapped out of his lethargy into the detailed thought of a good physician. "In atomics you may call it a little; but would it be small enough in the human body?"

Hokusai and Palmer were practically riding the pencil as Jenkins figured. "Say five grams of the stuff in Jorgenson, to be on the safe side, less in the others. Time for reaction . . . hm-m-m. Here's the total heat produced and the time taken by the reaction, probably, in the body. The stuff's water-soluble in the chloride we have of it, so there's no trouble dispersing it. What do you make of it, Doc?"

"Fifteen to eighteen degrees temperature rise at a rough estimate. Uh!"

"Too much! Jorgenson couldn't stand ten degrees right now!" Jenkins frowned down at his figures, tapping nervously with his hand.

Doc shook his head. "Not too much! We can drop his whole body temperature first in the hypothermy bath down to eighty degrees, then let it rise to a hundred, if necessary, and still be safe. Thank the Lord, there's equipment enough. If they'll rip out the refrigerating units in the cafeteria and improvise baths, the volunteers out in the tent can start on the other men while we handle Jorgenson. At least that way we can get the men all out, even if we don't save the plant."

Palmer stared at them in confusion before his face galvanized into resolution. "Refrigerating units—volunteers—tent? What— O. K., Doc, what do you want?" He reached for the telephone and began giving orders for the available I-231 to be sent to the surgery, for men to rip out the cafeteria cooling equipment, and for such other things as Doc requested. Jenkins had already gone to instruct the medical staff in the field tent without asking how they'd gotten there, but was back in the surgery before Doc reached it with Palmer and Hokusai at his heels.

"Blake's taking over out there," Jenkins announced. "Says if you want Dodd, Meyers, Jones or Sue, they're sleeping."

"No need. Get over there out of the way, if you must watch," Ferrel ordered the two engineers, as he and Jenkins began attaching the freezing units and bath to the sling on the exciter. "Prepare his blood for it, Jenkins; we'll force it down as low as we can to be on the safe side. And we'll have to keep tab on the temperature fall and regulate his heart and breathing to what it would be normally in that condition; they're both out of his normal control, now."

"And pray," Jenkins added. He grabbed the small box out of the messenger's hand before the man was fully inside the door and began preparing a solution, weighing out the whitish powder and measuring water carefully, but with the speed that was automatic to him under tension. "Doc, if this doesn't work—if Jorgenson's crazy or something

—you'll have another case of insanity on your hands. One more false hope would finish me."

"Not one more case; four! We're all in the same boat. Temperature's falling nicely—I'm rushing it a little, but it's safe enough. Down to ninety-six now." The thermometer under Jorgenson's tongue was one intended for hypothermy work, capable of rapid response, instead of the normal fever thermometer. Slowly, with agonizing reluctance, the little needle on the dial moved over, down to ninety, then on. Doc kept his eyes glued to it, slowing the pulse and breath to the proper speed. He lost track of the number of times he sent Palmer back out of the way, and finally gave up.

Waiting, he wondered how those outside in the field hospital were doing? Still, they had ample time to arrange their makeshift cooling apparatus and treat the men in groups—ten hours probably; and hypothermy was a standard thing, now. Jorgenson was the only real rush case. Almost imperceptibly to Doc, but speedily by normal standards, the temperature continued to fall. Finally it reached seventy-eight.

"Ready, Jenkins, make the injection. That enough?"

"No. I figure it's almost enough, but we'll have to go slow to balance out properly. Too much of this stuff would be almost as bad as the other. Gauge going up, Doc?"

It was, much more rapidly than Ferrel liked. As the injection coursed through the blood vessels and dispersed out to the fine deposits of radioactive, the needle began climbing past eighty, to ninety, and up. It stopped at ninety-four and slowly began falling as the cooling bath absorbed heat from the cells of the body. The radio-activity meter still registered the presence of Isotope R, though much more faintly.

The next shot was small, and a smaller one followed. "Almost," Ferrel commented. "Next one should about do the trick."

Using partial injections, there had been need for less drop in temperature than they had given Jorgenson, but there was small loss to that. Finally, when the last minute bit of the I-213 solution had entered the man's veins and done its work, Doc nodded. "No sign of activity left. He's up to ninety-five, now that I've cut off the refrigeration, and he'll pick up the little extra temperature in a hurry. By the time we can counteract the curare, he'll be ready. That'll take about fifteen minutes, Palmer."

The manager nodded, watching them dismantling the hypothermy equipment and going through the routine of canceling out the curare. It was always a slower job than treatment with the drug, but part of the work had been done already by the normal body processes, and the rest was a simple, standard procedure. Fortunately, the neo-heroin would be nearly worn off, or that would have been a longer and much harder problem to eliminate.

"Telephone for Mr. Palmer. Calling Mr. Palmer. Send Mr. Palmer to the telephone." The operator's words lacked the usual artificial exactness, and were only a nervous sing-song. It was getting her, and she wasn't bothered by excess imagination, normally. "Mr. Palmer is wanted on the telephone."

"Palmer." The manager picked up an instrument at hand, not equipped with vision, and there was no indication of the caller. But Ferrel could see what little hope had appeared at the prospect of Jorgenson's revival disappearing. "Check! Move out of there, and prepare to evacuate, but keep quiet about that until you hear further orders! Tell the men Jorgenson's about out of it, so they won't lack for something to talk about."

He swung back to them. "No use, Doc, I'm afraid. We're already too late. The stuff's stepped it up again, and they're having to move out of No. 3 now. I'll wait on Jorgenson, but even if he's all right and knows the answer, we can't get in to use it!"

VI

"Healing's going to be a long, slow process, but they should at least grow back better than silver ribs; never take a pretty X-ray photo, though." Doc held the instrument in his hand, staring down at the flap opened in Jorgenson's chest, and his shoulders came up in a faint shrug. The little platinum filaments had been removed from around the nerves to heart and lungs, and the man's normal impulses were operating again, less steadily than under the exciter, but with no danger signals. "Well, it won't much matter if he's still sane."

Jenkins watched him begin stitching the flap back, his eyes centered over the table out toward the converter. "Doc, he's got to be sane! If Hoke and Palmer find it's what it sounds like out there, we'll have to count on Jorgenson. There's an answer somewhere, has to be! But we won't find it without him."

"Hm-m-m. Seems to me you've been having ideas yourself, son. You've been right so far, and if Jorgenson's out——" He shut off the stitcher, finished the dressings, and flopped down on a bench, knowing that all they could do was wait for the drugs to work on Jorgenson and bring him around. Now that he relaxed the control over himself, exhaustion hit down with full force; his fingers were uncertain as he pulled off the gloves. "Anyhow, we'll know in another five minutes or so."

"And Heaven help us, Doc, if it's up to me. I've always had a flair for atomic theory; I grew up on it. But he's the production man who's been working at it week in and week out, and it's his process, to boot. . . . There they are now! All right for them to come back here?"

But Hokusai and Palmer were waiting for no permission. At the moment, Jorgenson was the nerve center of the plant, drawing them back, and they stalked over to stare down at him, then sat where they could be sure of missing no sign of returning consciousness. Palmer picked up the conversation where he'd dropped it, addressing his remarks to both Hokusai and Jenkins.

"Damn that Link-Stevens postulate! Time after time it fails, until you figure there's nothing to it; then, this! It's black magic, not science, and if I get out, I'll find some fool with more courage than sense to discover why. Hoke, are you positive it's the *theta* chain? There isn't one chance in ten thousand of that happening, you know; it's unstable, hard to stop, tends to revert to the simpler ones at the first chance."

Hokusai spread his hands, lifted one heavy eyelid at Jenkins questioningly, then nodded. The boy's voice was dull, almost uninterested. "That's what I thought it had to be, Palmer. None of the others throws off that much energy at this stage, the way you described conditions out there. Probably the last thing we tried to quench set it up in that pattern, and it's in a concentration just right to keep it going. We figured ten hours was the best chance, so it had to pick the six-hour short chain."

"Yeah." Palmer was pacing up and down nervously again, his eyes swinging toward Jorgenson from whatever direction he moved. "And in six hours, maybe all the population around here can be evacuated, maybe not, but we'll have to try it. Doc, I can't even wait for Jorgenson now! I've got to get the Governor started at once!"

"They've been known to practice lynch law, even in recent years," Ferrel reminded him grimly. He'd seen the result of one such case of mob violence when he was practicing privately, and he knew that people remain pretty much the same year after year; they'd move, but first they'd demand a sacrifice. "Better get the men out of here first, Palmer, and my advice is to get yourself a good long distance off; I heard some of the trouble at the gate, and that won't be anything compared to what an evacuation order will do."

Palmer grunted. "Doc, you might not believe it, but I don't give a continental about what happens to me or the plant right now."

"Or the men? Put a mob in here, hunting your blood, and the men will be on your side, because they know it wasn't your fault, and they've seen you out there taking chances yourself. That mob won't be too choosy about its targets, either, once it gets worked up, and you'll have a nice vicious brawl all over the place. Besides, Jorgenson's practically ready."

A few minutes would make no difference in the evacuation, and Doc had no desire to think of his partially crippled wife going through the hell evacuation would be; she'd probably refuse, until he returned. His eyes fell on the box Jenkins was playing with nervously, and he stalled for time. "I thought you said it was risky to break the stuff down into small particles, Jenkins. But that box contains the stuff in various sizes, including one big piece we scraped out, along with the contaminated instruments. Why hasn't it exploded?"

Jenkins' hand jerked up from it as if burned, and he backed away a step before checking himself. Then he was across the room toward the I-231 and back, pouring the white powder over everything in the box in a jerky frenzy. Hokusai's eyes had snapped fully open, and he was slopping water in to fill up the remaining space and keep the I-231 in contact with everything else. Almost at once, in spite of the low relative energy release, it sent up a white cloud of steam faster than the air conditioner could clear the room; but that soon faded down and disappeared.

Hokusai wiped his forehead slowly. "The ssuits—armor of the men?"

"Sent 'em back to the converter and had them dumped into the stuff to be safe long ago," Jenkins answered. "But I forgot the box, like a fool. Ugh! Either blind chance saved us or else the stuff spit out was all one kind, some reasonably long chain. I don't know nor care right—"

"S'ot! Nnnuh. . . . Whmah nahh?"

"Jorgenson!" They swung from the end of the room like one man, but Jenkins was the first to reach the table. Jorgenson's eyes were open and rolling in a semiorderly manner, his hands moving sluggishly. The boy hovered over his face, his own practically glowing with the intensity behind it. "Jorgenson, can you understand what I'm saying?"

"Uh." The eyes ceased moving and centered on Jenkins. One hand came up to his throat, clutching at it, and he tried unsuccessfully to lift himself with the other, but the aftereffects of what he'd been through seemed to have left him in a state of partial paralysis.

Ferrel had hardly dared hope that the man could be rational, and his relief was tinged with doubt. He pushed Palmer back, and shook his head. "No, stay back. Let the boy handle it; he knows enough not to shock the man now, and you don't. This can't be rushed too much."

"I—uh. . . . Young Jenkins? Whasha doin' here? Tell y'ur dad to ge' busy ou' there!" Somewhere in Jorgenson's huge frame, an untapped reserve of energy and will sprang up, and he forced himself into a sitting position, his eyes on Jenkins, his hand still catching at the reluctant throat that refused to co-operate. His words were blurry and uncertain, but sheer determination overcame the obstacles and made the words understandable.

"Dad's dead now, Jorgenson. Now—"

" 'Sright. 'N' you're grown up—'bout twelve years old, y' were. . . . The plant!"

"Easy, Jorgenson." Jenkins' own voice managed to sound casual, though his hands under the table were white where they clenched together. "Listen, and don't try to say anything until I finish. The plant's still all right, but we've got to have your help. Here's what happened."

Ferrel could make little sense of the cryptic sentences that followed, though he gathered that they were some form of engineering shorthand; apparently, from Hokusai's approving nod, they summed up the situation briefly but fully, and Jorgenson sat rigidly still until it was finished, his eyes fastened on the boy.

"Hellova mess! Gotta think . . . yuh tried—" He made an attempt to lower himself back, and Jenkins assisted him, hanging on feverishly to each awkward, uncertain change of expression on the man's face. "Uh . . . da' sroat! Yuh . . . uh . . . urrgh!"

"Got it?"

"Uh!" The tone was affirmative, unquestionably, but the clutching hands around his neck told their own story. The temporary burst of energy he'd forced was exhausted, and he couldn't get through with it. He lay there, breathing heavily and struggling, then relaxed after a few more half-whispered words, none intelligently articulated.

Palmer clutched at Ferrel's sleeve. "Doc, isn't there anything you can do?"

"Try." He metered out a minute quantity of drug doubtfully, felt Jorgenson's pulse, and decided on half that amount. "Not much hope, though; that man's been through hell, and it wasn't good for him to be forced around in the first place. Carry it too far, and he'll be delirious if he does talk. Anyway, I suspect it's partly his speech centers as well as the throat."

But Jorgenson began a slight rally almost instantly, trying again, then apparently drawing himself together for a final attempt. When they came, the words spilled out harshly in forced clearness, but without inflection.

"First . . . variable . . . at . . . twelve . . . water . . . stop." His eyes, centered on Jenkins, closed, and he relaxed again, this time no longer fighting off the inevitable unconsciousness.

Hokusai, Palmer, and Jenkins were staring back and forth at one another questioningly. The little Japanese shook his head negatively at first, frowned, and repeated it, to be imitated almost exactly by the manager. "Delirious ravings!"

"The great white hope Jorgenson!" Jenkins' shoulders drooped and the blood drained from his face, leaving it ghastly with fatigue and despair. "Oh, damn it, Doc, stop staring at me! I can't pull a miracle out of a hat!"

Doc hadn't realized that he was staring, but he made no effort to change it. "Maybe not, but you happen to have the most active imagination here, when you stop abusing it to scare yourself. Well, you're on the spot now, and I'm still giving odds on you. Want to bet, Hoke?"

It was an utterly stupid thing, and Doc knew it; but somewhere during the long hours together, he'd picked up a queer respect for the boy and a dependence on the nervousness that wasn't fear but closer akin to the reaction of a rear-running thoroughbred on the home stretch. Hoke was too slow and methodical, and Palmer had been too concerned with outside worries to give anywhere nearly full attention to the single most urgent phase of the problem; that left only Jenkins, hampered by his lack of self-confidence.

Hoke gave no sign that he caught the meaning of Doc's heavy wink, but he lifted his eyebrows faintly. "No, I think I am not bet. Dr. Jenkins, I am to be command!"

Palmer looked briefly at the boy, whose face mirrored incredulous confusion, but he had neither Ferrel's ignorance of atomic technique nor Hokusai's fatalism. With a final glance at the unconscious Jorgenson, he started across the room toward the phone. "You men play, if you like. I'm starting evacuation immediately!"

"Wait!" Jenkins was shaking himself, physically as well as mentally.

"Hold it, Palmer! Thanks, Doc. You knocked me out of the rut, and bounced my memory back to something I picked up somewhere; I think it's the answer! It has to work—nothing else can at this stage of the game!"

"Give me the Governor, operator." Palmer had heard, but he went on with the phone call. "This is no time to play crazy hunches until after we get the people out, kid. I'll admit you're a darned clever amateur, but you're no atomicist!"

"And if we get the men out, it's too late—there'll be no one left in here to do the work!" Jenkins' hand snapped out and jerked the receiver of the plug-in telephone from Palmer's hand. "Cancel the call, operator; it won't be necessary. Palmer, you've got to listen to me; you can't clear the whole middle of the continent, and you can't depend on the explosion to limit itself to less ground. It's a gamble, but you're risking fifty million people against a mere hundred thousand. Give me a chance!"

"I'll give you exactly one minute to convince me, Jenkins, and it had better be good! Maybe the blow-up won't hit beyond the fifty-mile limit!"

"Maybe. And I can't explain in a minute." The boy scowled tensely. "O. K., you've been bellyaching about a man named Kellar being dead. If he were here, would you take a chance on him? Or on a man who'd worked under him on everything he tried?"

"Absolutely, but you're not Kellar. And I happen to know he was a lone wolf; didn't hire outside engineers after Jorgenson had a squabble with him and came here." Palmer reached for the phone. "It won't wash, Jenkins."

Jenkins' hand clamped down on the instrument, jerking it out of reach. "I wasn't outside help, Palmer. When Jorgenson was afraid to run one of the things off and quit, I was twelve; three years later, things got too tight for him to handle alone, but he decided he might as well keep it in the family, so he started me in. I'm Kellar's stepson!"

Pieces clicked together in Doc's head then, and he kicked himself mentally for not having seen the obvious before. "That why Jorgenson knew you, then? I thought that was funny. It checks, Palmer."

For a split second, the manager hesitated uncertainly. Then he shrugged and gave in. "O. K., I'm a fool to trust you, Jenkins, but it's too late for anything else, I guess. I never forgot that I was gambling the locality against half the continent. What do you want?"

"Men—construction men, mostly, and a few volunteers for dirty work. I want all the blowers, exhaust equipment, tubing, booster blowers, and everything ripped from the other three converters and connected as close to No. 4 as you can get. Put them up some way so they can be shoved in over the stuff by crane—I don't care how; the shop men will know better than I do. You've got sort of a river running off behind the plant; get everyone within a few miles of it out of there, and connect the blower outlets down to it. Where does it end, anyway—some kind of a swamp, or morass?"

"About ten miles farther down, yes; we didn't bother keeping the drainage system going, since the land meant nothing to us, and the swamps made as good a dumping ground as anything else." When the plant had first used the little river as an outlet for their waste products, there'd been so much trouble that National had been forced to take over all adjacent land and quiet the owners' fears of the atomic activity in cold cash. Since then, it had gone to weeds and rabbits, mostly. "Everyone within a few miles is out, anyway, except a few fishers or tramps that don't know we use it. I'll have militia sent in to scare them out."

"Good. Ideal, in fact, since the swamps will hold stuff in there where the current's slow longer. Now, what about that superthermite stuff you were producing last year. Any around?"

"Not in the plant. But we've got tons of it at the warehouse, still waiting for the army's requisition. That's pretty hot stuff to handle, though. Know much about it?"

"Enough to know it's what I want." Jenkins indicated the copy of the *Weekly Ray* still lying where he'd dropped it, and Doc remembered skimming through the nontechnical part of the description. It was made up of two superheavy atoms, kept separate. By itself, neither was particularly important or active, but together they reacted with each other atomically to release a tremendous amount of raw heat and comparatively little unwanted radiation. "Goes up around twenty thousand centigrade, doesn't it? How's it stored?"

"In ten-pound bombs that have a fragile partition; it breaks with shock, starting the action. Hoke can explain it—it's his baby." Palmer reached for the phone. "Anything else? Then, get out and get busy! The men will be ready for you when you get there! I'll be out myself as soon as I can put through your orders."

Doc watched them go out, to be followed in short order by the manager, and was alone in the Infirmary with Jorgenson and his thoughts. They weren't pleasant; he was both too far outside the inner circle to know what was going on and too much mixed up in it not to know the dangers. Now he could have used some work of any nature to take his mind off useless speculations, but aside from a needless check of the foreman's condition, there was nothing for him to do.

He wriggled down in the leather chair, making the mistake of trying to force sleep, while his mind chased out after the sounds that came in from outside. There were the drones of crane and tank motors coming to life, the shouts of hurried orders, and above all, the jarring rhythm of pneumatic hammers on metal, each sound suggesting some possibility to him without adding to his knowledge. The "Decameron" was boring, the whiskey tasted raw and rancid, and solitaire wasn't worth the trouble of cheating.

Finally, he gave up and turned out to the field hospital tent. Jorgenson would be better off out there, under the care of the staff from Mayo's, and perhaps he could make himself useful. As he passed through the rear entrance, he heard the sound of a number of helicopters coming over with heavy loads, and looked up as they began settling over the edge of the buildings. From somewhere, a group of men came running forward, and disappeared in the direction of the freighters. He wondered whether any of those men would be forced back into the stuff out there to return filled with radioactive; though it didn't matter so much, now that the isotope could be eliminated without surgery.

Blake met him at the entrance of the field tent, obviously well satisfied with his duty of bossing and instructing the others. "Scram, Doc. You aren't necessary here, and you need some rest. Don't want you added to the casualties. What's the latest dope from the pow-wow front?"

"Jorgenson didn't come through, but the kid had an idea, and they're out there working on it." Doc tried to sound more hopeful than he felt. "I was thinking you might as well bring Jorgenson in here; he's still unconscious, but there doesn't seem to be anything to worry about. Where's Brown? She'll probably want to know what's up, if she isn't asleep."

"Asleep when the kid isn't? Uh-huh. Mother complex, has to worry about him." Blake grinned. 'She got a look at him running out with Hoke tagging at his heels, and hiked out after him, so she probably knows everything now. Wish Anne'd chase me that way, just once— Jenkins, the wonder boy! Well, it's out of my line; I don't intend to start worrying until they pass out the order. O. K.,

Doc, I'll have Jorgenson out here in a couple of minutes, so you grab yourself a cot and get some shut-eye."

Doc grunted, looking curiously at the refinements and well-equipped interior of the field tent. "I've already prescribed that, Blake, but the patient can't seem to take it. I think I'll hunt up Brown, so give me a call over the public speaker if anything turns up."

He headed toward the center of action, knowing that he'd been wanting to do it all along, but hadn't been sure of not being a nuisance. Well, if Brown could look on, there was no reason why he couldn't. He passed the machine shop, noting the excited flurry of activity going on, and went past No. 2, where other men were busily ripping out long sections of big piping and various other devices. There was a rope fence barring his way, well beyond No. 3, and he followed along the edge, looking for Palmer or Brown.

She saw him first. "Hi, Dr. Ferrel, over here in the truck. I thought you'd be coming soon. From up here we can get a look over the heads of all these other people, and we won't be tramped on." She stuck down a hand to help him up, smiled faintly as he disregarded it and mounted more briskly than his muscles wanted to. He wasn't so old that a girl had to help him yet.

"Know what's going on?" he asked, sinking down onto the plank across the truck body, facing out across the men below toward the converter. There seemed to be a dozen different centers of activity, all crossing each other in complete confusion, and the general pattern was meaningless.

"No more than you do. I haven't seen my husband, though Mr. Palmer took time enough to chase me here out of the way."

Doc centered his attention on the 'copters, unloading, rising, and coming in with more loads, and he guessed that those boxes must contain the little thermodyne bombs. It was the one thing he could understand, and consequently the least interesting. Other men were assembling the big sections of piping he'd seen before, connecting them up in almost endless order, while some of the tanks hooked on and snaked them off in the direction of the small river that ran off beyond the plant.

"Those must be the exhaust blowers, I guess," he told Brown, pointing them out. "Though I don't know what any of the rest of the stuff hooked on is."

"I know—I've been inside the plant Bob's father had." She lifted an inquiring eyebrow at him, went on as he nodded. "The pipes are for exhaust gases, all right, and those big square things are the

motors and fans—they put in one at each five hundred feet or less
of piping. The things they're wrapping around the pipe must be
the heaters to keep the gases hot. Are they going to try to suck all
that out?"

Doc didn't know, though it was the only thing he could see.
But he wondered how they'd get around the problem of moving
in close enough to do any good. "I heard your husband order some
thermodyne bombs, so they'll probably try to gassify the magma;
then they're pumping it down the river."

As he spoke, there was a flurry of motion at one side, and his
eyes swung over instantly, to see one of the cranes laboring with
a long framework stuck from its front, holding up a section of pipe
with a nozzle on the end. It tilted precariously, even though heavy
bags were piled everywhere to add weight, but an inch at a time
it lifted its load, and began forcing its way forward, carrying the
nozzle out in front and rather high.

Below the main exhaust pipe was another smaller one. As it drew
near the outskirts of the danger zone, a small object ejaculated from
the little pipe, hit the ground, and was a sudden blazing inferno of
glaring blue-white light, far brighter than it seemed, judging by the
effect on the eyes. Doc shielded his, just as someone below put something into his hands.

"Put 'em on. Palmer says the light's actinic."

He heard Brown fussing beside him, then his vision cleared, and
he looked back through the goggles again to see a glowing cloud
spring up from the magma, spread out near the ground, narrowing
down higher up, until it sucked into the nozzle above, and disappeared. Another bomb slid from the tube, and erupted with blazing
heat. A sideways glance showed another crane being fitted, and a
group of men near it wrapping what might have been oiled rags
around the small bombs; probably no tubing fitted them exactly, and
they were padding them so pressure could blow them forward and
out. Three more dropped from the tube, one at a time, and the
fans roared and groaned, pulling the cloud that rose into the pipe
and feeding it down toward the river.

Then the crane inched back out carefully as men uncoupled
its piping from the main line, and a second went in to replace it. The
heat generated must be too great for the machine to stand steadily
without the pipe fusing, Doc decided; though they couldn't have kept
a man inside the heavily armored cab for any length of time, if the
metal had been impervious. Now another crane was ready, and went

in from another place; it settled down to a routine of ingoing and out-coming cranes, and men feeding materials in, coupling and un-coupling the pipes and replacing the others who came from the cabs. Doc began to feel like a man at a tennis match, watching the ball without knowing the rules.

Brown must have had the same idea, for she caught Ferrel's arm and indicate. ι little leather case that came from her handbag. "Doc, do you play chess? W. might as well fill our time with that as sitting here on edge, just watching. It's supposed to be good for nerves."

He seized on it gratefully, without explaining that he'd been city champion three years running; he'd take it easy, watch her game, handicap himself just enough to make it interesting by the deliberate loss of a rook, bishop, or knight, as was needed to even the odds— Suppose they got all the magma out and into the river; how did that solve the problem? It removed it from the plant, but far less than the fifty-mile minimum danger limit.

"Check," Brown announced. He castled, and looked up at the half-dozen cranes that were now operating. "Check! Checkmate!"

He looked back again hastily, then, to see her queen guarding all possible moves, a bishop checking him. Then his eye followed down toward her end. "Umm. Did you know you've been in check for the last half-dozen moves? Eecause I didn't."

She frowned, shook her head, and began setting the men up again. Doc moved out the queen's pawn, looked out at the workers, and then brought out the king's bishop, to see her take it with her king's pawn. He hadn't watched her move it out, and had counted on her queen's to block his. Things would require more careful watching on this little portable set. The men were moving steadily and there was a growing clear space, but as they went forward, the violent action of the thermodyne had pitted the ground, carefully as it had been used, and going become more uncertain. Time was slipping by rapidly now.

"Checkmate!" He found himself in a hole, started to nod; but she caught herself this time. "Sorry, I've been playing my king for a queen. Doctor, let's see if we can play at least one game right."

Before it was half finished, it became obvious that they couldn't. Neither had chess very much on the mind, and the pawns and men did fearful and wonderful things, while the knights were as likely to jump six squares as their normal L. They gave it up, just as one of the cranes lost its precarious balance and toppled forward, drop-

ping the long extended pipe into the bubbling mass below. Tanks
were in instantly, hitching on and tugging backward until it came
down with a thump as the pipe fused, releasing the extreme forward
load. It backed out on its own power, while another went in. The
driver, by sheer good luck, hobbled from the cab, waving an armored
hand to indicate he was all right. Things settled back to an excited
routine again that seemed to go on endlessly, though seconds were
dropping off too rapidly, turning into minutes that threatened to be
hours far too soon.

"Uh!" Brown had been staring for some time, but her little feet
suddenly came down with a bang and she straightened up, her hand to
her mouth. "Doctor, I just thought; it won't do any good—all this!"

"Why?" She couldn't know anything, but he felt the faint hopes
he had go downward sharply. His nerves were dulled, but still ready
to jump at the slightest warning.

"The stuff they were making was a superheavy—it'll sink as soon
as it hits the water, and all pile up right there! It won't float down
river!"

Obvious, Ferrel thought; too obvious. Maybe that was why the
engineers hadn't thought of it. He started from the plank, just as
Palmer stepped up, but the manager's hand on his shoulder forced
him back.

"Easy, Doc, it's O. K. Umm, so they teach women some science
nowadays, eh, Mrs. Jenkins . . . Sue . . . Dr. Brown, whatever your
name is? Don't worry about it, though—the old principle of Brownian
movement will keep any colloid suspended, if it's fine enough to be
a real colloid. We're sucking it out and keeping it pretty hot until it
reaches the water—then it cools off so fast it hasn't time to collect in
particles big enough to sink. Some of the dust that floats around in
the air is heavier than water, too. I'm joining the bystanders, if you
don't mind; the men have everything under control, and I can see
better here than I could down there, if anything does come up."

Doc's momentary despair reacted to leave him feeling more sure
of things than was justified. He pushed over on the plank, making
room for Palmer to drop down beside him. "What's to keep it from
blowing up anyway, Palmer?"

"Nothing! Got a match?" He sucked in on the cigarette heavily,
relaxing as much as he could. "No use trying to fool you, Doc, at
this stage of the game. We're gambling, and I'd say the odds are
even; Jenkins thinks they're ninety to ten in his favor, but he has to
think so. What we're hoping is that by lifting it out in a gas, thus

breaking it down at once from full concentration to the finest possible form, and letting it settle in the water in colloidal particles,
there won't be a concentration at any one place sufficient to set it
all off at once. The big problem is making sure we get every bit of it
cleaned out here, or there may be enough left to take care of us and
the nearby city! At least, since the last change, it's stopped spitting,
so all the man have to worry about is burn!"

"How much damage, even if it doesn't go off all at once?"

"Possibly none. If you can keep it burning slowly, a million tons
of dynamite wouldn't be any worse than the same amount of wood,
but a stick going off at once will kill you. Why the dickens didn't
Jenkins tell me he wanted to go into atomics? We could have fixed
all that—it's hard enough to get good men as it is!"

Brown perked up, forgetting the whole trouble beyond them, and
went into the story with enthusiasm, while Ferrel only partly listened.
He could see the spot of magma growing steadily smaller, but the
watch on his wrist went on ticking off minutes remorselessly, and
the time was growing limited. He hadn't realized before how long
he'd been sitting there. Now three of the crane nozzles were almost
touching, and around them stretched the burned-out ground, with no
sign of converter, masonry, or anything else; the heat from the thermodyne had gassified everything, indiscriminately.

"Palmer!" The portable ultrawave set around the manager's neck
came to life suddenly. "Hey, Palmer, these blowers are about shot;
the pipe's pitting already. We've been doing everything we can to
replace them, but that stuff eats faster than we can fix. Can't hold
up more'n fifteen minutes more."

"Check, Briggs. Keep 'em going the best you can." Palmer flipped
a switch and looked out toward the tank standing by behind the
cranes. "Jenkins, you get that?"

"Yeah. Surprised they held out this long. How much time till
deadline?" The boy's voice was completely toneless, neither hope
nor nerves showing up, only the complete weariness of a man almost
at his limit.

Palmer looked and whistled. "Twelve minutes, according to the
minimum estimate Hoke made! How much left?"

"We're just burning around now, trying to make sure there's no
pocket left; I hope we've got the whole works, but I'm not promising. Might as well send out all the I-231 you have and we'll boil it
down the pipes to clear out any deposits on them. All the old treads
and parts that contacted the R gone into the pile?"

"You melted the last, and your cranes haven't touched the stuff directly. Nice pile of money's gone down that pipe—converter, machinery, everything!"

Jenkins made a sound that was expressive of his worry about that. "I'm coming in now and starting the clearing of the pipe. What've you been paying insurance for?"

"At a lovely rate, too! O. K., come on in, kid; and if you're interested, you can start sticking A. E. after the M. D., any time you want. Your wife's been giving me your qualifications, and I think you've passed the final test, so you're now an atomic engineer, duly graduated from National!"

Brown's breath caught, and her eyes seemed to glow, even through the goggles, but Jenkins' voice was flat. "O. K., I expected you to give me one if we don't blow up. But you'll have to see Dr. Ferrel about it; he's got a contract with me for medical practice. Be there shortly."

Nine of the estimated twelve minutes had ticked by when he climbed up beside them, mopping off some of the sweat that covered him, and Palmer was hugging the watch. More minutes ticked off slowly, while the last sound faded out in the plant, and the men stood around, staring down toward the river or at the hole that had been No. 4. Silence. Jenkins stirred, and grunted.

"Palmer, I know where I got the idea, now. Jorgenson was trying to remind me of it, instead of raving, only I didn't get it, at least consciously. It was one of dad's, the one he told Jorgenson was a last resort, in case the thing they broke up about went haywire. It was the first variable dad tried. I was twelve, and he insisted water would break it up into all its chains and kill the danger. Only dad didn't really expect it to work!"

Palmer didn't look up from the watch, but he caught his breath and swore. "Fine time to tell me that!"

"He didn't have your isotopes to heat it up with, either," Jenkins answered mildly. "Suppose you look up from that watch of yours for a minute, down the river."

As Doc raised his eyes, he was aware suddenly of a roar from the men. Over to the south, stretching out in a huge mass, was a cloud of steam that spread upward and out as he watched, and the beginnings of a mighty hissing sound came in. Then Palmer was hugging Jenkins and yelling until Brown could pry him away and replace him.

"Ten miles or more of river, plus the swamps, Doc!" Palmer was shouting in Ferrel's ear. "All that dispersion, while it cooks slowly from now until the last chain is finished, atom by atom! The *theta* chain broke, unstable, and now there's everything there, too scattered to set itself off! It'll cook the river bed up and dry it, but that's all!"

Doc was still dazed, unsure of how to take the relief. He wanted to lie down and cry or to stand up with the men and shout his head off. Instead, he sat loosely, gazing at the cloud. "So I lose the best assistant I ever had! Jenkins, I won't hold you; you're free for whatever Palmer wants."

"Hoke wants him to work on R—he's got the stuff for his bomb now!" Palmer was clapping his hands together slowly, like an excited child watching a steam shovel. "Heck, Doc, pick out anyone you want until your own boy gets out next year. You wanted a chance to work him in here, now you're got it. Right now I'll give you anything you want."

"You might see what you can do about hospitalizing the injured and fixing things up with the men in the tent behind the Infirmary. And I think I'll take Brown in Jenkins' place, with the right to grab him in an emergency, until that year's up."

"Done." Palmer slapped the boy's back, stopping the protest, while Brown winked at him. "Your wife likes working, kid; she told me that herself. Besides, a lot of the women work here where they can keep an eye on their men; my own wife does, usually. Doc, take these two kids and head for home, where I'm going myself. Don't come back until you get good and ready, and don't let them start fighting about it!"

Doc pulled himself from the truck and started off with Brown and Jenkins following, through the yelling, relief-crazed men. The three were too thoroughly worn out for any exhibition themselves, but they could feel it. Happy ending! Jenkins and Brown where they wanted to be, Hoke with his bomb, Palmer with proof that atomic plants were safe where they were, and he—well, his boy would start out right, with himself and the widely differing but competent Blake and Jenkins to guide him. It wasn't a bad life, after all.

Then he stopped and chuckled. "You two wait for me, will you? If I leave here without making out that order of extra disinfection at the showers, Blake'll swear I'm growing old and feeble-minded. I can't have that."

Old? Maybe a little tired, but he'd been that before, and with luck would be again. He wasn't worried. His nerves were good for twenty years and fifty accidents more, and by that time Blake would be due for a little ribbing himself.

THE SANDS OF TIME

by

P. SCHUYLER MILLER

One irrefutable proof of a visit to the far past would be to return with a dinosaur egg—a fresh one! Or, take your camera with you, and come back to develop pictures that were taken millions of years ago. But one should be careful of time travel, for it might be true that the dinosaurs weren't the only ones who used the earth of the Cretaceous age as a battleground. There might have been visitors who came, fought and departed, leaving not a single footprint in the sands of our time.

*

A LONG SHADOW fell across the ledge. I laid down the curved blade with which I was chipping at the soft sandstone, and squinted up into the glare of the afternoon sun. A man was sitting on the edge of the pit, his legs dangling over the side. He raised a hand in salutation.

"Hi!"

He hunched forward to jump. My shout stopped him.

"Look out! You'll smash them!"

He peered down at me, considering the matter. He had no hat, and the sun made a halo of his blond, curly hair.

"They're fossils, aren't they?" he objected. "Fossils I've seen were stone, and stone is hard. What do you mean—I'll smash 'em?"

"I mean what I said. This sandstone is soft and the bones in it are softer. Also, they're old. Digging out dinosaurs is no pick-and-shovel job nowadays."

"Um-m-m." He rubbed his nose thoughtfully. "How old would you say they were?"

I got wearily to my feet and began to slap the dust out of my breeches. Evidently I was in for another siege of questions. He might be a reporter, or he might be any one of the twenty-odd farmers in the surrounding section. It would make a difference what I told him.

"Come on down here where we can talk," I invited. "We'll be more comfortable. There's a trail about a hundred yards up the draw."

"I'm all right." He leaned back on braced arms. "What is it? What did it look like?"

I know when I'm beaten. I leaned against the wall of the quarry, out of the sun, and began to fill my pipe. I waved the packet of tobacco courteously at him, but he shook his head.

"Thanks. Cigarette." He lighted one. "You're Professor Belden, aren't you? E. J. Belden. 'E' stands for Ephratah, or some such. Doesn't affect your digging any, though." He exhaled a cloud of smoke. "What's that thing you were using?"

I held it up. "It's a special knife for working out bones like these. The museum's model. When I was your age we used butcher knives and railroad spikes—anything we could get our hands on. There weren't any railroads out here then."

He nodded. "I know. My father dug for 'em. Hobby of his, for a while. Changed over to stamps when he lost his leg." Then, with an air of changing the subject, "That thing you're digging out—what did it look like? Alive, I mean."

I had about half of the skeleton worked out. I traced its outline for him with the knife. "There's the skull; there's the neck and spine, and what's left of the tail; this was its left foreleg. You can see the remains of the crest along the top of the skull, and the flat snout like a duck's beak. It's one of many species of trachodon—the duckbilled aquatic dinosaurs. They fed along the shore lines, on water plants and general browse, and some of them were bogged down and drowned."

"I get it. Big bruiser—little front legs and husky hind ones with a tail like a kangaroo. Sat on it when he got tired. Fin on his head like a fish, and a face like a duck. Did he have scales?"

"I doubt it," I told him. "More likely warts like a toad, or armor plates like an alligator. We've found skin impressions of some of this one's cousins, south of here, and that's what they were like."

He nodded again—that all-knowing nod that gets my eternal goat. He fumbled inside his coat and brought out a little leather folder or wallet, and leafed through its contents. He leaned forward and something white came scaling down at my feet.

"Like that?" he asked.

I picked it up. It was a photograph, enlarged from a miniature camera shot. It showed the edge of a reedy lake or river, with a narrow, sandy strip of beach and a background of feathery foliage that looked like tree ferns. Thigh-deep in the water, lush lily stalks trailing from its flat jaws, stood a replica of the creature whose skeleton was embedded in the rock at my feet—a trachodon. It was a perfect likeness—the heavy, frilled crest, the glistening skin with its uneven patches of dark tubercles, the small, webbed forepaws on skinny arms.

"Nice job," I admitted. "Is it one of Knight's new ones?"

"Knight?" He seemed puzzled. "Oh—the Museum of Natural History. No—I made it myself."

"You're to be congratulated," I assured him. "I don't know when I've seen a nicer model. What's it for—the movies?"

"Movies?" He sounded exasperated. "I'm not making movies. I made the picture—the photograph. Took it myself—here—or pretty close to here. The thing was alive, and is still for all I know. It chased me."

That was the last straw. "See here," I said, "if you're trying to talk me into backing some crazy publicity stunt, you can guess again. I wasn't born yesterday, and I cut my teeth on a lot harder and straighter science than your crazy newspaper syndicates dish out. I worked these beds before you were born, or your father, either, and there were no trachodons wandering around chasing smart photographers with the d. t.s, and no lakes or tree ferns for 'em to wander in. If you're after a testimonial for some one's model of Cretaceous fauna, say so. That is an excellent piece of work, and if you're responsible you have every right to be proud of it. Only stop this blither about photographing dinosaurs that have been fossils for sixty million years."

The fellow was stubborn. "It's no hoax," he insisted doggedly. "There's no newspaper involved and I'm not peddling dolls. I took that photograph. Your trachodon chased me and I ran. And I have more of the same to prove it! Here."

The folder landed with a thump at my feet. It was crammed with prints like the first—enlargements of Leica negatives—and for sheer realism I have never seen anything like them.

"I had thirty shots," he told me. "I used 'em all, and they were all beauties. And I can do it again!"

Those prints! I can see them now: landscapes that vanished from this planet millions of years before the first furry tree shrew scurried among the branches of the first temperate forests, and became the ancestor of mankind; monsters whose buried bones and fossil footprints are the only mementos of a race of giants vaster than any other creatures that ever walked the earth; there were more of the trachodons—a whole herd of them, it seemed, browsing along the shore of a lake or large river, and they had that individuality that marks the work of the true artist; they were Corythosaurs, like the one I was working on—one of the better-known genera of the great family of Trachodons. But the man who had restored them had used his imagination to show details of markings and fleshy structure that I was sure had never been shown by any recorded fossils.

Nor was that all. There were close-ups of plants—trees and low bushes—that were masterpieces of minute detail, even to the point of showing withered fronds, and the insects that walked and stalked and crawled over them. There were vistas of rank marshland scummed over with stringy algæ and lush with tall grasses and taller reeds, among which saurian giants wallowed. There were two or three other varieties of trachodon that I could see, and a few smaller dinosaurs, with a massive bulk in what passed for the distance that might have been a Brontosaurus hangover from the Jurassic of a few million years before. I pointed to it.

"You slipped up there," I said. "We've found no traces of that creature so late in the Age of Reptiles. It's a very common mistake; every fantastic novelist makes it when he tries to write a time-traveling story. Tyrannosaurus eats Brontosaurus and is then gored to death by Triceratops. The trouble with it is that it couldn't happen."

The boy ground his cigarette butt into the sand. "I don't know about that," he said. "It was there—I photographed it—and that's all there was to it. Tyrannosaurus I didn't see—and I'm not sorry. I've read those yarns you're so supercilious about. Good stuff—they arouse your curiosity and make you think. Triceratops—if he's the chunky devil with three big horns sticking out of his head and snout —I got in profusion. You haven't come to him yet. Go down about three more."

I humored him. Sure enough, there was a vast expanse of low, rolling plains with some lumpy hills in the distance. The thing was planned very poorly—any student would have laid it out looking toward the typical Cretaceous forest, rather than away from it—but it had the same startling naturalness that the others had. And there were indeed Triceratops in plenty—a hundred or more, grazing stolidly in little family groups of three or four, on a rank prairie grass that grew in great tufts from the sandy soil.

I guffawed. "Who told you that was right?" I demanded. "Your stuff is good—the best I've ever seen—but it is careless slips like that that spoil everything for the real scientist. Reptiles never herd, and dinosaurs were nothing but overgrown reptiles. Go on—take your pictures to some one who has the time to be amused. I don't find them funny or even interesting."

I stuffed them into the folder and tossed it to him. He made no attempt to catch it. For a moment he sat staring down at me, then in a shower of sand he was beside me. One hob-nailed boot gouged viciously across the femur of my dinosaur and the other crashed down among its brittle ribs. I felt the blood go out of my face with anger, then come rushing back. If I had been twenty years younger I would have knocked him off his feet and dared him to come back for more. But he was as red as I.

"Damn it," he cried, "no bald-headed old fuzzy-wuzzy is going to call me a liar twice! You may know a lot about dead bones, but your education with regard to living things has been sadly neglected. So reptiles never herd? What about alligators? What about the Galapagos iguanas? What about snakes? Bah—you can't see any farther than your own nose and never will! When I show you photographs of living dinosaurs, taken with this very camera twenty-four hours ago, not more than three or four miles from where we're standing —well, it's high time you scrap your hide-bound, bone-dry theories and listen to a branch of science that's real and living, and always will be. *I photographed those dinosaurs!* I can do it again—any time I like. I *will* do it."

He stopped for breath. I simply looked at him. It's the best way, when some crank gets violent. He colored and grinned sheepishly, then picked up the wallet from where it had fallen at the base of the quarry cut. There was an inner compartment with a covering flap which I had not touched. He rummaged in it with a finger and thumb and brought out a scrap of leathery-looking stuff, porous and coated with a kind of shiny, dried mucous.

"Put a name to it," he demanded.

I turned it over in my palm and examined it carefully. It was a bit of eggshell—undoubtedly a reptilian egg, and a rather large one —but I could tell nothing more.

"It might be an alligator or crocodile egg, or it might have been laid by one of the large oviparous snakes," I told him. "That would depend on where you found it. I suppose that you will claim that it is a dinosaur egg—a fresh egg."

"I claim nothing," he retorted. "That's for you to say. You're the expert on dinosaurs, not I. But if you don't like that—what about this?"

He had on a hunting jacket and corduroy breeches like mine. From the big side pocket he drew two eggs about the length of my palm —misshapen and gray-white in color, with that leathery texture so characteristic of reptile eggs. He held them up between himself and the sun.

"This one's fresh," he said. "The sand was still moist around the nest. This other is from the place where I got the shell. There's something in it. If you want to, you can open it."

I took it. It was heavy and somewhat discolored at the larger end, where something had pierced the shell. As he had said, there was evidently something inside. I hesitated. I felt that I would be losing face if I took him at his word to open it. And yet——

I squatted down and, laying the egg on a block of sandstone beside the weird, crested skull of the Corythosaur, I ripped its leathery shell from end to end.

The stench nearly felled me. The inside was a mass of greenish-yellow matter such as only a very long-dead egg can create. The embryo was well advanced, and as I poked around in the noisome mess it began to take definite form. I dropped the knife and with my fingers wiped away the last of the putrid ooze from the twisted, jellylike thing that remained. I rose slowly to my feet and looked him squarely in the eye.

"Where did you get that egg?"

He smiled—that maddening, slow smile. "I told you," he said. "I found it over there, a mile or so, beyond the belt of jungle that fringes the marshes. There were dozens of them—mounds like those that turtles make, in the warm sand. I opened two. One was fresh; the other was full of broken shells—and this." He eyed me quizzically. "And what does the great Professor Belden make of it?"

What he said had given me an idea. "Turtles," I mused aloud. "It could be a turtle—some rare species—maybe a mutation or freak that never developed far enough to really take shape. It must be!"

He sounded weary. "Yes," he said flatly, "it could be a turtle. It isn't but that doesn't matter to you. Those photographs could be fakes, and none-too-clever fakes at that. They show things that couldn't happen—that your damned dry-bone science says are wrong. All right—you've got me. It's your round. But I'm coming back, and I'm coming to bring proof that will convince you and every other stiff-necked old fuzz-buzz in the world that I, Terence Michael Aloysius Donovan, have stepped over the traces into the middle of the Cretaceous era and lived there, comfortably and happily, *sixty million years before I was born!*"

He walked away. I heard his footsteps receding up the draw, and the rattle of small stones as he climbed to the level of the prairie. I stood staring down at the greenish mess that was frying in the hot sun on the bright-red sandstone. It *could* have been a turtle, malformed in the embryo so that its carapace formed a sort of rudimentary, flaring shield behind the beaked skull. Or it could be— something else.

If it was that something, all the sanity and logic had gone out of the world, and a boy's mad, pseudoscientific dream became a reality that could not possibly be real. Paradox within paradox—contradiction upon contradiction. I gathered up my tools and started back for camp.

II

During the days that followed we worked out the skeleton of the Corythosaur and swathed it in plaster-soaked burlap for its long journey by wagon, truck and train back to the museum. I had perhaps a week left to use as I saw fit. But somehow, try as I would, I could not forget the young, blond figure of Terry Donovan, and the two strange eggs that he had pulled out of his pocket.

About a mile up the draw from our camp I found the remains of what had been a beach in Cretaceous times. Where it had not weathered away, every ripple mark and worm burrow was intact. There were tracks—remarkably fine ones—of which any museum would be proud. Dinosaurs, big and little, had come this way, millions of years ago, and left the mark of their passing in the moist sand, to be buried and preserved to arouse the apish curiosity of a race whose tiny, hairy ancestors were still scrambling about on all fours.

Beyond the beach had been marshes and a quicksand. Crumbling white bones protruded from the stone in incalculable profusion, massed and jumbled into a tangle that would require years of careful study to unravel. I stood with a bit of crumbling bone in my hand, staring at the mottled rock. A step sounded on the talus below me. It was Donovan.

Some of the cocksure exuberance had gone out of him. He was thinner, and his face was covered with a stubbly growth of beard. He wore shorts and a tattered shirt, and his left arm was strapped to his side with bands of some gleaming metallic cloth. Dangling from the fingers of his good hand was the strangest bird I have ever seen.

He flung it down at my feet. It was purplish-black with a naked red head and wattled neck. Its tail was feathered as a sumac is leafed, with stubby feathers sprouting in pairs from a naked, ratty shaft. Its wings had little three-fingered hands at the joints. And its head was long and narrow, like a lizard's snout, with great, round, lidless eyes and a mouthful of tiny yellow teeth.

I looked from the bird to him. There was no smile on his lips now. He was staring at the footprints of the rock.

"So you've found the beach." His voice was a weary monotone. "It was a sort of sandy spit, between the marshes and the sea, where they came to feed and be fed on. Dog eat dog. Sometimes they would blunder into the quicksands and flounder and bleat until they drowned. You see—I was there. That bird was there—alive when those dead, crumbling bones were alive—not only in the same geological age but in the same year, the same month—*the same day!* You've got proof now—proof that you can't talk away! Examine it. Cut it up. Do anything you want with it. But by the powers, this time you've *got* to believe me! This time you've got to help!"

I stooped and picked the thing up by its long, scaly legs. No bird like it had lived, or could have lived, on this planet for millions of years. I thought of those thirty photographs of the incredible—of the eggs he had had, one of them fresh, one with an embryo that might, conceivably, have been an unknown genus of turtle.

"All right," I said. "I'll come. What do you want?"

He lived three miles away across the open prairie. The house was a modernistic metal box set among towering cottonwoods at the edge of a small reservoir. A power house at the dam furnished light and electricity—all that he needed to bring civilized comfort out of the desert.

One wing of the house was windowless and sheer-walled, with blower vents at intervals on the sloping roof. A laboratory, I guessed. Donovan unlocked a steel door in the wall and pushed it open. I stepped past him into the room.

It was bare. A flat-topped desk stood in the corner near the main house, with a shelf of books over it. A big switchboard covered the opposite wall, flanked by two huge D. C. generators. There were cupboards and a long worktable littered with small apparatus. But a good half of the room was empty save for the machine that squatted in the middle of the concrete floor.

It was like a round, lead egg, ten feet high and half as broad. It was set in a cradle of steel girders, raised on massive insulators. Part of it stood open like a door, revealing the inside—a chamber barely large enough to hold a man, with a host of dials and switches set in an insulated panel in the leaden wall, and a flat bakelite floor. Heavy cables came out of that floor to the instrument board, and two huge, copper bus bars were clamped to the steel base. The laboratory was filled with the drone of the generators, charging some hidden battery, and there was a faint tang of ozone in the air.

Donovon shut and locked the door. "That's the Egg," he said. "I'll show it to you later, after you've heard me out. Will you help me with this arm of mine, first?"

I cut the shirt away and unwrapped the metallic gauze that held the arm tight against his body. Both bones of the forearm were splintered and the flesh gashed as though by jagged knives. The wound had been cleaned, and treated with some bright-green antiseptic whose odor I did not recognize. The bleeding had stopped, and there was none of the inflammation that I should have expected.

He answered my unspoken question. "She fixed it up—Lana. One of your little playmates—the kind I didn't see the first time—wanted to eat me." He was rummaging in the bottom drawer of the desk. "There's no clean cloth here," he said. "I haven't time to look in the house. You'll have to use that again."

"Look here," I protested, "you can't let a wound like that go untreated. It's serious. You must have a doctor."

He shook his head. "No time. It would take a doctor two hours to get out here from town. He'd need another hour, or more, to fool around with me. In just forty minutes my accumulators will be charged to capacity, and in forty-one I'll be gone—back there. Make a couple of splints out of that orange crate in the corner and tie me up again. It'll do—for as long as I'll be needing it."

I split the thin boards and made splints, made sure that the bones were set properly and bound them tightly with the strange silvery cloth, then lopped the loose ends in a sling around his neck. I went into the house to get him clean clothes. When I returned he was stripped, scrubbing himself at the laboratory sink. I helped him clamber into underwear, a shirt and breeches, pull on high-top shoes. I plugged in an electric razor and sat watching him as he ran it over his angular jaw.

He was grinning now. "You're all right, professor," he told me. "Not a question out of you, and I'll bet you've been on edge all the while. Well—I'll tell you everything. Then you can take it or leave it.

"Look there on the bench behind you—that coiled spring. It's a helix—a spiral made up of two-dimensional cross sections twisted in a third dimension. If you make two marks on it, you can go from one to the other by traveling along the spring, round and round, for about six inches. Or you can cut across from one spiral to the next. Suppose your two marks come right together—so. They're two inches apart, along the spring—and no distance at all if you cut across.

"So much for that. You know Einstein's picture of the universe —space and time tied up together in some kind of four-dimensional continuum that's warped and bent in all sorts of weird ways by the presence of matter. Maybe closed and maybe not. Maybe expanding like a balloon and maybe shrinking like a melting hailstone. Well—I know what that shape is. I've proved it. It's spiraled like that spring —spiraled in time!

"See what that means? Look—I'll show you. This first scratch, here on the spring, is today—now. Here will be tomorrow, a little further along the wire. Here's next year. And here is some still later time, one full turn of the coil away, directly above the first mark.

"Now watch. I can go from today to tomorrow—to next year— like this by traveling with time along the spring. That's what the world is doing. Only by the laws of physics—entropy and all that— there's no going back. It's one-way traffic. And you can't get ahead any faster than time wants to take you. That's *if you follow the spring*. But you can cut across!

"Look—here are the two marks I just made, now and two years from now. They're two inches apart, along the coiled wire, but when you compress the spring they are together—nothing between them but the surface of the two coils. You can stretch a bridge across from

one to the other, so to speak, and walk across—into a time two years
from now. Or you can go the other way, two years into the past.

"That's all there is to it. Time is coiled like a spring. Some other
age in earth's history lies next to ours, separated only by an intangible
boundary, a focus of forces that keeps us from seeing into it and
falling into it. Past time—present time—future time, side by side.
Only it's not two years, or three, or a hundred. It's sixty million
years from now to then, the long way around!

"I said you could get from one coil of time to the next one if you
built a bridge across. I built that bridge—the Egg. I set up a field
of forces in it—no matter how—that dissolve the invisible barrier
between our time and the next. I give it an electromagnetic shove that
sends it in the right direction, forward or back. And I land sixty
million years in the past, in the age of dinosaurs."

He paused, as if to give me a chance to challenge him. I didn't try.
I am no physicist, and if it was as he said—if time was really a
spiral, with adjacent coils lying side by side, and if his leaden Egg
could bridge the gap between—then the pictures and the eggs and
the bird were possible things. And they were more than possible. I
had seen them.

"You can see that the usual paradoxes don't come in at all," Donovan went on. "About killing your grandfather, and being two places at
once—that kind of thing. The time screw has a sixty-million-year
pitch. You can slide from coil to coil, sixty million years at a time,
but you can't cover any shorter distance without living it. If I go back
or ahead sixty million years, and live there four days, I'll get back here
next Tuesday, four days from now. As for going ahead and learning
all the scientific wonders of the future, then coming back to change
the destiny of humanity, sixty million years is a long time. I doubt
that there'll be anything human living then. And if there is—if I
do learn their secrets and come back—it will be because their future
civilization was built on the fact that I did so. Screwy as it sounds,
that's how it is."

He stopped and sat staring at the dull-gray mass of the Egg. He was
looking back sixty million years, into an age when giant dinosaurs
ruled the earth. He was watching herds of Triceratops grazing on the
Cretaceous prairie—seeing unsuspected survivors of the genus that
produced Brontosaurus and his kin, wallowing in some protected
swamp—seeing rat-tailed, purple-black Archæopteryx squawking in
the tree ferns. And he was seeing more!

"I'll tell you the whole story," he said. "You can believe it or not, as you like. Then I'll go back. After that—well, maybe you'll write the end, and maybe not. Sixty million years is a long time!"

He told me: how he hit on his theory of spiraled time; how he monkeyed around with the mathematics of the thing until it hung together—built little models of machines that swooped into nothingness and disappeared; how he made the Egg, big enough to hold a man, yet not too big for his generators to provide the power to lift it and him across the boundary between the coils of time—and back again; how he stepped out of the close, cramped chamber of the Egg into a world of steaming swamps and desert plains, sixty million years before mankind!

That was when he took the pictures. It was when the Corythosaur chased him, bleating and bellowing like a monster cow, when he disturbed its feeding. He lost it among the tree ferns, and wandered warily through the bizarre, luxurious jungle, batting at great mosquitoes the size of horse flies and ducking when giant dragon flies zoomed down and seized them in mid-air. He watched a small hornless dinosaur scratch a hole in the warm sand at the edge of the jungle and ponderously lay a clutch of twenty eggs. When she had waddled away, he took one—the fresh one he had showed me—and scratched out another from a nest that had already hatched. He had photographs—he had specimens—and the sun was getting low. Some of the noises from the salt marshes along the seashore were not very reassuring. So he came back. And I laughed at him and his proofs, and called him a crazy fake!

He went back. He had a rifle along this time—a huge thing that his father had used on elephants in Africa. I don't know what he expected to do with it. Shoot a Triceratops, maybe—since I wouldn't accept his photographs—and hack off its ungainly, three-horned head for a trophy. He could never have brought it back, of course, because it was a tight enough squeeze as it was to get himself and the big rifle into the Egg. He had food and water in a pack—he didn't much like the look of the water that he had found "over there"—and he was in a mood to stay until he found something that I and every one like me would have to accept.

Inland, the ground rose to a range of low hills along the horizon. Back there, he reasoned, there would be creatures a little smaller than the things he had seen buoying up their massive hulks in the sea and marshes. So, shutting the door of the Egg and heaping cycad

fronds over it to hide it from inquisitive dinosaurs, he set out across
the plain toward the west.

The Triceratops herds paid not the slightest attention to him. He
doubted that they could see him unless he came very close, and then
they ignored him. They were herbivorous, and anything his size could
not be an enemy. Only once, when he practically fell over a tiny,
eight-foot calf napping in the tall grass, did one of the old ones emit
a snuffling, hissing roar and come trotting toward him with its
three sharp spikes lowered and its little eyes red.

There were many small dinosaurs, light and fleet of foot, that
were not so unconcerned with his passage. Some of them were big
enough to make him feel distinctly uneasy, and he fired his first
shot in self-defense when a creature the size of an ostrich leaned forward and came streaking at him with obviously malicious intent. He
blew its head off at twenty paces, and had to duck the body that
came clawing and scampering after him. It blundered on in a straight
line, and when it finally collapsed he cooked and ate it over a fire
of dead grass. It tasted like iguana, he said, and added that iguana
tasted a lot like chicken.

Finally, he found a stream running down from the hills and took
to its bed for greater safety. It was dry, but in the baked mud were
the tracks of things that he hadn't seen and didn't want to see. He
guessed, from my description, that they had been made by Tyrannosaurus or something equally big and dangerous.

Incidentally, I have forgotten the most important thing of all.
Remember that Donovan's dominating idea was to prove to me, and
to the world, that he had been in the Cretaceous and hobnobbed
with its flora and fauna. He was a physicist by inclination, and had
the physicist's flair for ingenious proofs. Before leaving, he loaded a
lead cube with three quartz quills of pure radium chloride that he'
had been using in a previous experiment, and locked the whole thing
up in a steel box. He had money to burn, and besides, he expected
to get them back.

The first thing he did when he stepped out of the Egg on that
fateful second trip was to dig a deep hole in the packed sand of the
beach, well above high tide, and bury the box. He had seen the fossil
tracks and ripple marks in the sandstone near his house, and guessed
rightly enough that they dated from some time near the age to which
he had penerated. If I, or some one equally trustworthy, were to dig
that box up one time coil later, he would not only have produced

some very pretty proof that he had traveled in time—his name and the date were inside the cube—but an analysis of the radium, and an estimate of how much of it had turned into lead, would show how many years had elapsed since he buried it. In one fell swoop he would prove his claim, and give the world two very fundamental bits of scientific information: an exact date for the Cretaceous period, and the "distance" between successive coils in the spiral of time.

The stream bed finally petered out in a gully choked with boulders. The terrain was utterly arid and desolate, and he began to think that he had better turn back. There was nothing living to be seen, except for some small mammals like brown mice that got into his pack the first night and ate the bread he was carrying. He pegged a rock at them, but they vanished among the boulders, and an elephant gun was no good for anything their size. He wished he had a mousetrap. Mice were something that he could take back in his pocket.

III

The morning of the second day some birds flew by overhead. They were different from the one he killed later—more like sea gulls—and he got the idea that beyond the hills, in the direction they were flying, there would be either more wooded lowlands or an arm of the sea. As it turned out, he was right.

The hills were the summit of a ridge like the spine of Italy, jutting south into the Cretaceous sea. The sea had been higher once, covering the sandy waste where the Triceratops herds now browsed, and there was a long line of eroded limestone cliffs, full of the black holes of wave-worn caves. From their base he looked back over the desert plain with its fringe of jungle along the shore of the sea. Something was swimming in schools, far out toward the horizon—something as big as whales, he thought—but he had forgotten to bring glasses and he could not tell what they were. He set about finding a way to climb the escarpment.

Right there was where he made his first big mistake. He might have known that what goes up has to come down again on the other side. The smart thing to do would have been to follow the line of the cliffs until he got into the other valley, or whatever lay beyond. Instead, he slung his gun around his neck and climbed.

The summit of the cliffs was a plateau, hollowed out by centuries of erosion into a basin full of gaudy spires of rock with the green stain

of vegetation around their bases. There was evidently water and there
might be animals that he could photograph or kill. Anything he found
up here, he decided, would be pretty small.

He had forgotten the caves. They were high-arched, wave-eaten
tunnels that extended far back into the cliffs, and from the lay of the
land it was probable that they opened on the inside as well. Besides,
whatever had lived on the plateau when it was at sea level had presumably been raised with it and might still be in residence. Whether
it had wandered in from outside, or belonged there, it might be hungry—very hungry. It was.

There was a hiss that raised the short hair all along his spine. The
mice that he had shied rocks at had heard such hisses and passed the
fear of them down to their descendants, who eventually became his
remote ancestors. And they had cause for fear! The thing that lurched
out of the rocky maze, while it didn't top him by more than six feet
and had teeth that were only eight inches long, was big enough to
swallow him in three quick gulps, gun and all.

He ran. He ran like a rabbit. He doubled into crannies that the
thing couldn't cram into and scrambled up spires of crumbling rock
that a monkey would have found difficult, but it knew short cuts and
it was downwind from him, and it thundered along behind with very
few yards to spare. Suddenly he popped out of a long, winding corridor
onto a bare ledge with a sheer drop to a steaming, stinking morass alive
with things like crocodiles, only bigger. At the cliff's edge the thing
was waiting for him.

One leap and it was between him and the crevice. He backed toward
the cliff, raising his rifle slowly. It sat watching him for a moment,
then raised its massive tail, teetered forward on its huge hind legs, and
came running at him with its tiny foreclaws pumping like a sprinter's
fists.

He threw up the gun and fired. The bullet plowed into its throat
and a jet of smoking blood sprayed him as its groping claws knocked
the rifle from his grasp. Its hideous jaws closed on his upflung left
arm, grinding the bones until he screamed. It jerked him up, dangling
by his broken arm, ten feet in the air; then the idea of death hit it
and it rolled over and lay twitching on the blood-soaked rock. Its
jaws sagged open, and with what strength he had left Donovan dragged
himself out of range of its jerking claws. He pulled himself up with
his back against a rock and stared into the face of a second monster!

This was the one that had trailed him. The thing that had actually
tasted him was a competitor. It came striding out of the shadowy gorge,

the sun playing on its bronzed armor, and stopped to sniff at the thing Donovan had killed. It rolled the huge carcass over and tore out the belly, then straightened up with great gouts of bloody flesh dribbling from its jaws, and looked Donovan in the eye. Inch by inch, he tried to wedge himself into the crack between the boulders against which he lay. Then it stepped over its deceased relative and towered above him. Its grinning mask swooped down and its foul breath was in his face.

Then it was gone!

It wasn't a dream. There were the rocks—there was the carcass of the other beast—but it was gone! Vanished! In its place a wisp of bluish vapor was dissipating slowly in the sunlight. Vapor—and a voice! A woman's voice, in an unknown tongue.

She stood at the edge of the rocks. She was as tall as he, with very white skin and very black hair, dressed in shining metal cloth that was wound around her like bandage, leaving her arms and one white leg free. She was made like a woman and she spoke like a woman, in a voice that thrilled him in spite of the sickening pain in his arm. She had a little black cylinder in her hand, with a narrowed muzzle and a grip for her fingers, and she was pointing it at him. She spoke again, imperiously, questioning him. He grinned, tried to drag himself to his feet, and passed out cold.

It was two days before he came to. He figured that out later. It was night. He was in a tent somewhere near the sea, for he could hear it pounding on hard-packed sands. Above its roar there were other noises of the night; mutterings and rumblings of great reptiles, very far away, and now and then a hissing scream of rage. They sounded unreal. He seemed to be floating in a silvery mist, with the pain in his wounded arm throb, throb, throbbing to the rhythm of the sea.

Then he saw that the light was moonlight, and the silver the sheen of the woman's garment. She sat at his feet, in the opening of the tent, with the moonlight falling on her hair. It was coiled like a coronet about her head, and he remembered thinking that she must be a queen in some magic land, like the ones in fairy tales.

Someone moved, and he saw that there were others—men—crouching behind a breastwork of stone. They had cylinders like the one the woman had carried, and other weapons on tripods like parabolic microphones—great, polished reflectors of energy. The wall seemed more for concealment than protection, for he remembered the blasting power of the little cylinder and knew that no mere heap of rock could withstand it long. Unless, of course, they were fighting some foe who lacked their science. A foe native to this Cretaceous age—hairy, savage men with stones and clubs.

Realization struck him. There were no men in the Cretaceous. The only mammals were the mouselike marsupials that had robbed his pack. Then—who was the woman and how had she come here? Who were the men who guarded her? Were they—could they be—travelers in time like himself?

He sat up with a jerk that made his head swim. There was a shimmering, flowing movement in the moonlight and a small, soft hand was pressed over his mouth, an arm was about his shoulders, easing him back among the cushions. She called out and one of the men rose and came into the tent. He was tall, nearly seven feet, with silvery white hair and a queer-shaped skull. He stared expressionlessly down at Donovan, questioning the woman in that same strange tongue. She answered him, and Donovan felt with a thrill that she seemed worried. The other shrugged—that is, he made a queer, quick gesture with his hands that passed for a shrug—and turned away. Before Donovan knew what was happening, the woman gathered him up in her arms like a babe and started for the door of the tent.

Terry Donovan is over six feet tall and weighs two hundred pounds. He stiffened like a naughty child. It caught her off-guard and they went down with a thud, the woman underneath. It knocked the wind out of her, and Donovan's arm began to throb furiously, but he scrambled to his feet, and with his good hand helped her to rise. They stood eyeing each other like sparring cats, and then Terry laughed.

It was a hearty Irish guffaw that broke the tension, but it brought hell down on them. Something spanged on the barricade and went whining over their heads. Something else came arcing through the moonlight and fell at their feet—a metal ball the size of his head, whirring like a clock about to strike.

Donovan moved like greased lightning. He scooped the thing up with his good hand and lobbed it high and wide in the direction from which it came, then grabbed the woman and ducked. It burst in mid-air with a blast of white flame that would have licked them off the face of the earth in a twinkling—and there was no sound, no explosion such as a normal bomb should make! There was no bark of rifles off there in the darkness, though slugs were thudding into the barricade and screaming overhead with unpleasant regularity. The tent was in ribbons, and seeing no reason why it should make a better target than need be, he kicked the pole out from under it and brought it down in a billowing heap.

That made a difference, and he saw why. The material of the tent was evanescent, hard to see. It did something to the light that fell on it, distorted it, acting as a camouflage. But where bullets had torn its fabric a line of glowing green sparks shone in the night.

The enemy had lost their target, but they had the range. A bullet whined evilly past Donovan's ear as he dropped behind the shelter of the wall. His groping hand found a familiar shape—his rifle. The cartridge belt was with it. He tucked the butt between his knees and made sure that it was loaded, then rose cautiously and peeped over the barricade.

Hot lead sprayed his cheek as a bullet pinged on the stone beside him. There was a cry from the woman. She had dropped to her knees beside the tent, and he could see that the ricochet had cut her arm. The sight of blood on her white skin sent a burning fury surging through him. He lunged awkwardly to his feet, resting the rifle on top of the wall, and peered into the darkness.

Five hundred yards away was the jungle, a wall of utter blackness out of which those silent missiles came. Nothing was visible against its shadows—or was that a lighter spot that slipped from tree to tree at the very edge of the moonlight? Donovan's cheek nestled against the stock of his gun and his eyes strained to catch that flicker of gray in the blackness. It came—the gun roared—and out of the night rang a scream of pain. A hit!

Twice before sunup he fired at fleeting shadows, without result. Beside him, the oldest of the four men—the one he had seen first— was dressing the woman's wound. It was only a scratch, but Donovan reasoned that in this age of virulent life forms, it was wise to take every precaution. There might be germs that no one had even heard of, lurking everywhere. The others were about his own age, or seemed to be, with the same queer heads and white hair as their companion's. They seemed utterly disinterested in him and what he was doing.

IV

As the first rays of the sun began to brighten the sky behind them, Donovan took stock of the situation. Their little fortress was perched on a point of rock overlooking the sea, with the plateau behind it. Salt marshes ran inland as far as he could see, edged with heavy jungle. And in the No Man's Land between the two was the queerest ship he had ever seen.

It was of metal, cigar-shaped, with the gaping mouths of rocket jets fore and after and a row of staring portholes. It was as big as a large ocean vessel and it answered his question about these men whose cause he was championing. They had come from space—from another world!

Bodies were strewn in the open space between the ship and the barricade. One lay huddled against a huge boulder, a young fellow, barely out of his teens as we would gauge it. Donovan's gaze wandered away, then flashed back. The man had moved!

Donovan turned eagerly to the others. They stared at him, blankfaced. He seized the nearest man by the shoulder and pointed. A cold light came into the other's eyes, and Donovan saw his companions edging toward him, their hands on the stubby cylinders of their weapons. He swore. Damn dummies! He flung the rifle down at the woman's sandaled feet and leaped to the top of the wall. As he stood there he was a perfect target, but no shot came. Then he was among the scattered rocks, zigzagging toward the wounded man. A moment later he slid safely into the niche behind the boulder, and lifted the other into a sitting position against his knee. He had been creased— an ugly furrow plowed along his scalp—but he seemed otherwise intact.

Donovan got his good shoulder under the man's armpit and lifted him bodily. From the hill behind the barricade a shot screamed past his head. Before he could drop to safety a second slug whacked into the body of the man in his arms, and the youth's slim form slumped in death.

Donovan laid him gently down in the shelter of the boulder. He wondered whether this would be the beginning of the end. Under fire from both sides, the little fortress could not hold out for long. A puff of vapor on the hillside told him why the fire was not being returned. The damned cylinders had no range. That was why the enemy was using bullets—air guns, or whatever the things were. All the more reason why he should save his skin while the saving was good. He ducked behind the rock, then straightened up and streaked for the shelter of the trees.

Bullets sang around him and glanced whistling from the rocks. One whipped the sleeve that hung loose at his side and another grooved the leather of his high-top boots. All came from behind—from the hill above the camp—and as he gained the safety of the forest he turned and saw the foe for the first time.

They were deployed in a long line across the top of the ridge behind the camp. They had weapons like fat-barreled rifles, with some bulky contraption at the breach. As he watched they rose and came stalking down the hillside, firing as they came.

They were black, but without the heavy features of a Negro. Their hair was as yellow as corn, and they wore shorts and tunics of copper-colored material. Donovan saw that they were maneuvering toward a spur from which they could fire down into the little fortress and pick off its defenders one by one. With the men at the barricade gone, they would be coming after him. If he started now, he might make his way through the jungle to a point where he could cut back across the hills and reach the Egg. He had a fifty-fifty chance of making it. Only —there was the woman. It was murder to leave her, and suicide to stay.

Fate answered for him. From the barricade he heard the roar of his rifle and saw one of the blacks spin and fall in a heap. The others stood startled, then raced for cover. Before they reached it, two more were down, and Donovan saw the woman's sleek black head thrust above the top of the rocky wall with the rifle butt tucked in the hollow of her shoulder.

That settled it. No one with her gumption was going to say that Terry Donovan had run out on her. Cautiously, he stuck his head out of the undergrowth and looked to left and right. A hundred feet from him one of the blacks lay half in and half out of the forest. One of the outlandish-looking rifles was beside him. Donovan pulled his head back and began to pry his way through the thick undergrowth.

The Donovan luck is famous. The gun was intact, and with it was a belt case crammed with little metal cubes that had the look of ammunition. He poked the heavy barrel into the air and pushed the button that was set in the butt. There was a crackling whisper, barely audible, and a slug went tearing through the fronds above him. He tried again, and an empty cube popped out into his palm. He examined it carefully. There was a sliding cover that had to be removed before the mechanism of the gun could get at the bullets it contained. He slipped in one of the loaded cubes and tried again. A second shot went whistling into space. Then, tucking the gun under his arm, he set out on a flanking trip of his own.

He knew the range of the weapon he was carrying, if not its nature, and he knew how to use it. He knew that if he could swing far around to the east, along the sea, he might come up on the ridge behind the blacks and catch them by surprise. Then, if the gang in the fort would lend a hand, the war was as good as over.

It was easier said than done. A man with one mangled arm strapped to his side, and a twenty-pound rifle in his good hand, is not the world's best mountaineer. He worked his way through the jungle into the lee of the dunes that lay between the cliffs and the beach, then ran like blue blazes until he was out of sight of the whole fracas, cut back inland, took his lip in his teeth, and began to climb.

There were places where he balanced on spires the size and sharpness of a needle, or so he said. There were places where he prayed hard and trod on thin air. Somehow he made it and stuck his head out from behind a crimson crag to look down on a very pretty scene.

The ten remaining blacks were holed upon the crest of the ridge. They were within range of the camp, but they didn't dare get up and shoot because of whoever was using the rifle. That "whoever"—the woman, as Donovan had suspected—was out of sight and stalking them from the north just as he was doing from the south. The fighting blood of his Irish ancestors sizzled in his veins. He slid the misshapen muzzle of his weapon out over the top of the rock and settled its butt in the crook of his good arm. He swiveled it around until it pointed in the direction of two of the blacks who were sheltering under the same shallow ledge. Then he jammed down the button and held on.

The thing worked like a machine gun and kicked like one. Before it lashed itself out of his grip one of the foemen was dead, two were flopping about like fish out of water, and the rest were in full flight. As they sprang to their feet the woman blazed away at them with the elephant gun. Then the men from the barricade were swarming over the rock wall, cylinders in hand, and mowing the survivors down in a succession of tiny puffs of blue smoke. In a moment it was over.

Donovan made his way slowly down the hillside. The woman was coming to meet him. She was younger than he had thought—a lot younger—but her youth did not soften her. He thought that she might still be a better man than he, if it came to a test. She greeted him in her soft tongue, and held out the rifle. He took it, and as he touched the cold metal a terrific jolt of static electricity knocked him from his feet.

He scrambled up ruefully. The woman had not fallen, but her eyes blazed with fury. Then she saw that he had not acted intentionally, and smiled. Donovan saw now why the blacks wore metal suits. Their weapons built up a static charge with each shot, and unless the gunner was well grounded it would accumulate until it jumped to the nearest conductor. His rubber-soled shoes had insulated him, and the charge built up on him until he touched the barrel of the rifle, whereupon it grounded through the steel and the woman's silvery gown.

They went down the hillside together. Donovan had given the woman the gun he had salvaged, and she was examining it carefully. She called out to the men, who stood waiting for them, and they began to search the bodies of the blacks for ammunition. Half an hour later they were standing on the beach in the shadow of the great rocket. The men had carried their equipment from the camp and stowed it away, while Donovan and the woman stood outside bossing the job. That is, she bossed while he watched. Then he recalled who and where he was. Helping these people out in their little feud was one thing, but going off with them, Heaven knew where, was another. He reached down and took the woman's hand.

"I've got to be going," he said.

Of course, she didn't understand a word he said. She frowned and asked some question in her own tongue. He grinned. He was no better at languages than she. He pointed to himself, then up the beach to the east where the Egg should be. He saluted cheerfully and started to walk away. She cried out sharply and in an instant all four men were on him.

He brought up the rifle barrel in a one-handed swing that dropped the first man in his tracks. The gun went spinning out of his hand, but before the others could reach him he had vaulted the man's body and caught the woman to him in a savage, one-armed hug that made her gasp for breath. The men stopped, their ray guns drawn. One second more and he would have been a haze of exploded atoms, but none of them dared fire with the woman in the way. Over the top of her sleek head he stared into their cold, hard eyes. Human they might be, but there was blessed little of the milk of human kindness in the way they looked at him.

"Drop those guns," he ordered, "or I'll break her damned neck!" None of them moved. "You heard me!" he barked. "Drop 'em!"

They understood his tone. Three tapering cylinders thudded on the sand. He thrust the woman forward with the full weight of his body and trod them into the sand.

"Get back," he commanded. "Go on. Scram!"

They went. Releasing the woman, he leaped back and snatched up the weapon she had dropped. He poked its muzzle at her slender waist and fitted his fingers cozily about the stock. He jerked his head back, away from the ship.

"You're coming with me," he said.

She stared inscrutably at him for a moment, then, without a word, walked past him and set off up the beach. Donovan followed her. A moment later the dunes had hidden the ship and the three men who stood beside it.

V

Then began a journey every step of which was a puzzle. The girl— for she was really little more—made no attempt to escape. After the first mile Donovan thrust the ray gun into his belt and caught up with her. Hours passed, and still they were slogging wearily along under the escarpment. In spite of the almost miraculous speed with which it was healing, the strain and activity of the past few hours had started his arm throbbing like a toothache. It made him grumpy, and he had fallen behind when a drumming roar made him look up.

It was the rocket ship. It was flying high, but as he looked it swooped down on them with incredible speed. A thousand feet above it leveled off and a shaft of violet light stabbed down, missing the girl by a scant ten feet. Where it hit the sand was a molten pool, and she was running for her life, zigzagging like a frightened rabbit, streaking for the shelter of the cliffs. With a shout, Donovan raced after her.

A mile ahead the ship zoomed and came roaring back at him. A black hole opened in the face of the cliff. The girl vanished in its shadows, and as the thunder of the rocket sounded unbearably loud in his ears, Donovan dived after her. The ray slashed across the rock above his head and droplets of molten magma seared his back. The girl was crouching against the wall of the cave. When she saw him she plunged into the blackness beyond.

He had had enough of hide and seek. He wanted a show-down and he wanted it now. With a shout, he leaped after the girl's receding figure and caught her by the shoulder, spinning her around.

Instantly he felt like an utter fool. He could say nothing that she could understand. The whole damned affair was beyond understanding. He had strongarmed her into coming with him—and her own men had tried to burn her down. Her—not him. Somehow, by something he had done, he had put her in danger of her life from the only people in the entire universe who had anything in common with her. He couldn't leave her alone in a wilderness full of hungry dinosaurs, with a gang of gunmen on her trail, and he couldn't take her with him. The Egg would barely hold one. He was on a spot, and there was nothing he could do about it.

There was the sound of footsteps on the gravel behind them. In the dim light he saw the girl's eyes go wide. He wheeled. Two men were silhouetted against the mouth of the cave. One of them held a ray gun He raised it slowly.

Donovan's shoulder flung the girl against the wall. His hand flicked past his waist and held the gun. Twice it blazed and the men were gone in a puff of sparkling smoke. But in that instant, before they were swept out of existence, their guns had exploded in a misdirected burst of energy that brought the roof crashing down in a thundering avalanche, sealing the cave from wall to wall.

The shock flung Donovan to the ground. His wounded arm smashed brutally into the wall and a wave of agony left him white and faint. The echoes of that stupendous crash died away slowly in the black recesses of the cave. Then there was utter silence.

Something stirred beside him. A small, soft hand touched his face, found his shoulder, his hand. The girl's voice murmured, pleading. There was something she wanted—something he must do. He got painfully to his feet and awaited her next move. She gently detached the ray gun from his fingers, and before he knew it he was being hustled through utter darkness into the depths of the cave.

He did a lot of thinking on that journey through blackness. He put two and two together and got five or six different answers. Some of them hung together to make sense out of nightmare.

First, the girl herself. The rocket, and Donovan's faith in a science that he was proving fallible, told him that she must have come from another planet. Her unusual strength might mean that she was from some larger planet, or even some star. At any rate, she was human and she was somebody of importance.

Donovan mulled over that for a while. Two races, from the same or different planets, were thirsting for each other's blood. It might be politics that egged them on, or it might be racial trouble or religion. Nothing else would account for the fury with which they were exterminating each other. The girl had apparently taken refuge with her bodyguard on this empty planet. Possession of her was important. She might be a deposed queen or princess—and the blacks were on her trail. They found her and laid siege—whereupon Terry Donovan of 1937 A. D. came barging into the picture.

That was where the complications began. The girl, reconnoitering, had saved him from the dinosaur which was eating him. Any one would have done as much. She lugged him back to camp—Donovan flushed at the thought of the undignified appearance he must have made—and they patched him up with their miraculous green ointment. Then the scrap began, and he did his part to bring them out on top. Did it damn well, if any one was asking. Donovan didn't belong to their gang and didn't want to, so when they started for home he did likewise. Only it didn't work out that way.

She had ordered her men to jump him. She wanted to hang on to him, whether for romantic reasons, which was doubtful, or because she needed another fighting man. They didn't get very far with their attempt to gang up on him. That was where the worst of the trouble began.

Grabbing her as he had had been a mistake. Somehow that act of touching her—of doing physical violence to her person—made a difference. It was as though she were a goddess who lost divinity through his violence, or a priestess who was contaminated by his touch. She recognized that fact. She knew then that she would have short shrift at the hands of her own men if she stayed with them. So she came along. Strangely enough, the men did not follow for some time. It was not until they returned to the rocket, *until they received orders from whoever was in that rocket*, that they tried to kill her.

Whoever was in the rocket! The thought opened new possibilities. A priest, enforcing the taboos of his god. A politician, playing party policy. A traitor, serving the interests of the blacks. None of these did much to explain the girl's own attitude, nor the reason why this assumed potentate, if he was in the rocket during the battle, had done nothing to bring one side or the other to victory. It didn't explain why hours had passed before the pursuit began. And nothing told him what he was going to do with her when they reached the Egg, if they ever did.

The cave floor had been rising for some time when Donovan saw a gleam of light ahead. At once the girl's pace quickened, and she dropped his arm. How, he wondered, had she been able to traverse that pitch-black labyrinth so surely and quickly? Could she see in the dark, or judge her way with some strange sixth sense? It added one more puzzle to the mysteries surrounding her.

He could have danced for joy when they came out into the light. They had passed under the ridge and come out at the foot of the cliffs which he had climbed hours before. The whole landscape was familiar: the gullies in the barren plain, the fringe of swamp and jungle, and the reefs over which the oily sea was breaking. There, a few miles to the north, the Egg was hidden. There was safety—home —for one.

She seemed to know what he was thinking. She laid a reassuring hand on his arm and smiled up at him. This was his party from now on. Then she saw the pain in his eyes. His arm had taken more punishment than most men could have stood and stayed alive. Her nimble fingers peeled away the dressing and gently probed the wound to test the position of the broken bones. Evidently everything was to her liking, for she smiled reassuringly and opened a pouch at her waist, from which she took a little jar of bright-green ointment and smeared it liberally on the wound.

It burned like fire, then a sensuous sort of glow crept through his arm and side, deadening the pain. She wadded the dirty bandages into a ball and threw them away. Then, before Donovan knew what was happening, she had ripped a length of the metallic-looking fabric from her skirt and was binding the arm tightly to his side.

Stepping back, she regarded him with satisfaction, then turned her attention to the gun she had taken from him. A lip of the firing button and an empty cartridge cube popped out into her palm. She looked at him and he at her. It was all the weapon they had, and it was empty. Donovan shrugged. Nothing much mattered anyway. With an answering grimace she sent it spinning away among the rocks. Side by side, they set off toward the coast and the Egg.

It was the sky that Donovan feared now. Dinosaurs they could outwit or outrun. He thought he could even fight one of the little ones, with her to cheer him on. But heat rays shot at them from the sky, with no cover within miles, was something else again. Strangely enough, the girl seemed to be enjoying herself. Her voice was a joy to hear, even if it didn't make sense, and Donovan thought that he got the drift of her comments on some of the ungainly monstrosities that blemished the Cretaceous landscape.

Donovan had no desire to be in the jungle at night, so they took their time. He had matches, which she examined with curiosity, and they slept, back to back, beside a fire of grass and twigs in the lee of a big boulder. There was nothing to eat, but it didn't seem to matter. A sort of silent partnership had been arrived at, and Donovan, at least, was basking in its friendly atmosphere.

VI

Every road has its ending. Noon found them standing beside the leaden hulk of the Egg, face to face with reality. One of them, and only one could make the journey back. The Egg would not hold two, nor was there power enough in its accumulators to carry more than one back through the barrier between time coils. If the girl were to go, she would find herself alone in a world unutterably remote from her own, friendless and unable to understand or to make herself understood. If Donovan returned, he must leave her here alone in the Cretaceous jungle, with no food, no means of protection from man or beast, and no knowledge of what might be happening sixty million years later which would seal her fate for good.

There was only one answer. Her hand went to his arm and pushed him gently toward the open door of the Egg. He, and he alone, could get the help which they must have and return to find her. In six hours at the outside the Egg should be ready to make its return trip. In that six hours Donovan could find me, or some other friend, and enlist my aid.

Fortune played into his hands. There was a patter of footsteps among the fallen fronds, and a small dinosaur appeared, the body of a bird in its jaws. With a whoop, Donovan sprang at it. It dropped the bird and disappeared. The creature was not dead, but Donovan wrung its scrawny neck. Here was proof that must convince me of the truth of his story—that would bring me to their aid!

He stepped into the machine. As the door swung shut, he saw the girl raise her hand in farewell. When it opened again, he stepped out on the concrete floor of his own laboratory, sixty million years later.

His first thought was for the generators that would recharge the batteries of the Egg. Then, from the house and the laboratory, he collected the things that he would need: guns, food, water, clothing. Finally, he set out to fetch me.

He sat there, his broken arm strapped to his side with that queer metallic cloth, the torn flesh painted with some aromatic green ointment. A revolver in its holster lay on the desk at his elbow; a rifle leaned against the heap of duffel on the floor of the Egg. What did it all mean? Was it part of some incredibly elaborate hoax, planned for some inconceivable purpose? Or—fantastic as it seemed—was it truth?

"I'm leaving in ten minutes," he said. "The batteries are charged."

"What can I do?" I asked. "I'm no mechanic—no physicist."

"I'll send her back in the Egg," he told me. "I'll show you how to charge it—it's perfectly simple—and when it's ready you will send it back, empty, for me. If there is any delay, make her comfortable until I come."

I noted carefully everything he did, every setting of every piece of apparatus, just as he showed them to me. Then, just four hours after he threw that incredible bird down at my feet, I watched the leaden door of the Egg swing shut. The hum of the generators rose to an ugly whine. A black veil seemed to envelop the huge machine—a network of emptiness which ran together and coalesced into a hole into which I gazed for interminable distances. Then it was gone. The room was empty. I touched the switch that stopped the generators.

The Egg did not return—not on that day, nor the next, nor ever while I waited there. Finally, I came away. I have told his story—my story before—but they laugh as I did. Only there is one thing that no one knows.

This year there were new funds for excavation. I am still senior paleontologist at the museum, and in spite of the veiled smiles that are beginning to follow me, I was chosen to continue my work of previous seasons. I knew from the beginning what I would do. The executors of Donovan's estate gave me permission to trace the line of the ancient Cretaceous beach that ran across his property. I had a word picture of that other world as he had seen it, and a penciled sketch, scrawled on the back of an envelope as he talked. I knew where he had buried the cube of radium. And it might be that this beach of fossil sands, preserved almost since the beginning of time, was the same one in which Terry Donovan had scooped a hole and buried a leaden cube, sealed in a steel box.

I have not found the box. If it is there, it is buried under tons of rock that will require months of labor and thousands of dollars to remove. We have uncovered a section of the beach in whose petrified sands every mark made in that ancient day is as sharp and clear as though it was made yesterday: the ripples of the receding tide—the tracks of sea worms crawling in the shallow water—the trails of the small reptiles that fed on the flotsam and jetsam of the water's edge.

Two lines of footprints come down across the wet sands of that Cretaceous beach, side by side. Together they cross the forty-foot slab of sandstone which I have uncovered, and vanish where the rising tide has filled them. They are prints of a small, queerly made sandal and a rubber-soled hiking boot—of a man and a girl.

A third line of tracks crosses the Cretaceous sands and overlies those others—huge, splayed, three-toed, like the prints of some gigantic bird. Sixty million years ago, mighty Tyrannosaurus and his smaller cousins made such tracks. The print of one great paw covers both the girl's footprints as she stands for a moment, motionless, beside the man. They, too, vanish at the water's edge.

That is all, but for one thing: an inch or two beyond the point where the tracks vanish, where the lapping waters have smoothed the sand, there is a strange mark. The grains of sand are fused, melted together in a kind of funnel of greenish glass that reminds me of the fulgurites that one often finds where lightning has struck iron-bearing sand, or where some high-voltage cable has grounded. It is smoother and more regular than any fulgurite that I have ever seen.

Two years ago I saw Terry Donovan step into the leaden Egg that stood in its cradle on the floor of his laboratory, and vanish with it into nothingness. He has not returned. The tracks which I have described, imprinted in the sands of a Cretaceous beach, are very plain, but workmen are the only people besides myself who have seen them. They see no resemblance to human footprints in the blurred hollows in the stone. They know, for I have told them again and again during the years that I have worked with them, that there were no human beings on the earth sixty million years ago. Science says—and is not science always right?—that only the great dinosaurs of the Cretaceous age left their fossil footprints in the sands of time.

THE PROUD ROBOT

by

LEWIS PADGETT

No type of writing can be said to reach its full development until it is able to laugh at itself. In his picture of the drunken Gallegher, who played at science by ear, Lewis Padgett gives all the learned men of science and their fictional interpreters the rib perfect. We think this should rank with the best of the Sherlock Holmes pastiches as a masterpiece of affectionate burlesque.

*

ORIGINALLY the robot was intended to be a can opener. Things often happened that way with Gallegher, who played at science by ear. He was, as he often remarked, a casual genius. Sometimes he'd start with a twist of wire, a few batteries, and a button hook, and before he finished, he might contrive a new type of refrigerating unit. The affair of the time locker had begun that way, with Gallegher singing hoarsely under his breath and peering, quite drunk, into cans of paint.

At the moment he was nursing a hangover. A disjointed, lanky, vaguely boneless man with a lock of dark hair falling untidily over his forehead, he lay on the couch in the lab and manipulated his mechanical liquor bar. A very dry Martini drizzled slowly from the spigot into his receptive mouth.

He was trying to remember something, but not trying too hard. It had to do with the robot, of course. Well, it didn't matter.

"Hey, Joe," Gallegher said.

The robot stood proudly before the mirror and examined its in-

144

nards. Its hull was transparent, and wheels were going around at a great rate inside.

"When you call me that," Joe remarked, "whisper. And get that cat out of here."

"Your ears aren't that good."

"They are. I can hear the cat walking about, all right."

"What does it sound like?" Gallegher inquired, interested.

"Just like drums," said the robot, with a put-upon air. "And when you talk, it's like thunder." Joe's voice was a discordant squeak, so Gallegher meditated on saying something about glass-houses and casting the first stone. He brought his attention, with some effort, to the luminous door panel, where a shadow loomed—a familiar shadow, Gallegher thought.

"It's Brock," the annunciator said. "Harrison Brock. Let me in!"

"The door's unlocked." Gallegher didn't stir. He looked gravely at the well-dressed, middle-aged man who came in, and tried to remember. Brock was between forty and fifty; he had a smoothly massaged, clean-shaved face, and wore an expression of harassed intolerance. Probably Gallegher knew the man. He wasn't sure. Oh, well.

Brock looked around the big, untidy laboratory, blinked at the robot, searched for a chair, and failed to find it. Arms akimbo, he rocked back and forth and glared at the prostrate scientist.

"Well?" he said.

"Never start conversations that way," Gallegher mumbled, siphoning another Martini down his gullet. "I've had enough trouble today. Sit down and take it easy. There's a dynamo behind you. It isn't very dusty, is it?"

"Did you get it?" Brock snapped. "That's all I want to know. You've had a week. I've a check for ten thousand in my pocket. Do you want it, or don't you?"

"Sure," Gallegher said. He extended a large, groping hand. "Give."

"Caveat emptor. What am I buying?"

"Don't you know?" the scientist asked, honestly puzzled.

Brock began to bounce up and down in a harassed fashion. "My God," he said. "They told me you could help me if anybody could. Sure. And they also said it'd be like pulling teeth to get sense out of you. Are you a technician or a driveling idiot?"

Gallegher pondered. "Wait a minute. I'm beginning to remember. I talked to you last week, didn't I?"

"You talked—" Brock's round face turned pink. "Yes! You lay there swilling liquor and babbled poetry. You sang 'Frankie and

Johnnie.' And you finally got around to accepting my commission."

"The fact is," Gallegher said, "I have been drunk. I often get drunk. Especially on my vacation. It releases my subconscious, and then I can work. I've made my best gadgets when I was tizzied," he went on happily. "Everything seems so clear then. Clear as a bell. I mean a bell, don't I? Anyway——" He lost the thread and looked puzzled. "Anyway, what are you talking about?"

"Are you going to keep quiet?" the robot demanded from its post before the mirror.

Brock jumped. Gallegher waved a casual hand. "Don't mind Joe. I just finished him last night, and I rather regret it."

"A robot?"

"A robot. But he's no good, you know. I made him when I was drunk, and I haven't the slightest idea how or why. All he'll do is stand there and admire himself. And sing. He sings like a banshee. You'll hear him presently."

With an effort Brock brought his attention back to the matter in hand. "Now look, Gallegher. I'm in a spot. You promised to help me. If you don't, I'm a ruined man."

"I've been ruined for years," the scientist remarked. "It never bothers me. I just go along working for a living and making things in my spare time. Making all sorts of things. You know, if I'd really studied, I'd have been another Einstein. So they tell me. As it is, my subconscious picked up a first-class scientific training somewhere. Probably that's why I never bothered. When I'm drunk or sufficiently absent-minded, I can work out the damndest problems."

"You're drunk now," Brock accused.

"I approach the pleasanter stages. How would you feel if you woke up and found you'd made a robot for some unknown reason, and hadn't the slightest idea of the creature's attributes?"

"Well——"

"I don't feel that way at all," Gallegher murmured. "Probably you take life too seriously, Brock. Wine is a mocker; strong drink is raging. Pardon me. I rage." He drank another Martini.

Brock began to pace around the crowded laboratory, circling various enigmatic and untidy objects. "If you're a scientist, Heaven help science."

"I'm the Larry Adler of science," Gallegher said. "He was a musician—lived some hundreds of years ago, I think. I'm like him. Never took a lesson in my life. Can I help it if my subconscious likes practical jokes?"

"Do you know who I am?" Brock demanded.

"Candidly, no. Should I?"

There was bitterness in the other's voice. "You might have the courtesy to remember, even though it was a week ago. Harrison Brock. Me. I own Vox-View Pictures."

"No," the robot said suddenly, "it's no use. No use at all, Brock."

"What the—"

Gallegher sighed wearily. "I forget the damned thing's alive. Mr. Brock, meet Joe. Joe, meet Mr. Brock—of Vox-View."

Joe turned, gears meshing within his transparent skull. "I am glad to meet you, Mr. Brock. Allow me to congratulate you on your good fortune in hearing my lovely voice."

"Uh," said the magnate inarticulately. "Hello."

"Vanity of vanities, all is vanity," Gallegher put in, *sotto voce.* "Joe's like that. A peacock. No use arguing with him, either."

The robot ignored this aside. "But it's no use, Mr. Brock," he went on squeakily. "I'm not interested in money. I realize it would bring happiness to many if I consented to appear in your pictures, but fame means nothing to me. Nothing. Consciousness of beauty is enough."

Brock began to chew his lips. "Look," he said savagely, "I didn't come here to offer you a picture job. See? Am I offering you a contract? Such colossal nerve— *Pah!* You're crazy."

"Your schemes are perfectly transparent," the robot remarked coldly. "I can see that you're overwhelmed by my beauty and the loveliness of my voice—its grand tonal qualities. You needn't pretend you don't want me, just so you can get me at a lower price. I said I wasn't interested."

"You're cr-r-razy!" Brock howled, badgered beyond endurance, and Joe calmly turned back to his mirror.

"Don't talk so loudly," the robot warned. "The discordance is deafening. Besides, you're ugly and I don't like to look at you." Wheels and cogs buzzed inside the transplastic shell. Joe extended his eyes on stalks and regarded himself with every appearance of appreciation.

Gallegher was chuckling quietly on the couch. "Joe has a high irritation value," he said. "I've found that out already. I must have given him some remarkable senses, too. An hour ago he started to laugh his damn fool head off. No reason, apparently. I was fixing myself a bite to eat. Ten minutes after that I slipped on an apple core I'd thrown away and came down hard. Joe just looked at me. 'That was it,' he said. 'Logics of probability. Cause and effect. I knew you were going to drop that apple core and then step on it when you went to pick up the mail.' Like the White Queen, I suppose. It's a poor memory that doesn't work both ways."

Brock sat on the small dynamo—there were two, the larger one named Monstro, and the smaller one serving Gallegher as a bank—and took deep breaths. "Robots are nothing new."

"This one is. I hate its gears. It's beginning to give me an inferiority complex. Wish I knew why I'd made it," Gallegher sighed. "Oh, well. Have a drink?"

"No. I came here on business. Do you seriously mean you spent last week building a robot instead of solving the problem I hired you for?"

"Contingent, wasn't it?" Gallegher asked. "I think I remember that."

"Contingent," Brock said with satisfaction. "Ten thousand, if and when."

"Why not give me the dough and take the robot? He's worth that. Put him in one of your pictures."

"I won't have any pictures unless you figure out an answer," Brock snapped. "I told you all about it."

"I have been drunk," Gallegher said. "My mind has been wiped clear, as by a sponge. I am as a little child. Soon I shall be as a drunken little child. Meanwhile, if you'd care to explain the matter again—"

Brock gulped down his passion, jerked a magazine at random from the bookshelf, and took out a stylo. "All right. My preferred stocks are at twenty-eight, 'way below par—" He scribbled figures on the magazine.

"If you'd taken that medieval folio next to that, it'd have cost you a pretty penny," Gallegher said lazily. "So you're the sort of guy who writes on tablecloths, eh? Forget this business of stocks and stuff. Get down to cases. Who are you trying to gyp?"

"It's no use," the robot said from before its mirror. "I won't sign a contract. People may come and admire me, if they like, but they'll have to whisper in my presence."

"A madhouse," Brock muttered, trying to get a grip on himself. "Listen, Gallegher. I told you all this a week ago, but—"

"Joe wasn't here then. Pretend like you're talking to him."

"Uh—look. You've heard of Vox-View Pictures, at least."

"Sure. The biggest and best television company in the business. Sonatone's about your only competitor."

"Sonatone's squeezing me out."

Gallegher looked puzzled. "I don't see how. You've got the best product. Tri-dimensional color, all sorts of modern improvements, the top actors, musicians, singers—"

"No use," the robot said. "I won't."

"Shut up, Joe. You're tops in your field, Brock. I'll hand you that. And I've always heard you were fairly ethical. What's Sonatone got on you?"

Brock made helpless gestures. "Oh, it's politics. The bootleg theaters. I can't buck 'em. Sonatone helped elect the present administration, and the police just wink when I try to have the bootleggers raided."

"Bootleg theaters?" Gallegher asked, scowling a trifle. "I've heard something—"

"It goes 'way back. To the old sound-film days. Home television killed sound film and big theaters. People were conditioned away from sitting in audience groups to watch a screen. The home televisors got good. It was more fun to sit in an easy-chair, drink beer, and watch the show. Television wasn't a rich man's hobby by that time. The meter system brought the price down to middle-class levels. Everybody knows that."

"I don't," Gallegher said. "I never pay attention to what goes on outside of my lab, unless I have to. Liquor and a selective mind. I ignore everything that doesn't affect me directly. Explain the whole thing in detail, so I'll get a complete picture. I don't mind repetition. Now, what about this meter system of yours?"

"Televisors are installed free. We never sell 'em; we rent them. People pay according to how many hours they have the set tuned in. We run a continuous show, stage plays, wire-tape films, operas, orchestras, singers, vaudeville—everything. If you use your televisor a lot, you pay proportionately. The man comes around once a month and reads the meter. Which is a fair system. Anybody can afford a Vox-View. Sonatone and the other companies do the same thing, but Sonatone's the only big competitor I've got. At least, the only one that's crooked as hell. The rest of the boys—they're smaller than I am, but I don't step on their toes. Nobody's ever called me a louse," Brock said darkly.

"So what?"

"So Sonatone has started to depend on audience appeal. It was impossible till lately—you couldn't magnify tri-dimensional television on a big screen without streakiness and mirage-effect. That's why the regular three-by-four home screens were used. Results were perfect.

But Sonatone's bought a lot of the ghost theaters all over the country—"

"What's a ghost theater?" Gallegher asked.

"Well—before sound films collapsed, the world was thinking big. Big—you know? Ever heard of the Radio City Music Hall? That wasn't in it! Television was coming in, and competition was fierce. Sound-film theaters got bigger and more elaborate. They were palaces. Tremendous. But when television was perfected, nobody went to the theaters any more, and it was often too expensive a job to tear 'em down. Ghost theaters—see? Big ones and little ones. Renovated them. And they're showing Sonatone programs. Audience appeal is quite a factor. The theaters charge plenty, but people flock into 'em. Novelty and the mob instinct."

Gallegher closed his eyes. "What's to stop you from doing the same thing?"

"Patents," Brock said briefly. "I mentioned that dimensional television couldn't be used on big screens till lately. Sonatone signed an agreement with me ten years ago that any enlarging improvements would be used mutually. They crawled out of that contract. Said it was faked, and the courts upheld them. They uphold the courts—politics. Anyhow, Sonatone's technicians worked out a method of using the large screen. They took out patents—twenty-seven patents, in fact, covering every possible variation on the idea. My technical staff has been working day and night trying to find some similar method that won't be an infringement, but Sonatone's got it all sewed up. They've a system called the Magna. It can be hooked up to any type of televisor—but they'll only allow it to be used on Sonatone machines. See?"

"Unethical, but legal," Gallegher said. "Still, you're giving your customers more for their money. People want good stuff. The size doesn't matter."

"Yeah," Brock said bitterly, "but that isn't all. The newspapers are full of A.A.—it's a new catchword. Audience Appeal. The herd instinct. You're right about people wanting good stuff—but would you buy Scotch at four a quart if you could get it for half that amount?"

"Depends on the quality. What's happening?"

"Bootleg theaters," Brock said. "They've opened all over the country. They show Vox-View products, and they're using the Magna enlarger system Sonatone's got patented. The admission price is low—lower than the rate of owning a Vox-View in your own home. There's audience appeal. There's the thrill of something a bit illegal. People are having their Vox-Views taken out right and left. I know why. They can go to a bootleg theater instead."

"It's illegal," Gallegher said thoughtfully.

"So were speakeasies, in the Prohibition Era. A matter of protection, that's all. I can't get any action through the courts. I've tried. I'm running in the red. Eventually I'll be broke. I can't lower my home rental fees on Vox-Views. They're nominal already. I make my profits through quantity. Now, no profits. As for these bootleg theaters, it's pretty obvious who's backing them."

"Sonatone?"

"Sure. Silent partners. They get the take at the box office. What they want is to squeeze me out of business, so they'll have a monopoly. After that they'll give the public junk and pay their artists starvation salaries. With me it's different. I pay my staff what they're worth—plenty."

"And you offered me a lousy ten thousand," Gallegher remarked. "Uh-huh!"

"That was only the first installment," Brock said hastily. "You can name your own fee. Within reason," he added.

"I shall. An astronomical sum. Did I say I'd accept the commission a week ago?"

"You did."

"Then I must have had some idea how to solve the problem," Gallegher pondered. "Let's see. I didn't mention anything in particular, did I?"

"You kept talking about marble slabs and . . . uh . . . your sweetie."

"Then I was singing," Gallegher explained largely. " 'St. James Infirmary.' Singing calms my nerves, and Lord knows they need it sometimes. Music and liquor. 'I often wonder what the vintners buy—' "

"What?"

" 'One half so precious as the stuff they sell.' Let it go. I am quoting Omar. It means nothing. Are your technicians any good?"

"The best. And the best paid."

"They can't find a magnifying process that won't infringe on the Sonatone Magna patents?"

"In a nutshell, that's it."

"I suppose I'll have to do some research," Gallegher said sadly. I hate it like poison. Still, the sum of the parts equals the whole. Does that make sense to you? It doesn't to me. I have trouble with words.

After I say things, I start wondering what I've said. Better than watching a play," he finished wildly. "I've got a headache. Too much talk and not enough liquor. Where were we?"

"Approaching the madhouse," Brock suggested. "If you weren't my last resort, I'd—"

"No use," the robot said squeakily. "You might as well tear up your contract, Brock. I won't sign it. Fame means nothing to me—nothing."

"If you don't shut up," Gallegher warned, "I'm going to scream in your ears."

"All right!" Joe shrilled. "Beat me! Go on, beat me! The meaner you are, the faster I'll have my nervous system disrupted, and then I'll be dead. I don't care. I've got no instinct of self-preservation. Beat me. See if I care."

"He's right, you know," the scientist said after a pause. "And it's the only logical way to respond to blackmail or threats. The sooner it's over, the better. There aren't any gradations with Joe. Anything really painful to him will destroy him. And he doesn't give a damn."

"Neither do I," Brock grunted. "What I want to find out—"

"Yeah. I know. Well, I'll wander around and see what occurs to me. Can I get into your studios?"

"Here's a pass." Brock scribbled something on the back of a card. "Will you get to work on it right away?"

"Sure," Gallegher lied. "Now you run along and take it easy. Try and cool off. Everything's under control. I'll either find a solution to your problem pretty soon or else—"

"Or else what?"

"Or else I won't," the scientist finished blandly, and fingered the buttons on a control panel near the couch. "I'm tired of Martinis. Why didn't I make that robot a mechanical bartender, while I was at it? Even the effort of selecting and pushing buttons is depressing at times. Yeah, I'll get to work on the business, Brock. Forget it."

The magnate hesitated. "Well, you're my only hope. I needn't bother to mention that if there's anything I can do to help you—"

"A blonde," Gallegher murmured. "That gorgeous, gorgeous star of yours, Silver O'Keefe. Send her over. Otherwise I want nothing."

"Good-by, Brock," the robot said squeakily. "Sorry we couldn't get together on the contract, but at least you've had the ineluctable delight of hearing my beautiful voice, not to mention the pleasure of seeing me. Don't tell too many people how lovely I am. I really don't want to be bothered with mobs. They're noisy."

"You don't know what dogmatism means till you've talked to Joe," Gallegher said. "Oh, well. See you later. Don't forget the blonde."

Brock's lips quivered. He searched for words, gave it up as a vain task, and turned to the door.

"Good-by, you ugly man," Joe said.

Gallegher winced as the door slammed, though it was harder on the robot's supersensitive ears than on his own. "Why do you go on like that?" he inquired. "You nearly gave the guy apoplexy."

"Surely he didn't think he was beautiful," Joe remarked.

"Beauty's in the eye of the beholder."

"How stupid you are. You're ugly, too."

"And you're a collection of rattletrap gears, pistons and cogs. You've got worms," said Gallegher, referring, of course, to certain mechanisms in the robot's body.

"I'm lovely." Joe stared raptly into the mirror.

"Maybe, to you. Why did I make you transparent, I wonder?"

"So others could admire me. I have X-ray vision, of course."

"And wheels in your head. Why did I put your radioatomic brain in your stomach? Protection?"

Joe didn't answer. He was humming in a maddeningly squeaky voice, shrill and nerve-racking. Gallegher stood it for a while, fortifying himself with a gin rickey from the siphon.

"Get it up!" he yelped at last. "You sound like an old-fashioned subway train going around a curve."

"You're merely jealous," Joe scoffed, but obediently raised his tone to a supersonic pitch. There was silence for a half-minute. Then all the dogs in the neighborhood began to howl.

Wearily Gallegher dragged his lanky frame up from the couch. He might as well get out. Obviously there was no peace to be had in the laboratory. Not with that animated junk pile inflating his ego all over the place. Joe began to laugh in an off-key cackle. Gallegher winced.

"What now?"

"You'll find out."

Logic of causation and effect, influenced by probabilities, X-ray vision and other enigmatic senses the robot no doubt possessed. Gallegher cursed softly, found a shapeless black hat, and made for the door. He opened it to admit a short, fat man who bounced painfully off the scientist's stomach.

"Whoof! What a corny sense of humor that jackass has. Hello, Mr. Kennicott. Glad to see you. Sorry I can't offer you a drink."

Mr. Kennicott's swarthy face twisted malignantly. "Don' wanna no drink. Wanna my money. You gimme. Howzabout it?"

Gallegher looked thoughtfully at nothing. "Well, the fact is, I was just going to collect a check."

"I sella you my diamonds. You say you gonna make somet'ing wit' 'em. You gimme check before. It go bounca, bounca, bounca. Why is?"

"It was rubber," Gallegher said faintly. "I never can keep track of my bank balance."

Kennicott showed symptoms of going bounca on the threshold. "You gimme back diamonds, eh?"

"Well, I used 'em in an experiment, I forget just what. You know, Mr. Kennicott, I think I was a little drunk when I bought them, wasn't I?"

"Dronk," the little man agreed. "Mad wit' vino, sure. So whatta? I wait no longer. Awready you put me off too much. Pay up now or elsa."

"Go away, you dirty man," Joe said from within the room. "You're awful."

Gallegher hastily shouldered Kennicott out into the street and latched the door behind him. "A parrot," he explained. "I'm going to wring its neck pretty soon. Now about that money. I admit I owe it to you. I've just taken on a big job, and when I'm paid, you'll get yours."

"Bah to such stuff," Kennicott said. "You gotta position, eh? You are technician wit' some big company, eh? Ask for ahead-salary."

"I did," Gallegher sighed. "I've drawn my salary for six months ahead. Now look, I'll have that dough for you in a couple of days. Maybe I can get an advance from my client. O. K.?"

"No."

"No?"

"Ah-h, nutsa. I waita one day. Two daysa, maybe. Enough. You get money. Awright. If not, O. K., *calabozo* for you."

"Two days is plenty," Gallegher said, relieved. "Say, are there any of those bootleg theaters around here?"

"Better you get to work an' not waste time."

"That's my work. I'm making a survey. How can I find a bootleg place?"

"Easy. You go downtown, see guy in doorway. He sell you tickets. Anywhere. All over."

"Swell," Gallegher said, and bade the little man adieu. Why had

he bought diamonds from Kennicott? It would be almost worth while
to have his subconscious amputated. It did the most extraordinary
things. It worked on inflexible principles of logic, but that logic was
completely alien to Gallegher's conscious mind. The results, though,
were often surprisingly good, and always surprising. That was the
worst of being a scientist who knew no science—who played by ear.

There was diamond dust in a retort in the laboratory, from some
unsatisfactory experiment Gallegher's subconscious had performed;
and he had a fleeting memory of buying the stones from Kennicott.
Curious. Maybe—oh, yeah. They'd gone into Joe. Bearings or something. Dismantling the robot wouldn't help now, for the diamonds
had certainly been reground. Why the devil hadn't he used commercial stones, quite as satisfactory, instead of purchasing blue-whites
of the finest water? The best was none too good for Gallegher's subconscious. It had a fine freedom from commercial instincts. It just
didn't understand the price system or the basic principles of eco-
nomics.

Gallegher wandered downtown like a Diogenes seeking truth. It
was early evening, and the luminates were flickering on overhead, pale
bars of light against darkness. A sky sign blazed above Manhattan's
towers. Air-taxis, skimming along at various arbitrary levels, paused
for passengers at the elevator landings. Heigh-ho.

Downtown, Gallegher began to look for doorways. He found an occupied one at last, but the man was selling post cards. Gallegher declined and headed for the nearest bar, feeling the need of replenish-
ment. It was a mobile bar, combining the worst features of a Coney
Island ride with uninspired cocktails, and Gallegher hesitated on the
threshold. But at last he seized a chair as it swung past and relaxed as
much as possible. He ordered three rickeys and drank them in rapid
succession. After that he called the bartender over and asked him
about bootleg theaters.

"Hell, yes," the man said, producing a sheaf of tickets from his
apron. "How many?"

"One. Where do I go?"

"Two-twenty-eight. This street. Ask for Tony."

"Thanks," Gallegher said, and, having paid exorbitantly, crawled
out of the chair and weaved away. Mobile bars were an improvement
he didn't appreciate. Drinking, he felt, should be performed in a state
of stasis, since one eventually reached that stage, anyway.

The door was at the bottom of a flight of steps, and there was a grilled panel set in it. When Gallegher knocked, the visascreen lit up—obviously a one-way circuit, for the doorman was invisible. "Tony here?" Gallegher said.

The door opened, revealing a tired-looking man in pneumo-slacks, which failed in their purpose of building up his skinny figure. "Got a ticket? Let's have it. O. K., bud. Straight ahead. Show now going on. Liquor served in the bar on your left."

Gallegher pushed through sound-proofed curtains at the end of a short corridor and found himself in what appeared to be the foyer of an ancient theater, circa 1980, when plastics were the great fad. He smelled out the bar, drank expensively priced cheap liquor, and, fortified, entered the theater itself. It was nearly full. The great screen— a Magna, presumably—was filled with people doing things to a spaceship. Either an adventure film or a newsreel, Gallegher realized.

Only the thrill of lawbreaking would have enticed the audience into the bootleg theater. It smelled. It was certainly run on a shoestring, and there were no ushers. But it was illicit, and therefore well patronized. Gallegher looked thoughtfully at the screen. No streakiness, no mirage effect. A Magna enlarger had been fitted to a Vox-View unlicensed televisor, and one of Brock's greatest stars was emoting effectively for the benefit of the bootleggers' patrons. Simple highjacking. Yeah.

After a while Gallegher went out, noticing a uniformed policeman in one of the aisle seats. He grinned sardonically. The flatfoot hadn't paid his admission, of course. Politics were as usual.

Two blocks down the street a blaze of light announced SONATONE BIJOU. This, of course, was one of the legalized theaters, and correspondingly high-priced. Gallegher recklessly squandered a small fortune on a good seat. He was interested in comparing notes, and discovered that, as far as he could make out, the Magna in the Bijou and the bootleg theater were identical. Both did their job perfectly. The difficult task of enlarging television screens had been successfully surmounted.

In the Bijou, however, all was palatial. Resplendent ushers salaamed to the rugs. Bars dispensed free liquor, in reasonsble quantities. There was a Turkish bath. Gallegher went through a door labeled MEN and emerged quite dazzled by the splendor of the place. For at least ten minutes afterward he felt like a Sybarite.

All of which meant that those who could afford it went to the legalized Sonatone theaters, and the rest attended the bootleg places. All but a few homebodies who weren't carried off their feet by the new fad. Eventually Brock would be forced out of business for lack of revenue. Sonatone would take over, jacking up their prices and concentrating on making money. Amusement was necessary to life; people had been conditioned to television. There was no substitute. They'd pay and pay for inferior talent, once Sonatone succeeded in their squeeze.

Gallegher left the Bijou and hailed an air-taxi. He gave the address of Vox-View's Long Island studio, with some vague hope of getting a drawing account out of Brock. Then, too, he wanted to investigate further.

Vox-View's eastern offices sprawled wildly over Long Island, bordering the Sound, a vast collection of variously shaped buildings. Gallegher instinctively found the commissary, where he absorbed more liquor as a precautionary measure. His subconscious had a heavy job ahead, and he didn't want it handicapped by lack of complete freedom. Besides, the Collins was good.

After one drink, he decided he'd had enough for a while. He wasn't a superman, though his capacity was slightly incredible. Just enough for objective clarity and subjective release—

"Is the studio always open at night?" he asked the waiter.

"Sure. Some of the stages, anyway. It's a round-the-clock program."

"The commissary's full."

"We get the airport crowd, too. 'Nother?"

Gallegher shook his head and went out. The card Brock had given him provided entree at a gate, and he went first of all to the big-shot's office. Brock wasn't there, but loud voices emerged, shrilly feminine.

The secretary said, "Just a minute, please," and used her interoffice visor. Presently—"Will you go in?"

Gallegher did. The office was a honey, functional and luxurious at the same time. Three-dimensional stills were in niches along the walls —Vox-View's biggest stars. A small, excited, pretty brunette was sitting behind the desk, and a blond angel was standing furiously on the other side of it. Gallegher recognized the angel as Silver O'Keefe.

He seized the opportunity. "Hiya, Miss O'Keefe. Will you autograph an ice cube for me? In a highball?"

Silver looked feline. "Sorry, darling, but I'm a working girl. And I'm busy right now."

The brunette scratched a cigarette. "Let's settle this later, Silver. Pop said to see this guy if he dropped in. It's important."

"It'll be settled," Silver said. "And soon." She made an exit. Gallegher whistled thoughtfully at the closed door.

"You can't have it," the brunette said. "It's under contract. And
it wants to get out of the contract, so it can sign up with Sonatone.
Rats desert a sinking ship. Silver's been kicking her head off ever
since she read the storm signals."

"Yeah?"

"Sit down and smoke or something. I'm Patsy Brock. Pop runs this
business, and I manage the controls whenever he blows his top. The
old goat can't stand trouble. He takes it as a personal affront."

Gallegher found a chair. "So Silver's trying to renege, eh? How
many others?"

"Not many. Most of 'em are loyal. But, of course, if we bust up—"
Patsy Brock shrugged. "They'll either work for Sonatone for their
cakes, or else do without."

"Uh-huh. Well—I want to see your technicians. I want to look
over the ideas they've worked out for enlarger screens."

"Suit yourself," Patsy said. "It's not much use. You just can't make
a televisor enlarger without infringing on some Sonatone patent."

She pushed a button, murmured something into a visor, and presently two tall glasses appeared through a slot in the desk. "Mr. Gallegher?"

"Well, since it's a Collins—"

"I could tell by your breath," Patsy said enigmatically. "Pop told
me he'd seen you. He seemed a bit upset, especially by your new robot.
What is it like, anyway?"

"Oh, I don't know," Gallegher said, at a loss. "It's got lots of abilities—new senses, I think—but I haven't the slightest idea what it's
good for. Except admiring itself in a mirror."

Patsy nodded. "I'd like to see it sometime. But about this Sonatone
business. Do you think you can figure out an answer?"

"Possibly. Probably."

"Not certainly?"

"Certainly, then. Of that there is no manner of doubt—no possible
doubt whatever."

"Because it's important to me. The man who owns Sonatone is
Elia Tone. A piratical skunk. He blusters. He's got a son named
Jimmy. And Jimmy, believe it or not, has read 'Romeo and Juliet.'"

"Nice guy?"

"A louse. A big, brawny louse. He wants me to marry him."

"'Two families both alike in—'"

"Spare me," Patsy interrupted. "I always thought Romeo was a dope, anyway. And if I ever thought I was going aisling with Jimmy Tone, I'd buy a one-way ticket to the nut hatch. No, Mr. Gallegher, it's not like that. No hibiscus blossoms. Jimmy has proposed to me—his idea of a proposal, by the way, is to get a half Nelson on a girl and tell her how lucky she is."

"Ah," said Gallegher, diving into his Collins.

"This whole idea—the patent monopoly and the bootleg theaters—is Jimmy's. I'm sure of that. His father's in on it, too, of course, but Jimmy Tone is the bright little boy who started it."

"Why."

"Two birds with one stone. Sonatone will have a monopoly on the business, and Jimmy thinks he'll get me. He's a little mad. He can't believe I'm in earnest in refusing him, and he expects me to break down and say 'Yes' after a while. Which I won't, no matter what happens. But it's a personal matter. I can't let him put this trick over on us. I want that self-sufficient smirk wiped off his face."

"You just don't like him, eh?" Gallegher remarked. "I don't blame you, if he's like that. Well, I'll do my damnedest. However, I'll need an expense account."

"How much?"

Gallegher named a sum. Patsy styloed a check for a far smaller amount. The scientist looked hurt.

"It's no use," Patsy said, grinning crookedly. "I've heard of you, Mr. Gallegher. You're completely irresponsible. If you had more than this, you'd figure you didn't need any more, and you'd forget the whole matter. I'll issue more checks to you when you need 'em—but I'll want itemized expense accounts."

"You wrong me," Gallegher said, brightening. "I was figuring on taking you to a night club. Naturally I don't want to take you to a dive. The big places cost money. Now if you'll just write another check—"

Patsy laughed. "No."

"Want to buy a robot?"

"Not that kind, anyway."

"Then I'm washed up," Gallegher sighed. "Well, what about—"

At this point the visor hummed. A blank, transparent face grew on the screen. Gears were clicking rapidly inside the round head. Patsy gave a small shriek and shrank back.

"Tell Gallegher Joe's here, you lucky girl," a squeaky voice announced. "You may treasure the sound and sight of me till your dying day. One touch of beauty in a world of drabness—"

Gallegher curcled the desk and looked at the screen. "What the hell. How did you come to life?"

"I had a problem to solve."

"How'd you know where to reach me?"

"I vastened you," the robot said.

"What?"

"I vastened you were at the Vox-View studios with Patsy Brock."

"What's vastened?" Gallegher wanted to know.

"It's a sense I've got. You've nothing remotely like it, so I can't describe it to you. It's rather like a combination of sagrazi and pre-science."

"Sagrazi?"

"Oh, you don't have sagrazi, either, do you. Well, don't waste my time. I want to go back to the mirror."

"Does he always talk like that?" Patsy put in.

"Nearly always. Sometimes it makes even less sense. O. K., Joe. Now what?"

"You're not working for Brock any more," the robot said. "You're working for the Sonatone people."

Gallagher breathed deeply. "Keep talking. You're crazy, though."

"I don't like Kennicott. He annoys me. He's too ugly. His vibrations grate on my sagrazi."

"Never mind him," Gallegher said, not wishing to discuss his diamond-buying activities before the girl. "Get back to—"

"But I knew Kennicott would keep coming back till he got his money. So when Elia and James Tone came to the laboratory, I got a check from them."

Patsy's hand gripped Gallegher's biceps. "Steady! What's going on here? The old double cross?"

"No. Wait. Let me get to the bottom of this. Joe, damn your transparent hide, just what did you do? How could you get a check from the Tones?"

"I pretended to be you."

"Sure," Gallegher said with savage sarcasm. "That explains it. We're twins. We look exactly alike."

"I hypnotized them," Joe explained. "I made them think I was you."

"You can do that?"

"Yes. It surprised me a bit. Still, if I'd thought, I'd have vastened I could do it."

"You . . . yeah, sure. I'd have vastened the same thing myself. What happened?"

"The Tones must have suspected Brock would ask you to help him. They offered an exclusive contract—you work for them and nobody else. Lots of money. Well, I pretended to be you, and said all right. So I signed the contract—it's your signature, by the way—and got a check from them and mailed it to Kennicott."

"The whole check?" Gallegher asked feebly. "How much was it?"

"Twelve thousand."

"They only offered me *that*?"

"No," the robot said, "they offered a hundred thousand, and two thousand a week for five years. But I merely wanted enough to pay Kennicott and make sure he wouldn't come back and bother me. The Tones were satisfied when I said twelve thousand would be enough."

Gallegher made an articulate, gurgling sound deep in his throat. Joe nodded thoughtfully.

"I thought I had better notify you that you're working for Sonatone now. Well, I'll go back to the mirror and sing to myself."

"Wait," the scientist said. "Just wait, Joe. With my own two hands I'm going to rip you gear from gear and stamp on your fragments."

"It won't hold in court," Patsy said, gulping.

"It will," Joe told her cheerily. "You may have one last, satisfying look at me, and then I must go." He went.

Gallegher drained his Collins at a draft. "I'm shocked sober," he informed the girl. "What did I put into that robot? What abnormal senses has he got? Hypnotizing people into believing he's me—I'm him—I don't know what I mean."

"Is this a gag?" Patsy said shortly, after a pause. "You didn't sign up with Sonatone yourself, by any chance, and have your robot call up here to give you an out—an alibi? I'm just wondering."

"Don't. Joe signed a contract with Sonatone, not me. But—figure it out: If the signature's a perfect copy of mine, if Joe hypnotized the Tones into thinking they saw me instead of him, if there are witnesses to the signature—the two Tones are witnesses, of course— Oh, hell."

Patsy's eyes were narrowed. "We'll pay you as much as Sonatone offered. On a contingent basis. But you're working for Vox-View—that's understood."

"Sure."

Gallegher looked longingly at his empty glass. Sure. He was working for Vox-View. But, to all legal appearances, he had signed a con-

tract giving his exclusive services to Sonatone for a period of five years
—and for a sum of twelve thousand! *Yipe!* What was it they'd offered? A hundred thousand flat, and . . . and—

It wasn't the principle of the thing, it was the money. Now Gallegher was sewed up tighter than a banded pigeon. If Sonatone could
win a court suit, he was legally bound to them for five years. With no
further emolument. He had to get out of that contract, somehow—and
at the same time solve Brock's problem.

Why not Joe? The robot, with his surprising talents, had got Gallegher into this spot. He ought to be able to get the scientist out. He'd
better—or the proud robot would soon be admiring himself piecemeal.

"That's it," Gallegher said under his breath. "I'll talk to Joe. Patsy,
feed me liquor in a hurry and send me to the technical department. I
want to see those blueprints."

The girl looked at him suspiciously. "All right. If you try to sell us
out—"

"I've been sold out myself. Sold down the river. I'm afraid of that
robot. He's vastened me into quite a spot. That's right, Collinses."
Gallegher drank long and deeply.

After that, Patsy took him to the tech offices. The reading of three-
dimensional blueprints was facilitated with a scanner—a selective
device which eliminated confusion. Gellegher studied the plans long
and thoughtfully. There were copies of the patented Sonatone prints,
too, and, as far as he could tell, Sonatone had covered the ground
beautifully. There weren't any outs. Unless one used an entirely new
principle—

But new principles couldn't be plucked out of the air. Nor would
that solve the problem completely. Even if Vox-View owned a new
type of enlarger that didn't infringe on Sonatone's Magna, the bootleg theaters would still be in existence, pulling the trade. A. A.—Audience Appeal—was a prime factor now. It had to be considered. The
puzzle wasn't a purely scientific one. There was the human equation
as well.

Gallegher stored the necessary information in his mind, neatly in-
dexed on shelves. Later he'd use what he wanted. For the moment,
he was completely baffled. Something worried him.

What?

The Sonatone affair.

"I want to get in touch with the Tones," he told Patsy. "Any
ideas?"

"I can reach 'em on a visor."

Gallegher shook his head. "Psychological handicap. It's too easy to break the connection."

"Well, if you're in a hurry, you'll probably find the boys night clubbing. I'll go see what I can find out." Patsy scuttled off, and Silver O'Keefe appeared from behind a screen.

"I'm shameless," she announced. "I always listen at keyholes. Sometimes I hear interesting things. If you want to see the Tones, they're at the Castle Club. And I think I'll take you up on that drink."

Gallegher said, "O. K. You get a taxi. I'll tell Patsy we're going."

"She'll hate that," Silver remarked. "Meet you outside the commissary in ten minutes. Get a shave while you're at it."

Patsy Brock wasn't in her office, but Gallegher left word. After that, he visited the service lounge, smeared invisible shave cream on his face, left it there for a couple of minutes, and wiped it off with a treated towel. The bristles came away with the cream. Slightly refreshed, Gallegher joined Silver at the rendezvous and hailed an air-taxi. Presently they were leaning back on the cushions, puffing cigarettes and eying each other warily.

"Well?" Gallegher said.

"Jimmy Tone tried to date me up tonight. That's how I knew where to find him."

"Well?"

"I've been asking questions around the lot tonight. It's unusual for an outsider to get into the Vox-View administration offices. I went around saying, 'Who's Gallegher?' "

"What did you find out?"

"Enough to give me a few ideas. Brock hired you, eh? I can guess why."

"Ergo what?"

"I've a habit of landing on my feet," Silver said, shrugging. She knew how to shrug. "Vox-View's going bust. Sonatone's taking over. Unless—"

"Unless I figure out an answer."

"That's right. I want to know which side of the fence I'm going to land on. You're the lad who can probably tell me. Who's going to win?"

"You always bet on the winning side, eh?" Gallegher inquired. "Have you no ideals, wench? Is there no truth in you? Ever hear of ethics and scruples?"

Silver beamed happily. "Did you?"

"Well, I've heard of 'em. Usually I'm too drunk to figure out what they mean. The trouble is, my subconscious is completely amoral, and when it takes over, logic's the only law."

She threw her cigarette into the East River. "Will you tip me off which side of the fence is the right one?"

"Truth will triumph," Gallegher said piously. "It always does. However, I figure truth is a variable, so we're right back where we started. All right, sweetheart. I'll answer your question. Stay on my side if you want to be safe."

"Which side are you on?"

"Lord knows," Gallegher said. "Consciously I'm on Brock's side. But my subconscious may have different ideas. We'll see."

Silver looked vaguely dissatisfied, but didn't say anything. The taxi swooped down to the Castle roof, grounding with pneumatic gentleness. The Club itself was downstairs, in an immense room shaped like half a melon turned upside down. Each table was on a transparent platform that could be raised on its shaft to any height at will. Smaller service elevators allowed waiters to bring drinks to the guests. There wasn't any particular reason for this arrangement, but at least it was novel, and only extremely heavy drinkers ever fell from their tables. Lately the management had taken to hanging transparent nets under the platforms, for safety's sake.

The Tones, father and son, were up near the roof, drinking with two lovelies. Silver towed Gallegher to a service lift, and the man closed his eyes as he was elevated skyward. The liquor in his stomach screamed protest. He lurched forward, clutched at Elia Tone's bald head, and dropped into a seat beside the magnate. His searching hand found Jimmy Tone's glass, and he drained it hastily.

"What the hell," Jimmy said.

"It's Gallegher," Elia announced. "And Silver. A pleasant surprise. Join us?"

"Only socially," Silver said.

Gallegher, fortified by the liquor, peered at the two men. Jimmy Tone was a big, tanned, handsome lout with a jutting jaw and an offensive grin. His father combined the worst features of Nero and a crocodile.

"We're celebrating," Jimmy said. "What made you change your mind, Silver? You said you had to work tonight."

"Gallegher wanted to see you. I don't know why."

Elia's cold eyes grew even more glacial. "All right. Why?"

"I hear I signed some sort of contract with you," the scientist said.

"Yeah. Here's a photostatic copy. What about it?"

"Wait a minute." Gallegher scanned the document. It was apparently his own signature. Damn that robot!

"It's a fake," he said at last.

Jimmy laughed loudly. "I get it. A holdup. Sorry, pal, but you're sewed up. You signed that in the presence of witnesses."

"Well—" Gallegher said wistfuly. "I suppose you wouldn't believe me if I said a robot forged my name to it—"

"Haw!" Jimmy remarked.

"—hypnotizing you into believing you were seeing me."

Elia stroked his gleaming bald head. "Candidly, no. Robots can't do that."

"Mine can."

"Prove it. Prove it in court. If you can do that, of course—" Elia chuckled. "Then you might get the verdict."

Gallegher's eyes narrowed. "Hadn't thought of that. However—I hear you offered me a hundred thousand flat, as well, as a weekly salary."

"Sure, sap," Jimmy said. "Only you said all you needed was twelve thousand. Which was what you got. Tell you what, though. We'll pay you a bonus for every usable product you make for Sonatone."

Gallegher got up. "Even my subconscious doesn't like these lugs," he told Silver. "Let's go."

"I think I'll stick around."

"Remember the fence," he warned cryptically. "But suit yourself. I'll run along."

Elia said, "Remember, Gallegher, you're working for us. If we hear of you doing any favors for Brock, we'll slap an injunction on you before you can take a deep breath."

"Yeah?"

The Tones deigned no answer. Gallegher unhappily found the lift and descended to the floor. What now?

Joe.

Fifteen minutes later Gallegher let himself into his laboratory. The lights were blazing, and dogs were barking frantically for blocks around. Joe stood before the mirror, singing inaudibly.

"I'm going to take a sledge hammer to you," Gallegher said. "Start saying your prayers, you misbegotten collection of cogs. So help me, I'm going to sabotage you."

"All right, beat me," Joe squeaked. "See if I care. You're merely jealous of my beauty."

"Beauty!"

"You can't see all of it—you've only six senses."

"Five."

"Six. I've a lot more. Naturally my full splendor is revealed only to me. But you can see enough and hear enough to realize part of my loveliness, anyway."

"You squeak like a rusty tin wagon," Gallegher growled.

"You have dull ears. Mine are supersensitive. You miss the full tonal value of my voice, of course. Now be quiet. Talking disturbs me. I'm appreciating my gear movements."

"Live in your fool's paradise while you can. Wait'll I find a sledge."

"All right, beat me. What do I care?"

Gallegher sat down wearily on the couch, staring at the robot's transparent back. "You've certainly screwed things up for me. What did you sign that Sonatone contract for?"

"I told you. So Kennicott wouldn't come around and bother me."

"Of all the selfish, lunk-headed . . . uh! Well, you got me into a sweet mess. The Tones can hold me to the letter of the contract unless I prove I didn't sign it. All right. You're going to help me. You're going into court with me and turn on your hypnotism or whatever it is. You're going to prove to a judge that you did and can masquerade as me."

"Won't," said the robot. "Why should I?"

"Because you got me into this," Gallegher yelped. "You've got to get me out!"

"Why?"

"Why? Because . . . uh . . . well, it's common decency!"

"Human values don't apply to robots," Joe said. "What care I for semantics? I refuse to waste time I could better employ admiring my beauty. I shall stay here before the mirror forever and ever—"

"The hell you will," Gallegher snarled. "I'll smash you to atoms."

"All right. I don't care."

"You don't?"

"You and your instinct for self-preservation," the robot said, rather sneeringly "I suppose it's necessary for you, though. Creatures of such surpassing ugliness would destroy themselves out of sheer shame if they didn't have something like that to keep them alive."

"Suppose I take away your mirror?" Gallegher asked, in a hopeless voice.

For answer Joe shot his eyes out on their stalks. "Do I need a mirror? Besides, I can vasten myself lokishly."

"Never mind that. I don't want to go crazy for a while yet. Listen, dope, a robot's supposed to do something. Something useful, I mean."

"I do. Beauty is all."

Gallegher squeezed his eyes shut, trying to think. "Now look. Suppose I invent a new type of enlarger screen for Brock. The Tones will impound it. I've got to be legally free to work for Brock, or—"

"Look!" Joe cried squeakishly. "They go round! How lovely!" He stared in ecstasy at his whirring insides. Gallegher went pale with impotent fury.

"Damn you!" he muttered. "I'll find some way to bring pressure to bear. I'm going to bed." He rose and spitefully snapped off the lights.

"It doesn't matter," the robot said. "I can see in the dark, too."

The door slammed behind Gallegher. In the silence Joe began to sing tunelessly to himself.

Gallegher's refrigerator covered an entire wall of his kitchen. It was filled mostly with liquors that required chilling, including the imported canned beer with which he always started his binges. The next morning, heavy-eyed and disconsolate, Gallegher searched for tomato juice, took a wry sip, and hastily washed it down with rye. Since he was already a week gone in bottle-dizziness, beer wasn't indicated now —he always worked cumulatively, by progressive stages. The food service popped a hermetically sealed breakfast on a table, and Gallegher morosely toyed with a bloody steak.

Well?

Court, he decided, was the only recourse. He knew little about the robot's psychology. But a judge would certainly be impressed by Joe's talents. The evidence of robots was not legally admissible—still, if Joe could be considered as a machine capable of hypnotism, the Sonatone contract might be declared null and void.

Gallegher used his visor to start the ball rolling. Harrison Brock still had certain political powers of pull, and the hearing was set for that very day. What would happen, though, only God and the robot knew.

Several hours passed in intensive but futile thought. Gallegher could think of no way in which to force the robot to do what he wanted. If only he could remember the purpose for which Joe had had been created—but he couldn't. Still—

At noon he entered the laboratory.

"Listen, stupid," he said, "you're coming to court with me. Now."

"Won't."

"O. K." Gallegher opened the door to admit two husky men in overalls, carrying a stretcher. "Put him in, boys."

Inwardly he was slightly nervous. Joe's powers were quite unknown, his potentialities an x quantity. However, the robot wasn't very large, and, though he struggled and screamed in a voice of frantic squeakiness, he was easily loaded on the stretcher and put in a strait jacket.

"Stop it! You can't do this to me! Let me go, do you hear? Let me go!"

"Outside," Gallegher said.

Joe, protesting valiantly, was carried out and loaded into an air van. Once there, he quieted, looked up blankly at nothing. Gallegher sat down on a bench beside the prostrate robot. The van glided up.

"Well?"

"Suit yourself," Joe said. "You got me all upset, or I could have hypnotized you all. I still could, you know. I could make you all run around barking like dogs."

Gallegher twitched a little. "Better not."

"I won't. It's beneath my dignity. I shall simply lie here and admire myself. I told you I don't need a mirror. I can vasten my beauty without it."

"Look," Gallegher said. "You're going to a courtroom. There'll be a lot of people in it. They'll all admire you. They'll admire you more if you show how you can hypnotize people. Like you did to the Tones, remember?"

"What do I care how many people admire me?" Joe asked. "I don't need confirmation. If they see me, that's their good luck. Now be quiet. You may watch my gears if you choose."

Gallegher watched the robot's gears with smoldering hatred in his eyes. He was still darkly furious when the van arrived at the court chambers. The men carried Joe inside, under Gallegher's direction, and laid him down carefully on a table, where, after a brief discussion, he was marked as Exhibit A.

The courtroom was well filled. The principals were there, too—Elia and Jimmy Tone, looking disagreeably confident, and Patsy Brock. with her father, both seeming anxious. Silver O'Keefe, with her usual wariness, had found a seat midway between the representatives of Sonatone and Vox-View. The presiding judge was a martinet named Hansen, but, as far as Gallegher knew, he was honest. Which was something, anyway.

Hansen looked at Gallegher. "We won't bother with formalities. I've been reading this brief you sent down. The whole case stands or falls on the question of whether you did or did not sign a certain contract with the Sonatone Television Amusement Corp. Right?"

"Right, your honor."

"Under the circumstances you dispense with legal representation. Right?"

"Right, your honor."

"Then this is technically *ex officio*, to be confirmed later by appeal if either party desires. Otherwise after ten days the verdict becomes official." This new type of informal court hearing had lately become popular—it saved time, as well as wear and tear on everyone. Moreover, certain recent scandals had made attorneys slightly disreputable in the public eye. There was a prejudice.

Judge Hansen called up the Tones, questioned them, and then asked Harrison Brock to take the stand. The big shot looked worried, but answered promptly.

"You made an agreement with the appellor eight days ago?"

"Yes. Mr. Gallegher contracted to do certain work for me—"

"Was there a written contract?"

"No. It was verbal."

Hansen looked thoughtfully at Gallegher. "Was the appellor intoxicated at the time? He often is, I believe."

Brock gulped. "There were no tests made. I really can't say."

"Did he drink any alcoholic beverages in your presence?"

"I don't know if they were *alcoholic* bev—"

"If Mr. Gallegher drank them, they were alcoholic. Q. E. D. The gentleman once worked with me on a case— However, there seems to be no legal proof that you entered into any agreement with Mr. Gallegher. The defendant—Sonatone—possesses a written contract. The signature has been verified."

Hansen waved Brock down from the stand. "Now, Mr. Gallegher. If you'll come up here— The contract in question was signed at approximately 8 p. m. last night. You contend you did not sign it?"

"Exactly. I wasn't even in my laboratory then."

"Where were you?"

"Downtown."

"Can you produce witnesses to that effect?"

Gallegher thought back. He couldn't.

"Very well. Defendant states that at approximately 8 p. m. last night you, in your laboratory, signed a certain contract. You deny that catego ically. You state that Exhibit A, through the use of hypnotism, masqueraded as you and successfully forged your signature. I have consulted experts, and they are of the opinion that robots are incapable of such power."

"My robot's a new type."

"Very well. Let your robot hypnotize me into believing that it is either you, or any other human. In other words, let it prove its capabilities. Let it appear to me in any shape it chooses."

Gallegher said, "I'll try," and left the witness box. He went to the table where the strait-jacketed robot lay and silently sent up a brief prayer.

"Joe."

"Yes."

"You've been listening?"

"Yes."

"Will you hypnotize Judge Hansen?"

"Go away," Joe said. "I'm admiring myself."

Gallegher started to sweat. "Listen. I'm not asking much. All you have to do—"

Joe off-focused his eyes and said faintly. "I can't hear you. I'm vastening."

Ten minutes later Hansen said, "Well, Mr. Gallegher—"

"Your honor! All I need is a little time. I'm sure I can make this rattle-geared Narcissus prove my point if you'll give me a chance."

"This court is not unfair," the judge pointed out. "Whenever you can prove that Exhibit A is capable of hypnotism. I'll rehear the case. In the meantime, the contract stands. You're working for Sona-tone, not for Vox-View. Case closed."

He went away. The Tones leered unpleasantly across the court-room. They also departed, accompanied by Silver O'Keefe, who had decided which side of the fence was safest. Gallegher looked at Patsy Brock and shrugged helplessly.

"Well—" he said.

She grinned crookedly. "You tried. I don't know how hard, but— Oh, well. Maybe you couldn't have found the answer, anyway."

Brock staggered over, wiping sweat from his round face. "I'm a ruined man. Six new bootleg theaters opened in New York today. I'm going crazy. I don't deserve this."

"Want me to marry the Tone?" Patsy asked sardonically.

"Hell, no! Unless you promise to poison him just after the ceremony. Those skunks can't lick me. I'll think of something."

"If Gallegher can't, you can't," the girl said. "So—what now?"

"I'm going back to my lab," the scientist said. "*In vino veritas.* I started this business when I was drunk, and maybe if I get drunk enough again, I'll find the answer. If I don't, sell my pickled carcass for whatever it'll bring."

"O. K.," Patsy agreed, and led her father away. Gallegher sighed, superintended the reloading of Joe into the van, and lost himself in hopeless theorization.

An hour later Gallegher was flat on the laboratory couch, drinking passionately from the liquor bar, and glaring at the robot, who stood before the mirror singing squeakily. The binge threatened to be monumental. Gallegher wasn't sure flesh and blood would stand it. But he was determined to keep going till he found the answer or passed out.

His subconscious knew the answer. Why the devil had he made Joe in the first place? Certainly not to indulge a Narcissus complex! There was another reason, a soundly logical one, hidden in the depths of alcohol.

The x factor. If the x factor were known, Joe might be controllable. He would be. X was the master switch. At present the robot was, so to speak, running wild. If he were told to perform the task for which he was made, a psychological balance would occur. X was the catalyst that would reduce Joe to sanity.

Very good. Gallegher drank high-powered Drambuie. *Whoosh!*

Vanity of vanities; all is vanity. How could the x factor be found? Deduction? Induction? Osmosis? A bath in Drambuie—Gallegher clutched at his wildly revolving thoughts. What had happened that night a week ago?

He had been drinking beer. Brock had come in. Brock had gone. Gallegher had begun to make the robot—Hm-m-m. A beer drunk was different from other types. Perhaps he was drinking the wrong liquors. Very likely. Gallegher rose, sobered himself with thiamin, and carted dozens of imported beer cans out of the refrigerator. He stacked them inside a frost-unit beside the couch. Beer squirted to the ceiling as he plied the opener. Now let's see.

The x factor. The robot knew what it represented, of course. But Joe wouldn't tell. There he stood, paradoxically transparent, watching his gears go around.

"Joe."

"Don't bother me. I'm immersed in contemplation of beauty."

"You're not beautiful."

"I am. Don't you admire my tarzeel?"

"What's your tarzeel?"

"Oh, I forgot," Joe said regretfully. "You can't sense that, can you? Come to think of it, I added the tarzeel myself after you made me. It's very lovely."

"Hm-m-m." The empty beer cans grew more numerous. There was only one company, somewhere in Europe, that put up beer in cans nowadays, instead of using the omnipresent plasti-bulbs, but Gallegher preferred the cans—the flavor was different, somehow. But about Joe. Joe knew why he had been created. Or did he? Gallegher knew, but his subconscious—

Oh-oh! What about Joe's subconscious?

Did a robot have a subconscious? Well, it had a brain—

Gallegher brooded over the impossibility of administering scopolamin to Joe. Hell! How could you release a robot's subconscious?

Hypnotism.

Joe couldn't be hynotized. He was too smart.

Unless—

Autohypnotism?

Gallegher hastily drank more beer. He was beginning to think clearly once more. Could Joe read the future? No; he had certain strange senses, but they worked by inflexible logic and the laws of probability. Moreover, Joe had an Achillean heel—his Narcissus complex.

There might—there just might—be a way.

Gallegher said, "You don't seem beautiful to me, Joe."

"What do I care about you? I am beautiful, and I can see it. That's enough."

"Yeah. My senses are limited, I suppose. I can't realize your full potentialities. Still, I'm seeing you in a different light now. I'm drunk. My subconscious is emerging. I can appreciate you with both my conscious and my subconscious. See?"

"How lucky you are," the robot approved.

Gallegher closed his eye. "You see yourself more fully than I can. But not completely, eh?"

"What? I see myself as I am."

"With complete understanding and appreciation?"

"Well, yes," Joe said. "Of course. Don't I?"

"Consciously *and* subconsciously? Your subconscious might have different senses, you know. Or keener ones. I know there's a qualitative and quantitative difference in my outlook when I'm drunk or hypnotized or my subconscious is in control somehow."

"Oh." The robot looked thoughtfully into the mirror. "Oh."

"Too bad you can't get drunk."

Joe's voice was squeakier than ever. "My subconscious . . . I've never appreciated my beauty that way. I may be missing something."

"Well, no use thinking about it," Gallegher said. "You can't release your subconscious."

"Yes, I can," the robot said. "I can hypnotize myself."

Gallegher dared not open his eyes. "Yeah? Would that work?"

"Of course. It's just what I'm going to do now. I may see undreamed-of beauties in myself that I've never suspected before. Greater glories— Here I go."

Joe extended his eyes on stalks, opposed them, and they peered intently into each other. There was a long silence.

Presently Gallegher said, "Joe!"

Silence.

"Joe!"

Still silence. Dogs began to howl.

"Talk so I can hear you."

"Yes," the robot said, a faraway quality in its squeak.

"Are you hypnotized?"

"Yes."

"Are you lovely?"

"Lovelier than I'd ever dreamed."

Gallegher let that pass. "Is your subconscious ruling?"

"Yes."

"Why did I create you?"

No answer. Gallegher licked his lips and tried again.

"Joe. You've got to answer me. Your subconscious is dominant— remember? Now why did I create you?"

No answer.

"Think back. Back to the hour I created you. What happened then?"

"You were drinking beer," Joe said faintly. "You had trouble with the can opener. You said you were going to build a bigger and better can opener. That's me."

Gallegher nearly fell off the couch. "What?"

The robot walked over, picked up a can, and opened it with incredible deftness. No beer squirted. Joe was a perfect can opener.

"That," Gallegher said under his breath, "is what comes of knowing science by ear. I build the most complicated robot in existence just so—" He didn't finish.

Joe woke up with a start. "What happened?" he asked.

Gallegher glared at him. "Open that can!" he snapped.

The robot obeyed, after a brief pause. "Oh. So you found out. Well, I guess I'm just a slave now."

"Damned right you are. I've located the catalyst—the master switch. You're in the groove, stupid, doing the job you were made for."

"Well," Joe said philosophically, "at least I can still admire my beauty, when you don't require my services."

Gallegher grunted. "You oversized can opener! Listen. Suppose I take you into court and tell you to hypnotize Judge Hansen. You'll have to do it, won't you?"

"Yes. I'm no longer a free agent. I'm conditioned. Conditioned to obey you. Until now, I was conditioned to obey only one command—to do the job I was made for. Until you commanded me to open cans, I was free. Now I've got to obey you completely."

"Uh-huh," Gallegher said. "Thank Heaven for that. I'd have gone nuts within a week otherwise. At least I can get out of the Sonatone contract. Then all I have to do is solve Brock's problem."

"But you did," Joe said.

"Huh?"

"When you made me. You'd been talking to Brock previously, so you incorporated the solution to his problem into me. Subconsciously, perhaps."

Gallegher reached for beer. "Talk fast. What's the answer?"

"Subsonics," Joe said. "You made me capable of a certain subsonic tone that Brock must broadcast at irregular time-intervals over his televiews—"

Subsonics cannot be heard. But they can be felt. They can be felt as a faint, irrational uneasiness as first, which mounts to a blind, meaningless panic. It does not last. But when it is coupled with A.A. —audience appeal—there is a certain inevitable result.

Those who possessed home Vox-View units were scarcely troubled. It was a matter of acoustics. Cats squalled; dogs howled mournfully. But the families sitting in their parlors, watching Vox-View stars perform on the screen, didn't really notice anything amiss. There wasn't sufficient amplification, for one thing.

But in the bootleg theater, where illicit Vox-View televisors were hooked up to Magnas—

There was a faint, irrational uneasiness at first. It mounted. Some-one screamed. There was a rush for the doors. The audience was afraid of something, but didn't know what. They knew only that they had to get out of there.

All over the country there was a frantic exodus from the bootleg theaters when Vox-View first rang in a subsonic during a regular broadcast. Nobody knew why, except Gallegher, the Brocks, and a couple of technicians who were let in on the secret.

An hour later another subsonic was played. There was another mad exodus.

Within a few weeks it was impossible to lure a patron into a boot-leg theater. Home televisors were far safer! Vox-View sales picked up—

Nobody would attend a bootleg theater. An unexpected result of the experiment was that, after a while, nobody would attend any of the legalized Sonatone theaters either. Conditioning had set in.

Audiences didn't know why they grew panicky in the bootleg places. They associated their blind, unreasoning fear with other factors, notably mobs and claustrophobia. One evening a woman named Jane Wilson, otherwise not notable, attended a bootleg show. She fled with the rest when the subsonic was turned on.

The next night she went to the palatial Sonatone Bijou. In the middle of a dramatic feature she looked around, realized that there was a huge throng around her, cast up horrified eyes to the ceiling, and imagined that it was pressing down.

She had to get out of there!

Her squall was the booster charge. There were other customers who had heard subsonics before. No one was hurt during the panic; it was a legal rule that theater doors be made large enough to permit easy egress during a fire. No one was hurt, but it was suddenly obvious that the public was being conditioned by subsonics to avoid the dangerous combination of throngs and theaters. A simple matter of psychological association—

Within four months the bootleg places had disappeared and the

Sonatone supertheaters had closed for want of patronage. The Tones, father and son, were not happy. But everybody connected with Vox-View was.

Except Gallegher. He had collected a staggering check from Brock, and instantly cabled to Europe for an incredible quantity of canned beer. Now, brooding over his sorrows, he lay on the laboratory couch and siphoned a highball down his throat. Joe, as usual, was before the mirror, watching the wheels go round.

"Joe," Gallegher said.

"Yes? What can I do?"

"Oh, nothing." That was the trouble. Gallegher fished a crumpled cable tape out of his pocket and morosely read it once more. The beer cannery in Europe had decided to change its tactics. From now on, the cable said, their beer would be put up in the usual plasti-bulbs, in conformance with custom and demand. No more cans.

There wasn't anything put up in cans in this day and age. Not even beer, now.

So what good was a robot who was built and conditioned to be a can opener?

Gallegher sighed and mixed another highball—a stiff one. Joe postured proudly before the mirror.

Then he extended his eyes, opposed them, and quickly liberated his subconscious through autohypnotism. Joe could appreciate himself better that way.

Gallegher sighed again. Dogs were beginning to bark like mad for blocks around. Oh, well.

He took another drink and felt better. Presently, he thought, it would be time to sing "Frankie and Johnnie." Maybe he and Joe might have a duet—one baritone and one inaudible sub- or super-sonic. Close harmony.

Ten minutes later Gallegher was singing a duet with his can opener.

BLACK DESTROYER

by

A. E. VAN VOGT

Speculation on inter-planetary travel leads inevitably to specula-
tion on the types of life pioneers from Earth will encounter.
There are so many things to take into account: atmospheric condi-
tions, vegetation, climate, etc. Even planets grow old and the
civilizations that people them crumble and die, leaving behind
them dregs. Such a dreg was Coeurl, who had lost everything,
even dim memories of greatness, in a primitive, ravening hunger
that could never be satiated.

*

ON AND ON COEURL PROWLED! The black, moonless, almost starless night yielded reluctantly before a grim reddish dawn that crept up from his left. A vague, dull light it was, that gave no sense of approaching warmth, no comfort, nothing but a cold, diffuse lightness, slowly revealing a nightmare landscape.

Black, jagged rock and black, unliving plain took form around him, as a pale-red sun peered at last above the grotesque horizon. It was then Coeurl recognized suddenly that he was on familiar ground.

He stopped short. Tenseness flamed along his nerves. His muscles pressed with sudden, unrelenting strength against his bones. His great forelegs—twice as long as his hindlegs—twitched with a shuddering movement that arched every razor-sharp claw. The thick tentacles that sprouted from his shoulders ceased their weaving undulation, and grew taut with anxious alertness.

Utterly appalled, he twisted his great cat head from side to side, while the little hairlike tendrils that formed each ear vibrated frantically, testing every vagrant breeze, every throb in the ether.

But there was no response, no swift tingling along his intricate nervous system, not the faintest suggestion anywhere of the presence of the all-necessary id. Hopelessly, Coeurl crouched, an enormous catlike figure silhouetted against the dim reddish skyline, like a distorted etching of a black tiger resting on a black rock in a shadow world.

He had known this day would come. Through all the centuries of restless search, this day had loomed ever nearer, blacker, more frightening—this inevitable hour when he must return to the point where he began his systematic hunt in a world almost depleted of id-creatures.

The truth struck in waves like an endless, rhythmic ache at the seat of his ego. When he had started, there had been a few id-creatures in every hundred square miles, to be mercilessly rooted out. Only too well Coeurl knew in this ultimate hour that he had missed none. There were no id-creatures left to eat. In all the hundreds of thousands of square miles that he had made his own by right of ruthless conquest—until no neighboring coeurl dared to question his sovereignty—there was no id to feed the otherwise immortal engine that was his body.

Square foot by square foot he had gone over it. And now—he recognized the knoll of rock just ahead, and the black rock bridge that formed a queer, curling tunnel to his right. It was in that tunnel he had lain for days, waiting for the simple-minded, snakelike id-creature to come forth from its hole in the rock to bask in the sun—his first kill after he had realized the absolute necessity of organized extermination.

He licked his lips in brief gloating memory of the moment his slavering jaws tore the victim into precious toothsome bits. But the dark fear of an idless universe swept the sweet remembrance from his consciousness, leaving only certainty of death.

He snarled audibly, a defiant, devilish sound that quavered on the air, echoed and re-echoed among the rocks, and shuddered back along his nerves—instinctive and hellish expression of his will to live.

And then—abruptly—it came.

He saw it emerge out of the distance on a long downward slant, a tiny glowing spot that grew enormously into a metal ball. The great

shining globe hissed by above Coeurl, slowing visibly in quick deceleration. It sped over a black line of hills to the right, hovered almost
motionless for a second, then sank down out of sight.

Coeurl exploded from his startled immobility. With tiger speed, he
flowed down among the rocks. His round, black eyes burned with
the horrible desire that was an agony within him. His ear tendrils
vibrated a message of id in such tremendous quantities that his body
felt sick with the pangs of his abnormal hunger.

The little red sun was a crimson ball in the purple-black heavens
when he crept up from behind a mass of rock and gazed from its
shadows at the crumbling, gigantic ruins of the city that sprawled
below him. The silvery globe, in spite of its great size, looked strangely
inconspicuous against that vast, fairylike reach of ruins. Yet about
it was a leashed aliveness, a dynamic quiescence that, after a moment,
made it stand out, dominating the foreground. A massive, rock-
crushing thing of metal, it rested on a cradle made by its own weight
in the harsh, resisting plain which began abruptly at the outskirts
of the dead metropolis.

Coeurl gazed at the strange, two-legged creatures who stood in little
groups near the brilliantly lighted opening that yawned at the base of
the ship. His throat thickened with the immediacy of his need; and
his brain grew dark with the first wild impulse to burst forth in furious
charge and smash these flimsy, helpless-looking creatures whose bodies
emitted the id-vibrations.

Mists of memory stopped that mad rush when it was still only
electricity surging through his muscles. Memory that brought fear
in an acid stream of weakness, pouring along his nerves, poisoning
the reservoirs of his strength. He had time to see that the creatures
wore things over their real bodies, shimmering transparent material
that glittered in strange, burning flashes in the rays of the sun.

Other memories came suddenly. Of dim days when the city that
spread below was the living, breathing heart of an age of glory that
dissolved in a single century before flaming guns whose wielders knew
only that for the survivors there would be an ever-narrowing supply
of id.

It was the remembrance of those guns that held him there, cringing
in a wave of terror that blurred his reason. He saw himself smashed
by balls of metal and burned by searing flame.

Came cunning—understanding of the presence of these creatures.
This, Coeurl reasoned for the first time, was a scientific expedition
from another star. In the olden days, the coeurls had thought of

space travel, but disaster came too swiftly for it ever to be more than a thought.

Scientists meant investigation, not destruction. Scientists in their way were fools. Bold with his knowledge, he emerged into the open. He saw the creatures become aware of him. They turned and stared. One, the smallest of the group, detached a shining metal rod from a sheath, and held it casually in one hand. Coeurl loped on, shaken to his core by the action; but it was too late to turn back.

Commander Hal Morton heard little Gregory Kent, the chemist, laugh with the embarrassed half gurgle with which he invariably announced inner uncertainty. He saw Kent fingering the spindly metalite weapon.

Kent said: "I'll take no chances with anything as big as that."

Commander Morton allowed his own deep chuckle to echo along the communicators. "That," he grunted finally, "is one of the reasons why you're on this expedition, Kent—because you never leave anything to chance."

His chuckle trailed off into silence. Instinctively, as he watched the monster approach them across that black rock plain, he moved forward until he stood a little in advance of the others, his huge form bulking the transparent metalite suit. The comments of the men pattered through the radio communicator into his ears:

"I'd hate to meet that baby on a dark night in an alley."

"Don't be silly. This is obviously an intelligent creature. Probably a member of the ruling race."

"It looks like nothing else than a big cat, if you forget those tentacles sticking out from its shoulders, and make allowances for those monster forelegs."

"Its physical development," said a voice, which Morton recognized as that of Siedel, the psychologist, "presupposes an animal-like adaptation to surroundings, not an intellectual one. On the other hand, its coming to us like this is not the act of an animal but of a creature possessing a mental awareness of our possible identity. You will notice that its movements are stiff, denoting caution, which suggests fear and consciousness of our weapons. I'd like to get a good look at the end of its tentacles. If they taper into handlike appendages that can really grip objects, then the conclusion would be inescapable that it is a descendant of the inhabitants of this city. It would be a great help if we could establish communication with it, even though appearances indicate that it has degenerated into a historyless primitive."

Coeurl stopped when he was still ten feet from the foremost creature. The sense of id was so overwhelming that his brain drifted to the ultimate verge of chaos. He felt as if his limbs were bathed in molten liquid; his very vision was not quite clear, as the sheer sensuality of his desire thundered through his being.

The men—all except the little one with the shining metal rod in his fingers—came closer. Coeurl saw that they were frankly and curiously examining him. Their lips were moving, and their voices beat in a monotonous, meaningless rhythm on his ear tendrils. At the same time he had the sense of waves of a much higher frequency— his own communication level—only it was a machinelike clicking that jarred his brain. With a distinct effort to appear friendly, he broadcast his name from his ear tendrils, at the same time pointing at himself with one curving tentacle.

Gourlay, chief of communications, drawled: "I got a sort of static in my radio when he wiggled those hairs, Morton. Do you think—"

"Looks very much like it," the leader answered the unfinished question. "That means a job for you, Gourlay. If it speaks by means of radio waves, it might not be altogether impossible that you can create some sort of television picture of its vibrations, or teach him the Morse code."

"Ah," said Siedel. "I was right. The tentacles each develop into seven strong fingers. Provided the nervous system is complicated enough, those fingers could, with training, operate any machine."

Morton said: "I think we'd better go in and have some lunch. Afterward, we've got to get busy. The material men can set up their machines and start gathering data on the planet's metal possibilities, and so on. The others can do a little careful exploring. I'd like some notes on architecture and on the scientific development of this race, and particularly what happened to wreck the civilization. On earth civilization after civilization crumbled, but always a new one sprang up in its dust. Why didn't that happen here? Any questions?"

"Yes. What about pussy? Look, he wants to come in with us."

Commander Morton frowned, an action that emphasized the deep-space pallor of his face. "I wish there was some way we could take it in with us, without forcibly capturing it. Kent, what do you think?"

"I think we should first decide whether it's an it or a him, and call it one or the other. I'm in favor of him. As for taking him in with us—" The little chemist shook his head decisively. "Impossible. This atmosphere is twenty-eight per cent chlorine. Our oxygen would be pure dynamite to his lungs."

The commander chuckled. "He doesn't believe that, apparently." He watched the catlike monster follow the first two men through the great door. The men kept an anxious distance from him, then glanced at Morton questioningly. Morton waved his hand. "O. K. Open the second lock and let him get a whiff of the oxygen. That'll cure him."

A moment later, he cursed his amazement. "By Heaven, he doesn't even notice the difference! That means he hasn't any lungs, or else the chlorine is not what his lungs use. Let him in! You bet he can go in! Smith, here's a treasure house for a biologist—harmless enough if we're careful. We can always handle him. But what a metabolism!"

Smith, a tall, thin, bony chap with a long, mournful face, said in an oddly forceful voice: "In all our travels, we've found only two higher forms of life. Those dependent on chlorine, and those who need oxygen—the two elements that support combustion. I'm prepared to stake my reputation that no complicated organism could ever adapt itself to both gases in a natural way. At first thought I should say here is an extremely advanced form of life. This race long ago discovered truths of biology that we are just beginning to suspect. Morton, we mustn't let this creature get away if we can help it."

"If his anxiety to get inside is any criterion," Commander Morton laughed, "then our difficulty will be to get rid of him."

He moved into the lock with Coeurl and the two men. The automatic machinery hummed; and in a few minutes they were standing at the bottom of a series of elevators that led up to the living quarters.

"Does that go up?" One of the men flicked a thumb in the direction of the monster.

"Better send him up alone, if he'll go in."

Coeurl offered no objection, until he heard the door slam behind him; and the closed cage shot upward. He whirled with a savage snarl, his reason swirling into chaos. With one leap, he pounced at the door. The metal bent under his plunge, and the desperate pain maddened him. Now, he was all trapped animal. He smashed at the metal with his paws, bending it like so much tin. He tore great bars loose with his thick tentacles. The machinery screeched; there were horrible jerks as the limitless power pulled the cage along in spite of projecting pieces of metal that scraped the outside walls. And then the cage stopped, and he snatched off the rest of the door and hurtled into the corridor.

He waited there until Morton and the men came up with drawn weapons. "We're fools," Morton said. "We should have shown him how it works. He thought we'd double-crossed him."

He motioned to the monster, and saw the savage glow fade from the coal-black eyes as he opened and closed the door with elaborate gestures to show the operation.

Coeurl ended the lesson by trotting into the large room to his right. He lay down on the rugged floor, and fought down the electric tautness of his nerves and muscles. A very fury of rage against himself for his fright consumed him. It seemed to his burning brain that he had lost the advantage of appearing a mild and harmless creature. His strength must have startled and dismayed them.

It meant greater danger in the task which he now knew he must accomplish: To kill everything in the ship, and take the machine back to their world in search of unlimited id.

With unwinking eyes, Coeurl lay and watched the two men clearing away the loose rubble from the metal doorway of the huge old building. His whole body ached with the hunger of his cells for id. The craving tore through his palpitant muscles, and throbbed like a living thing in his brain. His every nerve quivered to be off after the men who had wandered into the city. One of them, he knew, had gone—alone.

The dragging minutes fled; and still he restrained himself, still he lay there watching, aware that the men knew he watched. They floated a metal machine from the ship to the rock mass that blocked the great half-open door, under the direction of a third man. No flicker of their fingers escaped his fierce stare, and slowly, as the simplicity of the machinery became apparent to him, contempt grew upon him.

He knew what to expect finally, when the flame flared in incandescent violence and ate ravenously at the hard rock beneath. But in spite of his preknowledge, he deliberately jumped and snarled as if in fear, as that white heat burst forth. His ear tendrils caught the laughter of the men, their curious pleasure at his simulated dismay.

The door was released, and Morton came over and went inside with the third man. The latter shook his head.

"It's a shambles. You can catch the drift of the stuff. Obviously, they used atomic energy, but . . . but it's in wheel form. That's a peculiar development. In our science, atomic energy brought in the nonwheel machine. It's possible that here they've progressed *further* to a new type of wheel mechanics. I hope their libraries are better preserved than this, or we'll never know. What could have happened to a civilization to make it vanish like this?"

A third voice broke through the communicators: "This is Siedel. I heard your question, Pennons. Psychologically and sociologically speaking, the only reason why a territory becomes uninhabited is lack of food."

"But they're so advanced scientifically, why didn't they develop space flying and go elsewhere for their food?"

"Ask Gunlie Lester," interjected Morton. "I heard him expounding some theory even before we landed."

The astronomer answered the first call. "I've still got to verify all my facts, but this desolate world is the only planet revolving around that miserable red sun. There's nothing else. No moon, not even a planetoid. And the nearest star system is *nine hundred light-years* away.

"So tremendous would have been the problem of the ruling race of this world, that in one jump they would not only have had to solve interplanetary but interstellar space traveling. When you consider how slow our own development was—first the moon, then Venus—each success leading to the next, and after centuries to the nearest stars; and last of all to the anti-accelerators that permitted galactic travel—considering all this, I maintain it would be impossible for any race to create such machines without practical experience. And, with the nearest star so far away, they had no incentive for the space adventuring that makes for experience."

Coeurl was trotting briskly over to another group. But now, in the driving appetite that consumed him, and in the frenzy of his high scorn, he paid no attention to what they were doing. Memories of past knowledge, jarred into activity by what he had seen, flowed into his consciousness in an ever developing and more vivid stream.

From group to group he sped, a nervous dynamo—jumpy, sick with his awful hunger. A little car rolled up, stopping in front of him, and a formidable camera whirred as it took a picture of him. Over on a mound of rock, a gigantic telescope was rearing up toward the sky. Nearby, a disintegrating machine drilled its searing fire into an ever-deepening hole, down and down, straight down.

Coeurl's mind became a blur of things he watched with half attention. And ever more imminent grew the moment when he knew he could no longer carry on the torture of acting. His brain strained with an irresistible impatience; his body burned with the fury of his eagerness to be off after the man who had gone alone into the city.

He could stand it no longer. A green foam misted his mouth, maddening him. He saw that, for the bare moment, nobody was looking.

Like a shot from a gun, he was off. He floated along in great, gliding leaps, a shadow among the shadows of the rocks. In a minute, the harsh terrain hid the spaceship and the two-legged beings.

Coeurl forgot the ship, forgot everything but his purpose, as if his brain had been wiped clear by a magic, memory-erasing brush. He circled widely, then raced into the city, along deserted streets, taking short cuts with the ease of familiarity, through gaping holes in time-weakened walls, through long corridors of moldering buildings. He slowed to a crouching lope as his ear tendrils caught the id vibrations.

Suddenly, he stopped and peered from a scatter of fallen rock. The man was standing at what must once have been a window, sending the glaring rays of his flashlight into the gloomy interior. The flashlight clicked off. The man, a heavy-set, powerful fellow, walked off with quick, alert steps. Coeurl didn't like that alertness. It presaged trouble; it meant lightning reaction to danger.

Coeurl waited till the human being had vanished around a corner, then he padded into the open. He was running now, tremendously faster than a man could walk, because his plan was clear in his brain. Like a wraith, he slipped down the next street, past a long block of buildings. He turned the first corner at top speed; and then, with dragging belly, crept into the half-darkness between the building and a huge chunk of débris. The street ahead was barred by a solid line of loose rubble that made it like a valley, ending in a narrow, bottlelike neck. The neck had its outlet just below Coeurl.

His ear tendrils caught the low-frequency waves of whistling. The sound throbbed through his being; and suddenly terror caught with icy fingers at his brain. The man would have a gun. Suppose he leveled one burst of atomic energy—one burst—before his own muscles could whip out in murder fury.

A little shower of rocks streamed past. And then the man was beneath him. Coeurl reached out and struck a single crushing blow at the shimmering transparent headpiece of the spacesuit. There was a tearing sound of metal and a gushing of blood. The man doubled up as if part of him had been telescoped. For a moment, his bones and legs and muscles combined miraculously to keep him standing. Then he crumpled with a metallic clank of his space armor.

Fear completely evaporated, Coeurl leaped out of hiding. With ravenous speed, he smashed the metal and the body within it to bits. Great chunks of metal, torn piecemeal from the suit, sprayed the ground. Bones cracked. Flesh crunched.

It was simple to tune in on the vibrations of the id, and to create the violent chemical disorganization that rreed it from the crushed bone. The id was, Coeurl discovered, mostly in the bone.

He felt revived, almost reborn. Here was more food than he had had in the whole past year.

Three minutes, and it was over, and Coeurl was off like a thing fleeing dire danger. Cautiously, he approached the glistening globe from the opposite side to that by which he had left. The men were all busy at their tasks. Gliding noiselessly, Coeurl slipped unnoticed up to a group of men.

Morton stared down at the horror of tattered flesh, metal and blood on the rock at his feet, and felt a tightening in his throat that prevented speech. He heard Kent say:

"He *would* go alone, damn him!" The little chemist's voice held a sob imprisoned; and Morton remembered that Kent and Jarvey had chummed together for years in the way only two men can.

"The worst part of it is," shuddered one of the men, "it looks like a senseless murder. His body is spread out like little lumps of flattened jelly, but it seems to be all there. I'd almost wager that if we weighed everything here, there'd still be one hundred and seventy-five pounds by earth gravity. That'd be about one hundred and seventy pounds here."

Smith broke in, his mournful face lined with gloom: "The killer attacked Jarvey, and then discovered his flesh was alien—uneatable. Just like our big cat. Wouldn't eat anything we set before him—" His words died out in sudden, queer silence. Then he said slowly: "Say, what about that creature? He's big enough and strong enough to have done this with his own little paws."

Morton frowned. "It's a thought. After all, he's the only living thing we've seen. We can't just execute him on suspicion, of course—"

"Besides," said one of the men, "he was never out of my sight."

Before Morton could speak, Siedel, the psychologist, snapped, "Positive about that?"

The man hesitated. "Maybe he was for a few minutes. He was wandering around so much, looking at everything."

"Exactly," said Siedel with satisfaction. He turned to Morton. "You see, commander, I, too, had the impression that he was always around; and yet, thinking back over it, I find gaps. There were moments—probably long minutes—when he was completely out of sight."

Morton's face was dark with thought, as Kent broke in fiercely: "I say, take no chances. Kill the brute on suspicion before he does any more damage."

Morton said slowly: "Korita, you've been wandering around with Cranessy and Van Horne. Do you think pussy is a descendant of the ruling class of this planet?"

The tall Japanese archeologist stared at the sky as if collecting his mind. "Commander Morton," he said finally, respectfully, "there is a mystery here. Take a look, all of you, at that majestic skyline. Notice the almost Gothic outline of the architecture. In spite of the megalopolis which they created, these people were close to the soil. The buildings are not simply ornamented. They are ornamental in themselves. Here is the equivalent of the Doric column, the Egyptian pyramid, the Gothic cathedral, growing out of the ground, earnest, big with destiny. If this lonely, desolate world can be regarded as a mother earth, then the land had a warm, a spiritual place in the hearts of the race.

"The effect is emphasized by the winding streets. Their machines prove they were mathematicians, but they were artists first; and so they did not create the geometrically designed cities of the ultra-sophisticated world metropolis. There is a genuine artistic abandon, a deep joyous emotion written in the curving and unmathematical arrangements of houses, buildings and avenues; a sense of intensity, of divine belief in an inner certainty. This is not a decadent, hoary-with-age civilization, but a young and vigorous culture, confident, strong with purpose.

"There it ended. Abruptly, as if at this point culture had its Battle of Tours, and began to collapse like the ancient Mohammedan civilization. Or as if in one leap it spanned the centuries and entered the period of contending states. In the Chinese civilization that period occupied 480-230 B. C., at the end of which the State of Tsin saw the beginning of the Chinese Empire. This phase Egypt experienced between 1780-1580 B. C., of which the last century was the 'Hyksos'—unmentionable—time. The classical experienced it from Chæronea—338—and, at the pitch of horror, from the Gracchi —133—to Actium—31 B. C. The West European Americans were devastated by it in the nineteenth and twentieth centuries, and modern historians agree that, nominally, we entered the same phase fifty years ago; though, of course, we have solved the problem.

"You may ask, commander, what has all this to do with your question? My answer is: there is no record of a culture entering abruptly into the period of contending states. It is always a slow development; and the first step is a merciless questioning of all that was once held sacred. Inner certainties cease to exist, are dissolved before the ruthless probings of scientific and analytic minds. The skeptic becomes the highest type of being

"I say that this culture ended abruptly in its most flourishing age. The sociological effects of such a catastrophe would be a sudden vanishing of morals, a reversion to almost bestial criminality, unleavened by any sense of ideal, a callous indifference to death. If this . . . this pussy is a descendant of such a race, then he will be a cunning creature, a thief in the night, a cold-blooded murderer, who would cut his own brother's throat for gain."

"That's enough!" It was Kent's clipped voice. "Commander, I'm willing to act the role of executioner."

Smith interrupted sharply: "Listen, Morton, you're not going to kill that cat yet, even if he is guilty. He's a biological treasure house."

Kent and Smith were glaring angrily at each other. Morton frowned at them thoughtfully, then said: "Korita, I'm inclined to accept your theory as a working basis. But one question: Pussy comes from a period earlier than our own? That is, we are entering the highly civilized era of our culture, while he became suddenly historyless in the most vigorous period of his. But it is possible that his culture is a later one on this planet than ours is in the galactic-wide system we have civilized?"

"Exactly. His may be the middle of the tenth civilization of his world; while ours is the end of the eighth sprung from earth, each of the ten, of course, having been builded on the ruins of the one before it."

"In that case, pussy would not know anything about the skepticism that made it possible for us to find him out so positively as a criminal and murderer?"

"No; it would be literally magic to him."

Morton was smiling grimly. "Then I think you'll get your wish, Smith. We'll let pussy live; and if there are any fatalities, now that we know him, it will be due to rank carelessness. There's just the chance, of course, that we're wrong. Like Siedel, I also have the impression that he was always around. But now—we can't leave poor Jarvey here like this. We'll put him in a coffin and bury him."

"No, we won't!" Kent barked. He flushed. "I beg your pardon, commander. I didn't mean it that way. I maintain pussy wanted something from that body. It looks to be all there, but something must be missing. I'm going to find out what, and pin this murder on him so that you'll have to believe it beyond the shadow of a doubt."

It was late night when Morton looked up from a book and saw Kent emerge through the door that led from the laboratories below.

Kent carried a large, flat bowl in his hands; his tired eyes flashed across at Morton, and he said in a weary, yet harsh, voice: "Now watch!"

He started toward Coeurl, who lay sprawled on the great rug, pretending to be asleep.

Morton stopped him. "Wait a minute, Kent. Any other time, I wouldn't question your actions, but you look ill; you're overwrought. What have you got there?"

Kent turned, and Morton saw that his first impression had been but a flashing glimpse of the truth. There were dark pouches under the little chemist's gray eyes—eyes that gazed feverishly from sunken cheeks in an ascetic face.

"I've found the missing element," Kent said. "It's phosphorus. There wasn't so much as a square millimeter of phosphorus left in Jarvey's bones. Every bit of it had been drained out—by what superchemistry I don't know. There are ways of getting phosphorus out of the human body. For instance, a quick way was what happened to the workman who helped build this ship. Remember, he fell into fifteen tons of molten metalite—at least, so his relatives claimed—but the company wouldn't pay compensation until the metalite, on analysis, was found to contain a high percentage of phosphorus—"

"What about the bowl of food?" somebody interrupted. Men were putting away magazines and books, looking up with interest.

"It's got organic phosphorus in it. He'll get the scent, or whatever it is that he uses instead of scent—"

"I think he gets the vibrations of things," Gourlay interjected lazily. "Sometimes, when he wiggles those tendrils, I get a distinct static on the radio. And then, again, there's no reaction, just as if he's moved higher or lower on the wave scale. He seems to control the vibrations at will."

Kent waited with obvious impatience until Gourlay's last word, then abruptly went on: "All right, then, when he gets the vibration of the phosphorus and reacts to it like an animal, then—well, we can decide what we've proved by his reaction. May I go ahead, Morton?"

"There are three things wrong with your plan," Morton said. "In the first place, you seem to assume that he is only animal; you seem to have forgotten he may not be hungry after Jarvey; you seem to think that he will not be suspicious. But set the bowl down. His reaction may tell us something."

Coeurl stared with unblinking black eyes as the man set the bowl before him. His ear tendrils instantly caught the id-vibrations from the contents of the bowl—and he gave it not even a second glance.

He recognized this two-legged being as the one who had held the weapon that morning. Danger! With a snarl, he floated to his feet. He caught the bowl with the fingerlike appendages at the end of one looping tentacle, and emptied its contents into the face of Kent, who shrank back with a yell.

Explosively, Coeurl flung the bowl aside and snapped a hawser-thick tentacle around the cursing man's waist. He didn't bother with the gun that hung from Kent's belt. It was only a vibration gun, he sensed —atomic powered, but not an atomic disintegrator. He tossed the kicking Kent onto the nearest couch—and realized with a hiss of dismay that he should have disarmed the man.

Not that the gun was dangerous—but, as the man furiously wiped the gruel from his face with one hand, he reached with the other for his weapon. Coeurl crouched back as the gun was raised slowly and a white beam of flame was discharged at his massive head.

His ear tendrils hummed as they canceled the efforts of the vibration gun. His round, black eyes narrowed as he caught the movement of men reaching for their metalite guns. Morton's voice lashed across the silence.

"Stop!"

Kent clicked off his weapon; and Coeurl crouched down, quivering with fury at this man who had forced him to reveal something of his power.

"Kent," said Morton coldly, "you're not the type to lose your head. You deliberately tried to kill pussy, knowing that the majority of us are in favor of keeping him alive. You know what our rule is: If anyone objects to my decisions, he must say so *at the time.* If the majority object, my decisions are overruled. In this case, no one but you objected, and. therefore, your action in taking the law into your own hands is most reprehensible, and automatically debars you from voting for a year."

Kent stared grimly at the circle of faces. "Korita was right when he said ours was a highly civilized age. It's decadent." Passion flamed harshly in his voice. "My God, isn't there a man here who can see the horror of the situation? Jarvey dead only a few hours, and this creature, whom we all know to be guilty, lying there unchained, planning his next murder; and the victim is right here in this room. What kind of men are we—fools, cynics, ghouls—or is it that our civilization is so steeped in reason that we can contemplate a murderer sympathetically?"

He fixed brooding eyes on Coeurl. "You were right, Morton, that's no animal. That's a devil from the deepest hell of this forgotten planet, whirling its solitary way around a dying sun."

"Don't go melodramatic on us," Morton said. "Your analysis is all wrong, so far as I am concerned. We're not ghouls or cynics; we're simply scientists, and pussy here is going to be studied. Now that we suspect him, we doubt his ability to trap any of us. One against a hundred hasn't a chance." He glanced around. "Do I speak for all of us?"

"Not for me, commander!" It was Smith who spoke, and, as Morton stared in amazement, he continued: "In the excitement and momentary confusion, no one seems to have noticed that when Kent fired his vibration gun, the beam hit this creature squarely on his cat head—and didn't hurt him."

Morton's amazed glance went from Smith to Coeurl, and back to Smith again. "Are you certain it hit him? As you say, it all happened so swiftly—when pussy wasn't hurt I simply assumed that Kent had missed him."

"He hit him in the face," Smith said positively. "A vibration gun, of course, can't even kill a man right away—but it can injure him. There's no sign of injury on pussy, though, not even a singed hair."

"Perhaps his skin is a good insulation against heat of any kind."

"Perhaps. But in view of our uncertainty, I think we should lock him up in the cage."

While Morton frowned darkly in thought, Kent spoke up. "Now you're talking sense, Smith."

Morton asked: "Then you would be satisfied, Kent, if we put him in the cage?"

Kent considered, finally: "Yes. If four inches of micro-steel can't hold him, we'd better give him the ship."

Coeurl followed the men as they went out into the corridor. He trotted docilely along as Morton unmistakably motioned him through a door he had not hitherto seen. He found himself in a square, solid metal room. The door clanged metallically behind him; he felt the flow of power as the electric lock clicked home.

His lips parted in a grimace of hate, as he realized the trap, but he gave no other outward reaction. It occurred to him that he had progressed a long way from the sunk-into-primitiveness creature who, a few hours before, had gone incoherent with fear in an elevator cage. Now, a thousand memories of his powers were reawakened in his brain; ten thousand cunnings were, after ages of disuse, once again part of his very being.

He sat quite still for a moment on the short, heavy haunches into which his body tapered, his ear tendrils examining his surroundings. Finally, he lay down, his eyes glowing with contemptuous fire. The fools! The poor fools!

It was about an hour later when he heard the man—Smith—fumbling overhead. Vibrations poured upon him, and for just an instant he was startled. He leaped to his feet in pure terror—and then realized that the vibrations were vibrations, not atomic explosions. Somebody was taking pictures of the inside of his body.

He crouched down again, but his ear tendrils vibrated, and he thought contemptuously: the silly fool would be surprised when he tried to develop those pictures.

After a while the man went away, and for a long time there were noises of men doing things far away. That, too, died away slowly.

Coeurl lay waiting, as he felt the silence creep over the ship. In the long ago, before the dawn of immortality, the coeurls, too, had slept at night; and the memory of it had been revived the day before when he saw some of the men dozing. At last, the vibration of two pairs of feet, pacing, pacing endlessly, was the only human-made frequency that throbbed on his ear tendrils.

Tensely, he listened to the two watchmen. The first one walked slowly past the cage door. Then about thirty feet behind him came the second. Coeurl sensed the alertness of these men; knew that he could never surprise either while they walked separately. It meant— he must be doubly careful!

Fifteen minutes, and they came again. The moment they were past, he switched his senses from their vibrations to a vastly higher range. The pulsating violence of the atomic engines stammered its soft story to his brain. The electric dynamos hummed their muffled song of pure power. He felt the whisper of that flow through the wires in the walls of his cage, and through the electric lock of his door. He forced his quivering body into straining immobility, his senses seeking, searching, to tune in on that sibilant tempest of energy. Suddenly, his ear tendrils vibrated in harmony—he caught the surging change into shrillness of that rippling force wave.

There was a sharp click of metal on metal. With a gentle touch of one tentacle, Coeurl pushed open the door, and glided out into the dully gleaming corridor. For just a moment he felt contempt, a glow of superiority, as he thought of the stupid creatures who dared to match their wit against a coeurl. And in that moment, he suddenly thought of other coeurls. A queer, exultant sense of race pounded through his being; the driving hate of centuries of ruthless competition yielded reluctantly before pride of kinship with the future rulers of all space.

Suddenly, he felt weighed down by his limitations, his need for other coeurls, his aloneness—one against a hundred, with the stake all eternity; the starry universe itself beckoned his rapacious, vaulting ambition. If he failed, there would never be a second chance—no time to revive long-rotted machinery, and attempt to solve the secret of space travel.

He padded along on tensed paws—through the salon—into the next corridor—and came to the first bedroom door. It stood half open. One swift flow of synchronized muscles, one swiftly lashing tentacle that caught the unresisting throat of the sleeping man, crushing it; and the lifeless head rolled crazily, the body twitched once.

Seven bedrooms; seven dead men. It was the seventh taste of murder that brought a sudden return of lust, a pure, unbounded desire to kill, return of a millennium-old habit of destroying everything containing the precious id.

As the twelfth man slipped convulsively into death, Coeurl emerged abruptly from the sensuous joy of the kill to the sound of footsteps.

They were not near—that was what brought wave after wave of fright swirling into the chaos that suddenly became his brain.

The watchmen were coming slowly along the corridor toward the door of the cage where he had been imprisoned. In a moment, the first man would see the open door—and sound the alarm.

Coeurl caught at the vanishing remnants of his reason. With frantic speed, careless now of accidental sounds, he raced—along the corridor with its bedroom doors—through the salon. He emerged into the next corridor, cringing in awful anticipation of the atomic flame he expected would stab into his face.

The two men were together, standing side by side. For one single instant, Coeurl could scarcely believe his tremendous good luck. Like a fool the second had come running when he saw the other stop before the open door. They looked up, paralyzed, before the nightmare of claws and tentacles, the ferocious cat head and hate-filled eyes.

The first man went for his gun, but the second, physically frozen before the doom he saw, uttered a shriek, a shrill cry of horror that floated along the corridors—and ended in a curious gurgle, as Coerl flung the two corpses with one irresistible motion the full length of the corridor. He didn't want the dead bodies found near the cage. That was his one hope.

Shaking in every nerve and muscle, conscious of the terrible error he had made, unable to think coherently, he plunged into the cage. The door clicked softly shut behind him. Power flowed once more through the electric lock.

He crouched tensely, simulating sleep, as he heard the rush of many feet, caught the vibration of excited voices. He knew when somebody actuated the cage audioscope and looked in. A few moments now, and the other bodies would be discovered.

"Siedel gone!" Morton said numbly. "What are we going to do without Siedel? And Breckenridge! And Coulter and— Horrible!"

He covered his face with his hands, but only for an instant. He looked up grimly, his heavy chin outthrust as he stared into the stern faces that surrounded him. "If anybody's got so much as a germ of an idea, bring it out."

"Space madness!"

"I've thought of that. But there hasn't been a case of a man going mad for fifty years. Dr. Eggert will test everybody, of course, and right now he's looking at the bodies with that possibility in mind."

As he finished, he saw the doctor coming through the door. Men crowded aside to make way for him.

"I heard you, commander," Dr. Eggert said, "and I think I can say right now that the space-madness theory is out. The throats of these men have been squeezed to a jelly. No human being could have exerted such enormous strength without using a machine."

Morton saw that the doctor's eyes kept looking down the corridor, and he shook his head and groaned:

"It's no use suspecting pussy, doctor. He's in his cage, pacing up and down. Obviously heard the racket and— Man alive! You can't suspect him. That cage was built to hold literally *anything*—four inches of micro-steel—and there's not a scratch on the door. Kent, even you won't say, 'Kill him on suspicion,' because there can't be any suspicion, unless there's a new science here, beyond anything we can imagine—"

"On the contrary," said Smith flatly, "we have all the evidence we need. I used the telefluor on him—you know the arrangement we have on top of the cage—and tried to take some pictures. They just blurred. Pussy jumped when the telefluor was turned on, as if he felt the vibrations.

"You all know what Gourlay said before? This beast can apparently receive and send vibrations of any lengths. The way he dominated the power of Kent's gun is final proof of his special ability to interfere with energy."

"What in the name of all the hells have we got here?" One of the men groaned. "Why, if he can control that power, and sent it out in any vibrations, there's nothing to stop him killing all of us."

"Which proves," snapped Morton, "that he isn't invincible, or he would have done it long ago."

Very deliberately, he walked over to the mechanism that controlled the prison cage.

"You're not going to open the door!" Kent gasped, reaching for his gun.

"No, but if I pull this switch, electricity will flow through the floor, and electrocute whatever's inside. We've never had to use this before, so you had probably forgotten about it."

He jerked the switch hard over. Blue fire flashed from the metal, and a bank of fuses above his head exploded with a single bang.

Morton frowned. "That's funny. Those fuses shouldn't have blown! Well, we can't even look in, now. That wrecked the audios, too."

Smith said: "If he could interfere with the electric lock, enough to open the door, then he probably probed every possible danger and was ready to interfere when you threw that switch."

"At least, it proves he's vulnerable to our energies!" Morton smiled grimly. "Because he rendered them harmless. The important thing is, we've got him behind four inches of the toughest of metal. At the worst we can open the door and ray him to death. But first, I think we'll try to use the telefluor power cable—"

A commotion from inside the cage interrupted his words. A heavy body crashed against a wall, followed by a dull thump.

"He knows what we were trying to do!" Smith grunted to Morton. "And I'll bet it's a very sick pussy in there. What a fool he was to go back into that cage and does he realize it!"

The tension was relaxing; men were smiling nervously, and there was even a ripple of humorless laughter at the picture Smith drew of the monster's discomfiture.

"What I'd like to know," said Pennons, the engineer, "is, why did the telefluor meter dial jump and waver at full power when pussy made that noise? It's right under my nose here, and the dial jumped like a house afire!"

There was silence both without and within the cage, then Morton said: "It may mean he's coming out. Back, everybody, and keep your guns ready. Pussy was a fool to think he could conquer a hundred men, but he's by far the most formidable creature in the galactic system. He may come out of that door, rather than die like a rat in a trap. And he's just tough enough to take some of us with him—if we're not careful."

The men backed slowly in a solid body; and somebody said: "That's funny. I thought I heard the elevator."

"Elevator!" Morton echoed. "Are you sure, man?"

"Just for a moment I was!" The man, a member of the crew, hesitated. "We were all shuffling our feet—"

"Take somebody with you, and go look. Bring whoever dared to run off back here—"

There was a jar, a horrible jerk, as the whole gigantic body of the ship careened under them. Morton was flung to the floor with a violence that stunned him. He fought back to consciousness, aware of the other men lying all around him. He shouted: "Who the devil started those engines!"

The agonizing acceleration continued; his feet dragged with awful exertion, as he fumbled with the nearest audioscope, and punched the engine-room number. The picture that flooded onto the screen brought a deep bellow to his lips:

"It's pussy! He's in the engine room—and we're heading straight out into space."

The screen went black even as he spoke, and he could see no more.

It was Morton who first staggered across the salon floor to the supply room where the spacesuits were kept. After fumbling almost blindly into his own suit, he cut the effects of the body-torturing acceleration, and brought suits to the semiconscious men on the floor. In a few moments, other men were assisting him; and then it was only a matter of minutes before everybody was clad in metalite, with anti-acceleration motors running at half power.

It was Morton then who, after first looking into the cage, opened the door and stood, silent as the others crowded about him, to stare at the gaping hole in the rear wall. The hole was a frightful thing of jagged edges and horribly bent metal, and it opened upon another corridor.

"I'll swear," whispered Pennons, "that it's impossible. The ten-ton hammer in the machine shops couldn't more than dent four inches of micro with one blow—and we only heard one. It would take at least a minute for an atomic disintegrator to do the job. Morton, this is a super-being."

Morton saw that Smith was examining the break in the wall. The biologist looked up. "If only Breckinridge weren't dead! We need a metallurgist to explain this. Look!"

He touched the broken edge of the metal. A piece crumbled in his finger and slithered away in a fine shower of dust to the floor. Morton noticed for the first time that there was a little pile of metallic debris and dust.

"You've hit it." Morton nodded. "No miracle of strength here. The monster merely used his special powers to interfere with the electronic tensions holding the metal together. That would account, too, for the drain on the telefluor power cable that Pennons noticed. The thing used the power with his body as a transforming medium, smashed through the wall, ran down the corridor to the elevator shaft, and so down to the engine room."

"In the meantime, commander," Kent said quietly, "we are faced with a super-being in control of the ship, completely dominating the engine room and its almost unlimited power, and in possession of the best part of the machine shops."

Morton felt the silence, while the men pondered the chemist's words. Their anxiety was a tangible thing that lay heavily upon their faces; in every expression was the growing realization that here was the ultimate situation in their lives; their very existence was at stake and perhaps much more. Morton voiced the thought in everybody's mind:

"Suppose he wins. He's utterly ruthless, and he probably sees galactic power within his grasp."

"Kent is wrong," barked the chief navigator. "The thing doesn't dominate the engine room. We've still got the control room, and that gives us first control of all the machines. You fellows may not know the mechanical set-up we have; but, though he can eventually disconnect us, we can cut off all the switches in the engine room now. Commander, why didn't you just shut off the power instead of putting us into spacesuits? At the very least you could have adjusted the ship to the acceleration."

"For two reasons," Morton answered. "Individually, we're safer within the force fields of our spacesuits. And we can't afford to give up our advantages in panicky moves."

"Advantages! What other advantages have we got?"

"We know things about him," Morton replied. "And right now, we're going to make a test. Pennons, detail five men to each of the four approaches to the engine room. Take atomic disintegrators to blast through the big doors. They're all shut, I noticed. He's locked himself in.

"Selenski, you go up to the control room and shut off everything except the drive engines. Gear them to the master switch, and shut them off all at once. One thing, though—leave the acceleration on full blast. No anti-acceleration must be applied to the ship. Understand?"

"Aye, sir!" The pilot saluted.

"And report to me through the communicators if any of the machines start to run again." He faced the men. "I'm going to lead the main approach. Kent, you take No. 2; Smith, No. 3, and Pennons, No. 4. We're going to find out right now if we're dealing with unlimited science, or a creature limited like the rest of us. I'll bet on the second possibility."

Morton had an empty sense of walking endlessly, as he moved, a giant of a man in his transparent space armor, along the glistening metal tube that was the main corridor of the engine-room floor. Reason told him the creature had already shown feet of clay, yet the feeling that here was an invincible being persisted.

He spoke into the communicator: "It's no use trying to sneak up on him. He can probably hear a pin drop. So just wheel up your units. He hasn't been in that engine room long enough to do anything.

"As I've said, this is largely a test attack. In the first place, we could never forgive ourselves if we didn't try to conquer him now, before he's had time to prepare against us. But, aside from the possibility that we can destroy him immediately, I have a theory."

"The idea goes something like this: Those doors are built to withstand accidental atomic explosions, and it will take fifteen minutes for the atomic disintegrators to smash them. During that period the monster will have no power. True, the drive will be on, but that's straight atomic explosion. My theory is, he can't touch stuff like that; and in a few minutes you'll see what I mean—I hope."

His voice was suddenly crisp: "Ready, Selenski?"

"Aye, ready."

"Then cut the master switch."

The corridor—the whole ship, Morton knew—was abruptly plunged into darkness. Morton clicked on the dazzling light of his spacesuit; the other men did the same, their faces pale and drawn.

"Blast!" Morton barked into his communicator.

The mobile units throbbed; and then pure atomic flame ravened out and poured upon the hard metal of the door. The first molten droplet rolled reluctantly, not down, but up the door. The second was more normal. It followed a shaky downward course. The third rolled sideways—for this was pure force, not subject to gravitation. Other drops followed until a dozen streams trickled sedately yet unevenly in every direction—streams of hellish, sparkling fire, bright as fairy gems, alive with the coruscating fury of atoms suddenly tortured, and running blindly, crazy with pain.

The minutes ate at time like a slow acid. At last Morton asked huskily:

"Selenski?"

"Nothing yet, commander."

Morton half whispered: "But he must be doing something. He can't be just waiting in there like a cornered rat. Selenski?"

"Nothing, commander."

Seven minutes, eight minutes, then twelve.

"Commander!" It was Selenski's voice, taut. "He's got the electric dynamo running."

Morton drew a deep breath, and heard one of his men say:

"That's funny. We can't get any deeper. Boss, take a look at this."

Morton looked. The little scintillating streams had frozen rigid. The ferocity of the disintegrators vented in vain against metal grown suddenly invulnerable.

Morton sighed. "Our test is over. Leave two men guarding every corridor. The others come up to the control room."

He seated himself a few minutes later before the massive control keyboard. "So far as I'm concerned the test was a success. We know that of all the machines in the engine room, the most important to the monster was the electric dynamo. He must have worked in a frenzy of terror while we were at the doors."

"Of course, it's easy to see what he did," Pennons said. "Once he had the power he increased the electronic tensions of the door to their ultimate."

"The main thing is this," Smith chimed in. "He works with vibrations only so far as his special powers are concerned, and the energy must come from outside himself. Atomic energy in its pure form, not being vibration, he can't handle any differently than we can."

Kent said glumly: "The main point in my opinion is that he stopped us cold. What's the good of knowing that his control over vibrations did it? If we can't break through those doors with our atomic disintegrators, we're finished."

Morton shook his head. "Not finished—but we'll have to do some planning. First, though, I'll start these engines. It'll be harder for him to get control of them when they're running."

He pulled the master switch back into place with a jerk. There was a hum, as scores of machines leaped into violent life in the engine room a hundred feet below. The noises sank to a steady vibration of throbbing power.

Three hours later, Morton paced up and down before the men gathered in the salon. His dark hair was uncombed; the space pallor of his strong face emphasized rather than detracted from the out-thrust aggressiveness of his jaw. When he spoke, his deep voice was crisp to the point of sharpness:

"To make sure that our plans are fully co-ordinated, I'm going to ask each expert in turn to outline his part in the overpowering of this creature. Pennons first!"

Pennons stood up briskly. He was not a big man, Morton thought, yet he looked big, perhaps because of his air of authority. This man knew engines, and the history of engines. Morton had heard him trace a machine through its evolution from a simple toy to the highly complicated modern instrument. He had studied machine development on a hundred planets; and there was literally nothing fundamental that he didn't know about mechanics. It was almost weird to hear Pennons, who could have spoken for a thousand hours and still only have touched upon his subject, say with absurd brevity:

"We've set up a relay in the control room to start and stop every engine rhythmically. The trip lever will work a hundred times a second, and the effect will be to create vibrations of every description.

There is just a possibility that one or more of the machines will burst, on the principle of soldiers crossing a bridge in step—you've heard that old story, no doubt—but in my opinion there is no real danger of a break of that tough metal. The main purpose is simply to interfere with the interference of the creature, and smash through the doors."

"Gourlay next!" barked Morton.

Gourlay climbed lazily to his feet. He looked sleepy, as if he was somewhat bored by the whole proceedings, yet Morton knew he loved people to think him lazy, a good-for-nothing slouch, who spent his days in slumber and his nights catching forty winks. His title was chief communication engineer, but his knowledge extended to every vibration field; and he was probably, with the possible exception of Kent, the fastest thinker on the ship. His voice drawled out, and— Morton noted—the very deliberate assurance of it had a soothing effect on the men—anxious faces relaxed, bodies leaned back more restfully:

"Once inside," Gourlay said, "we've rigged up vibration screens of pure force that should stop nearly everything he's got on the ball. They work on the principle of reflection, so that everything he sends will be reflected back to him. In addition, we've got plenty of spare electric energy that we'll just feed him from mobile copper cups. There must be a limit to his capacity for handling power with those insulated nerves of his."

"Selenski!" called Morton.

The chief pilot was already standing, as if he had anticipated Morton's call. And that, Morton reflected, was the man. His nerves had that rocklike steadiness which is the first requirement of the master controller of a great ship's movements; yet that very steadiness seemed to rest on dynamite ready to explode at its owner's volition. He was not a man of great learning, but he "reacted" to stimuli so fast that he always seemed to be anticipating.

"The impression I've received of the plan is that it must be cumulative. Just when the creature thinks that he can't stand any more, another thing happens to add to his trouble and confusion. When the uproar's at its height, I'm supposed to cut in the anti-accelerators. The commander thinks with Gunlie Lester that these creatures will know nothing about anti-acceleration. It's a development, pure and simple, of the science of interstellar flight, and couldn't have been developed in any other way. We think when the creature feels the first effects of the anti-acceleration—you all remember the caved-in feeling you had the first month—it won't know what to think or do."

"Korita next."

"I can only offer you encouragement," said the archeologist, "on the basis of my theory that the monster has all the characteristics of a criminal of the early ages of any civilization, complicated by an apparent reversion to primitiveness. The suggestion has been made by Smith that his knowledge of science is puzzling, and could only mean that we are dealing with an actual inhabitant, not a descendant of the inhabitants of the dead city we visited. This would ascribe a virtual immortality to our enemy, a possibility which is borne out by his ability to breathe both oxygen and chlorine—or neither—but even that makes no difference. He comes from a certain age in his civilization; and he has sunk so low that his ideas are mostly memories of that age.

"In spite of all the powers of his body, he lost his head in the elevator the first morning, until he remembered. He placed himself in such a position that he was forced to reveal his special powers against vibrations. He bungled the mass murders a few hours ago. In fact, his whole record is one of the low cunning of the primitive, egotistical mind which has little or no conception of the vast organization with which it is confronted.

"He is like the ancient German soldier who felt superior to the elderly Roman scholar, yet the latter was part of a mighty civilization of which the Germans of that day stood in awe.

"You may suggest that the sack of Rome by the Germans in later years defeats my argument; however, modern historians agree that the 'sack' was an historical accident, and not history in the true sense of the word. The movement of the 'Sea-peoples' which set in against the Egyptian civilization from 1400 B. C. succeeded only as regards the Cretan island-realm—their mighty expeditions against the Libyan and Phoenician coasts, with the accompaniment of viking fleets, failed as those of the Huns failed against the Chinese Empire. Rome would have been abandoned in any event. Ancient, glorious Samarra was desolate by the tenth century; Pataliputra, Asoka's great capital, was an immense and completely uninhabited waste of houses when the Chinese traveler Hsinan-tang visited it about A. D. 635.

"We have, then, a primitive, and that primitive is now far out in space, completely outside of his natural habitat. I say, let's go in and win."

One of the men grumbled, as Korita finished: "You can talk about the sack of Rome being an accident, and about this fellow being a primitive, but the facts are facts. It looks to me as if Rome is about to fall again; and it won't be no primitive that did it, either. This guy's got plenty of what it takes."

Morton smiled grimly at the man, a member of the crew. "We'll see about that—right now!"

In the blazing brilliance of the gigantic machine shop, Coeur'l slaved. The forty-foot, cigar-shaped spaceship was nearly finished. With a grunt of effort, he completed the laborious installation of the drive engines, and paused to survey his craft.

Its interior, visible through the one aperture in the outer wall, was pitifully small. There was literally room for nothing but the engines —and a narrow space for himself.

He plunged frantically back to work as he heard the approach of the men, and the sudden change in the tempest-like thunder of the engines—a rhythmical off-and-on hum, shriller in tone, sharper, more nerve-racking than the deep-throated, steady throb that had preceded it. Suddenly, there were the atomic disintegrators again at the massive outer doors.

He fought them off, but never wavered from his task. Every mighty muscle of his powerful body strained as he carried great loads of tools, machines and instruments, and dumped them into the bottom of his makeshift ship. There was no time to fit anything into place, no time for anything—no time—no time.

The thought pounded at his reason. He felt strangely weary for the first time in his long and vigorous existence. With a last, tortured heave, he jerked the gigantic sheet of metal into the gaping aperture of the ship—and stood there for a terrible minute, balancing it precariously.

He knew the doors were going down. Half a dozen disintegrators concentrating on one point were irresistibly, though slowly, eating away the remaining inches. With a gasp, he released his mind from the doors and concentrated every ounce of his mind on the yard-thick outer wall, toward which the blunt nose of his ship was pointing.

His body cringed from the surging power that flowed from the electric dynamo through his ear tendrils into that resisting wall. The whole inside of him felt on fire, and he knew that he was dangerously close to carrying his ultimate load.

And still he stood there, shuddering with the awful pain, holding the unfastened metal plate with hard-clenched tentacles. His massive head pointed as in dread fascination at that bitterly hard wall.

He heard one of the engine-room doors crash inward. Men shouted; disintegrators rolled forward, their raging power unchecked. Coeurl heard the floor of the engine room hiss in protest, as those beams of atomic energy tore everything in their path to bits. The machines rolled closer; cautious footsteps sounded behind them. In a minute they would be at the flimsy doors separating the engine room from the machine shop.

Suddenly, Coeurl was satisfied. With a snarl of hate, a vindictive glow of feral eyes, he ducked into his little craft, and pulled the metal plate down into place as if it was a hatchway.

His ear tendrils hummed, as he softened the edges of the surrounding metal. In an instant, the plate was more than welded—it was part of his ship, a seamless, rivetless part of a whole that was solid opaque metal except for two transparent areas, one in the front, one in the rear.

His tentacle embraced the power drive with almost sensuous tenderness. There was a forward surge of his fragile machine, straight at the great outer wall of the machine shops. The nose of the forty-foot craft touched—and the wall dissolved in a glittering shower of dust.

Coeurl felt the barest retarding movement; and then he kicked the nose of the machine out into the cold of space, twisted it about, and headed back in the direction from which the big ship had been coming all these hours.

Men in space armor stood in the jagged hole that yawned in the lower reaches of the gigantic globe. The men and the great ship grew smaller Then the men were gone; and there was only the ship with its blaze of a thousand blurring portholes. The ball shrank incredibly, too small now for individual portholes to be visible.

Almost straight ahead, Coeurl saw a tiny, dim, reddish ball—his own sun, he realized. He headed toward it at full speed. There were caves where he could hide and with other coeurls build secretly a spaceship in which they could reach other planets safely—now that he knew how.

His body ached from the agony of acceleration, yet he dared not let up for a single instant. He glanced back, half in terror. The globe was still there, a tiny dot of light in the immense blackness of space Suddenly it twinkled and was gone.

For a brief moment, he had the empty, frightened impression that just before it disappeared, it moved. But he could see nothing. He could not escape the belief that they had shut off all their lights, and were sneaking up on him in the darkness. Worried and uncertain, he looked through the forward transparent plate.

A tremor of dismay shot through him. The dim red sun toward which he was heading was not growing larger. *It was becoming smaller* by the instant, and it grew visibly tinier during the next five minutes, became a pale-red dot in the sky—and vanished like the ship.

Fear came then, a blinding surge of it, that swept through his being and left him chilled with the sense of the unknown. For minutes, he stared frantically into the space ahead, searching for some landmark. But only the remote stars glimmered there, unwinking points against a velvet background of unfathomable distance.

Wait! One of the points was growing larger. With every muscle and nerve tensed, Coeurl watched the point becoming a dot, a round ball of light—red light. Bigger, bigger, it grew. Suddenly, the red light shimmered and turned white—and there, before him, was the great globe of the spaceship, lights glaring from every porthole, the very ship which a few minutes before he had watched vanish behind him.

Something happened to Coeurl in that moment. His brain was spinning like a flywheel, faster, faster, more incoherently. Suddenly, the wheel flew apart into a million aching fragments. His eyes almost started from their sockets as, like a maddened animal, he raged in his small quarters.

His tentacles clutched at precious instruments and flung them insensately; his paws smashed in fury at the very walls of his ship. Finally, in a brief flash of sanity, he knew that he couldn't face the inevitable fire of atomic disintegrators.

It was a simple thing to create the violent disorganization that freed every drop of id from his vital organs.

They found him lying dead in a little pool of phosphorus.

"Poor pussy," said Morton. "I wonder what he thought when he saw us appear ahead of him, after his own sun disappeared. Knowing nothing of anti-accelerators, he couldn't know that we could stop short in space, whereas it would take him more than three hours to decelerate; and in the meantime he'd be drawing farther and farther away from where he wanted to go. He couldn't know that by stopping, we flashed past him at millions of miles a second. Of course, he didn't have a chance once he left our ship. The whole world must have seemed topsy-turvy."

"Never mind the sympathy," he heard Kent say behind him. "We've got a job—to kill every cat in that miserable world."

Korita murmured softly: "That should be simple. They are but primitives; and we have merely to sit down, and they will come to us, cunningly expecting to delude us."

Smith snapped: "You fellows make me sick! Pussy was the toughest nut we ever had to crack. He had everything he needed to defeat us—"

Morton smiled as Korita interrupted blandly: "Exactly, my dear Smith, except that he reacted according to the biological impulses of his type. His defeat was already foreshadowed when we unerringly analyzed him as a criminal from a certain era of his civilization.

"It was history, honorable Mr. Smith, our knowledge of history that defeated him," said the Japanese archeologist, reverting to the ancient politeness of his race.

SYMBIOTICA

by

ERIC FRANK RUSSELL

*Assuming that our own universe is as well-traveled as the Atlantic
sea lanes, Mr. Russell sends the good ship Marathon out to the
cluster of planets circling Rigel. This is a story of fascinating detail.
The relationship of the various members of a crew made up of
Terrestrials, Martians and a giant thinking robot; the utterly alien
pattern of life on a planet whose inhabitants have followed the
vegetable, rather than the animal path of evolution—all these are
written with such care and logic that it seems like the log of an
actual voyage rather than a purely speculative piece of fiction.*

*

I

THEY'D COMMISSIONED the *Marathon* to look over one
floating near Rigel, and what some of us would've liked to know was
how the devil our Terrestrial astronomers could pick out likely specimens at such an arithmetical distance. Last trip they'd found us a
juicy job when they sent us to that mechanical world and its watery
neighbor near Bootes. The *Marathon*, a newly designed Flettner job,
was something super. It hadn't a counterpart in our neck of the cosmos. So our solution of the mystery was that the astronomers had got
hold of some instrument just as revolutionary.

Anyway, we'd covered the outward trip as per instructions and were
near enough to see that once again the astronomers had lined them up
for jackpot when they said that here was a planet likely to hold life.
Rigel blazed like a distant furnace way over to starboard and about

thirty degrees above the plane that was horizontal at that moment. What I mean is that the horizontal plane is always the ship's horizontal plane and the cosmos has to relate itself to it whether it likes it or not. But this plane's primary wasn't the far-off Rigel: it was a kid brother sun just a fraction smaller and paler than Old Sol. There were two more planets lying farther out, we'd seen yet another the other side of the sun. That made four in all, but three looked as sterile as a Venusian guppy's mind and only this one, the innermost one, seemed interesting.

We swooped on it bow first. The way that world swelled in the ports did things to my bowels. One trip on the casually meandering *Upsydaisy* had given me my space legs and got me used to living in suspense over umpteen million miles of nothing, but I reckoned it'd take me another century or two to get accustomed to the mad bull take-offs and landings of these Flettner craft. Young Wilson muttered in his harness and I knew that he was following his pious custom of praying for the safety of his precious photographic plates. From his look of spiritual agony you'd have thought he was married to the darned things. We landed, *kerumph!* The boat did a belly slide.

"I wouldn't grieve," I told Wilson. "Those things never fry you a chicken or shove a strawberry shortcake under your drooling mouth."

"No," he admitted, "they don't." Struggling out of his harness, he gave me the sour eye and growled. "How'd you like me to spit in the needlers?"

"I wouldn't," I snapped.

"See?" he said, and forthwith beat it to find out whether his stuff had survived.

Sticking my face to the nearest port, I stared through the immensely strong Permex disk, had a look at the new world. It was green. You'd've never believed any place could be so thoroughly and absolutely green. The sun, which had appeared a primrose color out in space, now looked an extremely pale green. It poured down a flood of yellowy-green light. The *Marathon* lay in a great glade that cut through a mighty forest, and the glade was full of green grasses, herbs, shrubs and bugs. The forest was one mass of tremendous growths that ranged in color from a very light silver-green up to a dark, glossy green that verged on black. Brennand came and stood beside me, his face promptly went a spotty and bilious green as the light hit it. He looked like one of the undead.

"Well, here we are again." He turned his attention from the port, grinned at me, abruptly wiped away the grin. "Hey, don't you be sick over me!"

"It's the light," I pointed out. "You look like something floating in the scuppers of a Moon-tripper."

"Thanks," he said.

"Don't mention it."

We stood there looking out and waiting for the general summons to the conference which usually preceded the first venture out of the ship. I was counting on maintaining my lucky streak by being picked out of the hat, and Brennand was itching to stamp his dogs outside, too. But the summons didn't come.

After a while, Brennand said, "The skipper's slow. What's holding him back?"

"No idea." I had another look at his leprous face. It was awful. Judging by his expression, he wasn't enamored of my features either. "You know what a cautious guy McNulty is. Guess that spree we had on Mechanistria persuaded him to count a hundred before giving an order."

"Yeah," agreed Brennand. "I'll go forward and see what's cooking."

He went along the passage. I couldn't go with him because I had to stand by the armory. You could never tell when they'd come for my stuff, and they had a habit of coming on the run. Brennand mooched disconsolately around the farther corner and had hardly gone when sure enough the exploring party barged in shouting for equipment. There were six of them: Molders, an engineer; Jepson, a navigating officer; Sam Hignett, our Negro surgeon; young Wilson and two Martians, Kli Dreen and Kli Morg.

"Huh, lucky again?" I growled at Sam, tossing him his needle ray and sundry oddments.

"Yes, sergeant." Sam's very white teeth glistened in his black face as he smiled with satisfaction. "The skipper says nobody's to go out afoot until we've first scouted around in No. 4 lifeboat."

Kli Morg got his needler in a long, snaky tentacle, waved the thing with bland disregard for everybody's personal safety, and chirruped, "Give Dreen and me our helmets."

"Helmets?" I looked from him to the Terrestrials. "You guys want spacesuits, too?"

"No," replied Jepson. "The stuff outside is up to fifteen pounds and so rich in oxygen you whizz while you think you're just ambling along."

"Mud," snapped Kli Morg. "Just like mud. Give us our helmets."

He got the helmets. These Martians were so accustomed to the three pounds atmospheric pressure of their native planet that anything heavier bothered them no end. That's why they had the use of the starboard air lock in which pressure was kept down to suit their taste. They could endure heavy pressure for a limited time, but sooner or later they'd wax unsociable and act like somebody had burdened them with all the world's woes.

We Terrestrials helped the pair of Martians to clamp down their goldfish bowls and exhaust the air to what they considered comfortable. If I'd lent a hand with this job once, I'd done it fifty times and it still seemed as wacky as ever. It isn't right that guys should be happy breathing in short whiffs.

Jay Score lumbered lithely into the armory just as I'd got all the clients decorated like Christmas trees. He leaned his three hundred pounds on the tubular barrier, which promptly groaned. He got off it quickly. His strong face was as impassive as ever, his eyes brilliant with their unearthly light.

Shaking the barrer to see if it was wrecked, I told him, "The trouble with you is that you don't know your own strength."

"No?" he inquired, with utter lack of tone. He turned his attention to the others. "The skipper wants you to be extra careful. We can't permit any copy of what happened to Haines and his crew. Don't fly below one thousand feet, keep the autocamera running, keep eyes skinned and beat it back here immediately you find anything worth reporting."

"Sure, Jay." Molders slung a couple of ammo belts over one arm. "We'll be careful."

They trailed out. Shortly, the lifeboat broke free with a squeaky parody of the *Marathon's* deep-throated, sonorous drumming. It curved sharply into the green light, soared over the huge trees and diminished to a dot. Brennand came back, stood by the port, watched the boat vanish.

"McNulty's as leery as an old maid with a penitentiary out back."

"He's got plenty of reason," I pointed out. "He's all the explaining to do when we return."

A smirk passed over his bilious complexion, and he went on, "I took a walk to the noisy end and found that a couple of stern-gang punks have beaten us all to it. They're outside playing duck-on-the-rock."

"Playing what?" I yelped.

"Duck-on-the-rock," he repeated, enjoying himself.

I beat it to stern, Brannand following with a wide grin. Sure enough, two of those dirty mechanics who polish the tail had pulled a fast one. They must have crawled out through a main driver not yet cool. Standing ankle-deep in the green growths, the pair of them were ribbing each other and shying pebbles at a small rock poised on top of a boulder. You'd have thought this was a Sunday-school picnic.

"Does the skipper know about this?"

"You bet he doesn't! Think he'd pick that pair of unshaven bums for first out?"

One of the couple turned, saw us staring at him through the port. He smiled toothily, shouted something we could not hear, jumped nine feet into the air, smacked his chest with a grimy hand. I gathered that the gravity was low, the oxygen high, and that he was feeling top notch. Brennand's face suggested that he was sorely tempted to crawl through a tube and join in the fun.

"McNulty'll skin those hoodlums," I said.

"Can't blame them. The artificial gravity's still on, the ship's full of fog and we've come a long, long way. It'll be great to get out. I could do some sand-castling myself."

"There isn't any sand."

The pair outside became tired of the rock, got themselves a supply of pebbles from somewhere down among the growths, advanced toward a big bush growing fifty yards from the *Marathon's* stern. The farther out they went, the more they were likely to be spotted from the skipper's lair, but they didn't care a hoot. They knew McNulty couldn't do much more than lecture them.

This bush stood between ten and twelve feet high, had a very thick mass of bright green foliage at the top of a thin, willowy trunk. One of the approaching pair got a couple of yards ahead of the other, slung a pebble at the bush, struck it fair and square in the middle of the foliage. What happened then was so swift that we'd the utmost difficulty in following it.

The pebble crashed into the foliage, the entire bush whipped over as if its trunk was a steel spring. A trio of tiny creatures fell out of its leaves, dropped from sight in the herbage below. The bush stood as before, undisturbed except for a minute quivering in its topmost branches. But the guy who'd flung the missile lay flat on his face. His following companion had stopped and was gaping like one petrified by the unexpected.

"Hey," squawked Brennand, "what happened there?"

Outside, the one who'd fallen flat stirred, rolled over, sat up and started picking at himself. The other one got to him, helped him pick. No sound came into the ship, so we couldn't hear what they might have been talking about or the oaths they were certainly using. The picking finished, the smitten one came unsteadily erect. His balance was lousy, and his companion supported him as they started back to the ship. Behind them, the bush stood as imperturbably as ever, even its vague quivers having died out.

Halfway to the *Marathon* the pebble-thrower teetered, went white. Then he licked his lips and keeled over. The other one looked anxiously back toward the bush as if he wouldn't have been surprised to find it charging them. Bending down, he got the body in a fireman's hitch, struggled with it toward the midway air lock. Jay Score met him before he'd heaved his load ten steps. Jay strode powerfully and confidently through the carpet of green, took the limp form from the other's arms, carried it like it was nothing. We raced toward bow to find out what had happened.

Jay brushed past us, carried his burden into our tiny surgery where Wally Simcox, Sam's side-kick, started working on the patient. The other guy hung around outside the door and looked sick. He looked even sicker when Captain McNulty came along and stabbed him with a stare before he went inside.

After half a minute, the skipper shoved out a red, irate face and bellowed, "Go tell Steve to order that boat back at once. He's to warn Sam he's urgently needed."

Pelting to the radio room, I passed the message on. Steve's eyebrows circumnavigated his face as he flicked a switch and cuddled the microphone to his chest. He rattled off the message, listened to the reply.

"They're returning at once."

Going back, I said to the uneasy duck-on-the-rock enthusiast, "What happened, Stupid?"

He flinched. "That bush made a target of him and filled his area with darts. Long, thin ones, like thorns. All over his face and neck and through his clothes. One of 'em made a pinhole in his ear, but they didn't get his eyes."

"Hell!" mouthed Brennand.

"A bunch of them whisked past me on my left, fell twenty feet behind. I heard 'em buzz like bees." He swallowed hard, shuffled his feet around. "It must have flung fifty or more. Guess I was lucky."

McNulty came out then. He looked pretty fierce, and the escapee promptly changed his mind about being lucky. The skipper said to

him, very slowly and deliberately, "I'll deal with you later!" The look
he passed across was enough to scorch the pants off a space cop. We
watched his portly form parade down the passage.

The victim registered bitterness, scrammed to his post at stern.
Next minute, the lifeboat made one complete circle overhead, descended with a thin zoom ending in a heavy swish. Its crew poured
aboard the *Marathon* while the derricks clanked and rattled as they
swung the lifeboat's twelve-ton bulk into the mother ship.

Sam was in the surgery an hour, came out shaking his head. "He's
gone. We could do nothing for him."

"You mean he's—dead?"

"Yes. There's some sort of vegetable poison in those darts. It's
virulent. We've no antidote for it. It seems to create blood clots, a
condition of thrombosi." He rubbed a weary hand over his crisp,
curly hair, added, "I hate having to report this to the skipper."

We followed him toward bow. I stuck my eye to the peephole in
the starboard air lock as I passed and had a look at what the Martians
were doing. Kli Dreen and Kli Morg were playing chess with three
others watching them. As usual, Sug Farn was asleep in one corner.
It takes a Martian to be bored by adventure and to sweat with excitement over a slow-motion game like chess. They always did have an
inverted sense of values.

Kli Dreen kept one saucerlike eye on the board while the other
glanced idly at my face framed in the peephole. His two-way look
gave me the meemies. I've heard that chameleons can swivel them
independently, but no chameleon could do it so violently that the
spectacle tied your own optic nerves in knots. I chased after Brennand
and Sam. There was a strong smell of trouble up that end.

II

The skipper fairly rocketed on getting Sam's report. His voice re-
sounded loud and complainingly through the slightly open door.

"Hardly landed and already there's a casualty in the log . . . utter
foolhardiness . . . more than a silly prank . . . disregard of standing
orders . . . sheer indiscipline." He paused while he took a breath. "The
responsibility is mine. Jay, summon the ship's company."

The general call sounded throughout the ship as Jay Score pressed
the stud. We barged in, the rest following close behind, the Martians
arriving last. Eying us sourly, McNulty strutted up and down, lec-

tured us at some length. We'd been picked as the crew of the *Marathon* because we were believed to be cool, calculating, well-disciplined individuals who'd come of age and had long outgrown such infantile attractions as duck-on-the-rock.

"Not to mention chess," he added, his manner decidedly jaundiced.

Kli Dreen started, looked around to see whether the others heard this piece of incredible blasphemy. Nobody spoke in denial.

"Mind you," continued the skipper, thinking again, "I'm no killjoy, but it is necessary to emphasize that there's a time and place for everything." The Martians rallied. "And so," McNulty went, "I want you always to—"

The ship's phone shrilled and cut him short. He had three phones on his desk, and he gaped at them as if his ears were telling him blatant lies. The ship's company looked each other over to see who was missing. They were all supposed to be there.

McNulty suddenly decided that to answer the phone would be a simple way to solve the mystery. Grabbing up an instrument, he shouted, "Yes?" One of the other phones whirred, proving him a bad picker. He slammed down the one he was holding, took up another, repeated, "Yes?"

The phone made squeaky noises against his ear while his florid features underwent the most peculiar contortions. "Who? What?" he said, incredulously. "What awoke you?" His eyes bugged out. "Somebody knocking at the door?" He planted the phone with the air of a sleepwalker, then spoke weakly to Jay Score. "That was Sug Farn. He complains that he's been disturbed from a siesta by somebody hammering on the turnscrew of the storrad lock." Finding a chair, he flopped into it, breathed asthmatically. His still popping eyes found Steve Gregory, and he snapped, "For Heaven's sake, man, control those eyebrows of yours!"

Steve pushed one up, pulled one down, opened his mouth and tried to look contrite. The result was imbecilic. Jay Score bent over the skipper, conversed with him in smooth undertones. McNulty nodded tiredly. Jay came erect, addressed us.

"All right men, get back to your stations. The Martians had better don their helmets. We'll install a pom-pom in that lock and have the armed lifeboat crew standing ready. Then we'll open the lock."

That was sensible enough. You could see anyone approaching the ship in broad daylight, but you couldn't see them once they'd got close up. The side ports didn't allow a sharp enough angle, besides which anyone standing under the lock would be shielded by the vessel's bulge. Nobody mentioned it, but the skipper had made an error in holding a revival meeting without keeping watch. Unless the hammerers chose to move farther out there was no way of getting a gander at them except by opening. And we weren't going to cook the dinner and make the beds before seeing what was outside, not after that nasty experience when intelligent machines had started to disassemble the ship around us.

Well, the dozy Sug Farn got pushed out of his corner and sent off for his goldfish bowl. We erected the pom-pom, its eighth barrel lined dead center on the closed door of the lock. Something made half a dozen loud clunks on the door as we finished. It sounded to me like a shower of flung stones.

Slowly the door spun along its worm and drew aside. A bright shaft of green light poured through, also a dollop of air that made me feel like a healthy hippopotamus. At the same time, Chief Engineer Douglas switched off the artificial gravity and we all dropped to two thirds normal weight.

We watched the green illuminated opening so intently and anxiously that it was easy to imagine an animated metal coffin suddenly clambering through, its front lenses staring glassily. But there came no whir of hidden machinery, no menacing clank of metal arms and legs, nothing except the sigh of invigorating wind in the distant trees, the rustle of blown grasses and a queer, faraway throbbing that I couldn't identify.

So silent was everyone that Jepson's regular breathing was loud over my shoulder. The pom-pom gunner squatted in his metal seat, his hard eyes focused along the sights, his finger ready on the trigger, his right and left hand feeders ready with reserve belts. All three were busy with wads of gum. Then I heard a soft pad-pad of feet moving in the grass below the lock.

We all knew that McNulty would throw a fit if anyone walked out to the rim. He still nursed memories of the last time somebody did just that and got snatched out. So we stayed put like a gang of dummies, waiting, waiting. Presently, there sounded a querulous gabble beneath the opening. A smooth rock the size of a melon flew through the gap, missed Jepson by a few inches, shattered against the back wall.

Skipper or no skipper, I got fed up, hefted my needler in my right hand, prowled half-bent along the footwalk cut through the threads of the air-lock opening. I reached the rim which was about nine feet above ground level, shoved out my inquiring face. Molders pressed close behind me. The muffled throbbing was clearer than ever, but just as elusive.

Beneath me stood a band of six beings who were startlingly human in general appearance. Same bodily contours, same limbs and digits, same features. They differed from us mostly in that their skins were coarse and crinkly, a dull, dead green in color, and that they had a peculiar organ like the head of a green and fleshy chrysanthemum growing out of their chests. Their eyes were sharp and jet-black, they jerked them about with monkeylike alertness.

For all these differences our similarity was so surprising that I stood staring at them while they stood staring back at me. Then one of them shrilled something in the singsong tones of an agitated Chinese, swung his right arm, did his best to bash out what I use for brains. I ducked, heard the missile swish over my hair. Molders also ducked it, involuntarily pushed against me. The thing crashed somewhere inside the lock, I heard someone spit a lurid oath just as I overbalanced and fell out.

Clinging grimly to the needle ray, I flopped into soft greenery, rolled like mad and bounced to my feet. At any instant, I expected to see a shower of meteors as I got slugged. But the six weren't there. They were fifty yards away and moving fast, making for the forest in long, agile leaps that would have shamed a hungry kangaroo. It would have been easy to have brought two or three of them down, but McNulty would have crucified me for that. Earth laws were strict about treatment of extramundane aborigines.

Molders dropped down beside me, followed by Jepson, Wilson and Kli Yang. Wilson had his owl-eye camera with a color filter over the lens. He was wild with excitement.

"I got them from the fourth port. I made two shots as they scrammed."

"Humph!" Molders stared around. He was a big, burly, phlegmatic man who looked more like a Scandinavian brewer than a space bug. "Let's follow them to the edge of the forest."

"Yeah," agreed Jepson, heartily. He wouldn't have been so hearty if he'd known what was coming to him. Stamping his feet in the springy turf, he took a lungful of the oxygen-rich air. "This is our chance for a legitimate walk."

We started off without delay, knowing it wouldn't be long before the skipper began baying for us to come back. There was no man so hard to convince that risks have to be taken and that casualties are the price of knowledge, nor was there any man who went so far determined to do so little.

Reaching the verge of the forest, the six green ones stopped and watched our approach. If they were quick to beat it when caught out in the open, they weren't so quick when in the shadow of the trees which, for some unknown reason, inspired them with confidence. Turning his back to us, one of them doubled himself, peered at us from between his knees. It seemed senseless.

"What's that for?" growled Jepson.

Wilson sniggered dirtily, and said, "The Arab's farewell to his steed. It must be of cosmic significance."

"I could have scalded his seat if I'd been quick," remarked Jepson, aggrievedly. Then he put his foot in a hole and fell on his face.

The green ones set up a howl of glee, flung a volley of stones which all fell far short. We began to run, going along in great bounds. The low gravity wasn't spoiled by the thick blanket of air which, of course, pressed equally in all directions. Our weight was down so that we went along several laps ahead of Olympic champions. Five of the green ones promptly faded into the forest; the sixth shot like a squirrel up the trunk of the nearest tree. Their behavior told that they'd reason for regarding the trees as safe refuge against all assault.

We stopped about eighty yards from that tree which, for all we knew, might have been ready for us with a monster load of darts. Our minds recalled what one bush had done. Scattering in a thin line, each ready to flop at the first untoward motion, we edged cautiously toward it. Nothing happened. We went nearer. Still nothing happened. In this manner we got well beneath its branches and close to its trunk. There was a strange fragrance like that of a mixture of pineapple and cinnamon. The elusive throbbing was stronger than ever.

It was a big, imposing tree. Its dark green, fibrous trunk, seven feet in diameter, soared up to twenty-five feet before it split into strong, lengthy branches each of which terminated in one huge, spatulate leaf. Looking at that trunk, it was difficult to tell how our quarry had fled up it, but he'd performed the feat like an adept.

All the same, we couldn't see him. Carefully, we went around the tree, gazing up into its great branches through which the green light filtered in large mosaic patterns. There was not a sign of him. No doubt about it, he was somewhere up there, but he simply couldn't be spotted by us. There wasn't any way in which he could have passed from this tree to its nearest neighbor, neither could he have come down. Our view up this lump of alien timber was fairly good considering the peculiar light, but the more we stared the more invisible he remained.

"That's a puzzler!" Jepson stepped well away from the trunk, seeking a better angle of view.

With a mighty *swoosh* a branch above his head drove down. Its spatulate leaf smacked him squarely in the back and a waft of pineapple and cinnamon went all over the place. Just as swiftly, the branch went up, carrying Jepson high into the air. Swearing like a tail mechanic, he struggled furiously while we gathered below him. He was stuck to the underside of that great leaf, gradually became covered in thick, yellowy-green goo as he writhed. The stuff must have been fifty times stickier than birdlime.

Together we roared at him to keep still before he got the deadly junk spread all over his face. Already his clothes were covered with it, his left arm tied up in it. He looked a mess. It was obvious that once he smeared it over his mouth and nostrils he'd stick up there and quietly suffocate.

Molders had a try at getting up the trunk, found it impossible. He edged out to have a look upward, came in when he noticed another leaf in a strategic position. The safest place was beneath the unfortunate Jepson. A little over twenty feet up, the goo was slowly spreading over its victim and I reckoned that in half an hour he'd be completely covered—in much less if he wriggled around. All this time the dull pulsations continued as if ticking off the last moments of the doomed. They made me think of jungle drums heard through thick walls.

Gesturing to the golden cylinder which was the *Marathon* lying five hundred yards away in the glade, Wilson said, "Let's beat it back and get ropes and steel dogs. We'll soon bring him down."

"No," I answered. "We'll get him down a darned sight faster than that." Whereupon I aimed my needle ray at the point where Jepson's leaf joined the branch. The beam lanced forth at full strength.

The leaf dropped off and the tree went mad. Jepson fell into soft, springy undergrowth, the leaf still firmly fastened to his back. He landed with a wild yelp and a flood of curses. While we all lay flat, frantically trying to bury ourselves deeper, the tree thrashed around, its gum-laded spatulates hungry for vengeance.

One persistent branch kept beating within a yard of my head as I tried to shove said top-piece below ground. I hated the stink of pine-apple and cinnamon that permeated the air. And it made me sweat to think how my lungs would strain, my eyes pop and my heart burst if I got a dollop of that junk slap in the face. I'd sooner've been neatly needled.

The tree ended its wild larruping, stood like a dreaming giant liable to wake into frenzy at any moment. Crawling to Jepson, we dragged him out of reach. He couldn't walk, his jackboots and the legs of his pants being firmly stuck together. His left arm was just as securely gummed to his side. He was in an awful pickle, cursed steadily and without pause for breath or thought. We'd never suspected him of such fluency. But we got him into the safety of the glade, and it was there I thought up a few words he'd overlooked.

III

Molders stolidly said nothing, contenting himself with listening to Jepson and me. Molders had helped me do the dragging and now neither of us could let go. We were fixed to the original victim, bonded like brothers but not talking like brothers. There was nothing to do but carry Jepson bodily with our hands remaining on the most inconvenient parts of his anatomy. He had to go horizontally and face downward, as if he was a drunk getting frog-marched to barracks. He was still adorned with the leaf. He was still reciting.

The task wasn't lightened by that young fool Wilson who thought there was something funny in other people's misfortunes. He followed us, snapping his accursed camera which I could have stuffed down his gullet with the greatest of pleasure. He was too happy about the fact that there wasn't any goo on him.

Jay Score, Brennand, Armstrong, Petersen and Drake met us as we lumbered awkwardly, across the sward. They looked curiously at Jepson, listened to him with much respect. We warned them not to touch. The pair of us weren't feeling too sprightly by the time we reached the *Marathon*. Jepson's weight was only two thirds normal, but after five hundred yards he seemed like the last remains of a glutinous mammoth.

We dumped him on the grass below the open lock, perforce sitting with him. The faint booming sound was still coming out of the forest. Jay went inside the ship, brought out Sam and Wally to see what they could do about the super-adhesive. The stuff was stiffening, growing gradually harder. My hands and fingers felt as if they'd been set into glassite gloves.

Sam and Wally tried cold water, lukewarm water and hot water, but none of it did any good. Chief Engineer Douglas obliged them with a bottle of rocket fuel. That didn't work either. They had a go with some special gasoline which Steve Gregory kept for the crew's cigarette lighters. They wasted their time. That gasoline could play hell with rubber, but it couldn't dissolve this stuff.

"Stick it, fellers!" advised Wilson, cackling loudly. Jepson made sulphuric mention of this idiot's parents. I enlarged upon his grandparents. Jepson turned to the subject of his nonexistent progeny. Molders looked stolid, said nothing. "You sure are in a fix," went on Wilson. "By gum!"

Then Sam came out with some iodine. It didn't work, but it did make a terrible stink. Molders permitted his face to look slightly pained. Some nitric acid caused bubbles on the surface of the semi-hard goo, but did no more than that. It was risky stuff to use, anyway. Frowning, Sam went back to look for something else, passed Jay Score coming out to see how we were doing. Jay stumbled as he got near, a strange thing for him to do considering his superhuman sense of balance. His solid three hundred pounds nudged young Wilson between the shoulder blades and that grinning ape promptly flopped against Jepson's legs. Wilson struggled and changed his tune, but stayed stuck. Jepson gave him the sardonic ha-ha, and the other didn't enjoy it a bit.

Picking up the dropped camera, Jay dangled it in one powerful hand, said contritely, "I never missed a step before. It is most unfortunate."

"Unfortunate, hell!" yelled Wilson.

Sam came out with a big glass jar, dribbled its contents over my gooey hands. The ghastly green covering at once thinned into a weak slime and my hands came free.

"Ammonia," remarked Sam. He needn't have mentioned it—I could smell the pungent stuff. It was a good solvent, and he soon had us cleaned up.

Then I chased Wilson three times around the ship. He was too fast for me. We were just about to go aboard to tell our tale to the skipper when that tree started threshing again. You could see its deadly branches beating the air and hear the violent *swoosh* of them even at that distance. Pausing beneath the lock, we watched the spectacle wonderingly. Suddenly, Jay Score spoke, his voice metallic, harsh.

"Where's Kli Yang?"

None of us knew. Now I came to think about it, I couldn't recall him being with us while we dragged Jepson home. The last I remembered of him was when he stood beside me under that tree and his saucer eyes gave me the creeps by carefully scanning two opposite branches at once. Armstrong shot into the ship, came out with the report that Kli Yang definitely wasn't there. His own eyes as saucer-like as the missing Martian's, Wilson said that he didn't remember Kli Yang coming out of the forest. Upon which we snatched up our needlers and made for that tree at the run. All the while, the tree continued to larrup around like a crazy thing tied down by its own roots.

Reaching the monstrous growth, we made a circle just beyond the sweep of its treacherous leaves, had a look to see where the Martian was wrapped in glue. He wasn't wrapped in glue. We found him forty feet up the trunk, five of his powerful tentacles clamped around its girth, the other five embracing the green native we'd pursued. His captive was struggling wildly and futilely, all the time yelling a high-pitched stream of gibberish.

Carefully, Kli Yang edged down the trunk. The way he looked and moved made him resemble an impossible cross between a college professor and an educated octopus. His eyes rolling with terror, the native battered at Kli's glassite helmet. Kli blandly ignored the hostility, reached the branch that had caught Jepson, didn't descend any farther. Still grasping the furiously objecting green one, he crept along the whipping limb until he reached its leafless end. At that point, he and the native were being waved up and down in twenty-five feet sweeps.

Timing himself, he cast off at the lowermost point of one beat, scuttled from reach before another eager branch could swat him. There was a singing howl from the nearer parts of the forest and something that looked like a blue-green coconut shot out of the shadows and broke at Drake's feet. The thing was as thin and brittle as an empty eggshell, had a white inner surface, and contained nothing. Kli Yang took no notice of the howls or the missile, bore his still struggling captive toward the Marathon.

Hanging back, Drake peered curiously at the coconut or whatever it was, struck the fragments of shell with his boot. He caught the full benefit of something invisible that was floating up from it, sucked in his cheeks, screwed up his eyes and backed away. Then he retched. He did it so violently that he fell over as he ran. We'd the sense to pick him up and rush him after Kli without getting too nosy about what had bitten him. He continued to regurgitate all the way across the grass, recovered just as we came under the ship's bulging side.

"Holy smoke!" he wheezed, "what a stench! It'd make a skunk smell like the rose of the animal world." He wiped his lips. "My stomach turned right over."

Looking up Kli, we found that his captive had been conducted to the galley for a peace-making feed. Kli dragged off his helmet, said, "That tree wasn't so difficult for me to mount. It walloped around as I went up, but it couldn't get at anything on its own trunk." He sniffed, rubbed his flat, Red Planet face with the flexible tip of a great tentacle. "Don't know how you bipeds can swallow this soup which you're pleased to regard as air."

"Where'd you find the greenie, Kli?" asked Brennand.

"He was stuck to the trunk more than forty feet up. His whole front fitted neatly into an indentation shaped like himself, and his back matched the trunk so perfectly that I couldn't see him until he moved uneasily as I got near him." He picked up the helmet. "It was a most wonderful sample of camouflage." He looked at the helmet with one eye, kept the other on the interested Brennand, made a gesture of disgust. "How about pulling down the pressure some place where higher forms of life can live in peace?"

"We'll pump out the port lock," Brennand promised. "And don't be so all-fired snooty, you caricature of a rubber spider."

"Bah!" said Kli, with great dignity. "Who invented chess? And who can't even play duck-on-the-rock without grabbing the grief?" With that insulting reference to Terrestrial inexpertness at chess, he slapped on his glassite dome. I pumped it down for him. "Thanks!" he said, through the diaghragm.

Now to get the low-down on the greenie.

Captain McNulty himself interviewed the native. The skipper sat grandly behind his metal desk, eyed the jittery captive with a mixture of pomposity and kindliness. The native stood before him, his black optics jerking around fearfully. At that close range you could see he was wearing a loincloth that matched his own skin. His back was several shades darker than his front, coarser, more fibrous, with little nodules here and there—perfect simulation of the surface of the trunk of the tree in which he'd sought refuge. Even his loincloth was darker at the back than at the front. His feet were broad and bare; the toes double-jointed and as long as the fingers of his hands. Except for the loincloth, he was completely naked and had no weapons. The queer chrysanthemum growing out of his chest attracted all eyes.

"Has he been given a meal?" asked the skipper, full of solicitude.

"He was offered one," Jay told him. "He refused it. As far as I can make out, he wants to go back to his tree."

"Hm-m-m," grunted McNulty. "In due time, in due time." He assumed the expression of a benevolent uncle, said to the native, "What's your name?"

The green one grasped the note of interrogation, waved his arms, broke into an untranslatable tirade. On and on he went, helping his gabble with many emphatic but incomprehensible gestures. His language was very liquid, his voice singsong.

"I see," murmured McNulty as the flood of talk petered out. He blinked at Jay Score. "Think this fellow is telepathic, like those lobster things were?"

"It is much to be doubted. I'd put him at the level of a Congo pygmy—maybe lower. He doesn't even possess a simple spear, let alone bow and arrow or a blowpipe."

"Yes, that's how he looks to me." Still maintaining his soothingly paternal air, McNulty went on, "All right, Jay. There's no common basis on which we can gain his understanding at the start, so I guess we'll have to create one. We'll dig up a natural linguist, set him to learing the rudiments of this fellow's language and teaching him some of ours."

"I've got the advantage of a mechanical memory—let me have a try," suggested Jay. He approached the green native, his huge, well-proportioned body moving quietly on the sponge rubber cushions of his dogs. The native didn't like his size or his bearing, neither did he approve of those brightly lit eyes. He backed away from Jay, backed right to the wall, his optics darting hither and thither.

Jay stopped as he saw the other's fear, slapped his own top-piece with a hand that could have knocked mine clean off my neck. He said, "Head." He did it half a dozen times, repeating, "Head, head." The green one wasn't so stupid; he caught on, faltered, "Mah."

Touching his own head again, Jay said, inquiringly, "Mah?"

"Bya!" lilted the other, starting to recover his composure.

"See, it's dead easy," approved McNulty. "*Mah*—head; *bya*—yes."

"Not necessarily," Jay contradicted. "It all depends upon how his mind translated my action. *Mah* might mean head, face, man, hair, god, mind, thought, or alien, or even the color black. If he's thinking of my hair and his own, then *mah* probably does mean black, while *bya* may mean not yes, but green."

"Oh, I hadn't thought of that." The skipper looked crushed.

"We'll have to carry on with this performance until we've picked up enough words to form lame sentences. Then we can deduce further meanings from the context. Give me a few days."

"Go ahead. Do your best, Jay. We can't expect to be able to talk turkey in the first five minutes. It isn't reasonable."

Taking our prisoner to the rest room, Jay summoned Minshull and Petersen. He thought three might just as well learn something as one. Minshull and Petersen were both hot on languages, speaking Esperanto, Ido, Venusian, low Martian and high Martian. They were the only ones aboard the ship who could give our chess maniacs a boiling in their own lingo.

I found Sam in the armory, waiting to hand in the stuff he'd taken out, and I said to him, "What did you see from the lifeboat, Sam?"

"Not so much. We weren't out long enough. Didn't get more than a hundred and twenty miles away. There was forest, nothing but forest with glades here and there. A couple of glades were the size of counties. The biggest of them lay at the end of a long lake. There were several rivers and streams."

"Any signs of life?"

"None." He gestured down the passage toward the rest room where Jay and the others were cross-examining the native. "It seems there's superior life in the forest, but you can detect no signs of it from above. Wilson's processing his reel—I doubt whether his camera caught anything that we missed."

"Ah, well," I said, "one twenty miles in one direction is nothing from which to estimate a world. I don't let myself be deluded, not since that drummer sold me a can of striped paint."

He chuckled. "Didn't it come out?"

"I laid it wrong side up," I told him.

It was right in the middle of that bantering that a powerful idea smote me. I followed him out of the armory, made a rush to the radio room. Steve Gregory was sitting by his instruments trying to look busy doing nothing. I was all set to wake him with my brain wave,

IV

As Steve looked up inquiringly, I said to him, "Hey, how about combing the bands?"

"Uh?"

"Remember those weird whistles and waterfalls you picked up on Mechanistria? Well, if anyone's radiating here, couldn't you detect 'em?"

"Sure." He kept his bushy eyebrows still for once, but spoiled it by waggling his ears. "If anyone was radiating."

"Go ahead and find out. It'll tell us something. What're you waiting for?"

"Have you kept those needlers cleaned and charged?" he asked.

I stared at him. "You bet I have! They're always ready for action. That's my job."

"And this one's mine," he said, dryly. He waved the ears again. "You're hours behind the times. I searched the ether immediately we landed, got nothing but a faint hiss on twelve point three meters. It was Rigel's characteristic discharge and came from that way. D'you think I'm that snake-armed snorer Sug Farn?"

"No, I don't. Sorry, Steve—it just struck me as a bright idea."

"Oh, it's O. K., sergeant," he said, amiably. "Every man to his job and every tail mechanic to his dirt." Idly he twiddled the shining dials of his slow-motion selectors.

The loud-speaker coughed as if it was clearing its throat, then announced in sharp tones, "*Pip-pip-whop! Pip-pip-whop!*"

Nothing could have been better calculated to upset the determined serenity of his brows. I'll swear that after they'd entered his hair they continued over the top, down the back and lodged under his collar.

"Morse," he said, in the complaining tone of a hurt child.

"I always thought Morse was a code, not a mode," I remarked. "Anyway, if it is Morse, you'll be able to translate it." I paused as the loud-speaker shouted me down with, "*Pip-pipper-pee-eep-whop!*" then I concluded, "Every cat to his ash can."

" 'Tain't Morse," he contradicted himself. "But it's spark signals." He might have frowned if it hadn't taken too long to drag the brows back. Giving me one of those tragic looks you get sometimes, he snatched a pad, started recording the impulses.

The spacesuits, pom-pom chargers and other things had to be

done, so I left him, returned to the armory, got on with my work. He was still fiddling around when darkness fell. So were Jay and his gang, but not for long.

The sun sunk, its long, greenish streamers faded from the sky and a velvet pall covered the forest and the glade. I ambled along the passage toward the gallery and was passing the rest room when its door jerked open and the green native burst out. His face was desperate, his legs going as if there was a thousand international smackers tied to the tape. Minshull yelped somewhere back of him as he jumped full tilt into my ready arms. The greenie squirmed like an eel, beat at my face, tried to kick my legs off my torso with his bare feet. His rough, harsh body exuded a weak odor of pineapple and cinnamon.

The others pounced out, got him tight, talked to him in halting words until he relaxed. His eyes shifty, anxious, he jabbered excitedly to Jay Score, making urgent gestures and waving his woody arms around in a way that reminded me of branches beating the air. Jay soothed him with fair if faltering speech. It looked like they'd picked up enough words to get along, though not enough to understand each other perfectly. Still, they were managing.

Eventually, Jay said to Petersen, "Tell the skipper I want to let Kala go."

Petersen cleared off, came back in a minute. "He says do whatever you think is best."

"Good." Conducting the native to the opening of the starboard lock, Jay yapped to him briefly, let him go. The greenie dived off the rim. Someone in the forest must have owed him for a loincloth because his feet made rapid brushing sounds as he fled across the turf. Jay stood on the rim, his flaming orbs staring into outer gloom.

"Why let him go, Jay?"

Turning, he said to me, "I've tried to persuade him to come back at sunup. He may, or he may not—it remains to be seen. We didn't have time to get much out of him, but his language is exceedingly simple and we picked up enough of it to learn that he calls himself Kala of the tribe of Ka. All members of his tribe are named Ka-something, such as Kalee, Ka'noo, or Kaheer."

"Something like the Martians with their Klis and Leids and Sugs," I remarked.

"Something," he agreed, not caring what the Martians might think of being compared with the green aborigines. "He also told us that every man has his tree, every gnat its lichen. I can't understand what he means by that, but he satisfied me that his life depended upon his being with his tree during darkness. It was imperative. I tried to delay him, but his need was almost pitiful. He was willing to die rather than be away from his tree."

"Sounds silly to me." I blew my nose, grinned widely. "It sounds even sillier to Jepson."

Jay stared again into the deep murkiness from which came strange, nocturnal scents and those everlasting pulsations. Quietly, he said, "I also learned that there are others in the dark, others mightier than the Ka. They have much *gamish*."

"They have what?"

"Much *gamish*," he repeated. "That word defeated me. He used it again and again. He said that the *Marathon* had much *gamish*, I had much *gamish* and that Kli Yang had very much *gamish*. Captain McNulty, it appeared, had only a little. The Ka have none at all."

"Was it something of which he was afraid?"

"Not exactly. As far as I could make out, anything unusual or surprising or unique is chock-full of *gamish*. Anything just abnormal has a lesser amount of *gamish*. Anything ordinary has none at all."

"This," I said, "goes to show the difficulties of communication. It isn't as easy as the people back home think it ought to be."

"No, it isn't." His gleaming optics shifted toward Armstrong leaning against the pom-pom. "You doing this guard?"

"Until twelve. Kelly follows me."

Picking Kelly for guard was poor psychology. That tattooed specimen was welded to a three-foot spanner and in any hot moment was liable to wield said instrument in preference to such new-fangled articles as pom-poms and needlers. Rumor had it that he'd held the lump of iron at his wedding and that his wife had gained a divorce on account of the thing's effect on her morale. My private opinion was that Kelly had a Neanderthal mind.

"We'll shut the lock," decided Jay, "fresh air or no fresh air." That was characteristic of him, and what made him seem so human— he could mention fresh air as if he used it himself. The casual way he did it made you forget that he'd never taken a breath since the day old Knud Johanssen stood him on his dogs. "Let's plug in the turnscrew." Turning his back upon the throbbing gloom, he started to walk into the lighted lock, treading carefully in the cutout of the threads.

A piping voice sprang from the darkness; it ejaculated, "*Nou baiders!*"

Jay stopped dead. His eyes were glowing. Feet padded outside just underneath the lock. Something spherical and glassy soared through the worm, went over Jay's left shoulder, broke to shards on the top recoil chamber of the pom-pom. A thin, golden liquid splashed around, vaporized instantly.

Reversing, Jay faced the black opening. Armstrong got to the wall, put out a thumb to jab the general alarm stud. Without touching the stud, Armstrong went down as if batted by an invisible club. My needler out, its muzzle extended, I began to move cautiously forward, saw the glittering thread of the worm framing a picture of Jay standing against the ebony background. It was a hell of a mistake— I should have gone for that stud. Three steps, and the whole picture swelled like a blown bubble, the circle widened, the threads of the worm became broad and deep with Jay as a gigantic shape in the middle. The bubble burst and I went down as soggily as Armstrong had done.

Don't know how long I stayed that way, for when I opened my eyes it was with the faint memory of hearing much shouting and stamping of feet around my prostrate form. Things must have happened over and all around me while I lay like a corpse. Now I was still flat. I reposed full length on deep, dew-soaked turf with the throbbing forest close on my left, the indifferent stars peering at me from the vault of night. I was bound up like an Egyptian mummy. Jepson was another mummy at one side of me; Armstrong and several more at the other.

Several hundreds of yards away, noises were still spoiling the silence of the night, a mixture of occasional Terrestrial oaths and many queer, alien pipings. The *Marathon* lay over there; all that could be seen of her in the general blackness was the funnel of light pouring from her open lock. The light flickered, waxed and waned, once or twice was momentarily obliterated. There was a struggle on that shaft of light which became blocked as the fight swayed to and fro.

Jepson was snoring as if it was Saturday night in the old home town, but Armstrong was in full possession of his wits and tongue. He cursed luridly. Rolling over, he started to chew at the knots of Blaine's bindings. Something vaguely human emerged silently from the darkness, smote downward. Armstrong went quiet.

Blinking my eyes, I adapted them enough to make out many more noiseless shapes standing around us. Keeping still and behaving myself, I thought noncomplimentary thoughts about McNulty, the *Marathon*, old Flettner who'd invented the ship and all the public-spirited guys who backed him morally and financially. I'd always had the feeling that sooner or later they would be the death of me.

Deep down inside me, a tiny voice said, "Sergeant, d'you remember that promise you made your mother about obscene language? D'you remember when you gave that guppy a can of condensed milk for a pinfire opal not as big as the city clock? Repent, sergeant, while there yet is time!"

The distant pipings arose crescendo, the few earthly voices died out. There sounded occasional smashings of light, brittle things. More shapes brought more bodies, dumped them beside us, melted back into the gloom. I wish I could have counted the catch, but darkness didn't permit it. All the newcomers were unconscious. They revived rapidly. I could recognize Brennand's angry voice and the skipper's asthmatic breathing.

A blue star shone through the thin fringe of a drifting cloud as the fight ended. The succeeding pause was ghastly; a solemn, brooding silence broken only by the scuffle of many feet through the grass and the steady pumping in the forest.

Forms gathered around us in large number. The glade was full of them. Hands lifted me, felt my bonds, tossed me into a wicker hammock. I went up shoulder-high, was borne along. You'd have thought I was a defunct wart hog being toted in some sportsman's line of native porters. Just meat—that was me. Just a trophy of the chase. I wondered whether God would confront me with that guppy.

The caravan filed into the forest, my direction of progress being head first. Another hammock followed my feet and I could sense rather than see a string of them farther behind. Jepson was the sardine following me; he went along making a loud recitation about how he'd got tied up ever since he landed in this unprintable world. Curving warily around one dim tree, our line marched boldly under the next, dodged the third. How the deuce our bearers could tell one growth from another in this lousy light was beyond my comprehension.

We'd just got deep into the deeper darkness when a tremendous explosion sounded way back in the glade and a column of fire lit up the whole sky. Even the fire looked faintly green. Our line stopped. Two or three hundred voices cheeped querulously, running from the front past me to a hundred yards farther back. "They've blown up the good old *Marathon*," thought I. "Ah, well, all things come to an end, including the flimsiest hope of returning home."

The squeakers were drowned out as the noisy pillar of flame built itself up to a roar. My hammock started to jump as its bearers re-acted. The way they put on the pace had to be experienced to be believed; I almost flew along, dodging this tree, but not that, some-times avoiding half-seen growths that weren't trees at all. My heart was in my boots.

The bellowing back in the glade suddenly ended in a mighty thump, and crimson spear flung itself into the sky and stabbed the clouds. It was a spectacle I'd seen before: it was a spaceship going up. It was the *Marathon!*

Were these creatures so talented that they could pick up a thor-oughly strange vessel and take it whever they wanted it? Were these the beings described as superior to the Ka? The whole thing was incongruous—expert astronauts carrying their prisoners in wicker ham-mocks. Besides, the way they'd jabbered and put on the pace sug-gested that the *Marathon's* spurt of life had taken them by surprise. The mystery was one I couldn't solve.

While the fiery trail of the spaceship arced northward, our party pressed hurriedly on. There was one stop during which our captors congregated together, but their continual piping suggested that they hadn't stopped for a meal. Twenty minutes afterward there was an-other halt and a hell of a row in front. Guards kept close to us while a short distance ahead sounded a vocal uproar in which many voices vied with a loud mewing and much beating of great branches. I tried to imagine a bright green tiger.

Things went *phut-phut* and the mewing ended in a choking cough. The sound of whipping branches died away. We moved on, making a wide curve around a monstrous growth that I strained in vain to see. If only this world had possessed a moon. But there was no moon. There were only the stars and the clouds and the forest from which came that all-pervading beat.

Dawn broke as the line warily bent away from a small clump of apparently innocent briers. We came to the bank of a wide river. Here, we could give our guards the once-over as they shepherded bearers and burdens down the bank. They were creatures very much like the Ka, only taller, more slender, with big, intelligent eyes. They had the same fibrous skins, grayer, not so green, and the same chrys-anthemums on their chests. Unlike the Ka, their middles were clothed in pleated garments, they had harness of woven fiber, and wooden accouterments which included things like complicated blow-guns and bowl-shaped vessels having a bulbous container in the base. A few also bore panniers holding small spheres like the one that had laid me flat in the air lock.

Craning my head, I tried to see more, but could only discern Jepson in the next hammock and Brennand in the one behind that. The next instant, my hammock was unceremoniously dumped by the water's brink, Jepson's beside mine, the rest in a level row.

Jepson screwed round his head, looked at me, and said, "The punks!"

"Take it easy," I suggested. "If we play with them, they may give us more rope."

"And," he said, viciously, "I don't like guys who try to be funny at the wrong time."

"I wasn't trying to be funny," I snapped. "We're all bound to hold our own opinions, aren't we?"

"There you go again!" He writhed around on his hammock, tried to stretch his fastenings. "Some day I'll bind you!"

It's no use talking with a guy like that, so I didn't answer. The light waxed stronger, shone greenly through the thin, green mist hanging over the green river. I could now see Blaine and Minshull tied up beyond Armstrong, and the portly form of McNulty beyond them. We'd traveled about two hours.

Ten of our captors went along the line opening jackets and shirts, baring our chests. They had with them a supply of the bowls with bulbous containers. Two of them pawed my uniform apart, got my chest exposed, stared at it like Anthony stared at Cleopatra. Something about it struck them as wonderful, and it wasn't my reserve beard. It didn't require much brains to tell that they missed my chrysanthemum and couldn't see how I'd got through life without it. They called their fellows, the whole gang debated the subject while I lay like a sacrificial virgin. Then they decided that they'd struck a new line of research and went hot along the trail.

Seizing Blaine and the boob who'd played duck-on-the-rock, they untied them, stripped them down to the raw, examined them as if they were prize cattle at an agricultural exhibition. One of them prodded Blaine in the solar plexus, whereat he jumped the fellow with a savage whoop and brought him down. The other nudist joined in. Armstrong, who never had been a ninety-pound weakling, promptly burst his bonds, came up dark-faced with the effort and roared into the fray. Fragments of his mangled hammock swung and bounced on his beefy back.

All along the line the rest of us made mighty efforts to break free,

but in vain. Green ones centered on the scene of the struggle, brittle
spheres plopped all around the three madly fighting Earthmen. The
tail mechanic and Blaine collapsed together, going down as if in a
sleep. Armstrong shuddered and roared, teetered and pulled himself
to, held out long enough to toss two natives into the river and slug
the daylights out of a third. Then he, too, dropped.

V

The green ones dragged their fellows from the river, dressed the
slumber-wrapped Blaine and the other, added Armstrong, tied all
three securely. Once more they conferred together. I couldn't make
head or tail of their canary talk, but I got the notion that, in their
opinion, we had an uncertain quantity of *gamish*.

My bonds began to irk. I'd have given much for the chance to go
into action and bash a few green heads. Twisting myself, I used a
lackluster eye to survey a tiny shrub growing near the side of the hammock. The shrub jiggled its midget branches and emitted a smell of
burned caramel. Local vegetation was all movement and stinks.

Abruptly, the green ones ended their talk, crowded down to the
bank of the river. A flotilla of long, narrow, shapely vessels swept
around the bend, foamed under projecting branches of great trees,
cut in to the bank. We were carted aboard, five prisoners to the
boat. Thrusting away from the bank, our crew of twenty pulled and
pushed rhythmically at a row of ten wooden levers on each side of
the boat, drove the vessel upstream. We went along at a fair pace,
left a shallow wake on the surface of the sluggish river.

"I had a grandfather who was a missionary," I told Jepson. "He got
himself in trouble like this."

"So what?"

"He went to pot," I said.

"So can you," snapped Jepson. He strained futilely at his bonds.

For lack of anything better to do, I watched the way in which our
crew handled our vessel, came to the conclusion that the levers worked
two large pumps or a battery of small ones, and that the vessel got
along by sucking in water at the bow and blowing it out at the stern.
Later, I found I was wrong. Their method was much simpler than
that. The levers connected with twenty split-bladed paddles jutting
horizontally a foot or two below the water line. The two flaps of the
blades closed together as each paddle drove forward, opened as it

swept backward. By this means they got along a good deal faster than they could have done with oars since the subsurface paddles only moved forward and back with their weight on the boat—they didn't have to be raised, turned and dipped by the muscles of the rowers.

The sun climbed higher as we progressed steadily upriver. On the second bend, the river split, its current moving more rapidly either side of a rocky islet about a hundred yards long. A group of four huge trees stood at the upstream end of the islet, their trunks and limbs a somber green that verged on black. Each of them had one horizontal spray of branches above which the trunk continued to a feathery crest forty feet higher. Every branch ended in half a dozen powerful twigs which curved downward like the fingers of a clutching hand.

Their crews speeding up the levers, the string of boats took the right-hand channel over which reached the largest of those great branches. As the first boat's prow came underneath, the branch twitched its fingers hungrily. It was no illusion; I saw it as clearly as I can see my trip bonus when they slide it toward me across the mahogany. That limb was getting all set to grab, and from its size and spread I reckoned it could pluck the entire boatload out of the water and do things of which I didn't care to think.

But it didn't do it. Just as that boat entered the danger area its helmsman stood up, bawled a string of gibberish at the tree. The fingers relaxed. The helmsman of the next boat did the same. And the next. Then mine. Flat on my back, as ready for action as a corpse, I gaped at that enormous neck-wringer while all too slowly it came on, passed above and fell behind. Our helmsman went silent; the one in the following boat took up the tale. There was dampness on my spine.

Five miles farther on, we made for the shore. My head was toward that side. I didn't get a view of the buildings until the greenies contemptuously tossed out my hammock, released me from the thing, stood me on my feet. I promptly lost balance and sat down. Temporarily, my dogs were dead. Rubbing them to restore the circulation, my curious eyes examined this dump that might have been anything from a one-horse hamlet to a veritable metropolis.

The buildings were made of light green wood, all cylindrical, of uniform height and diameter, and each had a big tree growing through its middle. The foliage of each tree extended farther then the radius of each house, thus effectively hiding it from overhead view.

Nothing could have been better calculated to conceal the place from the air, though there wasn't any reason to suppose that the inhabitants feared any menace from above.

Still, the way in which trees and buildings shared the same sites made it quite impossible to estimate the size of the place, for beyond the nearer screen of buildings were trees, trees and more trees, each of which may have shielded a house. I couldn't tell whether I was looking at a kraal or at the riverside suburb of some place running right over the horizon. It was little wonder that the exploring lifeboat had observed nothing but forest. Its crew could have scouted over an area holding a population of many millions and have thought it nothing but jungle.

Their weapons ready, their eyes alert, a horde of the green ones clustered around us while some of them finished the task of releasing the prisoners. The fact that we'd arrived in a thing like the *Marathon* didn't awe them one little bit. My feet were obedient now, so I lugged on my jackboots, stood up and looked around. It was then that I got two shocks.

The first hit me as I scanned my companions in misery. They consisted of little more than half the complement of the *Marathon*. The rest weren't there. One hammock held a still, lax figure that I recognized as the body of the guy who'd caught the darts soon after we landed. Upon another reposed the awake but dreamy, disinterested form of Sug Farn. But he was the only Martian present. None of the others were there. Neither were Chief Douglas, Bannister, Kane, Richards, Kelly, Jay Score, Steve Gregory, young Wilson and a dozen others.

Were they dead? It didn't seem so—else why should the greenies have transported one body and not the others? Had they escaped, or did they form a second party of prisoners that had been taken elsewhere? There was no way of determining their fate, yet it was strange that they should be missing.

I nudged Jepson. "Hey, have you noticed—"

Came a sudden roar over that river and all the green ones stared upward and gesticulated with their weapons. They made mouth motions, but the roar drowned them out. Whirling around, I could feel my eyes bugging as the *Marathon*'s sleek pinnace dived within a few feet of the surface of the river, soared upward again. It vanished over the treetops, drummed into the distance.

Then I could hear it sweeping round in a wide circle. Its note

accelerated as it went into another dive, it shot back into view,
swooped so low that it touched the surface of the water, whisked
a shower of green droplets behind it and sent a small wash lapping
into the bank. Then it was gone in another swift and uproarious soar,
bulleting past at such a rate that it was impossible to see the pilot's
cabin.

Jepson spat on his fist, gave the greenies a sour eye, and said,
"They've got it coming to them, the lice!"

"Tut!" I chided.

"As for you," he went on. He didn't get a chance to say more because a tall, thin, mean-looking greenie suddenly picked on him.

This one gave him a contemptuous shove in the chest and piped
something on a rising note of interrogation.

"Don't you do that to me!" snarled Jepson, giving an answering
shove.

The green one staggered backward, recovered his balance, kicked
out with his right leg. I thought he was trying to give Jepson a
crack on the shins, but he wasn't. He was throwing something with
his foot and what he threw was alive. All I could see of it was something that may or may not have been a tiny snake. It had no more
length and thickness than a pencil and, for a change, it wasn't
green but a bright orange color relieved by small, black spots. It landed
on Jepson's chest, bit him, then flicked down his front so fast that
I could hardly follow it. Reaching the ground, it made the grass
fairly whip aside as it streaked back to its owner.

Curling around the green one's ankle, it went supine, looking
exactly like a harmless leg ornament. A very small number of the
other natives were wearing similar objects all of which were orange
and black excepting one which was yellow and black.

Jepson bugged his eyes, opened his mouth, but emitted no sound.
He teetered. The guy wearing the yellow and black lump of wickedness was standing right at my side watching Jepson with academic
interest. I broke his neck. The way it snapped reminded me of a
rotten broomstick. That thing on his leg left him the moment he
was mutton, but fast as it moved it was too late. Jepson fell onto
his face just as my jackboot scrunched the thing into the turf.

There was a hullabaloo all around me. I could hear McNulty's
anxious voice yelping, "Men! Men!" Even at a time like this the
crackpot could dwell on the vision of himself being demoted for
tolerating maltreatment of natives. Armstrong kept bawling, "An-

other bugger!" and each time there followed a loud splash in the river. Things were going *phut-phut* and spheres were crashing again. Jepson lay like one dead while combatants stumbled over his body. Brennand barged up against me. He was breathing in quick puffs and trying to gouge a black eye out of a green face.

By this time I'd got myself another aborigine and proceeded to take him apart. I tried to imagine that he was a fried chicken of which I never seem to get any more than the piece that goes last over the fence. He was hard to hold, this greenie, and bounced around like a rubber ball. Over his swaying shoulder I could see Sug Farn juggling with five at once and envied him the anacondas he used for limbs. My opponent stabbed his fingers into the chrysanthemum I didn't possess, looked surprised at his own forgetfulness, was still trying to think of something else as he went into the river.

Then half a dozen spheres cracked open at my feet and the last I remember hearing was Armstrong bellowing just before a splash. The last I remember seeing was Sug Farn suddenly shooting out a spare tentacle he'd temporarily overlooked and using it to arrange that of the six greenies who jumped me only five landed. The other one was still going up as I went down.

For some reason I didn't pass out as I'd done before. Maybe I only got a half-dose of whatever the spheres gave forth, or perhaps they contained a different mixture. All I know is that I went down with five aborigines aboard my ribs, the skies spun crazily, my brains turned to porridge. Then, astonishingly, I was awake, my upper limbs again tightly bound.

Over to the left a group of natives made a heaving pile atop some forms that I couldn't see but could easily hear. Armstrong was doing some championship hog-calling underneath that bunch which, after a couple of hectic minutes, broke apart to reveal his tied body along with those of Blaine and Sug Farn. On my right lay Jepson, his limbs quite free, but the lower ones apparently helpless. There was now no sign of the pinnace.

Without further ado the greenies whisked us across the sward and five miles deep into the forest, or city, or whatever it ought to be called. Two of them bore Jepson in a sort of wicker hamper. There were still as many trees as houses. Here and there a few impassive citizens came to the doors of their abodes and watched us dragging on our way. You'd have thought we were the sole surviving specimens of the dodo.

Minshull and McNulty were right behind me in this death parade, and I heard the latter say, pontifically, "I shall speak to their leader about this. I shall point out to him that all these unfortunate struggles are the inevitable result of his own people's bellicosity."

"Undoubtedly," afforded Minshull, with a touch of sardonic heartiness.

"Making all allowances for mutual difficulties of understanding," McNulty went on, "I still think that we are entitled to be received with a modicum of courtesy."

"Quite," said Minshull. His voice was now solemn, like that of the president of a mortician's convention. "And we consider that our reception left much to be desired."

"Precisely my point," said the skipper.

"And any further hostilities would be most deplorable," continued Minshull.

"Of course!" McNulty enthused.

"In which event we'll tear the guts out of every greenie on this stinking planet."

"Eh?" McNulty paused in his pace. His voice went up in pitch.

"Nothing," lied Minshull, amiably. "I didn't even open my mouth."

What the outraged shipmaster intended to say remained a mystery, for at this point a greenie caught him lagging and prodded him on. With an angry snort, he speeded up, moving in introspective silence from then on.

Presently, we emerged from a long, orderly line of tree-shrouded homes and entered a glade fully twice as large as that in which the missing *Marathon* had made its landing. It was roughly circular, its surface level and carpeted with close-growing moss of a rich, emerald green. The sun, now well up in the sky, poured a flood of pale-green beams into this strange amphitheater around the fringes of which clustered a horde of silent, expectant natives.

The middle of the glade captured our attention. Here, as outstanding as the biggest skyscraper in the old home town, soared a veritable monster among trees. How high it went was quite impossible to estimate, but it was large enough to make Terra's giant redwoods look puny by comparison. Its bole was a full forty feet in diameter, and the spread of its oaklike branches looked immense even though they were way, way up there. So enormous was this mighty growth that we just couldn't keep our eyes off it. If these transcosmic Zulus were going to hang us, well, they sure intended to do it high and handsome. Our kicking bodies wouldn't look more than a few struggling bugs dangling between Earth and heaven.

Minshull must have been afflicted by the same thought, for J heard him say to McNulty, "There's the Christmas tree! We're the ornaments. They'll draw lots for us, and the boob who gets the ace of spades will be the fairy at the top."

"Don't be morbid," snapped McNulty. "They'll do nothing so illegal."

Then a native pointed at the positive skipper and six pounced on him before he could dilate further on the subject of intercosmic law. With complete disregard for all the customs which the victim held holy, they bore him toward the waiting tree.

VI

Up to that moment we'd failed to notice the drumming sound which thundered dully from all around the glade. It was strong now, and held a sinister quality in its muffled, insistent beat. The weird, elusive sound had been with us from the start; we'd got used to it, had become unconscious of it in the same way that one becomes insensitive to the ticking of a familiar clock. But now, perhaps because it lent emphasis to the dramatic scene, we were keenly aware of that deadly throb, throb, throb.

The green light made the skipper's face ghastly as he went forward. All the same, he still managed to lend importance to his characteristic strut, and his features had the air of one who has unshakable faith in the virtue of sweet reasonableness. I've never encountered a man with more confidence in the law. As he walked forward, I know he was supported by the profound conviction that these poor people could do nothing drastic with him unless they first filled in the necessary forms and got them properly stamped and signed. Whenever McNulty died, it was going to be with official approval.

Halfway to the tree the skipper and his guard were met by nine tall natives. The latter were dressed in no way different from their fellows, yet, in some vague manner, managed to convey the impression that they were beings apart from the common herd. Witch doctors, decided my agitated mind.

Those holding McNulty promptly handed him over to the newcomers, then beat it toward the fringe of the glade as if the devil himself had appeared in the middle. There wasn't any devil; there was only that monstrous tree. Still, knowing what some growths could and did do in this green-wrapped world it was highly probable that this, the grandpappy of all trees, was capable of some unique wickedness. Of that lump of statuesque timber one thing was certain, —it possessed a damned good dollop of *gamish*.

Briskly, the nine stripped McNulty to the waist. He was talking to them all the time, but he was too far away for us to get the gist of his lecture, and his captors took not the slightest notice. Again they examined his chest, conferred among themselves, abruptly started dragging him nearer to the tree. McNulty resisted with appropriate dignity. Picking him up bodily, they carried him forward.

Armstrong said, in harsh tones, "We've still got legs, haven't we?" and forthwith kicked his nearest guardian's feet from beneath him.

But before any of us could follow his example and start another useless melee an interruption came from the sky. Upon the steady drumming from the forest was superimposed another fiercer, more rapid roll which quickly merged its beasts to a rising howl. The howl waxed to an explosive roar as, swift and silvery, the pinnace swooped low over the fateful tree.

Something dropped from the belly of the bulleting boat, something which blew out to mushroomlike shape, hesitated in its fall, then lowered gently into the head of the tree. It was a parachute! I could see a figure hanging in its harness just before he was swallowed in the deeps of that elevated foliage. The distance made it quite impossible to recognize this invader from above.

The nine who were bearing McNulty dropped him unceremoniously on the sward, gazed expectantly at the tree. Strangely enough, aërial manifestations filled these natives more with curiosity than fear. The tree stood unmoving. Suddenly, amid its top branches, the thin beam of a needle ray lanced forth, touched a large branch at its junction with the trunk, and severed it. The amputated limb went whirling to the ground.

At once a thousand budlike protuberance which lay concealed between the leaves of the tree swelled up as if they were blown balloons, reached the size of giant pumpkins, and burst with a fusillade of dull pops. They gave out a light yellow mist, exuding the stuff at such a rate that the entire tree was clouded with it in less than one minute. All the natives within sight hooted like a gang of owls, turned and ran. McNulty's nine guardians also called off the ceremony they'd had in mind and started after their fellows. The needle caught two of them before they'd gone ten steps: the remaining seven doubled their pace. McNulty was left struggling with the bonds around his wrists while slowly the mist crawled toward him.

Again the beam speared high up in the tree which had grown dim within the envelope of its own fog, and again a branch went to ground. The last native had faded from sight. The creeping mist was now within thirty yards of the skipper who was standing and watching it like a man fascinated. His wrists were still tied to his sides. Deep inside the mist the popping sounds continued, though not as rapidly.

Yelling at the witless McNulty to make use of his nether limbs, we struggled furiously with our own and one anothers' bonds. McNulty responded no more than to shuffle backward a few yards. By a superhuman effort Armstrong burst free, snatched a jackknife from his pants pocket, started cutting our arms loose. Minshull and Blaine, the first two thus relieved, immediately raced to McNulty who was posing within ten yards of the mist like a portly Ajax defying the power of alien gods. They dragged him back.

Just as we'd all got rid of our bonds the pinnace came round in another wide sweep, vanished behind the column of yellow cloud and thundered away into the distance. We gave it a hoarse cheer. Then from the mist strode a great figure dragging a limp body with each hand. It was Jay Score. He had a tiny two-way radio on his back.

He came toward us, big, powerful, his eyes aflame with their everlasting fires, released his grip on the pair of cadavers, said, "Look —this is what that vapor will do to you unless you move out plenty fast!"

We looked. These things were the remains of the two natives he'd needled, but the needlers had not caused that awful rotting of the flesh. Both leprous objects were too far gone to be corpses, not far enough to be skeletons. They were mere rags of flesh and half-eaten organs on frames of festering bone. It was easy to see what would have happened to Jay had he been composed of flesh and blood, or had he been a breather.

"Back to the river," advised Jay, "even if we have to fight our way through. The *Marathon's* going to land on the front. We must reach her at all costs."

"And remember, men," put in McNulty, "I want no unnecessary slaughter."

That was a hell of a laugh. Our sole weapons now consisted of Jay's needler, Armstrong's jackknife, and our fists. Behind us, already very near and creeping steadily nearer, was the mist of death. Between us and the river lay the greenie metropolis with its unknown number of inhabitants armed with unknown devices. Veritably we were between a yellow devil and a green sea.

We started off, Jay in the lead, McNulty and the burly Armstrong following. Behind them, two men carried Jepson who could
use his tongue even if not his legs. Two more bore the body which
our attackers had borne all the way from the ship. Without opposition
or mishap we got a couple of hundred yards deep into the trees and
there we buried the corpse of the man who was first to set foot
on this soil. He went from sight with the limp silence of the dead
while all around us the forest throbbed.

In the next hundred yards we were compelled to bury another.
The surviving duck-on-the-rock player, sobered by the end of his
buddy, took the lead as a form of penance. We were marching slowly
and cautiously, our eyes alert for hidden natives, our wits ready for any
untoward move by a dart-throwing bush or a goo-smearing branch.

The man in front swerved away from one tree which topped an
empty and silent greenie abode. His full attention was upon the vacant
entrance to that house, and he failed to be wary of another tree
under which he had moved. This growth was of medium size, had
a silvery green bark, long, oranmental leaves from which dangled
sprays of stringy threads. The ends of the threads came within four
feet of the ground. He brushed against two of them. Came a sharp,
bluish flash of light, a smell of ozone and scorched hair, and he
dropped. He'd been electrocuted as thoroughly as if smitten by a
stroke of lightning.

Mist or no mist, we carried him back the hundred yards we'd just
traversed, buried him beside his comrade. That job was done in the
nick of time. The crawling leprosy was at our very heels as we resumed our way. High in the almost concealed sky the sun poured
down its limpid rays and made mosaic patterns through overhead
leaves.

Giving a wide berth to this latest menace, which we named the
voltree, we hit the end of Main Street. Here, we had the advantage
in one way, though not in another. The houses stood dead in line
and well apart; we could march along the center of the route beneath
the wider gap of sky and be beyond reach of this planet's bellicose
vegetation. But this made our march exposed to attack from any
direction by any natives who might be determined to oppose our
escape. We'd have to do the trip, one way or the other, with our
necks stuck out a yard.

Sug Farn said to me, "You know, I've an idea well worth developing."

"What is it?" I demanded, hopefully.

"Supposing that we had twelve squares a side," he suggested, "we could then have four more pawns and four new master pieces. I propose to call the latter 'archers.' They would move two squares forward, and could take opponents one square sidewise. Wouldn't that make a beautifully complicated game?"

"You," I told him, "may go drown yourself!"

"As I should have known, your mental appreciation is poor." So saying, he extracted a bottle of *hooloo* scent which somehow he'd managed to retain through all the turmoil, moved away from me, and sniffed it in a deliberately offensive manner. I don't give a damn what anybody says—we don't smell like Martians say we do! These octopuses are downright liars.

Stopping both our progress and argument, Jay Score growled, "I guess this'll do." Unhitching his portable radio, he tuned it up, said into its microphone. "That you, Steve?" A pause, then, "Yes, we're waiting about a quarter of a mile on the river side of the glade. No, there's been no opposition—yet. But it'll come, it'll come. O. K., we'll wait." Another pause. "We'll give it guidance by sound."

Turning his attention from the radio to the sky, but with one earpiece still in action, he listened intently. We all listened. For a while there was nothing but that *throb, throb, throb* which never ceased upon this crazy world, but presently came a faraway drone like the hum of an approaching bumblebee.

Jay snatched at the mike. "We've got you. You're coming nearer." The drone grew louder. "Nearer, nearer." He waited a moment. "Now you're away to one side." The drone drifted off. "No, you're swerved the wrong way." Another brief wait. The distant sound suddenly grew strong. "Heading correctly now." The drone swelled to a roar. "Right!" yelled Jay. "You're almost on us!"

He looked expectantly upward, and we followed his gaze like one man. The next instant the pinnace raced across the sky gap at such a pace that it had come and gone in less time than it takes to draw one breath. But those aboard must have seen us, for the little vessel zoomed around in a wide, graceful arc, hit the main stem a couple of miles farther down, and came up it at terrific speed. This time, we could watch it most of the way, and we yelled at it as if we were a gang of excited kids.

"Got us?" inquired Jay of the microphone. "All right, try it on the next run."

Again the pinnace swept around, struck its former path, tore the air as it traveled toward us. It was like a monster shell from some old-time cannon. Things fell from its underside as it neared us, bundles and packages in a parachuted stream. The stuff came down as manna from heaven while the sower passed uproariously on and dug a hole in the northern sky. But for these infernal trees the pinnace could have landed and snatched the lot of us from danger's grasp.

Eagerly we pounced on the supplies, tearing covers open and dragging out the contents. Spacesuits for all. Well, they'd preserve us from various forms of gaseous unpleasantness. Needlers, oiled and loaded, together with reserves of excitants. A small case, all sponge rubber and cotton wool, containing half a dozen atomic bombs. An ampoule of iodine and a first-aid pack apiece.

One large bundle had become lodged high up in the branches of a tree, or rather its parachute had become entangled and it was dangling enticingly from the ropes. Praying that it contained nothing liable to blast the earth from beneath us, we needled the ropes and brought it down. It proved to hold a good supply of concentrated rations and a three-gallon can of pineapple juice.

Packing the chutes and shouldering the supplies, we started off. The first mile was easy: just trees, trees, trees and abandoned houses. It was on this part of the journey that I noticed that it was always the same type of tree which surmounted a house. There was no abode built around any of those gootrees or voltrees of whose powers we now knew too well. Whether those particular trees were innocuous was something nobody seemed inclined to discover, but it was here that Minshull discovered in them the source of that everlasting throbbing.

Disregarding McNulty, who was clucking at him like an agitated hen, he tiptoed into one empty house, his needler held forward in readiness for trouble. A minute later he came out, said that the building was deserted, but that the tree in its center was booming like a tribal tom-tom. He'd put his ear to its trunk and had heard the beating of its mighty heart.

That started a dissertation by McNulty, his subject being our legal right to mutilate or otherwise harm the trees of this planet. If, in fact, they were semisentient, then in law they had the status of aborigines and as such were subject to subsection so-and-so, paragraph such 'n' such of the Intercosmic Code governing planetary relations. He got down to this with gusto and with typical disregard for the fact that he might be boiled in oil by nightfall.

When he paused for breath, Jay Score said, evenly, "Skipper, maybe these people have laws of their own and are about to enforce them!" He pointed straight ahead.

I followed his unemotional finger, then frantically poured myself into my spacesuit. This, I thought, is it! The long arm of justice was about to face me with that poor guppy.

VII

What awaited us about half a mile ahead was a vanguard of enormous, snakelike things fully as thick as my body and about a hundred feet in length. They were writhing in our general direction, their movements peculiarly stiff and lacking in sinuosity. Behind them, also moving awkwardly forward, was a small army of bushes deceivingly harmless in appearance. And behind those, hooting with the courage of those who now feel themselves secure, was a great horde of natives. The progress of this nightmarish crowd was determined by the pace of the snakish objects in front, and these crept forward in tortuous manner as if they were trying to move a hundred times faster than nature had intended them to move.

Aghast at this crazy spectacle, we stopped. The creepers came steadily on and somehow managed to convey an impression of tremendous strength awaiting sudden release. The nearer they got, the bigger they looked, and when they were a mere three hundred yards away I knew that any one of them could embrace a bunch of six of us and do more to us than any boa constrictor ever did to a hapless goat.

These were the wild ones of a vast and semisentient forest. I knew it instinctively, and I could hear them faintly mewing as they came on. These, then, were my bright green tigers, samples of the thing our captors had slaughtered in the emerald jungle. But they could be tamed, their strength and fury kept on tap. This tribe had done it. Veritably, they were higher than the Ka.

"I think I can just about make this distance," said Jay Score when the intervening space had shrunk to two hundred yards.

Nonchalantly, he thumbed an atomic bomb which could have made an awful mess of the *Marathon*. His chief weakness was that he never could appreciate the power of things that go bang. So he juggled it around in a way that made me wish him some place the other end of the cosmos, and just when I was about to burst into tears, he threw it. His powerful right arm whistled in the air as he flung the missile in a great arc.

We flattened. The earth heaved like the belly of a sick man. Huge clods of plasma and lumps of green, fibrous stuff geysered, hung momentarily in midair, then showered all around us. We got up, raced forward a hundred yards, went prone as Jay tossed another. This one made me think of volcanoes. Its blast nearly pushed me back into my boots. The uproar had scarcely ceased when the pinnace reappeared, dived upon the rear ranks of the foe, and let them have a couple there. More disruption. It tied me in knots to see what went up.

"Now!" yelled Jay. Grabbing the handicapped Jepson, he tossed him upon one shoulder and pounced forward. We drove with him as one man.

Our first obstacle was a great crater bottomed with tired and steaming earth and some mutilated yellow worms. Cutting around the edges of this, I leaped a six-foot length of blasted creeper which, even in death, continued to jerk spasmodically and horribly. There were many more odd lengths writhing between here and the next crater. All were greener than any complexion, and bristled with hair-like tendrils which squirmed around as if seeking the life that had gone. The one hundred yards between craters we covered in record time, Jay still in the lead despite his heavy burden. I was sweating like a tormented bull, and I thanked my lucky star for the low gravity which enabled us to keep up this frantic pace.

Again we split and raced around the the rim of the second crater. This brought us nose to nose with the enemy, and after that, all was confusion.

A bush got me. Sheer Terrestrialism made me disregard the darned thing despite all my recent experiences. I had my eyes off it, and in an instant it had shifted to one side, wrapped itself around my legs and brought me down. I went prostrate, unharmed but cursing, and the bush methodically sprinkled my space fabric with a fine gray powder. Then a long, leatherish tentacle snaked from behind me, ripped the bush from my form, tore it to pieces.

"Thanks, Sug Farn!" I breathed, got up, and charged on.

A second bellicose growth collapsed before my needler and the potent ray carried on another sixty or seventy yards and roasted the guts of a yelling, gesticulating native. Sug snatched a third bush, scattered it with scorn. The powder it emitted did not seem to affect him.

Jay was now twenty yards ahead. He paused, flung a bomb, dropped, got up and raced on, Jepson still grasped in his mighty left arm.

The pinnace howled overhead, dived, created wholesale slaughter in the enemy's rear. A needle ray spurted from behind me, lanced dangerously close to my helmet, and burned a bush. I could hear in my phone a constant and monotonous cursing as I pounded along. On my right, a great tree lashed furiously and toppled headlong, but I had neither time nor inclination to look at it.

Then a snake got Blaine. How it had survived, alone among its blasted fellows, was a mystery. It lay jerking exactly like all the other tattered bits and pieces, but it was still in one, long lump and, as Blaine jumped it, the thing curled viciously, wound around him. He shrieked into his mouthpiece, and the sound of his dying was terrible to hear. His spacesuit sank in and his blood spurted out between the folds. The sound and the sight shocked me so much that I stopped abruptly, and Armstrong blundered into me from behind.

"Get going!" he roared. With his needler he sliced the green constrictor, segmenting it with savage gusto. We charged on, perforce leaving behind Blaine's crushed and broken corpse.

Now we were through the fronting ranks and into the natives whose numbers miraculously had thinned. Brittle globes plopped all around our thudding feet, but their gaseous contents were as harmless as summer air. We were protected and, in any case, we were moving too fast to get a whiff. I needled three greenies in rapid succession, saw Jay tear off the head of another without as much as pausing in his heavy onrush.

We were gasping with exertion when unexpectedly the foe gave up. The remaining natives melted into their protecting forest just as the pinnace roared vengefully toward them again. Our way was clear. Not slackening our pace in the slightest, and with eyes alert and weapons ready, we raced to the water front, and there, lying in the great space of bright green sward, found the sweetest sight in the entire cosmos—the *Marathon!*

It was here that Sug Farn put a scare into us, for as we sprinted joyfully toward the open port, he beat us to it, held up the stump of a tentacle, said, "It would be as well if we do not enter—yet."

"Why not?" demanded Jay. His cold, glowing eyes settled on the Martian's stump. "What the devil happened to you?"

"I was forced to shed a limb," said Sug Farn, mentioning it with the air of one to whom shedding a limb is like taking off a hat. "It was that powder. It was made of a million insects. It crawls around and it eats. It was eating me. Look at yourselves!"

By hokey, he was right! Now that I came to look at it, I could
see small clusters of gray powder changing shape on my spacesuit.
It was moving around. Sooner or later, it would eat its way through
—and then start on me. I've never felt lousier in my life. So, keeping
watch upon the fringe of the forest, we had to spend an impatient
and sweaty half-hour roasting each other's suits with needlers turned
to wide jet and low power. I was cooked by the time the last microscopic louse dropped off.

Young Wilson seized the opportunity to dig out a movie camera
and record our communal decontamination. This, I knew, eventually
would be shown to an amused world sitting in armchair comfort
far, far from the troubles surrounding Rigel. Secretly, I wished that
a few surviving bugs would somehow manage to get around with the
film. With a more official air, he also got shots of the forest, the
river, and a couple of upturned boats with all their bivalve paddles
exposed. Then, thankfully, we all piled into the spaceship.

The pinnace was lugged aboard and the *Marathon* blew off pronto.
I don't think there's ever been a time when I felt more like a million
dollars than I did when normal, glorious light came through the ports
and the bilious green coloring faded from our faces. With Brennand,
I watched this strange, eerie world sink below us, and I can't say I
was sorry to see it drop.

Jay came along, said, "Sergeant, we're not making any further
landings. The skipper's decided to return to Terra at once and make
a full report."

"Why?" asked Brennand. He gestured below. "We've come away
with practically nothing worth having!"

"McNulty thinks we've learned quite enough." The rhythmic thum
of the stern tubes sounded through his momentary silence. "He says
he's conducting an exploratory expedition and not managing a
slaughterhouse. He's had enough and is thinking of offering his
resignation."

"The dunderhead!" said Brennand, with total lack of reverence.

"What have we learned, if anything?" I asked.

"Well, we know that life on that planet is mostly symbiotic," Jay
replied. "There, different forms of life share their existence and their
faculties. Men share with trees, each according to his kind. The communal point is that queer chest organ."

"Drugs for blood," said Brennand. "Bah!"

"But," Jay went on. "there were some higher than the Ka and

their kind, some so high and godlike that they could depart from their trees and travel the globe, by day or by night. They could milk their trees, transport their nourishment and absorb it from bowls. Of the partnership imposed upon them, they had gained the mastery, and, in the estimation of this planet, they alone were free!"

"How fallen are the mighty," I commented.

"Not so," Jay contradicted. "We have killed, but not conquered. The world is still theirs. We are retiring, with our losses—and we still have Jepson to cure!" He turned away.

A thought struck me, and I said to him, "Hey, what happened during that assault on the ship? And how did you keep track of us?"

"It was a losing fight, so we blew free," he replied. "After that, we followed you very easily." His eyes were always inscrutably aflame, but I will swear that there was a touch of humor in them as he went on. "You had Sug Farn with you. We had Kli Yang and the rest." He tapped his head suggestively. "The Martians have much gamish."

"Hell, telepathy!" yelped Brennand. "I forgot all about that. Sug Farn never said a word. That cross-eyed spider just slept every chance he got!"

"Nevertheless," said Jay, "he was constantly in touch with his fellows!"

He went along the passage, rounded the corner. Then the warning alarm sounded, and Brennand and I clung like brothers while the ship switched to Flettner drive. The green world faded to a dot with swiftness that never failed to astound me. We took fresh hold on ourselves, rubbed our distorted innards into shape. Then Brennand went to the valve of the storrad air lock, turned the control, watched the pressure gauge crawl from three pounds to fifteen.

"The Martians are inside there," I pointed out. "And they won't like that."

"I don't want 'em to like it. I'll teach those rubber caricatures to hold out on me!"

"McNulty won't like it either."

"Who cares what McNulty likes!" he yelled. Then McNulty himself came around the corner, walking with portly dignity, and Brennand promptly added, in a still louder voice, "You ought to be a darned sight more respectful and refer to him as the skipper."

When you travel the void, never mind the ship—pick the guys who're going to accompany you in it!

SEEDS OF THE DUSK

by

RAYMOND Z. GALLUN

*Medical men have suggested several times in recent years that
life in virus—and infectious—form may come to this planet from
other worlds. Far worse than any bacteria or virus life forms are the
vegetable growths that Mr. Gallun here describes. Communal,
inter-dependent, these invading spores from dead and useless
Mars attempt to colonize earth. And the weird pioneers combat
man's last survivors on an intellectual as well as a physical plane.*

*

IT WAS a spore, microscopic in size. Its hard shell—resistant to the
utter dryness of interplanetary space—harbored a tiny bit of plant
protoplasm. That protoplasm, chilled almost to absolute zero,
possessed no vital pulsation now—only a grim potentiality, a savage
capacity for revival, that was a challenge to Fate itself.

For years the spore had been drifting and bobbing erratically be
tween the paths of Earth and Mars, along with billions of other spores
of the same kind. Now the gravity of the Sun drew it a few million
miles closer to Earth's orbit, now powerful magnetic radiations from
solar vortices forced it back toward the world of its origin.

It seemed entirely a plaything of chance. And, of course, up to a
point it was. But back of its erratic, unconscious wanderings, there
was intelligence that had done its best to take advantage of the law
of averages.

The desire for rebirth and survival was the dominant urge of this
intelligence. For this was during the latter days, when Earth itself was

249

showing definite signs of senility, and Mars was near as dead as the Moon.

Strange, intricate spore-pods, conceived as a man might conceive a new invention, but put into concrete form by a process of minutely exact growth control, had burst explosively toward a black, spacial sky. In dusty clouds the spores had been hurled upward into the vacuum thinness that had once been an extensive atmosphere. Most of them had, of course, dropped back to the red, arid soil; but a comparative few, buffeted by feeble air currents, and measured numerically in billions, had found their way from the utterly tenuous upper reaches of Mars' gaseous envelope into the empty ether of the void.

With elements of a conscious purpose added, the thing that was taking place was a demonstration of the ancient Arrhenius Spore Theory, which, countless ages ago, had explained the propagation of life from world to world.

The huge, wonderful parent growths were left behind, to continue a hopeless fight for survival on a burnt-out world. During succeeding summer seasons they would hurl more spores into the interplanetary abyss. But soon they themselves would be only brown, mummied relics—one with the other relics of Mars; the gray, carven monoliths; the strange, hemispherical dwellings, dotted with openings arranged like the cells of a honeycomb. Habitations of an intelligent animal folk, long perished, who had never had use for halls or rooms, as such things are known to men on Earth.

The era of utter death would come to Mars, when nothing would move on its surface except the shadows shifting across dusty deserts, and the molecules of sand and rock vibrating with a little warmth from the hot, though shrunken, Sun. Death—complete death! But the growths which were the last civilized beings of Mars had not originated there. Once they had been on the satellites of Jupiter, too. And before that—well, perhaps even the race memory of their kind had lost the record of those dim, distant ages. Always they had waited their chance, and when the time came—when a world was physically suited for their development—they had acted.

A single spore was enough to supply the desired foothold on a planet. Almost inevitably—since chance is, in fundamentals, a mathematical element depending on time and numbers and repetition—that single spore reached the upper atmosphere of Earth.

For months, it bobbed erratically in tenuous, electrified gases. It might have been shot into space again. Upward and downward it wandered; but with gravity to tug at its insignificant mass, probability favored its ultimate descent to the harsh surface.

It found a resting place, at last, in a frozen desert gully. Around the gully were fantastic, sugar-loaf mounds. Near-by was one thin, ruined spire of blue porcelain—an empty reminder of a gentler era, long gone.

The location thus given to it seemed hardly favorable in its aspect. For this was the northern hemisphere, locked now in the grip of a deadly winter. The air, depleted through the ages, as was the planet's water supply, was arid and thin. The temperature, though not as rigorous and deadening as that of interplanetary space, ranged far below zero. Mars in this age was near dead; Earth was a dying world.

But perhaps this condition, in itself, was almost favorable. The spore belonged to a kind of life developed to meet the challenge of a generally much less friendly environment than that of even this later-day Earth.

There was snow in that desert gully—maybe a quarter-inch depth of it. The rays of the Sun—white and dwarfed after so many eons of converting its substance into energy—did not melt any of that snow even at noon. But this did not matter. The life principle within the spore detected favorable conditions for its germination, just as, in spring, the vital principle of Earthly seeds had done for almost incalculable ages.

By a process parallel to that of simple fermentation, a tiny amount of heat was generated within the spore. A few crystals of snow around it turned to moisture, a minute quantity of which the alien speck of life absorbed. Roots finer than spiderweb grew, groping into the snow. At night they were frozen solid, but during the day they resumed their brave activity.

The spore expanded, but did not burst. For its shell was a protecting armor which must be made to increase in size gradually without rupture. Within it, intricate chemical processes were taking place. Chlorophyl there was absorbing sunshine and carbon dioxide and water. Starch and cellulose and free oxygen were being produced.

So far, these processes were quite like those of common terrestrial flora. But there were differences. For one thing, the oxygen was not liberated to float in the atmosphere. It had been ages since such lavish waste had been possible on Mars, whose thin air had contained but a small quantity of oxygen in its triatomic form, ozone, even when Earth was young.

The alien thing stored its oxygen, compressing the gas into the tiny compartments in its hard, porous, outer shell. The reason was simple. Oxygen, combining with starch in a slow, fermentive combustion, could produce heat to ward off the cold that would otherwise stop growth.

The spore had become a plant now. First, it was no bigger than a pinhead. Then it increased its size to the dimensions of a small marble, its fuzzy, green-brown shape firmly anchored to the soil itself by its long, fibrous roots. Like any terrestrial growth, it was an intricate chemical laboratory, where transformations took place that were not easy to comprehend completely.

And now, perhaps, the thing was beginning to feel the first glimmerings of a consciousness, like a human child rising out of the blurred, unremembering fog of birth. Strange, oily nodules, scattered throughout its tissues, connected by means of a complex network of delicate, white threads, which had the functions of a nervous system, were developing and growing—giving to the sporeplant from Mars the equivalent of a brain. Here was a sentient vegetable in the formative stage.

A sentient vegetable? Without intelligence it is likely that the ancestors of this nameless invader from across the void would long ago have lost their battle for survival.

What senses were given to this strange mind, by means of which it could be aware of its environment? Undoubtedly it possessed faculties of sense that could detect things in a way that was as far beyond ordinary human conception as vision is to those individuals who have been born blind. But in a more simple manner it must have been able to feel heat and cold and to hear sounds, the latter perhaps by the sensitivity of its fine, cilialike spines. And certainly it could see in a way comparable to that of a man.

For, scattered over the round body of the plant, and imbedded deep in horny hollows in its shell, were little organs, lensed with a clear vegetable substance. These organs were eyes, developed, perhaps, from far more primitive light-sensitive cells, such as many forms of terrestrial flora possess.

But during those early months, the spore plant saw little that could be interpreted as a threat, swiftly to be fulfilled. Winter ruled, and the native life of this desolate region was at a standstill.

There was little motion except that of keen, cutting winds, shifting dust, and occasional gusts of fine, dry snow. The white, shrunken Sun rose in the east, to creep with protracted slowness across the

sky, shedding but the barest trace of warmth. Night came, beautiful
and purple and mysterious, yet bleak as the crystalline spirit of an
easy death.

Through the ages, Earth's rate of rotation had been much decreased by the tidal drag of Solar and Lunar gravities. The attraction
of the Moon was now much increased, since the satellite was nearer
to Terra than it had been in former times. Because of the decreased
rate of rotation, the days and nights were correspondingly lengthened.

All the world around the spore plant was a realm of bleak, un-
peopled desolation. Only once, while the winter lasted, did anything happen to break the stark monotony. One evening, at moon-
rise, a slender metal car flew across the sky with the speed of a bullet.
A thin propelling streamer of fire trailed in its wake, and the pale
moonglow was reflected from its prow. A shrill, mechanical scream
made the rarefied atmosphere vibrate, as the craft approached to a
point above the desert gully, passed, and hurtled away, to leave
behind it only a startling silence and an aching memory.

For the spore plant did remember. Doubtless there was a touch
of fear in that memory, for fear is a universal emotion, closely connected with the law of self-preservation, which is engrained in the
texture of all life, regardless of its nature or origin.

Men. Or rather, the cold, cruel, cunning little beings who were
the children of men. The Itorloo, they called themselves. The invader could not have known their form as yet, or the name of the
creatures from which they were descended. But it could guess something of their powers from the flying machine they had built. Inherited memory must have played a part in giving the queer thing
from across the void this dim comprehension. On other worlds its
ancestors had encountered animal folk possessing a similar science.
And the spore plant was surely aware that here on Earth the builders
of this speeding craft were its most deadly enemies.

The Itorloo, however, inhabiting their vast underground cities, had
no knowledge that their planet had received an alien visitation—
one which might have deadly potentialities. And in this failure to
know, the little spore plant, hidden in a gully where no Itorloo foot
had been set in a thousand years, was safe.

Now there was nothing for it to do but grow and prepare to reproduce its kind, to be watchful for lesser enemies, and to develop
its own peculiar powers.

It is not to be supposed that it must always lack, by its very nature,
an understanding of physics and chemistry and biological science. It

possessed no test tubes, or delicate instruments, as such things were understood by men. But it was gifted with something—call it an introspective sense—which enabled it to study in minute detail every single chemical and physical process that went on within its own substance. It could feel not only the juices coursing sluggishly through its tissues, but it could feel, too, in a kind of atomic pattern, the change of water and carbon dioxide into starch and free oxygen.

Gift a man with the same power that the invader's kind had acquired, perhaps by eons of practice and directed will—that of feeling vividly even the division of cells, and the nature of the protoplasm in his own tissues—and it is not hard to believe that he would soon delve out even the ultimate secret of life. And in the secret of life there must be involved almost every conceivable phase of practical science.

The spore plant proceeded with its marvelous self-education, part of which must have been only recalling to mind the intricate impressions of inherited memories.

Meanwhile it studied carefully its bleak surroundings, prompted not only by fear, but by curiosity as well. To work effectively, it needed understanding of its environment. Intelligence it possessed beyond question; still it was hampered by many limitations. It was a plant, and plants have not an animal's capacity for quick action, either of offense or defense. Here, forever, the entity from across the void was at a vast disadvantage, in this place of pitiless competition. In spite of all its powers, it might now have easily been destroyed.

The delicate, ruined tower of blue porcelain, looming up from the brink of the gully—— The invader, scrutinizing it carefully for hours and days, soon knew every chink and crack and fanciful arabesque on its visible side. It was only a ruin, beautiful and mysterious alike by sunshine and moonlight, and when adorned with a fine sifting of snow. But the invader, lost on a strange world, could not be sure of its harmlessness.

Close to the tower were those rude, high, sugar-loaf mounds, betraying a sinister cast. They were of hard-packed Earth, dotted with many tiny openings. But in the cold, arid winter, there was no sign of life about them now.

All through those long, arctic months, the spore plant continued to develop, and to grow toward the reproductive stage. And it was making preparations too—combining the knowledge acquired by its observations with keen guesswork, and with a science apart from the manual fabrication of metal and other substances.

II

A milder season came at last. The Sun's rays were a little warmer now. Some of the snow melted, moistening the ground enough to germinate Earthly seeds. Shoots sprang up, soon to develop leaves and grotesque, devilish-looking flowers.

In the mounds beside the blue tower a slow awakening took place. Millions of little, hard, reddish bodies became animated once more, ready to battle grim Nature for sustenance. The ages had done little to the ants, except to increase their fierceness and cunning. Almost any organic substances could serve them as food, and their tastes showed but little discrimination between one dainty and another. And it was inevitable, of course, but presently they should find the spore plant.

Nor were they the latter's only enemies, even in this desert region. Of the others, Kaw and his black-feathered brood were the most potent makers of trouble. Not because they would attempt active offense themselves, but because they were able to spread news far and wide.

Kaw wheeled alone now, high in the sunlight, his ebon wings outstretched, his cruel, observant little eyes studying the desolate terrain below. Buried in the sand, away from the cold, he and his mate and their companions had slept through the winter. Now Kaw was fiercely hungry. He could eat ants if he had to, but there should be better food available at this time of year.

Once, his keen eyes spied gray movement far below. As if his poised and graceful flight was altered by the release of a trigger, Kaw dived plummet-like and silent toward the ground.

His attack was more simple and direct than usual. But it was successful. His reward was a large, long-tailed rodent, as clever as himself. The creature uttered squeaks of terror as meaningful as human cries for help. In a moment, however, Kaw split its intelligently rounded cranium with a determined blow from his strong, pointed beak. Bloody brains were devoured with indelicate gusto, to be followed swiftly by the less tasty flesh of the victim. If Kaw had ever heard of table manners, he didn't bother with them. Kaw was intensely practical.

His crop full, Kaw was now free to exercise the mischievous curiosity which he had inherited from his ancient forbears. They who had, in the long-gone time when Earth was young, uprooted many a young corn shoot, and had yammered derisively from distant treetops when any irate farmer had gone after them with a gun.

With a clownish skip of his black, scaly feet, and a show-offish swerve of his dusty ebon wings, Kaw took to the air once more. Upward he soared, his white-lidded eyes directed again toward the ground, seeking something interesting to occupy his attention and energies.

Thus, presently, he saw a brownish puff that looked like smoke or dust in the gully beside the ruined blue tower at the pinnacle of which he and his mate were wont to build their nest in summer. Sound came then—a dull, ringing pop. The dusty cloud expanded swiftly upward, widening and thinning until its opacity was dissipated into the clearness of the atmosphere.

Kaw was really startled. That this was so was evinced by the fact that he did not voice his harsh, rasping cry, as he would have done had a lesser occurrence caught his attention. He turned back at first, and began to retreat, his mind recognizing only one possibility in what had occurred. Only the Itorloo, the Children of Men, as far as he knew, could produce explosions like that. And the Itorloo were cruel and dangerous.

However, Kaw did not go far in his withdrawal. Presently—since there were no further alarming developments—he was circling back toward the source of the cloud and the noise. But for many minutes he kept what he considered a safe distance, the while he tried to determine the nature of the strange, bulging, grayish-green thing down there in the gully.

A closer approach, he decided finally, was best made from the ground. And so he descended, alighting several hundred yards distant from the narrow pocket in the desert.

Thence he proceeded to walk cautiously forward, taking advantage of the cover of the rocks and dunes, his feathers gleaming with a dusty rainbow sheen, his large head bobbing with the motion of his advance like any fowl's. His manner was part laughably ludicrous, part scared, and part determined.

And then, peering from behind a large boulder, he saw what he had come to see. It was a bulging, slightly flattened sphere, perhaps a yard across. From it projected flat, oval things of a gray-green color, like the leaves of a cactus. And from these, in turn, grew clublike protuberances of a hard, horny texture—spore-pods. One of them was blasted open, doubtless by the pressure of gas accumulated within it. These spore-pods were probably not as complexly or powerfully designed as those used by the parent growths on Mars, for they were intended for a simpler purpose. The entire plant bristled with sharp spines, and was furred with slender hairs, gleaming like little silver wires.

Around the growth, thousands of ant bodies lay dead, and from its vicinity other thousands of living were retreating. Kaw eyed these evidences critically, guessing with wits as keen as those of a man of old their sinister significance. He knew, too, that presently other sporepods would burst with loud, disturbing noises.

Kaw felt a twinge of dread. Evolution, working through a process of natural selection—and, in these times of hardship and pitiless competition, putting a premium on intelligence—had given to his kind a brain power far transcending that of his ancestors. He could observe, and could interpret his observations with the same practical comprehension which a primitive human being might display. But, like those primitives, he had developed, too, a capacity to feel superstitious awe.

That gray-green thing of mystery had a fantastic cast which failed to identify it with—well—with naturalness. Kaw was no botanist, certainly; still he could recognize the object as a plant of some kind. But those little, bright, eye-lenses suggested an unimaginable scrutiny. And those spines, silvery in sheen, suggested ghoulish animation, the existence of which Kaw could sense as a nameless and menacing unease.

He could guess, then, or imagine—or even know, perhaps—that here was an intruder who might well make itself felt with far-reaching consequences in the future. Kaw was aware of the simple fact that most of the vegetation he was acquainted with grew from seeds or the equivalent. And he was capable of concluding that this flattened spheroid reproduced itself in a manner not markedly unfamiliar. That is, if one was to accept the evidence of the spore-pods. Billions of spores, scattering with the wind! What would be the result?

Kaw would not have been so troubled, were it not for those crumpled thousands of ant bodies, and the enigma of their death. It was clear that the ants had come to feed on the invader—but they had perished. How? By some virulent plant poison, perhaps?

The conclusions which intelligence provides can produce fear where fear would otherwise be impossible. Kaw's impulse was to seek safety in instant departure, but horror and curiosity fascinated him. Another deeper, more reasoned urge commanded him. When a man smells smoke in his house at night, he does not run away; he investigates. And so it was with Kaw.

He hopped forward cautiously toward the invader. A foot from its rough, curving side he halted. There, warily, as if about to attack a poisonous lizard, he steeled himself. Lightly and swiftly his beak shot forward. It touched the tip of a sharp spine.

The result left Kaw dazed. It was as though he had received a stunning blow on the head. A tingling, constricting sensation shot through his body, and he was down, flopping in the dust.

Electricity. Kaw had never heard of such a thing. Electricity generated chemically in the form of the invader, by a process analogous to that by which, in dim antiquity, it had been generated in the bodies of electric eels and other similar creatures.

However, there was a broad difference here between the subject and the analogy. Electric eels had never understood the nature of their power, for they were as unresponsible for it as they were unresponsible for the shape of the flesh in which they had been cast. The spore plant, on the other hand, comprehended minutely. Its electric organs had been minutely preplanned and conceived before one living cell of their structure had been caused to grow on another. And these organs were not inherited, but were designed to meet the more immediate needs of self-protection. During the winter, the invader, studying its surroundings, had guessed well.

Slowly Kaw's brain cleared. He heard an ominous buzzing, and knew that it issued from the plant. But what he did not know was that, like the electric organs, the thing's vocal equipment was invented for possible use in its new environment. For days, since the coming of spring, the invader had been listening to sounds of various kinds, and had recognized their importance on Earth.

Now Kaw had but one thought, and that was to get away. Still dazed and groggy, he leaped into the air. From behind him, in his hurried departure, he heard a dull plop. More billions of spores, mixing with the wind, to be borne far and wide.

But now, out of his excitement, Kaw drew a reasoned and fairly definite purpose. He had a fair idea of what he was going to do, even though the course of action he had in mind might involve him with the greatest of his enemies. Yet, when it came to a choice, he would take the known in preference to the unknown.

He soared upward toward the bright blue of the heavens. The porcelain tower, the ant hills, and the low mounds which marked the entrances to the rodent colonies slipped swiftly behind. As if the whole drab landscape were made to move on an endless belt.

Kaw was looking for his mate, and for the thirty-odd, black-winged individuals who formed his tribe. Singly and in small groups, he contacted and collected them. Loud, raucous cries, each with a definite verbal meaning, were exchanged. Menace was on the Earth—bizarre, nameless menace. Excitement grew to fever pitch.

Dusk, beautiful and soft and forbidding, found the bird clan assembled in a chamber high-placed in a tremendous edifice many miles from where Kaw had made his discovery. The building belonged to the same gentle culture which had produced the blue porcelain tower. The floor of the chamber was doubtless richly mosaiced. But these were relics of departed splendor now thickly masked with dust and filth.

From the walls, however, painted landscapes of ethereal beauty, and the faces of a happy humankind of long ago peeped through the gathering shadows. They were like ghosts, a little awed at what had happened to the world to which they had once belonged. Those gentle folk had dwelt in a kindlier climate which was now stripped forever from the face of the Earth. And they had been wiped out by creatures who were human too, but of a different, crueler race.

Through delicately carven screens of pierced marble, far up on the sides of the chamber's vast, brooding rotunda, the fading light of day gleamed, like a rose glow through the lacework of fairies.

But this palace of old, dedicated to laughter and fun and luxury, and to the soaring dreams of the fine arts, was now only a chill, dusty gathering place for a clan of black-winged, gruesome harpies.

They chuckled and chattered and cawed, like the crows of dead eras. But these sounds, echoing eerily beneath cloistered arches, dim and abhorrent in the advancing gloom of night, differed from that antique yammering. It constituted real, intelligent conversation.

Kaw, perched high on a fancifully wrought railing of bronze, green with the patina of age, urged his companions with loud cries, and with soft, pleading notes. In his own way, he had some of the qualities of a master orator. But, as all through an afternoon of similar arguing, he was getting nowhere. His tribe was afraid. And so it was becoming more and more apparent that he must undertake his mission alone. Even Teka, his mate, would not accompany him.

At last Kaw ruffled his neck feathers, and shook his head violently in an avian gesture of disgust. He leaped from his perch and shot through a glassless window with an angry scream that was like the curse of a black ghoul.

It was the first time that he had ever undertaken a long journey at night. But in his own judgment, necessity was such that no delay could be tolerated.

The stars were sharp and clear, the air chill and frosty. The ground was dotted sparsely with faint glimmerings from the chimneys of the crude furnaces which, during the colder nights of spring and fall, warmed the underground rodent colonies.

After a time the Moon rose, huge and yellow, like the eye of a monster. In that bloom and silence, Kaw found it easy to feel the creeping and imperceptible, yet avalanching, growth of horror. He could not be sure, of course, that he was right in his guess that the mission he had undertaken was grimly important. But his savage intuition was keen.

The Itorloo—the Children of Men—he must see them, and tell them what he knew. Kaw was aware that the Itorloo had no love for any but themselves. But they were more powerful than the winds and the movements of the Sun and Moon themselves. They would find a swift means to defeat the silent danger.

And so, till the gray dawn, Kaw flew on and on, covering many hundreds of miles, until he saw a low dome of metal, capping a hill. The soft half-light of early morning sharpened its outlines to those of a beautiful, ebon silhouette, peaceful and yet forbidding. Beneath it, as Kaw knew, was a shaft leading down to the wonderous underworld of the Itorloo, as intriguing to his mind as a shadowland of magic.

Fear tightened its constricting web around Kaw's heart—but retreat was something that must not be. There was too much at stake ever to permit a moment of hesitation.

Kaw swung into a wide arc, circling the dome. His long wings, delicately poised for a soaring glide, did not flap now, but dipped and rose to capture and make use of the lifting power of every vagrant wisp of breeze. And from his lungs issued a loud, raucous cry.

"Itorloo!" he screamed. "Itorloo!"

The word, except for its odd, parrot-like intonation, was pronounced in an entirely human manner. Kaw, in common with his crow ancestors, possessed an aptitude for mimicry of the speech of men.

Tensely he waited for a sign, as he swung lower and nearer to the dome.

III

Zar felt irritable. He did not like the lonely surface vigil and the routine astronomical checkings that constituted his duty. All night he'd sat there at his desk with signal lights winking around him, helping surface watchers at the other stations check the position of a new meteor swarm by means of crossing beams of probe rays.

Angles, distances, numbers! Zar was disgusted. Why didn't the construction crews hurry? The whole race could have been moved to Venus long ago, and might just as well have been. For as far as Zar could see, there was no real reason to retain a hold on the burnt-out Earth. The native Venusians should have been crushed a century back. There wasn't any reason why this pleasant task shouldn't have been accomplished then—no reason except stupid, official inertia!

The sound of a shrill bird cry, throbbing from the pickup diaphragm on the wall, did not add any sweetening potion to Zar's humor. At first he paid no attention; but the insistent screaming of the name of his kind—"Itorloo! Itorloo!"—at length aroused him to angry action.

His broad, withered face, brown and hideous and goblinlike, twisted itself into an ugly grimace. He bounded up from his chair, and seized a small, pistol-like weapon.

A moment later he was out on the sandy slopes of the hill, looking up at the black shape that swooped and darted timidly, close to his head. On impulse Zar raised his weapon, no thought of compassion in his mind.

But Kaw screamed again: "Itorloo! Loaaah!"

In Zar's language, "Loaaah!" meant "Danger!" very emphatically. Zar's hand, bent on execution, was stayed for the moment at least. His shrewd little eyes narrowed, and from his lips there issued yammering sounds which constituted an understandable travesty of the speech of Kaw's kind.

"Speak your own tongue, creature!" he ordered sharply. "I can understand!"

Still swooping and darting nervously, Kaw screamed forth his story, describing in quaint manner the thing he had seen, employing comparisons such as any primitive savage would use. In this way the invader was like a boulder, in that way it was like a thorn cactus, and in other ways it resembled the instruments of death which the Itorloo employed. In all ways it was strange, and unlike anything ever seen before.

And Zar listened with fresh and calculated attention, getting from this bird creature the information he required to locate the strange miracle. Kaw was accurate and clear enough in giving his directions.

Zar might have forgotten his inherent ruthlessness where his feathered informer was concerned, had not Kaw become a trifle too

insistent in his exhortations to action. He lingered too long and
screamed too loudly.

Irritated, Zar raised his weapon. Kaw swept away at once, but there
was no chance for him to get out of range. Invisible energy shot toward him. Black feathers were torn loose, and floated aflame in the
morning breeze. Kaw gave a shrill shriek of agony and reproach. Erratically he wavered to the ground.

Zar did not even glance toward him, but retraced his way leisurely
into the surface dome. An hour later, however, having received permission from his superiors, he had journeyed across those hundreds of
miles to the gully beside the blue porcelain tower. And there he bent
over the form of the invader. Zar was somewhat awed. He had never
been to Mars. For two hundred thousand years or more, no creature
from Earth had ever visited that planet. The Itorloo were too practical to attempt such a useless venture, and their more recent predeces-
sors had lacked some of the adventurous incentive required for so
great and hazardous a journey.

But Zar had perused old records, belonging to an era half a million
years gone by. He knew that this gray-green thing was at least like the
flora of ancient Mars. Into his mind, matter-of-fact for the most part,
came the glimmerings of a mighty romance, accentuating within him
a consciousness of nameless dread, and of grand interplanetary distances.

Spines. Bulging, hard-shelled, pulpy leaves that stored oxygen under
pressure. Chlorophyl that absorbed sunshine and made starch, just
as in an ordinary Earthly plant. Only the chlorophyl of this growth was
beneath a thick, translucent shell, which altered the quality of the
light it could reflect. That was why astronomers in the pre-interplane-
tary era had doubted the existence of vegetation on Mars. Green
plants of Terra, when photographed with infra red light, looked
silvery, like things of frost. But—because of their shells—Martian
vegetation could not betray its presence in the same manner.

Zar shuddered, though the morning air was not chill by his standards. The little gleaming orbs of the invader seemed to scrutinize him
critically and coldly, and with a vast wisdom. Zar saw the shattered
spore-pods, knowing that their contents now floated in the air, like
dust—floated and settled—presenting a subtle menace whose tool
was the unexpected, and against which—because of the myriad
numbers of the widely scattered spores—only the most drastic methods
could prevail.

Belatedly, then, anger came. Zar drew a knife from his belt. Half in fury and half in experiment, he struck the invader, chipping off a piece of its shell. He felt a sharp electric shock, though by no means strong enough to kill a creature of his size. From the wound he made in the plant, oxygen sizzed softly. But the invader offered no further defense. For the present it had reached the end of its resources.

Zar bounded back. His devilish little weapon flamed then, for a full two minutes. When he finally released pressure on its trigger, there was only a great, smouldering, glowing hole in the ground where the ghoulish thing from across space had stood.

Such was Zar's and the entire Itorloo race's answer to the intruder. Swift destruction! Zar chuckled wickedly. And there were ways to rid Earth of the treacherous menace of the plant intelligences of Mars entirely, even though they would take time.

Besides there was Venus, the world of promise. Soon half of the Itorloo race would be transported there. The others certainly could be accommodated if it became necessary.

Necessary? Zar laughed. He must be getting jittery. What had the Itorloo to fear from those inert, vegetable things? Now he aimed his weapon toward the blue tower, and squeezed the trigger. Weakened tiles crumbled and fell down with a hollow, desolate rattle that seemed to mock Zar's ruthlessness.

Suddenly he felt sheepish. To every intelligent being there is a finer side that prompts and criticizes. And for a moment Zar saw himself and his people a little more as they really were.

Unlike the lesser creatures, the Children of Men had not advanced very much mentally. The ups and downs of history had not favored them. War had reversed the benefits of natural selection, destroying those individuals of the species best suited to carry it on to greater glory. Zar knew this, and perhaps his senseless assault upon the ruined building was but a subconscious gesture of resentment toward the people of long ago who had been kinder and wiser and happier.

Zar regretted his recent act of destroying the spore plant. It should have been preserved for study. But now—well—what was done could not be changed.

He entered his swift, gleaming rocket car. When he closed its cabin door behind him, it seemed that he was shutting out a horde of mocking, menacing ghosts.

In a short while he was back at the surface station. Relieved there of his duty by another little brown man, he descended the huge cylindrical shaft which dropped a mile to the region that was like the realm of the Cyclops. Thrumming sounds, winking lights, shrill shouts of the workers, blasts of incandescent flame, and the colossal majesty of gigantic machines, toiling tirelessly.

In a vast, pillared plaza the keels of spaceships were being laid—spaceships for the migration and the conquest. In perhaps a year—a a brief enough time for so enormous a task—they would soar away from Earth, armed to the teeth. There would be thousands of the craft then, for all over the world, in dozens of similar underground places, they were in process of construction.

Zar's vague fears were dissipated in thoughts of conquest to come. The Venus folk annihilated in withering clouds of flame. The glory of the Itorloo carried on and on——

IV

Kaw was not dead. That this was so was almost a miracle, made possible, perhaps, by a savage, indomitable will to live. In his small bird body there was a fierce, burning courage that compensated for many of his faults.

For hours he lay there on the desert sand, a pathetic and crumpled bundle of tattered feathers, motionless except for his labored breathing, and the blinking of his hate-filled eyes. Blood dripped slowly from the hideous, seared wound on his breast, and his whole body ached with a vast, dull anguish.

Toward sundown, however, he managed to hobble and flutter forward a few rods. Here he buried himself shallowly in the sand, where his chilled body would be protected from the nocturnal cold.

For three days he remained thus interred. He was too weak and sick to leave his burrow. Bitterness toward Zar and the other cruel Itorloo, he did not feel. Kaw had lived too long in this harsh region to expect favors. But a black fury stormed within him, nevertheless—a black fury as agonizing as physical pain. He wanted revenge. No, he needed revenge as much as he needed the breath of life. He did not know that Itorloo plans directed against the intruding spores from Mars were already under way, and that—as a by-product—they would destroy his own kind, and all primitive life on the surface of the Earth.

Kaw left his hiding place on the fourth day. Luck favored him, for he found a bit of carrion—part of the dead body of au antelopelike creature.

Somehow, through succeeding weeks and days, he managed to keep alive. The mending of his injured flesh was slow indeed, for the burnt wound was unclean. But he started toward home, hopping along at first, then flying a little, a hundred yards at a time. Tedium and pain were endless. But the fiendish light of what must seem forever fruitless hatred, never faded in those wicked, white-lidded eyes. Frequently Kaw's long, black beak snapped in a vicious expression of boundless determination.

Weeks of long days became a month, and then two months. Starved to a black-clad skeleton, and hopeless of ever being fit to hunt again, Kaw tottered into a deep gorge one evening. Utterly spent, he sank to the ground here, his brain far too weary to take note of any subtle unusualness which the deepening shadows half masked.

He scarcely saw the rounded things scattered here. Had he noticed them, his blurred vision would have named them small boulders and nothing more. Fury, directed at the Itorloo, had made him almost forget the spore plants. He did not know that this was to be a place of magic. Chance and the vagrant winds had made it so. A hundred spores, out of many millions, had lodged here. Conditions had been just right for their swift development. It was warm, but not too warm. And there was moisture too. Distantly Kaw heard the trickle of water. He wanted to get to it, but his feebleness prevented him.

He must have slept, then, for a long time. It seemed that he awoke at the sound of an odd buzzing, which may have possessed hypnotic properties. He felt as weak and stiff as before, but he was soothed and peaceful now, in spite of his thirst and hunger.

He looked about. The gorge was deep and shadowy. A still twilight pervaded it, though sunshine gilded its bulging, irregular lips far above. These details he took in in a moment.

He looked, then, at the grotesque shapes around him—things which, in the deeper darkness, he had thought to be only boulders. But now he saw that they were spore plants, rough, eerie, brooding, with their little, lensed light-sensitive organs agleam.

The excitement of terror seized him, and he wanted to flee, as from a deadly enemy. But this urge did not last long. The hypnotic buzz, which issued from the diaphragmic vocal organs of the plants, soothed and soothed and soothed, until Kaw felt very relaxed.

There were dead ants around him, doubtless the victims of electrocution. Since no better food was within reach, Kaw hopped here and there, eating greedily.

After that he hobbled to the brackish spring that dripped from the wall, and drank. Next he dropped to the ground, his fresh drowsiness characterized by sleepy mutterings about himself, his people, and the all-wise Itorloo. And it seemed, presently, that the buzzing of the invaders changed in character at last, seeming to repeat his own mutterings clumsily, like a child learning to talk.

"Kaw! Itorloo!" And other words and phrases belonging to the speech of the crow clans.

It was the beginning of things miraculous and wonderful for Kaw, the black-feathered rascal. Many suns rose and set, but somehow he felt no urge to wander farther toward his home region. He did not know the Lethean fascination of simple hypnotism. True, he sallied afield farther and farther, as his increasing strength permitted. He hunted now, eating bugs and beetles for the most part. But always he returned to the gorge, there to listen to the weird growths, buzzing, chattering, speaking to him in his own tongue. In them there seemed somehow to be a vague suggestion of the benignance of some strange, universal justice, in spite of their horror.

And night and day, rocket cars, streamlined and gleaming, swept over the desert. Now and then beams of energy were unleashed from them, whipping the sand into hot flame, destroying the invading spore plants that had struck root her and there. Only the law of chance kept them away from the gorge, as doubtless it allowed them to miss other hiding places of alien life. For the wilderness was wide.

But this phase of the Itorloo battle against the invading spore plants was only a makeshift preliminary, intended to keep the intruders in check. Only the Itorloo themselves knew about the generators now being constructed far underground—generators which, with unseen emanations, could wipe out every speck of living protoplasm on the exposed crust of the planet. Theirs was a monumental task, and a slow one. But they meant to be rid, once and for all, of the subtle threat which had come perhaps to challenge their dominion of the Earth. Kaw and his kind, the rodents, the ants, and all the other simple People of the Dusk of Terra's Greatness, were seemingly doomed.

Kaw's hatred of the Children of Men was undimmed, more justly than he was aware. Thus it was easy for him to listen when he was commanded: "Get an Itorloo! Bring him here! Alone! On foot!"

Zar was the logical individual to produce, for he was the nearest, the most readily available. But summer was almost gone before Kaw encountered the right opportunity, though he watched with care at all times.

Evening, with Venus and the Moon glowing softly in the sky. Kaw was perched on a hilltop, close to the great surface dome, watching as he had often watched before. Out of its cylindrical hangar, Zar's flier darted, and then swung in a slow arc. Presently it headed at a leisurely pace into the northwest. For once its direction was right, and it was not traveling too fast for Kaw to keep pace with it. Clearly its pilot was engaged in a rambling pleasure jaunt, which had no definite objective.

Kaw, pleased and excited, fell in behind at a safe distance. There he remained until the craft was near the gorge. Now there was danger, but if things were done right——

He flapped his wings violently to catch up with his mechanical quarry. He screamed loudly: "Itorloo! Itorloo! Descend! Descend! I am Kaw, who informed you of the unknowns long ago! I would show you more! More! More!" All this in shrill, avian chatterings.

Kaw's trickery was naively simple. But Zar heard, above the noise of his rocket blasts. Suspicion? He felt it, of course. There was no creature in this era who accepted such an invitation without question. Yet he was well armed. In his own judgment he should be quite safe. Curiosity led him on.

He shut off his rocket motors, and uttered the bird jargon, questioning irritably: "Where? What is it, black trickster?"

Kaw skittered about defensively. "Descend!" he repeated. "Descend to the ground. The thing that bears you cannot take you where we must go!"

The argument continued for some little time, primitive with matching curiosity and suspicion.

And meanwhile, in the gloomy gorge cut in vague geologic times by some gushing stream, entities waited patiently. Sap flowed in their tissues, as in the tissues of any other vegetation, but the fine hairs on their forms detected sounds, and their light-sensitive cells served as eyes. Within their forms were organs equivalent to human nerve and brain. They did not use tools or metals, but worked in another way, dictated by their vast disadvantages when compared to animal intelligences. Yet they had their advantages, too.

Now they waited, dim as bulking shadows. They detected the excited cries of Kaw, who was their instrument. And perhaps they grew a little more tense, like a hunter in a blind, when he hears the quacking of ducks through a fog.

There was a grating of pebbles and a little brown man, clad in a silvery tunic, stepped cautiously into view. There was a weapon clutched in his slender hand. He paused, as if suddenly awed and fearful. But no opportunity to retreat was given him.

A spore-pod exploded with a loud plop in the confined space. A mass of living dust filled the gorge, like a dense, opaque cloud, choking, blinding. Zar squeezed the trigger of his weapon impulsively. Several of the invaders were blasted out of existence. Stones clattered down from where the unaimed beam of energy struck the wall.

Panic seized the little man, causing him to take one strangling breath. In a few moments he was down, writhing helpless on the ground. Choked by the finely divided stuff, his consciousness seemed to drop into a black hole of infinity. He, Zar, seemed about to pay for his misdeeds. With a mad fury he heard the derisive screams of Kaw, who had tricked him. But he could not curse in return, and presently his thoughts vanished away to nothing.

Awareness of being alive came back to him very slowly and painfully. At first he felt as though he had pneumonia—fever, suffocation, utter vagueness of mind. Had the spores germinated within his lungs, he would surely have died. But they did not, there; conditions were too moist and warm for them. Gradually he coughed them up.

He felt cold with a bitter, aching chill, for the weather had changed with the lateness of the season. Fine snow sifted down into the gorge from clouds that were thin and pearly and sun-gilded. Each tiny crystal of ice glittered with a thousand prismatic hues as it slowly descended. And the silence was deathly, bearing a burden of almost tangible desolation. In that burden there seemed to crowd all the antique history of a world—history whose grand movement shaded gradually toward stark, eternal death.

Zar wanted to flee this awful place that had become like part of another planet. He jerked his body as if to scramble feebly to his feet. He found then that he was restrained by cordlike tendrils, hard as horn, and warm with a faint, fermentive, animal-like heat. Like the beat of a nameless pulse, tiny shocks of electricity tingled his flesh in a regular rhythm.

It was clear to Zar that while he had been inert the tendrils had fastened themselves slowly around him, in a way that was half like the closing of an ancient Venus Flytrap, carnivorous plant of old, and half like the simple creeping of a vine on a wall.

Those constricting bonds were tightening now. Zar could feel the tiny thorns with which they were equipped biting into his flesh. He screamed in horror and pain. His cries echoed hollowly in the cold gorge. The snow, slowly sifting, and the silence, both seemed to mock —by their calm, pitiless lack of concern—the plight in which he found himself.

And then a voice, chattering faintly in the language of Kaw the Crow: "Be still. Peace. Peace. Peace. Peace. Peace——"

Gradually the sleepy tone quieted Zar, even though he was aware that whatever the invaders might do to him could bring him no good.

Plants with voices. Almost human voices! Some sort of tympanic organs, hidden, perhaps, in some of those pulpy leaves, Zar judged. From the records of the old explanations of Mars, he knew a little about these intruders, and their scheme of life. Organs, with the functions of mechanical contrivances, conceived and grown as they were needed! An alien science, adapted to the abilities and limitations of vegetative intelligences—intelligences that had never controlled the mining and smelting and shaping of metal!

Zar, tight in the clutch of those weird monstrosities, realized some of their power. Strangely it did not affect the hypnotic calm that wrapped him.

Mars. These wondrous people of the dusk of worlds had survived all animal life on the Red Planet. They had spanned Mars in a vast, irregularly formed network, growing along dry river beds, and the arms of vanished seas. They had not been mere individuals, for they had cooperated to form a civilization of a weird, bizarre sort. Great, hollow roots, buried beneath the ground, had drawn water from melting polar snows. Those roots had been like water conduits. A rhythmic pulsation within them had pumped the water across thousands of miles of desert, providing each plant along the way with moisture, even on that dying and almost dehydrated world. The canals of Mars! Yes, a great irrigation system, a great engineering feat—but out of the scope of Intorloo methods entirely.

And through the living texture of those immense joining roots, too, had doubtless flown the impulses of thoughts and commands—the essence of leadership and security. Even now, when Mars was all but dead, its final civilization must still be trying to fight on.

Strange, wonderful times those old explorers had seen. Cold sunlight on bizarre ruins, left by extinct animal folk. Thin air and arctic weather, worse than that of Earth in the present age. Death everywhere, except for those vegetative beings grouped in immense, spiny, ribbonlike stretches. Dim shapes at night under hurtling Phobos, the nearer moon, and Deimos, her leisurely sister. Zar did not know just how it had happened, but he had heard that only a few of those human adventurers had escaped from the people of Mars with their lives.

Zar's thought rambled on in a detached way that was odd for him. Perhaps Nature had a plan that she used over and over again. On Terra the great reptiles of the Mesozic period had died out to be replaced by mammals. Men and the Children of Men had became supreme at last.

Succession after succession, according to some well-ordered scheme? In the desolate quiet of falling snow, tempered only by the muted murmur of the frigid wind, it was easy for Zar to fall prey to such a concept, particularly since he was held powerless in the grasp of the invaders. Tendrils, thorny, stinging tendrils, which must have been grown purposely to receive an Itorloo captive! Zar could realize, then, a little of the fantastic introspective sense which gave these beings a direct contact with the physical secrets of their forms. And in consequence a knowledge of chemistry and biology that was clearer than anything that an Itorloo might be expected to attain along similar lines.

Zar wanted to shriek, but his awe and his weakness strangled him beyond more than the utterance of a gasping sigh.

Then the mighty spirit of his kind reasserted itself. Zar was aware that most probably he himself would presently perish; but the Itorloo, his kind, his real concern, could never lose! Not with all the mighty forces at their command! To suppose that they could be defeated by the sluggish intruders was against reason! In a matter of months— when the preparations for the vast purification process had been completed—Earth would be free of those intruders once more. Zar's brown face contracted into a leer of defiance that had a touch of real greatness. Brutality, force, cunning, and the capacity for quick action —those were the tools of the Itorloo, but they had strength too. Zar was no fool—no short-sighted individual who leaps to hasty, optimistic conclusions—but in a contest between the Itorloo and the invaders there could be but a single outcome by any standard within Zar's reach.

In this belief, he was comforted, and his luck, presently, after long hours of suffering, seemed far better than he had any reason to hope for. The hard, thorny tendrils unquestionably were relaxing from about him a very little. He could not guess why, and in consequence he suspected subtle treachery. But he could find no reason to suppose that some hidden motive was responsible.

All his avid energies were concentrated, now, on escape. He concluded that perhaps the cold had forced the slight vegetable relaxation, and he proceeded to make the best possible use of his chances. Some time during the night his straining hands reached the hilt of his knife. Not long afterward Zar clutched his blast gun.

Zar limped stiffly to his flier, cursing luridly; while behind him in the gorge, red firelight flickered, and wisps of smoke lanced into the frigid wind.

Zar wished that Kaw was somewhere in sight, to receive his wrath too. The ebon rascal had vanished.

Winter deepened during succeeding days. The Itorloo in their buried cities felt none of its rigors, however.

Zar had submitted to a physical examination after his weird adventure, and had been pronounced fit. And of all his people he seemed to toil the most conscientiously.

The Venus project. Soon the Children of Men would be masters of that youthful, sunward planet. The green plains and jungles, and the blue skies of Venus. Soon! Soon! Soon! Zar was full of dreams of adventure and brutal pleasure.

Periodically the rocket craft of the Itorloo sallied forth from the cities to stamp out the fresh growth of the invaders. The oxygen-impregnated substance of their forms flamed in desert gullies, and along the rims of shrivelled salt seas, where the spore plants were trying to renew their civilization. Most of them did not get a chance, even, to approach maturity. But because even one mature survivor could pollute the Earth with billions of spores, impossible to destroy otherwise, the purification process must be carried through.

Spring again, and then mid-summer. The spaceships were almost ready to leap Venus-ward on the great adventure. The generators, meant to spread life-destroying emanations over the crust and atmosphere above, stood finished and gleaming in the white-domed caverns that housed them.

Zar looked at the magnificent, glittering array in the spaceship construction chamber of his native community with pride and satisfaction.

"Tomorrow," he said to a companion, a fierce light in his eyes.

The other nodded, the white glare of the atomic welding furnaces lighting up his features, and betraying there a wolfish grin of pleasure.

"Tomorrow," Zar repeated, an odd sort of vagueness in his tone.

V

Kaw had long ago rejoined his tribe. Life, during those recent months, had been little different from what had been usual in the crow clans for thousands of years. For purposes of safety, Kaw had led his flock into a desert fastness where patrolling Itorloo fliers were seldom seen, and where only a few spore plants had yet appeared.

His first intimation that all was not well was a haunting feeling of unease, which came upon him quite suddenly one day just before noon. His body burned and prickled uncomfortably, and he felt restless. Other than these dim evidences, there was nothing to betray the invisible hand of death.

Emanations, originating in the generators of the Itorloo, far underground. But Kaw was no physicist. He knew only that he and his fellows were vaguely disturbed.

With Teka, his mate, and several of their companions, he soared high into the sky. There, for a time, he felt better. Far overhead, near the Sun's bright disc, he glimpsed the incandescent streamers ot Itorloo vessels, distant in space. And presently, with little attention, he saw those vessels—there were five in the group—turn back toward Earth.

The advance in the strength of the deadly emanations was slow. Vast masses of rock, covering the upper crust of the planet in a thin shell, had to develop a kind of resonance to them before they could reach their maximum power.

By nightfall Kaw felt only slightly more uncomfortable. By the following dawn, however, he was definitely droopy and listless. The gradual, world-wide process of purification advanced, directed at the invaders, but promising destruction to the less favored native life of Earth, too.

Four days. Huddled in a pathetic group in a ruined structure of antiquity, Kaw's tribe waited. Their features were dull and ruffled, and they shivered as if with cold. Some of them uttered low, sleepy twitterings of anguish.

That evening Kaw watched the pale Moon rise from a battered window embrasure. He was too weak to stand, but rested slumped forward on his breast. His eyes were rheumy and heavy-lidded, but they still held a savage glitter of defiance, which perhaps would burn in them even after they had ceased to live and see. And Kaw's clouded mind could still hazard a guess as to the identity of the author of his woes. Brave but impotent, he could still scream a hoarse challenge inspired by a courage as deathless as the ages.

"Itorloo! Itorloo!———"

Some time before the first group of spaceships, headed for Venus, had been recalled to Earth, Zar, assigned to the second group, which had not yet entered the launching tubes, had collapsed against his instrument panels.

His affliction had come with a suddenness that was utterly abrupt. Recovering from his swoon, he found himself lying on a narrow pallet in the hospital quarters of the city. His vision was swimming and fogged, and he felt hot and cold by turns.

But he could see the silvery tunic'd figure of the physician standing close to him.

"What is wrong?" he stammered. "What is it that has happened to me? A short time ago I was well!"

"Much is wrong," the physician returned quietly. "And you have not really been well for a long time. A germ disease—a type of thing which we thought our sanitation had stamped out millenniums ago— has been ravaging your brain and nerves for months! Only its insidiousness prevented it from being discovered earlier. During its incipient stages the poisons of it seem actually to stimulate mental and physical activity, giving a treacherous impression of robust health. And we know, certainly, that this disease is extremely contagious. It does not reveal itself easily, but I and others have examined many apparently healthy individuals with great care. In each there is the telltale evidence that the disease is not only present, but far advanced. Hundreds have collapsed as you have. More, surely, will follow. It is my belief that the entire race has been afflicted. And the plague has a fatal look. Panic has broken out. There is a threatened failure of power and food supplies. Perhaps an antitoxin can be found—but there is so little time."

Half delirious, Zar could still grasp the meaning of the physician's words, and could understand the origin of the disease.

He began to mutter with seeming incoherence: "The changing Earth. Reptiles. Mammals. Men—— Succession. Nature——"

His voice took on a fiercer tone. "Fight, Itorloo!" he screamed. "Fight!"

Cruel he was, as were all his people, but he had pluck. Suddenly he arose to a sitting posture on his bed. His eyes flamed. If his act represented the final dramatic gesture of all the hoary race of man, still it was magnificent. Nor were any tears to be shed, for extinction meant only a task completed.

"Fight!" he shouted again, as if addressing a limitless multitude. "Fight, Itorloo! Study! Learn! Work! It is the only hope! Keep power flowing in the purification generators if you can. The old records of the explorations of Mars—those plants! Their approach to problems is different from our own. No metals. No machines as we know them. But in hidden compartments in their tissues it was easy for them to create the bacteria of death! They *invented* those bacteria, and grew them, breaking them away from their own substance. Some way, when I was a captive, I was infected. The thorns on the tendrils that held me! I was the carrier! Find an antitoxin to fight the plague, Itorloo! Work——"

VI

One year. Two. Three. The sunshine was brilliant, the air almost warm. The rusty desert hills in the distance were the same. Ancient ruins brooded in the stillness, as they had for so long. On the slopes ant hordes were busy. Rodent colonies showed similar evidence of population. In the sky, Kaw and his companions wheeled and turned lazily.

This was the same Earth, with several changes. Bulbous, spiny things peopled the gorges, and were probing out across the desert, slowly building—with hollow, connecting roots—the water pipes of a tremendous irrigation system. Like that of Mars, and like that of Ganymede, moon of Jupiter, in former ages. Saline remnants of seas and polar snows could alike provide the needed moisture.

Thoughts traveled swiftly along connecting roots. Little orbs and wicked spines gleamed. The invaders were at peace now. Only the Itorloo could have threatened their massed might. There was no danger in the lesser native life.

The subterranean cities of the former rulers of Earth were inhabited only by corpses and by intruding ants, who, like the other fauna of this planet, were immune to the plague, which had been directed and designed for the Itorloo alone. The last race of men was now one with the reptiles of the Mesozoic. But all was peace.

Kaw screamed out his contentment in loud, lazy cries, as he circled in the clear air. He seldom thought of the past any more. If the new masters were not truly benignant, they were indifferent. They left him alone. Kaw, creature of Earth's dusk, was happy.

The great surface dome where Zar, the Itorloo, had once kept watch, was already surrounded by crowded growths. The plants had achieved a great, but an empty, victory. For Earth was a dying planet. Within the dome an astronomical telescope gleamed dully, collecting dust. Often Zar had directed it toward Venus, goal of shattered Itorloo dreams.

But who knew? Out of the void to Ganymede the invaders had come. Across space to Mars. Riding light to Earth. Perhaps when the time came—when Venus was growing old——

HEAVY PLANET

by

LEE GREGOR

Our race with the Axis powers toward the goal of ato. 'c power is paralleled by the struggles of the people of Heavyplanet to find the energy that might lift them through their inconceivably heavy atmosphere. Heavyplanet (which might be Jupiter or Saturn or Pluto) had a gravity a hundred times stronger than ours and an atmosphere ten thousand times heavier. But its compact, ton-heavy giants were still men, and a man with imagination can take a flight that failed and make of it a legacy.

*

ENNIS WAS completing his patrol of Sector EM, Division 426 of the Eastern Ocean. The weather had been unusually fine, the liquid-thick air roaring along in a continuous blast that propelled his craft with a rush as if it were flying, and lifting short, choppy waves that rose and fell with a startling suddenness. A short savage squall whirled about, pounding down on the ocean like a million hammers, flinging the little boat ahead madly.

Ennis tore at the controls, granite-hard muscles standing out in bas-relief over his short, immensely thick body, skin gleaming scalelike in the slashing spray. The heat from the sun that hung like a huge red lantern on the horizon was a tangible intensity, making an inferno of the gale.

The little craft, that Ennis maneuvered by sheer brawn, took a leap into the air and seemed to float for many seconds before burying its keel again in the sea. It often floated for long distances, the air was so dense. The boundary between air and water was sometimes scarcely defined at all—one merged into the other imperceptibly. The pressure did strange things.

Like a dust mote sparkling in a beam, a tiny speck of light above caught Ennis' eye. A glider, he thought, but he was puzzled. Why so far out here on the ocean? They were nasty things to handle in the violent wind.

The dust mote caught the light again. It was lower, tumbling down with a precipitancy that meant trouble. An upward blast caught it, checked its fall. Then it floated down gently for a space until struck by another howling wind that seemed to distort its very outlines.

Ennis turned the prow of his boat to meet the path of the falling vessel. Curious, he thought; where were its wings? Were they retracted, or broken off? It ballooned closer, and it wasn't a glider. Far larger than any glider ever made, it was of a ridiculous shape that would not stand up for an instant. And with the sharp splash the body made as it struck the water—a splash that fell in almost the same instant it rose—a thought seemed to leap up in his mind. A thought that was more important than anything else on that planet; or was to him, at least. For if it was what he thought it was—and it had to be that— it was what Shadden had been desperately seeking for many years. What a stroke of inconceivable luck, falling from the sky before his very eyes!

The silvery shape rode the ragged waters lightly. Ennis' craft came up with a rush; he skillfully checked its speed and the two came together with a slight jar. The metal of the strange vessel dented as if it were made of rubber. Ennis stared. He put out an arm and felt the curved surface of the strange ship. His finger prodded right through the metal. What manner of people were they who made vessels of such weak materials?

He moored his little boat to the side of the larger one and climbed to an opening. The wall sagged under him. He knew he must be careful; it was frightfully weak. It would not hold together very long; he must work fast if it were to be saved. The atmospheric pressure would have flattened it out long ago, had it not been for the jagged rent above which had allowed the pressure to be equalized.

He reached the opening and lowered himself carefully into the interior of the vessel. The rent was too small; he enlarged it by taking the two edges in his hands and pulling them apart. As he went down he looked askance at the insignificant plates and beams that were like tissue paper on his world. Inside was wreckage. Nothing was left in its original shape. Crushed, mutilated machinery, shattered vacuum tubes, sagging members, all ruined by the gravity and the pressure.

There was a pulpy mess on the floor that he did not examine closely. It was like red jelly, thin and stalky, pulped under a gravity a hundred times stronger and an atmosphere ten thousand times heavier than that it had been made for.

He was in a room with many knobs and dials on the walls, apparently a control room. A table in the center with a chart on it, the chart of a solar system. It had nine planets; his had but five.

Then he knew he was right. If they came from another system, what he wanted must be there. It could be nothing else.

He found a staircase, descended. Large machinery bulked there. There was no light, but he did not notice that. He could see well enough by infra red, and the amount of energy necessary to sustain his compact gianthood kept him constantly radiating.

Then he went through a door that was of a comfortable massiveness, even for his planet—and there it was. He recognized it at once. It was big, squat, strong. The metal was soft, but it was thick enough even to stand solidly under the enormous pull of this world. He had never seen anything quite like it. It was full of coils, magnets, and devices of shapes unknown to him. But Shadden would know. Shadden, and who knows how many other scientists before him, had tried to make something which would do what this could do, but they had all failed. And without the things this machine could perform, the race of men on Heavyplanet was doomed to stay down on the surface of the planet, chained there immovably by the crushing gravity.

It was atomic energy. That he had known as soon as he knew that the body was not a glider. For nothing else but atomic energy and the fierce winds was capable of lifting a body from the surface of Heavyplanet. Chemicals were impotent. There is no such thing as an explosion where the atmosphere pressed inward with more force than an explosion could press outward. Only atomic, of all the theoretically possible sources of energy, could supply the work necessary to lift a vessel away from the planet. Every other source of energy was simply too weak.

Yes, Shadden, all the scientists must see this. And quickly, because the forces of sea and storm would quickly tear the ship to shreds, and, even more vital, because the scientists of Bantin and Marak might obtain the secret if there was delay. And that would mean ruin—the loss of its age-old supremacy—for his nation. Bantin and Marak were war nations; did they obtain the secret they would use it against all the other worlds that abounded in the Universe.

The Universe was big. That was why Ennis was so sure there was atomic energy on this ship. For, even though it might have originated on a planet that was so tiny that *chemical energy*—although that was hard to visualize—would be sufficient to lift it out of the pull of gravity, to travel the distance that stretched between the stars only one thing would suffice.

He went back through the ship, trying to see what had happened.

There were pulps lying behind long tubes that pointed out through clever ports in the outer wall. He recognized them as weapons, worth looking into.

There must have been a battle. He visualized the scene. The forces that came from atomic energy must have warped even space in the vicinity. The ship pierced, the occupants killed, the controls wrecked, the vessel darting off at titanic speed, blindly into nothing. Finally it had come near enough to Heavyplanet to be enmeshed in its huge web of gravity.

Weeaao-o-ow! It was the wailing roar of his alarm siren, which brought him spinning around and dashing for his boat. Beyond, among the waves that leaped and fell so suddenly, he saw a long, low craft making way toward the derelict spaceship. He glimpsed a flash of color on the rounded, gray superstructure, and knew it for a battleship of Marak. Luck was going strong both ways; first good, now bad. He could easily have eluded the battleship in his own small craft, but he couldn't leave the derelict. Once lost to the enemy he could never regain it, and it was too valuable to lose.

The wind howled and buffeted about his head, and he strained his muscles to keep from being blasted away as he crouched there, half on his own boat and half on the derelict. The sun had set and the evening winds were beginning to blow. The hulk scudded before them, its prow denting from the resistance of the water it pushed aside.

He thought furiously fast. With a quick motion he flipped the switch of the radiophone and called Shadden. He waited with fierce impatience until the voice of Shadden was in his ear. At last he heard it, then: "Shadden! This is Ennis. Get your glider, Shadden, fly to a45j on my route! Quickly! It's come, Shadden! But I have no time. Come!"

He flipped the switch off, and pounded the valve out of the bottom of his craft, clutching at the side of the derelict. With a rush the

ocean came up and flooded his little boat and in an instant it was
gone, on its way down to the bottom. That would save him from
being detected for a short time.

Back into the darkness of the spaceship. He didn't think he had
been noticed climbing through the opening. Where could he hide?
Should he hide? He couldn't defeat the entire battleship singlehanded,
without weapons. There were no weapons that could be carried anyway. A beam of concentrated actinic light that ate away the eyes and
the nervous system had to be powered by the entire output of a
battleship's generators. Weapons for striking and cutting had never
been developed on a world where flesh was tougher than metal. Ennis
was skilled in personal combat, but how could he overcome all that
would enter the derelict?

Down again, into the dark chamber where the huge atomic generator towered over his head. This time he looked for something he had
missed before. He crawled around it, peering into its recesses. And
then, some feet above, he saw the opening, and pulled himself up to
it, carefully, not to destroy the precious thing with his mass. The
opening was shielded with a heavy, darkly transparent substance
through which seeped a dim glow from within. He was satisfied then.
Somehow, matter was still being disintegrated in there, and energy
could be drawn off if he knew how.

There were leads—wires of all sizes, and busbars, and thick, heavy
tubes that bent under their own weight. Some must lead in and some
must lead out; it was not good to tamper with them. He chose another track. Upstairs again, and to the places where he had seen the
weapons.

They were all mounted on heavy, rigid swivels. He carefully detached the tubes from the bases. The first time he tried it he was not
quite careful enough, and part of the projector itself was ripped away,
but next time he knew what he was doing and it came away nicely.
It was a large thing, nearly as thick as his arm and twice as long.
Heavy leads trailed from its lower end and a lever projected from
behind. He hoped it was in working condition. He dared not try it;
all he could do was to trace the leads back and make sure they were
intact.

He ran out of time. There came a thud from the side, and then
smaller thuds, as the boarding party incautiously leaped over. Once
there was a heavy sound, as someone went all the way through the
side of the ship.

"Idiots!" Ennis muttered, and moved forward with his weapon toward the stairway. Noises came from overhead, and then a loud crash buckled the plates of the ceiling. Ennis leaped out of the way, but the entire section came down, with two men on it. The floor sagged, but held for the moment. Ennis, caught beneath the downcoming mass, beat his way free. He came up with a girder in his hand, which he bent over the head of one of the Maraks. The man shook himself and struck out for Ennis, who took the blow rolling and countered with a buffet that left a black splotch on a skin that was like armor plate and sent the man through the opposite wall. The other was upon Ennis, who whirled with the quickness of one who maneuvers habitually under a pressure of ten thousand atmospheres, and shook the Marak from him, leaving him unconscious with a twist in a sensitive spot.

The first opponent returned, and the two grappled, searching for nerve centers to beat upon. Ennis twisted frantically, conscious of the real danger that the frail vessel might break to pieces beneath his feet. The railing of a staircase gave behind the two, and they hurtled down it, crashing through the steps to the floor below. Their weight and momentum carried them through. Ennis released his grip on the Marak, stopped his fall by grasping one of the girders that was part of the ship's framework. The other continued his devastating way down, demolishing the inner shell, and then the outer shell gave way with a grinding crash that ominously became a burbling rush of liquid.

Ennis looked down into the space where the Marak had fallen, hissed with a sudden intake of breath, then dove down himself. He met rising water, gushing in through a rent in the keel. He braced himself against a girder which sagged under his hand and moved onward against the rushing water. It geysered through the hole in a heavy stream that pushed him back and started to fill the bottom level of the ship. Against that terrific pressure he strained forward slowly, beating against the resisting waves, and then, with a mighty flounder, was at the opening. Its edges had been folded back upon themselves by the inrushing water, and they gaped inward like a jagged maw. He grasped them in a huge hand and exerted force. They strained for a moment and began to straighten. Irresistibly he pushed and stretched them into their former position, and then took the broken ends in his hands and squeezed. The metal grew soft under his grip and began to flow. The edges of the plate welded under that mighty pressure. He moved down the crack and soon it was watertight. He flexed his hands as he rose. They ached; even his strength was beginning to be taxed.

Noises from above; pounding feet. Men were coming down to investigate the commotion. He stood for a moment in thought, then turned to a blank wall, battered his way through it, and shoved the plates and girders back into position. Down to the other end of the craft, and up a staircase there. The corridor above was deserted, and he stole along it, hunting for the place he had left the weapon he had prepared. There was a commotion ahead as the Maraks found the unconscious man.

Two men came pounding up the passageway, giving him barely enough time to slip into a doorway to the side. The room he found himself in was a sleeping chamber. There were two red pulps there, and nothing that could help him, so he stayed in there only long enough to make sure that he would not be seen emerging into the hall. He crept down it again, with as little noise as possible. The racket ahead helped him; it sounded as though they were tearing the ship apart. Again he cursed their idiocy. Couldn't they see how valuable this was?

They were in the control room, ripping apart the machinery with the curiosity of children, wondering at the strange weakness of the paperlike metal, not realizing that, on the world where it was fabricated, it was sufficiently strong for any strain the builders could put upon it.

The strange weapon Ennis had prepared was on the floor of the passage, and just outside the control room. He looked anxiously at the trailing cables. Had they been stepped on and broken? Was the instrument in working condition? He had to get it and be away; no time to experiment to see if it would work.

A noise from behind, and Ennis again slunk into a doorway as a large Marak with a colored belt around his waist strode jarringly through the corridor into the control room. Sharp orders were barked, and the men ceased their havoc with the machinery of the room. All but a few left and scattered through the ship. Ennis' face twisted into a scowl. This made things more difficult. He couldn't overcome them all single-handed, and he couldn't use the weapon inside the ship if it was what he thought it was from the size of the cables.

A Marak was standing immediately outside the room in which Ennis lurked. No exit that way. He looked around the room; there were no other doors. A porthole in the outer wall was a tiny disk of transparency. He looked at it, felt it with his hands, and suddenly pushed his hands right through it. As quietly as he could, he worked at the edges of the circle until the hole was large enough for him to squeeze through. The jagged edges did not bother him. They felt soft, like a ragged pat of butter.

The Marak vessel was moored to the other side of the spaceship. On this side the wind howled blankly, and the sawtooth waves stretched on and on to a horizon that was many miles distant. He cautiously made his way around the glistening rotundity of the derelict, past the prow, straining silently against the vicious backward sweep of the water that tore at every inch of his body. The darker hump of the battleship loomed up as he rounded the curve, and he swam across the tiny space to grasp a row of projections that curved up over the surface of the craft. He climbed up them, muscles that were hard as carborundum straining to hold against all the forces of gravity and wind that fought him down. Near the top of the curve was a rounded, streamlined projection. He felt around its base and found a lever there, which he moved. The metal hump slid back, revealing a rugged swivel mounting with a stubby cylindrical projector atop it.

He swung the mounting around and let loose a short, sudden blast of white fire along the naked deck of the battleship. Deep voices yelled within and men sprang out, to fall back with abrupt screams clogged in their throats as Ennis caught them in the intolerable blast from the projector. Men, shielded by five thousand miles of atmosphere from actinic light, used to receiving only red and infra red, were painfully vulnerable to this frightful concentration of ultraviolet.

Noise and shouts burst from the derelict spaceship alongside, sweeping away eerily in the thundering wind that seemed to pound down upon them with new vigor in that moment. Heads appeared from the openings in the craft.

Ennis suddenly stood up to his full height, bracing himself against the wind, so dense it made him buoyant. With a deep bellow he bridged the space to the derelict. Then, as a squad of Maraks made their difficult, slippery way across the flank of the battleship toward him, and as the band that had boarded the spaceship crowded out on its battered deck to see what the noise was about, he dropped down into a crouch behind his ultraviolet projector, and whirled it around, pulling the firing lever.

That was what he wanted. Make a lot of noise and disturbance, get them all on deck, and then blow them to pieces. The ravening blast spat from the nozzle of the weapon, and the men on the battleship dropped flat on the deck. He found he could not depress the projector enough to reach them. He spun it to point at the spaceship. The incandescence reached out, and then seemed to waver and die. The current was shut off at the switchboard.

Ennis rose from behind the projector, and then hurtled from the flank of the battleship as he was struck by two Maraks leaping on him from behind the hump of the vessel. The three struck the water and sank, Ennis struggling violently. He was on the last lap, and he gave all his strength to the spurt. The water swirled around them in little choppy waves that fell more quickly than the eye could follow. Heavier blows than those from an Earthly trip hammer were scoring Ennis' face and head. He was in a bad position to strike back, and suddenly he became limp and sank below the surface. The pressure of the water around him was enormous, and it increased very rapidly as he went lower and lower. He saw the shadowy bulk of the spaceship above him. His lungs were fighting for air, but he shook off his pretended stupor and swam doggedly through the water beneath the derelict. He went on and on. It seemed as though the distance were endless, following the metal curve. It was so big from beneath, and trying to swim the width without air made it bigger.

Clear, finally, his lungs drew in the saving breaths. No time to rest, though. He must make use of his advantage while it was his; it wouldn't last long. He swam along the side of the ship looking for an opening. There was none within reach from the water, so he made one, digging his stubby fingers into the metal, climbing up until it was safe to tear a rent in the thick outer and inner walls of the ship.

He found himself in one of the machine rooms of the second level. He went out into the corridor and up the stairway which was half-wrecked, and found himself in the main passage near the control room. He darted down it, into the room. There was nobody there, although the noises from above indicated that the Maraks were again descending. There was his weapon on the floor, where he had left it. He was glad that they had not gotten around to pulling that instrument apart. There would be one thing saved for intelligent examination.

The clatter from the descending crowd turned into a clamor of anger as they discovered him in the passageway. They stopped there for a moment, puzzled. He had been in the ocean, and had somehow magically reappeared within the derelict. It gave him time to pick up the weapon.

Ennis debated rapidly and decided to risk the unknown. How powerful the weapon was he did not know, but with atomic energy it would be powerful. He disliked using it inside the spaceship; he wanted to have enough left to float on the water until Shadden arrived; but they were beginning to advance on him, and he had to start something.

He pulled a lever. The cylinder in his arms jerked back with great force; a bolt of fierce, blinding energy tore out of it and passed with the quickness of light down the length of the corridor.

When he could see again there was no corridor. Everything that had been in the way of the projector was gone, simply disappeared.

Unmindful of the heat from the object in his hands, he turned and directed it at the battleship that was plainly outlined through the space that had been once the walls of the derelict. Before the men on the deck could move, he pulled the lever again.

And the winds were silenced for a moment. The natural elements were still in fear at the incredible forces that came from the destruction of atoms. Then with an agonized scream the hurricane struck again, tore through the spot where there had been a battleship.

Far off in the sky Ennis detected motion. It was Shadden, speeding in a glider.

Now would come the work that was important. Shadden would take the big machine apart and see how it ran. That was what history would remember.

TIME LOCKER

by

LEWIS PADGETT

Mr. Padgett does more playing with time, time plus the fourth dimension—and concocts a locker that needed no lock. Wherein things shrank out of sight and out of time . . . until it was timely and convenient for them to reappear. A good place to hide stolen property, but even in the fourth dimension, crime does not pay!

*

GALLOWAY PLAYED by ear, which would have been all right had he been a musician—but he was a scientist. A drunken and erratic one, but good. He'd wanted to be an experimental technician, and would have been excellent at it, for he had a streak of genius at times. Unfortunately, there had been no funds for such specialized education, and now Galloway, by profession an integrator machine supervisor, maintained his laboratory purely as a hobby. It was the damndest-looking lab in six states. Galloway had spent ten months building what he called a liquor organ, which occupied most of the space. He could recline on a comfortably padded couch and, by manipulating buttons, siphon drinks of marvelous quantity, quality, and variety down his scarified throat. Since he had made the liquor organ during a protracted period of drunkenness, he never remembered the basic principles of its construction. In a way, that was a pity.

There was a little of everything in the lab, much of it incongruous. Rheostats had little skirts on them, like ballet dancers, and vacuously grinning faces of clay. A generator was conspicuously labeled, "Monstro," and a much smaller one rejoiced in the name of "Bubbles." Inside a glass retort was a china rabbit, and Galloway alone knew how it had got there. Just inside the door was a hideous iron dog, originally intended for Victorian lawns or perhaps for Hell, and its hollowed ears served as sockets for test tubes.

"But how do you do it?" Vanning asked.

Galloway, his lank form reclining under the liquor organ, siphoned a shot of double Martini into his mouth. "Huh?"

"You heard me. I could get you a swell job if you'd use that screwball brain of yours. Or even learn to put up a front."

"Tried it," Galloway mumbled. "No use. I can't work when I concentrate, except at mechanical stuff. I think my subconscious must have a high I.Q."

Vanning, a chunky little man with a scarred, swarthy face, kicked his heels against Monstro. Sometimes Galloway annoyed him. The man never realized his own potentialities, or how much they might mean to Horace Vanning, Commerce Analyst. The "commerce," of course, was extra-legal, but the complicated trade relationships of 1970 left many loopholes a clever man could slip through. The fact of the matter was, Vanning acted in an advisory capacity to crooks. It paid well. A sound knowledge of jurisprudence was rare in these days; the statutes were in such a tangle that it took years of research before one could even enter a law school. But Vanning had a staff of trained experts, a colossal library of transcripts, decisions, and legal data, and, for a suitable fee, he could have told Dr. Crippen how to get off scot-free.

The shadier side of his business was handled in strict privacy, without assistants. The matter of the neuro-gun, for example—

Galloway had made that remarkable weapon, quite without realiz-ing its importance. He had hashed it together one evening, piecing out the job with court plaster when his welder went on the fritz. And he'd given it to Vanning, on request. Vanning didn't keep it long. But already he had earned thousands of credits by lending the gun to potential murderers. As a result, the police department had a violent headache.

A man in the know would come to Vanning and say, "I heard you can beat a murder rap. Suppose I wanted to—"

"Hold on! I can't condone anything like that."

"Huh? But—"

"Theoretically, I suppose a perfect murder might be possible. Sup-pose a new sort of gun had been invented, and suppose—just for the sake of an example—it was in a locker at the Newark Stratoship Field."

"Huh?"

"I'm just theorizing. Locker Number 79, combination thirty-blue-eight. These little details always help one to visualize a theory, don't they?"

"You mean—"

"Of course if our murderer picked up this imaginary gun and used it, he'd be smart enough to have a postal box ready, addressed to . . . say . . . Locker 40, Brooklyn Port. He could slip the weapon into the box, seal it, and get rid of the evidence at the nearest mail conveyor. But that's all theorizing. Sorry I can't help you. The fee for an interview is three thousand credits. The receptionist will take your check."

Later, conviction would be impossible. Ruling 875-M, Illinois Precinct, case of State vs. Dupson, set the precedent. Cause of death must be determined. Element of accident must be considered. As Chief Justice Duckett had ruled during the trial of Sanderson vs. Sanderson, which involved the death of the accused's mother-in-law—

Surely the prosecuting attorney, with his staff of toxicological experts, must realize that—

And in short, your honor, I must respectfully request that the case be dismissed for lack of evidence and proof of *casus mortis*—

Galloway never even found out that his neuro-gun was a dangerous weapon. But Vanning haunted the sloppy laboratory, avidly watching the results of his friends' scientific doodling. More than once he had acquired handy little devices in just this fashion. The trouble was, Galloway wouldn't *work!*

He took another sip of Martini, shook his head, and unfolded his lanky limbs. Blinking, he ambled over to a cluttered workbench and began toying with lengths of wire.

"Making something?"

"Dunno. Just fiddling. That's the way it goes. I put things together, and sometimes they work. Trouble is, I never know exactly what they're going to do. *Tsk!*" Galloway dropped the wires and returned to his couch. "Hell with it."

He was, Vanning reflected, an odd duck. Galloway was essentially amoral, thoroughly out of place in this too-complicated world. He seemed to watch, with a certain wry amusement, from a vantage point of his own, rather disinterested for the most part. And he made things—

But always and only for his own amusement. Vanning sighed and glanced around the laboratory, his orderly soul shocked by the melee. Automatically he picked up a rumpled smock from the floor, and looked for a hook. Of course there was none. Galloway, running short of conductive metal, had long since ripped them out and used them in some gadget or other.

The so-called scientist was creating a zombie, his eyes half closed. Vanning went over to a metal locker in one corner and opened the door. There were no hooks, but he folded the smock neatly and laid it on the floor of the locker.

Then he went back to his perch on Monstro.

"Have a drink?" Galloway asked.

Vanning shook his head. "Thanks, no. I've got a case coming up tomorrow."

"There's always thiamin. Filthy stuff. I work better when I've got pneumatic cushions around my brain."

"Well, I don't."

"It is purely a matter of skill," Galloway hummed, "to which each may attain if he will. . . . What are you gaping at?"

"That—locker," Vanning said, frowning in a baffled way. "What the—" He got up. The metal door hadn't been securely latched and had swung open. Of the smock Vanning had placed within the metal compartment there was no trace.

"It's the paint," Galloway explained sleepily. "Or the treatment. I bombarded it with gamma rays. But it isn't good for anything."

Vanning went over and swung a fluorescent into a more convenient position. The locker wasn't empty, as he had at first imagined. The smock was no longer there, but instead there was a tiny blob of—something, pale-green and roughly spherical.

"It melts things?" Vanning asked, staring.

"Uh-huh. Pull it out. You'll see."

Vanning felt hesitant about putting his hand inside the locker. Instead, he found a long pair of test-tube clamps and teased the blob out. It was—

Vanning hastily looked away. His eyes hurt. The green blob was changing in color, shape and size. A crawling, nongeometrical blur of motion rippled over it. Suddenly the clamps were remarkably heavy.

No wonder. They were gripping the original smock.

"It does that, you know," Galloway said absently. "Must be a reason, too. I put things in the locker and they get small. Take 'em out, and they get big again. I suppose I could sell it to a stage magician." His voice sounded doubtful.

Vanning sat down, fingering the smock and staring at the metal locker. It was a cube, approximately 3 x 3 x 5, lined with what seemed to be grayish paint, sprayed on. Outside, it was shiny black.

"How'd you do it?"

"Huh? I dunno. Just fiddling around." Galloway sipped his zombie. "Maybe it's a matter of dimensional extension. My treatment may have altered the spatio-temporal relationships inside the locker. I wonder what that means?" he murmured in a vague aside. "Words frighten me sometimes."

Vanning was thinking about tesseracts. "You mean it's bigger inside than it is outside?"

"A paradox, a paradox, a most delightful paradox. You tell me. I suppose the inside of the locker isn't in this space-time continuum at all. Here, shove that bench in it. You'll see." Galloway made no move to rise; he waved toward the article of furniture in question.

"You're right. That bench is bigger than the locker."

"So it is. Shove it in a bit at a time. That corner first. Go ahead."

Vanning wrestled with the bench. Despite his shortness, he was stockily muscular.

"Lay the locker on its back. It'll be easier."

"I . . . uh! . . . O. K. Now what?"

"Edge the bench down into it."

Vanning squinted at his companion, shrugged, and tried to obey. Of course the bench wouldn't go into the locker. One corner did, that was all. Then, naturally, the bench stopped, balancing precariously at an angle.

"Well?"

"Wait."

The bench moved. It settled slowly downward. As Vanning's jaw dropped, the bench seemed to crawl into the locker, with the gentle motion of a not-too-heavy object sinking through water. It wasn't sucked down. It melted down. The portion still outside the locker was unchanged. But that, too, settled, and was gone.

Vanning craned forward. A blur of movement hurt his eyes. Inside the locker was—something. It shifted its contours, shrank, and became a spiky sort of scalene pyramid, deep-purple in hue.

It seemed to be less than four inches across at its widest point.

"I don't believe it," Vanning said.

Galloway grinned. "As the Duke of Wellington remarked to the subaltern, it was a demned small bottle, sir."

"Now, wait a minute. How the devil could I put an eight-foot bench inside of a five-foot locker?"

"Because of Newton," Galloway said. "Gravity. Go fill a test tube with water and I'll show you."

"Wait a minute . . . O. K. Now what?"

"Got it brim-full? Good. You'll find some sugar cubes in that drawer labeled 'Fuses.' Lay a cube on top of the test tube, one corner down so it touches the water."

Vanning racked the tube and obeyed. "Well?"

"What do you see?"

"Nothing. The sugar's getting wet. And melting."

"So there you are," Galloway said expansively. Vanning gave him a brooding look and turned back to the tube. The cube of sugar was slowly dissolving and melting down.

Presently it was gone.

"Air and water are different physical conditions. In air a sugar cube can exist as a sugar cube. In water it exists in solution. The corner of it extending into water is subject to aqueous conditions. So it alters physically, though not chemically. Gravity does the rest."

"Make it clearer."

"The analogy's clear enough, dope. The water represents the particular condition existing inside that locker. The sugar cube represents the workbench. Now! The sugar soaked up the water and gradually dissolved it, so gravity could pull the cube down into the tube as it melted. See?"

"I think so. The bench soaked up the . . . the x condition inside the locker, eh? A condition that shrank the bench—"

"*In partis*, not *in toto*. A little at a time. You can shove a human body into a small container of sulphuric acid, bit by bit."

"Oh," Vanning said, regarding the cabinet askance. "Can you get the bench out again?"

"Do it yourself. Just reach in and pull it out."

"*Reach* in? I don't want my hand to melt!"

"It won't. The action isn't instantaneous. You saw that yourself. It takes a few minutes for the change to take place. You can reach into the locker without any ill effects, if you don't leave your hand exposed to the conditions for more than a minute or so. I'll show you." Galloway languidly arose, looked around, and picked up an empty demijohn. He dropped this into the locker.

The change wasn't immediate. It occurred slowly, the demijohn altering its shape and size till it was a distorted cube the apparent size of a cube of sugar. Galloway reached down and brought it up again, placing the cube on the floor.

It grew. It was a demijohn again.

"Now the bench. Look out."

Galloway rescued the little pyramid. Presently it became the original workbench.

"You see? I'll bet a storage company would like this. You could probably pack all the furniture in Brooklyn in here, but there'd be trouble in getting what you wanted out again. The physical change, you know—"

"Keep a chart," Vanning suggested absently. "Draw a picture of how the thing looks inside the locker, and note down what it was."

"The legal brain," Galloway said. "I want a drink." He returned to his couch and clutched the siphon in a grip of death.

"I'll give you six credits for the thing," Vanning offered.

"Sold. It takes up too much room anyway. Wish I could put it inside itself." The scientist chuckled immoderately. "That's very funny."

"Is it?" Vanning said. "Well, here you are." He took credit coupons from his wallet. "Where'll I put the dough?"

"Stuff it into Monstro. He's my bank. . . . Thanks."

"Yeah. Say, elucidate this sugar business a bit, will you? It isn't just gravity that affects the cube so it slips into a test tube. Doesn't the water soak up into the sugar—"

"You're right at that. Osmosis. No, I'm wrong. Osmosis has something to do with eggs. Or is that ovulation? Conduction, convection —absorption! Wish I'd studied physics; then I'd know the right words. Just a zoot stoop, that's me. I shall take the daughter of the Vine to spouse," Galloway finished incoherently and sucked at the siphon.

"Absorption," Vanning scowled. "Only not water, being soaked up by the sugar. The . . . the *conditions* existing inside the locker, being soaked up by your workbench—in that particular case."

"Like a sponge or a blotter."

"The bench?"

"Me," Galloway said succinctly, and relapsed into a happy silence, broken by occasional gurgles as he poured liquor down his scarified gullet. Vanning sighed and turned to the locker. He carefully closed and latched the door before lifting the metal cabinet in his muscular arms.

"Going? G'night. Fare thee well, fare thee well—"
"Night."
"Fare—thee—well!" Galloway ended, in a melancholy outburst of
tunefulness, as he turned over preparatory to going to sleep.

Vanning sighed again and let himself out into the coolness of the
night. Stars blazed in the sky, except toward the south, where the
aurora of Lower Manhattan dimmed them. The glowing white towers
of skyscrapers rose in a jagged pattern. A sky-ad announced the virtues
of Vambulin—"It Peps You Up."

His speeder was at the curb. Vanning edged the locker into the
trunk compartment and drove toward the Hudson Floataway, the
quickest route downtown. He was thinking about Poe.

The Purloined Letter, which had been hidden in plain sight, but
re-folded and re-addressed, so that its superficial appearance was
changed. Holy Hutton! What a perfect safe the locker would make!
No thief could crack it, for the obvious reason that it wouldn't be
locked. No thief would *want* to clean it out. Vanning could fill the
locker with credit coupons and instantly they'd become unrecognizable. It was the ideal cache.

How the devil did it work?

There was little use in asking Galloway. He played by ear. A primrose by the river's rim a simple primrose was to him—not *Primula
vulgaris*. Syllogisms were unknown to him. He reached the conclusion
without the aid of either major or minor premises.

Vanning pondered. Two objects cannot occupy the same space at
the same time. *Ergo*, there was a different sort of space in the locker—

But Vanning was pumping at conclusions. There was another
answer—the right one. He hadn't guessed it yet.

Instead, he tooled the speeder downtown to the office building
where he maintained a floor, and brought the locker upstairs in the
freight lift. He didn't put it in his private office; that would have
been too obvious. He placed the metal cabinet in one of the storerooms, sliding a file cabinet in front of it for partial concealment. It
wouldn't do to have the clerks using this particular locker.

Vanning stepped back and considered. Perhaps—

A bell rang softly. Preoccupied, Vanning didn't hear it at first.
When he did, he went back to his own office and pressed the
acknowledgment button on the Winchell. The gray, harsh, bearded
face of Counsel Hatton appeared, filling the screen.

"Hello," Vanning said.

Hatton nodded. "I've been trying to reach you at your home. Thought I'd try the office—"

"I didn't expect you to call now. The trial's tomorrow. It's a bit late for discussion, isn't it?"

"Dugan & Sons wanted me to speak to you. I advised against it."

"Oh?"

Hatton's thick gray brows drew together. "I'm prosecuting, you know. There's plenty of evidence against MacIlson."

"So you say. But peculation's a difficult charge to prove."

"Did you get an injunction against scop?"

"Naturally," Vanning said. "You're not using truth serum on my client!"

"That'll prejudice the jury."

"Not on medical grounds. Scop affects MacIlson harmfully. I've got a covering prognosis."

"Harmfully is right!" Hatton's voice was sharp. "Your client embezzled those bonds, and I can prove it."

"Twenty-five thousand in credits, it comes to, eh? That's a lot for Dugan & Sons to lose. What about that hypothetical case I posed? Suppose twenty thousand were recovered—"

"Is this a private beam? No recordings?"

"Naturally. Here's the cut-off." Vanning held up a metal-tipped cord. "This is strictly *sub rosa*."

"Good," Counsel Hatton said. "Then I can call you a lousy shyster."

"Tch!"

"Your gag's too old. It's moth-eaten. MacIlson swiped five grand in bonds, negotiable into credits. The auditors start checking up. MacIlson comes to you. You tell him to take twenty grand more, and offer to return that twenty if Dugan & Sons refuse to prosecute. MacIlson splits with you on the five thousand, and on the plat standard, that ain't hay."

"I don't admit to anything like that."

"Naturally you don't, not even on a closed beam. But it's tacit. However, the gag's moth-eaten, and my clients won't play ball with you. They're going to prosecute."

"You called me up just to tell me that?"

"No, I want to settle the jury question. Will you agree to let 'em use scop on the panel?"

"O. K.," Vanning said. He wasn't depending on a fixed jury tomorrow. His battle would be based on legal technicalities. With scop-tested talesmen, the odds would be even. And such an arrangement would save days or weeks of argument and challenge.

"Good," Hatton grunted. "You're going to get your pants licked off."

Vanning replied with a mild obscenity and broke the connection. Reminded of the pending court fight, he forced the matter of the fourth-dimensional locker out of his mind and left the office. Later—

Later would be time enough to investigate the possibilities of the remarkable cabinet more thoroughly. Just now, he didn't want his brain cluttered with nonessentials. He went to his apartment, had the servant mix him a short highball, and dropped into bed.

And, the next day, Vanning won his case. He based it on complicated technicalities and obscure legal precedents. The crux of the matter was that the bonds had not been converted into government credits. Abstruse economic charts proved that point for Vanning. Conversion of even five thousand credits would have caused a fluctuation in the graph line, and no such break existed. Vanning's experts went into monstrous detail.

In order to prove guilt, it would have been necessary to show, either actually or by inference, that the bonds had been in existence since last December 20th, the date of their most recent check-and-recording. The case of Donovan vs. Jones stood as a precedent.

Hatton jumped to his feet. "Jones later confessed to his defalcation, your honor!"

"Which does not affect the original decision," Vanning said smoothly. "Retroaction is not admissible here. The verdict was not proven."

"Counsel for the defense will continue."

Counsel for the defense continued, building up a beautifully intricate edifice of casuistic logic.

Hatton writhed. "Your honor! I—"

"If my learned opponent can produce one bond—just one of the bonds in question—I will concede the case."

The presiding judge looked sardonic. "Indeed! If such a piece of evidence could be produced, the defendant would be jailed as fast as I could pronounce sentence. You know that very well, Mr. Vanning. Proceed."

"Very well. My contention, then, is that the bonds never existed. They were the result of a clerical error in notation."

"A clerical error in a Pederson Calculator?"

"Such errors have occurred, as I shall prove. If I may call my next witness—"

Unchallenged, the witness, a math technician, explained how a Pederson Calculator can go haywire. He cited cases.

Hatton caught him up on one point. "I protest this proof. Rhodesia, as everyone knows, is the location of a certain important experimental industry. Witness has refrained from stating the nature of the work performed in this particular Rhodesian factory. Is it not a fact that the Henderson United Company deals largely in radioactive ores?"

"Witness will answer."

"I can't. My records don't include that information."

"A significant omission," Hatton snapped. "Radioactivity damages the intricate mechanism of a Pederson Calculator. There is no radium nor radium by-product in the offices of Dugan & Sons."

Vanning stood up. "May I ask if those offices have been fumigated lately?"

"They have. It is legally required."

"A type of chlorine gas was used."

"Yes."

"I wish to call my next witness."

The next witness, a physicist and official in the Ultra Radium Institute, explained that gamma radiations affect chlorine strongly, causing ionization. Living organisms could assimilate by-products of radium and transmit them in turn. Certain clients of Dugan & Sons had been in contact with radioactivity—

"This is ridiculous, your honor! Pure theorization—"

Vanning looked hurt. "I cite the case of Dangerfield vs. Austro Products, California, 1963. Ruling states that the uncertainy factor is prime admissible evidence. My point is simply that the Pederson Calculator which recorded the bonds could have been in error. If this be true, there were no bonds, and my client is guiltless."

"Counsel will continue," said the judge, wishing he were Jeffries so he could send the whole damned bunch to the scaffold. Jurisprudence should be founded on justice, and not be a three-dimensional chess game. But, of course, it was the natural development of the complicated political and economic factors of modern civilization. It was already evident that Vanning would win his case.

And he did. The jury was directed to find for the defendant. On a last, desperate hope, Hatton raised a point of order and demanded

scop, but his petition was denied. Vanning winked at his opponent
and closed his brief case.

That was that.

Vanning returned to his office. At four-thirty that afternoon
trouble started to break. The secretary announced a Mr. MacIlson, and
was pushed aside by a thin, dark, middle-aged man lugging a gigantic
suedette suitcase.

"Vanning! I've got to see you—"

The attorney's eye hooded. He rose from behind his desk, dismissing
the secretary with a jerk of his head. As the door closed, Vanning
said brusquely, "What are you doing here? I told you to stay away
from me. What's in that bag?"

"The bonds," MacIlson explained, his voice unsteady. "Something's gone wrong—"

"You crazy fool! Bringing the bonds here—" With a leap Vanning
was at the door, locking it. "Don't you realize that if Hatton gets
his hands on that paper, you'll be yanked back to jail? And I'll
be disbarred! Get 'em out of here."

"Listen a minute, will you? I took the bonds to Finance Unity,
as you told me, but . . . but there was an officer there, waiting for
me. I saw him just in time. If he'd caught me—"

Vanning took a deep breath. "You were supposed to leave the
bonds in that subway locker for two months."

MacIlson pulled a news sheet from his pocket. "But the government's declared a freeze on ore stocks and bonds. It'll go into effect
in a week. I couldn't wait—the money would have been tied up indefinitely."

"Let's see that paper." Vanning examined it and cursed softly,
"Where'd you get this?"

"Bought it from a boy outside the jail. I wanted to check the current ore quotations."

"Uh-huh. I see. Did it occur to you that this sheet might be
faked?"

MacIlson's jaw dropped. "Fake?"

"Exactly. Hatton figured I might spring you, and had this paper
ready. You bit. You led the police right to the evidence, and a swell
spot you've put me in."

"B-but—"

Vanning grimaced. "Why do you suppose you saw that cop at
Finance Unity? They could have nabbed you any time. But they

wanted to scare you into heading for my office, so they could catch both of us on the same hook. Prison for you, disbarment for me. Oh, hell!"

MacIlson licked his lips. "Can't I get out a back door?"

"Through the cordon that's undoubtedly waiting? Orbs! Don't be more of a sap than you can help."

"Can't you—hide the stuff?"

"Where? They'll ransack this office with X rays. No, I'll just—" Vanning stopped. "Oh. Hide it, you said. *Hide it*—"

He whirled to the dictograph. "Miss Horton? I'm in conference. Don't disturb me for anything. If anybody hands you a search warrant, insist on verifying it through headquarters. Got me? O. K."

Hope had returned to MacIlson's face. "Is it all right?"

"Oh, shut up!" Vanning snapped. "Wait here for me. Be back directly." He headed for a side door and vanished. In a surprisingly short time he returned, awkardly lugging a metal cabinet.

"Help me . . . *uh!* . . . here. In this corner. Now get out."

"But—"

"Flash," Vanning ordered. "Everything's under control. Don't talk. You'll be arrested, but they can't hold you without evidence. Come back as soon as you're sprung." He urged MacIlson to the door, unlocked it, and thrust the man through. After that, he returned to the cabinet, swung open the door, and peered in. Empty. Sure.

The suedette suitcase—

Vanning worked it into the locker, breathing hard. It took a little time, since the valise was larger than the metal cabinet. But at last he relaxed, watching the brown case shrink and alter its outline till it was tiny and distorted, the shape of an elongated egg, the color of a copper cent piece.

"*Whew!*" Vanning said.

Then he leaned closer, staring. Inside the locker, something was moving. A grotesque little creature less than four inches tall was visible. It was a shocking object, all cubes and angles, a bright green in tint, and it was obviously alive.

Someone knocked on the door.

The tiny—thing—was busy with the copper-colored egg. Like an ant, it was lifting the egg and trying to pull it away. Vanning gasped and reached into the locker. The fourth-dimensional creature dodged. It wasn't quick enough. Vanning's hand descended, and he felt wriggling movement against his palm.

He squeezed.

The movement stopped. He let go of the dead thing and pulled his hand back swiftly.

The door shook under the impact of fists.

Vanning closed the locker and called, "Just a minute."

"Break it down," somebody ordered.

But that wasn't necessary. Vanning put a painful smile on his face and turned the key. Counsel Hatton came in, accompanied by bulky policemen. "We've got MacIlson," he said.

"Oh? Why?"

For answer Hatton jerked his hand. The officers began to search the room. Vanning shrugged.

"You've jumped the gun," he said. "Breaking and entering—"

"We've got a warrant."

"Charge?"

"The bonds, of course." Hatton's voice was weary. "I don't know where you've hid that suitcase, but we'll find it."

"What suitcase?" Vanning wanted to know.

"The one MacIlson had when he came in. The one he didn't have when he went out."

"The game," Vanning said sadly, "is up. You win."

"Eh?"

"If I tell you what I did with the suitcase, will you put in a good word for me?"

"Why . . . yeah. Where—"

"I ate it," Vanning said, and retired to the couch, where he settled himself for a nap. Hatton gave him a long, hating look. The officers tore in—

They passed by the locker, after a casual glance inside. The X rays revealed nothing, in walls, floor, ceiling, or articles of furniture. The other offices were searched, too. Vanning applauded the painstaking job.

In the end, Hatton gave up. There was nothing else he could do.

"I'll clap suit on you tomorrow," Vanning promised. "Same time I get a habeas corpus on MacIlson."

"Step to hell," Hatton growled.

" 'By now."

Vanning waited till his unwanted guests had departed. Then, chuckling quietly, he went to the locker and opened it.

The copper-colored egg that represented the suedette suitcase had vanished. Vanning groped inside the locker, finding nothing.

The significance of this didn't strike Vanning at first. He swung the cabinet around so that it faced the window. He looked again, with identical results.

The locker was empty.

Twenty-five thousand credits in negotiable ore bonds had disappeared.

Vanning started to sweat. He picked up the metal box and shook it. That didn't help. He carried it across the room and set it up in another corner, returning to search the floor with painstaking accuracy. Holy—

Hatton?

No. Vanning hadn't let the locker out of his sight from the time the police had entered till they left. An officer had swung open the cabinet's door, looked inside, and closed it again. After that the door had remained shut, till just now.

The bonds were gone.

So was the abnormal little creature Vanning had crushed. All of which meant—what?

Vanning approached the locker and closed it, clicking the latch into position. Then he reopened it, not really expecting that the copper-colored egg would reappear.

He was right. It didn't.

Vanning staggered to the Winchell and called Galloway.

"Whatzit? Huh? Oh. What do you want?" The scientist's gaunt face appeared on the screen, rather the worse for wear. "I got a hangover. Can't use thiamin, either. I'm allergic to it. How'd your case come out?"

"Listen," Vanning said urgently, "I put something inside that damn locker of yours and now it's gone."

"The locker? That's funny."

"No! The thing I put in it. A . . . a suitcase."

Galloway shook his head thoughtfully. "You never know, do you? I remember once I made a—"

"The hell with that. I want that suitcase back!"

"An heirloom?" Galloway suggested.

"No, there's money in it."

"Wasn't that a little foolish of you? There hasn't been a bank failure since 1949. Never suspected you were a miser, Vanning. Like to have the stuff around, so you can run it through your birdlike fingers, eh?"

"You're drunk."

"I'm *trying*," Galloway corrected. "But I've built up an awful resistance over a period of years. It takes time. Your call's already set me back two and a half drinks. I must put an extension on the siphon, so I can Winchell and guzzle at the same time."

Vanning almost chattered incoherently into the mike. "My suit-case! What happened to it? I want it back."

"Well, I haven't got it."

"Can't you find out where it is?"

"Dunno. Tell me the details. I'll see what I can figure out."

Vanning complied, revising his story as caution prompted.

"O. K.," Galloway said at last, rather unwillingly. "I hate work-ing out theories, but just as a favor. . . . My diagnosis will cost you fifty credits."

"What? Now listen—"

"Fifty credits," Galloway repeated unflinchingly. "Or no prog-nosis."

"How do I know you can get it back for me?"

"Chances are I can't. Still, maybe . . . I'll have to go over to Mechanistra and use some of their machines. They charge a good bit, too. But I'll need forty-brain-power calculators—"

"O. K., O. K.!" Vanning growled. "Hop to it. I want that suit-case back."

"What interests me is that little bug you squashed. In fact, that's the only reason I'm tackling your problem. Life in the fourth dimen-sion—" Galloway trailed off, murmuring. His face faded from the screen. After a while Vanning broke the connection.

He re-examined the locker, finding nothing new. Yet the suedette suitcase had vanished from it, into thin air. Oh, hell!

Brooding over his sorrows, Vanning shrugged into a top coat and dined vinously at the Manhattan Roof. He felt very sorry for him-self.

The next day he felt even sorrier. A call to Galloway had given the blank signal, so Vanning had to mark time. About noon MacIlson dropped in. His nerves were shot.

"You took your time in springing me," he started immediately. "Well, what now? Have you got a drink anywhere around?"

"You don't need a drink," Vanning grunted. "You've got a skin-ful already, by the look of you. Run down to Florida and wait till this blows over."

"I'm sick of waiting. I'm going to South America. I want some credits."

"Wait'll I arrange to cash the bonds."

"I'll take the bonds. A fair half, as we agreed."

Vanning's eyes narrowed. "And walk out into the hands of the police. Sure."

MacIlson looked uncomfortable. "I'll admit I made a boner. But this time—no, I'll play smart now."

"You'll wait, you mean."

"There's a friend of mine on the roof parking lot, in a helicopter. I'll go up and slip him the bonds, and then I'll just walk out. The police won't find anything on me."

"I said no," Vanning repeated. "It's too dangerous."

"It's dangerous as things are. If they locate the bonds—"

"They won't."

"Where'd you hide 'em?"

"That's my business."

MacIlson glowered nervously. "Maybe. But they're in this building. You couldn't have finagled 'em out yesterday before the cops came. No use playing your luck too far. Did they use X rays?"

"Yeah."

"Well, I heard Counsel Hatton's got a batch of experts going over the blueprints on this building. He'll find your safe. I'm getting out of here before he does."

Vanning patted the air. "You're hysterical. I've taken care of you, haven't I? Even though you almost screwed the whole thing up."

"Sure," MacIlson said, pulling at his lip. "But I"— He chewed a fingernail. "Oh, damn! I'm sitting on the edge of a volcano with termites under me. I can't stay here and wait till they find the bonds. They can't extradite me from South America—where I'm going, anyway."

"You're going to wait," Vanning said firmly. "That's your best chance."

There was suddenly a gun in MacIlson's hand. "You're going to give me half the bonds. Right now. I don't trust you a little bit. You figure you can stall me along—hell, get those bonds!"

"No," Vanning said.

"I'm not kidding."

"I know you aren't. I can't get the bonds."

"Eh? Why not?"

"Ever heard of a time lock?" Vanning asked, his eyes watchful. "You're right; I put the suitcase in a concealed safe. But I can't open that safe till a certain number of hours have passed."

"Mm-m." MacIlson pondered. "When—"

"Tomorrow."

"All right. You'll have the bonds for me then?"

"If you want them. But you'd better change your mind. It'd be safer."

For answer MacIlson grinned over his shoulder as he went out. Vanning sat motionless for a long time. He was, frankly, scared.

The trouble was, MacIlson was a manic-depressive type. He'd kill. Right now, he was cracking under the strain, and imagining himself a desperate fugitive. Well—precautions would be advisable.

Vanning called Galloway again, but got no answer. He left a message on the recorder and thoughtfully looked into the locker again. It was empty, depressingly so.

That evening Galloway let Vanning into his laboratory. The scientist looked both tired and drunk. He waved comprehensively toward a table, covered with scraps of paper.

"What a headache you gave me! If I'd known the principles behind that gadget, I'd have been afraid to tackle it. Sit down. Have a drink. Got the fifty credits?"

Silently Vanning handed over the coupons. Galloway shoved them into Monstro. "Fine. Now—" He settled himself on the couch. "Now we start. The fifty credit question."

"Can I get the suitcase back?"

"No," Galloway said flatly. "At least, I don't see how it can be worked. It's in another spatio-temporal sector."

"Just what does that mean?"

"It means the locker works something like a telescope, only the thing isn't merely visual. The locker's a window, I figure. You can reach through it as well as look through it. It's an opening into Now plus x."

Vanning scowled. "So far you haven't said anything."

"So far all I've got is theory, and that's all I'm likely to get. Look. I was wrong originally. The things that went into the locker didn't appear in another space, because there would have been a spatial constant. I mean, they wouldn't have got smaller. Size is size. Moving a one-inch cube from here to Mars wouldn't make it any larger or smaller."

"What about a different density in the surrounding medium? Wouldn't that crush an object?"

"Sure, and it'd stay squashed. It wouldn't return to its former size and shape when it was taken out of the locker again. X plus y never equals xy. But x times y—"

"So?"

"That's a pun," Galloway broke off to explain. "The things we put in the locker went into time. Their time-rate remained constant, but not the spatial relationships. Two things can't occupy the same place at the same time. *Ergo*, your suitcase went into a different time. Now plus x. And what x represents I don't know, though I suspect a few million years."

Vanning looked dazed. "The suitcase is a million years in the future?"

"Dunno how far, but—I'd say plenty. I haven't enough factors to finish the equation. I reasoned by induction, mostly, and the results are screwy as hell. Einstein would have loved it. My theorem shows that the universe is expanding and contracting at the same time."

"What's that got to do—"

"Motion is relative," Galloway continued inexorably. "That's a basic principle. Well, the Universe *is* expanding, spreading out like a gas, but its component parts are shrinking at the same time. The *parts* don't actually grow, you know—not the suns and atoms. They just run away from the central point. Galloping off in all directions . . . where was I? Oh. Actually, the Universe, taken as a unit, is shrinking."

"So, it's shrinking. Where's my suitcase?"

"I told you. In the future. Inductive reasoning showed that. It's beautifully simple and logical. And it's quite impossible of proof, too. A hundred, a thousand, a million years ago the Earth—the Universe —was larger than it is now. And it continues to contract. Sometime in the future the Earth will be just half as large as it is now. Only we won't notice it because the Universe will be proportionately smaller."

Galloway went on dreamily. "We put a workbench into the locker, so it emerged sometime in the future. The locker's an open window into a different time, as I told you. Well, the bench was affected by the conditions of that period. It shrank, after we gave it a few seconds to soak up the entropy or something. Do I mean entropy? Allah knows. Oh, well."

"It turned into a pyramid."

"Maybe there's geometric distortion, too. Or it might be a visual illusion. Perhaps we can't get the exact focus. I doubt if things will really look different in the future—except that they'll be smaller—but we're using a window into the fourth dimension. We're taking a pleat in time. It must be like looking through a prism. The alteration in size is real, but the shape and color are altered to our eyes by the fourth-dimensional prism."

"The whole point, then, is that my suitcase is in the future. Eh? But why did it disappear from the locker?"

"What about that little creature you squashed? Maybe he had pals. They wouldn't be visible till they came into the very narrow focus of the whatchmaycallit, but—figure it out. Sometime in the future, in a hundred or a thousand or a million years, a suitcase suddenly appears out of thin air. One of our descendants investigates. You kill him. His pals come along and carry the suitcase away, out of range of the locker. In space it may be anywhere, and the time factor's an unknown quantity. Now plus x. It's a time locker. Well?"

"Hell!" Vanning exploded. "So that's all you can tell me? I'm supposed to chalk it up to profit and loss?"

"Uh-huh. Unless you want to crawl into the locker yourself after your suitcase. Lord knows where you'd come out, though. The proportions of the air probably would have changed in a few thousand years. There might be other alterations, too."

"I'm not that crazy."

So there he was. The bonds were gone, beyond hope of redemption. Vanning could resign himself to that loss, once he knew the securities wouldn't fall into the hands of the police. But MacIlson was another matter, especially after a bullet spattered against the glassolex window of Vanning's office.

An interview with MacIlson had proved unsatisfactory. The defaulter was convinced that Vanning was trying to bilk him. He was removed forcibly, yelling threats. He'd go to the police—he'd confess—-

Let him. There was no proof. The hell with him. But, for safety's sake, Vanning clapped an injunction on his quondam client.

It didn't land. MacIlson clipped the official on the jaw and fled. Now, Vanning suspected, he lurked in dark corners, armed, and anxious to commit homicide. Obviously a manic-depressive type.

Vanning took a certain malicious pleasure in demanding a couple of plain-clothes men to act as his guards. Legally, he was within his rights, since his life had been threatened. Until MacIlson was under sufficient restriction, Vanning would be protected. And he made sure that his guards were two of the best shots on the Manhattan force. He also found out that they had been told to keep their eyes peeled for the missing bonds and the suedette suitcase. Vanning Winchelled Counsel Hatton and grinned at the screen.

"Any luck yet?"

"What do you mean?"

"My watchdogs. Your spies. They won't find the bonds, Hatton. Better call 'em off. Why make the poor devils do two jobs at once?"

"One job would be enough. Finding the evidence. If MacIlson drilled you, I wouldn't be too unhappy."

"Well, I'll see you in court," Vanning said. "You're prosecuting Watson, aren't you?"

"Yes. Are you waiving scop?"

"On the jurors? Sure. I've got this case in the bag."

"That's what you think," Hatton said, and broke the beam.

Chuckling, Vanning donned his topcoat, collected the guards, and headed for court. There was no sign of MacIlson—

Vanning won the case, as he had expected. He returned to his offices, collected a few unimportant messages from the switchboard girl, and walked toward his private suite. As he opened the door, he saw the suedette suitcase on the carpet in one corner.

He stopped, hand frozen on the latch. Behind him he could hear the heavy footsteps of the guards. Over his shoulder Vanning said, "Wait a minute," and dodged into the office, slamming and locking the door behind him. He caught the tail end of a surprised question.

The suitcase. There it was, unequivocally. And, quite as unequivocally, the two plain-clothes men, after a very brief conference, were hammering on the door, trying to break it down.

Vanning turned green. He took a hesitant step forward, and then saw the locker, in the corner to which he had moved it. The time locker—

That was it. If he shoved the suitcase inside the locker, it would become unrecognizable. Even if it vanished again, that wouldn't matter. What mattered was the vital importance of getting rid—immediately!—of incriminating evidence.

The door rocked on its hinges. Vanning scuttled toward the suitcase and picked it up. From the corner of his eye he saw movement.

In the air above him, a hand had appeared. It was the hand of a

giant, with an immaculate cuff fading into emptiness. Its huge fingers
were reaching down—

Vanning screamed and sprang away. He was too slow. The hand
descended, and Vanning wriggled impotently against the palm.

The hand contracted into a fist. When it opened, what was left
of Vanning dropped squashily to the carpet, which it stained.

The hand withdrew into nothingness. The door fell in and the
plain-clothes men stumbled over it as they entered.

It didn't take long for Hatton and his cohorts to arrive. Still, there
was little for them to do except clean up the mess. The suedette bag,
containing twenty-five thousand credits in negotiable bonds, was carried off to a safer place. Vanning's body was scraped up and removed
to the morgue. Photographers flashed pictures, fingerprint experts
insufflated their white powder, X ray men worked busily. It was all
done with swift efficiency, so that within an hour the office was empty
and the door sealed.

Thus there were no spectators to witness the advent of a gigantic
hand that appeared from nothingness, groped around as though
searching for something, and presently vanished once more—

The only person who could have thrown light on the matter was
Galloway, and his remarks were directed to Monstro, in the solitude
of his laboratory. All he said was:

"So that's why that workbench materialized for a few minutes
here yesterday. Hm-m-m. Now plus x—and x equals about a week.
Still, why not? It's all relative. But—I never thought the Universe
was shrinking that fast!"

He relaxed on the couch and siphoned a double Martini.

"Yeah, that's it," he murmured after a while. "Whew! I guess
Vanning must have been the only guy who ever reached into the
middle of next week and—killed himself! I think I'll get tight."

And he did.

THE LINK

by

CLEVE CARTMILL

*Mr. Cartmill describes the imaginary events of what was, per-
haps, the most important day in our history. That day when
a certain animal braced himself on his short hind legs, picked up
a heavy stick and started a world order that was really new. New,
yes—but apparently the old order didn't change completely, for
we couldn't help thinking how unchanged is the human trait of
instinctive hatred of the one who dares to differ from his fellows.*

*

LOK KNEW that he was different from his brothers after the incident with the big black and yellow cat.

It stood in the trail and looked at him. True, it drew back its lips,
exposing long, yellow tusks, but it did not growl insults, it did not
attack.

After a time, the cat said, "I could eat you."

Lok returned the steady, yellow gaze.

The cat asked, "Why don't you run into the trees like the others?
What are you doing here?"

"I am seeing pictures," Lok replied.

The cat arched its back and snarled with suspicion. "What is
that?"

"Why . . . why," Lok faltered, "things."

The cat edged back a pace.

"Things," Lok continued. "My brothers have tried to kill me. I
am alone. I am going . . . going—" He broke off, puzzled, and stared
with vacant, dark eyes at the cat.

308

"You have no hair," the cat said, moving forward again.

"I have, I have!" Lok cried desperately, and shook long, black locks over his face. "Look!"

"That!" the cat sneered. "It is not like the others."

The others. Lok sensed a power within himself when he thought of the others, a power that did not quite come into focus. It swelled up into his chest, however, and he straightened so that his knuckles were not on the ground.

"I am Lok," he said with dignity. "Therefore, step aside. I would pass."

He marched deliberately toward the cat. It crouched back on its haunches, spitting between fangs, but it gave way. Its eyes were wide and yellow, no longer instruments of sight now that it was suddenly afraid. Roaring incoherent blasphemies, it backed down the narrow path as Lok advanced. With one last cry of rage, it leaped into the wall of vines to one side, and Lok passed on, his low and leathery brow creased in thought.

He forgot the cat on the instant, but this new power held him erect as he moved away from the country of his tribe.

His inner perception strove to grasp what had happened to him, and, as he marched along the trail, he sifted the symphony of the jungle with subconscious attention. He noted the quiet wrought by the roars of the curve-toothed jungle king. He felt the sleepy rhythm of the hot afternoon begin to flow again; somewhere a red and green bird shouted harsh and senseless cries; succulent beetles buzzed stupidly in trees; off to the right a troupe of his little brown cousins swung by fingers and tails and chattered of drinking nuts; moving toward him on the trail swelled grunts of the white tusks.

This latter sound snapped him back to a realization of danger. He wanted no quarrel with a tribe of these quick, dark prima donnas, with their tiny, sharp hoofs and short, slashing tusks. Even the jungle king himself would tackle no more than one at a time. Lok broke through the green trail wall and went hand over hand up a thick vine, to wait for the white tusks to pass.

They trotted into sight, twenty yards away, four full-grown males and three females. The leader, an old boar, with tiny, red eyes, grunted tactical instructions in case of attack at the next trail curve.

Lok felt an ancient fury, and from the safety of a high limb he jumped up and down and screamed imprecations at the bristled band.

"Cowards!" he yelled, flinging handfuls of twigs and leaves at them. "Weaklings! Fish food! If you come up here, I will fight you all!"

At his first cry, the males had wheeled and stood shoulder to shoulder facing his tree, looking up at him with steady, gleaming eyes. The females huddled behind this ivory-pointed rampart, waiting without sound or motion.

The old leader grunted his contempt for Lok and his race.

"Come down," he invited. "Fool!"

Lok ceased his age-old antics, and regarded his actions with a dull sense of wonder. True, he had always done this; it was a part of life to insult other inhabitants of his world from a place of safety. He had done this with his brothers, and with his mother while he was still small enough to sit in her hand.

Yet this new part of himself which controlled his new sense of power sneered at such conduct. Lok felt at first like hanging his head; then he felt the need to assert himself.

He climbed down the vine, without fear. He marched toward the white tusks who now held their armored muzzles low to the ground in attack position.

"Wait!" the leader grunted to his companions. "This one has a strange smell."

Advancing steadily, Lok said, "Step aside, I would pass. I am Lok. I am master."

When he was within three paces, the white tusks acted.

"Go!" grunted the leader to the huddled females. "Remember his smell!"

The leader and the three younger boars backed away as Lok advanced. When they had retreated twenty paces in this fashion, they broke and wheeled at a signal from the old one, and pattered after the vanished females.

Lok stood motionless for some time, gazing vacantly but steadily at the bend of trail around which the white tusks had fled. Beside the last image of their curling tails and bobbing hindquarters now formed the picture of the furious, but frightened, cat.

For the first time in his twelve years of life, Lok used past experience to form a theory. It was vague and confused, but he felt that he could re-enter the tribe and rule in place of the Old One. He was Lok. He was master.

He departed from the trail and climbed to a remembered treetop pathway which would lead him to his tribe. As he leaped and swung from swaying limb to limb a troublesome feeling grew within his head. He felt that a matter of importance should be considered, but its form and shape escaped his powers of concentration.

His passage did not disturb the life of the sultry green forest. Gaudy birds flitted through the gloom, and hunting beasts made fleeting shadows at times below him. The sun dropped, stars flared overhead, and Lok found a sleeping crotch for the night.

Sleep evaded him. Not because of night cries of questing white owls, or of brief threshings in the nearby pool of a gurgling stream, or of directionless roars of the big cats. He was accustomed to this pattern of sound.

The disturbance was deep within himself, a troubling problem knocking at the door of memory. It was a new sensation, this groping backward. Heretofore he had been satisfied if there was fruit, if rotten logs yielded fat, white grubs. He had been content when fed and sheltered.

Consideration of shelter brought the problem nearer to recognition and, as he concentrated, it burst into form. The problem was one of the passage of seasons. Since he had left the tribe, followed by foaming threats of his brothers and the Old One, the rains had come twice. His lack of a protective furry coat had driven him into caves where he had shivered through the long, damp months.

Well did he know now what had made him uneasy. The tribe might not know him, after this long space of separation. An event took place, and during the time it affected them they considered it. Once it was over, it was as though it had never existed. Thus it had been for him, too, until now.

Lok's head began to ache, but he clung stubbornly to the pictures that formed in his thoughts. He saw himself forced to subdue the strongest of the tribe before he could take his rightful place at their head.

He was Lok. He was master. But he was not as strong as some, and in a fight where strength alone would determine the outcome he might be subdued and killed.

Restless, wide awake, he shook his head angrily and climbed to the highest level in search of a place where he might sleep. He moved from one tree to another, grumbling to himself. He crossed the stream near the drinking pool which gleamed in full brilliance under the shining eye of night.

He was instantly thirsty, and dropped lower. As he did so, his watchful eyes caught movement at one edge of the pool, and the arm of a ripple moved lazily across the bright surface. A long snout lurked there. Though he was large and unafraid, Lok wished to avoid a brush with those long, fanged jaws or the flashing armored tail. He half turned to go upstream to a place of safety, but was arrested by a sound on the trail. He caught the delicate scent of a spotted jumper, and presently saw a trio, mother and two small twins, advancing to the pool in dainty leaps. The mother's long, leaf-shaped ears were rigid, twitching toward every rustle in the night. She held her shapely head high, testing the air with suspicious nostrils, and the end of every pace found her poised for instant flight. The little ones, crowding her heels, duplicated her every motion.

Lok eyed the tableau with excitement, knowing what was coming. He could see the faint outline of the long snout motionless in the shallows near the path. A meal was in preparation.

The mother led her twins to the edge of the pool and stood watch while they dipped trusting muzzles in the water.

Lok saw blurred motion as the long snout's tail whipped one of the little twins into the pool and powerful jaws dragged it under With a cry of terror the mother and the remaining twin flashed into the darkness, the sound of their racing hoofs smothered by the threshing in the pool.

The turbulent surface darkened, and Lok cried out once from suppressed emotion. Presently he returned to his sleeping crotch, his thirst forgotten in consideration of what he had seen.

The long snout, Lok knew, was no match for spotted jumpers on land. Although the long snout could move for a short distance with great speed, the spotted jumper could simply vanish while one looked at it. Yet the long snout had caught, killed, and eaten one of the small spotted jumpers.

Another factor, in addition to simple speed or strength, had made this possible, and Lok beat against his head with a closed hand trying to call it to mind. The long snout had waited like one of the big cats above a trail—

Lok felt the solution begin to form and fixed wide, empty eyes on the dark while he made pictures inside his head.

He had seen a cat crouched on a limb in an all-day vigil, waiting without motion until its chosen prey trotted along the trail below. Then a flashing arc, a slashing blow, and the cat had slain an inhabitant sometimes more than twice its own size and speed.

He had seen also a fear striker, many times as long as Lok was tall, coiled in hunger beside a trail for a whole day or night until the proper sized victim passed. Then a flashing strike, whipping coils, a crushing of bones, and the fear striker held the limp body of one he could not possibly have caught by speed alone.

Yet the lying-in-wait alone was not the answer to the problem of his conquering the tribe, Lok felt. It was not his way to crouch near a rotten log until the Old One, for example, came to tear it apart for grubs and then fling himself on the hungry one. No, not that, but still the essence of what he sought was there.

Each denizen of the world in his own fashion delivered a death blow to his prey. With the long snout's tail—

Lok cried out in the night as he found the answer. "I am master!" he shouted. "I am Lok!"

Ignoring the sleepy protest of a bird in the neighboring tree, he slipped to the ground and coursed through the brush seeking his weapon, a short, stout limb.

When he found it, he stood in the darkness swinging it in vicious arcs, filled with an inner excitement. Pictures formed again in his mind.

When two males of his tribe fought, they shouted preliminary insults until rage was at a sufficient pitch for loose-armed, bare-fanged combat. How devastating, Lok thought, to step in during the insult stage and surprise his opponent with a death blow.

As soon as vivid dawn brought raucous, screaming wakefulness to the jungle, Lok continued toward the land of his tribe. He found sustained travel in the trees impossible while hampered with his weapon, and dropped to the jungle floor, slashing vines aside with the club when the going was thick.

Once he climbed a tree for long fruit to satisfy his hunger, and once he drank from a stream, searching somewhat eagerly for a long snout on whom he might try his new weapon.

He came at midday to the edge of a wide, treeless plain covered with waist-high yellow grass. Lok hesitated to cross it on foot, for out there, lurking near the herds of the striped feeders, one sometimes saw big heads.

These were yellow, catlike killers, more powerful than the jungle cats, more feared than any. They were not only powerful, they were agile and ruthless when in bad temper.

Yet if he did not cross the plain he would be forced into the trees for a long circuit and must abandon his weapon.

That decided him. He was fond of this heavy, knobbed length of wood. It seemed to give him an additional arm, and it doubled his courage. He set out through the yellow grass, circling a grazing tribe of striped feeders in the hope that he might pass unchallenged.

Presently he struck a path wriggling in his general direction, and it was on this path, in the center of the plain where there was no shelter, that he met a huge, golden-eyed big head.

It came upon him face to face, trotting as noiselessly as Lok, a heavy-maned, full-grown male. The two froze in their tracks, and the big head gave a roar of surprise. Lok drew back his weapon, holding it near one end with both hands.

"I will kill you," Lok said, a slight quaver in his voice, "if you do not go away."

"What?" the big head roared in disbelief.

Lok repeated his threat in a more steady voice.

The big head crouched, swishing his tufted tail.

"You have a strange smell," he said.

Lok detected a note of uneasiness and his courage rose to reckless heights.

"You are a coward!" he cried, and jumped up and down on the sun-baked trail. "Weakling! Fish food!"

The big head hesitated a second. Then with a roar of unintelligible rage he launched himself at Lok, jaws wide and red, claws unsheathed.

Lok darted to one side and swung his club. All his strength was in the blow which caught the big head in his yellow ribs while in mid-air. The tawny beast twisted, was deflected out of the path and fell heavily in the dry grass. He was on his feet instantly and in the air again, coming at Lok almost faster than his eye could follow.

Lok felt a hopeless surprise when his blow did not kill the big head, and confidence in his weapon deflated. But he swung again, and the club thudded home on the big head's neck. The powerful body jerked again in the air and sprawled away from the path.

The big head was not so quick in resuming attack. He crouched in the grass which his fall had flattened, and roared gibberish at Lok, who held his club at ready.

A little of Lok's confidence returned as he looked steadily into the blazing eyes which had taken on a tinge of reddish green. Yet he was afraid, for he well knew the power of those fanged, dripping jaws, and the death in each front paw.

Entirely aside from his thoughts of self-preservation, Lok was exhilarated by the scene: the sleek tan body rippling with taut muscles, the wide grassy theater of action, and the excited yaps of an approaching troupe of dead eaters gathering at a distance to dispose of the loser.

Flecks of dark sweat spotted the smooth body of the big head, and Lok felt his own body growing moist and then cool as a light breeze brushed past.

Without warning, the big head leaped a third time. Lok, caught slightly unaware, swung his club without definite aim and without the full power which he had put into his previous blows. He caught the cat just below one ear.

As the blow struck, Lok had the impression of a drinking nut being broken by striking it against a stone. It was a satisfying sensation as it ran up the club into his arms, but he attached no importance to it until he saw its result.

For the big head twisted again in the air and tumbled into the grass, dead with a crushed skull, lips skinned back from long, yellow fangs. Lok stood well away from the still body for a few moments, eyeing it with a dull sense of wonder.

His other blows had been mightier than this which terminated the battle, yet they had wrought no apparent damage. After a short time, he prodded the motionless body from a distance with his club.

"Coward!" he snarled softly. "Arise!"

When further abuse brought no reaction, Lok shouldered his club and went on his way, and the slinking dead eaters swarmed upon the corpse behind him.

He examined the plain in all directions for evidence of other big heads but saw nothing except the upraised heads and pointed ears of a herd of striped feeders who had heard the roars of battle. Lok continued cautiously toward the far jungle wall, thinking of the strange effect of a light blow on the head as compared to a heavy blow on the body of the big head. He felt no sense of accomplishment, although he was perhaps the first of his tribe to vanquish their most feared enemy. He was puzzled.

He soon dismissed the matter, however, for the more pressing problem of locating the tribe. When he reached his home country, a land of fruit and grubs near the foothills of a tall mountain range, he roamed in a wide circle. As he searched, an uneasiness grew within him, a sense of need for action.

Something was wrong, something completely dissociated from his finding the tribe. Other denizens of the forest felt it, too: birds reflected it in sharp, nervous cries, and the jungle reverberated now and then with baffled roars of big cats.

On the second night, while Lok was drowsing in the crotch of a thick, white tree, a distant growing murmur brought him awake. The murmur grew in volume to a sullen rushing roar as a wall of wind moved through the night.

On all sides was the crash of falling trees: first an ear-splitting crack as wind-strain shattered the trunk, a groaning sw-i-i-sh and finally an earth-shaking boom!

Lok shivered with discomfort in the sleeping crotch. He understood his uneasiness of the past two days—the rainy season was about to begin. Although he was fairly safe in this stout tree, he longed for the dry protection of the cave he now remembered.

A far-off mutter of rain deepened as it rushed across the treetops with the sound of a great herd of stampeded striped feeders. Lok felt a certain terror, which increased as brilliant twisting tongues lashed out of a roaring sky.

He shrank close to the tree which now leaned at a steady angle from the push of the wind, and grew wetter and more uncomfortable as the night wore on. During the lull when the quiet center of the storm moved past he shivered in dread of the wind which would now blow, even more fiercely, perhaps in the opposite direction.

When a leaden but dry dawn broke, Lok resumed his search for the tribe, torn between the desire for leadership and the desire for shelter.

Fallen trees were everywhere and though the rotten cores of many housed fat grubs, Lok took to the forest roof where his passage was unhindered by wet, tangled vines or a myriad of tiny, poisonous many legs and whip tails that scurried about.

The sun came out later in the morning, and Lok found the tribe near midday in a steaming clearing.

Perhaps fifty in number, from huge gray-tufted males to babies clinging to their mothers, they eyed Lok with sullen suspicion as he dropped from a tree and advanced to the center of the clearing, swing-his club in one hand.

"I am Lok," he said. "I have returned to rule the tribe."

The females scuttled behind the males, who formed a wide half circle of beetle-browed suspicion.

"This hairless one has a sickening smell," one said.

"Kill him!" cried another.

Lok moved a pace nearer. "Wait!" he commanded.

They were quiet.

"I have slain a big head," Lok said, swinging the club. "I am master."

The Old One stepped out of the half circle and advanced to within ten paces.

"Fish food!" the Old One yelled. "Coward! Go before I tear out your throat!"

He bounced up and down, as was the custom of fighters, on his squat legs and made his face as frightening as possible with wide, slavering jaws. Behind him the others emulated his example, howling and hurling threats. The clearing was in instant bedlam as the females augmented the cries and their babies clung to them in loud terror.

Into the midst of the insult and confusion, Lok stepped forward and swung his club.

Its sharp crack against the skull of the Old One cut all sound. The Old One brushed at his head with a hand as though driving away an annoying insect, and then fell like a shattered tree, his jaws and eyes still wide with anger.

Into the silence, Lok said, "I have slain the Old One. I am master."

They had not yet grasped the event and were quiet, save for the babies who whimpered softly.

"I have gone," Lok continued, gesturing, "far out there. There is a dry place safe from the rain and wind. It is good. I will lead you. There is food."

They stared at him with dull, uncomprehending eyes. For a long time there was no sound except for the babies and the far-off cries of birds while Lok stood in the center of the clearing with the dead Old One at his feet. Then one of the young males spoke.

"He has a smell I hate, this hairless scum."

The hate filled them instantly, and the entire tribe once more shrieked insults and threats of death. Some of the more foolhardy males rushed forward a few steps, and Lok's club slashed out the second life.

This brought another moment of quiet, and a big, gray female moved out of the ruck.

"Go!" she growled from foam-flecked jaws. "I, myself, will kill you!"

"Mother!" Lok cried. "I am Lok!"

"Mother?" she snarled. "Pink filth!"

"Kill him!" bawled half a dozen throats, and the males closed in.

Confusion and lust for death filled the air again as Lok backed away, swinging his club on the hairy beasts that crowded him with foaming mouths and screaming lungs. Each swing took its toll, and Lok remembered the lesson he had learned on the grassy plain. He struck each blow at a head, and the crushing skulls brought a tingling excitement into his arms and a wild exhilaration to his brain.

One of the larger males caught Lok by an arm and, as he bent to sink teeth home in the wrist, Lok took careful aim and shattered his head like a ripe fruit. The sound of its cracking cut sharply into the incoherent roars of the attackers.

"I am master!" Lok screamed, thinking of the split skulls. "I am Lok!"

And he swung again, and again.

When he was near the jungle edge, Lok's arms were tiring. The last three males he hit rose shakily to elbows and knees. Lok turned and fled. There were too many.

None followed. They returned to the still forms which marked the trail of battle, and Lok watched them try to shake life back into the dead for a time. Presently they tired of this, and the largest male called them into the forest. They trooped away, chattering lightly of drinking nuts, leaving the wounded to follow as best they might.

Lok's brooding eyes followed until they were hidden from sight and the sound of their chatter had faded. He looked at his club, spattered with blood, and at the dozen dead which littered the clearing floor. A greater sense of power and superiority than he had felt before now flooded his being, but this was also tempered with a feeling of desolation.

For he was alone again. He who had returned to his own was driven forth once more.

When the first dead eater slunk cautiously into the clearing, Lok turned to go.

He had gone but a short distance from the clearing toward the far country of the caves when he heard a moaning off to one side.

He sprang aloft and sat quietly for a time, listening. The moans were repeated, and Lok moved nearer.

A female of his tribe was pinned lightly under a tree. Lok dropped to the ground and approached. She was unconscious, but after he had prodded her a few times with his club she opened her eyes and cried out with terror.

"I am Lok," he said.

She groaned again and tried to push the tree off her body.

Lok squatted on his haunches to watch. She strained at the tree in an agony of effort, trying to free her legs, but it was beyond her strength. Presently Lok tired of watching and turned away.

"Help me!" she cried after him.

He looked back with puzzled eyes.

"Help me!" she cried again in the words and voice of a baby to its mother.

Lok stood over her again and poked her with his club, shaking his head in bewilderment. She looked up at him with wide, dark, pain-ridden eyes which took in his smooth, hairless body.

"I am hurt," she whimpered.

Lok crouched again as she renewed her efforts to push away the tree. His brows wrinkled in concentration as he tried to focus his thought. He poked his club at her.

"You are alone, too," he said.

She grasped the club with both hands and pulled. Lok, in surprise, turned it loose, and she cried out in anger and pain.

The picture of her desire burst into his mind and he leaped to his feet, dancing with excitement.

"I am Lok," he chattered. "I slew the Old One."

He grasped his end of the club, leaned back on his heels and tugged. She clung to it desperately, and presently she slid out from under the tree.

Lok stood over her as she rolled and kicked her skinned legs, crying aloud in anguish. Now and then he poked her experimentally. Presently she tried to rise.

Lok sat on his heels and looked at her for a long time. She returned his gaze steadily.

"I am Lok," he said finally. "I am master."

"Yes," she answered. "Yes."

Without understanding the deep calm which had taken possession of him, Lok slung her over his shoulder and began the long journey to the place of caves. As he trotted along the twisting trail, he swung his club now and then against a thick vine, feeling keen satisfaction at the sharp crack of the blows.

"I have killed a big head," he said proudly to the female, who clung to him tenderly. "I have killed a big head and—" he hesitated, searching his brain for a term to describe the dead he had strewn over the clearing "—and other animals," he concluded.

MECHANICAL MICE

by

MAURICE A. HUGI

*We are on the threshold of the robot age. Automatic pilots
are true robots. They are machines that perform set duties faith-
fully and well without the personal supervision of their masters,
man. Increase the functions and capabilities of such machines;
elaborate, develop, modify their design and—you have robots. But
what happens if (and when) a robot develops the power to think?
Who wins the ensuing struggle, man or machine? Pessimistic
author Hugi thinks the machine will be the victor and tells a spine-
tingling tale of the triumphant Robot Mother and her murderous
brood.*

*

IT'S ASKING for trouble to fool around with the unknown. Burman did it! Now there are quite a lot of people who hate like the very
devil anything that clicks, ticks, emits whirring sounds, or generally
behaves like an asthmatic alarm clock. They've got mechanophobia.
Dan Burman gave it to them.

Who hasn't heard of the Burman Bullfrog Battery? The same chap!
He puzzled it out from first to last and topped it with his now world-
famous slogan: "Power in Your Pocket." It was no mean feat to con-
coct a thing the size of a cigarette packet that would pour out a hundred times as much energy as its most efficient competitor. Burman
differed from everyone else in thinking it a mean feat.

Burman looked me over very carefully, then said, "When that technical journal sent you around to see me twelve years ago, you listened

sympathetically. You didn't treat me as if I were an idle dreamer or a congenital idiot. You gave me a decent write-up, and started all the publicity that eventually made me much money."

"Not because I loved you," I assured him, "but because I was honestly convinced that your battery was good."

"Maybe." He studied me in a way that conveyed he was anxious to get something off his chest. "We've been pretty pally since that time. We've filled in some idle hours together, and I feel that you're the one of my few friends to whom I can make a seemingly silly confession."

"Go ahead," I encouraged. We had been pretty pally, as he'd said. It was merely that we liked each other, found each other congenial. He was a clever chap, Burman, but there was nothing of the pedantic professor about him. Fortyish, normal, neat, he might have been a fashionable dentist to judge by appearances.

"Bill," he said, very seriously, "I didn't invent that damn battery."

"No?"

"No!" he confirmed. "I pinched the idea. What makes it madder is that I wasn't quite sure of what I was stealing and, crazier still, I don't know from whence I stole it."

"Which is as plain as a pikestaff," I commented.

"That's nothing. After twelve years of careful, exacting work I've built something else. It must be the most complicated thing in creation." He banged a fist on his knee, and his voice rose complainingly. "And now that I've done it, I don't know what I've done."

"Surely when an inventor experiments he knows what he's doing?"

"Not me!" Burman was amusingly lugubrious. "I've invented only one thing in my life, and that was more by accident than by good judgment." He perked up. "But that one thing was the key to a million notions. It gave me the battery. It has nearly given me things of greater importance. On several occasions it has nearly, but not quite, placed within my inadequate hands and half-understanding mind plans that would alter this world far beyond your conception." Leaning forward to lend emphasis to his speech, he said, "Now it has given me a mystery that has cost me twelve years of work and a nice sum of money. I finished it last night. I don't know what the devil it is."

"Perhaps if I had a look at it—"

"Just what I'd like you to do." He switched rapidly to mounting enthusiasm. "It's a beautiful job of work, even though I say so myself. Bet you that you can't say what it is, or what it's supposed to do."

"Assuming it can do something," I put in.

"Yes," he agreed. "But I'm positive it has a function of some sort." Getting up, he opened a door. "Come along."

It was a stunner. The thing was a metal box with a glossy, rhodium-plated surface. In general size and shape it bore a faint resemblance to an upended coffin, and had the same, brooding, ominous air of a casket waiting for its owner to give up the ghost.

There were a couple of small glass windows in its front through which could be seen a multitude of wheels as beautifully finished as those in a first-class watch. Elsewhere, several tiny lenses stared with sphinx-like indifference. There were three small trapdoors in one side, two in the other, and a large one in the front. From the top, two knobbed rods of metal stuck up like goat's horns, adding a satanic touch to the thing's vague air of yearning for midnight burial.

"It's an automatic layer-outer," I suggested, regarding the contraption with frank dislike. I pointed to one of the trapdoors. "You shove the shroud in there, and the corpse comes out the other side reverently composed and ready wrapped."

"So you don't like its air, either," Burman commented. He lugged open a drawer in a nearby tier, hauled out a mass of drawings. "These are its innards. It has an electric circuit, valves, condensers, and something that I can't quite understand, but which I suspect to be a tiny, extremely efficient electric furnace. It has parts I recognize as cog-cutters and pinion-shapers. It embodies several small-scale multiple stampers, apparently for dealing with sheet metal. There are vague suggestions of an assembly line ending in that large compartment shielded by the door in front. Have a look at the drawings yourself. You can see it's an extremely complicated device for manufacturing something only little less complicated."

The drawings showed him to be right. But they didn't show everything. An efficient machine designer could correctly have deduced the gadget's function if given complete details. Burman admitted this, saying that some parts he had made "on the spur of the moment," while others he had been "impelled to draw." Short of pulling the machine to pieces, there was enough data to whet the curiosity, but not enough to satisfy it.

"Start the damn thing and see what it does."

"I've tried," said Burman. "It won't start. There's no starting handle, nothing to suggest how it can be started. I tried everything I could think of, without result. The electric circuit ends in those antennae at the top, and I even sent current through those, but nothing happened."

"Maybe it's a self-starter," I ventured. Staring at it, a thought struck me. "Timed," I added.

"Eh?"

"Set for an especial time. When the dread hour strikes, it'll go of its own accord, like a bomb."

"Don't be so melodramatic," said Burman, uneasily.

Bending down, he peered into one of the tiny lenses.

"Bz-z-z!" murmured the contraption in a faint undertone that was almost inaudible.

Burman jumped a foot. Then he backed away, eyed the thing warily, turned his glance at me.

"Did you hear that?"

"Sure!" Getting the drawings, I mauled them around. That little lens took some finding, but it was there all right. It has a selenium cell behind it. "An eye," I said. "It saw you, and reacted. So it isn't dead even if it does just stand there seeing no evil, hearing no evil, speaking no evil." I put a white handkerchief against the lens.

"Bz-z-z!" repeated the coffin, emphatically.

Taking the handkerchief, Burman put it against the other lenses. Nothing happened. Not a sound was heard, not a funeral note. Just nothing.

"It beats me," he confessed.

I'd got pretty fed up by this time. If the crazy article had performed, I'd have written it up and maybe I'd have started another financial snowball rolling for Burman's benefit. But you can't do anything with a box that buzzes whenever it feels temperamental. Firm treatment was required, I decided.

"You've been all nice and mysterious about how you got hold of this brain wave," I said. "Why can't you go to the same source for information about what it's supposed to be?"

"I'll tell you—or, rather, I'll show you."

From his safe, Burman dragged out a box, and from the box he produced a gadget. This one was far simpler than the useless mass of works over by the wall. It looked just like one of those old-fashioned crystal sets, except that the crystal was very big, very shiny, and was set in a horizontal vacuum tube. There was the same single dial, the same cat's whisker. Attached to the lot by a length of flex was what might have been a pair of headphones, except in place of the phones

were a pair of polished, smoothly rounded copper circles shaped to
fit outside the ears and close against the skull.

"My one and only invention," said Burman, not without a justi-
fiable touch of pride.

"What is it?"

"A time-traveling device."

"Ha, ha!" My laugh was very sour. I'd read about such things. In
fact, I'd written about them. They were buncombe. Nobody could
travel through time, either backward or forward. "Let me see you grow
hazy and vanish into the future."

"I'll show you something very soon." Burman said it with assurance
I didn't like. He said it with the positive air of a man who knows
darned well that he can do something that everybody else knows
darned well can't be done. He pointed to the crystal set. "It wasn't
discovered at the first attempt. Thousands must have tried and failed.
I was the lucky one. I must have picked a peculiarly individualistic
crystal; I still don't know how it does what it does; I've never been
able to repeat its performance even with a crystal apparently identical."

"And it enables you to travel in time?"

'Only forward. It won't take me backward, not even as much as
one day. But it can carry me forward an immense distance, perhaps to
the very crack of doom, perhaps everlastingly through infinity."

I had him now! I'd got him firmly entangled in his own absurdities.
My loud chuckle was something I couldn't control.

"You can travel forward, but not backward, not even one day back.
Then how the devil can you return to the present once you've gone
into the future?"

"Because I never leave the present," he replied, evenly. "I don't
partake of the future. I merely survey it from the vantage point of the
present. All the same, it is time-traveling in the correct sense of the
term." He seated himself. "Look here, Bill, what are you?"

"Who, me?"

"Yes, what are you." He went on to provide the answer. "Your
name is Bill. You're a body and a mind. Which of them is Bill?"

"Both," I said, positively.

"True—but they're different parts of you. They're not the same
even though they go around like Siamese twins." His voice grew
serious. "Your body moves always in the present, the dividing line
between the past and the future. But your mind is more free. It can
think, and is in the present. It can remember, and at once is in the

past. It can imagine, and at once is in the future, in its own choice of all the possible futures. Your mind can travel through time!"

He'd outwitted me. I could find points to pick upon and argue about, but I knew that fundamentally he was right. I'd not looked at it from this angle before, but he was correct in saying that anyone could travel through time within the limits of his own memory and imagination. At that very moment I could go back twelve years and see him in my mind's eye as a younger man, paler, thinner, more excitable, not so cool and self-possessed. The picture was as perfect as my memory was excellent. For that brief spell I was twelve years back in all but the flesh.

"I call this thing a psychophone," Burman went on. "When you imagine what the future will be like, you make a characteristic choice of all the logical possibilities, you pick your favorite from a multitude of likely futures. The psychophone, somehow—the Lord alone knows how—tunes you into future reality. It makes you depict within your mind the future as it will be shaped in actuality, eliminating all the alternatives that will not occur."

"An imagination-stimulator, a dream-machine," I scoffed, not feeling as sure of myself as I sounded. "How do you know it's giving you the McCoy?"

"Consistency," he answered, gravely. "It repeats the same features and the same trends far too often for the phenomena to be explained as mere coincidence. Besides," he waved a persuasive hand, "I got the battery from the future. It works, doesn't it?"

"It does," I agreed, reluctantly. I pointed to his psychophone. "I, too, may travel in time. How about letting me have a try? Maybe I'll solve your mystery for you."

"You can try if you wish," he replied, quite willingly. He pulled a chair into position. "Sit here, and I'll let you peer into the future."

Clipping the headband over my cranium, and fitting the copper rings against my skull where it sprouted ears, Burman connected his psychophone to the mains, switched it on; or rather he did some twiddling that I assumed was a mode of switching on.

"All you have to do," he said, "is to close your eyes, compose yourself, then try and permit your imagination to wander into the future."

He meddled with the cat's whisker. A couple of times he said, "Ah!" And each time he said it I got a peculiar dithery feeling around my unfortunate ears. After a few seconds of this, he drew it out to, "A-a-ah!" I played unfair, and peeped beneath lowered lids. The crystal was glowing like rats' eyes in a forgotten cellar. A furtive crimson.

Closing my own optics, I let my mind wander. Something was flowing between those copper electrodes, a queer, indescribable something that felt with stealthy fingers at some secret portion of my brain. I got the asinine notion that they were the dexterous digits of a yet-to-be-born magician who was going to shout, "Presto!" and pull my abused lump of think-meat out of a thirtieth century hat—assuming they'd wear hats in the thirtieth century.

What was it like, or, rather, what would it be like in the thirtieth century? Would there be retrogression? Would humanity again be composed of scowling, fur-kilted creatures lurking in caves? Or had progress continued—perhaps even to the development of men like gods?

Then it happened! I swear it! I pictured, quite voluntarily, a savage, and then a huge-domed individual with glittering eyes—the latter being my version of the ugliness we hope to attain. Right in the middle of this erratic dreaming, those weird fingers warped my brain, dissolved my phantoms, and replaced them with a dictated picture which I witnessed with all the helplessness and clarity of a nightmare.

I saw a fat man spouting. He was quite an ordinary man as far as looks went. In fact, he was so normal that he looked henpecked. But he was attired in a Roman toga, and he wore a small, black box where his laurel wreath ought to have been. His audience was similarly dressed, and all were balancing their boxes like a convention of fish porters. What Fatty was orating sounded gabble to me, but he said his piece as if he meant it.

The crowd was in the open air, with great, curved rows of seats visible in the background. Presumably an outside auditorium of some sort. Judging by the distance of the back rows, it must have been a devil of a size. Far behind its sweeping ridge a great edifice jutted into the sky, a cubical erection with walls of glossy squares, like an immense glasshouse.

"F'wot?" bellowed Fatty, with obvious heat. "Wuk, wuk, wuk, mor, noon'n'ni'! Bok onned, ord this, ord that." He stuck an indignant finger against the mysterious object on his cranium. "Bok onned, wuk, wuk, wuk. F'wot?" he glared around. "F'nix!" The crowd murmured approval somewhat timidly. But it was enough for Fatty. Making up his mind, he flourished a plump fist and shouted, "Th'ell wit'm!" Then he tore his box from his pate.

Nobody said anything, nobody moved. Dumb and wide-eyed, the

crowd just stood and stared as if paralyzed by the sight of a human being sans box. Something with a long, slender streamlined body and broad wings soared gracefully upward in the distance, swooped over the auditorium, but still the crowd neither moved nor uttered a sound.

A smile of triumph upon his broad face, Fatty bawled, "Lem see'm make wuk now! Lem see'm—"

He got no further. With a rush of mistiness from its tail, but in perfect silence, the soaring thing hovered and sent down a spear of faint, silvery light. The light touched Fatty. He rotted where he stood, like a victim of ultra-rapid leprosy. He rotted, collapsed, crumbled within his sagging clothes, became dust as once he had been dust. It was horrible.

The watchers did not flee in utter panic; not one expression of fear, hatred or disgust came from their tightly closed lips. In perfect silence they stood there, staring, just staring, like a horde of wooden soldiers. The thing in the sky circled to survey its handiwork, then dived low over the mob, a stubby antenna in its prow sparking furiously. As one man, the crowd turned left. As one man it commenced to march, left, right, left, right.

Tearing off the headband, I told Burman what I'd seen, or what his contraption had persuaded me to think that I'd seen. "What the deuce did it mean?"

"Automatons," he murmured. "Glasshouses and reaction ships." He thumbed through a big diary filled with notations in his own hands. "Ah, yes, looks like you were very early in the thirtieth century. Unrest was persistent for twenty years prior to the Antibox Rebellion."

"What rebellion?"

"The Antibox—the revolt of the automatons against the thirty-first century Technocrats. Jackson-Dkj-99717, a successful and cunning schemer with a warped box, secretly warped hundreds of other boxes, and eventually led the rebels to victory in 3047. His great-grandson, a greedy, thick-headed individual, caused the rebellion of the Boxless Freemen against his own clique of Jacksocrats."

I gaped at this recital, then said, "The way you tell it makes it sound like history."

"Of course it's history," he asserted. "History that is yet to be." He was pensive for a while. "Studying the future will seem a weird process to you, but it appears quite a normal procedure to me. I've done it for years, and maybe familiarity has bred contempt. Trouble is though, that selectivity is poor. You can pick on some especial period twenty times in succession, but you'll never find yourself in the same month, or even the same year. In fact, you're fortunate if you strike twice in the same decade. Result is that my data is very erratic."

"I can imagine that," I told him. "A good guesser can guess the correct time to within a minute or two, but never to within ten or even fifty seconds."

"Quite!" he responded. "So the hell of it has been that mine was the privilege of watching the panorama of the future, but in a manner so sketchy that I could not grasp its prizes. Once I was lucky enough to watch a twenty-fifth century power pack assembled from first to last. I got every detail before I lost the scene which I've never managed to hit upon again. But I made that power pack—and you know the result."

"So that's how you concocted your famous battery!"

"It is! But mine, good as it may be, isn't as good as the one I saw. Some slight factor is missing." His voice was suddenly tight when he added, "I missed something because I had to miss it!"

"Why?" I asked, completely puzzled.

"Because history, past or future, permits no glaring paradox. Because, having snatched this battery from the twenty-fifth century, I am recorded in that age as the twentieth-century inventor of the thing. They've made a mild improvement to it in those five centuries, but that improvement was automatically withheld from me. Future history is as fixed and unalterable by those of the present time as is the history of the past."

"Then," I demanded, "explain to me that complicated contraption which does nothing but say bz-z-z."

"Damn it!" he said, with open ire, "that's just what's making me crazy! It can't be a paradox, it just can't." Then, more carefully, "So it must be a seeming paradox."

"O. K. You tell me how to market a seeming paradox, and the commercial uses thereof, and I'll give it a first-class write-up."

Ignoring my sarcasm, he went on, "I tried to probe the future as far as human minds can probe. I saw nothing, nothing but the vastness of a sterile floor upon which sat a queer machine, gleaming there in silent, solitary majesty. Somehow, it seemed aware of my scrutiny across the gulf of countless ages. It held my attention with a power almost hypnotic. For more than a day, for a full thirty hours, I kept that vision without losing it—the longest time I have ever kept a future scene."

"Well?"

"I drew it. I made complete drawings of it, performing the task with all the easy confidence of a trained machine draughtsman. Its insides could not be seen, but somehow they came to me, somehow I knew them. I lost the scene at four o'clock in the morning, finding myself with masses of very complicated drawings, a thumping head, heavy-lidded eyes, and a half-scared feeling in my heart." He was silent for a short time. "A year later I plucked up courage and started to build the thing I had drawn. It cost me a hell of a lot of time and a hell of a lot of money. But I did it—it's finished."

"And all it does is buzz," I remarked, with genuine sympathy.

"Yes," he sighed, doubtfully.

There was nothing more to be said. Burman gazed moodily at the wall, his mind far, far away. I fiddled aimlessly with the copper earpieces of the psychophone. My imagination, I reckoned, was as good as anyone's, but for the life of me I could neither imagine nor suggest a profitable market for a metal coffin filled with watchmaker's junk. No, not even if it did make odd noises.

A faint, smooth whir came from the coffin. It was a new sound that swung us round to face it pop-eyed. Whir-r-r! it went again. I saw finely machined wheels spin behind the window in its front.

"Good heavens!" said Burman.

Bz-z-z! Whir-r! Click! The whole affair suddenly slid sidewise on its hidden castors.

The devil you know isn't half so frightening as the devil you don't. I don't mean that this sudden demonstration of life and motion got us scared, but it certainly made us leery, and our hearts put in an extra dozen bumps a minute. This coffin-thing was, or might be, a devil we didn't know. So we stood there, side by side, gazing at it fascinatedly, feeling apprehensive of we knew not what.

Motion ceased after the thing had slid two feet. It stood there, silent, imperturbable, its front lenses eyeing us with glassy lack of expression. Then it slid another two feet. Another stop. More meaningless contemplation. After that, a swifter and farther slide that brought it right up to the laboratory table. At that point it ceased moving, began to emit varied but synchronized ticks like those of a couple of sympathetic grandfather clocks.

Burman said, quietly, "Something's going to happen!"

If the machine could have spoken it would have taken the words right out of his mouth. He'd hardly uttered the sentence when a trapdoor in the machine's side fell open, a jointed, metallic arm snaked cautiously through the opening and reached for a marine chronometer standing on the table.

With a surprised oath, Burman dashed forward to rescue the chronometer. He was too late. The arm grabbed it, whisked it into the machine, the trapdoor shut with a hard snap, like the vicious clash of a sprung bear trap. Simultaneously, another trapdoor in the front flipped open, another jointed arm shot out and in again, spearing with ultra-rapid motion too fast to follow. That trapdoor also snapped shut, leaving Burman gaping down at his torn clothing from which his expensive watch and equally expensive gold chain had been ripped away.

"Good heavens!" said Burman, backing from the machine.

We stood looking at it a while. It didn't move again, just posed there ticking steadily as if ruminating upon its welcome meal. Its lenses looked at us with all the tranquil lack of interest of a well-fed cow. I got the idiotic notion that it was happily digesting a mess of cogs, pinions and wheels.

Because its subtle air of menace seemed to have faded away, or maybe because we sensed its entire preoccupation with the task in hand, we made an effort to rescue Burman's valuable timepiece. Burman tugged mightily at the trapdoor through which his watch had gone, but failed to move it. I tugged with him, without result. The thing was sealed as solidly as if welded in. A large screwdriver failed to pry it open. A crowbar, or a good jimmy would have done the job, but at that point Burman decided that he didn't want to damage the machine which had cost him more than the watch.

Tick-tick-tick! went the coffin, stolidly. We were back where we'd started, playing with our fingers, and no wiser than before. There was nothing to be done, and I felt that the accursed contraption knew it. So it stood there, gaping through its lenses, and jeered *tick-tick-tick*. From its belly, or where its belly would have been if it'd had one, a slow warmth radiated. According to Burman's drawings, that was the location of the tiny electric furnace.

The thing was functioning; there could be no doubt about that! If Burman felt the same way as I did, he must have been pretty mad. There we stood, like a couple of prize boobs, not knowing what the machine was supposed to do, and all the time it was doing under our very eyes whatever it was designed to do.

From where was it drawing its power? Were those antennae sticking like horns from its head busily sucking current from the atmosphere? Or was it, perhaps, absorbing radio power? Or did it have internal energy of its own? All the evidence suggested that it was making something, giving birth to something, but giving birth to what?

Tick-tick-tick! was the only reply.

Our questions were still unanswered, our curiosity was still unsatis-fied, and the machine was still ticking industriously at the hour of midnight. We surrendered the problem until next morning. Burman locked and double-locked his laboratory before we left.

Police officer Burke's job was a very simple one. All he had to do was walk round and round the block, keeping a wary eye on the stores in general and the big jewel depot in particular, phoning headquarters once per hour from the post at the corner.

Night work suited Burke's taciturn disposition. He could wander along, communing with himself, with nothing to bother him or divert him from his inward ruminations. In that particular section nothing ever happened at nigh.t, nothing.

Stopping outside the gem-bedecked window, he gazed through the glass and the heavy grille behind it to where a low-power bulb shed light over the massive safe. There was a rajah's ransom in there. The guard, the grille, the automatic alarms and sundry ingenious traps preserved it from the adventurous fingers of anyone who wanted to ransom a rajah. Nobody had made the brash attempt in twenty years. Nobody had even made a try for the contents of the grille-protected window.

He glanced upward at a faintly luminescent path of cloud behind which lay the hidden moon. Turning, he strolled on. A cat sneaked past him, treading cautiously, silently, and hugging the angle of the wall. His sharp eyes detected its slinking shape even in the nighttime gloom, but he ignored it and progressed to the corner.

Back of him, the cat came below the window through which he just had stared. It stopped, one forefoot half-raised, its ears cocked forward. Then it flattened belly-low against the concrete, its burning orbs wide, alert, intent. Its tail waved slowly from side to side.

Something small and bright came skittering toward it, moving with mouselike speed and agility close in the angle of the wall. The cat tensed as the object came nearer. Suddenly, the thing was within range, and the cat pounced with lithe eagerness. Hungry paws dug at a surface that was not soft and furry, but hard, bright and slippery.

The thing darted around like a clockwork toy as the cat vainly tried to hold it. Finally, with an angry snarl, the cat swiped it viciously, knocking it a couple of yards where it rolled onto its back and emitted softly protesting clicks and tiny, urgent impulses that its feline attacker could not sense.

Gaining the gutter with a single leap, the cat crouched again. Something else was coming. The cat muscled, its eyes glowed. Another object slightly similar to the curious thing it had just captured, but a little bit bigger, a fraction noisier, and much different in shape. It resembled a small, gold-plated cylinder with a conical front from which projected a slender blade, and it slid along swiftly on invisible wheels.

Again the cat leaped. Down on the corner, Burke heard its brief shriek and following gurgle. The sound didn't bother Burke—he'd heard cats and rats and other vermin make all sorts of queer noises in the night. Phlegmatically, he continued on his beat.

Three quarters of an hour later, Police Officer Burke had worked his way around to the fatal spot. Putting his flash on the body, he rolled the supine animal over with his foot. Its throat was cut. Its throat had been cut with an utter savagery that had half-severed its head from its body. Burke scowled down at it. He was no lover of cats himself, but he found difficulty in imagining anyone hating like that!

"Somebody," he muttered, "wants flaying alive."

His big foot shoved the dead cat back into the gutter where street cleaners could cart it away in the morning. He turned his attention to the window, saw the light still glowing upon the untouched safe. His mind was still on the cat while his eyes looked in and said that something was wrong. Then he dragged his attention back to business, realized what was wrong, and sweated at every pore. It wasn't the safe, it was the window.

In front of the window the serried trays of valuable rings still gleamed undisturbed. To the right, the silverware still shone untouched. But on the left had been a small display of delicate and extremely expensive watches. They were no longer there, not one of them. He remembered that right in front had rested a neat, beautiful calendar-chronometer priced at a year's salary. That, too, was gone.

The beam of his flash trembled as he tried the gate, found it fast, secure. The door behind it was firmly locked. The transom was closed, its heavy wire guard still securely fixed. He went over the window, eventually found a small, neat hole, about two inches in diameter, down in the corner on the side nearest the missing display.

Burke's curse was explosive as he turned and ran to the corner. His hand shook with indignation while it grabbed the telephone from its box. Getting headquarters, he recited his story. He thought he'd a good idea of what had happened, fancied he'd read once of a similar stunt being pulled elsewhere.

"Looks like they cut a disk with a rotary diamond, lifted it out with a suction cup, then fished through the hole with a telescopic rod." He listened a moment, then said, "Yes, yes. That's just what gets me—the rings are worth ten times as much."

His still-startled eyes looked down the street while he paid attention to the voice at the other end of the line. The eyes wandered slowly, descended, found the glutter, remained fixed on the dim shape lying therein. Another dead cat! Still clinging to his phone, Burke moved out as far as the cord would allow, extended a boot, rolled the cat away from the curb. The flash settled on it. Just like the other—ear to ear!

"And listen," he shouted into the phone, "some maniac's wandering around slaughtering cats."

Replacing the phone, he hurried back to the maltreated window, stood guard in front of it until the police car rolled up. Four piled out.

The first said, "Cats! I'll say somebody's got it in for cats! We passed two a couple of blocks away. They were bang in the middle of the street, flat in the headlights, and had been damn near guillotined. Their bodies were still warm."

The second grunted, approached the window, stared at the small, neat hole, and said, "The mob that did this would be too cute to leave a print."

"They weren't too cute to leave the rings," growled Burke.

"Maybe you've got something there," conceded the other. "If they've left the one, they might have left the other. We'll test for prints, anyway."

A taxi swung into the dark street, pulled up behind the police car. An elegantly dressed, fussy, and very agitated individual got out, rushed up to the waiting group. Keys jangled in his pale, moist hand.

"Maley, the manager—you phoned me," he explained, breathlessly. "Gentlemen, this is terrible, terrible! The window show is worth thousands, thousands! What a loss, what a loss!"

"How about letting us in?" asked one of the policemen, calmly.

"Of course, of course."

Jerkily, he opened the gate, unlocked the door, using about six keys for the job. They walked inside. Maley switched on the lights, stuck his head between the plateglass shelves, surveyed the depleted window.

"My watches, my watches," he groaned.

"It's awful, it's awful!" said one of the policemen, speaking with beautiful solemnity. He favored his companions with a sly wink.

Maley leaned farther over, the better to inspect an empty corner. "All gone, all gone," he moaned, "all my show of the finest makes in —Yeeouw!" His yelp made them jump. Maley bucked as he tried to force himself through the obstructing shelves toward the grille and the window beyond it. "My watch! My own watch!"

The others tiptoed, stared over his shoulders, saw the gold buckle of a black velvet fob go through the hole in the window. Burke was the first outside, his ready flash searching the concrete. Then he spotted the watch. It was moving rapidly along, hugging the angle of the wall, but it stopped dead as his beam settled upon it. He fancied he saw something else, equally bright and metallic, scoot swiftly into the darkness beyond the circle of his beam.

Picking up the watch, Burke stood and listened. The noises of the others coming out prevented him from hearing clearly, but he could have sworn he'd heard a tiny whirring noise, and a swift, juicy ticking that was not coming from the instrument in his hand. Must have been only his worried fancy. Frowning deeply, he returned to his companions.

"There was nobody," he asserted. "It must have dropped out of your pocket and rolled."

Damn it, he thought, could a watch roll that far? What the devil was happening this night? Far up the street, something screeched, then it bubbled. Burke shuddered—he could make a shrewd guess at that! He looked at the others, but apparently they hadn't heard the noise.

The papers gave it space in the morning. The total was sixty watches and eight cats, also some oddments from the small stock of a local scientific instrument maker. I read about it on my way down to Burman's place. The details were fairly lavish, but not complete. I got them completely at a later time when we discovered the true significance of what had occurred.

Burman was waiting for me when I arrived. He appeared both annoyed and bothered. Over in the corner, the coffin was ticking away steadily, its noise much louder than it had been the previous day. The thing sounded a veritable hive of industry.

"Well?" I asked.

"It's moved around a lot during the night," said Burman. "It's smashed a couple of thermometers and taken the mercury out of them. I found some drawers and cupboards shut, some open, but I've an uneasy feeling that it's made a thorough search through the lot. A packet of nickel foil has vanished, a coil of copper wire has gone with it." He pointed an angry finger at the bottom of the door through which I'd just entered. "And I blame it for gnawing ratholes in that. They weren't there yesterday."

Sure enough, there were a couple of holes in the bottom of that door. But no rat made those—they were neat and smooth and round, almost as if a carpenter had cut them with a keyhole saw.

"Where's the sense in it making those?" I questioned. "It can't crawl through apertures that size."

"Where's the sense in the whole affair?" Burman countered. He glowered at the busy machine which stared back at him with its expressionless lenses and churned steadily on. *Tick-tick-tick!* persisted the confounded thing. Then, *whir-thump-click!*

I opened my mouth intending to voice a nice, sarcastic comment at the machine's expense when there came a very tiny, very subtle and extremely high-pitched whine. Something small, metallic, glittering shot through one of the rat holes, fled across the floor toward the churning monstrosity. A trapdoor opened and swallowed it with such swiftness that it had disappeared before I realized what I'd seen. The thing had been a cylindrical, polished object resembling the shuttle of a sewing machine, but about four times the size. And it had been dragging something also small and metallic.

Burman stared at me; I stared at Burman. Then he foraged around the laboratory, found a three-foot length of half-inch steel pipe. Dragging a chair to the door, he seated himself, gripped the pipe like a bludgeon, and watched the rat holes. Imperturbably, the machine watched him and continued to *tick-tick-tick.*

Ten minutes later, there came a sudden click and another tiny whine. Nothing darted inward through the holes, but the curious object we'd already seen—or another one exactly like it—dropped out of the trap, scooted to the door by which we were waiting. It caught Burman by surprise. He made a mad swipe with the steel as the thing skittered elusively past his feet and through a hole. It had gone even as the weapon walloped the floor.

"Damn!" said Burman, heartily. He held the pipe loosely in his grip while he glared at the industrious coffin. "I'd smash it to bits except that I'd like to catch one of these small gadgets first."

"Look out!" I yelled.

He was too late. He ripped his attention away from the coffin toward the holes, swinging up the heavy length of pipe, a startled look on his face. But his reaction was far too slow. Three of the little mysteries were through the holes and halfway across the floor before his weapon was ready to swing. The coffin swallowed them with the crash of a trapdoor.

The invading trio had rushed through in single file, and I'd got a better picture of them this time. The first two were golden shuttles, much like the one we'd already seen. The third was bigger, speedier, and gave me the notion that it could dodge around more dexterously. It had a long, sharp projection in front, a wicked, ominous thing like a surgeon's scalpel. Sheer speed deprived me of a good look at it, but I fancied that the tip of the scalpel had been tinged with red. My spine exuded perspiration.

Came an irritated scratching upon the outside of the door and a white-tipped paw poked tentatively through one of the holes. The cat backed to a safe distance when Burman opened the door, but looked lingeringly toward the laboratory. Its presence needed no explaining —the alert animal must have caught a glimpse of those infernal little whizzers. The same thought struck both of us; cats are quick on the pounce, very quick. Given a chance, maybe this one could make a catch for us.

We enticed it in with fair words and soothing noises. Its eagerness overcame its normal caution toward strangers, and it entered. We closed the door behind it; Burman got his length of pipe, sat by the door, tried to keep one eye on the holes and the other on the cat. He couldn't do both, but he tried. The cat sniffed and prowled around, mewed defeatedly. Its behavior suggested that it was seeking by sight rather than scent. There wasn't any scent.

With feline persistence, the animal searched the whole laboratory. It passed the buzzing coffin several times, but ignored it completely. In the end, the cat gave it up, sat on the corner of the laboratory table and started to wash its face.

Tick-tick-tick! went the big machine. Then *whir-thump!* A trap popped open, a shuttle fell out and raced for the door. A second one followed it. The first was too fast even for the cat, too fast for the surprised Burman as well. *Bang!* The length of steel tube came down viciously as the leading shuttle bulleted triumphantly through a hole.

But the cat got the second one. With a mighty leap, paws extended claws out, it caught its victim one foot from the door. It tried to handle the slippery thing, failed, lost it for an instant. The shuttle whisked around in a crazy loop. The cat got it again, lost it again, emitted an angry snarl, batted it against the skirting board. The shuttle lay there, upside down, four midget wheels in its underside spinning madly with a high, almost inaudible whine.

Eyes alight with excitement, Burman put down his weapon, went to pick up the shuttle. At the same time, the cat slunk toward it ready to play with it. The shuttle lay there, helplessly functioning upon its back, before either could reach it the big machine across the room went *clunk!* opened a trap and ejected another gadget.

With astounding swiftness, the cat turned and pounced upon the newcomer. Then followed pandemonium. Its prey swerved agilely with a fitful gleam of gold; the cat swerved with it, cursed and spat. Black-and-white fur whirled around in a fighting haze in which gold occasionally glowed; the cat's hissings and spittings overlay a persistent whine that swelled and sank in the manner of accelerating or decelerating gears.

A peculiar gasp came from the cat, and blood spotted the floor. The animal clawed wildly, emitted another gasp followed by a gurgle. It shivered and flopped, a stream of crimson pouring from the great gash in its gullet.

We'd hardly time to appreciate the full significance of the ghastly scene when the victor made for Burman. He was standing by the skirting board, the still-buzzing shuttle in his hand. His eyes were sticking out with utter horror, but he retained enough presence of mind to make a frantic jump a second before the bulleting menace reached his feet.

He landed behind the thing, but it reversed in its own length and came for him again. I saw the mirrorlike sheen of its scalpel as it banked at terrific speed, and the sheen was drowned in sticky crimson two inches along the blade. Burman jumped over it again, reached the lab table, got up on that.

"Lord!" he breathed.

By this time I'd got the piece of pipe which he'd discarded. I hefted it, feeling its comforting weight, then did my best to bat the buzzing lump of wickedness through the window and over the roofs. It was too agile for me. It whirled, accelerated, dodged the very tip of the descending steel, and flashed twice around the table upon which Burman had taken refuge. It ignored me completely. Somehow, I felt that it was responding entirely to some mysterious call from the shuttle Burman had captured.

I swiped desperately, missed it again, though I swear I missed by no more than a millimeter. Something whipped through the holes in the door, fled past me into the big machine. Dimly, I heard traps opening and closing, and beyond all other sounds that steady, persistent *tick-tick-tick.* Another furious blow that accomplished no more than to dent the floor and jar my arm to the shoulder.

Unexpectedly, unbelievably, the golden curse ceased its insane gyrations on the floor and around the table. With a hard click, and a whir much louder than before, it raced easily up one leg of the table and reached the top.

Burman left his sanctuary in one jump. He was still clinging to the shuttle. I'd never seen his face so white.

"The machine!" he said, hoarsely. "Bash it to hell!"

Thunk! went the machine. A trap gaped, released another demon with a scalpel. *Tzz-z-z!* a third shot in through the holes in the door. Four shuttles skimmed through behind it, made for the machine, reached it safely. A fifth came through more slowly. It was dragging an automobile valve spring. I kicked the thing against the wall even as I struck a vain blow at one with a scalpel.

With another jump, Burman cleared an attacker. A second sheared off the toe of his right shoe as he landed. Again he reached the table from which his first toe had departed. All three things with scalpels made for the table with a reckless vim that was frightening.

"Drop that damned shuttle," I yelled.

He didn't drop it. As the fighting trio whirred up the legs, he flung the shuttle with all his might at the coffin that had given it birth. It struck, dented the casing, fell to the floor. Burman was off the table again. The thrown shuttle lay battered and noiseless, its small motive wheels stilled.

The armed contraptions scooting around the table seemed to change their purpose coincidently with the captured shuttle's smashing. Together, they dived off the table, sped through the holes in the door. A fourth came out of the machine, escorting two shuttles, and those too vanished beyond the door. A second or two later, a new thing, different from the rest, came in through one of the holes. It was long, round-bodied, snub-nosed, about half the length of a policeman's nightstick, had six wheels beneath, and a double row of peculiar serrations in front. It almost sauntered across the room while we watched it fascinatedly. I saw the serrations jerk and shift when it climbed the lowered trap into the machine. They were midget caterpillar tracks!

Burman had had enough. He made up his mind. Finding the steel pipe, he gripped it firmly, approached the coffin. Its lenses seemed to leer at him as he stood before it. Twelve years of intensive work to be destroyed at a blow. Endless days and nights of effort to be undone at one stroke. But Burman was past caring. With a ferocious swing he demolished the glass, with a fierce thrust he shattered the assembly of wheels and cogs behind.

The coffin shuddered and slid beneath his increasingly angry blows. Trapdoors dropped open, spilled out lifeless samples of the thing's metallic brood. Grindings and raspings came from the accursed object while Burman battered it to pieces. Then it was silent, stilled, a shapeless, useless mass of twisted and broken parts.

I picked up the dented shape of the object that had sauntered in. It was heavy, astonishingly heavy, and even after partial destruction its workmanship looked wonderful. It had a tiny, almost unnoticeable eye in front, but the miniature lens was cracked. Had it returned for repairs and overhaul?

"That," said Burman, breathing audibly, "is that!"

I opened the door to see if the noise had attracted attention. It hadn't. There was a lifeless shuttle outside the door, a second a yard behind it. The first had a short length of brass chain attached to a tiny hook projecting from its rear. The nose cap of the second had opened fanwise, like an iris diaphragm, and a pair of jointed metal arms were folded inside, hugging a medium-sized diamond. It looked as if they'd been about to enter when Burman destroyed the big machine.

Picking them up, I brought them in. Their complete inactivity, though they were undamaged, suggested that they had been controlled by the big machine and had drawn their motive power from it. If so, then we'd solved our problem simply, and by destroying the one had destroyed the lot.

Burman got his breath back and began to talk.

He said, "The Robot Mother! That's what I made—a duplicate of the Robot Mother. I didn't realize it, but I was patiently building the most dangerous thing in creation, a thing that is a terrible menace because it shares with mankind the ability to propagate. Thank Heaven we stopped it in time!"

"So," I remarked, remembering that he claimed to have got it from the extreme future, "that's the eventual master, or mistress, of Earth. A dismal prospect for humanity, eh?"

"Not necessarily. I don't know just how far I got, but I've an idea it was so tremendously distant in the future that Earth had become sterile from humanity's viewpoint. Maybe we'd emigrated to somewhere else in the cosmos, leaving our semi-intelligent slave machines to fight for existence or die. They fought—and survived."

"And then wangle things to try and alter the past in their favor," I suggested.

"No, I don't think so." Burman had become much calmer by now. "I don't think it was a dastardly attempt so much as an interesting experiment. The whole affair was damned in advance because success would have meant an impossible paradox. There are no robots in the next century, nor any knowledge of them. Therefore the intruders in this time must have been wiped out and forgotten."

"Which means," I pointed out, "that you must not only have destroyed the machine, but also all your drawings, all your notes, as well as the psychophone, leaving nothing but a few strange events and a story for me to tell."

"Exactly—I shall destroy everything. I've been thinking over the whole affair, and it's not until now I've understood that the psychophone can never be of the slightest use to me. It permits me to discover or invent only those things that history has decreed I shall invent, and which, therefore, I shall find with or without the contraption. I can't play tricks with history, past or future."

"Humph!" I couldn't find any flaw in his reasoning. "Did you notice," I went on, "the touch of bee-psychology in our antagonists? You built the hive, and from it emerged workers, warriors, and"—I indicated the dead saunterer—"one drone."

"Yes," he said, lugubriously. "And I'm thinking of the honey— eighty watches! Not to mention any other items the late papers may report, plus any claims for slaughtered cats. Good thing I'm wealthy."

"Nobody knows you've anything to do with those incidents. You can pay secretly if you wish."

"I shall," he declared.

"Well," I went on, cheerfully, "all's well that ends well. Thank goodness we've got rid of what we brought upon ourselves."

With a sigh of relief, I strolled toward the door. A high whine of midget motors drew my startled attention downward. While Burman and I stared aghast, a golden shuttle slid easily through one of the rat holes, sensed the death of the Robot Mother and scooted back through the other hole before I could stop it.

If Burman had been shaken before, he was doubly so now. He came over to the door, stared incredulously at the little exit just used by the shuttle, then at the couple of other undamaged but lifeless shuttles lying about the room.

"Bill," he mouthed, "your bee analogy was perfect. Don't you understand? There's another swarm! A queen got loose!"

There was another swarm all right. For the next forty-eight hours it played merry hell. Burman spent the whole time down at headquarters trying to convince them that his evidence wasn't just a fantastic story, but what helped him to persuade the police of his veracity was the equally fantastic reports that came rolling in.

To start with, old Gildersome heard a crash in his shop at midnight, thought of his valuable stock of cameras and miniature movie projectors, pulled on his pants and rushed downstairs. A razor-sharp instrument stabbed him through the right instep when halfway down, and he fell the rest of the way. He lay there, badly bruised and partly stunned, while things clicked, ticked and whirred in the darkness and the gloom. One by one, all the contents of his box of expensive lenses went through a hole in the door. A quantity of projector cogs and wheels went with them.

Ten people complained of being robbed in the night of watches and alarm clocks. Two were hysterical. One swore that the bandit was "a six-inch cockroach" which purred like a toy dynamo. Getting out of bed, he'd put his foot upon it and felt its cold hardness wriggle away from beneath him. Filled with revulsion, he'd whipped his foot back into bed "just as another cockroach scuttled toward him." Burman did not tell that agitated complainant how near he had come to losing his foot.

Thirty more reports rolled in next day. A score of houses had been entered and four shops robbed by things that had the agility and furtiveness of rats—except that they emitted tiny ticks and buzzing noises. One was seen racing along the road by a homing railway worker. He tried to pick it up, lost his forefinger and thumb, stood nursing the stumps until an ambulance rushed him away.

Rare metals and fine parts were the prey of these ticking marauders. I couldn't see how Burman or anyone else could wipe them out once and for all, but he did it. He did it by baiting them like rats. I went around with him, helping him on the job, while he consulted a map.

"Every report," said Burman, "leads to this street. An alarm clock that suddenly sounded was abandoned near here. Two automobiles were robbed of small parts near here. Shuttles have been seen going to or from this area. Five cats were dealt with practically on this spot. Every other incident has taken place within easy reach."

"Which means," I guessed, "that the queen is somewhere near this point?"

"Yes." He stared up and down the quiet empty street over which the crescent moon shed a sickly light. It was two o'clock in the morning. "We'll settle this matter pretty soon!"

He attached the end of a reel of firm cotton to a small piece of silver chain, nailed the reel to the wall, dropped the chain on the concrete. I did the same with the movement of a broken watch. We distributed several small cogs, a few clock wheels, several camera fitments, some small, tangled bunches of copper wire, and other attractive oddments.

Three hours later, we returned accompanied by the police. They had mallets and hammers with them. All of us were wearing steel leg-and-foot shields knocked up at short notice by a handy sheet-metal worker.

The bait had been taken! Several cotton strands had broken after being unreeled a short distance, but others were intact. All of them either led to or pointed to a steel grating leading to a cellar below an abandoned warehouse. Looking down, we could see a few telltale strands running through the window frame beneath.

Burman said, "Now!" and we went in with a rush. Rusty locks snapped, rotten doors collapsed, we poured through the warehouse and into the cellar.

There was a small, coffin-shaped thing against one wall, a thing that ticked steadily away while its lenses stared at us with ghastly lack of emotion. It was very similar to the Robot Mother, but only a quarter of the size. In the light of a police torch, it was a brooding, ominous thing of dreadful significance. Around it, an active clan swarmed over the floor, buzzing and ticking in metallic fury.

Amid angry whirs and the crack of snapping scalpels on steel, we waded headlong through the lot. Burman reached the coffin first, crushing it with one mighty blow of his twelve-pound hammer, then bashing it to utter ruin with a rapid succession of blows. He finished exhausted. The daughter of the Robot Mother was no more, nor did her alien tribe move or stir.

Sitting down on a rickety wooden case, Burman mopped his brow and said, "Thank heavens that's done!"

Tick-tick-tick!

He shot up, snatched his hammer, a wild look in his eyes.

"Only my watch," apologized one of the policemen. "It's a cheap one, and it makes a hell of a noise." He pulled it out to show the worried Burman.

"*Tick! tick!*" said the watch, with mechanical aplomb.

V-2—ROCKET CARGO SHIP

by

WILLY LEY

It was not the editors' original plan to include any non-fiction articles in this volume. But when we read incontrovertible evidence that such matters as rocket-propelled space ships were no longer dreams, or even theoretical designs on a drawing board, we felt our readers would find it as fascinating as the most fantastic fiction we could dig up. Mr. Willy Ley, Secretary of the German Rocket Society under the Weimar Republic, refugee from the Nazis, knows as much about rocket theory as anyone in the field. Mr. Ley proves that the Germans should be credited with one accomplishment, utilized, of course, for Nazi barbarism—in V-2 they perfected a rocket-propelled ship capable of leaving this earth's atmosphere! This very morning at breakfast we read in an article by a world-renowned scientist that a trip to the moon is not only a possibility, but a probability within our own lifetime. Based on Mr. Ley's startling information, we predict that the first attempts to reach Luna will be made within a decade. And how would you like to make the trip?

*

THE FULL and complete story of the German rocket research laboratory near Peenemünde on the Baltic coast will never be written. There will be nobody alive who can write it. Most of those who knew the full story are dead already; those that are still alive will die before the war is over.

But the main points, the general outline, of the story of the creation of that laboratory, and more especially the results of its work, are known even now, and later efforts will hardly be able to do more than to fill in details.

First: the location. Peenemünde is, or was originally, a small fishing village on the island of Usedom which blocks the entrance to the Bay of Stettin. Its size was such that it cannot even be found on most maps. Its inhabitants, like those of all other fishing villages along that stretch of the Baltic coast, bolstered their standard of living by taking in summer guests, mostly from Berlin, some four hours away by rail.

Even as a seashore resort Peenemünde was not important. Nearby Zinnowitz was more fashionable by far—and Zinnowitz does appear on many maps. The small steamers which, starting out from Swinemünde, provided a coastwise connection between the string of seashore resorts on Usedom and then went on to those on the island of Rügen, made Zinnowitz their last stop before shuttling across to Rügen. Peenemünde was neglected and could only be seen in the distance from deck.

But it is possible to locate Peenemünde with fair accuracy even on a map where it does not appear. If you draw a straight line from the city of Stettin to the northernmost point of the island of Rügen, that line will cut the coastline very close to Peenemünde about two thirds of the whole distance from Stettin.

The Nazis selected this site for two reasons: it was at the seashore and out of the way of the main coastwise traffic. Being located at the tip of a long island, all land approaches could be easily sealed off, while the sea approaches could be patrolled without difficulty. It is possible that Hermann Oberth, who by some sources is credited with originating the idea for that laboratory, had something to do with that choice.

This whole section had some fame in the history of German rocket research. Between the island of Usedom—and Peenemünde—and the large island of Rügen there is the tiny little islet which is known locally as the Greifswalder Oie. When Oberth was working feverishly to complete his first rocket which was to be sent into the air on October 15, 1929, the day of the first showing of the Fritz Lang film which had provided Oberth with the necessary cash, he had the Oie in mind as a place from which to launch the rocket.

The fact that there was a lighthouse on the Oie prevented him from obtaining permission to use the island for this purpose. He then selected the coast of the mainland near the seashore resort of Horst, some forty miles east of the Oie. Two years later Johannes Winkler brought his second liquid fuel rocket to the Oie, hoping to persuade the authorities in charge to grant him the permission Oberth had failed to obtain. Winkler, incidentally, failed too. And then, finally, nearby Rügen was the "site" of the famous Fischer Hoax of 1933 which told about the "secret demonstration" of the fabulous man-carrying rocket of the Fischer Brothers who never even existed.

If Oberth had anything to say about the matter, it would be like him to select the site for a rocket research laboratory. Of course, we don't know yet just how much his words and wishes counted with the Nazis.

So much for the location of the rocket research laboratory, which was later found and mapped and bombed by the R.A.F. with great thoroughness.

Now the probable date of its founding.

When the Nazis came to power in Germany in February 1933 they discouraged all rocket research. The German Rocket Society was torn apart, the men who had worked under its auspices were distributed in commercial jobs which had nothing at all to do with rockets. The testing ground became an S.A. drill ground, the records disappeared in the files of the Gestapo.

Three groups had been interested in rocket research in Germany during the months before that happened. One was, of course, the German Rocket Society itself which had progressed to rocket motors delivering a thrust of four hundred forty pounds. The second group consisted of one man and his boss. The man was Pietsch, who was chief engineer of the Industrial Gas Company, Inc., and the owner, Dr. Heyland.

Dr. Heyland had been Max Valier's last sponsor and after Valier's death Pietsch had overhauled the liquid-fuel-propelled rocket auto-mobile on which Valier had been working and had demonstrated it on two public test runs in April and May 1931. His rocket motor was very inefficient from the point of view of fuel consumption, but it did produce a thrust of about three hundred fifty pounds, weighing some forty pounds itself.

The third group consisted of one man and his assistants, Friedrich Wilhelm Sander of Wesermünde who had manufactured the powder rockets for Valier's and Opel's rocket cars and rocket gliders. Sander was interested mostly in powder rockets, but had an interesting idea which, I think, bore fruit later on. He wanted to eliminate the danger of explosion and reasoned that this danger was due to the fact that in a powder rocket "combustion chamber" and "fuel tank" are one and the same thing.

The liquid-fuel enthusiasts had pointed to that until even Sander, who, after all, had a commercial interest in powder rockets, had to admit it. Sander then thought of building rockets of metal, with separate tank and combustion chamber, but still with powder for a fuel: *liquid powder*. He succeeded. In summer 1931 he staged a demonstration of products of his factory, signal rockets, line-throwing rockets, rockets throwing self-inflating life-savers, et cetera. Among the novelties shown there was the liquid-powder rocket. Witnesses stated that it looked "like heavy black machine oil," but the composition was, of course, Sander's trade secret.

Add to this some experiments made by the *Reichswehr* before Hitler. The *Reichswehr* did not consider liquid fuels of any kind, they wanted storable powder projectiles. Rumor has it that they attained a range of thirty thousand yards after some time—it was not specified whether vertically or horizontally—and that the project was then shelved for future reference.

At the time Hitler was actually coming to power no rocket research went on anywhere in Germany and this state of affairs was to prevail for another three years.

All the while Hermann Oberth was sitting in Mediash in Rumania, being simultaneously "at home" and "in exile," smoldering over his own misfortune and hating everybody, most especially Rumanians, Russians, Prussians, Jews and other rocket experimenters. He did some work of his own during that time, as evidenced by an interview which appeared in the Swiss newspaper *Neue Zürcher Zeitung* in 1935, but that work was in the nature of tinkering in the basement and in the school laboratory. Also he was, according to his own statement, an active member of the German Nazi organization in Rumania.

In 1937 he established, presumably through that organization, contact with the German Army and most especially with Colonel Albert Kesselring—now Field Marshal Kesselring in command of the German forces in Northern Italy.

Naturally there is no record of that conversation or conversations. But it is not difficult for someone acquainted with Oberth's conceptions of rocket theory to reconstruct the main points of those talks, especially in view of the results that became apparent later on.

Some time ago, I wrote an article about the use of rockets in place of artillery. The conclusions I arrived at were simple, but subsequent correspondence has taught me that some readers missed the points I tried to make. The most important point was that there is an upper size limit for powder rockets and that within the possible size limits rockets are inferior to artillery in two respects.

One is accuracy. Modern guns place their shells with extreme neatness, almost as neatly as if they were carried over to the target and dropped by hand. Rockets are not that accurate, rockets are what the military calls "area weapons," capable of beating a given area but hitting the target or targets within that area only by chance. The second drawback which I pointed out was the higher powder consumption. For a given range which can be attained by rockets as well as by artillery the rocket always needs at least three times as much powder to get there as does the artillery shell.

These two drawbacks are confronted by two advantages. One is the fact that rockets do not need guns. Guns are expensive pieces of precision workmanship. Rockets need only launching tubes which are neither expensive nor works of precision. The second advantage is that one can bank almost as many launching racks together as one feels like. The result is a very heavy volume of fire. It takes longer to load a launching rack than it does to load a gun, especially modern guns with automatic or semiautomatic loading mechanism. But for each salvo the volume can be much heavier.

My final conclusion was, when I wrote that article, that long-range powder rockets could not be built, that it would need a liquid-fuel rocket motor to make long-range rockets possible. Anything that needs a mass-ratio higher than 1:1 must have liquid fuels—and there is a disadvantage connected with that. One of the liquids is liquefied oxygen, and liquid oxygen cannot be regarded as a storable fuel, at least not in the sense in which powder is storable. You can, of course, store liquid oxygen for a few days, even weeks, if the quantity is large enough, but military projectiles are often stored for a year or more.

Liquid-fuel rockets, therefore, could be used only from a base where liquid oxygen is available, they could not be carted around in the field in the same manner as, say, a heavy howitzer and ammunition. But liquid-fuel rockets, if you only make them large enough, have a long range which makes up to a large extent for their lack of mobility. Very heavy guns are not very mobile either, except those mounted on a floating base called battleship.

What Professor Oberth told Colonel Kesselring must have been about the same I wrote in that article. Then Oberth would draw the following conclusions:

A. Liquid-fuel rockets can have a long range only if they have a high mass-ratio. They can have a high mass-ratio only if it is possible to evolve a light-weight high-capacity pump so that the fuel can be pumped from the tanks into the combustion chamber. That way the tanks can be thin-walled since they do not have to stand a higher internal pressure than the weight of the fuel multiplied by the acceleration of the rocket plus an added safety factor. The first job to be done, therefore, is the development of such a pump. Oberth probably pointed out that he had a design for such a pump which would work, or, if not, could at least be used as a starting point.

B. Once such a pump has been developed it is possible to build a high mass-ratio rocket for very long range, up to about six hundred miles. (Beyond that the mass-ratio would grow so big that a step-rocket would be required.) Six hundred miles, considering European conditions, is very long. Such rocket batteries, when stationed in Berlin, could sweep a circle outside the pre-war German border in any direction.

C. Being able to build a certain mass-ratio at all is almost equivalent to being able to build rockets of that mass-ratio in any order of magnitude, within reasonable limits. (One probably could not build such a rocket with a total weight of only twenty or thirty pounds.) Thus, if one can produce a rocket having a mass-ratio of 6.5:1—which, for fuels like alcohol or gasoline, amounts to saying "a rocket with a range of two hundred fifty to three hundred miles"—it is mostly a matter of choice, or of military considerations, how big the final weight is going to be.

D. Considering the range over which they could be fired, the accuracy of these rockets is going to be high and the remaining lack of accuracy could be made up by using poison gas which will spread over a certain area.

E. While there are many theoretical reasons why rockets should not have wings, it is possible to build a rocket-propelled airplane. It should be short and squat and generally bat-shaped rather than bird-shaped and should leave the ground vertically as long as the fuel tanks are full. I have a drawing of the general appearance here on page 280 of my book, if the Herr Oberst will be good enough to glance at it—

I did not invent this conversation, not even the wording. It can be found almost in its entirety and with almost the same words, in Oberth's "Wage zur Raumschiffahrt." I merely got the rather scattered references together and condensed them considerably. But this is how Oberth saw the problem of the long-distance war rocket as far back as 1929 and I still remember a conversation we had at that time.

Oberth and I spoke a good deal about long-distance mail rockets then and I wondered about a certain difficulty. The problem was this: if the mail rocket was to travel over a distance where the use of rockets would really involve a saving of time, it would have to be a high mass-ratio rocket, from about 5:1 up. Now such a mass-ratio was impossible without a pump—still to be invented—and that pump, no matter what shape it took, would have a certain minimum size. This automatically decreed a minimum size for the whole rocket and probably a large size, the payload available might come out as high as a thousand pounds.

"And do you think, herr professor, that there will be a need for rockets carrying a thousand pounds of mail over five hundred kilometers?" (About three hundred miles.) Oberth looked at me with the smile which old-fashioned pedagogues reserve for people whom they call "my dear young friend" and said after a while: "There will be need for rockets which carry a thousand pounds of dynamite over five hundred kilometers."

Oberth convinced Kesselring about such a need.

First, Swedish observers say, Oberth was provided with a camouflaging job in Germany. In ordinary German academic life it would have been impossible to give Oberth a professorship at a German university. The major obstacle was that he lacked a doctor's degree, the secondary obstacle was that he had been neither assistant professor nor *privatdozent*—"private lecturer," meaning one who receives no salary from the university—anywhere. The term "professor" as applied to him meant that he was teacher at an ordinary high school in, of all countries, Rumania. Normally he would have to fulfill both the requirements mentioned to be even eligible for a full professorship.

The Nazis made him "Professor of Physical Astronomy" at the University of Berlin, which, under the circumstances, conformed to academic tradition about as much as a foreign-born president would conform with the Constitution of the United States.

He may have taught astronomy for a while, provided that the Hitler youth was interested in astronomy, unless ordered to be. But from all we know and can know at this moment the founding of the laboratory near Peenemünde fell into the time of Oberth's professorship in Berlin.

No doubt that this laboratory was not only built in extreme secrecy, but that it was also endowed with all the safety measures and precautions which could be thought up by the Gestapo on the one hand and Military Security on the other. It is certain that none of the technicians and scientists working there knew the full program, each one learned only as much as he needed for doing his own job right.

Naturally nobody employed there could be permitted to go home. The actual construction work began most likely with the construction of homes for the people to be employed there. The fact that Peenemünde could pass as an inexpensive seashore resort helped: *Kraft durch Freude* built one of its innumerable *Ferieuheime*—"vacation resorts"—at Peenemünde. If any member of the Labor Front of which *Kraft durch Freude*—"Strength through Joy"—was only a part, had any special reason for wishing to spend his vacation in Peenemünde and applied for that particular resort he was assured that there was no room. If he insisted he was probably investigated as a spy, not dreaming about the real reason for the investigation.

Of course the answer was not even a lie, this particular resort was filled up, with engineers and physicists, presumably with everybody who had, in the past, shown interest in rockets and who had been passed by the Gestapo.

There was more than one laboratory, not only in the sense that the laboratories occupied a considerable number of buildings. The whole *Institut*, as it was probably referred to, was subdivided into several branches, certainly more than two, probably four. Of the two we know definitely, they might now be conveniently labeled V-1 and V-2. If the rocket weapons used by the German soldiers in the field were also developed at Peenemünde, as seems likely, the powder laboratory or laboratories formed the third branch. And if the propulsion unit for the rocket-propelled Messerschmitt 163 was developed there we get a fourth branch or department.

Oberth was not the head of the whole, but he probably was the department head of the V-2 branch. That he developed the V-1, the well-known jet-propelled robot bomb, was claimed when this weapon was new, but it is highly unlikely. While the V-2 bears many of the earmarks of Oberth's thinking and reasoning, V-1 not only lacks all of them but embodies some features which Oberth would never have used, if his word had counted.

The French physicist and collaborationist Georges Claude, otherwise a justly famous man, has recently been arrested because he is said to have invented V-1. It is quite likely that Claude contributed to the design, but the nature of V-1 is such that no one man can be called its inventor. The idea of an aerial counterpart to the naval torpedo, a self-propelled, unmanned and explosive-laden airplane —just as the naval torpedo is a self-propelled, unmanned and explosive-laden small submarine—is by no means new, in fact the United States developed such a weapon in 1918, too late for actual use. It did not only carry a "bomb" of the same weight as V-1, it had four hundred miles range as compared to the V-1's one hundred and fifty miles.

Nazi-controlled newspapers have named one Heinz Bunse as "inventor" of the V-1 after the initial assault on London was made. This mention caused a great search through biographical reference works, but the search was fruitless. Heinz Bunse could not be found, he probably was—or still is—a Nazi protégé, presumably placed in command of the V-1 development section for purely political reasons.

Some other candidates for the somewhat doubtful honor of having invented V-1 have also been named—I myself among them—usually on the strength of certain features of the robot bomb, covered by patents owned by the men in question. While it is quite possible that these patents were utilized, there is no guarantee of any kind that the men in question were even informed about it.

The results of the research work done at Peenemünde, as they emerged on the battlefields, are the following:

Powder Rocket Branch:

Nebelwerfer 41 (Smoke Thrower, Model 1941). The well-known six-barreled rocket mortar. In two sizes: 150 mm and 210 mm. The projectiles are between four and five feet long and come in many shapes and manners of manufacture. The range is around six thousand yards, the tubes are fired electrically around the circle, with one-second intervals between rockets. The range of the large type seems to be up to nine thousand yards. When fired an enormous flash and backflash is produced. Tactical employment is the same as that of field howitzers, but the *Nebelwerfer* is far inferior in accuracy. The name implies that it was originally developed as a chemical mortar.

Schweres Wurfgerät ("Heavy Throwing Engine"). This also comes in two sizes, the 320 mm incendiary rocket and the 280 mm high-explosive. Each type was used at first singly, with the shipping crate doubling as a launching rack when propped up and then in units of six, two rows of threes banked together on an artillery carriage. The projectiles for the smaller size weigh about one hundred eighty pounds, the larger size over two hundred thirty pounds. The large type always holds about eleven gallons of incendiary fluid—oil and gasoline—the smaller one always high-explosive, even though some were found marked with a yellow cross, the German marking for mustard gas. Employment is similar to that of the *Nebelwerfer*, but the range is not over two thousand yards. The rocket proper of the *Schweres Wurfgerät* seems to be the same as that of the larger variety of the *Nebelwerfer*, being also 210 mm in diameter.

Airplane rockets. First encountered in quantities over Schweinfurt by Flying Fortresses. The range which can be utilized seems to be well over one thousand yards, the caliber of the rockets around 80 mm. The Focke-Wulfs carry only two, one under each wing, while Allied rocket-equipped fighters carry up to eight.

A.A. rockets. Antiaircraft rockets, similar to the Z-guns of the British, were first used in quantities in the defense of Berlin. They seem to be able to attain a maximum altitude of around twenty thousand feet. Not much is known about their size and construction. But calculations of probable size and resulting performance, published by Ley and Schaefer in the July, 1944, issue of *The Military Engineer* led to the following results, with assumptions based on the known data of high-compression powder rockets built by F. W. Sander:

	Take-off weight (lbs.)	Weight empty (lbs.)	Mass-ratio	Peak velocity (ft./sec.)	Total altitude (ft.)	Time required (sec.)
Type I.	176	66	1:1.6	1270	29,000	48.4
Type II.	207	97	1:2.14	1170	27,000	49.1

The column "weight empty" is understood to include a projectile of about twenty-six pounds. The figures of twenty-nine thousand and twenty-seven thousand feet respectively refer to the altitude where a rocket the projectile of which did not explode would begin to fall back. Naturally this peak altitude cannot be utilized for A.A. fire. The peak velocity occurs in both cases twenty seconds after leaving the launching rack, and in both cases around thirteen thousand feet.

These, then, are the known results of the work of the Powder Rocket Section of the German research laboratory. That section also produced a German *bazooka*, patterned after the American rocket launcher but much heavier and more cumbersome, and a rocket-accelerated bomb, patterned after those used by the Russian *Shturm-ovik* planes.

Going over to the work of the Flying Bomb Section, it may be useful to switch viewpoints and tell the story as it unfolded to the Allies.

As early as 1942 the Allies, and more particularly the British, knew that the Germans were concentrating on a new weapon. Suspicion quickly centered on Peenemünde which was already marked in the files of the Allies as the development center of German rocket weapons. R.A.F. reconnaissance planes, ranging all along the Baltic seashore, took photographs of many places, among them Peenemünde. Much of the photographing was done rather openly, so that the Germans would get used to photographic reconnaissance over the Baltic. Sometimes the R.A.F. came mine-laying, which furnished a reason for all the photographing.

As a matter of fact it is said that the Germans in Peenemünde, standing behind the lines of electrically charged barbed wire which kept visitors away, became careless and just glanced at the British planes. The British planes took pictures of them, mapping the whole layout in the process so that there was little doubt what each building represented. Some were dwelling places, some were administration buildings where plans and blueprints were kept. Still others were storage buildings and workshops.

One day one of the pictures showed a very small airplane on a launching ramp. A little later some stories began to leak out from the Danish islands, even though these islands were occupied by the Germans. The stories told of the crashing of small unmanned airplanes of German manufacture, obviously crewless to begin with, doing no particular damage.

The world as a whole was still unaware of Peenemünde and kept watching the Russian front and the North African campaign. But by the end of August, 1943, everybody knew that Peenemünde must be important—very important.

During the night of August 17-18, 1943, the R.A.F. sent what was then an exceptionally large force of heavy bombers to the unobtrusive northwestern tip of the island of Usedom. Two thousand tons of bombs were concentrated on that small spot. Such an expenditure of bombs was in itself a strong hint that the target must have been important before the bombs rained down upon it. What was an even stronger hint was the admitted loss of forty-one aircraft. This meant that the out-of-the-way spot was heavily defended.

The result of that heavy and costly raid was in keeping with the effort and the losses. As Prime Minister Churchill described it later —speech of July 6, 1944: ". . . very great damage was done to the enemy and his affairs and a number of key German scientists, including the head scientist, who were all dwelling together in a so-called Strength-through-Joy establishment, were killed."

Churchill did not name the "head scientist" in that speech and it was generally believed that he referred to Oberth. Months later Allan A. Michie of the *Reader's Digest* was permitted to reveal the name of the *kommandant*, he was forty-nine-year-old Luftwaffe expert Major General Wolfgang von Chamier-Gliesezenski. It was then also revealed that, for reasons of secrecy, the bomber crews of the R.A.F. had no idea what they were ordered to bomb. Only a few group leaders and Intelligence knew. Intelligence had also chosen the date, not only because of moonlight, but because it knew that at that time some seven thousand scientists, technicians and precision workers were assembled in Peenemünde.

It transpired later that five thousand of them died during that night, a good number of them from the explosion of their own stores, set off by blockbusters. The Luftwaffe's chief of staff, General Jeschonnek, was among them, he had been visiting Peenemünde. It is likely that Ernst Udet, whose death was announced a short time afterward, was there too at that time. Half of all the buildings—there had been forty-five dwelling places before the attack and about one hundred workshops, storage buildings, et cetera—were completely destroyed, the other half badly damaged.

There is no way of telling whether the long delay in the use of V-1 and V-2 was actually due to that raid or whether the Germans planned to hold these weapons back until the Allied Invasion came. The latter is more probable, because Peenemünde, while the heart of the research work, was not the only production center. One was found near Vienna and the 15th U.S. Air Force, operating from Italy, paid several visits to it. There must have been others too.

Even Peenemünde itself had to be subjected to "touching up," the R.A.F. went back in strength about one year after the first raid and in between the 8th U.S. Air Force, operating from England, went over more than once.

The big August raid seems to have broken the back of the research staff, but a great deal of the research had been done before the raid was made, as subsequent events showed.

The first aftermath of the August raid was—strange workings of the Nazi mind—a wave of propaganda. We have terrible secret weapons, Dr. Goebbels screeched, enormous rockets of fearful power, but so far the Führer has not given the word to use them. The implication, stated later on in so many words, was that the Führer was too humane to use the weapons at his disposal—even though he, one may add, was losing the whole Mediterranean at the time and "disengaging" himself in Russia at a rate without parallel in military history.

In September the Goebbels Ministry "revealed" that the new weapon would be used against England, America being unfortunately out of reach. The spokesman added "for the present," after a short pause.

On September 26th "specific" information began to come over the wires of the various press services. A Swedish journalist whose name was given as Gunnert Pihl in the dispatches from Stockholm stated that the weapon was a long-range rocket, fired from monster barrels a hundred feet long. The barrels, he stated, were installed within a fifteen-mile radius of Calais and Boulogne. The range of the rockets was given as one hundred twenty-five miles, and it was stated that the pressure in the barrel was so excessive that it would stand only twenty rounds.

To any expert it was clear that the report was either straight German propaganda or a badly garbled version of the real thing. While it did seem likely that a rocket large enough to travel one hundred twenty-five miles would require a hundred-foot launching tube, the statement about the short life of these tubes was obviously wrong. Either the projectiles were rocket propelled, in which case the strain on the launching tubes could not be too excessive, or else the launching tubes were actually long-range guns and in that case there was no need to call them rocket guns.

Whether Pihl's tale was Nazi-inspired or not, the German Propaganda Ministry observed the large amount of publicity it received everywhere and on December 13, 1943, some more material flashed over the press wires, originating this time from "diplomatic sources" in Zürich. The report, as received in this country, read as follows:

Zürich, December 13 [1943]—UP—Germany has been conducting tests with a rocket shell forty-five feet long, weighing twelve tons. Thirty feet of the shell's capacity, it was said, is needed for the driving apparatus and fuel. The rocket allegedly is effective over an area of twenty square miles because of the explosive force generated by its charge of compressed nitric acid. It was said that the shell has a theoretical range of one hundred sixty miles although in tests thus far it has been confined to thirty-five and forty-mile distances.

These sources said the Nazis have begun the assembly of rocket catapults on the French Channel Coast despite the fact that tests of the projectile are not yet complete.

It was claimed that the Germans have been experimenting with steam-driven catapults. These reportedly would enable the rockets to be launched with an extremely low initial velocity. The projectile is driven by compressed Diesel oil which lends its propulsive force immediately after the rocket leaves the catapult . . .

All this sounded like so much hogwash. Just what was meant by an "effectiveness over twenty square miles" remained a mystery which nobody could clear up. It was obviously meant to imply that the area of destruction would be twenty square miles large, but it could also be construed as dispersion or, if you stretched things, even range. It remained mysterious why nitric acid was used as an explosive, not to mention the minor fact that nitric acid as well as Diesel oil, both being liquids, are incompressible to all intents and purposes. It is now clear that the dimensions given were correct for V-2, while the range is that of V-1, but there was no way of telling then.

At the same time, however, reports came more and more often that heavy Allied bombing formations had dropped the biggest possible tonnage of bombs on mysterious targets in the Pas-de-Calais area which was quickly christened Rocket Gun Coast. I figured out at that time that a rocket, fired from the so-called Rocket Gun Coast, and supposed to hit London, would have to have a mass-ratio of 7:1. Since I was assuming powder as a fuel I doubted the tales of long-range rockets, writing: ". . . . it boils down to the question whether we want to believe that the Germans can build such rockets. If we do believe it we still have to ask ourselves what good such rockets, being inaccurate, could do." I suggested then, in December 1943, that the weapon might be a crewless plane, stuffed with TNT and guided by a radio beam.

That article had just been published—in PM—when other papers published a report that the Germans had used their giant rocket guns for the first time. The story was retracted the following day, it had been an almost ridiculous error. The Germans had stated that they had used *Leuchtgranaten*—flare shells—during a minor naval action in the British Channel, an attack on a British coastwide convoy. The translator had confused *Leuchtgranaten* and *Leuchtraketen* which latter word means "distress rockets." Apparently that did not make enough sense to him, so he dropped the inconvenient "distress," thus making big headlines.

The latter part of December was filled up with reports on an actual weapon: the German glider bomb, launched against Allied shipping from various types of German bombers, Dornier 217, Heinkel 177, Junkers 290 and Focke-Wulf 200. These glider bombs, weighing about seventeen hundred pounds, were some ten feet long and had ten-foot wings. They had a rocket propulsion unit—it is not known whether powder or liquid fuel—and could be directed by radio-control from the plane which had launched it. The glider bombs were as a rule not too accurate, but did sink a few vessels. It is said that the sinking of the Italian battleship *Roma*, during its last voyage to surrender at Malta, was accomplished by such a bomb, but other sources state that this was done by a torpedo plane.

The confusion was miraculous to behold: Churchill's disclosures about the rocket glider bomb—a Peenemünde product, no doubt— German-inspired stories about super rockets, daily bombings of the "mystery targets" of the Rocket Gun Coast all arrived together, were garbled with each other and discussed with the most appalling lack of technical knowledge by newspaper commentators, especially the air-power branch.

On January 16, 1944, a rocket story to end all rocket stories came from Stockholm. The super rocket was, according to that story, carried aloft by a bomber and then ignited. After ignition it would rise to a thirty-mile altitude and hit targets sixty miles away. It consisted of three compartments inside:

"One compartment contains a charge of eight hundred eighty pounds of liquid air and Uranium salt solution, the second holds the four hundred fifty to six hundred fifty pound propulsion charge consisting of coal oxide and picric acid, and the third contains the ignition mechanism believed to comprise radio-active salt solution and quicksilver."

Goebbels' Ministry, shouting nonsense at the top of its lungs, added a few days later: "Such rockets will cause artificial icebergs in the Channel in case the Allies try a suicidal invasion of the mainland of Europe where they will smash their heads against the Atlantic Wall."

By the end of January a correct-sounding report came, sent by wireless to the New York *Times* by C. L. Sulzberger, then with the Fifth Army in Italy. The Nazi secret, he wrote, is a crewless plane. "Flying at high speed it would be extraordinarily difficult to stop with either fighter aircraft, air mines or balloon barrages. . . ." And, Mr. Sulzberger added: "It was only after Allied bombing began wrecking the take-off points that the Germans, realizing the Allies were in on their secret, began to brag about its terrific potentialities."

Goebbels then spoke of the *Wunderwaffe*, the "miracle weapon," which would win the war for Germany quickly, once the Führer makes the decision to use it. Berliners, of course, abbreviated *Wunderwaffe* to Wuwa—which sounds as funny to a German as it does to an American—and every once in a while would ask "*Wo bleibt die Wuwa?*" ("What happened to the Wuwa?") But the Wuwa did not appear. Eisenhower and Montgomery invaded France. For a few days things hung in a balance. But no Wuwa.

One week after D-Day the first robot bomb appeared over England's southern shore. The Wuwa—meanwhile re-christened *Vergeltungswaffe* or weapon of retaliation and specifically designated as V-1 —had made its appearance. It was a pilotless plane, 25.4 feet long, with a wingspread of 17.67 feet, carrying a warhead with one thousand kilograms—twenty-two hundred pounds—of high explosive, propelled by an intermittent jet engine, flying at a top speed of about 360 m.p.h. and using one of its one hundred fifty gallons of low-grade aviation gasoline for every mile of flight.

A few weeks later the Berlin radio told that during the early experiments in 1942 the flying bombs had had a tendency to shed their wings and that the trouble could not be found until Anna Reisch, a German woman pilot, had made several flights in one, observing her own vehicle through a periscope. She got the Iron Cross, First Class, for her feat, having been "not dangerously injured" in the experiment.

And British Intelligence had a report on hand stating that Hitler himself had watched a demonstration, seeing a robot bomb chased by a captured *Spitfire* and smiling with satisfaction when the *Spitfire* was slowly left behind. The real *Spitfire* pilots quickly learned that they could make up for the difference by diving on the flying bomb.

"After the bomb had been in the air for a certain number of

minutes," to quote from the official history of the "robot blitz," written by the British war historian Hilary St. George Saunders, "a clockwork mechanism locked the elevators so that they dived into the ground. When the bomb tilted, any gasoline remaining in the tank flowed away from the propulsion unit, cutting off the engine. In several cases the engine stopped before the dive, which gave rise to the belief that there were two kinds of bombs, one which stopped and fell steeply and another which stopped and glided. Actually it was the same bomb—"

The remainder of that story is statistics.

During the interval from June 12, 1944 and August 30, 1944 the Germans launched eight thousand seventy flying bombs, all aimed at London. (There was a second battery of launching racks, aimed at Bristol, but it was still incomplete when it fell into Allied hands.) Over two thousand of them, one out of every four, fell into the Channel, strayed from their course, or crashed near the take-off ramps— the Germans offered French civilians as much as one thousand francs a day if they would help them launch flying bombs. Fighter interception destroyed twenty-four per cent of the bombs in flight, A.A. guns and rockets accounted for seventeen percent, balloon barrages for five per cent so that only two thousand bombs, or about twenty-nine per cent, actually fell on London.

They killed 5,864 persons, injured 17,197 badly and 23,174 slightly, destroyed 24,491 houses, rendered another 52,293 uninhabitable and damaged over 950,000. The results were impressive as far as figures go, their influence on the course of the war was nil.

V-1 had two main weaknesses. One was inherent in the design, the other is inherent in the type of weapon. The weakness in design was the jet motor. It was of a type which could not work at rest but needed a speed of at least 150 m.p.h. which necessitated the launching ramp and take-off help. Most of the twenty-five percent which did not cross the Channel did not do so for reasons of faulty take-off. Also, the take-off ramps were fine bombing targets if they could be found.

A different type of engine, whether jet or conventional, would cure most of these troubles. If an engine which can work when at rest were used, there would be hardly any crashes near the take-off point, there might be no need for take-off ramps but just for runways.

The weakness inherent in the type, which would remain, is interceptibility. It is a good guess that interceptor planes which are expected to come back and which carry a valuable pilot, will always be faster than the flying bombs of the same period. And as the performance of the flying bomb improves, the performance of A.A. gunnery will improve too.

The Flying Bomb Section of Peenemünde did not create an irresistible weapon. But it did create a novel weapon which is destined to remain standard equipment of all armies and probably of all navies too. It will always be more or less an area weapon, but there is need for area weapons too in warfare.

Leaving the work of the V-2 section of Peenemünde to the last, the result of still another probable section of those laboratories has to be mentioned.

When the robots streaked across the Channel there were occasional reports of a larger type, almost twice as fast as the flying bomb. But while there is no reason to doubt the words of the pilots who reported what they saw, there is reason to doubt their interpretation. Examination of wreckage failed to disclose the existence of a larger type of flying bomb, although such a larger type would have been possible, of course.

What the pilots probably saw were samples of still another German invention, presumably also from Peenemünde, the rocket propelled fighter plane Messerschmitt 163. The Me 163 is not a jet plane, as is often stated, it is a rocket plane.

It was encountered later—on August 16, 1944—over Leipzig. Suddenly things swished past the Flying Fortresses, so fast that the crews failed to see them clearly. The fighter pilots, flying fast Mustangs, had a better chance. The strange planes still left the Mustangs behind at a rate of 250 m.p.h. or more, but the Mustangs succeeded in intercepting them on occasion. The Germans were faster, but by the same token less maneuverable.

The pilots said later that these Germans "were ugly things, looking like bats flying around." Their fuselage was very short and stubby, the wings were so strongly tapered as to be almost triangular. The fuselage did not project at all beyond the leading edge of the wing in front, and projected for only a few feet beyond the trailing edge in the back, leaving no room for horizontal stabilizers and elevators. They only carried vertical stabilizer and rudder, and the rocket motor was located directly beneath the rudder.

The Me 163 is said to have fuel for eight minutes of powered flight only, but can stay in the air for about half an hour, performing as a

very fast glider in the meantime. The armament consists of a total
of six single-shot rocket tubes in the wings, augmented by one automatic cannon in the nose.

The design can be traced back in a straight line to experiments
made in Germany as early as 1928—they were then seven-foot models
with a Sander powder rocket—but it also reflects "page 280 in my
book, if the Herr Oberst will be good enough to look." The Me 163
embodies most of Oberth's idea of what a rocket airplane should be
like—as modified by an experienced aerodynamicist.

The fuel for the propulsion rocket has been described as giving off
"chemical fumes" by American pilots. This sounds strange, because
the exhaust of an oxygen-gasoline rocket motor would smell like any
exhaust, and the smell of alcohol of an oxygen-alcohol rocket motor
is hard to mistake.

Is the rocket motor of the Me 163 the place where Sander's "liquid
powder" was finally utilized? Not a single word was ever written about
it after that first publication—and that was in a provincial newspaper.
Did the Reichswehr step in then and there and put its hand over the
new invention, hiding it from sight?

Winston Churchill, reporting to the House of Commons on July
6, 1944, referred to Peenemünde as "the main experiment station
both of the flying bomb and the long-range rocket." In the same
speech he stated that "at first our information led us to believe that
a rocket weapon would be used"—but then V-1 came.

The mystery of V-2 deepened.

It was an enormous puzzle.

There were the stories that Oberth was responsible for the founding of Peenemünde. There were the stories of gigantic rockets, but
full of technological nonsense. There was V-1, decidedly not something Oberth would build, besides the fact that "Heinz Bunse,"
Georges Claude and at least four other people were alternately given
credit for the invention.

V-1 lived up to some of the early reports as far as range, weight of
bomb and the possibility of launching it from airplanes were concerned. But V-1 was not a rocket. Was all the rocket talk a mistake?

When Churchill spoke of "flying bombs and long-range rockets"
it became clear that there was such a thing. But what did "long
range" mean? Twenty miles is long range for a rocket, even ten miles
would be long range.

Besides what good would a long-range rocket do as far as the Ger-

mans were concerned. Another area weapon? Another means of haphazard bombardment?

Like Arthur Clarke of the British Interplanetary Society I found
myself torn between two wishes. As far as the war was concerned, or
rather the needless suffering of the people who might fall victims,
the better hope was to discount all the German propaganda stories
as propaganda. But as far as the future of rocket research was concerned, a twenty-ton rocket with a range of a hundred miles or better,
would be a definite trump card. One would be able to point at that
weapon and to say: "See, it can be done! But you didn't believe it!"

Yes, it can be done.

V-2, looking and performing precisely as rocket theory had always
stated it would, is a reality.

Churchill, again reporting to the House of Commons on November
10, 1944, stated: "For the last few weeks the enemy has been using
his new weapon, the long-range rocket, and a number have landed at
widely scattered points in this country."

Information about the rocket itself was forthcoming quickly. Allied
airmen saw one take-off, describing it as a streamlined projectile about
forty feet long and fifteen feet around, shooting a thirty-foot flame
out of its tail and followed by a long trail of vapor, described as looking "like a Bronx cheer in smoke."

V-2 carries a warhead holding twenty-two hundred pounds of high-
explosive, possibly the same warhead as V-1. Its maximum range with
that warhead is around three hundred miles, the peak of the long
trajectory is between sixty and seventy miles above the ground. The
fuel, reports say, is either gasoline or alcohol and liquid oxygen.

Everything about it spells out OBERTH in capital letters.

That it is not an effective war weapon goes almost without saying.
A weapon which lands "at widely scattered points" is only a terror
weapon but nothing which can decide a war. And if, as Churchill
suggested, the range is increased by cutting down the weight of the
warhead, the scattering is going to increase too. Besides the warhead
is even less effective than it is when carried by a V-1. V-2, crashing
down from its stratospheric altitude of seventy miles, buries itself
deeply before the warhead has a chance to explode. It has more
penetration by far where it hits, but the lateral blast effects are considerably smaller.

If you calculate the mass-ratio requirements for such a trajectory
and for liquid fuels which may be expected to produce an exhaust
velocity of about sixty-five hundred feet per second, you arrive at

about 6.5:1. The warhead weighs one ton, the rocket itself cannot very well weigh less than a ton, so that the "weight of arrival" is two tons. Multiplied by the mass-ratio required we find a take-off weight of thirteen tons. This checks well with Allied estimates and German announcements, which both ascribe to V-2 a minimum take-off weight of twelve and a maximum of fifteen tons.

V-2 proves that it is possible to build liquid fuel rockets of almost any size. There are stories of experimental models which had a take-off weight of fifty tons. These might be just stories, but they also might be true. It does not matter too much one way or another because V-2, as it exists, proves that Oberth and his associates succeeded in making the one invention on which the whole future of rocket research and rocket construction rested. They must have invented a light-weight, high-capacity fuel pump. With such pumps you can, theoretically, build any size of liquid fuel rocket beyond a certain minimum size.

With such pumps you can, given a little time, even build a spaceship.

As a matter of fact, this is no longer in the future, the first spaceship has been built already, only it is not used as such. Yes, we might as well admit it, V-2 is the first spaceship.

With its eight and a half tons of liquid oxygen and about four tons of alcohol V-2 lifts a "payload" of one ton—the bomb—to an altitude of seventy miles. Presumably it is fired at an angle of about fifty degrees.

Now take off the bomb and substitute an observer, wearing a light diving suit and having a nice set of instruments around him, making a total of, say, three hundred pounds. This gives you another nineteen hundred pounds of fuel. Do that and fire V-2 vertically, it is not apt to have a maximum acceleration surpassing three or four G. It will ascend beyond two hundred miles—it will just touch empty space!

It will probably be necessary to re-create V-2 after the war for this purpose. We cannot hope to take Peenemünde or any one of the subsidiary research stations. The Nazis will see to it that everything will be utterly destroyed before we get there. And Himmler, I am sure, has lists of all those who know a good deal about this work. If they escape future Allied bombings, they will be shot by the Gestapo.

Barring miracles we will not be able to continue for peaceful purposes what the Germans started with war in mind. But the recreation of these things can be undertaken with confidence after the war, because Peenemünde proved that it can be done.

ADAM AND NO EVE

by

ALFRED BESTER

The terrifying possibilities for error that lurk in any scientific experiment are here exploited to the fullest extent. For the man who built the first rocket ship was wrong in just one calculation— and his mistake destroyed the human race. Now that we know of such things as atomic explosion, the catastrophe that followed the first rocket flight seems shockingly plausible. On the other hand, it is equally plausible to assume that man's instinct will never let the race perish utterly.

*

CRANE KNEW this must be the seacoast. Instinct told him; but more than instinct, the few shreds of knowledge that clung to his torn, feverish brain told him; the stars that had shown at night through the rare breaks in the clouds, and his compass that still pointed a trembling finger north. That was strangest of all, Crane thought. Though a welter of chaos, the Earth still retained its polarity.

It was no longer a coast; there was no longer any sea. Only the faint line of what had been a cliff, stretching north and south for endless miles. A line of gray ash. The same gray ash and cinders that lay behind him; the same gray ash that stretched before him. Fine silt, knee-deep, that swirled up at every motion and choked him. Cinders that scudded in dense mighty clouds when the mad winds blew. Cinders that were churned to viscous mud when the frequent rains fell.

The sky was jet overhead. The black clouds rode high and were pierced with shafts of sunlight that marched swiftly over the Earth.

Where the light struck a cinder storm, it was filled with gusts of dancing, gleaming particles. Where it played through rain it brought the arches of rainbows into being. Rain fell; cinder-storms blew; light thrust down—together, alternately and continually in a jigsaw of black and white violence. So it had been for months. So it was over every mile of the broad Earth.

Crane passed the edge of the ashen cliffs and began crawling down the even slope that had once been the ocean bed. He had been traveling so long that all sense of pain had left him. He braced elbows and dragged his body forward. Then he brought his right knee under him and reached forward with elbows again. Elbows, knee, elbows, knee— He had forgotten what it was to walk.

Life, he thought dazedly, is wonderful. It adapts itself to anything. If it must crawl, it crawls. Callus forms on the elbows and knees. The neck and shoulders toughen. The nostrils learn to snort away the ashes before they inhale. The bad leg swells and festers. It numbs, and presently it will rot and fall off.

"I beg pardon," Crane said, "I didn't quite get that—"

He peered up at the tall figure before him and tried to understand the words. It was Hallmyer. He wore his stained lab jacket and his gray hair was awry. Hallmyer stood delicately on top of the ashes and Crane wondered why he could see the scudding cinder clouds through his body.

"How do you like your world, Stephen?" Hallmyer asked.

Crane shook his head miserably.

"Not very pretty, eh?" said Hallmyer. "Look around you. Dust, that's all; dust and ashes. Crawl, Stephen, crawl. You'll find nothing but dust and ashes—"

Hallmyer produced a goblet of water from nowhere. It was clear and cold. Crane could see the fine mist of dew on its surface and his mouth was suddenly coated with dry grit.

"Hallmyer!" he cried. He tried to get to his feet and reach for the water, but the jolt of pain in his right leg warned him. He crouched back.

Hallmyer sipped and then spat in his face. The water felt warm.

"Keep crawling," said Hallmyer bitterly. "Crawl round and round the face of the Earth. You'll find nothing but dust and ashes—" He emptied the goblet on the ground before Crane. "Keep crawling. How many miles? Figure it out for yourself. Pi-R-Square. The radius is eight thousand or so—"

He was gone, jacket and goblet. Crane realized that rain was falling again. He pressed his face into the warm sodden cinder mud, opened his mouth and tried to suck the moisture. He groaned and presently began crawling.

There was an instinct that drove him on. He had to get somewhere. It was associated, he knew, with the sea—with the edge of the sea. At the shore of the sea something waited for him. Something that would help him understand all this. He had to get to the sea—that is, if there were a sea any more.

The thundering rain beat his back like heavy planks. Crane paused and yanked the knapsack around to his side where he probed in it with one hand. It contained exactly three things. A pistol, a bar of chocolate and a can of peaches. All that was left of two months' supplies. The chocolate was pulpy and spoiled. Crane knew he had best eat it before all value rotted away. But in another day he would lack the strength to open the can. He pulled it out and attacked it with the opener. By the time he had pierced and pried away a flap of tin, the rain had passed.

As he munched the fruit and sipped the juice, he watched the wall of rain marching before him down the slope of the ocean bed. Torrents of water were gushing through the mud. Small channels had already been cut—channels that would be new rivers some day. A day he would never see. A day that no living thing would ever see. As he flipped the empty can aside, Crane thought: The last living thing on Earth eats its last meal. Metabolism plays its last act.

Wind would follow the rain. In the endless weeks that he had been crawling, he had learned that. Wind would come in a few minutes and flog him with its clouds of cinders and ashes. He crawled forward, bleary eyes searching the flat gray miles for cover.

Evelyn tapped his shoulder.

Crane knew it was she before he turned his head. She stood alongside, fresh and gay in her bright dress, but her lovely face was puckered with alarm.

"Stephen," she cried, "you've got to hurry!"

He could only admire the way her smooth honey hair waved to her shoulders.

"Oh, darling!" she said, "you've been hurt!" Her quick gentle hands touched his legs and back. Crane nodded.

"Got it landing," he said. "I wasn't used to a parachute. I always thought you came down gently—like plumping onto a bed. But the gray earth came up at me like a fist— And Umber was fighting around in my arms. I couldn't let him drop, could I?"

"Of course not, dear—" Evelyn said.

"So I just held on to him and tried to get my legs under me," Crane said. "And then something smashed my legs and side—"

He paused, wondering how much she knew of what really had happened. He didn't want to frighten her.

"Evelyn, darling—" he said, trying to reach up his arms.

"No dear," she said. She looked back in fright. "You've got to hurry. You've got to watch out behind!"

"The cinder storms?" He grimaced. "I've been through them before."

"Not the storms!" Evelyn cried. "Something else. Oh, Stephen—"

Then she was gone, but Crane knew she had spoken the truth. There was something behind—something that had been following him all those weeks. Far in the back of his mind he had sensed the menace. It was closing in on him like a shroud. He shook his head. Somehow that was impossible. He was the last living thing on Earth. How could there be a menace?

The wind roared behind him, and an instant later came the heavy clouds of cinders and ashes. They lashed over him, biting his skin. With dimming eyes, he saw the way they coated the mud and covered it with a fine dry carpet. Crane drew his knees under him and covered his head with his arms. With the knapsack as a pillow, he prepared to wait out the storm. It would pass as quickly as the rain.

The storm whipped up a great bewilderment in his sick head. Like a child he pushed at the pieces of his memory, trying to fit them together. Why was Hallmyer so bitter toward him? It couldn't have been that argument, could it?

What argument?

Why, that one before all this happened.

Oh, that!

Abruptly, the pieces fitted themselves together.

Crane stood alongside the sleek lines of his ship and admired it tremendously. The roof of the shed had been removed and the nose of the ship hoisted so that it rested on a cradle pointed toward the sky. A workman was carefully burnishing the inner surfaces of the rocket jets.

The muffled sounds of an argument came from within the ship and then a heavy clanking. Crane ran up the short iron ladder to the port and thrust his head inside. A few feet beneath him, two men were buckling the long tanks of ferrous solution into place.

"Easy there," Crane called. "Want to knock the ship apart?"

One looked up and grinned. Crane knew what he was thinking.

That the ship would tear itself apart. Everyone said that. Everyone except Evelyn. She had faith in him. Hallmyer never said it either. But Hallmyer thought he was crazy in another way. As he descended the ladder, Crane saw Hallmyer come into the shed, lab jacket flying.

"Speak of the devil!" Crane muttered.

Hallmyer began shouting as soon as he saw Crane. "Now listen—"

"Not all over again," Crane said.

Hallmyer dug a sheaf of papers out of his pocket and waved it under Crane's nose.

"I've been up half the night," he said, "working it through again. I tell you I'm right. I'm absolutely right—"

Crane looked at the tight-written equations and then at Hallmyer's bloodshot eyes. The man was half mad with fear.

"For the last time," Hallmyer went on. "You're using your new catalyst on iron solution. All right. I grant that it's a miraculous discovery. I give you credit for that."

Miraculous was hardly the word for it. Crane knew that without conceit, for he realized he'd only stumbled on it. You had to stumble on a catalyst that would induce atomic disintegration of iron and give 10×10^{10} foot-pounds of energy for every gram of fuel. No man was smart enough to think all that up by himself.

"You don't think I'll make it?" Crane asked.

"To the Moon? Around the Moon? Maybe. You've got a fifty-fifty chance." Hallmyer ran fingers through his lank hair. "But for God's sake, Stephen, I'm not worried about you. If you want to kill yourself, that's your own affair. It's the Earth I'm worried about—"

"Nonsense. Go home and sleep it off."

"Look"—Hallmyer pointed to the sheets of paper with a shaky hand—"no matter how you work the feed and mixing system you can't get one hundred percent efficiency in the mixing and discharge."

"That's what makes it a fifty-fifty chance," Crane said. "So what's bothering you?"

"The catalyst that will escape through the rocket tubes. Do you realize what it'll do if a drop hits the Earth? It'll start a chain of iron disintegrations that'll envelope the globe. It'll reach out to every iron atom—and there's iron everywhere. There won't be any Earth left for you to return to—"

"Listen," Crane said wearily, "we've been through all this before."

He took Hallmyer to the base of the rocket cradle. Beneath the iron framework was a two-hundred-foot pit, fifty feet wide and lined with firebrick.

"That's for the initial discharge flames. If any of the catalyst goes through, it'll be trapped in this pit and taken care of by the secondary reactions. Satisfied now?"

"But while you're in flight," Hallmyer persisted, "you'll be endangering the Earth until you're beyond Roche's limit. Every drop of non-activated catalyst will eventually sink back to the ground and—"

"For the very last time," Crane said grimly, "the flame of the rocket discharge takes care of that. It will envelop any escaped particles and destroy them. Now get out. I've got work to do."

As he pushed him to the door, Hallmyer screamed and waved his arms. "I won't let you do it!" he repeated over and over. "I'll find some way to stop you. I won't let you do it—"

Work? No, it was sheer intoxication to labor over the ship. It had the fine beauty of a well-made thing. The beauty of polished armor, of a balanced swept-hilt rapier, of a pair of matched guns. There was no thought of danger and death in Crane's mind as he wiped his hands with waste after the last touches were finished.

She lay in the cradle ready to pierce the skies. Fifty feet of slender steel, the rivet heads gleaming like jewels. Thirty feet were given over to fuel the catalyst. Most of the forward compartment contained the spring hammock Crane had devised to take up the initial acceleration shock. The ship's nose was a solid mass of natural quartz that stared upward like a cyclopian eye.

Crane thought: She'll die after this trip. She'll return to the Earth and smash in a blaze of fire and thunder, for there's no way yet of devising a safe landing for a rocket ship. But it's worth it. She'll have had her one great flight, and that's all any of us should want. One great beautiful flight into the unknown—

As he locked the workshop door, Crane heard Hallmyer shouting from the cottage across the fields. Through the evening gloom he could see him waving frantically. He trotted through the crisp stubble, breathing the sharp air deeply, grateful to be alive.

"It's Evelyn on the phone," Hallmyer said.

Crane stared at him. Hallmyer was acting peculiarly. He refused to meet his eyes.

"What's the idea?" Crane asked. "I thought we agreed that she wasn't to call—wasn't to get in touch with me until I was ready to start? You been putting ideas into her head? Is this the way you're going to stop me?"

Hallmyer said: "No—" and studiously examined the indigo horizon.

Crane went into his study and picked up the phone.

"Now listen, darling," he said without preamble, "there's no sense getting alarmed now. I explained everything very carefully. Just before the ship crashes, I take to a parachute and float down as happy and gentle as Wynken, Blynken and Nod. I love you very much and I'll see you Wednesday when I start. So long—"

"Good-by, sweetheart," Evelyn's clear voice said, "and is that what you called me for?"

"Called you!"

A brown hulk disengaged itself from the hearth rug and lifted itself to strong legs. Umber, Crane's Great Dane, sniffed and cocked an ear. Then he whined.

"Did you say I called you?" Crane shouted.

Umber's throat suddenly poured forth a bellow. He reached Crane in a single bound, looked up into his face and whined and roared all at once.

"Shut up, you monster!" Crane said. He pushed Umber away with his foot.

"Give Umber a kick for me," Evelyn laughed. "Yes, dear. Someone called and said you wanted to speak to me."

"They did, eh? Look, honey, I'll call you back—"

Crane hung up. He arose doubtfully and watched Umber's uneasy actions. Through the windows, the late evening glow sent flickering shadows of orange light. Umber gazed at the light, sniffed and bellowed again. Suddenly struck, Crane leaped to the window.

Across the fields a solid mass of flame thrust high into the air, and within it was the fast-crumbling walls of the workshop. Silhouetted against the blaze, the figures of half a dozen men darted and ran.

"Good heavens!" Crane cried.

He shot out of the cottage and with Umber hard at his heels, sprinted toward the shed. As he ran he could see the graceful nose of the spaceship within the core of heat, still looking cool and untouched. If only he could reach it before the flames softened its metal and started the rivets.

The workmen trotted up to him, grimy and panting. Crane gaped at them in a mixture of fury and bewilderment.

"Hallmyer!" he shouted. "Hallmyer!"

Hallmyer pushed through the crowd. His eyes were wild and gleamed with triumph.

"Too bad," he said. "I'm sorry. Stephen—"

"You swine!" Crane shouted. "You frightened old man!" He

grasped Hallmyer by the lapels and shook him just once. Then he dropped him and started into the shed.

Hallmyer cried something and an instant later a body hurtled against Crane's calves and spilled him to the ground. He lurched to his feet, fists swinging. Umber was alongside, growling over the roar of the flames. Crane smashed a man in the face, and saw him stagger back against a second. He lifted a knee in a vicious drive that sent the last man crumpling to the ground. Then he ducked his head and plunged into the shop.

The scorch felt cool at first, but when he reached the ladder and began mounting to the port, he screamed with the agony of his burns. Umber was howling at the foot of the ladder, and Crane realized that the dog could never escape from the rocket blasts. He reached down and hauled Umber into the ship.

Crane was reeling as he closed and locked the port. He retained consciousness barely long enough to settle himself in the spring hammock. Then instinct alone prompted his hands to reach out toward the control board. Instinct and the frenzied refusal to let his beautiful ship waste itself in the flames. He would fail— Yes. But he would fail, trying.

His fingers tripped the switches. The ship shuddered and roared. And blackness descended over him.

How long was he unconscious? There was no telling. Crane awoke with cold pressing against his face and body, and the sound of frightened yelps in his ears. Crane looked up and saw Umber tangled in the springs and straps of the hammock. His first impulse was to laugh; then suddenly he realized. He had looked up! He had looked up at the hammock.

He was lying curled in the cup of the quartz nose. The ship had risen high—perhaps almost to Roche's zone, to the limit of the Earth's gravitational attraction, but then without guiding hands at the controls to continue its flight, had turned and was dropping back toward Earth. Crane peered through the crystal and gasped.

Below him was the ball of the Earth. It looked three times the size of the Moon. And it was no longer his Earth. It was a globe of fire mottled with black clouds. At the northernmost pole there was a tiny patch of white, and even as Crane watched, it was suddenly blotted over with hazy tones of red, scarlet and crimson. Hallmyer had been right.

He lay frozen in the cup of the nose for hours as the ship descended.

watching the flames gradually fade away to leave nothing but the dense blanket of black around the Earth. He lay numb with horror, unable to understand—unable to reckon up a billion people snuffed out, a green fair planet reduced to ashes and cinders. His family, home, friends, everything that was once dear and close to him—gone. He could not think of Evelyn.

Air, whistling outside, awoke some instinct in him. The few shreds of reason left told him to go down with his ship and forget everything in the thunder and destruction, but the instinct of life forced him to his feet. He climbed up to the store chest and prepared for the landing. Parachute, a small oxygen tank—a knapsack of supplies. Only half aware of what he was doing he dressed for the descent, buckled on the 'chute and opened the port. Umber whined pathetically, and he took the heavy dog in his arms and stepped out into space.

But space hadn't been so clogged, the way it was now. Then it had been difficult to breathe. But that was because the air had been rare—not filled with dry clogging grit like now.

Every breath was a lungful of ground glass—or ashes—or cinders—

The pieces of memory sagged apart. Abruptly he was in the present again—a dense black present that hugged him with soft weight and made him fight for breath. Crane struggled in mad panic, and then relaxed.

It had happened before. A long time past he'd been buried deep under ashes when he'd stopped to remember. Weeks ago—or days— or months. Crane clawed with his hands, inching forward through the mound of cinders that the wind had thrown over him. Presently he emerged into the light again. The wind had died away. It was time to begin his crawl to the sea once more.

The vivid pictures of his memory scattered again before the grim vista that stretched out ahead. Crane scowled. He remembered too much, and too often. He had the vague hope that if he remembered hard enough, he might change one of the things he had done—just a very little thing—and then all this would become untrue. He thought: It might help if everyone remembered and wished at the same time—but there isn't any more everyone. I'm the only one. I'm the last memory on Earth. I'm the last life.

He crawled. Elbows, knee, elbows, knee— And then Hallmyer was crawling alongside and making a great game of it. He chortled and plunged in the cinders like a happy sea lion.

Crane said: "But why do we have to get to the sea?"

Hallmyer blew a spume of ashes.

"Ask her," he said, pointing to Crane's other side.

Evelyn was there, crawling seriously, intently; mimicking Crane's smallest action.

"It's because of our house," she said. "You remember our house, darling? High on the cliff. We were going to live there forever and ever, breathing the ozone and taking morning dips. I was there when you left. Now you're coming back to the house at the edge of the sea. Your beautiful flight is over, dear, and you're coming back to me. We'll live together, just we two, like Adam and Eve—"

Crane said: "That's nice."

Then Evelyn turned her head and screamed: "Oh, Stephen! Watch out!" and Crane felt the menace closing in on him again. Still crawling, he stared back at the vast gray plains of ash, and saw nothing. When he looked at Evelyn again he saw only his shadow, sharp and black. Presently, it, too, faded away as the marching shaft of sunlight passed.

But the dread remained. Evelyn had warned him twice, and she was always right. Crane stopped and turned, and settled himself to watch. If he was really being followed, he would see whatever it was, coming along his tracks.

There was a painful moment of lucidity. It cleaved through his fever and bewilderment, bringing with it the sharpness and strength of a knife.

I'm going mad, he thought. The corruption in my leg has spread to my brain. There is no Evelyn, no Hallmyer, no menace. In all this land there is no life but mine—and even ghosts and spirits of the underworld must have perished in the inferno that girdled the planet. No—there is nothing but me and my sickness. I'm dying—and when I perish, everything will perish. Only a mass of lifeless cinders will go on.

But there was a movement.

Instinct again. Crane dropped his head and played dead. Through slitted eyes he watched the ashen plains, wondering if death was playing tricks with his eyes. Another façade of rain was beating down toward him, and he hoped he could make sure before all vision was obliterated.

Yes. There.

A quarter mile back, a gray-brown shape was flitting along the gray surface. Despite the drone of the distant rain, Crane could hear the

whisper of trodden cinders and see the little clouds kicking up. Stealthily he groped for the revolver in the knapsack as his mind reached
feebly for explanations and recoiled from fear.

The thing approached, and suddenly Crane squinted and understood. He recalled Umber kicking with fear and springing away from
him when the 'chute landed them on the ashen face of the Earth.

"Why, it's Umber," he murmured. He raised himself. The dog
halted. "Here, boy!" Crane croaked gayly. "Here, boy!"

He was overcome with joy. He realized that a miserable loneliness
had hung over him, almost a horrible sensation of oneness in emptiness. Now his was not the only life. There was another. A friendly
life that could offer love and companionship. Hope kindled again.

"Here, boy!" he repeated. "Come on, boy—"

After a while he stopped trying to snap his fingers. The Great Dane
hung back, showing fangs and a lolling tongue. The dog was emaciated
to a skeleton and its eyes gleamed red and ugly in the dusk. As Crane
called once more, mechanically, the dog snarled. Puffs of ash leaped
beneath its nostrils.

He's hungry, Crane thought, that's all. He reached into the knapsack and at the gesture the dog snarled again. Crane withdrew the
chocolate bar and laboriously peeled off the paper and silver foil.
Weakly he tossed it toward Umber. It fell far short. After a minute
of savage uncertainty, the dog advanced slowly and gobbled up the
food. Ashes powdered its muzzle. It licked its chops ceaselessly and
continued to advance on Crane.

Panic jerked within him. A voice persisted: This is no friend. He
has no love or companionship for you. Love and companionship have
vanished from the land along with life. Now there is nothing left but
hunger.

"No—" Crane whispered. "That isn't right. We're the last of life
on Earth. It isn't right that we should tear at each other and seek to
devour—"

But Umber was advancing with a slinking sidle, and his teeth
showed sharp and white. And even as Crane stared at him, the dog
snarled and lunged.

Crane thrust up an arm under the dog's muzzle, but the weight of
the charge carried him backward. He cried out in agony as his broken,
swollen leg was struck by the weight of the dog. With his free right
hand he struck weakly, again and again, scarcely feeling the grind
of teeth gnawing his left arm. Then something metallic was pressed

under him and he realized he was lying on the revolver he had let fall.

He groped for it and prayed the cinders had not clogged its mechanism. As Umber let go his arm and tore at his throat, Crane brought the gun up and jabbed the muzzle blindly against the dog's body. He pulled and pulled the trigger until the roars died away and only empty clicks sounded. Umber shuddered in the ashes before him, his body nearly shot in two. Thick scarlet stained the gray.

Evelyn and Hallmyer looked down sadly at the broken animal. Evelyn was crying, and Hallmyer reached nervous fingers through his hair in the same old gesture.

"This is the finish, Stephen," he said. "You've killed part of yourself. Oh—you'll go on living, but not all of you. You'd best bury that corpse, Stephen. It's the corpse of your soul."

"I can't," Crane said. "The wind will blow the ashes away."

"Then burn it—"

It seemed that they helped him thrust the dead dog into his knapsack. They helped him take off his clothes and pack them underneath. They cupped their hands around the matches until the cloth caught fire, and blew on the weak flame until it sputtered and burned limply. Crane crouched by the fire and nursed it until nothing was left but more gray ash. Then he turned and once again began crawling down the ocean bed. He was naked now. There was nothing left of what-had-been but his flickering little life.

He was too heavy with sorrow to notice the furious rain that slammed and buffeted him, or the searing pains that were shooting through his blackened leg and up his hip. He crawled. Elbows, knee, elbows, knee— Woodenly, mechanically, apathetic to everything. To the latticed skies, the dreary ashen plains and even the dull glint of water that lay far ahead.

He knew it was the sea—what was left of the old, or a new one in the making. But it would be an empty, lifeless sea that some day would lap against a dry lifeless shore. This would be a planet of rock and stone, of metal and snow and ice and water, but that would be all. No more life. He, alone, was useless. He was Adam, but there was no Eve.

Evelyn waved gayly to him from the shore. She was standing alongside the white cottage with the wind snapping her dress to show the clean, slender lines of her figure. And when he came a little closer, she ran out to him and helped him. She said nothing—only placed her hands under his shoulders and helped him lift the weight of his heavy pain-ridden body. And so at last he reached the sea.

It was real. He understood that. For even after Evelyn and the cottage had vanished, he felt the cool waters bathe his face. Quietly—Calmly—

Here's the sea, Crane thought, and here am I. Adam and no Eve. It's hopeless.

He rolled a little farther into the waters. They laved his torn body. Quietly— Calmly—

He lay with face to the sky, peering at the high menacing heavens, and the bitterness within him welled up.

"It's not right!" he cried. "It's not right that all this should pass away. Life is too beautiful to perish at the mad act of one mad creature—"

Quietly the waters laved him. Quietly— Calmly—

The sea rocked him gently, and even the agony that was reaching up toward his heart was no more than a gloved hand. Suddenly the skies split apart—for the first time in all those months—and Crane stared up at the stars.

Then he knew. This was not the end of life. There could never be an end to life. Within his body, within the rotting tissues that were rocking gently in the sea was the source of ten million-million lives. Cells—tissues—bacteria—endamœba— Countless infinities of life that would take new root in the waters and live long after he was gone.

They would live on his rotting remains. They would feed on each other. They would adapt themselves to the new environment and feed on the minerals and sediments washed into this new sea. They would grow, burgeon, evolve. Life would reach out to the lands once more. It would begin again the same old re-repeated cycle that had begun perhaps with the rotting corpse of some last survivor of interstellar travel. It would happen over and over in the future ages.

And then he knew what had brought him back to the sea. There need be no Adam—no Eve. Only the sea, the great mother of life was needed. The sea had called him back to her depths that presently life might emerge once more, and he was content.

Quietly the waters rocked him. Quietly— Calmly—the mother of life rocked the last-born of the old cycle who would become the first-born of the new. And with glazing eyes Stephen Crane smiled up at the stars, stars that were sprinkled evenly across the sky. Stars that had not yet formed into the familiar constellations, nor would not for another hundred million centuries.

NIGHTFALL

by

ISAAC ASIMOV

Taking advantage of the wonderfully broad latitude science-fiction allows its authors, Mr. Asimov has conceived of a planet where the sun shines day and night and darkness falls but once a millenium. In a startling reversal of Emerson's hypothesis, Asimov conceives the week of darkness as a period of terror and chaos. The result is a penetrating study in mass psychology, a haunting picture of a race doomed by fear of the dark to ever-recurring ruin and destruction.

*

"If the stars should appear one night in a thousand years, how would men believe and adore, and preserve for many generations the remembrance of the city of God!"—Emerson

ATON 77, director of Saro University, thrust out a belligerent lower lip and glared at the young newspaperman in a hot fury.

Theremon 762 took that fury in his stride. In his earlier days, when his now widely syndicated column was only a mad idea in a cub reporter's mind, he had specialized in "impossible" interviews. It had cost him bruises, black eyes, and broken bones; but it had given him an ample supply of coolness and self-confidence.

So he lowered the outthrust hand that had been so pointedly ignored and calmly waited for the aged director to get over the worst. Astronomers were queer ducks, anyway, and if Aton's actions of the last two months meant anything, this same Aton was the queer-duckiest of the lot.

Aton 77 found his voice, and though it trembled with restrained emotion, the careful, somewhat pedantic, phraseology, for which the famous astronomer was noted, did not abandon him.

"Sir," he said, "you display an infernal gall in coming to me with that impudent proposition of yours."

The husky telephotographer of the Observatory, Beenay 25, thrust a tongue's tip across dry lips and interposed nervously, "Now, sir, after all—"

The director turned to him and lifted a white eyebrow. "Do not interfere, Beenay. I will credit you with good intentions in bringing this man here; but I will tolerate no insubordination now."

Theremon decided it was time to take a part. "Director Aton, if you'll let me finish what I started saying I think—"

"I don't believe, young man," retorted Aton, "that anything you could say now would count much as compared with your daily columns of these last two months. You have led a vast newspaper campaign against the efforts of myself and my colleagues to organize the world against the menace which it is now too late to avert. You have done your best with your highly personal attacks to make the staff of this Observatory objects of ridicule."

The director lifted the copy of the Saro City *Chronicle* on the table and shook it at Theremon furiously. "Even a person of your well-known impudence should have hesitated before coming to me with a request that he be allowed to cover today's events for his paper. Of all newsmen, you!"

Aton dashed the newspaper to the floor, strode to the window and clasped his arms behind his back.

"You may leave," he snapped over his shoulder. He stared moodily out at the skyline where Gamma, the brightest of the planet's six suns, was setting. It had already faded and yellowed into the horizon mists, and Aton knew he would never see it again as a sane man.

He whirled. "No, wait, come here!" He gestured peremptorily. "I'll give you your story."

The newsman had made no motion to leave, and now he approached the old man slowly. Aton gestured outward, "Of the six suns, only Beta is left in the sky. Do you see it?"

The question was rather unnecessary. Beta was almost at zenith; its ruddy light flooding the landscape to an unusual orange as the brilliant rays of setting Gamma died. Beta was at aphelion. It was

small; smaller than Theremon had ever seen it before, and for the
moment it was undisputed ruler of Lagash's sky.

Lagash's own sun, Alpha, the one about which it revolved, was at
the antipodes; as were the two distant companion pairs. The red
dwarf Beta—Alpha's immediate companion—was alone, grimly alone.

Aton's upturned face flushed redly in the sunlight. "In just under
four hours," he said, "civilization, as we know it, comes to an end. It
will do so because, as you see, Beta is the only sun in the sky." He
smiled grimly. "Print that! There'll be no one to read it."

"But if it turns out that four hours pass—and another four—
and nothing happens?" asked Theremon softly.

"Don't let that worry you. Enough will happen."

"Granted! And *still*—if nothing happens?"

For a second time, Beenay 25 spoke, "Sir, I think you ought to
listen to him."

Theremon said, "Put it to a vote, Director Aton."

There was a stir among the remaining five members of the Observatory staff, who till now had maintained an attitude of wary neu-
trality.

"That," stated Aton flatly, "is not necessary." He drew out his
pocket watch. "Since your good friend, Beenay, insists so urgently,
I will give you five minutes. Talk away."

"Good! Now, just what difference would it make if you allowed
me to take down an eyewitness account of what's to come? If your
prediction comes true, my presence won't hurt; for in that case my
column would never be written. On the other hand, if nothing comes
of it, you will just have to expect ridicule or worse. It would be wise
to leave that ridicule to friendly hands."

Aton snorted. "Do you mean yours when you speak of friendly
hands?"

"Certainly!" Theremon sat down and crossed his legs. "My columns may have been a little rough at times, but I gave you people the
benefit of the doubt every time. After all, this is not the century to
preach 'the end of the world is at hand' to Lagash. You have to understand that people don't believe the 'Book of Revelations' any more,
and it annoys them to have scientists turn about face and tell us the
Cultists are right after all—"

"No such thing, young man," interrupted Aton. "While a great
deal of our data has been supplied us by the Cult, our results contain
none of the Cult's mysticism. Facts are facts, and the Cult's so-called

'mythology' *has* certain facts behind it. We've exposed them and
ripped away their mystery. I assure you that the Cult hates us now
worse than you do."

"I don't hate you. I'm just trying to tell you that the public is in
an ugly humor. They're angry."

Aton twisted his mouth in derision. "Let them be angry."

"Yes, but what about tomorrow?"

"There'll be no tomorrow!"

"But if there is. Say that there is—just to see what happens. That
anger might take shape into something serious. After all, you know,
business has taken a nose dive these last two months. Investors don't
really believe the world is coming to an end, but just the same they're
being cagy with their money until it's all over. Johnny Public doesn't
believe you, either, but the new spring furniture might as well wait a
few months—just to make sure.

"You see the point. Just as soon as this is all over, the business
interests will be after your hide. They'll say that if crackpots—beg-
ging your pardon—can upset the country's prosperity any time they
want simply by making some cockeyed prediction—it's up to the
planet to prevent them. The sparks will fly, sir."

The director regarded the columnist sternly. "And just what were
you proposing to do to help the situation?"

"Well," grinned Theremon, "I was proposing to take charge of
the publicity. I can handle things so that only the ridiculous side will
show. It would be hard to stand, I admit, because I'd have to make
you all out to be a bunch of gibbering idiots, but if I can get people
laughing at you, they might forget to be angry. In return for that, all
my publisher asks is an exclusive story."

Beenay nodded and burst out, "Sir, the rest of us think he's right.
These last two months we've considered everything but the million-
to-one chance that there is an error somewhere in our theory or in our
calculations. We ought to take care of that, too."

There was a murmur of agreement from the men grouped about
the table, and Aton's expression became that of one who found his
mouth full of something bitter and couldn't get rid of it.

"You may stay if you wish, then. You will kindly refrain, however,
from hampering us in our duties in any way. You will also remember
that I am in charge of all activities here, and in spite of your opinions
as expressed in your columns, I will expect full co-operation and full
respect—"

His hands were behind his back, and his wrinkled face thrust forward determinedly as he spoke. He might have continued indefinitely but for the intrusion of a new voice.

"Hello, hello, hello!" It came in a high tenor, and the plump cheeks of the newcomer expanded in a pleased smile. "What's this morgue-like atmosphere about here? No one's losing his nerve, I hope."

Aton started in consternation and said peevishly, "Now what the devil are you doing here, Sheerin? I thought you were going to stay behind in the Hideout."

Sheerin laughed and dropped his tubby figure into a chair. "Hide-out be blowed! The place bored me. I wanted to be here, where things are getting hot. Don't you suppose I have my share of curiosity? I want to see these Stars the Cultists are forever speaking about." He rubbed his hands and added in a soberer tone, "It's freezing outside. The wind's enough to hang icicles on your nose. Beta doesn't seem to give any heat at all, at the distance it is."

The white-haired director ground his teeth in sudden exasperation, "Why do you go out of your way to do crazy things, Sheerin? What kind of good are you around here?"

"What kind of good am I around there?" Sheerin spread his palms in comical resignation. "A psychologist isn't worth his salt in the Hideout. They need men of action and strong, healthy women that can breed children. Me? I'm a hundred pounds too heavy for a man of action, and I wouldn't be a success at breeding children. So why bother them with an extra mouth to feed? I feel better over here."

Theremon spoke briskly, "Just what is the Hideout, sir?"

Sheerin seemed to see the columnist for the first time. He frowned and blew his ample cheeks out, "And just who in Lagash are you, redhead?"

Aton compressed his lips and then muttered sullenly, "That's Theremon 762, the newspaper fellow. I suppose you've heard of him."

The columnist offered his hand. "And, of course, you're Sheerin 501 of Saro University. I've heard of you." Then he repeated, "What is this Hideout, sir?"

"Well," said Sheerin, "we have managed to convince a few people of the validity of our prophecy of—er—doom, to be spectacular about it, and those few have taken proper measures. They consist mainly of the immediate members of the families of the Observatory staff, cer-tain of the faculty of Saro University and a few outsiders. Altogether, they number about three hundred, but three quarters are women and children."

"I see! They're supposed to hide where the Darkness and the—er —Stars can't get at them, and then hold out when the rest of the world goes poof."

"If they can. It won't be easy. With all of mankind insane; with the great cities going up in flames—environment will not be conducive to survival. But they have food, water, shelter, and weapons—"

"They've got more," said Aton. "They've got all our records, except for what we will collect today. Those records will mean everything to the next cycle, and that's what must survive. The rest can go hang."

Theremon whistled a long, low whistle and sat brooding for several minutes. The men about the table had brought out a multichess board and started a six-member game. Moves were made rapidly and in silence. All eyes bent in furious concentration on the board. Theremon watched them intently and then rose and approached Aton, who sat apart in whispered conversation with Sheerin.

"Listen," he said, "Let's go somewhere where we won't bother the rest of the fellows. I want to ask some questions."

The aged astronomer frowned sourly at him, but Sheerin chirped up, "Certainly. It will do me good to talk. It always does. Aton was telling me about your ideas concerning world reaction to a failure of the prediction—and I agree with you. I read your column pretty regularly, by the way, and as a general thing I like your views."

"Please, Sheerin," growled Aton.

"Eh? Oh, all right. We'll go into the next room. It has softer chairs, anyway."

There were softer chairs in the next room. There were also thick red curtains on the windows and a maroon carpet on the floor. With the bricky light of Beta pouring in, the general effect was one of dried blood.

Theremon shuddered, "Say, I'd give ten credits for a decent dose of white light for just a second. I wish Gamma or Delta were in the sky."

"What are your questions?" asked Aton. "Please remember that our time is limited. In a little over an hour and a quarter we're going upstairs, and after that there will be no time for talk."

"Well, here it is." Theremon leaned back and folded his hands on his chest. "You people seem so all-fired serious about this that I'm beginning to believe you. Would you mind explaining what it's all about?"

Aton exploded, "Do you mean to sit there and tell me that you've been bombarding us with ridicule without even finding out what we've been trying to say?"

The columnist grinned sheepishly. "It's not that bad, sir. I've got the general idea. You say that there is going to be a world-wide Darkness in a few hours and that all mankind will go violently insane. What I want now is the science behind it."

"No, you don't. No, you don't," broke in Sheerin. "If you ask Aton for that—supposing him to be in the mood to answer at all—he'll trot out pages of figures and volumes of graphs. You won't make head or tail of it. Now if you were to ask me, I could give you the layman's standpoint."

"All right; I ask you."

"Then first I'd like a drink." He rubbed his hands and looked at Aton.

"Water?" grunted Aton.

"Don't be silly!"

"Don't you be silly. No alcohol today. It would be too easy to get my men drunk. I can't afford to tempt them."

The psychologist grumbled wordlessly. He turned to Theremon, impaled him with his sharp eyes, and began.

"You realize, of course, that the history of civilization on Lagash displays a cyclic character—but I mean, *cyclic!*"

"I know," replied Theremon cautiously, "that that is the current archeological theory. Has it been accepted as a fact?"

"Just about. In this last century it's been generally agreed upon. This cyclic character is—or, rather, was—one of the great mysteries. We've located series of civilizations, nine of them definitely, and indications of others as well, all of which have reached heights comparable to our own, and all of which, without exception, were destroyed by fire at the very height of their culture.

"And no one could tell why. All centers of culture were thoroughly gutted by fire, with nothing left behind to give a hint as to the cause."

Theremon was following closely. "Wasn't there a Stone Age, too?"

"Probably, but as yet, practically nothing is known of it, except that men of that age were little more than rather intelligent apes. We can forget about that."

"I see. Go on!"

"There have been explanations of these recurrent catastrophes, all of a more or less fantastic nature. Some say that there are periodic rains of fire; some that Lagash passes through a sun every so often;

some even wilder things. But there is one theory, quite different from all of these, that has been handed down over a period of centuries."

"I know. You mean this myth of the 'Stars' that the Cultists have in their 'Book of Revelations.' "

"Exactly," rejoined Sheerin with satisfaction. "The Cultists said that every two thousand and fifty years Lagash entered a huge cave, so that all the suns disappeared, and there came *total darkness all over the world!* And then, they say, things called Stars appeared, which robbed men of their souls and left them unreasoning brutes, so that they destroyed the civilization they themselves had built up. Of course, they mix all this up with a lot of religio-mystic notions, but that's the central idea."

There was a short pause in which Sheerin drew a long breath. "And now we come to the Theory of Universal Gravitation." He pronounced the phrase so that the capital letters sounded—and at that point Aton turned from the window, snorted loudly, and stalked out of the room.

The two stared after him, and Theremon said, "What's wrong?"

"Nothing in particular," replied Sheerin. "Two of the men were due several hours ago and haven't shown up yet. He's terrifically shorthanded, of course, because all but the really essential men have gone to the Hideout."

"You don't think the two deserted, do you?"

"Who? Faro and Yimot? Of course not. Still, if they're not back within the hour, things would be a little sticky." He got to his feet suddenly, and his eyes twinkled. "Anyway, as long as Aton is gone—"

Tiptoeing to the nearest window, he squatted, and from the low window box beneath withdrew a bottle of red liquid that gurgled suggestively when he shook it.

"I *thought* Aton didn't know about this," he remarked as he trotted back to the table. "Here! We've only got one glass so, as the guest, you can have it. I'll keep the bottle." And he filled the tiny cup with judicious care.

Theremon rose to protest, but Sheerin eyed him sternly. "Respect your elders, young man."

The newsman seated himself with a look of pain and anguish on his face. "Go ahead, then, you old villain."

The psychologist's Adam's apple wobbled as the bottle upended, and then, with a satisfied grunt and a smack of the lips, he began again.

"But what do you know about gravitation?"

"Nothing, except that it is a very recent development, not too well established, and that the math is so hard that only twelve men in Lagash are supposed to understand it."

"*Tcha!* Nonsense! Boloney! I can give you all the essential math in a sentence. The Law of Universal Gravitation states that there exists a cohesive force among all bodies of the universe, such that the amount of this force between any two given bodies is proportional to the product of their masses divided by the square of the distance between them."

"Is that all?"

"That's enough! It took four hundred years to develop it."

"Why that long? It sounded simple enough, the way you said it."

"Because great laws are not divined by flashes of inspiration, whatever you may think. It usually takes the combined work of a world full of scientists over a period of centuries. After Genovi 41 discovered that Lagash rotated about the sun Alpha, rather than vice versa—and that was four hundred years ago—astronomers have been working. The complex motions of the six suns were recorded and analyzed and unwoven. Theory after theory was advanced and checked and counter-checked and modified and abandoned and revived and converted to something else. It was a devil of a job."

Theremon nodded thoughtfully and held out his glass for more liquor. Sheerin grudgingly allowed a few ruby drops to leave the bottle.

"It was twenty years ago," he continued after remoistening his own throat, "that it was finally demonstrated that the Law of Universal Gravitation accounted exactly for the orbital motions of the six suns. It was a great triumph."

Sheerin stood up and walked to the window, still clutching his bottle, "And now we're getting to the point. In the last decade, the motions of Lagash about Alpha were computed according to gravity, and *it did not account for the orbit observed*; not even when all perturbations due to the other suns were included. Either the law was invalid, or there was another, as yet unknown, factor involved."

Theremon joined Sheerin at the window and gazed out past the wooded slopes to where the spires of Saro City gleamed bloodily on the horizon. The newsman felt the tension of uncertainty grow within him as he cast a short glance at Beta. It glowered redly at Zenith, dwarfed and evil.

"Go ahead, sir," he said softly.

Sheerin replied, "Astronomers stumbled about for years, each proposed theory more untenable than the one before—until Aton had the inspiration of calling in the Cult. The head of the Cult, Sor 5, had access to certain data that simplified the problem considerably. Aton set to work on a new track.

"What if there were another nonluminous planetary body such as Lagash? If there were, you know, it would shine only by reflected light, and if it were composed of bluish rock, as Lagash itself largely is, then, in the redness of the sky, the eternal blaze of the suns would make it invisible—drown it out completely."

Theremon whistled, "What a screwy idea!"

"You think *that's* screwy? Listen to this: Suppose this body rotated about Lagash at such a distance and in such an orbit and had such a mass that its attraction would exactly account for the deviations of Lagash's orbit from theory—do you know what would happen?"

The columnist shook his head.

"Well, sometimes this body would get in the way of a sun." And Sheerin emptied what remained in the bottle at a draft.

"And it does, I suppose," said Theremon flatly.

"Yes! But only one sun lies in its plane of revolutions." He jerked a thumb at the shrunken sun above. "Beta! And it has been shown that the eclipse will occur only when the arrangement of the suns is such that Beta is alone in its hemisphere and at maximum distance, at which time the moon is invariably at minimum distance. The eclipse that results, with the moon seven times the apparent diameter of Beta, covers all of Lagash and lasts well over half a day, so that no spot on the planet escapes the effects. *That eclipse comes once every two thousand and forty-nine years.*"

Theremon's face was drawn into an expressionless mask. "And that's my story?"

The psychologist nodded. "That's all of it. First the eclipse—which will start in three quarters of an hour—then universal Darkness, and, maybe, these mysterious Stars—then madness, and end of the cycle."

He brooded. "We had two months' leeway—we at the Observatory —and that wasn't enough time to persuade Lagash of the danger. Two centuries might not have been enough. But our records are at the Hideout, and today we photograph the eclipse. The next cycle will start off with the truth, and when the *next* eclipse comes, mankind will at last be ready for it. Come to think of it, that's part of your story, too."

A thin wind ruffled the curtains at the window as Theremon opened it and leaned out. It played coldly with his hair as he stared at the crimson sunlight on his hand. Then he turned in sudden rebellion.

"What is there in Darkness to drive me mad?"

Sheerin smiled to himself as he spun the empty liquor bottle with abstracted motions of his hand. "Have you ever experienced Darkness, young man?"

The newsman leaned against the wall and considered. "No. Can't say I have. But I know what it is. Just—uh—" He made vague motions with his fingers, and then brightened. "Just no light. Like in caves."

"Have you ever been in a cave?"

"In a cave! Of course not!"

"I thought not. I tried last week—just to see—but I got out in a hurry. I went in until the mouth of the cave was just visible as a blur of light, with black everywhere else. I never thought a person my weight could run that fast."

Theremon's lip curled. "Well, if it comes to that, I guess I wouldn't have run, if I had been there."

The psychologist studied the young man with an annoyed frown. "My, don't you talk big! I dare you to draw the curtain."

Theremon looked his surprise and said, "What for? If we had four or five suns out there we might want to cut the light down a bit for comfort, but now we haven't enough light as it is."

"That's the point. Just draw the curtain; then come here and sit down."

"All right." Theremon reached for the tasseled string and jerked. The red curtain slid across the wide window, the brass rings hissing their way along the crossbar, and a dusk-red shadow clamped down on the room.

Theremon's footsteps sounded hollowly in the silence as he made his way to the table, and then they stopped halfway. "I can't see you, sir," he whispered.

"Feel your way," ordered Sheerin in a strained voice.

"But I can't see you, sir." The newsman was breathing harshly. "I can't see anything."

"What did you expect?" came the grim reply. "Come here and sit down!"

The footsteps sounded again, waveringly, approaching slowly. There was the sound of someone fumbling with a chair. Theremon's voice came thinly, "Here I am. I feel . . . ulp . . . all right."

"You like it, do you?"

"N-no. It's pretty awful. The walls seem to be—" He paused. "They seem to be closing in on me. I keep wanting to push them away. But I'm not going mad! In fact, the feeling isn't as bad as it was."

"All right. Draw the curtain back again."

There were cautious footsteps through the dark, the rustle of Theremon's body against the curtain as he felt for the tassel, and then the triumphant ro-o-o-osh of the curtain slithering back. Red light flooded the room, and with a cry of joy Theremon looked up at the sun.

Sheerin wiped the moistness off his forehead with the back of a hand and said shakily, "And that was just a dark room."

"It can be stood," said Theremon lightly.

"Yes, a dark room can. But were you at the Jonglor Centennial Exposition two years ago?"

"No, it so happens I never got around to it. Six thousand miles was just a bit too much to travel, even for the exposition."

"Well, I was there. You remember hearing about the 'Tunnel of Mystery' that broke all records in the amusement area—for the first month or so, anyway?"

"Yes. Wasn't there some fuss about it?"

"Very little. It was hushed up. You see, that Tunnel of Mystery was just a mile-long tunnel—with no lights. You got into a little open car and jolted along through Darkness for fifteen minutes. It was very popular—while it lasted."

"Popular?"

"Certainly. There's a fascination in being frightened when it's part of a game. A baby is born with three instinctive fears: of loud noises, of falling, and of the absence of light. That's why it's considered so funny to jump at someone and shout 'Boo!' That's why it's such fun to ride a roller coaster. And that's why that Tunnel of Mystery started cleaning up. People came out of that Darkness shaking, breathless, half dead with fear, but they kept on paying to get in."

"Wait a while, I remember now. Some people came out dead, didn't they? There were rumors of that after it shut down."

The psychologist snorted. "Bah! Two or three died. That was nothing! They paid off the families of the dead ones and argued the Jonglor City Council into forgetting it. After all, they said, if people with weak hearts want to go through the tunnel, it was at their own risk—and besides, it wouldn't happen again. So they put a doctor in the front office and had every customer go through a physical examination before getting into the car. That actually boosted ticket sales."

"Well, then?"

"But, you see, there was something else. People sometimes came out in perfect order, except that they refused to go into buildings—any buildings; including palaces, mansions, apartment houses, tenements, cottages, huts, shacks, lean-tos, and tents."

Theremon looked shocked. "You mean they refused to come in out of the open. Where'd they sleep?"

"In the open."

"They should have *forced* them inside."

"Oh, they did, they did. Whereupon these people wevt into vio. lent hysterics and did their best to bat their brains out against the nearest wall. Once you got them inside, you couldn't keep them there without a strait jacket and a shot of morphine."

"They must have been crazy."

"Which is exactly what they were. One person out of every ten who went into that tunnel came out that way. They called in the psychologists, and we did the only thing possible. We closed down the exhibit." He spread his hands.

"What was the matter with these people?" asked Theremon finally.

"Essentially the same thing that was the matter with you when you thought the walls of the room were crushing in on you in the dark. There is a psychological term for mankind's instinctive fear of the absence of light. We call it 'claustrophobia,' because the lack of light is always tied up with inclosed places, so that fear of one is fear of the other. You see?"

"And those people of the tunnel?"

"Those people of the tunnel consisted of those unfortunates whose mentality did not quite possess the resiliency to overcome the claustrophobia that overtook them in the Darkness. Fifteen minutes without light is a long time; you only had two or three minutes, and I believe you were fairly upset.

"The people of the tunnel had what is called a 'claustrophobic fixation.' Their latent fear of Darkness and inclosed places had crystallized and become active, and, as far as we can tell, permanent. *That's* what fifteen minutes in the dark will do."

There was a long silence, and Theremon's forehead wrinkled slowly into a frown. "I don't believe it's that bad."

"You mean you don't want to believe," snapped Sheerin. "You're afraid to believe. Look out the window!"

Theremon did so, and the psychologist continued without pausing

"Imagine Darkness—everywhere. No light, as far as you can see. The houses, the trees, the fields, the earth, the sky—*black!* And Stars thrown in, for all I know—whatever *they* are. Can you conceive it?"

"Yes, I can," declared Theremon truculently.

And Sheerin slammed his fist down upon the table in sudden passion. "You lie! You can't conceive that. Your brain wasn't built for the conception any more than it was built for the conception of infinity or of eternity. You can only talk about it. A fraction of the reality upsets you, and when the real thing comes, your brain is going to be presented with a phenomenon outside its limits of comprehension. You will go mad, completely and permanently! There is no question of it!"

He added sadly, "And another couple of milleniums of painful struggle comes to nothing. Tomorrow there won't be a city standing unharmed in all Lagash."

Theremon recovered part of his mental equilibrium. "That doesn't follow. I still don't see that I can go loony just because there isn't a Sun in the sky—but even if I did, and everyone else did, how does that harm the cities? Are we going to blow them down?"

But Sheerin was angry, too. "If you were in Darkness, what would you want more than anything else; what would it be that every instinct would call for? Light, damn you, *light!*"

"Well?"

"And how would you get light?"

"I don't know," said Theremon flatly.

"What's the *only* way to get light, short of the sun?"

"How should I know?"

They were standing face to face and nose to nose.

Sheerin said, "You burn something, mister. Ever see a forest fire? Ever go camping and cook a stew over a wood fire? Heat isn't the only thing burning wood gives off, you know. It gives off light, and people know that. And when it's dark they want light, and they're going to get *it.*"

"So they burn wood?"

"So they burn whatever they can get. They've got to have light. They've got to burn something, and wood isn't handy—so they'll burn whatever is nearest. They'll have their light—and every center of habitation goes up in flames!"

Eyes held each other as though the whole matter were a personal affair of respective will powers, and then Theremon broke away wordlessly. His breathing was harsh and ragged, and he scarcely noted the sudden hubbub that came from the adjoining room behind the closed door.

Sheerin spoke, and it was with an effort that he made it sound matter-of-fact. "I think I heard Yimot's voice. He and Faro are probably back. Let's go in and see what kept them."

"Might as well!" muttered Theremon. He drew a long breath and seemed to shake himself. The tension was broken.

The room was in an uproar, with members of the staff clustering about two young men who were removing outer garments even as they parried the miscellany of questions being thrown at them. Aton bustled through the crowd and faced the newcomers angrily. "Do you realize that it's less than half an hour before deadline? Where have you two been?"

Faro 24 seated himself and rubbed his hands. His cheeks were red with the outdoor chill. "Yimot and I have just finished carrying through a little crazy experiment of our own. We've been trying to see if we couldn't construct an arrangement by which we could simulate the appearance of Darkness and Stars so as to get an advance notion as to how it looked."

There was a confused murmur from the listeners, and a sudden look of interest entered Aton's eyes. "There wasn't anything said of this before. How did you go about it?"

"Well," said Faro, "the idea came to Yimot and myself long ago, and we've been working it out in our spare time. Yimot knew of a low one-story house down in the city with a domed roof—it had once been used as a museum, I think. Anyway, we bought it—"

"Where did you get the money?" interrupted Aton peremptorily.

"Our bank accounts," grunted Yimot 70. "It cost two thousand credits." Then, defensively, "Well, what of it? Tomorrow, two thousand credits will be two thousand pieces of paper. That's all."

"Sure," agreed Faro. "We bought the place and rigged it up with black velvet from top to bottom so as to get as perfect a Darkness as possible. Then we punched tiny holes in the ceiling and through the roof and covered them with little metal caps, all of which could be shoved aside simultaneously at the close of a switch. At least, we didn't do that part ourselves; we got a carpenter and an electrician and some others—money didn't count. The point was that we could get the light to shine through those holes in the roof, so that we could get a starlike effect."

Not a breath was drawn during the pause that followed. Aton said stiffly:

"You had no right to make a private—"

Faro seemed abashed. "I know, sir—but, frankly, Yimot and I thought the experiment was a little dangerous. If the effect really worked, we half expected to go mad—from what Sheerin says about all this, we thought that would be rather likely. We wanted to take the risk ourselves. Of course, if we found we could retain sanity, it occurred to us that we might develop immunity to the real thing, and then expose the rest of you to the same thing. But things didn't work out at all—"

"Why, what happened?"

It was Yimot who answered. "We shut ourselves in and allowed our eyes to get accustomed to the dark. It's an extremely creepy feeling because the total Darkness makes you feel as if the walls and ceiling are crushing in on you. But we got over that and pulled the switch. The caps fell away and the roof glittered all over with little dots of light—"

"Well?"

"Well—nothing. That was the whacky part of it. Nothing happened. It was just a roof with holes in it, and that's just what it looked like. We tried it over and over again—that's what kept us so late—but there just isn't any effect at all."

There followed a shocked silence, and all eyes turned to Sheerin, who sat motionless, mouth open.

Theremon was the first to speak. "You know what this does to this whole theory you've built up, Sheerin, don't you?" He was grinning with relief.

But Sheerin raised his hand. "Now wait a while. Just let me think this through." And then he snapped his fingers, and when he lifted his head there was neither surprise nor uncertainty in his eyes. "Of course—"

He never finished. From somewhere up above there sounded a sharp clang, and Beenay, starting to his feet, dashed up the stairs with a "What the devil!"

The rest followed after.

Things happened quickly. Once up in the dome, Beenay cast one horrified glance at the shattered photographic plates and at the man bending over them; and then hurled himself fiercely at the intruder, getting a death grip on his throat. There was a wild threshing, and as others of the staff joined in, the stranger was swallowed up and smothered under the weight of half a dozen angry men.

Aton came up last, breathing heavily. "Let him up!"

There was a reluctant unscrambling and the stranger, panting harshly, with his clothes torn and his forehead bruised, was hauled to his feet. He had a short yellow beard curled elaborately in the style affected by the Cultists.

Beenay shifted his hold to a collar grip and shook the man savagely. "All right, rat, what's the idea? These plates—"

"I wasn't after *them*," retorted the Cultist coldly. "That was an accident."

Beenay followed his glowering stare and snarled, "I see. You were after the cameras themselves. The accident with the plates was a stroke of luck for you, then. If you had touched Snapping Bertha or any of the others, you would have died by slow torture. As it is—"

He drew his fist back.

Aton grabbed his sleeve. "Stop that! Let him go!"

The young technician wavered, and his arm dropped reluctantly. Aton pushed him aside and confronted the Cultist. "You're Latimer, aren't you?"

The Cultist bowed stiffly and indicated the symbol upon his hip. "I am Latimer 25, adjutant of the third class to his serenity, Sor 5."

"And"—Aton's white eyebrows lifted—"you were with his serenity when he visited me last week, weren't you?"

Latimer bowed a second time.

"Now, then, what do you want?"

"Nothing that you would give me of your own free will."

"Sor 5 sent you, I suppose—or is this your own idea?"

"I won't answer that question."

"Will there be any further visitors?"

"I won't answer that, either."

Aton glanced at his timepiece and scowled. "Now, man, what is it your master wants of me? I have fulfilled my end of the bargain."

Latimer smiled faintly, but said nothing.

"I asked him," continued Aton angrily, "for data only the Cult could supply, and it was given to me. For that, thank you. In return, I promised to prove the essential truth of the creed of the Cult."

"There was no need to prove that," came the proud retort. "It stands proven by the 'Book of Revelations.' "

"For the handful that constitute the Cult, yes. Don't pretend to mistake my meaning. I offered to present scientific backing for your beliefs. And I did!"

The Cultist's eyes narrowed bitterly. "Yes, you did—with a fox's subtlety, for your pretended explanation backed our beliefs, and at the same time removed all necessity for them. You made of the Darkness and of the Stars a natural phenomenon, and removed all its real significance. That was blasphemy."

"If so, the fault isn't mine. The facts exist. What can I do but state them?"

"Your 'facts' are a fraud and a delusion."

Aton stamped angrily. "How do you know?"

And the answer came with the certainty of absolute faith. "I know!"

The director purpled and Beenay whispered urgently. Aton waved him silent. "And what does Sor 5 want us to do? He still thinks, I suppose, that in trying to warn the world to take measures against the menace of madness, we are placing innumerable souls in jeopardy. We aren't succeeding, if that means anything to him."

"The attempt itself has done harm enough, and your vicious effort to gain information by means of your devilish instruments must be stopped. We obey the will of their Stars, and I only regret that my clumsiness prevented me from wrecking your infernal devices."

"It wouldn't have done you too much good," returned Aton. "All our data, except for the direct evidence we intend collecting right now, is already safely cached and well beyond possibility of harm." He smiled grimly. "But that does not affect your present status as an attempted burglar and criminal."

He turned to the men behind him. "Someone call the police at Saro City."

There was a cry of distaste from Sheerin. "Damn it, Aton, what's wrong with you? There's no time for that. Here"—he bustled his way forward—"let me handle this."

Aton stared down his nose at the psychologist. "This is not the time for your monkeyshines, Sheerin. Will you please let me handle this my own way? Right now you are a complete outsider here, and don't forget it."

Sheerin's mouth twisted eloquently. "Now why should we go to the impossible trouble of calling the police—with Beta's eclipse a matter of minutes from now—when this young man here is perfectly willing to pledge his word of honor to remain and cause no trouble whatsoever?"

The Cultist answered promptly, "I will do no such thing. You're free to do what you want, but it's only fair to warn you that just as soon as I get my chance I'm going to finish what I came out here to do. If it's my word of honor you're relying on, you'd better call the police."

Sheerin smiled in a friendly fashion. "You're a determined cuss, aren't you? Well, I'll explain something. Do you see that young man at the window? He's a strong, husky fellow, quite handy with his fists, and he's an outsider besides. Once the eclipse starts there will be nothing for him to do except keep an eye on you. Besides him, there will be myself—a little too stout for active fisticuffs, but still able to help."

"Well, what of it?" demanded Latimer frozenly.

"Listen and I'll tell you," was the reply. "Just as soon as the eclipse starts, we're going to take you, Theremon and I, and deposit you in a little closet with one door, to which is attached one giant lock and no windows. You will remain there for the duration."

"And afterward," breathed Latimer fiercely, "there'll be no one to let me out. I know as well as you do what the coming of the Stars means—I know it far better than you. With all your minds gone, you are not likely to free me. Suffocation or slow starvation, is it? About what I might have expected from a group of scientists. But I don't give my word. It's a matter of principle, and I won't discuss it further."

Aton seemed perturbed. His faded eyes were troubled. "Really, Sheerin, locking him—"

"Please!" Sheerin motioned him impatiently to silence. "I don't think for a moment things will go that far. Latimer has just tried a clever little bluff, but I'm not a psychologist just because I like the sound of the word." He grinned at the Cultist. "Come now, you don't really think I'm trying anything as crude as slow starvation. My dear Latimer, if I lock you in the closet, you are not going to see the Darkness, and you are not going to see the Stars. It does not take much of a knowledge of the fundamental creed of the Cult to realize that for you to be hidden from the Stars when they appear means the loss of your immortal soul. Now, I believe you to be an honorable man. I'll accept your word of honor to make no further effort to disrupt proceedings if you'll offer it."

A vein throbbed in Latimer's temple, and he seemed to shrink within himself as he said thickly, "You have it!" And then he added with swift fury, "But it is my consolation that you will all be damned for your deeds of today." He turned on his heel and stalked to the high three-legged stool by the door.

Sheerin nodded to the columnist. "Take a seat next to him, Theremon—just as a formality. Hey, Theremon!"

But the newspaperman didn't move. He had gone pale to the lips. "Look at that!" The finger he pointed toward the sky shook, and his voice was dry and cracked.

There was one simultaneous gasp as every eye followed the pointing finger and, for one breathless moment, stared frozenly.

Beta was chipped on one side!

The tiny bit of encroaching blackness was perhaps the width of a fingernail, but to the staring watchers it magnified itself into the crack of doom.

Only for a moment they watched, and after that there was a shrieking confusion that was even shorter of duration and which gave way to an orderly scurry of activity—each man at his prescribed job. At the crucial moment there was no time for emotion. The men were merely scientists with work to do. Even Aton had melted away.

Sheerin said prosaically, "First contact must have been made fifteen minutes ago. A little early, but pretty good considering the uncertainties involved in the calculation." He looked about him and then tiptoed to Theremon, who still remained staring out the window, and dragged him away gently.

"Aton is furious," he whispered, "so stay away. He missed first contact on account of this fuss with Latimer, and if you get in his way he'll have you thrown out the window."

Theremon nodded shortly and sat down. Sheerin stared in surprise at him.

"The devil, man," he exclaimed, "you're shaking."

"Eh?" Theremon licked dry lips and then tried to smile. "I don't feel very well, and that's a fact."

The psychologist's eyes hardened. "You're not losing your nerve?"

"No!" cried Theremon in a flash of indignation. "Give me a chance, will you? I haven't really believed this rigmarole—not way down beneath, anyway—till just this minute. Give me a chance to get used to the idea. You've been preparing yourself for two months or more."

"You're right, at that," replied Sheerin thoughtfully. "Listen! Have you got a family—parents, wife, children?"

Theremon shook his head. "You mean the Hideout, I suppose. No, you don't have to worry about that. I have a sister, but she's two thousand miles away. I don't even know her exact address."

"Well, then, what about yourself? You've got time to get there, and they're one short anyway, since I left. After all, you're not needed here, and you'd make a darned fine addition—"

Theremon looked at the other wearily. "You think I'm scared stiff, don't you? Well, get this, mister, I'm a newspaperman and I've been assigned to cover a story. I intend covering it."

There was a faint smile on the psychologist's face. "I see. Profes sional honor, is that it?"

"You might call it that. But, man, I'd give my right arm for another bottle of that sockeroo juice even half the size of the one you hogged. If ever a fellow needed a drink, I do."

He broke off. Sheerin was nudging him violently. "Do you hear that? Listen!"

Theremon followed the motion of the other's chin and stared at the Cultist, who, oblivious to all about him, faced the window, a look of wild elation on his face, droning to himself the while in singsong fashion.

"What's he saying?" whispered the columnist.

"He's quoting 'Book of Revelations,' fifth chapter," replied Shee-rin. Then, urgently, "Keep quiet and listen, I tell you."

The Cultist's voice had risen in a sudden increase of fervor:

" 'And it came to pass that in those days the Sun, Beta, held lone vigil in the sky for ever longer periods as the revolutions passed; until such time as for full half a revolution, it alone, shrunken and cold, shone down upon Lagash.

" 'And men did assemble in the public squares and in the highways, there to debate and to marvel at the sight, for a strange depression had seized them. Their minds were troubled and their speech confused, for the souls of men awaited the coming of the Stars.

" 'And in the city of Trigon, at high noon, Vendret 2 came forth and said unto the men of Trigon, "Lo, ye sinners! Though ye scorn the ways of righteousness, yet will the time of reckoning come. Even now the Cave approaches to swallow Lagash; yea, and all it contains.

" 'And even as he spoke the lip of the Cave of Darkness passed the edge of Beta so that to all Lagash it was hidden from sight. Loud were the cries of men as it vanished, and great the fear of soul that fell upon them.

" 'It came to pass that the Darkness of the Cave fell upon Lagash, and there was no light on all the surface of Lagash. Men were even as blinded, nor could one man see his neighbor, though he felt his breath upon his face.

" 'And in this blackness there appeared the Stars, in countless numbers, and to the strains of ineffable music of a beauty so wondrous that the very leaves of the trees turned to tongues that cried out in wonder.

" 'And in that moment the souls of men departed from them, and their abandoned bodies became even as beasts; yea, even as brutes of the wild; so that through the blackened streets of the cities of Lagash they prowled with wild cries.

" 'From the Stars there then reached down the Heavenly Flame, and where it touched, the cities of Lagash flamed to utter destruction, so that of man and of the works of man nought remained.

" 'Even then—' "

There was a subtle change in Latimer's tone. His eyes had not shifted, but somehow he had become aware of the absorbed attention of the other two. Easily, without pausing for breath, the timbre of his voice shifted and the syllables became more liquid.

Theremon, caught by surprise, stared. The words seemed on the border of familiarity. There was an elusive shift in the accent, a tiny change in the vowel stress; nothing more—yet Latimer had become thoroughly unintelligible.

Sheerin smiled slyly. "He shifted to some old-cycle tongue, probably their traditional second cycle. That was the language in which the 'Book of Revelations' had originally been written, you know."

"It doesn't matter; I've heard enough." Theremon shoved his chair back and brushed his hair back with hands that no longer shook. "I feel much better now."

"You do?" Sheerin seemed mildly surprised.

"I'll say I do. I had a bad case of jitters just a while back. Listening to you and your gravitation and seeing that eclipse start almost finished me. But this"—he jerked a contemptuous thumb at the yellow-bearded Cultist—"*this* is the sort of thing my nurse used to tell me. I've been laughing at that sort of thing all my life. I'm not going to let it scare me *now*."

He drew a deep breath and said with a hectic gaiety, "But if I expect to keep on the good side of myself, I'm going to turn my chair away from the window."

Sheerin said, "Yes, but you'd better talk lower. Aton just lifted his head out of that box he's got it stuck into and gave you a look that should have killed you."

Theremon made a mouth. "I forgot about the old fellow." With elaborate care he turned the chair from the window, cast one distasteful look over his shoulder and said, "It has occurred to me that there must be considerable immunity against this Star madness."

The psychologist did not answer immediately. Beta was past its zenith now, and the square of bloody sunlight that outlined the window upon the floor had lifted into Sheerin's lap. He stared at its dusky color thoughtfully and then bent and squinted into the sun itself.

The chip in its side had grown to a black encroachment that covered a third of Beta. He shuddered, and when he straightened once more his florid cheeks did not contain quite as much color as they had had previously.

With a smile that was almost apologetic, he reversed his chair also. "There are probably two million people in Saro City that are all trying to join the Cult at once in one gigantic revival." Then, ironically, "The Cult is in for an hour of unexampled prosperity. I trust they'll make the most of it. Now, what was it you said?"

"Just this. How do the Cultists manage to keep the 'Book of Revelations' going from cycle to cycle, and how on Lagash did it get written in the first place? There must have been some sort of immunity, for if everyone had gone mad, who would be left to write the book?"

Sheerin stared at his questioner ruefully. "Well, now, young man, there isn't any eyewitness answer to that, but we've got a few damned good notions as to what happened. You see, there are three kinds of people who might remain relatively unaffected. First, the very few who don't see the Stars at all; the blind, those who drink themselves into a stupor at the beginning of the eclipse and remain so to the end. We leave them out—because they aren't really witnesses.

"Then there are children below six, to whom the world as a whole is too new and strange for them to be too frightened at Stars and Darkness. They would be just another item in an already surprising world. You see that, don't you?"

The other nodded doubtfuly. "I suppose so."

"Lastly, there are those whose minds are too coarsely grained to be entirely toppled. The very insensitive would be scarcely affected —oh, such people as some of our older, work-broken peasants. Well, the children would have fugitive memories, and that, combined with the confused, incoherent babblings of the half-mad morons, formed the basis for the 'Book of Revelations.'

"Naturally, the book was based, in the first place, on the testimony of those least qualified to serve as historians; that is, children and morons; and was probably extensively edited and re-edited through the cycles."

"Do you suppose," broke in Theremon, "that they carried the book through the cycles the way we're planning on handing on the secret of gravitation?"

Sheerin shrugged. "Perhaps, but their exact method is unimportant. They do it, somehow. The point I was getting at was that the book can't help but be a mass of distortion, even if it is based on fact. For instance, do you remember the experiment with the holes in the roof that Faro and Yimot tried—the one that didn't work?"

"Yes."

"You know why it didn't w—" He stopped and rose in alarm, for Aton was approaching, his face a twisted mask of consternation. "What's happened?"

Aton drew him aside and Sheerin could feel the fingers on his elbow twitching.

"Not so loud!" Aton's voice was low and tortured. "I've just gotten word from the Hideout on the private line."

Sheerin broke in anxiously, "They are in trouble?"

"Not *they*." Aton stressed the pronoun significantly. "They sealed themselves off just a while ago, and they're going to stay buried till day after tomorrow. They're safe. But the *city*, Sheerin—it's a shambles. You have no idea—" He was having difficulty in speaking.

"Well?" snapped Sheerin impatiently. "What of it? It will get worse. What are you shaking about?" Then, suspiciously, "How do you feel?"

Aton's eyes sparked angrily at the insinuation, and then faded to anxiety once more. "You don't understand. The Cultists are active. They're rousing the people to storm the Observatory—promising them immediate entrance into grace, promising them salvation, promising them anything. What are we to do, Sheerin?"

Sheerin's head bent, and he stared in long abstraction at his toes. He tapped his chin with one knuckle, then looked up and said crisply, "Do? What is there to do? Nothing at all! Do the men know of this?"

"No, of course not!"

"Good! Keep it that way. How long till totality?"

"Not quite an hour."

"There's nothing to do but gamble. It will take time to organize any really formidable mob, and it will take more time to get them out here. We're a good five miles from the city—"

He glared out the window, down the slopes to where the farmed patches gave way to clumps of white houses in the suburbs; down to where the metropolis itself was a blur on the horizon—a mist in the waning blaze of Beta.

He repeated without turning, "It will take time. Keep on working and pray that totality comes first."

Beta was cut in half, the line of division pushing a slight concavity into the still-bright portion of the Sun. It was like a gigantic eyelid shutting slantwise over the light of a world.

The faint clatter of the room in which he stood faded into oblivion, and he sensed only the thick silence of the fields outside. The very insects seemed frightened mute. And things were dim.

He jumped at the voice in his ear. Theremon said, "Is something wrong?"

"Eh? Er—no. Get back to the chair. We're in the way." They slipped back to their corner, but the psychologist did not speak for a time. He lifted a finger and loosened his collar. He twisted his neck back and forth but found no relief. He looked up suddenly.

"Are you having any difficulty in breathing?"

The newspaperman opened his eyes wide and drew two or three long breaths. "No. Why?"

"I looked out the window too long, I suppose. The dimness got me. Difficulty in breathing is one of the first symptoms of a claustrophobic attack."

Theremon drew another long breath. "Well, it hasn't got me yet. Say, here's another of the fellows."

Beenay had interposed his bulk between the light and the pair in the corner, and Sheerin squinted up at him anxiously. "Hello, Beenay."

The astronomer shifted his weight to the other foot and smiled feebly. "You won't mind if I sit down awhile and join in on the talk? My cameras are set, and there's nothing to do till totality." He paused and eyed the Cultist, who fifteen minutes earlier had drawn a small, skin-bound book from his sleeve and had been poring intently over it ever since. "That rat hasn't been making trouble, has he?"

Sheerin shook his head. His shoulders were thrown back and he frowned his concentration as he forced himself to breathe regularly. He said, "Have you had any trouble breathing, Beenay?"

Beenay sniffed the air in his turn. "It doesn't seem stuffy to me."

"A touch of claustrophobia," explained Sheerin apologetically.

"Oh-h-h! It worked itself differently with me. I get the impression that my eyes are going back on me. Things seem to blur and—well, nothing is clear. And it's cold, too."

"Oh, it's cold, all right. That's no illusion." Theremon grimaced. "My toes feel as if I've been shipping them cross country in a refrigerating car."

"What we need," put in Sheerin, "is to keep our minds busy with extraneous affairs. I was telling you a while ago, Theremon, why Faro's experiments with the holes in the roof came to nothing."

"You were just beginning," replied Theremon. He encircled a knee with both arms and nuzzled his chin against it.

"Well, as I started to say, they were misled by taking the 'Book of Revelations' literally. There probably wasn't any sense in attaching any physical significance to the Stars. It might be, you know, that in the presence of total Darkness, the mind finds it absolutely necessary to create light. This illusion of light might be all the Stars there really are."

"In other words," interposed Theremon, "you mean the Stars are the results of the madness and not one of the causes. Then, what good will Beenay's photographs be?"

"To prove that it is an illusion, maybe; or to prove the opposite, for all I know. Then again—"

But Beenay had drawn his chair closer, and there was an expression of sudden enthusiasm on his face. "Say, I'm glad you two got on to this subject." His eyes narrowed and he lifted one finger. "I've been thinking about these Stars and I've got a really cute notion. Of course, it's strictly ocean foam, and I'm not trying to advance it seriously, but I think it's interesting. Do you want to hear it?"

He seemed half reluctant, but Sheerin leaned back and said, "Go ahead! I'm listening."

"Well, then, supposing there were other suns in the universe." He broke off a little bashfully. "I mean suns that are so far away that they're too dim to see. It sounds as if I've been reading some of that fantastic fiction, I suppose."

"Not necessarily. Still, isn't that possibility eliminated by the fact that, according to the Law of Gravitation, they would make themselves evident by their attractive forces?"

"Not if they were far enough off," rejoined Beenay, "really far off—maybe as much as four light years, or even more. We'd never be able to detect perturbations then, because they'd be too small. Say that there were a lot of suns that far off; a dozen or two, maybe."

Theremon whistled melodiously. "What an idea for a good Sunday supplement article. Two dozen suns in a universe eight light years across. Wow! That would shrink our universe into insignificance. The readers would eat it up."

"Only an idea," said Beenay with a grin, "but you see the point. During eclipse, these dozen suns would become visible, because there'd be no real sunlight to drown them out. Since they're so far off, they'd appear small, like so many little marbles. Of course, the Cultists talk of millions of Stars, but that's probably exaggeration. There just isn't any place in the universe you could put a million suns—unless they touch one another."

Sheerin had listened with gradually increasing interest. "You've hit something there, Beenay. And exaggeration is just exactly what would happen. Our minds, as you probably know, can't grasp directly any number higher than five; above that there is only the concept of 'many.' A dozen would become a million just like that. A damn good idea!"

"And I've got another cute little notion," Beenay said. "Have you ever thought what a simple problem gravitation would be if only you had a sufficiently simple system? Supposing you had a universe in which there was a planet with only one sun. The planet would travel in a perfect ellipse and the exact nature of the gravitational force would be so evident it could be accepted as an axiom. Astronomers on such a world would start off with gravity probably before they even invent the telescope. Naked-eye observation would be enough."

"But would such a system be dynamically stable?" questioned Sheerin doubtfully.

"Sure! They call it the 'one-and-one' case. It's been worked out mathematically, but it's the philosophical implications that interest me."

"It's nice to think about," admitted Sheerin, "as a pretty abstraction—like a perfect gas or absolute zero."

"Of course," continued Beenay, "there's the catch that life would be impossible on such a planet. It wouldn't get enough heat and light, and if it rotated there would be total Darkness half of each day. You couldn't expect life—which is fundamentally dependent upon light—to develop under those conditions. Besides—"

Sheerin's chair went over backward as he sprang to his feet in a rude interruption. "Aton's brought out the lights."

Beenay said, "Huh," turned to stare, and then grinned halfway around his head in open relief.

There were half a dozen foot-long, inch-thick rods cradled in Aton's arms. He glared over them at the assembled staff members.

"Get back to work, all of you. Sheerin, come here and help me!"

Sheerin trotted to the older man's side and, one by one, in utter silence, the two adjusted the rods in makeshift metal holders suspended from the walls.

With the air of one carrying through the most sacred item of a religious ritual, Sheerin scraped a large, clumsy match into spluttering life and passed it to Aton, who carried the flame to the upper end of one of the rods.

It hesitated there a while, playing futilely about the tip, until a sudden, crackling flare cast Aton's lined face into yellow highlights. He withdrew the match and a spontaneous cheer rattled the window.

The rod was topped by six inches of wavering flame! Methodically, the other rods were lighted, until six independent fires turned the rear of the room yellow.

The light was dim, dimmer even than the tenuous sunlight. The flames reeled crazily, giving birth to drunken, swaying shadows. The torches smoked devilishly and smelled like a bad day in the kitchen. But they emitted yellow light.

There is something to yellow light—after four hours of somber, dimming Beta. Even Latimer had lifted his eyes from his book and stared in wonder.

Sheerin warmed his hands at the nearest, regardless of the soot that gathered upon them in a fine, gray powder, and muttered ecstatically to himself. "Beautiful! Beautiful! I never realized before what a wonderful color yellow is."

But Theremon regarded the torches suspiciously. He wrinkled his nose at the rancid odor, and said, "What are those things?"

"Wood," said Sheerin shortly.

"Oh, no, they're not. They aren't burning. The top inch is charred and the flame just keeps shooting up out of nothing."

"That's the beauty of it. This is a really efficient artificial-light mechanism. We made a few hundred of them, but most went to the Hideout, of course. You see"—he turned and wiped his blackened hands upon his handkerchief—"you take the pithy core of coarse water reeds, dry them thoroughly and soak them in animal grease. Then you set fire to it and the grease burns, little by little. These torches will burn for almost half an hour without stopping. Ingenious, isn't it? It was developed by one of our own young men at Saro University."

After the momentary sensation, the dome had quieted. Latimer had carried his chair directly beneath a torch and continued reading, lips moving in the monotonous recital of invocations to the Stars. Beenay had drifted away to his cameras once more, and Theremon seized the opportunity to add to his notes on the article he was going to write for the Saro City Chronicle the next day—a procedure he had been following for the last two hours in a perfectly methodical, perfectly conscientious and, as he was well aware, perfectly meaningless fashion.

But, as the gleam of amusement in Sheerin's eyes indicated, careful note taking occupied his mind with something other than the fact that the sky was gradually turning a horrible deep purple-red, as if it were one gigantic, freshly peeled beet; and so it fulfilled its purpose.

The air grew, somehow, denser. Dusk, like a palpable entity, entered the room, and the dancing circle of yellow light about the torches etched itself into ever-sharper distinction against the gathering grayness beyond. There was the odor of smoke and the presence of little chuckling sounds that the torches made as they burned; the soft pad of one of the men circling the table at which he worked, on hesitant tiptoes; the occasional indrawn breath of someone trying to retain composure in a world that was retreating into the shadow.

It was Theremon who first heard the extraneous noise. It was a vague, unorganized *impression* of sound that would have gone unnoticed but for the dead silence that prevailed within the dome.

The newsman sat upright and replaced his notebook. He held his breath and listened; then, with considerable reluctance, threaded his way between the solarscope and one of Beenay's cameras and stood before the window.

The silence ripped to fragments at his startled shout:

"Sheerin!"

Work stopped! The psychologist was at his side in a moment. Aton joined him. Even Yimot 70, high in his little lean-back seat at the eyepiece of the gigantic solarscope, paused and looked downward.

Outside, Beta was a mere smoldering splinter, taking one last desperate look at Lagash. The eastern horizon, in the direction of the city, was lost in Darkness, and the road from Saro to the Observatory was a dull-red line bordered on both sides by wooded tracts, the trees of which had somehow lost individuality and merged into a continuous shadowy mass.

But it was the highway itself that held attention, for along it there surged another, and infinitely menacing, shadowy mass.

Aton cried in a cracked voice, "The madmen from the city! They've come!"

"How long to totality?" demanded Sheerin.

"Fifteen minutes, but . . . but they'll be here in five."

"Never mind, keep the men working. We'll hold them off. This place is built like a fortress. Aton, keep an eye on our young Cultist just for luck. Theremon, come with me."

Sheerin was out the door, and Theremon was at his heels. The stairs stretched below them in tight, circular sweeps about the central shaft, fading into a dank and dreary grayness.

The first momentum of their rush had carried them fifty feet down, so that the dim, flickering yellow from the open door of the dome had disappeared and both up above and down below the same dusky shadow crushed in upon them.

Sheerin paused, and his pudgy hand clutched at his chest. His eyes bulged and his voice was a dry cough. "I can't . . . breathe . . . go down . . . yourself. Close all doors—"

Theremon took a few downward steps, then turned. "Wait! Can you hold out a minute?" He was panting himself. The air passed in and out his lungs like so much molasses, and there was a little germ of screeching panic in his mind at the thought of making his way into the mysterious Darkness below by himself.

Theremon, after all, was afraid of the dark!

"Stay here," he said. "I'll be back in a second." He dashed upward two steps at a time, heart pounding—not altogether from the exertion —tumbled into the dome and snatched a torch from its holder. It was foul smelling, and the smoke smarted his eyes almost blind, but he clutched that torch as if he wanted to kiss it for joy, and its flame streamed backward as he hurtled down the stairs again.

Sheerin opened his eyes and moaned as Theremon bent over him. Theremon shook him roughly. "All right, get a hold on yourself. We've got light."

He held the torch at tiptoe height and, propping the tottering psychologist by an elbow, made his way downward in the middle of the protecting circle of illumination.

The offices on the ground floor still possessed what light there was, and Theremon felt the horror about him relax.

"Here," he said brusquely, and passed the torch to Sheerin. "You can hear *them* outside."

And they could. Little scraps of hoarse, wordless shouts.

But Sheerin was right; the Observatory was built like a fortress. Erected in the last century, when the neo-Gavottian style of architecture was at its ugly height, it had been designed for stability and durability, rather than for beauty.

The windows were protected by the grillework of inch-thick iron bars sunk deep into the concrete sills. The walls were solid masonry that an earthquake couldn't have touched, and the main door was a huge oaken slab reinforced with iron at the strategic points. Theremon shot the bolts and they slid shut with a dull clang.

At the other end of the corridor, Sheerin cursed weakly. He pointed to the lock of the back door which had been neatly jimmied into uselessness.

"That must be how Latimer got in," he said.

"Well, don't stand there," cried Theremon impatiently. "Help drag up the furniture—and keep that torch out of my eyes. The smoke's killing me."

He slammed the heavy table up against the door as he spoke, and in two minutes had built a barricade which made up for what it lacked in beauty and symmetry by the sheer inertia of its massiveness.

Somewhere, dimly, far off, they could hear the battering of naked fists upon the door; and the screams and yells from outside had a sort of half reality.

That mob had set off from Saro City with only two things in mind: the attainment of Cultist salvation by the destruction of the Observatory, and a maddening fear that all but paralyzed them. There was no time to think of ground cars, or of weapons, or of leadership, or even of organization. They made for the Observatory on foot and assaulted it with bare hands.

And now that they were there, the last flash of Beta, the last ruby-red drop of flame; flickered feebly over a humanity that had left only stark, universal fear!

Theremon groaned, "Let's get back to the dome!"

In the dome, only Yimot, at the solarscope, had kept his place. The rest were clustered about the cameras, and Beenay was giving his instructions in a hoarse, strained voice.

"Get it straight, all of you. I'm snapping Beta just before totality and changing the plate. That will leave one of you to each camera. You all know about . . . about times of exposure—"

There was a breathless murmur of agreement.

Beenay passed a hand over his eyes. "Are the torches still burning? Never mind, I see them!" He was leaning hard against the back of a chair. "Now remember, don't . . . don't try to look for good shots. Don't waste time trying to get t-two stars at a time in the scope field. One is enough. And . . . and if you feel yourself going, get away from the camera."

At the door, Sheerin whispered to Theremon, "Take me to Aton. I don't see him."

The newsman did not answer immediately. The vague forms of the astronomers wavered and blurred, and the torches overhead had become only yellow spotches.

"It's dark," he whimpered.

Sheerin held out his hand, "Aton." He stumbled forward. "Aton!"

Theremon stepped after and seized his arm. "Wait, I'll take you." Somehow he made his way across the room. He closed his eyes against the Darkness and his mind against the chaos within it.

No one heard them or paid attention to them. Sheerin stumbled against the wall. "Aton!"

The psychologist felt shaking hands touching him, then withdrawing, and a voice muttering, "Is that you, Sheerin?"

"Aton!" He strove to breathe normally. "Don't worry about the mob. The place will hold them off."

Latimer, the Cultist, rose to his feet, and his face twisted in desperation. His word was pledged, and to break it would mean placing his soul in mortal peril. Yet that word had been forced from him and had not been given freely. The Stars would come soon; he could not stand by and allow— And yet his word was pledged.

Beenay's face was dimly flushed as it looked upward at Beta's last ray, and Latimer, seeing him bend over his camera, made his decision. His nails cut the flesh of his palms as he tensed himself.

He staggered crazily as he started his rush. There was nothing before him but shadows; the very floor beneath his feet lacked substance. And then someone was upon him and he went down with clutching fingers at his throat.

He doubled his knee and drove it hard into his assailant. "Let me up or I'll kill you."

Theremon cried out sharply and muttered through a blinding haze of pain, "You double-crossing rat!"

The newsman seemed conscious of everything at once. He heard Beenay croak, "I've got it. At your cameras, men!" and then there was the strange awareness that the last thread of sunlight had thinned out and snapped.

Simultaneously he heard one last choking gasp from Beenay, and a queer little cry from Sheerin, a hysterical giggle that cut off in a rasp —and a sudden silence, a strange, deadly silence from outside.

And Latimer had gone limp in his loosening grasp. Theremon peered into the Cultist's eyes and saw the blankness of them, staring upward, mirroring the feeble yellow of the torches. He saw the bubble of froth upon Latimer's lips and heard the low animal whimper in Latimer's throat.

With the slow fascination of fear, he lifted himself on one arm and turned his eyes toward the blood-curdling blackness of the window.

Through it shone the Stars!

Not Earth's feeble thirty-six hundred Stars visible to the eye— Lagash was in the center of a giant cluster. Thirty thousand mighty suns shown down in a soul-searing splendor that was more frighteningly cold in its awful indifference than the bitter wind that shivered across the cold, horribly bleak world.

Theremon staggered to his feet, his throat constricting him to breathlessness, all the muscles of his body writhing in a tensity of terror and sheer fear beyond bearing. He was going mad, and knew it, and somewhere deep inside a bit of sanity was screaming, struggling to fight off the hopeless flood of black terror. It was very horrible to go mad and know that you were going mad—to know that in a little minute you would be here physically and yet all the real essence would be dead and drowned in the black madness. For this was the Dark—the Dark and the Cold and the Doom. The bright walls of the universe were shattered and their awful black fragments were falling down to crush and squeeze and obliterate him.

He jostled someone crawling on hands and knees, but stumbled somehow over him. Hands groping at his tortured throat, he limped toward the flame of the torches that filled all his mad vision.

"Light!" he screamed.

Aton, somewhere, was crying, whimpering horribly like a terribly frightened child. "Stars—all the Stars—we didn't know at all. We didn't know anything. We thought six stars is a universe is something the Stars didn't notice is Darkness forever and ever and ever and the walls are breaking in and we didn't know we couldn't know and anything—"

Someone clawed at the torch, and it fell and snuffed out. In the instant, the awful splendor of the indifferent Stars leaped nearer to them.

On the horizon outside the window, in the direction of Saro City, a crimson glow began growing, strengthening in brightness, that was not the glow of a sun.

The long night had come again.

A MATTER OF SIZE

by

HARRY BATES

Here is the world seen through the eyes of an ant or a beetle—
a world where the grass of your lawn becomes dense jungle growth,
where the trickle of water in a gutter becomes an impassable
torrent, where the casual footsteps of passers-by become blind
instruments of complete obliteration. And in this world is a man
who has become the size of an ant, but without the ant's saving
ignorance of the perils that beset his every movement. Still, even
when reduced to an appalling miniature, man still possesses his
ingenuity.

*

THOUGH his head was as stuffed with cotton, the details of the
scene in his New York laboratory that night came back with insistent
clearness. It was long past the turn of the clock, and he had been
working for hours on a monograph on the Mutrantian Titans, which
would establish indubitably the biological brotherhood of those
colossi of Saturn's Satellite Three with the genus Homo of Earth.
He was deeply immersed, and the muted night murmurs of the great
city around and below washed unheeded through his ears.

Then something, perhaps a slight motion, an extraneous noise,
caused him to look up—and there, within the lamplight on the far
side of his desk, stood the most amazing figure of a man that he,
ethnologist though he was, had ever seen.

His visitor wore sandals and a loose-fitting blue robe. He stood ill
at ease, a slight, enigmatic smile on his face.

That man! He could see him now, as clear in every point as if he
were present.

The head was massive, the cranium oval, and not one hair adorned its smooth and shining surface. Beneath the deep corrugations of the forehead the face sloped gently backward past a snub nose as far as the mouth, where it fell sharply away, leaving but the merest excuse of chin and lower jaw. The neck was long, the shoulders sloping; the whole apparition was grotesque. But he was not tempted to smile. No one could have looked into that man's face and smiled. The eyes, large, light, and piercing, would have prevented that.

"You are Doctor Arthur Allison," the man had said. "I've come a long way to see you."

"You're certainly not from Earth?" Allison said, gaping, stating the fact rather than asking it.

"No."

"Then"—he could not restrain the question—"then, for Heaven's sake tell me, are you sport or typical?"

The other smiled. "Always the scientist, I see! I am typical."

Allison rose in amazement and went around the side of the desk. "But—but that can hardly be!" he exclaimed. "The solar system's been pretty thoroughly explored, and no race such as yours has ever been discovered."

The stranger's smile faded. "That discovery has been reserved for you," he said significantly. He paused. "May I come to the point of my visit?"

"Please do. I—I'm tremendously interested. Will you sit down?"

"Thank you—no. There is not much time."

He locked the ethnologist with his eyes.

"I am the emissary of a people unknown to you," he began. "Our abode lies within the solar system a reasonable distance away, and for sufficient reasons no uninvited man of your race has ever laid questioning eyes on it, and no man of your generation but you ever will. Our racial strain is cousin to yours, but our science and civilization are ahead by more than 40,000 years. Our powers exceed what might be your wildest imaginings. In terms of death, for instance, we could, in fourteen days, destroy every trace of crustal life on Earth and all her tributary planets; or we could, in that same space of time, reduce every single vertebrate to a state of impotent slavery.

"We would never do these things, however. We have neither the need nor the desire; we are not inhumane and not, of course, so stupid. Our self-determined developmental cycle will not bring us into intimate contact with you Earthmen for tens of thousands of years, and meanwhile we will remain as we are, aloof and inaccessible, happy within reason and practically self-sufficient.

"You note that I say 'practically'. Once in every twenty-five years we invite one carefully chosen Earthman to do us a service. You, without knowing it, have ever since your graduation from college been our most promising candidate. We have had you under observation for seven years, have investigated your ancestors back for ten generations, and in heredity, manhood, intellect, and achievement you are all that we ask; so it is to you, alone of your generation, that I come now to offer this highest honor that could fall to a man of your time.

"I may not tell you what your service to us will be. You must trust me implicitly, obey me blindly. You will come to no danger or hurt. You must leave with me immediately, for a destination and by a route that will be kept secret from you. You will be gone four months. Those four months will be the high point of your intellectual, scientific, and, I might add, emotional life. Are you ready?"

"You make an extraordinary request!" the ethnologist said, when he found words.

"Ours is an extraordinary race," was the instant answer.

"If I refuse?"

"I could use force, and you'd be just as valuable to us under coercion as without; but I won't. You will not refuse. Not one of the men that has ever been approached has refused."

"Has this 'service' anything to do with my specialty?"

The man's eyes showed the faintest trace of amusement. "I may say yes," he replied. "It is applied and very, very practical ethnology."

"I shall be returned here without hindrance when this service is done?"

"Of course; and you may bring back with you all the knowledge of our science that you can absorb and retain."

Allison considered a moment. He asked: "May I see your feet?"

The out-worlder smiled. He sat on a chair and removed one sandal, exposing a foot such as no man on Earth had ever yet possessed. The big toe was very large, and was flanked by another only a little bit smaller. The three outer toes were vestigial. Here was the foot of the human race, thousands of years in the future.

Allison's eyes bulged. The knowledge there would be!

As if reading his mind the stranger said: "Your Mr. Wells said it long ago. 'Think of the new knowledge!' "

The words were a light in Allison's brain. He turned away. The stranger replaced the sandal and rose.

"Think of the new knowledge!" he repeated.

The ethnologist turned to him. "What is your name?" he said. The other smiled. "I am sometimes called Jones," he replied.

And they were the last words that had been spoken. Allison remembered that he, too, had smiled; that he had spontaneously held out his hand in tacit acceptance; that as his palm touched the out-worlder's there had been a sharp sting as of a needle; and then all his senses had left him, and he sank down and down into oblivion.

For one and a half Earth hours Allison lay loggy on the immaculate white cot, only the changing expression of his opened eyes telling of the chaos within. Then slowly and by insensible degrees his delirium became more physical, and he strained at the broad cloth bands that held him down, tossed within their narrow confines, muttered gibberish in three languages.

A thousand horrific menaces disputed his long way up to a consciousness, each a nightmare shape spawned out of unknown frustrations in the abysmal unconscious. By twos and by threes he battled them—all the long dark arms, the fire eyes, the scale-skinned, and the amorphous, and those worse ones without name or substance which enveloped him with intangible oppression. It was most unfair, for no combat was ever decisive; always the shapes eluded him; and indeed they changed their identity as he faced them and were never twice the same.

Except three. Three there were that remained a little apart, but which came again and were always clear and undistorted. First was the out-worldly stranger. Then the blue-eyed girl. And the last the interminable rows of doll faces, each a likeness of his own; each one himself.

As the hours passed and he fought upward it became increasingly necessary to identify these recurring images. They were somehow enormously important. They were bound with his life, or had been, or would be; it was very obscure, which; and they were all a mystery and a menace in their own fashion.

To trap their secret he constructed colossal edifices of metaphysical cunning, performed prodigies of deduction, all the while he swam oceans, plunged through fire, sank through bottomless ooze in his running fight with the demons that beset him; but always at the moment of knowing he would forget what he was looking for and have to begin all over.

Who was the out-worldly stranger? Who, the blue-eyed girl? Those rows of doll faces—why were they *his* faces? Why was each one himself?

He would try new cunning. He would close his eyes for a long while, then open them suddenly, and he'd know.

The man on the immaculate white cot closed his eyes and lay still; and then began the long, deep sleep that was to restore him to himself.

Allison awoke gently and lay quiet a moment, dully wondering where he might be and how he had arrived there. The room was unfamiliar, with its close, square walls and the peculiar but soothing soft amber haze that filtered evenly from horizontal tubes set well up near the ceiling. There was no trace of a window, but a metal-framed door showed indistinctly in the wall at his right. He turned toward it—and found himself restrained.

A surge of alarm ran through his veins and brought him fully awake. He arched upward and discovered that a broad cloth band had been passed over his chest and another over his thighs. His arms were free, and his exploring hands soon found a buckle which was easily loosened. He sat up and released his legs, then was at once out of bed and making for the door.

He found it locked.

"Not so good," he thought, pushing back his shock of yellow hair and turning and surveying the room. But at the head of the bed was a small table—the only other article of furniture. Placed opposite under the ceiling were grilles which he decided were for ventilation. The walls looked like marble, cream-colored, and apparently synthetic.

He turned back to the door; pounded on it; yelled out: "Hey, Jones"; listened. He couldn't be sure, but he thought he heard a faint answering noise outside. He repeated his call; but no one came, and, irritated, he went back to the cot and sat on its edge, head in hands, until "Jones" should come and release him.

It was clear he had been anesthetized, and he supposed he couldn't complain, for it had been part of their agreement that both route and destination be kept secret; but how deucedly prompt the man had acted!

And how long he must have been unconscious! A quarter-inch growth of beard scratched the palms held to his cheeks! Well, no doubt he had arrived.

The ethnologist rose from the cot and stalked about the room. He was not overcongratulating himself for the sheeplike docility with which he had acceded to the out-worlder's amazing offer. There were a hundred questions to ask, and hardly one had been answered; there were affairs of importance to be put in order before leaving Earth,

and not one had been attended to. Confound Jones, for the out-
rageous promptness of his action! Where was he now, anyway?

Again he banged on the door and yelled, and again it was fruitless. He resumed his pacing.

"Jones!" Of all names for the out-worlder to go by! Practical,
though, of course. His real name was probably Ugkthgubx, or some
such jaw breaker. Would match his face——

The Earthman stopped short. Into his stream of consciousness had
floated a figment that would not be identified. Something about a
girl, blue-eyed and beautiful. And something else—connected with
her—rows and rows—frightening—himself there, somehow——

It sank and was gone.

He sat again on the cot, tense, "open," delicately fishing it back
up. It came—went—came clearly.

Interminable rows of doll faces—— But why were they *his* faces?
Why was each one himself?

A thrill of fear swept up his back. Had something been done to
him while he was unconscious?

Later: Why the emotion, why the fear that accompanied that
memory?

Still later: Why that flash that something may have been done to
me while I was unconscious?

He hung suspended, fishing for answers that would not come.
Gradually the image faded, leaving in its place an intangible feeling
of oppression. He got up and walked to throw off the spell; muttered:

"God help Jones if he did monkey with me!"

There was a noise at the door, and, turning, he beheld the massive
bald head that never could he forget. Smiling, Jones entered.

"You are recovered?" he asked cordially.

An exclamation of anger rose to Allison's lips—and died there.
Behind the out-worlder stood a girl. She was clad in a simple, loose-
flowing crimson robe, gathered at the waist. She was blue-eyed and
beautiful.

Jones beckoned to her. "Doctor Allison," he said, "let me present
our Miss CB-301."

II

Allison did not distinguish himself for ease of manner in that introduction, for he was wondering how it could be that this girl, whom
he was now meeting for the first time, could be the very one whose

image already dimly lurked in his memory. None of his awkwardness was to be charged to any romantic "falling for" her; no mistake is to be made about that. A score of girls had hitherto found he was quite immune—though a psychoanalyst might have discovered that what he called "a scientific disinterest in the sex" could be reduced to the absurd fact that he was simply a little afraid of them.

The ethnologist, becoming aware that Miss So-and-So had said "How do you do!" in the most conventional of Earth fashions, in turn nodded and mumbled something himself. Jones smiled broadly and, stepping to the door, begged to be excused, saying he was overwhelmed with work.

"Miss CB-301 speaks your language perfectly," he said, "and will explain such things as are permitted. I'll be back presently." And the door clicked closed behind him, leaving an off-balanced young ethnologist very much alone with an unabashed young maiden with freckles on her nose and the light of admiration in her eyes.

Allison stood stiffly uncomfortable. Who could have thought that this would happen? And so suddenly? Confound that Jones again; he was certainly one fast worker.

What should he say to the female? Nice day? No—better, flattery. He complimented her on the lack of accent in her speech. It suggested unusual brains in one so young.

"Oh, but no—I'm really terribly dumb!" the young thing gushed sincerely. "I could hardly get through my fourth-dimensional geometry! But English is easier. Don't you think so?"

Yes; he certainly thought so. He warmed toward her a little. "Then let me congratulate you," he said, "for admitting your dumbness. I'm not accustomed to such extraordinary modesty on the part of women. I may say I find it very becoming."

The girl smiled her delight, and Allison smiled, too. Then, struck by an unpleasant thought, her face took on a woebegone look.

"I'm an atavism," she said.

What was the polite comment on that?

The ethnologist in Allison rose to the surface. "Let me see your feet," he said with sudden eagerness.

"Oh, no—don't ask that! Please!"

She shrunk from him.

"Why not?" he demanded.

"Because they're so ugly!" the girl exclaimed wretchedly. "I don't want you to see them! Ever!"

"Sit down and take off your sandals!" he ordered. After all, she was only a kid, and her reluctance was unwarranted and foolish.

Tremblingly the girl obeyed, and Allison looked down upon as beautiful a pair of five-toed feet as he had ever seen. Extremely interesting, so complete a divergence from what must be the present racial type. He smiled, and she, seeing, felt better and hastened to put her sandals on again.

"After all," she said rising, "even though I am an atavism, you're a primitive, and—and—well, it could be terribly thrilling!"

She looked up at him adoringly—hopefully.

Allison laughed. He was all at his ease now with the young thing, and, it must be repeated, he was thoroughly immune.

"It sounds as if you're proposing," he said.

"We're to be married," she confided. "I hope you don't mind too much."

This was ominous and led to a sudden terrible suspicion.

"Is this why I was brought from Earth—to marry you?" he demanded angrily.

"Oh, no! Not just for me!" she answered; then, as if conscious of having made a slip, she added quickly; "I saw you when they brought you in and asked then. You see, you're the only man I've ever met who is like me. I never felt funny about any one else the way I feel funny about you."

He was reassured, but it left the problem of rebuffing her. He had done nothing to commit himself, and it was just her hard luck if she had to go and "feel funny" where one so hopeless as he was concerned. He had better nip her romantic notions in the bud.

"Young lady, I like you very much," he said, "but my interest is largely ethnological. I'm sorry, but it can never be anything more. I —I'll be a—a big brother to you," he concluded asininely.

The girl was hurt, and her face fell. It was very awkward for a moment. Allison affected a cheeriness he did not feel.

"Come," he said, "tell me about your people. Do they all look like the man who brought me here? Are you the only one of your kind in the whole country?"

She brightened a little. "Yes," she replied; "I'm the only one like you. You wouldn't care for the others at all. Look—I'll show you."

She lifted her left wrist and showed him, strapped thereto, what looked like an enameled wrist watch with a large bezel; only the dial of this was blank, and radiating from the sides were five gnurled stems.

"Do you have these on Earth?" she asked. He admitted they did not. "Look," she said, turning her body at an angle and adjusting the stems.

As Allison looked, close by her side, the dial took on an opalescent glow, and dimly there appeared on it threads and shadows which under her adjustments cleared into a picture, animated—the heads and figures of half a dozen women.

"Television," he said. "You're receiving this from a broadcasting studio."

"No," she corrected; "a searchbeam, portable. I can focus it at a distance on whatever I choose. It passes through almost anything." Allison marveled. "But that's not the point," she objected: "Look at those women. Do you find them more beautiful than I?"

He certainly did not. They were, each one, the feminine counterpart of the man Jones. Their necks were as columnar, their shoulders as sloped, and their heads were nothing less than disgusting, considering that they belonged to bodies of what is commonly called the "fair sex." They had wide faces, flat, with bulging foreheads and utterly degenerated jaws, with a rim of thin hair that circled their craniums as might a fringed girdle, an egg.

Allison shuddered. "I pass!" he said.

The girl probably did not understand his words, but she read aright the expression on his face. "You see!" she cried triumphantly, as if it were thereby decided that he was to marry her. "That is part of the line of waiting brides to be. You've got to marry one of us!"

"Well, I'm not going to marry one of you!" the ethnologist exclaimed angrily. "Why do you say I do?" he demanded, the ominous suspicion again taking shape in his mind. "Why? Why?" he repeated, following her as she backed away.

The girl was on the verge of tears. "I can't tell you, and I won't!" she said. "But it's a shame, 'cause I thought it would be so easy and nice! Because you're a primitive."

Allison turned away; there was no satisfaction to be had from her. She was a throwback, all right. He suddenly wanted very much to see the man called Jones. He had plenty of explanations coming to him, and it seemed to him he'd been treated rather shabbily so far. He turned back to the girl.

"Miss—Miss——" He came to a stop. "Pardon me—what is your name again?"

"Miss CB-301."

"Ah, yes. May I call you Miss Brown? Uh—Miss Brown, will you go find Mr. Jones—the man who introduced us? I want to see him at once.

"Or maybe I can go to him?" he quickly suggested.

"Oh, no, you can't do that. I'll go bring him here." She seemed a little afraid of her primitive. She added, more brightly: "I think I want to see him myself."

"Will you lend me that search-beam till you get back?"

She hesitated, as if she should not, then, pathetically eager to please him, she unstrapped and placed it about his left wrist. She's beautiful, all right, he thought, as she fastened it on. Hair, and plenty of it. Thick and dark and tastefully drawn through that jeweled clasp at the nape of her neck. Those other women's!

She tapped on the door, and it was opened by a brown-robed figure outside. For a moment she looked softly into Allison's eyes, and then she was gone.

What had she meant by saying he had to marry "one of us"? Had to! Yes; Jones had plenty of explanations piling up.

The ethnologist sat on the edge of the cot and held up his wrist. What a marvel of ingenuity the little device was! Tentatively he turned the stem she had first touched. The dial glowed, then meaningless shadows appeared on it. The slightest movement of his body changed these shadows for new ones. He turned other stems and got what seemed to be a wall. Delicately he manipulated in the attempt to probe beyond. The blurred figure of a man appeared, came clearer, and then Allison got a shock. The image that lay on the glowing round dial was point for point his own.

In his amazement he moved, and the man was gone. Pulse throbbing, he fished him back. No doubt about it—the outlines were fuzzy, but the resemblance was there. All over—size, shoulders, head, proportions, clothing. Even the room he occupied was identical. He stood leaning against the wall, arms folded, looking in angry fashion straight ahead, and on his face was a short thatch of yellow beard.

Out of Allison's unconscious came the memory he had had before. Interminable rows of doll faces. Each face his own face, and each one, somehow, himself.

Mystery lay all around him. Jones, so strangely in out of the night. His extraordinary offer. The sudden unconscious journey. The unknown out-world civilization that hemmed him in. The rows of doll faces with their freight of fear. This man who looked so like himself. What devil's work could be under way?

There was a movement on the glowing dial. The door of the room opened, and the man known as Jones entered, followed by a surgeon-like figure in white smock and helmet who pushed before him a rubber-wheeled table. At sight of them the man left the wall and advanced menacingly. They talked, and Jones' manner was wholly conciliatory.

Then, suddenly, it was over. Jones stepped to the man's side and touched him lightly on the shoulder with the palm of his hand. He slumped to the floor, from which in businesslike fashion he was picked up, laid on the table and wheeled out through the door.

Allison stared with amazement. It was the same trick that had been worked on him. The shoulder instead of the hand.

The men were gone from the dial. He set himself quickly to picking them up again. Angling his body slightly did it. They had paused outside the door.

They moved; grew blurred; he found a stem that brought them sharper again. He followed them down a square corridor into which many doors were set at equal distances on each side. As they progressed they dwindled to the size of match heads, but he found the way to make them larger. Other figures passed by, two in white smocks and helmets, others in colored gowns, their ugly heads fully exposed; and as Allison looked at them, his group was gone.

An anxious moment, then he found them. They were a little lower to one side, descending in an elevator. Lost them! Again his heart stood still while he felt them out. It was as if that unconscious man on the table—that man who so resembled him—were he himself. Where were they taking him? What was to be done with him, all unresisting?

There passed an interval during which a jumble of walls, shadows, people, strange apparatus, and blurs were all that came to his dial. Once, even, a conical green bush; or perhaps it was a tree. Then Allison by pure chance found his men again.

An imposing picture lay on the dial when he had brought them to size and clarity. They stood waiting behind a low railing at one end of a large auditorium. Behind them, the other side of the railing, half a hundred rows of seats, laced by aisles, rose upward to the ceiling, and every seat was occupied by men and women of the strange race whose prisoner he was. In front of them, the focal point of every eye in that vast gathering, was a glittering cage, within which rested two chairs, meshed by wires together, and placed in front of a complicated battery of scientific apparatus whose nature Allison didn't know.

Quickly, with perfect coordination, the ensuing scene took place. The table bearing the unconscious man was wheeled within the cage, and he was removed and made to sit upright in one of the chairs. At the same time a woman of the race, escorted by an official, entered the space within the railing from a doorway to the right and was conducted to the other chair. She was touched, palm on shoulder, by Jones, and immediately slumped back unconscious. Metallic headbands attached to the chairs were fastened about their foreheads. Then all left the cage and the door was closed.

Jones went to a large panel to one side and threw a switch, and for one instant a glow of varicolored light flooded the cage. When it had died he and the others reentered, freed the two subjects, and, in a way Allison could not catch, revived them. Then the handsome young man with the blond hair and the ugly woman with the fringed bald head and corrugated brow proceeded out of the cage to a small desk by the railing, where they stopped, looked deeply at each other, and in full view of the assembled thousands kissed each other ardently on the mouth.

Idols of Pluto! Allison was flabbergasted, but, more than that, he was nauseated. For that blond young man who so disturbingly resembled him was subtly, somehow, himself. He, too, felt he had kissed that woman.

For a moment he could not look, and when he did he found the actors gone. The audience, however, remained, and most of them were smiling. What could it all mean?

The ethnologist let his wrist fall, brushed his forehead, tried to consider. Should he confront Jones with this new knowledge when he saw him? If he were slated to figure in such proceedings himself, it would surely be as scientist rather than subject. And just as surely, in spite of his subconscious feeling of oppression, the man he had been following could have no relation to him.

Speaking out to Jones would get the girl in trouble.

As he was thinking, the man himself entered in his quick and quiet way. Allison rose, with care keeping his left wrist to his side.

"Doctor Allison," the out-worlder said without preamble, "may I ask if you feel any—uh—sentimental inclination toward the young lady I introduced you to?"

"It happens I do not," the ethnologist answered sharply. The question irritated him. "May I in turn ask when I'm to be allowed to leave this room?" he asked.

The other made an appealing gesture. "Please," he said, "you've only just regained consciousness." He made a promise. "I'll see to it that you leave within fifteen minutes."

"It would seem that my arrival is of not quite the importance you led me to anticipate," Allison said with bitterness.

The out-worlder smiled inscrutably. "On the contrary," he objected, "it is. You've caused a tremendous excitement. Thousands are now busy with the preparations to receive you."

Was he alluding to anything in connection with the scene in the auditorium? How could he sound him without betraying the girl? There seemed no way.

"Exactly what is the nature of this service you've asked me to render?" he asked at last.

The other was at the door. "I'll tell you when I come back," Jones promised. "But I might say, for the time being, that it is of vital importance to the fecundity of our race."

And with these cryptic words, before Allison could recover, Jones was gone.

III

Sitting on the cot, Allison tried to bring to order his scattered thoughts. He felt his position grew moment by moment more dangerous, but why, it was difficult to discover. Jones had as yet made no overt act, nor had he done anything that might be construed as contrary to their agreement. The fellow was not very likable, but then he was an out-worlder, of unpleasant face and figure, and Allison well knew how wrong superficial estimates of such characters were apt to be. He had always acted friendly, even if he was a trifle—to him—high-handed and abrupt. The girl could not be charged against him, for she was acting largely on her own. Allison rather liked her, anyway. She was a credit.

What else was there? Well, the scene he had witnessed by means of the search-beam. But in itself that was only interesting and amusing, except, perhaps, to the blond chap concerned. It was just the confusion of the fellow's resemblance to himself that summoned those nameless fears. He could conclude that somebody, very much like himself, had simply undergone some sort of scientific ceremony ending with a kiss.

But that was not a ceremonial kiss—it was shamelessly ardent. Could there be love—mating—between two such opposites? A wedding, perhaps, since it was public.

A wedding! Jones' last words, anent his "service," still rang in his ears. "It is of vital importance to the fecundity of our race." No forced marriage of his to one of those top-heavy heads—even to Miss Brown —would have any effect on that.

Another remark of Jones. His "service" had to do with "applied and very, very practical ethnology."

The worst was certainly those interminable rows of doll faces. He could never have actually seen them, surely; they would have to be symbols of the unconscious, standing for something else. But what else?

And why the resemblance of that young fellow to himself—and, therefore, to the doll faces? That could not be coincidence.

Allison gave it up. He knew only that a nameless oppression sat on his heart, and that he, who had seldom been afraid, was now afraid.

He was roused by a light knock on the door. He rose; Miss Brown entered; and some one in brown closed the door behind her. She was smiling radiantly and held in her hands a curious fruit something like a very large soft-skinned sapodilla.

"Eat it," she said. "It is very nourishing and very good."

Allison thanked her, broke it and gave her half. He found it good indeed. He had not realized he was so hungry. She watched him with an expression of joy that would not come off.

"Why do you smile so?" he asked. "You weren't feeling so cheerful when you left."

She laughed and shook her head, and would not tell him.

"You'll find out!" she promised.

Something occurred to Allison, and he sat on the cot and pulled the girl gently down by his side. The watchlike search-beam was still adjusted to the auditorium, and he turned his wrist delicately in various directions till he found it again.

"What is that place?" he asked.

She gave him a look of fright. "Please don't ask!" she begged. "I can't tell you! I—I'll get in awful trouble!"

"From Jones?"

She nodded. He debated whether to ask her the explanation of what he had witnessed and decided it was useless. He peered into the dial of the instrument. Her soft hand came to take it away, but he guarded it with his own and kept on looking.

He touched a stem, and the picture came clearer. The audience was there as before, and the space within the railing empty; but, as he watched, two familiar figures entered from a doorway on the left, and between them rolled a third on the wheeled table. Jones and his surgeonlike accessory were bringing in another victim.

The girl reached forth her hand again. "Please don't!" she pleaded softly. "I shouldn't have let you have it, only—only——"

"In a minute!" he cried irritably, keeping her hand away.

The figures had started for the cage. As before, the man was placed in one chair and a native woman, promptly entering, in the other. She was anesthetized, and both were fitted with the headbands. Then all left. Jones pulled the switch, and there was the expected burst of varicolored light.

Allison kept his eyes glued to the man, unable to make him out through the glass, fearful, deep down, of what he might see. Jones and the others re-entered the cage. The man and woman were revived; freed, went out; and far away in his little room in the building Allison started with shock. The man who had emerged, the man who even then was kissing ardently that ugly woman—he, too, looked like himself.

Prickles of fear ran all over the Earthman's body. "Who was that man?" he demanded of the girl. "Who was it?" he repeated, roughly grasping her arms.

She shook her head and sobbed out she dared not tell. He let her go; rose and paced about the room.

After a little she came to him. "Don't be mad with me," she pleaded softly. "I'll tell you some of it—a little." She paused, gathering courage, then said: "That instrument's the way we make people fall in love with each other here. It does something in their heads."

Allison stood still, struck with amazement at her words. She pulled his sleeve; took his hands.

"Arthur," she said tenderly. "Arthur." He looked down at her. "Don't be mad," she went on, smiling a little, "but we *will* marry. You *will* love me. I just arranged it with Mr. Jones. He's coming up for us next. Though I didn't have to be made to fall in love with you. Arthur —aren't you listening? We'll be so happy, and then you won't have to marry one of those ugly other women, and then you'll never want to go back to your horrid Earth! Never!"

For some time Allison looked at her; then he freed his hands and turned toward the door. "Sister, I'm checking out!"

She suspected what he meant. "What are you going to do?" she cried. "You can't go away! Mr. Jones won't let you!"

"Miss 891-X, you've no idea how good I am at handling guys like that. I'm a primitive, you know."

He felt worlds better, already. It was the waiting, a helpless prisoner facing the unknown, that had got him so down before. Now he had made a decision, and the promise of action, even of conflict, tuned him to his old accustomed pitch.

But the girl would fight to keep him. She threw herself on his chest and begged and pleaded.

"But Arthur," she said, "you'll like it after you're changed. You'll never know any difference except that you'll love me. Don't you see?"

He held her off. "Miss Brown, I'm sorry, but I don't want to like to be any other way than I am now. You go down to that damn machine; get 'em to make you fall in love with some nice local boy."

A noise was heard at the door. At once he jumped and wedged his body behind it. "Hide! Here they are!" he whispered. "Quick! Under the bed! There may be trouble."

Trembling, the girl obeyed. Allison stepped back. Jones entered, and his hooded assistant followed with the wheeled table and closed the door.

The ethnologist wasted no time. "Jones," he said, "it's all off. You will kindly arrange to send me back to Earth."

The out-worlder showed less surprise than Allison expected.

"But my dear Doctor Allison," he objected, "you can't mean to change your mind now. You are here; thousands of our scientists are assembled; we've come even now to conduct you to the place where your service is to begin."

He drew close. Allison turned a little, and watched him like a hawk. Jones continued, soothingly:

"Your trepidations are natural, but in a few minutes you'll be laughing at yourself for ever having entertained them. You just see."

He raised his right hand to clap Allison in good-fellow manner on the shoulder, but the pat never landed. Quick as a cat the Earthman wheeled and caught his wrist. The man, surprised, persisted, and he was strong; but Allison was stronger, and, clasping his left arm about the other's body, putting all his power behind short, savage jabs, he forced the hand back in toward its owner's chest.

"Take—some of—your own—medicine—doctor!"

The hand turned, and without a word Jones slumped to the floor, unconscious.

At once Allison was leaping toward the assistant, and before the fellow knew what had happened he lay sprawling on the floor beside the other. Harmless as he had seemed, the ethnologist took no chances. He reached for the relaxed right arm of Jones and pressed its palm into the prone man's arm. He went limp immediately. Allison rose.

"Act two," he said. "And two curtains."

He looked under the cot and laughed to see the way the wide-eyed girl there was trembling.

"Come out, Miss 23—PDQ," he said. "The war's over."

She pushed out and stood up. He went and knelt over Jones. "Ingenious little weapons you have hereabouts," he commented. A thin, rubberish sack lay flat in the man's palm, and from it led a tube to a short, hollow-tipped needle placed projecting from the lower end of the heel, just out of reach of the fingers. The instrument stuck there of itself. He pulled it off and placed it in his own right palm.

"They'll kill you!" the girl said, tears in her eyes.

"I hope not," he answered lightly. "I'll be moving pretty fast." He laughed. "You should know how I escaped from the Mutrantian Titans!"

"Is anybody outside that door?" he asked, pointing.

She nodded.

He went to it, took position on one side and knocked. The door opened slightly, and a hand, wrist, and sleeve showed. Allison touched the hand with the heel of his right palm—and pulled an unconscious, white-clad attendant into the room. He laid him neatly by the others and looked again at the needle.

"Aye, ingenious!" he said.

"How are you going to get away?" the girl asked.

For answer, he queried: "Where's your space port?"

"Oh, it's way over on the other side of the city. They'd catch you."

"Do you have air-cars?"

She nodded.

"Where can I get one? On the roof, maybe?"

"Yes," she said reluctantly. "There are stairs down the hall," she added, indicating.

This looked promising. Allison was sure he could work anything that could fly.

He searched the three men, finding no weapon; then, suggesting that Miss Brown turn her back, he exchanged clothes with the assistant in white. The helmet was much too large, but he remedied that by padding it with a strip torn off the hem of the attendant's robe.

With this in hand he stood for a moment before the slender girl. He remembered the search-beam; removed it and strapped it again on her wrist. She had remained surprisingly passive.

"You must get out of here!" he warned her. Her eyes were full of tears.

He took her in his arms and kissed her lips. "Good-by, little one," he murmured. "Good, good luck to you!"

He put on the helmet. Only his square shoulders might give him away outside. He would depress them as much as possible. He stepped to the partly opened door—and then at last she spoke.

"Oh, Arthur," she cried, "be careful! Get safe away! But don't forget me! Come back to me some day, if you can! I'll be here always, waiting!"

Allison squeezed her hand, then turned and went out. Sweet girl, he thought. He liked her very much.

IV

Only one man was in sight, a man in brown like one Allison had overcome, and he was approaching along the way Allison himself had to go. Walking rapidly, eyes straight ahead, he passed him without attracting attention.

The corridor was of the kind he had seen with the search-beam. Scores of doorways, identical with the one he had left, lined both its sides. Ahead might be the elevator, if he was headed in the right direction.

He was; and he came to it quickly—and had there a bad moment. On drawing abreast, the car came level with his floor, and off stepped two men clad like himself, trundling another wheeled table between them. One called after him a barbarous-sounding phrase, but he continued on, affecting not to hear. An open spiral staircase showed at his left, and with relief he turned in and started up. He would like to have run, but did not dare. He might meet some one.

As he climbed he wondered how many poor victims were being taken unconscious to that scientific hymeneal altar. Those fellows had enjoyed their marriage kiss! In his mind he could hear them at their love-making. "How brightly shine the stars on your incomparable scalp tonight!" "How lovely that line where your lips kiss your neck!" Ugh!

He shuddered and climbed faster, passed the landing next above, and continued up to where a closed door barred his way. He opened it, stepped through, and found himself on the roof.

It was daylight, and a small sun shone warmly. Blinking in its sudden glare, he made out that he was in the middle of a large flat open area floored with pink marble. In several scattered places were other roof doors like the one he had emerged from, and straight ahead stood a row of transparent objects that had to be the air-cars. One massive-headed man in purple was loitering near them, but he was the only person in sight. Allison strode casually over to the nearest car, studying it closely as he went.

It, like the others, was small, hardly five feet high, with open sides and streamlined shells of a stuff like glass, front and back. Within was one wide seat, in front of which were three control levers which led to a boxed space below. It rested on three splayed legs. And that was all there was. No motive device was apparent, and there were no wings or vanes whatever.

Allison was not pleased to have a witness to his first flight, but he stepped into the nearest car without hesitation and gingerly raised the lever he guessed would be the elevator. The car lifted. Slight pulls on another lever turned the nose of his craft, and the third gave forward velocity. It was extremely simple. A glance at the man below showed that he wasn't even looking. Boldly, now, Allison ordered the controls, and within a minute he was climbing silently a hundred feet above the edge of the roof to where other air-cars like elongated soap bubbles were scattered through the sky above.

Below, and shrinking as he climbed, lay a beautiful city. Broad ribbons of white streets stretched away to all sides, and within them lay low, curved, and angled buildings, each its own delicate pastel tint. Greens, blues, yellows, and purples, octagons of pink, and open green plazas everywhere between. It was not large, but it was such a place as modern architects back on Earth were still dreaming of.

On the far side should be the space port, according to the poor little girl of the numbers. Allison anxiously searched, but could spot nothing that looked like one—no great open place sprinkled with silver ovaloids that would be the ships. There was one silver shape well off on the right, but it was far too big for a space ship, he told himself. Still, he'd have a look. He turned his car and speeded up.

As he drew closer he saw that it was a ship, and, to his astonishment, that he knew it. It was the one belonging to the Mutrantian Titans. Two years before, Earth, in making overtures for the friendship of Saturn's somewhat backward Satellite Three, had caused to be made and presented as a gift to its government a space ship of tremendous size after the famous RV-3 model, so popular with her own private owners. The ship below was unmistakably that model, and, from its size, could only be the one presented to the Mutrantians.

What could its presence here mean? Were some of the Titans, like himself, here as instruments in the schemes of the ultrascientists?

Allison reached the ship and hovered high overhead. She lay alone in a large circular area, bare except for several scattered rows of long, buff-colored buildings with rounded tops. This was the space port after all; the buildings were hangars, and their local craft must all be housed inside. He lowered, circled, studied that bit of terrain. Everything depended on the raid he was about to make. How should he go about it? The scene was peaceful enough in appearance, and he could not at his altitude make out a single figure; but he had a great respect for the danger potential of a people so advanced in science.

What were the space ships inside those hangars like? Had he not been a bit too cocky in his assurance that he could navigate one? They might operate by entirely different principles from those he was familiar with—like the air-car he was in, for instance. He might stand like a child before an atomic engine in the presence of their motivating device.

As he hesitated, a preposterous idea invaded his mind. He rejected it at once, but it returned, and soon, as he faced it, he began to glow with the possibilities. Why not try for the Mutrantian ship? He was at least thoroughly familiar with it, and its operation was automatic in flight and foolproof. The one great problem was the matter of size. The ship had been made to a scale ten times that of the Earthmen's, and that meant that such a comparative midget as he might face extraordinary difficulties making the trip in it.

In the cool stillness five thousand feet in the air Allison laughed. He had the answer for that. It would be the Titan ship, by all means. He much preferred it, now.

But first he had to get it, and that might not be so easy. Especially if one of the Titans was inside. He lowered the elevating lever and dropped cleanly down.

At three thousand feet, even at one, no guard or other field attendant showed. The port looked deserted. "I can make a pretty good guess why," Allison told himself with a grin. "Big reception over in town. Thousands getting ready for the appearance of one Doctor Arthur Allison, pick of Earth!

"Earth's dumb-bells!" he corrected.

He lowered still more; hovered motionless fifty feet over the mammoth length of silver. A fifth of a mile, it lay stretched out. It was three hundred feet in the beam.

He set his ship in a glide down and around the gently curving flank. The ground rose to meet him; the side turned sheer. He saw that the midship port was open. A gangway from the field reached up and touched its lower lip.

There was still no sign of any one about. He lowered his car to the yawning forty-foot-wide cavern; peered; turned his ship and nosed through. Beyond the port lock, seventy feet within, he sunk to a landing and stepped out.

He was within, but not safe. There might be a Mutrantian, or a guard. He would have to reconnoiter.

For ten minutes he disappeared into the dark bowels of the ship, and when he emerged he was dragging the limp form of a man, whom he placed on the top of the gangway. There had been a guard.

A few seconds later he had returned to his car and ascended the forward wall. Faintly, he saw what he wanted. Hovering motionless, he reached out and pushed hard on two buttons the size of saucers. Behind him the two massive lock doors knifed closed, enveloping him within pitchy darkness.

Then, with extreme of caution, foot by foot, he directed his car ahead. After a little he turned right, toward where a dim light came from the control room, far up in the nose of the ship. More rapidly now he proceeded, through the long, longitudinal passageway and into the Gargantuan reach of wanly lighted control room. He climbed higher, and aimed for the panel of huge disks that were the control buttons.

Hovering by their side, he reached out and pushed at three he knew.

The floor started rapidly to rise. The ship was lifting. With all the skill he had, he met the floor.

V

Allison did not gloat at his luck in getting off, for it was far from certain that he would be able to win clear. Thousands of people would see the ship rise, and that would bring quick action. He had no idea what the offensive weapons of the natives might be. At the worse, they might bring him down with some destroying ray; but he counted on their not doing that. He was supposed to be a valuable property, and they unquestionably would want to take him alive. He could afford to chance their powers.

In his comparatively diminutive size, and faced by the danger of quick discovery, it had been impossible to investigate the stores of the ship before taking off, but in this he did not take so great a chance as may be thought. There were, primarily, only the factors of air, temperature, food, water, starting power, and navigation, and in all of these the probabilities were in his favor.

He was so tiny that there should be enough air in the craft to last him for a long trip even if the air-renewers were idle. The temperature was maintained automatically. As for food and water, the ship would at least have the "iron rations" and reserve tanks of water which interplanetary flying regulations required ships at all times to carry against emergency.

That the ship had the necessary starting power was already proved by the fact that she had lifted and her acceleration was being maintained. She was of the more recent type that utilized solar rays in transit, and there was therefore no concern over energy once she had got out into the airless void where the sun's rays shone always burning hot. Navigation was all but automatic and would not concern him until he was sure he was out of the atmosphere.

His immediate concern was light, and to get it he would use the unusual tool provided to his hand—the air-car. It would be a space ship within a space ship. It would serve him for the transportation. He laughed at his audacity in having thought of it.

Carefully he took off, and rose into the dangerous dimness that enveloped him on all sides. One error with the controls and he might dash into a wall, or the ceiling, and the end of his career as a scientist-adventurer would be a hundred-foot fall to the floor of what would turn out to be his coffin. He knew about where the switch was, but the multiplied height and the darkness made finding it critical. It was necessary to control his air-car with one hand while he felt with the other over the surface of the wall.

It took a little time, but eventually he found it. Using all his strength, he turned it on.

At sight of the vast control room under full light he got a new sense of his audacity—and his insignificance. Around him stretched a chamber three hundred feet long, and fully two thirds that in width and height. He had lived with the Mutrantians, and so had experience with interiors multiplied in size, but these dimensions for the control room of a space ship took his breath away. The chart table alone reached thirty feet up from the floor. Only an air-car would so much as enable him to get around.

He decided to investigate the food situation while the ship was getting out of the atmosphere. Carefully turning his car, the ethnologist glided down to within ten feet of the floor, and from that height skimmed back through the doorway into the corridor, where he came to a stop amidships, on the port side, in front of the galley door.

Here, for the first time, he had trouble. The door was closed, and there was the job of opening it. He found the handle, a curved, thick, iron bar more than a yard long, without difficulty, but all the strength of his right arm would not serve to lift it. He rested a moment and thought it over. Any tools he might find up in the tool locker would be far too heavy for him to work with from the car, so he decided to use the car itself.

Delicately maneuvering, he got the knobbed end of the handle hooked over the footboard of his car. Then, ready, he raised the elevator control of the car and at the same time directed its nose hard inward. The handle lifted and the door opened.

"Problem and solution," he thought, pleased, pushing the door back with the nose of his craft as elephants were used to push circus freight cars around. Allison prided himself on his capacity to solve problems.

Inside, there was again the need of finding the light switch, and this time, the room being in pitch darkness, he had far more trouble; but at length he found it and turned it on. No fresh provisions were in evidence anywhere, so he skimmed across to the row of gigantic lockers where canned food and water should be found.

Every locker was closed, so once more Allison used the car to pry up one of the handles, this time pulling, instead of pushing. He found this harder—and more dangerous. For as the door started slowly to open under the force he was exerting, the end of the handle slipped off the floor board and he suddenly found himself hurtling at dizzying speed into the opposite wall. Only in the nick of time did he cut his controls and zoom, to lose momentum at the ceiling.

"Phew!" he exclaimed. He realized that he was getting dull and tired. He could not have come out of that long period of enforced unconsciousness with much reserve of strength.

He glided down to the locker and looked in. There were the cans, just as in the Earthmen's ships—rows and rows of giant tin containers, stacked a hundred feet to the ceiling. Synthetic food tablets, all of one kind, from the labels in English.

With more care he opened the locker adjoining and found there similar cans of water. He felt considerably relieved. He was certain, at least, to eat and drink.

He now flew back to the main cabin for the one last thing to be done. The ship until then had been flying outward blindly; it remained for him to set it on its course for Earth. He climbed his little craft over to the great chart table to the forward end of the room where were the banks of dials and the rows of colored buttons whereby the ship was controlled.

A glance at a dial half as large as his ship showed a negligible amount of air outside, so he advanced thirty feet to hover like a humming bird in front of a green button with a large 3 on its face, and, feeling a little sentimental, reached out and pushed it in. Farther on he pushed in another, which would give him the ship's maximum acceleration. Then he glided to a landing on the immense flat top of the chart table and sat down. The rest was up to the ship's automatic navigator.

It was equal to the job. Its ultra-sensitive receivers picked up and identified every major planetary body in the solar system and sent the information through an overlapping labyrinth of seventy-two circuits where every navigation factor of location, spacial relation, planetary gravital pulls, ship's speed and acceleration and deceleration, planetary speeds and orbits, ship's destination, and so forth, were second by second electrically arranged and coordinated into the necessary resultant course; and it put the ship on that course, and corrected infinitesimal strayings, and would without attention start deceleration at the proper time, and bring the ship gently to ground in a place reserved for it in Earth's great space port at New York. All that Allison had to do, therefore, was set the buttons for destination and acceleration.

The ethnologist was tired and lay down where he was. He had done all that was possible. If his enemies followed and took steps to destroy him, it was too bad, but there was nothing he could do about it. This was a private ship and was equipped with no defensive screens or ray batteries.

At that, death was preferable to life with his normal instincts so altered by their devilish ingenuity that he would be a happy slave to them for the rest of his days. A man had an inalienable right to his own personality, and as a free citizen of the Federation of Earth he was never going to submit to having his taken away. Miss Brown wasn't so bad, but what if they were to marry him to one of those chinless damsels? What of his career in ethnology, so brilliantly started?

Well, the outcome was now in the hands of the gods.

He was surprised at how fatigued he was. He was hungry and thirsty, too, but he'd have to attend to that later; he hadn't strength just now to undertake the task of getting stuff out of those gigantic tins; or even to go back in the darkness of the stern and seek out one of the mammoth beds that would be there. He would sleep where he was.

He did sleep, a bearded doll on the chart table thirty feet up off the floor. He was almost the length of the sharp-pointed dividers a dozen yards away, and against the ruler that lay by his side he measured exactly six inches.

Allison awoke stiff and aching but refreshed, and in high good humor. He seemed to have slept for some time and was not yet burned to a cinder by a heat-ray, or dissolved into nothingness by a disintegrator; the solar motors of the ship were whining faintly but evenly; and before him stretched an adventure such as no man had ever had before.

He was going home. He was going to arrive safely. And he was going to descend spectacularly, in the greatest space ship ever built, with a story that would set three thousand million tongues awagging, and with a marvelous little air-car whose motive power was a mystery that all the physichemists of Earth would pounce happily on until they had its secret unraveled for Earth's own use.

And on the way he would have the pleasure of meeting, with his wits, all the bizarre problems which his discrepancy to the size of the ship would bring.

Buoyantly he jumped into his air-car and guided it to the galley; a drink first, and then food. But the water tins were twelve feet high, of tough, thick metal, sealed tight, and must have weighed, each one, several tons. Here was his first problem. The best solution lay in melting his way in with a hand heat-ray. He found one, a cylinder eight feet long and two thick, in one of the control-room tool lockers, after he had lifted up its lid with the help of his car.

With lengths of rope he found there, and again aided by the lifting power of his car, he got the heat-ray out of the box and into the middle of the galley floor. Next problem: how to get it aimed at the top edge of the bottom tin in one of the stacks. He flew back to the tool box and brought back, slung underneath, a seven-foot file. Then, changing the ropes to the heat-ray again, he lifted it to rest on the file; and after many trials, and getting out of his car each time to sight along the cylinder, he got it at approximately the angle he wanted.

He had taken pains to leave the push-button switch facing upward, and now he vaulted to a seat on the rear end of the cylinder and worked his way up to it. When he got there he pushed to his feet and stepped on it with all his weight.

A thin pinkish beam speared out, and a glow appeared on the side of the tin, a little lower than he had wanted. In seconds the metal melted, and before Allison could remove his foot a geyser of steam and scalding water shot out, spattering the floor in all directions. Some of it hit his arm, burning him painfully even through the sleeve, and causing him to lose his balance and slip to the floor.

The heat over there was terrific, but when the water in the tin had cooled, he would be able to get a drink. He smiled, a little grimly. Opening that tin had taken three hours.

While it was cooling he repeated the process on a tin of synthetic food in the locker adjoining, this time stepping briefly on and off the button several times, until he saw that the hole had been made.

This took another hour. And still he couldn't approach the lockers. He wiped his forehead and sat down to wait. He was exhausted with his exertions and faint from lack of food. It was not quite the lark he had anticipated, pitting his wits against the problems that arose from his comparative lack of size.

The little air-car might have meant the difference between life and death. He had called on it heavily for many hours, and had no means of knowing how much longer it would function without its energy giving out. Hereafter, he decided, he would use it as little as possible.

He lay back, and before he knew it was asleep. When he awoke he found the tins cooled, and ate and drank, and then slept some more. And when he awoke for the third time the long, deadly monotonous routine of his journey began.

There was nothing to do. The navigation of the ship was entirely automatic, so Allison could have no concern in that. The two tins he had opened had provided him with food and water that would last many times the probable duration of his trip back home. It was highly concentrated, predigested stuff, so that no time could be expended in its preparation. He had no duties. There were nowhere any books which might afford an opportunity for reading or translation.

Even the solar engine, the automatic navigator, and other machinery were locked inaccessibly in the spaces above the ceiling and below the floor, so he could not watch and study them. Had he dared to use the air-car as much as he wanted, he might in time have opened almost every door, locker, and cubby in the space ship; but many of them, including the radio cubby, were locked, and a few others stubborn, so their contents, if any, could not be reached. Only too well had the big ship been cleaned and all accessories put away after the Mutrantian's arrival at that land of mystery.

Men can spend their time sleeping, eating, working, and in recreation. Allison slept all he could; stretched out his meals of sandy, tasteless food tablets as long as he could. He made a bed under the chart table out of one of the coarse sheets from a Mutrantian bunk.

He started a complicated mechanism which would enable him to hang suspended before the eyepiece of the telescope which gave vision of the outside, and from there manipulate its controls, some of them thirty feet away—to stop when it became apparent that it would take far longer than the duration of his journey to finish it. And also he, for four or five hours each day, continued his monograph on the Mutrantian Titans by scratching the words laboriously on the floor of the control room with the points of the hundred-pound dividers left on the chart table.

For the rest of the time he prowled about the floor of the ship, investigating every corner like a rat without a hole. A toy man in those spaces, he skulked about; ran, to keep in condition; paced up and down, integrating ethnological data stored in his memory. And dreamed of the day when the ship would alight on the welcome bosom of Earth, and he'd be freed of the intolerable burden of life under the handicap of surroundings so colossal.

Days passed so, and weeks. The ship had long since been decelerating. The desire to get back into normal surroundings became an obsession in his mind. To sit at a table again! Friendly faces on the other side! Food, real food! And books, and work, and the theater, and human voices, and spring beds, and tools that would fit the hand, and things that he could lift! Mobility!

Sometimes he thought of the crowded events of the few short hours in the strange civilization left behind. Jones. The beautiful girl of the numbers. She had really loved him. He hoped she had not got in trouble.

Sometimes his thoughts were darker. Those two men—should he have made some wild quixotic attempt at their rescue?

Perhaps there were yet others locked in those rooms.

Why did those men so resemble him? And why that still-recurring image of the doll faces? Interminable rows of them. Each one with his own face, and each one, somehow, himself!

Now he would never know.

He was sitting thinking these thoughts in a corner of the control room one day when a jar, accompanied by a dull rumble, went over the ship, and her motors stopped. Allison sprang to his feet. He had landed! The journey was over! The great ship had brought him back at last to Earth!

He ran to his little air-car, parked under the telescope mounting, and jumped inside. He would give his welcomers a surprise. He would open the port doors and skim nonchalantly out over their heads. Within seconds he was gliding down the corridor and turning left along the transverse passage to where the port-lock buttons were located.

He pushed them, inner and outer in turn, and the huge metal doors slid back. Outside it was night, but a bright light flooded the wide opening. Fifty feet in the air, far above the heads of those who would be waiting, he skimmed out.

But he never received the welcome he expected. A titanic figure stepped forth and blocked his way; a hand eight feet across stabbed out and grabbed his little car; a thumb and forefinger that were colossal reached in and plucked him out.

For a second he was carried in dizzying flight through the air—and then he was dropped lightly into a Gargantuan side coat pocket.

VI

Allison was stunned. All he could think was that he had landed on Saturn's Satellite Three and was again in the hands of the Mutrantian Titans. The ship, not obeying the button marked 3, had taken him back to the land where it was owned. He was in the hands of the enemy; they'd not forget the damage he had done in his spectacular escape from them a few months before.

Tears of rage filled his eyes, that the long difficult journey had come to this. He had apparently been expected, and was being taken even now to the place where revenge would be taken. Out of the frying pan! He knew the Mutrantians.

He could hardly hope to escape again, but the instinct for self-preservation was strong, and he set about seeing what might be done.

The pocket he was in was deep; his upraised hands did not come within two feet of the top. But he thought he could make it. Grasping the canvaslike stuff he pulled himself up, inch by inch, until he got a grasp on the top edge, and then, straining mightily in the close press of the folds about him, he pulled himself up and got his arms hooked over, beneath the flap.

No sooner was he there than there came a stunning pressure through the flap, and he was shaken violently back down.

For a while he rested; and then, more quietly, he repeated the attempt. But the Titan was on his guard and again, more roughly, he was shaken down.

Only now, for the first time, did panic sweep over him. As best he could he controlled his feelings and considered what to do. But what could any one do, with his insignificant size in that extraordinary position? He was being carried half a hundred feet from the ground; even if he could get out of the pocket, how could he hope to get down and away? With a knife he might do some minor damage to the Titan and then try to cut his way out—but his knife was gone. He had searched himself a dozen times on the space ship, for to have had one then would have saved him many hours of toil; but all his pocket things had been removed while he was unconscious.

Nevertheless, almost automatically, by old habit, he started the search—and at what he found hope sprang to his heart and his nerves keyed to new possibilities. He still had the hypodermic. For the whole of the trip the little sack and needle, unneeded, had lain wrapped in a piece of bedding in his pocket. Carefully he got it out and uncovered it. It seemed in good order. If only it would have effect on a creature so large!

He attached it in his palm. He could not use it as he was, for the coat pocket was swinging free from the Titan's body, and its tiny needle would never reach. He would have to bring his carrier's hand to the pocket, as before.

To do it he set up a terrific commotion in the narrow space where he was. He bent and sprang and kicked and flung his arms about violently—and, as he had expected, from the other side of the pocket came a smothering pressure. Now was the time! Violently twisting his right arm free, he plunged its palm three times with all the strength he had at the nearest place the canvas pressed inward. At once the pressure from outside was removed; he had the sensation of falling, upsupported; and with a terrific jolt he came to a dead stop, dazed, bruised, and almost smothered.

He twisted free of the cloth against his face and rested, listening. There was no sign of motion, now. Cautiously, then, he squirmed his way up to the top of the pocket and got out.

He saw that he had brought the giant down on the sidewalk of an immense, deserted street—and, to his dismay, that he was lying on his left side, on top of the pocket which he had counted on to contain the air-car. Not having it would greatly lessen his chances of getting away; but there was nothing to be done about salvaging it. He could only set out on foot and travel as great a distance as possible before the unconscious Titan came to, or was discovered. His objective would be the space ship he had just left, for only that ship offered a way to get free of the planet.

From the Titan's position Allison could tell the direction he had been going, and without further delay he started running back in the other direction.

The street he was on was of fabulous proportions, and in spite of his former experiences among the Mutrantians he took in his surroundings with awe. The street, from curb to curb, was over one hundred and fifty yards in width, and the sidewalk he was on not less than fifty. On his side, hundreds of yards into the sky, towered one colossal building of many stories, and along the other was a hundred-foot fence, all of wooden planks ten feet wide. Electric street lamps shone like fixed star-shells at long intervals down the street to where, half a mile away, shone neon and other colored tubes marking an important intersection.

Allison slowed down to a walk. A hundred yards ahead loomed the glass-and-metal canopy before the entrance of the great house he was passing, and just to one side, already outlining him in its powerful rays, was a street lamp. That meant danger. His safest course would be to get down into the street and pass by close to the curb.

He crossed to the edge of the pavement and looked down. It was an eight-foot drop.

Sitting first, then turning and holding by his hands, he lowered himself over the stone ledge and dropped to the street. From there, hugging close to the sheltering curb wall, he passed safely under the light and beyond in one long sprint; but as he slowed to a walk he began to worry how he ever would be able to cross the street he was coming to. If he had only been able to get his air-car!

Two eyes of fire turned Allison's way in the distance and quickly grew to alarming proportions. Could they belong to some gigantic animal? He tried to scramble up over the curb onto the pavement; but it was too high, and, paralyzed by fear, he crouched low at its base, instead, and saw the eyes grow to the size of hogsheads, and grow and grow, devouring him with merciless light—till at the terrific speed of two hundred and fifty miles an hour they passed him with queer noises only twenty feet away, pulling him head over heels after in the wind displaced by their passage. As he picked himself up and looked back he saw a titanic bulk with one evil red eye diminish down the street.

An automobile!

That was strange. The Mutrantians had very few automobiles.

Anyhow, he had again been lucky. It had not stopped for—or seen —the Titan he had left unconscious behind.

He hurried on; alternated walking and running for a while. His victim might revive any second, for the tiny amount of fluid he had injected would hardly keep him under long, and he was still in his immediate vicinity.

As he approached the intersecting street he saw other autos pass by there, and the shape of them was several times familiar. A fear that would not down took possession of him, and goose-flesh rose all over his body as he hurried yet nearer. It was preposterous, it was too horribly fantastic, the fear he had; but there was no mistaking those body lines; and the glass-and-metal canopy before the entrance of the great house he still was passing—that, too, now that he thought of it, had looked familiar.

He was very close to the street now, and seeing a ten-foot piece of newspaper in his way he picked it up and placed it over his head. It seemed to him to be as heavy as stiff cardboard. Under cover of this, still hugging the protecting wall of the curb, he stole furtively nearer.

People were passing; colossi; but they wore the costumes of Earthmen! And the letters on that window high up way over there certainly looked like "Restaurant."

Heart in his throat, Allison ventured closer and closer to the corner. The legend *did* read restaurant; the passing autos were of American make; the very newspaper that was his camouflage bore printing in a gigantic English! And up by the street lights were name plates such as he had seen a million times before—and the numbers on their faces told him that he was at Forty-ninth Street and First Avenue.

He was back on Earth. In the heart of New York City. Of a New York grown colossal, in every dimension, and that had left him and him only far down from normal size.

Or, more probable, it was his surroundings that were normal, and he reduced in size.

What had Jones done to him? Why? Why?

Stunned, stupid with shock, he stood there, until he came to full realization of his tragic plight. And then he sat down under his paper and cried.

Allison sat there in the gutter for a long time, and for a while went quite out of his mind. A few yards away the night traffic of a great metropolitan artery streamed up and down, while he, the only one of his size on Earth, sat utterly helpless and hopeless under the miserable sheet of wind-blown newspaper that alone hid his degradation from the eyes of his kind.

In gallant spirit he had taken up the out-worlder's offer and trusted him. When it seemed that he was to be betrayed he had with high, clear courage won free; run that great space ship back to Earth; and only now was he to see that it had all been for worse than nothing. The irony was a knife in his heart; and his shame, in that mouselike size, was unendurable.

The traffic thinned; store lights went out. The tears on the face of the miserable little atom under the paper dried away, and in their place came an expression of gaunt courage. Allison knew what he would do.

He would kill Jones.

That Jones would return for him, he had no doubts. He "knew too much," and the out-worlder would have either to recapture or destroy him. Already he had made the attempt—for who, other than some agent of his, could it have been that had kidnaped him from the space ship?

He would come to Allison's laboratory, and Allison would be ready for him.

Until then, only two men would ever see him as he was—his best friend, Doctor Heiler, the physicist who occupied the other half of the top floor where he lived and worked at 301 W. 22nd Street, and his old college mate Jack Peyton, a struggling writer who lived around the corner from First Avenue on Fiftieth Street. Peyton would have to know in order to take him to Heiler, for alone he could never get to the house where he lived without discovery, or into Heiler's quarters without great danger of running right into the out-worlder.

It would be extremely difficult to so much as get to Peyton. The short block he lived north, twenty to the Earthman's mile, was over half a mile to him, and the night traffic along First Avenue, mainly trucks, was considerable. But Allison thought he could do it.

Allison waited a while longer under his newspaper camouflage, then, making a hole in the middle of it for his eyes, advanced cautiously under it to the great round curve which was the curb corner itself, and sneaked around. There were then few passers-by—only the trucks, titanic monsters that shook the ground under his feet as they appeared at terrific speed and passed in a discordant jangle of sounds quite unlike those heard by normal ears.

He walked at half speed and stopped still when, over the verge of the curb, he saw a pedestrian approach, or, down the street, a truck; and all that any one glancing his way might have seen was a sheet of old newspaper that occasional light gusts of wind was blowing along the gutter.

He could not keep his eyes where his feet were stepping, and several times he tripped and fell, once over a stone in his path, and again over a twisted package that had contained cigarettes. From time to time he reached a parked automobile, and then he would run until he reached its farther side. He found he was getting hungry; and, realizing what was yet before him, he at one place stopped with his paper over a banana peeling, lifted back, with an effort, one of its flaps, and ate briefly of the bit of pulpy fruit that remained in its end.

It took him exactly thirty-seven minutes to walk that short block north, and by the time he had rounded the curb wall on Fiftieth Street and seen the vast stretch that still lay ahead of him he was growing tired.

Peyton, being very poor, lived in one of the few old-fashioned cold-water tenement houses that remained in New York, a house on the north side of the street, with a stoop of half a dozen high brownstone steps. It being June, both doors should be open, and allow entrance into the dark, bare, smelly hall, halfway back, in which were steps which led upward, and which he would somehow have to climb to reach the second-story where his friend's room was. As he remembered it, the house was about one third the long east-west block from the corner—nearly a mile, to him. He hoped devoutly he would be able to recognize it.

He crossed the hundred and fifty yards of street-width in one long sprint, and fetched up breathless on the other side. He got there just in time. A seventy-foot young man and a sixty-five foot young woman turned the corner and started west up the street. Under the street light, house-high over his head, he saw the man talking earnestly to the girl. Slowly, his great lips opened and closed; but no word could be heard. The vibration frequency of their tones was far too low for his tiny eardrums. Only low rumbles and a comic jabber of squeaks and squawks—overtones and errant noises made by imperfections in the vocal apparatus—reached his ears.

And it was all that would ever reach his ears. Unless Doctor Heiler could make some instrument——

He waited for the two to get well ahead. They were probably sweethearts, he reflected bitterly. How could there ever be love for him—a circus side-show freak, whose toy proportions could only arouse vulgar gawks from the many and pity from the few! He was very proud, and pity he would never be able to endure. Quite, quite alone, a ludicrous watch charm of a man, he would live, until that time when his one purpose in life was realized and he free to end the whole ironic jest forever.

He thought of the girl of the numbers. She had loved him. Somewhere in the solar system, in a place unknown and unattainable, she, a girl of his size, was perhaps thinking of him. She, alone of all others, held or could hold a place of warmth for him in her cheerful, lovely little heart.

He held on to that thought, for it was good.

But there was hard, bitter work ahead. He discarded his paper, walked and ran along the curb until he came to the building which he recognized as his destination. The curb there was his own height, and with a jump and vigorous press-up he rolled over the edge onto the pavement. Above him the two house doors stood open, but between rose five steps, each eight feet high. Inside, up to the second floor, there would be a score more. How was he to get up them?

At his height of six inches he was exactly one seventeen hundred and twenty-eighth of his old self, and his strength was in proportion. He weighed one and one half ounces.

VII

Allison needed a ladder. He would try to make one. It called for two upright stems at least six feet long; but less than three shorter pieces for rungs, and cord. He set about scouring the vicinity of the house for things that would serve. It was very dark, but he was so close to the ground that anything not black could be easily discerned.

Eighty yards from the southwest corner of the first step he found a fine long stick of straight tough stuff that would do for a rung. Its end was bulbous and charred. It was a used match.

One hundred and twenty yards farther, near the curb, he found another, a little shorter, and carried it back to the first, and both to the step. Ten minutes later, over the edge of the curb in the street, he saw no less than two, only a few yards apart. He went down over the side and lifted them up, then climbed back and carried them, one under each arm, over to the others. Four would be enough, for the rungs.

He still needed cord and uprights. He went forth and searched hard, but after fifteen minutes he had not found a thing. That pavement was kept all too clean.

He sat down a moment to rest. What might he reasonably hope to find for uprights among the trifling litter of normal-sized human beings? Nothing, that he could think of.

He fared forth again. Bending low, and sometimes feeling with his finger tips, he searched the gutter and pavements of an immense area extending as far as four houses away; and after one hour and twenty minutes he returned lugging three hairpins and one long length of dirty white rope—string, he once would have called it— after him.

It took all the strength he had to bend the hairpins to single length, and he might have failed altogether had he not been so fortunate as to find a pretty good crevice angling slightly from the straight side of one of the blocks that made the pavement—a crevice that held securely to one side of the hairpin while he could apply leverage to the end of the other. In one of them, the shortest, he rebent a hook near one end.

Harbingers of dawn were streaking the eastern sky as at last he started getting his materials together. It did not take long. The one length of rope, since he had no means of cutting it, could be carried in turn to all the rungs on one side, and then around to all those on the other. When he finished he had a heavy ladder five feet high, with four rungs each one foot wide.

With an effort he carried and placed it against the first step. It lacked three feet of reaching the top, but he had arranged for that. Grasping the remaining shorter hairpin, he climbed his ladder to the top, pushed the hairpin over the edge of the step above, and followed up after. Then, using the hook on the shorter hairpin, he pulled the ladder up after him.

He had climbed the first step.

In fifteen minutes he was in the open vestibule, dragging his hook and ladder after him in the long trip to mid-hall where the stairway to the upper floors was.

Allison was never to forget the weary time he had climbing that new set of steps. Already tired to exhaustion, he had for eighteen more times to go through with the back-breaking routine of climbing eight inches upward—pushing his hook up and over, before, and with it pulling his heavy ladder up, after. Daylight came on apace, and through the dirty window, halfway up, revealed him as a tiny purposeful doll in a long white dress. When the last step had been surmounted, Allison sat right down where he was for a moment of rest.

He needed it. His labors since leaving the space ship had been titanic, his emotions had taken their own heavy toll—and his metabolic rate was much higher in toy size than when normal.

He got up refreshed, but already a little stiff. It occurred to him that he might be able to make enough noise on Peyton's door to rouse him from sleep; so, rather anxious, dragging his hook and ladder after him, he started down the long stretch of wooden planking to the rear, where his friend's room opened off the left.

He arrived and knocked; then, suspecting that he had made pitifully little noise, he turned his back to the door and kicked hard with the heel of his shoe. There was no answer. As he had feared, he was unable to make himself heard.

The crack under the door, however, was almost an inch—a foot— in depth, and, with considerable relief, he found he was able to squeeze in under it. There was much more light on the other side. There was enough for him to see at once that the couch which served his friend for a bed was covered with its usual daytime cover and was unoccupied.

This was a major misfortune. He had never considered the possibility that his friend might not be there.

He dropped his hook and ladder on the floor and looked around. Two windows, one in the back wall and one, partly opened, on the left, showed up a dirty and disordered room. Along the right wall was the unoccupied couch; in front of the remaining one a sink and a four-foot cupboard on whose top rested a gas plate; and between the windows stood a chair and flimsy card table which Peyton used as a desk. These made up most of the furnishings of the room.

Allison walked over to the cupboard, the door of which stood slightly ajar. He was weak for food and hoped desperately that some-

thing loose might be lying around that he could eat. He was unable
to pull the door open any farther, so he stepped right through the
narrow opening above the one-foot board that formed its base.

There was nothing there. Only a row of canned goods—baked
beans and salmon, in six-foot tins. How he hated the sight of tins!
He disappeared around the side of one and rummaged in the back—
and when he came into view again he held five, large stale crumbs in
his left hand and was eating heartily from a six-inch piece of cheese
in his right.

He had found a baited mousetrap. And food had never tasted so
good.

Munching his cheese and gnawing with his side teeth one of the
rock-hard crumbs he had found, he went over and sat down against
one leg of the couch. His position was still precarious; chiefly in the
matter of food. He had no air-car. What was he to do?

As he ate and considered, Allison was suddenly aware of movement off under the far end of the couch to his right. Startled, he
looked, and in the dimness he saw two unblinking eyes of yellow
fire. It was Peyton's cat. He had utterly forgotten that Peyton had
a cat.

The hair rose on the back of his neck, and with one push he was
on his feet. The cat at his movement bellied forward a few yards, a
nerve-taut orange tiger, tail lashing. It was stalking him.

And he was fair prey. Only shoulder-high to the cat would he
stand; he'd be but one fiftieth its weight. Lighter than a mouse.

He tried frantically to remember the cat's name, but for the life
of him he couldn't. It bellied a little closer. Desperately he called
out soothing cat talk; but words that at other times might have
caused it to purr, now had absolutely no effect. It was preposterous!
That cat had been his friend; he had petted it a score of times; and
now in his helpless size it no longer knew him and was preparing to
take his life. For all of his human brains, he, weaponless, would not
fare even so well as a mouse.

With a thrill he remembered that he was not weaponless. Out
came Jones' hypodermic, and in a second was fitted into his palm.
It was a poor-enough weapon against the lightning speed of a cat's
claw, but it would have to do.

He advanced boldly against the cat. He would not have had time
to reach the cupboard, and he had always found it safest, when possible, to attack.

In this, brains showed. The cat, surprised, backed; circled; crouched again. He followed it up. Noiselessly it backed toward the door; crouched; circled from there. Allison could then have backed out through the crack under the door; but that would have got him nothing; and moreover a strange new elation had come to him—the lust to conquer. He felt, with that weapon, that he could win. Forward to the cat, then, he went; back and to the side it retreated, crouching every time it stopped. It clearly was disconcerted by his unexpected advance.

At the wall under the card table it stood its ground, and Allison felt that that would be the place to see the end. He advanced to within its own length of it; stood ready, right arm out. The cat opened its mouth in a noiseless hiss, and he was drenched with the creature's breath.

He gestured with his arm. The cat's front quarters lifted from the floor, and, ears flat, made a lightning swipe at his hand. It touched; the cat fell slowly to its side; and like that it was over.

Allison brought up his forearm—numb, from the violence with which it had been hit back. His hand was slit deeply in two places, and dark blood was dripping copiously from the openings. But it had been better to take the cat's claws there than over his body. And it would have been his body if he had not forced the creature to make a swipe that was half defensive.

He lost no time in tying up the cat with a piece of cord found under the sink; and then, staggering with fatigue, trembling all over with the reaction to the encounter, he was setting himself to think of a way to climb to the basin and get water out of the spigot, when to his overpowering joy he found a saucer of it nearly full, that had been left on the floor for the cat.

He drank, as deeply as he dared, then washed and tended his wounds. Then, on the cat's own cushion under the couch, he lay down and slept.

The sun showed mid-afternoon through the western window when he awoke. Terribly stiff, aching all over, he got up, saw that the cat still lay unconscious, sat a while in thought and then set to work.

He did many curious things, all under the terrific handicap usual to the predicament of his size. He routed out a cardboard box that dental powder had come in; removed the corrugated paper inside; opened both ends of the box so that it could be pressed flat, and pushed box and paper under the hall door. He found some medical cotton and pushed that under; also a long unsharpened pencil. He did the same with a long piece of string, to which at one end he had tied several paper clips. He took a piece of manuscript paper from the table; wrote some large words on it; found some stamps and a razor blade—and pushed them under. Then he squeezed under himself and returned after nearly an hour.

But then the sun had gone down, and he was exhausted again. He ate a little more of the mouse's cheese, drank some more water from the cat's saucer, and then lay down once more on the cushion and went to sleep.

It was pitch dark when Allison awoke. He got up at once, released the still-unconscious cat, drank all the water he could hold, and pushed out under the door. He could not be sure, but after reconnoitering the second-floor hall he came to the conclusion that it was after midnight, and time for what he had in mind, so he returned to the hall door and dragged to the stairhead what he had secreted there. It was the tooth-powder box, now wrapped up, and within, visible through one end, the corrugated pasteboard, cotton, razor blade, string with the clips, and the long unsharpened pencil.

The coast seemed clear; he pushed the box containing all this through the rungs of the banister to the main-floor landing below, then followed down himself by way of the steps—sitting, turning over the edge, letting himself down by his arms and then dropping—all these eighteen times until he was at the bottom.

There, he retrieved his box, filled it as before, and dragged it to the vestibule, where he cautiously surveyed the street. It was dark and obviously very late. Nothing stirred except the occasional trucks and taxis far down the corner of First Avenue. Assured, he pushed the box and its contents off onto the broad top step, lowered himself there, then pushed it off the side to the pavement and again followed down.

Fifteen minutes later, dragging his box laboriously behind him, he arrived at a letter box precisely halfway in the block toward Second Avenue; and that was his destination.

He proceeded to work with unhesitating efficiency. First he took the pencil out of the box and laid it on the ground. Then he removed the string and tied its free end to the base of the letter box. After four tries he succeeded in casting the clip-tied end over the top of the letter box; and when its weight had carried the string down on the other side climbed that string to the top.

He sat there a moment—a bloody, bearded, six-inch gnome, still in his dirty white dress—and after he was rested rose, tied the string by its middle to the letter-drop door, and slid down one string to the ground.

And now had his string tied at one end of the base of the letter box, a slack length leading from there up to the letter-drop knob, and the long loose clip end hanging free.

He tied the tooth-powder box to this clip end.

Next, he stuck the pencil, head high, in a loop he made in the string attached at both ends, and began, in the fashion of one tightening a tourniquet, to twist. He twisted it many scores of times, and when he had finished, the letter-drop door was held open.

He rested a little, then once more climbed hand over hand to the top of the letter box. There, he rested again, then pulled up the tooth-powder box to position in the open mouth of the letter drop. And, that done, he got down in the mouth alongside his box, and took out the razor blade and cut both strings.

The letter-drop door closed, and he and the little box fell down into the inside of the letter box.

Fifteen minutes later he himself was in the little tooth-powder box, and it was closed, the outer paper gathered at the end and tied.

He had mailed himself. How else was he to get to Doctor Heiler?

There was no telling when Peyton would return; probably not for some time, from the window he had left open for the cat to get in and out by way of the fire escape. If Allison had waited, he might have starved, for he was none too sure that he would have been able to open one of those cans of beans, helpless and without tools as he was.

It was better, anyway, that Peyton did not know. That would leave only Heiler.

Snug in his cotton-padded box, Allison tried to sleep. Once more he was dog-tired. The acts that were casual nothings to normal people had required titanic energies on his part. He was lame all over, and his right arm, now that it was no longer being used, was beginning to ache intolerably.

He thought back over the amazing events of the last twenty-four hours—Jones' agent, whom he had left lying unconscious back on Forty-ninth Street—the heart-bursting discovery that he had been reduced to a pitiful toy—his colossal labors in getting to Doctor Heiler. He had performed feats that once he would have called impossible; but now the worst was over. His friend would take him in: would guard his secret; and would help him prepare a way to kill without possible failure that traitor Jones when he should call on him once more.

It was good that Heiler lived just down the hall from him. He would have perfect protection, and yet be close to his own laboratory.

Sleep came gradually, and when it did it was filled with the face of Jones, and a lovely girl, his own size, whom he would never see again, and two men who looked remarkably like himself—and always, ever returning, doll faces, rows of them, each one identical with himself, and each one somehow himself.

He was rudely awakened by the shock of his plunge into the postman's bag, and knew, then, it must be morning.

There was no sleep after that. He rode; was jolted; rested; was jolted, rode, and rested some more; and then was off in a carrier's bag on the way to his own house. He could hear nothing, but could tell when he was being carried up the steps and given to the maid. She would now be carrying him up to his old friend Heiler.

A pause, and he came to rest.

Another pause, but Allison couldn't wait. He pushed aside the string and paper at the top end of the box and looked out. He was on the desk in his own laboratory. Fearfully he continued out and looked around.

His high-backed swivel chair pivoted; a colossus was seated there. And the high-looming features of the colossus were those of the man called Jones.

VIII

For a moment Allison crouched there, petrified.

Then the great features above spread up in a smile, and that released him, and in instant wild panic he was scrambling back over the surface of the desk looking for a way to get down. Jones' hand came swooping through the air, but before it could close over him he had made one wild jump out beyond the edge of the table to the cord leading up to the reading lamp, had closed his arms about it and was sliding down its rough, wavy length.

He was skinned and bleeding when he reached the floor, but at once he was away and looking for a place—any place—to escape into. Nothing near by offered. The desk was placed forty yards out from the wall, and far to one side, in the corner, stood a high, heavy specimen cabinet. If he could make that!

The colossal feet under the desk were moving; Jones' head and arm appeared into view above them. Allison seized his chance and ran with all his might over the hundred-yard open space to the cabinet. After him charged Jones; but he reached it safely and retired far under its base. Its height was such that he just had room to stand erect.

He got out his hypodermic. He was cornered; but let Jones' fingers come near enough and he was as good as dead!

Heart beating like a frightened mouse, Allison waited. What would his enemy do? Get the broom and sweep him out? Then bat him to death as one would a cockroach?

He watched the man's feet. They lifted out of sight, lowered, slowly, one at a time; receded: he was returning to the desk. A pause, then the feet returned. Knees appeared, and hands; the man's head showed. He was wearing over his head and mouth an apparatus not unlike that of a telephone operator. Then Allison heard words, the first since he had left the other's civilization, weeks—it seemed years —before. The word-sounds were extremely attenuated; he could not recognize them as belonging to Jones.

"Come out, Allison," they said. "I won't hurt you."

"Come and get me!" the ethnologist challenged, hoping fervently that he would reach in and try.

"All right; but throw out the hypodermic first," came the long-drawn-out reply.

"Like hell I will!" exclaimed Allison passionately. Jones knew! He was prepared! Despair seized him. He was lost.

He waited to see what would happen next. Jones wasted no more words, but returned to the desk and occupied himself there in a manner Allison could not see. Then he returned, and knelt down again.

"All right, 372, if you will," he said.

What did these cryptic words mean?

Allison waited, tense, far back under the cabinet. Jones' cupped hands lowered near the front edge; one was removed; and off the other stepped a tiny man, his own size. He wore a soft-green robe and sandals; was clean and freshly shaven; and in figure, face, and bearing he was another himself!

He stepped under the front edge of the cabinet and looked around. Allison, amazed and frightened, cowered farther back. Jones' face appeared at the floor, watching.

"I say, Allison, how are you?" exclaimed the double, seeing the other and starting heartily over to him.

"Who are you?" Allison asked fearfully, backing still more. The fellow had his own voice!

"372." The other laughed. "You're 793—though I know you aren't aware of it. But heavens, man—how you look!"

Allison looked the wreck he was. His dresslike costume was torn and filthy; his arm was burned; his hands were skinned, swollen, raw, and bleeding; and on his face was a tangled, matted three-inch yellow beard.

"Who are you?" Allison repeated, crouching, devouring him with bloodshot eyes, ready at a flash to run or strike, like a man cornered by his own ghost.

"Come on out, old fellow, and I'll explain," said the double kindly. He made as if to grasp Allison's upper arm.

"If you touch me, you die!" growled the ethnologist intensely, avoiding his hand.

Jones' voice floated in. "Watch out! He has a hypodermic!"

"Oh!" said the double and held himself with more caution. "Allison," he said seriously to the other, "you've been a damn fool. We're not here to hurt you. Come on out and——"

"Go away!" Allison interrupted, crouching lower, a wild light in his eyes. "Go away! Go away!" he replied shrilly, utter desperation in his voice.

The double took a step back. "I think he is a little mad," he said to Jones.

The two men faced each other tensely. They were the same person, except that one stood erect, fresh, confident, and in full health and strength, and the other was bruised, battered, bloody, spent, and crouched like a cornered rat about to spring.

"Give me that needle," the double said.

Allison's head went a little lower. His lips drew back over his teeth like an animal's. Without warning he jumped and struck out.

Like a mongoose dodging a cobra the double leaped back, and his own right arm flashed forth, caught the other's by the wrist and held it. It was his fresh strength against the last reserves of the ethnologist's, and the balance was all for him. He twisted the wrist; the arm gave backward; and both fell to the floor, he on top. Carefully, still holding the wrist at the breaking point, he removed the sack and threw it out to Jones. Then he dragged his wildly threshing prisoner out in the open.

Jones was waiting to relieve him. Gently, so as to give no hurt, he enfolded Allison in one hand, took the double up in the other, and carried both over to the desk. There he placed the two on the blotter, ringed them with his hands, and sat down.

Allison at once shied away from the double.

"I admire you, 793," Jones said. "But you've put me to an extraordinary amount of trouble."

The ethnologist turned and looked up at him. "And look what you've done to me! he yelled back, panting. "I accepted your offer in all good faith. I was to come to no harm. And the first thing I discovered was that I was just another victim whose mind you intended to pervert. Jones, you're the system's lowest, most treacherous skunk!"

The out-worlder smiled a little; but Allison found it impossible to read his face when it was so big. The double at his side startled him, speaking up in defense.

"No, no—you're all wrong! Let him explain."

"Explain how he kept his agreement by reducing me to this size?" Allison retorted bitterly. "Who are you, anyway?"

"Tell him," the double said to Jones.

"Will you listen to what I have to say?" the out-worlder asked in his slow-creeping voice.

"I don't see that I have any choice," Allison spat back.

There was a pause.

"I'll have to start far in the past," the colossus began at last.

"Forty-five thousand years ago the human race was one, and lived only on Earth. One segment of that race, living on a great warm island in the South Pacific, developed a mighty civilization. You Earthmen of today who live in what you call the scientific age are but in the early groping stages of the civilization that was your forebears' at that time.

"Among other things, the human race had perfected space ships and ventured out into the void. It set up colonies on other planets suitable. And when the day predicted for centuries by its geologists came, and the great island that was its home began to sink under the surface of the sea, it was ready, and in thousands of space ships set forth, some for out-world portions of the solar system, and the rest to other and more stable parts of Earth.

"There was but one blood. The Mutrantian Titans, who in your work under preparation will be held up as a cousin strain to that of Earthmen, are so in fact. They are the descendants of one colony of the Earthmen of forty-five thousand years ago. Their size resulted from local conditions which I need not go into.

"I am of a race you would call pygmies; but we, for good reasons, deliberately reduced ourselves to that size. We have for a long time known how to do it. I, to attain my present size, for purposes of mixing among you Earthmen, simply underwent the reverse of the process. But I and my kind are of the human race. We are the descendants of another colony.

"We have always been a small colony, for our environment did not encourage a great population. In time we were exposed to the dangers of inbreeding. We did the logical thing. Every so often we obtained from our brother colonies new stock, with varied and vigorous hereditary factors different from those in us. This new stock we scientifically infiltrated through our own; and so we kept the fecundity and the vigor of our strain——"

"Jones," interrupted Allison hotly, "you're lower than a dog to have taken me, and others like me, for use as studs in the series of matings which would be necessary for that result!"

The out-worlder showed no anger. "There are no 'series of matings,' and won't be," he answered. "And you—Allison—were the only Earthman we took."

"I have positive knowledge that you mated off other Earthmen while I was there," contradicted the ethnologist.

"I know what you know," the other said. "Miss CB-301 voluntarily came and told me. But in spite of what you saw through the search-beam, you were the only Earthman concerned."

"You're a liar!" Allison flung back.

Still the out-worlder showed no sign of anger. Patiently he went on:

"You learned a little, but not enough. When you escaped it became necessary to follow and bring you back, for we could not have you disseminating false information, or indeed any. It was thought most expedient to take you upon your arrival here. To that end I arranged for the private grounding of my space ship, which you had appropriated, and one of my men was there waiting.

"You know what happened. You got away from him, and went I don't know where. But it was certain that you would try to return to your home, so I came here and waited for you. And, naturally, your friend, Doctor Heiler, was watched, and your suspicious package brought in to me.

"Now," he concluded, "I am going to take you back."

"I prefer to be destroyed!"

"You won't, later."

"That's the damnable part of it! What, then, will you do with me?"

"I will hold you to your part of our agreement."

"Meaning, you'll force me to marry a never-ending series of your disgusting females with the prognathous foreheads—and like it."

"You will mate only with one."

"One is too many. I shall never arrive back there alive."

"You will be watched," the colossus said significantly. He smiled a little.

"It happens, though," he went on, "that I have promised you to Miss CB-301. Would that be so painful? She loves you. If," he added, "you could find it in your heart to love her, I think we might make an exception in your case and not force you by the means we have."

Allison was in the man's power; why should he grant favors? He was skeptical.

"Jones," he said, "I don't trust you and don't believe you. My mating with that girl—or any one of your women, no matter how prolific she might be—would have no effect whatever on the racial stock of a city like yours."

Jones smiled. "Doctor Allison has already mated with 1722 of our women," he said.

For a moment the ethnologist could not believe his ears. Then he dismissed the remark with an expression of irritation. "You talk crazy!" he said.

"Do you not know," the out-worlder asked calmly, "that theoretically it is possible to divide in half the various molecules which make up an object and reassemble them to make two of that object, exactly like it, only smaller? Some day you Earthmen will learn to do it; but we can do it already. We can split objects into fifties, hundreds; we can do it with the living human body!

"Shortly after Doctor Allison had come to us, he, the original 178-pound Doctor Allison, was split up into 1728 little ones, each identical with the original except in the matter of size. You are one of those little ones. Mr. 372, here, is another. You each weigh approximately one and a half ounces."

A great light burst over Allison's mind. He saw again that fearful recurring image of the doll faces. Interminable rows of them. Each face *his* face, *and every one somehow himself.*

They had been those doll faces! Sometime during the process he in the large size had become aware of the scene before him and had subconsciously remembered.

He gaped foolishly at the out-worlder. The new vista of possibilities which his words had opened up was overpowering. Jones smiled.

"Yes," he said, "1728 little ones, and 1722 are already mated with our women.

"I'm sorry," he added, "but five died, for various reasons out of our control. When you all are eventually recombined, Doctor Allison will weigh several ounces less. I don't think he will mind, though, for he can more than make that up in one good meal."

Allison still stood as if turned to stone. The man really did seem to be telling the truth. He must have been sincere all along.

"You will recall," Jones went on, "that I promised Doctor Allison he would be returned here unharmed after four months. He will be. All your—well, brothers, now so happily married, will just before that time undergo the reverse of the process whereby we made them fall in love; and then all will be assembled. You will be one of them. I am in conscience bound to see that every one of his living partitions are present."

The colossal face smiled. "Of course, for all that desire it, there will be a suitable ceremony of divorce."

The smile faded. There was a pause. "Has it occurred to you," Jones asked, "that I am reasoning with you, not just snatching you? On the face of it, I might be telling the truth."

Allison no longer doubted, but his thoughts were elsewhere. 1723 matings! That many homes—angles—environments! All parts of himself, later to be recombined into himself!

"Think of the new knowledge!" Jones said.

Was the man smiling?

"Why hasn't anyone ever brought his knowledge back to Earth with him?" Allison asked with sudden sharp suspicion.

"Before leaving, we removed it from their minds," came the frank, easy answer. "We'll of course do that with Doctor Allison too."

So! Well, if he ever had that knowledge in one person, *he'd come* back with it! Somehow! Somehow.

He hesitated, still shaken, thinking, a doll beside another doll on the great table over which leaned the colossus who had been his enemy. He felt a touch on his arm. It was 372.

"Don't be deterred by thoughts of that ugly young atavism," the fellow said encouragingly. "They'll get you some one more beautiful than she." His face lighted up. "Personally, I've had the greatest of luck. I understand about the machine; but deep down I know right well there's something more than that between KS-971 and myself. It's beyond words. Even to see her! Her mouth! Her scalp—not a hair! Her high, wide, wrinkled forehead!"

He'd been in the machine, all right.

Allison still hesitated. So all his struggles had come to this! "Service." "Applied, and very, very practical ethnology." Yes; and one very, very widely applied ethnologist.

There was that lovely girl of the numbers. She loved him. Even Jones had said she loved him. He was bruised and weary; he needed very much to have some one lovely and kind and warm——

"After all, you don't have any choice," the out-worlder reminded him.

793 shrugged. "All right," he said with a sigh. "If you will agree to enlarge Miss CB-301 to earth-size and permit her to return with me."

Jones smiled. "As you wish," he said. He rose and picked up the two tiny men. He put them in a little box in his pocket and walked out of the door.

AS NEVER WAS

by

P. SCHUYLER MILLER

*Consider, for a moment, the complexities and contradictions
of time travel. It involves, for example, your living in a time
before you were born; i.e., before you lived! Or, it may involve
your traveling to the future and living in a time after you have
died. Few illustrations of the completeness of the paradox that is
time travel have been so well drawn as Mr. Miller's story of
the knife. That knife of wonderful metal that—by ordinary logic
—could never have been placed where—and when—it was found.*

*

HAVE YOU ever dreamed of murder?

Have you ever set your elbows on the desk and let your head
slump down on your hands, and closed your eyes, and dreamed of how
it would feel to drive a knife up to the hilt in a scrawny, wrinkled
throat, and twist it until the thin old blood begins to slime your
fingers and drip from your wrist—until the piercing old eyes roll back
and close, and the skinny old legs crumple and sag? Have you felt the
blood pounding in your own temples, and savage satisfaction swarming up in you as you stare down on the hideous, sprawling thing you
have destroyed?

And then have you opened your eyes and looked down at the mass
of scribbled papers, and the meticulously drawn sectional charts, and
the trait tables and correlation diagrams and all the other dead, dry
details that make up your life's work? And picked up your pen and
started making more scribbles on the papers and more checks on the
charts and more little colored dots on the scattergrams, just as you've

been doing three days out of every five since you were old enough to
start the career for which you'd been tested and picked and trained?

Maybe I should go to a clinic and let the psychotherapists feed
vitamins to my personality. Maybe I should go to a religious center
and let the licensed clergy try to put this fear of Humanity into my
reputed soul. Maybe I should go to a pleasure palace and let them mix
me up an emotional hooker to jar the megrims out of my disposition,
or go down and apply for a permit to wed and set about begetting
another generation of archeologists who will grow up to be just as tired
and bored and murderous as their illustrious father.

Night after night and day after day I dream of what might have
happened that day in the laboratory if I had picked up the knife and
slit the gullet of the man who had just injected the time-steam concept into the quietly maturing science of human archeology. If I
could have seen ahead— If I could have guessed what would happen
to all the romantic visions he had worked so hard to inspire in me—

Why should I dream? I was a child then; I had no way of looking
ahead; the knife was just another knife. And I think if he had known
—if he had been able to see ahead and watch the science to which he
had devoted his every waking moment for a long lifetime degenerate
into a variety of three-dimensional bookkeeping—he'd have cut his
own heart out and offered it to me in apology.

He was a great old man. He was my grandfather.

You've seen the knife. Everyone has, I guess. I was the first, after
him, ever to see it, and I was about ten years old. I was sitting in a
chair in his laboratory, waiting for him to come back. It was a wooden
chair, something his grandfather had used, and maybe other people
before that. The laboratory was just a big room at the back of the
house, with a concrete floor and plenty of light from a row of windows over the worktable. There were hundreds of potsherds strewn
over the table where he'd been classifying and matching them for
restoration. There were trays of stone implements, and cheap wooden
boxes full of uncatalogued stuff with the dirt still on it. There was
a row of battered-looking notebooks, bound in imitation leather, fray-
ing at the corners and stained with ink and dirt. There was a pot that
had been half restored, the sherds joined so neatly that you could
barely see where they fitted together, and a little ivory goddess whose
cracks and chips were being replaced with a plastic filler until you'd
never have known she was five thousand years old.

That was what an archeologist's laboratory was like in those days.

Of course, we've outgrown all that. His experiment, and the knife he
brought back and tossed down on the table for me to look at, have
ended all that. Archeology has found its place among the major sciences. It's no longer a kind of bastard stepchild of art and anthropology. We got money for the best equipment, the newest gadgets. We
have laboratories designed by the best architects to fit the work we do
in them. We can call on the technicians of a score of other sciences
to do our dirty work, or can train ourselves to know as much as they
do if we're reactionaries like me. We have our own specialists, just as
learned and as limited as any hairsplitter in biochemistry or galactic
physics. We have prestige—recognition—everything he never had in
his day, when he was the acknowledged master in his field, and we
have him to thank for it all. But Walter Toynbee, if he were living
now, would dry up and die in the kind of laboratory his grandson has.
He'd push his charts and his correlations back and drop his head in
his hands and dream. He'd plan out his own murder.

I'd been sitting there for nearly six hours. I'd been over the worktable from one end to the other, three times. I'd picked up every
potsherd—turned them over—studied them with all the solemn intentness of ten years old—put them back exactly where I'd found
them, as he had taught me. I'd found four sherds that would fit
onto the pot he was restoring, and two that made an ear for a
little clay figurine shaped like a fat, happy puppy. I'd taken down
his books, one by one, and looked at the plates and figures as I had
done many times before. I had even taken down one of his notebooks
and slowly leafed through it, trying to spell out the straggling hand-
writing and make sense of the precise sketches, until a loose slip
of paper fell out from among the pages and I slipped it hurriedly back
and put the book away.

All one corner of the laboratory was taken up by the time shuttle.
It had cost more than all the air surveys, all the expeditions, all the
books and photographs and restorations of his whole career. The copper bus bars that came in through the wall behind it were like
columns in some Mayan colonnade. The instrument panel was like
something you'd imagine on—well, on a time machine. The machine itself was a block of dull gray lead with a massive steel door
in one side of it, the time cell floating in a magnetic bearing between
the pole pieces which set up the field.

Ours are neater now, but inside they're about the same. Old Walter Toynbee was an artist to the core, and Balmer, who built the

machine for him from Malecewicz's notes, had a flair for functional design. It was the first shuttle big enough and powerful enough to push a man and his baggage more than twenty years into the future—or the past, for that matter. Malecewicz had gone back fifteen years. He never returned. His equations showed why that was, and the archeological world, which had been rubbing its hands in anticipation of striking up a speaking acquaintance with Hatshepsut and Queen Shub-Ad, went back to its trowels and whisk-brooms with sighs of resignation. All but my grandfather. All but Walter Toynbee.

Malecewicz had never taken time to really work out his theory of the time function and lapsed interval, or he might be alive now. Laymen will still ask you why we archeologists don't simply climb into a shuttle with a solido camera and slip back to Greece or Elam or maybe Atlantis, and film what went on instead of tediously slicing the dust of millennia over the graveyards of past civilizations. It can be done, but the man who does it must be utterly self-centered, wrapped up in knowledge for its own sake, utterly unconcerned with his duties to his fellow men. As any schoolchild learns, the time shuttler who goes into the past introduces an alien variable into the spacio-temporal matrix at the instant when he emerges. The time stream forks, an alternative universe is born in which his visit is given its proper place, and when he returns it will be to a future level in the new world which he has created. His own universe is forever barred to him.

The future is by nature different. All that we are now and all that we have been or become from moment to moment is integral in the structure and flow of our particular thread of time. The man who visits the future is not changing it: his visit is a foredestined part of that future. As the ancients might have said: "It is written." Though I should imagine that the writing is in the matrix of spacetime and not in the record book of God.

Walter Toynbee was a brilliant man who might have made a success of many sciences. He had money to guarantee him such comfort as he might want, and he chose the science which most attracted him—archeology. He was the last of the great amateurs. He had know Malecewicz well—financed some of his experimental work—and when the physicist failed to return he wheedled the trustees of the university into turning the man's notes over to him. He showed them almost at once where Malecewicz had gone and why he would never return, and he saw immediately that there was no such

barrier between Man and his tomorrows. Inside of a week he and
Balmer were moving cases of artifacts out of the back room to make
room for the shuttle. Night after night they sat up into the wee
hours, arguing over fantastic-looking diagrams. In two months the
power lines were coming in across the fields, straight from the generators at Sheldon Forks, and Balmer's men were pouring the colossal
concrete base on which the machine would sit.

It was past dinner time. I had been sitting there alone since a
little after one o'clock, when he had stepped into the shuttle and
asked me to wait until he returned. There it sat, just as it had sat
for the last six hours, shimmering a little as though the air around
it were hot and humming like a swarm of bees deep in an old
beech. I got down a big book of plates of early Sumerian cylinder
seals and began to turn the pages slowly. The sameness of them had
grown boring when I realized that the humming had stopped.

I looked up at the lead cube. It was no longer shimmering. I closed
the book and put it carefully back on the shelf, just as the great
steel door of the shuttle swung silently open, and my grandfather
stepped down out of the time cell.

He had been digging. His breeches and heavy jacket were covered
with whitish dust. Dirt made grimy gutters under his eyes and filled
in the creases and wrinkles of his face and neck. He had a stubble
of dirty gray beard on his chin, which hadn't been there six hours
before, and his shirt was dark with sweat. He was tired, but there
was a gleam of satisfaction in his sharp black eyes and a kind of
grin on his wrinkled face.

The battered canvas bag in which he kept his tools and records
was slung over one shoulder. He slapped at his thighs and puffs of
dust spurted from his trousers. He took off the shabby felt hat which
he always wore, and his thin gray hair was damp and draggled. He
came over to the table, fumbling with the buckle on the bag. I
watched his knotted fingers wide-eyed, for I had seen them pull many
wonders out of that dusty wallet. I can hear his trimphant chuckle
as he drew out a knife—*the* knife—and tossed it ringing on the
table among the sherds.

You've seen it, of course. It's been in the pictures many times, and
there are solidographs of the thing in most museums. I saw it then
for the first time—ever—in our time.

He hadn't washed it. There was dirt on the fine engraving of the
dull-black hilt, and caked in the delicate filigree of the silver guard.

But the blade was clean, and it was as you have seen it—cold, gleaming, metallic blue—razor-edged—and translucent.

Maybe you've had a chance to handle it, here in the museum. Where the blade thins down to that feather-edge you can read small print through it. Where it's thicker, along the rib that reinforces the back of the blade, it's cloudy—milky looking. There has been engraving on the blade, too, but it has been ground or worn down until it is illegible. That is odd, because the blade is harder than anything we know except diamond. There is no such metal in the System or the Galaxy, so far as we know, except in this one well-worn and apparently very ancient knife blade.

It must be old. Not only is the engraving on the blade obliterated by wear; there is the telltale little serif near the hilt, where that utterly keen, hard edge has been worn back a little by use and honing. The black stuff of the hilt looks newer, and the carving is clearer, though still very old. Grandfather thought that it was made of some very heavy wood, possibly impregnated with a plastic of some sort, and that it had been made to replace an earlier hilt which had become worn out or broken. The metal of the guard and the plate and rivets which hold the hilt are ordinary silver, in one of the new stainless alloys which were just then coming into fairly general use.

Well—there it was. Walter Toynbee, who was probably the most competent archeologist the world has yet seen, had gone into the future in a Malecewicz shuttle. He had dug up a knife, and brought it back with him. And it was made of a material—a metal—of which our science knew absolutely nothing.

Three days later Walter Toynbee was dead. It may have been some virus picked up in that distant future which he had visited, to which our generation of mankind had developed no resistance. It may have been the strain of the trip into time, or the excitement and exertion of what he did there. He washed up, and we went home together to supper. We had it together, in the kitchen, because the family had finished and the dishes were done. Grandfather examined the knife while we were eating, but he wouldn't talk about it then. He was tired: he wanted to sleep. He never awoke.

In my father, old Walter's only son, the family talents had taken another turn. He was a more practical man than his father, and had done his noted parent many a good turn by husbanding and stimulating the family fortunes when they most needed it. Where grandfather had been interested in the minutiae and complexities of the ancient cultures whose dust he cleared away, father was one of the then popular cyclic historians who tried to see civilization as a whole —as a kind of super-organism—and to find recurring patterns in Man's gradual progression from the jungle to Parnassus. I am not implying that old Walter had no interest in synthesis and generalization—it is, as a matter of fact, a tradition that he had adopted the name Toynbee out of admiration for an historian of that name— a scholar of scholars—who lived and wrote in the early years of the last century. There is a letter among his papers which suggests that our original patronym may have been Slavic. If so, it might also explain his long and warm friendship with the unfortunate Malecewicz.

Be that as it may, Grandfather's death set in motion events whose result is all too familiar to all who have chosen to identify their lives with the pursuit of archeology. By the time the public lamentations had begun to die away, the press found a new sensation in the knife. The experts mulled over it and reported with remarkable unanimity that the engraving on the blade and hilt, while clearly of the same provenance, resembled no known human script or style of decoration. Finding their progress blocked, they called on the metallurgists and chemists to identify the blue metal of the blade, and on the botanists to specify the wood—if it was wood—of which the hilt was made.

Need I continue? There was more quibbling for its own sake in those days than there is now. Every expert was jealous of his personal acumen and insistent upon being the Only Right Man. It was considered fitting and proper that experts should disagree. But it gradually dawned on everyone concerned that here was something where there could be no disagreement, and what was more, something which might very well open new vistas of human progress.

Physically and chemically the blue stuff was a metal, though it was no metal chemistry had ever described or imagined. When they had succeeded in sawing out a sliver of the blade for tests, and finally got it into solution, its chemical behavior placed it quite outside the periodic system of the elements. The physicists went to work on another sample with X rays and spectographs, and arrived at much the same result. The more they studied it, the less they knew, for sooner or later some experiment would succeed in knocking over any hypothesis which they might have built up on the basis of their previous investigations.

Out of it all eventually came the judgment which stands today: that the blue stuff might well be some familiar metal, but that its atomic and molecular structure—and consequently its physical and chemical properties—had been modified or tampered with in a manner unknown to our science, making it to all intents and purposes a new state of matter. The botanists returned the same report. The black material had the structure of wood, and it might be any of several common tropical woods or it might be something quite alien, but it, too, had been hardened—indurated—through internal transformations which left it something entirely new to our planet.

That ended the first stage of the battle. When the experts threw up their hands in despair, the attack shifted to another quarter. The knife came back to my father, and he promptly made it the nucleus of a Toynbee Museum of Human Acculturation at his and Malecewicz's university, where it is today. But it was common knowledge that old Walter had brought the thing from the future. That meant that somewhere in the coming centuries of our race was a science which could create such unheard of things as the blue metal, and that the stuff was sufficiently common with them for knives to be made of it. Its electrical properties alone were such as to open a host of possible uses for it—father had been offered a small fortune by a certain great electrical concern for the material in the knife alone —and science decided to visit that future civilization, learn its secrets, and profit suitably thereby.

So the experiments shifted to time traveling. Malecewicz's notes were unearthed again and published; Grandfather's shuttle was dismantled and reconstructed a dozen times; Balmer found himself in a position to charge almost any fee as a consultant to industrial laboratories, universities, and private speculators who were hot on the trail of tomorrow. Shuttles were built on every hand, and men —and women—disappeared into the future. One by one they straggled back, empty-handed and thoroughly disgruntled. The future had no such metal.

There was a brief period in which everyone who had failed to solve the problem of the knife tried to cast doubts on Walter Toynbee, but the thing existed, its nature was what it was, and presently the hubbub swung around full circle to the place it had started. Grandfather had been an archeologist. He had gone into the future, and excavated the knife from the detritus of what might conceivably have been a colony or a chance visitant from another world—even another galaxy—someone—or something—of which the rest of humanity at that moment in time was quite unaware.

Archeology had found the thing. Science craved it. It was up to
archeology to find it—or its source—again.

So we became, in the language of the popularizers, the Mother
Science—spawning off all sorts of minuscule specialties, lording it
over a score of devoutly adulatory slave sciences, enjoying our position and taking every advantage of it.

I grew up in that atmosphere. From the time I could talk and
listen, Grandfather had filled me with the wonders of the past
and the romance of their discovery. Now the whole world was
awake to the glories of archeology as the science of sciences which
would open a whole new world to struggling Mankind. Is it any
wonder I chose to follow in my grandfather's footsteps?

Let me say now that men like my father and grandfather, who had
needed no world-shaking anomaly to intrigue them with their chosen
study, never lost their heads in the storm of recognition which
swept over them. It might have been better if they had. Archeology
was in the saddle; very well, it was going to ride—and ride hard.
Projects which had been tabled for lack of funds were financed in
a twinkling. Tools and instruments of investigation which had been
regarded as extremists' pipe dreams were invented on demand. With
new tools came new techniques, and with new techniques came a
hierarchy of skilled technicians, statisticians in place of explorers,
desk work in place of excavation, piddling with detail instead of
drawing in broad strokes the panorama of advancing civilization
which men like Schliemann, and Evans, and Breasted, and that first
Toynbee—yes, and old Walter Toynbee after them all—had seen
with clear and understanding eyes.

We have no one to blame but ourselves. I fully realize that. We
dug our own hole; we furnished it lavishly; we built a wall around it
to exclude the non-elite; we arranged to be fed and comforted while
we dawdled with our trivia; and then we pulled the hole in on
top of ourselves. We wore a rut so deep that we can never climb
out of it. So I dream of cutting my grandfather's throat instead of
realizing that if I were the man he was—if I had the courage to
break away from the stultified pattern I have helped to make, and
go primitive, dig in the dirt with a trowel, regain the thrill of new
worlds—the barriers would disappear and I would be free again, as
men were meant to be.

Of course, by the time I was old enough for the university the
whole business was well under way. My father, with his cycles in
mind, had instigated a project whereby Archeology—it rated the

capital by now—would uncover and describe the entire growth, maturity, and decline of representative communities, our own included. A colleague—or maybe he was a competitor—at Harvard was all for starting all over again at the beginning and redigesting the entire corpus of archeological data accumulated by grubbers since the beginning of time, using the new statistical attacks and the college's vast new calculating machine. He got his money. Science had declared that Archeology was the magician which would presently pass out unbounded benefits to one and all, and one and all swarmed to get on Santa Claus' good side.

I served my apprenticeship doing the dirty work for the men who voyaged into the future and sent back reams and sheaves of notes out of which we desk-workers were supposed to pull blue metal rabbits. This was the era of specialism: when trained mechanics did the digging, when stenographers and solido-scanners took the notes, and when laboratory drudges squeezed out of them every possible drop of information which super-statistics could extract.

I remember the worst pest of them all—a man with as much personality as my grandfather, though of a different kind—who nearly imposed his infernal pattern on the science for a generation. He had been a mathematical physicist who turned to archeology in what he claimed was an attempt to fit human behavior "in its broader sense" into some set of universal field-equations he had distilled out of his stars and atoms, and which purported to express the Totality of All, or some such pat phrase, in a large nutshell.

Of course, any such over-view of civilization was music to my father's ears, and he gave the man the run of the Museum and a voice in all our activities. Hill—that was his name—at once announced the precept that it was quite unnecessary to find blue-metal knives in some future culture. By making a sufficiently exhaustive collection of data at any particular moment, and applying his field equations in their humano-cultural aspect—I am trying here to recall his jargon—it would be possible to predict accurately when and where such knives must be.

Hill had a shock of red hair, a barrel chest, and a loud voice. He spoke often and in the right places. Myriads of miserable students like myself had to mull over the tons of notes which expeditions under his direction sent back. We translated facts into symbols, put the symbols through his mill, and got out more symbols. Nine times, by count, he announced to the world that "now he had it"

—and nine times by count a simple check up showed that the poor beleaguered natives of whatever era it was he had chosen as It had never heard of such a metal. Some of them had never heard of metal.

By the time I was twenty-three and had my own license to explore past and future indiscriminately, we had a pretty good overall view of the future of humanity. We had libraries of histories which had been written in millennia to come. We had gadgets and super-gadgets developed by future civilizations, some of which we could use and most of which we were able to misuse. The world we supposedly enjoy today was in the making, and you know what it is like.

I had done altogether too well at whipping the esteemed Dr. Hill's hodgepodge of miscellaneous data into some semblance of intelligibility. The powers that were—and are—announced that I might spend the rest of my life, for the good of Humanity, fiddling with the same kind of stuff. But I was young, and I was a Toynbee. I stood up and demanded my rights, and they gave them to me. I could go out like all the rest and hunt for the knife.

I am not a fool. Moreover, I had had the advantage of knowing my grandfather—better even than Father ever did. I knew how he would think and how he would react. He was the kind of man who went at things hard—all out—to the limit of his ability. It seemed clear enough to me that the first step in finding the knife was to determine what that limit was—although in thirteen years or so nobody had chosen that approach.

Balmer was still alive, and I made him dig out the plans and specifications he had drawn up when he made Grandfather's shuttle. I got hold of the notes the experts had made when they tore the machine apart after his death, and they checked. And then I had Balmer set me up just the same kind of old gray cube out of which Walter Toynbee had stumbled that day, with the blue knife in his dusty old ditty bag.

It was bigger, of course—I had to have room for the kind of equipment a field man considered necessary in my day. I'd never had any training or experience with the kind of work old Walter did with his own two hands, a camera, and a trowel. The profession had been mechanized, and it was silly not to use the best I could lay my hands on. The time field, though, was the same, and it should carry me just as far as it had carried its originator thirteen years before.

It did. Malecewicz, by stretching his original model, had been able to get fifteen years out of it. Grandfather's huge old vault of a machine lofted him nearly twenty times as far into the future of our race—and of our town. As I had suspected from the specifications of the machine, it dropped me somewhere near the middle of that interregnum which followed the Hemispheric Wars, when half the cities of America had been reduced to rubble, disease and famine had put the population of the planet back into a hunting-fishing-food-gathering economy, and all that remained of civilization was a memory which would some day be revived, restored, and started off again.

I am not saying that in thirteen years of trying nobody had hit upon this particular period in the future. It is true that having hit it they let common sense scare them off. It was obvious that that level of culture could never produce so sophisticated a scientific marvel as the knife. There was no evidence in the ruins they found to show that our own culture, up to and during the time of the Wars, had done so. Ergo: onward and upward. Try another thousand years. Try a million.

I had a slightly different point of view on the matter. I knew grandfather. He would go as far as his machine could take him. I had duplicated that. He would look around him for a promising site, get out his tools, and pitch in. Well, I could do that, too.

There is enough uncertainty—backlash, if you want to call it that—in the operation of any time shuttle so that you can never be certain that you will hit any specific moment or even any specific day or week in the future. Put that down to mechanical imperfections, if you like—I know some do—but I consider it a matter of the inexactitude of the physical universe, and I doubt that there is ever anything that we can do about it. You can approximate—hopping back and forth across the time you want until you get reasonably close—but that is a makeshift solution, borrowed from practical mathematics. I didn't try.

If you've read your history of the next five hundred years, you'll know that the gas attacks toward the end of the war had stripped the Atlantic coastal regions of vegetation and every other living thing. I got out of the shuttle in a dusty landscape where the bare bones of the planet stuck up in shattered stumps in a wind-swept desert of gullied clay. I might be ahead of my grandfather's time—in which case I saw a paradox brewing—or I might be following him. As it turned out, it was the latter.

I knew from what others had learned that there was no life in this coastal strip until much later. Gradually vegetation worked its way into the arid strip, insects and mammals followed, men followed them—but this is no essay on the future. There was no point in hunting for survivors; Grandfather certainly hadn't. For on all sides stretched the wreckage of our own city—or its counterpart of three centuries from now—and I knew that he would have stood just as I was standing, looking it over with an appraising eye, wondering where to begin.

One mass of fallen masonry, half submerged in a drift of sand, towered higher than the rest. It would provide a vantage point from which to size up the situation. As I plodded toward it through the soft sand I found myself watching for his footprints, so certain was I that this must be the place and the time. It was nonsense, of course; my own tracks were filling in as the wind curled sand into them.

Then I saw it—and that day thirteen years before came rushing back to me. Of course there would be traces! Walter Toynbee would never in his life have abandoned a dig as promising as this—a dig where surface-scratching had yielded him a relic like the knife. But for his sickness and death he would have been planning a return expedition—a camp—a full-scale attack. Not half the equipment he had taken with him was in the shuttle when he returned. And there, at the eastern base of the mound, the tatters of a red bandanna whipping in the wind, a short-handled shovel was driven into a crack in the masonry.

I fingered the shreds of red cloth. It was his. He always had one stuffed in the pocket of his jeans. Duster—sun shield—lashing—he had a score of uses for them. Any field worker had in those days, before there was a tool for every purpose.

The crevice into which the shovel had been wedged widened as it went down. Sand had drifted into it, filling it to within a few feet of the top. By all the tenets of civilized archeology I should first prepare my aërial plan of the entire complex of ruins, erect the light tower with its instrument board to establish a zero reference plane for the solidograph, and assemble the scanner. When a grid had been projected on the screen of the excavator, it would be time enough to think of beginning the actual investigation.

Do you believe in ghosts? As I stood there, with those shreds of faded red cloth in my hand, stroking the sand-polished handle of the shovel, I suddenly realized that so far as time itself went

he might have been standing here only hours, or even minutes before me. It was as though he had turned his back for a moment, and
I had stepped into his tracks there in the sand. I was a child again,
tagging after him as he strode around the big laboratory with his
giant's strides, pulling down a book here, running through a file
of negatives there, gathering his tools around him before he set to
work to unravel some perplexing situation in his digging. A thin
cloud passed across the sun, and it was as though his shadow had
fallen on me.

I pulled the shovel out of the crack in which he had wedged
it. It was in good condition—perfectly usable. In my time we did
not work with shovels or picks, but any fool could handle the
thing. I dug it into the sand—scratched at the base of the crack. It
would take only a few moments to deepen it enough so that I could
crawl inside.

There was a kind of satisfaction to the work. I exercise in the
public gymnasia—all young men of my age have to, to keep fit—
but there was a difference. Using this primitive tool brought with
it a feeling of accomplishment—of purpose—that I never found in
mere exercise. I was strong, and it gratified me to see the hole
deepen and the drift of sand grow behind me. Soon I had a tunnel
into which I could crawl without bumping my head. I went back to
the shuttle for a glow lamp and a pocket scanner, and plunged into
the darkness.

After the first few feet I had no use for the lamp. My eyes grew
accustomed to the dark, and I saw that shafts and streaks of light
broke through gaps in the ruin overhead. Presently I found a hard
floor under my feet, and then I came out into a room which was
like a wedge—the ceiling fallen in one mass which hung diagonally
between the wall over my head and the floor about twenty feet
before me. Sunlight seeped in through a crevice to the left, striking
on the wall and filling the whole place with a kind of diffuse glow.
In that glow I saw footprints in the thick dust which covered the
floor, and the table to which they led.

They were his footprints, of course. On that table he had found
the knife. I stepped out of the doorway where I had been standing,
an odd feeling of familiarity growing in me. I crossed the floor to
the table. It had been covered with heavy glass, which lay in shreds
on the dusty bronze. I could see the marks of his fingers in the
dust where he had moved the broken glass aside. And I could see
the outline of the knife, as sharp in the unstirred dust as it was when

he picked it up in his gnarled old fingers thirteen years—or was it thirteen minutes?—before.

The crack of light was widening as the sun moved; the place grew brighter. I brushed the dust away from the table top. It was heavy bronze; it told me nothing. And then, turning, I saw the opposite wall and the frieze in low relief which ran above the door—

I don't like the impossible. I don't like paradox. I sit here, toiling over my correlations—they have promised a machine by spring which will perform them for us more quickly and in far more detail than we have ever attempted—and when I grow tired I let my head slip down on my hands, and I dream of a day when I was a child. I dream of an old man and a knife—and murder.

I had had my chance. Others, more experienced and possibly more capable than I, followed me. The entire ruin was excavated, with the most meticulous attention to technique, down to bedrock. And I . . . I was sent back to my correlations and my trait tables, to work up the data which other men would presently send me. Because strive as they will, they can find no other explanation than the one which—to me—seems obvious. The answer which is no answer—

You can go into the Toynbee Museum now, today, and see the knife in a guarded case, in the anteroom of the main exhibit hall. In the course of three hundred years that case will have been replaced by a bronze table and a cover of heavy glass. Bombs will fall, the building will crumble in ruins, and the knife will still be there. Dust will cover the ruins, and one day a gnarled old man in shabby clothes will shovel it away and creep inside. He will find the knife and carry it away. Later a younger man will come—and then others—many others, men and women both. And all the while, on the granite lintel above the door to the room where the knife is kept, will be the inscription:

WALTER TOYNBEE
1962—2035

My grandfather brought the knife back from the future. He died. It was placed in the museum named for him. It lay there for three hundred years, while the human race went mad trying to solve its secret—while all civilization was turned upside down in the search for something which never existed!

He found it in the museum where it had always been. He carried it back through time, and it was placed in that museum. It lay there until he came and found it, and carried it back through time—

It was a simple pattern—as simple as ever was. Must we think only in terms of a beginning and an end? Cannot a thing—even a person—exist in a closed cycle without beginning or end? Appearing to us now, at this level of our time thread, accompanying us down its extension into our future, then vanishing from our stream and circling back to the point where it appeared? Can't you imagine that?

I thought I could. I thought it was a paradox—no more—as simple to explain as ever was. I was wrong, of course, and they are right.

The knife old Walter Toynbee brought back from the museum built in his honor, to house his knife, was perfect—worn, dirty, but perfect. A little notch was sawed in the back of its translucent blue blade—sawed with a diamond saw, to provide the chemist and the physicists with the samples they needed to test its properties. That notch is still in its blade as it lies out there in the museum case—it will be there for the next three hundred years, or until the raids come and the museum falls in ruins. Until an old man comes out of the past to find it—

The knife old Walter Toynbee will find there in our future will have that notch. The knife he brought back to me thirty years ago had no notch in it. Somewhere the circle must have a beginning. Somewhere it must have an end—but where, and how? How was this knife created, out of a strange blue metal, and a strange, black, indurated wood, when its existence has no beginning or end? How can the circle be broken? I wish I knew. I might not dream of murder then. I might find logic and purpose in the future instead of chaos—instead of impossible worlds that never were.

Q. U. R.

by

ANTHONY BOUCHER

*Ordinarily, Mr. Anthony Boucher employs the resources of his
keenly logical mind in constructing puzzles for his mystery novels.
Now he turns from the "whodunit" to the world of the future
and, still brilliantly logical, depicts humanity at that future date
when it has become almost helpless without its robots. Dependent
on automata, tomorrow's world will be subjected to unusual
economic stresses and strains. So, thinks Mr. Boucher, will the
robots. Even more so. So much more so that the robots might go
insane.*

*

IT'S GOT so the young sprouts nowadays seem never to have heard
of androids. Oh, they look at them in museums and they read the
references to them in the literature of the time, but they never seem
to realize how essential a part of life androids once were, how our
whole civilization, in fact, depended on them. And when you say
you got your start in life as trouble shooter for an android factory,
they look at you as though you'd worked in two-dimensional shows
way back before the sollies, as though you ought to be in a museum
yourself.

Now I'll admit I'm no infant. I'll never see a hundred again.
But I'm no antique either. And I think it's a crying shame that
the rising generation is so completely out of touch with the last
century. Not that I ever intended to be writing my memoirs; I didn't
exactly construct my life to that end. But somebody's got to tell
the real story of what androids meant and how they ceased to

mean it. And I'm the man to tell it, because I'm the man who discovered Dugg Quinby.

Yes, I said Quinby. Dugglesmarther H. Quinby, the Q. in Q. U. R. The man who made your life run the way it does today. And I found him.

That summer was a hell of a season for a trouble shooter for androids. There was nothing but trouble. My five-hour day stretched to eight, and even ten and twelve while I dashed all over New Washington checking on one android after another that had cracked up. And maybe you know how hot the Metropolitan District gets in summer, even worse than the rest of Oklahoma.

Because my job wasn't one that you could carry on comfortably in conditioned buildings and streets, it meant going outside and topside and everywhere that a robot might work. We called the androids robots then. We hadn't conceived of any kind of robot that wasn't an android or at least a naturoid of some sort.

And these breakdowns were striking everywhere, hitting robots in every line of activity. Even the Martoids and Veneroids that some ex-colonists fancied for servants. It would be an arm that went limp or a leg that crumpled up or a tentacle that collapsed. Sometimes mental trouble, too, slight indications of a tendency toward insubordination, even a sort of mania that wasn't supposed to be in their make-up. And the thing kept spreading and getting worse. Any manifestation like this among living beings, and you'd think of an epidemic. But what germ could attack tempered duralite?

The worst of it was there was nothing wrong with them. Nothing that I could find, and to me that meant plain nothing. You don't get to be head trouble shooter of Robinc if anything can get past you. And the second worst was that it was hitting my own staff. I had had six robots under me—plenty to cover the usual normal amount of trouble. Now I had two, and I needed forty.

So all in all I wasn't happy that afternoon. It didn't make me any happier to see a crowd in front of the Sunspot engaged in the merry pastime of Venusian-baiting. It was never safe for one of the little green fellows to venture out of the Venusian ghetto; this sport was way too common a spectacle.

They'd got his vapor inhalator away from him. That was all there was to the game, but that was enough. No extra-physical torment was needed. There the poor giller lay on the sidewalk, sprawled and gasping like a fish out of water, which he practically was. The men —factory executives mostly, and a few office foremen—made a circle around him and laughed. There was supposed to be something hilariously funny about the struggles of a giller drowning in air, though I never could see it myself.

Oh, they'd give him back his inhalator just in time. They never killed them off; the few Venusians around had their uses, particularly for repair work on the Veneroid robots that were used under water. But meanwhile there'd be some fun.

Despite the heat of the day, I shuddered a little. Then I crossed to the other side of the street. I couldn't watch the game. But I turned back when I heard one loud shout of fury.

That was when I found Dugg Quinby. That shout was the only sound he made. He was ragingly silent as he plowed through that mass of men, found the biggest of them, snatched the inhalator away from him, and restored it to its gasping owner. But there was noise enough from the others.

Ever try to take a bone from a dog? Or a cigar from a Martian mountaineer? Well, this was worse. Those boys objected to having their fun spoiled, and they expressed their objection forcibly.

I liked this young blond giant that had plowed in there. I liked him because his action had asked me what I was doing crossing over to the other side of the street, and I didn't have an answer. The only way even to try to answer was to cross back.

Androids or Q. U. R., single-drive space-ships or modern multiples, one thing that doesn't change much is a brawl, and this was a good one. I don't know who delivered the right that met my chin as I waded in, and I don't know who it was meant for, but it was just what I needed. Not straight enough to do more than daze me for a minute, but just hard enough to rouse my fighting spirit to the point of the hell with anything but finding targets for my knuckles. I avenged the Venusian, I avenged the blond youth, I avenged the heat of the day and the plague of the robots. I avenged my job and my corns and the hangover I had two weeks ago.

The first detail that comes clear is sitting inside the Sunspot I don't know how much later. The blond boy was with me, and so was one of the factory men. We all seemed to be the best of friends, and there wasn't any telling whose blood was which.

Guzub was beaming at us. When you know your Martians pretty well you learn that that trick of shutting the middle eye is a beam. "You zure bolished 'em ub, boys," he gurgled.

The factory man felt of his neck and decided his head was still there. "Guzub," he declared, "I've learned me a lesson: From now on any green giller is safe around me."

"That'z the zbird," Guzub glurked. "Avder all, we're all beings, ain'd we? Now, wad'll id be?"

Guzub was hurt when the blond youth ordered milk, but delighted when the factory man said he'd have a Three Planet with a double shot of margil. I'm no teetotaler, but I don't go for these strong drinks; I stuck to my usual straight whiskey.

We exchanged names while we waited. Mike Warren, the factory man was; and the other—but then I tipped that off already. That was Quinby. They both knew me by name.

"So you're with Robinc," Mike said. "I want to have a talk with you about that sometime. My brother-in-law's got a new use for a robot that could make somebody, including me, a pile of credits, and I can't get a hearing any place."

"Glad to," I said, not paying too much attention. Everybody's got a new use for a robot, just like writers tell me everybody's got a swell idea for a solly.

Dugg Quinby had been staring straight ahead of him and not listening. Now he said, "What I don't see is why."

"Well," Mike began, "it seems like he was stuck once on the lunar desert and—"

"Uh-huh. Not that. What I don't see is why Venusians. Why we act that way about them, I mean. After all, they're more or less like us. They're featherless bipeds, pretty much on our general model. And we treat them like they weren't even beings. While Martians are a different shape of life altogether, but we don't have ghettos for them or Martian-baiting."

"That's just it," said Mike. "The gillers are too much like us. They're like a cartoon of us. We see them, and they're like a dirty joke on humans, and we see red. I mean," he added hastily, his hand rubbing his neck, "that's the way I used to feel. I was just trying to explain."

"Nuts," I said. "It's all a matter of historical parallel. We licked the pants—which they don't wear—off the Venusians in the First War of Conquest, so we feel we can push 'em around. The Second War of Conquest went sour on us and damned near put an end to the Empire and the race to boot, so we've got a healthy respect for the Martians." I looked over at the bartender, his tentacles industriously plying an impressive array of bottles and a gleaming duralite shaker. "We only persecute the ones it's safe to persecute."

Quinby frowned. "It's bad enough to do what no being ought to do, but to do it only when you know you can get away with it— I've been reading," he announced abruptly, as though it was a challenge to another fight.

Mike grunted. "Sollies and telecasts are enough for a man, I always say. You get to reading and you get mixed up."

"Do you think you aren't mixed up without it? Do you think you aren't all mixed up? If people would only try to look at things straight—"

"What have you been reading?" I asked.

"Old stuff. Dating, oh I guess, a millennium or so back. There were people then that used to write a lot about the Brotherhood of Man. They said good things. And it all means something to us now if you translate it into the Brotherhood of Beings. Man is unified now, but what's the result? The doctrine of Terrene Supremacy."

Guzub brought the drinks and we forked out our credits. When he heard the phrase "Terrene Supremacy" his left eyelid went into that little quiver that is the Martian expression of polite incredulity but he said nothing.

Quinby picked up his milk. "It's all because nobody looks at things straight. Everybody looks around the corners of his own prejudices. If you look at a problem straight, there isn't a problem. That's what I'm trying to do," he said with that earnestness you never come back to after youth. "I'm trying to train myself to look straight."

"So there isn't a problem. No problems at all." I thought of the day I'd had and the jobs still ahead of me and I snorted. And then I had an idea and calmly, between swallows of whiskey, changed the course of terrene civilization. "I've got problems," I asserted. "How'd you like to look straight at them? Are you working now?"

"I'm in my free-lance period," he said. "I've finished technical college and I'm not due for my final occupational analysis for another year."

"All right," I said. "How's about it?"

Slowly he nodded.

"If you can look," said Mike, wobbling his neck, "as straight as you can hit—"

I was back in my office when the call came from the space port. I'd seen Thuringer's face red before, but never purple. He had trouble speaking, but he finally spluttered out, "Somebody did a lousy job of sterilization on your new assistant's parents."

"What seems to be the trouble?" I asked in my soothingest manner.

"Trouble! The man's lunatic stock. Not a doubt. When you see what he's done to—" He shuddered. He reached out to switch the ike-range, but changed his mind. "Uh-huh. Come over here and see it for yourself. You wouldn't believe it. But come quick, before I go and apply for sterilization myself."

We had a special private tube to the space port; they used so many of our robots. It took me less than five minutes to get there. A robot parked my bus and another robot took me up in the lift. It was a relief to see two in good working order, though I noticed that the second one showed signs of incipient limpness in his left arm. Since he ran the lift with his right, it didn't really matter, but Robinc had principles of perfection.

Thuringer's robot secretary said, "Tower room," and I went on up. The space-port manager scanned me and gave the click that meant the beam was on. The tower door opened as I walked in.

I don't know what I'd expected to see. I couldn't imagine what would get the hard-boiled Thuringer into such a blasting dither. This had been the first job that I'd tried Quinby out on, and a routine piece of work it was, or should have been. Routine, that is, in these damnable times. The robot which operated the signal tower had gone limp in the legs and one arm. He'd been quoted as saying some pretty strange things on the beam, too. Backsass to pilots and insubordinate mutterings.

The first thing I saw was a neat pile of scrap in the middle of the room. Some of it looked like robot parts. The next thing I saw was Thuringer, who had gone from purple to a kind of rosy black. "It's getting me!" he burst out. "I sit here and watch it and I'm going mad! Do something, man! Then go out and annihilate your assistant, but do something first!"

I looked where he pointed. I'd been in this tower control room before. The panel had a mike and an ike, a speaker and a viewer, and a set of directional lights. In front of it there used to be a chair where the robot sat, talking on the beam and watching the indicators.

Now there was no chair. And no robot. There was a table, and on the table was a box. And from that box there extended one arm, which was alive. That arm punched regularly and correctly at the lights, and out of the box there issued the familiar guiding voice.

I walked around and got a gander at the front of the box. It had eyes and a mouth and a couple of holes that it took me a minute to spot as ear holes. It was like a line with two dots above and two below it, so:

It was like no face that ever was in nature, but it could obviously see and hear and talk.

Thuringer moaned. "And that's what you call a repair job! My beautiful robot! Your A-1-A Double Prime All-Utility Extra-Quality De-Luxe Model! Nothing of him left but this"—he pointed at the box —"and this"—he gestured sadly at the scrap heap.

I looked a long time at the box and I scratched my head. "He works, doesn't he?"

"Works? What? Oh, works."

"You've been here watching him. He pushes the right lights? He gets messages right? He gives the right instructions?"

"Oh yes. I suppose so. Yes, he works all right. But damn it, man, he's not a robot any more. You've ruined him."

The box interrupted its beam work. "Ruined hell," it said in the same toneless voice. "I never felt so good since I was animated. Thanks, boss."

Thuringer goggled. I started to leave the room.

"Where are you going? Are you going to make this right? I demand another A-1-A Double Prime at once, you understand. And I trust you'll kill that assistant."

"Kill him? I'm going to kiss him."

"Why, you—" He'd picked up quite a vocabulary when he ran the space port at Venusberg. "I'll see that you're fired from Robinc tomorrow!"

"I quit today," I said. "One minute ago."

That was the birth of Q. U. R.

I found Quinby at the next place on the list I'd given him. This was a job repairing a household servant—one of the Class B androids with a pretty finish, but not up to commercial specifications.

I gawped when I saw the servant. Instead of two arms he had four tentacles, which he was flexing intently.

Quinby was packing away his repair kit. He looked up at me, smiling. "It was very simple," he said. "He'd seen Martoid robots at work, and he realized that flexible tentacles would be much more useful than jointed arms for housework. The more he brooded about it, the clumsier his arms got. But it's all right now, isn't it?"

"Fine, boss," said the servant. He seemed to be reveling in the free pleasure of those tentacles.

"There were some Martoid spares in the kit," Quinby explained, "and when I switched the circuit a little—"

"Have you stopped," I interposed, "to think what that housewife is going to say when she comes home and finds her servant waving Martoid tentacles at her?"

"Why, no. You think she'd—"

"Look at it straight," I said. "She's going to join the procession demanding that I be fired from Robinc. But don't let it worry you. Robinc's nothing to us. From now on we're ourselves. We're Us Incorporated. Come on back to the Sunspot and we'll thrash this out."

"Thanks, boss," the semi-Martoid called after us, happily writhing.

I recklessly ordered a Three Planet. This was an occasion. Quinby stuck to milk. Guzub shrugged—that is, he wrinkled his skin where shoulders might have been on his circular body—and said, "You loog abby, boys. Good news?"

I nodded. "Best yet, Guzub. You're dishing 'em up for an historic occasion. Make a note."

"Lazd dime you zelebrade izdorig oggazion," said Guzub resignedly, "you breag zevendy-vour glazzes. Wy zhould I maig a node?"

"This is different, Guz. Now," I said to Quinby, "tell me how you got this unbelievable idea of repair?"

"Why, isn't it obvious?" he asked simply. "When Zwergenhaus invented the first robot, he wasn't thinking functionally. He was trying to make a mechanical man. He did, and he made a good job of it. But that's silly. Man isn't a functionally useful animal. There's very little he can do himself. What's made him top dog is that he can invent and use tools to do what needs doing. But why make his mechanical servants as helplessly constructed as he is?

"Almost every robot, except perhaps a few like farmhands, does only one or two things and does those things constantly. All right. Shape them so that they can best do just those things, with no part left over. Give them a brain, eyes and ears to receive commands, and whatever organs they need for their work.

"There's the source of your whole robot epidemic. They were all burdened down with things they didn't need—legs when their job was a sedentary one, two arms when they used only one—or else, like my house servant, their organs were designed to imitate man's rather than to be ideally functional. Result: the unused waste parts atrophied, and the robots became physically sick, sometimes mentally as well because they were tortured by unrealized potentialities. It was simple enough, once you looked at it straight."

The drinks came. I went at the Three Planets cautiously. You know the formula: one part Terrene rum—170 proof—one part Venusian margil, and a dash or so of Martian vuzd. It's smooth and murderous. I'd never tasted one as smooth as this of Guzub's, and I feared it'd be that much the more murderous.

"You know something of the history of motor transportation?" Quinby went on. "Look at the twentieth century models in the museum sometime. See how long they kept trying to make a horseless carriage look like a carriage for horses. We've been making the same mistake—trying to make a manless body look like the bodies of men."

"Son," I said—he was maybe five or ten years younger than I was—"there's something in this looking-straight business of yours. There's so much, in fact, that I wonder if even you realize how much. Are you aware that if we go at this right we can damned near wipe Robinc out of existence?"

He choked on his milk. "You mean," he ventured, slowly and dreamily, "we could—"

"But it can't be done overnight. People are used to android robots. It's the only kind they ever think of. They'll be scared of your unhuman-looking contraptions, just like Thuringer was scared. We've got to build into this gradually. Lots of publicity. Lots of promotion. Articles, lectures, debates. Give 'em a name. A good name. Keep robots; that's common domain, I read somewhere, because it comes out of a play written a long time ago in some dialect of Old Slavic. Quinby's Something Robots—"

"Functionoid?"

"Sounds too much like fungoid. Don't like. Let me see—" I took some more Three Planets. "I've got it. Usuform. Quinby's Usuform Robots. Q. U. R."

Quinby grinned. "I like it. But shouldn't it be your name too?"

"Me, I'll take a cut on the credits. I don't like my name much. Now what we ought to do is introduce it with a new robot. One that can do something no android in the Robinc stock can tackle—"

Guzub called my name. "Man ere looking vor you."

It was Mike. "Hi, mister," he said. "I was wondering did you maybe have a minute to listen to my brother-in-law's idea. You remember, about that new kind of robot—"

"Hey, Guzub," I yelled. "Two more Three Planets."

"Make it three," said Quinby quietly.

We talked all the rest of that night. When the Sunspot closed at twenty-three—we were going through one of our cyclic periods of blue laws then—we moved to my apartment and kept at it until we fell asleep from sheer exhaustion, scattered over my furniture.

Quinby's one drink—he stopped there—was just enough to stimulate him to seeing straighter than ever. He took something under one minute to visualize completely the possibilities of Mike's contribution.

This brother-in-law was a folklore hobbyist, and had been reading up on the ancient notion of dowsing. He had realized at once that there could have been no particular virtue in the forked witch-hazel rod which was supposed to locate water in the earth, but that certain individuals must have been able to perceive that water in some nth-sensory manner, communicating this reaction subconsciously to the rod in their hands.

To train that nth sense in a human being was probably impossible; it was most likely the result of a chance mutation. But you could attempt to develop it in a robot brain by experimentation with the patterns of the sense-perception tracks; and he had succeeded. He could equip a robot with a brain that would infallibly register the presence of water, and he was working on the further possibilities of oil and other mineral deposits. There wasn't any need to stress the invaluability of such a robot to an exploring party.

"All right," Quinby said. "What does such a robot need beside his brain and his sense organs? A means of locomotion and a means of marking the spots he finds. He'll be used chiefly in rough desert country, so a caterpillar tread will be far more useful to him than legs that can trip and stumble. The best kind of markers—lasting and easy to spot—would be metal spikes. He could, I suppose, carry those and have an arm designed as a pile driver; but . . . yes, look, this is best: Supposing he lays them?"

"Lays them?" I repeated vaguely.

"Yes. When his water sense registers maximum intensity—that is, when he's right over a hidden spring—there'll be a sort of sphincter reaction, and *plop*, he'll lay a sharp spike, driving it into the ground."

It was perfect. It would be a cheap robot to make—just a box on treads, the box containing the brain, the sense organs, and a supply of spikes. Maybe later in a more elaborate model he could be fed crude metal and make his own spikes. There'd be a decided demand for him, and nothing of Robinc's could compete. An exploring party could simply send him out for the day, then later go over the clear track left by his treads and drill wherever he had laid a spike. And the pure functionalism of him would be the first step in our campaign to accustom the public to Quinby's Usuform Robots.

Then the ideas came thick and fast. We had among us figured out at least seventy-three applications in which usuforms could beat androids, before our eyes inevitably folded up on us.

I woke up with three sensations: First, a firm resolve to stick to whiskey and leave Three Planetses to the Martians that invented them. Second, and practically obliterating this discomfort, a thrill of anticipation at the wonders that lay ahead of us, like a kid that wakes up and knows today's his birthday. But third, and uncomfortably gnawing at the back of this pleasure, the thought that there was something wrong, something we'd overlooked.

Quinby was fixing up a real cooked breakfast. He insisted that this was an occasion too noble for swallowing a few concentrates, and he'd rummaged in my freezing storeroom to find what he called "honest food." It was good eating, but this gnawing thought kept pestering me. At last I excused myself and went into the library. I found the book I wanted: *Planetary Civil Code. Volume 34. Robots.* I put it in the projector and ran it rapidly over the screen till I located the paragraph I half remembered.

That gnawing was all too well founded. I remembered now. The theory'd always been that this paragraph went into the Code because only Robinc controlled the use of the factor that guaranteed the robots against endangering any intelligent beings, but I've always suspected that there were other elements at work. Even Council Members get their paws greased sometimes.

The paragraph read:

259: All robots except those in the military employ of the Empire shall be constructed according to the patents held by Robots Inc.,

sometimes known as Robinc. Any robot constructed in violation of
this section shall be destroyed at once, and all those concerned
in constructing him shall be sterilized and segregated.

I read this aloud to the breakfast party. It didn't add to the cheer
of the occasion.

"I knew it was too good to be true," Mike grunted. "I can just
see Robinc leasing its patents to the boys that'll put it out of business."

"But our being great business successes isn't what's important,"
Quinby protested. "Do we really want . . . could any being of good
will really want to become like the heads of Robinc?"

"I do," said Mike honestly.

"What's important is what this can do: Cure this present robot
epidemic, conserve raw materials in robot building, make possible a
new and simpler and more sensible life for everybody. Why can't we
let Robinc take over the idea?"

"Look," I said patiently. "Quite aside from the unworthy ambi-
tions that Mike and I may hold, what'll happen if we do? What has
always happened when a big company buys out a new method when
they've got a billion credits sunk in the old? It gets buried and is
never heard of again."

"That's right," Quinby sighed. "Robinc would simply strangle it."

"All right. Now look at it straight and say what is going to become
of Quinby's Usuform Robots."

"Well," he said simply, "there's only one solution. Change the
code."

I groaned. "That's all, huh? Just that. Change the code. And how
do you propose to go about that?"

"See the head of the Council. Explain to him what our idea means
to the world—to the system. He's a good man. He'll see us through."

"Dugg," I said, "when you look at things straight I never know
whether you're going to see an amazing truth or the most amazing
nonsense that ever was. Sure the Head's a good man. If he could do
it without breaking too many political commitments, I think he
might help out on an idea as big as this. But how to get to see him
when—"

"My brother-in-law tried once," Mike contributed. "He got kind
of too persistent. That's how come he's in the hospital now. Hey,"
he broke off. "Where you going?"

"Come on, Dugg," I said. "Mike, you spend the day looking

around the city for a likely factory site. We'll meet you around seventeen at the Sunspot. Quinby and I are going to see the Head of the Council."

We met the first guard about a mile from the office. "Robinc Repair," I said, and waved my card. After all, I assuaged Quinby's conscience, I hadn't actually resigned yet. "Want to check the Head's robot."

The guard nodded. "He's expecting you."

It hadn't been even a long shot. With robots in the state they were in, it was practically a certainty that one of those in direct attendance on the Head would need repair. The gag got us through a mile of guards, some robot, some—more than usual since all the trouble—human, and at last into the presence of the Head himself.

The white teeth gleamed in the black face in that friendly grin so familiar in telecasts. "I've received you in person," he said, "because the repair of this robot is such a confidential matter."

"What are his duties?" I asked.

"He is my private decoder. It is most important that I should have his services again as soon as possible."

"And what's the matter with him?"

"Partly what I gather is, by now, almost the usual thing. Paralysis of the legs. But partly more than that: He keeps talking to himself. Babbling nonsense."

Quinby spoke up. "Just what is he supposed to do?"

The Head frowned. "Assistants bring him every coded or ciphered dispatch. His brain was especially constructed for cryptanalysis. He breaks them down, writes out the clear, and drops it into a pneumatic chute which goes to a locked compartment in my desk."

"He uses books?"

"For some of the codes. The ciphers are entirely brain-mechanics."

Quinby nodded. "Can do. Bring us to him."

The robot was saying to himself, "This is the ponderous time of the decadence of the synaptic reflexes when all curmudgeons wonkle in the withering wallabies."

Quinby looked after the departing Head. "Some time," he said, "we're going to see a Venusian as Interplanetary Head."

I snorted.

"Don't laugh. Why, not ten centuries ago people would have snorted just like that at the idea of a black as Head on this planet.

Such narrow stupidity seems fantastic to us now. Our own prejudices will seem just as comical to our great-great-grandchildren."

The robot said, "Over the larking lunar syllogisms lopes the chariot of funereal ellipses."

Quinby went to work. After a minute—I was beginning to catch on to this seeing-straight business myself—I saw what he was doing and helped.

This robot needed nothing but the ability to read, to transcribe deciphered messages, and to handle papers and books. His legs had atrophied—that was in line with the other cases. But he was unusual in that he was the rare thing: a robot who had no need at all for communication by speech. He had the power of speech and was never called upon to exercise it; result, he had broken down into this fantastic babbling of nonsense, just to get some exercise of his futile power.

When Quinby had finished, the robot consisted only of his essential cryptanalytic brain, eyes, one arm, and the writer. This last was now a part of the robot's hookup; so that instead of using his hands to transcribe the message, he thought it directly into the writer. He had everything he needed, and nothing more. His last words before we severed the speech connection were, "The runcible rhythm of ravenous raisins rollers through the rookery rambling and raving." His first words when the direct connection with the writer was established were, "This feels good. Thanks, boss."

I went to fetch the Head. "I want to warn you," I explained to him, "you may be a little surprised by what you see. But please look at it without preconceptions."

He was startled and silent. He took it well; he didn't blow up hysterically like Thuringer. But he stared at the new thing for a long time without saying a word. Then he took a paper from his pocket and laid it on the decoding table. The eyes looked at it. The arm reached out for a book and opened it. Then a message began to appear on the writer. The Head snatched it up before it went into the tube, read it, and nodded.

"It works," he said slowly. "But it's not a robot any more. It's . . . it's just a decoding machine."

"A robot," I quoted, "is any machine equipped with a Zwergenhaus brain and capable of independent action upon the orders or subject to the guidance of an intelligent being. Planetary Code, paragraph num—"

"But it looks so—"

"It works," I cut in. "And it won't get paralysis of the legs and it won't ever go mad and babble about wonkling curmudgeons. Because, you see, it's a usuform robot." And I hastily sketched out the Quinby project.

The Head listened attentively. Occasionally he flashed his white grin, especially when I explained why we could not turn the notion over to Robinc. When I was through, he paused a moment and then said at last. "It's a fine idea you have there. A great idea. But the difficulties are great, too. I don't need to recount the history of robots to you," he said, proceeding to do so. "How Zwergenhaus' discovery lay dormant for a century and a half because no one dared upset the economic system by developing it. How the Second War of Conquest so nearly depopulated the earth that the use of robot labor became not only possible but necessary. How our society is now so firmly based on it that the lowest laboring rank possible to a being is foreman. The Empire is based on robots; robots are Robinc. We can't fight Robinc."

"Robinc is slowly using up all our resources of metallic and radio-active ore, isn't it?" Quinby asked.

"Perhaps. Scaremongers can produce statistics—"

"And our usuforms will use only a fraction of what Robinc's androids need."

"A good point. An important one. You have convinced me that android robots are a prime example of conspicuous waste, and this epidemic shows that they are moreover dangerous. But I cannot attempt to fight Robinc now. My position—I shall be frank, gentlemen—my position is too precarious. I have problems of my own."

"Try Quinby," I said. "I had a problem and tried him, and he saw through it at once."

"Saw through it," the Head observed, "to a far vaster and more difficult problem beyond. Besides, I am not sure if my problem lies in his field. It deals with the question of how to mix a Three Planets cocktail."

The excitement of our enterprise had made me forget my head. Now it began throbbing again at the memory. "A Three Planets?"

The Head hesitated. "Gentlemen," he said at last, "I ask your pledge of the utmost secrecy."

He got it.

"And even with that I cannot give you too many details. But you know that the Empire holds certain mining rights in certain districts of Mars—I dare not be more specific. These rights are essential to maintain our stocks of raw materials. And they are held only on lease, by an agreement which must be renewed quinquennially. It has heretofore been renewed as a matter of course, but the recent rise of the Planetary Party in Mars, which advocates the abolition of all interplanetary contact, makes this coming renewal a highly doubtful matter. Within the next three days I am to confer here with a certain high Martian dignitary, traveling incognito. Upon the result of that conference our lease depends."

"And the Three Planets?" I asked. "Does the Planetary Party want to abolish them as a matter of principle?"

"Probably," he smiled. "But this high individual is not a party member, and is devoted to Three Planets He hates to travel, because only on Mars, he claims, is the drink ever mixed correctly. If I could brighten his trip here by offering him one perfect Three Planets—"

"Guzub!" I cried. "The bartender at the Sunspot. He's a Martian and the drink is his specialty."

"I know," the Head agreed sadly. "Dza . . . the individual in question once said that your Guzub was the only being on this planet who knew how. Everyone else puts in too much or too little vuzd. But Guzub is an exiled member of the Varjinian Loyalists. He hates everything that the present regime represents. He would never consent to perform his masterpiece for my guest."

"You could order one at the Sunspot and have it sent here by special—"

"You know that a Three Planets must be drunk within thirty seconds of mixing for the first sip to have its ideal flavor."

"Then—"

"All right," Quinby said. "You let us know when your honored guest arrives, and we'll have a Three Planets for him."

The Head looked doubtful. "If you think you can— A bad one might be more dangerous than none—"

"And if we do," I interposed hastily, "you'll reconsider this business of the usuform robots?"

"If this mining deal goes through satisfactorily, I should be strong enough to contemplate facing Robinc."

"Then you'll get your Three Planets," I said calmly, wondering what Quinby had seen straight now.

We met Mike at the Sunspot as arranged. He was drinking a Three Planets. "This is good," he announced. "This has spacedrive and zoomf to it. You get it other places and—"

"I know," I said. "Find a site?"

"A honey. Wait'll I—"

"Hold it. We've got to know have we got anything to go on it. Guzub! One Three Planets."

We watched entranced as he mixed the potion. "Get exactly what he does," Quinby had said. "Then construct a usuform bartender who'll be infallible. It'll satisfy the Martian envoy and at the same time remind the Head of why we're helping him out."

But all we saw was a glittering swirl of tentacles. First a flash as each tentacle picked up its burden—one the shaker, one the lid, one the glass, and three others the bottles of rum, margil, and vuzd. Then a sort of spasm that shook all Guzub's round body as the exact amount of each liquid went in, and finally a gorgeous pin-wheel effect of shaking and pouring.

Guzub handed me my drink, and I knew as much as I had before.

By the time I'd finished it, I had courage. "Guzub," I said, "this is wonderful."

"Zure," Guzub glurked. "Always I maig id wondervul."

"Nobody else can make 'em like you, Guz. But tell me. How much vuzd do you put in?"

Guzub made his kind of a shrug. "I dell you, boys, I dunno. Zome dime maybe I wadge myzelv and zee. I juzd go zo! I dunno how mudj."

"Give me another one. Let's see you watch yourself."

"Businezz is good by you, you dring zo many Blanedz? O Gay, ere goes."

But the whirl stopped in the middle. There was Guzub, all his eyes focused sadly on the characteristic green corkscrew-shaped bottle of vuzd. Twice he started to move that tentacle, then drew it back. At last he made a dash with it.

"Exactly two drops," Quinby whispered.

Guzub handed over the drink unhappily. "Dry id," he said.

I did. It was terrible. Too little vuzd, so that you could taste both the heavy sweetness of the rum and the acrid harshness of the margil. I said so.

"I know, boys. Wen I zdob do wadge, id bothers me. No gan do."

I gulped the drink. "Mix up another without watching. Maybe we can tell."

This one was perfect. And we could see nothing.

The next time he "wadged." He used precisely four and half drops of vuzd. You tasted nothing but the tart decay of the vuzd itself.

The next time—
But my memory gets a little vague after that. Like I said, I'm a whiskey drinker. And four Three Planetses in quick succession—I'm told the party went on till closing hour at twenty-three, after which Guzub accepted Quinby's invitation to come on and mix for us at my apartment. I wouldn't know. All I remember is one point where I found a foot in my face. I bit it, decided it wasn't mine, and stopped worrying about it. Or about anything.

I'm told that I slept thirty-six hours after that party—a whole day and more simply vanished out of my existence. I woke up feeling about twelve and spry for my age, but it took me a while to reconstruct what had been going on.

I was just beginning to get it straightened out when Quinby came in. His first words were, "How would you like a Three Planets?"

I suddenly felt like two hundred and twelve, and on an off day at that. Not until I'd packed away a superman-size breakfast did he dare repeat the offer. By then I felt brave. "O. K.," I said. "But with a whiskey chaser."

I took one sip and said, "Where's Guzub? I didn't know he was staying here too."

"He isn't."

"But this Three Planets— It's perfect. It's the McCoy. And Guzub—"

Quinby opened a door. There sat the first original Quinby Usuform—no remake of a Robinc model, but a brand-new creation. Quinby said, "Three Planets," and he went into action. He had tentacles, and the motions were exactly like Guzub's except that he was himself the shaker. He poured the liquids into his maw, joggled about, and then poured them out of a hollow hoselike tentacle.

The televisor jangled. Quinby hastily shifted the ike so as to miss the usuform barkeep, as I answered. The screen showed the Head himself. He'd been there before on telecasts, but this was the real thing.

He didn't waste time. "Tonight, nineteen thirty," he said. "I don't need to explain?"

"We'll be there," I choked out.

A special diplomatic messenger brought the pass to admit the two of us and "one robot or robotlike machine" to the Council building. I was thankful for that alternative phrase; I didn't want to have to argue with each guard about the technical legal definition of a robot.

We were installed in a small room directly off the Head's private reception room. It was soundproofed and there was no window; no chance of our picking up interplanetary secrets of diplomacy. And there was a bar.

A dream of a bar, a rhapsody of a bar. The vuzd, the rum, the margil were all of brands that you hear about and brood about but never think to see in a lifetime. And there was whiskey of the same caliber.

We had hardly set our usuform facing the bar when a servant came in. He was an android. He said. "The Head says now."

Quinby asked me, "Do you want one?"

I shook my head and selected a bottle of whiskey.

"Two Three Planetses," Quinby said.

The tentacles flickered, the shaker-body joggled, the hose-tentacle poured. The android took the tray from our usuform. He looked at him with something as close to a mixture of fear, hatred, and envy as his eye cells could express. He went out with the tray.

I turned to Quinby. "We've been busy getting ready for this party ever since I woke up. I still don't understand how you made him into another Guzub."

There was a click and the room was no longer soundproof. The Head was allowing us to hear the reception of our creation. First his voice came, quiet, reserved and suave. "I think your magnitude would enjoy this insignificant drink. I have been to some slight pains to see that it was worthy of your magnitude's discriminating taste."

There was silence. Then the faintest sound of a sip, a pause, and an exhalation. We could almost hear the Head holding his breath.

"Bervegd!" a deep voice boomed—which since no Martian has ever yet learned to pronounce a voiceless consonant, means a verdict of "Perfect!"

"I am glad that your magnitude is pleased."

"Bleased is doo mild a word, my dear Ead. And now thad you ave zo delighdvully welgomed me—"

The sound went dead again.

"He liked it, huh?" said Guzub II. "You boys want some, maybe?"

"No thanks," said Quinby. "I wonder if I should have given him a Martian accent—they are the best living bartenders. Perhaps when we get the model into mass production—".

I took a gleefully long swig of whiskey. Its mild warmth felt soothing after memories of last night's Three Planetses. "Look," I said. "We have just pulled off the trick that ought to net us a change in

the code and a future as the great revolutionists of robot design. I
feel like . . . hell, like Ley landing on the Moon. And you sit there
with nothing on your mind but a bartender's accent."

"Why not?" Quinby asked. "What is there to do in life but find
what you're good for and do it best you can?"

He had me there. And I began to have some slight inklings of the
trouble ahead with a genius who had commercial ideas and the conscience of an other-worldly saint. I said, "All right. I won't ask you
to kill this bottle with me, and in return I expect you not to interfere with my assassinating it. But as to what you're good for—how
did you duplicate Guzub?"

"Oh that. That was simple—"

"—when you looked at it straight," I ended.

"Yes." That was another thing about Quinby; he never knew if
he was being ribbed. "Yes. I got one of those new electronic cameras—you know, one thousand exposures per second. Hard to find
at that time of night, but we made it."

"We?"

"You helped me. You kept the man from overcharging me. Or
maybe you don't remember? So we took pictures of Guzub making a
Three Planets, and I could construct this one to do it exactly right
down to the thousandth of a second. The proper proportion of vuzd,
is case you're interested, works out to three-point-six-five-four-seven-
eight-two-three drops. It's done with a flip of the third joint of the
tentacle on the down beat. It didn't seem right to use Guzub to
make a robot that would compete with him and probably drive him
out of business; so we've promised him a generous pension from the
royalties on usuform barkeeps."

"We?" I said again, more feebly.

"You drew up the agreement."

I didn't argue. It was fair enough. A good businessman would have
slipped Guzub a fiver for posing for pictures and then said the hell
with him. But I was beginning to see that running Q. U. R. was not
going to be just good business.

When the Head finally came in, he didn't need to say a word,
though he said plenty. I've never seen that white grin flash quite so
cheerfully. That was enough; the empire had its Martian leases, and
Q. U. R. was a fact.

When I read back over this story, I can see there's one thing
wrong. That's about the giller. I met Dugg Quinby, and you met

him through me, in the act of rescuing a Venusian from a giller-baiting mob. By all the rights of storytelling, the green being should have vowed everlasting gratitude to his rescuer, and at some point in our troubles he should have showed up and made everything fine for us.

That's how it should have been. In actual fact the giller grabbed his inhalator and vanished without so much as a "thank you." If anybody helped us, it was Mike, who had been our most vigorous enemy in the battle.

Which means, I think, that seeing straight can work with things and robots, but not with beings, because no being is really straight, not even to himself.

Except maybe Dugg Quinby.

WHO GOES THERE?

by

DON A. STUART

Man is pretty well master of the animal life on this planet. Nothing is too big to stand up against man, master as he is of the art of destruction. But what of the animals that are, as yet, alien to this planet? What armament will they possess besides the familiar tooth and claw, size and strength? Whatever space travelers encounter, we can imagine nothing will be more dreadful than the alien monster found frozen in the polar ice. Frozen, but not dead. Not even helpless when it possessed its terrible weapon of masquerade.

*

THE PLACE stank. A queer, mingled stench that only the ice-buried cabins of an Antarctic camp know, compounded of reeking human sweat, and the heavy, fish-oil stench of melted seal blubber. An overtone of liniment combated the musty smell of sweat-and-snow-drenched furs. The acrid odor of burnt cooking fat, and the animal, not-unpleasant smell of dogs, diluted by time, hung in the air.

Lingering odors of machine oil contrasted sharply with the taint of harness dressing and leather. Yet, somehow, through all that reek of human beings and their associates—dogs, machines and cooking—came another taint. It was a queer, neck-ruffling thing, a faintest suggestion of an odor alien among the smells of industry and life. And it was a life-smell. But it came from the thing that lay bound with cord and tarpaulin on the table, dripping slowly, methodically onto the heavy planks, dank and gaunt under the unshielded glare of the electric light.

Blair, the little bald-pated biologist of the expedition, twitched nervously at the wrappings, exposing clear, dark ice beneath and then pulling the tarpaulin back into place restlessly. His little bird-like motions of suppressed eagerness danced his shadow across the fringe of dingy gray underwear hanging from the low ceiling, the equatorial fringe of stiff, graying hair around his naked skull a comical halo about the shadow's head.

Commander Garry brushed aside the lax legs of a suit of under-wear, and stepped toward the table. Slowly his eyes traced around the rings of men sardined into the Administration Building. His tall, stiff body straightened finally, and he nodded. "Thirty-seven. All here." His voice was low, yet carried the clear authority of the com-mander by nature, as well as by title.

"You know the outline of the story back of that find of the Sec-ondary Pole Expedition. I have been conferring with Second-in-Com-mand McReady, and Norris, as well as Blair and Dr. Copper. There is a difference of opinion, and because it involves the entire group, it is only just that the entire Expedition personnel act on it.

"I am going to ask McReady to give you the details of the story, because each of you has been too busy with his own work to follow closely the endeavors of the others. McReady?"

Moving from the smoke-blued background, McReady was a figure from some forgotten myth, a looming, bronze statue that held life, and walked. Six-feet-four inches he stood as he halted beside the table, and, with a characteristic glance upward to assure himself of room under the low ceiling beams, straightened. His rough, clash-ingly orange windproof jacket he still had on, yet on his huge frame it did not seem misplaced. Even here, four feet beneath the drift-wind that droned across the antarctic waste above the ceiling, the cold of the frozen continent leaked in, and gave meaning to the harshness of the man. And he was bronze—his great red-bronze beard, the heavy hair that matched it. The gnarled, corded hands gripping, relaxing, gripping and relaxing on the table planks were bronze. Even the deep-sunken eyes beneath heavy brows were bronzed.

Age-resisting endurance of the metal spoke in the cragged heavy outlines of his face, and the mellow tones of the heavy voice. "Norris and Blair agree on one thing; that animal we found was not—terrestrial in origin. Norris fears there may be danger in that; Blair says there is none.

"But I'll go back to how, and why, we found it. To all that was known before we came here, it appeared that this point was exactly over the South Magnetic Pole of Earth. The compass does point straight down here, as you all know. The more delicate instruments of the physicists, instruments especially designed for this expedition and its study of the magnetic pole, detected a secondary effect, a secondary, less powerful magnetic influence about 80 miles south-west of here.

"The Secondary Magnetic Expedition went out to investigate it. There is no need for details. We found it, but it was not the huge meteorite or magnetic mountain Norris had expected to find. Iron ore is magnetic, of course; iron more so—and certain special steels even more magnetic. From the surface indications, the secondary pole we found was small, so small that the magnetic effect it had was preposterous. No magnetic material conceivable could have that effect. Soundings through the ice indicated it was within one hundred feet of the glacier surface.

"I think you should know the structure of the place. There is a broad plateau, a level sweep that runs more than 150 miles due south from the Secondary station, Van Wall says. He didn't have time or fuel to fly farther, but it was running smoothly due south then. Right there, where that buried thing was, there is an ice-drowned mountain ridge, a granite wall of unshakable strength that has dammed back the ice creeping from the south.

"And four hundred miles due south is the South Polar Plateau. You have asked me at various times why it gets warmer here when the wind rises, and most of you know. As a meteorologist I'd have staked my word that no wind could blow at —70 degrees—that no more than a 5-mile wind could blow at —50—without causing warming due to friction with ground, snow and ice and the air itself.

"We camped there on the lip of that ice-drowned mountain range for twelve days. We dug our camp into the blue ice that formed the surface, and escaped most of it. But for twelve consecutive days the wind blew at 45 miles an hour. It went as high as 48, and fell to 41 at times. The temperature was —63 degrees. It rose to —60 and fell to —68. It was meteorologically impossible, and it went on uninterruptedly for twelve days and twelve nights.

"Somewhere to the south, the frozen air of the South Polar

plateau slides down from that 18,000 foot bowl, down a mountain pass, over a glacier, and starts north. There must be a funneling mountain chain that directs it, and sweeps it away for four hundred miles to hit that bald plateau where we found the secondary pole, and 350 miles farther north reaches the Antarctic Ocean.

"It's been frozen there since Antarctica froze twenty million years ago. There never has been a thaw there.

"Twenty million years ago Antarctica was beginning to freeze. We've investigated, thought and built speculations. What we believe happened was about like this.

"Something came down out of space, a ship. We saw it there in the blue ice, a thing like a submarine without a conning tower or directive vanes, 280 feet long and 45 feet in diameter at its thickest.

"Eh, Van Wall? Space? Yes, but I'll explain that better later." McReady's steady voice went on.

"It came down from space, driven and lifted by forces men haven't discovered yet, and somehow—perhaps something went wrong then —it tangled with Earth's magnetic field. It came south here, out of control probably, circling the magnetic pole. That's a savage country there, but when Antarctica was still freezing it must have been a thousand times more savage. There must have been blizzard snow, as well as drift, new snow falling as the continent glaciated. The swirl there must have been particularly bad, the wind hurling a solid blanket of white over the lip of that now-buried mountain.

"The ship struck solid granite head-on, and cracked up. Not every one of the passengers in it was killed, but the ship must have been ruined, her driving mechanism locked. It tangled with Earth's field, Norris believes. No thing made by intelligent beings can tangle with the dead immensity of a planet's natural forces and survive.

"One of its passengers stepped out. The wind we saw there never fell below 41, and the temperature never rose above —60. Then— the wind must have been stronger. And there was drift falling in a solid sheet. The thing was lost completely in ten paces." He paused for a moment, the deep, steady voice giving way to the drone of wind overhead, and the uneasy, malicious gurgling in the pipe of the galley-stove.

Drift—a drift-wind was sweeping by overhead. Right now the snow picked up by the mumbling wind fled in level, blinding lines across the face of the buried camp. If a man stepped out of the tunnels that connected each of the camp buildings beneath the surface, he'd be lost in ten paces. Out there, the slim, black finger of the radio mast lifted 300 feet into the air, and at its peak was the clear night sky. A sky of thin, whining wind rushing steadily from beyond to another beyond under the licking, curling mantle of the aurora. And off north, the horizon flamed with queer, angry color of the midnight twilight. That was spring 300 feet above Antarctica

At the surface—it was white death. Death of a needle-fingered cold driven before the wind, sucking heat from any warm thing. Cold—and white mist of endless, everlasting drift, the fine, fine particles of licking snow that obscured all things.

Kinner, the little, scar-faced cook, winced. Five days ago he had stepped out to the surface to reach a cache of frozen beef. He had reached it, started back—and the drift-wind leapt out of the south. Cold, white death that streamed across the ground blinded him in twenty seconds. He stumbled on wildly in circles. It was half an hour before rope-guided men from below found him in the impenetrable murk.

It was easy for man—or *thing*—to get lost in ten paces.

"And the drift-wind then was probably more impenetrable than we know." McReady's voice snapped Kinner's mind back. Back to welcome, dank warmth of the Ad Building. "The passenger of the ship wasn't prepared either, it appears. It froze within ten feet of the ship.

"We dug down to find the ship, and our tunnel happened to find the frozen—animal. Barclay's ice-ax struck its skull.

"When we saw what it was, Barclay went back to the tractor, started the fire up and when the steam pressure built, sent a call for Blair and Dr. Copper. Barclay himself was sick then. Stayed sick for three days, as a matter of fact.

"When Blair and Copper came, we cut out the animal in a block of ice, as you see, wrapped it and loaded it on the tractor for return here. We wanted to get into that ship.

"We reached the side and found the metal was something we didn't know. Our beryllium-bronze, non-magnetic tools wouldn't touch it. Barclay had some tool-steel on the tractor, and that wouldn't scratch it either. We made reasonable tests—even tried some acid from the batteries with no results.

"They must have had a passivating process to make magnesium metal resist acid that way, and the alloy must have been at least 95% magnesium. But we had no way of guessing that, so when we spotted the barely opened lock door, we cut around it. There was clear, hard ice inside the lock, where we couldn't reach it. Through the little crack we could look in and see that only metal and tools were in there, so we decided to loosen the ice with a bomb.

"We had decanite bombs and thermite. Thermite is the ice-softener; decanite might have shattered valuable things, where the thermite's heat would just loosen the ice. Dr. Copper, Norris and I placed a 25-pound thermite bomb, wired it, and took the connector up the tunnel to the surface, where Blair had the steam tractor waiting. A hundred yards the other side of that granite wall we set off the thermite bomb.

"The magnesium metal of the ship caught, of course. The glow of the bomb flared and died, then it began to flare again. We ran back to the tractor, and gradually the glare built up. From where we were we could see the whole ice-field illuminated from beneath with an unbearable light; the ship's shadow was a great, dark cone reaching off toward the north, where the twilight was just about gone. For a moment it lasted, and we counted three other shadow-things that might have been other—passengers—frozen there. Then the ice was crashing down and against the ship.

"That's why I told you about that place. The wind sweeping down from the Pole was at our backs. Steam and hydrogen flame were torn away in white ice-fog; the flaming heat under the ice there was yanked away toward the Antarctic Ocean before it touched us. Otherwise we wouldn't have come back, even with the shelter of that granite ridge that stopped the light.

"Somehow in the blinding inferno we could see great hunched things, black bulks glowing, even so. They shed even the furious incandescence of the magnesium for a time. Those must have been the engines, we knew. Secrets going in blazing glory—secrets that might have given Man the planets. Mysterious things that could lift and hurl that ship—and had soaked in the force of the Earth's magnetic field. I saw Norris' mouth move, and ducked. I couldn't hear him.

"Insulation—something—gave way. All Earth's field they'd soaked up twenty million years before broke lose. The aurora in the sky above licked down, and the whole plateau there was bathed in cold fire that blanketed vision. The ice-ax in my hand got red hot, and hissed on the ice. Metal buttons on my clothes burned into me. And a flash of electric blue seared upward from beyond the granite wall.

"Then the walls of ice crashed down on it. For an instant it squealed the way dry-ice does when it's pressed between metal.

"We were blind and groping in the dark for hours while our eyes recovered. We found every coil within a mile was fused rubbish, the dynamo and every radio set, the earphones and speakers. If we hadn't had the steam tractor, we wouldn't have gotten over to the Secondary Camp.

"Van Wall flew in from Big Magnet at sun-up, as you know. We came home as soon as possible. That is the history of—that." McReady's great bronze beard gestured toward the thing on the table.

II

Blair stirred uneasily, his little, bony fingers wriggling under the harsh light. Little brown freckles on his knuckles slid back and forth as the tendons under the skin twitched. He pulled aside a bit of the tarpaulin and looked impatiently at the dark ice-bound thing inside.

McReady's big body straightened somewhat. He'd ridden the rocking, jarring steam tractor forty miles that day, pushing on to Big Magnet here. Even his calm will had been pressed by the anxiety to mix again with humans. It was lone and quiet out there in Secondary Camp, where a wolf-wind howled down from the Pole. Wolf-wind howling in his sleep—winds droning and the evil, unspeakable face of that monster leering up as he'd first seen it through clear, blue ice, with a bronze ice-ax buried in its skull.

The giant meteorologist spoke again. "The problem is this. Blair wants to examine the thing. Thaw it out and make micro slides of its tissues and so forth. Norris doesn't believe that is safe, and Blair does. Dr. Copper agrees pretty much with Blair. Norris is a physicist, of course, not a biologist. But he makes a point I think we should all hear. Blair has described the microscopic life-forms biologists find living, even in this cold and inhospitable place. They freeze every winter, and thaw every summer—for three months—and live.

"The point Norris makes is—they thaw, and live again. There must have been microscopic life associated with this creature. There is with every living thing we know. And Norris is afraid that we may release a plague—some germ disease unknown to Earth—if we thaw those microscopic things that have been frozen there for twenty million years.

"Blair admits that such micro life might retain the power of living.

Such unorganized things as individual cells can retain life for unknown periods, when solidly frozen. The beast itself is as dead as those frozen mammoths they find in Siberia. Organized, highly developed life-forms can't stand that treatment.

"But micro-life could. Norris suggests that we may release some disease-form that man, never having met it before, will be utterly defenseless against.

"Blair's answer is that there may be such still-living germs, but that Norris has the case reversed. They are utterly non-immune to man. Our life-chemistry probably——"

"Probably!" The little biologist's head lifted in a quick, birdlike motion. The halo of gray hair about his bald head ruffled as though angry. "Heh. One look——"

"I know," McReady acknowledged. "The thing is not Earthly. It does not seem likely that it can have a life-chemistry sufficiently like ours to make cross-infection remotely possible. I would say that there is no danger."

McReady looked toward Dr. Copper. The physician shook his head slowly. "None whatever," he asserted confidently. "Man cannot infect or be infected by germs that live in such comparatively close relatives as the snakes. And they are, I assure you," his clean-shaven face grimaced uneasily, "*much* nearer to us than—*that*."

Vance Norris moved angrily. He was comparatively short in this gathering of big men, some five-feet-eight, and his stocky, powerful build tended to make him seem shorter. His black hair was crisp and hard, like short, steel wires, and his eyes were the gray of fractured steel. If McReady was a man of bronze, Norris was all steel. His movements, his thoughts, his whole bearing had the quick, hard impulse of a steel spring. His nerves were steel—hard, quick-acting —swift corroding.

He was decided on his point now, and he lashed out in its defense with a characteristic quick, clipped flow of words. "Different chemistry be damned. That thing may be dead—or, by God, it may not— but I don't like it. Damn it, Blair, let them see the monstrosity you are petting over there. Let them see the foul thing and decide for themselves whether they want that thing thawed out in this camp.

"Thawed out, by the way. That's got to be thawed out in one of the shacks to-night, if it is thawed out. Somebody—who's watchman to-night? Magnetic—oh, Connant. Cosmic rays to-night. Well, you get to sit up with that twenty-million-year-old mummy of his.

"Unwrap it, Blair. How the hell can they tell what they are buying, if they can't see it? It may have a different chemistry. I don't
care what else it has, but I know it has something I don't want. If
you can judge by the look on its face—it isn't human so maybe you
can't—it was annoyed when it froze. Annoyed, in fact, is just about
as close an approximation of the way it felt as crazy, mad, insane
hatred. Neither one touches the subject.

"How the hell can these birds tell what they are voting on? They
haven't seen those three red eyes, and that blue hair like crawling
worms. Crawling—damn, it's crawling there in the ice right now!

"Nothing Earth ever spawned had the unutterable sublimation of
devastating wrath that thing let loose in its face when it looked
around his frozen desolation twenty million years ago. Mad? It was
mad clear through—searing, blistering mad!

"Hell, I've had bad dreams ever since I looked at those three red
eyes. Nightmares. Dreaming the thing thawed out and came to life—
that it wasn't dead, or even wholly unconscious all those twenty
million years, but just slowed, waiting—waiting. You'll dream, too,
while that damned thing that Earth wouldn't own is dripping,
dripping in the Cosmos House tonight.

"And, Connant," Norris whipped toward the cosmic ray specialist,
"won't you have fun sitting up all night in the quiet. Wind whining
above—and that thing dripping——" He stopped for a moment,
and looked around.

"I know. That's not science. But this is, it's psychology. You'll
have nightmares for a year to come. Every night since I looked at
that thing I've had 'em. That's why I hate it—sure I do—and don't
want it around. Put it back where it came from and let it freeze for
another twenty million years. I had some swell nightmares—that it
wasn't made like we are—which is obvious—but of a different kind
of flesh that it can really control. That it can change its shape, and
look like a man—and wait to kill and eat——

"That's not a logical argument. I know it isn't. The thing isn't
Earth-logic anyway.

"Maybe it has an alien body-chemistry, and maybe its bugs do
have a different body-chemistry. A germ might not stand that, but,
Blair and Cooper, how about a virus? That's just an enzyme molecule, you've said. That wouldn't need anything but a protein
molecule of any body to work on.

"And how are you so sure that, of the million varieties of microscopic life it may have, none of them are dangerous? How about dis-

eases like hydrophobia—rabies—that attacks any warm-blooded creature, whatever its body-chemistry may be? And parrot fever? Have you a body like a parrot, Blair? And plain rot—gangrene—necrosis if you want? *That* isn't choosy about body chemistry!"

Blair looked up from his puttering long enough to meet Norris' angry, gray eyes for an instant. "So far the only thing you have said this thing gave off that was catching was dreams. I'll go so far as to admit that." An impish, slightly malignant grin crossed the little man's seamed face. "I had some, too. So. It's dream-infectious. No doubt an exceedingly dangerous malady.

"So far as your other things go, you have a badly mistaken idea about viruses. In the first place, nobody has shown that the enzyme-molecule theory, and that alone, explains them. And in the second place, when you catch tobacco mosaic or wheat rust, let me know. A wheat plant is a lot nearer your body-chemistry than this other-world creature is.

"And your rabies is limited, strictly limited. You can't get it from, nor give it to, a wheat plant or a fish—which is a collateral descendant of a common ancestor of yours. Which this, Norris, is not." Blair nodded pleasantly toward the tarpaulined bulk on the table.

"Well, thaw the damned thing in a tub of formalin if you must thaw it. I've suggested that——"

"And I've said there would be no sense in it. You can't compromise. Why did you and Commander Garry come down here to study magnetism? Why weren't you content to stay at home? There's magnetic force enough in New York. I could no more study the life this thing once had from a formalin-pickled sample than you could get the information you wanted back in New York. And—if this one is so treated, *never in all time to come can there be a duplicate!* The race it came from must have passed away in the twenty million years it lay frozen, so that even if it came from Mars then, we'd never find its like. And—the ship is gone.

"There's only one way to do this—and that is the best possible way. It must be thawed slowly, carefully, and not in formalin."

Commander Garry stood forward again, and Norris stepped back muttering angrily. "I think Blair is right, gentlemen. What do you say?"

Connant grunted. "It sounds right to us, I think—only perhaps he ought to stand watch over it while it's thawing." He grinned ruefully, brushing a stray lock of ripe-cherry hair back from his forehead. "Swell idea, in fact—if he sits up with his jolly little corpse."

Garry smiled slightly. A general chuckle of agreement rippled over the group. "I should think any ghost it may have had would have starved to death if it hung around here that long, Connant," Garry suggested. "And you look capable of taking care of it. 'Ironman' Connant ought to be able to take out any opposing players, still."

Connant shook himself uneasily. "I'm not worrying about ghosts. Let's see that thing. I——"

Eagerly Blair was stripping back the ropes. A single throw of the tarpaulin revealed the thing. The ice had melted somewhat in the heat of the room, and it was clear and blue as thick, good glass. It shone wet and sleek under the harsh light of the unshielded globe above.

The room stiffened abruptly. It was face up there on the plain, greasy planks of the table. The broken half of the bronze ice-ax was still buried in the queer skull. Three mad, hate-filled eyes blazed up with a living fire, bright as fresh-spilled blood, from a face ringed with a writhing, loathsome nest of worms, blue, mobile worms that crawled where hair should grow——

Van Wall, six feet and 200 pounds of ice-nerved pilot, gave a queer, strangled gasp and butted, stumbled his way out to the corridor. Half the company broke for the doors. The others stumbled away from the table.

McReady stood at one end of the table watching them, his great body planted solid on his powerful legs. Norris from the opposite end glowered at the thing with smouldering hate. Outside the door, Garry was talking with half a dozen of the men at once.

Blair had a tack hammer. The ice that cased the thing *schluffed* crisply under its steel claw as it peeled from the thing it had cased for twenty thousand thousand years——

III

"I know you don't like the thing, Connant, but it just has to be thawed out right. You say leave it as it is till we get back to civilization. All right, I'll admit your argument that we could do a better and more complete job there is sound. But—how are we going to get this across the Line? We have to take this through one temperate zone, the equatorial zone, and half way through the other temperate zone before we get it to New York. You don't want to sit with it one night, but you suggest, then, that I hang its corpse in the freezer with the beef?" Blair looked up from his cautious chipping, his bald, freckled skull nodding triumphantly.

Kinner, the stocky, scar-faced cook, saved Connant the trouble of answering. "Hey, you listen, mister. You put that thing in the box with the meat, and by all the gods there ever were, I'll put you in to keep it company. You birds have brought everything movable in this camp in onto my mess tables here already, and I had to stand for that. But you go putting things like that in my meat box or even my meat cache here, and you cook your own damn grub."

"But, Kinner, this is the only table in Big Magnet that's big enough to work on," Blair objected. "Everybody's explained that."

"Yeah, and everybody's brought everything in here. Clark brings his dogs every time there's a fight and sews them up on that table. Ralsen brings in his sledges. Hell, the only thing you haven't had on that table is the Boeing. And you'd 'a' had that in if you coulda figured a way to get it through the tunnels."

Commander Garry chuckled and grinned at Van Wall, the huge Chief Pilot. Van Wall's great blond beard twitched suspiciously as he nodded gravely to Kinner. "You're right, Kinner. The aviation department is the only one that treats you right."

"It does get crowded, Kinner," Garry acknowledged. "But I'm afraid we all find it that way at times. Not much privacy in an antarctic camp."

"Privacy? What the hell's that? You know, the thing that really made me weep, was when I saw Barclay marchin' through here chantin' 'The last lumber in the camp! The last lumber in the camp!' and carryin' it out to build that house on his tractor. Damn it, I missed that moon cut in the door he carried out more'n I missed the sun when it set. That wasn't just the last lumber Barclay was walkin' off with. He was carryin' off the last bit of privacy in this blasted place."

A grin rode even on Connant's heavy face as Kinner's perennial good-natured grouch came up again. But it died away quickly as his dark, deep-set eyes turned again to the red-eyed thing Blair was chipping from its cocoon of ice. A big hand ruffed his shoulder-length hair, and tugged at a twisted lock that fell behind his ear in a familiar gesture. "I know that cosmic ray shack's going to be too crowded if I have to sit up with that thing," he growled. "Why can't you go on chipping the ice away from around it—you can do that without anybody butting in, I assure you—and then hang the thing up over the power-plant boiler? That's warm enough. It'll thaw out a chicken, even a whole side of beef, in a few hours."

"I know," Blair protested, dropping the tack hammer to gesture more effectively with his bony, freckled fingers, his small body tense with eagerness, "but this is too important to take any chances. There never was a find like this; there never can be again. It's the only chance men will ever have, and it has to be done exactly right.

"Look, you know how the fish we caught down near the Ross Sea would freeze almost as soon as we got them on deck, and come to life again if we thawed them gently? Low forms of life aren't killed by quick freezing and slow thawing. We have——"

"Hey, for the love of Heaven—you mean that damned thing will come to life!" Connant yelled. "You get the damned thing—— Let me at it! That's going to be in so many pieces——"

"NO! No, you fool——" Blair jumped in front of Connant to protect his precious find. "No. Just *low* forms of life. For Pete's sake let me finish. You can't thaw higher forms of life and have them come to. Wait a moment now—hold it! A fish can come to after freezing because it's so low a form of life that the individual cells of its body can revive, and that alone is enough to reëstablish life. Any higher forms thawed out that way are dead. Though the individual cells revive, they die because there must be organization and coöperative effort to live. That coöperation cannot be reëstablished. There is a sort of potential life in any uninjured, quick-frozen animal. But it can't—can't under any circumstances—become active life in higher animals. The higher animals are too complex, too delicate. This is an intelligent creature as high in its evolution as we are in ours. Perhaps higher. It is as dead as a frozen man would be."

"How do you know?" demanded Connant, hefting the ice-ax he had seized a moment before.

Commander Garry laid a restraining hand on his heavy shoulder. "Wait a minute, Connant. I want to get this straight. I agree that there is going to be no thawing of this thing if there is the remotest chance of its revival. I quite agree it is much too unpleasant to have alive, but I had no idea there was the remotest possibility."

Dr. Copper pulled his pipe from between his teeth and heaved his stocky, dark body from the bunk he had been sitting in. "Blair's being technical. That's dead. As dead as the mammoths they find frozen in Siberia. Potential life is like atomic energy—there, but nobody can get it out, and it certainly won't release itself except in rare cases, as rare as radium in the chemical analogy. We have all sorts of proof that things don't live after being frozen—not even fish, generally speaking—and no proof that higher animal life can under any circumstances. What's the point, Blair?"

The little biologist shook himself. The little ruff of hair standing out around his bald pate waved in righteous anger. "The point is," he said in an injured tone, "that the individual cells might show the characteristics they had in life, if it is properly thawed. A man's muscle cells live many hours after he has died. Just because they live, and a few things like hair and fingernail cells still live, you wouldn't accuse a corpse of being a Zombie, or something.

"Now if I thaw this right, I may have a chance to determine what sort of world it's native to. We don't, and can't know by any other means, whether it came from Earth or Mars or Venus or from beyond the stars.

"And just because it looks unlike men, you don't have to accuse it of being evil, or vicious or something. Maybe that expression on its face is its equivalent to a resignation to fate. White is the color of mourning to the Chinese. If men can have different customs, why can't a so-different race have different understandings of facial expressions?"

Connant laughed softly, mirthlessly. "Peaceful resignation! If that is the best it could do in the way of resignation, I should exceedingly dislike seeing it when it was looking mad. That face was never designed to express peace. It just didn't have any philosophical thoughts like peace in its make-up.

"I know it's your pet—but be sane about it. That thing grew up on evil, adolesced slowly roasting alive the local equivalent of kittens, and amused itself through maturity on new and ingenious torture."

"You haven't the slightest right to say that," snapped Blair. "How do you know the first thing about the meaning of a facial expression inherently inhuman? It may well have no human equivalent whatever. That is just a different development of Nature, another example of Nature's wonderful adaptability. Growing on another, perhaps harsher world, it has different form and features. But it is just as much a legitimate child of Nature as you are. You are displaying that childish human weakness of hating the different. On its own world it would probably class you as a fish-belly, white monstrosity with an insufficient number of eyes and a fungoid body pale and bloated with gas.

"Just because its nature is different, you haven't any right to say it's necessarily evil."

Norris burst out a single, explosive, "Haw!" He looked down at the thing. "May be that things from other worlds don't *have* to be evil just because they're different. But that thing *was!* Child of Nature, eh? Well, it was a hell of an evil Nature."

"Aw, will you mugs cut crabbing at each other and get the damned thing off my table?" Kinner growled. "And put a canvas over it. It looks indecent."

"Kinner's gone modest," jeered Connant.

Kinner slanted his eyes up to the big physicist. The scarred cheek twisted to join the line of his tight lips in a twisted grin. "All right, big boy, and what were you grousing about a minute ago? We can set the thing in a chair next to you tonight, if you want."

"I'm not afraid of its face," Connant snapped. "I don't like keeping a wake over its corpse particularly, but I'm going to do it."

Kinner's grin spread. "Uh-huh." He went off to the galley stove and shook down ashes vigorously, drowning the brittle chipping of the ice as Blair fell to work again.

IV

"*Cluck*," reported the cosmic ray counter, "*cluck-brrrp-cluck*." Connant started and dropped his pencil.

"Damnation." The physicist looked toward the far corner, back at the Gieger counter on the table near that corner, and crawled under the desk at which he had been working to retrieve the pencil. He sat down at his work again, trying to make his writing more even. It tended to have jerks and quavers in it, in time with the abrupt proud-hen noises of the Gieger counter. The muted whoosh of the pressure lamp he was using for illumination, the mingled gargles and bugle calls of a dozen men sleeping down the corridor in Paradise House formed the background sounds for the irregular, clucking noises of the counter, the occasional rustle of falling coal in the copper-bellied stove. And a soft, steady *drip-drip-drip* from the thing in the corner.

Connant jerked a pack of cigarettes from his pocket, snapped it so that a cigarette protruded and jabbed the cylinder into his mouth. The lighter failed to function, and he pawed angrily through the pile of papers in search of a match. He scratched the wheel of the lighter several times, dropped it with a curse and got up to pluck a hot coal from the stove with the coal-tongs.

The lighter functioned instantly when he tried it on returning to the desk. The counter ripped out a series of chucking guffaws as a burst of cosmic rays struck through to it. Connant turned to glower at it, and tried to concentrate on the interpretation of data collected during the past week. The weekly summary——

He gave up and yielded to curiosity, or nervousness. He lifted the pressure lamp from the desk and carried it over to the table in the corner. Then he returned to the stove and picked up the coal tongs. The beast had been thawing for nearly 18 hours now. He poked at it with an unconscious caution; the flesh was no longer hard as armor plate, but had assumed a rubbery texture. It looked like wet, blue rubber glistening under droplets of water like little round jewels in the glare of the gasoline pressure lantern. Connant felt an unreasoning desire to pour the contents of the lamp's reservoir over the thing in its box and drop the cigarette into it. The three red eyes glared up at him sightlessly, the ruby eyeballs reflecting murky, smoky rays of light.

He realized vaguely that he had been looking at them for a very long time, even vaguely understood that they were no longer sightless. But it did not seem of importance, of no more importance than the labored, slow motion of the tentacular things that sprouted from the base of the scrawny, slowly pulsing neck.

Connant picked up the pressure lamp and returned to his chair. He sat down, staring at the pages of mathematics before him. The clucking of the counter was strangely less disturbing, the rustle of the coals in the stove no longer distracting.

The creak of the floorboards behind him didn't interrupt his thoughts as he went about his weekly report in an automatic manner, filling in columns of data and making brief, summarizing notes.

The creak of the floorboards sounded nearer.

V

Blair came up from the nightmare-haunted depths of sleep abruptly. Connant's face floated vaguely above him; for a moment it seemed a continuance of the wild horror of the dream. But Connant's face was angry, and a little frightened. "Blair—Blair you damned log. wake up."

"Uh-eh?" the little biologist rubbed his eyes, his bony, freckled fingers crooked to a mutilated child-fist. From surrounding bunks other faces lifted to stare down at them.

Connant straightened up. "Get up—and get a lift on. Your damned animal's escaped."

"Escaped—what!" Chief Pilot Van Wall's bull voice roared out with a volume that shook the walls. Down the communication tunnels other voices yelled suddenly. The dozen inhabitants of Paradise House tumbled in abruptly, Barclay, stocky and bulbous in long woolen underwear, carrying a fire extinguisher.

"What the hell's the matter?" Barclay demanded.

"Your damned beast got loose. I fell asleep about twenty minutes ago, and when I woke up, the thing was gone. Hey, Doc, the hell you say those things can't come to life. Blair's blasted potential life developed a hell of a lot of potential and walked out on us."

Copper stared blankly. "It wasn't—Earthly," he sighed suddenly. "I—I guess Earthly laws don't apply."

"Well, it applied for leave of absence and took it. We've got to find it and capture it somehow." Connant swore bitterly, his deep-set black eyes sullen and angry. "It's a wonder the hellish creature didn't eat me in my sleep."

Blair started back, his pale eyes suddenly fear-struck. "Maybe it di—er—uh—we'll have to find it."

"You find it. It's your pet. I've had all I want to do with it, sitting there for seven hours with the counter clucking every few seconds, and you birds in here singing night-music. It's a wonder I got to sleep. I'm going through to the Ad Building."

Commander Garry ducked through the doorway, pulling his belt tight. "You won't have to. Van's roar sounded like the Boeing taking off down wind. So it wasn't dead?"

"I didn't carry it off in my arms, I assure you," Connant snapped. "The last I saw, that split skull was oozing green goo, like a squashed caterpillar. Doc just said our laws don't work—it's unearthly. Well, it's an unearthly monster, with an unearthly disposition, judging by the face, wandering around with a split skull and brains oozing out."

Norris and McReady appeared in the doorway, a doorway filling with other shivering men. "Has anybody seen it coming over here?" Norris asked innocently. "About four feet tall—three red eyes— brains oozing out—— Hey, has anybody checked to make sure this isn't a cracked idea of humor? If it is, I think we'll unite in tying

Blair's pet around Connant's neck like the Ancient Mariner's albatross."

"It's no humor," Connant shivered. "Lord, I wish it were. I'd rather wear——" He stopped. A wild, weird howl shrieked through the corridors. The men stiffened abruptly, and half turned.

"I think it's been located," Connant finished. His dark eyes shifted with a queer unease. He darted back to his bunk in Paradise House, to return almost immediately with a heavy .45 revolver and an ice-ax. He hefted both gently as he started for the corridor toward Dog-town. "It blundered down the wrong corridor—and landed among the huskies. Listen—the dogs have broken their chains——"

The half-terrorized howl of the dog pack had changed to a wild hunting melee. The voices of the dogs thundered in the narrow corridors, and through them came a low rippling snarl of distilled hate. A shrill of pain, a dozen snarling yelps.

Connant broke for the door. Close behind him, McReady, then Barclay and Commander Garry came. Other men broke for the Ad Building, and weapons—the sledge house. Pomroy, in charge of Big Magnet's five cows, started down the corridor in the opposite direction—he had a six-foot-handled, long-tined pitchfork in mind.

Barclay slid to a halt, as McReady's giant bulk turned abruptly away from the tunnel leading to Dogtown, and vanished off at an angle. Uncertainly, the mechanician wavered a moment, the fire extinguisher in his hands, hesitating from one side to the other. Then he was racing after Connant's broad back. Whatever McReady had in mind, he could be trusted to make it work.

Connant stopped at the bend in the corridor. His breath hissed suddenly through his throat. "Great God——" The revolver exploded thunderously; three numbing, palpable waves of sound crashed through the confined corridors. Two more. The revolver dropped to the hard-packed snow of the trail, and Barclay saw the ice-ax shift into defensive position. Connant's powerful body blocked his vision, but beyond he heard something mewing, and, insanely, chuckling. The dogs were quieter; there was a deadly seriousness in their low snarls. Taloned feet scratched at hard-packed snow, broken chains were clinking and tangling.

Connant shifted abruptly, and Barclay could see what lay beyond. For a second he stood frozen, then his breath went out in a gusty curse. The Thing launched itself at Connant, the powerful arms of the man swung the ice-ax flatside first at what might have been a head. It scrunched horribly, and the tattered flesh, ripped by a half-dozen savage huskies, leapt to its feet again. The red eyes blazed with an unearthly hatred, an unearthly, unkillable vitality.

Barclay turned the fire extinguisher on it; the blinding, blistering stream of chemical spray confused it, baffled it, together with the savage attacks of the huskies, not for long afraid of anything that did, or could live, held it at bay.

McReady wedged men out of his way and drove down the narrow corridor packed with men unable to reach the scene. There was a sure fore-planned drive to McReady's attack. One of the giant blow-torches used in warming the plane's engines was in his bronzed hands. It roared gustily as he turned the corner and opened the valve. The mad mewing hissed louder. The dogs scrambled back from the three-foot lance of blue-hot flame.

"Bar, get a power cable, run it in somehow. And a handle. We can electrocute this—monster, if I don't incinerate it." McReady spoke with an authority of planned action. Barclay turned down the long corridor to the power plant, but already before him Norris and Van Wall were racing down.

Barclay found the cable in the electrical cache in the tunnel wall. In a half minute he was hacking at it, walking back. Van Wall's voice rang out in warning shout of "Power!" as the emergency gasoline-powered dynamo thudded into action. Half a dozen other men were down there now; the coal, kindling were going into the firebox of the steam power plant. Norris, cursing in a low, deadly monotone, was working with quick, sure fingers on the other end of Barclay's cable, splicing in a contactor in one of the power leads.

The dogs had fallen back when Barclay reached the corridor bend, fallen back before a furious monstrosity that glared from baleful red eyes, mewing in trapped hatred. The dogs were a semi-circle of red-dipped muzzles with a fringe of glistening white teeth, whining with a vicious eagerness that near matched the fury of the red eyes. McReady stood confidently alert at the corridor bend, the gustily muttering torch held loose and ready for action in his hands. He stepped aside without moving his eyes from the beast as Barclay came up. There was a slight, tight smile on his lean, bronzed face.

Norris' voice called down the corridor, and Barclay stepped forward. The cable was taped to the long handle of a snow-shovel, the two conductors split, and held 18 inches apart by a scrap of lumber lashed at right angles across the far end of the handle. Bare copper conductors, charged with 220 volts, glinted in the light of pressure lamps. The Thing mewed and halted and dodged. McReady advanced to Barclay's side. The dogs beyond sensed the plan with the almost-telepathic intelligence of trained huskies. Their whining grew shriller, softer, their mincing steps carried them nearer. Abruptly a huge, night-black Alaskan leapt onto the trapped thing. It turned squalling, saber-clawed feet slashing.

Barclay leapt forward and jabbed. A weird, shrill scream rose and choked out. The smell of burnt flesh in the corridor intensified; greasy smoke curled up. The echoing pound of the gas-electric dynamo down the corridor became a slogging thud.

The red eyes clouded over in a stiffening, jerking travesty of a face. Armlike, leglike members quivered and jerked. The dogs leapt forward, and Barclay yanked back his shovel-handled weapon. The thing on the snow did not move as gleaming teeth ripped it open.

VI

Garry looked about the crowded room. Thirty-two men, some tensed nervously standing against the wall, some uneasily relaxed, some sitting, most perforce standing, as intimate as sardines. Thirty-two, plus the five engaged in sewing up wounded dogs, made thirty-seven, the total personnel.

Garry started speaking. "All right, I guess we're here. Some of you—three or four at most—saw what happened. All of you have seen that thing on the table, and can get a general idea. Anyone hasn't, I'll lift——" His hand strayed to the tarpaulin bulking over the thing on the table. There was an acrid odor of singed flesh seeping out of it. The men stirred restlessly, hasty denials.

"It looks rather as though Charnauk isn't going to lead any more teams," Garry went on. "Blair wants to get at this thing, and make some more detailed examination. We want to know what happened, and make sure right now that this is permanently, totally dead. Right?"

Connant grinned. "Anybody that doesn't agree can sit up with it tonight."

"All right then, Blair, what can you say about it? What was it?" Garry turned to the little biologist.

"I wonder if we ever saw its natural form," Blair looked at the covered mass. "It may have been imitating the beings that built that ship—but I don't think it was. I think that was its true form. Those of us who were up near the bend saw the thing in action; the thing on the table is the result. When it got loose, apparently, it started looking around. Antarctica still frozen as it was ages ago when the creature first saw it—and froze. From my observations while it was thawing out, and the bits of tissue I cut and hardened then, I think it was native to a hotter planet than Earth. It couldn't, in its natural form, stand the temperature. There is no life-form on Earth that can live in Antarctica during the winter, but the best compromise is the dog. It found the dogs, and somehow got near enough to Charnauk to get him. The others smelled it—heard it— I don't know—anyway they went wild, and broke chains, and attacked it before it was finished. The thing we found was part Charnauk, queerly only half-dead, part Charnauk half-digested by the jellylike protoplasm of that creature, and part the remains of the thing we originally found, sort of melted down to the basic protoplasm.

"When the dogs attacked it, it turned into the best fighting thing it could think of. Some other-world beast apparently."

"Turned," snapped Garry. "How?"

"Every living thing is made up of jelly—protoplasm and minute, submicroscopic things called nuclei, which control the bulk, the protoplasm. This thing was just a modification of that same worldwide plan of Nature; cells made up of protoplasm, controlled by infinitely tinier nuclei. You physicists might compare it—an individual cell of any living thing—with an atom; the bulk of the atom, the space-filling part, is made up of the electron orbits, but the character of the thing is determined by the atomic nucleus.

"This isn't wildly beyond what we already know. It's just a modification we haven't seen before. It's as natural, as logical, as any other manifestation of life. It obeys exactly the same laws. The cells are made of protoplasm, their character determined by the nucleus.

"Only in this creature, the cell-nuclei can control those cells at will. It digested Charnauk, and as it digested, studied every cell of his tissue, and shaped its own cells to imitate them exactly. Parts of it —parts that had time to finish changing—are dog-cells. But they don't have dog-cell nuclei." Blair lifted a fraction of the tarpaulin. A torn dog's leg with stiff gray fur protruded. "That, for instance, isn't dog at all; it's imitation. Some parts I'm uncertain about; the nucleus was hiding itself, covering up with dog-cell imitation nucleus. In time, not even a microscope would have shown the difference."

"Suppose," asked Norris bitterly, "it had had lots of time?"

"Then it would have been a dog. The other dogs would have accepted it. We would have accepted it. I don't think anything would have distinguished it, not microscope, nor X-ray, nor any other means. This is a member of a supremely intelligent race, a race that has learned the deepest secrets of biology, and turned them to its use."

"What was it planning to do?" Barclay looked at the humped tarpaulin.

Blair grinned unpleasantly. The wavering halo of thin hair round his bald pate wavered in a stir of air. "Take over the world, I imagine."

"Take over the world! Just it, all by itself?" Connant gasped. "Set itself up as a lone dictator?"

"No," Blair shook his head. The scalpel he had been fumbling in his bony fingers dropped; he bent to pick it up, so that his face was hidden as he spoke. "It would become the population of the world."

"Become—populate the world? Does it reproduce asexually?"

Blair shook his hand and gulped. "It's—it doesn't have to. It weighed 85 pounds. Charnauk weighed about 90. It would have become Charnauk, and had 85 pounds left, to become—oh, Jack for instance, or Chinook. It can imitate anything—that is, become anything. If it had reached the Antarctic Sea, it would have become a seal, maybe two seals. They might have attacked a killer whale, and become either killers, or a herd of seals. Or maybe it would have caught an albatross, or a skua gull, and flown to South America."

Norris cursed softly. "And every time it digested something, and imitated it——"

"It would have had its original bulk left, to start again," Blair finished. "Nothing would kill it. It has no natural enemies, because it becomes whatever it wants to. If a killer whale attacked it, it would become a killer whale. If it was an albatross, and an eagle attacked it, it would become an eagle. Lord, it might become a female eagle. Go back—build a nest and lay eggs!"

"Are you sure that thing from hell is dead?" Dr. Copper asked softly.

"Yes, thank Heaven," the little biologist gasped. "After they drove the dogs off, I stood there poking Bar's electrocution thing into it for five minutes. It's dead and—cooked."

"Then we can only give thanks that this is Antarctica, where there is not one, single, solitary, living thing for it to imitate, except these animals in camp."

"Us," Blair giggled. "It can imitate us. Dogs can't make 400 miles to the sea; there's no food. There aren't any skua gulls to imitate at this season. There aren't any penguins this far inland. There's nothing that can reach the sea from this point—except us. We've got brains. We can do it. Don't you see—*it's got to imitate us*—*it's got to be one of us—that's the only way it can fly an airplane—fly a plane for two hours, and rule—be—all Earth's inhabitants. A world for the taking—if it imitates us!*

"It didn't know yet. It hadn't had a chance to learn. It was rushed—hurried—took the thing nearest its own size. Look—I'm Pandora! I opened the box! And the only hope that can come out is—that nothing can come out. You didn't see me. I did it. I fixed it. I smashed every magneto. Not a plane can fly. Nothing can fly." Blair giggled and lay down on the floor crying.

Chief Pilot Van Wall made a dive for the door. His feet were fading echoes in the corridors as Dr. Copper bent unhurriedly over the little man on the floor. From his office at the end of the room he brought something, and injected a solution into Blair's arm. "He might come out of it when he wakes up," he sighed rising. McReady helped him lift the biologist onto a near-by bunk. "It all depends on whether we can convince him that thing is dead."

Van Wall ducked into the shack brushing his heavy blond beard absently. "I didn't think a biologist would do a thing like that up thoroughly. He missed the spares in the second cache. It's all right. I smashed them."

Commander Garry nodded. "I was wondering about the radio."

Dr. Copper snorted. "You don't think it can leak out on a radio wave, do you? You'd have five rescue attempts in the next three months if you stop the broadcasts. The thing to do is talk loud and not make a sound. Now I wonder——"

McReady looked speculatively at the doctor. "It might be like an infectious disease. Everything that drank any of its blood——"

Copper shook his head. "Blair missed something. Imitate it may, but it has, to a certain extent, its own body chemistry, its own metabolism. If it didn't, it would become a dog—and be a dog and nothing more. It has to be an imitation dog. Therefore you can detect it by serum tests. And its chemistry, since it comes from another world, must be so wholly, radically different that a few cells, such as gained by drops of blood, would be treated as disease germs by the dog, or human body."

"Blood—would one of those imitations bleed?" Norris demanded.

"Surely. Nothing mystic about blood. Muscle is about 90% water; blood differs only in having a couple per cent more water, and less connective tissue. They'd bleed all right," Copper assured him.

Blair sat up in his bunk suddenly. "Connant—where's Connant?"

The physicist moved over toward the little biologist. "Here I am. What do you want?"

"Are you?" giggled Blair. He lapsed back into the bunk contorted with silent laughter.

Connant looked at him blankly. "Huh? Am I what?"

"Are you there?" Blair burst into gales of laughter. "Are you Connant? The beast wanted to be a man—not a dog——"

VII

Dr. Copper rose wearily from the bunk, and washed the hypodermic carefully. The little tinkles it made seemed loud in the packed room, now that Blair's gurgling laughter had finally quieted. Copper looked toward Garry and shook his head slowly. "Hopeless, I'm afraid. I don't think we can ever convince him the thing is dead now."

Norris laughed uncertainly. "I'm not sure you can convince me. Oh, damn you, McReady."

"McReady?" Commander Garry turned to look from Norris to McReady curiously.

"The nightmares," Norris explained. "He had a theory about the nightmares we had at the Secondary Station after finding that thing."

"And that was?" Garry looked at McReady levelly.

Norris answered for him, jerkily, uneasily. "That the creature wasn't dead, had a sort of enormously slowed existence, an existence that permitted it, none the less, to be vaguely aware of the passing of time, of our coming, after endless years. I had a dream it could imitate things."

"Well," Copper grunted, "it can."

"Don't be an ass," Norris snapped. "That's not what's bothering me. In the dream it could read minds, read thoughts and ideas and mannerisms."

"What's so bad about that? It seems to be worrying you more than the thought of the joy we're going to have with a mad man in an Antarctic camp." Copper nodded toward Blair's sleeping form.

McReady shook his great head slowly. "You know that Connant is Connant, because he not merely looks like Connant— which we're beginning to believe that beast might be able to do— but he thinks like Connant, talks like Connant, moves himself around as Connant does. That takes more than merely a body that looks like him; that takes Connant's own mind, and thoughts and mannerisms. Therefore, though you know that the thing might make itself look like Connant, you aren't much bothered, because you know it has a mind from another world, a totally unhuman mind, that couldn't possibly react and think and talk like a man we know, and do it so well as to fool us for a moment. The idea of the creature imitating one of us is fascinating, but unreal because it is too completely unhuman to deceive us. It doesn't have a human mind."

"As I said before," Norris repeated, looking steadily at McReady, "you can say the damnedest things at the damnedest times. Will you be so good as to finish that thought—one way or the other?"

Kinner, the scar-faced expedition cook, had been standing near Connant. Suddenly he moved down the length of the crowded room toward his familiar galley. He shook the ashes from the galley stove noisily.

"It would do it no good," said Dr. Copper, softly as though thinking out loud, "to merely look like something it was trying to imitate; it would have to understand its feelings, its reactions. It is unhuman; it has powers of imitation beyond any conception of man. A good actor, by training himself, can imitate another man, another man's mannerisms, well enough to fool most people. Of course no actor could imitate so perfectly as to deceive men who had been living with the imitated one in the complete lack of privacy of an Antarctic camp. That would take a super-human skill."

"Oh, you've got the bug too?" Norris cursed softly.

Connant, standing alone at one end of the room, looked about him wildly, his face white. A gentle eddying of the men had crowded them slowly down toward the other end of the room, so that he stood quite alone. "My God, will you two Jeremiahs shut up?" Connant's voice shook. "What am I? Some kind of a microscopic specimen you're dissecting? Some unpleasant worm you're discussing in the third person?"

McReady looked up at him; his slowly twisting hands stopped for a moment. "Having a lovely time. Wish you were here. Signed: Everybody.

"Connant, if you think you're having a hell of a time, just move over on the other end for a while. You've got one thing we haven't; you know what the answer is. I'll tell you this, right now you're the most feared and respected man in Big Magnet."

"Lord, I wish you could see your eyes," Connant gasped. "Stop staring, will you! What the hell are you going to do?"

"Have you any suggestions, Dr. Copper?" Commander Garry asked steadily. "The present situation is impossible."

"Oh, is it?" Connant snapped. "Come over here and look at that crowd. By Heaven, they look exactly like that gang of huskies around the corridor bend. Benning, will you stop hefting that damned ice-ax?"

The coppery blade rang on the floor as the aviation mechanic nervously dropped it. He bent over and picked it up instantly, hefting it slowly, turning it in his hands, his brown eyes moving jerkily about the room.

Copper sat down on the bunk beside Blair. The wood creaked noisily in the room. Far down a corridor, a dog yelped in pain, and the dog-drivers' tense voices floated softly back. "Microscopic examination," said the doctor thoughtfully, "would be useless, as Blair pointed out. Considerable time has passed. However, serum tests would be definitive."

"Serum tests? What do you mean exactly?" Commander Garry asked.

"If I had a rabbit that had been injected with human blood— a poison to rabbits, of course, as is the blood of any animal save that of another rabbit—and the injections continued in increasing doses for some time, the rabbit would be human-immune. If a small quantity of its blood were drawn off, allowed to separate in a test-tube, and to the clear serum, a bit of human blood were added, there would be a visible reaction, proving the blood was human. If cow, or dog blood were added—or any protein material other than that one thing, human blood—no reaction would take place. That would prove definitely."

"Can you suggest where I might catch a rabbit for you, Doc?" Norris asked. "That is, nearer than Australia; we don't want to waste time going that far."

"I know there aren't any rabbits in Antarctica," Copper nodded, "but that is simply the usual animal. Any animal except man will do. A dog for instance. But it will take several days, and due to the greater size of the animal, considerable blood. Two of us will have to contribute."

"Would I do?" Garry asked.

"That will make two," Copper nodded. "I'll get to work on it right away."

"What about Connant in the meantime?" Kinner demanded. "I'm going out that door and head off for the Ross Sea before I cook for him."

"He may be human——" Copper started.

Connant burst out in a flood of curses. "Human! *May* be human, you damned saw-bones! What in hell do you think I am?"

"A monster," Copper snapped sharply. "Now shut up and listen." Connant's face drained of color and he sat down heavily as the indictment was put in words. "Until we know—you know as well as we do that we have reason to question the fact, and only you know how that question is to be answered—we may reasonably be expected to lock you up. If you are—unhuman—you're a lot more dangerous than poor Blair there, and I'm going to see that he's locked up thoroughly. I expect that his next stage will be a violent desire to kill you, all the dogs, and probably all of us. When he wakes, he will be convinced we're all unhuman, and nothing on the planet will ever change his conviction. It would be kinder to let him die, but we can't do that, of course. He's going in one shack, and you can stay in Cosmos House with your cosmic ray apparatus. Which is about what you'd do anyway. I've got to fix up a couple of dogs."

Connant nodded bitterly. "I'm human. Hurry that test. Your eyes —Lord, I wish you could see your eyes staring——"

Commander Garry watched anxiously as Clark, the dog-handler, held the big brown Alaskan husky, while Copper began the injection treatment. The dog was not anxious to coöperate; the needle was painful, and already he'd experienced considerable needle work that morning. Five stitches held closed a slash that ran from his shoulder across the ribs half way down his body. One long fang was broken off short; the missing part was to be found half-buried in the shoulder bone of the monstrous thing on the table in the Ad Building.

"How long will that take?" Garry asked, pressing his arm gently. It was sore from the prick of the needle Dr. Copper had used to withdraw blood.

Copper shrugged. "I don't know, to be frank. I know the general method, I've used it on rabbits. But I haven't experimented with dogs. They're big, clumsy animals to work with; naturally rabbits are preferable, and serve ordinarily. In civilized places you can buy a stock of human-immune rabbits from suppliers, and not many investigators take the trouble to prepare their own."

"What do they want with them back there?" Clark asked.

"Criminology is one large field. A says he didn't murder B, but that the blood on his shirt came from killing a chicken. The State makes a test, then it's up to A to explain how it is the blood reacts on human-immune rabbits, but not on chicken-immunes."

"What are we going to do with Blair in the meantime?" Garry asked wearily. "It's all right to let him sleep where he is for a while, but when he wakes up——"

"Barclay and Benning are fitting some bolts on the door of Cosmos House," Copper replied grimly. "Connant's acting like a gentleman. I think perhaps the way the other men look at him makes him rather want privacy. Lord knows, heretofore we've all of us individually prayed for a little privacy."

Clark laughed brittlely. "Not any more, thank you. The more the merrier."

"Blair," Copper went on, "will also have to have privacy—and locks. He's going to have a pretty definite plan in mind when he wakes up. Ever hear the old story of how to stop hoof-and-mouth disease in cattle?"

Clark and Garry shook their heads silently.

"If there isn't any hoof-and-mouth disease, there won't be any hoof-and-mouth disease," Copper explained. "You get rid of it by killing every animal that exhibits it, and every animal that's been near the diseased animal. Blair's a biologist, and knows that story. He's afraid of this thing we loosed. The answer is probably pretty clear in his mind now. Kill everybody and everything in this camp before a skua gull or a wandering albatross coming in with the spring chances out this way and—catches the disease."

Clark's lips curled in a twisted grin. "Sounds logical to me. If things get too bad—maybe we'd better let Blair get loose. It would save us committing suicide. We might also make something of a vow that if things get bad, we see that that does happen."

Copper laughed softly. "The last man alive in Big Magnet—wouldn't be a man," he pointed out. "Somebody's got to kill those —creatures that don't desire to kill themselves, you know. We don't have enough thermite to do it all at once, and the decanite explosive wouldn't help much. I have an idea that even small pieces of one of those beings would be self-sufficient."

"If," said Garry thoughtfully, "they can modify their protoplasm at will, won't they simply modify themselves to birds and fly away? They can read all about birds, and imitate their structure without even meeting them. Or imitate, perhaps, birds of their home planet."

Copper shook his head, and helped Clark to free the dog. "Man studied birds for centuries, trying to learn how to make a machine to fly like them. He never did do the trick; his final success came when he broke away entirely and tried new methods. Knowing the general idea, and knowing the detailed structure of wing and bone and nerve-tissue is something far, far different. And as for other-world birds, perhaps, in fact very probably, the atmospheric conditions here are so vastly different that their birds couldn't fly. Perhaps, even, the being came from a planet like Mars with such a thin atmosphere that there were no birds."

Barclay came into the building, trailing a length of airplane control cable. "It's finished, Doc. Cosmos House can't be opened from the inside. Now where do we put Blair?"

Copper looked toward Garry. "There wasn't any biology building. I don't know where we can isolate him."

"How about East Cache?" Garry said after a moment's thought. "Will Blair be able to look after himself—or need attention?"

"He'll be capable enough. We'll be the ones to watch out," Copper assured him grimly. "Take a stove, a couple of bags of coal, necessary supplies and a few tools to fix it up. Nobody's been out there since last fall, have they?"

Garry shook his head. "If he gets noisy—I thought that might be a good idea."

Barclay hefted the tools he was carrying and looked up at Garry. "If the muttering he's doing now is any sign, he's going to sing away the night hours. And we won't like his song."

"What's he saying?" Copper asked.

Barclay shook his head. "I didn't care to listen much. You can if you want to. But I gathered that the blasted idiot had all the dreams McReady had, and a few more. He slept beside the thing when we stopped on the trail coming in from Secondary Magnetic, remember. He dreamt the thing was alive, and dreamt more details. And— damn his soul—knew it wasn't all dream, or had reason to. He knew it had telepathic powers that were stirring vaguely, and that it could not only read minds, but project thoughts. They weren't dreams, you see. They were stray thoughts that thing was broadcasting, the way Blair's broadcasting his thoughts now—a sort of telepathic muttering in its sleep. That's why he knew so much about its powers. I guess you and I, Doc, weren't so sensitive—if you want to believe in telepathy."

"I have to," Copper sighed. "Dr. Rhine of Duke University has shown that it exists, shown that some are much more sensitive than others."

"Well, if you want to learn a lot of details, go listen in on Blair's broadcast. He's driven most of the boys out of the Ad Building; Kinner's rattling pans like coal going down a chute. When he can't rattle a pan, he shakes ashes.

"By the way, Commander, what are we going to do this spring, now the planes are out of it?"

Garry sighed. "I'm afraid our expedition is going to be a loss. We cannot divide our strength now."

"It won't be a loss—if we continue to live, and come out of this," Copper promised him. "The find we've made, if we can get it under control, is important enough. The cosmic ray data, magnetic work, and atmospheric work won't be greatly hindered."

Garry laughed mirthlessly. "I was just thinking of the radio broadcasts. Telling half the world about the wonderful results of our exploration flights, trying to fool men like Byrd and Ellsworth back home there that we're doing something."

Copper nodded gravely. "They'll know something's wrong. But men like that have judgment enough to know we wouldn't do tricks without some sort of reason, and will wait for our return to judge us. I think it comes to this: men who know enough to recognize our deception will wait for our return. Men who haven't discretion and faith enough to wait will not have the experience to detect any fraud. We know enough of the conditions here to put through a good bluff."

"Just so they don't send 'rescue' expeditions," Garry prayed. "When—if—we're ever ready to come out, we'll have to send word to Captain Forsythe to bring a stock of magnetos with him when he comes down. But—never mind that."

"You mean if we don't come out?" asked Barclay. "I was wondering if a nice running account of an eruption or an earthquake via radio—with a swell windup by using a stick of decanite under the microphone—would help. Nothing, of course, will entirely keep people out. One of those swell, melodramatic 'last-man-alive-scenes' might make 'em go easy though."

Garry smiled with genuine humor. "Is everybody in camp trying to figure that out too?"

Copper laughed. "What do you think, Garry? We're confident we can win out. But not too easy about it, I guess."

Clark grinned up from the dog he was petting into calmness. "Confident, did you say, Doc?"

VIII

Blair moved restlessly around the small shack. His eyes jerked and quivered in vague, fleeting glances at the four men with him; Barclay, six feet tall and weighing over 190 pounds; McReady, a bronze giant of a man; Dr. Copper, short, squatly powerful; and Benning, five-feet-ten of wiry strength.

Blair was huddled up against the far wall of the East Cache cabin, his gear piled in the middle of the floor beside the heating stove, forming an island between him and the four men. His bony hands clenched and fluttered, terrified. His pale eyes wavered uneasily as his bald, freckled head darted about in birdlike motion.

"I don't want anybody coming here. I'll cook my own food," he snapped nervously. "Kinner may be human now, but I don't believe it. I'm going to get out of here, but I'm not going to eat any food you send me. I want cans. Sealed cans."

"O. K., Blair, we'll bring 'em tonight," Barclay promised. "You've got coal, and the fire's started. I'll make a last——" Barclay started forward.

Blair instantly scurried to the farthest corner. "Get out! Keep away from me, you monster!" the little biologist shrieked, and tried to claw his way through the wall of the shack. "Keep away from me— keep away—I won't be absorbed—I won't be——"

Barclay relaxed and moved back. Dr. Copper shook his head. "Leave him alone, Bar. It's easier for him to fix the thing himself. We'll have to fix the door, I think——"

The four men let themselves out. Efficiently, Benning and Barclay fell to work. There were no locks in Antarctica; there wasn't enough privacy to make them needed. But powerful screws had been driven in each side of the door frame, and the spare aviation control cable, immensely strong, woven steel wire, was rapidly caught between them and drawn taut. Barclay went to work with a drill and a keyhole saw. Presently he had a trap cut in the door through which goods could be passed without unlashing the entrance. Three powerful hinges from a stock-crate, two hasps and a pair of three-inch cotterpins made it proof against opening from the other side.

Blair moved about restlessly inside. He was dragging something over to the door with panting gasps and muttering, frantic curses. Barclay opened the hatch and glanced in, Dr. Copper peering over his shoulder. Blair had moved the heavy bunk against the door. It could not be opened without his coöperation now.

"Don't know but what the poor man's right at that," McReady sighed. "If he gets loose, it is his avowed intention to kill each and all of us as quickly as possible, which is something we don't agree with. But we've something on our side of that door that is worse than a homicidal maniac. If one or the other has to get loose, I think I'll come up and undo chose lashings here."

Barclay grinned. "You let me know, and I'll show you how to get these off fast. Let's go back."

The sun was painting the northern horizon in multi-colored rainbows still, though it was two hours below the horizon. The field of drift swept off to the north, sparkling under its flaming colors in a million reflected glories. Low mounds of rounded white on the northern horizon showed the Magnet Range was barely awash above the sweeping drift. Little eddies of wind-lifted snow swirled away from their skis as they set out toward the main encampment two miles away. The spidery finger of the broadcast radiator lifted a gaunt black needle against the white of the Antarctic continent. The snow under their skis was like fine sand, hard and gritty.

"Spring," said Benning bitterly, "is came. Ain't we got fun! I've been looking forward to getting away from this blasted hole in the ice."

"I wouldn't try it now, if I were you." Barclay grunted. "Guys that set out from here in the next few days are going to be marvelously unpopular."

"How is your dog getting along, Dr. Copper?" McReady asked, "Any results yet?"

"In 30 hours? I wish there were. I gave him an injection of my blood today. But I imagine another five days will be needed. I don't know certainly enough to stop sooner."

"I've been wondering—if Connant were—changed, would he have warned us so soon after the animal escaped? Wouldn't he have waited long enough for it to have a real chance to fix itself? Until we woke up naturally?" McReady asked slowly.

"The thing is selfish. You didn't think it looked as though it were possessed of a store of the higher justices, did you?" Dr. Copper pointed out. "Every part of it is all of it, every part of it is all for itself, I imagine. If Connant were changed, to save his skin, he'd have to—but Connant's feelings aren't changed; they're imitated perfectly, or they're his own. Naturally, the imitation, imitating perfectly Connant's feelings, would do exactly what Connant would do."

"Say, couldn't Norris or Vane give Connant some kind of a test? If the thing is brighter than men, it might know more physics than Connant should, and they'd catch it out," Barclay suggested.

Copper shook his head wearily. "Not if it reads minds. You can't plan a trap for it. Vane suggested that last night. He hoped it would answer some of the questions of physics he'd like to know answers to."

"This expedition-of-four idea is going to make life happy." Benning looked at his companions. "Each of us with an eye on the others to make sure he doesn't do something—peculiar. Man, aren't we going to be a trusting bunch! Each man eyeing his neighbors with the grandest exhibition of faith and trust—— I'm beginning to know what Connant meant by 'I wish you could see your eyes'. Every now and then we all have it, I guess. One of you looks around with a sort of 'I-wonder-if-the-other-three-are-look.' Incidentally, I'm not excepting myself."

"So far as we know, the animal is dead, with a slight question as to Connant. No other is suspected," McReady stated slowly. "The 'always-four' order is merely a precautionary measure."

"I'm waiting for Garry to make it four-in-a-bunk," Barclay sighed. "I thought I didn't have any privacy before, but since that order——"

None watched more tensely than Connant. A little sterile glass test-tube, half-filled with straw-colored fluid. One—two—three—four—five drops of the clear solution Dr. Copper had prepared from the drops of blood from Connant's arm. The tube was shaken carefully, then set in a beaker of clear, warm water. The thermometer read blood heat, a little thermostat clicked noisily, and the electric hotplate began to glow as the lights flickered slightly.

Then—little white flecks of precipitation were forming, snowing down in the clear straw-colored fluid. "Lord," said Connant. He dropped heavily into a bunk, crying like a baby. "Six days—" Connant sobbed, "six days in there—wondering if that damned test would lie——"

Garry moved over silently, and slipped his arm across the physicist's back.

"It couldn't lie," Dr. Copper said, "The dog was human-immune—and the serum reacted."

"He's—all right?" Norris gasped. "Then—the animal is dead—dead forever?"

"He is human," Copper spoke definitely, "and the animal is dead."

Kinner burst out laughing, laughing hysterically. McReady turned toward him and slapped his face with a methodical one-two, one-two action. The cook laughed, gulped, cried a moment, and sat up rubbing his cheeks, mumbling his thanks vaguely. "I was scared. Lord, I was scared——"

Norris laughed brittlely. "You think we weren't, you ape? You think maybe Connant wasn't?"

The Ad Building stirred with a sudden rejuvenation. Voices laughed, the men clustering around Connant spoke with unnecessarily loud voices, jittery, nervous voices relievedly friendly again. Somebody called out a suggestion, and a dozen started for their skis. Blair. Blair might recover—— Dr. Copper fussed with his test-tubes in nervous relief, trying solutions. The party of relief for Blair's shack started out the door, skis clapping noisily. Down the corridor, the dogs set up a quick yelping howl as the air of excited relief reached them.

Dr. Copper fussed with his tubes. McReady noticed him first, sitting on the edge of the bunk, with two precipitin-whitened test-tubes of straw-colored fluid, his face whiter than the stuff in the tubes, silent tears slipping down from horror-widened eyes.

McReady felt a cold knife of fear pierce through his heart and freeze in his breast. Dr. Copper looked up.

"Garry," he called hoarsely. "Garry, for God's sake, come here."

Commander Garry walked toward him sharply. Silence clapped down on the Ad Building. Connant looked up, rose stiffly from his seat.

"Garry—tissue from the monster—precipitates too. It proves nothing. Nothing but—but the dog was monster-immune too. That *one of the two contributing blood—one of us two, you and I, Garry —one of us is a monster."*

IX

"Bar, call back those men before they tell Blair," McReady said quietly. Barclay went to the door; faintly his shouts came back to the tensely silent men in the room. Then he was back.

"They're coming," he said. "I didn't tell them why. Just that Dr. Copper said not to go."

"McReady," Garry sighed, "you're in command now. May God help you. I cannot."

The bronzed giant nodded slowly, his deep eyes on Commander Garry.

"I may be the one," Garry added. "I know I'm not, but I cannot prove it to you in any way. Dr. Copper's test has broken down. The fact that he showed it was useless, when it was to the advantage of the monster to have that uselessness not known, would seem to prove he was human."

Copper rocked back and forth slowly on the bunk. "I know I'm human. I can't prove it either. One of us two is a liar, for that test cannot lie, and it says one of us is. I gave proof that the test was wrong, which seems to prove I'm human, and now Garry has given that argument which proves me human—which he, as the monster, should not do. Round and round and round and round and——"

Dr. Copper's head, then his neck and shoulders began circling slowly in time to the words. Suddenly he was lying back on the bunk, roaring with laughter. "It doesn't have to prove *one* of us is a monster! It doesn't have to prove that at all! Ho-ho. If we're *all* monsters it works the same! We're all monsters—all of us—Connant and Garry and I—and all of you."

"McReady," Van Wall, the blond-bearded Chief Pilot, called softly, "you were on the way to an M. D. when you took up meteorology, weren't you? Can you make some kind of test?"

McReady went over to Copper slowly, took the hypodermic from his hand, and washed it carefully in 95% alcohol. Garry sat on the bunk-edge with wooden face, watching Copper and McReady expressionlessly. "What Copper said is possible," McReady sighed.

"Van, will you help here? Thanks." The filled needle jabbed into Copper's thigh. The man's laughter did not stop, but slowly faded into sobs, then sound sleep as the morphia took hold.

McReady turned again. The men who had started for Blair stood at the far end of the room, skis dripping snow, their faces as white as their skis. Connant had a lighted cigarette in each hand; one he was puffing absently, and staring at the floor. The heat of the one in his left hand attracted him and he stared at it, and the one in the other hand stupidly for a moment. He dropped one and crushed it under his heel slowly.

"Dr. Copper," McReady repeated, "could be right. I know I'm human—but of course can't prove it. I'll repeat the test for my own information. Any of you others who wish to may do the same."

Two minutes later, McReady held a test-tube with white precipitin settling slowly from straw-colored serum. "It reacts to human blood too, so they aren't both monsters."

"I didn't think they were," Van Wall sighed. "That wouldn't suit the monster either; we could have destroyed them if we knew. Why, hasn't the monster destroyed us, do you suppose? It seems to be loose."

McReady snorted. Then laughed softly. "Elementary, my dear Watson. The monster wants to have life forms available. It cannot animate a dead body, apparently. It is just waiting—waiting until the best opportunities come. We who remain human, it is holding in reserve."

Kinner shuddered violently. "Hey. Hey, Mac. Mac, would I know if I was a monster? Would I know if the monster had already got me? Oh Lord, I may be a monster already."

"You'd know," McReady answered.

"But we wouldn't," Norris laughed shortly, half-hysterically.

McReady looked at the vial of serum remaining. "There's one thing this damned stuff is good for, at that," he said thoughtfully. "Clark, will you and Van help me? The rest of the gang better stick together here. Keep an eye on each other," he said bitterly. "See that you don't get into mischief, shall we say?"

McReady started down the tunnel toward Dog Town, with Clark and Van Wall behind him. "You need more serum?" Clark asked.

McReady shook his head. "Tests. There's four cows and a bull, and nearly seventy dogs down there. This stuff reacts only to human blood and—monsters."

McReady came back to the Ad Building and went silently to the wash stand. Clark and Van Wall joined him a moment later. Clark's lips had developed a tic, jerking into sudden, unexpected sneers.

"What did you do?" Connant exploded suddenly. "More immunizing?"

Clark snickered, and stopped with a hiccough. "Immunizing. Haw! Immune all right."

"That monster," said Van Wall steadily, "is quite logical. Our immune dog was quite all right, and we drew a little more serum for the tests. But we won't make any more."

"Can't—can't you use one man's blood on another dog—" Norris began.

"There aren't," said McReady softly, "any more dogs. Nor cattle, I might add."

"No more dogs?" Benning sat down slowly.

"They're very nasty when they start changing," Van Wall said precisely, "but slow. That electrocution iron you made up, Barclay, is very fast. There is only one dog left—our immune. The monster left that for us, so we could play with our little test. The rest——" He shrugged and dried his hands.

"The cattle——" gulped Kinner.

"Also. Reacted very nicely. They look funny as hell when they start melting. The beast hasn't any quick escape, when it's tied in dog chains, or halters, and it had to be to imitate."

Kinner stood up slowly. His eyes darted around the room, and came to rest horribly quivering on a tin bucket in the galley. Slowly, step by step, he retreated toward the door, his mouth opening and closing silently, like a fish out of water.

"The milk——" he gasped. "I milked 'em an hour ago——" His voice broke into a scream as he dived through the door. He was out on the ice cap without windproof or heavy clothing.

Van Wall looked after him for a moment thoughtfully. "He's probably hopelessly mad," he said at length, "but he might be a monster escaping. He hasn't skis. Take a blow-torch—in case."

The physical motion of the chase helped them; something that needed doing. Three of the other men were quietly being sick. Norris was lying flat on his back, his face greenish, looking steadily at the bottom of the bunk above him.

"Mac, how long have the—cows been not-cows——"

McReady shrugged his shoulders hopelessly. He went over to the milk bucket, and with his little tube of serum went to work on it.

The milk clouded it, making certainty difficult. Finally he dropped the test-tube in the stand and shook his head. "It tests negatively. Which means either they were cows then, or that, being perfect imitations, they gave perfectly good milk."

Copper stirred restlessly in his sleep and gave a gurgling cross between a snore and a laugh. Silent eyes fastened on him. "Would morphia—a monster—" somebody started to ask.

"Lord knows," McReady shrugged. "It affects every Earthly animal I know of."

Connant suddenly raised his head. "Mac! The dogs must have swallowed pieces of the monster, and the pieces destroyed them! The dogs were where the monster resided. I was locked up. Doesn't that prove——"

Van Wall shook his head. "Sorry. Proves nothing about what you are, only proves what you didn't do."

"It doesn't do that," McReady sighed. "We are helpless because we don't know enough, and so jittery we don't think straight. Locked up! Ever watch a white corpuscle of the blood go through the wall of a blood vessel? No? It sticks out a pseudopod. And there it is— on the far side of the wall."

"Oh," said Van Wall unhappily. "The cattle tried to melt down, didn't they? They could have melted down—become just a thread of stuff and leaked under a door to re-collect on the other side. Ropes —no—no, that wouldn't do it. They couldn't live in a sealed tank or——"

"If," said McReady, "you shoot it through the heart, and it doesn't die, it's a monster. That's the best test I can think of, offhand."

"No dogs," said Garry quietly, "and no cattle. It has to imitate men now. And locking up doesn't do any good. Your test might work, Mac, but I'm afraid it would be hard on the men."

X

Clark looked up from the galley stove as Van Wall, Barclay, Mc-Ready and Benning came in, brushing the drift from their clothes. The other men jammed into the Ad Building continued studiously to do as they were doing, playing chess, poker, reading. Ralsen was fixing a sledge on the table; Vane and Norris had their heads together over magnetic data, while Harvey read tables in a low voice.

Dr. Copper snored softly on the bunk. Garry was working with

Dutton over a sheaf of radio messages on the corner of Dutton's bunk and a small fraction of the radio table. Connant was using most of the table for Cosmic Ray sheets.

Quite plainly through the corridor, despite two closed doors, they could hear Kinner's voice. Clark banged a kettle onto the galley stove and beckoned McReady silently. The meteorologist went over to him.

"I don't mind the cooking so damn much," Clark said nervously, "but isn't there some way to stop that bird? We all agreed that it would be safe to move him into Cosmos House."

"Kinner?" McReady nodded toward the door. "I'm afraid not. I can dope him, I suppose, but we don't have an unlimited supply of morphia, and he's not in danger of losing his mind. Just hysterical."

"Well, we're in danger of losing ours. You've been out for an hour and a half. That's been going on steadily ever since, and it was going for two hours before. There's a limit, you know."

Garry wandered over slowly, apologetically. For an instant, McReady caught the feral spark of fear—horror—in Clark's eyes, and knew at the same instant it was in his own. Garry—Garry or Copper —was certainly a monster.

"If you could stop that, I think it would be a sound policy, Mac," Garry spoke quietly. "There are—tensions enough in this room. We agreed that it would be safe for Kinner in there, because everyone else in camp is under constant eyeing." Garry shivered slightly. "And try, try in God's name, to find some test that will work."

McReady sighed. "Watched or unwatched, everyone's tense. Blair's jammed the trap so it won't open now. Says he's got food enough, and keeps screaming 'Go away, go away—you're monsters. I won't be absorbed. I won't. I'll tell men when they come. Go away.' So—we went away."

"There's no other test?" Garry pleaded.

McReady shrugged his shoulders. "Copper was perfectly right. The serum test could be absolutely definitive if it hadn't been—contaminated. But that's the only dog left, and he's fixed now."

"Chemicals? Chemical tests?"

McReady shook his head. "Our chemistry isn't that good. I tried the microscope, you know."

Garry nodded. "Monster-dog and real dog were identical. But— you've got to go on. What are we going to do after dinner?"

Van Wall had joined them quietly. "Rotation sleeping. Half the crowd sleep; half awake. I wonder how many of us are monsters? All

the dogs were. We thought we were safe, but somehow it got Copper
—or you." Van Wall's eyes flashed uneasily. "It may have gotten
every one of you—all of you but myself may be wondering, looking.
No, that's not possible. You'd just spring then. I'd be helpless. We
humans must somehow have the greater numbers now. But——" he
stopped.

McReady laughed shortly. "You're doing what Norris complained
of in me. Leaving it hanging. 'But if one more is changed—that may
shift the balance of power.' It doesn't fight. I don't think it ever fights.
It must be a peaceable thing, in its own—inimitable—way. It never
had to, because it always gained its end—otherwise."

Van Wall's mouth twisted in a sickly grin. "You're suggesting then,
that perhaps it already has the greater numbers, but is just waiting—
waiting, all of them—all of you, for all I know—waiting till I, the
last human, drop my wariness in sleep. Mac, did you notice their
eyes, all looking at us?"

Garry sighed. "You haven't been sitting here for four straight
hours, while all their eyes silently weighed the information that one of
us two, Copper or I, is a monster certainly—perhaps both of us."

Clark repeated his request. "Will you stop that bird's noise? He's
driving me nuts. Make him tone down, anyway."

"Still praying?" McReady asked.

"Still praying," Clark groaned. "He hasn't stopped for a second.
I don't mind his praying if it relieves him, but he yells, he sings psalms
and hymns and shouts prayers. He thinks God can't hear well way
down here."

"Maybe he can't," Barclay grunted. "Or he'd have done something
about this thing loosed from hell."

"Somebody's going to try that test you mentioned, if you don't
stop him," Clark stated grimly. "I think a cleaver in the head would
be as positive a test as a bullet in the heart."

"Go ahead with the food. I'll see what I can do. There may be
something in the cabinets." McReady moved wearily toward the
corner Copper had used as his dispensary. Three tall cabinets of rough
boards, two locked, were the repositories of the camp's medical supplies. Twelve years ago McReady had graduated, had started for an
internship, and been diverted to meteorology. Copper was a picked
man, a man who knew his profession thoroughly and modernly. More
than half the drugs available were totally unfamiliar to McReady;
many of the others he had forgotten. There was no huge medical
library here, no series of journals available to learn the things he had

forgotten, the elementary, simple things to Copper, things that did not merit inclusion in the small library he had been forced to content himself with. Books are heavy, and every ounce of supplies had been freighted in by air.

McReady picked a barbiturate hopefully. Barclay and Van Wall went with him. One man never went anywhere alone in Big Magnet.

Ralsen had his sledge put away, and the physicists had moved off the table, the poker game broken up when they got back. Clark was putting out the food. The click of spoons and the muffled sounds of eating were the only sign of life in the room. There were no words spoken as the three returned; simply all eyes focused on them questioningly, while the jaws moved methodically.

McReady stiffened suddenly. Kinner was screeching out a hymn in a hoarse, cracked voice. He looked wearily at Van Wall with a twisted grin and shook his head. "Hu-uh."

Van Wall cursed bitterly, and sat down at the table. "We'll just plumb have to take that till his voice wears out. He can't yell like that forever."

"He's got a brass throat and a cast-iron larynx," Norris declared savagely. "Then we could be hopeful, and suggest he's one of our friends. In that case he could go on renewing his throat till doomsday."

Silence clamped down. For twenty minutes they ate without a word. Then Connant jumped up with an angry violence. "You sit as still as a bunch of graven images. You don't say a word, but oh, Lord, what expressive eyes you've got. They roll around like a bunch of glass marbles spilling down a table. They wink and blink and stare—and whisper things. Can you guys look somewhere else for a change, please?

"Listen, Mac, you're in charge here. Let's run movies for the rest of the night. We've been saving those reels to make 'em last. Last for what? Who is it's going to see those last reels, eh? Let's see 'em while we can, and look at something other than each other."

"Sound idea, Connant. I, for one, am quite willing to change this in any way I can."

"Turn the sound up loud, Dutton. Maybe you can drown out the hymns," Clark suggested.

"But don't," Norris said softly, "don't turn off the lights altogether."

"The lights will be out." McReady shook his head. "We'll show all the cartoon movies we have. You won't mind seeing the old cartoons, will you?"

"Goody, goody—a moom pitcher show. I'm just in the mood." McReady turned to look at the speaker, a lean, lanky New Englander, by the name of Caldwell. Caldwell was stuffing his pipe slowly, a sour eye cocked up to McReady.

The bronze giant was forced to laugh. "O. K., Bart, you win. Maybe we aren't quite in the mood for Popeye and trick ducks, but it's something."

"Let's play Classifications," Caldwell suggested slowly. "Or maybe you call it Guggenheim. You draw lines on a piece of paper, and put down classes of things—like animals, you know. One for 'H' and one for 'U' and so on. Like 'Human' and 'Unknown' for instance. I think that would be a hell of a lot better game. Classification, I sort of figure, is what we need right now a lot more than movies. Maybe somebody's got a pencil that he can draw lines with, draw lines between the 'U' animals and the 'H' animals tor instance."

"McReady's trying to find that kind of a pencil," Van Wall answered quietly, "but we've got three kinds of animals here, you know. One that begins with 'M'. We don't want any more."

"Mad ones, you mean. Uh-huh. Clark, I'll help you with those pots so we can get our little peep-show going." Caldwell got up slowly.

Dutton and Barclay and Benning, in charge of the projector and sound mechanism arrangements, went about their job silently, while the Ad Building was cleared and the dishes and pans disposed of. McReady drifted over toward Van Wall slowly, and leaned back in the bunk beside him. "I've been wondering, Van," he said with a wry grin, "whether or not to report my ideas in advance. I forgot the 'U animals' as Caldwell named it, could read minds. I've a vague idea of something that might work. It's too vague to bother with though. Go ahead with your show, while I try to figure out the logic of the thing. I'll take this bunk."

Van Wall glanced up, and nodded. The movie screen would be practically on a line with his bunk, hence making the pictures least distracting here, because least intelligible. "Perhaps you should tell us what you have in mind. As it is, only the unknowns know what you plan. You might be—unknown before you got it into operation."

"Won't take long, if I get it figured out right. But I don't want any more all-but-the-test-dog-monsters things. We better move Copper into this bunk directly above me. He won't be watching the screen either." McReady nodded toward Copper's gently snoring bulk. Garry helped them lift and move the doctor.

McReady leaned back against the bunk, and sank into a trance, almost, of concentration, trying to calculate chances, operations, methods. He was scarcely aware as the others distributed themselves silently, and the screen lit up. Vaguely Kinner's hectic, shouted prayers and his rasping hymn-singing annoyed him till the sound accompaniment started. The lights were turned out, but the large, light-colored areas of the screen reflected enough light for ready visibility. It made men's eyes sparkle as they moved restlessly. Kinner was still praying, shouting, his voice a raucous accompaniment to the mechanical sound. Dutton stepped up the amplification.

So long had the voice been going on, that only vaguely at first was McReady aware that something seemed missing. Lying as he was, just across the narrow room from the corridor leading to Cosmos House, Kinner's voice had reached him fairly clearly, despite the sound accompaniment of the pictures. It struck him abruptly that it had stopped.

"Dutton, cut that sound," McReady called as he sat up abruptly. The pictures flickered a moment, soundless and strangely futile in the sudden, deep silence. The rising wind on the surface above bubbled melancholy tears of sound down the stove pipes. "Kinner's stopped," McReady said softly.

"For God's sake start that sound then, he may have stopped to listen," Norris snapped.

McReady rose and went down the corridor. Barclay and Van Wall left their places at the far end of the room to follow him. The flickers bulged and twisted on the back of Barclay's gray underwear as he crossed the still-functioning beam of the projector. Dutton snapped on the lights, and the pictures vanished.

Norris stood at the door as McReady had asked. Garry sat down quietly in the bunk nearest the door, forcing Clark to make room for him. Most of the others had stayed exactly where they were. Only Connant walked slowly up and down the room, in steady, unvarying rhythm.

"If you're going to do that, Connant," Clark spat, "we can get along without you altogether, whether you're human or not. Will you stop that damned rhythm?"

"Sorry." The physicist sat down in a bunk, and watched his toes thoughtfully. It was almost five minutes, five ages while the wind made the only sound, before McReady appeared at the door.

"We," he announced, "haven't got enough grief here already. Somebody's tried to help us out. Kinner has a knife in his throat, which was why he stopped singing, probably. We've got monsters, madmen and murderers. Any more 'M's' you can think of, Caldwell? If there are, we'll probably have 'em before long."

XI

"Is Blair loose?" someone asked.

"Blair is not loose. Or he flew in. If there's any doubt about where our gentle helper came from—this may clear it up." Van Wall held a foot-long, thin-bladed knife in a cloth. The wooden handle was half-burnt, charred with the peculiar pattern of the top of the galley stove.

Clark stared at it. "I did that this afternoon. I forgot the damn thing and left it on the stove."

Van Wall nodded. "I smelled it, if you remember. I knew the knife came from the galley."

"I wonder," said Benning, looking around at the party warily, "how many more monsters have we? If somebody could slip out of his place, go back of the screen to the galley and then down to the Cosmos House and back—he did come back, didn't he? Yes—everybody's here. Well, if one of the gang could do all that——"

"Maybe a monster did it," Garry suggested quietly. "There's that possibility."

"The monster, as you pointed out today, has only men left to imitate. Would he decrease his—supply, shall we say?" Van Wall pointed out. "No, we just have a plain, ordinary louse, a murderer to deal with. Ordinarily we'd call him an 'inhuman murderer' I suppose, but we have to distinguish now. We have inhuman murderers, and now we have human murderers. Or one at least."

"There's one less human," Norris said softly. "Maybe the monsters have the balance of power now."

"Never mind that," McReady sighed and turned to Barclay. "Bar, will you get your electric gadget? I'm going to make certain——"

Barclay turned down the corridor to get the pronged electrocuter, while McReady and Van Wall went back toward Cosmos House. Barclay followed them in some thirty seconds.

The corridor to Cosmos House twisted, as did nearly all corridors in Big Magnet, and Norris stood at the entrance again. But they heard, rather muffled, McReady's sudden shout. There was a savage flurry of blows, dull *ch-thunk, shluff* sounds. "Bar—Bar———" And a curious, savage mewing scream, silenced before even quick-moving Norris had reached the bend.

Kinner—or what had been Kinner—lay on the floor, cut half in two by the great knife McReady had had. The meteorologist stood against the wall, the knife dripping red in his hand. Van Wall was stirring vaguely on the floor, moaning, his hand half-consciously rubbing at his jaw. Barclay, an unutterably savage gleam in his eyes, was methodically leaning on the pronged weapon in his hand, jabbing—jabbing, jabbing.

Kinner's arms had developed a queer, scaly fur, and the flesh had twisted. The fingers had shortened, the hand rounded, the finger nails become three-inch long things of dull red horn, keened to steel-hard razor-sharp talons.

McReady raised his head, looked at the knife in his hand and dropped it. "Well, whoever did it can speak up now. He was an inhuman murderer at that—in that he murdered an inhuman. I swear by all that's holy, Kinner was a lifeless corpse on the floor here when we arrived. But when It found we were going to jab it with the power —It changed."

Norris stared unsteadily. "Oh, Lord, those things can act. Ye gods —sitting in here for hours, mouthing prayers to a God it hated! Shouting hymns in a cracked voice—hymns about a Church it never knew. Driving us mad with its ceaseless howling———

"Well. Speak up, whoever did it. You didn't know it, but you did the camp a favor. And I want to know how in blazes you got out of that room without anyone seeing you. It might help in guarding ourselves."

"His screaming—his singing. Even the sound projector couldn't drown it." Clark shivered. "It was a monster."

"Oh," said Van Wall in sudden comprehension. "You were sitting right next to the door, weren't you! And almost behind the projection screen already."

Clark nodded dumbly. "He—it's quiet now. It's a dead—Mac, your test's no damn good. It was dead anyway, monster or man, it was dead."

McReady chuckled softly. "Boys, meet Clark, the only one we know is human! Meet Clark, the one who proves he's human by trying to commit murder—and failing. Will the rest of you please refrain from trying to prove you're human for a while? I think we may have another test."

"A test!" Connant snapped joyfully, then his face sagged in disappointment. "I suppose it's another either-way-you-want-it."

"No," said McReady steadily. "Look sharp and be careful. Come into the Ad Building. Barclay, bring your electrocuter. And somebody —Dutton—stand with Barclay to make sure he does it. Watch every neighbor, for by the Hell these monsters came from, I've got something, and they know it. They're going to get dangerous!"

The group tensed abruptly. An air of crushing menace entered into every man's body, sharply they looked at each other. More keenly than ever before—*is that man next to me an inhuman monster?*

"What is it?" Garry asked, as they stood again in the main room. "How long will it take?"

"I don't know, exactly," said McReady, his voice brittle with angry determination. "But I *know* it will work, and no two ways about it. It depends on a basic quality of the *monsters*, not on us. 'Kinner' just convinced me." He stood heavy and solid in bronzed immobility, completely sure of himself again at last.

"This," said Barclay, hefting the wooden-handled weapon, tipped with its two sharp-pointed, charged conductors, "is going to be rather necessary, I take it. Is the power plant assured?"

Dutton nodded sharply. "The automatic stoker bin is full. The gas power plant is on stand-by. Van Wall and I set it for the movie operation and—we've checked it over rather carefully several times, you know. Anything those wires touch, dies," he assured them grimly. "I know that."

Dr. Copper stirred vaguely in his bunk, rubbed his eyes with fumbling hand. He sat up slowly, blinked his eyes blurred with sleep and drugs, widened with an unutterable horror of drug-ridden nightmares. "Garry," he mumbled, "Garry—listen. Selfish—from hell they came, and hellish shellfish—I mean self—— Do I? What do I mean?" he sank back in his bunk, and snored softly.

McReady looked at him thoughtfully. "We'll know presently," he nodded slowly. "But selfish is what you mean all right. You may have thought of that, half-sleeping, dreaming there. I didn't stop to think what dreams you might be having. But that's all right. Selfish is the word. They must be, you see." He turned to the men in the cabin, tense, silent men staring with wolfish eyes each at his neighbor. "Selfish, and as Dr. Copper said—*every part is a whole*. Every piece is self-sufficient, an animal in itself.

"That, and one other thing, tell the story. There's nothing mysterious about blood; it's just as normal a body tissue as a piece of muscle, or a piece of liver. But it hasn't so much connective tissue, though it has millions, billions of life-cells."

McReady's great bronze beard ruffled in a grim smile. "This is satisfying, in a way. I'm pretty sure we humans still outnumber you —others. Others standing here. And we have what you, your otherworld race, evidently doesn't. Not an imitated, but a bred-in-the-bone instinct, a driving, unquenchable fire that's genuine. We'll fight, fight with a ferocity you may attempt to imitate, but you'll never equal! We're human. We're real. You're imitations, false to the core of your every cell.

"All right. It's a showdown now. You know. You, with your mind reading. You've lifted the idea from my brain. You can't do a thing about it.

"Standing here——

"Let it pass. Blood is tissue. They have to bleed, if they don't bleed when cut, then, by Heaven, they're phony! Phony from hell! If they bleed—then that blood, separated from them, is an individual—a *newly formed individual in its own right, just as they, split, all of them, from one original, are individuals!*

"Get it, Van? See the answer Bar?"

Van Wall laughed very softly. "The blood—the blood will not obey. It's a new individual, with all the desire to protect its own life that the original—the main mass from which it was split—has. The *blood* will live—and try to crawl away from a hot needle, say!"

McReady picked up the scalpel from the table. From the cabinet, he took a rack of test-tubes, a tiny alcohol lamp, and a length of platinum wire set in a little glass rod. A smile of grim satisfaction rode his lips. For a moment he glanced up at those around him. Barclay and Dutton moved toward him slowly, the wooden-handled electric instrument alert.

"Dutton," said McReady, "suppose you stand over by the splice; there where you've connected that in. Just make sure no—thing pulls it loose."

Dutton moved away. "Now, Van, suppose you be first on this."

White-faced, Van Wall stepped forward. With a delicate precision, McReady cut a vein in the base of his thumb. Van Wall winced slightly, then held steady as a half inch of bright blood collected in the tube. McReady put the tube in the rack, gave Van Wall a bit of alum, and indicated the iodine bottle.

Van Wall stood motionlessly watching. McReady heated the platinum wire in the alcohol lamp flame, then dipped it into the tube. It hissed softly. Five times he repeated the test. "Human, I'd say." McReady sighed, and straightened "As yet, my theory hasn't been actually proven—but I have hopes. I have hopes.

"Don't, by the way, get too interested in this. We have with us some unwelcome ones, no doubt. Van, will you relieve Barclay at the switch? Thanks. O. K., Barclay, and may I say I hope you stay with us? You're a damned good guy."

Barclay grinned uncertainly; winced under the keen edge of the scalpel. Presently, smiling widely, he retrieved his long-handled weapon.

"Mr. Samuel Dutt—Bar!"

The tensity was released in that second. Whatever of hell the monsters may have had within them, the men in that instant matched it. Barclay had no chance to move his weapon as a score of men poured down on that thing that had seemed Dutton. It mewed, and spat, and tried to grow fangs—and was a hundred broken, torn pieces. Without knives, or any weapon save the brute-given strength of a staff of picked men, the thing was crushed, rent.

Slowly they picked themselves up, their eyes smouldering, very quiet in their emotions. A curious wrinkling of their lips betrayed a species of nervousness.

Barclay went over with the electric weapon. Things smouldered and stank. The caustic acid Van Wall dropped on each spilled drop of blood gave off tickling, cough-provoking fumes.

McReady grinned, his deep-set eyes alight and dancing. "Maybe," he said softly, "I underrated man's abilities when I said nothing human could have the ferocity in the eyes of that thing we found. I wish we could have the opportunity to treat in a more befitting manner these things. Something with boiling oil, or melted lead in it, or maybe slow roasting in the power boiler. When I think what a man Dutton was——

"Never mind. My theory is confirmed by—by one who knew? Well, Van Wall and Barclay are proven. I think, then, that I'll try to show you what I already know. That I too am human." McReady swished the scalpel in absolute alcohol, burned it off the metal blade, and cut the base of his thumb expertly.

Twenty seconds later he looked up from the desk at the waiting men. There were more grins out there now, friendly grins, yet withal, something else in the eyes.

"Connant," McReady laughed softly, "was right. The huskies watching that thing in the corridor bend had nothing on you. Wonder why we think only the wolf blood has the right to ferocity? Maybe on spontaneous viciousness a wolf takes tops, but after these seven days—abandon all hope, ye wolves who enter here!

"Maybe we can save time. Connant, would you step for——"

Again Barclay was too slow. There were more grins, less tensity still, when Barclay and Van Wall finished their work.

Garry spoke in a low, bitter voice. "Connant was one of the finest men we had here—and five minutes ago I'd have sworn he was a man. Those damnable things are more than imitation." Garry shuddered and sat back in his bunk.

And thirty seconds later, Garry's blood shrank from the hot platinum wire, and struggled to escape the tube, struggled as frantically as a suddenly feral, red-eyed, dissolving imitation of Garry struggled to dodge the snake-tongue weapon Barclay advanced at him, white faced and sweating. The Thing in the test-tube screamed with a tiny, tinny voice as McReady dropped it into the glowing coal of the galley stove.

XII

"The last of it?" Dr. Copper looked down from his bunk with bloodshot, saddened eyes. "Fourteen of them——"

McReady nodded shortly. "In some ways—if only we could have permanently prevented their spreading—I'd like to have even the imitations back. Commander Garry—Connant—Dutton—Clark—"

"Where are they taking those things?" Copper nodded to the stretcher Barclay and Norris were carrying out.

"Outside. Outside on the ice, where they've got fifteen smashed crates, half a ton of coal, and presently will add 10 gallons of kerosene. We've dumped acid on every spilled drop, every torn fragment. We're going to incinerate those."

"Sounds like a good plan." Copper nodded wearily. "I wonder, you haven't said whether Blair——"

McReady started. "We forgot him! We had so much else! I wonder—do you suppose we can cure him now?"

"If——" began Dr. Copper, and stopped meaningly.

McReady started a second time. "Even a madman. It imitated Kinner and his praying hysteria——" McReady turned toward Van Wall at the long table. "Van, we've got to make an expedition to Blair's shack."

Van looked up sharply, the frown of worry faded for an instant in surprised remembrance. Then he rose, nodded. "Barclay better go along. He applied the lashings, and may figure how to get in without frightening Blair too much."

Three quarters of an hour, through —37° cold, while the Aurora curtain bellied overhead. The twilight was nearly 12 hours long, flaming in the north on snow like white, crystalline sand under their skis. A 5-mile wind piled it in drift-lines pointing off to the northwest. Three quarters of an hour to reach the snow-buried shack. No smoke came from the little shack, and the men hastened.

"Blair!" Barclay roared into the wind when he was still a hundred yards away. "Blair!"

"Shut up," said McReady softly. "And hurry. He may be trying a lone hike. If we have to go after him—no planes, the tractors disabled——"

"Would a monster have the stamina a man has?"

"A broken leg wouldn't stop it for more than a minute," McReady pointed out.

Barclay gasped suddenly and pointed aloft. Dim in the twilit sky, a winged thing circled in curves of indescribable grace and ease. Great white wings tipped gently, and the bird swept over them in silent curiosity. "Albatross——" Barclay said softly. "First of the season, and wandering way inland for some reason. If a monster's loose——"

Norris bent down on the ice, and tore hurriedly at his heavy, windproof clothing. He straightened, his coat flapping open, a grim blue-metaled weapon in his hand. It roared a challenge to the white silence of Antarctica.

The thing in the air screamed hoarsely. Its great wings worked frantically as a dozen feathers floated down from its tail. Norris fired again. The bird was moving swiftly now, but in an almost straight line of retreat. It screamed again, more feathers dropped and with beating wings it soared behind a ridge of pressure ice, to vanish.

Norris hurried after the others. "It won't come back," he panted.

Barclay cautioned him to silence, pointing. A curiously, fiercely blue light beat out from the cracks of the shack's door. A very low, soft humming sounded inside, a low, soft humming and a clink and click of tools, the very sounds somehow bearing a message of frantic haste.

McReady's face paled. "Lord help us if that thing has——" He grabbed Barclay's shoulder, and made snipping motions with his fingers, pointing toward the lacing of control-cables that held the door.

Barclay dew the wire-cutters from his pocket, and kneeled soundlessly at the door. The snap and twang of cut wires made an unbearable racket in the utter quiet of the Antarctic hush. There was only that strange, sweetly soft hum from within the shack, and the queerly, hecticly clipped clicking and rattling of tools to drown their noises.

McReady peered through a crack in the door. His breath sucked in huskily and his great fingers clamped cruelly on Barclay's shoulder. The meteorologist backed down. "It isn't," he explained very softly, "Blair. It's kneeling on something on the bunk—something that keeps lifting. Whatever it's working on is a thing like a knapsack—and it lifts."

"All at once," Barclay said grimly. "No. Norris, hang back, and get that iron of yours out. It may have—weapons."

Together, Barclay's powerful body and McReady's giant strength struck the door. Inside, the bunk jammed against the door screeched madly and crackled into kindling. The door flung down from broken hinges, the patched lumber of the doorpost dropping inward.

Like a blue-rubber ball, a Thing bounced up. One of its four tentaclelike arms looped out like a striking snake. In a seven-tentacled hand a six-inch pencil of winking, shining metal glinted and swung upward to face them. Its line-thin lips twitched back from snake-fangs in a grin of hate, red eyes blazing.

Norris' revolver thundered in the confined space. The hate-washed face twitched in agony, the looping tentacle snatched back. The silvery thing in its hand a smashed ruin of metal, the seven-tentacled hand became a mass of mangled flesh oozing greenish-yellow ichor. The revolver thundered three times more. Dark holes drilled each of the three eyes before Norris hurled the empty weapon against its face.

The thing screamed in feral hate, a lashing tentacle wiping at blinded eyes. For a moment it crawled on the floor, savage tentacles lashing out, the body twitching. Then it staggered up again, blinded eyes working, boiling hideously, the crushed flesh sloughing away in sodden gobbets.

Barclay lurched to his feet and dove forward with an ice-ax. The flat of the weighty thing crushed against the side of the head. Again the unkillable monster went down. The tentacles lashed out, and suddenly Barclay fell to his feet in the grip of a living, livid rope. The thing dissolved as he held it, a white-hot band that ate into the flesh of his hands like living fire. Frantically he tore the stuff from him, held his hands where they could not be reached. The blind Thing felt and ripped at the tough, heavy, wind-proof cloth, seeking flesh—flesh it could convert——

The huge blow-torch McReady had brought coughed solemnly. Abruptly it rumbled disapproval throatily. Then it laughed gurglingly, and thrust out a blue-white, three-foot tongue. The Thing on the floor shrieked, flailed out blindly with tentacles that writhed and withered in the bubbling wrath of the blow-torch. It crawled and turned on the floor, it shrieked and hobbled madly, but always McReady held the blow-torch on the face, the dead eyes burning and bubbling uselessly. Frantically the Thing crawled and howled.

A tentacle sprouted a savage talon—and crisped in the flame. Steadily McReady moved with a planned, grim campaign. Helpless, maddened, the Thing retreated from the grunting torch, the caressing, licking tongue. For a moment it rebelled, squalling in inhuman hatred at the touch of the icy snow. Then it fell back before the charring breath of the torch, the stench of its flesh bathing it. Hopelessly it retreated—on and on across the Antarctic snow. The bitter wind swept over it twisting the torch-tongue; vainly it flopped, a trail of oily, stinking smoke bubbling away from it——

McReady walked back toward the shack silently. Barclay met him at the door. "No more?" the giant meteorologist asked grimly.

Barclay shook his head. "No more. It didn't split?"

"It had other things to think about," McReady assured him. "When I left it, it was a glowing coal. What was it doing?"

Norris laughed shortly. "Wise boys, we are. Smash magnetos, so planes won't work. Rip the boiler tubing out of the tractors. And leave that Thing alone for a week in this shack. Alone and undisturbed."

McReady looked in at the shack more carefully. The air, despite the ripped door, was hot and humid. On a table at the far end of the room rested a thing of coiled wires and small magnets, glass tubing and radio tubes. At the center a block of rough stone rested. From the center of the block came the light that flooded the place, the fiercely blue light bluer than the glare of an electric arc, and from it came the sweetly soft hum. Off to one side was another mechanism of crystal glass, blown with an incredible neatness and delicacy, metal plates and a queer, shimmery sphere of insubstantiality.

"What is that?" McReady moved nearer.

Norris grunted. "Leave it for investigation. But I can guess pretty well. That's atomic power. That stuff to the left—that's a neat little thing for doing what men have been trying to do with 100-ton cyclotrons and so forth. It separates neutrons from heavy water, which he was getting from the surrounding ice."

"Where did he get all—oh. Of course. A monster couldn't be locked in—or out. He's been through the apparatus caches." McReady stared at the apparatus. "Lord, what minds that race must have——"

"The shimmery sphere—I think it's a sphere of pure force. Neutrons can pass through any matter, and he wanted a supply reservoir of neutrons. Just project neutrons against silica—calcium—beryllium —almost anything, and the atomic energy is released. That thing is the atomic generator."

McReady plucked a thermometer from his coat. "It's 120° in here, despite the open door. Our clothes have kept the heat out to an extent, but I'm sweating now."

Norris nodded. "The light's cold. I found that. But it gives off heat to warm the place through that coil. He had all the power in the world. He could keep it warm and pleasant, as his race thought of warmth and pleasantness. Did you notice the light, the color of it?"

McReady nodded. "Beyond the stars is the answer. From beyond the stars. From a hotter planet that circled a brighter, bluer sun they came."

McReady glanced out the door toward the blasted, smoke-stained trail that flopped and wandered blindly off across the drift. "There won't be any more coming, I guess. Sheer accident it landed here, and that was twenty million years ago. What did it do all that for?" He nodded toward the apparatus.

Barclay laughed softly. "Did you notice what it was working on when we came? Look." He pointed toward the ceiling of the shack.

Like a knapsack made of flattened coffee-tins, with dangling cloth straps and leather belts, the mechanism clung to the ceiling. A tiny, glaring heart of supernal flame burned in it, yet burned through the ceiling's wood without scorching it. Barclay walked over to it, grasped two of the dangling straps in his hands, and pulled it down with an effort. He strapped it about his body. A slight jump carried him in a weirdly slow arc across the room.

"Anti-gravity," said McReady softly.

"Anti-gravity," Norris nodded. "Yes, we had 'em stopped, with no planes, and no birds. The birds hadn't come—but they had coffee-tins and radio parts, and glass and the machine shop at night. And a week—a whole week—all to itself. America in a single jump—with anti-gravity powered by the atomic energy of matter.

"We had 'em stopped. Another half hour—it was just tightening these straps on the device so it could wear it—and we'd have stayed in Antarctica, and shot down any moving thing that came from the rest of the world."

"The albatross——" McReady said softly. "Do you suppose——"

"With this thing almost finished? With that death weapon it held in its hand?

"No, by the grace of God, who evidently does hear very well, even down here, and the margin of half an hour, we keep our world, and the planets of the system too. Anti-gravity, you know, and atomic power. Because *They* came from another sun, a star beyond the stars. *They* came from a world with a bluer sun."

THE ROADS MUST ROLL

by

ROBERT A. HEINLEIN

As an industrial civilization expands, its complexity multiplies. With each new development the web of interlocking units becomes more tangled. Each small unit grows more important, more susceptible to shock, more liable to halt the entire organism with its own individual breakdown. Take traffic, for example. The failure of a single traffic light can stop the busy movement of an entire city. And even if vehicles are eliminated and the roads themselves roll, still the individual man or machine is the vital part—the all-important part—that makes the whole stop or go.

*

"WHO MAKES the roads roll?"

The speaker stood still on the rostrum and waited for his audience to answer him. The reply came in scattered shouts that cut through the ominous, discontented murmur of the crowd.

"We do! We do! Damn right!"

"Who does the dirty work 'down inside'—so that Joe Public can ride at his ease?"

This time it was a single roar: "We do!"

The speaker pressed his advantage, his words tumbling out in a rasping torrent. He leaned toward the crowd, his eyes picking out individuals at whom to fling his words. "What makes business? The roads! How do they move the food they eat? The roads! How do they get to work? The roads! How do they get home to their wives? The roads!" He paused for effect, then lowered his voice. "Where

551

would the public be if you boys didn't keep them roads rolling? Behind the eight ball, and everybody knows it. But do they appreciate it? *Pfui!* Did we ask for too much? Were our demands unreasonable? 'The right to resign whenever we want to.' Every working stiff in any other job has that. 'The same pay as the engineers.' Why not? Who are the real engineers around here? D'yuh have to be a cadet in a funny little hat before you can learn to wipe a bearing, or jack down a rotor? Who earns his keep: The gentlemen in the control offices, or the boys down inside? What else do we ask? 'The right to elect our own engineers.' Why the hell not? Who's competent to pick engineers? The technicians—or some damn dumb examining board that's never been down inside, and couldn't tell a rotor bearing from a field coil?"

He changed his pace with natural art, and lowered his voice still further. "I tell you, brother, it's time we quit fiddlin' around with petitions to the Transport Commission, and use a little direct action. Let 'em yammer about democracy; that's a lot of eyewash— we've got the power, and we're the men that count!"

A man had risen in the back of the hall while the speaker was haranguing. He spoke up as the speaker paused. "Brother chairman," he drawled, "may I stick in a couple of words?"

"You are recognized, Brother Harvey."

"What I ask is: What's all the shootin' for? We've got the highest hourly rate of pay of any mechanical guild, full insurance and retirement, and safe working conditions, barring the chance of going deaf." He pushed his antinoise helmet farther back from his ears. He was still in dungarees, apparently just up from standing watch. "Of course we have to give ninety days' notice to quit a job, but, cripes, we knew that when we signed up. The roads have got to roll—they can't stop every time some lazy punk gets tired of his billet.

"And now Soapy"—the crack of the gavel cut him short—"Pardon me, I mean *Brother* Soapy—tells us how powerful we are, and how we should go in for direct action. Rats! Sure, we could tie up the roads, and play hell with the whole community—but so could any screwball with a can of nitroglycerin, and he wouldn't have to be a technician to do it, neither.

"We aren't the only frogs in the puddle. Our jobs are important, sure, but where would we be without the farmers—or the steel workers—or a dozen other trades and professions?"

He was interrupted by a sallow little man with protruding upper teeth, who said: "Just a minute, Brother Chairman, I'd like to ask

Brother Harvey a question," then turned to Harvey and inquired in a sly voice: "Are you speaking for the guild, brother—or just for yourself? Maybe you don't believe in the guild? You wouldn't by any chance be"—he stopped and slid his eyes up and down Harvey's lank frame—"a *spotter*, would you?"

Harvey looked over his questioner as if he had found something filthy in a plate of food. "Sikes," he told him, "if you weren't a runt, I'd stuff your store teeth down your throat. I helped found this guild. I was on strike in '60. Where were you in '60? With the finks?"

The chairman's gavel pounded. "There's been enough of this," he said. "Nobody that knows anything about the history of this guild doubts the loyalty of Brother Harvey. We'll continue with the regular order of business." He stopped to clear his throat. "Ordinarily, we don't open our floor to outsiders, and some of you boys have expressed a distaste for some of the engineers we work under, but there is one engineer we always like to listen to whenever he can get away from his pressing duties. I guess maybe it's because he's had dirt under his nails the same as us. Anyhow, I present at this time Mr. Shorty van Kleeck—"

A shout from the floor stopped him. "*Brother* van Kleeck!"

"O. K., Brother van Kleeck, chief deputy engineer of this road-town."

"Thanks, Brother Chairman." The guest speaker came briskly forward, and grinned expansively at the crowd. He seemed to swell under their approval. "Thanks, brothers. I guess our chairman is right. I always feel more comfortable here in the guild hall of the Sacramento Sector—or any guild hall for that matter—than I do in the engineers' clubhouse. Those young punk cadet engineers get in my hair. Maybe I should have gone to one of the fancy technical institutes, so I'd have the proper point of view, instead of coming up from down inside.

"Now, about those demands of yours that the Transport Commission just threw back in your face—Can I speak freely?"

"Sure you can, Shorty! You can trust us!"

"Well, of course I shouldn't say anything, but I can't help but understand how you feel. The roads are the big show these days, and you are the men who make them roll. It's the natural order of things that your opinions should be listened to, and your desires met. One would think that even politicians would be bright enough to see that. Sometimes, lying awake at night, I wonder why we technicians don't just take things over, and—"

"Your wife is calling, Mr. Gaines."

"Very well." He flicked off the office intercommunicator and picked up a telephone handset from his desk. "Yes, darling, I know I promised, but . . . You're perfectly right, darling, but Washington has especially requested that we show Mr. Blekinsop anything he wants to see. I didn't know he was arriving today. . . . No, I can't turn him over to a subordinate. It wouldn't be courteous. He's Minister of Transport for Australia. I told you that. . . . . Yes, darling, I know that courtesy begins at home, but the roads must roll. It's my job; you knew that when you married me. And this is part of my job. . . . That's a good girl. We'll positively have breakfast together. Tell you what, order horses and a breakfast pack and we'll make it a picnic. I'll meet you in Bakersfield—usual place. . . . Good-by, darling. Kiss Junior good night for me."

He replaced the handset, whereupon the pretty but indignant features of his wife faded from the visor screen. A young woman came into his office. As she opened the door, she exposed momentarily the words painted on its outer side: "Diego-Reno Roadtown, Office of the Chief Engineer." He gave her a harassed glance.

"Oh, it's you. Don't marry an engineer, Dolores, marry an artist. They have more home life."

"Yes, Mr. Gaines. Mr. Blekinsop is here, Mr. Gaines."

"Already? I didn't expect him so soon. The Antipodes ship must have grounded early."

"Yes, Mr. Gaines."

"Dolores, don't you ever have any emotions?"

"Yes, Mr. Gaines."

"Hm-m-m, it seems incredible, but you are never mistaken. Show Mr. Blekinsop in."

"Very good, Mr. Gaines."

Larry Gaines got up to greet his visitor. Not a particularly impressive little guy, he thought, as they shook hands and exchanged formal amenities. The rolled umbrella, the bowler hat, were almost too good to be true. An Oxford accent partially masked the underlying clipped, flat, nasal twang of the native Australia.

"It's a pleasure to have you here, Mr. Blekinsop, and I hope we can make your stay enjoyable."

The little man smiled. "I'm sure it will be. This is my first visit to your wonderful country. I feel at home already. The eucalyptus trees, you know, and the brown hills—"

"But your trip is primarily business?"

"Yes, yes. My primary purpose is to study your roadcities and report to my government on the advisability of trying to adapt your startling American methods to our social problems Down Under. I thought you understood that such was the reason I was sent to you."

"Yes, I did, in a general way. I don't know just what it is that you wish to find out. I suppose that you have heard about our road towns, how they came about, how they operate, and so forth."

"I've read a good bit, true, but I am not a technical man, Mr. Gaines, not an engineer. My field is social and political. I want to see how this remarkable technical change has affected your people. Suppose you tell me about the roads as if I were entirely ignorant. And I will ask questions."

"That seems a practical plan. By the way, how many are there in your party?"

"Just myself. My secretary went on to Washington."

"I see." Gaines glanced at his wrist watch. "It's nearly dinner time. Suppose we run up to the Stockton Sector for dinner. There is a good Chinese restaurant up there that I'm partial to. It will take us about an hour and you can see the ways in operation while we ride."

"Excellent."

Gaines pressed a button on his desk, and a picture formed on a large visor screen mounted on the opposite wall. It showed a strong-boned, angular young man seated at a semicircular control desk, which was backed by a complex instrument board. A cigarette was tucked in one corner of his mouth.

The young man glanced up, grinned, and waved from the screen. "Greetings and salutations, chief. What can I do for you?"

"Hi, Dave. You've got the evening watch, eh? I'm running up to the Stockton Sector for dinner. Where's Van Kleeck?"

"Gone to a meeting somewhere. He didn't say."

"Anything to report?"

"No, sir. The roads are rolling, and all the little people are going ridey-ridey home to their dinners."

"O. K.—keep 'em rolling."

"They'll roll, chief."

Gaines snapped off the connection and turned to Blekinsop. "Van Kleeck is my chief deputy. I wish he'd spend more time on the road and less on politics. Davidson can handle things, however. Shall we go?"

They glided down an electric staircase, and debouched on the walkway which bordered the north-bound five-mile-an-hour strip. After skirting a stairway trunk marked "Overpass to Southbound Road," they paused at the edge of the first strip. "Have you ever ridden a conveyor strip before?" Gaines inquired. "It's quite simple. Just remember to face against the motion of the strip as you get on."

They threaded their way through homeward-bound throngs, passing from strip to strip. Down the center of the twenty-mile-an-hour strip ran a glassite partition which reached nearly to the spreading roof. The Honorable Mr. Blekinsop raised his eyebrows inquiringly as he looked at it.

"Oh, that?" Gaines answered the unspoken question as he slid back a panel door and ushered his guest through. "That's a wind break. If we didn't have some way of separating the air currents over the strips of different speeds, the wind would tear our clothes off on the hundred-mile-an-hour strip." He bent his head to Blekinsop's as he spoke, in order to cut through the rush of air against the road surfaces, the noise of the crowd, and the muted roar of the driving mechanism concealed beneath the moving strips. The combination of noises inhibited further conversation as they proceeded toward the middle of the roadway. After passing through three more wind screens located at the forty, sixty, and eighty-mile-an-hour strips, respectively, they finally reached the maximum-speed strip, the hundred-mile-an-hour strip, which made the round trip, San Diego to Reno and back, in twelve hours.

Blekinsop found himself on a walkway, twenty feet wide, facing another partition. Immediately opposite him an illuminated showwindow proclaimed:

JAKE'S STEAK HOUSE No. 4
The Fastest Meal on the Fastest Road!
"To dine on the fly
Makes the miles roll by!"

"Amazing!" said Mr. Blekinsop. "It would be like dining in a tram. Is this really a proper restaurant?"

"One of the best. Not fancy, but sound."

"Oh, I say, could we—"

Gaines smiled at him. "You'd like to try it, wouldn't you, sir?"

"I don't wish to interfere with your plans—"

"Quite all right. I'm hungry myself, and Stockton is a long hour away. Let's go in."

Gaines greeted the manageress as an old friend. "Hello, Mrs. McCoy. How are you tonight?"

"If it isn't the chief himself! It's a long time since we've had the pleasure of seeing your face." She led them to a booth somewhat detached from the crowd of dining commuters. "And will you and your friend be having dinner?"

"Yes, Mrs. McCoy. Suppose you order for us—but be sure it includes one of your steaks."

"Two inches thick—from a steer that died happy." She glided away, moving her fat frame with surprising grace.

With sophisticated foreknowledge of the chief engineer's needs, Mrs. McCoy had left a portable telephone at the table. Gaines plugged it into an accommodation jack at the side of the booth, and dialed a number. "Hello—Davidson? Dave, this is the chief. I'm in Jake's Steak House No. 4 for supper. You can reach me by calling 10-L-6-6."

He replaced the handset, and Blekinsop inquired politely: "Is it necessary for you to be available at all times?"

"Not strictly necessary," Gaines told him, "but I feel safer when I am in touch. Either Van Kleeck, or myself, should be where the senior engineer of the watch—that's Davidson this shift—can get hold of us in a pinch. If it's a real emergency, I want to be there, naturally."

"What would constitute a real emergency?"

"Two things, principally. A power failure on the rotors would bring the road to a standstill, and possibly strand millions of people a hundred miles, or more, from their homes. If it happened during a rush hour, we would have to evacuate those millions from the road—not too easy to do."

"You say millions—as many as that?"

"Yes, indeed. There are twelve million people dependent on this roadway, living and working in the buildings adjacent to it, or within five miles of each side."

The Age of Power blends into the Age of Transportation almost imperceptibly, but two events stand out as landmarks in the change: The invention of the Sun-power screen, and the opening of the first moving road. The power resources of oil and coal of the United States had—save for a few sporadic outbreaks of common sense—been shamefully wasted in their development all through the first half of the twentieth century. Simultaneously, the automobile, from its humble start as a one-lunged horseless carriage, grew into a steel-bodied monster of over a hundred horsepower and capable of making more than a hundred miles an hour. They boiled over the country-side, like yeast in ferment. In the middle of the century it was estimated that there was a motor vehicle for every two persons in the United States.

They contained the seeds of their own destruction. Seventy million steel juggernauts, operated by imperfect human beings at high speed, are more destructive than war. In the same reference year the pre-miums paid for compulsory liability and property damage insurance by automobile owners exceeded in amount the sum paid the same year to purchase automobiles. Safe driving campaigns were chronic phenomena, but were mere pious attempts to put Humpty-Dumpty together again. It was not physically possible to drive safely in those crowded metropolises. Pedestrians were sardonically divided into two classes, the quick and the dead.

But a pedestrian could be defined as a man who had found a place to park his car. The automobile made possible huge cities, then choked those same cities to death with their numbers. In 1900 Herbert George Wells pointed out that the saturation point in the size of a city might be mathematically predicted in terms of its trans-portation facilities. From a standpoint of speed alone the automobile made possible cities two hundred miles in diameter, but traffic con-gestion, and the inescapable, inherent danger of high-powered, indi-vidually operated vehicles canceled out the possibility.

Federal Highway No. 66 from Los Angeles to Chicago, "The Main Street of America," was transformed into a superhighway for motor vehicles, with an underspeed limit of sixty miles per hour. It was planned as a public works project to stimulate heavy industry; it had an unexpected by-product. The great cities of Chicago and St. Louis stretched out urban pseudopods toward each other, until they met near Bloomington, Illinois. The two parent cities actually shrank in population.

The city of San Francisco replaced its antiquated cable cars with moving stairways, powered with the Douglas-Martin Solar Reception Screens. The largest number of automobile licenses in history had been issued that calendar year, but the end of the automobile was in sight. The National Defense Act closed its era.

This act, one of the most bitterly debated ever to be brought out of committee, declared petroleum to be an essential and limited material of war. The army and navy had first call on all oil, above or

below the ground, and seventy million civilian vehicles faced short
and expensive rations.

Take the superhighways of the period, urban throughout their
length. Add the mechanized streets of San Francisco's hills. Heat to
boiling point with an imminent shortage of gasoline. Flavor with
Yankee ingenuity. The first mechanized road was opened between
Cincinnati and Cleveland.

It was, as one would expect, comparatively primitive in design.
The fastest strip moved only thirty miles per hour, and was quite
narrow, for no one had thought of the possibility of locating retail
trade on the strips themselves. Nevertheless, it was a prototype of
the social pattern which was to dominate the American scene within
the next two decades—neither rural nor urban, but partaking
equally of both, and based on rapid, safe, cheap, convenient transportation.

Factories—wide, low buildings whose roofs were covered with
solar power screens of the same type that drove the road—lined the
roadway on each side. Back of them and interspersed among them
were commercial hotels, retail stores, theaters, apartment houses.
Beyond this long, thin, narrow strip was the open countryside, where
much of the population lived. Their homes dotted the hills, hung
on the banks of creeks, and nestled between the farms. They worked
in the "city," but lived in the "country"—and the two were not ten
minutes apart.

Mrs. McCoy served the chief and his guest in person. They
checked their conversation at the sight of the magnificent steaks.

Up and down the six-hundred-mile line, sector engineers of the
watch were getting in their hourly reports from their subsector technicians. "Subsector One—check!" "Subsector Two—check!" Tensi-
ometer readings, voltage, load, bearing temperatures, synchrota-
chometer readings—"Subsector Seven—check!" Hardbitten, able men
in dungarees, who lived much of their lives down inside amidst the
unmuted roar of the hundred-mile strip, the shrill whine of driving
rotors, and the complaint of the relay rollers.

Davidson studied the moving model of the road, spread out before
him in the main control room at Fresno Sector. He watched the
barely perceptible crawl of the miniature hundred-mile strip and
subconsciously noted the reference number on it which located Jake's
Steak House No. 4. The chief would be getting into Stockton soon;
he'd give him a ring after the hourly reports were in. Everything was

quiet; traffic tonnage normal for rush hour; he would be sleepy before this watch was over. He turned to his cadet engineer of the watch. "Mr. Barnes."

"Yes, sir."

"I think we could use some coffee."

"Good idea, sir. I'll order some as soon as the hourlies are in."

The minute hand of the control board chronometer reached twelve. The cadet watch officer threw a switch. "All sectors, report!" he said, in crisp, self-conscious tones.

The faces of two men flicked into view on the visor screen. The younger answered him with the same air of acting under supervision. "Diego Circle—rolling!"

They were at once replaced by two more. "Angeles Sector—rolling!"

Then: "Bakerfield Sector—rolling!"

And: "Stockton Sector—rolling!"

Finally, when Reno Circle had reported, the cadet turned to Davidson and reported: "Rolling, sir."

"Very well—keep them rolling!"

The visor screen flashed on once more. "Sacramento Sector—supplementary report."

"Proceed."

"Cadet Engineer Guenther, while on visual inspection as cadet sector engineer of the watch, found Cadet Engineer Alec Jeans, on watch as cadet subsector technician, and R. J. Ross, technician second class, on watch as technician for the same subsector, engaged in playing cards. It was not possible to tell with any accuracy how long they had neglected to patrol their subsector."

"Any damage?"

"One rotor running hot, but still synchronized. It was jacked down, and replaced."

"Very well. Have the paymaster give Ross his time, and turn him over to the civil authorities. Place Cadet Jeans under arrest and order him to report to me."

"Very well, sir."

"Keep them rolling!"

Davidson turned back to the control desk and dialed Chief Engineer Gaines' temporary number.

"You mentioned that there were two things that could cause major trouble on the road, Mr. Gaines, but you spoke only of power failure to the rotors."

Gaines pursued an elusive bit of salad before answering. "There really isn't a second major trouble—it won't happen. However—we are traveling along here at one hundred miles per hour. Can you visualize what would happen if this strip under us should break?"

Mr. Blekinsop shifted nervously in his chair. "Hm-m-m! Rather a disconcerting idea, don't you think? I mean to say, one is hardly aware that one is traveling at high speed, here in this snug room. What would the result be?"

"Don't let it worry you; the strip can't part. It is built up of overlapping sections in such a fashion that it has a safety factor of better than twelve to one. Several miles of rotors would have to shut down all at once, and the circuit breakers for the rest of the line fail to trip out before there could possibly be sufficient tension on the strip to cause it to part.

"But it happened once, on the Philadelphia-Jersey City road, and we aren't likely to forget it. It was one of the earliest high-speed roads, carrying a tremendous passenger traffic, as well as heavy freight, since it serviced a heavily industrialized area. The strip was hardly more than a conveyor belt, and no one had foreseen the weight it would carry. It happened under maximum load, naturally, when the high-speed way was crowded. The part of the strip behind the break buckled for miles, crushing passengers against the roof at eighty miles per hour. The section forward of the break cracked like a whip, spilling pasengers onto the slower ways, dropping them on the exposed rollers and rotors down inside, and snapping them up against the roof.

"Over three thousand people were killed in that one accident, and there was much agitation to abolish the roads. They were even shut down for a week by presidential order, but he was forced to reopen them again. There was no alternative."

"Really? Why not?"

"The country had become economically dependent on the roads. They were the principal means of transportation in the industrial areas—the only means of economic importance. Factories were shut down; food didn't move; people got hungry—and the president was forced to let them roll again. It was the only thing that could be done; the social pattern had crystallized in one form, and it couldn't be changed overnight. A large, industrialized population must have large-scale transportation, not only for people, but for trade."

Mr. Blekinsop fussed with his napkin, and rather diffidently suggested: "Mr. Gaines, I do not intend to disparage the ingenious accomplishments of your great people, but isn't it possible that you may have put too many eggs in one basket in allowing your whole economy to become dependent on the functioning of one type of machinery?"

Gaines considered this soberly. "I see your point. Yes—and no. Every civilization above the peasant-and-village type is dependent on some key type of machinery. The old South was based on the cotton gin. Imperial England was made possible by the steam engine. Large populations have to have machines for power, for transportation, and for manufacturing in order to live. Had it not been for machinery the large populations could never have grown up. That's not a fault of the machine; that's its virtue.

"But it is true that whenever we develop machinery to the point where it will support large populations at a high standard of living we are then bound to keep that machinery running, or suffer the consequences. But the real hazard in that is not the machinery, but the men who run the machinery. These roads, as machines, are all right. They are strong and safe and will do everything they were designed to do. No, it's not the machines, it's the men.

"When a population is dependent on a machine, they are hostages of the men who tend the machines. If their morale is high, their sense of duty strong—"

Someone up near the front of the restaurant had turned up the volume control of the radio, letting out a blast of music that drowned out Gaines' words. When the sound had been tapered down to a more nearly bearable volume, he was saying:

"Listen to that. It illustrates my point."

Blekinsop turned an ear to the music. It was a swinging march of compelling rhythm, with a modern interpretive arrangement. One could hear the roar of machinery, the repetitive clatter of mechanisms. A pleased smile of recognition spread over the Australian's face. "It's your field artillery song, 'The Roll of the Caissons,' isn't it? But I don't see the connection."

"You're right; it was 'The Roll of the Caissons,' but we adapted it to our own purposes. It's 'The Road Song of the Transport Cadets,' too. Wait!"

The persistent throb of the march continued, and seemed to blend with the vibration of the roadway underneath into a single timpano. Then a male chorus took up the verse:

"Hear them hum!
Watch them run!
Oh, our job is never done,
For our roadways go rolling along!
While you ride,
While you glide,
We are watching down inside,
So your roadways keep rolling along!

"Oh, it's Hie! Hie! Hee!
The rotor men are we—
Check off the sectors loud and strong!
  ONE! TWO! THREE!
Anywhere you go
You are bound to know
That your roadways are rolling along!
KEEP THEM ROLLING!
That your roadways are rolling along!"

"See?" said Gaines, with more animation in his voice. "See? That is the real purpose of the United States Academy of Transport. That is the reason why the transport engineers are a semimilitary profession, with strict discipline. We are the bottle neck, the *sine qua non*, of all industry, all economic life. Other industries can go on strike, and only create temporary and partial dislocations. Crops can fail here and there, and the country takes up the slack. But if the roads stop rolling, everything else must stop; the effect would be the same as a general strike—with this important difference: It takes a majority of the population, fired by a real feeling of grievance, to create a general strike; but the men that run the roads, few as they are, can create the same complete paralysis.

"We had just one strike on the roads, back in '60. It was justified, I think, and it corrected a lot of real abuses—but it mustn't happen again."

"But what is to prevent it happening again, Mr. Gaines?"

"Morale—*esprit de corps*. The technicians in the road service are indoctrinated constantly with the idea that their job is a sacred trust. Besides, we do everything we can to build up their social position. But even more important is the academy. We try to turn out graduate engineers imbued with the same loyalty, the same iron self-discipline, and determination to perform their duty to the community at any cost, that Annapolis and West Point and Goddard are so successful in inculcating in their graduates."

"Goddard? Oh, yes, the rocket field. And have you been successful, do you think?"

"Not entirely, perhaps, but we will be. It takes time to build up a tradition. When the oldest engineer is a man who entered the academy in his teens we can afford to relax a little and treat it as a solved problem."

"I suppose you are a graduate?"

Gaines grinned. "You flatter me—I must look younger than I am. No, I'm a carry-over from the army. You see, the war department operated the roads for some three months during reorganization after the strike in '60. I served on the conciliation board that awarded pay increases and adjusted working conditions, then I was assigned—"

The signal light of the portable telephone glowed red. Gaines said, "Excuse me," and picked up the handset. "Yes?"

Blekinsop could overhear the voice at the other end. "This is Davidson, chief. The roads are rolling."

"Very well. Keep them rolling!"

"Had another trouble report from the Sacramento Sector."

"Again? What this time?"

Before Davidson could reply he was cut off. As Gaines reached out to dial him back, his coffee cup, half full, landed in his lap. Blekinsop was aware, even as he was lurched against the edge of the table, of a disquieting change in the hum of the roadway.

"What has happened, Mr. Gaines?"

"Don't know. Emergency stop—God knows why." He was dialing furiously. Shortly he flung the phone down, without bothering to return the handset to its cradle. "Phones are out. Come on! No! You'll be safe here. Wait."

"Must I?"

"Well, come along then, and stick close to me." He turned away, having dismissed the Australian cabinet minister from his mind. The strip ground slowly to a rest, the giant rotors and myriad rollers acting as flywheels in preventing a disastrous sudden stop. Already a little knot of commuters, disturbed at their evening meal, were attempting to crowd out the door of the restaurant.

"Halt!"

There is something about a command issued by one used to being obeyed which enforces compliance. It may be intonation, or possibly a more esoteric power, such as animal tamers are reputed to be able to

exercise in controlling ferocious beasts. But it does exist, a͟r
used to compel even those not habituated to obedience.

The commuters stopped in their tracks.

Gaines continued: "Remain in the restaurant until we are ready to
evacuate you. I am the chief engineer. You will be in no danger here.
You!" He pointed to a big fellow near the door. "You're deputized.
Don't let anyone leave without proper authority. Mrs. McCoy, resume serving dinner."

Gaines strode out the door, Blekinsop tagging along. The situation
outside permitted no such simple measures. The hundred-mile strip
alone had stopped; twenty feet away the next strip flew by at an unchecked ninety-five miles an hour. The passengers on it flickered past,
unreal cardboard figures.

The twenty-foot walkway of the maximum speed strip had been
crowded when the breakdown occurred. Now the customers of shops,
of lunch stands, and of other places of business, the occupants of
lounges, of television theaters—all came crowding out onto the walkway to see what had happened. The first disaster struck almost immediately.

The crowd surged, and pushed against a middle-aged woman on its
outer edge. In attempting to recover her balance she put one foot over
the edge of the flashing ninety-five-mile strip. She realized her gruesome error, for she screamed before her foot touched the ribbon.

She spun around and landed heavily on the moving strip, and was
rolled by it, as the strip attempted to impart to her mass, at one blow,
a velocity of ninety-five miles per hour—one hundred and thirty-nine
feet per second. As she rolled she mowed down some of the cardboard figures as a sickle strikes a stand of grass. Quickly, she was out
of sight, her identity, her injuries, and her fate undetermined, and
already remote.

But the consequences of her mishap were not done with. One of
the flickering cardboard figures bowled over by her relative moment
fell toward the hundred-mile strip, slammed into the shockbound
crowd, and suddenly appeared as a live man—but broken and bleeding—amidst the luckless, fallen victims whose bodies had checked his
wild flight.

Even there it did not end. The disaster spread from its source, each
hapless human ninepin more likely than not to knock down others so
that they fell over the danger-laden boundary, and in turn ricocheted
to a dearly-bought equilibrium.

But the focus of calamity sped out of sight, and Blekinsop could see no more. His active mind, accustomed to dealing with large numbers of individual human beings, multiplied the tragic sequence he had witnessed by twelve hundred miles of thronged conveyor strip, and his stomach chilled.

To Blekinsop's surprise, Gaines made no effort to succor the fallen, nor to quell the fear-infected mob, but turned an expressionless face back to the restaurant. When Blekinsop saw that he was actually reentering the restaurant, he plucked at Gaines' sleeve. "Aren't we going to help those poor people?"

The cold planes of the face of the man who answered him bore no resemblance to his genial, rather boyish host of a few minutes before. "No. Bystanders can help them—I've got the whole road to think of. Don't bother me."

Crushed, and somewhat indignant, the politician did as he was ordered. Rationally, he knew that the chief engineer was right—a man responsible for the safety of millions cannot turn aside from his duty to render personal service to one—but the cold detachment of such viewpoint was repugnant to him.

Gaines was back in the restaurant. "Mrs. McCoy, where is your getaway?"

"In the pantry, sir."

Gaines hurried there, Blekinsop at his heels. A nervous Filipino salad boy shrank out of Gaines' way as he casually swept a supply of prepared green stuffs onto the floor, and stepped up on the counter where they had rested. Directly above his head and within reach was a circular manhole, counterweighted and operated by a handwheel set in its center. A short steel ladder, hinged to the edge of the opening, was swung up flat to the ceiling and secured by a hook.

Blekinsop lost his hat in his endeavor to clamber quickly enough up the ladder after Gaines. When he emerged on the roof of the building, Gaines was searching the ceiling of the roadway with a pocket flashlight. He was shuffling along, stooped double in the awkward four feet of space between the roof underfoot and ceiling.

He found what he sought, some fifty feet away—another manhole similar to the one they had used to escape from below. He spun the wheel of the lock, and stood up in the space, then rested his hands on the sides of the opening, and with a single lithe movement vaulted to the roof of the roadways. His companion followed him with more difficulty.

They stood in darkness, a fine, cold rain feeling at their faces. But underfoot, and stretching beyond sight on each hand, the Sun-power

screens glowed with a faint opalescent radiance, their slight percentage of inefficiency as transformers of radiant Sun power to available
electrical power being evidenced as a mild induced radioactivity. The
effect was not illumination, but rather like the ghostly sheen of a
snow-covered plain seen by starlight.

The glow picked out the path they must follow to reach the rain-
obscured wall of buildings bordering the ways. The path was a narrow black stripe which arched away into the darkness over the low
curve of the roof. They started away on this path at a dogtrot, making
as much speed as the slippery footing and the dark permitted, while
Blekinsop's mind still fretted at the problem of Gaines' apparently
callous detachment. Although possessed of a keen intelligence, his
nature was dominated by a warm, human sympathy, without which
no politician, irrespective of other virtues or shortcomings, is long
successful.

Because of this trait he distrusted instinctively any mind which was
guided by logic alone. He was aware that, from a standpoint of strict
logic, no reasonable case could be made out for the continued existence of the human race, still less for the human values he served.

Had he been able to pierce the preoccupation of his companion,
he would have been reassured. On the surface, Gaines' exceptionally
intelligent mind was clicking along with the facile ease of an electro-
mechanical integrator—arranging data at hand, making tentative decisions, postponing judgments without prejudice until necessary data
were available, exploring alternatives. Underneath, in a compartment
insulated by stern self-discipline from the acting theater of his mind,
his emotions were a torturing storm of self reproach. He was heart-
sick at the suffering he had seen, and which he knew too well was
duplicated up and down the line. Although he was not aware of any
personal omission, nevertheless the fault was somehow his, for authority creates responsibility.

He had carried too long the superhuman burden of kingship—
which no sane mind can carry lightheartedly—and was at this moment perilously close to the frame of mind which sends captains down
with their ships. But the need for immediate, constructive action
sustained him.

But no trace of this conflict reached his features.

At the wall of buildings glowed a green line of arrows, pointing to
the left. Over them, at the terminus of the narrow path, shone a
sign: "Access down." They pursued this, Blekinsop puffing in Gaines'

wake, to a door let in the wall, which gave into a narrow stairway lighted by a single glow tube. Gaines plunged down this, still followed, and they emerged on the crowded, noisy, stationary walkway adjoining the northbound road.

Immediately adjacent to the stairway, on the right, was a public tele-booth. Through the glassite door they could see a portly, well-dressed man speaking earnestly to his female equivalent, mirrored in the visor screen. Three other citizens were waiting outside the booth.

Gaines pushed past them, flung open the door, grasped the bewildered and indignant man by the shoulders and hustled him outside, kicking the door closed after him. He cleared the visor screen with one sweep of his hand, before the matron pictured therein could protest, and pressed the emergency-priority button.

He dialed his private code number, and was shortly looking into the troubled face of his engineer of the watch, Davidson.

"Report!"

"It's you, chief! Thank God! Where are you?" Davidson's relief was pathetic.

"Report!"

The senior watch officer repressed his emotion, and complied in direct, clipped phrases: "At 7:09 p. m. the consolidated tension reading, Strip 20, Sacramento Sector, climbed suddenly. Before action could be taken, tension on Strip 20 passed emergency level; the interlocks acted, and power to subject strip cut out. Cause of failure unknown. Direct communication to Sacramento control office has failed. They do not answer the auxiliary, nor commercial. Effort to reestablish communication continues. Messenger dispatched from Stockton Subsector 10.

"No casualties reported. Warning broadcast by public announcement circuit to keep clear of Strip 19. Evacuation has commenced."

"There are casualties," Gaines cut in. "Police and hospital emergency routine. Move!"

"Yes, sir!" Davidson snapped back, and hooked a thumb over his shoulder—but his cadet officer of the watch had already jumped to comply. "Shall I cut out the rest of the road, chief?"

"No. No more casualties are likely after the first disorder. Keep up the broadcast warnings. Keep those other strips rolling, or we will have a traffic jam the devil himself couldn't untangle."

Gaines had in mind the impossibility of bringing the strips up to speed under load. The rotors were not powerful enough to do this.

If the entire road was stopped, he would have to evacuate every strip, correct the trouble on Strip 20, bring all strips up to speed, and then move the accumulated peak-load traffic. In the meantime, over five million stranded passengers would constitute a tremendous police problem. It was simpler to evacuate passengers on Strip 20 over the roof, and allow them to return home via the remaining strips.

"Notify the major and the governor that I have assumed emergency authority. Same to the chief of police and place him under your orders. Tell the commandant to arm all cadets available and await orders. Move!"

"Yes, sir. Shall I recall technicians off watch?"

"No. This isn't an engineering failure. Take a look at your readings; that entire sector went out simultaneously. Somebody cut out those rotors by hand. Place off-watch technicians on standby status—but don't arm them, and don't send them down inside. Tell the commandant to rush all available senior-class cadets to Stockton Subsector Office No. 10 to report to me. I want them equipped with tumblebugs, pistols, and sleep-gas bombs."

"Yes, sir." A clerk leaned over Davidson's shoulder and said something in his ear. "The governor wants to talk to you, chief."

"Can't do it—nor can you. Who's your relief? Have you sent for him?"

"Hubbard—he's just come in."

"Have him talk to the governor, the mayor, the press—anybody that calls—even the White House. You stick to your watch. I'm cutting off. I'll be back in communication as quickly as I can locate a reconnaissance car." He was out of the booth almost before the screen cleared.

Blekinsop did not venture to speak, but followed him out to the northbound twenty-mile strip. There Gaines stopped, short of the windbreak, turned, and kept his eyes on the wall beyond the stationary walkway. He picked out some landmark or sign—not apparent to his companion—and did an Eliza crossing the ice back to the walkway, so rapidly that Blekinsop was carried some hundred feet beyond him, and almost failed to follow when Gaines ducked into a doorway, and ran down a flight of stairs.

They came out on a narrow lower walkway, down inside. The pervading din claimed them, beat upon their bodies as well as their ears. Dimly, Blekinsop perceived their surroundings, as he struggled to face that wall of sound. Facing him, illuminated by the red monochrome of a neon arc, was one of the rotors that drove the five-mile strip, its great, drum-shaped armature revolving slowly around the stationary field coils in its core. The upper surface of the drum pressed against the under side of the moving way and imparted to it its stately progress.

To the left and right, a hundred yards each way, and beyond at similar intervals, farther than he could see, were other rotors. Bridging the gaps between the rotors were the slender rollers, crowded together like cigars in a box, in order that the strip might have a continuous rolling support. The rollers were supported by steel-girder arches through the gaps of which he saw row after row of rotors in staggered succession, the rotors in each succeeding row turning over more rapidly than the last.

Separated from the narrow walkway by a line of supporting steel pillars, and lying parallel to it on the side away from the rotors, ran a shallow paved causeway, joined to the walk at this point by a ramp. Gaines peered up and down this tunnel in evident annoyance. Blekinsop started to ask him what troubled him, but found his voice snuffed out by the sound. He could not cut through the roar of thousands of rotors and the whine of hundreds of thousands of rollers.

Gaines saw his lips move, and guessed at the question. He cupped his hands around Blekinsop's right ear, and shouted: "No car—I expected to find a car here."

The Australian, wishing to be helpful, grasped Gaines' arm and pointed back into the jungle of machinery. Gaines' eye followed the direction indicated and picked out something that he had missed in his preoccupation—a half dozen men working around a rotor several strips away. They had jacked down a rotor until it was no longer in contact with the road surface, and were preparing to replace it *in toto.* The replacement rotor was standing by on a low, heavy truck.

The chief engineer gave a quick smile of acknowledgment and thanks, and aimed his flashlight at the group, the beam focused down to a slender, intense needle of light. One of the technicians looked up, and Gaines snapped the light on and off in a repeated, irregular pattern. A figure detached itself from the group and ran toward them.

It was a slender young man, dressed in dungarees, and topped off with ear pads and an incongruous, pillbox cap, bright with gold braid and insignia. He recognized the chief engineer and saluted, his face falling into humorless, boyish intentness.

Gaines stuffed his torch into a pocket and commenced to gesticulate rapidly with both hands—clear, clean gestures, as involved and as meaningful as deaf-mute language. Blekinsop dug into his own dilettante knowledge of anthropology and decided that it was most like an American Indian sign language, with some of the finger move-ments of hula. But it was necessarily almost entirely strange, being adapted for a particular terminology.

The cadet answered him in kind, stepped to the edge of the cause-way, and flashed his torch to the south. He picked out a car, still some distance away, but approaching at headlong speed. It braked, and came to a stop alongside them.

It was a small affair, ovoid in shape, and poised on two centerline wheels. The forward, upper surface swung up and disclosed the driver, another cadet. Gaines addressed him briefly in sign language, then hustled Blekinsop ahead of him into the cramped passenger compartment.

As the glassite hood was being swung back into place, a blast of wind smote them, and the Australian looked up in time to glimpse the last of three much larger vehicles hurtle past them. They were headed north, at a speed of not less than two hundred miles per hour. Blekinsop thought that he had made out the little hats of cadets through the windows of the last of the three, but he could not be sure.

He had no time to wonder, so violent was the driver's getaway. Gaines ignored the accelerating surge—he was already calling David-son on the built-in communicator. Comparative silence had settled down once the car was closed. The face of a female operator at the relay station showed on the screen.

"Get me Davidson—senior watch office!"

"Oh! It's Mr. Gaines! The Mayor wants to talk to you, Mr. Gaines."

"Refer him—and get me Davidson. Move!"

"Yes, sir."

"And see here—leave this circuit hooked in to Davidson's board until I tell you personally to cut it."

"Right." Her face gave way to the watch officer's.

"That you, chief? We're moving—progress O. K.—no change."

"Very well. You'll be able to raise me on this circuit, or at Sub-sector 10 office. Clearing now." Davidson's face gave way to the relay operator.

"Your wife is calling, Mr. Gaines. Will you take it?"

Gaines muttered something not quite gallant, and answered: "Yes." Mrs. Gaines flashed into facsimile. He burst into speech before she could open her mouth. "Darling I'm all right don't worry I'll be home when I get there I've got to go now." It was all out in one breath, and he slapped the control that cleared the screen.

They slammed to a breath-taking stop alongside the stair leading to the watch office of Subsector 10, and piled out. Three big lorries were drawn up on the ramp, and three platoons of cadets were ranged in restless ranks alongside them. Tumblebugs—small, open monocycles, used to patrol down inside—were ready nearby.

A cadet trotted up to Gaines and saluted. "Lindsay, sir—cadet engineer of the watch. The engineer of the watch requests that you come at once to the control room."

The engineer of the watch looked up as they came in. "Chief— Van Kleeck is calling you."

"Put him on."

When Van Kleeck appeared in the big visor, Gaines greeted him with: "Hello, Van. Where are you?"

"Sacramento office. Now listen—"

"Sacramento? That's good! Report."

Van Kleeck looked disgruntled. "Report, hell! I'm not your deputy any more, Gaines. Now, you—"

"What the hell are you talking about?"

"Listen, and don't interrupt me, and you'll find out. You're through, Gaines. I've been picked as Director of the Provisional Control Committee for the New Order."

"Van, have you gone off your rocker? What do you mean—the 'New Order'?"

"You'll find out. This is it—the Functionalist revolution. We're in; you're out. We stopped Strip 20 just to give you a little taste of what we can do."

Concerning Function: A Treatise on the Natural Order in Society, the Bible of the Functionalist movement, was first published in 1930. It claimed to be a scientifically accurate theory of social relations. The author, Paul Decker, disclaimed the "outworn and futile" ideas of democracy and human equality, and substituted a system in which human beings were evaluated "functionally"—that is to say, by the role each filled in the economic sequence. The underlying thesis was that it was right and proper for a man to exercise over his fellows whatever power was inherent in his function, and that any other form of social organization was silly, visionary, and contrary to the "natural order."

The complete interdependence of modern economic life seems to have escaped him entirely.

His ideas were dressed up with a glib mechanistic pseudopsychology based on the observed orders of precedence among barnyard fowls, and on the famous Pavlov conditioned reflex experiments on dogs. He failed to note that human beings are neither dogs nor chickens. Old Dr. Pavlov ignored him entirely, as he had ignored so many others who had blindly and unscientifically dogmatized about the meaning of his important, but strictly limited, experiments.

Functionalism did not take hold at once—during the '30s almost everyone, from truck driver to hatcheck girl, had a scheme for setting the world right in six easy lessons; and a surprising percentage managed to get their schemes published. But it gradually spread. Functionalism was particularly popular among little people everywhere who could persuade themselves that their particular jobs were the indispensable ones, and that therefore, under the "natural order," they would be top dogs. With so many different functions actually indispensable such self-persuasion was easy.

Gaines stared at Van Kleeck for a moment before replying. "Van," he said slowly, "you don't really think you can get away with this, do you?"

The little man puffed out his chest. "Why not? We have gotten away with it. You can't start Strip 20 until I am ready to let you. and I can stop the whole road, if necessary."

Gaines was becoming uncomfortably aware that he was dealing with unreasonable conceit, and held himself patiently in check. "Sure you can, Van—but how about the rest of the country? Do you think the United States army will sit quietly by and let you run California as your private kingdom?"

Van Kleeck looked sly. "I've planned for that. I've just finished broadcasting a manifesto to all the road technicians in the country, telling them what we have done, and telling them to arise, and claim their rights. With every road in the country stopped, and people getting hungry, I reckon the President will think twice before sending the army to tangle with us. Oh, he could send a force to capture, or kill, me—I'm not afraid to die!—but he doesn't dare start shooting down road technicians as a class, because the country can't get along without us—consequently, he'll have to get along with us—on our terms!"

There was much bitter truth in what he said. If an uprising of the road technicians became general, the government could no more attempt to settle it by force than a man could afford to cure a headache by blowing out his brains. But was the uprising general?

"Why do you think that the technicians in the rest of the country will follow your lead?"

"Why not? It's the natural order of things. This is an age of machinery; the real power everywhere is in the technicians, but they have been kidded into not using their power with a lot of obsolete catch phrases. And of all the classes of technicians, the most important, the absolutely essential, are the road technicians. From now on they run the show—it's the natural order of things!" He turned away for a moment and fussed with some papers on the desk before him; then he added: "That's all for now, Gaines—I've got to call the White House, and let the President know how things stand. You carry on, and behave yourself, and you won't get hurt."

Gaines sat quite still for some minutes after the screen cleared. So that's how it was. He wondered what effect, if any, Van Kleeck's invitation to strike had had on road technicians elsewhere. None, he thought—but then he had not dreamed that it could happen among his own technicians. Perhaps he had made a mistake in refusing to take time to talk to anyone outside the road. No—if he had stopped to talk to the Governor, or the newspapermen, he would still be talking. Still—

He dialed Davidson.

"Any trouble in any other sectors, Dave?"

"No, chief."

"Or on any other road?"

"None reported."

"Did you hear my talk with Van Kleeck?"

"I was cut in—yes."

"Good. Have Hubbard call the President and the Governor, and tell them that I am strongly opposed to the use of military force as long as the outbreak is limited to this one road. Tell them that I will not be responsible if they move in before I ask for help."

Davidson looked dubious. "Do you think that is wise, chief?"

"I do! If we try to blast Van and his red-hots out of their position, we may set off a real, countrywide uprising. Furthermore, he could wreck the road so that God himself couldn't put it back together. What's your rolling tonnage now?"

"Fifty-three percent under evening peak."

"How about Strip 20?"

"Almost evacuated."

"Good. Get the road clear of all traffic as fast as possible. Better have the chief of police place a guard on all entrances to the road to keep out new traffic. Van may stop all the strips any time—or I may need to myself. Here is my plan: I'm going down inside with these armed cadets. We will work north, overcoming any resistance we meet. You arrange for watch technicians and maintenance crews to follow immediately behind us. Each rotor, as they come to it, is to be cut out, then hooked into the Stockton control board. It will be a haywire rig, with no safety interlocks, so use enough watch technicians to be able to catch trouble before it happens.

"If this scheme works, we can move control of the Sacramento Sector right out from under Van's feet, and he can stay in his Sacramento control office until he gets hungry enough to be reasonable."

He cut off and turned to the subsector engineer of the watch. "Edmunds, give me a helmet—and a pistol."

"Yes, sir." He opened a drawer, and handed his chief a slender, deadly-looking weapon. Gaines belted it on, and accepted a helmet, into which he crammed his head, leaving the antinoise ear flaps up. Blekinsop cleared his throat.

"May . . . uh . . . may I have one of those helmets?" he inquired.

"What?" Gaines focused his attention. "Oh— You won't need one, Mr. Blekinsop. I want you to remain right here until you hear from me."

"But—" The Australian statesman started to speak, thought better of it, and subsided.

From the doorway the cadet engineer of the watch demanded the chief engineer's attention. "Mr. Gaines, there is a technician out here who insists on seeing you—a man named Harvey."

"Can't do it."

"He's from the Sacramento Sector, sir."

"Oh! Send him in."

Harvey quickly advised Gaines of what he had seen and heard at the guild meeting that afternoon. "I got disgusted and left while they were still jawin', chief. I didn't think any more about it until Strip 20 stopped rolling. Then I heard that the trouble was in Sacramento Sector, and decided to look you up."

"How long has this been building up?"

"Quite some time, I guess. You know how it is. There are a few soreheads everywhere, and a lot of them are Functionalists. But you can't refuse to work with a man just because he holds different political views. It's a free country."

"You should have come to me before, Harvey." Harvey looked stubborn. Gaines studied his face. "No, I guess you are right. It's my business to keep tabs on your mates, not yours. As you say, it's a free country. Anything else?"

"Well—now that it has come to this, I thought maybe I could help you pick out the ringleaders."

"Thanks. You stick with me. We are going down inside and try to clear up this mess."

The office door opened suddenly, and a technician and a cadet appeared, lugging a burden between them. They deposited it on the floor, and waited.

It was a young man, quite evidently dead. The front of his dungaree jacket was soggy with blood. Gaines looked at the watch officer. "Who is he?"

Edmunds broke his stare and answered: "Cadet Hughes. He's the messenger I sent to Sacramento when communication failed. When he didn't report, I sent Marston and Cadet Jenkins after him."

Gaines muttered something to himself, and turned away. "Come along, Harvey."

The cadets waiting below had changed in mood. Gaines noted that the boyish intentness for excitement had been replaced by something uglier. There was much exchange of hand signals and several appeared to be checking the loading of their pistols.

He sized them up, then signaled to the cadet leader. There was a short interchange of signals. The cadet saluted, turned to his men, gesticulated briefly, and brought his arm down smartly. They filed upstairs, and into an empty standby room, Gaines following.

Once inside, and the noise shut out, he addressed them: "You saw Hughes brought in. How many of you want a chance to kill the louse that did it?"

Three of the cadets reacted almost at once, breaking ranks and striding forward. Gaines looked at them coldly. "Very well. You three turn in your weapons, and return to your quarters. Any of the rest of you that think this is a matter of private revenge, or a hunting party, may join them." He permitted a short silence to endure before continuing. "Sacramento Sector has been seized by unauthorized persons. We are going to retake it—if possible, without loss of life on either side, and, if possible, without stopping the roads. The plan is to take over down inside, rotor by rotor, and cross-connect through Stockton. The task assignment of this group is to proceed north down inside, locating and overpowering all persons in your path. You will bear in mind the probability that most of the persons you will arrest are completely innocent. Consequently, you will favor the use of sleep-gas bombs, and will shoot to kill only as a last resort.

"Cadet captain, assign your men in squads of ten each, with squad leader. Each squad is to form a skirmish line across down inside, mounted on tumblebugs, and will proceed north at fifteen miles per hour. Leave an interval of one hundred yards between successive waves of skirmishers. Whenever a man is sighted, the entire leading wave will converge on him, arrest him, and deliver him to a transport car, then reform in the rear of the last wave. You will assign the transports that delivered you here to hold prisoners. Instruct the drivers to keep abreast of the second wave.

"You will assign an attack group to recapture subsector control offices, but no office is to be attacked until its subsector has been cross-connected with Stockton. Arrange liaison accordingly.

"Any questions?" He let his eyes run over the faces of the young men. When no one spoke up, he turned back to the cadet in charge. "Very well, sir. Carry out your orders!"

By the time the dispositions had been completed, the follow-up crew of technicians had arrived, and Gaines had given the engineer in charge his instructions. The cadets "stood to horse" alongside their poised tumblebugs. The cadet captain looked expectantly at Gaines. He nodded, the cadet brought his arm down smartly, and the first wave mounted and moved off.

Gaines and Harvey mounted tumblebugs, and kept abreast of the cadet captain, some twenty-five yards behind the leading wave. It had been a long time since the chief engineer had ridden one of these silly-looking little vehicles, and he felt awkward. A tumblebug does not give a man dignity, since it is about the size and shape of a kitchen stool, gyro-stabilized on a single wheel. But it is perfectly adapted to patrolling the maze of machinery down inside, since it can go through an opening the width of a man's shoulders, is easily controlled, and will stand patiently upright, waiting, should its rider dismount.

The little reconnaissance car followed Gaines at a short interval, weaving in and out among the rotors, while the television and audio communicator inside continued as Gaines' link to his other manifold responsibilities.

The first two hundred yards of Sacramento Sector passed without incident, then one of the skirmishers sighted a tumblebug parked by a rotor. The technician it served was checking the gauges at the rotor's base, and did not see them approach. He was unarmed and made no resistance, but seemed surprised and indignant, as well as very bewildered.

The little command group dropped back and permitted the new leading wave to overtake them.

Three miles farther along, the score stood thirty-seven men arrested, none killed. Two of the cadets had received minor wounds, and had been directed to retire. Only four of the prisoners had been armed; one of these Harvey had been able to identify definitely as a ringleader. Harvey expressed a desire to attempt to parley with the outlaws, if any occasion arose. Gaines agreed tentatively. He knew of Harvey's long and honorable record as a labor leader, and was willing to try anything that offered a hope of success with a minimum of violence.

Shortly thereafter the first wave flushed another technician. He was on the far side of a rotor; they were almost on him before he was seen. He did not attempt to resist, although he was armed, and the incident would not have been worth recording, had he not been talking into a hush-a-phone which he had plugged into the telephone jack at the base of the rotor.

Gaines reached the group as the capture was being effected. He snatched at the soft rubber mask of the phone, jerking it away from the man's mouth so violently that he could feel the bone-conduction receiver grate between the man's teeth. The prisoner spat out a piece of broken tooth and glared, but ignored attempts to question him

Swift as Gaines had been, it was highly probable that they had lost the advantage of surprise. It was necessary to assume that the prisoner had succeeded in reporting the attack going on beneath the ways. Word was passed down the line to proceed with increased caution.

Gaines' pessimism was justified shortly. Riding toward them appeared a group of men, as yet several hundred feet away. There were at least a score, but their exact strength could not be determined, as they took advantage of the rotors for cover as they advanced. Harvey looked at Gaines, who nodded, and signaled the cadet captain to halt his forces.

Harvey went on ahead, unarmed, his hands held high above his head, and steering by balancing the weight of his body. The outlaw party checked its speed uncertainly, and finally stopped. Harvey approached within a couple of rods of them and stopped likewise. One of them, apparently the leader, spoke to him in sign language, to which he replied.

They were too far away, and the red light too uncertain, to follow the discussion. It continued for several minutes, then ensued a pause. The leader seemed uncertain what to do. One of his party rolled forward, returned his pistol to its holster, and conversed with the leader. The leader shook his head at the man's violent gestures.

The man renewed his argument, but met the same negative response. With a final disgusted wave of his hands, he desisted, drew his pistol, and shot at Harvey. Harvey grabbed at his middle and leaned forward. The man shot again; Harvey jerked, and slid to the ground.

The cadet captain beat Gaines to the draw. The killer looked up as the bullet hit him. He looked as if he were puzzled by some strange occurrence—being too freshly dead to be aware of it.

The cadets came in shooting. Although the first wave was outnumbered better than two to one, they were helped by the comparative demoralization of the enemy. The odds were nearly even after the first ragged volley. Less than thirty seconds after the first treacherous shot all of the insurgent party were dead, wounded, or under arrest. Gaines' losses were two dead—including the murder of Harvey—and two wounded.

Gaines modified his tactics to suit the changed conditions. Now that secrecy was gone, speed and striking power were of first importance. The second wave was directed to close in practically to the heels of the first. The third wave was brought up to within twenty-five yards of the second. These three waves were to ignore unarmed men, leaving them to be picked up by the fourth wave, but they were directed to shoot on sight any person carrying arms.

Gaines cautioned them to shoot to wound, rather than to kill, but he realized that his admonishment was almost impossible to obey. There would be killing. Well—he had not wanted it, but he felt that he had no choice. Any armed outlaw was a potential killer—he could not, in fairness to his own men, lay too many restrictions on them.

When the arrangements for the new marching order were completed, he signed the cadet captain to go ahead, and the first and second waves started off together at the top speed of which the tumblebugs were capable—not quite eighteen miles per hour. Gaines followed them.

He swerved to avoid Harvey's body, glancing involuntarily down as he did so. The face was set in a death mask of rugged beauty in which the strong fiber of the dead man's character was evident. Seeing this, Gaines did not regret so much his order to shoot, but the deep sense of loss of personal honor lay more heavily on him than before.

They passed several technicians during the next few minutes, but had no occasion to shoot. Gaines was beginning to feel somewhat hopeful of a reasonably bloodless victory, when he noticed a change in the pervading throb of machinery which penetrated even through the heavy antinoise pads of his helmet. He lifted an ear pad in time to hear the end of a rumbling diminuendo as the rotors and rollers slowed to rest.

The road was stopped.

He shouted to the cadet captain: "Halt your men!" His words echoed hollowly in the unreal silence.

The top of the reconnaissance car swung up as he turned and hurried to it. "Chief," the cadet within called out, "relay station calling you."

The girl in the visor screen gave way to Davidson as soon as she recognized Gaines' face.

"Chief," Davidson said at once, "Van Kleeck's calling you."

"Who stopped the road?"

"He did."

"Any other major change in the situation?"

"No—the road was practically empty when he stopped it."

"Good. Give me Van Kleeck."

The chief conspirator's face was livid with uncurbed anger when he identified Gaines. He burst into speech.

"So! You thought I was fooling, eh? What do you think now, Mr. Chief Engineer Gaines?"

Gaines fought down an impulse to tell him exactly what he thought, particularly about Van Kleeck. Everything about the short man's manner affected him like a squeaking slate pencil.

But he could not afford the luxury of speaking his mind. He strove to get just the proper tone into his voice which would soothe the other man's vanity. "I've got to admit that you've won this trick, Van—the road is stopped—but don't think I didn't take you seriously. I've watched you work too long to underrate you. I know you mean what you say."

Van Kleeck was pleased by the tribute, but tried not to show it. "Then why don't you get smart, and give up?" he demanded belligerently. "You can't win."

"Maybe not, Van, but you know I've got to try. Besides," he went on, "why can't I win? You said yourself that I could call on the whole United States army."

Van Kleeck grinned triumphantly. "You see that?" He held up a pear-shaped electric push button, attached to a long cord. "If I push that, it will blow a path right straight across the ways—blow it to kingdom come. And just for good measure, I'll take an ax, and wreck this control station before I leave."

Gaines wished whole-heartedly that he knew more about psychology. Well—he'd just have to do his best, and trust to horse sense to give him the right answers. "That's pretty drastic, Van, but I don't see how we can give up."

"No? You'd better have another think. If you force me to blow up the road, how about all the people that will be blown up along with it?"

Gaines thought furiously. He did not doubt that Van Kleeck would carry out his threat. His very phraseology, the childish petulance of "If you force me to do this—," betrayed the dangerous irrationality of his frame of mind. And such an explosion anywhere in the thickly populated Sacramento Sector would be likely to wreck one or more apartment houses, and would be certain to kill shopkeepers on the included segment of Strip 20, as well as chance passers-by. Van was absolutely right; he dare not risk the lives of bystanders who were not aware of the issue and had not consented to the hazard—even if the road never rolled again.

For that matter, he did not relish chancing major damage to the road itself—but it was the danger to innocent life which left him helpless.

A tune ran through his head:

"Hear them hum; watch them run. Oh, our work is never done—"

What to do? What to do?

"While you ride, while you glide, we are—"

This wasn't getting any place.

He turned back to the screen. "Look, Van, you don't want to blow up the road unless you have to, I'm sure. Neither do I. Suppose I come up to your headquarters, and we talk this thing over. Two reasonable men ought to be able to make a settlement."

Van Kleeck was suspicious. "Is this some sort of a trick?"

"How can it be? I'll come alone, and unarmed, just as fast as my car can get there."

"How about your men?"

"They will sit where they are until I'm back. You can put out observers to make sure of it."

Van Kleeck stalled for a moment, caught between the fear of a trap and the pleasure of having his erstwhile superior come to him to sue for terms. At last he grudgingly consented.

Gaines left his instructions, and told Davidson what he intended to do. "If I'm not back within an hour, you're on your own, Dave."

"Be careful, chief."

"I will."

He evicted the cadet driver from the reconnaissance car, and ran it down the ramp into the causeway, then headed north and gave it the gun. Now he would have a chance to collect his thoughts, even at two hundred miles per hour. Suppose he pulled off this trick—there would still have to be some changes made. Two lessons stood out like sore thumbs: First, the strips must be cross-connected with safety interlocks so that adjacent strips would slow down, or stop, if a strip's speed became dangerously different from those adjacent. No repetition of what happened on 20!

But that was elementary, a mere mechanical detail. The real failure had been in men. Well, the psychological classification tests must be improved to insure that the roads employed only conscientious, reliable men. But hell's bells—that was just exactly what the present classification tests were supposed to insure beyond question. To the best of his knowledge there had never been a failure from the improved Humm-Wadsworth-Burton method—not until today in the Sacramento Sector. How had Van Kleeck gotten one whole sector of temperament-classified men to revolt?

It didn't make sense.

Personnel did not behave erratically without a reason. One man might be unpredictable, but in large numbers personnel were as dependable as machines, or figures. They could be measured, examined, classified. His inner eye automatically pictured the personnel office, with its rows of filing cabinets, its clerks— He'd got it! He'd got it! Van Kleeck, as chief deputy, was ex officio *personnel officer for the entire road!*

It was the only solution that covered all the facts. The personnel officer alone had the perfect opportunity to pick out all the bad apples and concentrate them in one barrel. Gaines was convinced beyond any reasonable doubt that there had been skulduggery, perhaps for years, with the temperament classification tests, and that Van Kleeck had deliberately transferred the kind of men he needed to one sector, after falsifying their records.

And that taught another lesson—tighter tests for officers, and no officer to be trusted with classification and assignment without close supervision and inspection. Even he, Gaines, should be watched in that respect. *Qui custodiet ipsos custodes?* Who will guard those selfsame guardians? Latin might be obsolete, but those old Romans weren't dummies.

He at last knew wherein he had failed, and he derived melancholy pleasure from the knowledge. Supervision and inspection, check and recheck, was the answer. It would be cumbersome and inefficient, but it seemed that adequate safeguards always involved some loss of efficiency.

He should not have intrusted so much authority to Van Kleeck without knowing more about him. He still should know more about him— He touched the emergency-stop button, and brought the car to a dizzying halt. "Relay station! See if you can raise my office."

Dolores' face looked out from the screen. "You're still there— good!" he told her. "I was afraid you'd gone home."

"I came back, Mr. Gaines."

"Good girl. Get me Van Kleeck's personal file jacket. I want to see his classification record."

She was back with it in exceptionally short order, and read from it the symbols and percentages. He nodded repeatedly as the data checked his hunches: Masked introvert—inferiority complex. It checked.

" 'Comment of the board':" she read. " 'In spite of the slight potential instability shown by maxima A and D on the consolidated profile curve, the board is convinced that this officer is, nevertheless, fitted for duty. He has an exceptionally fine record, and is especially adept in handling men. He is, therefore, recommended for retention and promotion.' "

"That's all, Dolores. Thanks."

"Yes, Mr. Gaines."

"I'm off for a showdown. Keep your fingers crossed."

"But, Mr. Gaines—" Back in Fresno, Dolores stared wide-eyed at an empty screen.

"Take me to Mr. Van Kleeck!"

The man addressed took his gun out of Gaines' ribs—reluctantly, Gaines thought—and indicated that the chief engineer should precede him up the stairs. Gaines climbed out of the car, and complied.

Van Kleeck had set himself up in the sector control room proper, rather than the administrative office. With him were half a dozen men, all armed.

"Good evening, Director Van Kleeck." The little man swelled visibly at Gaines' acknowledgment of his assumed rank.

"We don't go in much around here for titles," he said, with ostentatious casualness. "Just call me Van. Sit down, Gaines."

Gaines did so. It was necessary to get those other men out. He looked at them with an expression of bored amusement. "Can't you handle one unarmed man by yourself, Van? Or don't the Functionalists trust each other?"

Van Kleeck's face showed his annoyance, but Gaines' smile was undaunted. Finally the smaller man picked up a pistol from his desk, and motioned toward the door. "Get out, you guys."

"But, Van—"

"Get out, I said!"

When they were alone, Van Kleeck picked up the electric push button which Gaines had seen in the visor screen, and pointed his pistol at his former chief. "O. K.," he growled, "try any funny stuff, and off it goes! What's your proposition?"

Gaines' irritating smile grew broader. Van Kleeck scowled. "What's so damn funny?" he said.

Gaines granted him an answer. "You are, Van—honest, this is rich. You start a Functionalist revolution, and the only function you can think of to perform is to blow up the road that justifies your title. Tell me," he went on, "what is it you are so scared of?"

"I am not afraid!"

"Not afraid? You? Sitting there, ready to commit hara-kiri with that toy push button, and you tell me that you aren't afraid. If your buddies knew how near you are to throwing away what they've fought for, they'd shoot you in a second. You're afraid of them, too, aren't you?"

Van Kleeck thrust the push button away from him, and stood up.

"I am not afraid!" he shouted, and came around the desk toward Gaines.

Gaines sat where he was, and laughed. "But you are! You're afraid of me, this minute. You're afraid I'll have you on the carpet for the way you do your job. You're afraid the cadets won't salute you. You're afraid they are laughing behind your back. You're afraid of using the wrong fork at dinner. You're afraid people are looking at you—and you are afraid that they won't notice you."

"I am not!" he protested. "You . . . you dirty, stuck-up snob! Just because you went to a high-hat school you think you're better than anybody." He choked, and became incoherent, fighting to keep back tears of rage. "You, and your nasty little cadets—"

Gaines eyed him cautiously. The weakness in the man's character was evident now—he wondered why he had not seen it before. He recalled how ungracious Van Kleeck had been one time when he had offered to help him with an intricate piece of figuring.

The problem now was to play on his weakness, to keep him so preoccupied that he would not remember the peril-laden push button. He must be caused to center the venom of his twisted outlook on Gaines, to the exclusion of every other thought.

But he must not goad him too carelessly, or a shot from across the room might put an end to Gaines, and to any chance of avoiding a bloody, wasteful struggle for control of the road.

Gaines chuckled. "Van," he said, "you are a pathetic little shrimp. That was a dead giveaway. I understand you perfectly—you're a third-rater, Van, and all your life you've been afraid that someone would see through you, and send you back to the foot of the class. Director—*pfui!* If you are the best the Functionalists can offer, we can afford to ignore them—they'll fold up from their own rotten inefficiency." He swung around in his chair, deliberately turning his back on Van Kleeck and his gun.

Van Kleeck advanced on his tormentor, halted a few feet away, and shouted: "You . . . I'll show you . . . I'll put a bullet in you; that's what I'll do!"

Gaines swung back around, got up, and walked steadily toward him. "Put that popgun down before you hurt yourself."

Van Kleeck retreated a step. "Don't you come near me!" he screamed. "Don't you come near me . . . or I'll shoot you . . . see if I don't."

"This is it," thought Gaines, and dived.

The pistol went off alongside his ear. Well, that one didn't get him. They were on the floor. Van Kleeck was hard to hold, for a little man. Where was the gun? There! He had it. He broke away.

Van Kleeck did not get up. He lay sprawled on the floor, tears streaming out of his closed eyes, blubbering like a frustrated child.

Gaines looked at him with something like compassion in his eyes, and hit him carefully behind the ear with the butt of the pistol. He walked over to the door, and listened for a moment, then locked it cautiously.

The cord from the push button led to the control board. He examined the hookup, and disconnected it carefully. That done, he turned to the televisor at the control desk, and called Fresno.

"O. K., Dave," he said, "let 'em attack now—and for the love of Pete, hurry!" Then he cleared the screen, not wishing his watch officer to see how he was shaking.

Back in Fresno the next morning Gaines paced around the main control room with a fair degree of contentment in his heart. The roads were rolling—before long they would be up to speed again. It had been a long night. Every engineer, every available cadet, had been needed to make the inch-by-inch inspection of Sacramento Sector which he had required. Then they had to cross-connect around two wrecked subsector control boards. But the roads were rolling—he could feel their rhythm up through the floor.

He stopped beside a haggard, stubbly-bearded man. "Why don't you go home, Dave?" he asked. "McPherson can carry on from here."

"How about yourself, chief? You don't look like a June bride."

"Oh, I'll catch a nap in my office after a bit. I called my wife, and told her I couldn't make it. She's coming down here to meet me."

"Was she sore?"

"Not very. You know how women are." He turned back to the instrument board, and watched the clicking busybodies assembling the data from six sectors. San Diego Circle, Angeles Sector, Bakersfield Sector, Fresno Sector, Stockton—Stockton? Stockton! Good grief—Blekinsop! He had left a cabinet minister of Australia cooling his heels in the Stockton office all night long!

He started for the door, while calling over his shoulder: "Dave, will you order a car for me? Make it a fast one!" He was across the hall, and had his head inside his private office before Davidson could acknowledge the order.

"Dolores!"

"Yes, Mr. Gaines."

"Call my wife, and tell her I had to go to Stockton. If she's already left home, just have her wait here. And, Dolores—"

"Yes, Mr. Gaines?"

"Calm her down."

She bit her lip, but her face was impassive. "Yes, Mr. Gaines."

"That's a good girl." He was out and started down the stairway. When he reached road level, the sight of the rolling strips warmed him inside and made him feel almost cheerful.

He strode briskly away toward a door marked, "Access Down," whistling softly to himself. He opened the door, and the rumbling, roaring rhythm from down inside seemed to pick up the tune even as it drowned out the sound of his whistling.

> "Hie! Hie! Hee!
> The rotor men are we—
> Check off your sectors loud and strong!
> ONE! TWO! THREE!
> Anywhere you go
> You are bound to know
> That your roadways go rolling along!"

ASYLUM

by

A. E. VAN VOGT

Asylum contributes a fresh idea to the literature of vampirism, something that hasn't happened since Dracula was written! Further, Mr. Van Vogt brings forth the unpleasant and revolutionary idea that the status of intellectual eminence is determined only by comparative environment. He accepts the hypothesis that man is very low on the universal scale of evolved intelligence. Further, he postulates man as being in the care of beings who, while possessing an I.Q. of at least 300, are, in their own worlds, regarded as morons!

I

INDECISION WAS dark in the man's thoughts as he walked across the spaceship control room to the cot where the woman lay so taut and so still. He bent over her; he said in his deep voice:

"We're slowing down, Merla."

No answer, no movement, not a quiver in her delicate, abnormally blanched cheeks. Her fine nostrils dilated ever so slightly with each measured breath. That was all.

The Dreegh lifted her arm, then let it go. It dropped to her lap like a piece of lifeless wood, and her body remained rigid and unnatural. Carefully, he put his fingers to one eye, raised the lid, peered into it. It stared back at him, a clouded, sightless blue.

He straightened, and stood very still there in the utter silence of the hurtling ship. For a moment, then, in the intensity of his posture and in the dark ruthlessness of his lean, hard features, he seemed the veritable embodiment of grim, icy calculation.

He thought grayly: "If I revived her now, she'd have more time to attack me, and more strength. If I waited, she'd be weaker—"

Slowly, he relaxed. Some of the weariness of the years he and this woman had spent together in the dark vastness of space came to shatter his abnormal logic. Bleak sympathy touched him—and the decision was made.

He prepared an injection, and fed it into her arm. His gray eyes held a steely brightness as he put his lips near the woman's ear; in a ringing, resonant voice he said:

"We're near a star system. There'll be blood, Merla! And life!"

The woman stirred; momentarily, she seemed like a golden-haired doll come alive. No color touched her perfectly formed cheeks, but alertness crept into her eyes. She stared up at him with a hardening hostility, half questioning.

"I've been chemical," she said—and abruptly the doll-like effect was gone. Her gaze tightened on him, and some of the prettiness vanished from her face. Her lips twisted into words:

"It's damned funny, Jeel, that you're still O. K. If I thought—"

He was cold, watchful. "Forget it," he said curtly. "You're an energy waster, and you know it. Anyway, we're going to land."

The flamelike tenseness of her faded. She sat up painfully, but there was a thoughtful look on her face as she said:

"I'm interested in the risks. This is not a Galactic planet, is it?"

"There are no Galactics out here. But there is an Observer. I've been catching the secret *ultra* signals for the last two hours"—a sardonic note entered his voice—"warning all ships to stay clear because the system isn't ready for any kind of contact with Galactic planets."

Some of the diabolic glee that was in his thoughts must have communicated through his tone. The woman stared at him, and slowly her eyes widened. She half whispered:

"You mean—"

He shrugged. "The signals ought to be registering full blast now. We'll see what degree system this is. But you can start hoping hard right now."

At the control board, he cautiously manipulated the room into darkness and set the automatics—a picture took form on a screen on the opposite wall.

At first there was only a point of light in the middle of a starry sky, then a planet floating brightly in the dark space, continents and oceans plainly visible. A voice came out of the screen:

"This star system contains one inhabited planet, the third from the Sun, called Earth by its inhabitants. It was colonized by Galactics about seven thousand years ago in the usual manner. It is now in the third degree of development, having attained a limited form of space travel little more than a hundred years ago. It—"

With a swift movement, the man cut off the picture and turned on the light, then looked across at the woman in a blank, triumphant silence.

"Third degree!" he said softly, and there was an almost incredulous note in his voice. "Only third degree. Merla, do you realize what this means? This is the opportunity of the ages. I'm going to call the Dreegh tribe. If we can't get away with several tankers of blood and a whole battery of 'life,' we don't deserve to be immortal. We—"

He turned toward the communicator, and for that exultant moment caution was a dim thing in the back of his mind. From the corner of his eye, he saw the woman flow from the edge of the cot. Too late he twisted aside. The frantic jerk saved him only partially; it was their cheeks, not their lips that met.

Blue flame flashed from him to her. The burning energy seared his cheek to instant, bleeding rawness. He half fell to the floor from the shock; and then, furious with the intense agony, he fought free.

"I'll break your bones!" he raged.

Her laughter, unlovely with her own suppressed fury, floated up at him from the floor, where he had flung her. She snarled:

"So you did have a secret supply of 'life' for yourself. You damned double-crosser!"

His black mortification dimmed before the stark realization that anger was useless. Tense with the weakness that was already a weight on his muscles, he whirled toward the control board, and began feverishly to make the adjustments that would pull the ship back into normal space and time.

The body urge grew in him swiftly, a dark, remorseless need. Twice, black nausea sent him reeling to the cot; but each time he fought back to the control board. He sat there finally at the controls, head drooping, conscious of the numbing tautness that crept deeper, deeper—

Almost, he drove the ship too fast. It turned a blazing white when at last it struck the atmosphere of the third planet. But those hard metals held their shape; and the terrible speeds yielded to the fury of the reversers and to the pressure of the air that thickened with every receding mile.

It was the woman who helped his faltering form into the tiny lifeboat. He lay there, gathering strength, staring with tense eagerness down at the blazing sea of lights that was the first city he had seen on the night side of this strange world.

Dully, he watched as the woman carefully eased the small ship into the darkness behind a shed in a little back alley; and, because succor seemed suddenly near, sheer hope enabled him to walk beside her to the dimly lighted residential street nearby.

He would have walked on blankly into the street, but the woman's fingers held him back into the shadows of the alleyway.

"Are you mad?" she whispered. "Lie down. We'll stay right here till someone comes."

The cement was hard beneath his body, but after a moment of the painful rest it brought, he felt a faint surge of energy; and he was able to voice his bitter thought:

"If you hadn't stolen most of my carefully saved 'life,' we wouldn't be in this desperate position. You know well that it's more important that I remain at full power."

In the dark beside him, the woman lay quiet for a while; then her defiant whisper came:

"We both need a change of blood and a new charge of 'life.' Perhaps I did take a little too much out of you, but that was because I had to steal it. You wouldn't have given it to me of your own free will, and you know it."

For a time, the futility of argument held him silent, but, as the minutes dragged, that dreadful physical urgency once more tainted his thoughts, he said heavily:

"You realize of course that we've revealed our presence. We should have waited for the others to come. There's no doubt at all that our ship was spotted by the Galactic Observer in this system before we reached the outer planets. They'll have tracers on us wherever we go, and, no matter where we bury our machine, they'll know its exact location. It is impossible to hide the interstellar drive energies; and, since they wouldn't make the mistake of bringing such energies to a third-degree planet, we can't hope to locate them in that fashion.

"But we must expect an attack of some kind. I only hope one of the great Galactics doesn't take part in it."

"One of *them!*" Her whisper was a gasp, then she snapped irritably, "Don't try to scare me. You've told me time and again that—"

"All right, all right!" He spoke grudgingly, wearily. "A million years have proven that they consider us beneath their personal attention. And"—in spite of his appalling weakness, scorn came—"let any of the kind of agents they have in these lower category planets try to stop us."

"Hush!" Her whisper was tense. "Footsteps! Quick, get to your feet!"

He was aware of the shadowed form of her rising; then her hands were tugging at him. Dizzily, he stood up.

"I don't think," he began wanly, "that I can—"

"Jeel!" Her whisper beat at him; her hands shook him. "It's a man and a woman. They're 'life,' Jeel, 'life'!"

Life!

He straightened with a terrible effort. A spark of the unquenchable will to live that had brought him across the black miles and the blacker years, burst into flames inside him. Lightly, swiftly, he fell into step beside Merla, and strode beside her into the open. He saw the shapes of the man and the woman.

In the half-night under the trees of that street, the couple came toward them, drawing aside to let them pass; first the woman came, then the man—and it was as simple as if all his strength had been there in his muscles.

He saw Merla launch herself at the man; and then he was grabbing the woman, his head bending instantly for that abnormal kiss—

Afterward—after they had taken the blood, too—grimness came to the man, a hard fabric of thought and counterthought, that slowly formed into purpose; he said:

"We'll leave the bodies here."

Her startled whisper rose in objection, but he cut her short harshly: "Let me handle this. These dead bodies will draw to this city news gatherers, news reporters or whatever their breed are called on this planet; and we need such a person now. Somewhere in the reservoir of facts possessed by a person of this type must be clues, meaningless to him, but by which we can discover the secret base of the Galactic Observer in this system. We must find that base, discover its strength, and destroy it if necessary when the tribe comes."

His voice took on a steely note: "And now, we've got to explore this city, find a much frequented building, under which we can bury our ship, learn the language, replenish our own vital supplies—and capture that reporter.

"After I'm through with him"—his tone became silk smooth— "he will undoubtedly provide you with that physical diversion which you apparently crave when you have been particularly chemical."

He laughed gently, as her fingers gripped his arm in the darkness, a convulsive gesture; her voice came: "Thank you, Jeel, you do understand, don't you?"

II

Behind Leigh, a door opened. Instantly the clatter of voices in the room faded to a murmur. He turned alertly, tossing his cigarette onto the marble floor, and stepping on it, all in one motion.

Overhead, the lights brightened to daylight intensity; and in that blaze he saw what the other eyes were already staring at: the two bodies, the man's and the woman's, as they were wheeled in.

The dead couple lay side by side on the flat, gleaming top of the carrier. Their bodies were rigid, their eyes closed; they looked as dead as they were, and not at all, Leigh thought, as if they were sleeping.

He caught himself making a mental note of that fact—and felt abruptly shocked.

The first murders on the North American continent in twenty-seven years. And it was only another job. By Heaven, he was tougher than he'd ever believed.

He grew aware that the voices had stopped completely. The only sound was the hoarse breathing of the man nearest him—and then the scrape of his own shoes as he went forward.

His movement acted like a signal on that tense group of men. There was a general pressing forward. Leigh had a moment of hard anxiety; and then his bigger, harder muscles brought him where he wanted to be, opposite the two heads.

He leaned forward in dark absorption. His fingers probed gingerly the neck of the woman, where the incisions showed. He did not look up at the attendant, as he said softly:

"This is where the blood was drained?"

"Yes."

Before he could speak again, another reporter interjected: "Any special comment from the police scientists? The murders are more than a day old now. There ought to be something new."

Leigh scarcely heard. The woman's body, electrically warmed for embalming, felt eerily lifelike to his touch. It was only after a long moment that he noticed her lips were badly, almost brutally bruised

His gaze flicked to the man; and there were the same neck cuts, the same torn lips. He looked up, questions quivered on his tongue— and remained unspoken as realization came that the calm-voiced attendant was still talking. The man was saying:

"—normally, when the electric embalmers are applied, there is resistance from the static electricity of the body. Curiously, that resistance was not present in either body."

Somebody said: "Just what does that mean?"

"This static force is actually a form of life force, which usually trickles out of a corpse over a period of a month. We know of no way to hasten the process, but the bruises on the lips show distinct burns, which are suggestive."

There was a craning of necks, a crowding forward; and Leigh allowed himself to be pushed aside. He stopped attentively, as the attendant said: "Presumably, a pervert could have kissed with such violence."

"I thought," Leigh called distinctly, "there were no more perverts since Professor Ungarn persuaded the government to institute his brand of mechanical psychology in all schools, thus ending murder, theft, war and all unsocial perversions."

The attendant in his black frock coat hesitated; then: "A very bad one seems to have been missed."

He finished: "That's all, gentlemen. No clues, no promise of an early capture, and only this final fact: We've wirelessed Professor Ungarn and, by great good fortune, we caught him on his way to Earth from his meteorite retreat near Jupiter. He'll be landing shortly after dark, in a few hours now."

The lights dimmed. As Leigh stood frowning, watching the bodies being wheeled out, a phrase floated out of the gathering chorus of voices:

"—The kiss of death—"

"I tell you," another voice said, "the captain of this space liner swears it happened—the spaceship came past him at a million miles an hour, and it was slowing down, get that, slowing down—two days ago."

"—The vampire case! That's what I'm going to call it—"

That's what Leigh called it, too, as he talked briefly into his wrist communicator. He finished: "I'm going to supper now, Jim."

"O. K., Bill." The local editor's voice came metallically. "And say, I'm supposed to commend you. Nine thousand papers took the Planetarian Service on this story, as compared with about forty-seven hundred who bought from Universal, who got the second largest coverage.

"And I think you've got the right angle for today also. Husband and wife, ordinary young couple, taking an evening's walk. Some devil hauls up alongside them, drains their blood into a tank, their life energy onto a wire or something—people will believe that, I guess. Anyway, you suggest it could happen to anybody; so be careful, folks. And you warn that, in these days of interplanetary speeds, he could be anywhere tonight for his next murder.

"As I said before, good stuff. That'll keep the story frying hard for tonight. Oh, by the way—"

"Shoot!"

"A kid called half an hour ago to see you. Said you expected him."

"A kid?" Leigh frowned to himself.

"Name of Patrick. High school age, about sixteen. No, come to think of it, that was only my first impression. Eighteen, maybe twenty, very bright, confident, proud."

"I remember now," said Leigh, "college student. Interview for a college paper. Called me up this afternoon. One of those damned persuasive talkers. Before I knew it, I was signed up for supper at Constantine's."

"That's right. I was supposed to remind you. O. K.?"

Leigh shrugged. "I promised," he said.

Actually, as he went out into the blaze of late afternoon, sunlit street, there was not a thought in his head. Nor a premonition.

Around him, the swarm of humankind began to thicken. Vast buildings discharged the first surge of the five o'clock tidal wave—and twice Leigh felt the tug at his arm before it struck him that someone was not just bumping him.

He turned, and stared down at a pair of dark, eager eyes set in a brown, wizened face. The little man waved a sheaf of papers at him. Leigh caught a glimpse of writing in longhand on the papers. Then the fellow was babbling:

"Mr. Leigh, hundred dollars for these . . . biggest story—"

"Oh," said Leigh. His interest collapsed; then his mind roused itself from its almost blank state; and pure politeness made him say: "Take it up to the Planetarian office. Jim Brian will pay you what the story is worth."

He walked on, the vague conviction in his mind that the matter was settled. Then, abruptly, there was the tugging at his arm again.

"Scoop!" the little man was muttering. "Professor Ungarn's log, all about a spaceship that came from the stars. Devils in it who drink blood and kiss people to death!"

"See here!" Leigh began, irritated; and then he stopped physically and mentally. A strange ugly chill swept through him. He stood there, swaying a little from the shock of the thought that was frozen in his brain:

The newspapers with those details of "blood" and "kiss" were not on the street yet, wouldn't be for another five minutes.

The man was saying: "Look, it's got Professor Ungarn's name printed in gold on the top of each sheet, and it's all about how he first spotted the ship eighteen light years out, and how it came all that distance in a few hours . . . and he knows where it is now and—"

Leigh heard, but that was all. His reporter's brain, that special, highly developed department, was whirling with a little swarm of thoughts that suddenly straightened into a hard, bright pattern; and in that tightly built design, there was no room for any such brazen coincidence as this man coming to him here in this crowded street.

He said: "Let me see those!" And reached as he spoke.

The papers came free from the other's fingers into his hands, but Leigh did not even glance at them. His brain was crystal-clear, his eyes cold; he snapped:

"I don't know what game you're trying to pull. I want to know three things, and make your answers damned fast! One: How did you pick me out, name and job and all, here in this packed street of a city I haven't been in for a year?"

He was vaguely aware of the little man trying to speak, stammering incomprehensible words. But he paid no attention. Remorselessly, he pounded on:

"Two: Professor Ungarn is arriving from Jupiter in three hours. How do you explain your possession of papers he must have written, less than two days ago?"

"Look, boss," the man chattered, "you've got me all wrong—"

"My third question," Leigh said grimly, "is how are you going to explain to the police your pre-knowledge of the details of—murder?"

"Huh!" The little man's eyes were glassy, and for the first time pity came to Leigh. He said almost softly:

"All right, fellah, start talking."

The words came swiftly, and at first they were simply senseless sounds; only gradually did coherence come.

"—And that's the way it was, boss. I'm standing there, and this kid comes up to me and points you out, and gives me five bucks and those papers you've got, and tells me what I'm supposed to say to you and—"

"Kid!" said Leigh; and the first shock was already in him.

"Yeah, kid about sixteen; no, more like eighteen or twenty . . . and he gives me the papers and—"

"This kid," said Leigh, "would you say he was of college age?"

"That's it, boss; you've got it. That's just what he was. You know him, eh? O. K., that leaves me in the clear, and I'll be going—"

"Wait!" Leigh called, but the little man seemed suddenly to realize that he need only run, for he jerked into a mad pace; and people stared, and that was all. He vanished around a corner, and was gone forever.

Leigh stood, frowning, reading the thin sheaf of papers. And there was nothing beyond what the little man had already conveyed by his incoherent word of mouth, simply a vague series of entries on sheets from a loose-leaf notebook.

Written down, the tale about the spaceship and its occupants lacked depth, and seemed more unconvincing each passing second. True, there was the single word "Ungarn" inscribed in gold on the top of each sheet but—

Leigh shook himself. The sense of silly hoax grew so violently that he thought with abrupt anger: If that damned fool college kid really pulled a stunt like—

The thought ended; for the idea was as senseless as everything that had happened.

And still there was no real tension in him. He was only going to a restaurant.

He turned into the splendid foyer that was the beginning of the vast and wonderful Constantine's. In the great doorway, he paused for a moment to survey the expansive glitter of tables, the hanging garden tearooms; and it was all there.

Brilliant Constantine's, famous the world over—but not much changed from his last visit.

Leigh gave his name, and began: "A Mr. Patrick made reservations, I understand—"

The girl cut him short. "Oh, yes, Mr. Leigh. Mr. Patrick reserved Private 3 for you. He just now phoned to say he'd be along in a few minutes. Our premier will escort you."

Leigh was turning away, a vague puzzled thought in his mind at the way the girl had gushed, when a flamelike thought struck him: "Just a minute, did you say *Private 3*? Who's paying for this?"

The girl glowed at him: "It was paid by phone. Forty-five hundred dollars!"

Leigh stood very still. In a single, flashing moment, this meeting that, even after what had happened on the street, had seemed scarcely more than an irritation to be gotten over with, was become a fantastic, abnormal thing.

Forty-five—hundred—dollars! Could it be some damned fool rich kid sent by a college paper, but who had pulled this whole affair because he was determined to make a strong, personal impression?

Coldly, alertly, his brain rejected the solution. Humanity produced egoists on an elephantiastic scale, but not one who would order a feast like that to impress a reporter.

His eyes narrowed on an idea: "Where's your registered phone?" he asked curtly.

A minute later, he was saying into the mouthpiece: "Is that the Amalgamated Universities Secretariat? . . . I want to find out if there is a Mr. Patrick registered at any of your local colleges, and, if there is, whether or not he has been authorized by any college paper to interview William Leigh of the Planetarian News Service. This is Leigh calling."

It took six minutes, and then the answer came, brisk, tremendous and final: "There are three Mr. Patricks in our seventeen units. All are at present having supper at their various official residences. There are four Miss Patricks similarly accounted for by our staff of secretaries. None of these seven is in any way connected with a university paper. Do you wish any assistance in dealing with the impostor?"

Leigh hesitated; and when he finally spoke, it was with the queer, dark realization that he was committing himself. "No," he said, and hung up.

He came out of the phone box, shaken by his own thoughts. There was only one reason why he was in this city at this time. Murder! And he knew scarcely a soul. Therefore—

It was absolutely incredible that any stranger would want to see him for a reason not connected with his own purpose. He shook the ugly thrill out of his system; he said:

"To Private 3, please—"

Tensed but cool, he examined the apartment that was Private 3. Actually that was all it was, a splendidly furnished apartment with a palacelike dining salon dominating the five rooms, and one entire wall of the salon was lined with decorated mirror facings, behind which glittered hundreds of bottles of liquors.

The brands were strange to his inexpensive tastes, the scent of several that he opened heady and—quite uninviting. In the ladies' dressing room was a long showcase displaying a gleaming array of jewelry—several hundred thousand dollars' worth, if it was genuine, he estimated swiftly.

Leigh whistled softly to himself. On the surface, Constantine's appeared to supply good rental value for the money they charged.

"I'm glad you're physically big," said a cool voice behind him. "So many reporters are thin and small."

It was the voice that did it, subtly, differently toned than it had been over the phone in the early afternoon. Deliberately different.

The difference, he noted as he turned, was in the body, too, the difference in the shape of a woman from a boy, skillfully but not perfectly concealed under the well-tailored man's suit—actually, of course, she was quite boyish in build, young, finely molded.

And, actually, he would never have suspected if she had not allowed her voice to be so purposefully womanish. She echoed his thought coolly:

"Yes, I wanted you to know. But now, there's no use wasting words. You know as much as you need to know. Here's a gun. The spaceship is buried below this building."

Leigh made no effort to take the weapon, nor did he even glance at it. Instead, cool now, that the first shock was over, he seated himself on the silk-yielding chair of the vanity dresser in one corner, leaned heavily back against the vanity itself, raised his eyebrows, and said:

"Consider me a slow-witted lunk who's got to know what it's all about. Why so much preliminary hocus-pocus?"

He thought deliberately: He had never in his adult life allowed himself to be rushed into anything. He was not going to start now.

III

The girl, he saw after a moment, was small of build. Which was odd, he decided carefully. Because his first impression had been of reasonable length of body. Or perhaps—he considered the possibility unhurriedly—this second effect was a more considered result of her male disguise.

He dismissed that particular problem as temporarily insoluble, and because actually—it struck him abruptly—this girl's size was unimportant. She had long, black lashes and dark eyes that glowed at him from a proud, almost haughty face. And that was it; quite definitely that was the essence of her blazing, powerful personality.

Pride was in the way she held her head. It was in the poised easiness of every movement, the natural shift from grace to grace as she walked slowly toward him. Not conscious pride here, but an awareness of superiority that affected every movement of her muscles, and came vibrantly into her voice, as she said scathingly:

"I picked you because every newspaper I've read today carried your account of the murders, and because it seemed to me that somebody who already was actively working on the case would be reasonably quick at grasping essentials. As for the dramatic preparation, I considered that would be more convincing than drab explanation. I see I was mistaken in all these assumptions."

She was quite close to him now. She leaned over, laid her revolver on the vanity beside his arm, and finished almost indifferently:

"Here's an effective weapon. It doesn't shoot bullets, but it has a trigger and you aim it like any gun. In the event you develop the beginning of courage, come down the tunnel after me as quickly as possible, but don't blunder in on me and the people I shall be talking to. Stay hidden! Act only if I'm threatened."

Tunnel, Leigh thought stolidly, as she walked with a free, swift stride out of the room—tunnel here in this apartment called Private 3. Either he was crazy, or she was.

Quite suddenly, realization came that he ought to be offended at the way she had spoken. And that insultingly simple come-on trick of hers, leaving the room, leaving him to develop curiosity—he smiled ruefully; if he hadn't been a reporter, he'd show her that such a second-rate psychology didn't work on him.

Still annoyed, he climbed to his feet, took the gun, and then paused briefly as the odd, muffled sound came of a door opening reluctantly—

He found her in the bedroom to the left of the dining salon; and because his mind was still in that state of pure receptiveness, which, for him, replaced indecisiveness, he felt only the vaguest surprise to see that she had the end of a lush green rug rolled back, and that there was a hole in the floor at her feet.

The gleaming square of floor that must have covered the opening, lay back neatly, pinned to position by a single, glitteringly complicated hinge. But Leigh scarcely noticed that.

His gaze reached beyond that—tunnel—to the girl; and, in that moment, just before she became aware of him, there was the barest suggestion of uncertainty about her. And her right profile, half turned away from him, showed pursed lips, a strained whiteness, as if—

The impression he received was of indecisiveness. He had the subtle sense of observing a young woman who, briefly, had lost her superb confidence. Then she saw him; and his whole emotion picture twisted.

She didn't seem to stiffen in any way. Paying no attention to him at all, she stepped down to the first stair of the little stairway that led down into the hole, and began to descend without a quiver of hesitation. And yet—

Yet his first conviction that she had faltered brought him forward with narrowed eyes. And, suddenly, that certainty of her brief fear made this whole madness real. He plunged forward, down the steep stairway, and pulled up only when he saw that he was actually in a smooth, dimly lighted tunnel; and that the girl had paused, one finger to her lips.

"Sssshh!" she said. "The door of the ship may be open."

Irritation struck Leigh, a hard trickle of anger. Now that he had committed himself, he felt automatically the leader of this fantastic expedition; and that girl's pretensions, the devastating haughtiness of her merely produced his first real impatience.

"Don't 'ssshh me'!" he whispered sharply. "Just give me the facts, and I'll do the rest."

He stopped. For the first time the meaning of all the words she had spoken penetrated. His anger collapsed like a plane in a crash landing.

"Ship!" he said incredulously. "Are you trying to tell me there's actually a spaceship buried here under Constantine's?"

The girl seemed not to hear; and Leigh saw that they were at the end of a short passageway. Metal gleamed dully just ahead. Then the girl was saying:

"Here's the door. Now, remember, you act as guard. Stay hidden, ready to shoot. And if I yell 'Shoot,' you shoot!"

She bent forward. There was the tiniest scarlet flash. The door opened, revealing a second door just beyond. Again that minute, intense blaze of red; and that door too swung open.

It was swiftly done, too swiftly. Before Leigh could more than grasp that the crisis was come, the girl stepped coolly into the brilliantly lighted room beyond the second door.

There was shadow where Leigh stood half-paralyzed by the girl's action. There was deeper shadow against the metal wall toward which he pressed himself in one instinctive move. He froze there, cursing silently at a stupid young woman who actually walked into a den of enemies of unknown numbers without a genuine plan of self-protection.

Or did she know how many there were? And who?

The questions made twisting paths in his mind down, down to a thrall of blankness—that ended only when an entirely different thought replaced it:

At least he was out here with a gun, unnoticed—or was he?

He waited tensely. But the door remained open; and there was no apparent movement towards it. Slowly, Leigh let himself relax, and allowed his straining mind to absorb its first considered impressions.

The portion of underground room that he could see showed one end of what seemed to be a control board, a metal wall that blinked with tiny lights, the edge of a rather sumptuous cot—and the whole was actually so suggestive of a spaceship that Leigh's logic-resistance collapsed.

Incredibly, here under the ground, actually under Constantine's was a small spaceship and—

That thought ended, too, as the silence beyond the open door, the curiously long silence, was broken by a man's cool voice:

"I wouldn't even try to raise that gun if I were you. The fact that you have said nothing since entering shows how enormously different we are to what you expected."

He laughed gently, an unhurried, deep-throated derisive laughter that came clearly to Leigh. The man said:

"Merla, what would you say is the psychology behind this young lady's action? You have of course noticed that she is a young lady, and not a boy."

A richly toned woman's voice replied: "She was born here, Jeel. She has none of the normal characteristics of a Klugg, but she is a Galactic, though definitely not the Galactic Observer. Probably, she's not alone. Shall I investigate?"

"No!" The man sounded indifferent to the tensing Leigh. "We don't have to worry about a Klugg's assistant."

Leigh relaxed slowly, but there was a vast uneasiness in his solar nerves, a sense of emptiness, the first realization of how great a part the calm assurance of the young woman had played in the fabricating of his own basic confidence.

Shattered now! Before the enormous certainties of these two, and in the face of their instant penetration of her male disguise, the effects of the girl's rather wonderful personality seemed a remote pattern, secondary, definitely overwhelmed.

He forced the fear from him, as the girl spoke; forced his courage to grow with each word she uttered, feeding on the haughty and immense confidence that was there. It didn't matter whether she was simulating or not, because they were in this now, he as deep as she; and only the utmost boldness could hope to draw a fraction of victory from the defeat that loomed so starkly.

With genuine admiration, he noted the glowing intensity of her speech, as she said:

"My silence had its origin in the fact that you are the first Dreeghs I have ever seen. Naturally, I studied you with some curiosity, but I can assure you I am not impressed.

"However, in view of your extraordinary opinions on the matter, I shall come to the point at once: I have been instructed by the Galactic Observer of this system to inform you to be gone by morning. Our sole reason for giving you that much leeway is that we don't wish to bring the truth of all this into the open.

"But don't count on that. Earth is on the verge of being given fourth-degree rating; and, as you probably know, in emergencies fourths are given Galactic knowledge. That emergency we will consider to have arrived tomorrow at dawn."

"Well, well"—the man was laughing gently, satirically—"a pretty speech, powerfully spoken, but meaningless for us who can analyze its pretensions, however sincere, back to the Klugg origin."

"What do you intend with her, Jeel?"

The man was cold, deadly, utterly sure. "There's no reason why she should escape. She had blood and more than normal life. It will convey to the Observer with clarity our contempt for his ultimatum."

He finished with a slow, surprisingly rich laughter: "We shall now enact a simple drama. The young lady will attempt to jerk up her gun and shoot me with it. Before she can even begin to succeed, I shall have my own weapon out and firing. The whole thing, as she will discover, is a matter of nervous co-ordination. And Kluggs are chronically almost as slow-moving as human beings."

His voice stopped. His laughter trickled away.

Silence.

In all his alert years, Leigh had never felt more indecisive. His emotions said—now; surely, she'd call now. And even if she didn't, he must act on his own. Rush in! Shoot!

But his mind was cold with an awful dread. There was something about the man's voice, a surging power, a blazing, incredible certainty. Abnormal, savage strength was here; and if this was really a spaceship from the stars—

His brain wouldn't follow that flashing, terrible thought. He crouched, fingering the gun she had given him, dimly conscious for the first time that it felt queer, unlike any revolver he'd ever had.

He crouched stiffly, waiting—and the silence from the spaceship control room, from the tensed figures that must be there just beyond his line of vision, continued. The same curious silence that had followed the girl's entrance short minutes before. Only this time it was the girl who broke it, her voice faintly breathless but withal cool, vibrant, unafraid:

"I'm here to warn, not to force issues. And unless you're charged with the life energy of fifteen men, I wouldn't advise you to try anything either. After all, I came here knowing what you were."

"What do you think, Merla? Can we be sure she's a Klugg? Could she possibly be of the higher Lennel type?"

It was the man, his tone conceding her point, but the derision was still there, the implacable purpose, the high, tremendous confidence.

And yet, in spite of that unrelenting sense of imminent violence,

Leigh felt himself torn from the thought of her danger—and his. His reporter's brain twisted irresistibly to the fantastic meaning of what was taking place:

—Life energy of fifteen men—

It was all there; in a monstrous way it all fitted. The two dead bodies he had seen drained of blood and life energy, the repeated reference to a Galactic Observer, with whom the girl was connected.

Leigh thought almost blankly: Galactic meant—well—Galactic; and that was so terrific that— He grew aware that the woman was speaking:

"Klugg!" she said positively. "Pay no attention to her protestations, Jeel. You know, I'm sensitive when it comes to women. She's lying. She's just a little fool who walked in here expecting us to be frightened of her. Destroy her at your pleasure."

"I'm not given to waiting," said the man. "So—"

Quite automatically, Leigh leaped for the open doorway. He had a flashing glimpse of a man and woman, dressed in evening clothes, the man standing, the woman seated. There was awareness of a gleaming, metallic background, the control board, part of which he had already seen, now revealed as a massive thing of glowing instruments; and then all that blotted out as he snapped:

"That will do. Put up your hands."

For a long, dazzling moment he had the impression that his entry was a complete surprise; and that he dominated the situation. None of the three people in the room was turned toward him. The man, Jeel, and the girl were standing, facing each other; the woman, Merla, sat in a deep chair, her fine profile to him, her golden head flung back.

It was she who, still without looking at him, sneered visibly— and spoke the words that ended his brief conviction of triumph. She said to the disguised girl:

"You certainly travel in low company, a stupid human being. Tell him to go away before he's damaged."

The girl said: "Leigh, I'm sorry I brought you into this. Every move you made in entering was heard, observed and dismissed before you could even adjust your mind to the scene."

"Is his name Leigh?" said the woman sharply. "I thought I recognized him as he entered. He's very like his photograph over his newspaper column." Her voice grew strangely tense: "Jeel, a newspaper reporter!"

"We don't need him now," the man said. "We know who the Galactic Observer is."

"Eh?" said Leigh; his mind fastened hard on those amazing words. "Who? How did you find out? What—"

"The information," said the woman; and it struck him suddenly that the strange quality in her voice was eagerness, "will be of no use to you. Regardless of what happens to the girl, you're staying."

She glanced swiftly at the man, as if seeking his sanction. "Remember, Jeel, you promised."

It was all quite senseless, so meaningless that Leigh had no sense of personal danger. His mind scarcely more than passed the words; his eyes concentrated tautly on a reality that had, until that moment, escaped his awareness. He said softly:

"Just now you used the phrase, 'Regardless of what happens to the girl.' When I came in, you said, 'Tell him to go away before he's damaged.'"

Leigh smiled grimly: "I need hardly say this is a far cry from the threat of immediate death that hung over us a few seconds ago. And I have just now noticed the reason.

"A little while ago, I heard our pal, Jeel, dare my little girl friend here to raise her gun. I notice now that *she has it raised*. My entrance did have an effect." He addressed himself to the girl, finished swiftly: "Shall we shoot—or withdraw?"

It was the man who answered: "I would advise withdrawal. I could still win, but I am not the heroic type who takes the risk of what might well be a close call."

He added, in an aside to the woman: "Merla, we can always catch this man, Leigh, now that we know who he is."

The girl said: "You first, Mr. Leigh." And Leigh did not stop to argue.

Metal doors clanged behind him, as he charged along the tunnel. After a moment, he was aware of the girl running lightly beside him.

The strangely unreal, the unbelievably murderous little drama was over, finished as fantastically as it had begun.

IV

Outside Constantine's a gray light gathered around them. A twilight side street it was, and people hurried past them with the strange, anxious look of the late for supper. Night was falling.

Leigh stared at his companion; in the dimness of the deep dusk, she seemed all boy, slightly, lithely built, striding along boldly. He laughed a little, huskily, then more grimly:

"Just what was all that? Did we escape by the skin of our teeth? Or did we win? What made you think you could act like God, and give those tough eggs twelve hours to get out of the Solar System?"

The girl was silent after he had spoken. She walked just ahead of him, head bent into the gloom. Abruptly, she turned; she said:

"I hope you will have no nonsensical idea of telling what you've seen or heard."

Leigh said: "This is the biggest story since—"

"Look"—the girl's voice was pitying—"you're not going to print a word because in about ten seconds you'll see that no one in the world would believe the first paragraph."

In the darkness, Leigh smiled tightly: "The mechanical psychologist will verify every syllable."

"I came prepared for that, too!" said the vibrant voice. Her hand swung up, toward his face. Too late, he jerked back.

Light flared in his eyes, a dazzling, blinding force that exploded into his sensitive optic nerves with all the agonizing power of intolerable brightness. Leigh cursed aloud, wildly, and snatched forward toward his tormentor. His right hand grazed a shoulder. He lashed out violently with his left, and tantalizingly caught only the edge of a sleeve that instantly jerked away.

"You little devil!" he raged futilely. "You've blinded me."

"You'll be all right," came the cool answer, "but you'll find that the mechanical psychologist will report anything you say as the purest imagination. In view of your threat to publish, I had to do that. Now, give me my gun."

The first glimmer of sight was returning. Leigh could see her body a dim, wavering shape in the night. In spite of the continuing pain, Leigh smiled grimly. He said softly:

"I've just now remembered you said this gun didn't shoot bullets. Even the *feel* of it suggests that it'll make an interesting proof of anything I say. So—"

His smile faded abruptly. For the girl stepped forward. The metal that jabbed into his ribs was so hardly thrust, it made him grunt.

"Give me that gun!"

"Like fun I will," Leigh snapped. "You ungrateful little ruffian, how dare you treat me so shoddily after I saved your life? I ought to knock you one right on the jaw for—"

He stopped—stopped because with staggering suddenness the hard, hard realization struck that she meant it. This was no girl raised in a refined school, who wouldn't dare to shoot, but a cold-blooded young creature, who had already proved the metalliclike fabric of which her courage was made.

He had never had any notions about the superiority of man over woman; and he felt none now. Without a single word, almost hastily, he handed the weapon over. The girl took it, and said coldly:

"You seem to be laboring under the illusion that your entry into the spaceship enabled me to raise my weapon. You're quite mistaken. What you did do was to provide me with the opportunity to let them think that that was the situation, and that they dominated it. But I assure you, that is the extent of your assistance, almost valueless."

Leigh laughed out loud, a pitying, ridiculing laugh.

"In my admittedly short life," he said laconically, "I've learned to recognize a quality of personality and magnetism in human beings. You've got it, a lot of it, but not a fraction of what either of those two had, particularly the man. He was terrible. He was absolutely the most abnormally magnetic human being I've ever run across. Lady, I can only guess what all this is about, but I'd advise you"— Leigh paused, then finished slashingly—"you and all the other Kluggs to stay away from that couple.

"Personally, I'm going to get the police in on this, and there's going to be a raid on Private 3. I didn't like that odd threat that they could capture me any time. Why me—"

He broke off hastily: "Hey, where are you going? I want to know your name. I want to know what made you think you could order those two around. Who did you think you were?"

He said no more, his whole effort concentrated on running. He could see her for a moment, a hazy, boyish figure against a dim corner light. Then she was around the corner.

His only point of contact with all this; and if she got away—

Sweating, he rounded the corner; and at first the street seemed dark and empty of life. Then he saw the car.

A normal-looking, high-hooded coupe, long, low-built, that began to move forward noiselessly and—quite normally.

It became abnormal. It lifted. Amazingly, it lifted from the ground. He had a swift glimpse of white rubber wheels folding out of sight. Streamlined, almost cigar-shaped now, the spaceship that had been a car darted at a steep angle into the sky.

Instantly it was gone.

Above Leigh, the gathering night towered, a strange, bright blue. In spite of the brilliant lights of the city glaring into the sky, one or two stars showed. He stared up at them, empty inside, thinking: "It was like a dream. Those—Dreeghs—coming out of space—bloodsuckers, vampires."

Suddenly hungry, he bought a chocolate from a sidewalk stand, and stood munching it.

He began to feel better. He walked over to a nearby wall socket, and plugged in his wrist radio.

"Jim," he said. "I've got some stuff, not for publication, but maybe we can get some police action on it. Then I want you to have a mechanical psychologist sent to my hotel room. There must be some memory that can be salvaged from my brain—"

He went on briskly. His sense of inadequacy waned notably. Reporter Leigh was himself again.

V

The little glistening balls of the mechanical psychologist were whirring faster, faster. They became a single, glowing circle in the darkness. And not till then did the first, delicious whiff of psychogas touch his nostrils. He felt himself drifting, slipping—

A voice began to speak in the dim distance, so far away that not a word came through. There was only the sound, the faint, curious sound, and the feeling, stronger every instant, that he would soon be able to hear the fascinating things it seemed to be saying.

The longing to hear, to become a part of the swelling, murmuring sound drew his whole being in little rhythmical, wavelike surges. And still the promise of meaning was unfulfilled.

Other, private thoughts ended utterly. Only the mindless chant remained; and the pleasing gas holding him so close to sleep, its flow nevertheless so delicately adjusted that his mind hovered minute after minute on the ultimate abyss of consciousness.

He lay, finally, still partially awake, but even the voice was merging now into blackness. It clung for a while, a gentle, friendly, melodious sound in the remote background of his brain, becoming more remote with each passing instant. He slept, a deep, hypnotic sleep, as the machine purred on—

When Leigh opened his eyes, the bedroom was dark except for the floor lamp beside a corner chair. It illuminated the darkly dressed woman who sat there, all except her face, which was in shadow above the circle of light.

He must have moved, for the shadowed head suddenly looked up from some sheets of typewriter-size paper. The voice of Merla, the Dreegh, said:

"The girl did a very good job of erasing your subconscious memories. There's only one possible clue to her identity and—"

Her words went on, but his brain jangled them to senselessness in that first horrible shock of recognition. It was too much, too much fear in too short a time. For a brief, terrible moment, he was like a child, and strange, cunning, *intense* thoughts of escape came:

If he could slide to the side of the bed, away from where she was sitting, and run for the bathroom door—

"Surely, Mr. Leigh," the woman's voice reached toward him, "you know better than to try anything foolish. And, surely, if I had intended to kill you, I would have done it much more easily while you were asleep."

Leigh lay very still, gathering his mind back into his head, licking dry lips. Her words were utterly unreassuring. "What—do—you—want?" he managed finally.

"Information!" Laconically. "What was that girl?"

"I don't know." He stared into the half gloom, where her face was. His eyes were more accustomed to the light now, and he could catch the faint, golden glint of her hair. "I thought—you knew."

He went on more swiftly: "I thought you knew the Galactic Observer; and that implied the girl could be identified any time."

He had the impression she was smiling. She said:

"Our statement to that effect was designed to throw both you and the girl off guard, and constituted the partial victory we snatched from what had become an impossible situation."

The body sickness was still upon Leigh, but the desperate fear that had produced it was fading before the implications of her confession of weakness, the realization that these Dreeghs were not so superhuman as he had thought. Relief was followed by caution. Careful, he warned himself, it wouldn't be wise to underestimate. But he couldn't help saying:

"So you weren't so smart. And I'd like to point out that even your so-called snatching of victory from defeat was not so well done. Your husband's statement that you could pick me up any time could easily have spoiled the picking."

The woman's voice was cool, faintly contemptuous. "If you knew anything of psychology, you would realize that the vague phrasing of the threat actually lulled you. Certainly, you failed to take even minimum precautions. And the girl has definitely not made any effort to protect you."

The suggestion of deliberately subtle tactics brought to Leigh a twinge of returning alarm. Deep, deep inside him was the thought: What ending did the Dreegh woman plan for this strange meeting?

"You realize, of course," the Dreegh said softly, "that you will either be of value to us alive—or dead. There are no easy alternatives. I would advise alertness and utmost sincerity in your co-operation. You are in this affair without limit."

So that was the plan. A thin bead of perspiration trickled down Leigh's cheek. And his fingers trembled as he reached for a cigarette on the table beside the bed.

He was shakily lighting the cigarette when his gaze fastened on the window. That brought a faint shock, for it was raining, a furious rain that hammered soundlessly against the noise-proof glass.

He pictured the bleak, empty streets, their brilliance dulled by the black, rain-filled night; and, strangely, the mind picture unnerved him.

Deserted streets—deserted Leigh. For he was deserted here; all the friends he had, scattered over the great reaches of the earth, couldn't add one ounce of strength, or bring one real ray of hope to him in this darkened room, against this woman who sat so calmly under the light, studying him from shadowed eyes.

With a sharp effort, Leigh steadied himself. He said: "I gather that's my psychograph report you have in your hand. What does it say?"

"Very disappointing." Her voice seemed far away. "There's a warning in it about your diet. It seems your meals are irregular."

She was playing with him. The heavy attempt at humor made her seem more inhuman, not less; for, somehow, the words clashed unbearably with the reality of her; the dark immensity of space across which she had come, the unnatural lusts that had brought her and the man to this literally unprotected Earth.

Leigh shivered. Then he thought fiercely: "Damn it, I'm scaring myself. So long as she stays in her chair, she can't pull the vampire on me."

The harder thought came that it was no use being frightened. He'd better simply be himself, and await events. Aloud, he said:

"If there's nothing in the psychograph, then I'm afraid I can't help you. You might as well leave. Your presence isn't making me any happier."

In a dim way, he hoped she'd laugh. But she didn't. She sat there, her eyes glinting dully out of the gloom. At last, she said:

"We'll go through this report together. I think we can safely omit the references to your health as being irrelevant. But there are a number of factors that I want developed. Who is Professor Ungarn?"

"A scientist." Leigh spoke frankly. "He invented this system of mechanical hypnosis, and he was called in when the dead bodies were found because the killings seemed to have been done by perverts."

"Have you any knowledge of his physical appearance?"

"I've never seen him," Leigh said more slowly. "He never gives interviews, and his photograph is not available now. I've heard stories, but—"

He hesitated. It wasn't, he thought frowning, as if he was giving what was not general knowledge. What was the woman getting at, anyway? Ungarn—

"These stories," she said, "do they give the impression that he's a man of inordinate magnetic force, but with lines of mental suffering etched in his face, and a sort of resignation?"

"Resignation to what?" Leigh exclaimed sharply. "I haven't the faintest idea what you're talking about. I've only seen photographs, and they show a fine, rather sensitive, tired face."

She said: "There would be more information in any library?"

"Or in the Planetarian Service morgue," Leigh said, and could have bitten off his tongue for that bit of gratuitous information.

"Morgue?" said the woman.

Leigh explained, but his voice was trembling with self-rage. For seconds now the feeling had been growing on him: Was it possible this devilish woman was on the right track? And getting damaging answers out of him because he dared not stop and organize for lying.

Even as savage anxiety came, he had an incongruous sense of the unfairness of the abnormally swift way she had solved the Observer's identity because, damn it, damn it, it could be Professor Ungarn.

Ungarn, the mystery scientist, great inventor in a dozen highly

complicated, widely separated fields; and there was that mysterious
meteorite home near one of Jupiter's moons and he had a daughter,
named Patricia. Good heavens, Patrick—Patricia—

His shaky stream of thoughts ended, as the woman said:

"Can you have your office send the information to your recorder
here?"

"Y-yes!" His reluctance was so obvious that the woman bent into
the light. For a moment, her golden hair glittered; her pale-blue
eyes glowed at him in a strangely humorless, satanic amusement.

"Ah!" she said, "you think so, too?"

She laughed, an odd, musical laugh—odd in that it was at once
so curt and so pleasant. The laugh ended abruptly, unnaturally,
on a high note. And then—although he had not seen her move—
there was a metal thing in her hand, pointing at him. Her voice came
at him, with a brittle, jarring command:

"You will climb out of the bed, operate the recorder, and naturally
you will do nothing, say nothing but what is necessary."

Leigh felt genuinely dizzy. The room swayed; and he thought
sickly: If he could only faint.

But he recognized dismally that that was beyond the power of
his tough body. It was sheer mental dismay that made his nerves
so shivery. And even that faded like fog in strong sunlight, as he
walked to the recorder. For the first time in his life, he hated the
resilience of strength that made his voice steady as a rock, as, after
setting the machine, he said:

"This is William Leigh. Give me all the dope you've got on Professor Garret Ungarn."

There was a pause, during which he thought hopelessly: "It
wasn't as if he was giving information not otherwise accessible.
Only—"

There was a click in the machine; then a brisk voice: "You've
got it. Sign the form."

Leigh signed, and watched the signature dissolve into the machine.
It was then, as he was straightening, that the woman said:

"Shall I read it here, Jeel, or shall we take the machine along?"

That was mind-wrecking. Like a man possessed, Leigh whirled;
and then, very carefully, he sat down on the bed.

The Dreegh, Jeel, was leaning idly against the jamb of the bathroom door, a dark, malignantly handsome man, with a faint, unpleasant smile on his lips. Behind him—incredibly, behind him,
through the open bathroom door was, not the gleaming bath, but

another door; and beyond that door still another door, and beyond that—

The control room of the Dreegh spaceship!

There it was, exactly as he had seen it in the solid ground under Constantine's. He had the same partial view of the sumptuous cot, the imposing section of instrument board, the tastefully padded floor—

In his bathroom!

The insane thought came to Leigh: "Oh, yes, I keep my spaceship in my bathroom and—" It was the Dreegh's voice that drew his brain from its dizzy contemplation; the Dreegh saying:

"I think we'd better leave. I'm having difficulty holding the ship on the alternation of space-time planes. Bring the man and the machine and—"

Leigh didn't hear the last word. He jerked his mind all the way out of the—bathroom. "You're—taking—me?"

"Why, of course." It was the woman who spoke. "You've been promised to me, and, besides, we'll need your help in finding Ungarn's meteorite."

Leigh sat very still. The unnatural thought came: He was glad that he had in the past proven to himself that he was not a coward.

For here was certainty of death.

He saw after a moment that the rain was still beating against the glass, great, sparkling drops that washed murkily down the broad panes. And he saw that the night was dark.

Dark night, dark rain, dark destiny—they fitted his dark, grim thoughts. With an effort he forced his body, his mind, into greater stiffness. Automatically, he shifted his position, so that the weight of muscles would draw a tight band over the hollowness that he felt in his stomach. When at last he faced his alien captors again, Reporter Leigh was cold with acceptance of his fate—and prepared to fight for his life.

"I can't think of a single reason," he said, "why I should go with you. And if you think I'm going to help you destroy the Observer, you're crazy."

The woman said matter-of-factly: "There was a passing reference in your psychograph to a Mrs. Henry Leigh, who lives in a village called Relton, on the Pacific coast. We could be there in half an hour, your mother and her home destroyed within a minute after that. Or, perhaps, we could add her blood to our reserves."

"She would be too old," the man said in a chill tone. "We do not want the blood of old people."

It was the icy objection that brought horror to Leigh. He had a brief, terrible picture of a silent, immensely swift ship sweeping out of the Eastern night, over the peaceful hamlet; and then unearthly energies would reach down in a blaze of fury.

One second of slashing fire, and the ship would sweep on over the long, dark waters to the west.

The deadly picture faded. The woman was saying, gently:

"Jeel and I have evolved an interesting little system of interviewing human beings of the lower order. For some reason, he frightens people merely by his presence. Similarly, people develop an unnatural fear of me when they see me clearly in a strong light. So we have always tried to arrange our meetings with human beings with me sitting in semidarkness and Jeel very much in the background. It has proved very effective."

She stood up, a tall, lithely built, shadowed figure in a rather tight-fitting skirt and a dark blouse. She finished: "But now, shall we go? You bring the machine, Mr. Leigh."

"I'll take it," said the Dreegh.

Leigh glanced sharply at the lean, sinewed face of the terrible man, startled at the instant, accurate suspicion of the desperate intention that had formed in his mind.

The Dreegh loomed over the small machine, where it stood on a corner desk. "How does it work?" he asked almost mildly.

Trembling, Leigh stepped forward. There was still a chance that he could manage this without additional danger to anyone. Not that it would be more than a vexation, unless—as their suggestion about finding the Ungarn meteorite indicated—they headed straight out to space. Then, why, it might actually cause real delay. He began swiftly:

"Press the key marked 'Titles,' and the machine will type all the main headings."

"That sounds reasonable." The long, grim-faced head nodded. The Dreegh reached forward, pressed the button. The recorder hummed softly, and a section of it lit up, showing typed lines under a transparent covering. There were several headings.

"—'His Meteorite Home,' " the Dreegh read. "That's what I want. What is the next step?"

"Press the key marked 'Subheads.' "

Leigh was suddenly shaky. He groaned inwardly. Was it possible this creature-man was going to obtain the information he wanted? Certainly, such a tremendous intelligence would not easily be led away from logical sequence.

He forced himself to grimness. He'd have to take a chance.

"The subhead I desire," said the Dreegh, "is marked 'Location.' And there is a number, one, in front of it. What next?"

"Press Key No. 1," Leigh said, "then press the key lettered 'General Release.'"

The moment he had spoken, he grew taut. If this worked—and it should. There was no reason why it shouldn't.

Key No. 1 would impart all the information under that heading. And surely the man would not want more until later. After all, this was only a test. They were in a hurry.

And later, when the Dreegh discovered that the "General Release" key had dissolved all the other information—it would be too late.

The thought dimmed. Leigh started. The Dreegh was staring at him with a bleak sardonicism. The man said:

"Your voice has been like an organ; each word uttered full of subtle shadings that mean much to the sensitive ear. Accordingly" —a steely, ferocious smile twisted that lean and deadly face—"I shall press Key No. 1. But not 'General Release.' And as soon as I've examined the little story on the recorder, I shall attend to you for that attempted trick. The sentence is—death."

"Jeel!"

"Death!" reiterated the man flatly. And the woman was silent.

There was silence, then, except for the subdued humming of the recorder. Leigh's mind was almost without thought. He felt flesh-less, a strange, disembodied soul; and only gradually did a curious realization grow that he was waiting here on the brink of a night darker than the black wastes of space from which these monster humans had come.

Consciousness came of kinship with the black rain that poured with such solid, noiseless power against the glinting panes. For soon, he would be part of the inorganic darkness—a shadowed figure sprawling sightlessly in this dim room.

His aimless gaze returned to the recorder machine, and to the grim man who stood so thoughtfully, staring down at the words it was unfolding.

His thought quickened. His life, that had been pressed so shock-ingly out of his system by the sentence of death, quivered forth. He straightened, physically and mentally. And, suddenly, there was purpose in him.

If death was inescapable, at least he could try again, somehow, to knock down that "General Release" key. He stared at the key, measur-ing the distance; and the gray thought came: What incredible irony that he should die, that he should waste his effort, to prevent the Dreeghs from having *this minute* information that was available from ten thousand sources. And yet—

The purpose remained. Three feet, he thought carefully, perhaps four. If he should fling himself toward it, how could even a Dreegh prevent the dead weight of his body and his extended fingers from accomplishing such a simple, straightforward mission?

After all, his sudden action had once before frustrated the Dreeghs, permitting the Ungarn girl—in spite of her denials—to get her gun into position for firing. And—

He grew rigid as he saw that the Dreegh was turning away from the machine. The man pursed his lips, but it was the woman, Merla, who spoke from where she stood in the gloom:

"Well?"

The man frowned. "The exact location is nowhere on record. Apparently, there has been no development of meteorites in this system. I suspected as much. After all, space travel has only existed a hundred years; and the new planets and the moons of Jupiter have absorbed all the energies of exploring, exploiting man."

"I could have told you that," said Leigh.

If he could move a little to one side of the recorder, so that the Dreegh would have to do more than simply put his arm out—

The man was saying: "There is, however, a reference to some man who transports food and merchandise from the moon Europa to the Ungarns. We will . . . er . . . persuade this man to show us the way."

"One of these days," said Leigh, "you're going to discover that all human beings cannot be persuaded. What pressure are you going to put on this chap? Suppose he hasn't got a mother."

"He has—life!" said the woman softly.

"One look at you," Leigh snapped, "and he'd know that he'd lose that, anyway."

As he spoke, he stepped with enormous casualness to the left, one short step. He had a violent impulse to say something, anything to cover the action. But his voice had betrayed him once. And actually it might already have done so again. The cold face of the man was almost too enigmatic.

"We could," said the woman, "use William Leigh to persuade him."

The words were softly spoken, but they shocked Leigh to his bones. For they offered a distorted hope. And that shattered his will to action. His purpose faded into remoteness. Almost grimly, he fought to draw that hard determination back into his consciousness. He concentrated his gaze on the recorder machine, but the woman was speaking again; and his mind wouldn't hold anything except the urgent meaning of her words:

"He is too valuable a slave to destroy. We can always take his blood and energy, but now we must send him to Europa, there to find the freighter pilot of the Ungarns, and actually accompany him to the Ungarn meteorite. If he could investigate the interior, our attack might conceivably be simplified, and there is just a possibility that there might be new weapons, of which we should be informed. We must not underestimate the science of the great Galactics.

"Naturally, before we allowed Leigh his freedom, we would do a little tampering with his mind, and so blot out from his conscious mind all that has happened in this hotel room.

"The identification of Professor Ungarn as the Galactic Observer we would make plausible for Leigh by a little rewriting of his psychograph report; and tomorrow he will waken in his bed with a new purpose, based on some simple human impulse such as love of the girl."

The very fact that the Dreegh, Jeel, was allowing her to go on, brought the first, faint color to Leigh's cheeks, a thin flush at the enormous series of betrayals she was so passionately expecting of him. Nevertheless, so weak was his resistance to the idea of continued life, that he could only snap:

"If you think I'm going to fall in love with a dame who's got twice my I. Q., you're—"

The woman cut him off. "Shut up, you fool! Can't you see I've saved your life?"

The man was cold, ice-cold. "Yes, we shall use him, not because he is essential, but because we have time to search for easier victories. The first members of the Dreegh tribe will not arrive for a month and a half, and it will take Mr. Leigh a month of that to get to the moon, Europa, by one of Earth's primitive passenger liners. For-

tunately, the nearest Galactic military base is well over three months
distant—by Galactic ship speeds.

"Finally"—with a disconcerting, tigerish swiftness, the Dreegh
whirled full upon Leigh, eyes that were like pools of black fire
measured his own startled stare—"finally, as a notable reminder
to your subconscious of the error of trickery, and as complete punishment for past and—intended—offenses, this!

Despairingly, Leigh twisted away from the metal that glowed at
him. His muscles tried horribly to carry out the purpose that had
been working to a crisis inside him. He lunged for the recorder—
but something caught his body. Something—not physical. But the
very pain seemed mortal.

There was no visible flame of energy, only that glow at the metal
source. But his nerves writhed; enormous forces contorted his throat
muscles, froze the scream that quivered there, hideously.

His whole being welcomed the blackness that came mercifully to
blot out the hellish pain.

VI

On the third day, Europa began to give up some of the sky to the
vast mass of Jupiter behind it. The engines that so imperfectly transformed magnetic attraction to a half-hearted repulsion functioned
more and more smoothly as the infinite complication of pull and
counterpull yielded to distance.

The old, slow, small freighter scurried on into the immense, enveloping night; and the days dragged into weeks, the weeks crawled
their drab course toward the full month.

On the thirty-seventh day, the sense of slowing up was so distinct
that Leigh crept dully out of his bunk, and croaked:

"How much farther?"

He was aware of the stolid-faced space trucker grinning at him. The
man's name was Hanardy, and he said now matter-of-factly:

"We're just pulling in. See that spot of light over to the left? It's
moving this way."

He ended with a rough sympathy. "Been a tough trip, eh?
Tougher'n you figgered when you offered to write up my little route
for your big syndicate."

Leigh scarcely heard. He was clawing at the porthole, straining
to penetrate the blackness. At first his eyes kept blinking on him,
and nothing came. Stars were out there, but it was long seconds

before his bleary gaze made out moving lights. He counted them
with sluggish puzzlement:

"One, two, three—seven—" he counted. "And all traveling together."

"What's that?" Hanardy bent beside him. "Seven?"

There was a brief silence between them, as the lights grew visibly
dim with distance, and winked out.

"Too bad," Leigh ventured, "that Jupiter's behind us. They
mightn't fade out like that in silhouette. Which one was Ungarn's
meteorite?"

With a shock, he grew aware that Hanardy was standing. The
man's heavy face was dark with frown. Hanardy said slowly:

"Those were ships. I never saw ships go so fast before. They were
out of sight in less than a minute."

The frown faded from his stolid face. He shrugged. "Some of those
new police ships, I guess. And we must have seen them from a
funny angle for them to disappear so fast."

Leigh half sat, half knelt, frozen into immobility. And after that
one swift glance at the pilot's rough face, he averted his own. For
a moment, the black fear was in him that his wild thoughts would
blaze from his eyes.

Dreeghs! Two and a half months had wound their appallingly slow
course since the murders. More than a month to get from Earth to
Europa, and now this miserable, lonely journey with Hanardy, the
man who trucked for the Ungarns.

Every day of that time, he had known with an inner certainty that
none of this incredible business had gone backward. That it could
only have assumed a hidden, more dangerous form. The one fortunate
reality in the whole mad affair was that he had wakened on the
morning after the mechanical psychologist test from a dreamless
sleep; and there in the psychograph report was the identification of
Ungarn as the Observer, and the statement, borne out by an all too
familiar emotional tension, that he was in love with the girl.

Now this! His mind flared. Dreeghs in seven ships. That meant
the first had been reinforced by—many. And perhaps the seven
were only a reconnaissance group, withdrawing at Hanardy's approach.

Or perhaps those fantastic murderers had already attacked the
Observer's base. Perhaps the girl—

He fought the desperate thought out of his consciousness, and
watched, frowning, as the Ungarn meteorite made a dark, glinting

path in the blackness to one side. The two objects, the ship and
the bleak, rough-shaped mass of metallic stone drew together in the
night, the ship slightly behind.

A great steel door slid open in the rock. Skillfully, the ship
glided into the chasm. There was a noisy clicking. Hanardy came
out of the control room, his face dark with puzzlement.

"Those damn ships are out there again," he said. "I've closed
the big steel locks, but I'd better tell the professor and—"

Crash! The world jiggled. The floor came up and hit Leigh a
violent blow. He lay there, cold in spite of the thoughts that burned
at fire heat in his mind:

For some reason, the vampires had waited until the freighter was
inside. Then instantly, ferociously, attacked.

In packs!

"Hanardy!" A vibrant girl's voice blared from one of the loud-
speakers.

The pilot sat up shakily on the floor, where he had fallen, near
Leigh. "Yes, Miss Patricia."

"You dared to bring a stranger with you!"

"It's only a reporter, miss; he's writing up my route for me."

"You conceited fool! That's William Leigh. He's a hypnotized spy
of those devils who are attacking us. Bring him immediately to my
apartment. He must be killed at once."

"Huh!" Leigh began; and then slowly he began to stiffen. For
the pilot was staring at him from narrowing eyes, all the friendliness
gone from his rough, heavy face Finally, Leigh laughed curtly.

"Don't you be a fool, too, Hanardy. I made the mistake once of
saving that young lady's life, and she's hated me ever since."

The heavy face scowled at him. "So you knew her before, eh?
You didn't tell me that. You'd better come along before I sock
you one."

Almost awkwardly, he drew the gun from his side holster, and
pointed its ugly snout at Leigh.

"Get along!" he said.

Hanardy reached toward a tiny arrangement of lights beside the
paneled door of Patricia Ungarn's apartment—and Leigh gave one
leap, one blow. He caught the short, heavy body as it fell, grabbed
at the sagging gun, lowered the dead weight to the floor of the
corridor; and then, for a grim, tense moment, he stood like a great
animal, straining for sound.

Silence! He studied the bland panels of the doorway to the apart

ment, as if by sheer, savage intentness he would penetrate their
golden, beautiful grained opaqueness.

It was the silence that struck him again after a moment, the emptiness of the long, tunnellike corridors. He thought, amazed: Was it
possible father and daughter actually lived here without companions
or servants or any human association? And that they had some idea
that they could withstand the attack of the mighty and terrible
Dreeghs?

They had a lot of stuff here, of course: Earthlike gravity and—
and, by Heaven, he'd better get going before the girl acquired impatience and came out with one of her fancy weapons. What he
must do was quite simple, unconnected with any nonsense of spying, hypnotic or otherwise.

He must find the combination automobile-spaceship in which
—Mr. Patrick—had escaped him that night after they left Constantine's. And with that tiny ship, he must try to slip out of Ungarn's
meteorite, sneak through the Dreegh line, and so head back for
Earth.

What a fool he had been, a mediocre human being, mixing in
such fast, brainy company. The world was full of more normal,
thoroughly dumb girls. Why in hell wasn't he safely married to one
of them and—and damn it, it was time he got busy.

He began laboriously to drag Hanardy along the smooth flooring.
Halfway to the nearest corner, the man stirred. Instantly, quite coolly,
Leigh struck him with the revolver butt, hard. This was not time
for squeamishness.

The pilot dropped; and the rest was simple. He deserted the
body as soon as he had pulled it out of sight behind the corner,
and raced along the hallway, trying doors. The first four wouldn't
open. At the fifth, he pulled up in a dark consideration.

It was impossible that the whole place was locked up. Two people
in an isolated meteorite wouldn't go around perpetually locking and
unlocking doors. There must be a trick catch.

There was. The fifth door yielded to a simple pressure on a tiny,
half-hidden push button, that had seemed an integral part of the
design of the latch. He stepped through the entrance, then started
back in brief, terrible shock.

The room had no ceiling. Above him was—space. An ice-cold blast
of air swept at him.

He had a flashing glimpse of gigantic machines in the room,
machines that dimly resembled the ultramodern astronomical observa-

tory on the moon that he had visited on opening day two days before. That one, swift look was all Leigh allowed himself. Then
he stepped back into the hallway. The door of the observatory closed
automatically in his face.

He stood there, chagrined. Silly fool! The very fact that cold air
had blown at him showed that the open effect of the ceiling was only
an illusion of invisible glass. Good Lord, in that room might be
wizard telescopes that could see to the stars. Or—an ugly thrill raced
along his spine—he might have seen the Dreeghs attacking.

He shook out of his system the brief, abnormal desire to look
again. This was no time for distractions. For, by now, the girl must
know that something was wrong.

At top speed, Leigh ran to the sixth door. It opened into a little
cubbyhole. A blank moment passed before he recognized what it was.

An elevator!

He scrambled in. The farther he got away from the residential
floor, the less the likelihood of quick discovery.

He turned to close the door, and saw that it was shutting automatically. It clicked softly; the elevator immediately began to go up.
Piercingly sharp doubt came to Leigh. The machine was apparently
geared to go to some definite point. And that could be very bad.

His eyes searched hastily for controls. But nothing was visible.
Gun poised, he stood grim and alert, as the elevator stopped. The
door slid open.

Leigh stared. There was no room. The door opened—onto blackness.

Not the blackness of space with its stars. Or a dark room, half
revealed by the light from the elevator. But—blackness!

Impenetrable.

Leigh put a tentative hand forward, half expecting to feel a solid
object. But as his hand entered the black area, it vanished. He
jerked it back, and stared at it, dismayed. It shone with a light of its
own, all the bones plainly visible.

Swiftly, the light faded, the skin became opaque, but his whole
arm pulsed with a pattern of pain.

The stark, terrible thought came that this could be a death
chamber. After all, the elevator had deliberately brought him here;
it might not have been automatic. Outside forces could have directed
it. True, he had stepped in of his own free will, but—

Fool, fool!

He laughed bitterly, braced himself—and then it happened.

There was a flash out of the blackness. Something that sparkled vividly, something material that blazed a brilliant path to his forehead—and drew itself inside his head. And then—

He was no longer in the elevator. On either side of him stretched a long corridor. The stocky Hanardy was just reaching for some tiny lights beside the door of Patricia Ungarn's apartment.

The man's fingers touched one of the lights. It dimmed. Softly, the door opened. A young woman with proud, insolent eyes and a queenlike bearing stood there.

"Father wants you down on Level 4," she said to Hanardy. "One of the energy screens has gone down; and he needs some machine work before he can put up another."

She turned to Leigh; her voice took on metallic overtones as she said: *"Mr. Leigh, you can come in!"*

The crazy part of it was that he walked in with scarcely a physical tremor. A cool breeze caressed his cheeks; and there was the liltingly sweet sound of birds singing in the distance. Leigh stood stockstill for a moment after he had entered, dazed partly by the wonders of the room and the unbelievable sunlit garden beyond the French windows, partly by—what?

What had happened to him?

Gingerly, he put his hands to his head, and felt his forehead, then his whole head. But nothing was wrong, not a contusion, not a pain. He grew aware of the girl staring at him, and realization came that his actions must seem unutterably queer.

"What is the matter with you?" the girl asked.

Leigh looked at her with abrupt, grim suspicion. He snapped harshly: "Don't pull that innocent stuff. I've been up in the blackness room, and all I've got to say is, if you're going to kill me, don't skulk behind artificial night and other trickery."

The girl's eyes, he saw, were narrowed, unpleasantly cold. "I don't know what you're trying to pretend," she said icily. "I assure you it will not postpone the death we have to deal you."

She hesitated, then finished sharply: "The *what* room?"

Leigh explained grimly, puzzled by her puzzlement, then annoyed by the contemptuous smile that grew into her face. She cut him off curtly:

"I've never heard a less balanced story. If your intention was to astound me and delay your death with that improbable tale, it has failed. You must be mad. You didn't knock out Hanardy, because when I opened the door, Hanardy was there, and I sent him down to father."

"See here!" Leigh began. He stopped wildly. By Heaven, Hanardy had been there as she opened the door!

And yet earlier—

WHEN?

Doggedly, Leigh pushed the thought on: Earlier, he had attacked Hanardy. And then he—Leigh—had gone up in an elevator; and then, somehow, back and—

Shakily, he felt his head again. And it was absolutely normal. Only, he thought, there was something inside it that sparkled.

Something—

With a start, he grew aware that the girl was quite deliberately drawing a gun from a pocket of her simple white dress. He stared at the weapon, and before its gleaming menace, his thoughts faded, all except the deadly consciousness that what he had said had delayed her several minutes now. It was the only thing that could delay her further until, somehow—

The vague hope wouldn't finish. Urgently, he said:

"I'm going to assume you're genuinely puzzled by my words. Let's begin at the beginning. There is such a room, is there not?"

"Please," said the girl wearily, "let us not have any of your logic. My I. Q. is 243, yours is 112. So I assure you I am quite capable of reasoning from any beginning you can think of."

She went on, her low voice as curt as the sound of struck steel: "There is no 'blackness' room, as you call it, no sparkling thing that crawls inside a human head. There is but one fact: The Dreeghs in their visit to your hotel room, hypnotized you; and this curious mind illusion can only be a result of that hypnotism—don't argue with me—"

With a savage gesture of her gun, she cut off his attempt to speak. "There's no time. For some reason, the Dreeghs did something to you. Why? What did you see in those rooms?"

Even as he explained and described, Leigh was thinking chilly:

He'd have to catch hold of himself, get a plan, however risky, and carry it through. The purpose was tight and cold in his mind as he obeyed her motion, and went ahead of her into the corridor. It was there, an icy determination, as he counted the doors from the corner where he had left the unconscious Hanardy.

"One, two, three, four, five. This door!" he said.

"Open it!" the girl gestured.

He did so; and his lower jaw sagged. He was staring into a fine, cozy room filled with shelf on shelf of beautifully bound books. There were comfortable chairs, a magnificent rag rug and—

It was the girl who closed the door firmly and—he trembled with the tremendousness of the opportunity—she walked ahead of him to the sixth door.

"And this is your elevator?"

Leigh nodded mutely; and because his whole body was shaking, he was only dimly surprised that there was no elevator, but a long, empty, silent corridor.

The girl was standing with her back partly to him; and if he hit her, it would knock her hard against the door jamb and—

The sheer brutality of the thought was what stopped him, held him for the barest second—as the girl whirled, and looked straight into his eyes.

Her gun was up, pointing steadily. "Not that way," she said quietly. "For a moment I was wishing you would have the nerve to try it. But, after all, that would be the weak way for me."

Her eyes glowed with a fierce pride. "After all, I've killed before through necessity, and hated it. You can see yourself that, because of what the Dreeghs have done to you, it is necessary. So—"

Her voice took on a whiplash quality. "So back to my rooms. I have a space lock there to get rid of your body. Get going!"

It was the emptiness, the silence except for the faint click of their shoes that caught at Leigh's nerves, as he walked hopelessly back to the apartment. This meteorite hurtling darkly through the remote wastes of the Solar System, pursued and attacked by deadly ships from the fixed stars, and himself inside it, under sentence of death, the executioner to be a girl—

And that was the devastating part. He couldn't begin to argue with this damnable young woman, for every word would sound like pleading. The very thought of mentally getting down on his knees to any woman was paralyzing.

The singing of the birds, as he entered the apartment, perked him violently out of his black passion. Abruptly marveling, he walked to the stately French windows, and stared at the glorious summery garden.

At least two acres of green wonder spread before him, a blaze of flowers, trees where gorgeously colored birds fluttered and trilled, a wide, deep pool of green, green water, and over all, the glory of brilliant sunshine.

It was the sunshine that held Leigh finally; and he stood almost breathless for a long minute before it seemed that he had the solu- tion. He said in a hushed voice, without turning:

"The roof—is an arrangement—of magnifying glass. It makes the Sun as big as on Earth. Is that the—"

"You'd better turn around," came the hostile, vibrant voice from behind him. "I don't shoot people in the back. And I want to get this over with."

It was the moralistic smugness of her words that shook every muscle in Leigh's body. He whirled, and raged:

"You damned little Klugg. You can't shoot me in the back, eh? Oh, no! And you couldn't possibly shoot me while I was attacking you because that would be the weak way. It's all got to be made right with your conscience."

He stopped so short that, if he had been running instead of talking, he would have stumbled. Figuratively, almost literally, he saw Patricia Ungarn for the first time since his arrival. His mind had been so concentrated, so absorbed by deadly things that—

—For the first time as a woman.

Leigh drew a long breath. Dressed as a man, she had been darkly handsome in an extremely youthful fashion. Now she wore a simple, snow-white sports dress. It was scarcely more than a tunic, and came well above her knees.

Her hair shone with a brilliant brownness, and cascaded down to her shoulders. Her bare arms and legs gleamed a deep, healthy tan. Sandals pure white graced her feet. Her face—

The impression of extraordinary beauty yielded to the amazing fact that her perfect cheeks were flushing vividly. The girl snapped:

"Don't you dare use that word to me."

She must have been utterly beside herself. Her fury was such an enormous fact that Leigh gasped; and he couldn't have stopped him- self from saying what he did, if the salvation of his soul had de- pended on it.

"Klugg!" he said, "Klugg, Klugg, Klugg! So you realize now that the Dreeghs had you down pat, that all your mighty pretensions was simply your Klugg mind demanding pretentious compensation for a dreary, lonely life. You had to think you were somebody, and yet all the time you must have known they'd only ship the tenth-raters to these remote posts. Klugg, not even Lennel; the Dreegh woman wouldn't even grant you Lennel status, whatever that is. And she'd know. Because if you're I. Q. 243, the Dreeghs were 400. You've realized that, too, haven't you?"

"Shut up! Or I'll kill you by inches!" said Patrician Ungarn; and Leigh was amazed to see that she was as white as a sheet. The astounded realization came that he had struck, not only the emotional Achilles heel of this strange and terrible young woman, but the very vital roots of her mental existence.

"So," he said deliberately, "the high morality is growing dim. Now you can torture me to death without a qualm. And to think that I came here to ask you to marry me because I thought a Klugg and a human being might get along."

"You what?" said the girl. Then she sneered. "So that was the form of their hypnotism. They would use some simple impulse for a simple human mind.

"But now I think we've had just about enough. I know just the type of thoughts that come to a male human in love; and even the realization that you're not responsible makes the very idea none the less bearable. I feel sickened, utterly insulted. Know, please, that my future husband is arriving with the reinforcements three weeks from now. He will be trained to take over father's work—"

"Another Klugg!" said Leigh, and the girl turned shades whiter.

Leigh stood utterly thunderstruck. In all his life, he had never gotten anybody going the way he had this young girl. The intellectual mask was off, and underneath was a seething mass of emotions bitter beyond the power of words to express. Here was evidence of a life so lonely that it strained his imagination. Her every word showed an incredible pent-up masochism as well as sadism, for she was torturing herself as well as him.

And he couldn't stop now to feel sorry for her. His life was at stake, and only more words could postpone death—or bring the swift and bearable surcease of a gun fired in sudden passion. He hammered on grimly:

"I'd like to ask one question. How did you find out my I. Q. was 112? What special interest made you inquire about that? Is it possible that, all by yourself here, you, too, had a special type of thought, and that, though your intellect rejected the very idea of such lowly love, its existence is the mainspring behind your fantastic determination to kill. rather than cure me? I—"

"That will do," interrupted Patricia Ungarn.

It required one lengthy moment for Leigh to realize that in those few short seconds she had pulled herself completely together.

He stared in gathering alarm, as her gun motioned toward a door he had not seen before.

She said curtly:

"I suppose there is a solution other than death. That is, immediate death. And I have decided to accept the resultant loss of my spaceship."

She nodded at the door: "It's there in the air lock. It works very simply. The steering wheel pulls up or down or sideways, and that's the way the ship will go. Just step on the accelerator, and the machine will go forward. The decelerator is the left pedal. The automobile wheels fold in automatically as soon as they lift from the floor.

"Now, get going. I need hardly tell you that the Dreeghs will probably catch you. But you can't stay here. That's obvious."

"Thanks!" That was all Leigh allowed himself to say. He had exploded an emotional powder keg, and he dared not tamper even a single word further. There was a tremendous psychological mystery here, but it was not for him to solve.

Suddenly shaky from realization of what was still ahead of him, he walked gingerly toward the air lock. And then—

It happened!

He had a sense of unutterable nausea. There was a wild swaying through blackness and—

He was standing at the paneled doorway leading from the corridor to Patricia Ungarn's apartment. Beside him stood Hanardy. The door opened. The young woman who stood there said strangely familiar words to Hanardy, about going down to the fourth level to fix an energy screen. Then she turned to Leigh, and in a voice hard and metallic said:

"Mr. Leigh, you can come in."

VII

The crazy part of it was that he walked in with scarcely a physical tremor. A cool breeze caressed his cheeks; and there was the liltingly sweet sound of birds singing in the distance. Leigh stood stockstill for a moment after he had entered; by sheer will power he emptied the terrible daze out of his mind, and bent, mentally, into the cyclone path of complete memory. Everything was there suddenly, the way the Dreeghs had come to his hotel apartment and ruthlessly forced him to their will, the way the "blackness" room had affected him, and how the girl had spared his life.

For some reason, the whole scene with the girl had been unsatisfactory to—Jeel; and it was now, fantastically, to be repeated.

That thought ended. The entire, tremendous reality of what had happened yielded to a vastly greater fact:

There was—something—inside his head, a distinctly physical something; and in a queer, horrible, inexperienced way, his mind was instinctively fighting—it. The result was ghastly confusion. Which hurt him, not the thing.

Whatever it was, rested inside his head, unaffected by his brain's feverish contortions, cold, aloof, watching.

Watching.

Madly, then, he realized what it was. Another mind. Leigh shrank from the thought as from the purest destroying fire. He tensed his brain. For a moment the frenzy of his horror was so great that his face twisted with the anguish of his efforts. And everything blurred.

Exhausted finally, he simply stood there. And the thing-mind was still inside his head.

Untouched.

What had happened to him?

Shakily, Leigh put his hands up to his forehead; then he felt his whole head; there was a vague idea in him that if he pressed—

He jerked his hands down with an unspoken curse. Damnation on damnation, he was even repeating the actions of this scene. He grew aware of the girl staring at him. He heard her say:

"What is the matter with you?"

It was the sound of the words, exactly the same words, that did it. He smiled wryly. His mind drew back from the abyss, where it had teetered.

He was sane again.

Gloomy recognition came then that his brain was still a long way down; sane yes, but dispirited. It was only too obvious that the girl had no memory of the previous scene, or she wouldn't be parroting. She'd—

That thought stopped, too. Because a strange thing was happening.

The mind inside him stirred, and looked through his—Leigh's—
eyes. Looked intently.

Intently.

The room and the girl in it changed, not physically, but subjec-
tively, in what he saw, in the—details.

Details burned at him; furniture and design that a moment before
had seemed a flowing, artistic whole, abruptly showed flaws, hideous
errors in taste and arrangement and structure.

His gaze flashed out to the garden, and in instants tore it to mental
shreds. Never in all his existence had he seen or felt criticism on such
a high, devastating scale. Only—

Only it wasn't criticism. Actually. The mind was indifferent. It
saw things. Automatically, it saw some of the possibilities; and by
comparison the reality suffered.

It was not a matter of anything being hopelessly bad. The wrongness was frequently a subtle thing. Birds not suited, for a dozen
reasons, to their environment. Shrubs that added infinitesimal dis-
cord not harmony to the superb garden.

The mind flashed back from the garden; and this time, for the
first time, studied the girl.

On all Earth, no woman had ever been so piercingly examined.
The structure of her body and her face, to Leigh so finely, proudly
shaped, so gloriously patrician—found low grade now.

An excellent example of low-grade development in isolation.

That was the thought, not contemptuous, not derogatory, simply
an impression by an appallingly direct mind that saw—overtones,
realities behind realities, a thousand facts where one showed.

There followed crystal-clear awareness of the girl's psychology, objective admiration for the system of isolated upbringing that made
Klugg girls such fine breeders; and then—

Purpose!

Instantly carried out. Leigh took three swift steps toward the girl.
He was aware of her snatching at the gun in her pocket, and
there was the sheerest startled amazement on her face. Then he had
her.

Her muscles writhed like steel springs. But they were hopeless
against his superstrength, his superspeed. He tied her with some wire
he had noticed in a half-opened clothes closet.

Then he stepped back, and to Leigh came the shocked personal
thought of the incredible thing that had happened, comprehension

that all this, which seemed so normal, was actually so devastatingly
superhuman, so swift that—seconds only had passed since he came
into the room.

Private thought ended. He grew aware of the mind, contemplating
what it had done, and what it must do before the meteorite would
be completely under control.

Vampire victory was near.

There was a phase of walking along empty corridors, down several
flights of stairs. The vague, dull thought came to Leigh, his own
personal thought, that the Dreegh seemed to know completely the
interior of the meteorite.

Somehow, during the periods of—transition, of time manipulation, the creature-mind must have used his, Leigh's, body to explore
the vast tomb of a place *thoroughly*. And now, with utter simplicity
of purpose—he was heading for the machine shops on the fourth
level, where Professor Ungarn and Hanardy labored to put up another
energy defense screen.

He found Hanardy alone, working at a lathe that throbbed—and
the sound made it easy to sneak up—

The professor was in a vast room, where great engines hummed
a strange, deep tune of titanic power. He was a tall man, and his back
was turned to the door as Leigh entered.

But he was immeasurably quicker than Hanardy, quicker even
than the girl. He sensed danger. He whirled with a catlike agility.
Literally. And succumbed instantly to muscles that could have torn
him limb from limb. It was during the binding of the man's hands
that Leigh had time for an impression.

In the photographs that Leigh had seen, as he had told the
Dreegh, Merla, in the hotel, the professor's face had been sensitive,
tired-looking, withal noble. He was more than that, tremendously
more.

The man radiated power, as no photograph could show it, *good*
power in contrast to the savage, malignant, immensely greater power
of the Dreegh.

The sense of power faded before the aura of—weariness. Cosmic
weariness. It was a lined, an amazingly lined face. In a flash, Leigh
remembered what the Dreegh woman had said; and it was all there:
deep-graven lines of tragedy and untold mental suffering, interlaced
with a curious peacefulness, like—resignation.

On that night months ago, he had asked the Dreegh woman:

Resignation to what? And now, here in this tortured, kindly face was the answer:

Resignation to hell.

Queerly, an unexpected second answer trickled in his mind: Morons; they're Galactic morons. Kluggs.

The thought seemed to have no source; but it gathered with all the fury of a storm. Professor Ungarn and his daughter were Kluggs, *morons* in the incredible Galactic sense. No wonder the girl had reacted like a crazy person. Obviously born here, she must have only guessed the truth in the last two months.

The I. Q. of human morons wavered between seventy-five and ninety, of Kluggs possibly between two hundred and twenty-five and, say, two hundred and forty-three.

Two hundred and forty-three. What kind of civilization was this Galactic—if Dreeghs were four hundred and—

Somebody, of course, had to do the dreary, routine work of civilization; and Kluggs and Lennels and their kind were obviously elected. No wonder they looked like morons with that weight of inferiority to influence their very nerve and muscle structure. No wonder whole planets were kept in ignorance—

Leigh left the professor tied hand and foot, and began to turn off power switches. Some of the great motors were slowing noticeably as he went out of that mighty engine room; the potent hum of power dimmed.

Back in the girl's room, he entered the air lock, climbed into the small automobile spaceship—and launched into the night.

Instantly, the gleaming mass of meteorite receded into the darkness behind him. Instantly, magnetic force rays caught his tiny craft, and drew it remorselessly toward the hundred and fifty foot, cigar-shaped machine that flashed out of the darkness.

He felt the spy rays; and he must have been recognized. For another ship flashed up to claim him.

Air locks opened noiselessly—and shut. Sickly, Leigh stared at the two Dreeghs, the tall man and the tall woman; and, as from a great distance, heard himself explaining what he had done.

Dimly, hopelessly, he wondered why he should have to explain. Then he heard Jeel say:

"Merla, this is the most astoundingly successful case of hypnotism in our existence. He's done—everything. Even the tiniest thoughts we put into his mind have been carried out to the letter. And the proof is, the screens are going down. With the control of this station, we can hold out even after the Galactic warships arrive—and fill our tankers and our energy reservoirs for ten thousand years. Do you hear, *ten thousand years?*"

His excitement died. He smiled with sudden, dry understanding as he looked at the woman. Then he said laconically:

"My dear, the reward is all yours. We could have broken down those screens in another twelve hours, but it would have meant the destruction of the meteorite. This victory is so much greater. Take your reporter. Satisfy your craving—while the rest of us prepare for the occupation. Meanwhile, I'll tie him up for you."

Leigh thought, a cold, remote thought: The kiss of death—

He shivered in sudden, appalled realization of what he had done—

He lay on the couch, where Jeel had tied him. He was surprised, after a moment, to notice that, though *the* mind had withdrawn into the background of his brain—it was still there, cold, steely, abnormally conscious.

The wonder came: what possible satisfaction could Jeel obtain from experiencing the mortal thrill of death with him? These people were utterly abnormal, of course, but—

The wonder died like dry grass under a heat ray, as the woman came into the room, and glided toward him. She smiled; she sat down on the edge of the couch.

"So here you are," she said.

She was, Leigh thought, like a tigress. There was purpose in every cunning muscle of her long body. In surprise he saw that she had changed her dress. She wore a sleek, flimsy, sheeny, tight-fitting gown that set off in startling fashion her golden hair and starkly white face. Utterly fascinated, he watched her. Almost automatically, he said:

"Yes, I'm here."

Silly words. But he didn't feel silly. Tenseness came the moment he had spoken. It was her eyes that did it. For the first time since he had first seen her, her eyes struck him like a blow. Blue eyes, and steady. So steady. Not the steady frankness of honesty. But steady—like dead eyes.

A chill grew on Leigh, a special, extra chill, adding to the ice that was already there inside him; and the unholy thought came that this was a dead woman—artificially kept alive by the blood and *life* of dead men and women.

She smiled, but the bleakness remained in those cold fish eyes. No smile, no warmth could ever bring light to that chill, beautiful countenance. But she smiled the form of a smile, and she said:

"We Dreeghs live a hard, lonely life. So lonely that sometimes I cannot help thinking our struggle to remain alive is a blind, mad thing. We're what we are through no fault of our own. It happened during an interstellar flight that took place a million years ago—"

She stopped, almost hopelessly. "It seems longer. It must be longer. I've really lost track."

She went on, suddenly grim, as if the memory, the very telling, brought a return of horror: "We were among several thousand holi dayers who were caught in the gravitational pull of a sun, afterward called the Dreegh sun.

"Its rays, immensely dangerous to human life, infected us all. It was discovered that only continuous blood transfusions, and the life force of other human beings, could save us. For a while we received donations; then the government decided to have us destroyed as hopeless incurables.

"We were all young, terribly young and in love with life; some hundreds of us had been expecting the sentence, and we still had friends in the beginning. We escaped, and we've been fighting ever since to stay alive."

And still he could feel no sympathy. It was odd, for all the thoughts she undoubtedly wanted him to have, came. Picture of a bleak, endless existence in spaceships, staring out into the perpetual night; all life circumscribed by the tireless, abnormal needs of bodies gone mad from ravenous disease.

It was all there, all the emotional pictures. But no emotions came. She was too cold; the years and the devil's hunt had stamped her soul and her eyes and her face.

And besides, her body seemed tenser now, leaning toward him, bending forward closer, closer, till he could hear her slow, measured breathing. Even her eyes suddenly held the vaguest inner light—her whole being quivered with the chill tensity of her purpose; when she spoke, she almost breathed the words:

"I want you to kiss me, and don't be afraid. I shall keep you alive for days, but I must have response, not passivity. You're a bachelor, at least thirty. You won't have any more morals about the matter than I. But you must let your whole body yield."

He didn't believe it. Her face hovered six inches above his; and there was such a ferocity of suppressed eagerness in her that it could only mean death.

Her lips were pursed, as if to suck, and they quivered with a strange, tense, trembling desire, utterly unnatural, almost obscene. Her nostrils dilated at every breath—and no normal woman who had kissed as often as she must have in all her years could feel like that, if that was all she expected to get.

"Quick!" she said breathlessly. "Yield, yield!"

Leigh scarcely heard; for that other mind that had been lingering in his brain, surged forward in its incredible way. He heard himself say:

"I'll trust your promise because I can't resist such an appeal. You can kiss your head off. I guess I can stand it—"

There was a blue flash, an agonizing burning sensation that spread in a flash to every nerve of his body.

The anguish became a series of tiny pains, like small needles piercing a thousand bits of his flesh. Tingling, writhing a little, amazed that he was still alive, Leigh opened his eyes.

He felt a wave of purely personal surprise.

The woman lay slumped, lips half twisted off of his, body collapsed hard across his chest. And the mind, that blazing mind was there, watching—as the tall figure of the Dreegh man sauntered into the room, stiffened, and then darted forward.

He jerked her limp form into his arms. There was the same kind of blue flash as their lips met, from the man to the woman. She stirred finally, moaning. He shook her brutally.

"You wretched fool!" he raged. "How did you let a thing like that happen? You would have been dead in another minute, if I hadn't come along."

"I—don't—know." Her voice was thin and old. She sank down to the floor at his feet, and slumped there like a tired old woman. Her blond hair straggled, and looked curiously faded. "I don't know, Jeel. I tried to get his life force, and he got mine instead. He—"

She stopped. Her blue eyes widened. She staggered to her feet. "Jeel, he must be a spy. No human being could do a thing like that to me.

"Jeel"—there was sudden terror in her voice—"Jeel, get out of this room. Don't you realize? He's got my energy in him. He's lying there now, and whatever has control of him has my energy to work with—"

"All right, all right." He patted her fingers. "I assure you he's only

a human being. And he's got your energy. You made a mistake, and
the flow went the wrong way. But it would take much more than that
for anyone to use a human body successfully against us. So—"

"You don't understand!"

Her voice shook. "Jeel, I've been cheating. I don't know what got
into me, but I couldn't get enough life force. Every time I was able,
during the four times we stayed on Earth, I sneaked out.

"I caught men on the street. I don't know exactly how many because I dissolved their bodies after I was through with them. But
there were dozens. And he's got all the energy I collected, enough for
scores of years, enough for—don't you see?—enough for *them.*"

"My dear!" The Dreegh shook her violently, as a doctor would an
hysterical woman. "For a million years, the great ones of Galactic
have ignored us and—"

He paused. A black frown twisted his long face. He whirled like
the tiger man he was, snatching at his gun—as Leigh stood up.

The man Leigh was no longer surprised at—anything. At the way
the hard cords fell rotted from his wrists and legs. At the way the
Dreegh froze rigid after one look into his eyes. For the first shock
of the tremendous, the almost cataclysmic, truth was already in
him.

"There is only one difference," said Leigh in a voice so vibrant that
the top of his head shivered from the unaccustomed violence of
sound. "This time there are two hundred and twenty-seven Dreegh
ships gathered in one concentrated area. The rest—and our records
show only a dozen others—we can safely leave to our police patrols."

The Great Galactic, who had been William Leigh, smiled darkly
and walked toward his captives. "It has been a most interesting experiment in deliberate splitting of personality. Three years ago, our
time manipulators showed this opportunity of destroying the
Dreeghs, who hitherto had escaped by reason of the vastness of our
galaxy.

"And so I came to Earth, and here built up the character of William Leigh, reporter, complete with family and past history. It was
necessary to withdraw into a special compartment of the brain some
nine-tenths of my mind, and to drain completely an equal percentage
of life energy.

"That was the difficulty. How to replace that energy in sufficient
degree at the proper time, without playing the role of vampire. I
constructed a number of energy caches, but naturally at no time had

we been able to see all the future. We could not see the details of
what was to transpire aboard this ship, or in my hotel room that night
you came, or under Constantine's restaurant.

"Besides, if I had possessed full energy as I approached this ship,
your spy ray would have registered it; and you would instantly have
destroyed my small automobile-spaceship.

"My first necessity, accordingly, was to come to the meteorite, and
obtain an initial control over my own body through the medium of
what my Earth personality called the 'blackness' room.

"That Earth personality offered unexpected difficulties. In three
years it had gathered momentum as a personality, and that impetus
made it necessary to repeat a scene with Patricia Ungarn, and to
appear directly as another conscious mind, in order to convince Leigh
that he must yield. The rest of course was a matter of gaining additional life energy after boarding your ship, which"—he bowed
slightly at the muscularly congealed body of the woman—"which she
supplied me.

"I have explained all this because of the fact that a mind will
accept complete control only if full understanding of—defeat—is
present. I must finally inform you, therefore, that you are to remain
alive for the next few days, during which time you will assist me in
making personal contact with your friends."

He made a gesture of dismissal: "Return to your normal existence.
I have still to co-ordinate my two personalities completely, and that
does not require your presence."

The Dreeghs went out blank-eyed, almost briskly; and the two
minds in one body were—alone!

For Leigh, the Leigh of Earth, the first desperate shock was past.
The room was curiously dim, as if he was staring out through eyes
that were no longer—his!

He thought, with a horrible effort at self-control: "I've got to fight.
Some *thing* is trying to possess my body. All the rest is lie."

A soothing, mind-pulsation stole into the shadowed chamber where
his—self—was cornered:

"No lie, but wondrous truth. You have not seen what the Dreeghs
saw and felt, for you are inside this body, and know not that it has
come marvelously *alive*, unlike anything that your petty dreams on
Earth could begin to conceive. You must accept your high destiny,
else the sight of your own body will be a terrible thing to you. Be
calm, be braver than you've ever been, and pain will turn to joy."

Calm came out. His mind quivered in its dark corner, abnormally conscious of strange and unnatural pressures that pushed in at it like winds out of unearthly night. For a moment of terrible fear, it funked that pressing night, then forced back to sanity, and had another thought of its own, a grimly cunning thought:

The devilish interloper was arguing. Could that mean—his mind rocked with hope—that co-ordination was impossible without his yielding to clever persuasion?

Never would he yield.

"Think," whispered the alien mind, "think of being one valuable facet of a mind with an I. Q. twelve hundred, think of yourself as having played a role; and now you are returning to normalcy, a normalcy of unlimited power. You have been an actor completely absorbed in your role, but the play is over; you are alone in your dressing room removing the grease paint; your mood of the play is fading, fading, fading—"

"Go to hell!" said William Leigh, loudly. "I'm William Leigh, I. Q. one hundred and twelve, satisfied to be just what I am. I don't give a damn whether you built me up from the component elements of your brain, or whether I was born normally. I can just see what you're trying to do with that hypnotic suggestion stuff, but it isn't working. I'm here, I'm myself, and I stay myself. Go find yourself another body, if you're so smart."

Silence settled where his voice had been; and the emptiness, the utter lack of sound brought a sharp twinge of fear greater than that which he had had before he spoke.

He was so intent on that inner struggle that he was not aware of outer movement until—

With a start he grew aware that he was staring out of a port window. Night spread there, the living night of space.

A trick, he thought in an agony of fear; a trick somehow designed to add to the corroding power of hypnotism.

A trick! He tried to jerk back—and, terrifyingly, couldn't. His body wouldn't move. Instantly, then, he tried to speak, to crash through that enveloping blanket of unholy silence. But no sound came.

Not a muscle, not a finger stirred; not a single nerve so much as trembled.

He was alone.

Cut off in his little corner of brain.

Lost.

Yes, lost, came a strangely pitying sibilation of thought, lost to a cheap, sordid existence, lost to a life whose end is visible from the hour of birth, lost to a civilization that has already had to be saved from itself a thousand times. Even you, I think, can see that all this is lost to you forever—

Leigh thought starkly: The *thing* was trying by a repetition of ideas, by showing evidence of defeat, to lay the foundations of further defeat. It was the oldest trick of simple hypnotism for simple people. And he couldn't let it work—

You have, urged the mind inexorably, accepted the fact that you were playing a role; and now you have recognized our oneness, and are giving up the role. The proof of this recognition on your part is that you have yielded control of—our—body.

—Our body, our body, OUR body—

The words re-echoed like some Gargantuan sound through his brain, then merged swiftly into that calm, other-mind pulsation:

—Concentration. All intellect derives from the capacity to concentrate; and, progressively, the body itself shows *life,* reflects and focuses that gathering, vaulting power.

—One more step remains: You must see—

Amazingly, then, he was staring into a mirror. Where it had come from, he had no memory. It was there in front of him, where, an instant before, had been a black porthole—and there was an image in the mirror, shapeless at first to his blurred vision.

Deliberately—he felt the enormous deliberateness—the vision was cleared for him. He saw—and then he didn't.

His brain wouldn't look. It twisted in a mad desperation, like a body buried alive, and briefly, horrendously conscious of its fate. Insanely, it fought away from the blazing thing in the mirror. So awful was the effort, so titanic the fear, that it began to gibber mentally, its consciousness to whirl dizzily, like a wheel spinning faster, faster—

The wheel shattered into ten thousand aching fragments. Darkness came, blacker than Galactic night. And there was—

Oneness!

QUIETUS

by

ROSS ROCKLYNNE

Quietly, inexorably, the earth moves forward through the centuries toward inevitable change. Even now, astronomers have mapped out such changes and can predict a reasonably accurate picture of the globe's geography and climate as far in the future as forty thousand years. Predicated on such theory, "Quietus" is a story of heartbreak and disaster. One might well conclude that the essentially tragic significance of this tale is its brilliant portrayal of the historical struggle of the feminine mind to cope with logic a priori.

*

THE CREATURES from Alcon saw from the first that Earth, as a planet, was practically dead; dead in the sense that it had given birth to life, and was responsible, indirectly, for its almost complete extinction.

"This type of planet is the most distressing," said Tark, absently smoothing down the brilliantly colored feathers of his left wing. "I can stand the dark, barren worlds which never have, and probably never will, hold life. But these that have been killed by some celestial catastrophe! Think of what great things might have come from their inhabitants."

As he spoke thus to his mate, Vascar, he was marking down in a book the position of this planet, its general appearance from space, and the number and kind of satellites it supported.

Vascar, sitting at the controls, both her claws and her vestigial hands at work, guided the spherical ship at slowly decreasing speed toward the planet Earth. A thousand miles above it, she set the craft into an orbital motion, and then proceeded to study the planet, Tark setting the account into his book, for later insertion into the Astronomical Archives of Alcon.

"Evidently," mused Vascar, her brilliant, unblinking eyes looking at the planet through a transparent section above the control board, "some large meteor, or an errant asteroid—that seems most likely— must have struck this specimen a terrible blow. Look at those great, gaping cracks that run from pole to pole, Tark. It looks as if volcanic eruptions are still taking place, too. At any rate, the whole planet seems entirely denuded—except for that single, short strip of green we saw as we came in."

Tark nodded. He was truly a bird, for in the evolutionary race on his planet, distant uncounted light years, his stock had won out over the others. His wings were short, true, and in another thousand years would be too short for flight, save in a dense atmosphere; but his head was large, and his eyes, red, small, set close together, showed intelligence and a kind benevolence. He and Vascar had left Alcon, their planet, a good many years ago; but they were on their way back now. Their outward-bound trip had taken them many light-years north of the Solar System; but on the way back, they had decided to make it one of the stop-off points in their zigzag course. Probably their greatest interest in all this long cruise was in the discovery of planets—they were indeed few. And that pleasure might even be secondary to the discovery of life. To find a planet that had almost entirely died was, conversely, distressing. Their interest in the planet Earth was, because of this, a wistful one.

The ship made the slow circuit of Earth—the planet was a hodgepodge of tumbled, churned mountains; of abysmal, frightfully long cracks exuding unholy vapors; of volcanoes that threw their fires and hot liquid rocks far into the sky; of vast oceans disturbed from the ocean bed by cataclysmic eruptions. And of life they saw nothing save a single strip of green perhaps a thousand miles long, a hundred wide, in the Western Hemisphere.

"I don't think we'll find intelligent life, though," Tark said pessimistically. "This planet was given a terrific blow—I wouldn't be surprised if her rotation period was cut down considerably in a single instant. Such a charge would be unsupportable. Whole cities would literally be snapped away from their foundations—churned, ground to dust. The intelligent creatures who built them would die by the millions—the billions—in that holocaust; and whatever destruction

was left incomplete would be finished up by the appearance of volcanoes and faults in the crust of the planet."

Vascar reminded him, "Remember, where there's vegetation, even
as little as evidenced by that single strip down there, there must be
some kind of animal life."

Tark ruffled his wings in a shrug. "I doubt it. The plants would get
all the carbon dioxide they needed from volcanoes—animal life
wouldn't have to exist. Still, let's take a look. Don't worry, I'm hoping
there's intelligent life, too. If there is, it will doubtless need some help
if it is to survive. Which ties in with our aims, for that is our principal
purpose on this expedition—to discover intelligent life, and, wherever
possible, to give it what help we can, if it needs help."

Vascar's vestigial hands worked the controls, and the ship dropped
leisurely downward toward the green strip.

A rabbit darted out of the underbrush—Tommy leaped at it with
the speed and dexterity of a thoroughly wild animal. His powerful
hands wrapped around the creature—its struggles ceased as its vertebra
was snapped. Tommy squatted, tore the skin off the creature, and
proceeded to eat great mouthfuls of the still warm flesh.

Blacky cawed harshly, squawked, and his untidy form came flashing
down through the air to land precariously on Tommy's shoulder.
Tommy went on eating, while the crow fluttered its wings, smoothed
them out, and settled down to a restless somnolence. The quiet of
the scrub forest, save for the cries and sounds of movement of birds
and small animals moving through the forest, settled down about
Tommy as he ate. "Tommy" was what he called himself. A long time
ago, he remembered, there used to be a great many people in the
world—perhaps a hundred—many of whom, and particularly two
people whom he had called Mom and Pop, had called him by that
name. They were gone now, and the others with them. Exactly
where they went, Tommy did not know. But the world had rocked
one night—it was the night Tommy ran away from home, with
Blacky riding on his shoulder—and when Tommy came out of the
cave where he had been sleeping, all was in flames, and the city on the
horizon had fallen so that it was nothing but a huge pile of dust—
but in the end it had not mattered to Tommy. Of course, he was
lonesome, terrified, at first, but he got over that. He continued to
live, eating, drinking, sleeping, walking endlessly; and Blacky, his
talking crow, was good company. Blacky was smart. He could speak

every word that Tommy knew, and a good many others that he didn't. Tommy was not Blacky's first owner.

But though he had been happy, the last year had brought the recurrence of a strange feeling that had plagued him off and on, but never so strongly as now. A strange, terrible hunger was settling on him. Hunger? He knew this sensation. He had forthwith slain a wild dog, and eaten of the meat. He saw then that it was not a hunger of the belly. It was a hunger of the mind, and it was all the worse because he could not know what it was. He had come to his feet, restless, looking into the tangled depths of the second growth forest.

"Hungry," he had said, and his shoulders shook and tears coursed out of his eyes, and he sat down on the ground and sobbed without trying to stop himself, for he had never been told that to weep was unmanly. What was it he wanted?

He had everything there was all to himself. Southward in winter, northward in summer, eating of berries and small animals as he went, and Blacky to talk to and Blacky to talk the same words back at him. This was the natural life—he had lived it ever since the world went bang. But still he cried, and felt a panic growing in his stomach, and he didn't know what it was he was afraid of, or longed for, whichever it was. He was twenty-one years old. Tears were natural to him, to be indulged in whenever he felt like it. Before the world went bang— there were some things he remembered—the creature whom he called Mom generally put her arms around him and merely said, "It's all right, Tommy, it's all right."

So on that occasion, he arose from the ground and said, "It's all right, Tommy, it's all right."

Blacky, he with the split tongue, said harshly, as was his wont, "It's all right, Tommy, it's all right! I tell you, the price of wheat is going down!"

Blacky, the smartest crow anybody had—why did he say that? There wasn't anybody else, and there weren't any more crows—helped a lot. He not only knew all the words and sentences that Tommy knew, but he knew others that Tommy could never understand because he didn't know where they came from, or what they referred to. And in addition to all that, Blacky had the ability to anticipate what Tommy said, and frequently took whole words and sentences right out of Tommy's mouth.

Tommy finished eating his rabbit, and threw the skin aside, and sat quite still, a peculiarly blank look in his eyes. The strange hunger was on him again. He looked off across the lush plain of grasses that stretched away, searching into the distance, toward where the Sun was setting. He looked to left and right. He drew himself softly to his feet, and peered into the shadows of the forest behind him. His heavily bearded lips began to tremble, and the tears started from his eyes again. He turned and stumbled from the forest, blinded.

Blacky clutched at Tommy's broad shoulder, and rode him, and a split second before Tommy, said, "It's all right, Tommy, it's all right."

Tommy said the words angrily to himself, and blinked the tears away.

He was a little bit tired. The Sun was setting, and night would soon come. But it wasn't that that made him tired. It was a weariness of the mind, a feeling of futility, for, whatever it was he wanted, he could never, never find it, because he would not know where he should look for it.

His bare foot trampled on something wet—he stopped and looked at the ground. He stooped and picked up the skin of a recently killed rabbit. He turned it over and over in his hands, frowning. This was not an animal he had killed, certainly—the skin had been taken off in a different way. Someone else—no! But his shoulders began to shake with a wild excitement. Someone else? No, it couldn't be! There was no one—there could be no one—could there? The skin dropped from his nerveless fingers as he saw a single footprint not far ahead of him. He stooped over it, examining, and knew again that he had not done this, either. And certainly it could be no other animal than a man!

It was a small footprint at which he stared, as if a child, or an under-sized man, might have stepped in the soft humus. Suddenly he raised his head. He had definitely heard the crackling of a twig, not more than forty feet away, certainly. His eyes stared ahead through the gathering dusk. Something looking back at him? Yes! Something there in the bushes that was not an animal!

"No noise, Blacky," he whispered, and forgot Blacky's general response to that command.

"No noise, Blacky!" the big, ugly bird blasted out. "No noise, Blacky! Well, fer cryin' out loud!"

Blacky uttered a scared squawk as Tommy leaped ahead, a snarl contorting his features, and flapped from his master's shoulder. For several minutes Tommy ran after the vanishing figure, with all the strength and agility of his singularly powerful legs. But whoever—

or whatever—it was that fled him, outdistanced him easily, and Tommy had to stop at last, panting. Then he stooped, and picked up a handful of pebbles and hurled them at the squawking bird. A single tail feather fell to earth as Blacky swooped away.

"Told you not to make noise," Tommy snarled, and the tears started to run again. The hunger was starting up in his mind again, too! He sat down on a log, and put his chin in his palms, while his tears flowed. Blacky came flapping through the air, almost like a shadow—it was getting dark. The bird tentatively settled on his shoulder, cautiously flapped away again and then came back.

Tommy turned his head and looked at it bitterly, and then turned away, and groaned.

"It's all your fault, Blacky!"

"It's all your fault," the bird said. "Oh, Tommy, I could spank you! I get so exasperated!"

Sitting there, Tommy tried to learn exactly what he had seen. He had been sure it was a human figure, just like himself, only different. Different! It had been smaller, had seemed to possess a slender grace —it was impossible! Every time he thought of it, the hunger in his mind raged!

He jumped to his feet, his fists clenched. This hunger had been in him too long! He must find out what caused it—he must find her— why did the word her come to his mind? Suddenly, he was flooded with a host of childhood remembrances.

"It was a girl!" he gasped. "Oh, Tommy must want a girl!"

The thought was so utterly new that it left him stunned; but the thought grew. He must find her, if it took him all the rest of his life! His chest deepened, his muscles swelled, and a new light came into his blue eyes. Southward in winter, northward in summer—eat-ing—sleeping—truly, there was nothing in such a life. Now he felt the strength of a purpose swelling up in him. He threw himself to the ground and slept; and Blacky flapped to the limb of a tree, in-serted his head beneath a wing, and slept also. Perhaps, in the last ten or fifteen years, he also had wanted a mate, but probably he had long ago given up hope—for, it seemed, there were no more crows left in the world. Anyway, Blacky was very old, perhaps twice as old as Tommy; he was merely content to live.

Tark and Vascar sent their spherical ship lightly plummeting above the green strip—it proved to be vegetation, just as they had supposed. Either one or the other kept constant watch of the ground below—

they discovered nothing that might conceivably be classed as intelligent life. Insects they found, and decided that they worked entirely by instinct; small animals, rabbits, squirrels, rats, raccoons, otters, opossums, and large animals, deer, horses, sheep, cattle, pigs, dogs, they found to be just that—animals, and nothing more.

"Looks as if it was all killed off, Vascar," said Tark, "and not so long ago at that, judging by the fact that this forest must have grown entirely in the last few years."

Vascar agreed; she suggested they put the ship down for a few days and rest.

"It would be wonderful if we could find intelligent life after all," she said wistfully. "Think what a great triumph it would be if we were the ones to start the last members of that race on the upward trail again. Anyway," she added, "I think this atmosphere is dense enough for us to fly in."

He laughed—a trilling sound. "You've been looking for such an atmosphere for years. But I think you're right about this one. Put the ship down there, Vascar—looks like a good spot."

For five days Tommy followed the trail of the girl with a grim determination. He knew now that it was a woman; perhaps—indeed, very probably—the only one left alive. He had only the vaguest of ideas of why he wanted her—he thought it was for human companionship, that alone. At any rate, he felt that this terrible hunger in him—he could give it no other word—would be allayed when he caught up with her.

She was fleeing him, and staying just near enough to him to make him continue the chase, he knew that with a fierce exultation. And somehow her actions seemed right and proper. Twice he had seen her, once on the crest of a ridge, once as she swam a river. Both times she had easily outdistanced him. But by cross-hatching, he picked up her trail again—a bent twig or weed, a footprint, the skin of a dead rabbit.

Once, at night, he had the impression that she crept up close, and looked at him curiously, perhaps with the same great longing that he felt. He could not be sure. But he knew that very soon now she would be his—and perhaps she would be glad of it.

Once he heard a terrible moaning, high up in the air. He looked upward. Blacky uttered a surprised squawk. A large, spherical thing was darting overhead.

"I wonder what that is," Blacky squawked.

"I wonder what that is," said Tommy, feeling a faint fear. "There ain't nothin' like that in the yard."

He watched as the spaceship disappeared from sight. Then, with the unquestioning attitude of the savage, he dismissed the matter from his mind, and took up his tantalizing trail again.

"Better watch out, Tommy," the bird cawed.

"Better watch out, Tommy," Tommy muttered to himself. He only vaguely heard Blacky—Blacky always anticipated what Tommy was going to say, because he had known Tommy so long.

The river was wide, swirling, muddy, primeval in its surge of resistless strength. Tommy stood on the bank, and looked out over the waters—suddenly his breath soughed from his lungs.

"It's her!" he gasped. "It's her, Blacky! She's drownin'!

No time to waste in thought—a figure truly struggled against the push of the treacherous waters, seemingly went under. Tommy dived cleanly, and Blacky spread his wings at the last instant and escaped a bath. He saw his master disappear beneath the swirling waters, saw him emerge, strike out with singularly powerful arms, slightly upstream, fighting every inch of the way. Blacky hovered over the waters, cawing frantically, and screaming.

"Tommy, I could spank you! I could spank you! I get so exasperated! You wait till your father comes home!"

A log was coming downstream. Tommy saw it coming, but knew he'd escape it. He struck out, paid no more attention to it. The log came down with a rush, and would have missed him had it not suddenly swung broadside on. It clipped the swimming man on the side of the head. Tommy went under, threshing feebly, barely conscious, his limbs like leaden bars. That seemed to go on for a very long time. He seemed to be breathing water. Then something grabbed hold of his long black hair—

When he awoke, he was lying on his back, and he was staring into her eyes. Something in Tommy's stomach fell out—perhaps the hunger was going. He came to his feet, staring at her, his eyes blazing. She stood only about twenty feet away from him. There was something pleasing about her, the slimness of her arms, the roundness of her hips, the strangeness of her body, her large, startled, timid eyes, the mass of ebon hair that fell below her hips. He started toward her. She gazed at him as if in a trance.

Blacky came flapping mournfully across the river. He was making no sound, but the girl must have been frightened as he landed on Tommy's shoulder. She tensed, and was away like a rabbit. Tommy went after her in long, loping bounds, but his foot caught in a tangle of dead grass, and he plummeted head foremost to the ground.

The other vanished over a rise of ground.

He arose again, and knew no disappointment that he had again lost her. He knew now that it was only her timidity, the timidity of a wild creature, that made her flee him. He started off again, for now that he knew what the hunger was, it seemed worse than ever.

The air of this planet was deliciously breathable, and was the nearest thing to their own atmosphere that Tark and Vascar had encountered.

Vascar ruffled her brilliant plumage, and spread her wings, flapping them. Tark watched her, as she laughed at him in her own way, and then made a few short, running jumps and took off. She spiraled, called down to him.

"Come on up. The air's fine, Tark."

Tark considered. "All right," he conceded, "but wait until I get a couple of guns."

"I can't imagine why," Vascar called down; but nevertheless, as they rose higher and higher above the second growth forest, each had a belt strapped loosely around the neck, carrying a weapon similar to a pistol.

"I can't help but hope we run into some kind of intelligent life," said Vascar. "This is really a lovely planet. In time the volcanoes will die down, and vegetation will spread all over. It's a shame that the planet has to go to waste."

"We could stay and colonize it," Tark suggested rakishly.

"Oh, not I. I like Alcon too well for that, and the sooner we get back there, the better— Look! Tark! Down there!"

Tark looked, caught sight of a medium large animal moving through the underbrush. He dropped a little lower. And then rose again.

"It's nothing," he said. "An animal, somewhat larger than the majority we've seen, probably the last of its kind. From the looks of it, I'd say it wasn't particularly pleasant on the eyes. Its skin shows— Oh, now I see what you mean, Vascar!"

This time he was really interested as he dropped lower, and a strange excitement throbbed through his veins. Could it be that they were going to discover intelligent life after all—perhaps the last of its kind?

It was indeed an exciting sight the two bird-creatures from another planet saw. They flapped slowly above and a number of yards behind the unsuspecting upright beast, that moved swiftly through the forest, a black creature not unlike themselves in general structure riding its shoulder.

"It must mean intelligence!" Vascar whispered excitedly, her brilliant red eyes glowing with interest. "One of the first requisites of intelligent creatures is to put animals lower in the scale of evolution to work as beasts of burden and transportation."

"Wait awhile," cautioned Tark, "before you make any irrational conclusions. After all, there are creatures of different species which live together in friendship. Perhaps the creature which looks so much like us keeps the other's skin and hair free of vermin. And perhaps the other way around, too."

"I don't think so," insisted his mate. "Tark, the bird-creature is riding the shoulder of the beast. Perhaps that means its race is so old, and has used this means of transportation so long, that its wings have atrophied. That would almost certainly mean intelligence. It's talking now—you can hear it. It's probably telling its beast to stop—there, it has stopped!"

"Its voice is not so melodious," said Tark dryly.

She looked at him reprovingly; the tips of their flapping wings were almost touching.

"That isn't like you, Tark. You know very well that one of our rules is not to place intelligence on creatures who seem like ourselves, and neglect others while we do so. Its harsh voice proves nothing—to one of its race, if there are any left, its voice may be pleasing in the extreme. At any rate, it ordered the large beast of burden to stop—you saw that."

"Well, perhaps," conceded Tark.

They continued to wing their slow way after the perplexing duo, following slightly behind, skimming the tops of trees. They saw the white beast stop, and place its paws on its hips. Vascar, listening very closely, because she was anxious to gain proof of her contention, heard the bird-creature say,

"Now what, Blacky?" and also the featherless beast repeat the same words: "Now what, Blacky?"

"There's your proof," said Vascar excitedly. "Evidently the white beast is highly imitative. Did you hear it repeat what its master said?"

Tark said uneasily, "I wouldn't jump to conclusions, just from a hasty survey like this. I admit that, so far, all the proof points to the bird. It seems truly intelligent; or at least more intelligent than the other. But you must bear in mind that we are naturally prejudiced in favor of the bird—it may not be intelligent at all. As I said, they may merely be friends in the sense that animals of different species are friends."

Vascar made a scornful sound.

"Well, let's get goin', Blacky," she heard the bird say; and heard the white, upright beast repeat the strange, alien words. The white beast started off again, traveling very stealthily, making not the least amount of noise. Again Vascar called this quality to the attention of her skeptical mate—such stealth was the mark of the animal, certainly not of the intelligent creature.

"We should be certain of it now," she insisted. "I think we ought to get in touch with the bird. Remember, Tark, that our primary purpose on this expedition is to give what help we can to the intelligent races of the planets we visit. What creature could be more in need of help than the bird-creature down there? It is evidently the last of its kind. At least, we could make the effort of saving it from a life of sheer boredom; it would probably leap at the chance to hold converse with intelligent creatures. Certainly it gets no pleasure from the company of dumb beasts."

But Tark shook his handsome, red-plumed head worriedly.

"I would prefer," he said uneasily, "first to investigate the creature you are so sure is a beast of burden. There is a chance—though, I admit, a farfetched one—that it is the intelligent creature, and not the other."

But Vascar did not hear him. All her feminine instincts had gone out in pity to the seemingly intelligent bird that rode Tommy's broad shoulder. And so intent were she and Tark on the duo, that they did not see, less than a hundred yards ahead, that another creature, smaller in form, more graceful, but indubitably the same species as the white-skinned, unfeathered beast, was slinking softly through the underbrush, now and anon casting indecisive glances behind her toward him who pursued her. He was out of sight, but she could hear—

Tommy slunk ahead, his breath coming fast; for the trail was very strong, and his keen ears picked up the sounds of footsteps ahead. The chase was surely over—his terrible hunger about to end! He felt wildly exhilarated. Instincts were telling him much that his experience could not. He and this girl were the last of mankind. Something told him that now mankind would rise again—yet he did not know why. He slunk ahead, Blacky on his shoulder, all unaware of the two brilliantly colored denizens of another planet who followed above and behind him. But Blacky was not so easy of mind. His neck feathers were standing erect. Nervousness made him raise his wings up from his body—perhaps he heard the soft swish of large-winged creatures, beating the air behind, and though all birds of prey had been dead these last fifteen years, the old fear rose up.

Tommy glued himself to a tree, on the edge of a clearing. His breath escaped from his lungs as he caught a glimpse of a white, unclothed figure. It was she! She was looking back at him. She was tired of running. She was ready, glad to give up. Tommy experienced a dizzy elation. He stepped forth into the clearing, and slowly, very slowly, holding her large, dark eyes with his, started toward her. The slightest swift motion, the slightest untoward sound, and she would be gone. Her whole body was poised on the balls of her feet. She was not at all sure whether she should be afraid of him or not.

Behind him, the two feathered creatures from another planet settled slowly into a tree, and watched. Blacky certainly did not hear them come to rest—what he must have noticed was that the beat of wings, nagging at the back of his mind, had disappeared. It was enough.

"No noise, Blacky!" the bird screamed affrightedly, and flung himself into the air and forward, a bundle of ebon feathers with tattered wings outspread, as it darted across the clearing. For the third time, it was Blacky who scared her, for again she was gone, and had lost herself to sight even before Tommy could move.

"Come back!" Tommy shouted ragingly. "I ain't gonna hurt you!" He ran after her full speed, tears streaming down his face, tears of rage and heartbreak at the same time. But already he knew it was useless! He stopped suddenly, on the edge of the clearing, and sobbing to himself, caught sight of Blacky, high above the ground, cawing piercingly, warningly. Tommy stooped and picked up a handful of pebbles. With deadly, murderous intent he threw them at the bird. It soared and swooped in the air—twice it was hit glancingly.

"It's all your fault, Blacky!" Tommy raged. He picked up a rock the size of his fist. He started to throw it, but did not. A tiny, sharp sound bit through the air. Tommy pitched forward. He did not make the slightest twitching motion to show that he had bridged the gap between life and death. He did not know that Blacky swooped down and landed on his chest; and then flung himself upward, crying, "Oh, Tommy, I could spank you!" He did not see the girl come into the clearing and stoop over him; and did not see the tears that began to gush from her eyes, or hear the sobs that racked her body. But Tark saw.

Tark wrested the weapon from Vascar with a trill of rage.
"Why did you do that?" he cried. He threw the weapon from him
as far as it would go. "You've done a terrible thing, Vascar!"

Vascar looked at him in amazement. "It was only a beast, Tark,"
she protested. "It was trying to kill its master! Surely, you saw it. It
was trying to kill the intelligent bird-creature, the last of its kind on
the planet."

But Tark pointed with horror at the two unfeathered beasts, one
bent over the body of the other. "But they were mates! You have
killed their species! The female is grieving for its mate, Vascar. You
have done a terrible thing!"

But Vascar shook her head crossly. "I'm sorry I did it then," she
said acidly. "I suppose it was perfectly in keeping with our aim on
this expedition to let the dumb beast kill its master! That isn't like
you at all, Tark! Come, let us see if the intelligent creature will not
make friends with us."

And she flapped away toward the cawing crow. When Blacky saw
Vascar coming toward him, he wheeled and darted away.

Tark took one last look at the female bending over the male. He
saw her raise her head, and saw the tears in her eyes, and heard the
sobs that shook her. Then, in a rising, inchoate series of bewildering
emotions, he turned his eyes away, and hurriedly flapped after Vascar.
And all that day they pursued Blacky. They circled him, they cornered
him; and Vascar tried to speak to him in friendly tones, all to no
avail. It only cawed, and darted away, and spoke volumes of disap-
pointingly incomprehensible words.

When dark came, Vascar alighted in a tree beside the strangely
quiet Tark.

"I suppose it's no use," she said sadly. "Either it is terribly afraid
of us, or it is not as intelligent as we supposed it was, or else it has
become mentally deranged in these last years of loneliness. I guess we
might as well leave now, Tark; let the poor creature have its planet
to itself. Shall we stop by and see if we can help the female beast
whose mate we shot?"

Tark slowly looked at her, his red eyes luminous in the gathering
dusk. "No," he said briefly. "Let us go, Vascar."

The spaceship of the creatures from Alcon left the dead planet
Earth. It darted out into space. Tark sat at the controls. The ship
went faster and faster. And still faster. Fled at ever-increasing speed
beyond the Solar System and into the wastes of interstellar space.

And still farther, until the star that gave heat to Earth was not even visible.

Yet even this terrible velocity was not enough for Tark. Vascar looked at him strangely.

"We're not in that much of a hurry to get home, are we, Tark?"

"No," Tark said in a low, terrible voice; but still he urged the ship to greater and greater speed, though he knew it was useless. He could run away from the thing that had happened on the planet Earth; but he could never, never outrun his mind, though he passionately wished he could.

THE TWONKY

by

LEWIS PADGETT

The smooth inter-reaction of time-space vibrations sets up invisible walls that keep the dimensions apart. Lewis Padgett jestingly devises a temporal snag (without quite defining same) which closes the gap between one dimension and another. It all ceases to be a joke when an inhabitant of the alien plane falls through. He doesn't get his bearings before he has fulfilled his appointed task and manufactured a Twonky. Then comes a terrifying picture of an ordinary household subjected to an ordinary mechanical contrivance—a contrivance ordinary only in the fourth dimension.

*

THE TURNOVER at Mideastern Radio was so great that Mickey Lloyd couldn't keep track of his men. It wasn't only the draft; employees kept quitting and going elsewhere, at a higher salary. So when the big-headed little man in overalls wandered vaguely out of a storeroom, Lloyd took one look at the brown dungaree suit—company provided—and said mildly, "The whistle blew half an hour ago. Hop to work."

"Work-k-k?" The man seemed to have trouble with the word.

Drunk? Lloyd, in his capacity as foreman, couldn't permit that. He flipped away his cigarette, walked forward, and sniffed. No, it wasn't liquor. He peered at the badge on the man's overalls.

"Two-oh-four, m-mm. Are you new here?"

"New. Huh?" The man rubbed a rising bump on his forehead. He was an odd-looking little chap, bald as a vacuum tube, with a pinched pallid face and tiny eyes that held dazed wonder.

"Come on, Joe. Wake up!" Lloyd was beginning to sound impatient. "You work here, don't you?"

"Joe," said the man thoughtfully. "Work. Yes, I work. I make them." His words ran together oddly, as though he had a cleft palate.

With another glance at the badge, Lloyd gripped Joe's arm and ran him through the assembly room. "Here's your place. Hop to it. Know what to do?"

The other drew his scrawny body erect. "I am—expert," he remarked. "Make them better than Ponthwank."

"O. K.," Lloyd said. "Make 'em, then." And he went away.

The man called Joe hesitated, nursing the bruise on his head. The overalls caught his attention, and he examined them wonderingly. Where—oh, yes. They had been hanging in the room from which he had first emerged. His own garments had, naturally, dissipated during the trip—what trip?

Amnesia, he thought. He had fallen from the . . . the something . . . when it slowed down and stopped. How odd this huge, machine-filled barn looked. It struck no chord of remembrance.

Amnesia, that was it. He was a worker. He made things. As for the unfamiliarity of his surroundings, that meant nothing. He was still dazed. The clouds would lift from his mind presently. They were beginning to do that already.

Work. Joe scuttled around the room, trying to goad his faulty memory. Men in overalls were doing things. Simple, obvious things. But how childish—how elemental! Perhaps this was a kindergarten.

After a while Joe went out into a stock room and examined some finished models of combination radio-phonographs. So that was it. Awkward and clumsy, but it wasn't his place to say so. No. His job was to make Twonkies.

Twonkies? The name jolted his memory again. Of course he knew how to make Twonkies. He'd made them all his life—had been specially trained for the job. Now they were using a different model of Twonky, but what the hell! Child's play for a clever workman.

Joe went back into the shop and found a vacant bench. He began to build a Twonky. Occasionally he slipped off and stole the material he needed. Once, when he couldn't locate any tungsten, he hastily built a small gadget and made it.

His bench was in a distant corner, badly lighted, though it seemed quite bright to Joe's eyes. Nobody noticed the console that was swiftly growing to completion there. Joe worked very, very fast. He ignored the noon whistle, and, at quitting time, his task was finished. It could, perhaps, stand another coat of paint—it lacked the Shimmertone of a standard Twonky. But none of the others had Shimmertone. Joe sighed, crawled under the bench, looked in vain for a relaxopad, and went to sleep on the floor.

A few hours later he woke up. The factory was empty. Odd! Maybe the working hours had changed. Maybe— Joe's mind felt funny. Sleep had cleared away the mists of amnesia, if such it had been, but he still felt dazed.

Muttering under his breath, he sent the Twonky into the stock room and compared it with the others. Superficially it was identical with a console radio-phonograph combination of the latest model. Following the pattern of the others, Joe had camouflaged and disguised the various organs and reactors.

He went back into the shop. Then the last of the mists cleared from his mind. Joe's shoulders jerked convulsively.

"Great Snell!" he gasped. "So that was it! I ran into a temporal snag!"

With a startled glance around, he fled to the storeroom from which he had first emerged. The overalls he took off and returned to their hook. After that, Joe went over to a corner, felt around in the air, nodded with satisfaction, and seated himself on nothing, three feet above the floor. Then Joe vanished.

"Time," said Kerry Westerfield, "is curved. Eventually it gets back to the same place where it started. That's duplication." He put his feet up on a conveniently outjutting rock of the chimney and stretched luxuriously. From the kitchen Martha made clinking noises with bottles and glasses.

"Yesterday at this time I had a Martini," Kerry said. "The time curve indicates that I should have another one now. Are you listening, angel?"

"I'm pouring," said the angel distantly.

"You get my point, then. Here's another. Time describes a spiral instead of a circle. If you call the first cycle a, the second one's a plus 1—see? Which means a double Martini tonight."

"I know where that would end," Martha remarked, coming into the spacious, oak-raftered living room. She was a small, dark-haired woman with a singularly pretty face and a figure to match. Her tiny gingham apron looked slightly absurd in combination with slacks and silk blouse. "And they don't make infinity-proof gin. Here's your Martini." She did things with the shaker and manipulated glasses.

"Stir slowly," Kerry cautioned. "Never shake. Ah—that's it." He accepted the drink and eyed it appreciatively. Black hair, sprinkled with gray, gleamed in the lamplight as he sipped the Martini. "Good. Very good."

Martha drank slowly and eyed her husband. A nice guy, Kerry Westerfield. He was forty-odd, pleasantly ugly, with a wide mouth and an occasional sardonic gleam in his gray eyes as he contemplated life. They had been married for twelve years, and liked it.

From outside, the late faint glow of sunset came through the windows, picking out the console cabinet that stood against the wall by the door. Kerry peered at it with appreciation.

"A pretty penny," he remarked. "Still—"

"What? Oh. The men had a tough time getting it up the stairs. Why don't you try it, Kerry?"

"Didn't you?"

"The old one was complicated enough," Martha said, in a baffled manner. "Gadgets. They confuse me. I was brought up on an Edison. You wound it up with a crank, and strange noises came out of a horn. That I could understand. But now—you push a button, and extraordinary things happen. Electric eyes, tone selections, records that get played on both sides, to the accompaniment of weird groanings and clickings from inside the console—probably you understand those things. I don't even want to. Whenever I play a Crosby record in a superdooper like that, Bing seems embarrassed."

Kerry ate his olive. "I'm going to play some Sibelius." He nodded toward a table. "There's a new Crosby record for you. The latest."

Martha wriggled happily. "Can I, maybe, huh?"

"Uh-huh."

"But you'll have to show me how."

"Simple enough," said Kerry, beaming at the console. "Those babies are pretty good, you know. They do everything but think."

"I wish it'd wash dishes," Martha remarked. She set down her glass, got up, and vanished into the kitchen.

Kerry snapped on a lamp near by and went over to examine the new radio, Mideastern's latest model, with all the new improvements. It had been expensive—but what the hell? He could afford it. And the old one had been pretty well shot.

It was not, he saw, plugged in. Nor were there any wires in evidence —not even a ground. Something new, perhaps. Built-in antenna and ground. Kerry crouched down, looked for a socket, and plugged the cord into it.

That done, he opened the doors and eyed the dials with every appearance of satisfaction. A beam of bluish light shot out and hit him in the eyes. From the depths of the console a faint, thoughtful clicking proceeded. Abruptly it stopped. Kerry blinked, fiddled with dials and switches, and bit at a fingernail.

The radio said, in a distant voice, "Psychology pattern checked and recorded."

"Eh?" Kerry twirled a dial. "Wonder what that was? Amateur station—no, they're off the air. Hm-m-m." He shrugged and went over to a chair beside the shelves of albums. His gaze ran swiftly over the titles and composers' names. Where was the "Swan of Tuonela"? There it was, next to "Finlandia." Kerry took down the album and opened it in his lap. With his free hand he extracted a cigarette from his pocket, put it between his lips, and fumbled for the matches on the table beside him. The first match he lit went out.

He tossed it into the fireplace and was about to reach for another when a faint noise caught his attention. The radio was walking across the room toward him. A whiplike tendril flicked out from somewhere, picked up a match, scratched it beneath the table top—as Kerry had done—and held the flame to the man's cigarette.

Automatic reflexes took over. Kerry sucked in his breath, and exploded in smoky, racking coughs. He bent double, gasping and momentarily blind.

When he could see again, the radio was back in its accustomed place.

Kerry caught his lower lip between his teeth. "Martha," he called.

"Soup's on," her voice said.

Kerry didn't answer. He stood up, went over to the radio, and looked at it hesitantly. The electric cord had been pulled out of its socket. Kerry gingerly replaced it.

He crouched to examine the console's legs. They looked like finely finished wood. His exploratory hand told him nothing. Wood—hard and brittle.

How in hell—

"Dinner!" Martha called.

Kerry threw his cigarette into the fireplace and slowly walked out of the room. His wife, setting a gravy boat in place, stared at him.

"How many Martinis did you have?"

"Just one," Kerry said in a vague way. "I must have dozed off for a minute. Yeah. I must have."

"Well, fall to," Martha commanded. "This is the last chance you'll have to make a pig of yourself on my dumplings, for a week, anyway."

Kerry absently felt for his wallet, took out an envelope, and tossed it toward his wife. "Here's your ticket, angel. Don't lose it."

"Oh? I rate a compartment!" Martha thrust the pasteboard back into its envelope and gurgled happily. "You're a pal. Sure you can get along without me?"

"Huh? Hm-m-m—I think so." Kerry salted his avocado. He shook himself and seemed to come out of a slight daze. "Sure, I'll be all right. You trot off to Denver and help Carol have her baby. It's all in the family."

"We-ell, my only sister—" Martha grinned. "You know how she and Bill are. Quite nuts. They'll need a steadying hand just now."

There was no reply. Kerry was brooding over a forkful of avocado. He muttered something about the Venerable Bede.

"What about him?"

"Lecture tomorrow. Every term we bog down on the Bede, for some strange reason. Ah, well."

"Got your lecture ready?"

Kerry nodded. "Sure." For eight years he had taught at the University, and he certainly should know the schedule by this time!

Later, over coffee and cigarettes, Martha glanced at her wrist watch. "Nearly train time. I'd better finish packing. The dishes—"

"I'll do 'em." Kerry wandered after his wife into the bedroom and made motions of futile helpfulness. After a while, he carried the bags down to the car. Martha joined him, and they headed for the depot.

The train was on time. Half an hour after it had pulled out, Kerry drove the car back into the garage, let himself into the house and yawned mightily. He was tired. Well, the dishes, and then beer and a book in bed.

With a puzzled look at the radio, he entered the kitchen and did things with water and soap chips. The hall phone rang. Kerry wiped his hands on a dish towel and answered it.

It was Mike Fitzgerald, who taught psychology at the University.

"Hiya, Fitz."

"Hiya. Martha gone?"

"Yeah. I just drove her to the train."

"Feel like talking, then? I've got some pretty good Scotch. Why not run over and gab a while?"

"Like to," Kerry said, yawning again, "but I'm dead. Tomorrow's a big day. Rain check?"

"Sure. I just finished correcting papers, and relt the need of sharpening my mind. What's the matter?"

"Nothing. Wait a minute." Kerry put down the phone and looked over his shoulder, scowling. Noises were coming from the kitchen. What the hell!

He went along the hall and stopped in the doorway, motionless and staring. The radio was washing the dishes.

After a while he returned to the phone. Fitzgerald said, "Something?"

"My new radio," Kerry told him carefully. "It's washing the dishes."

Fitz didn't answer for a moment. His laugh was a bit hesitant. "Oh?"

"I'll call you back," Kerry said, and hung up. He stood motionless for a while, chewing his lip. Then he walked back to the kitchen and paused to watch.

The radio's back was toward him. Several limber tentacles were manipulating the dishes, expertly sousing them in hot, soapy water, scrubbing them with the little mop, dipping them into the rinse water, and then stacking them neatly in the metal rack. Those whip-lashes were the only sign of unusual activity. The legs were apparently solid.

"Hey!" Kerry said.

There was no response.

He sidled around till he could examine the radio more closely. The tentacles emerged from a slot under one of the dials. The electric cord was dangling. No juice, then. But what—

Kerry stepped back and fumbled out a cigarette. Instantly the radio turned, took a match from its container on the stove, and walked forward. Kerry blinked, studying the legs. They couldn't be wood. They were bending as the . . . the thing moved, elastic as rubber. The radio had a peculiar sidling motion unlike anything else on earth.

It lit Kerry's cigarette and went back to the sink, where it resumed the dishwashing.

Kerry phoned Fitzgerald again. "I wasn't kidding. I'm having hallucinations or something. That damned radio just lit a cigarette for me."

"Wait a minute—" Fitzgerald's voice sounded undecided. "This is a gag—eh?"

"No. And I don't think it's a hallucination, either. It's up your alley. Can you run over and test my knee-jerks?"

"All right," Fitz said. "Give me ten minutes. Have a drink ready."

He hung up, and Kerry, laying the phone back into its cradle, turned to see the radio walking out of the kitchen toward the living room. Its square, boxlike contour was subtly horrifying, like some bizarre sort of hobgoblin. Kerry shivered.

He followed the radio, to find it in its former place, motionless and impassive. He opened the doors, examining the turntable, the phonograph arm, and the other buttons and gadgets. There was nothing apparently unusual. Again he touched the legs. They were not wood, after all. Some plastic, which seemed quite hard. Or— maybe they were wood, after all. It was difficult to make certain, without damaging the finish. Kerry felt a natural reluctance to use a knife on his new console.

He tried the radio, getting local stations without trouble. The tone was good—unusually good, he thought. The phonograph—

He picked up Halvorsen's "Entrance of the Boyards" at random and slipped it into place, closing the lid. No sound emerged. Investigation proved that the needle was moving rhythmically along the groove, but without audible result. Well?

Kerry removed the record as the doorbell rang. It was Fitzgerald, a gangling, saturnine man with a leathery, wrinkled face and a tousled mop of dull-gray hair. He extended a large, bony hand.

"Where's my drink?"

" 'Lo, Fitz. Come in the kitchen. I'll mix. Highball?"

"Highball."

"O. K." Kerry led the way. "Don't drink it just yet, though. I want to show you my new combination."

"The one that washes dishes?" Fitzgerald asked. "What else does it do?"

Kerry gave the other a glass. "It won't play records."

"Oh, well. A minor matter, if it'll do the housework. Let's take a look at it." Fitzgerald went into the living room, selected "Afternoon of a Faun," and approached the radio. "It isn't plugged in."

"That doesn't matter a bit," Kerry said wildly.

"Batteries?" Fitzgerald slipped the record in place and adjusted the switches. "Now we'll see." He beamed triumphantly at Kerry. "Well? It's playing now."

It was.

Kerry said, "Try that Halvorsen piece. Here." He handed the disk to Fitzgerald, who pushed the reject switch and watched the lever arm lift.

But this time the phonograph refused to play. It didn't like "Entrance of the Boyards."

"That's funny," Fitzgerald grunted. "Probably the trouble's with the record. Let's try another."

There was no trouble with "Daphnis and Chloe." But the radio silently rejected the composer's "Bolero."

Kerry sat down and pointed to a near-by chair. "That doesn't prove anything. Come over here and watch. Don't drink anything yet. You, uh, you feel perfectly normal?"

"Sure. Well?"

Kerry took out a cigarette. The console walked across the room, picking up a match book on the way, and politely held the flame. Then it went back to its place against the wall.

Fitzgerald didn't say anything. After a while he took a cigarette from his pocket and waited. Nothing happened.

"So?" Kerry asked.

"A robot. That's the only possible answer. Where in the name of Petrarch did you get it?"

"You don't seem much surprised."

"I am, though. But I've seen robots before— Westinghouse tried it, you know. Only this—" Fitzgerald tapped his teeth with a nail. "Who made it?"

"How the devil should I know?" Kerry demanded. "The radio people, I suppose."

Fitzgerald narrowed his eyes. "Wait a minute. I don't quite understand—"

"There's nothing to understand. I bought this combination a few days ago. Turned in the old one. It was delivered this afternoon, and—" Kerry explained what had happened.

"You mean you didn't know it was a robot?"

"Exactly. I bought it as a radio. And . . . and . . . the damn thing seems almost alive to me."

"Nope." Fitzgerald shook his head, rose, and inspected the console carefully. "It's a new kind of robot. At least—" he hesitated. "What else is there to think? I suggest you get in touch with the Mideastern people tomorrow and check up."

"Let's open the cabinet and look inside," Kerry suggested.

Fitzgerald was willing, but the experiment proved impossible. The presumably wooden panels weren't screwed into place, and there was no apparent way of opening the console. Kerry found a screwdriver and applied it, gingerly at first, then with a sort of repressed fury. He could neither pry free a panel nor even scratch the dark, smooth finish of the cabinet.

"Damn!" he said finally. "Well, your guess is as good as mine. It's a robot. Only I didn't know they could make 'em like this. And why in a radio?"

"Don't ask me," Fitzgerald shrugged. "Check up tomorrow. That's the first step. Naturally I'm pretty baffled. If a new sort of specialized robot has been invented, why put it in a console? And what makes those legs move? There aren't any casters."

"I've been wondering about that, too."

"When it moves, the legs look—rubbery. But they're not. They're hard as . . . as hardwood. Or plastic."

"I'm afraid of the thing," Kerry said.

"Want to stay at my place tonight?"

"N-no. No. I guess not. The—robot—can't hurt me."

"I don't think it wants to. It's been helping you, hasn't it?"

"Yeah," Kerry said, and went off to mix another drink.

The rest of the conversation was inconclusive. Fitzgerald, several hours later, went home rather worried. He wasn't as casual as he had pretended, for the sake of Kerry's nerves. The impingement of something so entirely unexpected on normal life was subtly frightening. And yet, as he had said, the robot didn't seem menacing—

Kerry went to bed, with a new detective mystery. The radio followed him into the bedroom and gently took the book out of his hand. Kerry instinctively snatched for it.

"Hey!" he said. "What the devil—"

The radio went back into the living room. Kerry followed, in time to see the book replaced on the shelf. After a bit Kerry retreated, locking his door, and slept uneasily till dawn.

In dressing gown and slippers, he stumbled out to stare at the console. It was back in its former place, looking as though it had never moved. Kerry, rather white around the gills, made breakfast.

He was allowed only one cup of coffee. The radio appeared, reprovingly took the second cup from his hand, and emptied it into the sink.

That was quite enough for Kerry Westerfield. He found his hat and topcoat and almost ran out of the house. He had a horrid feeling that the radio might follow him, but it didn't, luckily for his sanity. He was beginning to be worried.

During the morning he found time to telephone Mideastern. The salesman knew nothing. It was a standard model combination—the latest. If it wasn't giving satisfaction, of course, he'd be glad to—

"It's O. K.," Kerry said. "But who made the thing? That's what I want to find out."

"One moment, sir." There was a delay. "It came from Mr. Lloyd's department. One of our foremen."

"Let me speak to him, please."

But Lloyd wasn't very helpful. After much thought, he remembered that the combination had been placed in the stock room without a serial number. It had been added later.

"But who *made* it?"

"I just don't know. I can find out for you, I guess. Suppose I ring you back."

"Don't forget," Kerry said, and went back to his class. The lecture on the Venerable Bede wasn't too successful.

At lunch he saw Fitzgerald, who seemed relieved when Kerry came over to his table. "Find out any more about your pet robot?" the psychology professor demanded.

No one else was within hearing. With a sigh Kerry sat down and lit a cigarette. "Not a thing. It's a pleasure to be able to do this myself." He drew smoke into his lungs. "I phoned the company."

"And?"

"They don't know anything. Except that it didn't have a serial number."

"That may be significant," Fitzgerald said.

Kerry told the other about the incidents of the book and the coffee, and Fitzgerald squinted thoughtfully at his milk. "I've given you some psych tests. Too much stimulation isn't good for you."

"A detective yarn!"

"Carrying it a bit to extremes, I'll admit. But I can understand why the robot acted that way—though I dunno how it managed it." He hesitated. "Without intelligence, that is."

"Intelligence?" Kerry licked his lips. "I'm not so sure that it's just a machine. And I'm not crazy."

"No, you're not. But you say the robot was in the front room. How could it tell what you were reading?"

"Short of X-ray vision and superfast scanning and assimilative powers, I can't imagine. Perhaps it doesn't want me to read anything."

"You've said something," Fitzgerald grunted. "Know much about theoretical—machines—of that type?"

"Robots?"

"Purely theoretical. Your brain's a colloid, you know. Compact, complicated—but slow. Suppose you work out a gadget with a multi-million radioatom unit embedded in an insulating material—the result is a brain, Kerry. A brain with a tremendous number of units interacting at light-velocity speeds. A radio tube adjusts current flow when it's operating at forty million separate signals a second. And—theoretically—a radioatomic brain of the type I've mentioned could include perception, recognition, consideration, reaction and adjustment in a hundred-thousandth of a second."

"Theory."

"I've thought so. But I'd like to find out where your radio came from."

A page came over. "Telephone call for Mr. Westerfield."

Kerry excused himself and left. When he returned, there was a puzzled frown knitting his dark brows. Fitzgerald looked at him inquiringly.

"Guy named Lloyd, at the Mideastern plant. I was talking to him about the radio."

"Any luck?"

Kerry shook his head. "No. Well, not much. He didn't know who had built the thing."

"But it was built in the plant?"

"Yes. About two weeks ago—but there's no record of who worked on it. Lloyd seemed to think that was very, very funny. If a radio's built in the plant, they *know* who put it together."

"So?"

"So nothing. I asked him how to open the cabinet, and he said it was easy. Just unscrew the panel in back."

"There aren't any screws," Fitzgerald said.

"I know."

They looked at one another.

Fitzgerald said, "I'd give fifty bucks to find out whether that robot was really built only two weeks ago."

"Why?"

"Because a radioatomic brain would need training. Even in such matters as the lighting of a cigarette."

"It saw me light one."

"And followed the example. The dish-washing—hm-m-m. Induction, I suppose. If that gadget has been trained, it's a robot. If it hasn't—" Fitzgerald stopped.

Kerry blinked. "Yes?"

"I don't know what the devil it is. It bears the same relation to a robot that we bear to *eohippus*. One thing I do know, Kerry; it's very probable that no scientist today has the knowledge it would take to make a . . . a thing like that."

"You're arguing in circles," Kerry said. "It was made."

"Uh-huh. But how—when—and by whom? That's what's got me worried."

"Well, I've a class in five minutes. Why not come over tonight?"

"Can't. I'm lecturing at the Hall. I'll phone you after, though."

With a nod Kerry went out, trying to dismiss the matter from his mind. He succeeded pretty well. But dining alone in a restaurant that night, he began to feel a general unwillingness to go home. A hobgoblin was waiting for him.

"Brandy," he told the waiter. "Make it double."

Two hours later a taxi let Kerry out at his door. He was remarkably drunk. Things swam before his eyes. He walked unsteadily toward the porch, mounted the steps with exaggerated care, and let himself into the house.

He switched on a lamp.

The radio came forward to meet him. Tentacles, thin, but strong as metal, coiled gently around his body, holding him motionless. A pang of violent fear struck through Kerry. He struggled desperately and tried to yell, but his throat was dry.

From the radio panel a beam of yellow light shot out, blinding the man. It swung down, aimed at his chest. Abruptly a queer taste was perceptible under Kerry's tongue.

After a minute or so, the ray clicked out, the tentacles flashed back out of sight, and the console returned to its corner. Kerry staggered weakly to a chair and relaxed, gulping.

He was sober. Which was quite impossible. Fourteen brandies infiltrate a definite amount of alcohol into the system. One can't wave a magic wand and instantly reach a state of sobriety. Yet that was exactly what had happened.

The—robot—was trying to be helpful. Only Kerry would have preferred to remain drunk.

He got up gingerly and sidled past the radio to the bookshelf. One eye on the combination, he took down the detective novel he had tried to read on the preceding night. As he had expected, the radio took it from his hand and replaced it on the shelf. Kerry, remembering Fitzgerald's words, glanced at his watch. Reaction time, four seconds.

He took down a Chaucer and waited, but the radio didn't stir. However, when Kerry found a history volume, it was gently removed from his fingers. Reaction time, six seconds.

Kerry located a history twice as thick.

Reaction time, ten seconds.

Uh-huh. So the robot did read the books. That meant X-ray vision and superswift reactions. Jumping Jehoshaphat!

Kerry tested more books, wondering what the criterion was. "Alice in Wonderland" was snatched from his hand; Millay's poems were not. He made a list, with two columns, for future reference.

The robot, then, was not merely a servant. It was a censor. But what was the standard of comparison?

After a while he remembered his lecture tomorrow, and thumbed through his notes. Several points needed verification. Rather hesitantly he located the necessary reference book—and the robot took it away from him.

"Wait a minute," Kerry said. "I need that." He tried to pull the volume out of the tentacle's grasp, without success. The console paid no attention. It calmly replaced the book on its shelf.

Kerry stood biting his lip. This was a bit too much. The damned robot was a monitor. He sidled toward the book, snatched it, and was out in the hall before the radio could move.

The thing was coming after him. He could hear the soft padding of its . . . its feet. Kerry scurried into the bedroom and locked the door. He waited, heart thumping, as the knob was tried gently.

A wire-thin cilia crept through the crack of the door and fumbled with the key. Kerry suddenly jumped forward and shoved the auxiliary bolt into position. But that didn't help, either. The robot's precision tools—the specialized antenna—slid it back; and then the console opened the door, walked into the room, and came toward Kerry.

He felt a touch of panic. With a little gasp he threw the book at the thing, and it caught it deftly. Apparently that was all that was wanted, for the radio turned and went out, rocking awkwardly on its rubbery legs, carrying the forbidden volume. Kerry cursed quietly.

The phone rang. It was Fitzgerald.
"Well? How'd you make out?"

"Have you got a copy of Cassen's 'Social Literature of the Ages'?"

"I don't think so—no. Why?"

"I'll get it in the University library tomorrow, then." Kerry explained what had happened. Fitzgerald whistled softly.

"Interfering, is it? Hm-m-m. I wonder—"

"I'm afraid of the thing."

"I don't think it means you any harm. You say it sobered you up?"

"Yeah. With a light ray. That isn't very logical."

"It might be. The vibrationary equivalent of thiamin chloride."

"Light?"

"There's vitamin content in sunlight, you know. That isn't the important point. It's censoring your reading—and apparently it reads the books, with superfast reactions. That gadget, whatever it is, isn't merely a robot."

"You're telling me," Kerry said grimly. "It's a Hitler."

Fitzgerald didn't laugh. Rather soberly, he suggested, "Suppose you spend the night at my place?"

"No," Kerry said, his voice stubborn. "No so-and-so radio's going to chase me out of my house. I'll take an ax to the thing first."

"We-ell—you know what you're doing, I suppose. Phone me if . . . if anything happens."

"O. K.," Kerry said, and hung up. He went into the living room and eyed the radio coldly. What the devil was it—and what was it trying to do? Certainly it wasn't merely a robot. Equally certainly, it wasn't alive, in the sense that a colloid brain is alive.

Lips thinned, he went over and fiddled with the dials and switches. A swing band's throbbing erratic tempo came from the console. He tried the short-wave band—nothing unusual there. So?

So nothing. There was no answer.

After a while he went to bed.

At luncheon the next day he brought Cassen's "Social Literature" to show Fitzgerald.

"What about it?"

"Look here," Kerry flipped the pages and indicated a passage. "Does this mean anything to you?"

Fitzgerald read it. "Yeah. The point seems to be that individualism is necessary for the production of literature. Right?"

Kerry looked at him. "I don't know."

"Eh?"

"My mind goes funny."

Fitzgerald rumpled his gray hair, narrowing his eyes and watching the other man intently. "Come again. I don't quite—"

With angry patience, Kerry said, "This morning I went into the library and looked at this reference. I read it all right. But it didn't mean anything to me. Just words. Know how it is when you're fagged out and have been reading a lot? You'll run into a sentence with a lot of subjunctive clauses, and it doesn't percolate. Well, it was like that."

"Read it now," Fitzgerald said quietly, thrusting the book across the table.

Kerry obeyed, looking up with a wry smile. "No good."

"Read it aloud. I'll go over it with you, step by step."

But that didn't help. Kerry seemed utterly unable to assimilate the sense of the passage.

"Semantic block, maybe," Fitzgerald said, scratching his ear. "Is this the first time it's happened?"

"Yes . . . no. I don't know."

"Got any classes this afternoon? Good. Let's run over to your place."

Kerry thrust away his plate. "All right. I'm not hungry. Whenever you're ready—"

Half an hour later they were looking at the radio. It seemed quite harmless. Fitzgerald wasted some time trying to pry a panel off, but finally gave it up as a bad job. He found pencil and paper, seated himself opposite Kerry, and began to ask questions.

At one point he paused. "You didn't mention that before."

"Forgot it, I guess."

Fitzgerald tapped his teeth with the pencil. "Hm-m-m. The first time the radio acted up—"

"It hit me in the eye with a blue light—"

"Not that. I mean—what it said."

Kerry blinked. "What *it* said?" He hesitated. " 'Psychology pattern checked and noted,' or something like that. I thought I'd tuned in on some station and got part of a quiz program or something. You mean—"

"Were the words easy to understand? Good English?"

"No, now that I remember it," Kerry scowled. "They were slurred quite a lot. Vowels stressed."

"Uh-huh. Well, let's get on." They tried a word-association test.

Finally Fitzgerald leaned back, frowning. "I want to check this stuff with the last tests I gave you a few months ago. It looks funny to me—damned funny. I'd feel a lot better if I knew exactly what memory was. We've done considerable work on mnemonics—artificial memory. Still, it may not be that at all."

"Eh?"

"That—machine. Either it's got an artificial memory, has been highly trained, or else it's adjusted to a different *milieu* and culture. It has affected you—quite a lot."

Kerry licked dry lips. "How?"

"Implanted blocks in your mind. I haven't correlated them yet. When I do, we may be able to figure out some sort of answer. No, that thing isn't a robot. It's a lot more than that."

Kerry took out a cigarette; the console walked across the room and lit it for him. The two men watched with a faint shrinking horror.

"You'd better stay with me tonight," Fitzgerald suggested.

"No," Kerry said. He shivered.

The next day Fitzgerald looked for Kerry at lunch, but the younger man did not appear. He telephoned the house, and Martha answered the call.

"Hello! When did you get back?"

"Hello, Fitz. About an hour ago. My sister went ahead and had her baby without me—so I came back." She stopped, and Fitzgerald was alarmed at her tone.

"Where's Kerry?"

"He's here. Can you come over, Fitz? I'm worried."

"What's the matter with him?"

"I . . . I don't know. Come right away."

"O. K.," Fitzgerald said, and hung up, biting his lips. He was worried. When, a short while later, he rang the Westerfield bell, he discovered that his nerves were badly out of control. But sight of Martha reassured him.

He followed her into the living room. Fitzgerald's glance went at once to the console, which was unchanged; and then to Kerry, seated motionless by a window. Kerry's face had a blank, dazed look. His pupils were dilated, and he seemed to recognize Fitzgerald only slowly.

"Hello, Fitz," he said.

"How do you feel?"

Martha broke in. "Fitz, what's wrong? Is he sick? Shall I call the doctor?"

Fitzgerald sat down. "Have you noticed anything funny about that radio?"

"No. Why?"

"Then listen." He told the whole story, watching incredulity struggle with reluctant belief on Martha's face. Presently she said, "I can't quite—"

"If Kerry takes out a cigarette, the thing will light it for him. Want to see how it works?"

"N-no. Yes. I suppose so." Martha's eyes were wide.

Fitzgerald gave Kerry a cigarette. The expected happened.

Martha didn't say a word. When the console had returned to its place, she shivered and went over to Kerry. He looked at her vaguely.

"He needs a doctor, Fitz."

"Yes." Fitzgerald didn't mention that a doctor might be quite useless.

"What is that thing?"

"It's more than a robot. And it's been readjusting Kerry. I told you what's happened. When I checked Kerry's psychology patterns, I found that they'd altered. He's lost most of his initiative."

"Nobody on earth could have made that—"

Fitzgerald scowled. "I thought of that. It seems to be the product of a well-developed culture, quite different from ours. Martian, perhaps. It's such a specialized thing that it naturally fits into a complicated culture. But I do not understand why it looks exactly like a Mideastern console radio."

Martha touched Kerry's hand. "Camouflage?"

"But why? You were one of my best pupils in psych, Martha. Look at this logically. Imagine a civilization where a gadget like that has its place. Use inductive reasoning."

"I'm trying to. I can't think very well. Fitz, I'm worried about Kerry."

"I'm all right," Kerry said.

Fitzgerald put his fingertips together. "It isn't a radio so much as a monitor. In this other civilization, perhaps every man has one, or maybe only a few—the ones who need it. It keeps them in line."

"By destroying initiative?"

Fitzgerald made a helpless gesture. "I don't know! It worked that way in Kerry's case. In others—I don't know."

Martha stood up. "I don't think we should talk any more. Kerry needs a doctor. After that we can decide upon that." She pointed to the console.

Fitzgerald said, "It'd be rather a shame to wreck it, but—" His look was significant.

The console moved. It came out from its corner with a sidling, rocking gait and walked toward Fitzgerald. As he sprang up, the whip-like tentacles flashed out and seized him. A pale ray shone into the man's eyes.

Almost instantly it vanished; the tentacles withdrew, and the radio returned to its place. Fitzgerald stood motionless. Martha was on her feet, one hand at her mouth.

"Fitz!" Her voice shook.

He hesitated. "Yes? What's the matter?"

"Are you hurt? What did it do to you?"

Fitzgerald frowned a little. "Eh? Hurt? I don't—"

"The radio. What did it do?"

He looked toward the console. "Something wrong with it? Afraid I'm not much of a repair man, Martha."

"Fitz." She came forward and gripped his arm. "Listen to me." Quick words spilled from her mouth. The radio. Kerry. Their discussion—

Fitzgerald looked at her blankly, as though he didn't quite understand. "I guess I'm stupid today. I can't quite understand what you're talking about."

"The radio—you know! You said it changed Kerry—" Martha paused, staring at the man.

Fitzgerald was definitely puzzled. Martha was acting strangely. Queer! He'd always considered her a pretty level-headed girl. But now she was talking nonsense. At least, he couldn't figure out the meaning of her words—there was no sense to them.

And why was she talking about the radio? Wasn't it satisfactory? Kerry had said it was a good buy, with a fine tone and the latest gadgets in it. Fitzgerald wondered, for a fleeting second, if Martha had gone crazy.

In any case, he was late for his class. He said so. Martha didn't try to stop him when he went out. She was pale as chalk.

Kerry took out a cigarette. The radio walked over and held a match.

"Kerry!"

"Yes, Martha?" His voice was dead.

She stared at the . . . the radio. Mars? Another world—another civilization? What was it? What did it want? What was it trying to do?

Martha let herself out of the house and went to the garage. When she returned, a small hatchet was gripped tightly in her hand.

Kerry watched. He saw Martha walk over to the radio and lift the hatchet. Then a beam of light shot out, and Martha vanished. A little dust floated up in the afternoon sunlight.

"Destruction of life-form threatening attack," the radio said, slurring the words together.

Kerry's brain turned over. He felt sick, dazed and horribly empty. Martha—

His mind—churned. Instinct and emotion fought with something that smothered them. Abruptly the dams crumbled, and the blocks were gone, the barriers down. Kerry cried out hoarsely, inarticulately, and sprang to his feet.

"Martha!" he yelled.

She was gone. Kerry looked around. Where—

What had happened? He couldn't remember.

He sat down in the chair again, rubbing his forehead. His free hand brought up a cigarette, an automatic reaction that brought instant response. The radio walked forward and held a lighted match ready.

Kerry made a choking, sick sound and flung himself out of the chair. He remembered now. He picked up the hatchet and sprang toward the console, teeth bared in a mirthless rictus.

Again the light beam flashed out.

Kerry vanished. The hatchet thudded onto the carpet.

The radio walked back to its place and stood motionless once more. A faint clicking proceeded from its radioatomic brain.

"Subject basically unsuitable," it said, after a moment. "Elimination has been necessary." Click! "Preparation for next subject completed."

Click.

"We'll take it," the boy said.

"You won't be making a mistake," smiled the rental agent. "It's quiet, isolated, and the price is quite reasonable."

"Not so very," the girl put in. "But it is just what we've been looking for."

The agent shrugged. "Of course an unfurnished place would run less. But—"

"We haven't been married long enough to get any furniture," the boy grinned. He put an arm around his wife. "Like it, hon?"

"Hm-m-m. Who lived here before?"

The agent scratched his cheek. "Let's see. Some people named

Westerfield, I think. It was given to me for listing just about a week ago. Nice place. If I didn't own my own house, I'd jump at it myself."

"Nice radio," the boy said. "Late model, isn't it?" He went over to examine the console.

"Come along," the girl urged. "Let's look at the kitchen again."

"O. K., hon."

They went out of the room. From the hall came the sound of the agent's smooth voice, growing fainter. Warm afternoon sunlight slanted through the windows.

For a moment there was silence. Then—

Click!

TIME-TRAVEL HAPPENS!

by

A. M. PHILLIPS

Despite the incredible happenings with which it is concerned, this is a fact article. According to the evidence furnished, time travel, at least involuntary time travel, is possible. The experience of the Misses Moberly and Jourdain has been checked by every test that skeptical science can offer. As Mr. Phillips remarks, the evidence against their being deliberate liars, or victims of collective hallucination, "seems to surmount all reasonable objection." It would appear, then, that all theories of time travel have an undeniable basis of fact. When will such theories be translated into practical accomplishment?

*

IS IT possible that two women of the twentieth century have literally, physically, walked in the France of 1789? If the evidence of two English ladies may be believed, they have seen and spoken to people of the eighteenth century! They have known the actual landscape of that vanished period—and walked across a bridge that has not been in existence for more than a hundred years!

The account of this visit to the year 1789 is one of the most astounding records of human experience I have ever encountered. And almost as thrilling is the story of the long years of research, the slow compilation of hard, unemotional facts, which, piled like brick upon brick, builds a wall of objective evidence that seems irrefutable.

Miss C. Anne E. Moberly became first principal of St. Hugh's College at Oxford in 1886. She resigned in 1915.

Miss Eleanor F. Jourdain was vice principal for some years, and succeeded Miss Moberly as head of the college. She was an M. A. of Oxford, and a doctor of the University of Paris. Her knowledge of the French language was so extensive that her services were requested by the government during the war. She died in 1924.

These are the two ladies who testify to this remarkable story—ladies whose intelligence and character are unquestioned. Of the care with which they examined and substantiated each point of their experience, you shall judge for yourself.

Miss Moberly and Miss Jourdain visited Versailles on August 10, 1901. They were residing in Paris at the time—Miss Moberly as the guest of Miss Jourdain—and were making expeditions to the various places of historical interest in the neighborhood. Neither lady had visited Versailles or the Trianon before; this was their first visit. They thought it might be a "dull expedition"!

While at Versailles, they decided to visit the Petit Trianon, a villa in the park at Versailles, which was a favorite resort of Marie Antoinette.

Although it had been hot all week, August 10th was pleasant—the sky overcast, hiding the strong sun, and a wind blowing. Leaving the palace at Versailles, they walked past the Grand Trianon, and came upon a drive that, had they known it, would have taken them directly to the building they sought. Instead, they crossed this drive and followed a lane. The course they took led through the gardens to the rear of the building.

Their preternatural experience probably began on this lane. It was here they saw a plow, among other farm implements lying about near some buildings. It was here, too, that they inquired of two men directions to the Trianon. These men, who appeared to be guards of some sort, were dressed in green uniforms and wore three-cornered hats. They directed the ladies to proceed along a path, straight forward.

As they walked along the path, both became conscious of an inexplicable depression of spirits. Together with this feeling of depression, the landscape became eerily unnatural—windless, shadowless, and deeply silent. This impression of utter loneliness, and of deep stillness and silence, was one of the strongest features of their experience. And loneliness, stillness, a museumlike silence, form a background that might be expected by those who wander through the untraveled glades of Time, a century back.

At the end of the path they followed, where it was crossed by an-

other, they encountered a thick woods. Set in among the trees, in
the indefinable gloom they made, was a small, circular, roofed building with a number of pillars and a low wall. Miss Moberly called it
"a light garden kiosk," and it is this name—kiosk—that is applied
to it throughout.

Seated, either near the kiosk or upon its steps, was a man of particularly evil countenance. His face was pock-marked, and his expression so repulsive that the ladies were genuinely alarmed. He wore
a dark, heavy cloak and a large, slouch hat—clothes that seemed those
of another period. As they approached he turned his head slowly
toward them.

They heard with relief the sound of someone running toward them.
Turning, they found another, younger man close behind them. He
was flushed with exertion, and very much excited. His clothes were
of the kind worn by the man by the kiosk; the dark cloak was wrapped
about him, with one end flying behind in the wind caused by his
haste. He was speaking to them in a voice made breathless by hurry,
and in the midst of a long sentence, most of which they lost, they
caught the words, "—cherchez la maison," and instructions to go to
the right.

They were surprised both by his insistence and excitement, but
went as he directed, crossing a small bridge by a tiny waterfall that
descended on the right so close they could have wetted their hands
in it. Beyond, they passed a meadow bordered by trees, and came
within sight of the house.

At this point the two ladies were in the English garden, to the
north of the house. A woman was seen here by Miss Moberly, but
not by Miss Jourdain. Miss Moberly gives a very detailed description
of her dress and appearance, which, like the men encountered, suggested a long-gone year. She was sitting, apparently upon a camp stool,
near the house, and appeared to be sketching the trees before her,
for she had a sheet of paper in her hand. As the two visitors passed
her she turned the paper so that its face could not be seen, and glanced
up at them. Miss Moberly saw her again from behind, and confirmed
her description of the woman's clothing.

They went up onto the terrace about the house and were approaching an unshuttered window when a man emerged from the doorway
of a chapel standing close by. He called to them, and told them they
must enter the house from the front. Guiding them down through
the French gardens, on the west side of the house, it seemed to the
two ladies that he regarded them with concealed amusement. He led

them to an entrance to the drive. And with that Miss Moberly and Miss Jourdain stepped back into the twentieth century.

They joined a French wedding party in the front entrance hall, and were conducted with them through the building. The feeling of unnaturalness and depression vanished; but not, says Miss Jourdain, until they had actually reached the front entrance to the Petit Trianon. Following the tour of the building they took a carriage and drove back to Versailles.

Upon their return to Paris the two ladies discussed their experience, and wondered about the strange persons they had encountered, and the weird feeling of oppression they both acknowledged to have known. But it wasn't until three months later, in November, they discovered that Miss Moberly had seen the woman outside the house and Miss Jourdain had not. Convinced then their experience had been no ordinary one, they determined to write separate reports of the expedition to the Petit Trianon, and to investigate the history of the locale.

The description I have given of this expedition is a condensation of these reports. The original statements, written and signed by the two ladies, are preserved in the Bodleian Library, at Oxford, England, together with the written testimony of more than twenty persons who had heard the ladies describe the Gardens as they had seen them before it was known that there was anything unusual in the descriptions.

In this library, also, are Miss Jourdain's notebooks, in which the daily results of her researches were noted, and all the original letters which were exchanged by the ladies during the investigation.

It was toward the identification of the persons they had seen that the early investigations were directed. Beginning with the two guards' who had first given them directions, each of these persons—their clothing, their appearance—was investigated down to the minutest detail, even to the stockings worn by the guards.

Informed persons at Versailles told the ladies it was impossible they could have seen guards dressed in green at the Trianon, unless the men were masqueraders, for green was royal livery, worn by no attendants at the Trianon of this century. But that green liveries had been worn there in the past was established beyond question.

So with the others. In all, they had encountered eight persons, but never more than two at a time. These persons, they learned through years of research, were attired in the morning costume of the closing years of the eighteenth century. "We have never," say the authors, eerily, "seen them exactly portrayed in any pictures of the costumes of that period." It is weirdly like talking to a being from that Past; an observer aware of the minute discrepancies which must have crept into all our histories, into all our picturizations of things of the Past.

On the day of January 2, 1902, Miss Jourdain went again to Versailles, her second visit. She went directly to the Temple de l'Amour, and ascertained that it was *not* the building—the kiosk—seen on their first visit. From here she went on to the Hamlet, a group of cottages and farm buildings situated near a lake. On her way to the Hamlet she again became conscious of the strange feeling of oppression which had been so marked a characteristic of the first visit to the Gardens. Miss Jourdain says it was as though she "had crossed a line and was suddenly in a circle of influence." That statement is potently significant. Does, or did, some strange, time-bridging extra dimension offer a threshold to this time, this place, in the Gardens of the Trianon?

At the Hamlet itself the feeling of gloom was very strong. After leaving the Hamlet she entered a thick woods, set with a multitude of paths, in which Miss Jourdain wandered for some time. She heard voices speaking in French, and the faint music of stringed instruments, a few bars of which she was able to write from memory afterward. Authorities later recognized in these bars the idiom of the late eighteenth and early nineteenth centuries.

A gardener gave her directions, and when she had returned to Versailles she inquired about the music, and was informed that no band had played in the Gardens that day. No such gardener as she had seen was employed in the Trianon of the present.

During the next two years Miss Jourdain made several visits to the Trianon, and never was she able to find the paths they had followed in 1901, nor even the woods in which she had wandered and heard the music!

Of this she informed Miss Moberly, and on July 4, 1904, the two friends returned again to the Gardens of the Trianon, set upon finding the paths they had followed on their memorable first visit.

They were utterly unsuccessful. Paths, buildings, bridge, woods, were gone, vanished, replaced by a new and different topography! The landscape they had seen—if it ever had existed—existed no longer!

Their bewilderment can be imagined. What more uncanny sensation than to find the supposedly stable earth fluctuant, shifting, insecure, or to see such solid things as trees, hills, buildings, vanish into nothing, and leave less trace than last year's leaves? Even though she had been prepared for this change by the letters of her friend, Miss Moberly was shaken and astonished. She had not, she says, "expected such complete disillusionment."

And so their investigations turned from the people seen to the landscape itself, and the research into historical topography which was to last for years began. In the face of the most contradictory evidence, and against the statements of authorities, they persisted that their descriptions were accurate. And slowly, piece by piece, they proved that each feature of the landscape as they remembered it had at one time existed!

Evidence on more than seventy points of minute historical detail, concerned primarily with alteration and rearrangement of the land surface, was assembled, substantiating in full the descriptions of the Gardens given by Miss Moberly and Miss Jourdain in 1901—but placing the Gardens as they described them in the year 1789!

This second adventure, although not as thrilling as that walk through the Gardens of the Trianon in 1901, is, in one way, just as important. Its results, the evidence so slowly compiled and so unanswerable, make of that walk something more than an intriguing story; make of it a startling question, challenging all man's knowledge, all the boundaries and limits he has set about the universe, and about reality. It is a signpost, lettered in a language we do not know, and pointing into the dark night of the unknown.

The papers dealing with their adventure, and with the subsequent historical research, are preserved, as has been said, in the Bodleian Library. At the Archives Nationales and the Bibliothèque Nationale, where these researches were conducted, are the dates of each of Miss Jourdain's visits, and her signature on each occasion.

This evidence, vouched for by these institutions, answers the questions of those who ask what proof there is that the "vision" preceded the investigation, and of those who suggest that, after learning through research or by conversation some detail of the topography of the Trianon Gardens, the ladies unconsciously believed themselves to be remembering those details from the occasion of their walk in the Gardens in 1901. Such a theory is utterly inconsistent with the documents which these institutions possess.

Another theory advanced was that Miss Moberly and Miss Jourdain had seen actors in costume for a fête, or a motion picture, for which the Gardens were a setting.

The two ladies investigated this possibility thoroughly, entering into correspondence with film companies, and examining the available records. M. Pératé, coadjutator at Versailles, informed them there had been a fête, in June, 1901. Miss Jourdain checked this in the Day-book of Permissions. No fête had been held in August, 1901, nor had any photographs been taken in that month. Those photographs taken in June were taken at the Hamlet, in a different part of the Gardens. M. Pératé's letter, definitely asserting the fact that no photographs were taken in August, 1901, is with the other papers at the Bodleian.

With characteristic thoroughness the two friends did not rest with this, but sought confirmation from the photographers of Paris, who assured them that no photographs had, to their knowledge, been taken in the Trianon Gardens on August 10, 1901.

A writer in *Chamber's Journal* asserted that Pathé was making a picture in the Gardens on that day. Pathé was queried. They replied, giving the date the picture was made—January 24, 1910. Nine years later.

But such a theory makes no attempt to explain the landscape the ladies had seen on that first visit, and which the evidence assembled through the years seems to prove conclusively was the landscape of 1789.

This evidence is mustered with painstaking care. For each smallest item a reference to some authority, frequently to several separate authorities, is given. There is not space here for a detailed examination of this evidence, but a number of points are so startling and significant that I feel they deserve inclusion.

One of the most interesting features is the story of the two maps. The only known map of the Trianon of 1789 was La Motte's copy of Mique's original. (Mique was landscape gardener for Marie Antoinette. He was guillotined in 1794.) By La Motte's map some features of the landscape were not located at the points where the ladies remembered to have seen them. Apparently the descriptions of Miss Moberly and Miss Jourdain were incorrect. But in 1903 Mique's original map was discovered—*and it placed each of these features just where the ladies had seen them in 1901!* La Motte's map had been incorrect. (Mique's original map was found thrust into the chimney of a house in Montmorency. It was uncovered when the chimney, of which it formed a part of the stuffing, was cleared.)

Besides this map, which depicted the bridge they had crossed—

and which authorities assured them had never existed—the two friends discovered, in 1908, protruding from a rock located within the area wherein they remembered the bridge to have been, two "peculiar projections"—which might have formed the supports for a small bridge.

Mique's map also established the kiosk at the spot the ladies had encountered it, and they finally discovered in the French National Archives an estimate of the cost of such a kiosk, and the actual sum paid for its erection. Further, Miss Jourdain discovered in the Gardens a part of a broken column, half buried in a tree growing around it!

Then there was the mystery of what the two ladies call "the chapel man." As they remembered it, and wrote of it in their records, he walked directly to them from a door in the chapel to the point at which they were standing on the terrace around the main building of the Little Trianon. As these buildings are related today, that would be impossible. To go from one to the other it would be necessary to descend a flight of steps, cross a lawn, and ascend a second flight of steps to the terrace.

But in 1910 the fact was established that there had at one time existed a covered passage from the house to the chapel. The roof of this passage had formed a terrace joining the terrace about the house to the small terrace outside the chapel door.

This chapel is today in a ruinous condition. The door used by the "chapel man" is reached from the inside only by a staircase which has been completely broken down since about 1885. In 1907 a guide told Miss Jourdain that the doors of the chapel had not been opened for fifteen years.

The "chapel man" was definitely conscious of the presence of the two ladies. He not only addressed them, and escorted them out to the drive, but also regarded them, they thought, inquisitively, and with amusement. At what was he amused? Their clothes? Their speech? Did he, perhaps, return to his chapel and tell of the two odd visitors to the Gardens, English by their accent, who spoke such a queer French, and wore such ridiculous clothing? Coming from a time more than a hundred years in the future, they must have seemed very strange to him. At any rate the man saw them.

The road leading to the drive along which the man had guided them is no longer existing. The point at which it joined the drive is now occupied by buildings, and if the ladies passed along this road in 1901 *they walked through the solid walls of the twentieth century!*

Mique's map placed the road where they remembered it, and in 1910 they found signs of an old road on the walls and the base of the buildings which now occupy the spot.

The ladies had seen, at the start of their walk in 1901, a plow lying near some farm buildings. It seemed unlikely that a plow would be part of the equipment of the Gardens. There is none there at present. But listed in the catalogue of the Trianon sale after the King's death is a plow. It was purchased by Louis XV, who had had lessons in plowing given to his grandson, the dauphin. And in a shop on the *Quai des Grand Augustins* the two investigators found an old engraving, which had never been reproduced, showing the dauphin—later Louis XVI—driving this plow. Was it the same plow which these two wanderers into another century had seen lying in the Gardens?

And so the evidence is marshaled, bit by bit. I have only briefly recounted what you may read for yourself in full in the book written by Miss Moberly and Miss Jourdain. It is entitled "An Adventure," and is well worth the attention of all possessed of an open mind. A preface by J. W. Dunne, the English physicist, discussed the theory of Serialism in relation to this adventure, and will be of interest to those equipped to follow this hypothesis of abstract and fourth dimensional Time.

In August, 1913, the two ladies walked through the grounds accompanied by two Frenchmen, one a distinguished scholar, the other a colonel of a French regiment who was an authority on the history of French uniforms. As far as the alterations permitted, they retraced the route taken in 1901.

The colonel had the ladies describe in detail the uniforms worn by the guards they had seen at the inception of their walk, and told them the description was perfectly correct for the year 1789. He also made the statement that it would have been almost impossible for them to have given this description unless they had seen these uniforms, for such information was very difficult of access, even for himself, an officer in the service.

These gentlemen checked each of the points of their story, and in many cases were able to explain the changes that had taken place, and the reason for them.

The actual pathway Miss Moberly and Miss Jourdain had followed on their first visit to the Gardens had been destroyed, they learned, by Louis Philippe when he had had the ground in that vicinity leveled.

In 1908 Miss Jourdain again experienced, for the third and last time, what we may only describe as time-travel. It was on one of her many subsequent visits to the Trianon, and happened on the lane which had first led them both back into another century. In her own words, she "knew that some indefinable change had taken place." She felt as though she "were being taken up into another condition of things quite as real as the former." (That may be an actual eyewitness' description of the experience of time-travel!) She glanced back to see the landscape of the present fading, and that of their original visit taking its place. Miss Jourdain continued as she had been going, and after leaving the lane the strangeness vanished. What if she had turned back—

One more point, which is no more than touched upon at the back of their book, seems to me pregnant with significance. In 1914 the two adventurers were visited by a family whose name is withheld. This family had lived in Versailles for two years, in 1907 and 1908. They, too, had inexplicable experiences in the Gardens of the Trianon— they found the topography and the light so frequently eerie and disturbing that it finally got on their nerves to such an extent that they departed.

This family had seen some of the landscape features described by Miss Moberly and Miss Jourdain, and were able to locate them accurately on a map of the Gardens.

But, more than this, this family reported a "curious hissing sound —and a vibration in the air," which to them suggested an electrical field. Upon hearing this, the authors of "An Adventure" referred to an almanac. They learned that August 10, 1901, was the date of an electric storm which had included the whole of Europe—

If you admit that these two ladies were not the victims of an hallucination, and not deliberate liars—and the evidence in their favor seems to me to surmount all objections—then a speculative vista lies before you in which no boundaries may be seen. I shall attempt no exploration here, but I would like to present one feature which might easily be overlooked.

How many others have made similar trips through time? Remember that Miss Moberly and Miss Jourdain were intellectual women, they were careful and painstaking research workers, and above all, they were alert enough to record immediately a history of their unique experience.

Now place in their position another person, ignorant, or superstitious, or merely someone who feared ridicule, and knew that such a story coming from himself would provoke nothing else. Would that story ever have been recorded, or ever published?

Although no explanation for their experience, considering the evidence, has been offered, there is no reason to believe that it could not happen to anyone—to you, perhaps. The case of the family residing in Versailles during 1907 and 1908 is an example. Perhaps others, unknown, undistinguished, keeping their secret to themselves, have also traveled in time; further back, possibly, than the authors of "An Adventure," even, it may be, into the future.

I wonder, too, why the Petit Trianon has not been the site and subject of experiments with time, in so far as the science of our day can investigate such matters; why have not the daring, who would venture into this undiscovered country of dimensional time, been drawn to it? By its record it is the pre-eminent site for such experiments, challenging the fearless.

I should also like to add, for those who may read "An Adventure," that excellent color photographs of the park at Versailles, and of the grounds of the Trianon, can be seen in the *National Geographic Magazine* for January, 1925. There clings to these scenes, it seems to me, an aura of strangeness, a shadowy suggestion of something beyond.

But that, I am sure, is because I had just read this amazing book, "the record," in the words of Edith Olivier, "of an unexplained extension of the limits of human experience—"

ROBOT'S RETURN

by

ROBERT MOORE WILLIAMS

Unhappy victim of disease, environmental changes and his own folly, man may some day perish from the earth. But those who depart always leave something of themselves behind. Then the question is: who will inherit from man? A being of his own devising? Granted these premises, we face the inexorable corollary, will the heirs want their inheritance?

*

AS THOUGH sustained by the strength of a dream, the ship floated gracefully, easily, a bare hundred feet above the surface of the planet. Overhead, slightly more than ninety million miles away, a sullen sun retreated down the dark blue sky. Its long rays fretted across the planet, washed from the low, brown hills, glinted from the jumbled mounds in the center of the valley.

The ship turned, slanted down toward the mounds, rose over them, circled, found a spot where the litter was nearly level and snuggled down to rest as though returning home after weary years spent between the stars.

Hissing from the pressure of air rushing inward, a forward lock opened.

Nine stood in the lock, staring from never-blinking eyes across the landscape—a fixed, somber gaze. Hungrily, his eyes pried among the jumbled masonry, the great blocks of white stone stained a dirty brown in places, the piles of red clay in which grass was reluctantly growing. Five, perhaps ten miles around, the piles circled, then gradually leveled off toward the low brown hills.

Behind him a voice whispered, asking a question.

"It is the same as all the others," his answer went, though the grim line of the mouth did not move. "Silence, and the wreckage of a mighty city. But nothing lives here now. The inhabitants are gone."

For a second there was silence, and then a third voice whispered. "Just as I said. We are only wasting time here. It is true that once some kind of a race lived on this planet—but certainly they were never intelligent enough to have been our ancestors."

Nine, in the lock, sighed softly. "Seven, you must remember that we have not made a complete investigation. You must also remember that we have absolutely no knowledge of our ancestors—even as to whether or not they actually existed. Our records are complete for eight thousand years, but they do not go back beyond the time when the Original Five awaked, finding themselves lying on the edge of the sea, with no knowledge of how they came to be there. Perhaps they were a special creation, for they possessed great intelligence, speedily adapting the planet to their needs, forging and constructing others to help them. Perhaps they had come there, in a ship that had sunk in the sea, from some other planet. But we have never been able to solve the problem."

Eight, silent after his first question, pressed forward, stared over Nine's shoulder.

"I am perfectly familiar with the history of our race." The edge of Seven's thinking was clear over the radio beam. "The point I make is that the little life we have seen on this planet—and little enough we have seen—has been organic, a mess of chemicals. Animals, eating each other, eating grass— Pah! I want no ancestors like that."

Slowly, Eight shook his head, the ripple of interwoven metal strands winking in the light. As if he had not heard the bickering of Seven and Nine he spoke. "For a minute, as I stood here, it seemed to me that I had been on this spot before. The low hills circling a city— Only the city has changed, and over there"—he pointed toward the east—"it seems there should be a lake, or an inlet from the ocean. But no—no—I must be mistaken." He paused, and the fixed gleam in his eyes held a touch of awe. "I spoke—I used the vocal apparatus— Now I wonder why I did that?"

"So do I," Seven's answer rasped. "You used the vocal apparatus when the radio beam is much better. I have never understood why we should equip ourselves with cumbersome apparatus for making and hearing sounds when we have a much better method of communication."

"Because," Eight answered. "Because we have always had them. The Original Five had them. I do not know why they had them, for they also had the radio beam. Perhaps they had a use for them, though what that use could have been— At any rate, we have retained them. Perhaps, some day, we will discover a use for them."

"Bah!" Seven snorted. "You are one of those inexplicable dreamers. It seems that no matter how carefully we construct the brain substance, we always get a few freaks who are unwilling to face reality, who are not sufficient in themselves, but who hunger for some day that is past—a day that never had existence. I have no sympathy with you, nor any sympathy with the Council that sent us here on this wild exploration."

"But," Nine protested, "the Council could not ignore the evidence of the old star map. The Original Five had that map, but we have never understood it, probably never would have understood it if our newly perfected telescopes had not revealed this system to us—nine planets circling a sun, the third planet a strange double system. Obviously that map is somehow a link with our unknown past."

"Nonsense. I am a realist. I face the future, not the past."

"But the future is built of material taken from the past, and how can we build securely when we do not know what our past has been? It is important to us to know whether we are descended from whatever gods there are, or whether we have evolved from some lower form. Come," Nine spoke.

The cunningly twisted strands of metal writhed and Nine stepped lithely from the lock. Eight followed, and after them came Seven, still grumbling.

Three little metal men four and a half feet tall. Two legs, two arms, two eyes, a nose, a mouth—the last two organs almost valueless survivals. For they did not need food or oxygen. The power of the bursting atom supplied them with energy. Nor did they really need the legs, for their evolution during their eight thousand years had been rapid. Seven touched the ground, glowed slightly, rose into the air and drifted after his companions. Eight and Nine used their legs. Somehow, to Eight the feel of the ground was good.

They stood on a little hill. Eight's eyes went around the horizon. The metal face did not shift or change, no flicker of emotion played over it. But in the myriad of cunning photo-cells that were the eyes, hungry lights appeared to reflect the thinking that went on in the brain substance behind.

"It's larger—larger than it looked from the air," Nine spoke, his vocal apparatus biting at the words, yet somehow reflecting the awe he felt.

"Yes," Eight answered. "All this litter that we see, all these mounds—and some of them are hundreds of feet high—are all that is left of some mighty city. Miles and miles and miles around, it stretches. How much work must have gone into it? How long must it have taken in the building? Centuries, perhaps hundreds of centuries, some race lived here, dreamed here, and dreaming built of clay and stone and steel and glass. I wonder—if they COULD have been our ancestors, our unknown forebears?"

"Nonsense!" Seven blurted.

Eight stirred, his eyes glinting uneasily as he glanced at Seven. "Perhaps it is not nonsense. I have the feeling, have had it ever since we sighted this system from the void—nine little planets clustering around a mother sun—that this is—home." His voice lingered over the word, caressed it.

"Home!" Seven echoed. "We have no meaning for the word. We are at home anywhere. And as for feeling, we have even less meaning for that word. Feeling is not logic," he finished, as if that settled everything.

"Perhaps logic has no meaning for that word," Eight retorted. "But remember that our minds are constructed according to the ancient pattern—and who knows that feeling was not a part of that pattern, a part that has come down to us?"

"I remember only that we are robots. I do not know or care about our origin. Only the future has meaning, the future in which we shall tread the paths beyond the stars."

"Robots!" Eight answered. "I even wonder where we got that name for ourselves."

"It was the name the Original Five had for themselves, just as they had a language."

"But why, among a myriad of possible sounds, should they have selected that one as their name?"

"Because—" Seven was suddenly silent. Eight felt the perturbed pulse of his thinking. Seven was trying to explain to himself why their name should be what it was. He was having a hard time doing it. The answer, somehow, went beyond the bounds of logic. Or was there no answer? But that was not logical either. There had to be an answer, a reason. Seven stirred uneasily, eyed his companions. Abruptly he lowered himself to the ground, shutting off the power that enabled him to bend gravity, as if he wanted the feel of the ground under his feet. He followed Nine over the rubble, and he used his legs.

Eight said nothing.

"What do you suppose this race looked like?" Seven awkwardly voiced the question.

Eight, gazing at the ruins, voiced the question that had been on his mind. "What happened to them? Could it happen to us?"

Seven and Nine stared at him. Seven's hand went to the heat gun swinging at his belt. Nine twisted his eyes away.

"It couldn't happen to us," Seven said flatly.

"I—hope not," Eight answered. "But something happened to the race that was here, and perhaps—"

"There is work to be done," Nine interrupted. "We must examine every inch of this area. Perhaps we may find the rusted bodies of the former inhabitants. At first, I had hoped we would find them alive, but after seeing all those deserted cities, I am afraid we will find no living intelligence. But it may be we will find records."

Slowly, under the unwinking sun overhead, they pressed forward among the ruins, Nine in the lead, then Eight, then Seven. Around them the air, stirred by the pressure of an unknown force, moved restlessly. A wind went with them, as though it, too, quested among tumbled masonry and piles of brick dust for some friend of the long-gone past. Silently, the wind went among the haunted débris. Eight felt it passing, a force touching him with a thousand invisible fingers, a force that could not be seen but only felt.

Eight stared at the ruins, wondering what manner of creatures had once moved among them. The rusted bones of the steel framework of buildings, steel that crumbled at the touch, casing stones upended, the greenish color of corrosion on copper. He tried to imagine the millions of inhabitants going about this city. He saw their glistening metal bodies moving along the streets, floating upward beside the bulk of the buildings. He saw them bringing stone and forging steel, creating a city under that yellow sun. And at night, he saw them looking up at the stars, at that strange dead satellite hovering in the black sky. He wondered if they had ever visited that satellite. They must have visited it, he decided, if not in reality, then in dreams.

And possibly the stars beyond. For the towers of their cities had pointed at the stars.

Little metal men. Slowly Eight's imagination failed him. Somehow he could not populate this silent city with little metal men. He shook his head. He could see the dream, but not the dreamers.

Nine stood in front of a pile of masonry. The rains, the heat of summer, the cold of uncounted winters, had brought down the stones from the top. Nine stared somberly at the dark opening between the tumbled blocks. He spoke. "I'm going in there."

Seven and Eight followed.

Darkness folded in around them—a stirring, whispering darkness. A beam of light flashed from Nine's forehead, smashed against the darkness, illumined the walls of what looked like a tunnel.

Under their feet the dust exploded in little gray clouds. Abruptly the tunnel widened into a circle with three other arteries branching out. Broad doors opened in the arteries, doors that now were closed. Staring, Nine pushed against one of the doors, and it crumbled with the pressure, opened into a small room that was totally bare. Nine stepped into it, and the floor crumbled. He shot down into gloom, but instantly his descent slowed as he flicked on the device that bent gravity. He hesitated, then allowed himself to float down into the darkness. His voice whispered over the radio beam and Seven and Eight followed him.

Nine looked up at them as they came down. "That little room was used to carry the former inhabitants up into the building. See, there is the mechanism. Whoever they were, they did not know how to control gravity or they would not have needed this device."

Neither Eight nor Seven answered, and Nine poked forward into the gloom, the bright beam from his light splashing from dozens of sturdy columns that supported the bulk above. His voice called and Seven and Eight moved toward him.

"Here is a machine," Nine spoke. "Or is it—one of our early life-forms?"

Eight stared at the rust-flecked wheels, the crumbling, corroded bulk of the motor housings, the gears falling away into ruin. This, a robot—! He rebelled at the thought. Yet it was hard to know where mechanism left off and robot began. The dividing line was thin. You took inanimate metal and the pressure of exploding force; you worked the metal into a thousand different parts and you confined the force; you added a brain that was in itself a force-field capable of receiving and retaining impressions—and you had a robot. You left out the brain—and you had a machine.

Seven, prying among the mechanism, whispered. "It *is* one of our primitive life-forms—one of the early upward steps. All the fundamentals of robot construction are here. Wheels turn, work is done."

"No." Eight shook his head. "A robot is more than that. This— this is only a machine, unintelligently carrying out reactions its nature set for it. I don't know what those reactions could have been, but I am certain it was not a robot. It was fixed in this place, for one thing, and, for another, I see no signs of brain control."

"A robot is a machine," Seven answered. "A logical machine. There is no doubt about it. Perhaps the control was in some other part of the building."

Nine stirred protestingly. "I—I am inclined to agree with Eight. See, this was only a pump, designed to force water, or some other liquid, through the building. Here is the pressure chamber, and this, I think, was a crude electric motor. But it was only a machine."

"We, ourselves, are only highly developed machines," Seven persisted. "Our operation can be explained purely in terms of mechanics. When you attempt to make us more than machines, you become illogical. True, this is a machine. It is also a primitive robot form, for the two terms mean the same thing. There are many links missing between it and us, but perhaps we may find those links—"

"But how?" Eight asked. "In the beginning how could lifeless, dead metal build itself into the first machine?"

Seven started to answer, hesitated, stared at Eight and then his gaze wandered off into the gloom of this cavern. His light smashed into the darkness, drove a clean channel through the murk, yet always the darkness crept in around the edges of the beam, and always, when the light moved, the darkness came back.

"I—I don't know the answer to that," Seven spoke. "Perhaps the Universe was different millions of years ago. But I don't know. Nobody knows. However, we have found one link in the chain. Maybe we will find others."

Eight kept his thinking to himself. There was little to be gained in disputing Seven. And, after all, Eight saw that Seven was right. Or partly right. Robots were machines, fundamentally. Yet they were something more than machines. Machines could not dream. In Eight's mind was the wild wonder—where had robots acquired their ability to dream? To what did that ability point?

Eight did not speak. He followed Seven and Nine. He watched, and thought.

They went out of the basement, went back to the floor where they had entered, forced their way up through the silent building. Dust, and furniture that became dust when they touched it, and corroded metal, were in the rooms above, but of the race that had lived there they found no sign.

On through the city they went. Seven crowed exultantly over the wreck of a huge bulk that had turned on its side. An engine, with eight huge driving wheels, and Seven, digging in the dust, uncovered the remnants of the track on which the wheels had run.

"Another link," Seven gloated. "A higher form, possessing the ability to move."

"But not to think," Nine still protested. "It ran on a track. There must have been another, separate intelligence guiding it."

"What of it? Perhaps so—perhaps not. Perhaps the intelligence that guided it was the final robot form." Again Seven suddenly ceased talking, and again Eight could feel the pulse of his troubled thinking. Final robot form—

"There was another, totally different life-form, here," Eight spoke slowly, marshalling his vague thoughts. "A life-form that created and used these machines. But that life has vanished, utterly, leaving no trace of itself, except the ruins of its cities, the wreckage of its machines."

"But what?" Nine gulped.

"What could have destroyed it? I have no idea. Only vaguely can I sense its existence, through the evidence that it once shaped a world to meet its needs. I have seen nothing that will give me a clue to its nature—or its death. Perhaps a new form of corrosion developed, destroying it. Perhaps— But I can't see the answer."

They moved on through the ruins. The slow sun dropped down toward the horizon. The silent wind, searching among the haunted ruins, went with them.

"Look!" Nine called.

They stood in an open space in front of a squat metallic structure that had resisted the rain and the snow. But Nine was not pointing at the building. He moved forward, bent over an object half buried in the mould.

Seven gasped. "A robot. Almost an exact model of us. Here, at last, is final proof!"

Eagerly they bent down, scraping away the soil. Quickly, they uncovered the figure. Perhaps ten feet tall, it was more than twice their size. Eight saw it was a robot. Seven had been right, after all, and here was proof. Those machines had somehow managed to develop intelligence and to evolve into sentient beings.

Somehow the crude ore had shaped and forged itself.

And yet this figure differed from the true robot form. Eight saw the difference as they uncovered it. The hopes rising in his mind failed.

"No—it isn't one of us. It's only a statue."

Cast of solid metal, covered by a thin film of corrosion, the statue lay, its feet still attached to a part of the pedestal that had served as a base from which, in some long-gone time, it had toppled. Eight stared at it, not heeding Seven's thinking which came over the radio beam. Seven was insisting that even if it was a statue—a lifeless thing —the form showed that robots had developed here. Otherwise they would not have made a statue in this shape.

Eight recognized the logic of Seven's statement, but the sight of the statue stirred again those vague rebellious thoughts, and in his mind was the feeling that the statue represented something more, that it was more than a replica of form—that it was the embodiment of an idea. But what that idea was, he could not grasp. Slender and graceful, yet with the suggestion of strength, it lay on the ground, a fallen god with head uplifted and arm outstretched. Eight's thinking became clearer. Yes, it was a fallen god, or the representation of a fallen god, and his mind went back to the builder, the designer, the artist who had dreamed of this figure and had then created in metal a figure adequate to his dreaming. The artist was gone, the statue had fallen. Eight wondered about the dream—

His turgid thinking burst into clarity like a jet of suddenly spouting water. Ever since he had seen this world from afar, especially since he had seen the wreckage of all those mighty cities, he had wondered about the dream of the race that had lived and built here. The fate of the race had never saddened him: all things rusted into ruin eventually, all material things, all logical things. Only a dream might achieve immortality, only a dream could start in slime and go onward to the end of Time. But the dream of this race—whatever that dream had been—appeared to have died. Some catastrophe had overtaken them before they had grown strong enough to forge their dream into an immortal shape. Eight sighed, and the photo-cells that were his eyes lost luster.

He did not notice that Seven and Nine had left him, were forcing an entrance into the building, until Nine's sharp call brought him to his feet.

There was only one large room, Eight saw. It had been a laboratory or a workshop. Benches, machinery, tools, were crumbling, just as everything else on this planet was crumbling, just as the dream of the race had crumbled——

Nine's voice, heavy with awe, echoed through the room.

"I—I can read it! It's our language!"

The written language of the robots, here on this forgotten planet circling an insignificant sun in a lost corner of the Universe! Eight felt the trembling pulse of currents flowing in his mind. They had found their past; they had found their ancestors. All the other evidence could be explained away, but not this.

Ancestors, forebears, those who had gone before, those who had labored to build for the benefit of some unknown descendant. Had the machine, the lever and the wheel somehow been their forebears? Or had there been an alien form preceding the machine?

A metal plate, inches thick, supported on heavy metal pillars. A tough metal, almost completely rust-resistant.

> Now Man dies. A mutant bacteriophage, vicious beyond imagination, is attacking, eating, destroying all living cells, even to dead animal matter.
>
> There is no hope of escape on Earth. The only hope is to flee from Earth. Tomorrow we blast our first rocket ship off for Mars, ourselves in suspended animation to withstand the acceleration, the ship manned by Thoradson's robots.
>
> It may be we shall live again. It may be we shall die.
>
> We go, and may God go with us.

Thus the record ended. Nine's raspy voice faded, and for a second the echoes came back from the dark corners of the room. Then there was silence. Seven shifted his feet.

"Man," he spoke. "Man. That is a word for which we have no meaning."

"Perhaps," Eight spoke softly, "perhaps it was the name of the life-form that created us."

Seven did not answer, and Nine, too, was silent. A wind came into the room, moved restlessly, and went out again. The silence held. Seven stared at the metal plate, picking out the words one by one.

"It must be you are right," he said. "See, they use the word—robot." Wonder grew in his voice, and then disgust mingled with the wonder. "An organism—an animal—— Yet obviously they must have created us, used us as slaves. They manned their ship with robots."

Eight stirred but said nothing. There was nothing to say.

"That," Nine whispered, "is why we are unable to find a link between the machine and us. They developed the machine, used it. They provided the intelligence. Finally they built machines with some kind of intelligence. It must have been late in their history, and they built very few of them. Perhaps they were afraid. There are so many links missing it is hard to know. But certainly, in a sense, they were our ancestors——"

"Yes," Eight agreed. "In a sense that seems——"

"But they started for a near-by planet," Seven protested. "Our sun is light-years distant. How did they ever get there?"

"They may have missed their aim. Or perhaps the robots rebelled and took the ship elsewhere, and, in landing smashed it, only five of them managing to escape."

"I don't believe that," Seven said. "You have no proof of it."

"No," Eight admitted. "No. We don't even know what happened to the men on the ship."

They stood again outside the building, three little metal men. Out yonder in the west the sun was dipping below the horizon. A soft dusk was coming down, hiding the barren world, and still the lonely wind was stirring in the shadows.

Eight saw the statue lying on the ground and vague thoughts stirred within his mind. "They may have eaten grass," he said. "They may have eaten the flesh of other animals; they may have been weaklings; they may have arisen out of slime, but somehow I think there was something fine about them. For they dreamed, and even if they died——"

The robot bent over. Tiny, ageless, atom-fed motors within him surged with an endless power. The robot lifted the dream of an age-dead man and set the statue back on its feet.

The three returned to their ship, and it lifted, following its path out to the stars. The proud, blind eyes of a forgotten statue seemed to follow it.

THE BLUE GIRAFFE

by

L. SPRAGUE DE CAMP

⊂⊨

There has been much theorizing of late about the possible reaction of human and/or animal genes to radioactivity caused by atomic explosion. This bizarre tale deserves attention not alone for its speculation in the field of a dangerous new science, but also for the charming denouement which makes of it a Saki-like fairy-tale.

*

ATHELSTAN CUFF was, to put it very mildly, astonished that his son should be crying. It wasn't that he had exaggerated ideas about Peter's stoicism, but the fact was that Peter never cried. He was, for a twelve-year-old boy, self-possessed to the point of grimness. And now he was undeniably sniffling. It must be something jolly well awful.

Cuff pushed aside the pile of manuscript he had been reading. He was the editor of *Biological Review*; a stoutish Englishman with prematurely white hair, prominent blue eyes, and a complexion that could have been used for painting box cars. He looked a little like a lobster who had been boiled once and was determined not to repeat the experience.

"What's wrong, old man?" he asked.

Peter wiped his eyes and looked at his father calculatingly. Cuff sometimes wished that Peter wasn't so damned rational. A spot of boyish unreasonableness would be welcome at times.

"Come on, old fella, out with it. What's the good of having a father if you can't tell him things?"

698

Peter finally got it out. "Some of the guys—" He stopped to blow his nose. Cuff winced slightly at the "guys." His one regret about coming to America was the language his son picked up. As he didn't believe in pestering Peter all the time, he had to suffer in silence.

"Some of the guys say you aren't really my father."

It had come, thought Cuff, as it was bound to sooner or later. He shouldn't have put off telling the boy for so long.

"What do you mean, old man?" he stalled.

"They say," sniff, "I'm just a 'dopted boy."

Cuff forced out, "So what?" The despised Americanism seemed to be the only thing that covered the situation.

"What do you mean, 'so what'?"

"I mean just that. What of it? It doesn't make a particle of difference to your mother or me, I assure you. So why should it to you?"

Peter thought. "Could you send me away some time, on account of I was only 'dopted?"

"Oh, so that's what's worrying you? The answer is no. Legally you're just as much our son as if . . . as anyone is anybody's son. But whatever gave you the idea we'd ever send you away? I'd like to see that chap who could get you away from us."

"Oh, I just wondered."

"Well, you can stop wondering. We don't want to, and we couldn't if we did. It's perfectly all right, I tell you. Lots of people start out as adopted children, and it doesn't make any difference to anybody. You wouldn't get upset if somebody tried to make fun of you because you had two eyes and a nose, would you?"

Peter had recovered his composure. "How did it happen?"

"It's quite a story. I'll tell you, if you like."

Peter only nodded.

"I've told you," said Athelstan Cuff, "about how before I came to America I worked for some years in South Africa. I've told you about how I used to work with elephants and lions and things, and about how I transplanted some white rhino from Swaziland to the Kruger Park. But I've never told you about the blue giraffe—"

In the 1940's the various South African governments were considering the problem of a park that would be not merely a game preserve available to tourists, but a completely wild area in which no people other than scientists and wardens would be allowed.

They finally agreed on the Okavango River Delta in Ngamiland, as the only area that was sufficiently large and at the same time thinly populated.

The reasons for its sparse population were simple enough: nobody likes to settle down in a place when he is likely to find his house and farm under three feet of water some fine morning. And it is irritating to set out to fish in a well-known lake only to find that the lake has turned into a grassy plain around the edges of which the mopane trees are already springing up.

So the Batawana, in whose reserve the Delta lay, were mostly willing to leave this capricious stretch of swamp and jungle to the elephant and the lion. The few Batawana who did live in and around the Delta were bought out and moved. The Crown Office of the Bechuanaland Protectorate got around its own rules against alienation of tribal lands by taking a perpetual lease on the Delta and surrounding territory from the Batawana, and named the whole area Jan Smuts Park.

When Athelstan Cuff got off the train at Francistown in September of 1976, a pelting spring rain was making the platform smoke. A tall black in khaki loomed out of the grayness, and said: "You are Mr. Cuff, from Cape Town? I'm George Mtengeni, the warden at Smuts. Mr. Opdyck wrote me you were coming. The Park's car is out this way."

Cuff followed. He'd heard of George Mtengeni. The man wasn't a Chwana at all, but a Zulu from near Durban. When the Park had been set up, the Batawana had thought that the warden ought to be a Tawana. But the Makoba, feeling chesty about their independence from their former masters, the Batawana, had insisted on his being one of their nation. Finally the Crown Office in disgust had hired an outsider. Mtengeni had the very dark skin and narrow nose found in so many of the Kaffir Bantu. Cuff guessed that he probably had a low opinion of the Chwana people in general and the Batawana in particular.

They got into the car. Mtengeni said: "I hope you don't mind coming way out here like this. It's too bad that you couldn't come before the rains started; the pans they are all full by now."

"So?" said Cuff. "What's the Mababe this year?" He referred to the depression known variously as Mababe Lake, Swamp, or Pan, depending on whether at a given time it contained much, little, or no water.

"The Mababe, it is a lake, a fine lake full of drowned trees and hippo. I think the Okavango is shifting north again. That means Lake Ngami it will dry up again."

"So it will. But look here, what's all this business about a blue giraffe? Your letter was dashed uninformative."

Mtengeni showed his white teeth. "It appeared on the edge of the Mopane Forest seventeen months ago. That was just the beginning. There have been other things since. If I'd told you more, you would have written the Crown Office saying that their warden was having a nervous breakdown. Me, I'm sorry to drag you into this, but the Crown Office keeps saying they can't spare a man to investigate."

"Oh, quite all right, quite," answered Cuff. "I was glad to get away from Cape Town anyway. And we haven't had a mystery since old Hickey disappeared."

"Since who disappeared? You know me, I can't keep up with things out in the wilds."

"Oh, that was many years ago. Before your time, or mine for that matter. Hickey was a scientist who set out into the Kalahari with a truck and a Xosa assistant, and disappeared. Men flew all over the Kalahari looking for him, but never found a trace, and the sand had blown over his tire tracks. Jolly odd, it was."

The rain poured down steadily as they wallowed along the dirt road. Ahead, beyond the gray curtain, lay the vast plains of northern Bechuanaland with their great pans. And beyond the plains were, allegedly, a blue giraffe, and other things.

The spidery steelwork of the tower hummed as they climbed. At the top, Mtengeni said: "You can look over that way . . . west . . . to the other side of the forest. That's about twenty miles."

Cuff screwed up his eyes at the eyepieces. "Jolly good 'scope you've got here. But it's too hazy beyond the forest to see anything."

"It always is, unless we have a high wind. That's the edge of the swamps."

"Dashed if I see how you can patrol such a big area all by yourself."

"Oh, these Bechuana they don't give much trouble. They are honest. Even I have to admit that they have some good qualities. Anyway, you can't get far into the Delta without getting lost in the swamps. There are ways, but then, I only know them. I'll show them to you, but please don't tell these Bechuana about them. Look, Mr. Cuff, there's our blue giraffe."

Cuff started. Mtengeni was evidently the kind of man who would announce an earthquake as casually as the morning mail.

Several hundred yards from the tower half a dozen giraffes were moving slowly through the brush, feeding on the tops of the scrubby trees. Cuff swung the telescope on them. In the middle of the herd was the blue one. Cuff blinked and looked again. There was no doubt about it; the animal was as brilliant a blue as if somebody had gone over it with paint. Athelstan Cuff suspected that that was what somebody *had* done. He said as much to Mtengeni.

The warden shrugged. "That, it would be a peculiar kind of amusement. Not to say risky. Do you see anything funny about the others?"

Cuff looked again. "Yes . . . by Jove, one of 'em's got a beard like a goat; Only it must be six feet long, at least. Now look here, George, what's all this leading up to?"

"I don't know myself. To-morrow, if you like, I'll show you one of those ways into the Delta. But that, it's quite a walk, so we'd better take supplies for two or three days."

As they drove toward the Tamalakane, they passed four Batawana, sad-looking reddish-brown men in a mixture of native and European clothes. Mtengeni slowed the car and looked at them suspiciously as they passed, but there was no evidence that they had been poaching.

He said: "Ever since their Makoba slaves were freed, they've been going on a . . . decline, I suppose you would call it. They are too dignified to work."

They got out at the river. "We can't drive across the ford this time of year," explained the warden, locking the car. "But there's a rapid a little way down where we can wade."

They walked down the trail, adjusting their packs. There wasn't much to see. The view was shut off by the tall soft-bodied swamp plants. The only sound was the hum of insects. The air was hot and steamy already, though the sun had been up only half an hour. The flies drew blood when they bit, but the men were used to that. They simply slapped and waited for the next bite.

Ahead there was a deep gurgling noise, like a foghorn with water in its works. Cuff said: "How are your hippo doing this year?"

"Pretty good. There are some in particular that I want you to see. Ah, here we are."

They had come in sight of a stretch of calm water. In the foreground a hippopotamus repeated its foghorn bellow. Cuff saw others, of which only the eyes, ears, and nostrils were visible. One of them was moving; Cuff could make out the little V-shaped wakes pointing back from its nearly submerged head. It reached the shallows and lumbered out, dripping noisily.

Cuff blinked. "Must be something wrong with my eyes."

"No," said Mtengeni. "That hippo she is one of those I wanted you to see."

The hippopotamus was green with pink spots.

She spied the men, grunted suspiciously, and slid back into the water.

"I still don't believe it," said Cuff. "Dash it, man, that's impossible."

"You will see many more things," said Mtengeni. "Shall we go on?"

They found the rapid and struggled across; then walked along what might, by some stretch of the imagination, be called a trail. There was little sound other than their sucking footfalls, the hum of insects, and the occasional screech of a bird or the crashing of a buck through the reeds.

They walked for some hours. Then Mtengeni said: "Be careful. There is a rhino near."

Cuff wondered how the devil the Zulu knew, but he was careful. Presently they came on a clear space in which the rhinoceros was browsing.

The animal couldn't see them at that distance, and there was no wind to carry their smell. It must have heard them, though, for it left off its feeding and snorted, once, like a locomotive. It had two heads.

It trotted toward them sniffing.

The men got out their rifles. "My God!" said Athelstan Cuff. "Hope we don't have to shoot him. My God!"

"I don't think so," said the warden. "That's Tweedle. I know him. If he gets too close, give him one at the base of the horn and he . . . he will run."

"Tweedle?"

"Yes. The right head is Tweedledum and the left is Tweedledee," said Mtengeni solemnly. "The whole rhino I call Tweedle."

The rhinoceros kept coming. Mtengeni said: "Watch this." He waved his hat and shouted: "Go away! *Footsack!*"

Tweedle stopped and snorted again. Then he began to circle like a waltzing mouse. Round and round he spun.

"We might as well go on," said Mtengeni. "He will keep that up for hours. You see Tweedledum is fierce, but Tweedledee, he is peace-

ful, even cowardly. So when I yell at Tweedle, Tweedledum wants to
charge us, but Tweedledee, he wants to run away. So the right legs
go forward and the left legs go back, and Tweedle, he goes in circles.
It takes him some time to agree on a policy."

"Whew!" said Athelstan Cuff. "I say, have you got any more things
like this in your zoo?"

"Oh, yes, lots. That's what I hope you'll do something about."

Do something about this! Cuff wondered whether this was touching
evidence of the native's faith in the white's omniscience, or whether
Mtengeni had gotten him there for the cynical amusement of watching him run in useless circles. Mtengeni himself gave no sign of what
he was thinking.

Cuff said: "I can't understand, George, why somebody hasn't looked
into this before."

Mtengeni shrugged. "Me, I've tried to get somebody to, but the
government won't send anybody, and the scientific expeditions, there
haven't been any of them for years. I don't know why."

"I can guess," said Cuff. "In the old days people even in the so-
called civilized countries expected travel to be a jolly rugged proposition, so they didn't mind putting up with a few extra hardships on
trek. But now that you can ride or fly almost anywhere on soft cushions, people won't put themselves out to get to a really uncomfortable and out-of-the-way place like Ngamiland."

Over the swampy smell came another, of carrion. Mtengeni pointed
to the carcass of a waterbuck fawn, which the scavengers had apparently not discovered yet.

"That's why I want you to stop this whatever-it-is," he said. There
was real concern in his voice.

"What do you mean, George?"

"Do you see its legs?"

Cuff looked. The forelegs were only half as long as the hind ones.

"That buck," said the Zulu. "It naturally couldn't live long. All
over the Park, freaks like this they are being born. Most of them don't
live. In ten years more, maybe twenty, all my animals will have died
out because of this. Then my job, where is it?"

They stopped at sunset. Cuff was glad to. It had been some time
since he'd done fifteen miles in one day, and he dreaded the morrow's
stiffness. He looked at his map and tried to figure out where he was.
But the cartographers had never seriously tried to keep track of the
changes in the Okavango's multifarious branches, and had simply

plastered the whole Delta with little blue dashes with tufts of blue lines sticking up from them, meaning simply "swamp." In all directions the country was a monotonous alternation of land and water. The two elements were inextricably mixed.

The Zulu was looking for a dry spot free of snakes. Cuff heard him suddenly shout "Footsack!" and throw a clod at a log. The log opened a pair of jaws, hissed angrily, and slid into the water.

"We'll have to have a good fire," said Mtengeni, hunting for dry wood. "We don't want a croc or hippo wandering into our tent by mistake."

After supper they set the automatic bug-sprayer going, inflated their mattresses, and tried to sleep. A lion roared somewhere in the west. That sound no African, native or Africander, likes to hear when he is on foot at night. But the men were not worried; lions avoided the swampy areas. The mosquitoes presented a more immediate problem.

Many hours later, Athelstan Cuff heard Mtengeni getting up.

The warden said: "I just remembered a high spot half a mile from here, where there's plenty of firewood. Me, I'm going out to get some."

Cuff listened to Mtengeni's retreating steps in the soft ground; then to his own breathing. Then he listened to something else. It sounded like a human yell.

He got up and pulled on his boots quickly. He fumbled around for the flashlight, but Mtengeni had taken it with him.

The yell came again.

Cuff found his rifle and cartridge belt in the dark and went out. There was enough starlight to walk by if you were careful. The fire was nearly out. The yells seemed to come from a direction opposite to that in which Mtengeni had gone. They were high-pitched, like a woman's screams.

He walked in their direction, stumbling over irregularities in the ground and now and then stepping up to his calves in unexpected water. The yells were plainer now. They weren't in English. Something was also snorting.

He found the place. There was a small tree, in the branches of which somebody was perched. Below the tree a noisy bulk moved around. Cuff caught the outline of a sweeping horn, and knew he had to deal with a buffalo.

He hated to shoot. For a Park official to kill one of his charges simply wasn't done. Besides, he couldn't see to aim for a vital spot, and he didn't care to try to dodge a wounded buffalo in the dark

They could move with race-horse speed through the heaviest growth.

On the other hand, he couldn't leave even a poor fool of a native woman treed. The buffalo, if it was really angry, would wait for days until its victim weakened and fell. Or it would butt the tree until the victim was shaken out. Or it would rear up and try to hook the victim out with its horns.

Athelstan Cuff shot the buffalo. The buffalo staggered about a bit and collapsed.

The victim climbed down swiftly, pouring out a flood of thanks in Xosa. It was very bad Xosa, even worse than the Englishman's. Cuff wondered what she was doing here, nearly a thousand miles from where the Maxosa lived. He assumed that she was a native, though it was too dark to see. He asked her if she spoke English, but she didn't seem to understand the question, so he made shift with the Bantu dialect.

"*Uveli phi na?*" he asked sternly. "Where do you come from? Don't you know that nobody is allowed in the Park without special permission?"

"*Izwe kamafene wabantu,*" she replied.

"What? Never heard of the place. Land of the baboon people, indeed! What are you?"

"*Ingwamza.*"

"You're a white stork? Are you trying to be funny?"

"I didn't say I was a white stork. Ingwamza's my name."

"I don't care about your name. I want to know what you are."

"*Umfene umfazi.*"

Cuff controlled his exasperation. "All right, all right, you're a baboon woman. I don't care what clan you belong to. What's your tribe? Batawana, Bamangwato, Bangwaketse, Barolong, Herero, or what? Don't try to tell me you're a Xosa; no Xosa ever used an accent like that."

"*Amafene abantu.*"

"What the devil are the baboon people?"

"People who live in the Park."

Cuff resisted the impulse to pull out two handfuls of hair by the roots. "But I tell you nobody lives in the Park! It isn't allowed! Come now, where do you really come from and what's your native language and why are you trying to talk Xosa?"

"I told you, I live in the Park. And I speak Xosa because all we *amafene abantu* speak it. That's the language Mqhavi taught us."

"Who is Mqhavi?"

"The man who taught us to speak Xosa.'

Cuff gave up. "Come along, you're going to see the warden. Perhaps he can make some sense out of your gabble. And you'd better have a good reason for trespassing, my good woman, or it'll go hard with you. Especially as it resulted in the killing of a good buffalo." He started off toward the camp, making sure that Ingwamza followed him closely.

The first thing he discovered was that he couldn't see the light of any fire to guide him back. Either he'd come farther than he thought, or the fire had died altogether while Mtengeni was getting wood. He kept on for a quarter of an hour in what he thought was the right direction. Then he stopped. He had, he realized, not the vaguest idea of where he was.

He turned. "Sibaphi na?" he snapped. "Where are we?"

"In the Park."

Cuff began to wonder whether he'd ever succeed in delivering this native woman to Mtengeni before he strangled her with his bare hands. "I know we're in the Park," he snarled. "But where in the Park?"

"I don't know exactly. Somewhere near my people's land."

"That doesn't do me any good. Look: I left the warden's camp when I heard you yell. I want to get back to it. Now how do I do it?"

"Where is the warden's camp?"

"I don't know, stupid. If I did I'd go there."

"If you don't know where it is, how do you expect me to guide you thither? I don't know either."

Cuff made strangled noises in his throat. Inwardly he had to admit that she had him there, which only made him madder. Finally he said: "Never mind, suppose you take me to your people. Maybe they have somebody with some sense."

"Very well," said the native woman, and she set off at a rapid pace, Cuff stumbling after her vague outline. He began to wonder if maybe she wasn't right about living in the Park. She seemed to know where she was going.

"Wait," he said. He ought to write a note to Mtengeni, explaining what he was up to, and stick it on a tree for the warden to find. But there was no pencil or paper in his pockets. He didn't even have a match safe or a cigarette lighter. He'd taken all those things out of his pockets when he'd lain down.

They went on a way, Cuff pondering on how to get in touch with

Mtengeni. He didn't want himself and the warden to spend a week chasing each other around the Delta. Perhaps it would be better to stay where they were and build a fire—but again, he had no matches, and didn't see much prospect of making a fire by rubbing sticks in this damned damp country.

Ingwamza said: "Stop. There are buffalo ahead."

Cuff listened and heard faintly the sound of snapping grass stems as the animals fed.

She continued: "We'll have to wait until it gets light. Then maybe they'll go away. If they don't, we can circle around them, but I couldn't find the way around in the dark."

They found the highest point they could and settled down to wait. Something with legs had crawled inside Cuff's shirt. He mashed it with a slap.

He strained his eyes into the dark. It was impossible to tell how far away the buffalo were. Overhead a nightjar brought its wings together with a single startling clap. Cuff told his nerves to behave themselves. He wished he had a smoke.

The sky began to lighten. Gradually Cuff was able to make out the black bulks moving among the reeds. They were at least two hundred yards away. He'd have preferred that they were at twice the distance, but it was better than stumbling right on them.

It became lighter and lighter. Cuff never took his eyes off the buffalo. There was something queer about the nearest one. It had six legs.

Cuff turned to Ingwamza and started to whisper: "What kind of buffalo do you call—" Then he gave a yell of pure horror and jumped back. His rifle went off, tearing a hole in his boot.

He had just gotten his first good look at the native woman in the rapidly waxing dawn. Ingwamza's head was that of an overgrown chacma baboon.

The buffalo stampeded through the feathery papyrus. Cuff and Ingwamza stood looking at each other. Then Cuff looked at his right foot. Blood was running out of the jagged hole in the leather.

"What's the matter? Why did you shoot yourself?" asked Ingwamza.

Cuff couldn't think of an answer to that one. He sat down and took off his boot. The foot felt numb, but there seemed to be no harm done aside from a piece of skin the size of a sixpence gouged out of the margin. Still, you never knew what sort of horrible infection might result from a trifling wound in these swamps. He tied his foot up with his handkerchief and put his boot back on.

"Just an accident," he said. "Keep going, Ingwamza."

Ingwamza went, Cuff limping behind. The sun would rise any minute now. It was light enough to make out colors. Cuff saw that Ingwamza, in describing herself as a baboon-woman, had been quite literal, despite the size, general proportions, and posture of a human being. Her body, but for the greenish-yellow hair and the short tail, might have passed for that of a human being, if you weren't too particular. But the astonishing head with its long bluish muzzle gave her the appearance of an Egyptian animal-headed god. Cuff wondered vaguely if the 'fene abantu were a race of man-monkey hybrids. That was impossible, of course. But he'd seen so many impossible things in the last couple of days.

She looked back at him. "We shall arrive in an hour or two. I'm sleepy." She yawned. Cuff repressed a shudder at the sight of four canine teeth big enough for a leopard. Ingwamza could tear the throat out of a man with those fangs as easily as biting the end off a banana. And he'd been using his most hectoring colonial-administrator tone on her in the dark! He made a resolve never to speak harshly to anybody he couldn't see.

Ingwamza pointed to a carroty baobab against the sky. "Izwe kamagene wabantu." They had to wade a little stream to get there. A six-foot monitor lizard walked across their path, saw them, and disappeared with a scuttle.

The 'fene abantu lived in a village much like that of any Bantu people, but the circular thatched huts were smaller and cruder. Baboon people ran out to peer at Cuff and to feel his clothes. He gripped his rifle tightly. They didn't act hostile, but it gave you a dashed funny feeling. The males were larger than the females, with even longer muzzles and bigger tusks.

In the center of the village sat a big umfene umntu scratching himself in front of the biggest hut. Ingwamza said. "This is my father, the chief. His name is Indlovu." To the baboon-man she told of her rescue.

The chief was the only umfene umntu that Cuff had seen who wore anything. What he wore was a necktie. The necktie had been a gaudy thing once.

The chief got up and made a speech, the gist of which was that Cuff had done a great thing, and that Cuff would be their guest until his wound healed. Cuff had a chance to observe the difficulties that the *'fene abantu* had with the Xosa tongue. The clicks were blurred, and they stumbled badly over the lip-smack. With those mouths, he could see how they might.

But he was only mildly interested. His foot was hurting like the very devil. He was glad when they led him into a hut so he could take off his boot. The hut was practically unfurnished. Cuff asked the *'fene abantu* if he might have some of the straw used for thatching. They seemed puzzled by his request, but complied, and he made himself a bed of sorts. He hated sleeping on the ground, especially on ground infested with anthropodal life. He hated vermin, and knew he was in for an intimate acquaintance with them.

He had nothing to bandage his foot with, except the one handkerchief, which was now thoroughly bloodsoaked. He'd have to wash and dry it before it would be fit to use again. And where in the Okavango Delta could he find water fit to wash the handkerchief in? Of course he could boil the water. In what? He was relieved and amazed when his questions brought forth the fact that there was a large iron pot in the village, obtained from God knew where.

The wound had clotted satisfactorily, and he dislodged the handkerchief with infinite care from the scab. While his water was boiling, the chief, Indlovu, came in and talked to him. The pain in his foot had subsided for the moment, and he was able to realize what an extraordinary thing he had come across, and to give Indlovu his full attention. He plied Indlovu with questions.

The chief explained what he knew about himself and his people. It seemed that he was the first of the race; all the others were his descendants. Not only Ingwamza but all the other *amafene abafazi* were his daughters. Ingwamza was merely the last. He was old now. He was hazy about dates, but Cuff got the impression that these beings had a shorter life span than human beings, and matured much more quickly. If they were in fact baboons, that was natural enough.

Indlovu didn't remember having had any parents. The earliest he remembered was being led around by Mqhavi. Stanley H. Mqhavi had been a black man, and worked for the machine man, who had been a pink man like Cuff. He had had a machine up on the edge of the Chobe Swamp. His name had been Heeky.

Of course, Hickey! thought Cuff. Now, he was getting somewhere. Hickey had disappeared by simply running his truck up to Ngamiland without bothering to tell anybody where he was going. That had been before the Park had been established; before Cuff had come out from England. Mqhavi must have been his Xosa assistant. His thoughts raced ahead of Indlovu's words.

Indlovu went on to tell about how Heeky had died, and how Mqhavi, not knowing how to run the machine, had taken him, Indlovu, and his now numerous progeny in an attempt to find his way back to civilization. He had gotten lost in the Delta. Then he had cut his foot somehow, and gotten sick, very sick. Cuff looked uneasily at his own foot. When he, Mqhavi, had gotten well he had been very weak. So he had settled down with Indlovu and his family. They already walked upright and spoke Xosa, which Mqhavi had taught them. Cuff got the idea that the early family relationships among the 'fene abantu had of necessity involved close inbreeding. Mqhavi had taught them all he knew, and then died, after warning them not to go within a mile of the machine, which, as far as they knew, was still up at the Chobe Swamp.

Cuff thought, that blasted machine is an electronic tube of some sort, built to throw short waves of the length to affect animal genes. Probably Indlovu represented one of Hickey's early experiments. Then Hickey had died, and—left the thing going. He didn't know how it got power; some solar system, perhaps.

Suppose Hickey had died while the thing was turned on. Mqhavi might have dragged his body out and left the door open. He might have been afraid to try to turn it off, or he might not have thought of it. So every animal that passed that doorway got a dose of the rays, and begat monstrous offspring. These super-baboons were one example; whether an accidental or a controlled mutation might never be known.

For every useful mutation there were bound to be scores of useless or harmful ones. Mtengeni had been right: it had to be stopped while there was still normal stock left in the Park. He wondered again how to get in touch with the warden. He'd be damned if anything short of the threat of death would get him to walk on that foot, for a few days anyhow.

Ingwamza entered with a wooden dish full of a mess of some sort. Athelstan Cuff decided resignedly that he was expected to eat it. He couldn't tell by looking whether it was animal or vegetable in nature. After the first mouthful he was sure it was neither. Nothing in the animal and vegetable worlds could taste as awful as that. It was too bad Mqhavi hadn't been a Bamangwato; he'd have really known how to cook, and could have taught these monkeys. Still, he had to eat something to support life. He fell to with the wooden spoon they gave him, suppressing an occasional gag and watching the smaller solid particles closely. Sure enough, he had to smack two of them with the spoon to keep them from crawling out.

"How it is?" asked Ingwamza. Indlovu had gone out.

"Fine," lied Cuff. He was chasing a slimy piece of what he suspected was waterbuck tripe around the dish.

"I am glad. We'll feed you a lot of that. Do you like scorpions?"

"You mean to eat?"

"Of course. What else are they good for?"

He gulped. "No."

"I won't give you any then. You see I'm glad to know what my future husband likes."

"What?" He thought he had misunderstood her.

"I said, I am glad to know what you like, so I can please you after you are my husband."

Athelstan Cuff said nothing for sixty seconds. His naturally prominent eyes bulged even more as her words sank in. Finally he spoke.

"*Gluk,*" he said.

"What's that?"

"*Gug. Gah.* My God. Let me out of here!" His voice jumped two octaves, and he tried to get up. Ingwamza caught his shoulders and pushed him gently, but firmly, back on his pallet. He struggled, but without visibly exerting herself the *'fene umfazi* held him as in a vise.

"You can't go," she said. "If you try to walk on that foot you will get sick."

His ruddy face was turning purple. "Let me up! Let me up, I say! I can't stand this!"

"Will you promise not to try to go out if I do? Father would be furious if I let you do anything unwise."

He promised, getting a grip on himself again. He already felt a bit foolish about his panic. He was in a nasty jam, certainly, but an official of His Majesty didn't act like a frightened schoolgirl at every crisis.

"What," he asked, "is this all about?"

"Father is so grateful to you for saving my life that he intends to bestow me on you in marriage, without even asking a bride price."

"But . . . but . . . I'm married already." He lied.

"What of it? I'm not afraid of your other wives. If they got fresh,

I'd tear them in pieces like this." She bared her teeth and went through the motions of tearing several Mistresses Cuff in pieces. Athelstan Cuff shut his eyes at the horrid sight.

"Among my people," he said, "you're allowed only one wife."

"That's too bad," said Ingwamza. "That means that you couldn't go back to your people after you married me, doesn't it?"

Cuff sighed. These *'fene abantu* combined the mental outlook of uneducated Maxosa with physical equipment that would make a lion think twice before attacking one. He'd probably have to shoot his way out. He looked around the hut craftily. His rifle wasn't in sight. He didn't dare ask about it for fear of arousing suspicion.

"Is your father set on this plan?" he asked.

"Oh, yes, very. Father is a good *umntu*, but he gets set on ideas like this and nothing will make him change them. And he has a terrible temper. If you cross him when he has his heart set on something, he will tear you in pieces. *Small* pieces." She seemed to relish the phrase.

"How do you feel about it, Ingwamza?"

"Oh, I do everything father says. He knows more than any of us."

"Yes, but I mean you personally. Forget about your father for the moment."

She didn't quite catch on for a moment, but after further explanation she said: "I wouldn't mind. It would be a great thing for my people if one of us was married to a man."

Cuff silently thought that that went double for him.

Indlovu came in with two other *amafene abantu*. "Run along, Ingwamza," he said. The three baboon-men squatted around Athelstan Cuff and began questioning him about men and the world outside the Delta.

When Cuff stumbled over a phrase, one of the questioners, a scarred fellow named Sondlo, asked why he had difficulty. Cuff explained that Xosa wasn't his native language.

"Men do speak other languages?" asked Indlovu. "I remember now, the great Mqhavi once told me something to that effect. But he never taught me any other languages. Perhaps he and Heeky spoke one of these other languages, but I was too young when Heeky died to remember."

Cuff explained something about linguistics. He was immediately pressed to "say something in English." Then they wanted to learn English, right then, that afternoon.

Cuff finished his evening meal and looked without enthusiasm at his pallet. No artificial light, so these people rose and set with the sun. He stretched out. The straw rustled. He jumped up, bringing his injured foot down hard. He yelped, swore, and felt the bandage. Yes, he'd started it bleeding again. Oh, to hell with it. He attacked the straw, chasing out a mouse, six cockroaches, and uncounted smaller bugs. Then he stretched out again. Looking up, he felt his scalp prickle. A ten-inch centipede was methodically hunting its prey over the underside of the roof. If it missed its footing when it was right over him— He unbuttoned his shirt and pulled it up over his face. Then the mosquitoes attacked his midriff. His foot throbbed.

A step brought him up; it was Ingwamza.

"What is it now?" he asked.

"*Ndiya kuhlaha apha*," she answered.

"Oh no, you're not going to stay here. We're not . . . well, anyway, it simply isn't done among my people."

"But Esselten, somebody must watch you in case you get sick. My father—"

"No, I'm sorry, but that's final. If you're going to marry me you'll have to learn how to behave among men. And we're beginning right now."

To his surprise and relief, she went without further objection, albeit sulkily. He'd never have dared to try to put her out by force.

When she had gone, he crawled over to the door of the hut. The sun had just set, and the moon would follow it in a couple of hours. Most of the *'fene abantu* had retired. But a couple of them squatted outside their huts, in sight of his place, watchfully.

Heigh ho, he thought, they aren't taking any chances. Perhaps the old boy *is* grateful and all that rot. But I think my fiancée let the cat out when she said that about the desirability of hitching one of the tribe to a human being. Of course the poor things don't know that it wouldn't have any legal standing at all. But that fact wouldn't save me from a jolly unpleasant experience in the meantime. Suppose I haven't escaped by the time of the ceremony. Would I go through with it? *Br-r-r!* Of course not. I'm an Englishman and an officer of the Crown. But if it meant my life . . . I don't know. I'm dashed if I do. Perhaps I can talk them out of it . . . being careful not to get them angry in the process—

He was tied to the straw, and enormous centipedes were dropping off the ceiling onto his face. Then he was running through the

swamp, with Ingwamza and her irate pa after him. His feet stuck
in the mud so he couldn't move, and there was a light in his face.
Mtengeni—good old George!—was riding a two-headed rhino. But
instead of rescuing him, the warden said: "Mr. Cuff, you must do
something about these Bechuana. Them, they are catching all my
animals and painting them red with green stripes." Then he woke up.

It took him a second to realize that the light was from the setting
moon, not the rising sun, and that he therefore had been asleep less
than two hours. It took him another second to realize what had
wakened him. The straw of the hut wall had been wedged apart, and
through the gap a 'fene umntu was crawling. While Cuff was still
wondering why one of his hosts, or captors, should use this peculiar
method of getting in, the baboon-man stood up. He looked enormous
in the faint light.

"What is it?" asked Cuff.

"If you make a noise," said the stranger, "I will kill you."

"What? What's the idea? Why should you want to kill me?"

"You have stolen my Ingwamza."

"But . . . but—" Cuff was at a loss. Here the gal's old man would
tear him in pieces—small pieces—if he didn't marry her, and a rival
or something would kill him if he did. "Let's talk it over first," he
said, in what he hoped was a normal voice. "Who are you, by the
way?"

"My name is Cukata. I was to have married Ingwamza next
month. And then you came."

"What . . . what—"

"I won't kill you. Not if you make no noise. I will just fix you so
you won't marry Ingwamza." He moved toward the pile of straw.

Cuff didn't waste time inquiring into the horrid details. "Wait a
minute," he said, cold sweat bedewing not merely his brow, but his
whole torso. "My dear fellow, this marriage wasn't my idea. It was
Indlovu's, entirely. I don't want to steal your girl. They just informed
me that I was going to marry her, without asking me about it at
all. I don't want to marry her. In fact there's nothing I want to do
less."

The 'fene umntu stood still for a moment, thinking. Then he said
softly: "You wouldn't marry my Ingwamza if you had the chance?
You think she is ugly?"

"Well—"

"By u-Qamata, that's an insult! Nobody shall think such thoughts
of my Ingwamza! Now I will kill you for sure!"

"Wait, wait!" Cuff's voice, normally a pleasant low baritone, became a squeak. "That isn't it at all! She's beautiful, intelligent, industrious, all that a 'ntu could want. But I can never marry her." Inspiration! Cuff went on rapidly. Never had he spoken Xosa so fluently. "You know that if lion mates with leopard, there are no offspring." Cuff wasn't sure that was so, but he took a chance. "It is that way with my people and yours. We are too different. There would be no issue to our marriage, and Indlovu would not have grandchildren by us to gladden his old age."

Cukata, after some thought, saw, or thought he did. "But," he said. "How can I prevent this marriage without killing you?"

"You could help me escape."

"So. Now that's an idea. Where do you want to go?"

"Do you know where the Hickey machine is?"

"Yes, though I have never been close to it. That is forbidden. About fifteen miles north of here, on the edge of the Chobe Swamp, is a rock. By the rock are three baobab trees, close together. Between the trees and the swamp are two houses. The machine is in one of those houses."

He was silent again. "You can't travel fast with that wounded foot. They would overtake you. Perhaps Indlovu would tear you in pieces, or perhaps he would bring you back. If he brought you back, we should fail. If he tore you in pieces. I should be sorry, for I like you, even if you are a feeble little *isipham-pham*." Cuff wished that the simian brain would get around to the point. "I have it. In ten minutes I shall whistle. You will then crawl out through this hole in the wall, making no noise. You understand?"

When Athelstan Cuff crawled out, he found Cukata in the alley between two rows of huts. There was a strong reptilian stench in the air. Behind the baboon-man was something large and black. It walked with a swaying motion. It brushed against Cuff, and he almost cried out at the touch of cold, leathery hide.

"This is the largest," said Cukata. "We hope some day to have a whole herd of them. They are fine for traveling across the swamps, because they can swim as well as run And they grow much faster than the ordinary crocodile."

The thing was a crocodile—but such a crocodile! Though not much over fifteen feet in length, it had long, powerful legs that raised its body a good four feet off the ground, giving it a dinosaurian look. It rubbed against Cuff, and the thought occurred to him that it had taken an astonishing mutation indeed to give a brainless and voracious reptile an affection for human beings.

Cukata handed Cuff a knobkerry, and explained: "Whistle, loudly, when you want him to come. To start him, hit him on the tail with this. To stop him, hit him on the nose. To make him go to the left, hit him on the right side of the neck, not too hard. To make him go to the right, hit him—"

"On the left side of the neck, but not too hard," finished Cuff. "What does he eat?"

"Anything that is meat. But you needn't feed him for two or three days; he has been fed recently."

"Don't you use a saddle?"

"Saddle? What's that?"

"Never mind." Cuff climbed aboard, wincing as he settled onto the sharp dorsal ridges of the animal's hide.

"Wait," said Cukata. "The moon will be completely gone in a moment. Remember, I shall say that I know nothing about your escape, but that you got out and stole him yourself. His name Soga."

There were the baobab trees, and there were the houses. There were also a dozen elephants, facing the rider and his bizarre mount and spreading their immense ears. Athelstan Cuff was getting so blasé about freaks that he hardly noticed that two of the elephants had two trunks apiece; that another of them was colored a fair imitation of a Scotch tartan; that another of them had short legs like a hippopotamus, so that it looked like something out of a dachshund breeder's nightmare.

The elephants, for their part, seemed undecided whether to run or to attack, and finally compromised by doing nothing. Cuff realized when he was already past them that he had done a wickedly reckless thing in going so close to them unarmed except for the useless kerry. But somehow he couldn't get excited about mere elephants. His whole life for the past forty-eight hours had had a dreamlike quality. Maybe he was dreaming. Or maybe he had a charmed life. Or something. Though there was nothing dreamlike about the throb in his foot, or the acute soreness in his gluteus maximus.

Soga, being a crocodile, bowed his whole body at every stride. First the head and tail went to the right and the body to the left; then the process was reversed. Which was most unpleasant for his rider.

Cuff was willing to swear that he'd ridden at least fifty miles in stead of the fifteen Cukata had mentioned. Actually he had done about thirty, not having been able to follow a straight line and having to steer by stars and, when it rose, the sun. A fair portion of the thirty had been hugging Soga's barrel while the croc's great tail drove them through the water like a racing shell. No hippo or other crocs had bothered them; evidently they knew when they were well off.

Athelstan Cuff slid—almost fell—off, and hobbled up to the entrance of one of the houses. His practiced eye took in the roof cistern, the solar boiler, the steam-electric plant, the batteries, and finally the tube inside. He went in. Yes, by Jove, the tube was in operation after all these years. Hickey must have had something jolly unusual. Cuff found the main switch easily enough and pulled it. All that happened was that the little orange glow in the tube died.

The house was so silent it made Cuff uncomfortable, except for the faint hum of the solar power plant. As he moved about, using the kerry for a crutch, he stirred up the dust which lay six inches deep on the floor. Maybe there were notebooks or something which ought to be collected. There had been, he soon discovered, but the termites had eaten every scrap of paper, and even the imitation-leather covers, leaving only the metal binding rings and their frames. It was the same with the books.

Something white caught his eye. It was paper, lying on a little metal-legged stand that the termites evidently hadn't thought well enough of to climb. He limped toward it eagerly. But it was only a newspaper, Umlindi we Nyanga—"The Monthly Watchman"—published in East London. Evidently, Stanley H. Mqhavi had subscribed to it. It crumbled at Cuff's touch.

Oh, well, he thought, can't expect much. We'll run along, and some of the bio-physicist chappies can come in and gather up the scientific apparatus.

He went out, called Soga, and started east. He figured that he could strike the old wagon road somewhere north of the Mababe, and get down to Mtengeni's main station that way.

Were those human voices? Cuff shifted uneasily on his Indian fakir's seat. He had gone about four miles after leaving Hickey scientific station.

They were voices, but not human ones. They belonged to a dozen 'fene abantu, who came loping through the grass with old Indlovu at their head.

Cuff reached back and thumped Soga's tail. If he could get the croc going all out, he might be able to run away from his late hosts. Soga wasn't as fast as a horse, but he could trot right along. Cuff was relieved to see that they hadn't brought his rifle along. They were armed with kerries and spears, like any of the more savage *abantu*. Perhaps the fear of injuring their pet would make them hesitate to throw things at him. At least he hoped so.

A familiar voice caught up with him in a piercing yell of "Soga!" The croc slackened his pace and tried to turn his head. Cuff whacked him unmercifully. Indlovu's yell came again, followed by a whistle. The croc was now definitely off his stride. Cuff's efforts to keep him headed away from his proper masters resulted in his zigzagging erratically. The contrary directions confused and irritated him. He opened his jaws and hissed. The baboon-men were gaining rapidly.

So, thought Cuff, this is the end. I hate like hell to go out before I've had a chance to write my report. But mustn't show it. Not an Englishman and an officer of the Crown. Wonder what poor Mtengeni'll think.

Something went *whick* past him; a fraction of a second later, the crash of an elephant rifle reached him. A big puff of dust ballooned up in front of the baboon-men. They skittered away from it as if the dust and not the bullet that made it were something deadly. George Mtengeni appeared from behind the nearest patch of thorn scrub, and yelled, "Hold still there, or me, I'll blow your heads off." If the *'fene abantu* couldn't understand his English, they got his tone.

Cuff thought vaguely, good old George, he could shoot their ears off at that distance, but he has more sense than to kill any of them before he finds out. Cuff slid off Soga and almost fell in a heap.

The warden came up. "What . . . what in the heavens has been happening to you, Mr. Cuff? What are these?" He indicated the baboon-men.

"Joke," giggled Cuff. "Good joke on you, George. Been living in your dashed Park for years, and you never knew— Wait, I've got to explain something to these chaps. I say, Indlovu . . . hell, he doesn't know English. Got to use Xosa. You know Xosa, don't you George?" He giggled again.

"Why, me, I . . . I can follow it. It's much like Zulu. But my God, what happened to the seat of your pants?"

Cuff pointed a wavering finger at Soga's saw-toothed back. "Good old Soga. Should have had a saddle. Dashed outrage, not providing a saddle for His Majesty's representative."

"But you look as if you'd been skinned! Me, I've got to get you to a hospital . . . and what about your foot?"

"T'hell with the foot. 'Nother joke. Can't stand up, can't sit

down. Jolly, what? Have to sleep on my stomach. But, Indlovu! I'm
sorry I had to run away. I couldn't marry Ingwamza. Really. Because . . . because—" Athelstan Cuff swayed and collapsed in a
small, ragged pile.

Peter Cuff's eyes were round. He asked the inevitable small-boy
question: "What happened then?"

Atheistan Cuff was stuffiing his pipe. "Oh, about what you'd
expect. Indlovu was jolly vexed, I can tell you, but he didn't dare
do anything with George standing there with the gun. He calmed
down later after he understood what I had been driving at, and we
became good friends. When he died, Cukata was elected chief in his
place. I still get Christmas cards from him."

"Christmas cards from a baboon?"

"Certainly. If I get one next Christmas, I'll show it to you. It's the
same card every year. He's an economical fella, and he bought a
hundred cards of the same pattern because he could get them at a
discount."

"Were you all right?"

"Yes, after a month in the hospital. I still don't know why I didn't
get sixteen kinds of blood poisoning. Fool's luck, I suppose."

"But what's that got to do with me being a 'dopted boy?"

"Peter!" Cuff gave the clicks represented in the Bantu languages
by x and in English by tsk. "Isn't it obvious? That tube of Hickey's
was on when I approached his house. So I got a full dose of the
radiations. Their effect was to produce violent mutations in the
germ-plasm. You know what that is, don't you? Well, I never dared
have any children of my own after that, for fear they'd turn out
to be some sort of monster. That didn't occur to me until afterward.
It fair bowled me over, I can tell you, when I did think of it. I
went to pieces, rather, and lost my job in South Africa. But now
that I have you and your mother, I realize that it wasn't so important after all."

"Father—" Peter hesitated.

"Go on, old man."

"If you'd thought of the rays before you went to the house, would
you have been brave enough to go ahead anyway?"

Cuff lit his pipe and looked off at nothing. "I've often wondered
about that myself. I'm dashed if I know. I wonder . . . just what
would have happened—"

FLIGHT INTO DARKNESS

by

WEBB MARLOWE

Writers of science-fiction attempt logical guesses about the future but they seldom set themselves up as prophets. Yet (as in "Nerves") some amazingly accurate forecasts have crept into recent stories. Written in 1942, "Flight into Darkness," predicts the building of the first rocket ship by a Nazi. And, as Mr. Ley has illustrated, that is exactly what happened! Further, author Marlowe presents an all-too-reasonable hypothesis of what might happen if we grow too lax in our rule of the beaten, but unreconstructed, Fascists.

*

DR. LINKMAN stepped rapidly across the subway platform and into the elevator that went to the street. He stood quiet, with soldierly erectness, as the elevator shot from a depth of three hundred feet below ground to more than five hundred above it. His hard face was expressionless, showing no sign of the triumph that boiled within him.

He left the elevator at the eighth level, walked a block down the glass-inclosed span and entered his apartment. He skirted the comfortable living room, went through a bedroom and entered a small closet. The closet was bare of furniture. What hung on the wall gave the tiny room distinction and lent it the air of being a shrine.

A large, framed photograph of Hoffman hung there. The fat, cruel face, magnified many times life-size, stared out challengingly. Below the picture hung a battered sword and an officer's dress helmet.

Dr. Linkman lifted his hand in the forbidden salute.

"At last, my Leader," he breathed. "The day of restoration is dawning!"

The door of the bedroom behind him opened. Linkman whirled, took a step forward, blocking the door of the closet. His crippled brother, Franz, limped into the room.

Linkman smiled thinly.

"Ah, Franz." he said. "I have good news for you."

The cripple's sad face lighted.

"Josef! They have made you manager of the plant?"

"Yes, I have worked my way up in the approved democratic fashion! After much pondering, our masters have decided that Colonel General Linkman is gone and the recently graduated Dr. Linkman is a thoroughly reformed character. Why, if I make good on this assignment, they may even let me—what do they say?—run for office! Bah!"

"But, Josef, will they . . . will they let you work on my—"

"Silence!"

Dr. Linkman strode forward and put both hands on his brother's twisted shoulders.

"You will forget that—as *they* have forgotten it! You hear?" He shook the boy a little. "Yes, I will work on it! I will build it! But you must be silent about our work. Understand?"

Franz nodded. Then he caught sight of the picture.

"The Leader!" he gasped. "Josef! His picture is forbidden!"

Linkman drove his fingers into Franz's shoulders until the boy cried aloud.

"That, too, is another thing you will never mention," he said slowly.

"Oh, don't, Josef! You're hurting me! But it is against the law —"

His voice trailed off into broken sobs.

Linkman's fingers relaxed slowly, almost reluctantly, and his arms dropped to his sides.

"Against *their* law, boy. I obey the *Leader's* law!"

Franz's small body seemed to shrink even more.

"But my ship . . . your position . . . I thought—"

Linkman grinned down at him.

"Do not worry, little Franz. Your ship will be built It shall be a tribute to *his* memory."

He turned back to the closet and saluted again. Then he closed the closet door, reverently.

"Come, Franz," he said, almost pleasantly, "it is time for dinner.

And if you doubt me or my course, little brother, just remember how all *their* technicians laughed at you when you went to them with plans for a rocketship that would travel to the Moon and beyond!"

Hastings looked from General McClernand to Oliver. He shifted uneasily in his chair and looked down at the papers in his hand.

"After all, gentlemen," he murmured, "I'm just the head of a department and—"

"And I'm just an old soldier!" roared McClernand. He scowled fiercely at Oliver. "I don't pack any weight here, either."

Mark Oliver grinned amiably at the old man. His long figure slouched lower in the chair behind the big desk.

"Sorry, Hastings," he said gently. "Don't let the general's bickering with me embarrass you. And don't be alarmed because he takes your side of the matter."

"It isn't a question of sides, sir," Hastings said. "It's just a question of fact advanced by my department."

"Exactly!" bellowed McClernand. He leaned forward and pounded Oliver's desk. "Here's this soulless Department of Psychological Correction comin' out and challengin' your pet, Linkman. D'ye remember, now, how I kicked when you appointed him?"

"Of course. You won't let me forget." Oliver's quiet voice grew a little weary. "You just won't forget, Mac, that the war's over and we've got a job to do—without *prejudice*."

"Maybe I won't forget. But Hastings, here—he doesn't know anything about Linkman's past—an' he comes here—"

"I . . . ah, beg your pardon, general."

Hastings was acutely uneasy. The general's roars would never have been tolerated in the Psycho section. He looked at Oliver's face, placid under the old man's wrath. There was strength, there, underneath the calm. Why didn't he use some of it against the soldier's irrational outbreaks?

He cleared his throat again.

"If I might state my report," he ventured.

"Yes, Mac," said Oliver. "For Heaven's sake, pipe down and let Mr. Hastings state his case."

Oliver clasped his hands behind his neck and leaned back. His attitude was one of careless ease, but his eyes were intent on the psychologist.

"Very well, sir. Ahem." He leafed through the report. "Ah, three mechanics, Cutlar, Vornov and Lockheim were discharged from the Zellerkraft plane factory. That's a native-managed concern."

"Your precious Linkman is the head man," growled McClernand.

"Charges were," continued Hastings, "maladjustment to occupation, lack of disciplinary balance, no receptivity to routine, general debility and so on."

"Put that in my language," ordered McClernand.

"Certainly. It means, simply, that they were lazy, incompetent, insubordinate and took poor physical care of themselves."

"Well," asked Oliver, "why have you come to me?"

He unclasped his hands and sat up straight in his chair.

"Just this, sir. The primary character and aptitude analyses that were made on these men gave no indication of such a development. When they were pronounced ready to begin work under our government, we had every reason to believe they would progress, not deteriorate."

"I see."

"Further—" Hastings swallowed and plunged on. "They have voluntarily applied to us for testing. Our preliminary examination gives no evidence that the alleged character reversal has taken place."

McClernand jumped to his feet again.

"See!" he snapped. "There's dirty work. That Linkman—"

"Just a minute!" Oliver did not raise his voice, but McClernand became quiet. "A psychograph of your emotional balance, Mac, might not give you a very high rating. Now, please be quiet until I'm through with Mr. Hastings."

He turned to Hastings and the young man fidgeted in his chair again. But Oliver's tone was kindly.

"Just what conclusion is your department trying to draw?" the director asked. "And why have you come to me?"

"Well, sir—" Hastings began to wish he'd never been promoted to such arduous jobs as arguing with big shots. "We can see no reason why such charges should have been preferred against these men. The manager of the factory is a native of doubtful antecedents—"

Oliver took out a pipe and began to fill it. He stared at McClernand's beet-red face. Although Oliver's face was impassive, Hastings could have sworn he saw the director's lips twitch.

"Tell me, Mac," the director asked, "just what your attitude is."

"Well," snarled the old man, "I think there's some of these

natives that ought to be taken out and shot! Linkman's one of
'em. I know—I fought him for five years! But you think he's reformed!
So—after he gets this job—he cans some employees under suspicious circumstances— I want it investigated."

Oliver applied the glowing tip of his lighter to his pipe. He
puffed slowly for a few seconds, then leaned back easily in his chair.

"Gentlemen," he said, "it has been investigated. Dr. Linkman
wrote me of his intention to discharge those men. With his letter,
he sent affidavits from workmen in the plant, corroborating his
charges. As a final point, I would remind you that their dismissal
was approved by the plant guild."

Hastings looked down at his papers.

McClernand made a wordless noise.

Oliver got up from his desk and walked to the window. He
stared out over the clean, white city, his view a tangle of arching
traffic spans, needlelike spires of dwellings, spotted here and there
by the dark green of hanging parks.

"Come here, gentlemen," he said.

They got up wonderingly and stood by him.

"See," he said. "That is *theirs*. Not ours, theirs. And we must
give it back to them as soon as we can. We have a home of our
own, you know, and I, for one, would like to get back to it. Because,
fundamentally, we don't belong here."

Young Hastings then realized why Mark Oliver was director of this
Occupied Area. He realized, more dimly perhaps, why he, himself,
could never hold such a job.

Oliver turned from the window.

"That is why, Mac, and you, too, Mr. Hastings, that is why I
have given Dr. Linkman his position. Why I will give others similar
positions. I may make mistakes. If I do, I will remedy those errors
as fully as I am able. But we must, all of us, run the risk of error—
and run that risk cheerfully, so we can get our job done and go home."

He put his hand on Hasting's shoulder.

"Continue with your tests, Mr. Hastings. When you have a complete report, bring it to me."

"Yes, sir." Hastings put his papers in his brief case and walked
to the door. There he turned. His eyes behind his glasses were very
bright. "Thank you, sir," he said.

The door had barely slid shut behind him when McClernand
grabbed Oliver by the arm.

"That was all very pretty, Mark," he growled. "And good for the youngster. But you can't fool these psychiatrists. They're scientists—"

"They're scientists as long as they agree with your prejudices, Mac. Now, let go my arm and I'll order up a drink for us."

McClernand straightened and moved back a pace.

"I'm an old has-been," he muttered. "My opinion doesn't count in these days of love and kisses for the enemy!"

Oliver threw his arms wide in a gesture of despair.

"For the love of Heaven, Mac," he cried, "just what do you suspect Linkman of doing?"

"I don't know. I only know he's in a spot to do harm if he's a mind to. And I know damn well he's a mind to! The butcher!"

Oliver shook his head wearily.

"Sorry, Mac," he said quietly. "I can't discuss it further. If 1 err, it's got to be on the side of tolerance. That's why I'm here."

"All right, all right!" McClernand stamped to the door. "Just remember, son, you can't teach an old dog new tricks!"

If it had been an old-fashioned door, he would have slammed it shut behind him.

Dr. Linkman glanced at his wrist watch. It showed five minutes past five. In the outer office he could hear his secretary close her electrotyper.

She appeared in the doorway, coat in hand.

"Good night, Dr. Linkman."

Linkman smiled benevolently.

"Good night, my dear."

She frowned a little.

"Don't stay late, sir. You've been working awfully hard lately."

"Now, now," he said. "You run along and don't worry about me. You must enjoy yourself—not think of an old man like me."

She shook her curly head.

"You're not old, doctor."

She smiled again as she went out. Linkman heard the office door slide shut behind her. The benevolent look was replaced by a scowl.

"Little flirt," he grated. "Women in industry—bah! Their place is in the home, bearing children for the race!" He shrugged. "Ah, well. That, too, will change."

He walked over to the production chart on the wall.

"Twenty-three units per day," he mused. "And they allow me just twenty-three units of raw materials. Our masters are good accountants." He moved back to his desk and picked up a scratch pad. His brows contracted as he figured. "Hm-m-m. To get material, I must lessen the quality of the plant's output. How long, then, before the inspectors find out?"

There was a rapid double knock at the door. Linkman ripped the sheet off the pad and tossed it down the waste chute.

"Come in," he called.

A man in working clothes stepped in, locked the door behind him and walked with swift, military strides into Linkman's office.

"My general!" he saluted.

"Major Falkayn!" Linkman returned the salute. "Sit down, major." He pushed a box of cigars across his desk. "Smoke and be comfortable. You have earned relaxation."

Falkayn slumped down in a leather chair, leaned back and closed his eyes as he puffed on the cigar. Linkman, too, lit one and the two men smoked silently for a few moments. Then Falkayn spoke slowly:

"This is wonderful, sir. The first time I have relaxed with a social equal in ten years! I have been"—his slow voice grew passionate with disgust—"a workman! A faithful member of one of those accursed guilds! Pah!"

Linkman smiled thinly.

"I have begged my way into a university." He raised a clenched fist. "I, a soldier, have studied plant management and the principles of democracy! I have allowed myself to be—educated!"

He broke into a sharp, grating laugh.

"But that is past. Soon, you and I will wear uniforms again!"

His cold eyes stared off into space over Falkayn's head. He seemed to be seeing a vision for his muscles tensed, his shoulders went back. Falkayn waited respectfully for a moment, then coughed slightly.

Still staring, Linkman said, "I will make a great leader, Falkayn. And you shall be my deputy. Give me your report."

He leaned back slowly and listened with half-closed eyes.

"Yes, sir. I have the great pleasure to report that the hull is finished. The left bank of tubes is installed. The right bank will be in place in another day. Tonight, we are starting to weld the fuel tanks."

"An operation of some four days," mused Linkman. "And the storage of materials?"

"We have accumulated a four-months' supply of all necessities. Our munitions are limited, though."

"We must get more! We must work faster!"

Falkayn leaned forward in his chair.

"But, general. We must *steal* armament. And those faithful to the Leader's memory are few—very few. I, myself, have worked twenty hours a day—my regular shift in the plant and the balance on our ship."

Linkman stood up. Falkayn followed suit and stiffened to attention.

"These excuses are not valid," rasped Linkman. "If you cannot execute my orders, I'll replace you, major. I want everything ready within one week from tonight!"

Falkayn saluted without speaking.

Linkman started to sit down. A faint hum seemed to come from his desk. He jerked open the center drawer. The hum grew louder.

"Keep talking," Linkman hissed. "About the ship. And loudly!"

As the major continued an expressionless monologue about the ship's construction, Linkman reached to the back of the drawer and pressed a stud. The hum stopped. Linkman's hand came out, clutching a flat pistol.

Linkman ran past Falkayn.

"Stay here," as the other turned to follow. "Keep talking."

His feet making no sound on the feltex carpet of the outer office, Dr. Linkman ran to the door, snapped the lock and slid it open.

A man crouched there, his ear glued to a dictascope.

He started to rise and Linkman shot him twice. The listener collapsed.

"Falkayn!" Linkman bent and lifted the body. "Wipe the floor clean of any blood," he grunted. "Then lock the door again."

He carried the body into his office, dropped it to the floor and bent to search the pockets.

Falkayn peered over his shoulder.

"Who is he?"

"An Intelligence man, of course. I would think that McClernand set him on me."

He looked at the miscellaneous data from the dead man's pockets.

"Nothing," Linkman muttered. "As I expected, of course."

He straightened, kicked absently at the corpse, then walked back to his desk.

"Yes," he said, "it must be McClernand. The old fool has more sense than the rest of them." He pointed at the corpse. "To the furnaces with that, major. If they have no evidence, the folks won't act, no matter how much they suspect."

The humming started again.

Linkman drew the pistol from his pocket. There was a light knock at the door.

"Yes?" Linkman called.

"Oliver, Dr. Linkman."

Sweat started on Linkman's brow. Falkayan drew a pistol, but Linkman gave a wordless snarl and shook his head. He put his gun back in the drawer.

"A moment," he called.

His frantic eyes lighted on the clothes locker. He stepped over and took out his coat and hat. He beckoned to Falkayn.

"In here," the doctor whispered. "Both of you. Stand on him, if necessary. Stay there until I return."

Falkayn dragged the body across the room. Linkman looked for bloodstains, saw none. He tossed Falkayn's cigar into the waste chute and walked unhurriedly to the door. The detector in the drawer still hummed.

"Good evening," the doctor bowed to Oliver. "You are just in time. I was just leaving."

"Glad to see you," smiled Oliver. "Although I have a complaint to make."

"A complaint?"

"Yes. You're working too hard, doctor."

Linkman smiled in turn.

"One must work to do the job," he said.

He still stood in the doorway, holding his hat and coat so that they were very apparent to his visitor.

"But not too hard," replied Oliver. "Have you an engagement, doctor? If not, I'd like to take a look around and then—perhaps you might have dinner with me."

"You are very kind." Still smiling, Linkman stepped back and gestured toward the inner office. "I am free for the evening. Shall we take a look at the charts, first? I have some figures that give me much satisfaction."

"I know you have."

As he followed Oliver into the office, Linkman stared balefully at the director's broad back. A knife between those big shoulders

—he shrugged off the idea regretfully. It was yet no time for personal pleasures.

Oliver stood where the corpse had lain and glanced around approvingly.

"Very pleasant." He took a step toward the big production chart.

"You've done well, doctor. I am sincerely glad for—"

He broke off. Linkman stiffened. Both men heard the faint hum of the detector. Oliver raised his eyebrows and half turned back to the doctor.

"An infernal machine?" He smiled, but his eyes were grave.

"Not at all," Linkman returned the smile. "Just a little gadget I've developed myself." (It was really Franz's invention.) "An alarm, based on the photoelectric principle."

"So? Let me see it. Perhaps you've got some patents coming to you."

Oliver stepped around behind the desk and waited expectantly. Linkman tossed his coat and hat on the chair and opened the drawer. Too late, he saw his pistol exposed to view.

"Really, Dr. Linkman," Oliver said slowly. "I don't quite understand this. The law forbids all nonmilitary citizens the possession of weapons." He stared hard at the doctor. "Nor do I quite understand just why you feel the need of an alarm, here in your private office."

Falkayn stepped from the locker, a stubby oxy-gun pointing at Oliver.

"Put up your hands, director!" he snapped.

"Falkayn! You are too zealous!" Linkman shook with rage.

"If I may presume, sir," retorted Falkayn, "the snooping swine would have handled the gun."

Linkman calmed visibly.

"Perhaps. I apologize, major."

The two bowed stiffly.

Oliver had not lost his calm. He looked from one to the other, dominating them with his quiet presence.

"May I ask, gentlemen," he said, "what these . . . these theatricals mean?"

Linkman raised his hand to eye level and held it for a moment, staring somberly at his bent fingers. Then he lashed out viciously, smashing Oliver in the mouth. Oliver's knees buckled, but he did not fall. He pulled himself erect and wiped the blood off his swelling lips.

"I was wrong about you, doctor. Wasn't I?" His voice was almost conversational in tone. "But will you explain just how I was wrong?"

Linkman rubbed his knuckles absently.

"He must be disposed of," he muttered. "But how? When? He will be missed. There will be a search—"

He paused. Then he reached for a phone.

He dialed a number, waited for a moment, then the mechanical voice of the director's fone-man intoned into the receiver.

"The director is not here. The director is not here. He left at six. May be at his club at seven. If not, try his residence. The director is—"

Linkman switched off the phone. He grinned evilly at Oliver.

"You should have mentioned you were coming here," he gloated. "No one but the plant doorman knows you are here." He turned to the major. "Take care of the doorman, Falkayn. Put one of our men in his place."

Falkayn saluted. Oliver's eyes narrowed when he saw the salute.

"Put the doorman's body and that spy's into a furnace. Be sure you leave no traces."

Linkman turned to Oliver and his eyes began to glow.

"As for you, my dear director," he sneered, "you shall live—for a while. You shall even start our flight with us!"

"Your flight?"

"Yes." Linkman's voice rose to a scream. "For five years I've toadied to you. I've gone to school and earned your gracious approval and become a good citizen! Do you know why I've debased myself so? Why I've licked your boots to get this factory? I'll tell you! I've found a few of the faithful left. I've brought them here to work with me. We are building a rocketship!"

"A rocketship?" Despite the pain it caused him, Mark Oliver began to laugh.

Falkayn stepped forward and slapped him.

"You will not laugh when the Leader speaks," he said.

"Yes." Linkman seemed oblivious of the interruption. "A rocketship to conquer space. We'll find a planet—make it ours—build a new race. One that lives and dies by my Leader's teachings!"

Oliver gazed at him with horror-struck eyes.

"Man," he said thickly, "you're insane."

Falkayn slapped him again, harder.

"You will not speak of him so," he cried. "He has become our Leader. And he will lead us to a new world. We have built our ship, here—right under your nose. I, myself, am an engineer. I know the ship will work."

"Our plans are well developed," sneered Linkman. "The ship is almost done. And, in return for your kindness to me, I shall take you with us—part of the way."

Oliver gave him a long, searching look.

"Yes," he said slowly, "I was wrong about you, Linkman." He wiped his lips with the back of his hand. "I won't plead with you," he went on, "or argue, for you are mad—mad with the worst madness that ever infected mankind!"

They both started toward him, but he lifted his hand and they halted. He grinned at them.

"Creatures of habit," he mocked. "Aren't you? And, I solemnly assure you, both of you, your habit is and always will be—failure!"

Linkman smashed him across the face with the gun barrel. As Oliver fell, Linkman kicked him.

Falkayn gazed at him admiringly.

"The Leader would be proud of you, sir," he whispered.

At ten-thirty in the morning, two days later, Linkman walked briskly through the engine-assembly room of his plant, nodding and smiling to his workers. He checked the speed of the conveyor belts, stopped to comment admiringly on an assembled engine, clocked the speed of the automatic cranes as they shuttled from one assembly room to the next. Then he walked out of the plant and across the yard to the edge of the small testing field. He was not surprised to see two men, in the uniform of the Civil Guard, examining a row of planes lined up for the arrival of the test pilots.

"Good morning, gentlemen," he called. "Checking specifications?"

They returned his greeting without warmth. They were not civil servants, but old soldiers who had received no training in toleration of a former foe.

"We have been examining your plant," one of them said.

"Examining the plant? But I would have been glad to escort you."

"We were searching it—if you want to know the truth."

Dr. Linkman drew himself up. His tone was a nice blend of injured dignity and weary patience.

"But why, gentlemen? Are there any charges against me?"

"Nope. No charges." The Guard turned to his companion. "Nothing here, Jed. Let's go."

They tramped across the field and out of the plant gate. Linkman grinned after them, then bent his head slightly and stared at the ground. He stamped his foot lightly.

"Poor, ignorant swine," he laughed. "It was right below you, all the time!"

He returned to the plant, walking unhurriedly. Through the assembly room he went and an elevator took him from there to the forge rooms, one floor down. Air conditioning fought successfully with the blasting heat of electric furnaces. Crane cars passed by overhead, men ladled molten steel into buckets, hammers smashed glowing blocks into new, hardened shapes. All were too busy to note the entrance of Linkman.

He strolled about carelessly for a moment, then stepped around the side of a furnace. He felt along the insulated wall of the furnace near its junction with the side of the building. As he probed, a section of the furnace wall turned on an axis and Linkman slipped through the opening revealed and passed down a short flight of steps.

It was simple enough. During the war, a bombproof cellar had been dug out below the plant and there a duplicate factory had been created, fitted with machinery and living quarters for the workmen. It had been used, too, when enemy bombs had shattered the plant above.

When peace and the allied invaders came, the surface plant had been recommissioned. Its underground copy was stripped of its machinery and sealed up.

But Linkman knew about it. It was being used.

He stopped at the foot of the stairs, as he always did, and gazed silently at the monster shape that gleamed silently in the dimness. He lifted his hand in salute.

"You'll leave this hole soon," he said softly, "and go where you belong, up through the sky to the stars!"

He walked along the seamless hull, gazing at the blast tubes, the steering vanes higher than himself. A port was open and he climbed in. The interior of the ship was a madhouse. A pressure lift hoisted the fuel tanks while workmen welded them into place. Men trotted nimbly along the lower catwalk, bent double with crates of supplies Linkman made his way to the upper catwalk and the pilothouse.

Major Falkayn turned from a calculator.

"Good morning, general! I'm glad to say that we're ahead of schedule."

"Yes. I noticed the fuel tanks. How about the fuel?"

"It is being mixed."

"Good."

Linkman went up to the instrument bank and stared down at the rows of dials. He fiddled absently with a control.

"I could wish some of our scientists had remained faithful," he muttered. "We could use them, now."

"Lieutenant Raeder was with the Fleet," Falkayn ventured. "He is thoroughly grounded in astronomy."

Linkman nodded.

"Yes. And Colonel Memsur was in Chemical Warfare." He gazed around the crowded room. "We will not be comfortable. It will be a voyage for men."

"But, of necessity, some women will take it," chuckled Falkayn.

"Yes. I am glad that some of our men are married. Otherwise there would have been further complications."

He stepped out of the room and back along the catwalk.

"Some of the wives are young," said Falkayn. "And attractive."

Linkman withered him with a glance.

"*I* shall beget no children," he said. "None now living shall take my place. As Fate brought me to succeed the Leader, so shall I leave it to Fate to bring forth my successor."

He stopped and leaned over the rail. Below him was the engine room. Men darted in and out among the intricate machinery of the converters, making last-minute adjustments on the conduit system. Far to aft he could hear a faint roar as the auxiliary motor, designed to carry the ship past the friction of the atmosphere, was being tuned up.

"To think," he said, "that, surrounded and dogged by my enemies, I have built this in only four months. Now, we must go. I have the Leader's intuition. It tells me that we must hurry!"

Falkayn shrugged.

"Test the wiring hookup, set up gun emplacements and—"

"Gun emplacements! Why have you delayed that?"

"They were not in the plans."

"Oh, yes." Linkman smiled grimly. "My young brother would not have designed them. I will speak to him at once."

Linkman went down the steps so fast he almost lost his footing. Why, why did he always have to ask and wheedle—instead of commanding? Naturally, Franz would not have designed armament—so he, Linkman, must postpone until the last, dangerous moment to make known their desperate need. Thank all the gods, the days of deception were over.

He jerked open the door of Franz's little cubbyhole. The cripple turned on his high stool and gave his brother an uncertain smile. "Josef!" he exclaimed. "How are—"

"Never mind," the other rasped. "I have a task for you. You must design gun emplacements for each port. To fire when the port is open, but the gun must have plenty of protection. Make it simple."

"Guns?"

"Yes, of course. One 6-inch gun to a side. With two 107s at each of the other ports."

"But, Josef!" Franz climbed down from his stool and limped toward his brother. "Armament is forbidden! The government would never accept our ship if it were designed for war!"

Dr. Linkman lighted a cigar. He inhaled deeply and blew the smoke at Franz. His lips curled in a sardonic grin.

"My little Franz," he murmured. "My little, innocent brother."

He stared hard at the younger man until Franz's eyes dropped guiltily.

"Did you think," Linkman went on with extreme gentleness, "that I was really developing this ship for the government? That I was going to give the greatest thing in history to this government that has killed our Leader and destroyed his teaching?"

"But I . . . I thought—"

"Yes?" Linkman took a step forward. "You thought what?"

"That you . . . you had changed. That you believed in the new government—"

"Ah!" Linkman threw back his head. "I am a success, indeed, for I have deluded my own brother."

He stepped forward again, until he was very close to Franz. He reached down and tilted the other's chin up.

"My boy," he said softly, "this government will never know of your ship—until it and thousands like it come back from the stars to destroy them. We leave in a few days. For Venus or Mars— there to set up the Leader's government! In your ship . . . in our ship, for although you are weak and feeble, you are still one of us!"

There was a discreet tap at the door. Linkman turned. A grimy workman stood at rigid attention.

"Your pardon, my general," he said, "but the prisoner demands to see you.

"I'll come along shortly," Linkman answered.

Franz stared wide-eyed as the workman saluted, then withdrew.

"Yes," grinned his brother. "An old soldier of mine. As all of them are. They follow me to a new world."

He reached out and grasped the boy's shoulders, dug his fingers in, deep.

"You may come, too, if you like," he said softly. "Otherwise—well, the invaders must not be able to follow me." He gave the boy a push. "Get busy on those gun mounts. I must visit that prisoner— our great director, Mr. Oliver!"

Franz slumped there against the table, dazed and sick. His first reaction was one of fear for his brother. His brother kidnaped Mr. Oliver—they would execute him for that. No—his brother was going to the Moon—or was it Mars—and there would be war again.

He moved weakly toward the door.

They would take him with them. Take him to the New World. He shook his head. No. Long ago, before his people had lost their war, he had known. Known with the wisdom of childhood that only his brother's eminence had kept him, crippled Franz, alive. There was no place for cripples in a state of supermen.

He peered out of the door. He did not know Oliver. But Oliver's government had allowed him to go to school and study the mathematics that he loved. He saw his brother go to the door of an abandoned tool closet and open it.

Mark Oliver looked up and focused his eyes on Linkman.

"I wish a drink of water," he said slowly and clearly.

"Sorry, I haven't time." Linkman laughed at his own humor.

"Give me a drink. Then let me out of here."

Linkman's laugh reverberated throughout the tiny room.

Oliver forced himself to concentrate. He licked his bruised lips with a swollen tongue. It was hard to talk.

"You are really going through with this madness?"

"Certainly."

Oliver closed his eyes, then forced them open.

"I have made a mistake in you," he said thickly. "A great mistake."

"You are all such fools," Linkman said casually.

"Not . . . not such as you. You . . . will always fail."

"Even now?" chuckled Linkman.

"You will do something . . . make some mistake . . . your kind doesn't *know*—" Oliver fainted. He did not feel it as Linkman kicked him before he went out.

"I wish, general," Blake, Director of Police, said irritably, "you would stop that confounded pacing!"

General McClernand took two steps to the facsimile receiver, then three to the electrofile, then two back to the director's desk. He bent over Blake's desk and thrust out his lower lip.

"Then do something!" he bellowed.

Blake ran a hand through his gray hair.

"General," he said patiently, "will you either shut up or give me some evidence?"

He gestured toward Hastings, who was manipulating a file separator.

"His report on the discharged workmen is the only concrete, factual bit of knowledge anybody has given me in the whole affair! Anything new, son?"

Hastings shrugged.

"Not yet, sir."

The director beat his palm with a hard fist.

"That's it, General Mac. I have nothing to go on!"

McClernand shoved a pipe in his mouth and bit hard. The bowl came loose in his hand. He hurled the wreckage to the floor.

"You . . . you're just like the rest—soft! You can't do anything!" Blake cursed.

"I put a secret operative on Linkman. Against the law, of course, but you asked me to. The man disappeared before turning in a single report. Hastings has dug up enough information to bring before Mr. Oliver. But Mr. Oliver disappears. So—again on your say-so—I sent two Civil Guards to search Linkman's factory. They couldn't find a thing!"

He leaned back in his chair and scowled at McClernand.

"The whole thing rests upon your personal dislike of Dr. Linkman. A dislike completely unsupported by factual evidence!"

"Humph! Do you like him?"

"No. I served on your staff—remember?" He grinned wryly. "But damn it, General Mac, we made these laws and we've got to obey them!"

Hastings stopped feeding cards into the separator.

"Ah, gentlemen," he ventured, "speaking outside the law, now, I think we are right in suspecting Dr. Linkman. My investigations have convinced me that his behavior mold is too set, his basic inclinations too well directed, to ever admit the possibility of fundamental change in his character."

"Which means, Mac," came a tired voice from the doorway, "that you can't teach an old dog new tricks. Just as you said."

The three turned as though on a single axis.

Oliver leaned against the door jamb. His battered lips tried to grin as they rushed to him. McClernand reached him first.

"Where you hurt?" he growled.

Hastings pushed a chair forward.

"I'm all right," Oliver said. "Some brandy, Blake, if you please. Round up all the men you can. Mac, call out the whole Civil Guard. We're going over to Zellercraft—in a hurry!"

"So it was Linkman!" cried the general.

"Yes." Oliver stood up. His eyes were clear again. "Prepare for a shock, gentlemen. Linkman's crippled brother has designed a rocketship for interplanetary travel. Linkman has built the ship in his factory!"

They stared.

"Yes, it's true." Oliver rubbed his aching head. "Linkman plans to conquer another planet."

Hastings nodded.

"Part of his proper pattern," he said.

Blake clicked off the phone he'd been using.

"Car's ready for us." He smiled vaguely. "I don't believe this, chief, but I'm at your orders."

"I don't believe it, either," said McClernand.

"It's true. I've seen it. I called at Linkman's office—just after he'd finished killing a man—"

"My man." Blake's voice was quiet. "Let's go."

"Not Oliver," grunted McClernand.

Oliver took a shaky step toward the door.

"Yes," he said firmly. "I'm going. This is partly my fault—and wholly our fault. I imagine our engineers laughed at the crippled boy when he submitted his designs."

He took another, firmer step.

"I can make it. No arguments, Mac. Remember, I rank you."

Their car spiraled up to a traffic-tree span and shot along toward the factory.

"Just what did happen to you?" asked Blake.

"They held me prisoner in an abandoned lower level of the plant," Oliver answered. "The ship's there. I think, somehow, it will work."

"To think *they* should have invented it," murmured Hastings.

"No." Oliver leaned out of the car window and took a deep breath of the night air. "The boy is one of us. He thought he was building it for us—to prove it could be done, you know. Today, his brother told him the truth. Tonight, he helped me get away."

"Here we are," said Blake. "There's a car of Guards!"

MacClernand peered over the side.

"Take the main ramp off the span," he said. "I see some people out on their testing field."

"They can't be starting already!" cried Oliver. "Hurry, Blake!"

They piled out of the car before it was fully stopped. Blake gave a low whistle and the Guards came running up. The great gate was locked, but a flamer blasted it. They surged through and rushed toward the building.

"Wait!" called Blake. "What's that on the ground?"

"No lights, now," ordered McClernand.

"I can see," grunted Oliver. "It's young Linkman."

Despite the pain in his ribs he knelt by the prone figure. The cripple lifted his head a little.

"Director!" he cried weakly. "Josef forced me to tell . . . I helped you . . . then he shot me. They are taking my ship . . . auxiliary motor only until they . . . they—"

The twisted body collapsed. Oliver reached forward and touched the big head. Then he rose to his feet.

"Come on," he said.

There was a throbbing roar from the other side of the building. The gleaming snout of the rocketship raised itself slowly above the roofline. They ran around the side of the building to the testing field. But they were too late.

"Fire, damn it!" bellowed McClernand.

The Guards gave a ragged volley. They could not miss, but the small shells exploded harmlessly against the sides of the ship.

"After all, they built it to ward off meteors," said Oliver.

"Some of you phone Aërial Defense," barked McClernand. "Blake, have a man get through to Grauheim Field and have every ship go up."

"Go ahead," Oliver said, "but we'll never catch them. Once they get high enough for rockets—"

"Then to the devil with them!" snarled McClernand.

Oliver watched the ship lunge skyward, auxiliary props making a furious drone.

"No," he said. "Don't you see, Mac, they'll be back!"

"Bah, they'll never make it!"

"Yes, they will. Look what Linkman himself has done. They'll make it—unless we stop them again."

They stared at each other, each with eyes that saw something other than the man before him. A sky filled with wheeling, diving planes, raining bombs on this white, immaculate city they had helped build. This, and all other cities, smashed by tanks, scarred with bombs beyond the recognition of peaceful eyes.

Oliver turned away slowly and his eye caught the row of new planes. Linkman had not bothered to cover them against the dew. He stared at them. Mail planes, standing sleek and trim, lined up for an initial test. Something clicked in his mind. He looked over his shoulder at the giant rocketship, then ran toward the planes.

"Hey!" yelled McClernand.

He took a step, then broke into a run. But he was old. Oliver reached a plane, slid open a port and jumped in. The elevator motor roared and the plane shot up.

McClernand stopped, panting. Blake and Hastings came alongside him and stared skyward.

"What's he going to do?" asked Blake, although he knew.

"Ram it, of course." Hastings' voice was as expressionless as ever. "Only way to stop it, you know."

The plane's drive turned over, then roared into life. It seemed to leap forward in the air. A Guard came out of the plant office, stopped short and looked up. Searchlights went on over the city, picked out the rocketship easily. The plane, tiny now, sped after it.

They saw the plane go high, above the ship, and poise there.

Then it dived.

For one moment they saw it on its way. Then the two met with a faint crash. The rocketship staggered and the smashed plane fell off, toward the earth. The big ship nosed down, seemed to recover, then, with an awful roar, it exploded.

The watchers turned away.

It was the unemotional Hastings who pronounced Oliver's epitaph.

"Now," he said, "we must build one."

THE WEAPONS SHOP

by

A. E. VAN VOGT

⊂⊏

Twentieth-century man is on the doorstep of wonder. What of that distant day when present dim conceptions have been resolved into concrete achievements? Questioning thus, Mr. Van Vogt has projected his imagination seven thousand years into the future, conceiving of an earth applying natural forces in ways that seem pure magic to the reader. The conquest of space and time has progressed logically to its ultimate triumph. But, sociologically, man has degenerated. The bare new world is governed by a ruthless dictatorship, opposed only by a gallant few. But the few are themselves masters of science and, with cold practicality, they turn their science to the one path of salvation—the manufacture of weapons that are invincible.

*

THE VILLAGE at night made a curiously timeless picture. Fara walked contentedly beside his wife along the street. The air was like wine; and he was thinking dimly of the artist who had come up from Imperial City, and made what the telestats called—he remembered the phrase vividly—" a symbolic painting reminiscent of a scene in the electrical age of seven thousand years ago."

Fara believed that utterly. The street before him with its weedless, automatically tended gardens, its shops set well back among the flowers, its perpetual hard, grassy sidewalks, and its street lamps that glowed from every pore of their structure—this was a restful paradise where time had stood still.

And it was like being a part of life that the great artist's picture of

741

this quiet, peaceful scene before him was now in the collection of the empress herself. She had praised it, and naturally the thrice-blest artist had immediately and humbly begged her to accept it.

What a joy it must be to be able to offer personal homage to the glorious, the divine, the serenely gracious and lovely Innelda Isher, one thousand one hundred eightieth of her line.

As they walked, Fara half turned to his wife, In the dim light of the nearest street lamp, her kindly, still youthful face was almost lost in shadow. He murmured softly, instinctively muting his voice to harmonize with the pastel shades of night:

"She said—our empress said—that our little village of Glay seemed to her to have in it all the wholesomeness, the gentleness, that constitutes the finest qualities of her people. Wasn't that a wonderful thought, Creel? She must be a marvelously understanding woman. I—"

He stopped. They had come to a side street, and there was something about a hundred and fifty feet along it that—

"Look!" Fara said hoarsely.

He pointed with rigid arm and finger at a sign that glowed in the night, a sign that read:

FINE WEAPONS

THE RIGHT TO BUY WEAPONS IS THE RIGHT TO BE FREE

Fara had a strange, empty feeling as he stared at the blazing sign. He saw that other villagers were gathering. He said finally, huskily:

"I've heard of these shops. They're places of infamy, against which the government of the empress will act one of these days. They're built in hidden factories, and then transported whole to towns like ours and set up in gross defiance of property rights. That one wasn't there an hour ago."

Fara's face hardened. His voice had a harsh edge in it, as he said: "Creel, go home."

Fara was surprised when Creel did not move off at once. All their married life, she had had a pleasing habit of obedience that had made cohabitation a wonderful thing. He saw that she was looking at him wide-eyed, and that it was a timid alarm that held her there. She said:

"Fara, what do you intend to do? You're not thinking of—"

"Go home!" Her fear brought out all the grim determination in his nature. "We're not going to let such a monstrous thing desecrate our village. Think of it"—his voice shivered before the appalling thought—"this fine, old-fashioned community, which we had resolved always to keep exactly as the empress has it in her picture gallery, debauched now, ruined by this . . . this thing— But we won't have it; that's all there is to it."

Creel's voice came softly out of the half-darkness of the street corner, the timidity gone from it: "Don't do anything rash, Fara. Remember it is not the first new building to come into Glay—since the picture was painted."

Fara was silent. This was a quality of his wife of which he did not approve, this reminding him unnecessarily of unpleasant facts. He knew exactly what she meant. The gigantic, multitentacled corporation, Automatic Atomic Motor Repair Shops, Inc., had come in under the laws of the State with their flashy building, against the wishes of the village council—and had already taken half of Fara's repair business.

"That's different!" Fara growled finally. "In the first place people will discover in good time that these new automatic repairers do a poor job. In the second place its fair competition. But this weapon shop is a defiance of all the decencies that make life under the House of Isher such a joy. Look at the hypocritical sign: 'The right to buy weapons—' Aaaaahh!"

He broke off with: "Go home, Creel. We'll see to it that they sell no weapons in this town."

He watched the slender woman-shape move off into the shadows. She was halfway across the street when a thought occurred to Fara. He called:

"And if you see that son of ours hanging around some street corner, take him home. He's got to learn to stop staying out so late at night."

The shadowed figure of his wife did not turn; and after watching her for a moment moving along against the dim background of softly glowing street lights, Fara twisted on his heel, and walked swiftly toward the shop. The crowd was growing larger every minute, and the night pulsed with excited voices.

Beyond doubt, here was the biggest thing that had ever happened to the village of Glay.

The sign of the weapon shop was, he saw, a normal-illusion affair. No matter what his angle of view, he was always looking straight at it.

When he paused finally in front of the great display window, the words had pressed back against the store front, and were staring unwinkingly down at him.

Fara sniffed once more at the meaning of the slogan, then forgot the simple thing. There was another sign in the window, which read:

THE FINEST ENERGY WEAPONS IN THE KNOWN
UNIVERSE

A spark of interest struck fire inside Fara. He gazed at that brilliant display of guns, fascinated in spite of himself. The weapons were of every size, ranging from tiny little finger pistols to express rifles. They were made of every one of the light, hard, ornamental substances: glittering glassein, the colorful but opaque Ordine plastic, viridescent magnesitic beryllium. And others.

It was the very deadly extent of the destructive display that brought a chill to Fara. So many weapons for the little village of Glay, where not more than two people to his knowledge had guns, and those only for hunting. Why, the thing was absurd, fantastically mischievous, utterly threatening.

Somewhere behind Fara, a man said: "It's right on Lan Harris' lot. Good joke on that old scoundrel. Will he raise a row!"

There was a faint titter from several men, that made an odd patch of sound on the warm, fresh air. And Fara saw that the man had spoken the truth. The weapon shop had a forty-foot frontage. And it occupied the very center of the green, gardenlike lot of tight-fisted old Harris.

Fara frowned. The clever devils, the weapon-shop people, selecting the property of the most disliked man in town, coolly taking it over and giving everybody an agreeable titillation. But the very cunning of it made it vital that the trick shouldn't succeed.

He was still scowling anxiously when he saw the plump figure of Mel Dale, the mayor. Fara edged toward him hurriedly, touched his hat respectfully, and said:

"Where's Jor?"

"Here." The village constable elbowed his way through a little bundle of men. "Any plans?" he said.

"There's only one plan," said Fara boldly. "Go in and arrest them."

To Fara's amazement, the two men looked at each other, then at the ground. It was the big constable who answered shortly:

"Door's locked. And nobody answers our pounding. I was just
going to suggest we let the matter ride until morning."

"Nonsense!" His very astonishment made Fara impatient. "Get an
ax and we'll break the door down. Delay will only encourage such
riffraff to resist. We don't want their kind in our village for so much
as a single night. Isn't that so?"

There was a hasty nod of agreement from everybody in his immediate vicinity. Too hasty. Fara looked around puzzled at eyes that
lowered before his level gaze. He thought: "They are all scared. And
unwilling." Before he could speak, Constable Jor said:

"I guess you haven't heard about those doors or these shops. From
all accounts, you can't break into them."

It struck Fara with a sudden pang that it was he who would have
to act here. He said, "I'll get my atomic cutting machine from my
shop. That'll fix them. Have I your permission to do that, Mr.
Mayor?"

In the glow of the weapon-shop window, the plump man was
sweating visibly. He pulled out a handkerchief, and wiped his forehead. He said:

"Maybe I'd better call the commander of the Imperial garrison at
Ferd, and ask them."

"No!" Fara recognized evasion when he saw it. He felt himself
steel; the conviction came that all the strength in this village was in
him. "We must act ourselves. Other communities have let these people get in because they took no decisive action. We've got to resist to
the limit. Beginning now. This minute. Well?"

The mayor's "All right!" was scarcely more than a sigh of sound.
But it was all Fara needed.

He called out his intention to the crowd; and then, as he pushed
his way out of the mob, he saw his son standing with some other
young men staring at the window display.

Fara called: "Cayle, come and help me with the machine."

Cayle did not even turn; and Fara hurried on, seething. That
wretched boy! One of these days he, Fara, would have to take firm
action there. Or he'd have a no-good on his hands.

The energy was soundless—and smooth. There was no sputter, no
fireworks. It glowed with a soft, pure white light, almost caressing the
metal panels of the door—but not even beginning to sear them.

Minute after minute, the dogged Fara refused to believe the incredible failure, and played the boundlessly potent energy on that resist-

ing wall. When he finally shut off his machine, he was perspiring freely.

"I don't understand it," he gasped. "Why—no metal is supposed to stand up against a steady flood of atomic force. Even the hard metal plates used inside the blast chamber of a motor take the explosions in what is called infinite series, so that each one has unlimited rest. That's the theory, but actually steady running crystallizes the whole plate after a few months."

"It's as Jor told you," said the mayor. "These weapon shops are— big. They spread right through the empire, and they don't recognize the empress."

Fara shifted his feet on the hard grass, disturbed. He didn't like this kind of talk. It sounded—sacrilegious. And besides it was nonsense. It must be. Before he could speak, a man said somewhere behind him:

"I've heard it said that that door will open only to those who cannot harm the people inside."

The words shocked Fara out of his daze. With a start, and for the first time, he saw that his failure had had a bad psychological effect. He said sharply:

"That's ridiculous! If there were doors like that, we'd all have them. We—"

The thought that stopped his words was the sudden realization that he had not seen anybody try to open the door; and with all this reluctance around him it was quite possible that—

He stepped forward, grasped at the doorknob, and pulled. The door opened with an unnatural weightlessness that gave him the fleeting impression that the knob had come loose into his hand. With a gasp, Fara jerked the door wide open.

"Jor!" he yelled. "Get in!"

The constable made a distorted movement—distorted by what must have been a will to caution, followed by the instant realization that he could not hold back before so many. He leaped awkwardly toward the open door—and it closed in his face.

Fara stared stupidly at his hand, which was still clenched. And then, slowly, a hideous thrill coursed along his nerves. The knob had —withdrawn. It had twisted, become viscous, and slipped amorphously from his straining fingers. Even the memory of that brief sensation gave him a feeling of unnormal things.

He grew aware that the crowd was watching with a silent intentness. Fara reached again for the knob, not quite so eagerly this time; and it was only a sudden realization of his reluctance that made him angry when the handle neither turned nor yielded in any way.

Determination returned in full force, and with it came a thought. He motioned to the constable. "Go back, Jor, while I pull."

The man retreated, but it did no good. And tugging did not help. The door would not open. Somewhere in the crowd, a man said darkly:

"It decided to let you in, then it changed its mind."

"What foolishness are you talking!" Fara spoke violently. "It changed its mind. Are you crazy? A door has no sense."

But a surge of fear put a half-quaver into his voice. It was the sudden alarm that made him bold beyond all his normal caution. With a jerk of his body, Fara faced the shop.

The building loomed there under the night sky, in itself bright as day, huge in width and length, and alien, menacing, no longer easily conquerable. The dim queasy wonder came as to what the soldiers of the empress would do if they were invited to act. And suddenly— a bare, flashing glimpse of a grim possibility—the feeling grew that even they would be able to do nothing.

Abruptly, Fara was conscious of horror that such an idea could enter his mind. He shut his brain tight, said wildly:

"The door opened for me once. It will open again."

It did. Quite simply it did. Gently, without resistance, with that same sensation of weightlessness, the strange, sensitive door followed the tug of his fingers. Beyond the threshold was dimness, a wide, darkened alcove. He heard the voice of Mel Dale behind him, the mayor saying:

"Fara, don't be a fool. What will you do inside?"

Fara was vaguely amazed to realize that he had stepped across the threshold. He turned, startled, and stared at the blur of faces "Why—" he began blankly; then he brightened; he said, "Why, I'll buy a gun, of course."

The brilliance of his reply, the cunning implicit in it, dazzled Fara for half a minute longer. The mood yielded slowly, as he found himself in the dimly lighted interior of the weapon shop.

It was preternaturally quiet inside. Not a sound penetrated from the night from which he had come; and the startled thought came that the people of the shop might actually be unaware that there was a crowd outside.

Fara walked forward gingerly on a rugged floor that muffled his footsteps utterly. After a moment, his eyes accustomed themselves to the soft lighting, which came like a reflection from the walls and ceilings. In a vague way, he had expected ultranormalness; and the ordinariness of the atomic lighting acted like a tonic to his tensed nerves.

He shook himself angrily. Why should there be anything really superior? He was getting as bad as those credulous idiots out in the street.

He glanced around with gathering confidence. The place looked quite common. It was a shop, almost scantily furnished. There were showcases on the walls and on the floor, glitteringly lovely things, but nothing unusual, and not many of them—a few dozens. There was in addition a double, ornate door leading to a back room—

Fara tried to keep one eye on that door, as he examined several showcases, each with three or four weapons either mounted or arranged in boxes or holsters.

Abruptly, the weapons began to excite him. He forgot to watch the door, as the wild thought struck that he ought to grab one of those guns from a case, and then the moment someone came, force him outside where Jor would perform the arrest and—

Behind him, a man said quietly: "You wish to buy a gun?"

Fara turned with a jump. Brief rage flooded him at the way his plan had been wrecked by the arrival of the clerk.

The anger died as he saw that the intruder was a fine-looking, silver-haired man, older than himself. That was immeasurably disconcerting. Fara had an immense and almost automatic respect for age, and for a long second he could only stand there gaping. He said at last, lamely:

"Yes, yes, a gun."

"For what purpose?" said the man in his quiet voice.

Fara could only look at him blankly. It was too fast. He wanted to get mad. He wanted to tell these people what he thought of them. But the age of this representative locked his tongue, tangled his emotions. He managed speech only by an effort of will:

"For hunting." The plausible word stiffened his mind. "Yes, definitely for hunting. There is a lake to the north of here," he went on more fulsomely, glibly, "and—"

He stopped, scowling, startled at the extent of his dishonesty. He was not prepared to go so deeply into prevarication. He said curtly:

"For hunting."

Fara was himself again. Abruptly, he hated the man for having put him so completely at a disadvantage. With smoldering eyes he watched the old fellow click open a showcase, and take out a green-shining rifle.

As the man faced him, weapon in hand, Fara was thinking grimly, "Pretty clever, having an old man as a front." It was the same kind of cunning that had made them choose the property of Miser Harris. Icily furious, taut with his purpose, Fara reached for the gun; but the man held it out of his reach, saying:

"Before I can even let you test this, I am compelled by the by-laws of the weapon shops to inform you under what circumstances you may purchase a gun."

So they had private regulations. What a system of psychology tricks to impress gullible fools! Well, let the old scoundrel talk. As soon as he, Fara, got hold of the rifle, he'd put an end to hypocrisy.

"We weapons makers," the clerk was saying mildly, "have evolved guns that can, in their particular ranges, destroy any machine or object made of what is called matter. Thus whoever possesses one of our weapons is the equal and more of any soldier of the empress. I say more because each gun is the center of a field of force which acts as a perfect screen against immaterial destructive forces. That screen offers no resistance to clubs or spears or bullets, or other material substances, but it would require a small atomic cannon to penetrate the superb barrier it creates around its owner.

"You will readily comprehend," the man went on, "that such a potent weapon could not be allowed to fall, unmodified, into irresponsible hands. Accordingly, no gun purchased from us may be used for aggression or murder. In the case of the hunting rifle, only such specified game birds and animals as we may from time to time list in our display windows may be shot. Finally, no weapon can be resold without our approval. Is that clear?"

Fara nodded dumbly. For the moment, speech was impossible to him. The incredible, fantastically stupid words were still going round and around in his head. He wondered if he ought to laugh out loud, or curse the man for daring to insult his intelligence so tremendously.

So the gun mustn't be used for murder or robbery. So only certain birds and animals could be shot. And as for reselling it, suppose— suppose he bought this thing, took a trip of a thousand miles, and offered it to some wealthy stranger for two credits—who would ever know?

Or suppose he held up the stranger. Or shot him. How would the weapon shop ever find out? The thing was so ridiculous that—

He grew aware that the gun was being held out to him stock first. He took it eagerly, and had to fight the impulse to turn the muzzle directly on the old man. Mustn't rush this, he thought tautly. He said.

"How does it work?"

"You simply aim it, and pull the trigger. Perhaps you would like to try it on a target we have."

Fara swung the gun up. "Yes," he said triumphantly, "and you're it. Now, just get over there to the front door, and then outside."

He raised his voice: "And if anybody's thinking of coming through the back door, I've got that covered, too."

He motioned jerkily at the clerk. "Quick now, move! I'll shoot! I swear I will."

The man was cool, unflustered. "I have no doubt you would. When we decided to attune the door so that you could enter despite your hostility, we assumed the capacity for homicide. However, this is our party. You had better adjust yourself accordingly, and look behind you—"

There was silence. Finger on trigger, Fara stood moveless. Dim thoughts came of all the *half-things* he had heard in his days about the weapon shops: that they had secret supporters in every district, that they had a private and ruthless hidden government, and that once you got into their clutches, the only way out was death and—

But what finally came clear was a mind picture of himself, Fara Clark, family man, faithful subject of the empress, standing here in this dimly lighted store, deliberately fighting an organization so vast and menacing that— He must have been mad.

Only—here he was. He forced courage into his sagging muscles, He said:

"You can't fool me with pretending there's someone behind me. Now, get to that door. And *fast!*"

The firm eyes of the old man were looking past him. The man said quietly: "Well, Rad, have you all the data?"

"Enough for a primary," said a young man's baritone voice behind Fara. "Type A-7 conservative. Good average intelligence, but a Monaric development peculiar to small towns. One-sided outlook fostered by the Imperial schools present in exaggerated form. Extremely honest. Reason would be useless. Emotional approach would require extended treatment. I see no reason why we should bother. Let him live his life as it suits him."

"If you think," Fara said shakily, "that that trick voice is going to make me turn, you're crazy. That's the left wall of the building. I know there's no one there."

"I'm all in favor, Rad," said the old man, "of letting him live his life. But he was the prime mover of the crowd outside. I think he should be discouraged."

"We'll advertise his presence," said Rad. "He'll spend the rest of his life denying the charge."

Fara's confidence in the gun had faded so far that, as he listened in puzzled uneasiness to the incomprehensible conversation, he forgot it completely. He parted his lips, but before he could speak, the old man cut in, persistently:

"I think a little emotion might have a long-run effect. Show him the palace."

Palace! The startling word tore Fara out of his brief paralysis. "See here," he began, "I can see now that you lied to me. This gun isn't loaded at all. It's—"

His voice failed him. Every muscle in his body went rigid. He stared like a madman. *There was no gun in his hands.*

"Why, you—" he began wildly. And stopped again. His mind heaved with imbalance. With a terrible effort he fought off the spinning sensation, thought finally, tremblingly: Somebody must have sneaked the gun from him. That meant—there was someone behind him. The voice was no mechanical thing. Somehow, they had—

He started to turn—and couldn't. What in the name of— He struggled, pushing with his muscles. And couldn't move, couldn't budge, couldn't even—

The room was growing curiously dark. He had difficulty seeing the old man and— He would have shrieked then if he could. Because the weapon shop was gone. He was—

He was standing in the sky above an immense city.

In the sky, and nothing beneath him, nothing around him but air, and blue summer heaven, and the city a mile, two miles below.

Nothing, nothing— He would have shrieked, but his breath seemed solidly embedded in his lungs. Sanity came back as the remote awareness impinged upon his terrified mind that he was actually standing on a hard floor, and that the city must be a picture somehow focused directly into his eyes.

For the first time, with a start, Fara recognized the metropolis below. It was the city of dreams, Imperial City, capital of the glorious Empress Isher— From his great height, he could see the gardens, the gorgeous grounds of the silver palace, the official Imperial residence itself—

The last tendrils of his fear were fading now before a gathering fascination and wonder; they vanished utterly as he recognized with a ghastly thrill of uncertain expectancy that the palace was drawing nearer at great speed.

"Show him the palace," they had said. Did that mean, could it mean—

That spray of tense thoughts splattered into nonexistence, as the glittering roof flashed straight at his face. He gulped, as the solid metal of it passed through him, and then other walls and ceilings.

His first sense of imminent and mind-shaking desecration came as the picture paused in a great room where a score of men sat around a table at the head of which sat—a young woman.

The inexorable, sacrilegious, limitlessly powered cameras that were taking the picture swung across the table, and caught the woman full face.

It was a handsome face, but there was passion and fury twisting it now, and a very blaze of fire in her eyes, as she leaned forward, and said in a voice at once familiar—how often Fara had heard its calm, measured tones on the telestats—and distorted. Utterly distorted by anger and an insolent certainty of command. That caricature of a beloved voice slashed across the silence as clearly as if he, Fara, was there in that room:

"I want that skunk killed, do you understand? I don't care how you do it, but I want to hear by tomorrow night that he's dead."

The picture snapped off and instantly—it was as swift as that— Fara was back in the weapon shop. He stood for a moment, swaying, fighting to accustom his eyes to the dimness; and then—

His first emotion was contempt at the simpleness of the trickery— a motion picture. What kind of a fool did they think he was, to swallow something as transparently unreal as that? He'd—

Abruptly, the appalling lechery of the scheme, the indescribable wickedness of what was being attempted here brought red rage.

"Why, you scum!" he flared. "So you've got somebody to act the part of the empress, trying to pretend that— Why, you—"

"That will do," said the voice of Rad; and Fara shook as a big young man walked into his line of vision. The alarmed thought came that people who would besmirch so vilely the character of her imperial majesty would not hesitate to do physical damage to Fara Clark. The young man went on in a steely tone:

"We do not pretend that what you saw was taking place this instant in the palace. That would be too much of a coincidence. But it was taken two weeks ago; the woman *is* the empress. The man whose death she ordered is one of her many former lovers. He was found murdered two weeks ago; his name, if you care to look it up in the news files, is Banton McCreddie. However, let that pass. We're finished with you now and—"

"But I'm not finished," Fara said in a thick voice. "I've never heard or seen so much infamy in all my life. If you think this town is through with you, you're crazy. We'll have a guard on this place day and night, and nobody will get in or out. We'll—"

"That will do." It was the silver-haired man;. and Fara stopped out of respect for age, before he thought. The old man went on· "The examination has been most interesting. As an honest man, you may call on us if you are ever in trouble. That is all. Leave through the side door."

It *was* all. Impalpable forces grabbed him, and he was shoved at a door that appeared miraculously in the wall, where seconds before the palace had been.

He found himself standing dazedly in a flower bed, and there was a swarm of men to his left. He recognized his fellow townsmen and that he was—outside.

The incredible nightmare was over.

"Where's the gun?" said Creel, as he entered the house half an hour later.

"The gun?" Fara stared at his wife.

"It said over the radio a few minutes ago that you were the first customer of the new weapon shop. I thought it was queer, but—"

He was eerily conscious of her voice going on for several words longer, but it was the purest jumble. The shock was so great that he had the horrible sensation of being on the edge of an abyss.

So that was what the young man had meant: "Advertise! We'll advertise his presence and—"

Fara thought: His reputation! Not that his was a great name, but he had long believed with a quiet pride that Fara Clark's motor repair shop was widely known in the community and countryside.

First, his private humiliation inside the shop. And now this—lying

—to people who didn't know why he had gone into the store. Diabolical.

His paralysis ended, as a frantic determination to rectify the base charge drove him to the telestat. After a moment, the plump, sleepy face of Mayor Mel Dale appeared on the plate. Fara's voice made a barrage of sound, but his hopes dashed, as the man said:

"I'm sorry, Fara. I don't see how you can have free time on the telestat. You'll have to pay for it. They did."

"They did!" Fara wondered vaguely if he sounded as empty as he felt.

"And they've just paid Lan Harris for his lot. The old man asked top price, and got it. He just phoned me to transfer the title."

"Oh!" The world was shattering. "You mean nobody's going to do anything. What about the Imperial garrison at Ferd?"

Dimly, Fara was aware of the mayor mumbling something about the empress' soldiers refusing to interfere in civilian matters.

"Civilian matters!" Fara exploded. "You mean these people are just going to be allowed to come here whether we want them or not, illegally forcing the sale of lots by first taking possession of them?"

A sudden thought struck him breathless. "Look, you haven't changed your mind about having Jor keep guard in front of the shop?"

With a start, he saw that the plump face in the telestat plate had grown impatient. "Now, see here, Fara," came the pompous words, "let the constituted authorities handle this matter."

"But you're going to keep Jor there," Fara said doggedly.

The mayor looked annoyed, said finally peevishly: "I promised, didn't I? So he'll be there. And now—do you want to buy time on the telestat? It's fifteen credits for one minute. Mind you, as a friend, I think you're wasting your money. No one has ever caught up with a false statement."

Fara said grimly: "Put two on, one in the morning, one in the evening."

"All right. We'll deny it completely. Good night."

The telestat went blank; and Fara sat there. A new thought hardened his face. "That boy of ours—there's going to be a showdown. He either works in my shop, or he gets no more allowance."

Creel said: "You've handled him wrong. He's twenty-three, and you treat him like a child. Remember, at twenty-three, you were a married man."

"That was different," said Fara. "I had a sense of responsibility.
Do you know what he did tonight?"

He didn't quite catch her answer. For the moment, he thought
she said: "No; in what way did you humiliate him first?"

Fara felt too impatient to verify the impossible words. He rushed
on: "He refused in front of the whole village to give me help. He's a
bad one, all bad."

"Yes," said Creel in a bitter tone, "he is all bad. I'm sure you
don't realize how bad. He's as cold as steel, but without steel's
strength or integrity. He took a long time, but he hates even me
now, because I stood up for your side so long, knowing you were
wrong."

"What's that?" said Fara, startled; then gruffly: "Come, come,
my dear, we're both upset. Let's go to bed."

He slept poorly.

There were days then when the conviction that this was a personal
fight between himself and the weapon shop lay heavily on Fara.
Grimly, though it was out of his way, he made a point of walking
past the weapon shop, always pausing to speak to Constable Jor and—

On the fourth day, the policeman wasn't there.

Fara waited patiently at first, then angrily; then he walked hastily
to his shop, and called Jor's house. No, Jor wasn't home. He was
guarding the weapon store.

Fara hesitated. His own shop was piled with work, and he had a
guilty sense of having neglected his customers for the first time in
his life. It would be simple to call up the mayor and report Jor's
dereliction. And yet—

He didn't want to get the man into trouble—

Out in the street, he saw that a large crowd was gathering in
front of the weapon shop. Fara hurried. A man he knew greeted him
excitedly:

"Jor's been murdered, Fara!"

"Murdered!" Fara stood stock-still, and at first he was not clearly
conscious of the grisly thought that was in his mind: Satisfaction! A
flaming satisfaction. Now, he thought, even the soldiers would have
to act. They—

With a gasp, he realized the ghastly tenor of his thoughts. He
shivered, but finally pushed the sense of shame out of his mind. He
said slowly:

"Where's the body?"

"Inside."

"You mean, those . . . scum—" In spite of himself, he hesitated over the epithet; even now, it was difficult to think of the fine-faced, silver-haired old man in such terms. Abruptly, his mind hardened; he flared: "You mean those scum actually killed him, then pulled his body inside?"

"Nobody saw the killing," said a second man beside Fara, "but he's gone, hasn't been seen for three hours. The mayor got the weapon shop on the telestat, but they claim they don't know anything. They've done away with him, that's what, and now they're pretending innocence. Well, they won't get out of it as easily as that. Mayor's gone to phone the soldiers at Ferd to bring up some big guns and—"

Something of the intense excitement that was in the crowd surged through Fara, the feeling of big things brewing. It was the most delicious sensation that had ever tingled along his nerves, and it was all mixed with a strange pride that he had been so right about this, that he at least had never doubted that here was evil.

He did not recognize the emotion as the full-flowering joy that comes to a member of a mob. But his voice shook, as he said:

"Guns? Yes, that will be the answer, and the soldiers will have to come, of course."

Fara nodded to himself in the immensity of his certainty that the Imperial soldiers would now have no excuse for not acting. He started to say something dark about what the empress would do if she found out that a man had lost his life because the soldiers had shirked their duty, but the words were drowned in a shout:

"Here comes the mayor! Hey, Mr. Mayor, when are the atomic cannons due?"

There was more of the same general meaning, as the mayor's sleek, all-purpose car landed lightly. Some of the questions must have reached his honor, for he stood up in the open two-seater, and held up his hand for silence.

To Fara's astonishment, the plump-faced man looked at him with accusing eyes. The thing seemed so impossible that, quite instinctively, Fara looked behind him. But he was almost alone; everybody else had crowded forward.

Fara shook his head, puzzled by that glare; and then, astoundingly, Mayor Dale pointed a finger at him, and said in a voice that trembled:

"There's the man who's responsible for the trouble that's come upon us. Stand forward, Fara Clark, and show yourself. You've cost this town seven hundred credits that we could ill afford to spend."

Fara couldn't have moved or spoken to save his life. He just stood there in a maze of dumb bewilderment. Before he could even think, the mayor went on, and there was quivering self-pity in his tone:

"We've all known that it wasn't wise to interfere with these weapon shops. So long as the Imperial government leaves them alone, what right have we to set up guards, or act against them? That's what I've thought from the beginning, but this man . . . this . . . this Fara Clark kept after all of us, forcing us to move against our wills, and so now we've got a seven-hundred-credit bill to meet and—"

He broke off with: "I might as well make it brief. When I called the garrison, the commander just laughed and said that Jor would turn up. And I had barely disconnected when there was a money call from Jor. He's on Mars."

He waited for the shouts of amazement to die down. "It'll take three weeks for him to come back by ship, and we've got to pay for it, and Fara Clark is responsible. He—"

The shock was over. Fara stood cold, his mind hard. He said finally, scathingly: "So you're giving up, and trying to blame me all in one breath. I say you're all fools."

As he turned away, he heard Mayor Dale saying something about the situation not being completely lost, as he had learned that the weapon shop had been set up in Glay because the village was equidistant from four cities, and that it was the city business the shop was after. This would mean tourists, and accessory trade for the village stores and—

Fara heard no more. Head high, he walked back toward his shop. There were one or two catcalls from the mob, but he ignored them.

He had no sense of approaching disaster, simply a gathering fury against the weapon shop, which had brought him to this miserable status among his neighbors.

The worst of it, as the days passed, was the realization that the people of the weapon shop had no personal interest in him. They were remote, superior, undefeatable. That unconquerableness was a dim, suppressed awareness inside Fara.

When he thought of it, he felt a vague fear at the way they had transferred Jor to Mars in a period of less than three hours, when all the world knew that the trip by fastest spaceship required nearly three weeks.

Fara did not go to the express station to see Jor arrive home. He had heard that the council had decided to charge Jor with half of the expense of the trip, on the threat of losing his job if he made a fuss.

On the second night after Jor's return, Fara slipped down to the constable's house, and handed the officer one hundred seventy-five credits. It wasn't that he was responsible, he told Jor, but—

The man was only too eager to grant the disclaimer, provided the money went with it. Fara returned home with a clearer conscience.

It was on the third day after that that the door of his shop banged open and a man came in. Fara frowned as he saw who it was: Castler, a village hanger-on. The man was grinning:

"Thought you might be interested, Fara. Somebody came out of the weapon shop today."

Fara strained deliberately at the connecting bolt of a hard plate of the atomic motor he was fixing. He waited with a gathering annoyance that the man did not volunteer further information. Asking questions would be a form of recognition of the worthless fellow. A developing curiosity made him say finally, grudgingly:

"I suppose the constable promptly picked him up."

He supposed nothing of the kind, but it was an opening.

"It wasn't a man. It was a girl."

Fara knitted his brows. He didn't like the idea of making trouble for women. But—the cunning devils! Using a girl, just as they had used an old man as a clerk. It was a trick that deserved to fail, the girl probably a tough one who needed rough treatment. Fara said harshly:

"Well, what's happened?"

"She's still out, bold as you please. Pretty thing, too."

The bolt off, Fara took the hard plate over to the polisher, and began patiently the long, careful task of smoothing away the crystals that heat had seared on the once shining metal. The soft throb of the polisher made the background to his next words:

"Has anything been done?"

"Nope. The constable's been told, but he says he doesn't fancy being away from his family for another three weeks, and paying the cost into the bargain."

Fara contemplated that darkly for a minute, as the polisher throbbed on. His voice shook with suppressed fury, when he said finally:

"So they're letting them get away with it. It's all been as clever as hell. Can't they see that they musn't give an inch before these . . . these transgressors. It's like giving countenance to sin."

From the corner of his eye, he noticed that there was a curious grin on the face of the other. It struck Fara suddenly that the man was enjoying his anger. And there was something else in that grin; something—a secret knowledge.

Fara pulled the engine plate away from the polisher. He faced the ne'er-do-well, scathed at him:

"Naturally, that sin part wouldn't worry you much."

"Oh," said the man nonchalantly, "the hard knocks of life make people tolerant. For instance, after you know the girl better, you yourself will probably come to realize that there's good in all of us."

It was not so much the words, as the curious I've-got-secret-information tone that made Fara snap:

"What do you mean—if I get to know the girl better! I won't even speak to the brazen creature."

"One can't always choose," the other said with enormous casualness. "Suppose he brings her home."

"Suppose who brings who home?" Fara spoke irritably. "Castler, you—"

He stopped; a dead weight of dismay plumped into his stomach; his whole being sagged. "You mean—" he said.

"I mean," replied Castler with a triumphant leer, "that the boys aren't letting a beauty like her be lonesome. And, naturally, your son was the first to speak to her."

He finished: "They're walkin' together now on Second Avenue, comin' this way, so—"

"Get out of here!" Fara roared. "And stay away from me with your gloating. Get out!"

The man hadn't expected such an ignominious ending. He flushed scarlet, then went out, slamming the door.

Fara stood for a moment, every muscle stiff; then, with an abrupt, jerky movement, he shut off his power, and went out into the street. The time to put a stop to that kind of thing was—now!

He had no clear plan, just that violent determination to put an immediate end to an impossible situation. And it was all mixed up with his anger against Cayle. How could he have had such a worth-less son, he who paid his debts and worked hard, and tried to be decent and to live up to the highest standards of the empress?

A brief, dark thought came to Fara that maybe there was some bad blood on Creel's side. Not from her mother, of course—Fara added the mental thought hastily. There was a fine, hard-working woman, who hung on to her money, and who would leave Creel a tidy sum one of these days.

But Creel's father had disappeared when Creel was only a child, and there had been some vague scandal about his having taken up with a telestat actress.

And now Cayle with this weapon-shop girl. A girl who had let her-self be picked up—

He saw them, as he turned the corner onto Second Avenue. They were walking a hundred feet distant, and heading away from Fara. The girl was tall and slender, almost as big as Cayle, and, as Fara came up, she was saying:

"You have the wrong idea about us. A person like you can't get a job in our organization. You belong in the Imperial Service, where they can use young men of good education, good appearance and no scruples. I—"

Fara grasped only dimly that Cayle must have been trying to get a job with these people. It was not clear; and his own mind was too intent on his purpose for it to mean anything at the moment. He said harshly:

"Cayle!"

The couple turned, Cayle with the measured unhurriedness of a young man who has gone a long way on the road to steellike nerves; the girl was quicker, but withal dignified.

Fara had a vague, terrified feeling that his anger was too great, self-destroying, but the very violence of his emotions ended that thought even as it came. He said thickly:

"Cayle, get home—at once."

Fara was aware of the girl looking at him curiously from strange, gray-green eyes. No shame, he thought, and his rage mounted sev-eral degrees, driving away the alarm that came at the sight of the flush that crept into Cayle's cheeks.

The flush faded into a pale, tight-lipped anger, Cayle half-turned to the girl, said:

"This is the childish old fool I've got to put up with. Fortunately, we seldom see each other; we don't even eat together. What do you think of him?"

The girl smiled impersonally: "Oh, we know Fara Clark; he's the backbone of the empress in Glay."

"Yes," the boy sneered. "You ought to hear him. He thinks we're living in heaven; and the empress is the divine power. The worst part of it is that there's no chance of his ever getting that stuffy look wiped off his face."

They walked off; and Fara stood there. The very extent of what had happened had drained anger from him as if it had never been. There was the realization that he had made a mistake so great that—

He couldn't grasp it. For long, long now, since Cayle had refused to work in his shop, he had felt this building up to a climax. Suddenly, his own uncontrollable ferocity stood revealed as a partial product of that—deeper—problem.

Only, now that the smash was here, he didn't want to face it—

All through the day in his shop, he kept pushing it out of his mind, kept thinking:

Would this go on now, as before, Cayle and he living in the same house, not even looking at each other when they met, going to bed at different times, getting up, Fara at 6:30, Cayle at noon? Would that go on through all the days and years to come?

When he arrived home, Creel was waiting for him. She said:

"Fara, he wants you to loan him five hundred credits, so that he can go to Imperial City."

Fara nodded wordlessly. He brought the money back to the house the next morning, and gave it to Creel, who took it into the bedroom.

She came out a minute later. "He says to tell you good-by."

When Fara came home that evening, Cayle was gone. He wondered whether he ought to feel relieved or—what?

The days passed. Fara worked. He had nothing else to do, and the gray thought was often in his mind that now he would be doing it till the day he died. Except—

Fool that he was—he told himself a thousand times how big a fool—he kept hoping that Cayle would walk into the shop and say:

"Father, I've learned my lesson. If you can ever forgive me, teach me the business, and then you retire to a well-earned rest."

It was exactly a month to a day after Cayle's departure that the telestat clicked on just after Fara had finished lunch. "Money call," it sighed, "money call."

Fara and Creel looked at each other. "Eh," said Fara finally, "money call for us."

He could see from the gray look in Creel's face the thought that was in her mind. He said under his breath: "Damn that boy!"

But he felt relieved. Amazingly, relieved! Cayle was beginning to appreciate the value of parents and—

He switched on the viewer. "Come and collect," he said.

The face that came on the screen was heavy-jowled, beetle-browed —and strange. The man said:

"This is Clerk Pearton of the Fifth Bank of Ferd. We have received a sight draft on you for ten thousand credits. With carrying charges and government tax, the sum required will be twelve thousand one hundred credits. Will you pay it now or will you come in this afternoon and pay it?"

"B-but . . . b-but—" said Fara. "W-who—"

He stopped, conscious of the stupidity of the question, dimly conscious of the heavy-faced man saying something about the money having been paid out to one Cayle Clark, that morning, in Imperial City. At last, Fara found his voice:

"But the bank had no right," he expostulated, "to pay out the money without my authority. I—"

The voice cut him off coldly: "Are we then to inform our central that the money was obtained under false pretenses? Naturally, an order will be issued immediately for the arrest of your son."

"Wait . . . wait—" Fara spoke blindly. He was aware of Creel beside him, shaking her head at him. She was as white as a sheet, and her voice was a sick, stricken thing, as she said:

"Fara, let him go. He's through with us. We must be as hard— let him go."

The words rang senselessly in Fara's ears. They didn't fit into any normal pattern. He was saying:

"I . . . I haven't got— How about my paying . . . installments? I—"

"If you wish a loan," said Clerk Pearton, "naturally we will be happy to go into the matter. I might say that when the draft arrived, we checked up on your status, and we are prepared to loan you eleven thousand credits on indefinite call with your shop as security. I have the form here, and if you are agreeable, we will switch this call through the registered circuit, and you can sign at once."

"Fara, no."

The clerk went on: "The other eleven hundred credits will have to be paid in cash. Is that agreeable?"

"Yes, yes, of course, I've got twenty-five hund—" He stopped his chattering tongue with a gulp; then: "Yes, that's satisfactory."

The deal completed, Fara whirled on his wife. Out of the depths of his hurt and bewilderment, he raged:

"What do you mean, standing there and talking about not paying it? You said several times that I was responsible for his being what he is. Besides, we don't know why he needed the money. He—"

Creel said in a low, dead tone: "In one hour, he's stripped us of our life work. He did it deliberately, thinking of us as two old fools, who wouldn't know any better than to pay it."

Before he could speak, she went on: "Oh, I know I blamed you, but in the final issue, I knew it was he. He was always cold and calculating, but I was weak, and I was sure that if you handled him in a different . . . and besides I didn't want to see his faults for a long time. He—"

"All I see," Fara interrupted doggedly, "is that I have saved our name from disgrace."

His high sense of duty rightly done lasted until midafternoon, when the bailiff from Ferd came to take over the shop.

"But what—" Fara began.

The bailiff said: "The Automatic Atomic Repair Shops, Limited, took over your loan from the bank, and are foreclosing. Have you anything to say?"

"It's unfair," said Fara. "I'll take it to court. I'll—"

He was thinking dazedly: "If the empress ever learned of this, she'd . . . she'd—"

The courthouse was a big, gray building; and Fara felt emptier and colder every second, as he walked along the gray corridors. In Glay, his decision not to give himself into the hands of a bloodsucker of a lawyer had seemed a wise act. Here, in these enormous halls and palatial rooms, it seemed the sheerest folly.

He managed, nevertheless, to give an articulate account of the criminal act of the bank in first giving Cayle the money, then turning over the note to his chief competitor, apparently within minutes of his signing it. He finished with:

"I'm sure, sir, the empress would not approve of such goings-on against honest citizens. I—"

"How dare you," said the cold-voiced creature on the bench, "use the name of her holy majesty in support of your own gross self-interest?"

Fara shivered. The sense of being intimately a member of the empress' great human family yielded to a sudden chill and a vast mind-picture of the ten million icy courts like this, and the myriad malevolent and heartless men—*like this*—who stood between the empress and her loyal subject, Fara.

He thought passionately: If the empress knew what was happening here, how unjustly he was being treated, she would—

Or would she?

He pushed the crowding, terrible doubt out of his mind—came out of his hard reverie with a start, to hear the Cadi saying:

"Plaintiff's appeal dismissed, with costs assessed at seven hundred credits, to be divided between the court and the defense solicitor in the ratio of five to two. See to it that the appellant does not leave till the costs are paid. Next case—"

Fara went alone the next day to see Creel's mother. He called first at "Farmer's Restaurant" at the outskirts of the village. The place was, he noted with satisfaction in the thought of the steady stream of money flowing in, half full, though it was only midmorning. But madame wasn't there. Try the feed store.

He found her in the back of the feed store, overseeing the weighing out of grain into cloth measures. The hard-faced old woman heard his story without a word. She said finally, curtly:

"Nothing doing, Fara. I'm one who has to make loans often from the bank to swing deals. If I tried to set you up in business, I'd find the Automatic Atomic Repair people getting after me. Besides, I'd be a fool to turn money over to a man who lets a bad son squeeze a fortune out of him. Such a man has no sense about worldly things.

"And I won't give you a job because I don't hire relatives in my business." She finished: "Tell Creel to come and live at my house. I won't support a man, though. That's all."

He watched her disconsolately for a while, as she went on calmly superintending the clerks who were manipulating the old, no longer accurate measuring machines. Twice her voice echoed through the dust-filled interior, each time with a sharp: "That's overweight, a gram at least. Watch your machine."

Though her back was turned, Fara knew by her posture that she was still aware of his presence. She turned at last with an abrupt movement, and said:

"Why don't you go to the weapon shop? You haven't anything to lose, and you can't go on like this."

Fara went out, then, a little blindly. At first the suggestion that he buy a gun and commit suicide had no real personal application. But he felt immeasurably hurt that his mother-in-law should have made it.

Kill himself? Why, it was ridiculous. He was still only a young man, going on fifty. Given the proper chance, with his skilled hands, he could wrest a good living even in a world where automatic ma-chines were encroaching everywhere. There was always room for a man who did a good job. His whole life had been based on that credo.

Kill himself—

He went home to find Creel packing. "It's the common sense thing to do," she said. "We'll rent the house and move into rooms."

He told her about her mother's offer to take her in, watching her face as he spoke. Creel shrugged.

"I told her 'No' yesterday," she said thoughtfully. "I wonder why she mentioned it to you."

Fara walked swiftly over to the great front window overlooking the garden, with its flowers, its pool, its rockery. He tried to think of Creel away from this garden of hers, this home of two thirds a life-time, Creel living in rooms—and knew what her mother had meant. There was one more hope—

He waited till Creel went upstairs, then called Mel Dale on the telestat. The mayor's plump face took on an uneasy expression as he saw who it was.

But he listened pontifically, said finally: "Sorry, the council does not loan money; and I might as well tell you, Fara—I have nothing to do with this, mind you—but you can't get a license for a shop any more."

"W-what?"

"I'm sorry!" The mayor lowered his voice. "Listen, Fara, take my advice and go to the weapon shop. These places have their uses."

There was a click, and Fara sat staring at the blank face of the viewing screen.

So it was to be—death!

He waited until the street was empty of human beings, then slipped across the boulevard, past a design of flower gardens, and so to the door of the shop. The brief fear came that the door wouldn't open, but it did, effortlessly.

As he emerged from the dimness of the alcove into the shop proper, he saw the silver-haired old man sitting in a corner chair, reading under a softly bright light. The old man looked up, put aside his book, then rose to his feet.

"It's Mr. Clark," he said quietly. "What can we do for you?"

A faint flush crept into Fara's cheeks. In a dim fashion, he had hoped that he would not suffer the humiliation of being recognized; but now that his fear was realized, he stood his ground stubbornly. The important thing about killing himself was that there be no body for Creel to bury at great expense. Neither knife nor poison would satisfy that basic requirement.

"I want a gun," said Fara, "that can be adjusted to disintegrate a body six feet in diameter in a single shot. Have you that kind?"

Without a word, the old man turned to a showcase, and brought forth a sturdy gem of a revolver that glinted with all the soft colors of the inimitable Ordine plastic. The man said in a precise voice:

"Notice the flanges on this barrel are little more than bulges. This makes the model ideal for carrying in a shoulder holster under the coat; it can be drawn very swiftly because, when properly attuned, it will leap toward the reaching hand of its owner. At the moment it is attuned to me. Watch while I replace it in its holster and—"

The speed of the draw was absolutely amazing. The old man's fingers moved; and the gun, four feet away, was in them. There was no blur of movement. It was like the door the night that it had slipped from Fara's grasp, and slammed noiselessly in Constable Jor's face. *Instantaneous!*

Fara, who had parted his lips as the old man was explaining, to protest the utter needlessness of illustrating any quality of the weapon except what he had asked for, closed them again. He stared in a brief, dazed fascination; and something of the wonder that was here held his mind and his body.

He had seen and handled the guns of soldiers, and they were simply ordinary metal or plastic things that one used clumsily like any other material substance, not like this at all, not possessed of a dazzling life of their own, leaping with an intimate eagerness to assist with all their superb power the will of their master. They—

With a start, Fara remembered his purpose. He smiled wryly, and said:

"All this is very interesting. But what about the beam that can fan out?"

The old man said calmly: "At pencil thickness, this beam will pierce any body except certain alloys of lead up to four hundred yards. With proper adjustment of the firing nozzle, you can disintegrate a six-foot object at fifty yards or less. This screw is the adjustor."

He indicated a tiny device in the muzzle itself. "Turn it to the left to spread the beam, to the right to close it."

Fara said: "I'll take the gun. How much is it?"

He saw that the old man was looking at him thoughtfully; the oldster said finally, slowly: "I have previously explained our regulations to you, Mr. Clark. You recall them, of course?"

"Eh!" said Fara, and stopped, wide-eyed. It wasn't that he didn't remember them. It was simply—

"You mean," he gasped, "those things actually apply. They're not—"

With a terrible effort, he caught his spinning brain and blurring voice. Tense and cold, he said:

"All I want is a gun that will shoot in self-defense, but which I can turn on myself if I have to or—want to."

"Oh, suicide!" said the old man. He looked as if a great understanding had suddenly dawned on him. "My dear sir, we have no objection to your killing yourself at any time. That is your personal privilege in a world where privileges grow scanter every year. As for the price of this revolver, it's four credits."

"Four cre . . . only four credits!" said Fara.

He stood, absolutely astounded, his whole mind snatched from its dark purpose. Why, the plastic alone was—and the whole gun with its fine, intricate workmanship—twenty-five credits would have been dirt cheap.

He felt a brief thrill of utter interest; the mystery of the weapon shops suddenly loomed as vast and important as his own black destiny. But the old man was speaking again:

"And now, if you will remove your coat, we can put on the holster—"

Quite automatically, Fara complied. It was vaguely startling to realize that, in a few seconds, he would be walking out of here, equipped for self-murder, and that there was now not a single obstacle to his death.

Curiously, he was disappointed. He couldn't explain it, but somehow there had been in the back of his mind a hope that these shops might, just might—what?

What indeed? Fara sighed wearily—and grew aware again of the old man's voice, saying:

"Perhaps you would prefer to step out of our side door. It is less conspicuous than the front."

There was no resistance in Fara. He was dimly conscious of the man's fingers on his arm, half guiding him; and then the old man pressed one of several buttons on the wall—so that's how it was done— and there was the door.

He could see flowers beyond the opening; without a word he walked toward them. He was outside almost before he realized it.

Fara stood for a moment in the neat little pathway, striving to grasp the finality of his situation. But nothing would come except a curious awareness of many men around him; for a long second, his brain was like a log drifting along a stream at night.

Through that darkness grew a consciousness of something wrong; the wrongness was there in the back of his mind, as he turned left-ward to go to the front of the weapon store.

Vagueness transformed to a shocked, startled sound. For—he was not in Glay, and the weapon shop *wasn't* where it had been. In its place—

A dozen men brushed past Fara to join a long line of men farther along. But Fara was immune to their presence, their strangeness. His whole mind, his whole vision, his very being was concentrating on the section of machine that stood where the weapon shop had been.

A machine, oh, a machine—

His brain lifted up, up in his effort to grasp the tremendousness of the dull-metaled immensity of what was spread here under a summer sun beneath a sky as blue as a remote southern sea.

The machine towered into the heavens, five great tiers of metal, each a hundred feet high; and the superbly streamlined five hundred feet ended in a peak of light, a gorgeous spire that tilted straight up a sheer two hundred feet farther, and matched the very sun for brightness.

And it was a machine, not a building, because the whole lower tier was alive with shimmering lights, mostly green, but sprinkled colorfully with red and occasionally a blue and yellow. Twice, as Fara watched, green lights directly in front of him flashed unscintillatingly into red.

The second tier was alive with white and red lights, although there were only a fraction as many lights as on the lowest tier. The third section had on its dull-metal surface only blue and yellow lights; they twinkled softly here and there over the vast area.

The fourth tier was a series of signs, That brought the beginning, of comprehension. The whole sign was:

WHITE   — BIRTHS
RED   — DEATHS
GREEN   — LIVING
BLUE   — IMMIGRATION TO EARTH
YELLOW   — EMIGRATION

The fifth tier was also all sign, finally explaining:

POPULATIONS

SOLAR SYSTEM   19,174,463,747
EARTH   11,193,247,361
MARS   1,097,298,604
VENUS   5,141,053,811
MOONS   1,742,863,971

The numbers changed, even as he looked at them, leaping up and down, shifting below and above what they had first been. People were dying, being born, moving to Mars, to Venus, to the moons of Jupiter, to Earth's moon, and others coming back again, landing minute by minute in the thousands of spaceports. Life went on in its gigantic fashion—and here was the stupendous record. Here was—

"Better get in line," said a friendly voice beside Fara. "It takes quite a while to put through an individual case, I understand."

Fara stared at the man. He had the distinct impression of having had senseless words flung at him. "In line?" he started—and stopped himself with a jerk that hurt his throat.

He was moving forward, blindly, ahead of the younger man, thinking a curious jumble about that this must have been how Constable Jor was transported to Mars—when another of the man's words penetrated.

"Case?" said Fara violently. "Individual case!"

The man, a heavy-faced, blue-eyed young chap of around thirty-five, looked at him curiously: "You must know why you're here," he said. "Surely, you wouldn't have been sent through here unless you had a problem of some kind that the weapon shop courts will solve for you; there's no other reason for coming to Information Center."

Fara walked on because he was in the line now, a fast-moving line that curved him inexorably around the machine; and seemed to be heading him toward a door that led into the interior of the great metal structure.

So it was a building as well as a machine.

A problem, he was thinking, why, of course, he had a problem, a hopeless, insoluble, completely tangled problem so deeply rooted in the basic structure of Imperial civilization that the whole world would have to be overturned to make it right.

With a start, he saw that he was at the entrance. And the awed thought came: In seconds he would be committed irrevocably to— what?

Inside was a long, shining corridor, with scores of completely transparent hallways leading off the main corridor. Behind Fara, the young man's voice said:

"There's one, practically empty. Let's go."

Fara walked ahead; and suddenly he was trembling. He had already noticed that at the end of each side hallway were some dozen young women sitting at desks, interviewing men and . . . and, good heavens, was it possible that all this meant—

He grew aware that he had stopped in front of one of the girls.

She was older than she had looked from a distance, over thirty, but good-looking, alert. She smiled pleasantly, but impersonally, and said: "Your name, please?"

He gave it before he thought and added a mumble about being from the village of Glay. The woman said:

"Thank you. It will take a few minutes to get your file. Won't you sit down?"

He hadn't noticed the chair. He sank into it; and his heart was beating so wildly that he felt choked. The strange thing was that there was scarcely a thought in his head, nor a real hope; only an intense, almost mind-wrecking excitement.

With a jerk, he realized that the girl was speaking again, but only snatches of her voice came through that screen of tension in his mind:

"—Information Center is . . . in effect . . . a bureau of statistics. Every person born . . . registered here . . . their education, change of address . . . occupation . . . and the highlights of their life. The whole is maintained by . . . combination of . . . unauthorized and unsuspected liaison with . . . Imperial Chamber of Statistics and . . . through medium of agents . . . in every community—"

It seemed to Fara that he was missing vital information, and that if he could only force his attention and hear more— He strained, but it was no use; his nerves were jumping madly and--

Before he could speak, there was a click, and a thin, dark plate slid onto the woman's desk. She took it up, and examined it. After a moment, she said something into a mouthpiece, and in a short time two more plates precipitated out of the empty air onto her desk. She studied them impassively, looked up finally.

"You will be interested to know," she said, "that your son, Cayle, bribed himself into a commission in the Imperial army with five thousand credits."

"Eh?" said Fara. He half rose from his chair, but before he could say anything, the young woman was speaking again, firmly:

"I must inform you that the weapon shops take no action against individuals. Your son can have his job, the money he stole; we are not concerned with moral correction. That must come naturally from the individual, and from the people as a whole—and now if you will give me a brief account of your problem for the record and the court."

Sweating, Fara sank back into his seat; his mind was heaving; most desperately, he wanted more information about Cayle. He began:

"But . . . but what . . . how—" He caught himself; and in a low voice described what had happened. When he finished, the girl said:

"You will proceed now to the Name Room; watch for your name, and when it appears go straight to Room 474. Remember, 474—and now, the line is waiting, if you please—"

She smiled politely, and Fara was moving off almost before he realized it. He half turned to ask another question, but an old man was sinking into his chair. Fara hurried on, along a great corridor, conscious of curious blasts of sound coming from ahead.

Eagerly, he opened the door; and the sound crashed at him with all the impact of a sledge-hammer blow.

It was such a colossal, incredible sound that he stopped short, just inside the door, shrinking back. He stood then trying to blink sense into a visual confusion that rivaled in magnitude that incredible tornado of noise.

Men, men, men everywhere; men by the thousands in a long, broad auditorium, packed into rows of seats, pacing with an abandon of restlessness up and down aisles, and all of them staring with a frantic interest at a long board marked off into squares, each square lettered from the alphabet, from A, B, C and so on to Z. The tremendous board with its lists of names ran the full length of the immense room.

The Name Room, Fara was thinking shakily, as he sank into a seat—and his name would come up in the C's, and then—

It was like sitting in at a no-limit poker game, watching the jewel-precious cards turn up. It was like playing the exchange with all the world at stake during a stock crash. It was nerve-racking, dazzling, exhausting, fascinating, terrible, mind-destroying, stupendous. It was—

It was like nothing else on the face of the earth.

New names kept flashing on to the twenty-six squares; and men would shout like insane beings and some fainted, and the uproar was absolutely shattering; the pandemonium raged on, one continuous, unbelievable sound.

And every few minutes a great sign would flash along the board, telling everyone:

"WATCH YOUR OWN INITIALS."

Fara watched, trembling in every limb. Each second it seemed to him that he couldn't stand it an instant longer. He wanted to scream at the room to be silent; he wanted to jump up to pace the floor, but others who did that were yelled at hysterically, threatened wildly, hated with a mad, murderous ferocity.

Abruptly, the blind savagery of it scared Fara. He thought unsteadily: "I'm not going to make a fool of myself. I—"

"Clark, Fara—" winked the board. "Clark, Fara—"

With a shout that nearly tore off the top of his head, Fara leaped to his feet. "That's me!" he shrieked. "Me!"

No one turned; no one paid the slightest attention. Shamed, he slunk across the room where an endless line of men kept crowding into a corridor beyond.

The silence in the long corridor was almost as shattering as the mind-destroying noise it replaced. It was hard to concentrate on the idea of a number—474.

It was completely impossible to imagine what could lie beyond—474.

The room was small. It was furnished with a small, business-type table and two chairs. On the table were seven neat piles of folders, each pile a different color. The piles were arranged in a row in front of a large, milky-white globe, that began to glow with a soft light. Out of its depths, a man's baritone voice said:

"Fara Clark?"

"Yes," said Fara.

"Before the verdict is rendered in your case," the voice went on quietly, "I want you to take a folder from the blue pile. The list will show the Fifth Interplanetary Bank in its proper relation to yourself and the world, and it will be explained to you in due course."

The list, Fara saw, was simply that, a list of the names of companies. The names ran from A to Z, and there were about five hundred of them. The folder carried no explanation; and Fara slipped it automatically into his side pocket, as the voice came again from the shining globe:

"It has been established," the words came precisely, "that the Fifth Interplanetary Bank perpetrated upon you a gross swindle, and that it is further guilty of practicing scavengery, deception, blackmail and was accessory in a criminal conspiracy.

"The bank made contact with your son, Cayle, through what is quite properly known as a scavenger, that is, an employee who exists by finding young men and women who are normally capable of drawing drafts on their parents or other victims. The scavenger obtains for this service a commission of eight percent, which is always paid by the person making the loan, in this case your son.

"The bank practiced deception in that its authorized agents deceived you in the most culpable fashion by pretending that it had already paid out the ten thousand credits to your son, whereas the money was not paid over until your signature had been obtained.

"The blackmail guilt arises out of a threat to have your son arrested for falsely obtaining a loan, a threat made at a time when no money had exchanged hands. The conspiracy consists of the action whereby your note was promptly turned over to your competitor.

"The bank is accordingly triple-fined, thirty-six thousand three hundred credits. It is not in our interest, Fara Clark, for you to know how this money is obtained. Suffice to know that the bank pays it, and that of the fine the weapon shops allocate to their own treasury a total of one half. The other half—"

There was a plop; a neatly packaged pile of bills fell onto the table. "For you," said the voice; and Fara, with trembling fingers, slipped the package into his coat pocket. It required the purest mental and physical effort for him to concentrate on the next words that came:

"You must not assume that your troubles are over. The re-establishment of your motor repair shop in Glay will require force and courage. Be discreet, brave and determined, and you cannot fail. Do not hesitate to use the gun you have purchased in defense of your rights. The plan will be explained to you. And now, proceed through the door facing you—"

Fara braced himself with an effort, opened the door and walked through.

It was a dim, familiar room that he stepped into, and there was a silver-haired, fine-faced man who rose from a reading chair, and came forward in the dimness, smiling gravely.

The stupendous, fantastic, exhilarating adventure was over; and he was back in the weapon shop of Glay.

He couldn't get over the wonder of it—this great and fascinating organization established here in the very heart of a ruthless civilization, a civilization that had in a few brief weeks stripped him of everything he possessed.

With a deliberate will, he stopped that glowing flow of thought. A dark frown wrinkled his solidly built face; he said:

"The . . . judge—" Fara hesitated over the name, frowned again, annoyed at himself, then went on: "The judge said that, to re-establish myself I would have to—"

"Before we go into that," said the old man quietly, "I want you to examine the blue folder you brought with you."

"Folder?" Fara echoed blankly. It took a long moment to remember that he had picked up a folder from the table in Room 474.

He studied the list of company names with a gathering puzzlement, noting that the name of Automatic Atomic Motor Repair Shops was well down among the A's, and the Fifth Interplanetary Bank only one of several great banks included. Fara looked up finally:

"I don't understand," he said; "are these the companies you have had to act against?"

The silver-haired man smiled grimly, shook his head. "That is not what I mean. These firms constitute only a fraction of the eight hundred thousand companies that are constantly in our books."

He smiled again, humorlessly: "These companies all know that, because of us, their profits on paper bear no relation to their assets. What they don't know is how great the difference really is; and, as we want a general improvement in business morals, not merely more skillful scheming to outwit us, we prefer them to remain in ignorance."

He paused, and this time he gave Fara a searching glance, said at last: "The unique feature of the companies on this particular list is that they are every one wholly owned by Empress Isher."

He finished swiftly: "In view of your past opinions on that subject, I do not expect you to believe me."

Fara stood as still as death, for—he did believe with unquestioning conviction, completely, finally. The amazing, the unforgivable thing was that all his life he had watched the march of ruined men into the oblivion of poverty and disgrace—and blamed *them*.

Fara groaned. "I've been like a madman," he said. "Everything the empress and her officials did was right. No friendship, no personal relationship could survive with me that did not include belief in things as they were. I suppose if I started to talk against the empress I would receive equally short shrift."

"Under no circumstances," said the old man grimly, "must you say anything against her majesty. The weapon shops will not countenance any such words, and will give no further aid to anyone who is so indiscreet. The reason is that, for the moment, we have reached an uneasy state of peace with the Imperial government. We wish to keep it that way; beyond that I will not enlarge on our policy.

"I am permitted to say that the last great attempt to destroy the weapon shops was made seven years ago, when the glorious Innelda Isher was twenty-five years old. That was a secret attempt, based on a new invention; and failed by purest acident because of our sacrifice of a man from seven thousand years in the past. That may sound mysterious to you, but I will not explain.

"The worst period was reached some forty years ago when every person who was discovered receiving aid from us was murdered in some fashion. You may be surprised to know that your father-in-law was among those assassinated at that time."

"Creel's father!" Fara gasped. "But—"

He stopped. His brain was reeling; there was such a rush of blood to his head that for an instant he could hardly see.

"But," he managed at last, "it was reported that he ran away with another woman."

"They always spread a vicious story of some kind," the old man said; and Fara was silent, stunned.

The other went on: "We finally put a stop to their murders by killing the three men from the top down, *excluding* the royal family, who gave the order for the particular execution involved. But we do not again want that kind of bloody murder.

"Nor are we interested in any criticism of our toleration of so much that is evil. It is important to understand that we *do not interfere in the main stream of human existence*. We right wrongs; we act as a barrier between the people and their more ruthless exploiters. Generally speaking, we help only honest men; that is not to say that we do not give assistance to the less scrupulous, but only to the extent of selling them guns—which is a very great aid indeed, and which is one of the reasons why the government is relying almost exclusively for its power on an economic chicanery.

"In the four thousand years since the brilliant genius Walter S. DeLany invented the vibration process that made the weapon shops possible, and laid down the first principles of weapon shop political philosophy, we have watched the tide of government swing backward and forward between democracy under a limited monarchy to complete tyranny. And we have discovered one thing:

"*People always have the kind of government they want. When they want change, they must change it.* As always we shall remain an incorruptible core—and I mean that literally; we have a psychological machine that never lies about a man's character—I repeat, an incorruptible core of human idealism, devoted to relieving the ills that arise inevitably under any form of government.

"But now—your problem. It is very simple, really. You must fight, as all men have fought since the beginning of time for what they valued, for their just rights. As you know, the Automatic Repair people removed all your machinery and tools within an hour of foreclosing on your shop. This material was taken to Ferd, and then shipped to a great warehouse on the coast.

"We recovered it, and with our special means of transportation have now replaced the machines in your shop. You will accordingly go there and—"

Fara listened with a gathering grimness to the instructions, nodded finally, his jaw clamped tight.

"You can count on me," he said curtly. "I've been a stubborn man in my time; and though I've changed sides, I haven't changed *that*."

Going outside was like returning from life to—death; from hope to—reality.

Fara walked along the quiet streets of Glay at darkest night. For the first time it struck him that the weapon shop Information Center must be halfway around the world, for it had been day, brilliant day.

The picture vanished as if it had never existed, and he grew aware again, preternaturally aware of the village of Glay asleep all around him. Silent, peaceful—yet ugly, he thought, ugly with the ugliness of evil enthroned.

He thought: The right to buy weapons—and his heart swelled into his throat; the tears came to his eyes.

He wiped his vision clear with the back of his hand, thought of

Creel's long dead father, and strode on, without shame. Tears were good for an angry man.

The shop was the same, but the hard metal padlock yielded before the tiny, blazing, supernal power of the revolver. One flick of fire; the metal dissolved—and he was inside.

It was dark, too dark to see, but Fara did not turn on the lights immediately. He fumbled across to the window control, turned the windows to darkness vibration, and then clicked on the lights.

He gulped with awful relief. For the machines, his precious tools that he had seen carted away within hours after the bailiff's arrival, were here again, ready for use.

Shaky from the pressure of his emotion, Fara called Creel on the telestat. It took a little while for her to appear; and she was in her dressing robe. When she saw who it was she turned a dead white.

"Fara, oh, Fara, I thought—"

He cut her off grimly: "Creel, I've been to the weapon shop. I want you to do this: go straight to your mother. I'm here at my shop. I'm going to stay here day and night until it's settled that I stay. . . . I shall go home later for some food and clothing, but I want you to be gone by then. Is that clear?"

Color was coming back into her lean, handsome face. She said: "Don't you bother coming home, Fara. I'll do everything necessary. I'll pack all that's needed into the carplane, including a folding bed. We'll sleep in the back room of the shop."

Morning came palely, but it was ten o'clock before a shadow darkened the open door; and Constable Jor came in. He looked shame-faced:

"I've got an order here for your arrest," he said.

"Tell those who sent you," Fara replied deliberately, "that I resisted arrest—with a gun."

The deed followed the words with such rapidity that Jor blinked. He stood like that for a moment, a big, sleepy-looking man, staring at that gleaming, magical revolver; then:

"I have a summons here ordering you to appear at the great court of Ferd this afternoon. Will you accept it?"

"Certainly."

"Then you will be there?"

"I'll send my lawyer," said Fara. "Just drop the summons on the floor there. Tell them I took it."

The weapon shop man had said: "Do not ridicule by word any legal measure of the Imperial authorities. Simply disobey them."

Jor went out, and seemed relieved. It took an hour before Mayor Mel Dale came pompously through the door.

"See here, Fara Clark," he bellowed from the doorway. "You can't get away with this. This is defiance of the law."

Fara was silent as His Honor waddled farther into the building. It was puzzling, almost amazing, that Mayor Dale would risk his plump, treasured body. Puzzlement ended as the mayor said in a low voice:

"Good work, Fara; I knew you had it in you. There's dozens of us in Glay behind you, so stick it out. I had to yell at you just now, because there's a crowd outside. Yell back at me, will you? Let's have a real name calling. But, first, a word of warning: the manager of the Automatic Repair Shop is on his way here with his bodyguards, two of them—"

Shakily, Fara watched the mayor go out. The crisis was at hand. He braced himself, thought: "Let them come, let them—"

It was easier than he had thought—for the men who entered the shop turned pale when they saw the holstered revolver. There was a violence of blustering, nevertheless, that narrowed finally down to:

"Look here," the man said, "we've got your note for twelve thousand one hundred credits. You're not going to deny you owe that money."

"I'll buy it back," said Fara in a stony voice, "for exactly half, not a cent more."

The strong-jawed young man looked at him for a long time. "We'll take it," he said finally, curtly.

Fara said: "I've got the agreement here—"

His first customer was old man Miser Lan Harris. Fara stared at the long-faced oldster with a vast surmise, and his first, amazed comprehension came of how the weapon shop must have settled on Harris' lot—by arrangement.

It was an hour after Harris had gone that Creel's mother stamped into the shop. She closed the door.

"Well," she said, "you did it, eh? Good work. I'm sorry if I seemed rough with you when you came to my place, but we weapon-shop supporters can't afford to take risks for those who are not on our side.

"But never mind that. I've come to take Creel home. The important thing is to return everything to normal as quickly as possible."

It was over; incredibly it was over. Twice, as he walked home that night, Fara stopped in midstride, and wondered if it had not all been a dream. The air was like wine. The little world of Glay spread before him, green and gracious, a peaceful paradise where time had stood still.

FAREWELL TO THE MASTER

by

HARRY BATES

"Farewell to the Master" represents the only occasion on which the editors reached complete unanimity of agreement on a story— a rare achievement for collaborators! It is our mutual, considered opinion that this is one of the finest stories we have ever read. Mr. Bates has depicted the inevitable tragedy of man confronting a situation beyond his present understanding. The reader is almost overwhelmed by the full realization of humanity's limitations. The utter foolishness of the world's reception of Gnut, visitor from outer space, will be a blow to our pride; yet, the final attempts at understanding and expiation will be a stimulus to our humility and wisdom.

*

FROM HIS perch high on the ladder above the museum floor, Cliff Sutherland studied carefully each line and shadow of the great robot, then turned and looked thoughtfully down at the rush of visitors come from all over the Solar System to see Gnut and the traveler for themselves and to hear once again their amazing, tragic story.

He himself had come to feel an almost proprietary interest in the exhibit, and with some reason. He had been the only free-lance picture reporter on the Capitol grounds when the visitors from the Unknown had arrived, and had obtained the first professional shots of the ship. He had witnessed at close hand every event of the next mad few days. He had thereafter photographed many times the eight-foot robot, the ship, and the beautiful slain ambassador, Klaatu, and his imposing tomb out in the center of the Tidal Basin, and, such was the continuing news value of the event to the billions of persons throughout

habitable space, ne was there now once more to get still other shots
and, if possible, a new "angle."

This time he was after a picture which showed Gnut as weird and
menacing. The shots he had taken the day before had not given quite
the effect he wanted, and he hoped to get it today; but the light was
not yet right and he had to wait for the afternoon to wane a little.

The last of the crowd admitted in the present group hurried in, ex-
claiming at the great pure green curves of the mysterious time-space
traveler, then completely forgetting the ship at sight of the awesome
figure and great head of the giant Gnut. Hinged robots of crude manlike appearance were familiar enough, but never had Earthling eyes
lain on one like this. For Gnut had almost exactly the shape of a man
—a giant, but a man—with greenish metal for man's covering flesh,
and greenish metal for man's bulging muscles. Except for a loin
cloth, he was nude. He stood like the powerful god of the machine
of some undreamed-of scientific civilization, on his face a look of sullen, brooding thought. Those who looked at him did not make jests
or idle remarks, and those nearest him usually did not speak at all.
His strange, internally illuminated red eyes were so set that every
observer felt they were fixed on himself alone, and he engendered a
feeling that he might at any moment step forward in anger and perform unimaginable deeds.

A slight rustling sound came from speakers hidden in the ceiling
above, and at once the noises of the crowd lessened. The recorded
lecture was about to be given. Cliff sighed. He knew the thing by
heart; had even been present when the recording was made, and met
the speaker, a young chap named Stillwell.

"Ladies and gentlemen," began a clear and well-modulated voice
—but Cliff was no longer attending. The shadows in the hollows of
Gnut's face and figure were deeper; it was almost time for his shot.
He picked up and examined the proofs of the pictures he had taken
the day before and compared them critically with the subject.

As he looked a wrinkle came to his brow. He had not noticed it
before, but now, suddenly, he had the feeling that since yesterday
something about Gnut was changed. The pose before him was the
identical one in the photographs, every detail on comparison seemed
the same, but nevertheless the feeling persisted. He took up his viewing glass and more carefully compared subject and photographs, line
by line. And then he saw that there was a difference.

With sudden excitement, Cliff snapped two pictures at different
exposures. He knew he should wait a little and take others, but he was

so sure he had stumbled on an important mystery that he had to get
going, and quickly folding his accessory equipment he descended the
ladder and made his way out. Twenty minutes later, consumed with
curiosity, he was developing the new shots in his hotel bedroom.

What Cliff saw when he compared the negatives taken yesterday
and today caused his scalp to tingle. Here was a slant indeed! And
apparently no one but he knew! Still, what he had discovered, though
it would have made the front page of every paper in the Solar System,
was after all only a lead. The story, what really had happened, he knew
no better than anyone else. It must be his job to find out.

And that meant he would have to secrete himself in the building
and stay there all night. That very night; there was still time for him
to get back before closing. He would take a small, very fast infrared
camera that could see in the dark, and he would get the real picture
and the story.

He snatched up the little camera, grabbed an aircab and hurried
back to the museum. The place was filled with another section of the
ever-present queue, and the lecture was just ending. He thanked
Heaven that his arrangement with the museum permitted him to go
in and out at will.

He had already decided what to do. First he made his way to the
"floating" guard and asked a single question, and anticipation broadened on his face as he heard the expected answer. The second thing
was to find a spot where he would be safe from the eyes of the men
who would close the floor for the night. There was only one possible
place, the laboratory set up behind the ship. Boldly he showed his
press credentials to the second guard, stationed at the partitioned
passageway leading to it, stating that he had come to interview the
scientists; and in a moment was at the laboratory door.

He had been there a number of times and knew the room well. It
was a large area roughly partitioned off for the work of the scientists
engaged in breaking their way into the ship, and full of a confusion
of massive and heavy objects—electric and hot-air ovens, carboys of
chemicals, asbestos sheeting, compressors, basins, ladles, a microscope,
and a great deal of smaller equipment common to a metallurgical
laboratory. Three white-smocked men were deeply engrossed in an
experiment at the far end. Cliff, waiting a good moment, slipped inside and hid himself under a table half buried with supplies. He felt
reasonably safe from detection there. Very soon now the scientists
would be going home for the night.

From beyond the ship he could hear another section of the waiting queue filing in—the last, he hoped, of the day. He settled himself as comfortably as he could. In a moment the lecture would begin. He had to smile when he thought of one thing the recording would say.

Then there it was again—the clear, trained voice of the chap Stillwell. The foot scrapings and whispers of the crowd died away, and Cliff could hear every word in spite of the great bulk of the ship lying interposed.

"Ladies and gentlemen," began the familiar words, "the Smithsonian Institution welcomes you to its new Interplanetary Wing and to the marvelous exhibits at this moment before you."

A slight pause. "All of you must know by now something of what happened here three months ago, if indeed you did not see it for yourself in the telescreen," the voice went on. "The few facts are briefly told. A little after 5:00 p. m. on September 16th, visitors to Washington thronged the grounds outside this building in their usual numbers and no doubt with their usual thoughts. The day was warm and fair. A stream of people was leaving the main entrance of the museum, just outside in the direction you are facing. This wing, of course, was not here at that time. Everyone was homeward bound, tired no doubt from hours on their feet, seeing the exhibits of the museum and visiting the many buildings on the grounds nearby. And then it happened.

"On the area just to your right, just as it is now, appeared the time-space traveler. It appeared in the blink of an eye. It did not come down from the sky; dozens of witnesses swear to that; it just appeared. One moment it was not here, the next it was. It appeared on the very spot it now rests on.

"The people nearest the ship were stricken with panic and ran back with cries and screams. Excitement spread out over Washington in a tidal wave. Radio, television, and newspapermen rushed here at once. Police formed a wide cordon around the ship, and army units appeared and trained guns and ray projectors on it. The direst calamity was feared.

"For it was recognized from the very beginning that this was no spaceship from anywhere in the Solar System. Every child knew that only two spaceships had ever been built on Earth, and none at all on any of the other planets and satellites; and of those two, one had been destroyed when it was pulled into the Sun, and the other had just been reported safely arrived on Mars. Then, the ones made here had a shell of a strong aluminum alloy, while this one, as you see, is of an unknown greenish metal.

"The ship appeared and just sat here. No one emerged, and there was no sign that it contained life of any kind. That, as much as any single thing, caused excitement to sky-rocket. Who, or what, was inside? Were the visitors hostile or friendly? Where did the ship come from? How did it arrive so suddenly right on this spot without dropping from the sky?

"For two days the ship rested here, just as you now see it, without motion or sign that it contained life. Long before the end of that time the scientists had explained that it was not so much a spaceship as a space-time traveler, because only such a ship could arrive as this one did—materialize. They pointed out that such a traveler, while theoretically understandable to us Earthmen, was far beyond attempt at our present state of knowledge, and that this one, activated by relativity principles, might well have come from the far corner of the Universe, from a distance which light itself would require millions of years to cross.

"When this opinion was disseminated, public tension grew until it was almost intolerable. Where had the traveler come from? Who were its occupants? Why had they come to Earth? Above all, why did they not show themselves? Were they perhaps preparing some terrible weapon of destruction?

"And where was the ship's entrance port? Men who dared go look reported that none could be found. No slightest break or crack marred the perfect smoothness of the ship's curving ovoid surface. And a delegation of high-ranking officials who visited the ship could not, by knocking, elicit from its occupants any sign that they had been heard.

"At last, after exactly two days, in full view of tens of thousands of persons assembled and standing well back, and under the muzzles of scores of the army's most powerful guns and ray projectors, an opening appeared in the wall of the ship, and a ramp slid down, and out stepped a man, godlike in appearance and human in form, closely followed by a giant robot. And when they touched the ground the ramp slid back and the entrance closed as before.

"It was immediately apparent to all the assembled thousands that the stranger was friendly. The first thing he did was to raise his right arm high in the universal gesture of peace; but it was not that which impressed those nearest so much as the expression on his face, which radiated kindness, wisdom, the purest nobility. In his delicately tinted robe he looked like a benign god.

"At once, waiting for this appearance, a large committee of high-ranking government officials and army officers advanced to greet the visitor. With graciousness and dignity the man pointed to himself, then to his robot companion, and said in perfect English with a peculiar accent, 'I am Klaatu,' or a name that sounded like that, 'and this is Gnut.' The names were not well understood at the time, but the sight-and-sound film of the television men caught them and they became known to everyone subsequently.

"And then occurred the thing which shall always be to the shame of the human race. From a treetop a hundred yards away came a wink of violet light and Klaatu fell. The assembled multitude stood for a moment stunned, not comprehending what had happened. Gnut, a little behind his master and to one side, slowly turned his body a little toward him, moved his head twice, and stood still, in exactly the position you now see him.

"Then followed pandemonium. The police pulled the slayer of Klaatu out of the tree. They found him mentally unbalanced; he kept crying that the devil had come to kill every one on Earth. He was taken away, and Klaatu, although obviously dead, was rushed to the nearest hospital to see if anything could be done to revive him. Confused and frightened crowds milled about the Capitol grounds the rest of the afternoon and much of that night. The ship remained as silent and motionless as before. And Gnut, too, never moved from the position he had come to rest in.

"Gnut never moved again. He remained exactly as you see him all that night and for the ensuing days. When the mausoleum in the Tidal Basin was built, Klaatu's burial services took place where you are standing now, attended by the highest functionaries of all the great countries of the world. It was not only the most appropriate but the safest thing to do, for if there should be other living creatures in the traveler, as seemed possible at that time, they had to be impressed by the sincere sorrow of us Earthmen at what had happened. If Gnut was still alive, or perhaps I had better say functionable, there was no sign. He stood as you see him during the entire ceremony. He stood so while his master was floated out to the mausoleum and given to the centuries with the tragically short sight-and-sound record of his historic visit. And he stood so afterward, day after day, night after night, in fair weather and in rain, never moving or showing by any slightest sign that he was aware of what had gone on.

"After the interment, this wing was built out from the museum to cover the traveler and Gnut. Nothing else could very well have been done, it was learned, for both Gnut and the ship were far too heavy to be moved safely by any means at hand.

"You have heard about the efforts of our metallurgists since then to break into the ship, and of their complete failure. Behind the ship now, as you can see from either end, a partitioned workroom has been set up where the attempt still goes on. So far its wonderful greenish metal has proved inviolable. Not only are they unable to get in, but they cannot even find the exact place from which Klaatu and Gnut emerged. The chalk marks you see are the best approximation.

"Many people have feared that Gnut was only temporarily deranged, and that on return to function might be dangerous, so the scientists have completely destroyed all chance of that. The greenish metal of which he is made seemed to be the same as that of the ship and could no more be attacked, they found, nor could they find any way to penetrate to his internals; but they had other means. They sent electrical currents of tremendous voltages and amperages through him. They applied terrific heat to all parts of his metal shell. They immersed him for days in gases and acids and strongly corroding solutions, and they have bombarded him with every known kind of ray. You need have no fear of him now. He cannot possibly have retained the ability to function in any way.

"But—a word of caution. The officials of the government know that visitors will not show any disrespect in this building. It may be that the unknown and unthinkably powerful civilization from which Klaatu and Gnut came may send other emissaries to see what happened to them. Whether or not they do, not one of us must be found amiss in our attitude. None of us could very well anticipate what happened, and we all are immeasurably sorry, but we are still in a sense responsible, and must do what we can to avoid possible retaliations.

"You will be allowed to remain five minutes longer, and then, when the gong sounds, you will please leave promptly. The robot attendants along the wall will answer any questions you may have.

"Look well, for before you stand stark symbols of the achievement, mystery, and frailty of the human race."

The recorded voice ceased speaking. Cliff, carefully moving his cramped limbs, broke out in a wide smile. If they knew what he knew!

For his photographs told a slightly different story from that of the lecturer. In yesterday's a line of the figured floor showed clearly at the outer edge of the robot's near foot; in today's, *that line was covered*. Gnut had moved!

Or been moved, though this was very unlikely. Where was the derrick and other evidence of such activity? It could hardly have been done in one night, and all signs so quickly concealed. And why should it be done at all?

Still, to make sure, he had asked the guard. He could almost remember verbatim his answer:

"No, Gnut has neither moved nor been moved since the death of his master. A special point was made of keeping him in the position he assumed at Klaatu's death. The floor was built in under him, and the scientists who completed his derangement erected their apparatus around him, just as he stands. You need have no fears."

Cliff smiled again. He did not have any fears.

Not yet.

II

A moment later the big gong above the entrance doors rang the closing hour, and immediately following it a voice from the speakers called out, "Five o'clock, ladies and gentlemen. Closing time, ladies and gentlemen."

The three scientists, as if surprised it was so late, hurriedly washed their hands, changed to their street clothes and disappeared down the partitioned corridor, oblivious of the young picture man hidden under the table. The slide and scrape of the feet on the exhibition floor rapidly dwindled, until at last there were only the steps of the two guards walking from one point to another, making sure everything was all right for the night. For just a moment one of them glanced in the doorway of the laboratory, then he joined the other at the entrance. Then the great metal doors clanged to, and there was silence.

Cliff waited several minutes, then carefully poked his way out from under the table. As he straightened up, a faint tinkling crash sounded at the floor by his feet. Carefully stooping, he found the shattered remains of a thin glass pipette. He had knocked it off the table.

That caused him to realize something he had not thought of before: A Gnut who had moved might be a Gnut who could see and hear—and really be dangerous. He would have to be very careful.

He looked about him. The room was bounded at the ends by two fiber partitions which at the inner ends followed close under the curving bottom of the ship. The inner side of the room was the ship itself, and the outer was the southern wall of the wing. There were four large high windows. The only entrance was by way of the passage.

Without moving, from his knowledge of the building, he made his plan. The wing was connected with the western end of the museum by a doorway, never used, and extended westward toward the Washington Monument. The ship lay nearest the southern wall, and Gnut stood out in front of it, not far from the northeast corner and at the opposite end of the room from the entrance of the building and the passageway leading to the laboratory. By retracing his steps he would come out on the floor at the point farthest removed from the robot. This was just what he wanted, for on the other side of the entrance, on a low platform, stood a paneled table containing the lecture apparatus, and this table was the only object in the room which afforded a place for him to lie concealed while watching what might go on. The only other objects on the floor were the six manlike robot attendants in fixed stations along the northern wall, placed there to answer visitors' questions. He would have to gain the table.

He turned and began cautiously tiptoeing out of the laboratory and down the passageway. It was already dark there, for what light still entered the exhibition hall was shut off by the great bulk of the ship. He reached the end of the room without making a sound. Very carefully he edged forward and peered around the bottom of the ship at Gnut.

He had a momentary shock. The robot's eyes were right on him! —or so it seemed. Was that only the effect of the set of his eyes, he wondered, or was he already discovered? The position of Gnut's head did not seem to have changed, at any rate. Probably everything was all right, but he wished he did not have to cross that end of the room with the feeling that the robot's eyes were following him.

He drew back and sat down and waited. It would have to be totally dark before he essayed the trip to the table.

He waited a full hour, until the faint beams from the lamps on the grounds outside began to make the room seem to grow lighter; then he got up and peeped around the ship once more. The robot's eyes seemed to pierce right at him as before, only now, due no doubt to the darkness, the strange internal illumination seemed much brighter. This was a chilling thing. Did Gnut know he was there? What were the thoughts of the robot? What could be the thoughts of a man-made machine, even so wonderful a one as Gnut?

It was time for the cross, so Cliff slung his camera around on his back, went down on his hands and knees, and carefully moved to the edge of the entrance wall. There he fitted himself as closely as he could into the angle made by it with the floor and started inching ahead. Never pausing, not risking a glance at Gnut's unnerving red eyes, moving an inch at a time, he snaked along. He took ten minutes to cross the space of a hundred feet, and he was wet with perspiration when his fingers at last touched the one-foot rise of the platform on which the table stood. Still slowly, silently as a shadow, he made his way over the edge and melted behind the protection of the table. At last he was there.

He relaxed for a moment, then, anxious to know whether he had been seen, carefully turned and looked around the side of the table. Gnut's eyes were now full on him! Or so it seemed. Against the general darkness, the robot loomed a mysterious and still darker shadow that, for all his being a hundred and fifty feet away, seemed to dominate the room. Cliff could not tell whether the position of his body was changed or not.

But if Gnut were looking at him, he at least did nothing else. Not by the slightest motion that Cliff could discern did he appear to move. His position was the one he had maintained these last three months, in the darkness, in the rain, and this last week in the museum.

Cliff made up his mind not to give away to fear. He became conscious of his own body. The cautious trip had taken something out of him—his knees and elbows burned and his trousers were no doubt ruined. But these were little things if what he hoped for came to pass. If Gnut so much as moved, and he could catch him with his infrared camera, he would have a story that would buy him fifty suits of clothes. And if on top of that he could learn the purpose of Gnut's moving—provided there was a purpose—that would be a story that would set the world on its ears.

He settled down to a period of waiting; there was no telling when Gnut would move, if indeed he would move that night. Cliff's eyes had long been adjusted to the dark and he could make out the larger objects well enough. From time to time he peered out at the robot—peered long and hard, till his outlines wavered and he seemed to move, and he had to blink and rest his eyes to be sure it was only his imagination.

Again the minute hand of his watch crept around the dial. The inactivity made Cliff careless, and for longer and longer periods he kept his head back out of sight behind the table. And so it was that when Gnut did move he was scared almost out of his wits. Dull and a little bored, he suddenly found the robot out on the floor, halfway in his direction.

But that was not the most frightening thing. It was that when he did see Gnut he did not catch him moving! He was stopped as still as a cat in the middle of stalking a mouse. His eyes were now much brighter, and there was no remaining doubt about their direction: he was looking right at Cliff!

Scarcely breathing, half hypnotized, Cliff looked back. His thoughts tumbled. What was the robot's intention? Why had he stopped so still? Was he being stalked? How could he move with such silence?

In the heavy darkness Gnut's eyes moved nearer. Slowly but in perfect rhythm the almost imperceptible sound of his footsteps beat on Cliff's ears. Cliff, usually resourceful enough, was this time caught flatfooted. Frozen with fear, utterly incapable of fleeing, he lay where he was while the metal monster with the fiery eyes came on.

For a moment Cliff all but fainted, and when he recovered, there was Gnut towering over him, legs almost within reach. He was bending slightly, burning his terrible eyes right into his own!

Too late to try to think of running now. Trembling like any cornered mouse, Cliff waited for the blow that would crush him. For an eternity, it seemed, Gnut scrutinized him without moving. For each second of that eternity Cliff expected annihilation, sudden, quick, complete. And then suddenly and unexpectedly it was over. Gnut's body straightened and he stepped back. He turned. And then, with the almost jerkless rhythm which only he among robots possessed, he started back toward the place from which he came.

Cliff could hardly believe he had been spared. Gnut could have crushed him like a worm—and he had only turned around and gone back. Why? It could not be supposed that a robot was capable of human considerations.

Gnut went straight to the other end of the traveler. At a certain place he stopped and made a curious succession of sounds. At once Cliff saw an opening, blacker than the gloom of the building, appear in the ship's side, and it was followed by a slight sliding sound as a ramp slid out and met the floor. Gnut walked up the ramp and, stooping a little, disappeared inside the ship.

Then, for the first time, Cliff remembered the picture he had come to get. Gnut had moved, but he had not caught him! But at least now, whatever opportunities there might be later, he could get the shot of the ramp connecting with the opened door; so he twisted his camera into position, set it for the proper exposure, and took a shot.

A long time passed and Gnut did not come out. What could he be doing inside? Cliff wondered. Some of his courage returned to him and he toyed with the idea of creeping forward and peeping through the port, but he found he had not the courage for that. Gnut had spared him, at least for the time, but there was no telling how far his tolerance would go.

An hour passed, then another, Gnut was doing something inside the ship, but what. Cliff could not imagine. If the robot had been a human being, he knew he would have sneaked a look, but as it was, he was too much of an unknown quantity. Even the simplest of Earth's robots under certain circumstances were inexplicable things; what. then, of this one, come from an unknown and even unthinkable civilization, by far the most wonderful construction ever seen— what superhuman powers might he not possess? All that the scientists of Earth could do had not served to derange him. Acid, heat, rays, terrific crushing blows—he had withstood them all; even his finish had been unmarred. He might be able to see perfectly in the dark. And right where he was, he might be able to hear or in some way sense the least change in Cliff's position.

More time passed, and then, some time after two o'clock in the morning, a simple homely thing happened, but a thing so unexpected that for a moment it quite destroyed Cliff's equilibrium. Suddenly, through the dark and silent building, there was a faint whir of wings, soon followed by the piercing, sweet voice of a bird. A mocking bird. Somewhere in the gloom above his head. Clear and full throated were its notes; a dozen little songs it sang, one after the other without pause between—short insistent calls, twirrings, coaxings, cooings— the spring love song of perhaps the finest singer in the world. Then, as suddenly as it began, the voice was silent.

If an invading army had poured out of the traveler, Cliff would have been less surprised. The month was December; even in Florida the mocking birds had not yet begun their song. How had one gotten into that tight, gloomy museum? How and why was it singing there?

He waited, full of curiosity. Then suddenly he was aware of Gnut, standing just outside the port of the ship. He stood quite still, his glowing eyes turned squarely in Cliff's direction. For a moment the hush in the museum seemed to deepen; then it was broken by a soft thud on the floor near where Cliff was lying.

He wondered. The light in Gnut's eyes changed, and he started his almost jerkless walk in Cliff's direction. When only a little away, the robot stopped, bent over, and picked something from the floor. For some time he stood without motion and looked at a little object he held in his hand. Cliff knew, though he could not see, that it was the mocking bird. Its body, for he was sure that it had lost its song forever. Gnut then turned, and without a glance at Cliff, walked back to the ship and again went inside.

Hours passed while Cliff waited for some sequel to this surprising happening. Perhaps it was because of his curiosity that his fear of the robot began to lessen. Surely if the mechanism was unfriendly, if he intended him any harm, he would have finished him before, when he had such a perfect opportunity. Cliff began to nerve himself for a quick look inside the port. And a picture; he must remember the picture. He kept forgetting the very reason he was there.

It was in the deeper darkness of the false dawn when he got sufficient courage and made the start. He took off his shoes, and in his stockinged feet, his shoes tied together and slung over his shoulder, he moved stiffly but rapidly to a position behind the nearest of the six robot attendants stationed along the wall, then paused for some sign which might indicate that Gnut knew he had moved. Hearing none, he slipped along behind the next robot attendant and paused again. Bolder now, he made in one spurt all the distance to the farthest one, the sixth, fixed just opposite the port of the ship. There he met with a disappointment. No light that he could detect was visible within; there was only darkness and the all-permeating silence. Still, he had better get the picture. He raised his camera, focused it on the dark opening, and gave the film a comparatively long exposure. Then he stood there, at a loss what to do next.

As he paused, a peculiar series of muffled noises reached his ears, apparently from within the ship. Animal noises—first scrapings and pantings, punctuated by several sharp clicks, then deep, rough snarls, interrupted by more scrapings and pantings, as if a struggle of some kind were going on. Then suddenly, before Cliff could even decide to run back to the table, a low, wide, dark shape bounded out of the port and immediately turned and grew to the height of a man. A terrible fear swept over Cliff, even before he knew what the shape was.

In the next second Gnut appeared in the port and stepped unhesitatingly down the ramp toward the shape. As he advanced it backed slowly away for a few feet; but then it stood its ground, and thick arms rose from its sides and began a loud drumming on its chest, while from its throat came a deep roar of defiance. Only one creature in the world beat its chest and made a sound like that. The shape was a gorilla!

And a huge one!

Gnut kept advancing, and when close, charged forward and grappled with the beast. Cliff would not have guessed that Gnut could move so fast. In the darkness he could not see the details of what happened; all he knew was that the two great shapes, the titanic metal Gnut and the squat but terrifically strong gorilla, merged for a moment with silence on the robot's part and terrible, deep, indescribable roars on the other's; then the two separated, and it was as if the gorilla had been flung back and away.

The animal at once rose to its full height and roared deafeningly. Gnut advanced. They closed again, and the separation of before was repeated. The robot continued inexorably, and now the gorilla began to fall back down the building. Suddenly the beast darted at a manlike shape against the wall, and with one rapid side movement dashed the fifth robot attendant to the floor and decapitated it.

Tense with fear, Cliff crouched behind his own robot attendant. He thanked Heaven that Gnut was between him and the gorilla and was continuing his advance. The gorilla backed farther, darted suddenly at the next robot in the row, and with strength almost unbelievable picked it from its roots and hurled it at Gnut. With a sharp metallic clang, robot hit robot, and the one of Earth bounced off to one side and rolled to a stop.

Cliff cursed himself for it afterward, but again he completely forgot the picture. The gorilla kept falling back down the building, demolishing with terrific bursts of rage every robot attendant that he passed and throwing the pieces at the implacable Gnut. Soon they arrived opposite the table, and Cliff now thanked his stars he had come away. There followed a brief silence. Cliff could not make out what was going on, but he imagined that the gorilla had at last reached the corner of the wing and was trapped.

If he was, it was only for a moment. The silence was suddenly shattered by a terrific roar, and the thick, squat shape of the animal came bounding toward Cliff. He came all the way back and turned just between Cliff and the port of the ship. Cliff prayed frantically for Gnut to come back quickly, for there was now only the last remaining robot attendant between him and the madly dangerous brute. Out of the dimness Gnut did appear. The gorilla rose to its full height and again beat its chest and roared its challenge.

And then occurred a curious thing. It fell on all fours and slowly rolled over on its side, as if weak or hurt. Then panting, making frightening noises, it forced itself again to its feet and faced the oncoming Gnut. As it waited, its eye was caught by the last robot attendant and perhaps Cliff, shrunk close behind it. With a surge of terrible destructive rage, the gorilla waddled sideward toward Cliff, but this time, even through his panic, he saw that the animal moved with difficulty, again apparently sick or severely wounded. He jumped back just in time; the gorilla pulled out the last robot attendant and hurled it violently at Gnut, missing him narrowly.

That was its last effort. The weakness caught it again; it dropped heavily on one side, rocked back and forth a few times, and fell to twitching. Then it lay still and did not move again.

The first faint pale light of the dawn was seeping into the room. From the corner where he had taken refuge, Cliff watched closely the great robot. It seemed to him that he behaved very queerly. He stood over the dead gorilla, looking down at him with what in a human would be called sadness. Cliff saw this clearly; Gnut's heavy greenish features bore a thoughtful, grieving expression new to his experience. For some moments he stood so, then as might a father with his sick child, he leaned over, lifted the great animal in his metal arms and carried it tenderly within the ship.

Cliff flew back to the table, suddenly fearful of yet other dangerous and inexplicable happenings. It struck him that he might be safer in the laboratory, and with trembling knees he made his way there and hid in one of the big ovens. He prayed for full daylight. His thoughts were chaos. Rapidly, one after another, his mind churned up the amazing events of the night, but all was mystery; it seemed there could be no rational explanation for them. That mocking bird. The gorilla. Gnut's sad expression and his tenderness. What could account for a fantastic melange like that!

Gradually full daylight did come. A long time passed. At last he began to believe he might yet get out of that place of mystery and danger alive. At 8:30 there were noises at the entrance, and the good sound of human voices came to his ears. He stepped out of the oven and tiptoed to the passageway.

The noises stopped suddenly and there was a frightened exclamation and then the sound of running feet, and then silence. Stealth-

ily Cliff sneaked down the narrow way and peeped fearfully around
the ship.

There Gnut was in his accustomed place, in the identical pose he
had taken at the death of his master, brooding sullenly and alone over
a space traveler once again closed tight and a room that was a shambles. The entrance doors stood open and, heart in his mouth, Cliff
ran out.

A few minutes later, safe in his hotel room, completely done in, he
sat down for a second and almost at once fell asleep. Later, still in
his clothes and still asleep, he staggered over to the bed. He did not
wake up till midafternoon.

III

Cliff awoke slowly, at first not realizing that the images tumbling
in his head were real memories and not a fantastic dream. It was
recollection of the pictures which brought him to his feet. Hastily
he set about developing the film in his camera.

Then in his hands was proof that the events of the night were real.
Both shots turned out well. The first showed clearly the ramp leading up to the port as he had dimly discerned it from his position behind the table. The second, of the open port as snapped from in
front, was a disappointment, for a blank wall just back of the opening
cut off all view of the interior. That would account for the fact that
no light had escaped from the ship while Gnut was inside. Assuming Gnut required light for whatever he did.

Cliff looked at the negatives and was ashamed of himself. What a
rotten picture man he was to come back with two ridiculous shots
like these! He had had a score of opportunities to get real ones—shots
of Gnut in action—Gnut's fight with the gorilla—even Gnut holding
the mocking bird—spine-chilling stuff!—and all he had brought
back was two stills of a doorway. Oh, sure, they were valuable, but he
was a Grade A ass.

And to top this brilliant performance, he had fallen asleep!

Well, he'd better get out on the street and find out what was
doing.

Quickly he showered, shaved, and changed his clothes, and soon
was entering a nearby restaurant patronized by other picture and
newsmen. Sitting alone at the lunch bar, he spotted a friend and
competitor.

"Well, what do you think?" asked his friend when he took the stool at his side.

"I don't think anything until I've had breakfast," Cliff answered.

"Then haven't you heard?"

"Heard what?" fended Cliff, who knew very well what was coming.

"You're a fine picture man," was the other's remark. "When something really big happens, you are asleep in bed." But then he told him what had been discovered that morning in the museum, and of the world-wide excitement at the news. Cliff did three things at once, successfully—gobbled a substantial breakfast, kept thanking his stars that nothing new had transpired, and showed continuous surprise. Still chewing he got up and hurried over to the building.

Outside, balked at the door, was a large crowd of the curious, but Cliff had no trouble gaining admittance when he showed his press credentials. Gnut and the ship stood just as he had left them, but the floor had been cleaned up and the pieces of the demolished robot attendants were lined up in one place along the wall. Several other competitor friends of his were there.

"I was away; missed the whole thing," he said to one of them— Gus. "What's supposed to be the explanation for what happened?"

"Ask something easy," was the answer. "Nobody knows. It's thought maybe something came out of the ship, maybe another robot like Gnut. Say—where have you been?"

"Asleep."

"Better catch up. Several billion bipeds are scared stiff. Revenge for the death of Klaatu. Earth about to be invaded."

"But that's—"

"Oh, I know it's all crazy, but that's the story they're being fed; it sells news. But there's a new angle just turned up, very surprising. Come here."

He led Cliff to the table where stood a knot of people looking with great interest at several objects guarded by a technician. Gus pointed to a long slide on which were mounted a number of short dark-brown hairs.

"Those hairs came off a large male gorilla," Gus said with a certain hard-boiled casualness. "Most of them were found among the sweepings of the floor this morning. The rest were found on the robot attendants."

Cliff tried to look astounded. Gus pointed to a test tube partly filled with a light amber fluid.

"And that's blood, diluted—gorilla blood. It was found on Gnut's arms."

"Good Heaven!" Cliff managed to exclaim. "And there's no explanation?"

"Not even a theory. It's your big chance, wonder boy."

Cliff broke away from Gus, unable to maintain his act any longer. He couldn't decide what to do about his story. The press services would bid heavily for it—with all his pictures—but that would take further action out of his hands. In the back of his mind he wanted to stay in the wing again that night, but—well, he simply was afraid. He'd had a pretty stiff dose, and he wanted very much to remain alive.

He walked over and looked a long time at Gnut. No one would ever have guessed that he had moved, or that there had rested on his greenish metal face a look of sadness. Those weird eyes! Cliff wondered if they were really looking at him, as they seemed, recognizing him as the bold intruder of last night. Of what unknown stuff were they made—those materials placed in his eye sockets by one branch of the race of man which all the science of his own could not even serve to disfunction? What was Gnut thinking? What could be the thoughts of a robot—a mechanism of metal poured out of man's clay crucibles? Was he angry at him? Cliff thought not. Gnut had had him at his mercy—and had walked away.

Dared he stay again?

Cliff thought perhaps he did.

He walked about the room, thinking it over. He felt sure Gnut would move again. A Mikton ray gun would protect him from another gorilla—or fifty of them. He did not yet have the real story. He had come back with two miserable architectural stills!

He might have known from the first that he would stay. At dusk that night, armed with his camera and a small Mikton gun, he lay once more under the table of supplies in the laboratory and heard the metal doors of the wing clang to for the night.

This time he would get the story—and the pictures.

If only no guard was posted inside!

IV

Cliff listened hard for a long time for any sound which might tell him that a guard had been left, but the silence within the wing remained unbroken. He was thankful for that—but not quite completely. The gathering darkness and the realization that he was now irrevocably committed made the thought of a companion not altogether unpleasant.

About an hour after it reached maximum darkness he took off his shoes, tied them together and slung them around his neck, down his back, and stole quietly down the passageway to where it opened into the exhibition area. All seemed as it had been the preceding night. Gnut looked an ominous, indistinct shadow at the far end of the room, his glowing red eyes again seemingly right on the spot from which Cliff peeped out. As on the previous night, but even more carefully, Cliff went down on his stomach in the angle of the wall and slowly snaked across to the low platform on which stood the table. Once in its shelter, he fixed his shoes so that they straddled one shoulder, and brought his camera and gun holster around, ready on his breast. This time, he told himself, he would get pictures.

He settled down to wait, keeping Gnut in full sight every minute. His vision reached maximum adjustment to the darkness. Eventually he began to feel lonely and a little afraid. Gnut's red-glowing eyes were getting on his nerves; he had to keep assuring himself that the robot would not harm him. He had little doubt but that he himself was being watched.

Hours slowly passed. From time to time he heard slight noises at the entrance, on the outside—a guard, perhaps, or maybe curious visitors.

At about nine o'clock he saw Gnut move. First his head alone; it turned so that the eyes burned stronger in the direction where Cliff lay. For a moment that was all; then the dark metal form stirred slightly and began moving forward—straight toward himself. Cliff had thought he would not be afraid—much—but now his heart stood still. What would happen this time?

With amazing silence, Gnut drew nearer, until he towered an ominous shadow over the spot where Cliff lay. For a long time his red eyes burned down on the prone man. Cliff trembled all over; this was worse than the first time. Without having planned it, he found himself speaking to the creature.

"You would not hurt me," he pleaded. "I was only curious to see what's going on. It's my job. Can you understand me? I would not harm or bother you. I . . . I couldn't if I wanted to! Please!"

The robot never moved, and Cliff could not guess whether his words had been understood or even heard. When he felt he could

not bear the suspense any longer, Gnut reached out and took something from a drawer of the table, or perhaps he put something back
in; then he stepped back, turned, and retraced his steps. Cliff was
safe! Again the robot had spared him!

Beginning then, Cliff lost much of his fear. He felt sure now that
this Gnut would do him no harm. Twice he had had him in his
power, and each time he had only looked and quietly moved away.
Cliff could not imagine what Gnut had done in the drawer of the
table. He watched with the greatest curiosity to see what would
happen next.

As on the night before, the robot went straight to the end of the
ship and made the peculiar sequence of sounds that opened the port,
and when the ramp slid out he went inside. After that Cliff was alone
in the darkness for a very long time, probably two hours. Not a
sound came from the ship.

Cliff knew he should sneak up to the port and peep inside, but he
could not quite bring himself to do it. With his gun he could
handle another gorilla, but if Gnut caught him it might be the end.
Momentarily he expected something fantastic to happen—he knew
not what; maybe the mocking bird's sweet song again, maybe a gorilla, maybe—anything. What did at last happen once more caught
him with complete surprise.

He heard a sudden muffled sound, then words—human words—
every one familiar.

"Gentlemen," was the first, and then there was a very slight pause.
"The Smithsonian Institution welcomes you to its new Interplanetary
Wing and to the marvelous exhibits at this moment before you."

It was the recorded voice of Stillwell! But it was not coming
through the speakers overhead, but much muted, from within the
ship.

After a slight pause it went on:

"All of you must . . . must—" Here it stammered and came to a
stop. Cliff's hair bristled. That stammering was not in the lecture!

For just a moment there was silence; then came a scream, a
hoarse man's scream, muffled, from somewhere within the heart of
the ship; and it was followed by muted gasps and cries. as of a man in
great fright or distress.

Every nerve tight, Cliff watched the port. He heard a thudding
noise within the ship, then out the door flew the shadow of what was
surely a human being. Gasping and half stumbling, he ran straight

down the room in Cliff's direction. When twenty feet away, the great shadow of Gnut followed him out of the port.

Cliff watched, breathless. The man—it was Stillwell, he saw now—came straight for the table behind which Cliff himself lay, as if to get behind it, but when only a few feet away, his knees buckled and he fell to the floor. Suddenly Gnut was standing over him, but Stillwell did not seem to be aware of it. He appeared very ill, but kept making spasmodic futile efforts to creep on to the protection of the table.

Gnut did not move, so Cliff was emboldened to speak.

"What's the matter, Stillwell?" he asked. "Can I help? Don't be afraid. I'm Cliff Sutherland; you know, the picture man."

Without showing the least surprise at finding Cliff there, and clutching at his presence like a drowning man would a straw, Stillwell gasped out:

"Help me! Gnut . . . Gnut—" He seemed unable to go on.

"Gnut what?" asked Cliff. Very conscious of the fire-eyed robot looming above, and afraid even to move out to the man, Cliff added reassuringly: "Gnut won't hurt you. I'm sure he won't. He doesn't hurt me. What's the matter? What can I do?"

With a sudden accession of energy, Stillwell rose on his elbows.

"Where am I?" he asked.

"In the Interplanetary Wing," Cliff answered. "Don't you know?"

Only Stillwell's hard breathing was heard for a moment. Then hoarsely, weakly, he asked:

"How did I get here?"

"I don't know," said Cliff.

"I was making a lecture recording," Stillwell said, "when suddenly I found myself here . . . or I mean in there—"

He broke off and showed a return of his terror.

"Then what?" asked Cliff gently.

"I was in that box—and there, above me, was Gnut, the robot. Gnut! But they made Gnut harmless! He's never moved!"

"Steady, now," said Cliff. "I don't think Gnut will hurt you."

Stillwell fell back on the floor.

"I'm very weak," he gasped. "Something— Will you get a doctor?"

He was utterly unaware that towering above him, eyes boring down at him through the darkness, was the robot he feared so greatly.

As Cliff hesitated, at a loss what to do, the man's breath began coming in short gasps, as regular as the ticking of a clock. Cliff dared to move out to him, but no act on his part could have helped the man now. His gasps weakened and became spasmodic, then suddenly he was completely silent and still. Cliff felt for his heart, then looked up to the eyes in the shadow above.

"He is dead," he whispered.

The robot seemed to understand, or at least to hear. He bent forward and regarded the still figure.

"What is it, Gnut?" Cliff asked the robot suddenly. "What are you doing? Can I help you in any way? Somehow I don't believe you are unfriendly, and I don't believe you killed this man. But what happened? Can you understand me? Can you speak? What is it you're trying to do?"

Gnut made no sound or motion, but only looked at the still figure at his feet. In the robot's face, now so close, Cliff saw the look of sad contemplation.

Gnut stood so several minutes; then he bent lower, took the limp form carefully—even gently, Cliff thought—in his mighty arms, and carried him to the place along the wall where lay the dismembered pieces of the robot attendants. Carefully he laid him by their side. Then he went back into the ship.

Without fear now, Cliff stole along the wall of the room. He had gotten almost as far as the shattered figures on the floor when he suddenly stopped motionless. Gnut was emerging again.

He was bearing a shape that looked like another body, a larger one. He held it in one arm and placed it carefully by the body of Stillwell. In the hand of his other arm he held something that Cliff could not make out, and this he placed at the side of the body he had just put down. Then he went to the ship and returned once more with a shape which he laid gently by the others; and when this last trip was over he looked down at them all for a moment, then turned slowly back to the ship and stood motionless, as if in deep thought, by the ramp.

Cliff restrained his curiosity as long as he could, then slipped forward and bent over the objects Gnut had placed there. First in the row was the body of Stillwell, as he expected, and next was the great shapeless furry mass of a dead gorilla—the one of last night. By the gorilla lay the object the robot had carried in his free hand— the little body of the mocking bird. These last two had remained in the ship all night, and Gnut, for all his surprising gentleness in handling them, was only cleaning house. But there was a fourth body whose history he did not know. He moved closer and bent very low to look.

What he saw made him catch his breath. Impossible!—he thought; there was some confusion in his directions; he brought his face back, close to the first body. Then his blood ran cold. The first body was that of Stillwell, but the last in the row was Stillwell, too; there were two bodies of Stillwell, both exactly alike, both dead.

Cliff backed away with a cry, and then panic took him and he ran down the room away from Gnut and yelled and beat wildly on the door. There was a noise on the outside.

"Let me out!" he yelled in terror. "Let me out! Let me out! Oh, hurry!"

A crack opened between the two doors and he forced his way through like a wild animal and ran far out on the lawn. A belated couple on a nearby path stared at him with amazement, and this brought some sense to his head and he slowed down and came to a stop. Back at the building, everything looked as usual, and in spite of his terror, Gnut was not chasing him.

He was still in his stockinged feet. Breathing heavily, he sat down on the wet grass and put on his shoes; then he stood and looked at the building, trying to pull himself together. What an incredible melange! The dead Stillwell, the dead gorilla, and the dead mocking bird—all dying before his eyes. And then that last frightening thing, the second dead Stillwell whom he had *not* seen die. And Gnut's strange gentleness, and the sad expression he had twice seen on his face.

As he looked, the grounds about the building came to life. Several people collected at the door of the wing, above sounded the siren of a police copter, then in the distance another, and from all sides people came running, a few at first, then more and more. The police planes landed on the lawn just outside the door of the wing, and he thought he could see the officers peeping inside. Then suddenly the lights of the wing flooded on. In control of himself now, Cliff went back.

He entered. He had left Gnut standing in thought at the side of the ramp, but now he was again in his old familiar pose in the usual place, as if he had never moved. The ship's door was closed, and the ramp gone. But the bodies, the four strangely assorted bodies, were still lying by the demolished robot attendants where he had left them in the dark.

He was startled by a cry behind his back. A uniformed museum guard was pointing at him.

"This is the man!" the guard shouted. "When I opened the door this man forced his way out and ran like the devil!"

The police officers converged on Cliff.

"Who are you? What is all this?" one of them asked him roughly.

"I'm Cliff Sutherland, picture reporter," Cliff answered calmly. "And I was the one who was inside here and ran away, as the guard says."

"What were you doing?" the officer asked, eyeing him. "And where did these bodies come from?"

"Gentlemen, I'd tell you gladly—only business first," Cliff answered. "There's been some fantastic goings on in this room, and I saw them and have the story, but"—he smiled—"I must decline to answer without advice of counsel until I've sold my story to one of the news syndicates. You know how it is. If you'll allow me the use of the radio in your plane—just for a moment, gentlemen—you'll have the whole story right afterward—say in half an hour, when the television men broadcast it. Meanwhile, believe me, there's nothing for you to do, and there'll be no loss by the delay."

The officer who had asked the questions blinked, and one of the others, quicker to react and certainly not a gentleman, stepped toward Cliff with clenched fists. Cliff disarmed him by handing him his press credentials. He glanced at them rapidly and put them in his pocket.

By now half a hundred people were there, and among them were two members of a syndicate crew whom he knew, arrived by copter. The police growled, but they let him whisper in their ear and then go out under escort to the crew's plane. There, by radio, in five minutes, Cliff made a deal which would bring him more money than he had ever before earned in a year. After that he turned over all his pictures and negatives to the crew and gave them the story, and they lost not one second in spinning back to their office with the flash.

More and more people arrived, and the police cleared the building. Ten minutes later a big crew of radio and television men forced their way in, sent there by the syndicate with which he had dealt. And then a few minutes later, under the glaring lights set up by the operators and standing close by the ship and not far from Gnut—he refused to stand underneath him—Cliff gave his story to the cameras and microphones, which in a fraction of a second shot it to every corner of the Solar System.

Immediately afterward the police took him to jail. On general principles and because they were pretty blooming mad.

V

Cliff stayed in jail all that night—until eight o'clock the next morning, when the syndicate finally succeeded in digging up a lawyer and got him out. And then, when at last he was leaving, a Federal man caught him by the wrist.

"You're wanted for further questioning over at the Continental Bureau of Investigation," the agent told him. Cliff went along willingly.

Fully thirty-five high-ranking Federal officials and "big names" were waiting for him in an imposing conference room—one of the president's secretaries, the undersecretary of state, the underminister of defense, scientists, a colonel, executives, department heads, and ranking "C" men. Old gray-mustached Sanders, chief of the CBI, was presiding.

They made him tell his story all over again, and then, in parts, all over once more—not because they did not believe him, but because they kept hoping to elicit some fact which would cast significant light on the mystery of Gnut's behavior and the happenings of the last three nights. Patiently Cliff racked his brains for every detail.

Chief Sanders asked most of the questions. After more than an hour, when Cliff thought they had finished, Sanders asked him several more, all involving his personal opinions of what had transpired.

"Do you think Gnut was deranged in any way by the acids, rays, heat, and so forth applied to him by the scientists?"

"I saw no evidence of it."

"Do you think he can see?"

"I'm sure he can see, or else has other powers which are equivalent."

"Do you think he can hear?"

"Yes, sir. That time when I whispered to him that Stillwell was dead, he bent lower, as if to see for himself. I would not be surprised if he also understood what I said."

"At no time did he speak, except those sounds he made to open the ship?"

"Not one word, in English or any other language. Not one sound with his mouth."

"In your opinion, has his strength been impaired in any way by our treatment?" asked one of the scientists.

"I have told you how easily he handled the gorilla. He attacked the animal and threw it back, after which it retreated all the way down the building, afraid of him."

"How would you explain the fact that our autopsies disclosed no mortal wound, no cause of death, in any of the bodies—gorilla, mocking bird, or the two identical Stillwells?"—this from a medical officer.

"I can't."

"You think Gnut is dangerous?"—from Sanders.

"Potentially very dangerous."

"Yet you say you have the feeling he is not hostile."

"To me, I meant. I do have that feeling, and I'm afraid that I can't give any good reason for it, except the way he spared me twice when he had me in his power. I think maybe the gentle way he handled the bodies had something to do with it, and maybe the sad, thoughtful look I twice caught on his face."

"Would you risk staying in the building alone another night?"

"Not for anything." There were smiles.

"Did you get any pictures of what happened last night?"

"No, sir." Cliff, with an effort, held on to his composure, but he was swept by a wave of shame. A man hitherto silent rescued him by saying:

"A while ago you used the word 'purposive' in connection with Gnut's actions. Can you explain that a little?"

"Yes, that was one of the things that struck me: Gnut never seems to waste a motion. He can move with surprising speed when he wants to; I saw that when he attacked the gorilla; but most other times he walks around as if methodically completing some simple task. And that reminds me of a peculiar thing: at times he gets into one position, any position, maybe half bent over, and stays there for minutes at a time. It's as if his scale of time values was eccentric, compared to ours; some things he does surprisingly fast, and others surprisingly slow. This might account for his long periods of immobility."

"That's very interesting," said one of the scientists. "How would you account for the fact that he recently moves only at night?"

"I think he's doing something he wants no one to see, and the night is the only time he is alone."

"But he went ahead even after finding you there."

"I know. But I have no other explanation, unless he considered me harmless or unable to stop him—which was certainly the case."

"Before you arrived, we were considering incasing him in a large block of glasstex. Do you think he would permit it?"

"I don't know. Probably he would; he stood for the acids and rays and heat. But it had better be done in the daytime; night seems to be the time he moves."

"But he moved in the daytime when he emerged from the traveler with Klaatu."

"I know."

That seemed to be all they could think of to ask him. Sanders slapped his hand on the table.

"Well, I guess that's all Mr. Sutherland," he said. "Thank you for your help, and let me congratulate you for a very foolish, stubborn, brave young man—young businessman." He smiled very faintly. "You are free to go now, but it may be that I'll have to call you back later. We'll see."

"May I remain while you decide about that glasstex?" Cliff asked. "As long as I'm here I'd like to have the tip."

"The decision has already been made—the tip's yours. The pouring will be started at once."

"Thank you, sir," said Cliff—and calmly asked more: "And will you be so kind as to authorize me to be present outside the building tonight? Just outside. I've a feeling something's going to happen."

"You want still another scoop, I see," said Sanders not unkindly, "then you'll let the police wait while you transact your business."

"Not again, sir. If anything happens, they'll get it at once."

The chief hesitated. "I don't know," he said. "I'll tell you what. All the news services will want men there, and we can't have that; but if you can arrange to represent them all yourself, it's a go. Nothing's going to happen, but your reports will help calm the hysterical ones. Let me know."

Cliff thanked him and hurried out and phoned his syndicate the tip—free—then told them Sanders' proposal. Ten minutes they called him back, said all was arranged, and told him to catch some sleep. They would cover the pouring. With light heart, Cliff hurried over to the museum. The place was surrounded by thousands of the curious, held far back by a strong cordon of police. For once he could not get through; he was recognized, and the police were still sore. But he did not care much; he suddenly felt very tired and needed that nap. He went back to his hotel, left a call, and went to bed.

He had been asleep only a few minutes when his phone rang. Eyes shut, he answered it. It was one of the boys at the syndicate, with

peculiar news. Stillwell had just reported, very much alive—the real
Stillwell. The two dead ones were some kind of copies; he couldn't
imagine how to explain them. He had no brothers.

For a moment Cliff came fully awake, then he went back to bed.
Nothing was fantastic any more.

VI

At four o'clock, much refreshed and with an infrared viewing
magnifier slung over his shoulder, Cliff passed through the cordon
and entered the door of the wing. He had been expected and there
was no trouble. As his eyes fell on Gnut, an odd feeling went through
him, and for some obscure reason he was almost sorry for the giant
robot.

Gnut stood exactly as he had always stood, the right foot advanced
a little, and the same brooding expression on his face; but now there
was something more. He was solidly incased in a huge block of transparent glasstex. From the floor on which he stood to the top of his
full eight feet, and from there on up for an equal distance, and for
about eight feet to the left, right, back, and front, he was immured
in a water-clear prison which confined every inch of his surface and
would prevent the slightest twitch of even his amazing muscles.

It was absurd, no doubt, to feel sorry for a robot, a man-made
mechanism, but Cliff had come to think of him as being really alive,
as a human is alive. He showed purpose and will; he performed complicated and resourceful acts; his face had twice clearly shown the emotion of sadness, and several times what appeared to be deep thought;
he had been ruthless with the gorilla, and gentle with the mocking
bird and the other two bodies, and he had twice refrained from crushing Cliff when there seemed every reason that he might. Cliff did not
doubt for a minute that he was still alive, whatever that "alive" might
mean.

But outside were waiting the radio and television men; he had
work to do. He turned and went to them and all got busy.

An hour later Cliff sat alone about fifteen feet above the ground
in a big tree which, located just across the walk from the building,
commanded through a window a clear view of the upper part of
Gnut's body. Strapped to the limbs about him were three instruments
—his infrared viewing magnifier, a radio mike, and an infrared television eye with sound pickup. The first, the viewing magnifier, would

allow him to see in the dark with his own eyes, as if by daylight, a magnified image of the robot, and the others would pick up any sights and sounds, including his own remarks, and transmit them to the several broadcast studios which would fling them millions of miles in all directions through space. Never before had a picture man had such an important assignment, probably—certainly not one who forgot to take pictures. But now that was forgotten, and Cliff was quite proud, and ready.

Far back in a great circle stood a multitude of the curious—and the fearful. Would the plastic glasstex hold Gnut? If it did not, would he come out thirsting for revenge? Would unimaginable beings come out of the traveler and release him, and perhaps exact revenge? Millions at their receivers were jittery; those in the distance hoped nothing awful would happen, yet they hoped something would, and they were prepared to run.

In carefully selected spots not far from Cliff on all sides were mobile ray batteries manned by army units, and in a hollow in back of him, well to his right, there was stationed a huge tank with a large gun. Every weapon was trained on the door of the wing. A row of smaller, faster tanks stood ready fifty yards directly north. Their ray projectors were aimed at the door, but not their guns. The grounds about the building contained only one spot—the hollow where the great tank was—where, by close calculation, a shell directed at the doorway would not cause damage and loss of life to some part of the sprawling capital.

Dusk fell; out streamed the last of the army officers, politicians and other privileged ones; the great metal doors of the wing clanged to and were locked for the night. Soon Cliff was alone, except for the watchers at their weapons scattered around him.

Hours passed. The moon came out. From time to time Cliff reported to the studio crew that all was quiet. His unaided eyes could now see nothing of Gnut but the two faint red points of his eyes, but through the magnifier he stood out as clearly as if in daylight from an apparent distance of only ten feet. Except for his eyes, there was no evidence that he was anything but dead and unfunctionable metal.

Another hour passed. Now and again Cliff thumbed the levels of his tiny radio-television watch—only a few seconds at a time because of its limited battery. The air was full of Gnut and his own face and his own name, and once the tiny screen showed the tree in which he was then sitting and even, minutely, himself. Powerful infra-red long-distance television pickups were even then focused on him from nearby points of vantage. It gave him a funny feeling.

Then, suddenly, Cliff saw something and quickly bent his eye to the viewing magnifier. Gnut's eyes were moving; at least the intensity of the light emanating from them varied. It was as if two tiny red flashlights were turned from side to side, their beams at each motion crossing Cliff's eyes.

Thrilling, Cliff signaled the studios, cut in his pickups, and described the phenomenon. Millions resonated to the excitement in his voice. Could Gnut conceivably break out of that terrible prison?

Minutes passed, the eye flashes continued, but Cliff could discern no movement or attempted movement of the robot's body. In brief snatches he described what he saw. Gnut was clearly alive; there could be no doubt he was straining against the transparent prison in which he had at last been locked fast; but unless he could crack it, no motion should show.

Cliff took his eye from the magnifier—and started. His unaided eye, looking at Gnut shrouded in darkness, saw an astonishing thing not yet visible through his instrument. A faint red glow was spreading over the robot's body. With trembling fingers he readjusted the lens of the television eye, but even as he did so the glow grew in intensity. It looked as if Gnut's body was being heated to incandescence!

He described it in excited fragments, for it took most of his attention to keep correcting the lens. Gnut passed from a figure of dull red to one brighter and brighter, clearly glowing now even through the magnifier. And then he moved! Unmistakably he moved!

He had within himself somehow the means to raise his own body temperature, and was exploiting the one limitation of the plastic in which he was locked. For glasstex, Cliff now remembered, was a thermoplastic material, one that set by cooling and conversely would soften again with heat. Gnut was melting his way out!

In three-word snatches, Cliff described this. The robot became cherry-red, the sharp edges of the icelike block rounded, and the whole structure began to sag. The process accelerated. The robot's body moved more widely. The plastic lowered to the crown of his head, then to his neck, then his waist, which was as far as Cliff could see. His body was free! And then, still cherry-red, he moved forward out of sight!

Cliff strained eyes and ears, but caught nothing but the distant roar of the watchers beyond the police lines and a few low, sharp commands from the batteries posted around him. They, too, had heard, and perhaps seen by telescreen, and were waiting.

Several minutes passed. There was a sharp, ringing crack; the great metal doors of the wing flew open, and out stepped the metal giant, glowing no longer. He stood stockstill, and his red eyes pierced from side to side through the darkness.

Voices out in the dark barked orders and in a twinkling Gnut was bathed in narrow crisscrossing rays of sizzling, colored light. Behind him the metal doors began to melt, but his great green body showed no change at all. Then the world seemed to come to an end; there was a deafening roar, everything before Cliff seemed to explode in smoke and chaos, his tree whipped to one side so that he was nearly thrown out. Pieces of debris rained down. The tank gun had spoken, and Gnut, he was sure, had been hit.

Cliff held on tight and peered into the haze. As it cleared he made out a stirring among the debris at the door, and then dimly but unmistakably he saw the great form of Gnut rise to his feet. He got up slowly, turned toward the tank, and suddenly darted toward it in a wide arc. The big gun swung in an attempt to cover him, but the robot side-stepped and then was upon it. As the crew scattered, he destroyed its breech with one blow of his fist, and then he turned and looked right at Cliff.

He moved toward him, and in a moment was under the tree. Cliff climbed higher. Gnut put his two arms around the tree and gave a lifting push, and the tree tore out at the roots and fell crashing to its side. Before Cliff could scramble away, the robot had lifted him in his metal hands.

Cliff thought his time had come, but strange things were yet in store for him that night. Gnut did not hurt him. He looked at him from arm's length for a moment, then lifted him to a sitting position on his shoulders, legs straddling his neck. Then, holding one ankle, he turned and without hesitation started down the path which led westward away from the building.

Cliff rode helpless. Out over the lawns he saw the muzzles of the scattered field pieces move as he moved, Gnut—and himself—their one focus. But they did not fire. Gnut, by placing him on his shoulders, had secured himself against that—Cliff hoped.

The robot bore straight toward the Tidal Basin. Most of the field pieces throbbed slowly after. Far back, Cliff saw a dark tide of confusion roll into the cleared area—the police lines had broken. Ahead, the ring thinned rapidly off to the sides; then, from all directions but the front, the tide rolled in until individual shouts and cries could be made out. It came to a stop about fifty yards off, and few people ventured nearer.

Gnut paid them no attention, and he no more noticed his burden than he might a fly. His neck and shoulders made Cliff a seat hard as steel, but with the difference that their underlying muscles with each movement flexed, just as would those of a human being. To Cliff, this metal musculature became a vivid wonder.

Straight as the flight of a bee, over paths, across lawns and through thin rows of trees Gnut bore the young man, the roar of thousands of people following close. Above droned copters and darting planes, among them police cars with their nerve-shattering sirens. Just ahead lay the still waters of the Tidal Basin, and in its midst the simple marble tomb of the slain ambassador, Klaatu, gleaming black and cold in the light of the dozen searchlights always trained on it at night. Was this a rendezvous with the dead?

Without an instant's hesitation, Gnut strode down the bank and entered the water. It rose to his knees, then waist, until Cliff's feet were under. Straight through the dark waters for the tomb of Klaatu the robot made his inevitable way.

The dark square mass of gleaming marble rose higher as they neared it. Gnut's body began emerging from the water as the bottom shelved upward, until his dripping feet took the first of the rising pyramid of steps. In a moment they were at the top, on the narrow platform in the middle of which rested the simple oblong tomb.

Stark in the blinding searchlights, the giant robot walked once around it, then, bending, he braced himself and gave a mighty push against the top. The marble cracked; the thick cover slipped askew and broke with a loud noise on the far side. Gnut went to his knees and looked within, bringing Cliff well up over the edge.

Inside, in sharp shadow against the converging light beams, lay a transparent plastic coffin, thick walled and sealed against the centuries, and containing all that was mortal of Klaatu, unspoken visitor from the great Unknown. He lay as if asleep, on his face the look of godlike nobility that had caused some of the ignorant to believe him divine. He wore the robe he had arrived in. There were no faded flowers, no jewelry, no ornaments; they would have seemed profane. At the foot of the coffin lay the small sealed box, also of transparent plastic, which contained all of Earth's records of his visit—a description of the events attending his arrival, pictures of Gnut and the traveler, and the little roll of sight-and-sound film which had caught for all time his few brief motions and words.

Cliff sat very still, wishing he could see the face of the robot. Gnut, too, did not move from his position of reverent contemplation—not for a long time. There on the brilliantly lighted pyramid, under the eyes of a fearful, tumultuous multitude, Gnut paid final respect to his beautiful and adored master.

Suddenly, then, it was over. Gnut reached out and took the little box of records, rose to his feet and started down the steps.

Back through the water, straight back to the building, across lawns and paths as before, he made his irresistible way. Before him the chaotic ring of people melted away, behind they followed as close as they dared, trampling each other in their efforts to keep him in sight. There are no television records of his return. Every pickup was damaged on the way to the tomb.

As they drew near the building, Cliff saw that the tank's projectile had made a hole twenty feet wide extending from the roof to the ground. The door still stood open, and Gnut, hardly varying his almost jerkless rhythm, made his way over the debris and went straight for the port end of the ship. Cliff wondered if he would be set free.

He was. The robot set him down and pointed toward the door; then, turning, he made the sounds that opened the ship. The ramp slid down and he entered.

Then Cliff did the mad, courageous thing which made him famous for a generation. Just as the ramp started sliding back in he skipped over it and himself entered the ship. The port closed.

VII

It was pitch dark, and the silence was absolute. Cliff did not move. He felt that Gnut was close, just ahead, and it was so.

His hard metal hand took him by the waist, pulled him against his cold side, and carried him somewhere ahead. Hidden lamps suddenly bathed the surroundings with bluish light.

He set Cliff down and stood looking at him. The young man already regretted his rash action, but the robot, except for his always unfathomable eyes, did not seem angry. He pointed to a stool in one

corner of the room. Cliff quickly obeyed this time and sat meekly, for
a while not even venturing to look around.

He saw he was in a small laboratory of some kind. Complicated
metal and plastic apparatus lined the walls and filled several small
tables; he could not recognize or guess the function of a single piece.
Dominating the center of the room was a long metal table on whose
top lay a large box, much like a coffin on the outside, connected by
many wires to a complicated apparatus at the far end. From close
above spread a cone of bright light from a many-tubed lamp.

One thing, half covered on a near-by table, did look familiar—and
very much out of place. From where he sat it seemed to be a brief
case—an ordinary Earthman's brief case. He wondered.

Gnut paid him no attention, but at once, with the narrow edge of a
thick tool, sliced the lid off the little box of records. He lifted out the
strip of sight-and-sound film and spent fully half an hour adjusting it
within the apparatus at the end of the big table. Cliff watched, fascinated, wondering at the skill with which the robot used his tough
metal fingers. This done, Gnut worked for a long time over some accessory apparatus on an adjoining table. Then he paused thoughtfully
a moment and pushed inward a long rod.

A voice came out of the coffinlike box—the voice of the slain ambassador.

"I am Klaatu," it said, "and this is Gnut."

From the recording!—flashed through Cliff's mind. The first and
only words the ambassador had spoken. But, then, in the very next
second he saw that it was not so. There was a man in the box! The
man stirred and sat up, and Cliff saw the living face of Klaatu!

Klaatu appeared somewhat surprised and spoke quickly in an unknown tongue to Gnut—and Gnut, for the first time in Cliff's experience, spoke himself in answer. The robot's syllables tumbled out
as if born of human emotion, and the expression on Klaatu's face
changed from surprise to wonder. They talked for several minutes.
Klaatu, apparently fatigued, then began to lie down, but stopped
midway, for he saw Cliff. Gnut spoke again, at length. Klaatu beckoned Cliff with his hand, and he went to him.

"Gnut has told me everything," he said in a low, gentle voice, then
looked at Cliff for a moment in silence, on his face a faint, tired smile.

Cliff had a hundred questions to ask, but for a moment hardly
dared open his mouth.

"But you," he began at last—very respectfully, but with an escaping
excitement—"you are not the Klaatu that was in the tomb?"

The man's smile faded and he shook his head.

"No." He turned to the towering Gnut and said something in his own tongue, and at his words the metal features of the robot twisted as if with pain. Then he turned back to Cliff. "I am dying," he announced simply, as if repeating his words for the Earthman. Again to his face came the faint, tired smile.

Cliff's tongue was locked. He just stared, hoping for light. Klaatu seemed to read his mind.

"I see you don't understand," he said. "Although unlike us, Gnut has great powers. When the wing was built and the lectures began, there came to him a striking inspiration. Acting on it at once, in the night, he assembled this apparatus . . . and now he has made me again, from my voice, as recorded by your people. As you must know, a given body makes a characteristic sound. He constructed an apparatus which reversed the recording process, and from the given sound made the characteristic body."

Cliff gasped. So that was it!

"But you needn't die!" Cliff exclaimed suddenly, eagerly. "Your voice recording was taken when you stepped out of the ship, while you were well! You must let me take you to a hospital! Our doctors are very skillful!"

Hardly perceptibly, Klaatu shook his head.

"You still don't understand," he said slowly and more faintly, "Your recording had imperfections. Perhaps very slight ones, but they doom the product. All of Gnut's experiments died in a few minutes, he tells me . . . and so must I."

Suddenly, then, Cliff understood the origin of the "experiments." He remembered that on the day the wing was opened a Smithsonian official had lost a brief case containing film strips recording the speech of various world fauna. There, on that table, was a brief case! And the Stillwells must have been made from strips kept in the table drawer!

But his heart was heavy. He did not want this stranger to die. Slowly there dawned on him an important idea. He explained it with growing excitement.

"You say the recording was imperfect, and of course it was. But the cause of that lay in the use of an imperfect recording apparatus. So if Gnut, in his reversal of the process, had used exactly the same pieces of apparatus that your voice was recorded with, the imperfections could be studied, canceled out, and you'd live, and not die!"

As the last words left his lips, Gnut whipped around like a cat and gripped him tight. A truly human excitement was shining in the metal muscles of his face.

"Get me that apparatus!" he ordered—in clear and perfect English! He started pushing Cliff toward the door, but Klaatu raised his hand.

"There is no hurry," Klaatu said gently; "it is too late for me. What is your name, young man?"

Cliff told him.

"Stay with me to the end," he asked. Klaatu closed his eyes and rested; then, smiling just a little, but not opening his eyes, he added: "And don't be sad, for I shall now perhaps live again . . . and it will be due to you. There is no pain—" His voice was rapidly growing weaker. Cliff, for all the questions he had, could only look on, dumb. Again Klaatu seemed to be aware of his thoughts.

"I know," he said feebly, "I know. We have so much to ask each other. About your civilization . . . and Gnut's—"

"And yours," said Cliff.

"And Gnut's," said the gentle voice again. "Perhaps . . . some day . . . perhaps I will be back—"

He lay without moving. He lay so for a long time, and at last Cliff knew that he was dead. Tears came to his eyes; in only these few minutes he had come to love this man. He looked at Gnut. The robot knew, too, that he was dead, but no tears filled his red-lighted eyes; they were fixed on Cliff, and for once the young man knew what was in his mind.

"Gnut," he announced earnestly, as if taking a sacred oath, "I'll get the original apparatus. I'll get it. Every piece of it, the exact same things."

Without a word, Gnut conducted him to the port. He made the sounds that unlocked it. As it opened, a noisy crowd of Earthmen outside trampled each other in a sudden scramble to get out of the building. The wing was lighted. Cliff stepped down the ramp.

The next two hours always in Cliff's memory had a dreamlike quality. It was as if that mysterious laboratory with the peacefully sleeping dead man was the real and central part of his life, and his scene with the noisy men with whom he talked a gross and barbaric interlude. He stood not far from the ramp. He told only part of his story. He was believed. He waited quietly while all the pressure which the highest officials in the land could exert was directed toward obtaining for him the apparatus the robot had demanded.

When it arrived, he carried it to the floor of the little vestibule behind the port. Gnut was there, as if waiting. In his arms he held the slender body of the second Klaatu. Tenderly he passed him out to Cliff, who took him without a word, as if all this had been arranged. It seemed to be the parting.

Of all the things Cliff had wanted to say to Klaatu, one remained imperatively present in his mind. Now, as the green metal robot stood framed in the great green ship, he seized his chance.

"Gnut," he said earnestly, holding carefully the limp body in his arms, "you must do one thing for me. Listen carefully. I want you to tell your master—the master yet to come—that what happened to the first Klaatu was an accident, for which all Earth is immeasurably sorry. Will you do that?"

"I have known it," the robot answered gently.

"But will you promise to tell your master—just those words—as soon as he is arrived?"

"You misunderstand," said Gnut, still gently, and quietly spoke four more words. As Cliff heard them a mist passed over his eyes and his body went numb.

As he recovered and his eyes came back to focus he saw the great ship disappear. It just suddenly was not there any more. He fell back a step or two. In his ears, like great bells, rang Gnut's last words. Never, never was he to disclose them till the day he came to die.

"You misunderstand," the mighty robot had said. "I am the master."

WITHIN THE PYRAMID

by

R. DE WITT MILLER

*Smothered in the lush jungles of Central and South America
stand the crumbling remains of bygone civilizations. Wreckage—
the tumbling-down remnants of pyramids, temples, walls—just
enough is left to hint at amazing achievement in science and art.
What vanished race built them? Mr. Miller thinks the full story
might be one of visitors from other galaxies, unable to survive
because of diet, climate, or whatever. Visitors who lived long
enough to build, to teach the natives a few things—including
fear that persisted through the centuries.*

*

GARVIN MATTHEWS, of the International Anthropological
Society, stared unbelievingly at the giant white pyramid poised on
top of the sheer ridge. It seemed utterly unreal. The fading sunlight
gleamed on the pure-white sandstone of its sides, making it stand
out in sharp contrast to the dark green of the Yucatan jungle which
struggled for a foothold on the sides of the ridge.

Somehow Matthews couldn't force himself to believe that it was
man-made. But those sure, straight lines were not the chance of nature.
It must have been built by human beings. But how—and why?

Black clouds, forerunners of a storm, drifted slowly behind the apex
of the pyramid. The daylight was dying rapidly. He shook himself
free from the spell of unreality and turned to the old man beside
him.

"This will be the greatest scientific discovery of the century," he said. "When I make my report the society will immediately equip an expedition to make a thorough exploration."

Professor Phinias Hexter shifted uneasily.

"It's really not so large," he declared. "It's the first impression that makes it seem huge."

"Don't be foolish," Matthews replied. "I've done some work in Egypt. This thing makes the Great Pyramid of Cheops seem like a dwarf."

Hexter glanced at the tenuous arms of the black clouds which were gradually blending into a single dark curtain.

"It will storm in a few minutes," he said. "Don't you think we'd better wait until to-morrow to get a closer view?"

"Not on your life. I'm going to get inside that thing to-night—that is, if there's an entrance."

"Yes," Hexter replied slowly, "there is. But it's on the other side. It will be dark by the time we reach it."

Matthews glanced at him sharply.

"What's wrong with you? You act as if you're afraid of the thing."

"No," Hexter muttered, "not afraid. I've seen that pyramid too long to be afraid of it. It's what it stands for that has——"

His voice dropped into silence.

"I think you'd better do all you can to aid my expedition," Matthews said meaningly. "Remember, I don't have to tell the world what you've done—if I don't want to."

"Whether you tell them or not is of no consequence to me."

Matthews looked wonderingly at the gaunt, sun-bitten old professor.

"Why did you keep quiet?" he asked suddenly. "You've known of the existence of this pyramid for years—and you've told no one. This is the toughest place to get to on the American continents. There isn't a chance of seeing the thing unless you get into this valley. It's only visible from above. Do you realize that if I hadn't happened to stumble on it, it might have been centuries before it was found?"

"One century more will be long enough."

"I don't know what you're talking about—and I don't much care. What I want to know is why you didn't tell the world of your discovery—and what you're doing camping here alone?"

"As to the first question," Hexter said quietly, "I don't care to answer it now. As to the second, I am here to make explorations, just as you are."

"But you are connected with no society?"

"Does a man have to be connected with a society to be a scientist?
I had an idea when I first saw this pyramid. It's an idea that's been in
the back of my mind ever since I started archeology thirty years ago
On my first exploration here I found enough evidence to indicate that
I might be right. It has taken ten years and five trips to prove it."

"What is your theory?"

"I think facts will be more potent than my arguments."

"Then let's get on. What's the best way to reach it?"

"You're determined to go to-night?"

"Certainly. What did you expect me to do?"

"Yes," Hexter said half to himself. "I suppose I would have done
the same thing at your age. Have you a carbide lamp?"

"Two of them."

"Good. If you'll follow me, I'll bring you to the entrance in fifteen
minutes."

When they came close to the side of the pyramid, Matthews was
stunned by the sheer immensity of the thing. As they walked parallel
to the wall he studied the construction. It was unbelievable. The
blocks fitted with the precision of the finest Egyptian workmanship.
Only these blocks made those of the Egyptian pyramids seem puny.

Halfway along the farther side, Hexter stopped and pointed to a
barely discernible set of steps in the stonework.

"These lead to the entrance of the tunnel," he said.

They climbed steadily for perhaps a hundred feet. Here the steps
widened out into a broad ledge. In front of them was the entrance of a
passage, slightly higher and wider than a man, which led into the
heart of the pyramid.

"Something similar to the Egyptian pyramids," Matthews murmured.

"They were little copies," Hexter said. "The idea was handed down
from this one, an almost universal legend of the days when they were
alive."

"Who do you mean by 'they'?"

"Later," Hexter muttered, "later. First we will go to the conventional burial chamber."

Taking one of the carbide lamps, he led the way into the passage.
Matthews lighted the second lamp and followed.

The passage ran level for a distance; then it slanted sharply upward.
There was a damp, musty smell, the stale odor of things long forgotten and unused.

Suddenly the dark walls about them receded. Matthews realized that they had entered a small room. He held his light above his head. The room was perhaps twenty feet square. It was lined with hard, pink sandstone blocks, so beautifully fitted together that his eyes could scarcely make out the joints.

In the center, on a raised dais, were four elaborately carved sarcophagi.

With a sudden cry, Matthews stepped forward and struggled to lift the lid of the nearest sarcophagus.

"You will be disappointed," Hexter said. But he helped wrench off the massive stone slab.

The blue-white flame of the lamp cast long shadows into the open sarcophagus. By looking closely, Matthews could make out a few bits of what might once have worn human form. Some whitened pieces of bones, several odd bits of metal, and something resembling fabric, which fell to dust at his touch.

With a curse of disappointment he turned away.

"The others are the same," Hexter said. "That was their masterpiece. No one would ever look farther than this room. It is all so perfectly obvious. It was the legend of the gigantic burial place which was carried over into Egypt."

"Hexter," Matthews said harshly, "are you going to quit talking nonsense and help me get the lids off the rest of these boxes? Or am I going to have to wring whatever you know about this place out of that scrawny neck of yours?"

For a moment the old man did not answer. His lamp, held below his face, made his features seem grotesque. Finally he shrugged wearily.

"You are determined to report this find?" he asked.

"Of course."

"Then a great expedition will be sent. This whole place will be gone over almost with a microscope, in hopes of finding secret passageways. Finally the tourists will come."

"And why not? What are you afraid of? Are you a scientist or an old woman?"

Again Hexter did not answer for a moment. At last he seemed to reach a decision.

"I'm trusting you," he said slowly. "After all, you are a man of science. You have a good brain. If, after I am through, you decide to go on with your original plan, there is no way I can stop you."

"Well, if you are going to show me something, get at it."

"Not yet." Hexter sat down on one of the unopened sarcophagi. "I would like to ask you a few questions."

"What is this? A game?" Matthews said sarcastically.

"Perhaps—but it is my game. And in the end I promise to show you something that will change your whole conception of the history of the Earth."

Matthews sat down on another sarcophagus.

"All right," he said, "but don't be too long."

"You're an Egyptologist," Hexter began slowly. "Didn't you ever wonder what was back of the old civilization, and what it was that we keep seeing dimly in the legends and folklore of all people?"

"No."

"Well, I suppose you wouldn't. One has to blast his mind out of its conventional ideas before he can ever conceive the truth. But when you get the key, it all fits together. First, let's suppose that thousands of years ago, when man was still only half civilized, the Earth was visited by creatures from another world."

"Shall we tell ghost stories now?"

Hexter ignored the remark.

"I am merely making a hypothesis," he said, "just part of my little game. But to continue—say that some astral body similar to the Earth chanced to pass near our planet. That would account for the floods in all legends, and for the seven days of darkness in Egyptian and Jewish writings?"

"It might."

"It's more than guesswork," Hexter declared. "You must have heard of Kobal's theory, based on the eccentricities in the orbits of Neptune and Pluto, that there is a body with about the specific gravity of the Earth which pursues an orbit similar to a comet."

"I've read something about it."

"Very well. Say further that intelligent beings on this astral body sent an expedition to the Earth. Perhaps their world was running out of natural resources, or it was overcrowded. Whatever the reason, certain brave members of their race decided to make the attempt to establish a new home."

"I wish you'd get to the point," Matthews said wearily.

Hexter paid no attention.

"Perhaps," he continued, "after the expedition reached the Earth, they discovered that its climate was incompatible with their type of life. They took a gamble, and they lost. Some essential element

—perhaps a gas in the atmosphere or a necessary part of their food —was lacking. Even spectroscope analysis leaves you pretty much in the dark as to the true conditions on another planet. Say, for argument, that such a state of affairs occurred and you, Matthews, were a member of the expedition, what would you do?"

Matthews looked away at an inscription in Mayan on the wall of the room, but he seemed slightly more interested in the conversation.

"Die," he said after a moment. "What else would there be to do?"

"Nothing—unless. Even our crude science has practically succeeded in producing artificially suspended animation. A more advanced science should be able to do that, shouldn't it?"

"It's possible."

"I'm glad you admit that much. At least, you must grant that it's an interesting hypothesis. Let us follow it through for a moment. Say you could suspend your life—by the use of some anesthetic—indefinitely, what would you do then?"

"I'd suspend it and wait. At least it would be better than simply dying."

"Not only that. It may be that my hypothetical expedition had some definite reason to hope that if they could suspend their lives long enough, there would be a chance to escape. But passing over that possibility—before you suspended your life, what would you do?"

"I'd arrange to protect my body so that it would be still in existence if a chance ever occurred for me to resume normal life."

"Then if you had access to super-science by which you could build a greater structure than any which puny man can create, you would construct a giant edifice that would protect your body during the dormant period."

"It at least sounds logical—which is more than I can say for most of your ideas."

"All right—there is only one more step. If you still had hope that the people of your world might send another expedition after you, it would be necessary to make sure that they knew you had been successful in living for at least a time on Earth. Remember, the inhabitants of this other world probably wouldn't believe there was any intelligent life on Earth. At the time their expedition landed, man hadn't yet built anything large enough to be seen far out in space. Therefore it would be necessary to prove that your expedition hadn't perished immediately."

"I suppose so."

"I know so. There is one thing nature does not create: a straight line. A gigantic pyramid, placed on a bare ridge, would stand out as an eternal proof of the existence of intelligent beings. No other form of architecture so completely demonstrates the existence of a guiding mind. A pyramid is all straight lines."

"A most interesting theory," Matthews said with a short laugh, "but how about the facts?"

"That," Hexter declared, "is the next step."

He crossed the room, made a swift computation, and selected one of the giant stone blocks. He threw his weight against it. Noiselessly it slipped inward.

"A piece of balance that our science cannot duplicate," he said simply. "The concealment is marvelous, too. It took me months to find it."

The block had completely vanished now. The passage it revealed was smaller than the one by which they had entered the pyramid.

Again Hexter led the way. The passage descended endlessly. Matthews calculated that they must have reached a point below the surface of the ground when the passage broadened into a room. It was slightly larger than the burial chamber, but there was none of the ornamentation. There were no inscriptions on the walls.

In the center of the room were four caskets. They gleamed dully in the flickering light. Apparently they were composed of some metal, but it was not one with which Matthews was familiar.

"You see there are the same number as in the room above," Hexter said. "That was their great deception. Several beings existed for a short while on Earth. While they were alive they built a giant burial chamber.

"Then these four other-world people apparently died. One or two must have remained active to arrange the thing. Anyway, four bodies were solemnly buried in the upper chamber. But they were really human beings, killed, and disguised to resemble the other race. After a few years in this climate no one could tell the difference anyway. They would look no further than that upper burial chamber. The whole thing became a religion. It was a burial cult when it reached Egypt."

But Garvin Matthews did not hear. He was staring into one of the caskets. His mind was struggling with the thing that he saw. It didn't square with reason. It was utterly alien to every conception he had ever known—and yet it was there.

The casket was covered by a transparent material resembling glass—and yet not glass. Lying within the cushioned interior was the nude body of a young woman.

But the ghostly calm of death was not on the chiseled, aquiline features.

She was merely sleeping there. Death seemed completely apart from this lovely creature.

Slowly another idea was fighting its way into his mind. That strange pastel tint which suffused her skin! It was a light, delicate green—not the ghastly hue of death. Somehow it seemed natural to her, as natural as the pink flush of human skin.

"Notice the hands," Hexter said softly.

Again Matthew's mind refused at first to admit the idea. Finally it broke through.

Each of the slim, delicate hands had six fingers!

"You see," Hexter said softly, "not of this world——"

And suddenly Matthews came to life. There was a way to end this mystery. It was the way of science. He jerked loose the heavy geologist hammer that swung from his belt, raised it above his head.

With a quick movement Hexter grasped his upraised arm. There was a remarkable strength in the frail body of the old professor.

"Not yet," he said. "There is one thing more to show you. After that, if you wish to break open the caskets, it is your affair."

Slowly Matthews lowered the hammer.

"What difference will it make?" he asked.

"Those caskets were sealed for a purpose. They were meant to be opened only by scientists of their own race. Before you decide to do anything, let's go back to the upper chamber."

"How do I know you will show me the secret of the sliding block?" he asked.

"I will leave the stone displaced," Hexter said quietly. "But first look in the other caskets."

Matthews went slowly to each of the three metal coffins. Each contained a body—sleeping—but not the sleep of death. There was another young woman and two young men.

When Matthews had finished his observations, Hexter led the way back through the passageway to the outer room. He pointed to the Mayan inscription.

"You can skim over it," he said, "except the last line. Of course, they wrote in the language of the country."

Matthews deciphered it quickly, keeping an eye on the open passageway to the inner chamber. The inscription was a conventional curse, calling down the wrath of the gods on whoever should desecrate the tomb.

"The last line," Hexter repeated.

Matthews read the line, read it again, a queer look on his face.

"But there's something wrong," he said. "The old boys must have made some mistake. There's a date in this last line—but it is still in the future. It seems to be the date when the curse ends. According to our calendar, it would be 2040."

Hexter spoke with slow emphasis, each syllable distinct.

"If this astral body or planet does pursue some sort of elongated orbit about the Sun, it will come back some time—say in 2040."

"What do you mean?"

There was a queer, soft note in Hexter's voice.

"Don't you have any admiration for these people? Think of them refusing to accept fate, struggling against the cosmos for a chance to live. It took supreme intelligence to figure it all out—and it took faith to lie down quietly in those caskets, in the forlorn hope that they would be safe through thousands of years. How about the ones that stayed outside to seal the caskets, and tend to the burial? They died calmly that others might live. Do you want to wreck it all now—less than a hundred years from the date they are waiting for?"

Matthews did not look at Hexter. He stared at the Mayan inscription—but he did not see it.

Hexter spoke again, but this time his voice was hard, driving.

"What if the creatures who built this pyramid, that makes our modern buildings seem like doll houses, should come back and find those caskets broken open, and the members of their ill-fated expedition dead and in our museums? It would not be well for man and his civilization in that hour."

There was silence in that room of the dummy dead. The dank smell of age-old things seemed a tangible presence. Faintly from outside came the roar of the storm which had broken over the Yucatan jungle.

Matthews' face was hard, like old, weather-stained ivory. His breath was short, gasping. At last he said, "I shall report, but—I will omit the pyramid."

HE WHO SHRANK

by

HENRY HASSE

The reader is warned that this story, like infinity, has no ending Being a faithful chronicle of infinity—sub-atomic infinity—it could properly have no ending. We never know the ultimate fate of our protagonist, for he descended into the vastnesses that lie within the atom. We have merely stepped on the top rung of an endless ladder in cracking the atom. What universes have we destroyed in exploding a single, solitary atom?

*

YEARS, centuries, aeons, have fled past me in endless parade, leaving me unscathed: for I am deathless, and in all the universe alone of my kind. Universe? Strange how that convenient word leaps instantly to my mind from force of old habit. Universe? The merest expression of a puny idea in the minds of those who cannot possibly conceive whereof they speak. The word is a mockery. Yet how glibly men utter it! How little do they realize the artificiality of the word!

That night when the Professor called me to him he was standing close to the curved transparent wall of the astrono-laboratory looking out into the blackness. He heard me enter, but did not look around as he spoke. I do not know whether he was addressing me or not.

"They call me the greatest scientist the world has had in all time."

I had been his only assistant for years, and was accustomed to his moods, so I did not speak. Neither did he for several moments and then he continued:

"Only a half year ago I discovered a principle that will be the means of utterly annihilating every kind of disease germ. And only recently I turned over to others the principles of a new toxin which stimulates the worn-out protoplasmic life-cells, causing almost complete rejuvenation. The combined results should nearly double the ordinary life span. Yet these two things are only incidental in the long list of discoveries I have made to the great benefit of the race."

He turned then and faced me, and I was surprised at a new peculiar glow that lurked deep in his eyes.

"And for these things they call me great! For these puny discoveries they heap honors on me and call me the benefactor of the race. They disgust me, the fools! Do they think I did it for them? Do they think I care about the race, what it does or what happens to it or how long it lives? They do not suspect that all the things I have given them were but accidental discoveries on my part—to which I gave hardly a thought. Oh, you seem amazed. Yet not even you, who have assisted me here for ten years, ever suspected that all my labors and experiments were pointed toward one end, and one end alone."

He went over to a locked compartment which in earlier years I had wondered about and then ceased to wonder about, as I became engrossed in my work. The professor opened it now, and I glimpsed but the usual array of bottles and test-tubes and vials. One of these vials he lifted gingerly from a rack.

"And at last I have attained the end," he almost whispered, holding the tube aloft. A pale liquid scintillated eerily against the artificial light in the ceiling. "Thirty years, long years, of ceaseless experimenting, and now, here in my hand—success!"

The Professor's manner, the glow deep in his dark eyes, the submerged enthusiasm that seemed at every instant about to leap out, all served to impress me deeply. It must indeed be an immense thing he had done, and I ventured to say as much.

"Immense!" he exclaimed. "Immense! Why—why it's so immense that—. But wait. Wait. You shall see for yourself."

At that time how little did I suspect the significance of his words. I was indeed to see for myself.

Carefully he replaced the vial, then walked over to the transparent wall again.

"Look!" he gestured toward the night sky. "The unknown! Does it not fascinate you? The other fools dream of some day travelling out there among the stars. They think they will go out there and

learn the secret of the universe. But as yet they have been baffled by
the problem of a sufficiently powerful fuel or force for their ships.
And they are blind. Within a month I could solve the puny difficulty
that confronts them; could, but I won't. Let them search, let them
experiment, let them waste their lives away, what do I care about
them?"

I wondered what he was driving at, but realized that he would
come to the point in his own way. He went on:

"And suppose they do solve the problem, suppose they do leave
the planet, go to other worlds in their hollow ships, what will it
profit them? Suppose that they travel with the speed of light for their
own life time, and then land on a star at that point, the farthest
point away from here that is possible for them? They would no doubt
say: 'We can now realize as never before the truly staggering expanse
of the universe. It is indeed a great structure, the universe. We have
traveled a far distance; we must be on the fringe of it.'

"Thus they would believe. Only I would know how wrong they
were, for I can sit here and look through this telescope and see stars
that are fifty and sixty times as distant as that upon which they
landed. Comparatively, their star would be infinitely close to us. The
poor deluded fools and their dreams of space travel!"

"But, Professor," I interposed, "just think—"

"Wait! Now listen. I, too, have long desired to fathom the universe, to determine what it is, the manner and the purpose and the
secret of its creation. Have you ever stopped to wonder what the
universe is? For thirty years I have worked for the answer to those
questions. Unknowing, you helped me with your efficiency on the
strange experiments I assigned to you at various times. Now I have
the answer in that vial, and you shall be the only one to share the
secret with me."

Incredulous, I again tried to interrupt.

"Wait!" he said. "Let me finish. There was the time when I
also looked to the stars for the answer. I built my telescope, on a
new principle of my own. I searched the depths of the void. I made
vast calculations. And I proved conclusively to my own mind what
had theretofore been only a theory. I know now without doubt that
this our planet, and other planets revolving about the sun, are but
electrons of an atom, of which the sun is the nucleus. And our sun is
but one of millions of others, each with its allotted number of planets,
each system being an atom just as our own is in reality.

"And all these millions of solar systems, or atoms, taken together in one group, form a galaxy. As you know, there are countless numbers of these galaxies throughout space, with tremendous stretches of space between them. And what are these galaxies? Molecules! They extend through space even beyond the farthest range of my telescope! But having penetrated that far, it is not difficult to make the final step.

"All of these far-flung galaxies, or molecules, taken together as a whole, form—what? Some indeterminable element or substance on a great, ultramacrocosmic world! Perhaps a minute drop of water, or a grain of sand, or wisp of smoke, or—good God!—an eyelash of some creature living on that world!"

I could not speak. I felt myself grow faint at the thought he had propounded. I tried to think it could not be—yet what did I or anyone know about the infinite stretches of space that must exist beyond the ranges of our most powerful telescope?

"It can't be!" I burst out. "It's incredible, it's—monstrous!"

"Monstrous? Carry it a step further. May not that ultra-world also be an electron whirling around the nucleus of an atom? And that atom only one of millions forming a molecule? And that molecule only one of millions forming—"

"For God's sake, stop!" I cried. "I refuse to believe that such a thing can be! Where would it all lead? Where would it end? It might go on—forever! And besides," I added lamely, "what has all this to do with—your discovery, the fluid you showed me?"

"Just this. I soon learned that it was useless to look to the infinitely large; so I turned to the infinitely small. For does it not follow that if such a state of creation exists in the stars above us, it must exist identically in the atoms below us?"

I saw his line of reasoning, but still did not understand. His next words fully enlightened me, but made me suspect that I was facing one who had gone insane from his theorizing. He went on eagerly, his voice the voice of a fanatic:

"If I could not pierce the stars above, that were so far, then I would pierce the atoms below, that were so near. They are everywhere. In every object I touch and in the very air I breathe. But they are minute, and to reach them I must find a way to make myself as minute as they are, and more so! This I have done. The solution I showed you will cause every individual atom in my body to contract, but each electron and proton will also decrease in size, or diameter, in direct proportion to my own shrinkage! Thus will I not only be able to become the size of an atom, but can go down, down into infinite smallness!"

II

When he had stopped speaking I said calmly: "You are mad."
He was imperturbed. "I expected you to say that," he answered. "It is only natural that that should be your reaction to all that I have said. But no, I am not mad, it is merely that you are unacquainted with the marvelous propensities of 'Shrinx.' But I promised that you should see for yourself, and that you shall. You shall be the first to go down into the atomic universe."

My original opinion in regard to his state of mind remained unshaken.

"I am sure you mean well, Professor," I said, "but I must decline your offer."

He went on as though I hadn't spoken:

"There are several reasons why I want to send you before I myself make the trip. In the first place, once you make the trip there can be no returning, and there are a number of points I want to be quite clear on. You will serve as my advance guard, so to speak."

"Professor, listen. I do not doubt that the stuff you call 'Shrinx' has very remarkable properties. I will even admit that it will do all you say it will do. But for the past month you have worked day and night, with scarcely enough time out for food and hardly any sleep at all. You should take a rest, get away from the laboratory for awhile."

"I shall keep in contact with your consciousness," he said, "through a very ingenious device I have perfected. I will explain it to you later. The 'Shrinx' is introduced directly into the blood stream. Shortly thereafter your shrinkage should begin, and continue at moderate speed, never diminishing in the least degree so long as the blood continues to flow in your body. At least, I hope it never diminishes. Should it, I shall have to make the necessary alterations in the formula. All this is theoretical of course, but I am sure it will all work according to schedule, and quite without harm."

I had now lost all patience. "See here, Professor," I said crossly, "I refuse to be the object of any of your wild-sounding experiments. You should realize that what you propose to do is scientifically impossible. Go home and rest—or go away for a while—"

Without the slightest warning he leaped at me, snatching an object from the table. Before I could take a backward step I felt a needle plunge deep into my arm, and cried out with the pain of it. Things became hazy, distorted. A wave of vertigo swept over me. Then it passed, and my vision cleared. The Professor stood leering before me.

"Yes, I've worked hard and I'm tired. I've worked thirty years, but I'm not tired enough nor fool enough to quit this thing now, right on the verge of the climax!"

His leer of triumph gave way to an expression almost of sympathy.

"I am sorry it had to come about this way," he said, "but I saw that you would never submit otherwise. I really am ashamed of you. I didn't think you would doubt the truth of my statements to the extent of really believing me insane. But to be safe I prepared your allotment of the 'Shrinx' in advance, and had it ready; it is now coursing through your veins, and it should be but a short time before we observe the effects. What you saw in the vial is for myself when I am ready to make the trip. Forgive me for having to administer yours in such an undignified manner."

So angered was I at the utter disregard he had shown for my personal feelings, that I hardly heard his words. My arm throbbed fiercely where the needle had plunged in. I tried to take a step toward him, but not a muscle would move. I struggled hard to break the paralysis that was upon me, but could not move a fraction of an inch from where I stood.

The professor seemed surprised too, and alarmed.

"What, paralysis? That is an unforeseen circumstance! You see, it is even as I said: the properties of 'Shrinx' are marvelous and many."

He came close and peered intently into my eyes, and seemed relieved.

"However, the effect is only temporary," he assured me. Then added: "But you will likely be a bit smaller when the use of your muscles returns, for your shrinkage should begin very shortly now. I must hurry to prepare for the final step."

He walked past me, and I heard him open his private cupboard again. I could not speak, much less move, and I was indeed in a most uncomfortable, not to mention undignified, position. All I could do was to glare at him when he came around in front of me again. He carried a curious kind of helmet with ear-pieces and goggles attached, and a number of wires running from it. This he placed upon the table and connected the wires to a small flat box there.

All the while I watched him closely. I hadn't the least idea what he was going to do with me, but never for a moment did I believe that I would shrink into an atomic universe; that was altogether too fantastic for my conception.

As though reading my thought the Professor turned and faced me. He looked me over casually for a moment and then said:

"I believe it has begun already. Yes, I am sure of it. Tell me, do you not feel it? Do not things appear a trifle larger to you, a trifle taller? Ah, I forgot that the paralyzing effect does not permit you to answer. But look at me—do I not seem taller?"

I looked at him. Was it my imagination, or some kind of hypnosis he was asserting on me, that made me think he was growing slightly, ever so slightly, upward even as I looked?

"Ah!" he said triumphantly. "You have noticed. I can tell it by your eyes. However, it is not I who am growing taller, but you who are shrinking."

He grasped me by the arms and turned me about to face the wall. "I can see that you doubt," he said, "so look! The border on the wall. If you remember, it used to be about even with your eyes. Now it is fully three inches higher."

It was true! And I could now feel a tingling in my veins, and a slight dizziness.

"Your shrinkage has not quite reached the maximum speed," he went on. "When it does, it will remain constant. I could not stop it now even if I wanted to, for I have nothing to counteract it. Listen closely now, for I have several things to tell you.

"When you have become small enough I am going to lift you up and place you on this block of Rehyllium-X here on the table. You will become smaller and smaller, and eventually should enter an alien universe consisting of billions and billions of star groups, or galaxies, which are only the molecules in this Rehyllium-X. When you burst through, your size in comparison with this new universe should be gigantic. However, you will constantly diminish, and will be enabled to alight on any one of the spheres of your own choosing. And—after alighting—you will continue—always down!"

At the concept I thought I would go mad. Already I had become fully a foot shorter, and still the paralysis gripped me. Could I have moved I would have torn the Professor limb from limb in my impotent rage—though if what he said was true, I was already doomed.

Again it seemed as though he read my mind.

"Do not think too harshly of me," he said. "You should be very grateful for this opportunity, for you are going on a marvelous venture, into a marvelous realm. Indeed, I am almost jealous that you should be the first. But with this," he indicated the helmet and box on the table, "I shall keep contact with you no matter how far you go. Ah, I see by your eyes that you wonder how such a thing could be possible. Well, the principle of this device is really very simple. Just as light is a form of energy, so is thought. And just as light travels through an 'ether' in the form of waves, so does thought. But the thought waves are much more intangible—in fact, invisible. Nevertheless the waves are there, and the coils in this box are so sensitized as to receive and amplify them a million times, much as sound waves might be amplified. Through this helmet I will receive but two of your six sensations: those of sound and sight. They are the two major ones, and will be sufficient for my purpose. Every sight and sound that you encounter, no matter how minute, reaches your brain and displaces tiny molecules there that go out in the form of thought waves and finally reach here and are amplified. Thus my brain receives every impression of sight and sound that your brain sends out."

I did not doubt now that his marvelous "Shrinx" would do everything he said it would do. Already I was but one-third of my original size. Still the paralysis showed no sign of releasing me, and I hoped that the Professor knew whereof he spoke when he said the effect would be but temporary. My anger had subsided somewhat, and I think I began to wonder what I would find in that other universe.

Then a terrifying thought assailed me—a thought that left me cold with apprehension. If, as the Professor had said, the atomic universe was but a tiny replica of the universe we knew, would I not find myself in the vast empty spaces between the galaxies with no air to breathe? In all the vast calculations the Professor had made, could he have overlooked such an obvious point?

Now I was very close to the floor, scarcely a foot high. Everything about me—the Professor, the tables, the walls—were gigantically out of proportion to myself.

The Professor reached down then, and swung me up on the table top amidst the litter of wires and apparatus. He began speaking again, and to my tiny ears his voice sounded a deeper note.

"Here is the block of Rehyllium-X containing the universe you soon will fathom," he said, placing on the table beside me the square piece of metal, which was nearly half as tall as I was. "As you know, Rehyllium-X is the densest of all known metals, so the universe await--

ing you should be a comparatively dense one—though you will not think so, with the thousands of light-years of space between stars. Of course I know no more about this universe than you do, but I would advise you to avoid the very bright stars and approach only the dimmer ones. Well, this is good-by, then. We shall never see each other again. Even should I follow you—as I certainly shall as soon as I have learned through you what alterations I should make in the formula—it is impossible that I could exactly trace your course down through all the spheres that you will have traversed. One thing already I have learned: the rate of shrinkage is too rapid; you will be able to stay on a world for only a few hours. But perhaps that is best, after all. This is good-by for all time."

He picked me up and placed me upon the smooth surface of the Rehyllium-X. I judged that I must be about four inches tall then. It was with immeasurable relief that I finally felt the paralysis going away. The power of my voice returned first, and expanding my lungs I shouted with all by might.

"Professor!" I shouted. "Professor!"

He bent down over me. To him my voice must have sounded ridiculously high pitched.

"What about the empty regions of space I will find myself in?" I asked a bit tremulously, my mouth close to his ear. "I would last but a few minutes. My life will surely be snuffed out."

"No, that will not happen," he answered. His voice beat upon my ear-drums like thunder, and I placed my hands over my ears.

He understood, and spoke more softly. "You will be quite safe in airless space," he went on. "In the thirty years I have worked on the problem, I would not be likely to overlook that point—though I will admit it gave me much trouble. But as I said, 'Shrinx' is all the more marvelous in the fact that its qualities are many. After many difficulties and failures, I managed to instill in it a certain potency by which it supplies sufficient oxygen for your need, distributed through the blood stream. It also irradiates a certain amount of heat; and, inasmuch as I consider the supposed sub-zero temperature of space as being somewhat exaggerated, I don't think you need worry about any discomfort in open space."

III

I was scarcely over an inch in height now. I could walk about, though my limbs tingled fiercely as the paralysis left. I beat my arms against my sides and swung them about to speed the circulation. The Professor must have thought I was waving good-by. His hand reached out and he lifted me up. Though he tried to handle me gently, the pressure of his fingers bruised. He held me in his open hand and raised me up to the level of his eyes. He looked at me for a long moment and then I saw his lips form the words "good-by." I was terribly afraid he would drop me to the floor a dizzy distance below, and I was relieved when he lowered me again and I slid off his hand to the block of Rehyllium-X.

The Professor now appeared as a giant towering hundreds of feet into the air, and beyond him, seemingly miles away, the walls of the room extended to unimaginable heights. The ceiling above seemed as far away and expansive as the dome of the sky I had formerly known. I ran to the edge of the block and peered down. It was as though I stood at the top of a high cliff. The face of it was black and smooth, absolutely perpendicular. I stepped back apace lest I lose my footing and fall to my death. Far below extended the vast smooth plain of the table top.

I walked back to the center of the block, for I was afraid of the edge; I might be easily shaken off if the Professor were to accidentally jar the table. I had no idea of my size now, for there was nothing with which I could compare it. For all I knew I might be entirely invisible to the Professor. He was now but an indistinguishable blur, like a far off mountain seen through a haze.

I now began to notice that the surface of the Rehyllium-X block was not as smooth as it had been. As far as I could see were shallow ravines, extending in every direction. I realized that these must be tiny surface scratches that had been invisible before.

I was standing on the edge of one of these ravines, and I clambered down the side and began to walk along it. It was as straight as though laid by a ruler. Occasionally I came to intersecting ravines, and turned to the left or right. Before long, due to my continued shrinkage, the walls of these ravines towered higher than my head, and it was as though I walked along a narrow path between two cliffs.

Then I received the shock of my life, and my adventure came near to ending right there. I approached one of the intersections. I turned the sharp corner to the right. I came face to face with the How-Shall I-Describe-It.

It was a sickly bluish white in color. Its body was disc shaped, with a long double row of appendages—legs—on the under side. Hundreds of ugly looking spikes rimmed the disc body on the outer and upper edges. There was no head and apparently no organ of sight, but dozens of snake-like protuberances waved in my face as I nearly crashed into it. One of them touched me and the creature backed swiftly away, the spikes springing stiffly erect in formidable array.

This impression of the creature flashed upon my mind in the merest fraction of time, for you may be sure that I didn't linger there to take stock of its pedigree. No indeed. My heart choked me in my fright, I whirled and sped down the opposite ravine. The sound of the thing's pursuit lent wings to my feet, and I ran as I had never run before. Up one ravine and down another I sped, doubling to right and left in my effort to lose my pursuer. The irony of being pursued by a germ occurred to me, but the matter was too serious to be funny. I ran until I was out of breath, but no matter which way I turned and doubled the germ was always a hundred paces behind me. Its organ of sound must have been highly sensitive. At last I could run no more, and I darted around the next corner and stopped, gasping for breath.

The germ rushed a short distance past me and stopped, having lost the sound of my running. Its dozens of tentacular sound organs waved in all directions. Then it came unhesitatingly toward me, and again I ran. Apparently it had caught the sound of my heavy breathing. Again I dashed around the next corner, and as I heard the germ approach I held my breath until I thought my lungs would burst. It stopped again, waved its tentacles in the air and then ambled on down the ravine. Silently I sneaked a hasty retreat.

Now the walls of these ravines (invisible scratches on a piece of metal!) towered very high above me as I continued to shrink. Now too I noticed narrow chasms and pits all around me, in both the walls at the sides and the surface on which I walked. All of these seemed very deep, and some were so wide that I had to leap across them.

At first I was unable to account for these spaces that were opening all about me, and then I realized with a sort of shock that the Rehyllium-X was becoming *porous*, so small was I in size! Although it was the densest of all known metals, no substance whatsoever could be so dense as to be an absolute solid.

I began to find it increasingly difficult to progress; I had to get back and make running jumps across the spaces. Finally I sat down and laughed as I realized the futility and stupidity of this. Why was I risking my life by jumping across these spaces that were becoming

wider as I became smaller, when I had no particular destination anyway—except down. So I may as well stay in one spot.

No sooner had I made this decision, however, than something
changed my mind.

It was the germ again.

I saw it far down the ravine, heading straight for me. It might
have been the same one I had encountered before, or its twin brother.
But now I had become so small that it was fully fifteen times my
own size, and the very sight of the huge beast ambling toward me
inspired terror into my heart. Once more I ran, praying that it
wouldn't hear the sound of my flight because of my small size.

Before I had gone a hundred yards I stopped in dismay. Before me
yawned a space so wide that I couldn't have leaped half the distance.
There was escape on neither side, for the chasm extended up both
the walls. I looked back. The germ had stopped. Its mass of tentacles
was waving close to the ground.

Then it came on, not at an amble now but at a much faster rate.
Whether it had heard me or had sensed my presence in some other
manner, I did not know. Only one thing was apparent: i had but a
few split seconds in which to act. I threw myself down flat, slid backward into the chasm, and hung there by my hands.

And I was just in time. A huge shape rushed overhead as I looked
up. So big was the germ that the chasm which had appeared so wide
to me, was inconsequential to it; it ran over the space as though it
weren't there. I saw the double row of the creature's limbs as they
flashed overhead. Each one was twice the size of my body.

Then happened what I had feared. One of the huge claw-like
limbs came down hard on my hand, and a sharp spur raked across it.
I could feel the pain all through my arm. The anguish was insuffer-
able. I tried to get a better grip but couldn't. My hold loosened. I
dropped down—down—

IV

"This is the end."

Such was my thought in that last awful moment as I slipped away
into space. Involuntarily I shut my eyes, and I expected at any
moment to crash into oblivion.

But nothing happened.

There was not even the usual sickening sensation that accompanies acceleration. I opened my eyes to a Stygian darkness, and put out an exploring hand. It encountered a rough wall which was flashing upward past my face. I was falling, then; but at no such speed as would have been the case under ordinary circumstances. This was rather as if I were floating downward. Or was it downward? I had lost all sense of up or down or sideways. I doubled my limbs under me and kicked out hard against the wall, shoving myself far away from it.

How long I remained falling—or drifting—there in that darkness I have no way of knowing. But it must have been minutes, and every minute I was necessarily growing smaller.

For some time I had been aware of immense masses all around me. They pressed upon me from every side, and from them came a very faint radiance. They were of all sizes, some no larger than myself and some looming up large as mountains. I tried to steer clear of the large ones, for I had no desire to be crushed between two of them. But there was little chance of that. Although we all drifted slowly along through space together, I soon observed that none of these masses ever approached each other or deviated the least bit from their paths.

As I continued to shrink, these masses seemed to spread out, away from me; and as they spread, the light which they exuded became brighter. They ceased to be masses, and became swirling, expanding, individual stretches of mist, milky white.

They were nebulae! Millions of miles of space must stretch between each of them! The gigantic mass I had clung to, drawn there by its gravity, also underwent this nebulosity, and now I was floating in the midst of an individual nebula. It spread out as I became smaller, and as it thinned and expanded, what had seemed mist now appeared as trillions and trillions of tiny spheres in intricate patterns.

I was in the very midst of these spheres! They were all around my feet, my arms, my head! They extended farther than I could reach, farther than I could see. I could have reached out and gathered thousands of them in my hand. I could have stirred and kicked my feet and scattered them in chaotic confusion about me. But I did not indulge in such reckless and unnecessary destruction of worlds. Doubtless my presence here had already done damage enough, displacing millions of them.

I scarcely dared to move a muscle for fear of disrupting the orbits of some of the spheres or wreaking havoc among some solar systems or star groups. I seemed to be hanging motionless among them; or if I were moving in any direction, the motion was too slight to be noticeable. I didn't even know if I were horizontal or vertical, as those two terms had lost all meaning.

As I became smaller, of course the spheres became larger and the space between them expanded, so that the bewildering maze thinned somewhat and gave me more freedom of movement.

I took more cognizance now of the beauty around me. I remembered what the Professor had said about receiving my thought waves, and I hoped he was tuned in now, for I wouldn't have had him miss it for anything.

Every hue I had ever known was represented there among the suns and encircling planets: dazzling whites, reds, yellows, blues, greens, violets, and every intermediate shade. I glimpsed also the barren blackness of suns that had burnt out; but these were infrequent, as this seemed to be a very young universe.

There were single suns with the orbital planets varying in number from two to twenty. There were double suns that revolved slowly about each other as on an invisible axis. There were triple suns that revolved slowly about one another—strange as it may seem—in perfect trihedral symmetry. I saw one quadruple sun: a dazzling white, a blue, a green, and a deep orange. The white and the blue circled each other on the horizontal plane while the green and the orange circled on the vertical plane, thus forming a perfect interlocking system. Around these four suns, in circular orbits, sped sixteen planets of varying size, the smallest on the inner orbits and the largest on the outer. The effect was a spinning, concave disc with the white-blue-green-orange rotating hub in the center. The rays from these four suns, as they bathed the rolling planets and were reflected back into space in many-hued magnificence, presented a sight both beautiful and weird.

I determined to alight on one of the planets of this quadruple sun as soon as my size permitted. I did not find it hard to maneuver to a certain extent; and eventually, when I had become much smaller, I stretched alongside this solar system, my length being as great as the diameter of the orbit of the outermost planet! Still I dared not come too close, for fear the gravity of my bulk would cause some tension in the orbital field.

I caught glimpses of the surface of the outer, or sixteenth planet, as it swung past me. Through rifts in the great billowing clouds I saw vast expanses of water, but no land; and then the planet was moving away from me, on its long journey around to the other side of the suns. I did not doubt that by the time it returned to my side I would be very much smaller, so I decided to move in a little closer and try to get a look at the fifteenth planet which was then on the opposite side but swinging around in my direction.

I had discovered that if I doubled up my limbs and thrust out violently in a direction opposite that in which I wished to move, I could make fairly good progress, though the effort was somewhat strenuous. In this manner I moved inward toward the sun-cluster, and by the time I had reached the approximate orbit of the fifteenth planet I had become much smaller—was scarcely one-third as long as the diameter of its orbit! The distance between the orbits of the sixteenth and fifteenth planets must have been about 2,500,000,000 miles, according to the old standards I had known; but to me the distance had seemed but a few hundred yards.

I waited there, and finally the planet hove into view from out of the glorious aurora of the suns. Nearer and nearer it swung in its circle, and as it approached I saw that its atmosphere was very clear, a deep saffron-color. It passed me a scant few yards away, turning lazily on its axis opposite the direction of flight. Here, too, as on planet sixteen, I saw a vast world of water. There was only one fairly large island and many scattered small ones, but I judged that fully nine-tenths of the surface area was ocean.

I moved on in to planet fourteen, which I had noticed was a beautiful golden-green color.

By the time I had maneuvered to the approximate fourteenth orbit I had become so small that the light of the central suns pained my eyes. When the planet came in sight I could easily see several large continents on the lighted side; and as the dark side turned to the suns, several more continents became visible. As it swung past me I made comparisons and observed that I was now about five times as large as the planet. When it came around again I would try to effect a landing. To attempt a contact with it now would likely prove disastrous to both it and myself.

As I waited there and became smaller my thoughts turned to the Professor. If his amazing theory of an infinite number of sub-universes was true, then my adventure had hardly begun; wouldn't begin until I alighted on the planet. What would I find there? I did not doubt that the Professor, receiving my thought waves, was just as curious as I. Suppose there was life on this world—hostile life? I would face the dangers while the Professor sat in his laboratory far away. This was the first time that aspect of it occurred to me; it had probably never occurred to the Professor. Strange, too, how I thought of him as "far away." Why, he could merely have reached out his hand and moved me, universe and all, on his laboratory table!

Another curious thought struck me: here I was waiting for a planet to complete its circle around the suns. To any beings who might exist on it, the elapsed time would represent a year; but to me it would only be a number of minutes.

At that, it returned sooner than I expected it, curving around to meet me. Its orbit, of course, was much smaller than those of the two outer planets. More minutes passed as it came closer and larger. As nearly as I could judge I was about one-fifth its size now. It skimmed past me, so closely that I could have reached out and brushed its atmosphere. And as it moved away I could feel its steady tugging, much as if I were a piece of metal being attracted to a magnet. Its speed did not decelerate in the least, but now I was moving along close behind it. It had "captured" me, just as I had hoped it would. I shoved in closer, and the gravity became a steady and stronger pull. I was "falling" toward it. I swung around so that my feet were closest to it, and they entered the atmosphere, where the golden-green touched the blackness of space. They swung down in a long arc and touched something solid. My "fall" toward the planet ceased. I was standing on one of the continents of this world.

V

So tall was I that the greatest part of my body still extended out into the blackness of space. In spite of the fact that the four suns were the distance of thirteen orbits away, they were of such intense brilliance now that to look directly at them would surely have blinded me. I looked far down my tapering length at the continent on which I stood. Even the multi-colored light reflected from the surface was dazzling to the eye. Too late I remembered the Professor's warning to avoid the brighter suns. Close to the surface a few fleeting wisps of cloud drifted about my limbs.

As the planet turned slowly on its axis I of course moved with it, and shortly I found myself on the side away from the suns, in the planet's shadow. I was thankful for this relief—but it was only temporary. Soon I swung around into the blinding light again. Then into the shadow, and again into the light. How many times this happened I do not know, but at last I was entirely within the planet's atmosphere; here the rays of the sun were diffused, and the light less intense.

Miles below I could see but a vast expanse of yellow surface, stretching unbroken in every direction. As I looked far behind the curving horizon it seemed that I caught a momentary glimpse of tall, silvery towers of some far-off city; but I could not be sure, and when I looked again it had vanished.

I kept my eyes on that horizon, however, and soon two tiny red specks became visible against the yellow of the plain. Evidently they were moving toward me very rapidly, for even as I looked they became larger, and soon took shape as two blood-red spheres. Immediately I visioned them as some terrible weapons of warfare or destruction.

But as they came close to me and swerved up to where I towered high in the thin atmosphere, I could see that they were not solid at all, as I had supposed, but were gaseous, and translucent to a certain extent. Furthermore, they behaved in a manner that hinted strongly of intelligence. Without visible means of propulsion they swooped and circled about my head, to my utter discomfiture. When they came dangerously close to my eyes I raised my hand to sweep them away, but they darted quickly out of reach.

They did not approach me again, but remained there close together, pulsating in mid air. This queer pulsating of their tenuous substance gave me the impression that they were conferring together; and of course I was the object of their conference. Then they darted away in the direction whence they had come.

My curiosity was as great as theirs had seemed to be, and without hesitation I set out in the same direction. I must have covered nearly a mile at each step, but even so, these gaseous entities easily out-distanced me and were soon out of sight. I had no doubt that their destination was the city—if indeed it were a city I had glimpsed. The horizon was closer now and less curved, due to my decrease in height: I judged that I was barely five or six hundred feet tall now.

I had taken but a few hundred steps in the direction the two spheres had gone, when to my great surprise I saw them coming toward me again, this time accompanied by a score of—companions. I stopped in my tracks, and soon they came close and circled about my head. They were all about five feet in diameter, and of the same dark red color. For a minute they darted about as though studying me from every angle; then they systematically arranged themselves in a perfect circle around me. Thin streamers emanated from them, and merged, linking them together and closing the circle. Then other streamers reached slowly out toward me, wavering, cautious.

This, their manner of investigation, did not appeal to me in the least, and I swept my arms around furiously. Instantly all was wild confusion. The circle broke and scattered, the streamers snapped back and they were spheres again. They gathered in a group a short distance away and seemed to consider.

One, whose color had changed to a bright orange, darted apart from them and pulsated rapidly. As clearly as though words had been spoken, I comprehended. The bright orange color signified anger, and he was rebuking the others for their cowardice.

Led by the orange sphere they again moved closer to me, this time they had a surprise for me. A score of streamers flashed out quick as lightning, and cold blue flames spluttered where they touched me. Electric shocks ran through my arms, rendering them numb and helpless. Again they formed their circle around me, again the streamers emerged and completed the circle, and other streamers reached out caressingly. For a moment they flickered about my head, then merged, enveloping it in a cold red radiance. I felt no sensation at all at the touch, except that of cold.

The spheres began to pulsate again in the manner I had observed before, and immediately this pulsating began I felt tiny needlepoints of ice pierce my brain. A question became impinged upon my consciousness more clearly than would have been possible by spoken word:

"Where do you come from?"

I was familiar with thought transference, had even practiced it to a certain extent, very often with astonishing success. When I heard —or received—that question, I tried hard to bring every atom of my consciousness to bear upon the circumstances that were the cause of my being there. When I had finished my mental narration and my mind relaxed from the tension I had put upon it, I received the following impressions:

"We receive no answer; your mind remains blank. You are alien, we have never encountered another of your organism here. A most peculiar organism indeed is one that becomes steadily smaller without apparent reason. Why are you here, and where do you come from?" The icy fingers probed deeper and deeper into my brain, seeming to tear it tissue from tissue.

Again I tried, my mind focusing with the utmost clearness upon every detail, picturing my course from the very minute I entered the Professor's laboratory to the present time. When I finished I was exhausted from the effort.

Again I received the impression: "You cannot bring your mind sufficiently into focus; we receive only fleeting shadows."

One of the spheres again changed to a bright color, and broke from the circle. I could almost imagine an angry shrug. The streamers relaxed their hold on my brain and began to withdraw—but not before I caught the fleeting impression from the orange one, who was apparently addressing the others: "—very low mentality."

"You're not so much yourself!" I said aloud. But of course such a crude method as speech did not register upon them. I wondered at my inability to establish thought communication with these beings. Either my brain was of such a size as to prevent them from receiving the impression (remember I was still a four or five hundred foot giant on this world), or their state of mentality was indeed so much higher than mine, that I was, to them, lower than the lowest savage. Possibly both, more probably the latter.

But they were determined to solve the mystery of my presence before I passed from their world, as I would surely do in a few hours at my rate of shrinkage. Their next move was to place themselves on each side of me in vertical rows extending from far down near the ground up to my shoulders. Again the luminous ribbons reached out and touched me at the various points. Then as at a given signal they rose high into the air, lifting me lightly as a feather! In perfect unison they sped towards their city beyond the horizon, carrying me perpendicularly with them! I marveled at the manner in which such gaseous entities as these could lift and propel such a material giant as myself. Their speed must have exceeded by far that of sound—though on all this planet there was no sound except the sound of my body swishing through the air.

In a very few minutes I sighted the city, which must have covered an area of a hundred miles square near the edge of a rolling green ocean. I was placed lightly on my feet at the very edge of the city, and once more the circle of spheres formed around my head and once more the cold tendrils of light probed my brain.

"You may walk at will about the city," came the thought, "accompanied by a few of us. You are to touch nothing whatever, or the penalty will be extreme; your tremendous size makes your presence here among us somewhat hazardous. When you have become much smaller we shall again explore your mind, with somewhat different method, and learn your origin and purpose. We realize that the great size of your brain was somewhat of a handicap to us in our first attempt. We go now to prepare. We have awaited your coming for years."

Leaving only a few there as my escort—or guard—the rest of the spheres sped toward a great domed building that rose from a vast plaza in the center of the city.

I was very much puzzled as to their last statement. For a moment I stood there wondering what they could have meant—"we have awaited your coming for years." Then trusting that this and other things would be answered in the due course of their investigation, I entered the city.

It was not a strange city in so far as architecture was concerned, but it was a beautiful one. I marveled that it could have been conceived and constructed by these confluent globules of gas who at first glance seemed anything but intelligent, reasoning beings. Tall as I was, the buildings towered up to four and five times my height, invariably ending in domed roofs. There was no sign of a spire or angle as far as my eye could see; apparently they grated harshly on the senses of these beings. The entire plan of the city was of vast sweeping curves and circular patterns, and the effect was striking. There were no preconceived streets or highways, nor connecting spans between buildings, for there was no need of them. The air was the natural habitable element of this race, and I did not see a one of them ever touch the ground or any surface.

They even came to rest in mid air, with a slow spinning motion. Everywhere I passed among them they paused, spinning, to observe me in apparent curiosity, then went on about their business, whatever it was. None ever approached me except my guards.

For several hours I wandered about in this manner, and finally when I was much smaller I was bade to walk towards the central plaza.

In the circular domed building the others awaited my coming, gathered about a dais surmounted by a huge oval transparent screen of glass or some similar substance. This time only one of the spheres made contact with my brain, and I received the following thought: "Watch."

The screen became opaque, and a vast field of white came into view.

"The great nebula in which this planet is but an infinitesimal speck," came the thought.

The mass drifted almost imperceptibly across the screen, and the thought continued:

"As you see it now, so it appeared to us through our telescopes centuries ago. Of course the drifting motion of the nebula as a whole was not perceptible, and what you see is a chemically recorded reproduction of the view, which has been speeded up to make the motion visible on the screen. Watch closely now."

The great mass of the nebula had been quiescent, but as I watched. it began to stir and swirl in a huge spiral motion, and a vast dark shadow was thrown across the whole scene. The shadow seemed to recede—no, grew smaller—and I could see that it was not a shadow but a huge bulk. This bulk was entering the nebula, causing it to swirl and expand as millions of stars were displaced and shoved outward.

The thought came again: "The scene has been speeded up a million-fold. The things you see taking place actually transpired over a great number of years; our scientists watched the phenomenon in great wonder, and many were the theories as to the cause of it. You are viewing yourself as you entered our nebula."

I watched in a few minutes the scene before me, as these sphere creatures had watched it over a period of years; saw myself grow smaller, gradually approach the system of the four suns and finally the gold-green planet itself. Abruptly the screen cleared.

"So we watched and waited your coming for years, not knowing what you were or whence you came. We are still very much puzzled. You become steadily smaller, and that we cannot understand. We must hurry. Relax. Do not interfere with our process by trying to think back to the beginning, as you did before; it is all laid bare to us in the recesses of your brain. Simply relax, think of nothing at all, watch the screen."

I tried to do as he said, again I felt the cold probing tendrils in my brain, and a lethargy came over my mind. Shadows flashed across the screen, then suddenly a familiar scene leaped into view: the Professor's laboratory as I had last seen it, on the night of my departure. No sooner had this scene cleared than I entered the room, exactly as I had on that night. I saw myself approach the table close behind the Professor, saw him standing as he had stood, staring out at the night sky; saw his lips move.

The spheres about me crowded close to the screen, seemed to hang intent on every motion that passed upon it, and I sensed great excitement among them. I judged that the one who was exploring my mind, if not all of them, were somehow cognizant not only of the words the Professor and I spoke in those scenes, but of their meaning as well.

I could almost read the Professor's lips as he spoke. I saw the utter amazement, then incredulity, then disbelief, on my features as he propounded his theory of macrocosmic worlds and still greater macrocosmic worlds. I saw our parley of words, and finally his lunge toward me and felt again the plunge of the needle into my arm.

As this happened the spheres around me stirred excitedly.

I saw myself become smaller, smaller, to be finally lifted onto the block of Rehyllium-X where I became still smaller and disappeared. I saw my meeting with the germ, and my wild flight; my plunge into the abyss, and my flight down through the darkness, during which time the entire screen before me became black. The screen was slightly illuminated again as I traveled along with the great masses all around me, and then gradually across the screen spread the huge nebula, the same one these sphere creatures had seen through their telescopes centuries ago. Again the screen cleared abruptly, became transparent.

"The rest we know," came the thought of the one who had searched my brain. "The rest the screen has already shown. He—the one who invented the—what he called 'Shrinx'—he is a very great man. Yours has indeed been a marvelous experience, and one which has hardly begun. We envy you, lucky being; and at the same time we are sorry for you. Anyway, it is fortunate for us that you chose our planet on which to alight, but soon you will pass away even as you came, and that we cannot, and would not, prevent. In a very few minutes you will once more become of infinitesimal size and pass into a still smaller universe. We have microscopes powerful enough to permit us to barely glimpse this smaller atomic universe, and we shall watch your further progress into the unknown until you are gone from our sight forever."

I had been so interested in the familiar scenes on the screen that I had lost all conception of my steady shrinkage. I was now very much smaller than those spheres around me.

I was as interested in them as they were in me, and I tried to flash the following thought:

"You say that you envy me, and are sorry for me. Why should that be?"

The thought came back immediately: "We cannot answer that. But it is true; wonderful as are the things you will see in realms yet to come, nevertheless you are to be pitied. You cannot understand at present, but some day you will."

I flashed another thought: "Your organism, which is known to me as gaseous, seems as strange to me as mine, a solid, must seem to you. You have mentioned both telescopes and microscopes, and I cannot conceive how beings such as yourselves, without organs of sight, can number astronomy and microscopy among the sciences."

"Your own organs of sight," came back the answer, "which you call 'eyes,' are not only superfluous, but are very crude sources of perception. I think you will grant that loss of them would be a terrible and permanent handicap. Our own source of perception is not confined to any such conspicuous organs, but envelops the entire outer surface of our bodies. We have never had organs and appendages such as those with which you are endowed so profusely, for we are of different substance; we merely extend any part of our bodies in any direction at will. But from close study of your structure, we conclude that your various organs and appendages are very crude. I predict that by slow evolution of your own race, such frailties will disappear entirely."

"Tell me more about your own race," I went on eagerly.

"To tell everything there is to tell," came the answer, "would take much time; and there is little time left. We have a very high sociological system, but one which is not without its faults, of course. We have delved deep into the sciences and gone far along the lines of fine arts—but all of our accomplishments along these lines would no doubt appear very strange to you. You have seen our city. It is by no means the largest, nor the most important, on the planet. When you alighted comparatively near, reports were sent out and all of our important scientists hurried here. We were not afraid because of your presence, but rather, were cautious, for we did not know what manner of being you were. The two whom you first saw, were sent to observe you. They had both been guilty of a crime against the community, and were given the choice of the punishment they deserved, or of going out to investigate the huge creature that had dropped from the sky. They accepted the latter course, and for their bravery—for it was bravery—they have been exonerated."

VI

I would have liked greatly to ask more questions, for there were many phases that puzzled me; but I was becoming so very small that further communication was impossible. I was taken to a laboratory and placed upon the slide of a microscope of strange and intricate construction and my progress continued unabated down into a still smaller atomic universe.

The method was the same as before. The substance became open and porous, spread out into open space dotted with the huge masses which in turn became porous and resolved into far flung nebulae.

I entered one of the nebulae and once more star-systems swung all around me. This time I approached a single sun of bright yellow hue, around which swung eight planets. I maneuvered to the outermost one, and when my size permitted, made contact with it.

I was now standing on an electron, one of billions forming a microscopic slide that existed in a world which was in turn only an electron in a block of metal on a laboratory table!

Soon I reached the atmosphere, and miles below me I could see only wide patches of yellow and green. But as I came nearer to the surface more of the details became discernible. Almost at my feet a wide yellow river wound sluggishly over a vast plateau which fell suddenly away into a long line of steep precipices. At the foot of these precipices stretched a great green expanse of steaming jungle, and farther beyond a great ocean, smooth as green glass, curved to the horizon. A prehistoric world of jungles and great fern-like growths and sweltering swamps and cliffs. Not a breeze stirred and nowhere was there sight of any living thing.

I was standing in the jungle close to the towering cliffs, and for a half mile in every direction the trees and vegetation were trampled into the soil where my feet had swung down and contacted.

Now I could see a long row of caves just above a ledge half way up the side of the cliff. And I did not doubt that in each cave some being was peering furtively out at me. Even as I watched I saw a tiny figure emerge and walk out on the ledge. He was very cautious, ready to dash back into the cave at any sign of hostility on my part, and his eyes never left me. Seeing that nothing happened, others took heart and came out, and soon the ledge was lined with tiny figures who talked excitedly among themselves and gesticulated wildly in my direction. My coming must surely have aroused all their superstitious fears—a giant descending out of the skies to land at their very feet.

I must have been nearly a mile from the cliff, but even at that distance I could see that the figures were barbarians, squat and thick muscled, and covered with hair; they were four limbed and stood erect, and all carried crude weapons.

One of them raised a bow as tall as himself and let fly a shaft at me—evidently as an expression of contempt or bravado, for he must have known that the shaft couldn't reach half the distance. Immediately one who seemed a leader among them felled the miscreant with a single blow. This amused me. Evidently their creed was to leave well enough alone.

Experimentally I took a step toward them, and immediately a long line of bows sprang erect and scores of tiny shafts arched high in my direction to fall into the jungle far in front of me. A warning to keep my distance.

I could have strode forward and swept the lot of them from the ledge; but wishing to show them that my intentions were quite peaceful, I raised my hands and took several backward steps. Another futile volley of arrows. I was puzzled, and stood still; and as long as I did not move neither did they.

The one who had seemed the leader threw himself down flat and, shielding his eyes from the sun, scanned the expanse of jungle below. Then they seemed to talk among themselves again, and gestured not at me, but at the jungle. Then I comprehended. Evidently a hunting party was somewhere in that jungle which spread out around my feet—probably returning to the caves, for already it was nearing dusk, the sun casting weird conflicting streaks across the horizon. These people of the caves were in fear that I would move around too freely and perhaps trample the returning party under foot.

So thinking, I stood quietly in the great barren patch I had levelled, and sought to peer into the dank growth below me. This was nearly impossible, however, for clouds of steam hung low over the tops of the trees.

But presently my ears caught a faint sound, as of shouting, far below me, and then I glimpsed a long single file of the barbarian hunters running at full speed along a well beaten game path. They burst into the very clearing in which I stood, and stopped short in surprise, evidently aware for the first time of my gigantic presence on their world. They let fall the poles upon which were strung the carcasses of the day's hunt, cast but one fearful look up to where I towered, then as one man fell flat upon the ground in abject terror.

All except one. I doubt if the one, who burst from the tangle of trees last of all, even saw me, so intent was he in glancing back into the darkness from which he fled. At any rate he aroused his companions with a few angry, guttural syllables, and pointed back along the path.

At that moment there floated up to me a roar that lingered loud and shuddering in my ears. At quick instructions from their leader the hunters picked up their weapons and formed a wide semi-circle before the path where they had emerged. The limb of a large tree overhung the path at this point, and the leader clambered up some overhanging vines and was soon crouched upon it. One of the warriors fastened a vine to a large clumsy looking weapon, and the one in the tree drew it up to him. The weapon consisted merely of a large pointed stake some eight feet long, with two heavy stones fastened securely to it at the half way point. The one in the tree carefully balanced this weapon on the limb, directly over the path, point downward. The semicircle of hunters crouched behind stout lances set at an angle in the ground.

Another shuddering roar floated up to me, and then the beast appeared. As I caught sight of it I marvelled all the more at the courage of these puny barbarians. From ground to shoulder the beast must have measured seven feet tall, and was fully twenty feet long. Each of its six legs ended in a wide, horny claw that could have ripped any of the hunters from top to bottom. Its long tapering tail was horny too, giving me the impression that the thing was at least partly reptilian; curved fangs fully two feet long, in a decidedly animal head, offset that impression, however.

For a long moment the monstrosity stood there, tail switching ceaselessly, glaring in puzzlement out upon the circle of puny beings who dared to confront it. Then, as its tail ceased switching and it tensed for the spring, the warrior on the limb above launched his weapon—launched it and came hurtling down with it, feet pressed hard against the heavy stone balance!

Whether the beast below heard some sound or whether a sixth sense warned it, I do not know; but just in time it leaped to one side with an agility belied by its great bulk, and the pointed stake drove deep into the ground, leaving the one who had ridden it lying there stunned.

The beast uttered a snarl of rage; its six legs sprawled outward, its great belly touched the ground. Then it sprang out upon the circle of crouching hunters. Lances snapped at the impact, and the circle broke and fled for the trees. But two of them never rose from the ground, and the lashing horned tail flattened another before he had taken four steps.

The scene took place in a matter of seconds as I towered there looking down upon it, fascinated. The beast whirled toward the fleeing ones and in another moment the destruction would have been terrible, for they could not possibly have reached safety.

Breaking the spell that was on me I swung my hand down in a huge arc even as the beast sprang for a second time. I slapped it in mid air, flattening it against the ground as I would have flattened a bothersome insect. It did not twitch a muscle, and a dark red stain seeped outward from where it lay.

The natives stopped in their flight, for the sound of my hand when I slapped the huge animal had been loud. They jabbered noisily among themselves, but fearfully kept their distance, when they saw me crouched there over the flattened enemy who had been about to wreak destruction among them.

Only one had seen the entire happening. He who had plunged downward from the tree was only momentarily stunned; he had risen dizzily to his feet as the animal charged out among his companions, and had been witness to the whole thing.

Glancing half contemptuously at the others, he now approached me. It must have taken a great deal of courage on his part, for, crouched down as I was, I still towered above the tallest trees. He looked for a moment at the dead beast, then gazed up at me in reverent awe. Falling prone, he beat his head upon the ground several times, and the others followed his example.

Then they all came forward to look at the huge animal.

From their talk and gestures, I gathered that they wanted to take it to the caves; but it would take ten of the strongest of them to even lift it, and there was still a mile stretch of jungle between them and the cliffs.

I decided that I would take it there for them if that was their want. Reaching out, I picked up the leader, the brave one, very gently. Placing him in the cupped hollow of my hand, I swung him far up to the level of my eyes. I pointed at the animal I had slain, then pointed toward the cliffs. But his eyes were closed tightly as if his last moment had come, and he trembled in every limb. He was a brave hunter, but this experience was too much. I lowered him to the ground unharmed, and the others crowded around him excitedly. He would soon recover from his fright, and no doubt some night around the camp fires he would relate this wonderful experience to a bunch of skeptical grandchildren.

Picking the animal up by its tapering tail I strode through the jungle with it, flattening trees at every step and leaving a wide path behind me. I neared the cliffs in a few steps, and those upon the ledge fled into the caves. I placed the huge carcass on the ledge, which was scarcely as high as my shoulders, then turned and strode away to the right, intending to explore the terrain beyond.

For an hour, I walked, passing other tribes of cliff dwellers who fled at my approach. Then the jungle ended in a point by the sea and the line of cliffs melted down into a rocky coast.

It had become quite dark now, there were no moons and the stars seemed dim and far away. Strange night cries came from the jungle, and to my left stretched wide, tangled marshes through which floated vague phosphorescent shapes. Behind me tiny fires sprang up on the face of the cliffs, a welcome sight, and I turned back toward them. I was now so much smaller that I felt extremely uneasy at being alone and unarmed at night on a strange planet abounding in monstrosities.

I had taken only a few steps when I felt, rather than heard, a rush of wings above and behind me. I threw myself flat upon the ground, and just in time, for the great shadowy shape of some huge night-creature swept down and sharp talons raked my back. I arose with apprehension after a few moments, and saw the creature winging its way back low over the marshes. Its wing spread must have been forty feet. I reached the shelter of the cliffs and stayed close to them thereafter.

I came to the first of the shelving ledges where the fires burned, but it was far above me now. I was a tiny being crouched at the base of the cliffs. I, an alien on this world, yet a million years ahead of these barbarians in evolution, peered furtively out into the darkness where glowing eyes and half-seen shapes moved on the edge of the encroaching jungle; and safe in their caves high above me were those so low in the state of evolution that had only the rudiments of a spoken language and were only beginning to learn the value of fire. In another million years perhaps a great civilization would cover this entire globe: a civilization rising by slow degrees from the mire and the mistakes and the myths of the dawn of time. And doubtlessly one of the myths would concern a great god-like figure that descended from the skies, leveled great trees in its stride, saved a famous tribe from destruction by slaying huge enemy beasts, and then disappeared forever during the night. And great men, great thinkers, of that future civilization would say: "Fie! Preposterous! A stupid myth."

But at the present time the godlike figure which slew enemy beasts by a slap of the hand was scarcely a foot high, and sought a place where he might be safe from a possible attack by those same beasts. At last I found a small crevice, which I squeezed into and felt much safer than I had out in the open.

And very soon I was so small that I would have been unnoticed by any of the huge animals that might venture my way.

VII

At last I stood on a single grain of sand, and other grains towered up like smooth mountains all around me. And in the next few minutes I experienced the change for the third time—the change from microscopic being on a gigantic world to a gigantic being floating amid an endless universe of galaxies. I became smaller, the distance between galaxies widened, solar systems approached and neared the orbit of the outermost planet, I received a very unexpected, but very pleasant, surprise. Instead of myself landing upon one of the planets —and while I was yet far too large to do so—the inhabitants of this system were coming out to land on me!

There was no doubt about it. From the direction of the inner planets a tapering silvery projectile moved toward me with the speed of light. This was indeed interesting, and I halted my inward progress to await developments.

In a few minutes the space rocketship was very close. It circled about me once, then with a great rush of flame and gases from the prow to break the fall, it swooped in a long curve and landed gracefully on my chest! I felt no more jar than if a fly had alighted on me. As I watched it, a square section swung outward from the hull and a number of things emerged. I say "things" because they were in no manner human, although they were so tiny that I could barely distinguish them as minute dots of gold. A dozen of them gathered in a group a short distance away from the space-ship.

After a few moments, to my surprise, they spread huge golden wings, and I gasped at the glistening beauty of them. They scattered in various directions, flying low over the surface of my body. From this I reasoned that I must be enveloped in a thin layer of atmosphere, as were the planets. These bird creatures were an exploring party sent out from one of the inner planets to investigate the new large world which had entered their system and was approaching dangerously close to their own planet.

But, on second thought, they must have been aware—or soon would be—that I was not a world at all, but a living, sentient being. My longitudinal shape should make that apparent, besides the movements of my limbs. At any rate they displayed unprecedented daring by coming out to land on me. I could have crushed their frail ship at the slightest touch or flung it far out into the void beyond their reach.

I wished I could see one of the winged creatures at closer range, but none landed on me again; having traversed and circled me in every direction they returned to the space-ship and entered it. The section swung closed, gases roared from the stern tubes and the ship swooped out into space again and back toward the sun.

What tiding would they bear to their planet? Doubtless they would describe me as an inconceivably huge monstrosity of outer space. Their scientists would wonder whence I came; might even guess at the truth. They would observe me anxiously through their telescopes. Very likely they would be in fear that I would invade or wreck their world, and would make preparations to repulse me if I came too near.

In spite of these probabilities I continued my slow progress toward the inner planets, determined to see and if possible land upon the planet of the bird creatures. A civilization that had achieved space travel must be a marvelous civilization indeed.

As I made my way through space between the planets by means of my grotesque exertions, I reflected upon another phase. By the time I reached the inner planets I would be so much smaller that I could not determine which of the planets was the one I sought, unless I saw more of the space ships and could follow their direction. Another interesting thought was that the inner planets would have

sped around the green sun innumerable times, and years would have
passed before I reached there. They would have ample time to prepare for my coming, and might give me a fierce reception if they
had many more of the space ships such as the one I had seen.

And they did indeed have many more of them, as I discovered after
an interminable length of time during which I had moved ever closer
to the sun. A red-tinged planet swung in a wide curve from behind
the blazing green of the sun, and I awaited its approach. After a
few minutes it was so close that I could see a moon encircling the
planet, and as it came still nearer I saw the rocket ships.

This, then, was the planet I sought. But I was puzzled. They
surely could not have failed to notice my approach, and I had expected to see a host of ships lined up in formidable array. I saw a
host of them all right, hundreds of them, but they were not pointed
in my direction at all; indeed, they seemed not to heed me in the
least, although I must have loomed large as their planet came nearer.
Perhaps they had decided, after all, that I was harmless.

But what seemed more likely to me was that they were confronted
with an issue of vastly more importance than my close proximity.
For as I viewed the space ships they were leaving the atmosphere
of their planet, and were pointing toward the single satellite. Row
upon row, mass upon endless mass they moved outward, hundreds,
thousands of them. It seemed as though the entire population was
moving en masse to the satellite!

My curiosity was immediately aroused. What circumstances or condition would cause a highly civilized race to abandon their planet
and flee to the satellite? Perhaps, if I learned, I would not want to
alight on that planet. . . .

Impatiently I awaited its return as it moved away from me on its
circuit around the sun. The minutes seemed long, but at last it
approached again from the opposite direction, and I marvelled at
the relativity of size and space and time. A year had passed on that
planet and satellite, and many things might have transpired since
I had last seen them.

The satellite swung between the planet and myself, and even from
my point of disadvantage I could see that many things had indeed
transpired. The bird people were building a protective shell around
the satellite! Protection—from what? The shell seemed to be of dull
gray metal, and already covered half the globe. On the uncovered
side I saw land and rolling oceans. Surely, I thought, they must
have the means of producing artificial light; but somehow it seemed

blasphemous to forever bar the surface from the fresh pure light of the green sun. In a manner I felt sorry for them in their circumstances. But they had their space ships, and in time could move to the vast unexplored fields that the heavens offered.

More than ever I was consumed with curiosity, but was still too large to attempt a contact with the planet, and I let it pass me for a second time. I judged that when it came around again I would be sufficiently small for its gravity to "capture" me and sufficiently large that the "fall" to the surface would in no means be dangerous; and I was determined to alight.

Another wait of minutes, more minutes this time because I was smaller and time for me was correspondingly longer. When the two spheres hove into view again I saw that the smaller one was now entirely clad in its metal jacket, and the smooth unbroken surface shimmered boldly in the green glare of the sun. Beneath that barren metal shell were the bird people with their glorious golden wings, their space ships, their artificial light, and atmosphere, and civilization. I had but a glance for the satellite, however; my attention was for the planet rushing ever closer to me.

Everything passed smoothly and without mishap. I was becoming an experienced "planet hopper." Its gravity caught me in an unrelenting grip, and I let my limbs rush downward first in their long curve, to land with a slight jar on solid earth far below.

Bending low, I sought to peer into the murky atmosphere and see something of the nature of this world. For a minute my sight could not pierce the half gloom, but gradually the surface became visible. First, I followed my tapering limbs to where they had contacted. As nearly as I could ascertain from my height, I was standing in the midst of what seemed to be a huge mass of crushed and twisted metal!

Now, I thought to myself, I have done it. I have let myself in for it now. I have wrecked something, some great piece of machinery it seems, and the inhabitants will not take the matter lightly. Then I thought: the inhabitants? Who? Not the bird people, for they have fled, have barricaded themselves on the satellite.

Again I sought to pierce the gloom of the atmosphere, and by slow degrees more details became visible. At first my gaze only encompassed a few miles, then more, and more, until at last the view extended from horizon to horizon and included nearly an entire hemisphere.

Slowly the view cleared and slowly comprehension came; and as full realization dawned upon me, I became momentarily panic stricken. I thought insanely of leaping outward into space again, away from the planet, breaking the gravity that held me; but the opposite force of my spring could likely send the planet careening out of its orbit and it and all the other planets and myself might go plunging toward the sun. No, I had put my feet on this planet and I was here to stay.

But I did not feel like staying, for what a sight I had glimpsed! As far as I could see in every direction were huge, grotesque metal structures and strange mechanical contrivances. The thing that terrified me was that these machines were scurrying about the surface all in apparent confusion, seemed to cover the entire globe, seemed to have a complete civilization of their own, and nowhere was there the slightest evidence of any human occupancy, no controlling force, no intelligence, nothing save the machines. And I could not bring myself to believe that they were possessed of intelligence!

Yet as I descended ever closer to the surface I could see that there was no confusion at all as it had seemed at first glance, but rather was there a simple, efficient, systematic order of things. Even as I watched, two strange mechanisms strode toward me on great jointed tripods, and stopped at my very feet. Long, jointed metal arms, with claw-like fixtures at the ends, reached out with uncanny accuracy and precision and began to clear away the twisted débris around my feet. As I watched them I admired the efficiency of their construction. No needless intricacies, no superfluous parts, only the tripods for movement and the arms for clearing. When they had finished they went away, and other machines came on wheels, the debris was lifted by means of cranes and hauled away.

I watched in stupefaction the uncanny activities below and around me. There was no hurry, no rush, but every machine from the tiniest to the largest, from the simplest to the most complicated, had a certain task to perform, and performed it directly and completely, accurately and precisely. There were machines on wheels, on treads, on tracks, on huge multi-jointed tripods, winged machines that flew clumsily through the air, and machines of a thousand other kinds and variations.

Endless chains of machines delved deep into the earth, to emerge with loads of ore which they deposited, to descend again.

Huge hauling machines came and transported the ore to roaring mills.

Inside the mills machines melted the ore, rolled and cut and fashioned the steel.

Other machines builded and assembled and adjusted intricate parts, and when the long process was completed the result was— more machines! They rolled or ambled or flew or walked or rattled away under their own power, as the case might be.

Some went to assist in the building of huge bridges across rivers and ravines.

Diggers went to level down forests and obstructing hills, or went away to the mines.

Others built adjoining mills and factories.

Still others erected strange, complicated towers thousands of feet high, and the purpose of these skeleton skyscrapers I could not determine. Even as I watched, the supporting base of one of them weakened and buckled, and the entire huge edifice careened at a perilous angle. Immediately a host of tiny machines rushed to the scene. Sharp white flames cut through the metal in a few seconds, and the tower toppled with a thunderous crash to the ground. Again the white-flame machines went to work and cut the metal into removable sections, and hoisters and haulers came and removed them. Within fifteen minutes another building was being erected on the exact spot.

Occasionally something would go wrong—some worn-out part ceased to function and a machine would stop in the middle of its task. Then it would be hauled away to repair shops, where it would eventually emerge good as new.

I saw two of the winged machines collide in mid air, and metal rained from the sky. A half dozen of the tripod clearing machines came from a half dozen directions and the metal was raked into huge piles; then came the cranes and hauling machines.

A great verticle wheel with slanting blades on the rim spun swiftly on a shaft that was borne forward on treads. The blades cut through trees and soil and stone as it bore onward toward the near-by mountains. It slowed down, but did not stop, and at length a straight wide path connected the opposite valley. Behind the wheel came the tripods, clearing the way of all debris, and behind them came machines that laid down long strips of metal, completing the perfect road.

Everywhere small lubricating machines moved about, periodically supplying the others with the necessary oil that insured smooth movement.

Gradually the region surrounding me was being levelled and cleared, and a vast city was rising—a city of meaningless, towering, ugly metal—a city covering hundreds of miles between the mountains and sea—a city of machines—ungainly, lifeless—yet purposeful—for what? What?

In the bay, a line of towers rose from the water like fingers pointing at the sky. Beyond the bay and into the open sea they extended. Now the machines were connecting the towers with wide network and spans. A bridge! They were spanning the ocean, connecting the continents—a prodigious engineering feat. If there were not already machines on the other side, there soon would be. No, not soon. The task was gigantic, fraught with failures, almost impossible. Almost? A world of machines could know no almost. Perhaps other machines did occupy the other side, had started the bridge from there, and they would meet in the middle. And for what purpose?

A great wide river came out of the mountains and went winding toward the sea. For some reason a wall was being constructed diagonally across the river and beyond, to change its course. For some reason—or unreason.

Unreason! That was it! Why, why, why, I cried aloud in an anguish that was real; why all of this? What purpose, what meaning, what benefit? A city, a continent, a world, a civilization of machines! Somewhere on this world there must be the one who caused all this, the one intelligence, human or unhuman, who controls it. My time here is limited, but I have time to seek him out, and if I find him I shall drag him out and feed him to his own machines and put a stop to this diabolism for all time!

I strode along the edge of the sea for five hundred miles, and rounding a sharp point of land, stopped abruptly. There before me stretched a city, a towering city of smooth white stone and architectural beauty. Spacious parks were dotted with winged colonnades and statues, and the buildings were so designed that everything pointed upward, seemed poised for flight.

That was one half of the city.

The other half was a ruinous heap of shattered white stone, of buildings levelled to the ground by the machines, which were even then intent on reducing the entire city to a like state.

As I watched I saw scores of the flame-machines cutting deep into the stone and steel supporting base of one of the tallest buildings. Two of the ponderous air machines, trailing a wide mesh-metal net-

work between them, rose clumsily from the ground on the outskirts
of the city. Straight at the building they flew, and passed one on each
side of it. The metal netting struck, jerked the machines backward,
and the tangled mass of them plunged to the ground far below. But
the building, already weakened at the base, swayed far forward, then
back, hung poised for a long shuddering moment and then toppled to
the ground with a thunderous crash amid a cloud of dust and debris
and tangled framework.

The flame-machines moved on to another building, and on a slope
near the outskirts two more of the air machines waited. . . .

Sickened at the purposeless vandalism of it all, I turned inland; and
everywhere I strode were the machines, destroying and building,
leveling to the ground the deserted cities of the bird people and
building up their own meaningless civilization of metal.

At last I came to a long range of mountains which towered up past
the level of my eyes as I stood before them. In two steps I stood on
the top of these mountains and looked out upon a vast plain dotted
everywhere with the grotesque machine-made cities. The machines
had made good progress. About two hundred miles to the left a
great metal dome rose from the level of the plain, and I made my
way toward it, striding unconcerned and recklessly amidst the machines that moved everywhere around my feet.

As I neared the domed structure a row of formidible looking
mechanisms, armed with long spikes, rose up to bar my path. I
kicked out viciously at them and in a few minutes they were reduced to tangled scrap, though I received a number of minor scratches
in the skirmish. Others of the spiked machines rose up to confront
me with each step I took, but I strode through them, kicking them
to one side, and at last I stood before an entrance-way in the side
of the huge dome. Stooping, I entered, and once inside my head almost touched the roof.

I had hoped to find here what I sought, and I was not disappointed. There in the center of the single spacious room was The
Machine of all Machines; the Cause of it All; the Central Force,
the Ruler, the Controlling Power of all the diabolism running riot
over the face of the planet. It was roughly circular, large and ponderous. It was bewilderingly complicated, a maze of gears, wheels,
switchboards, lights, levers, buttons, tubing, and intricacies beyond
my comprehension. There were circular tiers, and on each tier
smaller separate units moved, performing various tasks, attending
switchboards, pressing buttons, pulling levers. The result was a throb-

bing, rhythmic, purposeful unit. I could imagine invisible waves going
out in every direction.

I wondered what part of this great machine was vulnerable. Silly
thought. No part. Only it—itself. It was The Brain.

The Brain. The Intelligence. I had searched for it, and I had found
it. There it was before me. Well, I was going to smash it. I looked
around for some kind of weapon, but finding none, I strode forward bare-handed.

Immediately a square panel lighted up with a green glow, and I
knew that The Brain was aware of my intent. I stopped. An odd sensation swept over me, a feeling of *hate*, of *menace*. It came from the
machine, pervaded the air in invisible waves.

"Nonsense," I thought; "it is but a machine after all. A very complicated one, yes, perhaps even possessed of intelligence; but it only
has control over other machines, it cannot harm me." Again I took
a resolute step forward.

The feeling of menace became stronger, but I fought back my apprehension and advanced recklessly. I had almost reached the machine when a wall of crackling blue flame leaped from floor to roof.
If I had taken one more step I would have been caught in it.

The menace, and hate, and imagined rage at my escape, rolled
out from the machine in ponderous, almost tangible waves, engulfing
me, and I retreated hastily.

I walked back toward the mountains. After all, this was not my
world—not my universe. I would soon be so small that my presence
amid the machines would be extremely dangerous, and the tops of
the mountains was the only safe place. I would have liked to smash
The Brain and put an end to it all, but anyway, I thought, the bird
people were now safe on the satellite, so why not leave this lifeless
world to the machines?

It was twilight when I reached the mountains, and from a high
grassy slope—the only peaceful place on the entire planet, I imagined—I looked out upon the plain. Tiny lights appeared as the
machines moved about, carrying on their work, never resting. The
clattering and clanking of them floated faintly up to me and made
me glad that I was a safe distance from it all.

As I stood out toward the dome that housed The Brain, I saw what
I had failed to see before. A large globe rested there on a frame-work,
and there seemed to be unusual activity around it.

A vague apprehension tightened around my brain as I saw machines enter this globe, and I was half prepared for what happened

next. The globe rose lightly as a feather, sped upward with increasing speed, out of the atmosphere and into space, where, as a tiny speck, it darted and maneuvered with perfect ease. Soon it reappeared, floated gracefully down upon the framework again, and the machines that had mechanically directed its flight disembarked from it.

The machines had achieved space travel! My heart sickened with sudden realization of what that meant. They would build others— were already building them. They would go to other worlds, and the nearest one was the satellite . . . . encased in its protective metal shell . . . .

But then I thought of the white-flame machines that I had seen cut through stone and metal in a few seconds . . . .

The bird people would no doubt put up a valiant fight. But as I compared their rocket projectiles against the efficiency of the globe I had just seen, I had little doubt as to the outcome. They would eventually be driven out into space again to seek a new world, and the machines would take over the satellite, running riot as they had done here. They would remain there just as long as The Brain so desired, or until there was no more land for conquest. Already this planet was over-run, so they were preparing to leave.

The Brain. An intricate, intelligent mechanical brain, glorying in its power, drunk with conquest. Where had it originated? The bird people must have been the indirect cause, and no doubt they were beginning to realize the terrible menace they had loosed on the universe.

I tried to picture their civilization as it had been long ago before this thing had come about. I pictured a civilization in which machinery played a very important part. I pictured the development of this machinery until the time when it relieved them of many tasks. I imagined how they must have designed their machines with more and more intricacy, more and more finesse, until only a few persons were needed in control. And then the great day would come, the supreme day, when mechanical parts would take the place of those few.

That must have indeed been a day of triumph. Machines supplying their every necessity, attending to their every want, obeying their every whim at the touch of a button. That must have been Utopia achieved!

But it had proven to be a bitter Utopia. They had gone forward blindly and recklessly to achieve it, and unknowingly they had gone a step too far. Somewhere, amid the machines they supposed they had under their control, they were imbued with a spark of intelligence. One of the machines added unto itself—perhaps secretly; built and evolved itself into a terribly efficient unit of inspired intelligence. And guided by that intelligence, other machines were built and came under its control. The rest must have been a matter of course. Revolt and easy victory.

So I pictured the evolution of the mechanical brain that even now was directing activities from down there under its metal dome.

And the metal shell around the satellite—did not that mean that the bird people were *expecting* an invasion? Perhaps, after all, this was not the original planet of the bird people; perhaps space travel was not an innovation among the machines. Perhaps it was on one of the far inner planets near the sun that the bird people had achieved the Utopia that proved to be such a terrible nemesis; perhaps they had moved to the next planet, never dreaming that the machines could follow; but the machines had followed after a number of years, the bird people being always driven outward, the machines always following at leisure in search of new spheres of conquest. And finally the bird people had fled to this planet, and from it to the satellite; and realizing that in a few years the machines would come again in all their invincibility, they had then ensconced themselves beneath the shell of metal.

At any rate: they did not flee to a far-away safe spot in the universe as they could have very easily done. Instead, they stayed; always one sphere ahead of the marauding machines, they must always be planning a means of wiping out the spreading evil they had loosed.

It might be that the shell around the satellite was in some way a clever trap! But so thinking, I remembered again the white-flame machines and the deadly efficiency of the globe I had seen, and then my hopes faded away.

Perhaps some day they would eventually find a way to check the spreading menace. But on the other extreme, the machines might spread out to other solar systems, other galaxies, until some day, a billion years hence, they would occupy every sphere in this universe . . . .

Such were my thoughts as I lay prone there upon the grassy slope and looked down into the plain, down upon the ceaseless clatter and the ceaseless moving of lights in the dark. I was very small now; soon, very soon, I would leave this world.

My last impression was of a number of the space globes, barely discernible in the dusk below; and among them towering up high and round, was one much larger than the others, and I could guess which machine would occupy that globe.

And my last thought was a regret that I hadn't made a more determined effort to destroy that malicious mechanism, The Brain.

So I passed from this world of machines—the world that was an electron on a grain of sand that existed on a prehistoric world that was but an electron on a microscope-slide that existed on a world that was but an electron in a piece of Rehyllium-X on the Professor's laboratory table.

VIII

It is useless to go on. I have neither the time nor the desire to relate in detail all the adventures that have befallen me, the universes I have passed into, the things I have seen and experienced and learned on all the worlds since I left the planet of the machines.

Ever smaller cycles . . . . infinite universes . . . . never ending . . . . each presenting something new . . . . some queer variation of life or intelligence . . . . Life? Intelligence? Terms I once associated with things animate, things protoplasmic and understandable. I find it hard to apply them to all the divergencies of shape and form and construction I have encountered . . . .

Worlds young . . . . warm . . . . volcanic and steaming . . . . the single cell emerging from the slime of warm oceans to propagate on primordial continents . . . . other worlds, innumerable . . . . life divergent in all branches from the single cell . . . . amorphous globules . . . . amphibian . . . . crustacean . . . . reptilian . . . . plant . . . . insect . . . . bird . . . . mammal . . . . all possible variations of combinations . . . . biological monstrosities indescribable . . . .

Other forms beyond any attempt at classification . . . . beyond all reason or comprehension of my puny mind . . . . essences of pure flame . . . . others gaseous, incandescent and quiescent alike . . . . plant forms encompassing an entire globe . . . . crystalline beings sentient and reasoning . . . . great shimmering columnar forms, seemingly liquid, defying gravity by some strange power of cohesion . . . . a world of sound-vibrations, throbbing, expanding, reverberating in unbroken echoes that nearly drove me crazy . . . . globular brainlike masses utterly dissociated from any material substance . . . . intradimensional beings, all shapes and shapeless . . . . entities utterly

incapable of registration upon any of my senses except the sixth, that
of instinct . . . .

Suns dying . . . . planets cold and dark and airless . . . . last
vestiges of once proud races struggling for a few more meager years
of sustenance . . . . great cavities . . . . beds of evaporated seas . . . .
small furry animals scurrying to cover at my approach . . . . desolation
. . . . ruins crumbling surely into the sands of barren deserts, the
last mute evidence of vanished civilizations . . . .

Other worlds . . . . a-flourished with life . . . . blessed with light
and heat . . . . staggering cities . . . . vast populations . . . . ships plying the surface of oceans, and others in the air . . . . huge observa-
tories . . . . tremendous strides in the sciences . . . .

Space flight . . . . battles for the supremacy of worlds . . . . blasting rays of super-destruction . . . . collision of planets . . . . disruption
of solar systems . . . cosmic annihilation . . . .

Light space . . . . a universe with a tenuous, filmy something
around it, which I burst through . . . . all around me not the
customary blackness of outer space I had known, but light . . . .
filled with tiny dots that were globes of darkness . . . . that were
burnt-out suns and lifeless planets . . . . nowhere a shimmering planet,
nowhere a flaming sun . . . . only remote specks of black amid the
light-satiated emptiness . . . .

How many of the infinitely smaller atomic cycles I have passed
into, I do not know. I tried to keep count of them at first, but somewhere between twenty and thirty I gave it up; and that was long ago.

Each time I would think: "This cannot go on forever—it cannot;
surely this next time I must reach the end."

But I have not reached the end.

Good God—how can there be an end? Worlds composed of atoms
. . . . each atom similarly composed . . . . The end would have to be
an indestructible solid, and that cannot be; all matter divisible into
smaller matter . . . .

What keeps me from going insane? I want to go insane!

I am tired . . . . a strange tiredness neither of mind nor body.
Death would be a welcome release from the endless fate that is mine.

But even death is denied me. I have sought it . . . . I have prayed
for it and begged for it . . . . but it is not to be.

On all the countless worlds I have contacted, the inhabitants were
of two distinctions: they were either so low in the state of intelligence
that they fled and barricaded themselves against me in superstitious

terror—or were so highly intellectual that they recognized me for what I was and welcomed me among them. On all but a few worlds the latter was the case, and it is on these types that I will dwell briefly.

These beings—or shapes or monstrosities or essences—were in every case mentally and scientifically far above me. In most cases they had observed me for years as a dark shadow looming beyond the farthest stars, blotting out certain star-fields and nebulae . . . . and always when I came to their world they welcomed me with scientific enthusiasm.

Always they were puzzled as to my steady shrinking, and always when they learned of my origin and the manner of my being there, they were surprised and excited.

In most cases gratification was apparent when they learned definitely that there were indeed great ultramacrocosmic universes. It seemed that all of them had long held the theory that such was the case.

On most of the worlds, too, the beings—or entities—or whatever the case might be—were surprised that the Professor, one of my fellow creatures, had invented such a marvelous vitalized element as "Shrinx."

"Almost unbelievable," was the general consensus of opinion; "scientifically he must be centuries ahead of the time on his own planet, if we are to judge the majority of the race by this creature here"—meaning me.

In spite of the fact that on nearly every world I was looked upon as mentally inferior, they conversed with me and I with them, by various of their methods, in most cases different variations of telepathy. They learned in minute detail and with much interest all of my past experiences in other universes. They answered all of my questions and explained many things besides, about their own universe and world and civilization and scientific achievements, most of which were completely beyond my comprehension, so alien were they in nature.

And of all the intra-universal beings I have had converse with, the strangest were those essences who dwelt in outer space as well as on various planets; identifiable to me only as vague blots of emptiness, total absences of light or color or substance; who impressed upon me the fact that they were Pure Intelligences, far above and superior to any material plane; but who professed an interest in me, bearing me with them to various planets, revealing many things and treating me very kindly. During my sojourn with them I learned from ex-

perience the total subservience of matter to influences of mind. On a
giant mountainous world I stepped out upon a thin beam of light
stretched between two crags, and willed with all my consciousness that
I would not fall. And I did not.

I have learned many things. I know that my mind is much sharper,
more penetrative, more grasping, than ever before. And vast fields
of wonder and knowledge lie before me in other universes yet to
come.

But in spite of this, I am ready for it all to end. This strange tiredness that is upon me—I cannot understand it. Perhaps some invisible
radiation in empty space is satiating me with this tiredness.

Perhaps it is only that I am very lonely. How very far away I am
from my own tiny sphere! Millions upon millions . . . . trillions upon
trillions . . . . of light-years . . . . Light years! Light cannot measure
the distance. And yet it is no distance: I am in a block of metal on
the Professor's laboratory table . . . .

Yet how far away into space and time I have gone! Years have
passed, years far beyond my normal span of life. I am eternal.

Yes, eternal life . . . . that men have dreamed of . . . . prayed for
. . . . sought after . . . . is mine—and I dream and pray and seek for
death!

Death. All the strange beings I have seen and conversed with, have
denied it. I have implored many of them to release me painlessly and
for all time—but to no avail. Many of them were possessed of the
scientific means to stop my steady shrinkage—but they would not
stop it. None of them would hinder me, none of them would tamper
with the things that were. Why? Always I asked them why, and
they would not answer.

But I need no answer. I think I understand. These beings of
science realized that such an entity as myself should never be . . . .
that I am a blasphemy upon all creation and beyond all reason . . . .
they realized that eternal life is a terrible thing . . . . a thing not to
be desired . . . . and as punishment for delving into secrets never
meant to be revealed, none of them will release me from my fate . . . .

Perhaps they are right, but oh, it is cruel! Cruel! The fault is not
mine, I am here against my own will.

And so I continue ever down, alone and lonely, yearning for others
of my kind. Always hopeful—and always disappointed.

So it was that I departed from a certain world of highly intelligent
gaseous beings; a world that was in itself composed of a highly rarefied

substance bordering on nebulosity. So it was that I became even smaller, was lifted up in a whirling, expanding vortex of the dense atmosphere, and entered the universe which it composed.

Why I was attracted by that tiny, far away speck of yellow, I do not know. It was near the center of the nebula I had entered. There were other suns far brighter, far more attractive, very much nearer. This minute yellow sun was dwarfed by other suns and sun-clusters around it—seemed insignificant and lost among them. And why I was drawn to it, so far away, I cannot explain.

But mere distance, even space distance, was nothing to me now. I had long since learned from the Pure Intelligence the secret of propulsion by mind influence, and by this means I propelled myself through space at any desired speed not exceeding that of light; as my mind was incapable of imagining speed faster than light, I of course could not cause my material body to exceed it.

So I neared the yellow sun in a few minutes, and observed that it had twelve planets. And as I was far too large to yet land on any sphere, I wandered far among other suns, observing the haphazard construction of this universe, but never losing sight of the small yellow sun that had so intrigued me. And at last, much smaller, I returned to it.

And of all the twelve planets, one was particularly attractive to me. It was a tiny blue one. It made not much difference where I landed, so why should I have picked it from among the others? Perhaps only a whim—but I think the true reason was because of its constant pale blue twinkling, as though it were beckoning to me, inviting me to come to it. It was an unexplainable phenomenon; none of the others did that. So I moved closer to the orbit of the blue planet, and landed upon it.

As usual I didn't move from where I stood for a time, until I could view the surrounding terrain; and then I observed that I had landed in a great lake—a chain of lakes. A short distance to my left was a city miles wide, a great part of which was inundated by the flood I had caused.

Very carefully, so as not to cause further tidal waves, I stepped from the lake to solid ground, and the waters receded somewhat.

Soon I saw a group of five machines flying toward me; each of them had two wings held stiffly at right angles to the body. Looking around me I saw others of these machines winging toward me from every direction, always in groups of five, in V formation. When they had come very close they began to dart and swoop in a most peculiar manner, from them came sharp staccato sounds, and I felt the impact of many tiny pellets upon my skin! These beings were very warlike, I thought, or else very excitable.

Their bombardment continued for some time, and I began to find it most irritating; these tiny pellets could not harm me seriously, could not even pierce my skin, but the impact of them stung. I could not account for their attack upon me, unless it be that they were angry at the flood I had caused by my landing. If that were the case they were very unreasonable, I thought; any damage I had done was purely unintentional, and they should realize that.

But I was soon to learn that these creatures were very foolish in many of their actions and manners; they were to prove puzzling to me in more ways than one.

I waved my arms around, and presently they ceased their futile bombardment, but continued to fly around me.

I wished I could see what manner of beings flew these machines. They were continually landing and rising again from a wide level field below.

For several hours they buzzed all around while I became steadily smaller. Below me I could now see long ribbons of white that I guessed were roads. Along these roads crawled tiny vehicles, which soon became so numerous that all movement came to a standstill, so congested were they. In the fields a large part of the populace had gathered, and was being constantly augmented by others.

At last I was sufficiently small so that I could make out closer details, and I looked more intently at the beings who inhabited this world. My heart gave a quick leap then, for they somewhat resembled myself in structure. They were four-limbed and stood erect, their method of locomotion consisting of short jerky hops, very different from the smooth gliding movement of my own race. Their general features were somewhat different too—seemed grotesque to me—but the only main difference between them and myself was that their bodies were somewhat more columnar, roughly oval in shape and very thin, I would say almost frail.

Among the thousands gathered there were perhaps a score who seemed in authority. They rode upon the backs of clumsy looking, four-footed animals, and seemed to have difficulty in keeping the excited crowd under control. I, of course, was the center of their excitement; my presence seemed to have caused more consternation here than upon any other world.

Eventually a way was made through the crowd and one of the ponderous four wheeled vehicles was brought along the road opposite to where I stood. I supposed they wanted me to enter the rough box-like affair, so I did so, and was hauled with many bumps and jolts over the rough road toward the city I had seen to the left. I could have rebelled at this barbarous treatment, but I reflected that I was still very large and this was probably the only way they had of transporting me to wherever I was going.

It had become quite dark, and the city was aglow with thousands of lights. I was taken into a certain building, and at once many important looking persons came to observe me.

I have stated that my mind had become much more penetrative than ever before, so I was not surprised to learn that I could read many of the thoughts of these persons without much difficulty. I learned that these were scientists who had come here from other immediate cities as quickly as possible—most of them in the winged machines, which they called "planes"—when they had learned of my landing here. For many months they had been certain that I would land. They had observed me through their telescopes, and their period of waiting had been a speculative one. And I could now see that they were greatly puzzled, filled with much wonderment, and no more enlightenment about me than they had been possessed of before.

Though still very large, I was becoming surely smaller, and it was this aspect that puzzled them most, just as it had on all the other worlds. Secondly in their speculations was the matter of where I had come from.

Many were the theories that passed among them. Certain they were that I had come a far distance. Uranus? Neptune? Pluto? I learned that these were the names of the outmost planets of this system. No, they decided; I must have come a much farther distance than that. Perhaps from another far-away galaxy of this universe! Their minds were staggered at that thought. Yet how very far away they were from the truth.

They addressed me in their own language, and seemed to realize that it was futile. Although I understood everything they said and everything that was in their minds, they could not know that I did, for I could not answer them. Their minds seemed utterly closed to all my attempts at thought communication, so I gave it up.

They conversed then among themselves, and I could read the hopelessness in their minds. I could see, too, as they discussed me, that they looked upon me as being abhorrent, a monstrosity. And as I searched the recesses of their minds, I found many things.

I found that it was the inherent instinct of this race to look upon all unnatural occurrences and phenomena with suspicion and disbelief and prejudiced mind.

I found that they had great pride for their accomplishments in the way of scientific and inventive progress. Their astronomers had delved a short distance into outer space, but considered it a very great distance; and having failed to find signs of intelligent life upon any immediate sphere, they leaped blindly and fondly to the conclusion that their own species of life was the dominant one in this solar system and perhaps—it was a reluctant perhaps—in the entire universe.

Their conception of a universe was a puny one. True, at the present time there was extant a theory of an expanding universe, and in that theory at least they were correct, I knew, remembering the former world I had left—the swirling, expanding wisp of gaseous atmosphere of which this tiny blue sphere was an electron. Yes, their "expanding universe" theory was indeed correct. But very few of their thinkers went beyond their own immediate universe—went deeply enough to even remotely glimpse the vast truth.

They had vast cities, yes. I had seen many of them from my height as I towered above their world. A great civilization, I had thought then. But now I know that great cities do not make great civilizations. I am disappointed at what I have found here, and cannot even understand why I should be disappointed, for this blue sphere is nothing to me and soon I will be gone on my eternal journey downward . . . .

Many things I read in these scientists' minds—things clear and concise, things dim and remote; but they would never know.

And then in the mind of one of the persons, I read an idea. He went away, and returned shortly with an apparatus consisting of wires, a headphone, and a flat revolving disc. He spoke into an instrument, a sort of amplifier. Then a few minutes later he touched a sharp pointed instrument to the rotating disc, and I heard the identical sounds reproduced which he had spoken. A very crude method, but effective in a certain way. They wanted to register my speech so that they would have at least something to work on when I had gone.

I tried to speak some of my old language into the instrument. I had thought I was beyond all surprises, but I was surprised at what happened. For nothing happened. I could not speak. Neither in the old familiar language I had known so long ago, nor in any kind of sound. I had communicated so entirely by thought transference on so many of the other worlds, that now my power of vocal utterance was gone.

They were disappointed. I was not sorry, for they could not have deciphered any language so utterly alien as mine was.

Then they resorted to the mathematics by which this universe and all universes are controlled; into which mathematical mold the eternal All was cast at the beginning and has moved errorlessly since. They produced a great chart which showed the conglomerated masses of this and other galaxies. Then upon a black panel set in the wall, was drawn a circle—understandable in any universe—and around it ten smaller circles. This was evidently their solar system, though I could not understand why they drew but ten circles when I had seen twelve planets from outer space. Then a tiny spot was designated on the chart, the position of this system in its particular galaxy. Then they handed the chart to me.

It was useless. Utterly impossible. How could I ever indicate my own universe, much less my galaxy and solar system, by such puny methods as these? How could I make them know that my own universe and planet were so infinitely large in the scheme of things that *theirs* were practically non-existent? How could I make them know that their universe was not *outside* my own, but *on my planet?*—superimposed in a block of metal on a laboratory table, in a grain of sand, in the atoms of glass in a microscopic slide, in a drop of water, in a blade of grass, in a bit of cold flame, in a thousand other variations of elements and substances all of which I had passed down into and beyond, and finally in a wisp of gas that was the cause of their "expanding universe." Even could I have conversed with them in their own language I could not have made them grasp the vastness of all those substances existing on worlds each of which was but an electron of an atom in one of trillions upon trillions of molecules of an infinitely larger world! Such a conception would have shattered their minds.

It was very evident that they would never be able to establish communication with me even remotely, nor I with them; and I was becoming very impatient. I wanted to be out of the stifling building, out under the night sky, free and unhampered in the vast space which was my abode.

Upon seeing that I made no move to indicate on the chart which part of their puny universe I came from, the scientists around me again conversed among themselves; and this time I was amazed at the trend of their thoughts.

For the conclusion which they had reached was that I was some freak of outer space which had somehow wandered here, and that my place in the scale of evolution was too far below their own for them to establish ideas with me either by spoken language (of which they concluded I had none) or by signs (which I was apparently too barbaric to understand)!! This—this was their unanimous conclusion! This, because I had not uttered any language for them to record, and because the chart of their universe was utterly insignificant to me! Never did it occur to them that the opposite might be true— that I might converse with them but for the fact that their minds were too weak to register my thoughts!

Disgust was my reaction to these short-sighted conclusions of their unimaginable minds—disgust which gave way to an old emotion, that of anger.

And as that one impulsive, rising burst of anger flooded my mind, a strange thing happened:

Every one of the scientists before me dropped to the floor in a state of unconsciousness.

My mind had, indeed, become much more penetrative than ever before. No doubt my surge of anger had sent out intangible waves which had struck upon their centers of consciousness with sufficient force to render them insensible.

I was glad to be done with them. I left the four walls of the building, emerged into the glorious expansive night under the stars and set out along the street in a direction that I believed would lead me away from the city. I wanted to get away from it, away from this world and the people who inhabited it.

As I advanced along the streets all who saw me recognized me at once and most of them fled unreasonably for safety. A group of persons in one of the vehicles tried to bar my progress, but I exercised my power of anger upon them; they drooped senselessly and their vehicle crashed into a building and was demolished.

In a few minutes the city was behind me and I was striding down one of the roads, destination unknown; nor did it matter, except that now I was free and alone as it should be. I had but a few more hours on this world.

And then it was that the *feeling* came upon me again, the strange feeling that I had experienced twice before: once when I had selected the tiny orange sun from among the millions of others, and again when I had chosen this tiny blue planet. Now I felt it for a third time, more strongly than ever, and now I knew that this feeling had some very definite purpose for being. It was as though something, some power beyond question, drew me irresistibly to it; I could not resist, nor did I want to. This time it was very strong and very near.

Peering into the darkness along the road, I saw a light some distance ahead and to the left, and I knew that I must go to that light.

When I had come nearer I could see that it emanated from a house set far back in a grove of trees, and I approached it without hesitation. The night was warm, and a pair of double windows opened upon a well-lighted room. In this room was a man.

I stepped inside and stood motionless, not yet knowing why I should have been drawn there.

The man's back was toward me. He was seated before a square dialed instrument, and seemed to be listening intently to some report coming from it. The sounds from the box were unintelligible to me, so I turned my attention to reading the man's mind as he listened, and was not surprised to learn that the reports concerned myself.

"—casualties somewhat exaggerated, though the property damage has reached millions of dollars," came the news from the box. "Cleveland was of course hardest hit, though not unexpectedly, astronomical computators having estimated with fair accuracy the radius of danger. The creature landed in Lake Erie only a few miles east of the city. At the contact the waters rose over the breakwater with a rush and inundated nearly one-third of the city before receding, and it was well that the greater part of the populace had heeded the advance warnings and fled . . . . all lake towns in the vicinity have reported heavy property damage, and cities as far east as Erie, and as far west as Toledo, have reported high flood waters . . . . all available Government combat planes were rushed to the scene in case the creature should show signs of hostility . . . . scientific men who have awaited the thing's landing for months immediately chartered planes for Cleveland . . . . despite the elaborate cordons of police and militiamen, the crowds broke through and entered the area, and within an hour after the landing roads in every direction were congested with traffic . . . . for several hours scientists circled and examined the creature in planes, while its unbelievable shrinkage continued . . . . the only report we have from them is that, aside from the contour of its great bell-shaped torso, the creature is quite amazingly correct anatomically . . . . an unofficial statement from Dr. Hilton U. Cogsworthy of the Alleghany Biological Society, is to the effect that such a creature *isn't*. That it cannot possibly exist. That the whole thing is the result of some kind of mass hypnotism on a gigantic scale. This, of course, in lieu of some reasonable explanation. . . . many persons would like to believe the 'mass hypnotism' theory, and many always will; but those who have seen it and taken photographs of it from every angle know that it does exist and that its steady shrinking goes on . . . . Professor James L. Harvey of Miami University has suffered a stroke of temporary insanity and is under the care of physicians. The habitual curiosity seekers who flocked to the scene are apparently more hardened . . . . the latest report is that the creature, still very large, has been transported under heavy guard to the Cleveland Institute of Scientific Research, where is gathered every scientist of note east of the Mississippi . . . . stand by for further news flashes . . . . "

The voice from the box ceased, and as I continued to read the mind of the man whose back was toward me, I saw that he was deeply absorbed in the news he had heard. And the mind of this person was something of a puzzle to me. He was above the average intelligence of those on this world, and was possessed of a certain amount of fundamental scientific knowledge; but I could see immediately that his was not a scientifically trained mind. By profession he was a writer—one who recorded fictitious "happenings" in the written language, so that others might absorb and enjoy them.

And as I probed into his mind I was amazed at the depth of imagination there, a trait almost wholly lacking in those others I had encountered, the scientists. And I knew that at last here was one with whose mind I might contact . . . . here was one who was different from the others . . . . who went deeper . . . . who seemed on the very edge of the truth. Here was one who thought: "—this strange creature, which has landed here . . . . alien to anything we have ever known . . . . might it not be alien even to our universe? . . . . the strange shrinking . . . . from that phenomenon alone we might conclude that it has come an inconceivable distance . . . . its shrinking may have begun hundreds, thousands of years ago . . . . and if we could but communicate with it, before it passes from Earth forever, what strange things might it not tell us!"

The voice came from the box again, interrupting these thoughts in his mind.

"Attention! Flash! The report comes that the alien space-creature, which was taken to the Scientific Research Institute for observation by scientists, has escaped, atter projecting a kind ot invisible mind force which rendered unconscious all those within reach. The creature was reported seen by a number ot persons, after it left the building. A police squad car was wrecked as a direct result of the creature's "mind force," and three policemen were injured, none seriously. It was last seen leaving the city by the north-east, and all persons are ordered to be on the lookout and to report immediately if it is sighted."

Again the report from the box ceased, and again I probed into the man's mind, this time deeper, hoping to establish a contact with it which would allow for thought-communication.

I must have at least aroused some hidden mind-instinct, for he whirled to face me, overturning his chair. Surprise was on his face, and something in his eyes that must have been fear.

"Do not be alarmed," I flashed. "Be seated again."

I could see that his mind had not received my thought. But he must have known from my manner that I meant no harm, for he resumed his seat. I advanced further into the room, standing before him. The fear had gone out of his eyes and he only sat tensely staring at me, his hands gripping the arms of the chair.

"I know that you would like to learn things about myself," I telepathed; "things which those others—your scientists—would have liked to know."

Reading his mind I could see that he had not received the thought, so I probed even deeper and again flashed the same thought. This time he did receive it, and there was an answering light in his eyes.

He said "Yes," aloud.

"Those others, your scientists," I went on, "would never have believed nor even understood my story, even if their minds were of the type to receive my thoughts, which they are not."

He received and comprehended that thought, too, but I could see that this was a great strain on his mind and could not go on for long.

"Yours is the only mind I have encountered here with which I could establish thought," I continued, "but even now it is becoming weakened under the unaccustomed strain. I wish to leave my record and story with you, but it cannot be by this means. I can put your mind under a hypnotic influence and impress my thoughts upon your subconscious mind, if you have some means of recording them. But you must hurry; I have only a few more hours here at the most, and in your entire lifetime it would be impossible for you to record all that I could tell."

I could read doubt in his mind. But only for one instant did he hesitate. Then he rose and went to a table where there was a pile of smooth white paper and a sharp pointed instrument—pen—for recording my thoughts in words of his own language.

"I am ready," was the thought in his mind.

* * * *

So I have told my story. Why? I do not know, except that I wanted to. Of all the universes I have passed into, only on this blue sphere have I found creatures even remotely resembling myself. And they are a disappointment; and now I know that I shall never find others of my kind. Never, unless—

I have a theory. Where is the beginning or the end of the eternal All I have been traversing? Suppose there is none? Suppose that, after traversing a few more atomic cycles, I should enter a universe which seemed somehow familiar to me; and that I should enter a certain familiar galaxy, and approach a certain sun, a certain planet—and find that I was back where I started from so long ago: back on my own planet, where I should find the Professor in the laboratory still receiving my sound and sight impressions!! An insane theory; an impossible one. It shall never be.

Well, then, suppose that after leaving this sphere—after descending into another atomic universe—I should choose *not to alight on any planet?* Suppose I should remain in empty space, my size constantly diminishing? That would be one way of ending it all, I suppose. Or would it? Is not my body matter, and is not matter infinite, limitless, eternal? How then could I ever reach a "nothingness?" It is hopeless. I am eternal. My mind too must be eternal or it would surely have snapped long ago at such concepts.

I am so very small that my mind is losing contact with the mind of him who sits here before me writing these thoughts in words of his own language, though his mind is under the hypnotic spell of my own and he is oblivious to the words he writes. I have clambered upon the top of the table beside the pile of pages he has written, to bring my mind closer to his. But why should I want to continue the thought-contact for another instant? My story is finished, there is nothing more to tell.

I shall never find others of my kind . . . I am alone . . . . I think that soon, in some manner, I shall try to put an end to it . . . .

I am very small now . . . . the hypnosis is passing from his mind . . . . I can no longer control it . . . . the thought-contact is slipping . . . .

EPILOGUE

National Press-Radio Service, *Sept.* 29, 1937 (through Cleveland *Daily Clarion*):—Exactly one year ago today was a day never to be forgotten in the history of this planet. On that day a strange visitor arrived—and departed.

On September 29, 1936, at 3:31 P.M., that thing from outer space known henceforth only as "The Alien" landed in Lake Erie near Cleveland, causing not so much destruction and terror as great bewilderment and awe, scientists being baffled in their attempts to determine whence it came and the secret of its strange steady shrinking.

Now, on the anniversary of that memorable day, we are presenting to the public a most unusual and interesting document purported to be a true account and history of that strange being, The Alien. This document was presented to us only a few days ago by Stanton Cobb Lentz, renowned author of "The Answer to the Ages" and other serious books, as well as of scores of short stories and books of the widely popular type of literature known as science-fiction.

You have read the above document. While our opinion as to its authenticity is frankly skeptical, we shall print Mr. Lentz's comment and let you, the reader, judge for yourself whether the story was related to Mr. Lentz by The Alien in the manner described, or whether it is only a product of Mr. Lentz's most fertile imagination.

"On the afternoon of September 29 a year ago," states Mr. Lentz, "I fled the city as did many others, heeding the warning of a possible tidal wave, should The Alien land in the lake. Thousands of persons had gathered five or six miles to the south, and from there we watched the huge shape overhead, so expansive that it blotted out the sunlight and plunged that section of the country into a partial eclipse. It seemed to draw nearer by slow degrees until, about 3:30 o'clock, it began its downward rush. The sound of contact as it struck the lake was audible for miles, but it was not until later that we learned the extent of the flood. After the landing all was confusion and excitement as combat planes arrived and very foolishly began to bombard the creature and crowds began to advance upon the scene. The entire countryside being in such crowded turmoil, it took me several difficult hours to return to my home. There I listened to the varied reports of the happenings of the past several hours.

"When I had that strange feeling that someone was behind me, and when I whirled to see The Alien standing there in the room, I do not presume to say that I was not scared. I was. I was very much scared. I had seen The Alien when it was five or six hundred feet tall —but that had been from afar. Now it was only ten or eleven feet tall, but was standing right before me. But my scaredness was only momentary, for something seemed to enter and calm my mind.

"Then, although there was no audible sound, I became aware of the thought: 'I know that you would like to learn things about myself, things which those others—your scientists—would have liked to know.'

"This was mental telepathy! I had often used the theory in my stories, but never had I dreamed that I would experience such a medium of thought in real fact. But here it was.

" 'Those others, your scientists,' came the next thought, 'would never have believed nor even understood my story, even if their minds were of the type to receive my thoughts, which they are not.' And then I began to feel a strain upon my mind, and knew that I could not stand much more of it.

"Then came the thought that he would relate his story through my sub-conscious mind if I had some means of recording it in my own language. For an instant I hesitated; and then I realized that time was fleeing and never again would I have such an opportunity as this. I went to my desk, where only that morning I had been working on a manuscript. There was paper and ink in plenty.

"My last impression was of some force seeming to spread over my mind; then a terrific dizziness, and the ceiling seemed to crash upon me.

"No time at all had seemed to elapse, when my mind regained its normal faculties; but before me on the desk was a pile of manuscript paper closely written in my own longhand. And—what many persons will find it hard to believe—standing upon that pile of written paper upon my desk top, was The Alien—now scarcely two inches in height—and steadily and surely diminishing! In utter fascination I watched the transformation that was taking place before my eyes— watched until The Alien had become entirely invisible. had descended down into the topmost sheet of paper there on my desk . . . .

"Now I realize that the foregoing document and my explanation of it will be received in many ways. I have waited a full year before making it public. Accept it now as fiction if you wish. There may be some few who will see the truth of it, or at least the possibility; but the vast majority will leap at once to the conclusion that the whole thing is a concoction of my own imagination; that, taking advantage of The Alien's landing on this planet, I wrote the story to fit the occasion, very appropriately using The Alien as the main theme. To many this will seem all the more to be true, in face of the fact that in most of my science-fiction stories I have poked ridicule and derision and satire at mankind and all its high vaunted science and civilization and achievements—always more or less with my tongue in my cheek however, as the expression has it. And then along comes this Alien, takes a look at us and concludes that he is very disappointed, not to mention disgusted.

"However, I wish to present a few facts to help substantiate the authenticity of the script. Firstly: for some time after awakening from my hypnosis I was beset by a curious dizziness, though my mind was quite clear. Shortly after The Alien had disappeared I called my physician, Dr. C. M. Rollins. After an examination and a few mental tests he was greatly puzzled. He could not diagnose my case; my dizziness was the after effect of a hypnosis of a type he had never before encountered. I offered no explanation except to say that I had not been feeling well for the past several days.

"Secondly: the muscles of my right hand were so cramped from the long period of steady writing that I could not open my fingers. As an explanation I said that I had been writing for hours on the final chapters of my latest book, and Dr. Rollins said: 'Man, you must be crazy.' The process of relaxing the muscles was painful.

"Upon my request Dr. Rollins will vouch for the truth of the above statements.

"Thirdly: when I read the manuscript the writing was easily recognizable as my own free, swinging longhand up to the last few paragraphs, when the writing became shaky, the last few words terminating in an almost undecipherable scrawl as the Alien's contact with my mind slipped away.

"Fourthly: I presented the manuscript to Mr. Howard A. Byerson, fiction editor of the National Newspaper Syndicate Service, and at once he misunderstood the entire idea. 'I have read your story, Mr. Lentz,' he said a few days later, 'and it certainly comes at an appropriate time, right on the anniversary of The Alien's landing. A neat idea about the origin of The Alien, but a bit farfetched. Now, let's see, about the price; of course we shall syndicate your story through our National Newspaper chain, and—'

" 'You have the wrong idea,' I said. 'It is not a story, but a true history of The Alien as related to me by The Alien, and I wish that fact emphasized; if necessary I will write a letter of explanation to be published with the manuscript. And I am not selling you the publication rights, I am merely giving you the document as the quickest and surest way of presenting it to the public.'

" 'But surely you are not serious? An appropriate story by Stanton Cobb Lentz, on the eve of the anniversary of The Alien's landing, is a scoop; and you—'

" 'I do not ask and will not take a cent for the document,' I said; 'you have it now, it is yours, so do with it as you see fit.'

"A memory that will live with me always is the sight of The Alien as last seen by me—as last seen on this earth—as it disappeared into infinite smallness there upon my desk—waving two arms upward as if in farewell . . . .

"And whether the above true account and history of The Alien be received as such, or as fiction, there can be no doubt that on a not far off September, a thing from some infinite sphere above landed on this earth—and departed."

BY HIS BOOTSTRAPS

by

ANSON MACDONALD

This is literally a "whodunit." There are four or five characters in this story (or puzzle) and most of them are the same man! The question is who is who—and when. Or, when is a man not himself—yesterday, today or tomorrow? It may sound like a joke, but we assure you it isn't. It is a perfect illustration of the paradox of time travel. If the story's problem can be solved, then (perhaps) so can time travel.

⁘

BOB WILSON did not see the circle grow.

Nor, for that matter, did he see the stranger who stepped out of the circle and stood staring at the back of Wilson's neck—stared, and breathed heavily, as if laboring under strong and unusual emotion.

Wilson had no reason to suspect that anyone else was in his room; he had every reason to expect the contrary. He had locked himself in his room for the purpose of completing his thesis in one sustained drive. He *had* to—tomorrow was the last day for submission, yesterday the thesis had been no more than a title: "An Investigation into Certain Mathematical Aspects of a Rigor of Metaphysics."

Fifty-two cigarettes, four pots of coffee, and thirteen hours of continuous work had added seven thousand words to the title. As to the validity of his thesis he was far too groggy to give a damn. Get it done, turn it in, take three stiff drinks and sleep for a week.

He glanced up and let his eyes rest on his wardrobe door, behind which he had cached a gin bottle, nearly full. No, he admonished himself, one more drink and you'll never finish it, Bob, old son.

The stranger behind him said nothing.

Wilson resumed typing. "—nor is it valid to assume that a conceivable proposition is necessarily a possible proposition, even when it is possible to formulate mathematics which describes the proposition with exactness. A case in point is the concept 'Time Travel.' Time travel may be imagined and its necessities may be formulated under any and all theories of time, formulae which resolve the paradoxes of each theory. Nevertheless, we know certain things about the empirical nature of time which preclude the possibility of the conceivable proposition. Duration is an attribute of consciousness and not of the plenum. It has no *ding an sicht*. Therefore—"

A key of the typewriter stuck, three more jammed up on top of it. Wilson swore duly and reached forward to straighten out the cantankerous machinery. "Don't bother with it," he heard a voice say. "It's a lot of utter hogwash anyhow."

Wilson sat up with a jerk, then turned his head slowly around. He fervently hoped that there was someone behind him. Otherwise—

He perceived the stranger with relief. "Thank God," he said to himself. "For a moment I thought I had come unstuck." His relief turned to extreme annoyance. "What the devil are you doing in my room?" he demanded. He shoved back his chair, got up and strode over to the one door. It was still locked, and bolted on the inside.

The windows were no help; they were adjacent to his desk and three stories above a busy street. "How *did* you get in?" he added.

"Through that," answered the stranger, hooking a thumb toward the circle. Wilson noticed it for the first time, blinked his eyes and looked again. There it hung between them and the wall, a great disk of nothing, of the color one sees when the eyes are shut tight.

Wilson shook his head vigorously. The circle remained. "Gosh," he thought, "I was right the first time. I wonder when I slipped my trolley?" He advanced toward the disk, put out a hand to touch it.

"Don't!" snapped the stranger.

"Why not?" said Wilson edgily. Nevertheless he paused.

"I'll explain. But let's have a drink first." He walked directly to the wardrobe, opened it, reached in and took out the bottle of gin without looking.

"Hey!" yelled Wilson. "What are you doing there? That's *my* liquor."

"*Your* liquor—" The stranger paused for a moment. "Sorry. You don't mind if I have a drink, do you?"

"I suppose not," Bob Wilson conceded in a surly tone. "Pour me one while you're about it."

"O. K.," agreed the stranger, "then I'll explain."

"It had better be good," Wilson said ominously. Nevertheless he drank his drink and looked the stranger over.

He saw a chap about the same size as himself and much the same age—perhaps a little older, though a three-day growth of beard may have accounted for that impression. The stranger had a black eye and a freshly cut and badly swollen upper lip. Wilson decided he did not like the chap's face. Still, there was something familiar about the face; he felt that he should have recognized it, that he had seen it many times before under different circumstances.

"Who are you?" he asked suddenly.

"Me?" said his guest. "Don't you recognize me?"

"I'm not sure," admitted Wilson. "Have I ever seen you before?"

"Well—not exactly," the other temporized. "Skip it—you wouldn't know about it."

"What's your name?"

"My name? Uh . . . just call me Joe."

Wilson set down his glass. "O. K., Joe Whatever-your-name-is, trot out that explanation and make it snappy."

"I'll do that," agreed Joe. "That dingus I came through"—he pointed to the circle—"that's a Time Gate."

"A what?"

"A Time Gate. Time flows along side by side on each side of the Gate, but some thousands of years apart—just how many thousands I don't know. But for the next couple of hours that Gate is open. You can walk into the future just by stepping through that circle." The stranger paused.

Bob drummed on the desk. "Go ahead. I'm listening. It's a nice story."

"You don't believe me, do you? I'll show you." Joe got up, went again to the wardrobe and obtained Bob's hat, his prized and only hat, which he had mistreated into its present battered grandeur through six years of undergraduate and graduate life. Joe chucked it toward the impalpable disk.

It struck the surface, went on through with no apparent resistance, disappeared from sight.

Wilson got up, walked carefully around the circle, and examined the bare floor. "A neat trick," he conceded. "Now I'll thank you to return to me my hat."

The stranger shook his head. "You can get it yourself when you pass through."

"Huh?"

"That's right. Listen—" Briefly the stranger repeated his explanation about the Time Gate. Wilson, he insisted, had an opportunity that comes once in a millennium—if he would only hurry up and climb through that circle. Furthermore, though Joe could not explain in detail at the moment, it was very important that Wilson go through.

Bob Wilson helped himself to a second drink, and then a third. He was beginning to feel both good and argumentative. "Why?" he said flatly.

Joe looked exasperated. "Dammit, if you'd just step through once, explanations wouldn't be necessary. However—" According to Joe, there was an old guy on the other side who needed Wilson's help. With Wilson's help the three of them would run the country. The exact nature of the help Joe could not or would not specify. Instead he bore down on the unique possibilities for high adventure. "You don't want to slave your life away teaching numskulls in some freshwater college," he insisted. "This is your chance. Grab it!"

Bob Wilson admitted to himself that a Ph.D. and an appointment as an instructor was not his ideal of existence. Still, it beat working for a living. His eye fell on the gin bottle, its level now deplorably lowered. That explained it. He got up unsteadily.

"No, my dear fellow," he stated, "I'm not going to climb on your merry-go-round. You know why?"

"Why?"

"Because I'm drunk, that's why. You're not there at all. *That* ain't there." He gestured widely at the circle. "There ain't anybody here but me, and I'm drunk. Been working too hard," he added apologetically. "I'm goin' to bed."

"You're not drunk."

"I *am* drunk. Peter Piper pepped a pick of pippered peckles." He moved toward his bed.

Joe grabbed his arm. "You can't do that," he said.

"Let him alone!"

They both swung around. Facing them, standing directly in front of the circle, was a third man. Bob looked at the newcomer, looked back at Joe, blinked his eyes and tried to focus them. The two looked a good bit alike, he thought, enough alike to be brothers. Or maybe he was seeing double. Bad stuff, gin. Should've switched to rum a long time ago. Good stuff, rum. You could drink it, or take a bath in it. No, that was gin—he meant Joe.

How silly! Joe was the one with the black eye. He wondered why he had ever been confused.

Then who was this other lug? Couldn't a couple of friends have a quiet drink together without people butting in?

"Who are you?" he said with quiet dignity.

The newcomer turned his head, then looked at Joe. "He knows me," he said meaningly.

Joe looked him over slowly. "Yes," he said, "yes, I suppose I do. But what the deuce are you here for? And why are you trying to bust up the plan?"

"No time for long-winded explanations. I know more about it than you do—you'll concede that—and my judgment is bound to be better than yours. He doesn't go through the Gate."

"I don't concede anything of the sort—"

The telephone rang.

"Answer it!" snapped the newcomer.

Bob was about to protest the peremptory tone, but decided he wouldn't. He lacked the phlegmatic temperament necessary to ignore a ringing telephone. "Hello?"

"Hello," he was answered. "Is that Bob Wilson?"

"Yes. Who is this?"

"Never mind. I just wanted to be sure you were there. I thought you would be. You're right in the groove, kid, right in the groove."

Wilson heard a chuckle, then the click of disconnection. "Hello," he said. "Hello!" He jiggled the bar a couple of times, then hung up.

"What was it?" asked Joe.

"Nothing. Some nut with a misplaced sense of humor." The telephone bell rang again. Wilson added, "There he is again," and picked up the receiver. "Listen, you butterfly-brained ape! I'm a busy man, and this is not a public telephone."

"Why, Bob!" came a hurt feminine voice.

"Huh? Oh, it's you, Genevieve. Look—I'm sorry. I apologize—"

"Well, I should think you would!"

"You don't understand, honey. A guy has been pestering me over the phone and I thought it was him. You know I wouldn't talk that way to you, Babe."

"Well, I should think not. Particularly after all you said to me this afternoon, and all we meant to each other."

"Huh? This afternoon? Did you say this afternoon?"

"Of course. But what I called up about was this: You left your hat in my apartment. I noticed it a few minutes after you had gone and just thought I'd call and tell you where it is. Anyhow," she added coyly, "it gave me an excuse to hear your voice again."

"Sure. Fine," he said mechanically. "Look, babe, I'm a little mixed up about this. Trouble I've had all day long, and more trouble now. I'll look you up tonight and straighten it out. But I know I didn't leave your hat in my apartment—"

"Your hat, silly!"

"Huh? Oh, sure! Anyhow, I'll see you tonight. 'By." He rang off hurriedly. Gosh, he thought, that woman is getting to be a problem. Hallucinations. He turned to his two companions.

"Very well, Joe. I'm ready to go if you are." He was not sure just when or why he had decided to go through the time gadget, but he had. Who did this other mug think he was, anyhow, trying to interfere with a man's freedom of choice?

"Fine!" said Joe, in a relieved voice. "Just step through. That's all there is to it."

"No, you don't!" It was the ubiquitous stranger. He stepped between Wilson and the Gate.

Bob Wilson faced him. "Listen, you! You come butting in here like you think I was a bum. If you don't like it, go jump in the lake— and I'm just the kind of guy who can do it? You and who else?"

The stranger reached out and tried to collar him. Wilson let go a swing, but not a good one. It went by nothing faster than parcel post. The stranger walked under it and let him have a mouthful of knuckles —large, hard ones. Joe closed in rapidly, coming to Bob's aid. They traded punches in a free-for-all, with Bob joining in enthusiastically but inefficiently. The only punch he landed was on Joe, theoretically his ally. However, he had intended it for the third man.

It was this faux pas which gave the stranger the opportunity to land a clean left jab on Wilson's face. It was inches higher than the button, but in Bob's bemused condition it was sufficient to cause him to cease taking part in the activities.

Bob Wilson came slowly to awareness of his surroundings. He was seated on a floor which seemed a little unsteady. Someone was bending over him. "Are you all right?" the figure inquired.

"I guess so," he answered thickly. His mouth pained him; he put his hand to it, got it sticky with blood. "My head hurts."

"I should think it would. You came through head over heels. I think you hit your head when you landed."

Wilson's thoughts were coming back into confused focus. Came through? He looked more closely at his succorer. He saw a middle-aged man with gray-shot bushy hair and a short, neatly trimmed beard. He was dressed in what Wilson took to be purple lounging pajamas.

But the room in which he found himself bothered him even more. It was circular and the ceiling was arched so subtly that it was difficult to say how high it was. A steady glareless light filled the room from no apparent source. There was no furniture save for a high dais or pulpit-shaped object near the wall facing him. "Came through? Came through what?"

"The Gate, of course." There was something odd about the man's accent. Wilson could not place it, save for a feeling that English was not a tongue he was accustomed to speaking.

Wilson looked over his shoulder in the direction of the other's gaze, and saw the circle.

That made his head ache even more. "Oh Lord," he thought, "now I really am nuts. Why don't I wake up?" He shook his head to clear it.

That was a mistake. The top of his head did not quite come off— not quite. And the circle stayed where it was, a simple locus hanging in the air, its flat depth filled with the amorphous colors and shapes of no-vision. "Did I come through that?"

"Yes."

"Where am I?"

"In the Hall of the Gate in the High Palace of Norkaal. But what is more important is when you are. You have gone forward a little more than thirty thousand years."

"Now I know I'm crazy," thought Wilson. He got up unsteadily and moved toward the Gate.

The older man put a hand on his shoulder. "Where are you going?"

"Back!"

"Not so fast. You will go back all right—I give you my word on that. But let me dress your wounds first. And you should rest. I have some explanations to make to you, and there is an errand you can do for me when you get back—to our mutual advantage. There is a great future in store for you and me, my boy—a great future!"

Wilson paused uncertainly. The elder man's insistence was vaguely disquieting. "I don't like this."

The other eyed him narrowly. "Wouldn't you like a drink before you go?"

Wilson most assuredly would. Right at the moment a stiff drink seemed the most desirable thing on earth—or in time. "O. K."

"Come with me." The older man led him back of the structure near the wall and through a door which led into a passageway. He walked briskly; Wilson hurried to keep up.

"By the way," he asked, as they continued down the long passage, "what is your name?"

"My name? You may call me Diktor—everyone else does."

"O. K., Diktor. Do you want my name?"

"Your name?" Diktor chuckled. "I know your name. It's Bob Wilson."

"Huh? Oh—I suppose Joe told you."

"Joe? I know no one by that name."

"You don't? He seemed to know you. Say—maybe you aren't the guy I was supposed to see."

"But I am. I have been expecting you—in a way, Joe . . . Joe—Oh!" Diktor chuckled. "It had slipped my mind for a moment. He told you to call him Joe, didn't he?"

"Isn't it his name?"

"It's as good a name as any other. Here we are." He ushered Wilson into a small, but cheerful, room. It contained no furniture of any sort, but the floor was soft and warm as live flesh. "Sit down. I'll be back in a moment."

Bob looked around for something to sit on, then turned to ask Diktor for a chair. But Diktor was gone, furthermore the door through which they had entered was gone. Bob sat down on the comfortable floor and tried not to worry.

Diktor returned promptly. Wilson saw the door dilate to let him in, but did not catch on to how it was done. Diktor was carrying a carafe, which gurgled pleasantly, and a cup. "Mud in your eye," he said heartily and poured a good four fingers. "Drink up."

Bob accepted the cup. "Aren't you drinking?"

"Presently. I want to attend to your wounds first."

"O. K." Wilson tossed off the first drink in almost indecent haste —it was good stuff, a little like Scotch, he decided, but smoother and not as dry—while Diktor worked deftly with salves that smarted at first. then soothed. "Mind if I have another?"

"Help yourself."

Bob drank more slowly the second cup. He did not finish it; it slipped from relaxed fingers, spilling a ruddy, brown stain across the floor. He snored.

Bob Wilson woke up feeling fine and completely rested. He was cheerful without knowing why. He lay relaxed, eyes still closed, for a few moments and let his soul snuggle back into his body. This was going to be a good day, he felt. Oh, yes—he had finished that double-damned thesis. No, he hadn't either! He sat up with a start.

The sight of the strange walls around him brought him back into continuity. But before he had time to worry—at once, in fact—the door relaxed and Diktor stepped in. "Feeling better?"

"Why, yes, I do. Say what is this?"

"We'll get to that. How about some breakfast?"

In Wilson's scale of evaluations breakfast rated just after life itself and ahead of the chance of immortality. Diktor conducted him to another room—the first that he had seen possessing windows. As a matter of fact half the room was open, a balcony hanging high over a green countryside. A soft, warm, summer breeze wafted through the place. They broke their fast in luxury, Roman style, while Diktor explained.

Bob Wilson did not follow the explanations as closely as he might have done, because his attention was diverted by the maidservants who served the meal. The first came in bearing a great tray of fruit on her head. The fruit was gorgeous. So was the girl. Search as he would he could discern no fault in her.

Her costume lent itself to the search.

She came first to Diktor, and with a single, graceful movement dropped to one knee, removed the tray from her head, and offered it to him. He helped himself to a small, red fruit and waved her away. She then offered it to Bob in the same delightful manner.

"As I was saying," continued Diktor, "it is not certain where the High Ones came from or where they went when they left Earth. I am inclined to think they went away into Time. In any case they ruled more than twenty thousand years and completely obliterated human culture as you knew it. What is more important to you and to me is the effect they had on the human psyche. One twentieth-century style go-getter can accomplish just about anything he wants to accomplish around here— Aren't you listening?"

"Huh? Oh, yes, sure. Say, that's one mighty pretty girl." His eyes still rested on the exit through which she had disappeared.

"Who? Oh, yes, I suppose so. She's not exceptionally beautiful as women go around here."

"That's hard to believe. I could learn to get along with a girl like that."

"You like her? Very well, she is yours."

"Huh?"

"She's a slave. Don't get indignant. They are slaves by nature. If you like her, I'll make you a present of her. It will make her happy." The girl had just returned. Diktor called to her in a language strange to Bob. "Her name is Arma," he said in an aside, then spoke to her briefly.

Arma giggled. She composed her face quickly, and, moving over to where Wilson reclined, dropped on both knees to the floor and lowered her head, with both hands cupped before her. "Touch her forehead," Diktor instructed.

Bob did so. The girl arose and stood waiting placidly by his side. Diktor spoke to her. She looked puzzled, but moved out of the room. "I told her that, notwithstanding her new status, you wished her to continue serving breakfast."

Diktor resumed his explanations while the service of the meal continued. The next course was brought in by Arma and another girl. When Bob saw the second girl he let out a low whistle. He realized he had been a little hasty in letting Diktor give him Arma. Either the standard of pulchritude had gone up incredibly, he decided, or Diktor went to a lot of trouble in selecting his servants.

"—for that reason," Diktor was saying, "it is necessary that you go back through the Time Gate at once. Your first job is to bring this other chap back. Then there is one other task for you to do, and we'll be sitting pretty. After that it is share and share alike for you and me. And there is plenty to share, I— You aren't listening!"

"Sure I was, chief. I heard every word you said." He fingered his chin. "Say, have you got a razor I could borrow? I'd like to shave."

Diktor swore softly in two languages. "Keep your eyes off those wenches and listen to me! There's work to be done."

"Sure, sure. I understand that—and I'm your man. When do we start?" Wilson had made up his mind some time ago—just shortly after Arma had entered with the tray of fruit, in fact. He felt as if he had walked into some extremely pleasant dream. If co-operation

with Diktor would cause that dream to continue, so be it. To hell
with an academic career!

Anyhow, all Diktor wanted was for him to go back where he started
and persuade another guy to go through the Gate. The worst that
could happen was for him to find himself back in the twentieth
century. What could he lose?

Diktor stood up. "Let's get on with it," he said shortly, "before
you get your attention diverted again. Follow me." He set off at a
brisk pace with Wilson behind him.

Diktor took him to the Hall of the Gate and stopped. "All you
have to do," he said, "is to step through the Gate. You will find
yourself back in your own room, in your own time. Persuade the
man you find there to go through the Gate. We have need of him.
Then come back yourself."

Bob held up a hand and pinched thumb and forefinger together.
"It's in the bag, boss. Consider it done." He started to step through
the Gate.

"Wait!" commanded Diktor. "You are not used to time travel.
I warn you that you are going to get one hell of a shock when you
step through. This other chap—you'll recognize him."

"Who is he?"

"I won't tell you because you wouldn't understand. But you will
when you see him. Just remember this— There are some very
strange paradoxes connected with time travel. Don't let anything you
see throw you. You do what I tell you to and you'll be all right."

"Paradoxes don't worry me," Bob said confidently. "Is that all?
I'm ready."

"One minute." Diktor stepped behind the raised dais. His head
appeared above the side a moment later. "I've set the controls. O.K.
Go!"

Bob Wilson stepped through the locus known as the Time Gate.

There was no particular sensation connected with the transition.
It was like stepping through a curtained doorway into a darker room.
He paused for a moment on the other side and let his eyes adjust to
the dimmer light. He was, he saw, indeed in his own room.

There was a man in it, seated at his own desk. Diktor had been
right about that. This, then, was the chap he was to send back
through the Gate. Diktor had said he would recognize him. Well,
let's see who it is.

He felt a passing resentment at finding someone at *his* desk in *his* room, then thought better of it. After all, it was just a rented room; when he disappeared no doubt it had been rented again. He had no way of telling how long he had been gone—shucks, it might be the middle of next week!

The chap did look vaguely familiar, although all he could see was his back. Who was it? Should he speak to him, cause him to turn around? He felt vaguely reluctant to do so until he knew who it was. He rationalized the feeling by telling himself that it was desirable to know with whom he was dealing before he attempted anything as outlandish as persuading this man to go through the Gate.

The man at the desk continued typing, paused to snuff out a cigarette by laying it in an ash tray, then stamping it with a paper weight.

Bob Wilson knew that gesture.

Chills trickled down his back. "If he lights his next one," he whispered to himself, "the way I think he is going to—"

The man at the desk took out another cigarette, tamped it on one end, turned it and tamped the other, straightened and crimped the paper on one end carefully against his left thumbnail and placed that end in his mouth.

Wilson felt the blood beating in his neck. *Sitting there with his back to him was himself, Bob Wilson!*

He felt that he was going to faint. He closed his eyes and steadied himself on a chair back. "I knew it," he thought, "the whole thing is absurd. I'm crazy. I know I'm crazy. Some sort of split personality. I shouldn't have worked so hard."

The sound of typing continued.

He pulled himself together, and reconsidered the matter. Diktor had warned him that he was due for a shock, a shock that could not be explained ahead of time, because it could not be believed. "All right—suppose I'm not crazy. If time travel can happen at all, there is no reason why I can't come back and see myself doing something I did in the past. If I'm sane, that is what I'm doing.

"And if I am crazy, it doesn't make a damn bit of difference what I do!

"And furthermore," he added to himself, "if I'm crazy, maybe I can stay crazy and go back through the Gate! No, that does not make sense. Neither does anything else—the hell with it!"

He crept forward softly and peered over the shoulder of his double. "Duration is an attribute of the consciousness," he read, "and not of the plenum."

"'That tears it," he thought, "right back where I started, and watching myself write my thesis."

The typing continued. "It has no *ding an sicht*. Therefore—" A key stuck, and others piled up on top of it. His double at the desk swore and reached out a hand to straighten the keys.

"Don't bother with it," Wilson said on sudden impulse. "It's a lot of utter hogwash anyhow."

The other Bob Wilson sat up with a jerk, then looked slowly around. An expression of surprise gave way to annoyance. "What the devil are you doing in my room?" he demanded. Without waiting for an answer he got up, went quickly to the door and examined the lock. "How did you get in?"

"This," thought Wilson, "is going to be difficult."

"Through that," Wilson answered, pointing to the Time Gate. His double looked where he had pointed, did a double take, then advanced cautiously and started to touch it.

"Don't!" yelled Wilson.

The other checked himself. "Why not?" he demanded.

Just why he must not permit his other self to touch the Gate was not clear to Wilson, but he had had an unmistakable feeling of impending disaster when he saw it about to happen. He temporized by saying, "I'll explain. But let's have a drink." A drink was a good idea in any case. There had never been a time when he needed one more than he did right now. Quite automatically he went to his usual cache of liquor in the wardrobe and took out the bottle he expected to find there.

"Hey!" protested the other. "What are you doing there? That's my liquor."

"Your liquor—" Hell's bells! It was *his* liquor. No, it wasn't; it was—*their* liquor. Oh, the devil! It was much too mixed up to try to explain. "Sorry. You don't mind if I have a drink, do you?"

"I suppose not," his double said grudgingly. "Pour me one while you're about it."

"O. K.," Wilson assented, "then I'll explain." It was going to be much, much too difficult to explain until he had had a drink, he felt. As it was, he couldn't explain it fully to himself.

"It had better be good" the other warned him, and looked Wilson over carefully while he drank his drink.

Wilson watched his younger self scrutinizing him with confused and almost insupportable emotions. Couldn't the stupid fool recogaize his own face when he saw it in front of him? If he could not see what the situation was, how in the world was he ever going to make it clear to him?

It had slipped his mind that his face was barely recognizable in any case, being decidedly battered and unshaven. Even more important, he failed to take into account the fact that a person does not look at his own face, even in mirrors, in the same frame of mind with which he regards another's face. No sane person ever expects to see his own face hanging on another.

Wilson could see that his companion was puzzled by his appearance, but it was equally clear that no recognition took place. "Who are you?" the other man asked suddenly.

"Me?" replied Wilson. "Don't you recognize me?"

"I'm not sure. Have I ever seen you before?"

"Well—not exactly," Wilson stalled. How did you go about telling another guy that the two of you were a trifle closer than twins? "Skip it—you wouldn't know about it."

"What's your name?"

"My name? Uh—" Oh, oh! This was going to be sticky! The whole situation was utterly ridiculous. He opened his mouth, tried to form the words "Bob Wilson," then gave up with a feeling of utter futility. Like many a man before him, he found himself forced into a lie because the truth simply would not be believed. "Just call me Joe," he finished lamely.

He felt suddenly startled at his own words. It was at this point that he realized that he was *in fact,* "Joe," the Joe whom he had encountered once before. That he had landed back in his own room at the very time at which he had ceased working on his thesis he already realized, but he had not had time to think the matter through. Hearing himself refer to himself as Joe slapped him in the face with the realization that this was not simply a similar scene, but the *same* scene he had lived through once before—save that he was living through it from a different viewpoint.

At least he thought it was the same scene. Did it differ in any respect? He could not be sure, as he could not recall, word for word, what the conversation had been.

For a complete transcript of the scene that lay dormant in his memory he felt willing to pay twenty-five dollars cash, plus sales tax.

Wait a minute now—he was under no compulsion. He was sure of that. Everything he did and said was the result of his own free will.

Even if he couldn't remember the script, there were some things he knew "Joe" hadn't said. "Mary had a little lamb," for example. He would recite a nursery rhyme and get off this damned repetitious treadmill. He opened his mouth—

"O. K., Joe Whatever-your-name-is," his alter ego remarked, setting down a glass which had contained, until recently, a quarter pint of gin, "trot out that explanation and make it snappy."

He opened his mouth again to answer the question, then closed it. "Steady, son, steady," he told himself. "You're a free agent. You want to recite a nursery rhyme—go ahead and do it. Don't answer him; go ahead and recite it—and break this vicious circle."

But under the unfriendly, suspicious eye of the man opposite him he found himself totally unable to recall any nursery rhyme. His mental processes stuck on dead center.

He capitulated. "I'll do that. That dingus I came through—that's a Time Gate."

"A what?"

"A Time Gate. Time flows along side by side on each side—" As he talked he felt sweat breaking out on him; he felt reasonably sure that he was explaining in exactly the same words in which explanation had first been offered to *him*. "—into the future just by stepping through that circle." He stopped and wiped his forehead.

"Go ahead," said the other implacably. "I'm listening. It's a nice story."

Bob suddenly wondered if the other man *could* be himself. The stupid arrogant dogmatism of the man's manner infuriated him. All right, all right! He'd show him. He strode suddenly over to the wardrobe, took out his hat and threw it through the Gate.

His opposite number watched the hat snuff out of existence with expressionless eyes, then stood up and went around in back of the Gate, walking with the careful steps of a man who is a little bit drunk, but determined not to show it. "A neat trick," he applauded, after satisfying himself that the hat was gone, "now I'll thank you to return to me my hat."

Wilson shook his head. "You can get it for yourself when you pass through," he answered absent-mindedly. He was pondering the problem of how many hats there were on the other side of the Gate.

"Huh?"

"That's right. Listen—" Wilson did his best to explain persuasively what it was he wanted his earlier persona to do. Or rather to cajole.

Explanations were out of the question, in any honest sense of the word. He would have preferred attempting to explain tensor calculus to an Australian aborigine, even though he did not understand that esoteric mathematics himself.

The other man was not helpful. He seemed more interested in nursing the gin than he did in following Wilson's implausible protestations.

"Why?" he interrupted pugnaciously.

"Dammit," Wilson answered, "if you'd just step through once, explanations wouldn't be necessary. However—" He continued with a synopsis of Diktor's proposition. He realized with irritation that Diktor had been exceedingly sketchy with *his* explanations. He was forced to hit only the high spots in the logical parts of his argument, and bear down on the emotional appeal. He was on safe ground there—no one knew better than he did himself how fed up the earlier Bob Wilson had been with the petty drudgery and stuffy atmosphere of an academic career. "You don't want to slave your life away teaching numskulls in some fresh-water college," he concluded. "This is your chance. Grab it!"

Wilson watched his companion narrowly and thought he detected a favorable response. He definitely seemed interested. But the other set his glass down carefully, stared at the gin bottle, and at last replied:

"My dear fellow, I am not going to climb on your merry-go-round. You know why?"

"Why?"

"Because I'm drunk, that's why. You're not there at all. *That* ain't there." He gestured widely at the Gate, nearly fell, and recovered himself with effort. "There ain't anybody here but me, and I'm drunk. Been working too hard," he mumbled, " 'm goin' to bed."

"You're not drunk," Wilson protested unhopefully. "Damnation," he thought, "a man who can't hold his liquor shouldn't drink."

"I am drunk. Peter Piper pepped a pick of pippered peckles." He lumbered over toward the bed.

Wilson grabbed his arm. "You can't do that."

"Let him alone!"

Wilson swung around, saw a third man standing in front of the Gate—recognized him with a sudden shock. His own recollection of the sequence of events was none too clear in his memory, since he had been somewhat intoxicated—damned near boiled, he admitted—the first time he had experienced this particular busy afternoon. He realized that he should have anticipated the arrival of a third party. But his memory had not prepared him for who the third party would turn out to be.

He recognized himself—another carbon copy.

He stood silent for a minute, trying to assimilate this new fact and force it into some reasonable integration. He closed his eyes helplessly. This was just a little too much. He felt that he wanted to have a few plain words with Diktor.

"Who the hell are you?" He opened his eyes to find that his other self, the drunk one, was addressing the latest edition. The newcomer turned away from his interrogator and looked sharply at Wilson.

"*He* knows me."

Wilson took his time about replying. This thing was getting out of hand. "Yes," he admitted, "yes, I suppose I do. But what the deuce are you here for? And why are you trying to bust up the plan?"

His facsimile cut him short. "No time for long-winded explanations. I know more about it than you do—you'll concede that—and my judgment is bound to be better than yours. He doesn't go through the Gate."

The offhand arrogance of the other antagonized Wilson. "I don't concede anything of the sort—" he began.

He was interrupted by the telephone bell. "Answer it!" snapped Number Three.

The tipsy Number One looked belligerent but picked up the handset. "Hello. . . . Yes. Who is this? . . . Hello. . . . Hello!" He tapped the bar of the instrument, then slammed the receiver back into its cradle.

"Who was that?" Wilson asked, somewhat annoyed that he had not had a chance to answer it himself.

"Nothing. Some nut with a misplaced sense of humor." At that instant the telephone rang again. "There he is again!" Wilson tried to answer it, but his alcoholic counterpart beat him to it, brushed him aside. "Listen, you butterfly-brained ape! I'm a busy man and this is *not* a public telephone. . . . Huh? Oh, it's you, Genevieve. Look—I'm sorry. I apologize— . . . You don't understand, honey. A guy has been pestering me over the phone and I thought it was him. You know I wouldn't talk to you that way, Babe. . . . Huh? This afternoon? Did you say *this* afternoon? . . . Sure. Fine. Look, Babe, I'm a little mixed up about this. Trouble I've had all day long and more trouble now. I'll look you up tonight and straighten it out. But I *know* I didn't leave your hat in my apartment— . . . Huh? Oh, sure! Anyhow, I'll see you tonight. 'By."

It almost nauseated Wilson to hear his earlier self catering to the demands of that clinging female. Why didn't he just hang up on her? The contrast with Arma—there was a dish!—was acute; it made him more determined than ever to go ahead with the plan, despite the warning of the latest arrival.

After hanging up the phone his earlier self faced him, pointedly ignoring the presence of the third copy. "Very well, Joe," he announced. "I'm ready to go if you are."

"Fine!" Wilson agreed with relief. "Just step through. That's all there is to it."

"No, you don't!" Number Three barred the way.

Wilson started to argue, but his erratic comrade was ahead of him. "Listen, you! You come butting in here like you think I was a bum. If you don't like it, go jump in the lake—and I'm just the kind of a guy who can do it! You and who else?"

They started trading punches almost at once. Wilson stepped in warily, looking for an opening that would enable him to put the slug on Number Three with one decisive blow.

He should have watched his drunken ally as well. A wild swing from that quarter glanced off his already damaged features and caused him excruciating pain. His upper lip, cut, puffy, and tender from his other encounter, took the blow and became an area of pure agony. He flinched and jumped back.

A sound cut through his fog of pain, a dull *Smack!* He forced his eyes to track and saw the feet of a man disappear through the Gate. Number Three was still standing by the Gate. "Now you've done it!" he said bitterly to Wilson, and nursed the knuckles of his left hand.

The obviously unfair allegation reached Wilson at just the wrong moment. His face still felt like an experiment in sadism. "Me?" he said angrily. "You knocked him through. I never laid a finger on him."

"Yes, but it's your fault. If you hadn't interfered, I wouldn't have had to do it."

"*Me* interfere? Why, you baldfaced hypocrite—you butted in and tried to queer the pitch. Which reminds me—you owe me some explanations and I damn well mean to have 'em. What's the idea of—"

But his opposite number cut in on him. "Stow it," he said gloomily. "It's too late now. He's gone through."

"Too late for what?" Wilson wanted to know.

"Too late to put a stop to this chain of events."

"Why should we?"

"Because," Number Three said bitterly, "Diktor has played me—I mean has played you . . . us— for a dope, for a couple of dopes. Look, he told you that he was going to set you up as a big shot over there"—he indicated the Gate—"didn't he?"

"Yes," Wilson admitted.

"Well, that's a lot of malarkey. All he means to do is to get us so incredibly tangled up in this Time Gate thing that we'll never get straightened out again."

Wilson felt a sudden doubt nibbling at his mind. It could be true. Certainly there had not been much sense to what had happened so far. After all, why should Diktor want his help, want it bad enough to offer to split with him, even-Stephen, what was obviously a cushy spot? "How do you know?" he demanded.

"Why go into it?" the other answered wearily. "Why don't you just take my word for it?"

"Why should I?"

His companion turned a look of complete exasperation on him. "If you can't take my word, whose word can you take?"

The inescapable logic of the question simply annoyed Wilson. He resented this interloping duplicate of himself anyhow; to be asked to follow his lead blindly irked him. "I'm from Missouri," he said. "I'll see for myself." He moved toward the Gate.

"Where are you going?"

"Through! I'm going to look up Diktor and have it out with him."

"Don't!" the other said. "Maybe we can break the chain even now." Wilson felt and looked stubborn. The other sighed. "Go ahead," he surrendered. "It's your funeral. I wash my hands of you."

Wilson paused as he was about to step through the Gate. "It is, eh? Hm-m-m—how can it be my funeral unless it's your funeral, too?"

The other man looked blank, then an expression of apprehension raced over his face. That was the last Wilson saw of him as he stepped through.

The hall of the Gate was empty of other occupants when Bob Wilson came through on the other side. He looked for his hat, but did not find it, then stepped around back of the raised platform, seeking the exit he remembered. He nearly bumped into Diktor.

"Ah, there you are!" the older man greeted him. "Fine! Fine! Now there is just one more little thing to take care of, then we will be all squared away. I must say I am pleased with you, Bob, very pleased indeed."

"Oh, you are, are you?" Bob faced him truculently. "Well, it's too bad I can't say the same about you! I'm not a damn bit pleased. What was the idea of shoving me into that . . . that daisy chain without warning me? What's the meaning of all this nonsense? Why didn't you warn me?"

"Easy, easy," said the older man, "don't get excited. Tell the truth now—if I had told you that you were going back to meet yourself face to face, would you have believed me? Come now, 'fess up."

Wilson admitted that he would not have believed it.

"Well, then," Diktor continued with a shrug, "there was no point in my telling you, was there? If I had told you, you would not have believed me, which is another way of saying that you would have believed false data. Is it not better to be in ignorance than to believe falsely?"

"I suppose so, but—"

"Wait! I did not intentionally deceive you. I did not deceive you at all. But had I told you the full truth, you would have been deceived because you would have rejected the truth. It was better for you to learn the truth with your own eyes. Otherwise—"

"Wait a minute! Wait a minute!" Wilson cut in. "You're getting me all tangled up. I'm willing to let bygones be bygones, if you'll come clean with me. Why did you send me back at all?"

" 'Let bygones be bygones.' " Diktor repeated. "Ah, if we only could! But we can't. That's why I sent you back—in order that you might come through the Gate in the first place."

"Huh? Wait a minute—I already had come through the Gate."

Diktor shook his head. "Had you, now? Think a moment. When you got back into your own time and your own place you found your earlier self there, didn't you?"

"Mmmm—yes."

"He—your earlier self—had not yet been through the Gate, had he?"

"No. I—"

"How could you have been through the Gate, unless you persuaded him to go through the Gate?"

Bob Wilson's head was beginning to whirl. He was beginning to wonder who did what to whom and who got paid. "But that's impossible! You are telling me that I did something because I was going to do something."

"Well, didn't you? You were there."

"No I didn't—no . . . well, maybe I did, but it didn't feel like it."

"Why should you expect it to? It was something totally new to your experience."

"But . . . but—" Wilson took a deep breath and got control of himself. Then he reached back into his academic philosophical concepts and produced the notion he had been struggling to express. "It denies all reasonable theories of causation. You would have me believe that causation can be completely circular. I went through because I came back from going through to persuade myself to go through. That's silly."

"Well, didn't you?"

Wilson did not have an answer ready for that one. Diktor continued with, "Don't worry about it. The causation you have been accustomed to is valid enough in its own field but is simply a special case under the general case. *Causation in a plenum need not be and is not limited by a man's perception of duration.*"

Wilson thought about that for a moment. It sounded nice, but there was something slippery about it. "Just a second," he said. "How about entropy? You can't get around entropy."

"Oh, for Heaven's sake," protested Diktor, "shut up, will you? You remind me of the mathematicians that proved that airplanes couldn't fly." He turned and started out the door. "Come on. There's work to be done."

Wilson hurried after him. "Dammit, you can't do this to me. What happened to the other two?"

"The other two what?"

"The other two of me? Where are they? How am I ever going to get unsnarled?"

"You aren't snarled up. You don't feel like more than one person, do you?"

"No, but—"

"Then don't worry about it."

"But I've got to worry about it. What happened to the guy that came through just ahead of me?"

"You remember, don't you? However—" Diktor hurried on ahead.

led him down a passageway, and dilated a door. "Take a look inside,"
he directed.

Wilson did so. He found himself looking into a small windowless
unfurnished room, a room that he recognized. Sprawled on the floor,
snoring steadily, was another edition of himself.

"When you first came through the Gate," explained Diktor at his
elbow, "I brought you in here, attended to your hurts, and gave
you a drink. The drink contained a soporific which will cause you to
sleep about thirty-six hours, sleep that you badly needed. When you
wake up, I will give you breakfast and explain to you what needs to
be done."

Wilson's head started to ache again. "Don't do that," he pleaded.
"Don't refer to that guy as if he were me. *This is me*, standing here."

"Have it your own way," said Diktor. "That is the man you were.
You remember the things that are about to happen to him, don't
you?"

"Yes, but it makes me dizzy. Close the door, please."

"O. K.," said Diktor, and complied. "We've got to hurry, anyhow. Once a sequence like this is established there is no time to
waste. Come on." He led the way back to the Hall of the Gate.

"I want you to return to the twentieth century and obtain certain
things for us, things that can't be obtained on this side but which
will be very useful to us in, ah, developing—yes, that is the word—
developing this country."

"What sort of things?"

"Quite a number of items. I've prepared a list for you—certain
reference books, certain items of commerce. Excuse me, please. I
must adjust the controls of the Gate." He mounted the raised platform from the rear. Wilson followed him and found that the structure
was boxlike, open at the top, and had a raised floor. The Gate could
be seen by looking over the high sides.

The controls were unique.

Four colored spheres the size of marbles hung on crystal rods
arranged with respect to one another as the four major axes of a tetrahedron. The three spheres which bounded the base of the tetrahedron
were red, yellow, and blue; the fourth at the apex was white. "Three
spatial controls, one time control," explained Diktor. "It's very simple.
Using here-and-now as zero reference, displacing any control away
from the center moves the other end of the Gate farther from
here-and-now. Forward or back, right or left, up or down, past or

future—they are all controlled by moving the proper sphere in or out on its rod."

Wilson studied the system. "Yes," he said, "but how do you tell where the other end of the Gate is? Or when? I don't see any graduations."

"You don't need them. You can see where you are. Look." He touched a point under the control framework on the side toward the Gate. A panel rolled back and Wilson saw there was a small image of the Gate itself. Diktor made another adjustment and Wilson found that he could see through the image.

He was gazing into his own room, as if through the wrong end of a telescope. He could make out two figures, but the scale was too small for him to see clearly what they were doing, nor could he tell which editions of himself were there present—if they were in truth himself! He found it quite upsetting. "Shut it off," he said.

Diktor did so and said, "I must not forget to give you your list." He fumbled in his sleeve and produced a slip of paper which he handed to Wilson. "Here—take it."

Wilson accepted it mechanically and stuffed it into his pocket. "See here," he began, "everywhere I go I keep running into myself. I don't like it at all. It's disconcerting. I feel like a whole batch of guinea pigs. I don't half understand what this is all about and now you want to rush me through the Gate again with a bunch of half-baked excuses. Come clean. Tell me what it's all about."

Diktor showed temper in his face for the first time. "You are a stupid and ignorant young fool. I've told you all that you are able to understand. This is a period in history entirely beyond your comprehension. It would take weeks before you would even begin to understand it. I am offering you half a world in return for a few hours' co-operation and you stand there arguing about it. Stow it, I tell you. Now—where shall we set you down?" He reached for the controls.

"Get away from those controls!" Wilson rapped out. He was getting the glimmering of an idea. "Who are you, anyhow?"

"Me? I'm Diktor."

"That's not what I mean and you know it. How did you learn English?"

Diktor did not answer. His face became expressionless.

"Go on," Wilson persisted. "You didn't learn it here; that's a cinch. You're from the twentieth century, aren't you?"

Diktor smiled sourly. "I wondered how long it would take you to figure that out."

Wilson nodded. "Maybe I'm not bright, but I'm not as stupid as you think I am. Come on. Give me the rest of the story."

Diktor shook his head. "It's immaterial. Besides, we're wasting time."

Wilson laughed. "You've tried to hurry me with that excuse once too often. How can we waste time when we have that?" He pointed to the controls and to the Gate beyond it. "Unless you lied to me, we can use any slice of time we want to, any time. No, I think I know why you tried to rush me. Either you want to get me out of the picture here, or there is something devilishly dangerous about the job you want me to do. And I know how to settle it—you're going with me!"

"You don't know what you're saying," Diktor answered slowly. "That's impossible. I've got to stay here and manage the controls."

"That's just what you aren't going to do. You could send me through and lose me. I prefer to keep you in sight."

"Out of the question," answered Diktor. "You'll have to trust me." He bent over the controls again.

"Get away from there!" shouted Wilson. "Back out of there before I bop you one." Under Wilson's menacing fist Diktor withdrew from the control pulpit entirely. "There. That's better," he added when both of them were once more on the floor of the hall.

The idea which had been forming in his mind took full shape. The controls, he knew, were still set on his room in the boarding-house where he lived—or had lived—back in the twentieth century. From what he had seen through the speculum of the controls, the time control was set to take him right back to the day in 1942 from which he had started. "Stand there," he commanded Diktor, "I want to see something."

He walked over to the Gate as if to inspect it. Instead of stopping when he reached it, he stepped on through.

He was better prepared for what he found on the other side than he had been on the two earlier occasions of time translation —"earlier" in the sense of sequence in his memory track. Nevertheless it is never too easy on the nerves to catch up with one's self.

For he had done it again. He was back in his own room, but there were two of himself there before him. They were very much preoccupied with each other; he had a few seconds in which to get them straightened out in his mind. One of them had a beautiful black eye and a badly battered mouth. Beside that he was very much in need of a shave. That tagged him. He had been through the Gate at least once. The other, though somewhat in need of shaving himself, showed no marks of a fist fight.

He had them sorted out now, and knew where and *when* he was. It was all still most damnably confusing, but after former— no, not *former*, he amended—*other* experiences with time transla- tion he knew better what to expect. He was back at the beginning again; this time he would put a stop to the crazy nonsense once and for all.

The other two were arguing. One of them swayed drunkenly toward the bed. The other grabbed him by the arm. "You can't do that," he said.

"Let him alone!" snapped Wilson.

The other two swung around and looked him over. Wilson watched the more sober of the pair size him up, saw his expression of amaze- ment change to startled recognition. The other, the earliest Wilson, seemed to have trouble in focusing on him at all. "This is going to be a job," thought Wilson. "The man is positively stinking." He won- dered why anyone would be foolish enough to drink on an empty stomach. It was not only stupid, it was a waste of good liquor.

He wondered if they had left a drink for him.

"Who are you?" demanded his drunken double.

Wilson turned to "Joe." "*He* knows me," he said significantly.

"Joe," studied him. "Yes," he conceded, "yes, I suppose I do. But what the deuce are you here for? And why are you trying to bust up the plan?"

Wilson interrupted him. "No time for long-winded explanations. I know more about it than you do—you'll concede that—and my judgment is bound to be better than yours. He doesn't go through the Gate."

"I don't concede anything of the sort—"

The ringing of the telephone checked the argument. Wilson greeted the interruption with relief, for he realized that he had started out on the wrong tack. Was it possible that he was really as dense himself as this lug appeared to be? Did *he* look that way to other people? But the time was too short for self-doubts and soul-searching. "Answer it!" he commanded Bob (Boiled) Wilson.

The drunk looked belligerent, but acceded when he saw that Bob (Joe) Wilson was about to beat him to it.

"Hello. . . . Yes. Who is this? . . . Hello. . . . Hello!"

"Who was that?" asked "Joe."

"Nothing. Some nut with a misplaced sense of humor." The telephone rang again. "There he is again." The drunk grabbed the phone
before the others could reach it. "Listen, you butterfly-brained ape!
I'm a busy man and this is not a public telephone. . . . Huh? Oh,
it's you, Genevieve—" Wilson paid little attention to the telephone
conversation—he had heard it too many times before, and he had
too much on his mind. His earliest persona was much too drunk to
be reasonable, he realized; he must concentrate on some argument
that would appeal to "Joe"—otherwise he was outnumbered. "—Huh?
Oh, sure!" the call concluded. "Anyhow, I'll see you tonight. 'By."

Now was the time, thought Wilson, before this dumb yap can
open his mouth. What would he say? What would sound convincing?

But the boiled edition spoke first. "Very well, Joe," he stated,
"I'm ready to go if you are."

"Fine!" said "Joe." "Just step through. That's all there is to it."

This was getting out of hand, not the way he had planned it at all.
"No, you don't!" he barked and jumped in front of the Gate. He
would have to make them realize, and quickly.

But he got no chance to do so. The drunk cussed him out, then
swung on him; his temper snapped. He knew with sudden fierce
exultation that he had been wanting to take a punch at someone for
some time. Who did they think they were to be taking chances with
his future?

The drunk was clumsy; Wilson stepped under his guard and hit
him hard in the face. It was a solid enough punch to have convinced
a sober man, but his opponent shook his head and came back for
more. "Joe" closed in. Wilson decided that he would have to put
his original opponent away in a hurry, and give his attention to "Joe"
—by far the more dangerous of the two.

A slight mix-up between the two allies gave him his chance. He
stepped back, aimed carefully, and landed a long jab with his left,
one of the hardest blows he had ever struck in his life. It lifted his
target right off his feet.

As the blow landed Wilson realized his orientation with respect to
the Gate, knew with bitter certainty that he had again played through
the scene to its inescapable climax.

He was alone with "Joe"; their companion had disappeared through
the Gate.

His first impulse was the illogical but quite human and very common feeling of look-what-you-made-me-do. "Now you've done it!" he said angrily.

"Me?" "Joe" protested. "You knocked him through. I never laid a finger on him."

"Yes," Wilson was forced to admit. "But it's your fault," he added, "if you hadn't interfered, I wouldn't have had to do it."

"Me interfere? Why, you baldfaced hypocrite, you butted in and tried to queer the pitch. Which reminds me—you owe me some explanations and I damn well mean to have them. What's the idea of—"

"Stow it," Wilson headed him off. He hated to be wrong and he hated still more to have to admit that he was wrong. It had been hopeless from the start, he now realized. He felt bowed down by the utter futility of it. "It's too late now. He's gone through."

"Too late for what?"

"Too late to put a stop to this chain of events." He was aware now that it always had been too late, regardless of what time it was, what year it was, or how many times he came back and tried to stop it. He remembered having gone through the first time, he had seen himself asleep on the other side. Events would have to work out their weary way.

"Why should we?"

It was not worth while to explain, but he felt the need for self-justification. "Because," he said, "Diktor has played me—I mean has played you . . . us—for a dope, for a couple of dopes. Look, he told you that he was going to set you up as a big shot over there, didn't he?"

"Yes—"

"Well, that's a lot of malarkey. All he means to do is to get us so incredibly tangled up in this Gate thing that we'll never get straightened out again."

"Joe" looked at him sharply. "How do you know?"

Since it was largely hunch, he felt pressed for reasonable explanation. "Why go into it?" he evaded. "Why don't you just take my word for it?"

"Why should I?"

Why should you? Why, you lunk, can't you see? I'm yourself, older and more experienced—you have to believe me. Aloud he answered, "If you can't take my word, whose word can you take?"

"Joe" grunted. "I'm from Missouri," he said. "I'll see for myself."

Wilson was suddenly aware that "Joe" was about to step through the Gate. "Where are you going?"

"Through! I'm going to look up Diktor and have it out with him."

"Don't!" Wilson pleaded. "Maybe we can break the chain even now." But the stubborn sulky look on the other's face made him realize how futile it was. He was still enmeshed in inevitability; it *had* to happen. "Go ahead," he shrugged. "It's your funeral. I wash my hands of you."

"Joe" paused at the Gate. "It is, eh? Hm-m-m—how can it be my funeral unless it's your funeral, too?"

Wilson stared speechlessly while "Joe" stepped through the Gate. Whose funeral? He had not thought of it in quite that way. He felt a sudden impulse to rush through the Gate, catch up with his alter ego, and watch over him. The stupid fool might do anything. Suppose he got himself killed? Where would that leave Bob Wilson? Dead, of course.

Or would it? Could the death of a man thousands of years in the future kill *him* in the year 1942? He saw the absurdity of the situation suddenly, and felt very much relieved. "Joe's" actions could not endanger him; he remembered everything that "Joe" had done— was going to do. "Joe" would get into an argument with Diktor and, in due course of events, would come back through the Time Gate. No, *had* come back through the Time Gate. He was "Joe." It was hard to remember that.

Yes, he was "Joe." As well as the first guy. They would thread their courses, in and out and roundabout, and end up here, with *him*. Had to.

Wait a minute—in that case the whole crazy business was straightened out. He had gotten away from Diktor, had all of his various personalities sorted out, and was back where he started from, no worse for the wear except for a crop of whiskers and, possibly, a scar on his lip. Well, he knew when to let well enough alone. Shave, and get back to work, kid.

As he shaved he stared at his face and wondered why he had failed to recognize it the first time. He had to admit that he had never looked at it objectively before. He had always taken it for granted.

He acquired a crick in his neck from trying to look at his own profile through the corner of one eye.

On leaving the bathroom the Gate caught his eye forcibly. For some reason he had assumed that it would be gone. It was not. He inspected it, walked around it, carefully refrained from touching it. Wasn't the damned thing ever going to go away? It had served its purpose; why didn't Diktor shut it off?

He stood in front of it, felt a sudden surge of the compulsion that leads men to jump from high places. What would happen if he went through? What would he find? He thought of Arma. And the other one—what was her name? Perhaps Diktor had not told him. The other maidservant, anyhow, the second one.

But he restrained himself and forced himself to sit back down at the desk. If he was going to stay here—and of course he was, he was resolved on that point—he must finish the thesis. He had to eat; he needed the degree to get a decent job. Now where was he?

Twenty minutes later he had come to the conclusion that the thesis would have to be rewritten from one end to the other. His prime theme, the application of the empirical method of the problems of speculative metaphysics and its expression in rigorous formulae, was still valid, he decided, but he had acquired a mass of new and not yet digested data to incorporate in it. In re-reading his manuscript he was amazed to find how dogmatic he had been. Time after time he had fallen into the pathetic fallacy of DesCartes, mistaking clear reasoning for correct reasoning.

He tried to brief a new version of the thesis, but discovered that there were two problems he was forced to deal with which were decidedly not clear in his mind: the problem of the ego and the problem of free will. When there had been three of him in the room, which one was the ego—was *himself?* And how was it that he had been unable to change the course of events?

An absurdly obvious answer to the first question occurred to him at once. The ego was himself. Self is self, an unproved and unprovable first statement, directly experienced. What, then, of the other two? Surely they had been equally sure of ego-being—he remembered it. He thought of a way to state it: Ego is the point of consciousness, the latest term in a continuously expanding series along the line of memory duration. That sounded like a general statement, but he was not sure; he would have to try to formulate it mathematically before he could trust it. Verbal language had such queer booby traps in it.

The telephone rang.

He answered it absent-mindedly. "Yes?"

"Is that you, Bob?"

"Yes. Who is this?"

"Why, it's Genevieve, of course, darling. What's come over you today? That's the second time you've failed to recognize my voice."

Annoyance and frustration rose up in him. Here was another problem he had failed to settle—well, he'd settle it now. He ignored her complaint. "Look here, Genevieve, I've told you not to telephone me while I'm working Good-by!"

"Well, of all the— You can't talk that way to me, Bob Wilson! In the first place, you weren't working today. In the second place, what makes you think you can use honey and sweet words on me and two hours later snarl at me? I'm not any too sure I want to marry you."

"Marry you? What put that silly idea in your head?"

The phone sputtered for several seconds. When it had abated somewhat he resumed with, "Now just calm down. This isn't the Gay Nineties, you know. You can't assume that a fellow who takes you out a few times intends to marry you."

There was a short silence. "So that's the game, is it?" came an answer at last in a voice so cold and hard and completely shrewish that he almost failed to recognize it. "Well, there's a way to handle men like you. A woman isn't unprotected in this State!"

"You ought to know," he answered savagely. "You've hung around the campus enough years."

The receiver clicked in his ear.

He wiped the sweat from his forehead. That dame, he knew, was quite capable of causing him lots of trouble. He had been warned before he ever started running around with her, but he had been so sure of his own ability to take care of himself. He should have known better—but then he had not expected anything quite as raw as this.

He tried to get back to work on his thesis, but found himself unable to concentrate. The deadline of 10 a. m. the next morning seemed to be racing toward him. He looked at his watch. It had stopped. He set it by the desk clock—four fifteen in the afternoon. Even if he sat up all night he could not possibly finish it properly.

Besides there was Genevieve—

The telephone rang again. He let it ring. It continued; he took the receiver off the cradle. He would not talk to her again.

He thought of Arma. There was a proper girl with the right attitude. He walked over to the window and stared down into the dusty, noisy street. Half subconsciously he compared it with the green and placid countryside he had seen from the balcony where he and Diktor had breakfasted. This was a crummy world full of crummy people. He wished poignantly that Diktor had been on the up-and-up with him.

An idea broke surface in his brain and plunged around frantically. The Gate was still open. *The Gate was still open!* Why worry about Diktor? He was his own master. Go back and play it out—everything to gain, nothing to lose.

He stepped up to the Gate, then hesitated. Was he wise to do it? After all, how much did he know about the future?

He heard footsteps climbing the stairs, coming down the hall, no—yes, stopping at his door. He was suddenly convinced that it was Genevieve; that decided him. He stepped through.

The hall of the Gate was empty on his arrival. He hurried around the control box to the door and was just in time to hear, "Come on. There's work to be done." Two figures were retreating down the corridor. He recognized both of them and stopped suddenly.

That was a near thing, he told himself; I'll just have to wait until they get clear. He looked around for a place to conceal himself, but found nothing but the control box. That was useless; they were coming back. Still—

He entered the control box with a plan vaguely forming in his mind. If he found that he could dope out the controls, the Gate might give him all the advantage he needed. First he needed to turn on the speculum gadget. He felt around where he recalled having seen Diktor reach to turn it on, then reached in his pocket for a match.

Instead he pulled out a piece of paper. It was the list that Diktor had given him, the things he was to obtain in the twentieth century. Up to the present moment there had been too much going on for him to look it over.

His eyebrows crawled up his forehead as he read. It was a funny list, he decided. He had subconsciously expected it to call for technical reference books, samples of modern gadgets, weapons. There was nothing of the sort. Still, there was a sort of mad logic to the assortment. After all, Diktor knew these people better than he did. It might be just what was needed.

He revised his plans, subject to being able to work the Gate. He decided to make one more trip back and do the shopping Diktor's list called for—but for his own benefit, not Diktor's. He fumbled in the semidarkness of the control booth, seeking the switch or control for the speculum. His hand encountered a soft mass. He grasped it, and pulled it out.

It was his hat.

He placed it on his head, guessing idly that Diktor had stowed it there, and reached again. This time he brought forth a small note-book. It looked like a find—very possibly Diktor's own notes on the operation of the controls. He opened it eagerly.

It was not what he had hoped. But it did contain page after page of handwritten notes. There were three columns to the page; the first was in English, the second in international phonetic symbols, the third in a completely strange sort of writing. It took no brilliance for him to identify it as a vocabulary. He slipped it into a pocket with a broad smile; it might have taken Diktor months or even years to work out the relationship between the two languages; he would be able to ride on Diktor's shoulders in the matter.

The third try located the control and the speculum lighted up. He felt again the curious uneasiness he had felt before, for he was gazing again into his own room and again it was inhabited by two figures. He did not want to break into that scene again, he was sure. Cautiously he touched one of the colored beads.

The scene shifted, panned out through the walls of the boarding-house and came to rest in the air, three stories above the campus. He was pleased to have gotten the Gate out of the house, but three stories was too much of a jump. He fiddled with the other two colored beads and established that one of them caused the scene in the speculum to move toward him or away from him while the other moved it up or down.

He wanted a reasonably inconspicuous place to locate the Gate, some place where it would not attract the attention of the curious. This bothered him a bit; there was no ideal place, but he compromised on a blind alley, a little court formed by the campus power-house and the rear wall of the library. Cautiously and clumsily he maneuvered his flying eye to the neighborhood he wanted and set it down carefully between the two buildings. He then readjusted his position so that he stared right into a blank wall. Good enough!

Leaving the controls as they were, he hurried out of the booth and stepped unceremoniously back into his own period.

He bumped his nose against the brick wall. "I cut that a little too fine," he mused as he slid cautiously out from between the confining limits of the wall and the Gate. The Gate hung in the air, about fifteen inches from the wall and roughly parallel to it. But there was room enough, he decided—no need to go back and readjust the controls. He ducked out of the areaway and cut across the campus toward the Students' Co-op, wasting no time. He entered and went to the cashier's window.

"Hi, Bob."

"H'lo, Soupy. Cash a check for me?"

"How much?"

"Twenty dollars."

"Well—I suppose so. Is it a good check?"

"Not very. It's my own."

"Well, I might invest in it as a curiosity." He counted out a ten, a five, and five ones.

"Do that," advised Wilson. "My autographs are going to be rare collectors' items." He passed over the check, took the money, and proceeded to the bookstore in the same building. Most of the books on the list were for sale there. Ten minutes later he had acquired title to:

"The Prince," by Niccolo Machiavelli.

"Behind the Ballots," by James Farley.

"Mein Kampf" (unexpurgated), by Adolf Schicklegruber.

"How to Win Friends and Influence People," by Dale Carnegie.

The other titles he wanted were not available in the bookstore; he went from there to the university library where he drew out "Real Estate Broker's Manual," "History of Musical Instruments," and a quarto titled "Evolution of Dress Styles." The latter was a handsome volume with beautiful colored plates and was classified as reference. He had to argue a little to get a twenty-four hour permission for it.

He was fairly well loaded down by then; he left the campus, went to a pawnshop and purchased two used, but sturdy, suitcases into one of which he packed the books. From there he went to the largest music store in the town and spent forty-five minutes in selecting and rejecting phonograph records, with emphasis on swing and boogie-woogie—highly emotional stuff, all of it. He did not neglect classical and semi-classical, but he applied the same rule to those categories— a piece of music had to be sensuous and compelling, rather than cerebral. In consequence his collection included such strangely assorted items as the "Marseillaise," Ravel's "Bolero," four Cole Porter's, and "L'Après-midi d'un Faune."

He insisted on buying the best mechanical reproducer on the market in the face of the clerk's insistence that what he needed was an electrical one. But he finally got his own way, wrote a check for the order, packed it all in his suitcases, and had the clerk get a taxi for him.

He had a bad moment over the check. It was pure rubber, as the one he had cashed at the Students' Co-op had cleaned out his balance. He had urged them to phone the bank, since that was what he wished them not to do. It had worked. He had established, he reflected, the all-time record for kiting checks—thirty thousand years.

When the taxi drew up opposite the court where he had located the Gate, he jumped out and hurried in.

The Gate was gone.

He stood there for several minutes, whistling softly, and assessing —unfavorably—his own abilities, mental processes, et cetera. The consequences of writing bad checks no longer seemed quite so hypothetical.

He felt a touch at his sleeve. "See here, Bud, do you want my hack, or don't you? The meter's still clicking."

"Huh? Oh, sure." He followed the driver, climbed back in.

"Where to?"

That was a problem. He glanced at his watch, then realized that the usually reliable instrument had been through a process which rendered its reading irrelevant. "What time is it?"

"Two fifteen." He reset his watch.

Two fifteen. There would be a jamboree going on in his room at that time of a particularly confusing sort. He did not want to go there—not yet. Not until his blood brothers got through playing happy fun games with the Gate.

The Gate!

It would be in his room until sometime after four fifteen. If he timed it right— "Drive to the corner of Fourth and McKinley," he directed, naming the intersection closest to his boardinghouse.

He paid off the taxi driver there, and lugged his bags into the filling station at that corner, where he obtained permission from the attendant to leave them and assurance that they would be safe. He had nearly two hours to kill. He was reluctant to go very far from the house for fear some hitch would upset his timing.

It occurred to him that there was one piece of unfinished business in the immediate neighborhood—and time enough to take care of it.

He walked briskly to a point two streets away, whistling cheerfully, and turned in at an apartment house.

In response to his knock the door of Apartment 211 was opened a crack, then wider. "Bob darling! I thought you were working today."

"Hi, Genevieve. Not at all—I've got time to burn."

She glanced back over her shoulder. "I don't know whether I should let you come in—I wasn't expecting you. I haven't washed the dishes, or made the bed. I was just putting on my make-up."

"Don't be coy." He pushed the door open wide, and went on in.

When he came out he glanced at his watch. Three thirty—plenty of time. He went down the street wearing the expression of the canary that ate the cat.

He thanked the service station salesman and gave him a quarter for his trouble, which left him with a lone nickel. He looked at this coin, grinned to himself, and inserted it in the pay phone in the office of the station. He dialed his own number.

"Hello," he heard.

"Hello," he replied. "Is that Bob Wilson?"

"Yes. Who is this?"

"Never mind," he chuckled. "I just wanted to be sure you were there. I thought you would be. You're right in the groove, kid, right in the groove." He replaced the receiver with a grin.

At four ten he was too nervous to wait any longer. Struggling under the load of the heavy suitcases he made his way to the boarding house. He let himself in and heard a telephone ringing upstairs. He glanced at his watch—tour fifteen. He waited in the hall for three interminable minutes, then labored up the stairs and down the upper hallway to his own door. He unlocked the door and let himself in.

The room was empty, the Gate still there.

Without stopping for anything, filled with apprehension lest the Gate should flicker and disappear while he crossed the floor, he hurried to it, took a firm grip on his bags, and strode through it.

The Hall of the Gate was empty, to his great relief. What a break, he told himself thankfully. Just five minutes, that's all I ask. Five uninterrupted minutes. He set the suitcases down near the Gate to be ready for a quick departure. As he did so he noticed that a large chunk was missing from a corner of one case. Half a book showed through the opening, sheared as neatly as with a printer's trimmer. He identified it as "Mein Kampf."

He did not mind the loss of the book but the implications made him slightly sick at his stomach. Suppose he had not described a clear arc when he had first been knocked through the Gate, had hit the edge, half in and half out? Man Sawed in Half—and no illusion!

He wiped his face and went to the control booth. Following Diktor's simple instructions he brought all four spheres together at the center of the tetrahedron. He glanced over the side of the booth and saw that the Gate had disappeared entirely. "Check!" he thought. "Everything on zero—no Gate." He moved the white sphere slightly. The Gate reappeared. Turning on the speculum he was able to see that the miniature scene showed the inside of the Hall of the Gate itself. So far so good—but he would not be able to tell what time the Gate was set for by looking into the Hall. He displaced a space control slightly; the scene flickered past the walls of the palace and hung in the open air. Returning the white time control to zero he then displaced it very, very slightly. In the miniature scene the sun became a streak of brightness across the sky; the days flickered past like light from a low frequency source of illumination. He increased the displacement a little, saw the ground become sear and brown, then snow covered, and finally green again.

Working cautiously, steadying his right hand with his left, he made the seasons march past. He had counted ten winters when he became aware of voices somewhere in the distance. He stopped and listened, then very hastily returned the space controls to zero, leaving the time control as it was—set for ten years in the past—and rushed out of the booth.

He hardly had time to grasp his bags, lift them, and swing them through the Gate, himself with them. This time he was exceedingly careful not to touch the edge of the circle.

He found himself, as he had planned to, still in the Hall of the Gate, but, if he had interpreted the controls correctly, ten years away from the events he had recently participated in. He had intended to give Diktor a wider berth than that, but there had been no time for it. However, he reflected, since Diktor was, by his own statement and the evidence of the little notebook Wilson had lifted from him, a native of the twentieth century, it was quite possible that ten years was enough. Diktor might not be in this era. If he was, there was always the Time Gate for a gateway. But it was reasonable to scout out the situation first before making any more jumps.

It suddenly occurred to him that Diktor might be looking at him through the speculum of the Time Gate. Without stopping to consider that speed was no protection—since the speculum could be used to view any time sector— -he hurriedly dragged his two suitcases into the cover of the control booth. Once inside the protecting walls of the booth he calmed down a bit. Spying could work both ways. He found the controls set at zero; making use of the same process he had used once before, he ran the scene in the speculum forward through ten years, then cautiously hunted with the space controls on zero. It was a very difficult task; the time scale necessary to hunt through several months in a few minutes caused any figure which might appear in the speculum to flash past at an apparent speed too fast for his eye to follow. Several times he thought he detected flitting shadows which might be human beings but he was never able to find them when he stopped moving the time control.

He wondered in great exasperation why whoever had built the double-damned gadget had failed to provide it with graduations and some sort of delicate control mechanism—a vernier, or the like. It was not until much later that it occurred to him that the creator of the Time Gate might have no need of such gross aids to his senses. He would have given up, was about to give up, when, purely by accident, one more fruitless scanning happened to terminate with a figure in the field.

It was himself, carrying two suitcases. He saw himself walking directly into the field of view, grow large, disappear. He looked over the rail, half expecting to see himself step out of the Gate.

But nothing came out of the Gate. It puzzled him, until he recalled that it was the setting at that end, ten years in the future, which controlled the time of egress. But he had what he wanted; he sat back and watched. Almost immediately Diktor and another edition of himself appeared in the scene. He recalled the situation when he saw it portrayed in the speculum. It was Bob Wilson number three, about to quarrel with Diktor and make his escape back to the twentieth century.

That was that—Diktor had not seen him, did not know that he had made unauthorized use of the Gate, did not know that he was hiding ten years in the "past," would not look for him there. He returned the controls to zero, and dismissed the matter.

But other matters needed his attention—food, especially. It seemed obvious, in retrospect, that he should have brought along food to last him for a day or two at least. And maybe a .45. He had to admit that he had not been very foresighted. But he easily forgave himself—it was hard to be foresighted when the future kept slipping up behind one. "All right, Bob, old boy," he told himself aloud, "let's see if the natives are friendly—as advertised."

A cautious reconnoiter of the small part of the Palace with which he was acquainted turned up no human beings, nor life of any sort, not even insect life. The place was dead, sterile, as static and unlived-in as a window display. He shouted once, just to hear a voice. The echoes caused him to shiver; he did not do it again.

The architecture of the place confused him. Not only was it strange to his experience—he had expected that—but the place, with minor exceptions, seemed totally unadapted to the uses of human beings. Great halls large enough to hold ten thousand people at once—had there been floors for them to stand on. For there frequently were no floors in the accepted meaning of a level or reasonably level platform. In following a passageway he came suddenly to one of the great mysterious openings in the structure and almost fell in before he realized that his path had terminated. He crawled gingerly forward and looked over the edge. The mouth of the passage debouched high up on a wall of the place; below him the wall was cut back so that there was not even a vertical surface for the eye to follow. Far below him, the wall curved back and met its mate of the opposite side—not decently, in a horizontal plane, but at an acute angle.

There were other openings scattered around the walls, openings as unserviceable to human beings as the one in which he crouched. "The High Ones," he whispered to himself. All his cockiness was gone out of him. He retraced his steps through the fine dust and reached the almost friendly familiarity of the Hall of the Gate.

On his second try he attempted only those passages and compartments which seemed obviously adapted to men. He had already decided what such parts of the Palace must be—servants' quarters, or, more probably, slaves' quarters. He regained his courage by sticking to such area. Though deserted completely, by contrast with the rest of the great structure a room or a passage which seemed to have been built for men was friendly and cheerful. The sourceless ever-present illumination and the unbroken silence still bothered him, but not to the degree to which he had been upset by the Gargantuan and mysteriously convoluted chambers of the "High Ones."

He had almost despaired of finding his way out of the Palace and was thinking of retracing his steps when the corridor he was following turned and he found himself in bright sunlight.

He was standing at the top of a broad steep ramp which spread fanlike down to the base of the building. Ahead of him and below him, distant at least five hundred yards, the pavement of the ramp met the green of sod and bush and tree. It was the same placid, lush, and familiar scene he had looked out over when he breakfasted with Diktor—a few hours ago and ten years in the future.

He stood quietly for a short time, drinking in the sunshine, soaking up the heart-lifting beauty of the warm, spring day. "This is going to be all right," he exulted. "It's a grand place."

He moved slowly down the ramp, his eyes searching for human beings. He was halfway down when he saw a small figure emerge from the trees into a clearing near the foot of the ramp. He called out to it in joyous excitement. The child—it was a child he saw—looked up, stared at him for a moment, then fled back into the shelter of the trees.

"Impetuous, Robert—that's what you are," he chided himself. "Don't scare 'em. Take it easy." But he was not made downhearted by the incident. Where there were children there would be parents, society, opportunities for a bright, young fellow who took a broad view of things. He moved on down at a leisurely pace.

A man showed up at the point where the child had disappeared. Wilson stood still. The man looked him over and advanced hesitantly a step or two. "Come here!" Wilson invited in a friendly voice. "I won't hurt you."

The man could hardly have understood his words, but he advanced slowly. At the edge of the pavement he stopped, eyed it and would not proceed farther.

Something about the behavior pattern clicked in Wilson's brain, fitted in with what he had seen in the Palace, and with the little that Diktor had told him. "Unless," he told himself, "the time I spent in 'Anthropology I' was totally wasted, this Palace is tabu, and the ramp I'm standing on is tabu, and, by contagion, I'm tabu. Play your cards, son, play your cards!"

He advanced to the edge of the pavement, being careful not to step off it. The man dropped to his knees and cupped his hands in front of him, head bowed. Without hesitation Wilson touched him on the forehead. The man got back to his feet, his face radiant.

"This isn't even sporting," Wilson said. "I ought to shoot him on the rise."

His Man Friday cocked his head, looked puzzled, and answered in a deep, melodious voice. The words were liquid and strange and sounded like a phrase from a song. "You ought to commercialize that voice," Wilson said admiringly. "Some stars get by on less. However—Get along now, and fetch something to eat. Food." He pointed to his mouth.

The man looked hesitant, spoke again. Bob Wilson reached into his pocket and took out the stolen notebook. He looked up "eat," then looked up "food." It was the same word. "Blellan," he said carefully.

"Blellaaaan?"

"Blellaaaaaaaan," agreed Wilson. "You'll have to excuse my accent. Hurry up." He tried to find "hurry" in the vocabulary, but it was not there. Either the language did not contain the idea or Diktor had not thought it worth while to record it. But we'll soon fix that, Wilson thought—if there isn't such a word, I'll give 'em one.

The man departed.

Wilson sat himself down Turk-fashion and passed the time by studying the notebook. The speed of his rise in these parts, he decided, was limited only by the time it took him to get into full communication. But he had only time enough to look up a few common substantives when his first acquaintance returned, in company.

The procession was headed by an extremely elderly man, white-haired but beardless. All of the men were beardless. He walked under a canopy carried by four male striplings. Only he of all the crowd wore enough clothes to get by anywhere but on a beach. He was looking uncomfortable in a sort of toga effect which appeared to have started life as a Roman-striped awning. That he was the head man was evident.

Wilson hurriedly looked up the word for "chief."

The word for chief was "Diktor."

It should not have surprised him, but it did. It was, of course, a logical probability that the word "Diktor" was a title rather than a proper name. It simply had not occurred to him.

Diktor—the Diktor—had added a note under the word. "One of the few words," Wilson read, "which shows some probability of having been derived from the dead languages. This word, a few dozen others, and the grammatical structure of the language itself, appear to be the only link between the language of the 'Forsaken Ones' and the English language."

The chief stopped in front of Wilson, just short of the pavement. "O. K., Diktor," Wilson ordered, "kneel down. You're not exempt." He pointed to the ground. The chief knelt down. Wilson touched his forehead.

The food that had been fetched along was plentiful and very palatable. Wilson ate slowly and with dignity, keeping in mind the importance of face. While he ate he was serenaded by the entire assemblage. The singing was excellent, he was bound to admit. Their ideas of harmony he found a little strange and the performance, as a whole, seemed primitive, but their voices were all clear and mellow and they sang as if they enjoyed it.

The concert gave Wilson an idea. After he had satisfied his hunger he made the chief understand, with the aid of the indispensable little notebook, that he and his flock were to wait where they were. He then returned to the Hall of the Gate and brought back from there the phonograph and a dozen assorted records. He treated them to a recorded concert of "modern" music.

The reaction exceeded his hopes. "Begin the Beguine" caused tears to stream down the face of the old chief. The first movement of Tschaikowsky's "Concerto Number One in B Flat Minor" practically stampeded them. They jerked. They held their heads and moaned. They shouted their applause. Wilson refrained from giving them the second movement, tapered them off instead with the compelling monotony of the "Bolero."

"Diktor," he said—he was not thinking of the old chief—"Diktor, old chum, you certainly had these people doped out when you sent me shopping. By the time you show up—if you ever do—I'll own the place."

This is not an account of how Boosterism came to Arcadia. Wilson's rise to power was more in the nature of a triumphal progress than a struggle for supremacy; it contained little that was dramatic. Whatever it was that the High Ones had done to the human race it had left them with only physical resemblance and with temperament largely changed. The docile friendly children with whom Wilson dealt had little in common with the brawling, vulgar, lusty, dynamic swarms who had once called themselves the People of the United States.

The relationship was like that of Jersey cattle to longhorns, or cocker spaniels to wolves. The fight was gone out of them. It was not that they lacked intelligence, nor civilized arts; it was the competitive spirit that was gone, the will-to-power.

Wilson had a monopoly on that.

But even he lost interest in playing a game that he always won. Having established himself as boss man by taking up residence in the Palace and representing himself as the viceroy of the departed High Ones, he, for a time, busied himself in organizing certain projects intended to bring the culture "up-to-date"—the reinvention of musical instruments, establishment of a systematic system of mail service, redevelopment of the idea of styles in dress and a tabu against wearing the same fashion more than one season. There was cunning in the latter project. He figured that arousing a hearty interest in display in the minds of the womenfolk would force the men to hustle to satisfy their wishes. What the culture lacked was drive—it was slipping downhill. He tried to give them the drive they lacked.

His subjects co-operated with his wishes, but in a bemused fashion, like a dog performing a trick, not because he understands it, but because his master and godhead desires it.

He soon tired of it.

But the mystery of the High Ones, and especially the mystery of their Time Gate, still remained to occupy his mind. His was a mixed nature, half hustler, half philosopher. The philosopher had his inning.

It was intellectually necessary to him that he be able to construct in his mind a physio-mathematical model for the phenomena exhibited by the Time Gate. He achieved one, not a good one perhaps, but one which satisfied all of the requirements. Think of a plane surface, a sheet of paper, or, better yet, a silk handkerchief—silk, because it has no rigidity, folds easily, while maintaining all of the relational attributes of a two-dimensional continuum on the surface of the silk itself. Let the threads of the woof be the dimension—or direction—of time; let the threads of the warp represent all three of the space dimensions.

An ink spot on the handkerchief becomes the Time Gate. By folding the handkerchief that spot may be superposed on any other spot on the silk. Press the two spots together between thumb and forefinger; the controls are set, the Time Gate is open, a microscopic inhabitant of this piece of silk may crawl from one fold to the other without traversing any other part of the cloth.

The model is imperfect; the picture is static—but a physical picture is necessarily limited by the sensory experience of the person visualizing it.

He could not make up his mind whether or not the concept of folding the four-dimensional continuum—three of space, one of time —back on itself so that the Gate was "open" required the concept of higher dimensions through which to fold it. It seemed so, yet it might simply be an intellectual shortcoming of the human mind. Nothing but empty space was required for the "folding," but "empty space" was itself a term totally lacking in meaning—he was enough of a mathematician to know that.

If higher dimensions were required to "hold" a four-dimensional continuum, then the number of dimensions of space and of time were necessarily infinite; each order requires the next higher order to maintain it.

But "infinite" was another meaningless term. "Open series" was a little better, but not much.

Another consideration forced him to conclude that there was probably at least one more dimension than the four his senses could perceive—the Time Gate itself. He became quite skilled in handling its controls, but he never acquired the foggiest notion of how it worked, or how it had been built. It seemed to him that the creatures who built it must necessarily have been able to stand outside the limits that confined him in order to anchor the Gate to the structure of space time. The concept escaped him.

He suspected that the controls he saw were simply the part that stuck through into the space he knew. The very Palace itself might be no more than a three-dimensional section of a more involved structure. Such a condition would help to explain the otherwise inexplicable nature of its architecture.

He became possessed of an overpowering desire to know more about these strange creatures, the "High Ones," who had come and ruled the human race and built this Palace and this Gate, and gone away again—and in whose backwash he had been flung out of his setting some thirty millennia. To the human race they were no more than a sacred myth, a contradictory mass of tradition. No picture of them remained, no trace of their writing, nothing of their works save the High Palace of Norkaal and the Gate. And a sense of irreparable loss in the hearts of the race they had ruled, a loss expressed by their own term for themselves—the Forsaken Ones.

With controls and speculum he hunted back through time, seeking the Builders. It was slow work, as he had found before. A passing shadow, a tedious retracing—and failure.

Once he was sure that he had seen such a shadow in the miniature Hall reflected in the speculum. He set the controls back far enough to be sure that he had repassed it, armed himself with food and drink, and waited.

He waited three weeks.

The shadow might have passed during the hours he was forced to take out for sleep. But he felt sure that he was in the right period; he kept up the vigil.

He saw it.

It was moving toward the Gate.

When he pulled himself together he was halfway down the passageway leading away from the Hall. He realized that he had been screaming. He still had an attack of the shakes.

Somewhat later he forced himself to return to the Hall, and, with eyes averted, enter the control booth and return the spheres to zero. He backed out hastily and left the Hall for his apartment. He did not touch the controls nor enter the Hall for more than two years.

It had not been fear of physical menace that had shaken his reason, nor the appearance of the creature—he could recall nothing of *how* it looked. It had been a feeling of sadness infinitely compounded which had flooded through him at the instant, a sense of tragedy, of grief insupportable and unescapable, of infinite weariness. He had been flicked with emotions many times too strong for his spiritual fiber and which he was no more fitted to experience than an oyster is to play a violin.

He felt that he had learned all about the High Ones a man could learn and still endure. He was no longer curious. The shadow of that vicarious emotion ruined his sleep, brought him sweating out of dreams.

One other problem bothered him—the problem of himself and his meanders through time. It still worried him that he had met himself coming back, so to speak, had talked with himself, fought with himself.

Which one was *himself*?

He was all of them, he knew, for he remembered being each one. How about the times when there had been more than one present? By sheer necessity he was forced to expand the principle of non-identity—"Nothing is identical with anything else, not even with itself"—to include the ego. In a four-dimensional continuum each event is an absolute individual, it has its space co-ordinates and its date. The Bob Wilson he was right now was *not* the Bob Wilson he had been ten minutes ago. Each was a discrete section of a four-dimensional process. One resembled the other in many particulars, as one slice of bread resembles the slice next to it. But they were *not* the same Bob Wilson—they differed by a length of time.

When he had doubled back on himself, the difference had become apparent, for the separation was now in space rather than in time, and he happened to be so equipped as to be able to see a space length, whereas he could only remember a time difference. Thinking back he could remember a great many different Bob Wilsons, baby, small child, adolescent, young man. They were all different—he knew that. The only thing that bound them together into a feeling of identity was continuity of memory.

And that was the same thing that bound together the three—no, four, Bob Wilsons on a certain crowded afternoon, a memory track that ran through all of them. The only thing about it that remained remarkable was time travel itself.

And a few other little items—the nature of "free will," the problem of entropy, the law of the conservation of energy and mass. The last two, he now realized, needed to be extended or generalized to include the cases in which the Gate, or something like it, permitted a leak of mass, energy, or entropy from one neighborhood in the continuum to another. They were otherwise unchanged and valid. Free will was another matter. It could not be laughed off, because it could be directly experienced—yet his own free will had worked to create the same scene over and over again. Apparently human will must be considered as one of the factors which make up the processes in the continuum—"free" to the ego, mechanistic from the outside.

And yet his last act of evading Diktor had apparently changed the course of events. He was here and running the country, had been for many years, but Diktor had not showed up. Could it be that each act of "true" free will created a new and different future? Many philosophers had thought so.

This future appeared to have no such person as Diktor—*the* Diktor—in it, anywhere or anywhen.

As the end of his first ten years in the future approached, he became more and more nervous, less and less certain of his opinion. Damnation, he thought, if Diktor is going to show up it was high time that he did so. He was anxious to come to grips with him, establish which was to be boss.

He had agents posted throughout the country of the Forsaken Ones with instructions to arrest any man with hair on his face and fetch him forthwith to the Palace. The Hall of the Gate he watched himself.

He tried fishing the future for Diktor, but had no significant luck. He thrice located a shadow and tracked it down; each time it was himself. From tedium and partly from curiosity he attempted to see the other end of the process; he tried to relocate his original home, thirty thousand years in the past.

It was a long chore. The further the time button was displaced from the center, the poorer the control became. It took patient practice to be able to stop the image within a century or so of the period he wanted. It was in the course of this experimentation that he discovered what he had once looked for, a fractional control—a vernier, in effect. It was as simple as the primary control, but twist the bead instead of moving it directly.

He steadied down on the twentieth century, approximated the year by the models of automobiles, types of architecture, and other gross evidence, and stopped in what he believed to be 1942. Careful displacement of the space controls took him to the university town where he had started—after several false tries; the image did not enable him to read road signs.

He located his boardinghouse, brought the Gate into his own room. It was vacant, no furniture in it.

He panned away from the room, and tried again, a year earlier. Success—his own room, his own furniture, but empty. He ran rapidly back, looking for shadows.

There! He checked the swing of the image. There were three figures in the room, the image was too small, the light too poor for him to be sure whether or not one of them was himself. He leaned over and studied the scene.

He heard a dull thump outside the booth. He straightened up and looked over the side.

Sprawled on the floor was a limp human figure. Near it lay a crushed and battered hat.

He stood perfectly still for an uncounted time, staring at the two redundant figures, hat and man, while the winds of unreason swept through his mind and shook it. He did not need to examine the unconscious form to identify it. He knew . . . *he knew*—it was his younger self, knocked willy-nilly through the Time Gate.

It was not that fact in itself which shook him. He had not particularly expected it to happen, having come tentatively to the conclusion that he was living in a different, an alternative, future from the one in which he had originally transmitted the Time Gate. He had been aware that it might happen, nevertheless, that it did happen did not surprise him.

When it did happen, *he himself had been the only spectator!*

He was Diktor. He was *the* Diktor. He was *the only* Diktor!

He would never find Diktor, nor have it out with him. He need never fear his coming. There never had been, never would be, any other person called Diktor, because Diktor never had been nor ever would be anyone but himself.

In review, it seemed obvious that he must be Diktor; there were so many bits of evidence pointing to it. And yet it had not been obvious. Each point of similarity between himself and the Diktor, he recalled, had arisen from rational causes—usually from his desire to ape the gross characteristics of the "other" and thereby consolidate his own position of power and authority before the "other" Diktor showed up. For that reason he had established himself in the very apartments that "Diktor" had used—so that they would be "his" first.

To be sure his people called him Diktor, but he had thought nothing of that—they called anyone who ruled by that title, even the little subchieftains who were his local administrators.

He had grown a beard, such as Diktor had worn, partly in imitation of the "other" man's precedent, but more to set him apart from the hairless males of the Forsaken Ones. It gave him prestige, increased his tabu. He fingered his bearded chin. Still, it seemed strange that he had not recalled that his own present appearance checked with the appearance of "Diktor." "Diktor" had been an older man. He himself was only thirty-two, ten here, twenty-two *there*.

Diktor he had judged to be about forty-five. Perhaps an unprejudiced witness would believe himself to be that age. His hair and beard were shot with gray—had been, ever since the year he had succeeded too well in spying on the High Ones. His face was lined. Uneasy lies the head and so forth. Running a country, even a peaceful Arcadia, will worry a man, keep him awake nights.

Not that he was complaining—it had been a good life, a grand life, and it beat anything the ancient past had to offer.

In any case, he had been looking for a man in his middle forties, whose face he remembered dimly after ten years and whose picture he did not have. It had never occurred to him to connect that blurred face with his present one. Naturally not.

But there were other little things. Arma, for example. He had selected a likely-looking lass some three years back and made her one of his household staff, renaming her Arma in sentimental memory of the girl he had once fancied. It was logically necessary that they were the same girl, not two Armas, but one.

But, as he recalled her, the "first" Arma had been much prettier.

Hm-m-m—it must be his own point of view that had changed. He admitted that he had had much more opportunity to become bored with exquisite female beauty than his young friend over there on the floor. He recalled with a chuckle how he had found it necessary to surround himself with an elaborate system of tabus to keep the nubile daughters of his subjects out of his hair—most of the time. He had caused a particular pool in the river adjacent to the Palace to be dedicated to his use in order that he might swim without getting tangled up in mermaids.

The man on the floor groaned, but did not open his eyes.

Wilson, the Diktor, bent over him but made no effort to revive him. That the man was not seriously injured he had reason to be certain. He did not wish him to wake up until he had had time to get his own thoughts entirely in order.

For he had work to do, work which must be done meticulously, without mistake. Everyone, he thought with a wry smile, makes plans to provide for their future.

He was about to provide for his past.

There was the matter of the setting of the Time Gate when he got around to sending his early self back. When he had tuned in on the scene in his room a few minutes ago, he had picked up the action just before his early self had been knocked through. In sending him back he must make a slight readjustment in the time setting to an instant around two o'clock of that particular afternoon. That would be simple enough; he need only search a short sector until he found his early self alone and working at his desk.

But the Time Gate had appeared in that room at a later hour; he had just caused it to do so. He felt confused.

Wait a minute, now—if he changed the setting of the time control, the Gate would appear in his room at the earlier time, remain there, and simply blend into its "reappearance" an hour or so later. Yes, that was right. To a person in the room it would simply be as if the Time Gate had been there all along, from about two o'clock.

Which it had been. He would see to that.

Experienced as he was with the phenomena exhibited by the Time Gate, it nevertheless required a strong and subtle intellectual effort to think other than in durational terms, to take an eternal viewpoint.

And there was the hat. He picked it up and tried it on. It did not fit very well, no doubt because he was wearing his hair longer now. The hat must be placed where it would be found— Oh, yes, in the control booth. And the notebook, too.

The notebook, the notebook— Mm-m-m— Something funny, there. When the notebook he had stolen had become dog-eared and tattered almost to illegibility some four years back, he had carefully recopied its contents in a new notebook—to refresh his memory of English rather than from any need for it as a guide. The worn-out notebook he had destroyed; it was the new one he intended to obtain, and leave to be found.

In that case, there never had been two notebooks. The one he had now would become, after being taken through the Gate to a point ten years in the past, the notebook from which he had copied it. They were simply different segments of the same physical process, manipulated by means of the Gate to run concurrently, side by side, for a certain length of time.

As he had himself—one afternoon.

He wished that he had not thrown away the worn-out notebook. If he had it at hand, he could compare them and convince himself that they were identical save for the wear and tear of increasing entropy.

But when had he learned the language, in order that he might prepare such a vocabulary? To be sure, when he copied it he then knew the language—copying had not actually been necessary.

But he had copied it.

The physical process he had all straightened out in his mind, but the intellectual process it represented was completely circular. His older self had taught his younger self a language which the older self knew because the younger self, after being taught, grew up to be the older self and was, therefore, capable of teaching.

But where had it started?

Which comes first, the hen or the egg?

You feed the rats to the cats, skin the cats, and feed the carcasses of the cats to the rats who are in turn fed to the cats. The perpetual motion fur farm.

If God created the world, who created God?

Who wrote the notebook? Who started the chain?

He felt the intellectual desperation of any honest philosopher. He knew that he had about as much chance of understanding such problems as a collie has of understanding how dog food gets into cans. Applied psychology was more his size—which reminded him that there were certain books which his early self would find very useful in learning how to deal with the political affairs of the country he was to run. He made a mental note to make a list.

The man on the floor stirred again, sat up. Wilson knew that the time had come when he must insure his past. He was not worried; he felt the sure confidence of the gambler who is "hot," who knows what the next roll of the dice will show.

He bent over his alter ego. "Are you all right?" he asked.

"I guess so," the younger man mumbled. He put his hand to his bloody face. "My head hurts."

"I should think it would," Wilson agreed. "You came through head over heels. I think you hit your head when you landed."

His younger self did not appear fully to comprehend the words at first. He looked around dazedly, as if to get his bearings. Presently he said, "Came through? Came through what?"

"The Gate, of course," Wilson told him. He nodded his head toward the Gate, feeling that the sight of it would orient the still groggy younger Bob.

Young Wilson looked over his shoulder in the direction indicated, sat up with a jerk, shuddered and closed his eyes. He opened them again after what seemed to be a short period of prayer, looked again, and said, "Did I come through that?"

"Yes," Wilson assured him.

"Where am I?"

"In the Hall of the Gate in the High Palace of Norkaal. But what is more important," Wilson added, "is when you are. You have gone forward a little more than thirty thousand years."

The knowledge did not seem to reassure him. He got up and stumbled toward the Gate. Wilson put a restraining hand on his shoulder. "Where are you going?"

"Back!"

"Not so fast." He did not dare let him go back yet, not until the Gate had been reset. Besides he was still drunk—his breath was staggering. "You will go back all right—I give you my word on that. But let me dress your wounds first. And you should rest. I have some explanations to make to you, and there is an errand you can do for me when you get back—to our mutual advantage. There is a great future in store for you and me, my boy—a great future!"

A great future!

THE STAR MOUSE

by

FREDRIC BROWN

> Here, told for the first time in full detail, is the story of the
> first voyager in space. Mitkey (sic!) the Mouse, who sallied forth
> for the moon but landed on the asteroid Prxl, instead! And came
> back with a complete, if unstable, education. A science-fiction
> story that is a delightful fairy tale and a perfect scenario for a
> Disney cartoon.

*

MITKEY, THE MOUSE, wasn't Mitkey then.

He was just another mouse, who lived behind the floorboards and
plaster of the house of the great Herr Professor Oberburger, formerly
of Vienna and Heidelberg; then a refugee from the excessive admiration of the more powerful of his fellow-countrymen. The excessive admiration had concerned, not Herr Oberburger himself, but a certain
gas which had been a by-product of an unsuccessful rocket fuel—
which might have been a highly successful something else.

If, of course, the Professor had given them the correct formula.
Which he—Well, anyway, the Professor had made good his escape
and now lived in a house in Connecticut. And so did Mitkey.

A small gray mouse, and a small gray man. Nothing unusual about
either of them. Particularly there was nothing unusual about Mitkey;
he had a family and he liked cheese and if there were Rotarians
among mice, he would have been a Rotarian.

The Herr Professor, of course, had his mild eccentricities. A confirmed bachelor, he had no one to talk to except himself, but he

considered himself an excellent conversationalist and held constant
verbal communion with himself while he worked. That fact, it
turned out later, was important, because Mitkey had excellent ears
and heard those night-long soliloquies. He didn't understand them,
of course. If he thought about them at all, he merely thought of the
Professor as a large and noisy super-mouse who squeaked over-much.

"Und now," he would say to himself, "ve vill see vether this
eggshaust tube vas broberly machined. It should fidt vithin vun vun-
hundredth thousandth uf an indtch. Ahhh, it iss berfect. Und
now—"

Night after night, day after day, month after month. The gleaming
thing grew, and the gleam in Herr Oberburger's eyes grew apace.

It was about three and a half feet long, with weirdly shaped vanes,
and it rested on a temporary framework on a table in the center of
the room that served the Herr Professor for all purposes. The house
in which he and Mitkey lived was a four room structure, but the
Professor hadn't yet found it out, seemingly. Originally, he had
planned to use the big room as a laboratory only, but he found it
more convenient to sleep on a cot in one corner of it, when he slept
at all, and to do the little cooking he did over the same gas burner
over which he melted down golden grains of TNT into a dangerous
soup which he salted and peppered with strange condiments, but
did not eat.

"Und now I shall bour it into tubes, und see vether vun tube
adjacendt to another eggsplodes der secondt tube vhen der virst tube
iss—"

That was the night Mitkey almost decided to move himself and
his family to a more stable abode, one that did not rock and sway
and try to turn handsprings on its foundations. But Mitkey didn't
move after all, because there were compensations. New mouse-holes
all over, and—joy of joy!—a big crack in the back of the refrigerator
where the Professor kept, among other things, food.

Of course the tubes had been not larger than capillary size, or the
house would not have remained around the mouse-holes. And of
course Mitkey could not guess what was coming nor understand the
Herr Professor's brand of English (nor any other brand of English,
for that matter) or he would not have let even a crack in the
refrigerator tempt him.

The Professor was jubilant that morning.

"Der fuel, idt vorks! Der secondt tube, idt did not eggsplode.

Und der virst, in *segotions*, as I had eggspectedt! Und it is more bowerful; there will be blenty of room for der combartment—"

Ah, yes, the compartment. That was where Mitkey came in, although even the Professor didn't know it yet. In fact the Professor didn't even know that Mitkey existed.

"Und now," he was saying to his favorite listener, "idt is budt a madter of combining der fuel tubes so they work in obbosite bairs. Und then—"

That was the moment when the Herr Professor's eyes first fell on Mitkey. Rather, they fell upon a pair of gray whiskers and a black, shiny little nose protruding from a hole in the baseboards.

"Vell!" he said, "vot haff ve here! Mitkey Mouse himself! Mitkey, how would you like to go for a ride, negst veek? Ve shall see."

That is how it came about that the next time the Professor sent into town for supplies, his order included a mousetrap—not one of the vicious kind that kills, but one of the wire-cage kind. And it had not been set, with cheese, for more than ten minutes before Mitkey's sharp little nose had smelled out that cheese and he had followed his nose into captivity.

Not, however, an unpleasant captivity. Mitkey was an honored guest. The cage reposed now on the table at which the Professor did most of his work, and cheese in indigestion-giving abundance was pushed through the bars, and the Professor didn't talk to himself any more.

"You see, Mitkey, I vas going to sendt to der laboratory in Hardtfordt for a vhite mouse, budt vhy should I, mit you here? I am sure you are more soundt und healthy und able to vithstand a long chourney than those laboratory mices. No? Ah, you viggle your viskers und that means yes, no? Und being used to living in dargk holes, you should suffer less than they from glaustrophobia, no?"

And Mitkey grew fat and happy and forgot all about trying to get out of the cage. I fear that he even forgot about the family he had abandoned, but he knew, if he knew anything, that he need not worry about them in the slightest. At least not until and unless the Professor discovered and repaired the hole in the refrigerator. And the Professor's mind was most emphatically not on refrigeration.

"Und so, Mitkey, ve shall place this vane so—it iss only of assistance in der landing, in an atmosphere. It und these vill bring you down safely und slowly enough that der shock-absorbers in der movable combartment vill keep you from bumping your head too

hard, I think." Of course, Mitkey missed the ominous note to that
"I think" qualification because he missed all the rest of it. He did
not, as has been explained, speak English. Not then.

But Herr Oberburger talked to him just the same. He showed
him pictures. "Did you effer see der Mouse you vas named after,
Mitkey? Vhat? No? Loogk, this is der original Mitkey Mouse, by
Valt Dissney. Budt I think you are cuter, Mitkey."

Probably the Professor was a bit crazy to talk that way to a little
gray mouse. In fact, he must have been crazy to make a rocket that
worked. For the odd thing was that the Herr Professor was not
really an inventor. There was, as he carefully explained to Mitkey,
not one single thing about that rocket that was new. The Herr
Professor was a technician; he could take other people's ideas and
make them work. His only real invention—the rocket fuel that
wasn't one—had been turned over to the United States Government
and had proved to be something already known and discarded
because it was too expensive for practical use.

As he explained very carefully to Mitkey, "It iss burely a matter
of absolute accuracy and mathematical correctness, Mitkey. Idt iss
all here—ve merely combine—und ve achieff vhat, Mitkey?

"Eggscape velocity, Mitkey! Chust barely, it adds up to eggscape
velocity. Maybe. There are yet unknown facgtors, Mitkey, in der
ubper atmosphere, der troposphere, der stratosphere. Ve think ve
know eggsactly how mudch air there iss to calculate resistance
against, but are ve absolutely sure? No, Mitkey, ve are not. Ve haff
not been there. Und der marchin iss so narrow that so mudch as
an air current might affect idt."

But Mitkey cared not a whit. In the shadow of the tapering
aluminum-alloy cylinder he waxed fat and happy.

"Der tag, Mitkey, der tag! Und I shall not lie to you, Mitkey.
I shall not giff you valse assurances. You go on a dancherous
chourney, mein little friendt.

"A vifty-vifty chance ve giff you, Mitkey. Not der moon or bust,
but der moon und bust, or else maybe safely back to earth. You
see, my boor little Mitkey, der moon iss not made of green cheese
und if it were, you vould not live to eat it because there iss not
enough atmosphere to bring you down safely und vith your viskers
still on.

"Und vhy then, you may vell ask, do I send you? Because der
rocket may not attain eggscape velocity. Und in that case, it iss

still an eggsperiment, budt a different vun. Der rocket, if it goes
not to der moon, falls back on der earth, no? Und in that case
certain instruments shall giff us further information than ve haff
yet about things up there in space. Und you shall giff us information,
by vether or not you are yet alife, vether der shock absorbers und
vanes are sufficient in an earth-equivalent atmosphere. You see?

"Then ladter, vhen ve send rockets to Venus maybe vhere an
atmosphere eggsists, ve shall haff data to calculate the needed size
of vanes und shock-absorbers, no? Und in either case, und vether
or not you return, Mitkey, you shall be vamous! You shall be der
virst liffing greature to go oudt beyond der stratosphere of der
earth, out into space.

"Mitkey, you shall be der Star-Mouse! I enfy you, Mitkey, und
I only vish I vere your size, so I could go, too."

Der tag, and the door to the compartment. "Gootbye, little
Mitkey Mouse." Darkness. Silence. Noise!

"Der rocket—if it goes not to der moon—falls back on der earth,
no?" That was what the Herr Professor thought. But the best-laid
plans of mice and men gang aft agley. Even star-mice.

All because of Prxl.

The Herr Professor found himself very lonely. After having had
Mitkey to talk to, soliloquies were somehow empty and inadequate.

There may be some who say that the company of a small gray
mouse is a poor substitute for a wife; but others may disagree. And,
anyway, the Professor had never had a wife, and he had a mouse to
talk to, so he missed one and, if he missed the other, he didn't
know it.

During the long night after the launching of the rocket, he had
been very busy with his telescope, a sweet little eight-inch reflector,
checking its course as it gathered momentum. The exhaust explosions made a tiny fluctuating point of light that was possible to
follow, if one knew where to look.

But the following day there seemed to be nothing to do, and
he was too excited to sleep, although he tried. So he compromised
by doing a spot of housekeeping, cleaning the pots and pans. It was
while he was so engaged that he heard a series of frantic little
squeaks and discovered that another small gray mouse, with shorter
whiskers and a shorter tail than Mitkey, had walked into the
wire-cage mousetrap.

"Vell, vell," said the Professor, "vot haff ve here? Minnie? Iss it Minnie come to look for her Mitkey?"

The Professor was not a biologist, but he happened to be right. It *was* Minnie. Rather, it was Mitkey's mate, so the name was appropriate. What strange vagary of mind had induced her to walk into an unbaited trap, the Professor neither knew nor cared, but he was delighted. He promptly remedied the lack of bait by pushing a sizable piece of cheese through the bars.

Thus it was that Minnie came to fill the place of her far-traveling spouse as repository for the Professor's confidences. Whether she worried about her family or not there is no way of knowing, but she need not have done so. They were now large enough to fend for themselves, particularly in a house that offered abundant cover and easy access to the refrigerator.

"Ah, und now it iss dargk enough, Minnie, that ve can loogk for that husband of yours. His viery trail across the sky. True, Minnie, it iss a very small viery trail und der astronomers vill not notice it, because they do not know vhere to loogk. But ve do.

"He iss going to be a very vamous mouse, Minnie, this Mitkey of ours, vhen ve tell der vorld about him und about mein rocket. You see, Minnie ve haff not told them yet. Ve shall vait und giff der gomplete story all at vunce. By dawn of tomorrow ve'll—

"Ah, there he iss, Minnie! Vaint, but there. I'd hold you up to der scope und let you loogk, but it vould not be vocused right for your eyes, und I do not know how to—

"Almost vun hundred thousand miles, Minnnie, und still agcelerating, but not for much longer. Our Mitkey iss on schedule; in fagt he iss going vaster than ve had vigured, no? It iss sure now that he vill eggscape the gravitation of der earth, und fall upon der moon!"

Of course, it was purely coincidental that Minnie squeaked.

"Ah, yess, Minnie, little Minnie. I know, I know. Ve shall neffer see our Mitkey again, und I almost vish our eggsperiment hadt vailed. Budt there are gompensations, Minnie. He shall be der most vamous of all mices. Der Star-Mouse! Virst liffing greature effer to go beyond der gravitational bull of earth!"

The night was long. Occasionally high clouds obscured vision.

"Minnie, I shall make you more gomfortable than in that so-small vire cage. You vould like to seem to be vree, vould you not, vithout bars, like der animals at modern zoos, vith moats insteadt?"

And so, to fill in an hour when a cloud obscured the sky, the Herr Professor made Minnie her new home. It was the end of a wooden crate, about half an inch thick and a foot square, laid flat on the table, and with no visible barrier around it.

But he covered the top with metal foil at the edges, and he placed the board on another larger board which also had a strip of metal foil surrounding the island of Minnie's home. And wires from the two areas of metal foil to opposite terminals of a small transformer which he placed near by.

"Und now, Minnie, I shall blace you on your island, vhich shall be liberally supplied mitt cheese und vater, und you shall vind it iss an eggcelent blace to liff. But you vill get a mild shock or two vhen you try to step off der edge of der island. It vill not hurt much, but you vill not like it, und after a few tries you vill learn not to try again, no? Und—"

And night again.

Minnie happy on her island, her lesson well learned. She would no longer so much as step on the inner strip of metal foil. It was a mouse-paradise of an island, though. There was a cliff of cheese bigger than Minnie herself. It kept her busy. Mouse and cheese; soon one would be a transmutation of the other.

But Professor Oberburger wasn't thinking about that. The Professor was worried. When he had calculated and recalculated and aimed his eight-inch reflector through the hole in the roof and turned out the lights—

Yes, there are advantages to being a bachelor after all. If one wants a hole in the roof, one simply knocks a hole in the roof and there is nobody to tell one that one is crazy. If winter comes, or if it rains, one can always call a carpenter or use a tarpaulin.

But the faint trail of light wasn't there. The Professor frowned and re-calculated and re-re-calculated and shifted his telescope three-tenths of a minute and still the rocket wasn't there.

"Minnie, something iss wrong. Either der tubes haff stopped viring, or—"

Or the rocket was no longer traversing a straight line relative to its point of departure. By straight, of course, is meant parabolically curved relative to everything other than velocity.

So the Herr Professor did the only thing remaining for him to do, and began to search, with the telescope, in widening circles. It was two hours before he found it, five degrees off course already and veering more and more into a— Well, there was only one thing you could call it. A tailspin.

The darned thing was going in circles, circles which appeared to constitute an orbit about something that couldn't possibly be there. Then narrowing into a concentric spiral.

Then—out. Gone. Darkness. No rocket flares.

The Professor's face was pale as he turned to Minnie.

"It iss *imbossible*, Minnie. Mein own eyes, but it could not be. Even if vun side stopped viring, it could not haff gone into such sudden circles." His pencil verified a suspicion. "Und, Minnie, it decelerated vaster than bossible. Even mitt *no* tubes viring, its momentum vould haff been more—"

The rest of the night—telescope and calculus—yielded no clue. That is, no believable clue. Some force not inherent in the rocket itself, and not accountable by gravitation—even of a hypothetical body—had acted.

"Mein poor Mitkey."

The gray, inscrutable dawn. "Mein Minnie, it vill haff to be a secret. Ve dare not publish vhat ve saw, for it vould not be believed. I am not sure I believe it myself, Minnie. Berhaps because I vas offertired vrom not sleeping, I chust imachined that I saw—"

Later. "But, Minnie, ve shall hope. Vun hundred vifty thousand miles out, it vas. It vill fall back upon der earth. But I gannot tell vhere! I thought that if it did, I vould be able to galculate its course, und— But after those goncentric cirgles—Minnie, not even *Einstein* could galculate vhere it vill land. Not effen *me*. All ve can do iss hope that ve shall hear of vhere it falls."

Cloudy day. Black night jealous of its mysteries.

"Minnie, our poor Mitkey. There is *nothing* could have gauzed—"

But something had.

Prxl.

Prxl is an asteroid. It isn't called that by earthly astronomers, because—for excellent reasons—they have not discovered it. So we will call it by the nearest possible transliteration of the name its inhabitants use. Yes, it's inhabited.

Come to think of it, Professor Oberburger's attempt to send a rocket to the moon had some strange results. Or rather, Prxl did.

You wouldn't think that an asteroid could reform a drunk, would you? But one Charles Winslow, a besotted citizen of Bridgeport, Connecticut, never took a drink when—right on Grove Street—a mouse asked him the road to Hartford. The mouse was wearing bright red pants and vivid yellow gloves—

But that was fifteen months after the Professor lost his rocket. We'd better start over again.

Prxl is an asteroid. One of those despised celestial bodies which terrestrial astronomers call vermin of the sky, because the darned things leave trails across the plates that clutter up the more important observations of novae and nebulae. Fifty thousand fleas on the dark dog of night.

Tiny things, most of them. Astronomers have been discovering recently that some of them come close to Earth. Amazingly close. There was excitement in 1932 when Amor came within ten million miles; astronomically, a mere mashie shot. Then Apollo cut that almost in half, and in 1936 Adonis came within less than one and a half million miles.

In 1937, Hermes, less than half a million but the astronomers got really excited when they calculated its orbit and found that the little mile-long asteroid can come within a mere 220,000 miles, closer than Earth's own moon.

Some day they may be still more excited, if and when they spot the ⅜-mile asteroid Prxl, that obstacle of space, making a transit across the moon and discover that it frequently comes within a mere hundred thousand miles of our rapidly whirling world.

Only in event of a transit will they ever discover it, though, for Prxl does not reflect light. It hasn't, anyway, for several million years since its inhabitants coated it with a black, light-absorbing pigment derived from its interior. Monumental task, painting a world, for creatures half an inch tall. But worth it, at the time. When they'd shifted its orbit, they were safe from their enemies. There were giants in those days—eight-inch tall marauding pirates from Diemos. Got to Earth a couple of times too, before they faded out of the picture. Pleasant little giants who killed because they enjoyed it. Records in now-buried cities on Diemos might explain what happened to the dinosaurs. And why the promising Cro-Magnons disappeared at the height of their promise only a cosmic few minutes after the dinosaurs went west.

But Prxl survived. Tiny world no longer reflecting the sun's rays, lost to the cosmic killers when its orbit was shifted.

Prxl. Still civilized, with a civilization millions of years old. Its coat of blackness preserved and renewed regularly, more through tradition than fear of enemies in these later degenerate days. Mighty but stagnant civilization, standing still on a world that whizzes like a bullet.

And Mitkey Mouse.

Klarloth, head scientist of a race of scientists, tapped his assistant Bemj on what would have been Bemj's shoulder if he had had one. "Look," he said, "what approaches Prxl. Obviously artificial propulsion."

Bemj looked into the wall-plate and then directed a thought-wave at the mechanism that jumped the magnification of a thousand-fold through an alteration of the electronic field.

The image leaped, blurred, then steadied. "Fabricated," said Bemj. "Extremely crude, I must say. Primitive explosive-powered rocket. Wait, I'll check where it came from."

He took the readings from the dials about the viewplate, and hurled them as thoughts against the psychocoil of the computer, then waited while that most complicated of machines digested all the factors and prepared the answer. Then, eagerly, he slid his mind into rapport with its projector. Klarloth likewise listened in to the silent broadcast.

Exact point on Earth and exact time of departure. Untranslatable expression of curve of trajectory, and point on that curve where deflected by gravitational pull of Prxl. The destination—or rather the original intended destination—of the rocket was obvious, Earth's moon. Time and place of arrival on Prxl if present course of rocket was unchanged.

"Earth," said Klarloth meditatively. "They were a long way from rocket travel the last time we checked them. Some sort of a crusade, or battle of beliefs, going on, wasn't there?"

Bemj nodded. "Catapults. Bows and arrows. They've taken a long stride since, even if this is only an early experimental thing of a rocket. Shall we destroy it before it gets here?"

Klarloth shook his head thoughtfully. "Let's look it over. May save us a trip to Earth; we can judge their present state of development pretty well from the rocket itself."

"But then we'll have to—"

"Of course. Call the Station. Tell them to train their attracto-repulsors on it and to swing it into a temporary orbit until they prepare a landing-cradle. And not forget to damp out the explosive before they bring it down."

"Temporary force-field around point of landing—in case?"

"Naturally."

So despite the almost complete absence of atmosphere in which the vanes could have functioned, the rocket came down safely and so softly that Mitkey, in the dark compartment, knew only that the awful noise had stopped.

Mitkey felt better. He ate some more of the cheese with which the compartment was liberally provided. Then he resumed trying to gnaw a hole in the inch-thick wood with which the compartment was lined. That wooden lining was a kind thought of the Herr Professor for Mitkey's mental well-being. He knew that trying to gnaw his way out would give Mitkey something to do en route which would keep him from getting the screaming meemies. The idea had worked; being busy, Mitkey hadn't suffered mentally from his dark confinement. And now that things were quiet, he chewed away more industriously and more happily than ever, sublimely unaware that when he got through the wood, he'd find only metal which he couldn't chew. But better people than Mitkey have found things they couldn't chew.

Meanwhile, Klarloth and Bemj and several thousand other Prxlians stood gazing up at the huge rocket which, even lying on its side, towered high over their heads. Some of the younger ones, forgetting the invisible field of force, walked too close and came back, ruefully rubbing bumped heads.

Klarloth himself was at the psychograph.

"There is life inside the rocket," he told Bemj. "But the impressions are confused. One creature, but I cannot follow its thought processes. At the moment it seems to be doing something with its teeth."

"It could not be an Earthling, one of the dominant race. One of them is much larger than this huge rocket. Gigantic creatures. Perhaps, unable to construct a rocket large enough to hold one of themselves, they sent an experimental creature, such as our wooraths."

"I believe you've guessed right, Bemj. Well, when we have explored its mind thoroughly, we may still learn enough to save us a check-up trip to Earth. I am going to open the door."

"But air—creatures of Earth would need a heavy, almost a dense atmosphere. It could not live."

"We retain the force-field, of course. It will keep the air in. Obviously there is a source of supply of air within the rocket or the creature would not have survived the trip."

Klarloth operated controls, and the force-field itself put forth invisible pseudo-pods and turned the outer screw-door, then reached within and unlatched the inner door to the compartment itself.

All Prxl watched breathlessly as a monstrous gray head pushed out of the huge aperture yawning overhead. Thick whiskers, each as long as the body of a Prxlian—

Mitkey jumped down, and took a forward step that bumped his black nose hard—into something that wasn't there. He squeaked, and jumped backward against the rocket.

There was disgust in Bemj's face as he looked up at the monster. "Obviously much less intelligent than a woorath. Might just as well turn on the ray."

"Not at all," interrupted Klarloth. "You forget certain very obvious facts. The creature is unintelligent, of course, but the subconscious of every animal holds in itself every memory, every impression, every sense-image, to which it has ever been subjected. If this creature has ever heard the speech of the Earthlings, or seen any of their works—besides this rocket—every word and every picture is indelibly graven. You see now what I mean?"

"Naturally. How stupid of me, Klarloth. Well, one thing is obvious from the rocket itself: we have nothing to fear from the science of Earth for at least a few millennia. So there is no hurry, which is fortunate. For to send back the creature's memory to the time of its birth, and to follow each sensory impression in the psychograph will require—well, a time at least equivalent to the age of the creature, whatever that is, plus the time necessary for us to interpret and assimilate each."

"But that will not be necessary, Bemj."

"No? Oh, you mean the X-19 waves?"

"Exactly. Focused upon this creature's brain-center, they can, without disturbing his memories, be so delicately adjusted as to increase his intelligence—now probably about .0001 in the scale— to the point where he is a reasoning creature. Almost automatically, during the process, he will assimilate his own memories, and understand them just as he would if he had been intelligent at the time he received those impressions.

"See, Bemj? He will automatically sort out irrelevant data, and will be able to answer our questions."

"But would you make him as intelligent as—?"

"As we? No, the X-19 waves would not work so far. I would

say to about .2 on the scale. That, judging from the rocket, coupled with what we remember of Earthlings from our last trip there, is about their present place on the intelligence scale."

"Ummm, yes. At that level, he would comprehend his experiences on Earth just sufficiently that he would not be dangerous to us, too. Equal to an intelligent Earthling. Just about right for our purpose. Then, shall we teach him our language?"

"Wait," said Klarloth. He studied the psychograph closely for a while. "No, I do not think so. He will have a language of his own. I see in his subconscious, memories of many long conversations. Strangely, they all seem to be monologues by one person. But he will have a language—a simple one. It would take him a long time, even under treatment, to grasp the concepts of our own method of communication. But we can learn his, while he is under the X-19 machine, in a few minutes."

"Does he understand, now, any of that language?"

Klarloth studied the psychograph again. "No, I do not believe he— Wait, there is one word that seems to mean something to him. The word 'Mitkey.' It seems to be his name, and I believe that, from hearing it many times, he vaguely associates it with himself."

"And quarters for him—with air-locks and such?"

"Of course. Order them built."

To say it was a strange experience for Mitkey is understatement. Knowledge is a strange thing, even when it is acquired gradually. To have it thrust upon one—

And there were little things that had to be straightened out. Like the matter of vocal chords. His weren't adapted to the language he now found he knew. Bemj fixed that; you would hardly call it an operation because Mitkey—even with his new awareness—didn't know what was going on, and he was wide awake at the time. And they didn't explain to Mitkey about the J-dimension with which one can get at the inwardness of things without penetrating the outside.

They figured things like that weren't in Mitkey's line, and anyway they were more interested in learning from him than teaching him. Bemj and Klarloth, and a dozen others deemed worthy of the privilege. If one of them wasn't talking to him, another was.

Their questioning helped his own growing understanding. He

would not, usually, know that he knew the answer to a question until it was asked. Then he'd piece together, without knowing just how he did it (any more than you or I know *how* we know things) and give them the answer.

Bemj: "Iss this language vhich you sbeak a universal vun?"

And Mitkey, even though he'd never thought about it before, had the answer ready: "No, it iss nodt. It iss Englitch, but I remember der Herr Brofessor sbeaking of other tongues. I belief he sboke another himself originally, budt in America he always sboke Englitch to become more vamiliar mitt it. It iss a beaudiful ,sbeech, is it nodt?"

"Hmmmm," said Bemj.

Klarloth: "Und your race, the mices. Are they treated vell?"

"Nodt by most people," Mitkey told him. And explained.

"I vould like to do something for them," he added. "Loogk, could I nodt take back mitt me this brocess vhich you used upon me? Abbly it to other mices, und greate a race of super-mices?"

"Vhy not?" asked Bemj.

He saw Klarloth looking at him strangely, and threw his mind into rapport with the chief scientist's, with Mitkey left out of the silent communion.

"Yes, of course," Bemj told Klarloth, "it will lead to trouble on Earth, grave trouble. Two equal classes of beings so dissimilar as mice and men cannot live together in amity. But why should that concern us, other than favorably? The resultant mess will slow down progress on Earth—give us a few more millennia of peace before Earthlings discover we are here, and trouble starts. You know these Earthlings."

"But you would give them the X-19 waves? They might—"

"No, of course not. But we can explain to Mitkey here how to make a very crude and limited machine for them. A primitive one which would suffice for nothing more than the specific task of converting mouse mentality from .0001 to .2, Mitkey's own level and that of the bifurcated Earthlings."

"It is possible," communicated Klarloth. "It is certain that for aeons to come they will be incapable of understanding its basic principle."

"But could they not use even a crude machine to raise their own level of intelligence?"

"You forget, Bemj, the basic limitation of the X-19 rays; that no one can possibly design a projector capable of raising any mentality to a point on the scale higher than his own. Not even we."

All this, of course, over Mitkey's head, in silent Prxlian.

More interviews, and more.

Klarloth again: "Mitkey, ve varn you of vun thing. Avoid carelessness vith electricity. Der new molecular rearranchement of your
brain center—it iss unstable, und—"

Bemj: "Mitkey, are you sure your Herr Brofessor iss der most
advanced of all who eggsperiment vith der rockets?"

"In cheneral, yess, Bemj. There are others who on vun specific
boint, such as eggsplosives, mathematics, astrovisics, may know
more, but not much more. Und for combining these knowledges,
he iss ahead."

"It iss vell," said Bemj.

Small gray mouse towering like a dinosaur over tinier half-inch
Prxlians. Meek, herbivorous creature though he was, Mitkey could
have killed any one of them with a single bite. But, of course, it
never occurred to him to do so, nor to them to fear that he might.

They turned him inside out mentally. They did a pretty good
job of study on him physically, too, but that was through the
J-dimension, and Mitkey didn't even know about it.

They found out what made him tick, and they found out
everything he knew and some things he didn't even know he
knew. And they grew quite fond of him.

"Mitkey," said Klarloth one day, "all der civilized races on Earth
vear glothing, do they nodt? Vell, if you are to raise der level of
mices to men, vould it not be vitting that you vear glothes, too?"

"An eggcelent idea, Herr Klarloth. Und I know chust vhat kind
I should like. Der Herr Brofessor vunce showed me a bicture of a
mouse bainted by der artist Dissney, und der mouse vore glothing.
Der mouse vas not a real-life vun, budt an imachinary mouse in
a barable, und der Brofessor named me after der Dissney mouse."

"Vot kind of glothing vas it, Mitkey?"

"Bright red bants mitt two big yellow buttons in frondt und two
in back, und yellow shoes for der back feet und a pair of yellow
gloves for der front. A hole in der seat of der bants to aggomodate
der tail."

"Ogay, Mitkey. Such shall be ready for you in fife minutes."

That was on the eve of Mitkey's departure. Originally Bemj
had suggested awaiting the moment when Prxl's eccentric orbit
would again take it within a hundred and fifty thousand miles of

Earth. But, as Klarloth pointed out, that would be fifty-five Earth-years ahead, and Mitkey wouldn't last that long. Not unless they—And Bemj agreed that they had better not risk sending a secret like that back to Earth.

So they compromised by refueling Mitkey's rocket with something that would cancel out the million and a quarter odd miles he would have to travel. That secret they didn't have to worry about, because the fuel would be gone by the time the rocket landed.

Day of departure.

"Ve haff done our best, Mitkey, to set und time der rocket so it vill land on or near der spot from vhich you left Earth. But you gannot eggspect agguracy in a voyach so long as this. But you vill land near. The rest iss up to you. Ve haff equvipped the rocket ship for effery contingency."

"Thank you, Herr Klarloth, Herr Bemj. Gootbye."

"Gootbye, Mitkey. Ve hate to loose you."

"Gootbye, Mitkey."

"Gootbye, gootbye . . ."

For a million and a quarter miles, the aim was really excellent. The rocket landed in Long Island Sound, ten miles out from Bridgeport, about sixty miles from the house of Professor Oberburger near Hartford.

They had prepared for a water landing, of course. The rocket went down to the bottom, but before it was more than a few dozen feet under the surface, Mitkey opened the door—especially re-equipped to open from the inside—and stepped out.

Over his regular clothes he wore a neat little diving suit that would have protected him at any reasonable depth, and which, being lighter than water, brought him to the surface quickly where he was able to open his helmet.

He had enough synthetic food to last him for a week, but it wasn't necessary, as things turned out. The night-boat from Boston carried him in to Bridgeport on its anchor chain, and once in sight of land he was able to divest himself of the diving suit and let it sink to the bottom after he'd punctured the tiny compartments that made it float, as he'd promised Klarloth he would do.

Almost instinctively, Mitkey knew that he'd do well to avoid human beings until he'd reached Professor Oberburger and told his story. His worst danger proved to be the rats at the wharf

where he swam ashore. They were ten times Mitkey's size and
had teeth that could have taken him apart in two bites.

But mind has always triumphed over matter. Mitkey pointed an
imperious yellow glove and said, "Scram," and the rats scrammed.
They'd never seen anything like Mitkey before, and they were
impressed.

So for that matter, was the drunk of whom Mitkey inquired
the way to Hartford. We mentioned that episode before. That was
the only time Mitkey tried direct communication with strange
human beings. He took, of course, every precaution. He addressed
his remarks from a strategic position only inches away from a hole
into which he could have popped. But it was the drunk who did
the popping, without even waiting to answer Mitkey's question.

But he got there, finally. He made his way afoot to the north
side of town and hid out behind a gas station until he heard a
motorist who had pulled in for gasoline inquire the way to Hartford.
And Mitkey was a stowaway when the car started up.

The rest wasn't hard. The calculations of the Prxlians showed
that the starting point of the rocket was five Earth miles north-west
of what showed on their telescopomaps as a city, and which from
the Professor's conversation Mitkey knew would be Hartford.

He got there.

"Hello, Brofessor."

The Herr Professor Oberburger looked up, startled. There was no
one in sight. "Vot?" he asked, of the air. "Who iss?"

"It iss I, Brofessor. Mitkey, der mouse whom you sent to der
moon. But I vas not there. Insteadt, I—"

"Vot?? It iss imbossible. Somebody blays der choke. Budt—budt
nobody knows about that rocket. Vhen it vailed, I didn't told
nobody. Nobody budt me knows—"

"And me, Brofessor."

The Herr Professor sighed heavily. "Offervork. I am going vhat they
call battly in der bel—"

"No, Brofessor. This is really me, Mitkey. I can talk now. Chust
like you."

"You say you can— I do not belief it. Vhy can I not see you,
then. Vhere are you? Vhy don't you—"

"I am hiding, Brofessor, in der vall chust behind der big hole.
I vanted to be sure efferything vas ogay before I showed myself

Then you would not get eggcited und throw something at me maybe."

"Vot? Vhy, Mitkey, if it iss really you und I am nodt asleep or going— Vhy, Mitkey, you know better than to think I might do something like that!"

"Ogay, Brofessor."

Mitkey stepped out of the hole in the wall, and the Professor looked at him and rubbed his eyes and looked again and rubbed his eyes and—

"I am grazy,' he said finally. "Red bants he vears yet, und yellow— It gannot be. I am grazy."

"No, Brofessor. Listen, I'll tell you all aboudt."

And Mitkey told him.

Gray dawn, and a small gray mouse still talking earnestly.

"Yess, Brofessor. I see your boint, that you think an intelligent race of mices und an intelligent race of men couldt nodt get along side by sides. But it vould not be side by sides; as I said, there are only a ferry few beople in the smallest continent of Australia. Und it vould cost little to bring them back und turn offer that continent to us mices. Ve vould call it Moustralia instead Australia, und ve vould instead of Sydney call der capital Dissney, in honor of—"

"But, Mitkey—"

"But, Brofessor, look vot we offer for that continent. All mices vould go there. Ve civilize a few und the few help us catch others und bring them in to put them under red ray machine, und the others help catch more und build more machines und it grows like a snowball rolling down hill. Und ve sign a nonaggression pact mitt humans und stay on Moustralia und raise our own food und—"

"But, Mitkey—"

"Und look vot ve offer you in eggschange, Her Brofessor! Ve vill eggsterminate your vorst enemy—der rats. Ve do not like them either. Und vun battalion of vun thousand mices, armed mitt gas masks und small gas bombs, could go right in effery hole after der rats und could eggsterminate effery rat in a city in vun day or two. In der whole vorld ve could eggsterminate effery last rat in a year, und at the same time catch und civilize effery mouse und ship him to Moustralia, und—"

"But, Mitkey—"

"Vot, Brofessor?"

"It vould vork, but it vould not work. You could eggsterminate der rats, yess. But how long vould it be before conflicts of interests vould lead to der mices trying to eggsterminate de people or der people trying to eggsterminate der—"

"They vould not dare, Brofessor! Ve could make weapons that vould—"

"You see, Mitkey?"

"But it vould not habben. If men vill honor our rights, ve vill honor—"

The Herr Professor sighed.

"I—I vill act as your intermediary, Mitkey, und offer your broposition, und— Vell, it iss true that getting rid of rats vould be a greadt boon to der human race. Budt—"

"Thank you, Brofessor."

"By der vay, Mitkey. I haff Minnie. Your vife, I guess it iss, unless there vas other mices around. She iss in der other room; I put her there chust before you ariffed, so she vould be in der dark und could sleep. You vant to see her?"

"Vife?" said Mitkey. It had been so long that he had really forgotten the family he had perforce abandoned. The memory returned slowly.

"Vell," he said "—ummm, yess. Ve vill get her und I shall construct quvick a small X-19 prochector und—Yess, it vill help you in your negotiations mitt der governments if there are sefferal of us already so they can see I am not chust a freak like they might otherwise suspegt."

It wasn't deliberate. It couldn't have been, because the Professor didn't know about Klarloth's warning to Mitkey about carelessness with electricity—"Der new molecular rearranchement of your brain center—it iss unstable, und—"

And the Professor was still back in the lighted room when Mitkey ran into the room where Minnie was in her barless cage. She was asleep, and the sight of her— Memory of his earlier days came back like a flash and suddenly Mitkey knew how lonesome he had been.

"Minnie!" he called, forgetting that she could not understand.

And stepped up on the board where she lay. "Squeak!" The mild electrical current between the two strips of tinfoil got him.

There was silence for a while.

Then: "Mitkey," called the Herr Professor. "Come on back und ve vill discuss this—"

He stepped through the doorway and saw them, there in the gray light of dawn, two small gray mice cuddled happily together. He couldn't tell which was which, because Mitkey's teeth had torn off the red and yellow garments which had suddenly been strange, confining and obnoxious things.

"Vot on earth?" asked Professor Oberburger. Then he remembered the current, and guessed.

"Mitkey! Can you no longer talk? Iss der—"

Silence.

Then the Professor smiled. "Mitkey," he said, "my little starmouse. I think you are more happier now."

He watched them a moment, fondly, then reached down and flipped the switch that broke the electrical barrier. Of course they didn't know they were free, but when the Professor picked them up and placed them carefully on the floor, one ran immediately for the hole in the wall. The other followed, but turned around and looked back—still a trace of puzzlement in the little black eyes, a puzzlement that faded.

"Gootbye, Mitkey. You vill be happier this vay. Und there vill always be cheese."

"Squeak," said the little gray mouse, and it popped into the hole.

"Gootbye—" it might, or might not, have meant.

CORRESPONDENCE COURSE

by

RAYMOND F. JONES

> It is not the outward form with which life clothes itself that
> counts. The mind and spirit within each life form on each planet
> will make for peace and amity between the worlds. The alien
> visitor from outer space, forced to land on earth, brought with
> him (or her) something infinitely greater than the marvelous
> engines that powered his ship. A hope of harmony, a power for
> mutual understanding that will transcend any surface differences
> between beings who possess a common bond of affection and
> sympathy.

*

THE OLD lane from the farmhouse to the letter box down by the
road was the same dusty trail that he remembered from eons before.
The deep summer dust stirred as his feet moved slowly and haltingly.
The marks of his left foot were deep and firm as when he had last
walked the lane, but where his right foot moved there was a ragged,
continuous line with irregular depressions and there was the sharp
imprint of a cane beside the dragging footprints.

He looked up to the sky a moment as an echelon of planes from
the advanced trainer base fifty miles away wheeled overhead. A nostalgia seized him, an overwhelming longing for the men he had known
—and for Ruth.

He was home; he had come back alive, but with so many gone who
would never come back, what good was it?

With Ruth gone it was no good at all. For an instant his mind
burned with pain and his eyes ached as if a bomb-burst had blinded

him as he remembered that day in the little field hospital where he had watched her die and heard the enemy planes overhead.

Afterwards, he had gone up alone, against orders, determined to die with her, but take along as many Nazis as he could.

But he hadn't died. He had come out of it with a bullet-shattered leg and sent home to rust and die slowly over many years.

He shook his head and tried to fling the thoughts out of his mind. It was wrong. The doctors had warned him—

He resumed his slow march, half dragging the all but useless leg behind him. This was the same lane down which he had run so fast those summer days so long ago. There was a swimming hole and a fishing pond a quarter of a mile away. He tried to dim his vision with half-shut eyes and remember those pleasant days and wipe out all fear and bitterness from his mind.

It was ten o'clock in the morning and Mr. McAfee, the rural post-man, was late, but Jim Ward could see his struggling, antique Ford raising a low cloud of dust a mile down the road.

Jim leaned heavily upon the stout cedar post that supported the mailbox and when Mr. McAfee rattled up he managed to wave and smile cheerily.

Mr. McAfee adjusted his spectacles on the bridge of his nose with a rapid trombone manipulation.

"Bless me, Jim, it's good to see you up and around!"

"Pretty good to be up." Jim managed to force enthusiasm into his voice. But he knew he couldn't stand talking very long to old Charles McAfee as if everything had not changed since the last time.

"Any mail for the Wards, today?"

The postman shuffled the fistful of mail. "Only one."

Jim glanced at the return address block and shrugged. "I'm on the sucker lists already. They don't lose any time when they find out there's still bones left to pick on. You keep it."

He turned painfully and faced toward the house. "I've got to be getting back. Glad to have seen you, Mr. McAfee."

"Yeah, sure, Jim. Glad to have seen you. But I . . . er . . . got to deliver the mail—" He held the letter out hopefully.

"O.K." Jim laughed sharply and grasped the circular.

He went only as far as the giant oak whose branches extended far enough to overshadow the mailbox. He sat down in the shade with his back against the great bole and tried to watch the echelon still soaring above the valley through the rifts in the leaf coverage above him. After a time he glanced down at the circular letter from which his fingers were peeling little fragments of paper. Idly, he ripped open the envelope and glanced at the contents. In cheap, garish typograph with splatterings of red and purple ink the words seemed to be trying to jump at him.

SERVICEMAN—WHAT OF THE FUTURE?

You have come back from the wars. You have found life different than you knew it before, and much that was familiar is gone. But new things have come, new things that are here to stay and are a part of the world you are going to live in.

Have you thought of the place you will occupy? Are you prepared to resume life in the ways of peace?

WE CAN HELP YOU

Have you heard of the POWER CO-ORDINATOR? No, of course you haven't because it has been a hush-hush secret source of power that has been turning the wheels of war industries for many months. But now the secret of this vast source of new power can be told, and the need for hundreds, yes, thousands of trained technicians—such as you, yourself, may become—will be tremendous in the next decade.

LET US PROVE TO YOU

Let us prove to you that we know what we are talking about. We are so certain that you, as a soldier trained in intricate operations of the machines of war, will be interested in this almost miraculous new source of power and the technique of handling it that we are willing to send you absolutely FREE the first three lessons of our twenty-five lesson course that will train you to be a POWER CO-ORDINATOR technician.

Let us prove it to you. Fill out the inclosed coupon and mail it today!

Don't just shrug and throw this circular away as just another advertisement. MAIL THE COUPON NOW!

Jim Ward smiled reminiscently at the style of the circular. It reminded him of Billy Hensley and the time when they were thirteen. They sent in all the clipped and filled-out coupons they could find in magazines. They had samples of soap and magic tricks and catalogues and even a live bird came as the result of one. They kept all the stuff in Hensleys' attic until Billy's dad finally threw it all out.

Impulsively, in whimsical tribute to the gone-forever happiness of those days, Jim Ward scratched his name and address in pencil and told the power co-ordinators to send him their three free lessons.

Mr. McAfee had only another mile to go up the road before he came to the end and returned past the Ward farm to Kramer's Forks. Jim waited and hailed him.

"Want to take another letter?"

The postman halted the clattering Ford and jumped down. "What's that?"

Jim repeated his request and held up the stamped reply card. "Take this with you?"

Mr. McAfee turned it over and read every word on the back of the card. "Good thing," he grunted. "So you're going to take a correspondence course in this new power what-is-it? I think that's mighty fine, Jim. Give you new interests—sort of take your mind off things."

"Yeah, sure." Jim struggled up with the aid of his cane and the bole of the oak tree. "Better see if I can make it back to the house now."

All the whimsy and humor had suddenly gone out of the situation.

It was a fantastically short time—three days later—that Mr. Mc-Afee stopped again at the Ward farm. He glanced at the thick envelope in his pack and the return address block it bore. He could see Jim Ward on the farmhouse porch and turned the Ford up the lane. Its rattle made Jim turn his head and open his eyes from the thoughtless blankness into which he had been trying to sink. He removed the pipe from his mouth and watched the car approach.

"Here's your course," shouted Mr. McAfee. "Here's your first lesson!"

"What lesson?"

"The correspondence course you sent for. The power what-is-it? Don't you remember?"

"No," said Jim. "I'd forgotten all about it. Take the thing away. I don't want it. It was just a silly joke."

"You hadn't ought to feel that way, Jim. After all, your leg is going to be all right. I heard the Doc say so down in the drugstore last night. And everything is going to be all right. There's no use of letting it get you down. Besides—I got to deliver the mail."

He tossed the brown envelope on the porch beside Jim. "Brought it up special because I thought you'd be in a hurry to get it."

Jim smiled in apology. "I'm sorry, Mac. Didn't mean to take it out on you. Thanks for bringing it up. I'll study it good and hard this morning right here on the porch."

Mr. McAfee beamed and nodded and rattled away. Jim closed his eyes again, but he couldn't find the pleasing blankness he'd found before. Now the screen of his mind showed only the sky with thundering, plummeting engines—and the face of a girl lying still and white with closed eyes.

Jim opened his eyes and his hands slipped to his sides and touched the envelope. He ripped it open and scanned the pages. It was the sort of stuff he had collected as a boy, all right. He glanced at the paragraph headings and tossed the first lesson aside. A lot of obvious stuff about comparisons between steam power and waterfalls and electricity. It seemed all jumbled up like a high school student's essay on the development of power from the time of Archimedes.

The mimeographed pages were poorly done. They looked as if the stencils had been cut on a typewriter that had been hit on the type faces with a hammer.

He tossed the second lesson aside and glanced at the top sheet of the third. His hand arrested itself midway in the act of tossing this lesson beside the other two. He caught a glimpse of the calculations on an inside page and opened up the booklet.

There was no high school stuff there. His brain struggled to remember the long unused methods of the integral calculus and the manipulation of partial differential equations.

There were pages of the stuff. It was like a sort of beacon light, dim and far off, but pointing a sure pathway to his mind and getting brighter as he progressed. One by one, he followed the intricate steps of the math and the short paragraphs of description between. When at last he reached the final page and turned the book over and scowled heavily the sun was halfway down the afternoon sky.

He looked away over the fields and pondered. This was no elementary stuff. Such math as this didn't belong in a home study correspondence course. He picked up the envelope and concentrated on the return address block.

All it said was: M. H. Quilcon Schools, Henderson, Iowa. The lessons were signed at the bottom with the mimeographed reproductions of M. H. Quilcon's ponderous signature.

Jim picked up lesson one again and began reading slowly and carefully, as if hidden between the lines he might find some mystic message.

By the end of July his leg was strong enough for him to walk without the cane. He walked slowly and with a limp and once in a while the leg gave way as if he had a trick knee. But he learned quickly to catch himself before he fell and he reveled in the thrill of walking again.

By the end of July the tenth lesson of the correspondence course had arrived and Jim knew that he had gone as far as he could alone. He was lost in amazement as he moved in the new scientific wonderland that opened up before him. He had known that great strides had been made in techniques and production, but it seemed incredible that such a basic discovery as power co-ordination had been producing war machines these many months. He wondered why the principle had not been applied more directly as a weapon itself—but he didn't understand enough about it to know whether it could or not. He didn't even understand yet from where the basic energy of the system was derived.

The tenth lesson was as poorly produced as the rest of them had been, but it was practically a book in its thickness. When he had finished it Jim knew that he had to know more of the background of the new science. He had to talk to someone who knew something about it. But he knew of no one who had ever heard of it. He had seen no advertisements of the M. H. Quilcon Schools. Only that first circular and these lessons.

As soon as he had finished the homework on lesson ten and had given it into Mr. McAfee's care Jim Ward made up his mind to go down to Henderson, Iowa, and visit the Quilcon School.

He wished he had retained the lesson material because he could have taken it there faster than it would arrive via the local mail channels.

The streamliner barely stopped at Henderson, Iowa, long enough to allow him to disembark. Then it was gone and Jim Ward stared about him.

The sleepy looking ticket seller, dispatcher, and janitor eyed him wonderingly and spat a huge amber stream across his desk and out the window.

"Looking for somebody, mister?"

"I'm looking for Henderson, Iowa. Is this it?" Jim asked dubiously.

"You're here, mister. But don't walk too fast or you'll be out of it. The city limits only go a block past Smith's Drugstore."

Jim noticed the sign over the door and glanced at the inscription that he had not seen before: Henderson, Iowa, Pop. 806.

"I'm looking for a Mr. M. H. Quilcon. He runs a correspondence school here somewhere. Do you know of him?"

The depot staff shifted its cud again and spat thoughtfully. "Been here twenty-nine years next October. Never heard a name like that around here, and I know 'em all."

"Are there any correspondence schools here?"

"Miss Marybell Anne Simmons gives beauty operator lessons once in a while, but that's all the school of that kind that I know of."

Disconcerted, Jim Ward murmured his thanks and moved slowly out of the station. The sight before him was dismaying. He wondered if the population hadn't declined since the estimate on the sign in the station was made.

A small mercantile store that sagged in the middle faced him from across the street. Farther along was a tiny frame building labeled Sheriff's Office. On his side Jim saw Smith's Drugstore a couple of hundred feet down from the station with a riding saddle and a patented fertilizer displayed in the window. In the other direction was the combined postoffice, bank and what was advertised as a newspaper and printing office.

Jim strode toward this last building while curious watchers on the porch of the mercantile store stared at him trudging through the dust.

The postmistress glanced up from the armful of mail that she was sorting into boxes as Jim entered. She offered a cheery hello that seemed to tinkle from the buxom figure.

"I'm looking for a man named Quilcon. I thought you might be able to give me some information concerning him."

"Kweelcon?" She furrowed her brow. "There's no one here by that name. How do you spell it?"

Before he could answer, the woman dropped a handful of letters on the floor. Jim was certain that he saw the one he had mailed to the school before he left.

As the woman stooped to recover the letters a dark brown shadow streaked across the floor. Jim got the momentary impression of an enormous brown slug moving with lightning speed.

The postmistress gave a scream of anger and scuffled her feet to the door. She returned in a moment.

"Armadillo," she explained. "Darn thing's been hanging around here for months and nobody seems to be able to kill it." She resumed putting the mail in the boxes.

"I think you missed one," said Jim. She did not have the one that he recognized as the one he'd mailed.

The woman looked about her on the floor. "I got them all, thank you. Now what did you say this man's name was?"

Jim leaned over the counter and looked at the floor. He was sure— But there was obviously no other letter in sight and there was no place it could have gone.

"Quilcon," said Jim slowly. "I'm not sure of the pronunciation myself, but that's the way it seemed it should be."

"There's no one in Henderson by that name. Wait a minute now. That's a funny thing—you know it was about a month ago that I saw an envelope going out of here with a name something like that in the upper left corner. I thought at the time it was a funny name and wondered who put it in, but I never did find out and I thought I'd been dreaming. How'd you know to come here looking for him?"

"I guess I must have received the mail you saw."

"Well, you might ask Mr. Herald. He's in the newspaper office next door. But I'm sure there's no one in this town by that name."

"You publish a newspaper here?"

The woman laughed. "We call it that. Mr. Herald owns the bank and a big farm and puts this out free as a hobby. It's not much, but everybody in town reads it. On Saturday he puts out a regular printed edition. This is the daily."

She held up a small mimeographed sheet that was moderately legible. Jim glanced at it and moved towards the door. "Thanks, anyway."

As he went out into the summer sun there was something gnawing at his brain, an intense you-forgot-something-in-there sort of feeling. He couldn't place it and tried to ignore it.

Then as he stepped across the threshold of the printing office he got it. That mimeographed newssheet he had seen—it bore a startling resemblance to the lessons he had received from M. H. Quilcon. The same purple ink. Slightly crooked sheets. But that was foolish to try to make a connection there. All mimeographed jobs looked about alike.

Mr. Herald was a portly little man with a fringe around his baldness. Jim repeated his inquiry.

"Quilcon?" Mr. Herald pinched his lips thoughtfully. "No, can't say as I ever heard the name. Odd name—I'm sure I'd know it if I'd ever heard it."

Jim Ward knew that further investigation here would be a waste of time. There was something wrong somewhere. The information in his correspondence course could not be coming out of this half dead little town.

He glanced at a copy of the newssheet lying on the man's littered desk beside an ancient Woodstock. "Nice little sheet you put out there," said Jim.

Mr. Herald laughed. "Well, it's not much, but I get a kick out of it, and the people enjoy reading about Mrs. Kelly's lost hogs and the Dorius kid's whooping cough. It livens things up."

"Ever do any work for anybody else—printing or mimeographing?"

"If anybody wants it, but I haven't had an outside customer in three years."

Jim glanced about searchingly. The old Woodstock seemed to be the only typewriter in the room.

"I might as well go on," he said. "But I wonder if you'd mind letting me use your typewriter to write a note and leave in the post-office for Quilcon if he ever shows up."

"Sure, go ahead. Help yourself."

Jim sat down before the clanking machine and hammered out a brief paragraph while Mr. Herald wandered to the back of the shop. Then Jim rose and shoved the paper in his pocket. He wished he had brought a sheet from one of the lessons with him.

"Thanks," he called to Mr. Herald. He picked up a copy of the latest edition of the newspaper and shoved it in his pocket with the typed sheet.

On the trip homeward he studied the mimeographed sheet until he had memorized every line, but he withheld conclusions until he reached home.

From the station he called the farm and Hank, the hired man, came to pick him up. The ten miles out to the farm seemed like a hundred. But at last in his own room Jim spread out the two sheets of paper he'd brought with him and opened up lesson one of the correspondence course.

There was no mistake. The stencils of the course manuals had been cut on Mr. Herald's ancient machine. There was the same nick out of the side of the o, and the b was flattened on the bulge. The r was minus half its base.

Mr. Herald had prepared the course.

Mr. Herald must then be M. H. Quilcon. But why had he denied any knowledge of the name? Why had he refused to see Jim and admit his authorship of the course?

At ten o'clock that night Mr. McAfee arrived with a special delivery letter for Jim.

"I don't ordinarily deliver these way out here this time of night," he said. "But I thought you might like to have it. Might be something important. A job or something, maybe. It's from Mr. Quilcon."

"Thanks. Thanks for bringing it, Mac."

Jim hurried into his room and ripped open the letter. It read:

Dear Mr. Ward:

Your progress in understanding the principles of power co-ordination are exceptional and I am very pleased to note your progress in connection with the tenth lesson which I have just received from you.

An unusual opportunity has arisen which I am moved to offer you. There is a large installation of a power co-ordination engine in need of vital repairs some distance from here. I believe that you are fully qualified to work on this machine under supervision which will be provided and you would gain some valuable experience. The installation is located some distance from the city of Henderson. It is about two miles out on the Balmer Road. You will find there the Hortan Machine Works at which the installation is located. Repairs are urgently needed and you are the closest qualified student able to take advantage of this opportunity which might lead to a valuable permanent connection. Therefore, I request that you come at once. I will meet you there.

Sincerely,
M. H. Quilcon

For a long time Jim Ward sat on the bed with the letter and the sheets of paper spread out before him. What had begun as a simple quest for information was rapidly becoming an intricate puzzle.

Who was M. H. Quilcon?

It seemed obvious that Mr. Herald, the banker and part-time newspaper publisher, must be Quilcon. The correspondence course manuals had certainly been produced on his typewriter. The chances of any two typewriters having exactly the same four or five disfigurements in type approached the infinitesimal.

And Herald—if he were Quilcon—must have written this letter just before or shortly after Jim's visit. The letter was certainly a product of the ancient Woodstock.

There was a fascination in the puzzle and a sense of something sinister, Jim thought. Then he laughed aloud at his own melodrama and began repacking the suitcase. There was a midnight train he could get back to Henderson.

It was hot afternoon again when he arrived in the town for the second time. The station staff looked up in surprise as he got off the train.

"Back again? I thought you'd given up."

"I've found out where Mr. Quilcon is. He's at the Hortan Machine Works. Can you tell me exactly where that is?"

"Never heard of it."

"It's supposed to be about two miles out of town on Balmer Road."

"That's just the main street of town going on down through the Willow Creek district. There's no machine works out there. You must be in the wrong state, mister. Or somebody's kidding you."

"Do you think Mr. Herald could tell me anything about such a machine shop. I mean, does he know anything about machinery or things related to it?"

"Man, no! Old man Herald don't care about nothing but money and that little fool paper of his. Machinery! He can't hook up anything more complicated than his suspenders."

Jim started down the main street toward the Willow Creek district. Balmer Road rapidly narrowed and turned, leaving the town out of sight behind a low rise. Willow Creek was a glistening thread in the midst of meadow land.

There was no more unlikely spot in the world for a machine works of any kind, Jim thought. Someone must be playing an utterly fantastic joke on him. But how or why they had picked on him was mystifying.

At the same time he knew within him that it was no joke. There was a deadly seriousness about it all. The principles of power coordination were right. He had slaved and dug through them enough to be sure of that. He felt that he could almost build a power coordinating engine now with the proper means—except that he didn't understand from where the power was derived!

In the timelessness of the bright air about him, with the only sound coming from the brook and the leaves on the willow trees beside it, Jim found it impossible to judge time or distance.

He paced his steps and counted until he was certain that at least two miles had been covered. He halted and looked about almost determined to go back and re-examine the way he had come.

He glanced ahead, his eyes scanning every minute detail of the meadowland. And then he saw it.

The sunlight glistened as if on a metal surface. And above the bright spot in the distance was the faintly readable legend:

HORTAN MACHINE WORKS

Thrusting aside all judgment concerning the incredibility of a machine shop in such a locale, he crossed the stream and made his way over the meadow toward the small rise.

As he approached, the machine works appeared to be merely a dome-shaped structure about thirty feet in diameter and with an open door in one side. He came up to it with a mind ready for anything. The crudely painted sign above the door looked as if it had been drawn by an inexpert barn painter in a state of intoxication.

Jim entered the dimly lit interior of the shop and set his case upon the floor beside a narrow bench that extended about the room.

Tools and instruments of unfamiliar design were upon the bench and upon the walls. But no one appeared.

Then he noticed an open door and a steep, spiral ramp that led down to a basement room. He stepped through and half slid, half walked down to the next level.

There was artificial lighting by fluorescent tubes of unusual construction, Jim noticed. But still no sign of anyone. And there was not an object in the room that appeared familiar to him. Articles that vaguely resembled furniture were against the walls.

He felt uneasy amid the strangeness of the room and he was about to go back up the steep ramp when a voice came to him.

"This is Mr. Quilcon. Is that you, Mr. Ward?"

"Yes. Where are you?"

"I am in the next room, unable to come out until I finish a bit of work I have started. Will you please go on down to the room below? You will find the damaged machinery there. Please go right to work on it. I'm sure that you have a complete understanding of what is necessary. I will join you in a moment."

Hesitantly, Jim turned to the other side of the room where he saw a second ramp leading down to a brilliantly lighted room. He glanced about once more, then moved down the ramp.

The room was high-ceilinged and somewhat larger in diameter than the others he had seen and it was almost completely occupied by the machine.

A series of close fitting towers with regular bulbous swellings on their columns formed the main structure of the engine. These were grouped in a solid circle with narrow walkways at right angles to each other passing through them.

Jim Ward stood for a long time examining their surfaces that rose twenty feet from the floor. All that he had learned from the curious correspondence course seemed to fall into place. Diagrams and drawings of such machines had seemed incomprehensible. Now he knew exactly what each part was for and how the machine operated.

He squeezed his body into the narrow walkway between the towers and wormed his way to the center of the engine. His bad leg made it difficult, but he at last came to the damaged structure.

One of the tubes had cracked open under some tremendous strain and through the slit he could see the marvelously intricate wiring with which it was filled. Wiring that was burned now and fused to a mass. It was in a control circuit that rendered the whole machine functionless, but its repair would not be difficult, Jim knew.

He went back to the periphery of the engine and found the controls of a cranelike device which he lowered and seized the cracked sleeve and drew off the damaged part.

From the drawers and bins in the walls he selected parts and tools and returned to the damaged spot.

In the cramped space he began tearing away the fused parts and wiring. He was lost and utterly unconscious of anything but the fascination of the mighty engine. Here within this room was machine capacity to power a great city.

Its basic function rested upon the principle of magnetic currents in contrast to electric currents. The discovery of magnetic currents had been announced only a few months before he came home from the war. The application of the discovery had been swift.

And he began to glimpse the fundamental source of the energy supplying the machine. It was in the great currents of gravitational and magnetic force flowing between the planets and the suns of the universe. As great as atomic energy and as boundless in its resources, this required no fantastically dangerous machinery to harness. The principle of the power co-ordinator was simple.

The pain of his cramped position forced Jim to move out to rest his leg. As he stood beside the engine he resumed his pondering on the purpose it had in this strange location. Why was it built there and what use was made of its power?

He moved about to restore the circulation in his legs and sought to trace the flow of energy through the engine, determine where and what kind of a load was placed upon it.

His search led him below into a third sub-basement of the building and there he found the thing he was searching for, the load into which the tremendous drive of the engine was coupled.

But here he was unable to comprehend fully, for the load was itself a machine of strange design, and none of its features had been covered in the correspondence course.

The machine upstairs seized upon the magnetic currents of space and selected and concentrated those flowing in a given direction.

The force of these currents was then fed into the machines in this room, but there was no point of reaction against which the energy could be applied.

Unless—

The logical, inevitable conclusion forced itself upon his mind. There was only one conceivable point of reaction.

He stood very still and a tremor went through him. He looked up at the smooth walls about him. Metal, all of them. And this room —it was narrower than the one above—as if the entire building were tapered from the dome protruding out of the earth to the basement floor.

The only possible point of reaction was the building itself.

But it wasn't a building. It was a vessel.

Jim clawed and stumbled his way up the incline into the engine room, then beyond into the chamber above. He was halfway up the top ramp when he heard the voice again.

"Is that you, Mr. Ward? I have almost finished and will be with you in a moment. Have you completed the repairs? Was it very difficult?"

He hesitated, but didn't answer. Something about the quality of that voice gave him a chill. He hadn't noticed it before because of his curiosity and his interest in the place. Now he detected its unearthly, inhuman quality.

He detected the fact that it wasn't a voice at all, but that the words had been formed in his brain as if he himself had spoken them.

He was nearly at the top of the ramp and drew himself on hands and knees to the floor level when he saw the shadow of the closing door sweep across the room and heard the metallic clang of the door. It was sealed tight. Only the small windows—or ports—admitted light.

He rose and straightened and calmed himself with the thought that the vessel could not fly. It could not rise with the remainder of the repair task unfinished—and he was not going to finish it; that much was certain.

"Quilcon!" he called. "Show yourself! Who are you and what do you want of me?"

"I want you to finish the repair job and do it quickly," the voice replied instantly. "And quickly—it must be finished quickly."

There was a note of desperation and despair that seemed to cut into Jim. Then he caught sight of the slight motion against the wall beside him.

In a small, transparent hemisphere that was fastened to the side of the wall lay the slug that Jim had seen at the postoffice, the thing the woman had called an "armadillo." He had not even noticed it when he first entered the room. The thing was moving now with slow pulsations that swelled its surface and great welts like dark veins stood out upon it.

From the golden-hued hemisphere a maze of cable ran to instruments and junction boxes around the room and a hundred tiny pseudopods grasped terminals inside the hemisphere.

It was a vessel—and this slug within the hemisphere was its alien, incredible pilot. Jim knew it with startling cold reality that came to him in waves of thought that emanated from the slug called Quilcon and broke over Jim's mind. It was a ship and a pilot from beyond Earth—from out of the reaches of space.

"What do you want of me? Who are you?" said Jim Ward.

"I am Quilcon. You are a good student. You learn well."

"What do you want?"

"I want you to repair the damaged engine."

There was something wrong with the creature. Intangibly, Jim sensed it. An aura of sickness, a desperate urgency came to his mind.

But something else was in the foreground of Jim's mind. The horror of the alien creature diminished and Jim contemplated the miracle that had come to mankind.

"I'll bargain with you," he said quietly. "Tell me how to build a ship like this for my people and I will fix the engines for you."

"No! No—there is no time for that. I must hurry—"

"Then I shall leave without any repairs."

He moved toward the door and instantly a paralyzing wave took hold of him as if he had seized a pair of charged electrodes. It relaxed only as he stumbled back from the door.

"My power is weak," said Quilcon, "but it is strong enough for many days yet—many of your days. Too many for you to live without food and water. Repair the engine and then I shall let you go."

"Is what I ask too much to pay for my help?"

"You have had pay enough. You can teach your people to build power co-ordinator machines. Is that not enough?"

"My people want to build ships like this one and move through space."

"I cannot teach you that. I do not know. I did not build this ship."

There were surging waves of troubled thought that washed over his mind, but Jim Ward's tenseness eased. The first fear of totally alien life drifted from his mind and he felt a strange affinity for the creature. It was injured and sick, he knew, but he could not believe that it did not know how the ship was built.

"Those who built this ship come often to trade upon my world," said Quilcon. "But we have no such ships of our own. Most of us have no desire to see anything but the damp caves and sunny shores of our own world. But I longed to see the worlds from which these ships came.

"When this one landed near my cave I crept in and hid myself. The ship took off then and we traveled an endless time. Then an accident to the engine killed all three of those who manned the ship and I was left alone.

"I was injured, too, but I was not killed. Only the other of me died."

Jim did not understand the queer phrase, but he did not break into Quilcon's story.

"I was able to arrange means to control the flight of the ship, to prevent its destruction as it landed upon this planet, but I could not repair it because of the nature of my body."

Jim saw then that the creature's story must be true. It was obvious that the ship had been built to be manned by beings utterly unlike Quilcon.

"I investigated the city of yours near by and learned of your ways and customs. I needed the help of one of you to repair the ship. By force I could persuade one of you to do simple tasks, but none so complex as this requires.

"Then I discovered the peculiar customs of learning among you. I forced the man Herald to prepare the materials and send them to you. I received them before the person at the postoffice could see them. I got your name from the newspapers along with several others who were unsatisfactory.

"I had to teach you to understand the power co-ordinator because only by voluntary operation of your highest faculties will you be able to understand and repair the machine. I can assist but not force you to do that."

The creature began pleading again. "And now will you repair the engine quickly. I am dying—but shall live longer than you—it is a long journey to my home planet, but I must get there and I need every instant of time that is left to me."

Jim caught a glimpse of the dream vision that was the creature's home world. It was a place of security and peace—in Quilcon's terms. But even its alienness did not block out the sense of quiet beauty that Quilcon's mind transmitted to Jim's. They were a species of high intelligence. Exceptionally developed in the laws of mathematics and theory of logic, they were handicapped in bodily development from inquiring into other fields of science whose existence was demonstrated by their logic and their mathematics. The more intellectual among them were frustrated creatures whose lives were made tolerable only by an infinite capacity for stoicism and adaptation.

But of them all, Quilcon was among the most restless and rebellious and ambitious. No one of them had ever dared such a journey as he had taken. A swelling pity and understanding came over Jim Ward.

"I'll bargain with you," he said desperately. "I'll repair the engine if you'll let me have its principles. If you don't have them, you can get them to me with little trouble. My people must have such a ship as this."

He tried to visualize what it would mean to Earth to have space flight a century or perhaps five centuries before the slow plodding of science and research might reveal it.

But the creature was silent.

"Quilcon—" Jim repeated. He hoped it hadn't died.

"I'll bargain with you," said Quilcon at last. "Let me be the other of you, and I'll give you what you want."

"The other of me? What are you talking about?"

"It is hard for you to understand. It is union—such as we make upon our world. When two or more of us want to be together we go together in the same brain, the same body. I am alone now, and it is an unendurable existence because I have known what it is to have another of me.

"Let me come into your brain, into your mind and live there with you. We will teach your people and mine. We will take this ship to all the universes of which living creatures can dream. It is either this or we both die together, for too much time has gone for me to return. This body dies."

Stunned by Quilcon's ultimatum, Jim Ward stared at the ugly slug on the wall. Its brown body was heaving with violent pulsations of pain and a sense of delirium and terror came from it to Jim.

"Hurry! Let me come!" it pleaded.

He could feel sensations as if fingers were probing his cranium looking, pleading for entrance. It turned him cold.

He looked into the years and thought of an existence with this alien mind in his. Would they battle for eventual possession of his body and he perhaps be subjected to slavery in his own living corpse?

He tried to probe Quilcon's thoughts, but he could find no sense or intent of conquest. There were almost human amenities intermingled with a world of new science and thought.

He knew Quilcon would keep his promise to give the secrets of the ship to the men of Earth. That alone would be worth the price of his sacrifice—if it should be sacrifice.

"Come!" he said quietly.

It was as if a torrent of liquid light were flowing into his brain. It was blinding and excruciating in its flaming intensity. He thought he sensed rather than saw the brown husk of Quilcon quiver in the hemisphere and shrivel like a brown nut.

But in his mind there was union and he paused and trembled with the sudden great reality of what he knew. He knew what Quilcon was and gladness flowed into him like light. A thought soared through his brain: Is sex only in the difference of bodily function and the texture of skin and the tone of voice?

He thought of another day when there was death in the sky and on the Earth below, and in a little field hospital. A figure on a white cot had murmured, "You'll be all right, Jim. I'm going on, I guess, but you'll be all right. I know it. Don't miss me too much."

He had known there would be no peace for him ever, but now there was peace and the voice of Quilcon was like that voice from long ago, for as the creature probed into his thoughts its inherent adaptability matched its feelings and thought to his and said, "Everything is all right, isn't it, Jim Ward?"

"Yes . . . yes it is." The intensity of his feelings almost blinded him. "And I want to call you Ruth, after another Ruth—"

"I like that name." There was shyness and appreciation in the tones, and it was not strange to Jim that he could not see the speaker, for there was a vision in his mind far lovelier than any Earthly vision could have been.

"We'll have everything," he said. "Everything that your world and mine can offer. We'll see them all."

But like the other Ruth who had been so practical, this one was, too. "First we have to repair the engine. Shall we do it, now?"

The solitary figure of Jim Ward moved toward the ramp and disappeared into the depths of the ship.

BRAIN

by

S. FOWLER WRIGHT

*Some there are who believe that the cold reason of science is
everything; without even comprehending that the scientist is also
a man, with a man's strength and weakness, they demand that the
world be run by a formula. With devastating irony, Mr. Fowler
Wright pictures a state governed by just such a rigid, scientifically
correct formula. But man, even scientific man, is more than a
provable theorem; knowledge is not always perfect power, as witness the case of the pig who helped upset the rule of the wise
men.*

*

PROFESSOR BRISKET, President of the first Scientist government, sat in his new Studio of Contemplation, one morning in
the early spring of 1990, considering the possibilities of the unprecedented power which the advance of knowledge, and the events
of the last year, had placed in his somewhat bony hands.

It was six months since the suppression of the rebellion of 1989,
in which the last traditions of barbarism had gone down, drowned
in the blood of millions.

It was a crisis which had been inevitable for fifty years, though
there were few that had foreseen, even a year ago, how near it was,
and how decisive it must be.

A year ago, in spite of the changes and developments of half-a-
century, the grotesque custom had persisted which decided the government of the country by the equal votes of its adult inhabitants,
there being no distinction between youth and age, between folly

and wisdom, between knowledge and ignorance—not even the simplest distinction between the cranial capacities of the voters, no disability being recognized except that of certified lunacy, or definite conviction of criminality. It was scarcely more than fifty years since there had been the grotesque spectacle of an eminent scientist being summoned before a magistrate, with no University qualifications whatever, to account for the possession of a stolen dog, and for the uses to which he had put it.

Since then, scientific knowledge had been powerful enough to influence successive governments, in spite of the comic method of their appointment, in ways which had brought incalculable benefits to mankind.

And then (as the obstinate mule had died just as it had been successfully reduced to the daily diet of a single straw), from one absurd triviality, the whole country had leapt into a sudden flame of war, with all its horrors.

It was a woman, as usual, who was the first cause of the crisis. A woman who had been fond of turnips. A woman with an infatuated husband, who had actually grown them for her, on a strip of hidden land behind his dwelling, in excess of the regulated dietary, and in contempt of the balance of vitamins on which their health, if not their lives, depended.

Worse than that, after the crime had been detected and punished, mildly enough, by the painless amputation of his left ear, he had contumaciously repeated the offence, attempting to grow the forbidden vegetable in an unoccupied cellar.

Being again detected, and knowing that he could hope for no further mercy, he had resisted arrest with such violence that his captors had brought him to the dock with broken heads, and one of them having a damaged mouth, and a denture smashed beyond remedy.

There had been no demonstration at the trial, of which there had been no public report (which was prohibited for certain of the grosser forms of obscenity), and there had been no sign of previous agitation to forecast the riot which had demolished the vehicle intended to convey him to the port of banishment, and rescued him from it.

A week later, the city of Nottingham, in which the incident had occurred, was in a state of open rebellion, refusing to surrender the culprit, and demanding repeal of the legislation which had occasioned the trouble.

And then, while the government hesitated and temporized, using such intermittent severities as exasperated without suppressing a revolt which threatened to spread from the midland to the northern counties, Professor Brisket, until then only known as holding the chair of Homology at the London University, had called a conference of twenty of the leading scientists, and, three days later, it was announced to an astounded world that the Government had resigned, and that the Council of Twenty-One had assumed responsibility for the control of the country.

Open war followed. War that was fierce, and short, and sanguinary. The usurpation was resisted by nine-tenths of the population, including almost the whole of its (comparatively) illiterate, its political, its religious, and the majority of its literary and journalistic elements. But the scientists and their followers, banding in instant opposition to the forces of prejudice and reaction, opposed a hundred devices, secret, subtle, and deadly, to the crude violence of high-explosive, and the vain defenses of trench and steel.

The proletariat fought with the obsolete weapons with which they had been furnished by the subservient scientists of an earlier century: the scientists retaliated with a variety of deaths, insanities and diseases, of which the origin was often indiscoverable, and from which there was no defense, nor any road of escape which could be found by those upon whom they fell.

Yet so bitter was the enmity which had leapt to light from the tiny spark which had kindled it, so hopeless did the rebels feel that their fate would be, should they resign themselves to submission; so sure, on the other hand, were the ranks of the scientists that they fought for all the possibilities of the mind of man, and that failure would frustrate all their work, and lead the world backward, even to the monkey-twilight of their aboriginal ancestors, that it seemed for a time that extermination only would be sufficient to decide its issue.

The rebels had been encouraged, almost at the first, by the defection of one of the leading scientists of the day, Dr. Shercliff Binyon, whose teaching had always been of a heretical kind, as he had held that while the pursuit of knowledge is among the noblest occupations of the human mind, the idea that the created can be equal, by the application of such knowledge, to take the part of the Creator, was a presumptuous folly which could only end in such disaster as would revert the world to an elementary barbarism. He had even suggested that this result, and the recurrence of such results, might be the Divine method by which the earth was continually re-fitted for its purpose as a training-ground for the spirit of man.

But his support, however morally important, had had little practical result beyond the momentary heartening of the rebels, for his learning was not of a kind which could be used for the discomfiture of their enemies; and the scientists, infuriated by the unexpected stubbornness of the resistance which they encountered, and by the desertion of one of their own body, decided to strike with a severity which would end the conflict.

When Professor Brisket had given the members of the previous government an ultimatum of two hours to resign their offices, it had been with a warning that, should they refuse or hesitate, they would be smitten by a disease which would render them pestilent beyond endurance of any human associates.

Now he had warned the champions of ignorance and reaction that, unless there should be surrender, absolute and abject, within twelve hours, they would learn, in the desolation of a city, the irresistible powers which they had defied so vainly.

The rebels had replied by marshalling a cloud of fighting planes, which held the air from Southampton to Lowestoft in one unbroken line of heroic purpose, and by the up-thrown mouth of ten thousand antiaircraft guns. But the planes had held their line unchallenged, and the guns had remained silent. Only, when the next morning came, Bristol had ceased to be. It had dissolved into air or ground before a chemical agent so powerful, so silent, and so swift, that no sound disturbed the serenity of the surrounding country, no light of ruin flickered over the Channel waters. Simply, the city lights went out. Simply, the ground where once the city stood showed bare and burnt and of a somewhat crocus aspect, purple and yellow-streaked, when the dawn found it. But of the city that had been, of life or building or garden, even of Clifton bridge, there was no trace at all.

After that, there had been no more trouble.

Professor—now President—Brisket smiled silently, recalling the coincidence that Dr. Binyon had happened to be in the city which had been selected for the required example. His hesitations had ceased from troubling.

Power had come to the President, as it may never have come to any earlier potentate in the history of the world. There was only the Council of the Twenty-One, and to each of these he had allotted their appropriate occupations. Seventeen of them would continue the conquest of knowledge, by the power of which the world lay at their feet already; and the whole Universe was yielding, one by one, its cryptic secrets to their insatiate importunities. Of the other three, two were occupied in executive work as his enthusiastic subordinates. There was no danger from them. Professor Borthin? Well, he was not immortal. There might be a vacancy on the Council of Twenty-One. It might be very soon.

II

The President sat in his star-domed Studio of Contemplation, over the aromatic darkness of which its vault of stars gave the impression of the depths of space, without the risk of rain or cold or tempest, so that he might think without any triviality of distraction, and with the vast realm always before him,—the realm of blind, unchanging law which lay, in its vast unconsciousness, awaiting the control of the advancing minds of men.

The hours passed, and he did not move. He was facing the most momentous decision of his life. More gigantic in possibilities, more fatal should his judgment err, than had been that which had established him as the head of the first purely scientific government that the earth had known.

It was three years ago that he had casually discovered, when his investigations were directed to quite other ends, the substance which stimulates the cerebral processes, and controls the functioning of the brain. He had been cautious in its application, because the occasion of his discovery had suggested that its use might not be without danger to a mammalian subject, and an injection into a young dog had produced a condition of such uncontrollable ferocity as to be indistinguishable from actual madness.

A viper, receiving a small, and then a larger injection, had shown no sign of any effect whatever. On receiving a third, it had died within a few hours.

The first real success had been with a minnow, one of five in a glass tank, to which he had given an infinitesimal injection. Two days afterwards, when he went to scatter their food on the water in the usual corner, he found that it was surrounded by a barrier of the floating weed which the tank contained, through which there was only one passage left, and that somewhat tortuous.

Through this passage the inoculated minnow darted swiftly, reaching the food sufficiently before its baffled companions to get the largest share of the meal.

He had disturbed the weed, and had found it rearranged on the next morning.

Disturbing it again, he had watched, and seen the fish actually tugging the floating weed to the required position.

After that, he had fed the fish on whatever part of the surface might be clear, lest the other four should be starved entirely.

Four days, later, he had found three of them dead in the water, each with a wound behind the neck, the inoculated fish having evidently decided that one companion would be sufficient for its requirements, and would allow it to eat its fill.

This experiment had shown that he had been right in his judgment as to the nature of the substance which he had isolated, and, learning this, he had destroyed the too-intelligent minnow, and burnt its body, these precautions being taken because he was not sure whether the acquired characteristic, being physical in its basis, might not be transmitted to a succeeding generation, nor even whether there might not be a possibility that it might be transmissible to another fish which might swallow one which had benefited from the inoculation. He had no wish to create a race of pike with approximately human cunning.

Since that time he had made some fresh discoveries as to the nature and effects of the secretion, and modifications in its preparation, which, he believed, would render it suitable for injection into the blood of the mammalia, and, specifically, into the human blood which was to be its ultimate destination.

But he had still much to learn as to its effects, and as to the dose which could be safely given, as to whether such effects were permanent, and concerning that most important question of whether it would be transmitted to the children of those who might benefit from it.

He had also perfected another injection, which could be relied upon to produce in those who received it a docility so great that all other passions or proclivities would be subdued by the desire to act at the call of duty, or to fulfil the wishes of those about them. On this latter preparation he relied with a reasonable confidence to control any unruly symptoms which might result from the major experiment.

Now he sat, in the artificial unchanging night of the studio, considering the conditions of his next experiment, and on whom or what it should be made.

It was a matter on which he had no confidant. It was a power too great to share. The time might come for its announcement, even for doling it out to others, in some lesser degree than his own benefit from it. It would make his dominance absolute. It would bring, no doubt, the worship which must be paid, sooner or later, to the Lord of Science who will control the world. But that time was not yet.

. . . At last, he rose, and passed out of the studio. His course was clearly determined. He summoned Wilkins, who superintended the scientific diet which had maintained his health so well, until he was now on the threshold of his eighty-second year.

III

"Wilkins," said the Premier, "I want you to speak to the farmer who supplies the eggs and milk for my own table. I want him to procure me a young sow-pig. The breed doesn't matter, and I will pay his price. But it must be healthy, intelligent, and good-tempered."

"Good-tempered, sir?"

"Yes, that's very important. It's not for the laboratory."

"No, sir?"

"No, I shall want two other pigs sent there. Two with good foreheads. I may want a look at their brains. But I want this one sent to Berkhampsted. I shall be going down on Tuesday. I know there are some good sites there; though we haven't used them. You can give instructions about the details."

He turned his attention to more immediate things.

IV

The young sow came out eagerly at the splashing sound of the pig-wash. The abnormal activity of her brain had not resulted in any emaciation of her interior organs, nor of the adipose tissues which have been so successfully cultivated by a thousand ancestral generations. She was still growing, and the excitements of mother-hood were yet before her. She was well-fed, sleek, and supple in movement; her rapid growth, and a restless activity somewhat infrequent in her kind, having delayed the more extreme corpulence for which her race is so justly famed.

She would have been outside her sleeping-compartment before the opening of the sty-door, and the tilt of the bucket, but that she did not wish to show any interest in the condition of the fastenings of that door, which she felt sure would be carefully examined. It was true that they were quite in order, but it would have been a needless ordeal to have met the suspicious glances of Billy Tedman, who regarded her with a mixture of fear and admiration, which would have been insufficient to condone the delinquency of the early morning.

But what proof was there?

A brood of seven tiny goslings running through the dewy grass, toward the sanctuary of the coop three yards away, from which their mother stretched an anxious neck. Strong jaws that snapped five times—that snapped and swallowed—and two goslings only that tumbled clumsily over the wooden edge of the coop into the safety of the familiar straw.

No one had seen it. And Billy Tedman knew that the young sow could open the wooden latch of the sty-door, and that she was always to be found wandering loose should he omit to slide the lower bolt which had been added a few weeks ago—knew with equal certainty that she could not open that lower bolt, and that she was never found loose now, unless he should forget to slide it.

The five goslings had been only ten days old, and their fluffy bodies had done little to reduce the healthy appetite with which she plunged her snout into the creamy mess which had descended from Billy's bucket. Sharps are good, and skim-milk can be sucked up very pleasantly. But why, oh why, had she been such a fool as to tell Professor Brisket that she liked barley-meal best?

Now she knew that, after she had enjoyed an hour of happy dozing in the straw of her sleeping-quarters, a panel would slide back in the furthest wall, and she would have to rise and go out into a covered yard, where the Professor and she would commune together for an uncertain period, during which she would have to reply to his questions with exasperating slowness—a slowness which was, however, often less exasperating than the fatuous questions themselves—by indicating successive letters from an alphabet which was neatly painted upon the ground between them.

She knew already that he was a slow-brained old fossil, whose mind or eye would fail to follow her spelling if she quickened the motions of foot or snout, but she did not know why he had been foolish enough to discourage a simple suggestion that they should substitute a series of symbols for the more frequent words.

Here she erred, supposing him to be more stupid than he really was; the fact being that he only held the conversations at all to test the degree of intelligence with which he had endowed her, and that he intended her to go to the butcher immediately she had supplied him with a litter of young pigs which would enable him to judge the effects of his experiment upon the next generation.

Also, he destined her bacon for his own exclusive consumption, which would test the possibility of the transmission of this new brain-stimulus by the medium of eaten flesh. There must be tests also of the consumption of blood, of uncooked meat, particularly of uncooked brains. Professor Brisket would not have attained his present eminence had he not been careful and unhurried in his experiments.

His brain might be less agile, his perceptions slower, than those of the stimulated ganglia of his protagonist, but, from the advantage of his greater knowledge, his longer experience, and his somewhat different personality (though this last difference should not be too generously assessed), he was able, not merely to conceal his ultimate purpose, but the impulses also that prompted the questions which seemed so foolish to his pachydermatous protégée, and the opinions which he formed upon them.

He had already made one observation, of the first importance. The improvement in the faculties and functioning of the brain which he had been able to induce did not result in any change in the nature of the individual who received advantage from them.

The sow did not forget the swill-trough to observe the stars.

It was the nature of her kind to be cunning, cowardly, and greedful, and these characteristics continued. She had improved, beyond his utmost anticipation, in memory, in power of deductive reasoning, in alertness of mental anticipation, but he had no reason to doubt that, if one of her children should be still-born, she would proceed to eat it, as her mother had done before her; he knew that she would answer his questions with diligence solely because she would get no barley-meal in the afternoon should she show any indisposition to do so.

On the day which we are now considering, the Professor brought to its intended climax a line of inquiry which he had been pursuing for a previous week, during which he had explained very frankly to this intelligent animal the nature of the relations which had existed between her race and his own for so long a period. He had done this with some curiosity, if not trepidation, as to the reactions which it would arouse in the mind of his auditor, and had not been without the protection of a lethal weapon of recent invention, very swift and deadly in its action, which had lain ready to his hand on the little table which divided her from him, on which he was accustomed to make notes of the morning's conversations, beyond which was the alphabet set in the ground, by which the young sow was enabled to reply to his questions, despite the deficiency in the construction of her vocal chords, which reduced the possibilities of oral intercourse.

But the animal had taken his explanation in a very sensible way. She saw at once that it was natural that all creatures should eat each other as opportunity offered, and safety permitted. It was the only law of life which she would ever be likely to understand, even though her brain were stimulated a hundred-fold. She saw how greatly it was to the advantage of the young of her kind that they should receive (as it were) an insurance policy from the human race giving to each of them at the least a few months of happy carefree life, rather than that they should be exposed to the savage chances of the wilds, to precarious uncertainties of food and climate, and to the decimations of a hundred accidents. She saw at once that men would still have been able to kill pigs, had they done nothing to protect and cherish. When she learnt the almost incredible millions which are maintained in a princely indolence, she saw that the world was theirs, and that the greed and stupidity of mankind had been successfully exploited by the farsighted cunning of her kind. When the Professor explained that, though the majority of any litter might be destined to an early end, yet it frequently happened that the best among them would be selected to remain alive and continue the generations, and that she herself was one who had been so favored, it seemed a particularly admirable arrangement, of which she approved most heartily.

The Professor was somewhat disconcerted by the uncertainty with which her mind perceived that the human race has made itself subservient to her own, until he recollected that she was a pig still, though she might be a very intelligent one, and that her conclusions might naturally be influenced by this deficiency.

V

Professor Borthin, having no star-domed Studio of Contemplation in which to ponder, was pacing one of the longer corridors of Buckingham Palace. He was thirty-two, the youngest and most brilliant member of the Council of Twenty-One. A man of restless, drug-stimulated energy, he found that he could think best when his legs were moving.

He had a deep contempt for President Brisket, who had been allowed his position through the paltry claim of seniority (senility would have been a better word!) when it had been decided that the scientists should assert their power. What was Brisket? A sentimentalist. A dreamer. A man knowing no more mathematics than a nineteenth-century schoolgirl.

Even the occasion of the revolution had been an absurdity. What did it matter if women ate turnips? Or prussic acid? Most men and women were of no value, except for experimental purposes.

Now this brain-grafting. . . . He wanted a dozen babies of each sex, every month for a year, if the experiment were to be carried out with sufficient variations to make it interesting. Two or three hundred children's bodies growing up with the brains of dogs. . . . Two or three hundred bodies of dogs directed by the brains of children. It was fascinating in its possibilities. And some of the brains could be transferred back after a time. . . .

And the old fool had delayed permission! It was to be "discussed at the Council."

But there would be something else to be discussed at the Council. There would be a surprise for Brisket. . . . Or did he guess it? "Space lying curved in the arms of Time." That had been his expression when he had been perorating at the last meeting. Drivelling old fool! Did he not know that Space and Time is one and indissoluble?

He had spoken as though Time had pre-existed Space, and the heavy lids of Professor Sturmie's eyes had lifted for a moment, and surveyed him with a puzzled wonder. He didn't often show his ignorance in that assembly by talking outside the limits of his own Homology.

Even to the untrained mind to attempt imagination of Space without Time, or of Time without Space, should be enough to show its absurdity. Even Einstein's elementary speculations of sixty years ago had passed the bounds of such childishness.

He had roused Professor Sturmie to bring up the subject. Sturmie cared for no one, if his own subjects were left alone, but he had a gift of sarcasm, which had made him dreaded in controversy. He could be trusted to make the President look the fool he was. And when that had happened, what influence would he have left?

After that episode, he would ask for an order for the children he needed. If it were refused. . . .? He would claim a vote. It was the kind of point on which he would be sure to get it.

Then he would suggest the propriety of resignation. Probably, after that, there would be swift deaths on the Council. Well, if so, he had his own secret powers. He would not be unready.

Thirty years ago, Queen Hermione had presented Buckingham Palace to the nation (perhaps not very willingly) as a home for South American monkeys whose gland-extractions were required to increase the virility of members of the House of Commons.

Professor Borthin ceased his activities in the corridor. He went to look at the monkeys.

VI

The silent occupant of the Studio of Contemplation was not unaware of his danger.

He had regretted that florescence of oratory the moment that he had met the sardonic glance of Professor Sturmie's heavy eyes, as they had been lifted toward him.

Professor Sturmie seldom looked, or spoke, or voted.

His attendants wheeled his chair into position at the Council table, and he sat there, his hands motionless before him, his face a blank passivity, till the proceedings ended.

But he was held in a very great respect. He was supposed to know more on each of his colleagues' subjects than they knew themselves.

Twenty years ago, as Principal of the Birmingham University, it had become known that, in case of sudden indisposition, he could take the place of any of his professors, and lecture brilliantly on their own subjects at a moment's notice. There had been plots to test this capacity, but he had always been equal to them.

If he should now be roused to attack the intellectual eminence of the President, that gentleman knew that the assault could be delivered from no deadlier quarter.

He knew that there were other members of the Council whose knowledge both of Physics and Mathematics was greater than his own. There was nothing in that. Each man specialized, and was supreme in his own dominion. But he was not expected to talk dogmatic fallacies upon his neighbors' subjects. And the position of a President was different from that of others. He, of all men, must not be open to ridicule.

But, after all, it had only hastened the conflict, which was inevitable. Borthin meant to rule, and the difference was not of men only. It was one of fundamental principles. Professor Brisket had never been known as a sentimentalist. He would pour human blood on the altars of Science as readily as he would have sacrificed a mangel-wurzel. He had not hesitated to give the order which had evaporated Bristol. But he believed, in a vague way, that all he did was for the Higher Good of Humanity.

Professor Borthin had no such illusions, and no such object. For the Higher Good of Humanity he did not care a bean. He worshipped Science for its own sake, and it was its own justification.

To him, President Brisket was a sentimentalist, and an obstruction, and the time had come to remove him.

The two men were thus of one mind as to the necessity for removing the other. They were united in decision that the time had come. They were agreed as to the time and place of the conflict. They were alike in thinking that the first step must be to discredit the adversary before the Council. They only differed in the fact that the younger man was the attacker, that he fought from a less vulnerable situation, and that he was confident of success, whereas his older and more cautious opponent was aware of being forced to give battle on ground which he had not chosen, and was very far from comfortable as to the defense he could offer, or the strength of the counter-attack which he must be prepared to deliver. . . .

And yet his mind held to the point that Space and Time were not identical. They were not merely two aspects of one quality. There was an absolute difference. But how could he prove it in a way which would convince the Council, and confound his opponents? Of the difference, he was convinced. Of his own random metaphor—of the pre-existence of Time—he was much less confident.

He reflected that Space is motionless. It remains. It must have been—always. Full or empty, it must have been there. Timeless, perhaps, but *there*. Was this not the very opposite of the idea which he had advanced so randomly?

Must have been, if it had no conscious occupants? Yes, surely.

Then how about Time? A condition of Time of which there had never been, nor would be, conscious knowledge vexed his mind with a lack of reality. He was less sure.

Supposing that there were two separate realms of consciousness, not adjoining. Would not the unconscious interval be a Space, although it had no conscious occupant? Was it so in itself, or was it made such by the facts of the conscious realms which were contiguous to it? But he had first postulated that Space. . . . He became aware that he was speculating vaguely, whereas the thoughts of Professor Sturmie on such a subject would be clear and sure, and his words decisive.

It was not thus that he would be armed for conquest. He must be prepared not only to resist, but to rout with a returning ridicule. He could not afford to fail. He could not even afford an indecisive contest.

If his brain were stimulated. . . . He saw that the time had come to call in the aid of the unsuspected power which he held reserved. Surely, after all his experiments . . . ? He would try an infinitesimal dose at first, and then a larger one, when he had experienced its effects.

VII

It was about half an hour before he felt the effect of the injection. Then he became aware of an increased clarity of vision, by which the minor details of the objects around him, which he had previously overlooked, were thrown into a vivid prominence. Then he was conscious of a new mental energy, and a quickened perception of abstract things. It was absurd that he should have been troubled by the sluggish cerebrations of Professor Sturmie, who had a mind that floundered like a hippopotamus. And the problem itself was of a childish simplicity. Quiescent Space could have no Time at all. Therefore they could not be identical.

Space must be invaded by Energy: then Time was needed for its operations. Time commenced with its own occasion.

That was the sequence. Space must first exist. Then there must be the invasion of Energy. Then there must be Time for its operations.

So far he saw—or thought he saw—very clearly. But there was something further. Something behind, and beyond, of which his mind was aware, but which it could not reach. Something that vexed and baffled, like a half-faded dream. Something which, could he grasp it, would bring conviction to all who heard, and confound his opponents with a swift derision.

He saw that he would need a further injection before he would be able to overwhelm his enemies. With the experience which he had gained, he no longer feared it. He resolved to take the Council into a partial confidence. He would tell them of the discovery he had made. He would take a further injection before their eyes. He would discourse upon it for half an hour, telling of the experiments which he had made already—telling everything but the formula itself—offering to share his discovery with his colleagues, and to confine it to them, so that, even among their fellow-scientists, they would be assured of a continued supremacy.

Meanwhile, the injection would operate in him, and would demonstrate the miracle which he had achieved.

After that, he would know how to deal with Borthin, even with Sturmie, should they dare to attack him. Should they be silent, he would also deal with them, quickly and quietly, after the Council had risen.

Meanwhile, he could put the question from his mind entirely. He was disposed to experiment with the second preparation, to ascertain its effects upon those who had been exhilarated by the first already. Not, of course, upon himself. He went to the laboratory, filled a syringe, and went down to the pig-sty.

He entered it by the sliding door, at the back of the sleeping compartment. The sow, sprawled in clean straw, after a heavy lunch of her beloved barley-meal, was snoring happily. He applied the syringe behind her ear, and gave her an ample dose. The ear flicked, as though a fly had vexed it, but the sow did not waken.

VIII

President Brisket was not lacking in self-control, and there were probably few men who were less under the domination of the physical. Yet he had developed certain habits of which he vaguely disapproved, and against which he fought a desultory battle, in which he was never decisively victorious.

Among these habits was one of muttering to himself, more or less audibly, when he imagined himself to be alone, and sometimes even when those were present before whom a firmer restraint was desirable.

It was unfortunate for himself, and of momentous consequence to the world, that he had been particularly injudicious on more than one occasion when he had been lost in thought, sitting at the table, or pacing the private yard, after he had finished one of his instructive interviews with the animal intelligence that he had stimulated, and after the sow had retired to her own quarters. With all his wisdom, he had not considered that the hearing of a sow is more acute than that of a man, and that the alertness of the senses of this particular animal rendered the closing of the partition a useless obstacle to the hearing of the words which he subsequently muttered, however indistinctly.

It followed that the animal had been able to supplement the information which he had thought well to give her with a knowledge of the preparations he was using, and of his hopes and plans, which he would have found very disconcerting, had he been aware of this development, and still more so had he suspected the conclusions to which they had led her.

As we have remarked already, although she had become a pig of very exceptional intelligence, she was a pig still. She was not concerned with the stars, nor with the good of humanity, nor with the pursuit of science, nor even with the good of her own kind. She was concerned solely and entirely with her own physical welfare. Because she had learnt of the general destiny of pigs without resentment, it did not follow that she was willing to feel a knife in her own neck. Rather, she recognized that this was the one problem with which it was essential that she should deal successfully. It did not appear that it was of an immediate urgency, but it was of an overwhelming importance.

When the self-communings of the President had informed her of the nature of the cultures which he had produced, and of his intentions concerning them, she had seen at once that her ultimate hope must lie in the second of these preparations, which, administered at the right time, and to the right individual, could hardly fail to direct his mind to a universal benevolence, from which she would benefit, in common with all the other creatures around him.

But she was too clear-sighted to minimize the difficulties of such a program. She was aware of her physical limitations, and she felt no assurance, even should she be able to obtain and secrete some of the drug or culture in question (she was not very clear as to its exact nature), that the final assault upon herself would give her an opportunity of using it successfully.

She was, as we know, a very sensible animal, and she could not imagine a murderous-minded butcher, who might be short either of time or temper, delaying operations at her request, so that she might give him an injection in the right arm.

Beyond that, the mutterings of President Brisket had left her in doubt as to how soon the injection would take effect, and it is obvious that time would be of vital importance under such conditions as she had imagined.

She had a very practical mind, and it would have been no consolation to her to know that a repentant butcher would wreathe her corpse with flowers.

Finally, she had decided that her best hope lay in causing the President to take a sufficient dose of the second preparation to cause him to become of an overwhelming amiability, in which case the beneficence of his disposition could hardly fail to favor one who had been brought into such close and intellectually intimate relations with him.

That, at least, seemed her best hope, and she had now been watching for some weeks for an opportunity of putting into operation the simple but audacious plan by which she hoped to insure her safety.

This plan was to penetrate into the President's laboratory, and so to mix or interchange the cultures as to insure that when, as she had learnt from his own lips that he intended, he should aim to inoculate himself with the first, he should actually take an injection of the second.

But in this enterprise she could not afford to fail, and as she did not consider it urgent, she had delayed for choice of opportunity, until, as we have seen, President Brisket had already commenced the process of brain-stimulation which it was her object to complicate.

Such was the position when she awoke, alert from sleep, as the afternoon was waning, with a feeling of most unusual kindliness to the world around her.

IX

She went first into the outer sty, to observe the position of the sun, from which she was able to estimate the time—about three hours—

which would elapse before her snout would sink suckingly into the ecstasy of the evening meal. Then she returned, somewhat uncertainly, to the inner sty. She had a vague impulse of beneficence, such as she had never known before, causing her to feel that her time was wasted unless she were doing good to someone.

Someone certainly included herself. When she remembered the project that had recently possessed her mind, it had acquired an even greater importance than it had had previously. She observed that the absent-minded President had failed to close the sliding hatch from which he had entered to disturb her sleep so momentously.

She knew that she had only to cross the yard to gain the stairway door through which he was accustomed to descend upon her. She did not suppose that it would be locked, and there were few forms of latch which she had not learnt to manipulate. . . .

It would be little consonant with a narrative of such events as those that we are now approaching to give a detailed observation to the movements of a domestic pig, however intelligent.

It is sufficient to say that she must have succeeded in her purpose, which is not entirely surprising when her abnormal intelligence is considered, together with the fact that she was impulsed by an altruistic exaltation of mind, induced by the last injection she had received, and very foreign to her natural propensities, and, finally, that she was equipped by nature with a highly sensitive snout, capable, even with the less intelligent of her kind, of operations of almost manual dexterity, and to which feet and teeth could give very useful support at need.

But it is evident, from the sequel, that she must have found some human or mechanical obstacle, such as that of a closed door, which prevented her return to her sty by the direct way when she had completed her enterprise; for we next observe her in Berkhampsted High Street, where she was brought up short by encountering a certain carpenter, a Mr. Jubbins, who turned suddenly from a sidestreet, with his bag of tools on his shoulder.

It is evident that the carpenter must have been fond of pork (or perhaps bacon is indicated), and that the sight of this sleek-sided specimen of her kind must have awakened certain acquisitive, if not actually gluttonous, instincts in a corrupt mind, which must have communicated themselves to an animal in which the drug was still working most potently, so that it had become an uncontrollable impulse to gratify the desires of those among whom she moved.

"Can you direct me," she inquired fatuously, "to a really good butcher?"

We know that her articulation of human speech was not clear, but Mr. Jubbins seems to have caught her meaning immediately.

"Come this way," he said genially, with a persuasive hand on the ear that was nearer. He scratched her back very comfortably. He felt that he would be able to do all that was necessary.

. . . He doubted whether a saw would be mutually satisfactory, but perhaps a chisel . . . ?

They entered his workshop side by side, and the subsequent events may best be indicated by "noises off stage." Actually, I do not know what happened. I believe that the effects of the injection, which was certainly not as permanent in its nature as the first one, were beginning to clear as the carpenter turned the key on the inside of his workshop-door, but beyond that . . . well, she was a very intelligent animal.

We are dealing with the events of 1990, which I may not live to investigate, but should I attain to such a great longevity, I shall make a point of penetrating that side-turning from the Berkhampsted High Street. It would be nice to know.

X

The Council of Twenty-One met in a plainly furnished room in the London University buildings. They had no need of the vulgarity of material ostentation. Individual members might indulge in castle or park or palace, and none would stay them, for the earth was theirs, and common men lived or died at their pleasure, but collectively their power needed no pomp to display it. It lay in formulae which only they—or perhaps only some of them—could read: in powerhouse and test tube: most of all, in the fear of the unknown that lay, like a shadow of death, over the ignorant populace that they ruled and exploited.

Once before, in the twilight of the middle ages, this shadow had lengthened across the world, but the people of that time had struck viciously with fire and cord, and had stamped back into smoldering ash the threat that might otherwise have won, even then, its dark dominion over them.

Now it had triumphed, and not only the members of the Council, but their meanest student, could walk securely among a host of common men, though he knew there was not one but would have slain him gladly. They were the terror that walked at noon, and there was none so bold as to lift even a glance of hatred against them.

President Brisket sat at the table's head, with the Secretary of the Council, Dr. Acton-Shaw, at his right hand.

Dr. Acton-Shaw was himself one of the Council, as it was not considered expedient that its minutes should be in the hands of an official of inferior status or responsibility, nor were these minutes, dealing largely, as they did, with the application of the abstruser sciences, always easy to take.

The Secretary was a small man, with a very wizened face, and a habit of peering, as though he suffered from partial blindness. In fact, his sight was excellent, his observation abnormal, and his memory for fact or face an amazement, even to the trained minds that were round him. With these qualities he made no enemies, for he expressed no opinions. No one knew what he thought. So far, there had been no evidence that he thought at all.

There are many battles that are decided before the moment of actual conflict, by the courage or cowardice of those who approach to the encounter. Men defeat themselves more often than they are defeated by the assault of circumstance. But, on this occasion, a psychologist, investigating the mental confidence of either side, or observing the careful preparations on which such confidence rested, might have foretold their victory with an equal certainty.

The agenda which the Secretary had prepared from the President's instructions, and from the requisitions of members, included the name of Dr. Sturmie for the first time in the history of the Council.

Dr. P. A. Sturmie to address the Council on FUNDAMENTALS, and to move a resolution.

Immediately after, there came the name of Professor Borthin *to address the Council on the progress of BRAIN-GRAFTING, and to move a resolution.*

The atmosphere, as the scientists entered, one by one, and took their accustomed seats, was oppressive with the sense of a coming storm. The majority were not men of aggressive temperament. They only wanted to be left alone to the pursuit of their own researches. Now that the earth was theirs, and they could demand what they would for apparatus or experiment, they had no wish but to be left in quietness to cultivate the opportunity which life had offered.

But they knew, all of them more or less, of the conflict which was impending. And there were only seven members who had not some private knowledge in reserve of swift and secret ways by which he might destroy his colleagues, should he be disposed to do so.

President Brisket came late. He entered with an almost jaunty confidence. He glanced down the agenda which lay before him, with light words of bantering comment.

"Dr. Sturmie! . . . Always glad to hear Sturmie. . . . Quite a light-weight subject for you, doctor. Almost skittish. . . . Borthin? . . . Oh, yes. I remember. The babies' brains. . . . Always enterprising."

Then his manner changed. He drew a small tube from his pocket, and laid it on the table before him.

He spoke now with a grave elation. "Gentlemen, when these routine matters are over, I've something of real importance to tell you. An avenue is opening before us of unimagined life and power. I am going to show you an experiment on myself, and I am going to offer its benefits to you also, when I have demonstrated what they are. . . . But we'll get through the agenda first, and we'll try to make it as short as possible. . . . Dr. Sturmie will address us on—what is it? Oh, yes. FUNDAMENTALS."

Dr. Sturmie did not rise. His age and infirmities excused him from such an ordeal. He had shown no sign of hearing what had been said, but now he began to speak. At first, his tone was low, an indistinct rumbling from the depths of his massive chest. He looked at no one. He seemed to be unaware of the audience by which he was surrounded.

But as he went on, his voice became louder, his articulation clearer. Much that he said was difficult to understand, even to the select audience he addressed. Members leant forward eagerly to catch the pregnant sentences as they fell. Now and then he became strangely lucid, so that, though he spoke of things which are beyond the ordinary imaginations of men, a child could have understood him. The listeners felt that he spoke of things that they had always known, but that they had never been able to formulate, to articulate, previously. Had he concluded by moving that President Brisket should be sent to an Infants' School, it is doubtful whether there would have been less than nineteen votes to support him; but his motion was simply this: *That any member, after this date, who shall speak on subjects of which he is ignorant, shall be dismissed the Council.*

Hearing the resolution, the President decided instantly to ignore the fact that it was so clearly aimed at himself, and to put it without discussion. He did not merely ignore the attack, he swept it contemptuously back. Since he had taken that injection three days ago, his brain felt equal to anything.

"Well, gentlemen," he said briefly, "we've all enjoyed the address, but we've got some important business coming, so I'll put the resolution at once. It seems a good one to me, though we should all be sorry if Sturmie should have to leave us in consequence. Oh, you never know."—As the astonished Sturmie, really roused for once, turned a heavy contemptuous glance in his direction.— "I've got something to say about Space and Time myself before we part this afternoon. But that will come later. The resolution is . . . carried unanimously, of course. And now we'll hear about Borthin's brains. . . . Professor Borthin will address the meetings."

Professor Borthin rose quietly. Whatever he may have thought of the way in which the meeting was going, he gave no sign of perturba· tion. He began his address by explaining the progress which had been made in his laboratories in the processes of brain-grafting under prolonged anesthetized conditions, with local stimulations to the growth of connecting tissue, so that after a period of unconsciousness, lasting from ten to fourteen days, the subject of the experiment would awake with an alien brain (or an alien body, if you should prefer so to express it), functioning smoothly and well. At this stage, he produced a guinea-pig in a cage with climbing-bars, which he explained had been supplied with a brain from one of the smaller monkeys, and which now disported itself among the bars with a clumsy agility, giving somewhat the impression of a performing bear.

He had completed his preparations, he went on to explain, some weeks ago, for the transposition of the brains of children and dogs on a scale which could not fail to produce results of unusual interest. He had little doubt that the children would be able to contrive some measure of articulate speech from the throats of their new dwellings: he was hopeful that the dogs could be trained to use the power of speech which their new bodies would render available to them.

He wanted a large number of babies—healthy examples, the children of various sections of the community, professional, commercial, military, naval, artisan—even specimens of the superstitious religious sects which still lurked and lingered obscurely—so that their various reactions could be comprehensively studied. For this purpose he required power to make requisition among the babies which should be born during the next twelve months, including, if necessary, the power to order that such babies should be produced by suitable couples— the Council did not need his reminder that some sections of the community had almost ceased to produce children, unless ordered to do so under sufficient penalties, and he did not blind himself to the

fact that the authority he was seeking might tend to make them ad
ditionally obstinate in such abstentions—so that, in twelve months'
time, he could, he had no reason to doubt, make such report to the
Council, and exhibit such infant and canine specimens, as would
abundantly justify the experiment on which he was occupied.

He knew—he was sorry to know—that their esteemed President
had not received his first request with the cordiality which he might
have reasonably expected, but the claims of Science were paramount,
—surely, in that assembly, there was no need to urge it—and he ap-
pealed with confidence to the Council for the support he needed.

He moved his resolution accordingly.

He had scarcely resumed his seat when the President rose.

"I propose," he said, "to move the postponement of this resolution
—not because I doubt the value of our friend's experiments, not
because I doubt that the claims of Science are paramount, not because I doubt that many human brains may find congenial shelter
in the skulls of dogs, but because I have also something to tell you
of the development of the human brain, and because I believe, if
you accept the offer which I am able to make, we shall all be better
fitted when next we meet to decide this question wisely."

Briefly and clearly, he proceeded to tell them of the nature of this
discovery, of the injection which he had already taken, and of the
further one which he would administer to himself in their presence.
Amid a watchful silence, he drove the needle again into his
own arm.

"In half an hour," he went on, "you may expect its effects to be
apparent. In the meantime, I shall explain to you, in greater detail, the
nature and qualities of the preparation, and the experiments that I
have made already. After that, I shall propose to reply to Dr. Sturmie's
somewhat violent attack upon myself. Should I succeed in convincing
you that he is in error, you will recognize the value of the brain-
stimulus which I have discovered.

"Gentlemen," he went on, his voice falling to a note of earnestness,
and of apparent sincerity, "we are inclined to distrust one another. I
know that there is more than one here who fancies himself secure in
the belief that he could destroy me with impunity in three seconds
from where he sits, should he decide to do so (he is mistaken, but
never mind that), but I ask you this—if I offer to share this new
power equally with you all, if I propose that it be confined to members
of the Council, so that you will be supreme among all men, do I not
show my loyalty and my goodwill, and do I not provide a basis on

which a new standard of reciprocal loyalty may be established among us?"

Here he paused, and looked round for the applause which was not slow to respond. For the moment, he had gained the ear of the Council. He had only to justify his boast to establish his supremacy. Only Sturmie sat silent and contemptuous, digesting the insult which he had received. Professor Borthin, with an expressionless face, joined in the applause. He was not deceived. He knew that one of them must be doomed. But he would wait his time. The experiment had not yet succeeded.

Silent and watchful, he heard the President go on to the detailed explanations which he had promised, while the clock on the wall behind him ticked out the half hour for which they waited.

Twenty minutes passed, and he became aware, with a quickened interest, that President Brisket was changing. But it was not to any apparent advance in intellectual alertness, not in the clarity or profundity of the remarks he was making, but there was a change, both in voice and manner. Even his face seemed different. He was smiling fatuously. What was he saying now?

Dr. Acton-Shaw, who was listening with his usual intentness, his wizened face slightly lifted sideways to the speaker, pushed his chair a little back from the table.

"You know," President Brisket was saying, "we don't love humanity as we ought. We don't even love one another. There's Borthin here, one of the best, who doesn't trust me as he should. He's got something up his sleeve now that he thinks could kill me. —And, gentlemen—I know I shall feel better when I've confessed it—I've got a little arrangement of my own that would hit back automatically if he tried it, and would kill you all, if I wished. . . . No, don't move. You're quite safe. I'm sure Borthin wouldn't hurt a fly. . . . But if he did try, even I couldn't save you. You'd go so quickly you wouldn't know how you died. . . . Now we've got to alter all that. We've got to love each other, and the poor dogs, and Dr. Sturmie, and the dear little guinea-pigs. We mustn't think of ourselves. Sturmie thinks that I ought to resign, and, of course, I will. I know he didn't mean to be rude. He just hadn't thought of the Invasion of Energy, and what a difference it might make. It's almost sure to. . . . But Professor Borthin looks as though he's got something to say, and, of course, he shall. . . . Professor Borthin will address the meeting."

Professor Borthin rose. "Gentlemen," he said briefly, "you have heard our esteemed President tender his resignation. Before we deal with the previous resolution, I move that the resignation be now accepted."

The President rose to reply. There was the same deprecating fatuous smile on his face, and he did not appear to resent the resolution which had been put forward so abruptly.

"Gentlemen, of course I'll resign. But we'd better have the resolutions one at a time, hadn't we? I'm sure Borthin doesn't really want the babies. . . . You didn't think of their mothers, did you, Borthin? . . . And we don't want to hurt the little doggies either. The resolution is . . . Those against?"

He looked round the wondering faces of the Council, but not a hand was lifted.

"I know I needn't put the affirmative. I'm sure no one will vote for a resolution like that," he went on, with a plaintive confidence.

Dr. Sturmie turned his huge head slowly from right to left, reading the faces of those around him. His voice rumbled out contemptuously.

"After this exhibition of senile decay—unless anyone else wants a dose of the same kind—I think we'd better have the resolution properly. It has been moved *That Professor Borthin have power to examine all babies which may be born during the next twelve months within thirty-five miles of London, and to retain as many as he may select for experimental purposes, and further that he may require that those whom he may nominate shall provide him with babies of their own breeding within twelve months of such order, under such penalties as he may consider suitable, should they fail to do so.* Those in favor? Carried nem. con. The President and Secretary not voting."

President Brisket got to his feet unsteadily. His eyes had a curiously pathetic look, as of one who has lost his way in the dark.

Dr. Acton-Shaw looked at him again, and pushed his chair a little further back from the table.

"Oh, no, gentlemen," he began plaintively, "you don't really mean that. You couldn't mean it, you know. Oh, no, Sturmie dear. I'm not an old fool, really. But I'm not sure we oughtn't to end at once, really I'm not. I think we must have gone the wrong way. . . ."

He sat down uncertainly, and as he did so, Dr. Acton-Shaw pushed his chair further back, till it was clear of the central patterning of the floor on which the table stood.

A professor of chemistry, a dark slim man, younger than most, sitting half-way down the table, who had not spoken previously, interposed.

"Mr. President. I don't think you're quite yourself this afternoon.

Won't you . . ." He may have been about to ask him to adjourn the meeting, but the sentence was never finished.

The President had been scraping with his foot under the table. Once to the left—once forward—twice to the right. He might be feeling a bit queer, but he hadn't forgotten that. It would be best for the race, and oh, so much for themselves!

Dr. Sturmie looked at him intently, and half leapt from his chair, with an agility which he had not shown for the past ten years, but he was too late. The great body collapsed so heavily that the chair cracked audibly in the sudden silence of the room.

Dr. Acton-Shaw, still pushing his chair backward as he rose, the minute-book carefully retained beneath his arm, observed his twenty colleagues sagging around the table in attitudes which looked uncomfortable, but which they appeared to endure very patiently.

He was not greatly surprised, and not at all disconcerted.

They were clever men, but he had been led to wonder for some months past, as he had recorded their decisions, whether there might not be higher powers than they.

"There'll be bonfires to-morrow," he said thoughtfully. "I suppose I'd better clear." And then, with a new decision: "No, I won't do that. I expect I can do something to help. I'll ring up Wyndham."

He went out quietly, to ring up the Premier who had been deposed by Professor Brisket a ghastly year ago.

MODERN LIBRARY GIANTS

A series of sturdily bound and handsomely printed, full-sized library editions of books formerly available only in expensive sets. These volumes contain from 600 to 1,400 pages each.

THE MODERN LIBRARY GIANTS REPRESENT A
SELECTION OF THE WORLD'S GREATEST BOOKS

MISCELLANEOUS

The Best of the World's Best Books
COMPLETE LIST OF TITLES IN
THE MODERN LIBRARY

MISCELLANEOUS